THERE IS ONLY WAR

It is the 41st millennium and mankind stands on the brink of destruction. For ten thousand years the Imperium has endured, constantly beset by the enemy without and the traitor within. Aliens, daemons and the servants of dark, bloodthirsty gods seek to bring about the ruination of mankind, and only a few brave souls defend the common man – the brave soldiers of the Imperial Guard and the mighty Space Marines foremost amongst them. As battle is joined on a million worlds and death claims all but the most lucky or skilled, one truth shines out above all: in the grim darkness of the far future, there is only war.

More Warhammer 40,000 from Black Library

SPACE MARINES
An anthology of short stories about the defenders of humanity, the Space Marines.
Edited by Christian Dunn, Nick Kyme and Lindsey Priestley

• **BLACK LIBRARY CLASSICS** •

FIRST AND ONLY
A Gaunt's Ghosts novel
Dan Abnett

NIGHTBRINGER
An Ultramarines novel
Graham McNeill

ARMAGEDDON
Contains the novel *Helsreach* and the novella *Blood and Fire*.
Aaron Dembski-Bowden

DAMNOS
Contains the novel *Fall of Damnos* and the novella *Spear of Macragge*
Nick Kyme

BLOOD IN THE MACHINE
A Space Marine Battles audio drama
Andy Smillie

VEIL OF DARKNESS
A Space Marine Battles audio drama
Nick Kyme

THE HORUS HERESY®

Book 1: HORUS RISING
Dan Abnett

Book 2: FALSE GODS
Graham McNeill

Book 3: GALAXY IN FLAMES
Ben Counter

There are many more Space Marine Battles and Horus Heresy titles available. Visit blacklibrary.com to purchase the full range.

A WARHAMMER 40,000 ANTHOLOGY

THERE IS ONLY WAR

Edited by
Christian Dunn
Nick Kyme
Lindsey Priestley

BLACK LIBRARY

A Black Library Publication

*All stories in this book have been previously published
in print, eBook or audio drama formats.*

First published in Great Britain in 2013 by
Black Library,
Games Workshop Ltd.,
Willow Road,
Nottingham, NG7 2WS, UK.

10 9 8 7 6 5 4 3 2 1

Cover illustration by Hardy Fowler.

© Games Workshop Limited 2013. All rights reserved.

Black Library, the Black Library logo, The Horus Heresy, The Horus Heresy logo, The Horus Heresy eye device, Space Marine Battles, the Space Marine Battles logo, Warhammer 40,000, the Warhammer 40,000 logo, Games Workshop, the Games Workshop logo and all associated brands, names, characters, illustrations and images from the Warhammer 40,000 universe are either ®, ™ and/or © Games Workshop Ltd 2000-2013, variably registered in the UK and other countries around the world. All rights reserved.

A CIP record for this book is available from the British Library.

UK ISBN 13: 978 1 84970 394 9
US ISBN 13: 978 1 84970 395 6

No part of this publication may be reproduced, stored in a retrieval system, or transmitted in any form or by any means, electronic, mechanical, photocopying, recording or otherwise, without the prior permission of the publishers.

This is a work of fiction. All the characters and events portrayed in this book are fictional, and any resemblance to real people or incidents is purely coincidental.

See Black Library on the internet at
www.blacklibrary.com

Find out more about Games Workshop
and the world of Warhammer 40,000 at
www.games-workshop.com

Printed and bound by CPI Group (UK) Ltd, Croydon, CR0 4YY

It is the 41st millennium. For more than a hundred centuries the Emperor has sat immobile on the Golden Throne of Earth. He is the master of mankind by the will of the gods, and master of a million worlds by the might of his inexhaustible armies. He is a rotting carcass writhing invisibly with power from the Dark Age of Technology. He is the Carrion Lord of the Imperium for whom a thousand souls are sacrificed every day, so that he may never truly die.

Yet even in his deathless state, the Emperor continues his eternal vigilance. Mighty battlefleets cross the daemon-infested miasma of the warp, the only route between distant stars, their way lit by the Astronomican, the psychic manifestation of the Emperor's will. Vast armies give battle in His name on uncounted worlds. Greatest amongst his soldiers are the Adeptus Astartes, the Space Marines, bio-engineered super-warriors. Their comrades in arms are legion: the Imperial Guard and countless Planetary Defence Forces, the ever-vigilant Inquisition and the tech-priests of the Adeptus Mechanicus to name only a few. But for all their multitudes, they are barely enough to hold off the ever-present threat from aliens, heretics, mutants - and worse.

To be a man in such times is to be one amongst untold billions. It is to live in the cruellest and most bloody regime imaginable. These are the tales of those times. Forget the power of technology and science, for so much has been forgotten, never to be re-learned. Forget the promise of progress and understanding, for in the grim dark future there is only war. There is no peace amongst the stars, only an eternity of carnage and slaughter, and the laughter of thirsting gods.

CONTENTS

One Hate – *Aaron Dembski-Bowden*	9
Kraken – *Chris Wraight*	37
The Iron Without – *Graham McNeill*	75
Deus ex Mechanicus – *Andy Chambers*	101
Pestilence – *Dan Abnett*	121
Torment – *Anthony Reynolds*	139
Cold Trade – *Andy Hoare*	163
The Relic – *Jonathan Green*	189
Faces – *Matthew Farrer*	217
Beneath the Flesh – *Andy Smillie*	243
Even Unto Death – *Mike Lee*	279
Orphans of the Kraken – *Richard Williams*	295
Black Dawn – *C L Werner*	335
Unforgiven – *Graham McNeill*	357
Shadow Knight – *Aaron Dembski-Bowden*	373
Survivor – *Steve Parker*	385
Emperor's Deliverance – *Nick Kyme*	425
The Last Detail – *Paul Kearney*	439
Master Imus's Transgression – *Dan Abnett*	463
The Long Games at Carcharias – *Rob Sanders*	475
Helion Rain – *George Mann*	509
Echoes of the Tomb – *Sandy Mitchell*	535
Voidsong – *Henry Zou*	553
We Are One – *John French*	577

Bitter End – *S P Cawkwell*	597
Apostle's Creed – *Graham McNeill*	615
Mistress Baeda's Gift – *Braden Campbell*	651
Flesh – *Chris Wraight*	669
Twelve Wolves – *Ben Counter*	705
Suffer Not the Unclean to Live – *Gav Thorpe*	721
The Lives of Ferag Lion-Wolf – *Barrington J Bayley*	743
Snares and Delusions – *Matthew Farrer*	753
Gate of Souls – *Mike Lee*	773
The Wrath of Khârn – *William King*	785
The Returned – *James Swallow*	795
A Good Man – *Sandy Mitchell*	825
Hell Night – *Nick Kyme*	847
At Gaius Point – *Aaron Dembski-Bowden*	883
Midnight on the Street of Knives – *Andy Chambers*	903
The Carrion Anthem – *David Annandale*	921
Playing Patience – *Dan Abnett*	939

ONE HATE

Aaron Dembski-Bowden

I am the future of my Chapter.

My masters and mentors often tell me this. They say I, and those like me, hold the Chapter's soul in our hands. We wear the black, and we are the beating heart of a reborn brotherhood.

It is our duty to remember. We are charged to recall the traditions that came before the moment when our Chapter stood on the edge of extinction.

My name is Argo. In a Chapter with few remaining relics, I am blessed above my brothers in the tools of war in my possession.

My armour was born when the Imperium was born – repaired, amended and maintained in the centuries since by generations of warriors, slaves, servitors and serfs. My bolter roared on the battlefields of the Horus Heresy, and has been carried in the red-marked hands of thirty-seven Astartes since the day of its forging. Each of their names is etched into the dark iron of the weapon, along with the name of the world that claimed their lives. The eyes of my helm have stared out onto ten thousand wars, and seen a million of Mankind's foes die.

Around my neck is a gift from the Ecclesiarchy of Holy Terra: an aquila symbol of priceless worth and imbued with the warding secrets of a technology almost lost to time. My armour is black, for I am death itself. My helm is the skull of every man that died in every battle fought by my Chapter in the ten millennia since our founding.

More than that, my face is the victorious leer of the dying Emperor.

And why am I charged with this responsibility? Why do I wear the black?

Because I hate. I hate more than my brothers, and my hatred runs blacker, deeper, purer than theirs.

One hate stands above all others. One hate that burns in our blood and barks from the mouths of five hundred bolters when we stand together in war. It is a hatred with many names: the greenskin, the ork, the kine.

To us, they are simply the Enemy.

We are the Crimson Fists, the shield-hand of Dorn, and we have survived extinction when all others would have fallen into worthless memory. Our hatred takes us across the stars in service to the Throne.

And now it brings us to Syral.

Syral. A lone orb around a diminutive sun, on the edge of Segmentum Tempestus.

The single celestial child of a red star that was taking thousands of years to die. The sun's waning would take thousands of years before its eventual expiration, and the planet it warmed was still of great use to the Imperium.

Syral was an agri-world, with the globe's landmasses given over to expansive and fertile continents of foodstuffs and livestock. Syral's great oceans were similarly plundered by Imperial need. Beneath their dark surface, the tides concealed hydroponics facilities the size of cities, harvesting the edible wealth of the depths. As a planet, Syral had but one colossal purpose: to export a system's worth of food ready for purchase by the worlds nearby that lacked such natural bounty. Syral fed three hive-worlds, from the spires of the rich to the slums of the destitute, as well as several Imperial Navy fleets and regiments of the Imperial Guard warring in nearby crusades.

From space, Syral was the blue-green of mankind's ancestral memory, as if drawn from an artist's imaginings of the impious ages of Old Terra. However, the face of a world can change a great deal in a year.

'The Fists are back.'

Lord General Ulviran looked at Major Dace, who had spoken those words. With his thin face, ice-blue eyes and aquiline nose, the lord general was a natural when it came to bestowing withering looks on those among his staff that disappointed him. He gave one of those glances to Dace now. The major looked away, suitably chastised.

The gunship sat idle, as it had for several minutes now, its landing stanchions and velocity thrusters still hissing with occasional jets of steam as they released flight pressure and settled into repose. Across the side of this midnight-blue vulture of a vessel, an engraved symbol stared back at the horde of Guardsmen that waited. A clenched fist, as red and dark as good wine.

The gunship's forward ramp lowered like a mouth opening. Ulviran was put in mind – as he always was when seeing an Astartes Thunderhawk – of a great steel bird of prey. When its forward ramp lowered, just beneath the cockpit window, the bird seemed to roar with the sound of whining hydraulics.

'I count four,' Major Dace said, making this his second most obvious observation that day. Four armoured forms, each more than a head taller than a normal man, tramped down the clanking ramp.

'Just four...' the major added a moment later. Ulviran would gladly have shot him, had he been able to think of a reason to do so. Not even a good reason, just a legal one. Dace was an asset on the battlefield, but at staff meetings his dullard observations were a tedium his fellow officers could easily do without.

The Astartes made no move to approach the crowd of Guardsmen. They stood as still as statues, monstrous bolters held to their eagle-emblazoned chests. Ulviran took stock of the situation. The Astartes were back, and it was not the time to stand around gawping. Control. The scene warranted control. Maybe there could be some dignity salvaged from this whole tawdry development. Having the Astartes arrive would be a cause for celebration right enough, but Ulviran recalled every single word in the missive he'd composed to Chapter Master Kantor of the Crimson Fists. Begging was the only word for it, really. He'd begged for aid, and here it was: deliverance once more. He was not a man who enjoyed resorting to begging. It had galled him even as he'd dictated the distress call.

Ulviran strode forward to meet the giants as they stood stone-still in the shadow of their avian gunship. He noted with unnoticeable displeasure that the heavy bolter turrets on the Thunderhawk's wing tips panned across the camp, as if seeking threats even amongst Imperial forces. Did the Fists not even consider the Guard capable of holding their own base camp secure against the enemy? In that moment, deliverance or not, the lord general hated their damned arrogance.

'Welcome back,' he said to the first of the Astartes, who was undoubtedly the commander of this small team.

The warrior looked at the lord general, his snarling visored helm turning down to regard the human. This close, no more than an arm's length from the towering warriors, Ulviran felt his gums ache from the pressuring hum of the squad's power armour. The whine of energy was more tactile than audible, making his eyes water and prickling the skin on the back of his neck. He swallowed as the Astartes made the sign of the aquila, the warrior's gauntleted hands forming the salute and banging against his armoured chest. Even the smallest of movements made their armour joints purr in a low mechanical snarl.

Ulviran returned the salute. His neck hurt a little, looking up like this, and he unwillingly flinched when the Astartes spoke.

'With all due respect,' the voice was a crackling, vox-distorted growl, far deeper than a normal man's, 'why are you addressing me?'

Ulviran hadn't expected this level of disrespect, nor this degree of informality. He was a lord general, after all. Planets lived and died by his tactical expertise.

The general took in the details of the warrior's armour. The suit was the blue of a starless midnight sky, trimmed in places with a bold red, nowhere more noticeable than the clenched fist on the warrior's shoulder pad. A scroll detailing oaths and matters of unknowable honour was draped from the warrior's other shoulder pad, moving slightly in the gentle wind. Hanging from a thick chain that had been made into a bandolier, oversized, misshapen skulls knocked quietly together as the Astartes moved. From the pronounced lower jaws and brutish bone structure, Ulviran knew they were the skulls of orks. In life, they'd been big orks, most likely leaders among their bestial kind. In death, they were impressive trophies.

This Astartes was clearly the leader of the squad. None of the others wore trophies to match.

'I am addressing you because I assumed you were in command.' He adopted the tone of one speaking to a small child, which his men would have found both laughable and insane had they heard. The thrill of authority over these giants rushed through the lord general's blood. He would, after all, brook no disrespect.

'Do I look like a brother-captain to you?' the Astartes asked, and Ulviran wondered if the warrior's vox-speakers made his voice into a growl, or if it was naturally that low.

Ulviran nodded in response to the question. He was determined not to be intimidated.

'To my eyes, yes, you do.'

'Well, I'm not.' Here the Astartes looked to his fellows. 'Not yet, anyway.' Ulviran heard something at the edge of his hearing – a series of quiet clicks coming from the helms of the armoured men. He assumed, quite correctly, that they were laughing with each other over a private vox-channel.

The Astartes draped in skulls, chains and scrolls detailing his many victories inclined his head at one of the others.

'He's the sergeant.'

Ulviran turned to face this next one, making the sign of the aquila once more.

Before the lord general could speak, this next Astartes – who was clad in a blood-coloured toga draped around his armour – shook his helmed head.

'No, lord general,' the Astartes intoned, his voice as much a mechanical rumble as the first one's had been. 'You do not address me, either.'

Ulviran's patience was reaching its end.

'Then who am I to address?'

The robed warrior nodded in the direction of the Thunderhawk, at the newest arrival striding down the ramp. This Astartes was clad in plate of charcoal-black, and even without much knowledge of Astartes technology it was clear to Ulviran that the dark suit of power armour was an antique, dating back centuries – probably even millennia. The black warrior's helmed face was a grinning skull, the red eye lenses lending it a daemonic cast as he looked left and right, surveying the landing site.

Ulviran swallowed, unaware of how his Adam's apple bobbed and betrayed his nervousness. *Throne,* he thought. *A Chaplain.*

The Astartes in the red toga offered the lord general a slight bow.

'You address him.'

In private, they discussed Syral. The Chaplain stalked around the large table with its map-covered surface. Here in the lord general's command room, aboard his personal Baneblade, *The Indomitable Will,* the human and the Astartes shared words away from the ears of others.

'We handed you this world four months ago.'

Those words chilled the lord general's blood. They were an insult, certainly, but they were also an unarguable truth.

'Circumstances change, Brother-Chaplain.' And they had. Ork reinforcements had come in flooding waves, washing the western hemisphere in a tide of greenskin invaders. The Imperium's easy victory, largely bought by the surgical strikes of the Crimson Fists four months before, was nothing more than a pleasant memory and a tale of what might have been. The Imperial Guard had been falling back ever since.

The Chaplain's vox-voice was edged by growls, as if the man spoke at an octave almost too low for words.

'You are losing Syral,' the Astartes said. His skullish face stared at the human across the room.

'I know better than to argue that assessment,' came the lord general's reply. 'I'd wager that I see it clearer than you, for I've been watching it happen for months.'

Ulviran watched as the Chaplain reached up to his helm and pulled the release catches on his armoured collar. With a serpentine hiss of venting pressure, the locks disengaged and the Astartes removed his skulled helmet, reverently lifting it then laying it on the table before him. Its red eyes were dimmed now the helm was detached from the armour's power supply, but they still glared at the lord general in dull accusation.

'I am not here to chastise you, lord general.'

Ulviran smiled to hear the warrior's true voice. It was deep and resonant, but with a gentility shaping the words. The Chaplain was, by the lord general's best guess, close to thirty years of age, but with the Astartes it was almost impossible to tell. He didn't even know for certain if they *did* age; he'd always taken the trope for granted that one determined a Space Marine's age by the scars on their flesh and the inscriptions etched into their armour.

Had this Astartes been allowed to grow as a normal man, he might have been considered handsome. Even as the product of intensive genetic enhancement since puberty, the Chaplain was a fair example of his kind. The Astartes was almost two heads taller than a normal man, with features and body mass to match, but Ulviran saw something undeniably human within the warrior's dark-blue eyes and the half-smile he wore.

The lord general liked him immediately. For Ulviran, who prided himself on being a fine reader of men, this was a rare development.

'Brother-Chaplain–'

'Argo,' he interrupted. 'My name is Argo.'

'As you wish. I must ask you, Argo, how did you respond so quickly to our…' he didn't want to say *to our plea*, '…to our request for reinforcement?'

Argo met his gaze. The half-smile left his face, and the warrior's eyes narrowed. The silence that followed the general's question bordered on becoming awkward.

'Just good fortune,' the Chaplain said at last, the smile returning. 'We were close to the system.'

'I see. And are you alone?'

The Chaplain spread his hands in beneficence. One gauntlet was the same coal black as the warrior's armour. The other, his left, was painted blood red in keeping with the traditions of his Chapter.

'I bring with me the brothers of Squad Demetrian, of the Fifth Battle Company.'

'Yourself and four others. Nothing more?'

'The Chapter serfs and servitors responsible for the flight and maintenance of our Thunderhawk.'

'No more Astartes.' It was a statement of resignation, not a question.

'As you say,' the Chaplain offered a shallow but sincere bow, 'no more Astartes.'

Ulviran was noticeably ill at ease. 'As much as I thank the Throne and your Chapter Master for any assistance the Fists offer, especially so quickly, I had hoped for a… bolder show of support.'

'Hope is the first step on the road to disappointment. Four months ago, we broke the Enemy's back here. I assume you recall the date.'

'I do. The men still speak of it. They call it Vengeance Night.'

'Very apt. We left the enemy reeling, lord general. We left them bloody, their armies shattered from our assaults across the globe. I was at the Siege of the Cantorial Palace. I was part of the strike force that destroyed the palace itself, and I was there when Brother Imrich of the Fifth took the head of Warlord Golgorrad in the battle amongst the smoking rubble. We are back, lord general, and I humbly suggest you be grateful for even the small blessing one squad of our Chapter represents.'

'I am grateful, to you and your Chapter Master.'

'Good. I apologise for any harshness in my tone. Now, let us talk of strategy.' The Chaplain pointed with his red hand at the largest map spread across the table. 'Southspire, the capital city, unless I am mistaken.'

'You are not.'

'And, according to the sensor sweeps made by my Thunderhawk as we broke orbit, the city – and the site of the Cantorial Palace at the city's heart – is once more in the hands of the enemy.'

'It is.'

Argo's blue eyes met Ulviran's, drilling into the officer with an unblinking lack of mercy.

'So when do we take it back?'

The interior bay of the Thunderhawk echoed with Argo's footfalls, his clanking tread ringing from the iron skin of the inert machinery stored there. Chapter serfs in robes of deep blue stepped aside, making the sign of the aquila as he passed. Argo nodded to each one in kind, whispering benedictions for them all. They thanked him and moved about the business of attending to the gunship's innards and readying the stored machinery. Argo's eyes raked along the heavy digging equipment stored in the hold, and his mood turned black.

Squad Demetrian was training. He heard them long before he saw them. Climbing a ladder to the next deck, Argo thumped the door release to the communal 'quarters', a room where Astartes remained strapped in flight seats when the gunship took to the skies. In the small usable space between the twin rows of seats, two of Squad Demetrian duelled in full armour.

The two warriors could not have been less alike. His armour draped in scrolls of his deeds, bone tokens of fallen foes, and the skulls of seven orks hanging from his chain bandolier, Imrich was a whirlwind of movement. Kicks, punches, elbow thrusts, headbutts – all thrown into a duel with shortswords, added between the moves of the clashing blades.

Opposing him was Toma, embodying pure economy of motion. Where Imrich's fury twinned with his skill, Toma's movements were calculated to the finest degree by a lightning mind that drove his vicious combat reflexes. His blade snapped into position to block and thrust in a silver blur, stopping precisely at each twist, never overbalancing, never overreaching, with Toma never giving ground.

'I'll wear you down, Deathwatch,' Imrich teased. Their gladius blades locked again, and the two helms glared at each other only half a metre apart.

Toma said nothing. Displayed on the polished iron of his unique shoulder pad was the stylised symbol of the Holy Inquisition. He always fought in silence. His recent return from three years in the specialist Ordo Xenos Deathwatch Chapter hadn't changed that.

The fight came to an end when Argo cleared his throat. Disengaging from one another, Imrich and Toma resheathed their blades.

'I had you, Deathwatch.' Imrich saluted his opponent with his clenched left fist against his heart.

'Sure you did, hero.' Toma's voice was toneless as he returned the gesture.

'I had you.'

'The day you have me is the day the Emperor rises from the Throne and dances all night long.'

Brother-Sergeant Demetrian silenced them both with a fist pounded against the metal wall.

'News, Brother-Chaplain?' the sergeant asked.

Argo removed his helm and gave them his half-smile. 'They think we're here in answer of a distress call.'

The squad looked at the Chaplain, awaiting further explanation. Now this had their interest up.

'You didn't tell them the truth,' said Demetrian. The veteran's scarred face was a map of battles fought across a hundred systems. Both his gauntlets were crimson; he'd served time in the Crusade Company among the best of the best, and on the knee of his armour, a Black Templar cross was proudly displayed. The Declates Crusade, when the Templars and the Fists broke ranks to fight in mixed units, was a point of great honour for both Chapters. Demetrian had been there. A roll of his honours was recorded in acid-etched lettering on a gold tablet in the Chapter's fortress-monastery back home on Rynn's World.

Argo nodded. 'I thought it best to retain the illusion of our compliance. The truth would breed animosity.'

'No surprise,' Demetrian's words were as clipped and to the point as ever. 'The plan remains the same?'

'We fight until the Cantorial Palace. Then we do the duty entrusted to us. I saw the maps of Southspire and the enemy's forces spread across the sector. A new warlord leads the enemy on the far side of the city, and the Guard ready for their last attempt at a big push. The city itself is flooded with roaming bands of foes.'

'Numbers?'

'Thousands within the city. Tens of thousands at the edge, where the warlord waits.'

'I like those odds,' Imrich said. They all heard the smile in his words, even from behind his helm.

Argo shook his head. 'This is not a war we can win without the Guard.'

Now Toma spoke up. He sat in one of the restraining seats, meticulously dismantling and cleaning the sacred bolter given to him by the Ordo Xenos during his tenure in the Inquisitorial kill-teams.

'Will the Guard win this war without us?'

Argo shrugged. 'We have our orders.'

Toma pressed on. 'And once we leave?'

'The Emperor protects,' the Chaplain replied.

Imrich's skulls rattled as he turned. 'So we flee a war that the Imperium is losing? I don't like the thought of running from the kine.'

'Duly noted, but Chapter Master Kantor was clear in his priorities,' Argo said. 'And you will do penance for your disrespect of the Enemy, Brother Imrich.'

It was a matter of small shame among some of the Crimson Fists that they referred to the greenskins as *kine*. On Rynn's World, another agri-world, it was slang for 'cattle'.

'Yes, Brother-Chaplain,' Imrich growled.

'Hate the inhuman, slaughter the impure, and praise the Emperor above all. But always respect the foe.'

'Yes, Brother-Chaplain.' Imrich wanted to insist Argo stopped quoting the litanies at him. Instead he bowed his head. He knew better than to apologise.

'When do we move out?' Demetrian cut in.

'Tomorrow night, the Guard will advance,' Argo said, as he held his golden aquila medallion in his red-fingered gauntlet. 'And we advance with them.'

Dawn found Argo in the cockpit of the Thunderhawk, still in his armour. He sat in one of the command thrones, his elbows on his knees, staring out of the window. He had not slept. He was Astartes. He barely needed sleep.

Toma came to him as he mused on the coming battle. The quiet warrior was a powerful credit to the squad, and Argo – who was over a century younger than the Deathwatch specialist – always welcomed his presence. He suspected it would not be long before the captain of the Fifth selected Toma for promotion into the Crusade Company, or to lead his own squad into the field of war.

'Another dawn, Brother-Chaplain.' Toma took the command throne next to Argo, sitting and holding his helm in his hands. The Deathwatch had aged him, Argo saw. New scars, faded from fast treatment but still noticeable, pitted the warrior's cheek and temple.

'Acid burns,' Argo said, gesturing with a gloved hand, his black one. 'The Deathwatch kept you busy.'

'I can't say,' Toma replied. His face was as expressive as stone.

'Can't or won't?' Argo asked, already knowing the answer.

'Both.'

'The Ordo Xenos keeps its secrets close.'

'It does.' Toma's expression was edged with thought as he replayed hazy recollections, little more than echoes, through his mind. Oaths had been sworn. Promises were made. Memories were torn from the mind by psyk-enhanced meditation and the ungentle scouring of arcane machinery.

It was the first time Argo had seen his fellow Fist's neutral mask slip, and he found it fascinating.

'We go to war today,' the Chaplain said. 'We are a poor portion of the Fifth's strength, but we are the Fifth nevertheless. In the fires of war, we are forged. And yet I sense a burden on your soul, brother.'

Toma nodded. This was why he had come.

'It's Vayne.'

Brother-Apothecary Vayne was in the Thunderhawk's confined apothecarion, little more than an operating table and racks of monitoring equipment fastened to the small room's walls. Already prepared for the battle tonight, he was in full armour with one exception: his head was bare. The white-faced helm that marked him as an Apothecary rested on the surgery table, and this was the first thing Argo saw as he entered. The second thing was Vayne himself, adjusting data readouts on his arm-mounted narthecium. As Argo watched, several surgical spikes and knives snapped back into the bulky medical unit housed on Vayne's forearm.

Vayne eventually turned to the sound of thrumming power armour, though his enhanced senses would have detected the Chaplain's approach long before he came into the room.

'Argo,' he said in subdued greeting.

'Vayne,' the Chaplain nodded back.

The atmosphere between the two men was nothing short of ugly. Seven years before, they'd served together as novices in Nochlitan's Scout squad. Seven years since the final trials to become Astartes, when Argo had been chosen to wear the black, and Vayne the white.

A Chaplain and an Apothecary drawn from the same Scout unit. Sergeant Nochlitan, who like Demetrian had served admirably in the Crusade Company among the Chapter's elite, had been honoured by Chapter Master Kantor himself for honing such excellence in a novice squad.

With the Chapter still in its perilous rebuilding stage, the finest warriors of the Crimson Fists were often charged with the duty of training novice squads. It was no shame to step away from the First Company to the role of Scout-sergeant, and Nochlitan was one of the most respected.

Beyond a few scars, Argo looked no different. The same could not be said for the Apothecary. Half of Vayne's face was gone, replaced by cold, smooth steel shaped to resemble his features. Despite its artistry, the exquisite workmanship was clear evidence of a terrible wound that had almost been Vayne's death. Vayne's left eye, an augmetic lens of synthetic scarlet crystal, whirred in its circular socket as the Apothecary focused his gaze on the Chaplain.

'You're looking well,' he remarked. Argo didn't reply. He watched as Vayne limped around the surgical table, and considered the rest of the Apothecary's newly-restored body.

Daemon-fire had done this to Vayne, during the Cleansing of Chiaro two months before. Fresh from the victory on Syral and the destruction of the Cantorial Palace, the Crimson Fists had entered the warp for several weeks to reach Chiaro, answering a call for aid by the planetary governor. Mutant cults were spreading in the rotting industrial sectors of his world. A true purge was needed to stamp the problem out, after the local defence forces had failed to quell the matter.

The Fists had not failed. It took a month and was not without casualties, but their duty was done. The rest of the strike force returned to Rynn's World at the behest of Chapter Master Kantor. Argo and Squad Demetrian had returned to Syral aboard the support cruiser *Vigil*.

It had been a cold, quiet journey back to Syral. They were the only Astartes on board, except for a single Apothecary from the Fifth Company that remained to preside over Vayne's injuries – and act in his stead if the younger man died.

Vayne had suffered as the servitors and his potential replacement rebuilt his body. He was almost certain to die, given the massive burns sustained and their initial refusal to heal. The Chapter would lose a gifted healer in a time when the Fists most desperately needed to reclaim and preserve their fighting strength. Had Vayne died, it would have been a true loss.

From shoulder to fingertips, his left arm was augmetic. It connected internally to the bionic sections of his spine and collarbone, purring in a smooth hiss of expensive augmentation that Argo's keen hearing could detect even underneath the background hum of their power armour. As with his left arm, so too was his left leg bionic – from hip to toes. The augmentations were still new, still untested in battle, and although Argo doubted a normal human could discern the minute inconsistencies in Vayne's gait and posture, to Astartes senses it registered as a subtle but noticeable hitch in his stride. A limp.

It was temporary, until the augmetics aligned with Vayne's body patterns and wholly fused with his biorhythms. The leg ended in a splayed claw of a foot for enhanced stability: a cross of blackened metal that connected to the well-armoured ankle joint and the heavy musculature of the bionic shin and calf above.

'Your attitude is beginning to create strain within your squad,' Argo began. 'I am told you are melancholic.'

Vayne scowled. His false eye hummed in its socket as it tried to conform to his facial expression.

'Brother-Sergeant Demetrian has said nothing.'

'You were saved because you have value to the Chapter. You stand in high regard for your skills. Why are you unbalanced by wounds which heal even as we speak?'

Vayne watched his own crimson left gauntlet close and open, repeating the motion several times. It was his bionic arm, and feeling was slow in returning.

'I trained a lifetime in my own body. Now I fight in someone else's.'

'It is still your body.'

'Not yet. There is acclimatisation to come.'

'Then you will acclimatise. There is no more to say.'

'You don't see? This is not false pathos, Argo. I was perfect before, made in the Emperor's image in accordance with his ancient and most sacred designs.'

'You still are.'

'No. I am a simulacrum.' He clenched his augmetic hand into a numb fist. 'I am the best imitation we are capable of creating. I am no longer perfect.'

'Our brothers in the Iron Hands would dispute that diagnosis.'

Vayne scoffed. 'Those uninspired slaves of the Mechanicum? They make war at the pace of toothless old men.'

'If you resort to insults against our brother Chapters, I will lose my temper as well as my patience.'

'My point is that I am no Iron Hand. And I have no wish to be some half-flesh imitation Astartes.'

'You will acclimatise,' Argo stepped forward, taking Vayne's helm from the table and looking down at the white faceplate.

'Even so, until then I am a liability to my brothers.'

Argo handed his friend the helmet and shook his head. 'You are petulant beyond my comprehension. Only in death does duty end. We are the Fists. We are the shield-hand of Dorn. We do not weep and cower from battle because of pain or fear or worries of what might yet be. We fight and die because we were made to fight and die.'

Vayne took the helm and smiled without humour. Half of his face didn't follow the expression.

'What amuses you?'

'You are blind, Argo. You may preserve the soul of our Chapter, but I preserve its body. I harvest the gene-seed of the fallen, and I ensure the wounded will fight again. So listen to me, *brother*. I fear nothing but allowing my failures to harm my brethren. I am not at peak performance, and I am unused to the wounds I still wear under this armour. That is the source of my unbalance.'

'You lose your own argument. You fear to let down your brothers because your battle skills are hindered for a short while. Vayne, you are harming your brothers far more with your withdrawn attitude and the bitterness leaking from your every word. You are eroding their trust in you, and destroying their confidence.'

Argo's battle-collar pulsed a single blip. He tensed his neck, activating the pearl-like vox-bead attached to his throat, which picked up the vibrations of his vocal chords.

'Brother-Chaplain Argo. Speak.'

'Brother-Chaplain,' it was Lord General Ulviran. 'I have a request to ask you and your warriors.'

'I will be with you shortly,' Argo said, and killed the link. The silence between Argo and Vayne returned.

'Your point is taken,' Vayne conceded. 'I will not allow my melancholy to taint my squad any longer.'

'That is all I demand.' Argo was already turning to leave.

'I remember a time when you could not make such demands of me, Argo.'

'I remember a time when I did not need to make them.'

The Fists shed blood before the Guard's night-time advance. Under Ulviran's request, Argo and Demetrian led the squad into the shattered remains of the city's western sector.

In the minutes leading up to deployment, Argo had gathered the warriors together in the shadow of their Thunderhawk. Dozens of Guardsmen around the camp looked on, dallying about their business while they watched the Astartes soldiers perform their rite. The Fists ignored them all.

With his gladius, Argo sliced the palms of each warrior's left hand. They, in turn, pressed their bleeding hands against the chest piece of the Fist next to them.

Imrich rested his hand on the embossed silver eagle decorating Toma's breastplate. The Larraman cells in his blood scabbed and sealed the gash quickly, but not before his palm left a dark smear on Toma's Imperial symbol.

'My life for you,' Imrich said, then removed his hand and fastened his helm. Toma was next, pressing his bleeding hand against Vayne's breastplate.

'My life for you,' the Deathwatch veteran said, before donning his own helm. Vayne forced a smile. He had to perform the rite with his remaining flesh hand, his right instead of his left, and did so without complaint.

When it came to the Chaplain's turn, Argo rested his hand on Demetrian's armour, as tradition necessitated the officiating Chaplain to honour the ranking officer.

'My life for you,' Argo said. A moment later, his senses were submerged in the audiovisual chaos of his battle helm. On the eye lens displays, he saw the flickering readouts of the squad's vital signs, communication runes, lists of vox-channels, sight-altering lens options, thermo-conditional and local atmospheric readouts, and a cluster of information pertaining to the myriad functions of his armour.

All of the information added up to one thing.

'Ready,' he voxed to the others, blink-clicking most of the lens displays into transparency.

'Ready,' they voxed back. They'd started walking then, loping strides that emitted a chorus of mechanical growls from their armour joints.

The Guardsmen parted like a split sea as the Astartes neared them.

With blood on their Imperial eagles, the Crimson Fists went to war.

That had been three hours ago. The Fists took a Guard Chimera troop transport to the city limits, and were advancing through the western edge of Southspire. It was a scouting run, and progress was predicted – by Lord General Ulviran – to be fast. Intelligence had pinned enemy resistance in this section of the city to be minimal. Only at the city's centre was resistance expected to pick up.

Intelligence had been wrong about that.

Argo crouched in the ruins of what had once been an Administratum building, where hundreds of barely-educated wage slaves typed their lives away into cogitators that amassed Syral's exportation data. Pressed against a wall half tumbled down months ago from Imperial Basilisk shelling, the Chaplain waited unmoving, listening to the thrum of his power armour and the sounds of several foes breathing nearby.

Roaming bands of greenskins claimed this part of the city. Squad Demetrian had abandoned the Chimera long before, in favour of stalking through the ruins and clearing a path for the Guard's advance tonight.

Argo heard the xenos trampling closer, around the corner. They muttered to each other in their guttural, swinish tongue. The Chaplain tasted bile in his mouth. Their inhumanity repelled him.

He heard the bestial things pause in their lazy search, heard them snuffing at the air and grunting. They had his scent, he was sure of it, and his blood ran hot as he clenched his short combat sword in one hand, his bolter in the other.

At his hip hung his deactivated crozius arcanum, the symbolic weapon of his role in the Chapter. Capped by an eagle-shaped maul fashioned from blackened adamantium, it was a fearsome bludgeon when sheathed in its crackling power field. Argo's crozius had belonged to Ancient Amentus, one of the first Crimson Fist Chaplains; a founder of the Chapter from when the primarch divided the Imperial Fists Legion ten millennia before. Upon an arm-length haft of dark metal, the inscription *Traitor's Bane* was written in High Gothic.

He treasured the relic weapon, which still felt unfamiliar in his fists even after seven years. Against detritus such as these greenskins, his gladius was more than enough to suffice. He would not let the filthy blood of weakling xenos mar an honourable weapon dating back to the Great Crusade.

The first of the creatures, alert now, came around the corner. In its fists was a collection of scrap that evidently served the greenskin as a firearm. Argo surged to his feet, superhuman reflexes enhanced even further by his armour, and before the ork could utter a sound, it was falling backwards with the hilt of the Chaplain's gladius protruding from its eye socket.

Argo rounded the corner to meet the others head-on and his bolter barked, spitting detonating shells into green flesh. Eleven of them. Each hulking figure was momentarily outlined by a flicker of light in his helm's vision, cycling through target locks. But eleven was too many, even for an Astartes. In a flashing moment of anger, Argo cursed himself for not listening carefully to their breathing and trying to discern their numbers. It was his failing, he knew. He'd acted in rage, and now it was going to kill him.

The brutish creatures ran at him even as they took fire, massive fists gripping jagged axes that were pieced together from vehicle parts and industrial machinery. Argo's bolter cut down three orks as his targeting reticule flitted between weak points in the greenskins' piecemeal armour.

'You dare exist in mankind's galaxy!' Argo's bolter spat its last shell which destroyed an ork from the jaw up. He clamped the weapon to his thigh with its magnetic seal and threw his fist forward, shattering the forehead of the first greenskin to come in range. 'Die! Die knowing the Crimson Fists will cleanse the stars of your taint!'

Axes slashed towards him, which Argo weaved to avoid. A step back took him within reach of the first ork he'd felled, and he snatched up his gladius from the wretch's skull. Rivulets of dark blood slid along the silver blade, and the Astartes grinned behind his death's head mask.

'Come, alien filth. I am Argo, son of Rogal Dorn, and I am your death.'

The mob of orks ran in and Argo met them, the primarch's name on his lips.

'Break left.'

The voice crackled over the vox and Argo obeyed instantly, throwing himself into a roll that scattered a dust cloud in the ruins of the building. He came up, blade in hand, just as the speaker joined him in the fight.

The midday sun flashed from Toma's iron shoulder guard as he hammered the greenskins from behind. His bolter disgorged a stream of shells that exploded on impact in bursts of clear, hissing liquid. As he fired one-handed, he plunged his gladius into the throat of the closest greenskin, giving it a savage twist to half-sever the creature's head. Four of the orks fell back, the horrendously potent acid from Toma's prized bolt rounds overriding even the orkish resilience to pain as it ate through their flesh like holy fire.

All of this happened before Argo's two hearts had time to beat twice.

The last two orks leapt at the Fists to die in futility. Toma impaled the first through the chest, shattered its face with a brutal headbutt, and fired a single bolt at point-blank range into the alien's temple. The skull gave way in a shower of gore as the explosive shell performed its sacred function. Gobbets of flesh and bone hissed as they span away, eaten by the mutagenic acid in Toma's Inquisition-sanctioned ammunition.

Argo grappled with the second ork, his gauntlets wrapped around the thing's throat as it broke its thick nails scrabbling at his armour. He bore the howling greenskin to the ground, his weighty armour crushing the life from its chest as he strangled it in trembling fists.

'Die…'

The ork's answer was to roar voicelessly, its red eyes burning with rage. The Astartes grinned in mimicry of his helm and leaned close to the thing's face. His voice was a whisper through his vox-speakers.

'I *hate* you.'

Toma stood to the side, reloading his bolter and scanning the ruins for more foes. Argo's skulled face pressed against the choking ork's forehead. Orkish sweat left dark smears against his bone-cream faceplate.

'This is the Emperor's galaxy.' With a final surge of effort, he squeezed with all his strength. Vertebrae popped and cracked under the pressure. 'Mankind's galaxy. *Our* galaxy. Know that, as your worthless life ends.'

'Brother-Chaplain…' Toma said.

Argo barely heard. He let the creature fall dead and rose to his feet, savouring the taste of copper, bitter and hot, on his tongue. His rage had not killed him, after all. The enemy lay dead in great numbers.

'Brother-Chaplain,' Toma repeated.

'What?' Argo unclasped his bolter, reloading it now with the proper litany to the machine-spirit within.

There was a moment when Argo was sure Toma would say something; chide him for letting his fury get the better of him and lead him into reckless combat. Despite the break with tradition and authority, Argo would have accepted the criticism from a warrior like Toma.

Toma said nothing, but the silence passing between the two Astartes was laden with meaning.

'Report,' Argo said to break the quiet.

'Imrich and Vayne report their section is clear now. Brother-Sergeant Demetrian reports the same.'

'Resistance?'

'Vayne and Demetrian described it as savage.'

'And Imrich?'

'He described it as thrilling.'

Argo nodded. He was running low on ammunition, and knew the others must be as well.

'Prepare for a withdrawal.'

As Toma voxed Argo's orders to the others, the young Chaplain looked out across the ruined city. Small by Imperial standards – large settlements were rare on an agri-world – yet the focus of so much destruction.

On the other side of Southspire, the new warlord waited with the bulk of his horde. And in the heart of the city, the broken remains of the Cantorial Palace: the Fists' true goal, surrounded by foes.

Argo's blood boiled as he spat a curse behind his mask. He wanted to press on. The palace was no more than a handful of hours away, but resistance from the roaming warbands was intense. With another squad of Astartes, just five more men, he'd have taken the chance. But alone, it was suicide.

'What's that noise?' Toma said.

Argo levelled his bolter. He'd heard it, too. Drums. The music of primitives, echoing across the city like the pounding heartbeat of an angry god.

'It's a warning.'

The Imperial Guard advanced that night, and the weather turned bitter as if the heavens recognised the humans' intent.

Basilisks softened up the way ahead with relentless bombardments each hour. Ulviran was content to endure this halting advance, frequently cutting forward progress to establish another artillery barrage that took an age to set up. He pored over maps and holo-displays in his Baneblade's command room as Imperial guns pounded their own city into dust.

The big push consisted of the surviving elements of the Radimir Third Rifles, Seventh Irregulars and Ninth Armoured. These were the so-called 'Revenants', named for the many times Radimir had replaced entire regiments due to losses against the greenskins in Segmentum Tempestus. Rebirth at the precipice of extinction was a blessing familiar to the Crimson Fists, and the Chapter had fought well with the soldiers of Radimir countless times across the centuries.

Hundreds of Guardsmen clad in the gunmetal grey of the Radimir Revenants marched alongside rattling Sentinels in the vanguard of the assault, flanked by Leman Russ battle tanks in half a dozen variants. Radimir was close to being a forge world in terms of its armoured exports. No Revenant regiment ever went to war short of armour support.

The bulk of Ulviran's forces followed the vanguard: six thousand men including a detachment of storm troopers serving as his ceremonial guard, riding alongside his Baneblade in eight black-painted Chimeras.

At the rear of this main force came the artillery: Griffons and Basilisks, their punishing guns stowed and locked until the next time Ulviran brought the column to a halt and ordered them to set up a shelling storm kilometres ahead.

Last of all came the rearguard, made of the lord general's veteran Guard squads interspersed with auxiliary units, medical transports and supply trucks.

The Fists' Thunderhawk gunship remained back at the abandoned base camp at the city's edge, ready to be summoned. For a short while, until Argo scattered them, Squad Demetrian marched in the vanguard of the force, forming the vicious tip of the Imperium's conquering blade. In scything rain and howling winds, as the elements battered down upon the miserable Imperial advance, the war to retake Southspire began. The Fists soon bled away into the night, leaving Argo alone.

Major Dace, who had been present in the Baneblade's command room when Argo reported the Fists' scouting run, couldn't resist voxing the Chaplain now. Argo's suit insulated him from the noise of the rain slashing against his ceramite armour, and he tensed his throat to activate his vox-bead as it chimed.

'Brother-Chaplain Argo. Speak.'

'This is Major Dace of the Revenants.' Argo smiled as he heard the voice. The ritual processes that had moulded his body like clay, forming him into an Astartes, had given him a memory close to eidetic. It was known by most Imperial commanders who worked with Astartes that Space Marines possessed preternatural capacities for instant recollection.

'Have we met?' Argo asked with his half-smile in place. He didn't let his amusement leak into his voice. It had the desired effect; Dace's feathers were ruffled.

'I don't see your foretold resistance, Brother-Chaplain. All is quiet on the advance, is it not?'

'I can still hear the drums,' Argo noted. And he could, setting a distant rhythmic percussion to the thunder grinding across the sky.

'I can't,' Dace said.

'You are comfortably hidden in a tank, major.' Argo closed the link and added, 'And you are only human.'

The Fists had been killing greenskins their entire unnaturally long lives. Ulviran, no stranger to the orkish hordes himself, trusted Argo's belief that the drums pounded as a challenge to the Imperials. The new warlord, a curse upon his black heart, knew they were coming, and the drums of war beat to show he welcomed the coming bloodshed. The storm swallowed their noise now. Only the Astartes could make it out, and it was dimmed even to their senses.

'Ulviran to all units,' crackled the lord general's hourly message. 'Dig in for bombardment. Shelling to commence in thirty minutes.'

Argo bit back a curse. Too slow, much too slow. His thoughts were plagued by the Thunderhawk full of digging equipment back at the base.

'Brother-Chaplain?'

The communication rune that flashed on his reddish lens display was, thankfully, not Dace. Imrich's vital signs registered as almost a kilometre ahead.

'How goes the scouting, Brother Imrich?'

'Lord,' Imrich responded, speaking quietly and clearly. 'I've found the kine.'

'So have I, sir.' This was Vayne, a kilometre to the west.

'Contact,' voxed Demetrian. His readouts pinned him in the south.

Argo looked over his shoulder, at the procession of ocean-grey tanks with rain sluicing off their hulls.

'Numbers?' he asked them all over the squad's shared channel. The weather was banishing vox integrity, masking all the words in a haze of crackles and hisses.

'I count over a thousand, easily,' Vayne said. 'Perhaps two.'

'Same,' added Demetrian.

'I've got more. I've got lots more.' Imrich sounded overjoyed. But then, knowing Imrich, he probably was. 'Twice that number, I'm sure of it. If we hear from Toma,' Imrich added, 'we're in a world of trouble.'

The Deathwatch specialist had been sent to the south, stalking a good distance behind the rearguard.

The vox clicked live again. 'Brother-Chaplain, come in.' said Toma. The rest of his message was cut off by Imrich's delighted laughter.

With a cold feeling of metallic-tasting finality in his throat, Argo voxed the lord general.

Ulviran listened without hesitation. He ignored Dace's complaints and pulled the column into a still-advancing defensive spread that, admirably, took less than half an hour to form. No small feat for that many soldiers and vehicles. The organisational aspects of war were where Ulviran most prided himself. An orderly army was a victorious one. The faster orders were obeyed, the more men survived. It was a simple mathematic he liked, and had a talent for putting it into practice.

'The shelling,' Argo voxed to him, 'is doing nothing. The warlord has put significant force into the city against us, and the horde ahead is falling back to draw us in.'

Ulviran glared down at the hololithic display of the city projected onto the large table. His Baneblade rumbled as it rolled on.

'We're surrounded.'

'If we stop now, lord general, we will be. The pincers will close around us the moment we halt. If we push on at speed, we can make it to the Cantorial Palace and engage the forward elements before the rest of the noose can close around our throats.'

Ulviran liked that. Turn the ambush into an attack.

'Strike first, strike hard, and prepare to repel the rest of the attackers once the main force is crushed.' It sounded good. It sounded right. But…

'I am going purely on your word for this, Brother-Chaplain.'

'Good,' the Astartes replied, and ended the link.

'The Cantorial Palace?' voxed Demetrian.

'Yes. Squad, form up. We're taking the prize.'

The Cantorial Palace had been the seat of the planetary governor, and a masterpiece of gothic design; as skeletally, broodingly Imperial as would be expected.

All that remained was a series of shattered walls and a small mountain of rubble, where once battlements and ridged towers had risen around a central bastion. The previous greenskin warlord had claimed it as his lair, until the Crimson Fists had dissuaded him of the notion four months ago. Refuting his claim of ownership involved razing the building to the ground with infiltrating sappers, and even then, the gigantic xenos clad in its primitive power armour had survived to claw itself free from the smoking rubble.

Imrich had battled the warlord in the stone wreckage, finally taking its head after a long and bloody duel. He wore Warlord Golgorrad's skull on his bandolier, giving it pride of place on his chest.

The ork forces of this nameless new warlord evidently favoured the former site of battle. It was to be the anvil upon which the Imperial forces would be crushed by the flanking hordes.

Ulviran's army did not march sedately to a doom surrounded by foes. Time was of the essence, and the Revenants powered on to meet the larger force ahead. Men held to the side of speeding tanks and rode atop vehicle roofs. Within the hour, the Guard spilled with overwhelming force into the great plaza district where the Cantorial Palace's bones jutted from the ground.

The armoured fist of the Revenant advance crashed into the scattered greenskin lines. Rubble rained down as tanks unleashed the fury of their cannons, and a staccato chorus of heavy bolter fire filled the air between the thunder of main guns. Lacking entrenchments, the orks countercharged the armoured column, finding walls of Imperial Guard coming to meet them. Las-fire sliced across the night, illuminating the battlefield like some hellish pre-dawn in scarlet sunlight.

The rain lashed down on troopers in cold-weather gear as they fired in disciplined ranks, and the orks still came on in a roaring wave that drowned out the sound of thunder above.

Imperial records came to know this battle as the Night of the Axe, when the Radimir regiments on Syral were decimated by the hordes of xenos creatures they faced. Losses stood at forty-six per cent, utterly damning Lord General Ulviran's planned big push to face the new warlord that still lay in wait on the other side of the city. The Guard was bloody and beaten, and although thousands survived the assault, it was nowhere near enough to storm the warlord's position with any hope of success. The Radimir's one slim hope of survival on the kine-infested world – to strike the warlord down and cast the hordes into disarray – was gone. In turning the ambush into an attack of their own, the Guard had delayed their destruction but not avoided it.

However, for the purposes of the Crimson Fists, the Night of the Axe was neither the most critical juncture in the war for Syral, nor was it even recorded in their rolls of honour despite the harvest of lives reaped by Squad Demetrian of the Fifth Company.

The Fists, in true Astartes autonomy, had a sacred duty of their own to perform. This came to light the following morning, as the broken Guard made to move on from the scene of slaughter.

The sector was a mess of bloodshed and battle fallout. The corpses of thousands of orks and humans lay scattered over a square kilometre of annihilated urban terrain. The air thrummed with the growl of engines, frequently split by the cries of wounded men ringing out as they were tended by medics or died in agony, unfound among the charnel chaos that littered the ground.

Argo walked among the dead, gladius plunging down to end the lives of any greenskins that still drew breath. He listened to the general vox-channel as he performed his bloody work, making a mental note of casualties suffered by the Guard. He knew they were sure to be destroyed if they pressed on to face the warlord, just as surely as they'd be destroyed when the warlord's armies came hunting for them. He felt a moment of pity for the Guard. The Revenants were brave souls who'd always stood their ground in the face of the enemy. It was a shame to see them expire like this, in utter futility.

But the Fists would be long gone by then.

As he approached the edge of the colossal vista of rubble that made up the bones of the Cantorial Palace, he activated his vox and sent the signal he'd ached to send since his arrival. A single acknowledgement blip was the only answer he received, and the only answer he required.

Squad Demetrian stood a short distance from the lord general's Baneblade, honouring their wargear through daily prayer and muttered rituals. There they remained, ignoring the Guard all around, until thrusters shrieked in the sky above.

'What in the name of hell is that doing here?' Lord General Ulviran asked Major Dace as they looked up at the dark shape coming in to land with a howl of engines. The two officers left the cooling shadows of the command tank and approached the Astartes. Behind the warriors, throwing up a blizzard of dust, their Thunderhawk kissed the rubble-strewn ground and settled on its clawed stanchion feet.

'Are you leaving?' Ulviran demanded of Argo, aghast as he shouted above the cycling-down engines.

'No.'

'Then what–'

'Move aside, lord general,' the Chaplain said. 'We need room for our equipment. And if you would be so kind as to move your Baneblade, it would be appreciated.'

Dace, a short and rotund example of Radimir manhood, drew himself up to his unimpressive full height. 'We move out within the hour! You can't do... whatever it is you're doing.'

'Yes,' Argo said, 'I can.' His skullish helm glared down at the fat man. 'And if you try to stop me, I will kill you.'

To his credit, Dace did a fine job at appearing unmoved by the vox-growled threat.

'We have orders from Segmentum Command, and the Crimson Fists must abide by them.'

'That's an amusing fiction,' Argo smiled, knowing the humans couldn't see his expression. 'Feel free to entertain that fantasy as you get out of our way.'

Ulviran looked stricken, like he'd just taken a gut wound. He watched in mute sickness as servitors and robed serfs unloaded portable industrial equipment down the Thunderhawk's ramp.

'If you do not move aside,' Argo said with false patience in his voice, 'the Thunderhawk lander coming from orbit with more equipment will be forced to destroy your Baneblade to make room to land.'

'Equipment?' Dace was indignant. 'For what?'

It was Ulviran who answered. He'd seen the drills and clawed scoops on the machinery being unloaded.

'Digging...' The lord general's face was wrinkled in thought.

Argo favoured the officers with a bow. 'Yes. Digging. Now move aside, if you please.'

Defeated and confused, the two men backed away. Dace was red-faced and scowling, Ulviran subdued and voxing orders to make room for further Astartes landings.

When the Guard left just under an hour later, three Thunderhawks were nested in the ruins of the Cantorial Palace, each one freed of its cargo of servitors, serfs and machinery.

'They're heading west,' Imrich nodded towards the rolling Guard column.

'Then they'll die well,' the Chaplain snapped, and his hand cut through the air in a gesture to the work crews.

Drills ground into stone, scoops clawed piles of rubble aside, and the slaves of the Crimson Fists Chapter began to dig.

It took three days to make the first discovery.

By this time, the Guard was nearing the edge of Southspire, mere hours from their final encounter with the greenskin warlord. The Fists remained at the Cantorial Palace, silently admiring the Revenants' decision to die on the offensive, rather than retreat and die in their makeshift fort-camp.

Three days had passed since the Guard rolled out.

Three days of random sieges and petty assaults punctuating the sunlit hours and the long nights. Although the orks had been crushed in the area, wandering bands of savages still attacked the Crimson Fists' position. Each of the attempts made by the snorting, roaring mobs were met with torrents of heavy bolter fire from the grounded Thunderhawks and the seasoned killing prowess of Squad Demetrian as they maintained a perimeter vigil day and night, never resting, never sleeping.

On the evening of the third day, as the dull sun fell below the horizon, one of the serfs cried out. He'd found something, and the Astartes came running.

The first boy was dead.

His Scout's armour was largely intact, as was his body. Vayne was the one to lift the corpse from its rubble grave, treating it with all due honour as he laid it out on the ground by the first Thunderhawk. Argo came over once the examinations were complete to intone the Rite of Blessed Release. He knelt by the body, pressing his slit palm to the slain boy's forehead and leaving a smear of blood that mixed with the dirt on the child's dusty face.

'Novice Frael,' Vayne consulted his narthecium, tapping at the keypad as he examined the readout. 'Age thirteen, initial stages of implantation.'

'There's very little decay,' Argo observed in a soft voice.

'No. Blood and tissue samples indicate he died three or four days ago. My guess would be the day before we arrived.'

'Four months,' Argo whispered, looking back over the rubble. 'He was under there for *four months*, and we were three days too late. That…'

'What?' Vayne closed his narthecium and reset the data display. Surgical cutting tools snicked back into his bracer.

'That isn't… fair,' Argo finished. He knew how foolish the words sounded.

'If he'd been fully human,' Vayne said, 'he'd have died in the first two weeks. Thirst. Starvation. Trauma. It was a miracle his initial implantations even allowed him to survive this long. Almost sixteen weeks, Argo. That's worthy of the rolls of honour itself.'

They'd avoided discussing the odds up until now. It was a mission none of the squad expected to fulfil with anything approaching glory.

'Sixteen weeks.' Argo closed his eyes, though his helm stared at Vayne, its gaze unbroken.

'Even without the sus-an membrane,' Vayne was tapping keys on his narthecium bracer, 'our physiology will allow the slowing of the metabolism and the near-cessation of many bio-functions. It is still within the edge of prospective boundaries that an Astartes from the gene-seed of Rogal Dorn could survive the duration.'

Argo nodded. Full Astartes could survive, could *potentially* survive. That, however, wasn't the true issue. The Chaplain looked over his shoulder, where the corpse of the young novice lay.

'Kine,' snapped the vox. 'Kine at the south perimeter.'

Argo and Vayne were already running. 'That's penance for you, Imrich.'

'Yes, Brother-Chaplain. I'll do it right after we kill these whoreson aliens who've taken such umbrage at my trophies.'

* * *

The second body was discovered fifty metres away, two hours later. It was a dry husk, deep in waterless decay, and it took Vayne several minutes to identify the corpse as Novice Amadon, age fifteen, at the secondary stage of Astartes implantation.

'He's been dead for months,' Vayne said, without needing to point out the crushed ribcage and severed right leg. Scraps of Scout armour still clung to the dry fleshy remnants. 'He was killed when the palace fell.'

The Chaplain was conducting the funerary rite on Novice Amadon when the first survivor was found.

'Argo,' the vox crackled live with Vayne's excited voice. 'Blood of the primarch, Argo, come over here now.'

Argo clenched his teeth. 'A moment, please.' He pressed his cut palm to the ruined corpse's skull.

'Argo, *now*.'

The Chaplain forced his twin hearts to slow in their beat as he suppressed his eagerness and finished the rite. Such things were a matter of tradition. Such things mattered, and the dead must be respected for their sacrifice. After what seemed an age, he rose to his feet and moved over to where Vayne and Demetrian were helping the survivor from the rubble.

His targeting reticule outlined the figure in a flash, indicating a failed lock-on. A runic symbol flashed onto his retinas. Gene-seed failsafe. Target denied.

The figure was bone-thin, on shaking legs. Argo's lens display conceded to a passive lock on the emaciated wraith, and at first all he saw was the digital displays of low-pulsing life signs under the figure's name. He couldn't believe anyone, even an Astartes, could be that weak and still live.

The name registered at last, a moment before Vayne and Demetrian brought the figure close enough to recognise. Hollow-cheeked, sunken-eyed and looking more dead than alive, the older Astartes grinned when he saw Argo. The Chaplain didn't miss the resemblance between the survivor's wasted face and his own skull helm.

'Who have you found?' Imrich voxed, sounding annoyed to be missing the discovery.

Argo tried to speak but couldn't form the words. It was Vayne who answered.

'Nochlitan. We found Scout-sergeant Nochlitan.'

The skeletal figure, the sergeant responsible for training both Argo and Vayne in the same squad, kept grinning as he took in the hulking form of Argo's black battle armour.

'Hello, my boy,' Nochlitan said, and his voice was strong despite a scratchy edge and the veteran's shivering limbs. 'You took your damn time.'

'We... We didn't know...'

'I can see why they made you a Chaplain with oratory like that.' The sergeant paused to cough, a dry rasp of a sound that brought blood to his lips. 'Now stop standing around slack-jawed and save the rest of my boys.'

Three of them had survived. Three of the ten.

It was enough to justify the mission – far more than enough. A single Fist novice would have justified the risk. For four months they had survived in the rubble, and they each emerged as wasted husks, life-signs barely flickering on Vayne's narthecium. Nochlitan was the only one with the power of speech remaining to him. The two novices, in their ruined armour, were little more than tangles of withered limbs, barely breathing, drifting in and out of silent delirium.

The squad had been entombed since the Cantorial Palace had fallen. Nochlitan's Scout squad were embattled in the undercroft as the explosives ticked towards detonation, and had been unable to escape the blast area.

Seven dead. Three alive. A small but blessed victory, torn from the jaws of catastrophe.

As the servitors stored the digging equipment and the serfs readied the Thunderhawks for orbital flight, Argo sat with Nochlitan in the modest apothecarion. Vayne tended to the two novices, neither one older than sixteen.

'Dorn's holy hand,' Nochlitan said, fixing the Chaplain with his grey eyes. 'What happened to Vayne?'

'A daemon.'

'Is it dead?'

'Of course it's dead.'

'Yes, of course. You see that one there?' Nochlitan waved a weak hand in the direction of the stretcher next to him. 'That's Novice Zefaray.'

Zefaray wheezed into a rebreather mask that covered half of his face. Lines of angry tissue marked his temples and neck, where veins stood out like lightning streaks.

Argo watched the boy's laboured breathing. Zefaray was the Scout squad's Epistolary candidate, marked by the Chapter Librarium for the power of his psychic gift.

'He will be greatly honoured by Chapter Master Kantor for this,' the Chaplain said.

'Damn right he will. Almost killed him, you know. Day and night, screaming into the warp and hoping one of the Librarium would hear. We were trapped close to one another. He would whisper and mutter, speaking of how he was riding a hundred minds to reach one we could trust so many systems away.'

Argo didn't know what to say. It was a psychic feat of incredible strength. When one of the Chapter's Epistolaries had reported the weak yet crazed contact, it had been all the incentive the Chapter's highest echelons had needed. A recovery operation was mounted immediately.

'Great things ahead for him,' Nochlitan grinned. 'Did you find my bolter, boy?'

They hadn't. It showed on Argo's face.

'Ah, well.' Nochlitan lay back on the stretcher, plugged into an array of tubes and wires. 'I'll miss that weapon, without a doubt. It was a fine gun. A fine gun. I killed a genestealer patriarch genus with that bolter. Tore its head clean off.'

'We'll be taking off in a few minutes. The *Vigil* waits in orbit. Once aboard, we make haste to Rynn's World as soon as we break away from Syral.'

Nochlitan sat up again, trembling and overtaxing his remaining strength as his glare speared Argo's eyes.

'You told me the Radimir were still here. Still advancing on this new warlord.'

'They are. They'll engage the enemy's main force this afternoon, if initial projections were correct.'

'You'd abandon the Revenants? Boy, what's wrong with you?'

'Please don't call me "boy", sir. Chapter Master Kantor–'

'Pedro Kantor, blessings upon my old friend, isn't here, my boy. You are. And by Dorn's holy hand, you want to face the Emperor one day knowing you ran from this fight?'

'The odds are... beyond overwhelming. Everything we came to achieve would be void if we die in this battle.'

Nochlitan grasped at Argo's bracer, clenching the smooth black ceramite in a thin-fingered claw that shook as if palsied.

'You are the future of this Chapter.' His grey eyes were the colour of summer storms. 'You shape the path these novices will one day walk.'

Argo rose to his feet, letting his mentor's hand slip from his arm, and left the room without a word.

The Thunderhawk screamed across the night sky, its downward thrusters kicking in as it hovered four hundred metres high. Its wing-mounted bolters aimed at the ground, barking in an unremitting stream. The servitors slaved to the weapons didn't even need to aim. They couldn't miss the horde below: a sea of green skin and chattering weapons, ringing a diminished cluster of grey.

The Revenants' last stand.

The guns cut out after a minute, autoloaders cycling but not opening fire again. On the ground, the armoured divisions of the Radimir kept up their onslaught against the ork host in the city's ruins, and Ulviran watched the Crimson Fist gunship as it stayed aloft, out of enemy fire range.

'It's the Fists,' Dace said, and Ulviran smiled to himself at the man's painfully obvious statement. *Good old Dace. No better man to die with.*

'We did well, Dace. Almost reached that bastard warlord, eh?'

'We did fine, sir.' The major was still looking up at the sky, ignoring the war hammering around him.

'So what are the Fists doing, exactly?' the lord general asked. 'My eyes aren't what they once were.'

'They're...'

Argo's lens displays registered the altitude as he fell. The ground soared up fast in his red-tinted vision, and he clutched his sword and bolter tightly, blink-clicking the propulsion icon at the edge of his sight. The weighty jump pack on his back fired in a roaring kick, slowing his descent, but he still landed with jarring force ahead of the others.

He hit the ground running and his weapons sang. Left and right, he slashed his gladius into flesh and fired a relentless stream from his bolter, clearing a space around him in the thick of the churning orkish tide.

Toma was next, thudding to the ground and repeating Argo's lethal sprint. Then Demetrian, then Vayne. Imrich was last, much to his gall. The others, whirling and killing, heard his curses as they started without him.

Twenty metres ahead of them through the ocean of writhing orkish flesh, unmistakeable in salvaged armour that swelled his form to the size of an Astartes Dreadnought, was the greenskin warlord.

Imrich landed and opened up his bolter, running for the brute.

'He's mine!' he voxed to the others. 'That skull is mine!'

In two gauntleted fists, one red, one black, the ancient weapon *Traitor's Bane* was wreathed in coruscating waves of sparking force. The relic mace smashed aside three orks in a single swing, sending their broken forms to the ground still twitching with energy.

'No.' Argo stopped screaming the Litanies of Hate, drawing breath to reply to Imrich and the squad behind him.

'The kine lord is *mine.*'

KRAKEN

Chris Wraight

He wore their names on his armour. The words had been graven deeply; a parting gift from the Iron Priest before he'd left Fenris. Nearly a centimetre deep, now crusted with the filth of years, just like the rest of him.

Eight names: four on the right side of his dented breastplate, four on the left. One was barely legible, scraped away by some massive, crunching impact a long time ago. The others were all faded, or obscured by burn marks, or bisected with scratches.

He remembered them all anyway. They came to him when he slept, whispering to him in old voices. He saw their faces, looming up out of the dark well of memory, their flesh still marked by tattoos, scars and studs. Sometimes they were angry, sometimes mournful. Their purpose in appearing, so he'd realised, was always the same: to urge him on, to stir him into action.

And so he never rested, not truly. He respected the demands of his vocation and kept moving. Oaths had been sworn, and they bound him more tightly than bands of adamantium. One world after another, blurring into a morass of sense impressions; some cold, some hot, all struggling, all playing their tiny part in the galaxy-wide war that had long since ceased to have boundaries.

It would have been easy to lose his sense of significance in all of that. It would have been easy, after twenty years of it, to give in to the darkness that lurked behind his eyes and forget the faces. He'd seen it happen to mortals. Their mouths drooped, their eyes went dull, even as they still clutched their weapons and made a show of walking toward the enemy.

Then, as sure as ice follows fire, they died.

That was why he had the names put on his armour. The carvings would continue to fade or sustain damage, but some mark would always be there, some small impression to register what had once been lives as vital as his life.

And as long as there were marks to remind him, he would not slope off into despair. He would keep moving, seeking the final trial that would restore lost honour and still the whispers in the dark.

One world after another, blurring into a morass of sense impressions; some cold, some hot. None that made much of an impression on his sullen mind; since their wars gave no opportunity to achieve the goal he craved.

None, that was, until the last of them.

None of those worlds made an impression on Aj Kvara until, following the eddies of fate, he came to Lyses, and the raw beauty of it stirred even his old, cold soul.

Morren Oen shaded his eyes against the morning glare, squinting as the green light flashed from the waves. Fifty metres below him, the downdraft of the flyer's four rotors churned the water.

There shouldn't even have been water down there. There should have been several thousand tons of dirt-grey plasteel, designation Megaera VI, humming with life and machinery. There should have been lights blinking along the smoothly curved tidewalls to beckon the flyer down to land, and the low grind of algal processors working their way through the endless harvest.

Instead there was a thin skin of floating debris bobbing on the emerald water. He saw a plastic hopper tumble by, rolling amid a web of tangled fibres. Below the surface, there were dark shadows, perhaps the outlines the struts and flotation booms, still half-operative even after the main structure had gone down.

'Emperor,' he swore, sweeping the scene of devastation for something, some sign of resistance or survival.

Four other flyers hung low over the water, each one full of men with lasguns. They pointed their barrels uselessly down at the debris. Whatever had happened to Megaera VI had moved on long before they got there.

Preja Eim leaned a long way over the edge of the flyer's open-sided crew bay and took a few more picts. Her auburn hair fluttered in the warm breeze, catching on the upturned collar of her uniform.

'Have enough yet?' asked Oen, turning away from the view and leaning back against the juddering metal of his seat-back.

Eim carried on clicking.

'Information,' she said, her face screwed up in concentration. 'There might be something. Some clue.'

Oen looked at her wearily. She was so young. Her freckled skin looked healthy in the sun, almost translucent. Perhaps, once, he'd been as enthusiastic in his work.

For the first time since joining up, he felt too old. Forty years of service on Lyses, rising steadily through the ranks, had taken its toll. Rejuve was expensive, and he had other commitments that prevented him splashing out. And so he felt the skin of his jawline sag a little and his stomach bulge out over his heavy old regimental belt. Watching Eim made him feel worse. It reminded him of what he had been, and how long ago that was.

'Snap away,' he said. 'Don't think you'll get anything we haven't already scanned for.'

He looked out aimlessly, keeping his hand over his eyes. The curve of the ocean ran unbroken across the horizon, deep green and smooth. The pale rose sky shimmered above it, warmed by the diffuse light of both suns.

Oen was used to the view of open seas. All of Lyses was open seas. All of it, that was, except for the floating hubs, strewn across the endless ocean like motes of dust, separated by thousands of kilometres and gently drifting.

And they were being picked off, one by one. That thought, when he chose to entertain it, was quite thrillingly disquieting.

'Procurator,' came a voice over his earpiece.

'Go ahead,' said Oen, welcoming the distraction. Whatever news there was, it was unlikely to make him feel worse.

'Grid Nine have a comm-signal. Ship entering the orbital exclusion zone. The hails all check out, but they thought you ought to know.'

'Nice of them. Why, especially?'

'It's not in-system, nor Navy. They think it might be Adeptus Astartes, but they're not sure.'

At the mention of the magic triplet of syllables, *as-tar-tes*, Oen felt his heart miss a beat. He didn't know whether that was born of fear or excitement. Probably a bit of both.

'They're not sure? What are they not sure about?'

'Perhaps you'd better get back to Nyx, procurator. They're not going to try to stop it, and by the time you get back it'll be in geostat.'

'Fine. Keep them quiet until I get there. We're just about done here.'

The link broke. By then Eim had stopped taking picts and was looking intently at the wreckage.

'No signs of explosions,' she murmured, watching the pieces float by. 'It's like some giant hand just... pulled it apart.'

'Did you hear all that?' asked Oen, ignoring her. 'We're going back in. You can take another flyer out here if you want to keep at it.'

Eim looked at him, and her freckled face was wide-eyed. There was a strangely childlike look of desolation in them.

'What's doing this, procurator? Why can't we stop it?'

'If I knew that, do you not think I'd have ordered something more potent than overflights?' He smiled, trying to be reassuring, and knowing he'd probably failed. 'Listen, the distress signals have been picked up. Trust in grace, Eim. There's probably a whole company of Space Marines lining up on Nyx as we speak, and, believe me, there's no more impressive sight in the Emperor's own galaxy.'

He slumped in the chair in the reception chamber, leaning both hands on the only table, smelling like old meat. His scraggly beard spilled over the breastplate of his enormous armour, snarled and tangled. Grey streaks shot through it, making him look like an old, sick man.

Do they get old? thought Oen, observing him through the one-way plexiglass viewport in the corridor outside. *Would they die of age, if given long enough?*

Accounts of the newcomer's landing from atmospheric control had been garbled. One transmission implied that the newcomer had blasted his way through the upper defensive cordon without warning, while another, from a low-order servitor-controlled station, indicated nothing but impeccable orbital manners.

One way or another, though, he'd gotten through, and his ship, now standing five hundred metres up on the landing stages, was like nothing Oen had ever seen – dirty, angular, covered in plasma burns and with a blocky aquila picked out in bronze on the sloping nose. It didn't look big enough for inter-system travel, though it must have been, since its occupant certainly wasn't from Lyses.

From the look of it the ship's crew was entirely composed of servitors. They were strange looking creatures, with clunking servos and spikes and animal bones hanging from their pearl-white flesh. They'd stayed on board the ship after the pilot had stomped down the landing ramp, which Oen couldn't be too sorry about. Not that the pilot was any less strange.

'I thought you said...' began Eim, gazing through the viewer, fascinated. Her query trailed off.

Oen knew what she meant.

'I've been told they vary,' he said, rather stiffly. 'The only picts I saw were from a rogue trader who'd run a squadron out through Ultramar. Those ones were... different.'

Eim nodded slowly, running her eyes over the bulky figure sitting at the metal desk on the other side of the viewport.

His head was bare and bald. A knotwork tattoo ran across the tanned flesh from behind one ear, over the skull and down toward one eye. His face seemed to have several metal studs in it, each one a slightly different shape. His armour was pale grey, like dirty snow, and had carvings all over it. The lettering wasn't standard Gothic – it was angular and close-typed, covered in marks and bisected with slashes like those made by animal claws.

Oen had imagined the armour of a Space Marine to be clean, polished and flawless, just like the ones in the devotional holos sent out by the Ecclesiarchy's Office of Truth Distribution. He'd imagined bronze shoulder-guards and bright cobalt breastplates glimmering under the white lumens.

He hadn't imagined the mess, and the dirt. He certainly hadn't imagined the smell.

'Finished gawping?'

Both Oen and Eim jumped. He'd spoken. The words were thickly accented, as if Low Gothic were a foreign language, and muffled by the dividing wall. He hadn't looked up. His strange yellow eyes remained fixed on his loosely clasped hands.

Oen readied himself, shot Eim a reassuring glance, and went round the corner to open the door. As he entered the room, the newcomer looked up at him.

'I'm sorry, lord,' said Oen, bowing before taking a seat opposite. 'Standard observational procedure. We have to be careful.'

The newcomer, massive in his armour, gazed at him with a profoundly disinterested expression on his savage face. He didn't smile. His scarred and tattooed features looked almost incapable of smiling.

'A pointless gesture,' he said quietly. 'If I'd wanted to kill you, you'd be dead already. But since you've started, observe away.'

Oen swallowed. The newcomer's voice was worryingly deep, underlined with a permanent, breathy growl and made eerie by the unusual pronunciation.

'Do you have, er, a designation? Something I can use for the reports?'

'A designation?'

'A title, lord. Something I can–'

The huge figure leaned back, and Oen could see the metal chair flex under the huge strain.

'I am a Space Wolf, Procurator Morren Oen,' he said. As he spoke, Oen caught sight of long, yellow fangs flashing out from behind the hairy lips. 'Have you heard of us?'

Oen shook his head meekly. He felt his heart beating a little too quickly. Something about the man in front of him made it very hard to retain composure.

Except he wasn't a *man*. Not like Oen was a man, anyway.

'Good,' said the newcomer. 'Probably for the best.'

Oen cleared his throat, trying to remain something close to professional.

'And your name, lord?'

'My name is Kvara.'

Oen nodded. He was aware he was gesturing too much, but he couldn't stop it.

'I'd expected... more of you.'

That had come out wrong. Kvara looked at him with amusement. His eyes were circles of gold. Animal's eyes, lodged in a lined, worn and battered face.

'You do not need more of us. One of us is more than enough.'

Oen nodded again.

'Quite so,' he said, casting around for something more intelligent to say.

Kvara stepped in then, tiring of Oen's stammering enquiries.

'The data in your sending was clear,' he said. As he spoke, he lifted a gauntlet and flexed the fingers of it absently. Oen stared at it, distracted by the casual, supple movement. 'You've lost five of your harvester stations in five local months. No survivors, no readings. Nothing but debris. Something is coming out of the water. A beast.'

Kvara let his gauntlet fall to the tabletop with a dull clang.

'I have hunted beasts before.'

'We've men assigned to this already,' Oen said. 'I'd hoped that–'

'That I might join them?' Kvara shook his head. 'No. Tell your men to stand down. In this, as in everything, I work alone.'

Oen looked up into the golden eyes, and thought about protesting. Perhaps this... *Space Wolf* didn't know how big a hub harvester was. Anything that could take down one of those things must be massive, far bigger than the flyer he'd returned to Nyx in. The security detail he'd had on alert for three months consisted of nine hundred men, and he'd been considering expanding it.

'I'm not sure–'

'You're not sure I can handle whatever it is you've got attacking your people,' said Kvara. 'You're not sure something looking as dishevelled and terrible as me could do much more than get himself killed.'

He leaned forward, and the metal of the table bowed under the pressure of his forearms. Oen recoiled, feeling the hot meat-breath wash over him.

'This is not about you, Morren Oen,' whispered Kvara, taking a cold pleasure in running his tongue around the words. 'This has nothing to do with you.'

Oen tried to hold the gaze from those animal eyes, and failed. He looked down at the rivets on the table, ashamed of himself.

'I need a flyer,' said Kvara, sitting back. 'Fastest you have. Then you can forget about me, and forget about your problem.'

Oen nodded for a third time. Being in the presence of Kvara was intensely tiring. He found himself happy to do almost anything to get the encounter over with.

'It will be done, lord,' he said, knowing that, whatever he'd expected to get out of that first meeting, he'd failed badly. 'I'll get straight on it.'

* * *

Eim looked sympathetic as Oen emerged from the room. She placed a hand lightly on his shoulder.

'How'd it go?'

Oen shrugged and smiled wryly.

'Not what I expected,' he said, shaking off the hand and walking down the corridor. He went quickly, keen to be out of there. 'Though I don't really know what I thought would happen.'

Eim trotted after him, looking up anxiously.

'How many of them have come?'

'Just him.'

'You're joking.'

'No.'

Eim snorted.

'I'll get the 'paths sending again.'

'That may not be necessary.'

'Of course it'll be necessary,' said Eim, scowling. 'We need men. There must be Guard somewhere within range – they'd send a whole company soon enough if they thought tithe production was about to fall.'

Oen halted, looking thoughtful. Now that he was out of Kvara's intimidating presence, he was beginning to think more clearly.

'He doesn't think he needs help.'

'That's his problem. I mean, did you *see* what he looked like?'

'Right up close,' said Oen, ruefully. 'It wasn't pretty.'

Eim shook her head irritably.

'*One!*' she snorted. 'I didn't think they ever worked on their own. I thought they came in squads – you know, like you see on the holos.'

Oen shrugged.

'So did I,' he said. 'Maybe different types have different ways. He's a Space Wolf. Heard of them?'

Eim shook her head.

'Nice name,' she said. 'Suits his looks.'

'Careful what you say,' warned Oen, looking over his shoulder and back down the corridor. 'His hearing's very good.'

'Okay, okay.' Eim sighed, and ran a weary hand through her hair. 'But, procurator, this is the last thing we needed. We lose another hub, and we'll miss the next quota even if I keep the crews on triple rotation. For a minute there I was daring to hope we'd find a way out of this.'

This time it was Oen who put a reassuring hand on her shoulder.

'You never know,' he said. 'He may be more impressive than he looks.'

He leaned closer to her, and lowered his voice.

'He's taking a flyer out, soon as I can requisition one,' he said, covering his mouth. 'And, whatever he says, I want it tracked and a team placed ready for rapid deployment, just in case he finds anything. Can you do that?'

Eim shot him a tolerant, affectionate look.

'Sure I can,' she said. 'Just in case.'

The flyer skimmed low over the ocean, casting a deep green shadow on the waves. Kvara drove it hard, irritated by the lack of the explosive speed he was used to. One engine was already burning close to capacity, and the dashboard in front of him was active with red warning runes.

Kvara ignored them and concentrated on the view from the cockpit. Lyses stretched away in every direction, formless and empty, a wasteland of pure water and pure sky. The first sun was up, and the arc of the atmosphere was bleached salmon pink. The ocean was calm, veined with lines of white where the massive swells rolled under him.

It was pristine. In an Imperium where the hand of man fell heavily on everything it touched, Lyses was a rare jewel. In its inviolability it reminded Kvara of Fenris. On the death world, everything below the Asaheim parallel was barely touched by humanity. Lyses was more benign, but had the same vast, untouched quality.

Despite everything, that spoke to his soul. It had been a long time since anything had done that, and he found the experience, on the whole, uncomfortable.

There is one objective left, one mission, one task. Remember it.

He pushed the flyer down further, skimming it barely a man's height above the waves. Spray flashed down the sleek flanks of the machine, spinning and frothing as he banked around in a long arc. Then he powered it up, sweeping along the trajectory the procurator had given him. For a moment, just a moment, he could have been back on a *drekkar*, relishing the steep pitch and yaw of the heavy wooden hull as it ploughed through the endlessly violent seas of his home.

But Lyses was too beautiful for that. Too beautiful, and too forgiving.

Below him, the algal blooms began to intensify. Deep green and cloudy, they hung just below the surface, bathed by the light of the sun. They extended for hundreds of kilometres, a vast mat of nutrient-rich matter, stuffed with proteins.

It was for them that mankind had come to Lyses, to suck up the endless stream of life-giving algae, to process it into foodstuffs ready to be transported off-world to the famished hives and forges elsewhere in the sector. Hub harvesters, mobile floating industrial behemoths, prowled the waters endlessly, slowly ploughing furrows through the infinite bounty, dragging it up and packing it into billions upon billions of dried and pressed pellets ready for transport to gigantic processing manufactoria on other planets.

According to the records Kvara had accessed in Nyx, Lyses hadn't had a serious security incident for over five hundred years. The harvesters had just kept on going, criss-crossing the ocean, working the algae and scooping it into their maw-like hoppers, as if it would go on forever.

But nothing lasted forever – everything decayed, everything was tainted.

Kvara allowed himself a grunt of cynical satisfaction. A world without strife was an affront to his battle-hardened sensibilities. All that could exist in such a place was softness, and softness opened the door to corruption.

The blooms grew ever thicker as the flyer sped on. The green darkened, forming a solid mass under the waves. If things had been working properly, he guessed, it would never have been left to become so overgrown.

A green rune blinked on the forward scanner. Kvara sat back in the pilot's seat, cramped in his bulky armour, and watched the ruin of the hub approach. He came in low, observing the way the broken struts still speared up from the waves.

The harvester had been massive. Wreckage littered the surface for a square kilometre or more, floating on the gentle swell or lodged in thick knots of algae. Kvara applied the air brakes, swivelling the engines forward to arrest his speed and achieve a low hover. He flicked a dial on the dashboard, and the bubble-cockpit slid back.

Warm, softly fragranced air rolled over him. The smell of the algae was rich and faintly sweet. Kvara hauled himself out of the seat and leaned over the side. His weight caused the flyer to tip violently and the engines whined as they compensated.

He narrowed his eyes, poring over the debris. No burn marks or signs of explosions marked the surfaces. Where the plasteel was broken, it looked like it had been snapped cleanly. Other pieces had the jagged evidence of claw-rakes on them.

Kvara studied each piece carefully, spending time observing the angle of the impacts, the force used, the frequency of them.

Is it worthy? Is it enough?

Early signs were promising. He felt a tremor of excitement in his hearts, and swiftly suppressed it. There had been too many disappointments for him to start thinking along those lines.

Keeping the cockpit-bubble open, Kvara sat back in the pilot's seat and started a slow circle of the wreckage. As he did so, he abstracted his mind from the particular, and drifted into the general.

There were huge channels gouged through the algae blooms, marking the passage of something truly massive. Though there were several of them, Kvara had the sense that only one beast had made them.

Prey.

He closed his eyes, just as he would have done on Fenris where the spirits of hunter and hunted intertwined closely, haunting the high mountain airs and staining the unbroken snow.

I see you. I see your path. I will follow it, and then comes the test.

He saw the trail of the beast in his mind, just as if it were a herd of *konungur*, twisting away into possible futures. He saw it plunge down into the frigid depths, as dark as the void of space, writhing along the jagged ocean floor.

He opened his eyes. Below him, a wide furrow in the algal carpet stretched off into the distance, jagging back and forth.

I see you.

Kvara nudged the flyer after it, following the trail. As he did during every hunt, he put himself in the mind of his prey, imagining the mental processes of the beast and the strange, sluggish thoughts in that giant mind. He had learned to do it with such acuity that, for a moment at least, he might have been one himself.

As he travelled, his certainty grew. He powered the flyer back into full propulsion.

Kvara sat back, eyes half-closed, the warm wind racing past him. He let his instincts play loose, running down the prey, chasing after it as if a physical scent had lodged in his nostrils.

It was the same then as it had always been. For a moment, the hunt took over, the quest became everything.

In simpler, harsher times, that was all there had been.

In the past that was now faded and hard to recall, he had lived for nothing else.

I see you.

The *drekkar* took a heavy hit and buckled over to starboard. It rolled across the heavy, gun-grey sea, lashed by the torrential rain. The deluge lanced down from the low cloud line, spears of liquid that bounced and rattled from the deck.

Everything moved. Waves crashed against the high flanks and cascaded down the deck, as cold as mountain-ice and hard as bullwhips. The masts screamed against the rigging, taut with ice crystals and shivering.

'I see you!' roared Thenge, bounding up to the prow with his long, white pelt in tow.

Olekk and Regg followed him, clasping tight to the railing, their boots slipping on the sodden deck-boards. Each one of them carried a long spear in their hands, crowned with a biting edge ground out of the iron by the priests.

Lighting flickered across the northern sky, followed by the crack, roll and boom of thunder.

Fenrys was angry, just as ever, and the seas boiled with that anger.

Aj Kvara hung from the high foremast by one hand, swaying far out over the water as the ship tilted and tipped. He hadn't seen anything but the driving rain and riot of moving water.

He swore to himself, and hurried down the rigging. If Thenge had seen something from the prow, then his eyes had been the keener. That was bad. Kvara's youth was supposed to be his advantage.

Then, before he was halfway to the deck, the sea off to port boiled up in a mass of bubbles and lashing, slapping fronds.

'Here it comes!' yelled Rakki, his voice high with excitement. From somewhere else in the longship, furious laughter broke out. Kvara dropped to the deck, grabbed a spear and raced to the side.

Ahead of them, breaking the surface a dozen fathoms off, something vast and black slipped above the turmoil of the waves before sloping back down again. Kvara saw a glossy shell, pock-marked with barnacles, rolling away from the pursuing hunters and diving smoothly. A geyser of water puffed up as the beast exhaled and drew in more air.

'*Hvaluri*!' roared Olekk, laughing like the others.

Kvara felt excitement spur up within him, and he leaned further over, craning for another glimpse. The *drekkar* carried over thirty warriors. Taking a *hvaluri* would feed them and their families for weeks, as well as providing much else of value to the tribe.

'Faster!' Kvara shouted, up at old Rakki who was master of the ship.

The big man, one-eyed and scar-faced, glared back at him from the tiller.

'You hunt!' he blurted, outraged. 'I sail!'

The creature broke the surface again, closer that time, sweeping up through the choppy water and letting out a muffled bellow of anger.

Maggr was still up in the rigging, and was first to throw. His spear shot down through the rain, spinning on its axis. It hit hard, burying the jagged iron blade deep into the *hvaluri*'s armoured hide. The beast roared and went down again.

'*Hjolda*!' Maggr bellowed, balling his fists and sending his face red with fervour.

Other spears shot down, missing the target and splashing into the walls of moving water.

Kvara bided his time, waiting for the *hvaluri* to surface again. The ship slipped steeply down a precipitous leading wave, wallowing at the base of it before climbing up the next one. The deck rolled and swung like a berserker's axe-lunge, testing the warriors' precarious footing. They braced themselves against the ropes, edging closer to the tilting side of the ship, peering into the storm-lashed murk for a glimpse of the prey they hunted.

'Round left!' bellowed Thenge, getting frustrated and reaching for a second throwing spear.

The *drekkar* shivered as its prow came across, buffeted by the crashing seas. The skinsails, those hadn't been furled against the storm, stretched out taut, making the ship race through the spray like a loosed crossbow bolt.

'I have it!' crowed Olekk, leaping up on to the sharply pitching rail and taking aim.

Something long and sinuous flashed out of the water, lashing across at Olekk with spiked barbs and dragging him over.

There was no scream. He was gone in an instant, pulled down into the icy depths from which no living man ever returned.

Kvara ran across the deck, springing up to where Olekk had been standing. He had a brief glimpse of black tentacles thrashing in the water, covering a foaming patch of dark red before that was swept astern by the racing sea.

He hurled his spear down, but the edge of the ship bucked wildly, sending his aim wide.

'Skítja,' he swore, jumping down and reaching for another spear.

Then the *drekkar* shuddered heavily, as if something vast had hit it from below. Thenge lost his footing and sprawled across the deck like a drunkard. The whole ship shot up, briefly thrown clear of the waves, before crashing back down again, snapping whole lengths of rigging and making the loose ropes flail like scourges.

Maggr jumped from the broken ropes, still flushed from his success, and barrelled up to the prow, leaping over the grappling form of Thenge.

'Ha!' he crowed, grabbing two throwing spears and taking the lead warrior's place.

Kvara chuckled at the presumption of it, leaping away from the rolling edge and grabbing a fresh spear of his own.

Everyone was still laughing and roaring – the ragged, caustic laugh of hunters gripped by the manic touch of the kill-urge. The whole ship was febrile with it, spilling over with savage, raw energy.

'I *want* this kill,' spat Kvara. His blond hair had come loose of its plaits, and lashed round his clean, ruddy face in the wind. He grinned as he spoke, and his white teeth flashed in the storm.

'Then throw quicker, lad,' said Maggr, taking up a spearing position and scouring the churning waves.

It came up again then, huge and glistening. Kvara saw a single eye the size of his chest, as round as the moon and grey like an oyster. It glared at them, burning with bestial hatred and fury.

He didn't hesitate. Fast as a whip-snap, Kvara hurled the spear. It whistled through the air, striking straight through the heart of the eye. The shaft trembled, and it lodged fast.

The *hvaluri* bellowed, its roars making the water drum and vibrate, before rolling heavily away from the boat.

'It won't go down!' shouted Thenge, back on his feet and braced for another throw. 'Not now!'

Kvara raced to fetch another spear. His heart was thumping with glorious, brutal energy. Every muscle ached, every sinew was taut, but his heart sang.

I speared the eye! I did it!

The creature reared up, thundering out of the boiling sea, throwing water across its hunched, gnarled back in huge tumbling sheets.

'Morkai!' swore Regg, hurling a spear at it and somehow managing to miss.

The beast was massive, at least the size of the *drekkar* and much, much heavier. It thrashed around in a wallow of agony, the spears still protruding from its body. A huge shell of barnacle-crusted blackness rolled around, crowned with spines and bone-ridges. A mass of tentacles flashed out from under the skirts of the shell, twisting and writhing like a nest of prehensile tongues. Spray shot out, splattering against the masts and cascading down on to the warriors.

'Too close!' warned Rakki, heaving on the tiller.

The ship came round, but not quickly enough. Tentacles shot out, latching on to the railings and dragging the *drekkar* back. It tilted heavily, listing over nearly to the tipping point.

Thenge lost his footing again, raging and cursing as he slipped down the steepling deck. A tentacle spun out, clamping on to his ankle and gripping tight. He grabbed his axe from his belt and hacked down, severing it cleanly and freeing himself.

Other warriors charged, hurling their spears at the exposed underbelly of the beast. Some of the blades bit deep, disappearing into the forest of thrashing members, provoking fresh roars of pain. The sea frothed with a thick black sludge as the monster began to bleed. Some of it splashed out across Kvara's face, hot and salty.

'It'll drag us down!' shouted Rakki, toiling uselessly at the tiller.

More tentacles latched on to the ship, some reaching all the way across to the far side. The *drekkar* listed further, and water began to lap across the lower edge of the deck, washing up across the already drenched planks.

Thenge raced over to the nearest tendril, hacking away with his axe. He cut through it sharply, but two more fronds quickly whipped across. All across the ship, warriors swapped their throwing spears for short-handled axes and began chopping frantically at the strangling lengths of tentacle. Even as they worked, the ship slipped further down, dragged through the mountainous swell by the wounded beast.

Kvara drew his throwing arm back, only to feel a viscous, slimy wall of flesh hit him full in the face. He crashed back heavily, cracking his head on something unyielding on the way down. He had the blurred impression of a black tube the width of his arm snaking across his field of vision and falling over him. A hot wash of pain ran through his skull, and he felt blood running down the back of his neck.

Acting on instinct, he swept up his spear, still grasped in his right hand, shoving the blade of it up through the tentacle. It carved through sweetly, separating it into two pieces. The broken-off end continued to writhe on its own, jerking and spasming across the sodden wood.

Kvara staggered to his feet. The ship was going down. Waves rushed up the tilted deck, flooding into the hold below. For every tentacle the warriors slashed apart, more shot out, wrapping the *drekkar* in a morass of dripping, slippery tendrils.

'*Hjolda!*' he roared, grabbing his axe from his belt and throwing his arms back in challenge.

The beast loomed up at him, sweeping up out of the waves and roaring its own booming call of anger.

Kvara sprinted down the listing deck, leaping over the bodies of the fallen and veering past the flickering ends of searching tentacles, ignoring the hammering pain in his head. He ran straight at the huge domed shell, hacking away the snaking tubes of meat as they swept into his path.

It felt like he was running down a cliff-edge, straight into the depths of the bottomless ocean. He could see the bulk of the *hvaluri* below him, wallowing in a messy broth of broken spars and bloody water.

He leapt, flying away from the ship and through the air, plummeting for a moment, his long hair streaming behind him and his axe held high.

Then he landed, crunching on to the shell of the beast, feeling the hard surface flex from the impact.

He nearly skidded straight across it and over the far side, but managed to clutch at a bone-ridge with his trailing hand. He yanked to a halt, nearly blinded with spray and buffeted by the gusting wind.

The creature let out a deafening roar and hauled itself further out of the boiling sea. Tentacles shot up, trailing across its shell, reaching out to rip him from its back and hurl him into the water.

Kvara pulled himself to his knees, balancing precariously on the bucking, rolling curve, hacking at any tentacles that reached him. Blood still ran from his head wound, making him dizzy. Through the clouds of spray, he could just make out the *drekkar* rolling away, righting itself as the hold of the tentacles was released.

Kvara batted away a flailing length of tentacle, then slammed the axe-head down. It cracked open the shell, plunging deep into the translucent, sticky matter beneath.

The beast bellowed, thrashing and yawing in the waves. Jets of black ink spouted up, splashing across Kvara's chest. He pulled the axe free, drew it up and chopped down again. The blade cracked open a new wound, shattering the beast's armoured covering and tearing up the soft flesh beneath. More ink welled up, boiling hot and fizzing.

Kvara kept attacking it, ripping up the outer layers and burying the axe-head deep into the yielding blubber beneath. The tentacles lashed out, feebly now. The cries of the beast became plaintive rather than angry. Gouts of black murk pumped from its wounds, turning the roiling waves dark and viscous.

Kvara heard a heavy crunch close by. He looked up and saw Thenge by his side, scrabbling for purchase on the shell before getting to his knees. The big warrior grinned at him, an axe in each hand.

'Brave work, pup!' he laughed, whirling the blades in his hands before hacking them down. 'We'll make you a man yet!'

Then the two of them got to work, gripping the tilting shell and hacking it open, burrowing down, slicing through the hide of the beast, breaking up what remained of the hard barrier between them and the pulpy mass beneath. Out of the corner of his eye, Kvara saw the grappling hooks fly out from the *drekkar*, latching on the foundering creature, ready to haul it to the side of the ship. Other warriors were preparing to make the leap across, brandishing hooks and cleavers.

Kvara kept his head down after that, working hard. His pain at the back of his head wouldn't abate, though it didn't stop him working.

Amid all of it, he still grinned. He couldn't help himself. The flush of victory ran through his veins, keeping his arms moving and giving his legs the strength to hold him in position.

This is my kill, he thought as he hacked away furiously, trying not to let his stupid, childish grin show too much.

My kill.

A day later and the storm lessened in its fury, though the seas ran hard for much longer. The *drekkar* made heavy work of it, labouring in the deep swell. The central mast still stood but much of the rigging had been ripped away. Several holes had been punched below the waterline, and no matter how fast the crew bailed it out, the bilges sloshed with seawater where the makeshift repairs had been hammered on.

Aside from Olekk, three other warriors had been dragged over the edge. That was a heavy toll for the tribe, though the scale of the prize compensated for that. The meat of the *hvaluri* would keep them fed for many months once the women had smoked and salted it. The tough shell would provide tools for them and the beast's blood would be distilled into both fuel and food.

The ship ran low in the water, laden down with every piece of hide and blubber the warriors could fit aboard. It stank of the sea, acrid and salty, but no one minded that. It was a good haul, worth setting out across the blade-dark ocean for.

As they neared home Thenge sat with Kvara in the prow, chewing on a long piece of sinew and letting the grease run down his beard.

'Feeling better?' he asked good-naturedly.

Kvara nodded. He'd broken his arm on the leap back to the ship after the *hvaluri* had given up the fight, much to the raucous amusement of the rest of the crew. Even after it had been bound up with a rough splint, it still ached – not that he would ever show it.

His head was the worst of it. He didn't dare to get it looked at by the priests. The blood still oozed thickly from the wound, and the pain grew with every passing hour. His vision was beginning to blur. It wasn't healing.

'I mean what I say,' said Thenge, jabbing his finger at the blond warrior. 'That was brave. The test of manhood awaits, and you're ready.'

Kvara took up a string of sinew himself and chewed on it.

'Not sure?' asked Thenge.

'I'll do it,' he said. 'Not now.'

Thenge snorted.

'Why wait?'

Kvara looked away from him, down the longship where the rest of the crew laboured. They were his people, the ones he'd lived with all his short life. They'd never made him feel anything less than part of their world. The test of manhood – the long, solitary hunt across the icy wastes, daunted him. He didn't fear death, and certainly didn't fear danger, but something about the ordeal made him hang back.

He would do it, but not soon. The time wasn't right.

'I don't know,' he said, truthfully enough. He took another bite of the sinew, feeling the slippery flesh slide around his mouth. The action of eating dulled the pain slightly. 'I'm not ready.'

He looked up then, up at the grey walls of cloud that shrouded Fenrys. In a rare break, where the sheets of occlusion gave way slightly, he thought he saw something up there, shadowing them. A huge bird, perhaps, but its profile was strangely angular. It seemed to hang motionless in the air.

'Perhaps you're not ready to be out on your own,' said Thenge, resignedly.

Kvara nodded, not really paying attention. His head was getting worse. The clouds closed back together, hiding whatever it was that he'd seen.

'Yes,' he said. 'Perhaps that's right.'

Kvara ran his finger over the names on his armour. The snow-grey metal was softened in Lyses's warm light. Even the blade marks, the scorches and the dents looked a little less jagged.

He didn't need to read the names in order to remember them. They were carved on to his mind just as deeply as they were etched into the ceramite.

Mór, his thick-set face framed by black, dense sideburns. Dark hair, pale skin, like a vision of an underverse spectre with the sardonic humours to match.

Grimbjard Lek, the polar opposite. Sunny, blond, his mouth twitching up into a wicked smile at the first excuse. He'd killed with a smile on his face, that one, glorying the Allfather with every swing of his axe.

Vrakk, the one they'd all called Backhand, bulky and blunt with his powerfist thrumming, a dirty fighter but useful enough to make up for it.

Aerjak and Rann, brothers-in-arms, inseparable and possessed of that uncanny awareness of the other's state. Kvara had always had Aerjak down for the Rune Priests. He'd had a strange way about him, something tied to the wyrd, for all the good it had done him on Deneth Teros.

Frorl, the blade-master, swinging his frostblade with that unconscious, mocking ease, disdaining ranged weapons for the thrill of disruptors and steel-edge.

Rijal Svensson, wiry and fast, quick to anger and equally quick to laugh, his nose broken so many times that it had almost been not worth bothering with. He'd never accepted augmetic replacements, preferring to keep the stub of gristle and bone-shards in place to remind him not to get carried away.

Finally, Beorth, the quiet one. Only happy when hoisting his heavy bolter into position or at the controls of something huge and slung with big guns. He'd have been a Long Fang before he made Grey Hunter, if they'd let him. He'd laughed rarely, never sharing the coarse jokes the rest of them let spill from their profane lips, but when he had done, that rolling, rich, mirthful rumble had made Kvara grin unconsciously along with him.

Beorth had been the hardest, out of all of them. He'd been the one they'd never noticed unless he wasn't there.

Kvara let his armoured finger trace out the names, clicking softly as it passed over the runic grooves.

Perhaps you're not ready to be out on your own.

A warning light blinked on the dashboard. Kvara snapped out of his memories and took in the data.

The hub was in visual range and racing towards him fast. It was a small installation, a few hundred metres in diameter on the surface and crowned with a couple of comms towers, a few landing stages and a squat ops centre. Lights still blinked at the summit, flashing piercingly in the heat of day. The algae stretched away from it, sparse in patches and thick in others. Four lines of oily smoke rose from the harvester processing nodes, indicating that it was still working.

Kvara's face wrinkled in disapproval. He could smell the thick stench of promethium already, a low-grade variant, greasy and sour.

His armoured fingers ran over the console, keying in the landing codes from the databank Oen had uploaded to the flyer. A pict over to his left immediately updated with the response. The protective cover of one of the landing stages withdrew, unfurling like an iron rosebud, and he banked the flyer towards it.

Nothing obviously wrong.

He touched the flyer down on the platform and jumped down from the open cockpit. Smoke poured from one of the engines, and the others wound down slowly, as if their bearings had been ground away.

Kvara strode across the apron, unconsciously checking his weapons. The bolt pistol at his waist was fully loaded and primed with the appropriate blessing. Blood, his own blood, ceremonially stained the muzzle. Across his back was strapped Djalik, his blade. It was a short, stabbing sword, notched and serrated along one of the cutting edges and with inset runes lodged under the bronze-lined hilt. Over the years the metal had been dulled with burns from the weapon's disruptor field, making it as dark as charcoal.

Kvara sniffed the air, going watchfully. Everything was quiet. The installation barely moved on the placid waters. The warm wind blew across the towers and manufactoria units, washing over the grey plasteel in an endless, placid sigh.

Ahead of him, two doors slid soundlessly open, opening the way into the hub's interior. Orange lights blinked on, illuminating a bare, clean corridor. Everything smelled of the algae – a mulchy, briny tang that lingered at the back of the throat.

Kvara paused before entering, taking a final look across the hub. Aside from the low growl of automating processors, all was calm. The green waters lapped softly at the flanks of the harvester, a hundred metres down from the landing platforms.

Where are the men?

Reluctantly, having got used to the clean, unfiltered taste of the air, Kvara retrieved his battered helm from its mag-lock and screwed it in place. The balmy atmosphere of Lyses disappeared, replaced by the filtered, sterile environment of his armour-shell.

Kvara took up his bolt pistol, and breathed a prayer, the same prayer he'd uttered during every quest since Deneth Teros.

Allfather, deliver me from safety and bring me into peril.

Then he walked inside.

'Where is he now?'

'Alecto XI. He's landed.'

'That's a long way from the last site. Have we got anything from the crew?'

'Nothing. Not a thing.'

'When was the last transmit?'

'Uh, hang on.'

Eim steadied herself against the sway of the flyer. It was a big one, capable of spending several days out over the water and accommodating a full assault company. She didn't like using craft that big – their judder and yaw, as well as the fuel-tinged air, made her nauseous, and the grunts got restive cooped up in the holds.

'We don't have anything from them for six days, ma'am.'

Eim turned to the comms officer and raised an eyebrow.

'Why wasn't that picked up? They're meant to be checking in daily.'

The comms officer, a grey-faced man with deep-sunk eyes and an unfortunate overbite, shrugged apologetically.

'There are a lot to monitor.'

Eim swore and rubbed her eyes with the balls of his fists. Throne of Earth, she felt tired. Oen would owe her for this when she got back.

'Okay, run a scan. Check for anything.'

'I can't see... Whoa. I really don't know... what is that?'

Eim pushed him aside and leaned over the augur console. As she watched the shapes clarify, she felt a sudden, cold thrill shudder through her body.

'How close are we to him?'

'A long way. Procurator Oen insisted on a range of–'

'Forget that. We're going in. Signal Nyx, but don't wait for a response.'

She turned away from the comms officer and looked out across the cramped bridge space. Other officers looked up from their stations. Their expressions had switched from mild boredom into nervous expectation.

'Get the men armed and ready to deploy,' she said, speaking to the company commander, a squat, low-browed man called Frehis Aerem. 'All squads, assault order, ready to drop on my word.'

Eim looked back at the console before he'd had a chance to respond. As she watched the augur line sweep round for another pass, she felt her heart start to thump faster within her chest.

'Damn you, Oen,' she muttered, shaking her head as she watched the data stream in. 'You let him go out there – this is on *your* conscience.'

The corridors were quiet and lit only by dim orange light. Every metre of them was pristine, scrubbed clean and glistening. Octagonal hatches appeared at regular intervals along the walls, all closed. Kvara tried one of the handles, and it clicked against the bolt lock. He punched through the mechanism, cracking the handle, and the hatch swung open.

The chamber on the far side was empty. There was a desk, two metal chairs, a scale model of the harvester station on a sideboard. More orange light flickered from a semi-functional lumen, catching the jewels in a cheap devotional image of some primarch or other. No one was inside and, from the sterile smell of it, no one had been inside for some time.

Kvara turned back, walking through the network of corridors. Despite his heavy boots, his footfalls were soft. The power armour hummed – a low, grinding noise at the edge of mortal hearing – the only thing that broke the dense fog of silence.

Kvara paused, inclining his head, listening carefully. For a second, there was a trace sound, right on the edge of his audible range. Nothing he could latch on to, and not enough data for the helm to augment.

He started walking again, keeping his pistol held high. The grey hair along the back of his neck stood erect, brushing against the collar of his armour. He could feel his thick blood pumping vigorously around his bulky frame. His awareness had sharpened up, causing his muscles to loosen and his pupils to dilate. He heard his own breathing resonate within the helm, close and hot.

I come for you. You know I am here.

At the end of the corridor was another intersection. He waited again, watching, listening, absorbing.

Show yourself.

The lights blew.

The corridor plunged into darkness. Something raced up out of the shadows, phenomenally fast, scrabbling on the metal floor as it came.

In the nanosecond before Kvara's helm compensated, it swerved around the corner and out at him. A hellish face, obscenely long and crested, lashed up out of the dark.

Kvara loosed two bolts, aiming fast. They impacted with a crack and flash of light, shattering a brittle shell. High screams, alien screams, echoed from the walls.

More of them arrived, leaping over the fallen outrider. Jointed limbs clattered over metal, flashing ice-white as more bolt-flares lit them up. They came in a tangled rush, jostling each other, jaws wide and biting.

Kvara pulled back, firing all the time. His arm moved only by fractions, picking out target after target, cracking apart the growing swarm of xenos creatures. The intersection clogged quickly with smashed shells and oozing pulp, but he kept coolly firing.

Just as the ammo counter ran down, the onslaught ceased. The last of the chittering screams died away, leaving a pile of twisted, snapped and cracked shells in front of him.

Kvara ejected the old magazine, slammed a fresh one into the pistol housing and drew his blade with his left hand. Djalik's disruptor field fizzed into life, throwing an electric blue aura out from the cutting edge.

He strode out into the intersection, wading through a swamp of broken, twitching carcasses, watching for more of the xenos to come at him.

He knew what they were. He'd fought such beasts on a dozen worlds.

Hormagaunts, the Imperium called them.

Kvara liked fighting tyranids. Unlike Traitors, for whom he could feel nothing but a blind, disgusted fury, or the greenskins, which were contemptible, tyranids were a force he could respect.

They were pure. They suffered from neither fear nor corruption nor fatigue. Like the native beasts of his own world, they lashed out with an unsullied primal aggression, driven to kill out of hammered-in instinct and never stopping until death took them or the task was completed.

They saw him as prey. He saw them as prey. That made things even.

Ahead of Kvara the corridor opened out into a wide, square room. Banks of equipment were arranged in long rows, all still clean and unsullied. Across them lay the bodies of the hub's crew, very much not clean and unsullied.

They had been ripped open. Their bodies, what was left of them, hung in glistening loops of gristle and sinew all across the room. A few had tried to get out, running for the double doors on the far side of the space.

The trails of blood, as thick and dark as engine oil, didn't reach very far. The corpses still had looks of horrified surprise on their faces – those, at any rate, who still had faces.

Kvara swept the room with his pistol. The lights were still down, and his helm picked the outlines of the bodies in fuzzy grey light.

He sensed them coming before his armour's equipment did. A skittering, scraping run, muffled by the closed doors to the corridor beyond, punctuated by the high-pitched rattle of xenos vocal cords. They were racing toward him – dozens of them, maybe more.

Kvara grinned.

The doors burst apart, thrown aside by a press of straining bodies. Blurred xenos outlines, skeletal and reptilian, swarmed through the gap and into the room, screaming at him with stretched-wide jaws, pouring over the surfaces in a rolling wave of needle-teeth and hooked claws.

'*Fenrys!*'

Kvara charged straight back at them, leaping over a slumped pile of eviscerated bodies and bringing his blade round in a wide, blistering arc. He hurled himself into the tide, loosing volleys of bolt-fire that flashed out in the dark like storm lightning.

They came on, lashing out at him, and he shattered their talons. They leapt up to maul him, and he broke their snapping jaws. He spun round, shifting from one foot to another, punching out, slicing back with the blade, firing all the while. Scrawny xenos bodies smashed apart, bursting open and spraying fluid across his whirling, gyrating armour.

More of them poured in through the broken doors, streaming into the chamber and leaping up to make contact with him. They bounded over the bodies of their own dead, desperate to draw blood.

Kvara smashed his pistol-hand round, caving in a swollen xenos skull, before sending two more rounds spinning into two more targets, jabbing up with the blade and hauling it back through the entrails of another flailing monster.

They were all over him, tearing and screaming, but he was faster, bigger and stronger. As they howled with agonised frustration, he grunted with coarse satisfaction. His gauntlets were heavy and sticky with fluids, but he kept them moving. The liquid splattered over his breastplate, dousing the graven names under layers of filth.

He had been bred to do this. There was nothing left for him but this. Only in such work could his soul find a measure of peace even as his body pushed itself to the extremes of performance.

He was back where he belonged. Back in the fight.

'Kvara!'

Mór's voice was strained over the comm, broken up by the crackle of ordnance. Huge, thumping crashes distorted the feed.

'Position, brother,' snapped Kvara, running hard, feeling the sweat run down his temple.

'Rann… all gone…'

And that was it. The comm spat a fog of static. Kvara kept running, keeping his head low, weaving through the rubble. Solid rounds fizzed over his head, impacting against the rockcrete and showering him with rubble.

Blood of Russ – where are they?

He sensed a detonation to his left, and leapt clear. The already ruined wall exploded, hurling out an orb of fire and rusty shrapnel. The blast wave threw him from his feet, slamming him into the nearside bulwark. His armour crunched through it, tearing up the stone and showering him in dust.

'Position!' he spat, righting himself and breaking into a run again.

Nothing but hissing came over the comm. The fractured sky of Deneth Teros rumbled with electric storms, and a fork of violet lightning licked the burning horizon.

'Lek. Svensson. *Position*.'

He ducked down again and starting to run. Above him, huge artillery trails lanced between the shells of the spires, exploding in a cacophony of overlaid, shuddering booms.

The static mocked him, and he blinked the feed closed. Far ahead of him, the city core was tearing itself apart. A vast hab-spire, hundreds of metres tall and crested with jagged towers, toppled over with eerie, magisterial slowness. Already broken open by a hundred major impacts, the walls imploded as it crashed down amongst the ruins, throwing up a bow wave of burning dust. The screams of those inside were lost in the ripping, flickering wind, burned away by the igniting promethium in the air.

Kvara raced across a narrow transit corridor, dodging the smoking craters and leaping over the lines of barbed stranglewire. Explosive rounds followed him, puffing up as they hit the tarmac. Since he'd left Vrakk, coughing up his own blood in the gutter with his lower body on the other side of the street, Kvara's tactical display had showed nothing but interference. The location runes of his pack all showed blank.

We're being torn apart.

He spotted movement, right on the edge of his left visual field, and swerved after it. Something – something big – ducked under a huge, low-hanging metal beam.

Kvara fired. The bolts screamed off into the fire-flecked murk, exploding as they demolished the beam in a cloud of spinning metal shards.

Then he was running again, leaping past smoking mortar holes and sweeping around smouldering heaps of twisted slag. He hadn't killed it. He'd have known if he had killed it.

Warned by some inner sense, he skidded to a halt, dropping down to a crouch.

A ball of plasma seared out of the gloom, missing by centimetres, slamming into the wall behind him. Kvara lurched forward, feeling the heat as another plasma bolt flew across his back.

He rolled to one side, bringing up his pistol and firing blind. The bolts connected with something, there was a shrill shriek, and the plasma torrent ceased.

Kvara sprang up, bounding after the source of the noise, ducking and swooping across the broken ground. As he went, his senses processed a thousand minor events in every direction – Guardsmen howling and weeping with fear and pain, juddering fire from dug-in positions over by the refineries, the grind and crack of armoured formations coming up from the transit hub along what remained of the Joslynssbahn. He processed those sounds, but did nothing about them. Everything was focussed on the elusive shadow, the shape that stayed one step ahead, the shape that had come among them and summoned blood.

Kvara tore round the shell of a burned-out Chimera, tasting the sweet taste of the hunt in his cloyed saliva.

Ahead, two hundred metres, he saw it again, dark between clouds of engine smoke. Huge, edged with spikes, loping like a maddened devil of the Helwinter. Corruption rolled from its carapace in a stink of oily shadow.

It turned, and eyes the colour of newborn flesh blazed at him.

Kvara fired as he ran, loosing a rolling column of explosive rounds and zigzagging through the broken remnants of the 576th Armoured Falchions.

The bolts connected, and the creature rocked back on huge, cloven feet. It cast aside a charred and broken plasma cannon and reached for a glittering blade. A scream sliced through the air, echoing in nightmarish polyphony.

Kvara didn't slow down. The pistol clicked empty, and he cast it aside, drawing up his blade Rothgeril and activating the lashing disruptors.

The thing he faced had once been a man. After that, it had been a Space Marine. After that, it had become a living altar of sadism, a prophet of the darkest corner of insanity and depravity in a galaxy already drenched in it.

Its armour, a grotesque blasphemy of Tactical Dreadnought plate, had burst out and split from the pulsing flesh beneath. Translucent tumours swelled up in the cracks, glowing and leaking and trembling. A face – part helm-grille, part skeletal rictus – grinned out from under a cowl of whip-curl bronze snakes. Eldritch energy rippled across the warped ceramite like meltwater. Blood flecked and speckled the pale pink tracery, boiling and hissing as the raw ether touched it and recoiled.

Kvara swung the blade low, driving it with frightening speed and precision. He could sense the acuity of his own movements, and gloried in it. Every nanometre of his body was straining for the kill. His hearts thudded, his blood raged, his lungs burned with a cleansing pain.

The blades clashed, and a boom of power discharged, throwing Kvara back and blunting his charge. The monster reared over him, pulling its pulsing sword-edge round for another blow.

Kvara pulled away, opening up a narrow space and spinning round to build up fresh momentum. The creature sliced its own blade across at him, tearing the very air itself asunder and leaving a trail of agonised matter in its wake.

Kvara ducked under it, feeling the charged edge tear a chunk from his backpack. He thrust up, ignoring the sickly stench of filth that poured from the corrupted horror, grabbing the hilt of Rothgeril two-handed.

The sword bit deep, blazing like a field of stars as it crashed through the distorted ceramite and warp-addled flesh.

Then it was hauled away, dragged from his hands by a wrench so hard that Kvara lost his feet and was dragged, face-down, into the ash and dust of the ruined city. He recovered instantly, rolling away to evade the downward killing plunge before jumping back to his feet and backing away, disgusted at how easily his weapon had been taken from him.

Now the creature held two swords. One, its own, blazed with sick, overripe energy. The other, Kvara's, held upside-down by the blade-tip. The beast's long fingers squeezed through the furious disruptor field, bleeding dark purple blood where Rothgeril's biting edge sunk deep into its twisted flesh.

It laughed, and the sound was like the screaming of children.

Weaponless, Kvara clenched his gauntlets and snarled, ready for the onslaught. The creature was nearly twice his height, mutated and imbued with the essence of the Ruinous Powers. The Grey Hunter gazed up at it through red helm lenses, fearless and desperate, judging whether any blow he landed could do any damage to such a monster, tensing to sell his life with as much blood and fire as could still be mustered.

But not yet. A hurricane of heavy bolter fire slammed into the towering monster, smashing up the twisted armour and churning deep into the rose-pink muscle. It reeled, flailing against the bludgeoning hail of exploding projectiles.

Beorth limped out of the roiling clouds, his underslung bolter thundering from his two-handed grip. The comm-link was still a hiss of nothing. In broken bursts, Kvara could only hear a strangled, desperate sound from Beorth's feed.

The man, the big man, was *roaring*.

'A blade, brother!' shouted Kvara, stretching out a hand imploringly.

Beorth ignored him. He strode toward the staggering creature, firing all the while, ripping the armour-shell free of its sickening sigils and unholy signs. His own armour was as black as night, burned and rent open, and blood still poured from a dozen mortal wounds. He walked on regardless, massive and implacable, pouring a steady stream of withering, searing destruction from the red-hot muzzle of his huge weapon.

The monster waded through it, clawing at the bolts even as they punched into it, blowing shards from its armour and spraying plumes of purple. It staggered toward Beorth, screaming the whole time in a paroxysm of outrage and madness.

Then it leapt, streaming out in trails of blood and shell-discharge, arms outstretched and jaws open. It crashed into Beorth, knocking them both to the ground and rolling over. It savaged at his neck, tore at the cracks in his armour, stamped down with cloven hooves on to his prone limbs.

Kvara raced after them, pouncing on to the back of the creature. He grabbed the ornate lip of its armour and heaved, pulling it away from Beorth. The horror snarled and lashed round, trying to throw him off. Kvara clung on, digging his fingers deep into the exposed flesh under the ceramite, tearing it up and pulling it out in strips.

Beorth clambered back to his feet, drawing his blade. The heavy bolter thudded to the floor, spent and smoking.

The creature of Chaos threw Kvara off, hurling him to one side and swinging the twin swords down at his prone body. Kvara rolled away, evading them by centimetres, before Beorth charged back, slashing with his own combat blade, whirling and dancing with all the skill of Frorl.

Together, the two of them rocked back and forth, hacking and blocking. The Traitor was reeling now, weeping blood in rivulets down its shattered armour. Beorth's left arm hung limply by his side, awkwardly twisted, his every move radiating agony.

Kvara lurched to his feet in time to witness his brother's sword knocked away with a vicious swipe from the Traitor's warp-tainted blade. It spun away, glittering in the firelight, clattering across the stone. Spurred on by desperation, Kvara scrambled after it, grabbing the hilt just as it came to rest.

He whirled back round, only to see the creature break Beorth's neck with a final, horrifying lunge. The huge warrior was hoisted into the air and cast aside with a sickening crunch of bone.

Then it turned to Kvara, and grinned.

Kvara ignited the disruptor on Beorth's blade, barely noticing the runes signifying 'Djalik' along the blade. It felt light in his hand, balanced the way a combat sword should be.

'For the Allfather,' Kvara breathed softly, staring at the murderer of his pack, sensing the death-spirit locked tight in the killing blade.

The creature charged at him, both swords flailing, but its movements were jerky and erratic. Massive wounds had opened out across its body from Beorth's onslaught, all bleeding torrents.

Kvara darted forward, ducking under the first incoming swipe before jabbing up with the point of Djalik, twisting as the edge punched up through the outstretched chin of the Traitor.

The point cleaved cleanly, thrusting up through bone and brain. The monster, impaled on the lashing, spitting energy blade, jerked like a marionette, lashing out blindly with its twin weapons.

Huge fists battered Kvara, buffeting him from either side, but he remained firm. He fed power to Djalik's disruptors, and the creature's head bulged, cracked, and exploded.

A rain of pulp and bone shot outward, blinding Kvara and sending him reeling backwards again. Disorientated, he stumbled, landing heavily on his back. A sharp pain radiated from his side, and he caught sight of the Traitor's blade lodged in his torso. Runes flashed red across his helm display, giving him a tediously thorough summary of just how badly hurt that made him.

The headless body of the Traitor toppled, thudding dully against the tortured earth of Deneth Teros. Tendrils of warp-matter flickered across its ruined corpse, dancing like grave-sprites.

Still on his back, Kvara grabbed hold of the corrupted blade, gritted his teeth, and pulled. It came free with a wet squelch, dragging strands of muscle and skin with it through the jagged gash in his armour. He could feel the poison in the wound already, hot and boiling away like a swarm of insects. He tried to rise, and failed. Blood was leaking out of him freely, defying the clotting agents in his body. His vision blurred, going black, and his head fell back against the hot soil.

Above him, the sky was scored with trails of fire. As if from far away, he heard the rush and clamour of warfare. The ground trembled underfoot as huge war engines trundled toward one another. High up in the dark skies, black silhouettes of drop-ships hung, shaky in the heatwash from their labouring engines.

Kvara watched it all mutely, feeling paralysis creep up to his lips. He could feel his consciousness slipping away, even as his ravaged body rallied against the poison frothing in his blood.

'Position...' he murmured, automatically, repeating the word he'd used so often over the last hour, feeling the bitter futility of it even as his mind lost its grip on the world of the senses.

Beorth was dead. Vrakk was dead. Rann and Aerjak had died together, just as they had surely been fated to do. The pack – all of them – were dead.

Kvara felt a solitary tear of rage run down his burned cheek. He wanted to take his helm off, to taste the air of the world that had done this, but his hands no longer obeyed his commands.

Night closed in on him, the night of oblivion. The last thing he saw was the helm display, functional and stark. The eight runes, eight identifier marks, were all blank, like empty holes into the void.

All dead.

The thought burned at his mind even as it retreated in nothingness. It stabbed at him, far sharper than the wound in his side, sharper than the many wounds across his battle-worn body, sharper than the knowledge, coming to him even as lost everything else, that he was equal to the poisons, and that this would not be the last fight he would live to see.

That didn't matter. For the first time since coming off the ice and taking the Helix, that didn't matter.

Nothing mattered.

All dead.

'This is your choice.'

'I have made it.'

'Not yet. You need more time.'

'My decision won't change.'

'It may. I've seen it before.'

The eyes in the dark were red and slanted. If he had died, he would have expected eyes like those.

But he hadn't died, not physically. The eyes behind those lenses were like his. They were sunk deep into a black wolf skull mask with teeth set around the helm-grille.

Around him, the isolation chamber of the *Vrafnki* hummed with the grind of sub-warp travel. He didn't know where it was going, or how long it would be in transit. Much still had to be explained to him, though he was in no hurry to ask for information.

'It's a privilege, not a right,' said the Rune Priest, though less harshly than he might have done.

Kvara let his head sink back to the metal surface of the medicae cot. Every part of him still ached. His blood felt painfully hot, as if he'd been given a transfusion of molten lead.

'With all respect, lord,' he said, working his swollen lips painfully, 'I don't believe you. It's never been refused.'

For a moment, the skull mask remained static. Then a low, grating chuckle broke out from behind the black armour.

'Maybe.'

The mask drew closer, looming over him, coming to within a few centimetres of his face. Kvara looked up through the translucent mask of the medicae shroud with the one eye that still worked. He felt the soft pulse of the machinery around him, cycling his blood, working his hearts, filling his lungs, keeping him shackled to life.

'What do you think taking the lone path will be like, Hunter?' he asked. 'How long do you think it will take to find a prize big enough to extinguish your grief? When we pulled you from the ice, as near to death as you are now, you'd killed a *hvaluri*. How much bigger would your beast have to be, Aj Kvara, before its death would be enough?'

Kvara smiled grimly.

'When I was a child, I dreamed of killing a *krakken*. That's what I thought it took to become a Sky Warrior.'

'Then you are a fool. The *krakken* cannot be killed.'

'But Jarl Engir–'

'The *krakken* cannot be killed. It will tear at the roots of the world for eternity, weakening them, making them frail.'

The Rune Priest withdrew his skull mask. Kvara closed his eye. He felt the drugs in his system dragging him back to unconsciousness, and fought against it.

'It can be killed,' he said, feeling his words slur. 'I know it, and you know it. Everything that lives can be killed.'

He kept moving, heading down, ever down, fighting through the hormagaunts as they swarmed up from the lower levels, relishing every wave of them as they crashed and broke against his armour. Djalik was slick with their fluid, as was the muzzle of his bolt pistol, now dangerously low on ammunition.

The creatures had come from below. They'd run up the sensor shafts from the underwater sections, fast and silent. The human crew would have had no warning – no time even to send off a panicked transmission before the living wall of teeth and claws ripped into them. Before Kvara had arrived they'd been dispersing again, falling back down in scattered packs, making way for the monster whose appearance they'd heralded. Only his intervention had stirred them again, rousing them back into the slavering, indignant fury they'd shown before.

Now, once again, their numbers had been thinned. Kvara wheeled around smoothly, knocking three of the creatures bodily into the chamber walls. Two thumped wetly against the plasteel, slumping to the floor. The other managed to get up, and he grabbed it, snapping its neck with a contemptuous twist.

The floor rocked as something collided with the outside wall. The collisions were getting more violent, and he braced himself against them. A hormagaunt, one of the last remaining, skittered into the chamber and threw itself at him. Kvara cracked his fist into its oncoming jaws, not bothering to use the blade.

The chamber lurched again, and a crack snaked across the wall. Kvara backed away from it, running a quick check over his armour's integrity seals, knowing full well that he was several hundred metres below sea level.

The structure around him groaned and the walls began to bulge inwards. The cracks grew, as if something huge and prehensile had wrapped itself around the chamber and was pulling tight.

Kvara braced himself, gauging from the creaks and snaps of breaking struts how big the thing outside was.

The walls bulged further, breaking into a lattice of fractures, then broke. Seawater, opaque with bubbles, cascaded in, hitting him hard and knocking him off balance. Kvara thrust himself upward, kicking out against the sudden influx, rotating in the torrent and lashing out with his blade. Its edge connected with something viscous and mobile, snagging on it before cutting through.

He kept moving, pushing out from the rapidly disintegrating walls, powering through the rushing water. More tendrils snaked inside, thrashing after him. As he moved, he fought against a dizzying whirl of disorientation. Everything was in motion, frothing and racing. Water poured rapidly into what remained of the chamber's outer casing, rushing up to waist-height, then shoulder-height, then over his head.

Through a blurred curtain of moving water Kvara saw a huge length of sucker-clad skin race past him, ripping away a length of armour-casing from the hub's exterior. He kicked himself toward it. As he pushed off the crumbling floor gave way entirely, dissolving into a bubbling foam of broken mesh and cladding. More water bloomed up from under it, chasing out the last of the chamber's air in a glistening bubble.

Kvara brought Djalik round in a curve, aiming at the tentacle snaking through the breach. The blade sliced into it cleanly, and a huge cry echoed throughout the water – a shuddering, booming bellow of pain.

Then the last remnants of the chamber caved in, bringing with them a fresh deluge of churning, bloody water from all directions. Kvara ducked down under a collapsing wall section, lurching away from it in slow motion even as he fell down deeper, supported now by nothing but collapsing struts and spars. He tumbled into the centre of the zone of destruction, dragged further into the abyss as the metal around him was crushed and whipped into nothing more than splinters.

The last of the air shot up in columns of glittering silver, leaving him plummeting through rapidly darkening seawater. His helm-visor partially compensated, rendering the scene around him into a riot of false-colour targets.

Kvara spun away from the forest of needle-thin sensor prongs jutting below the disintegrating harvester, still falling rapidly, still trying to get some kind of lock on the creature that was doing this. He had a vague impression of something vast moving just above him. He spun cumbersomely on to his back and fired upward. The bolts shot through the water leaving long trails of bubbles. A series of muffled thuds rang out and impact shocks rippled through the water.

Then Kvara hit the algae. He was dragged into a sticky, cloying morass of thick vegetation. It grasped at him, pulling on his limbs. He twisted around again, slicing out with his blade to clear it, still falling deeper. He reached out with his bolter-arm, ready to fire upward again, only to have a tentacle shoot down and lash round his wrist, wrenching it out of position.

With a violent jerk, he stopped falling. The algae rolled away from him and more tendrils snaked down, grabbing him and pulling him back up. He cut himself free, only for more suckers to grab on. Kvara felt his second heart thumping hard. His breath echoed, fast and regular, in the enclosed space of his helm.

He looked up, and saw the creature in full for the first time. A huge serrated crest of armour reared up in the gloom, ridged and pocked with barnacles. Jaws protruded from under the crest, lined with flashing lines of needle teeth. A massive torso, segmented and flexible, hung down from a spike-ringed neck. Tentacles flowed out from joints along the torso, writhing in the water as if they had sentience of their own. A long tail trailed back into the depths, terminated with a scorpion-like sting. The beast's hide was glossy and streamlined, and it moved through the water with a ponderous, muscular grace.

As Kvara stared up at it, struggling against the tendrils that clutched at him, its huge jaws opened to reveal several flicking tongues, each one the length of his forearm. Six multi-jointed arms uncurled out from the forest of tentacles, stretching out to grab at him. As Kvara saw the claws extend toward him, he remembered the shattered pieces of plasteel floating on the water.

He wrenched his bolt pistol free of the tentacles and fired straight at the creature's looming face. The rounds shot off through the water, leaving trails of bubbles in their wake.

With a mighty whiplash movement, the leviathan surged away from them, evading the projectiles with a sinuous ease. While it was moving, Kvara brought his blade to bear, severing the tendrils that still bound him and breaking free of their hold.

He dropped deeper, spinning around as his heavy armour dragged him down. The creature swam around and swept down after him, undulating through the blooms of algae like a colossal sea-serpent of Fenrisian myth.

Kvara tried to control his cartwheeling descent and failed. The thick liquid dragged at his limbs and the turbulence buffeted him. The wrecked hub was now far above him and out of his eyeline. Even with his helm lenses compensating, it was hard to make out much through the murk other than the vast serrated shadow pursuing him.

Then he reached the bottom. The sea floor rushed up at him, dark and jagged. Huge rocks, each as sharp as butcher's knives and many metres high, cut up into the fog of algae. Kvara arched his back, missing the tip of the nearest stalagmite by a finger's width. He spun away from it and collided with the flank of another one. As he rebounded clear, he managed to mag-lock his blade and stretch out with his free hand. His fingers clutched at the sharp edge of another rock column and he clamped his gauntlet tightly over the rock. His body swung after it, crashing into the unyielding stone and grinding to a standstill.

The stalagmite held him, and his boots lodged firm against a narrow ledge on the stone. Locking himself in place with his free hand, Kvara swung his pistol up again and loosed another volley of bolts.

The creature had been close on his tail the whole time – too close to evade the point-blank shots. The bolts span into its bony crest, detonating once they penetrated the hard casing and exploding with a series of blunt thuds. The beast screamed and jerked sharply back up, sending a backdraught of water washing over him.

He spotted the tail sweeping round at him almost too late. Kvara pressed himself back against the rock-edge and the bulbous sting swam past just in front of him, lashing furiously as it passed.

Then the creature was coming at him again, surging through the water, multiple arms outstretched. Kvara squeezed the trigger again, but the pistol jammed.

Spitting a curse, he let it drop and brought his blade up. His movements were as fast as he could make them in the thick soup of algae, but still too slow, too cumbersome. The first tentacles clamped on to his weapon-arm, pinning him back to the rock. Then more shot out, wrapping themselves around his midriff. They squeezed tight, and Kvara felt his breastplate flex under the pressure.

A clawed hand reached for him, aimed at his head. Kvara managed to pull himself out of its path, wrestling hard against the drag of the tendrils. The beast's talons smashed into the rock behind him, shattering it and sending a cloud of dust floating out and up.

Kvara felt the first crack on his armour even before the warning runes started to flash. It ran transverse across the list of names on his right side, breaking up the inscriptions.

Then the creature went for him again, this time at his torso. Kvara kicked back against the rock, pushing himself upwards. He wrenched his blade-arm free and lashed out at the tendrils around him, briefly clearing a space to operate in. He struck deep, cutting into solid flesh and staining the water with the beast's dark blood, before rolling away and down, sliding down the sheer rock in a flurry of kicked-up dust.

But the beast was far faster, and the abyss was its element. It shot after him, moving with unhurried undulations. The creature's outstretched claws grasped at him, gouging new rents in the ceramite of his backpack where they made contact. More warning indicators flared red across his lens display.

Kvara rolled clumsily on to his back, swinging his blade round and slashing at the scrabbling talons. The beast clutched its claws back up away from the flashing blade before punching them back down after it had swept across. Talons punched down, through Kvara's guard, cutting into his trailing leg like a stud being shot into leather.

Kvara grimaced, wrenching his leg away as the flesh punctured. The leg-plate cracked open, leaving clouds of blood in the water behind him. Valves shut closed at his knee socket and his armour's greave filled with water as the rents in the ceramite spun apart.

The creature swooped in closer, black against the shadow of the deep waters. Off-balanced and unsighted, Kvara crashed and wheeled down the sheer face of the pinnacle. He hit a jutting outcrop in mid-spin that arched his spine and sent him reeling in the opposite direction. Then he collided with another wall of rock face-first, cracking his weakened breastplate further. For a second he could see nothing but flashes of red light. He swung out blindly as he fell further and the sword bit into pursuing claws, darkening the water with the beast's oil-black blood.

Then his boots connected with something solid and his dizzying plummet thumped abruptly to a halt. His vision cleared, though he could feel blood running down the inside of his helm. The cracks in his plate were leaking water and it sloshed around, freezing and pressurised, in the cavities between his skin and the armour.

He was lodged in a narrow cleft between two sheer peaks of rock. Frustrated for a moment, the beast scratched frantically at the pinnacles above him, pulling them apart to get at him. One elongated talon stabbed down clean through the gap, carving through the protection of his upraised sword-arm and severing it nearly clean through.

Kvara roared with pain, watching helplessly as his blade floated free of his control. Blood ballooned out from the wound, pluming in jets through the water.

Another claw shot down through the narrow cleft, reaching for his head and shoulders. Dizzy with pain and incipient shock, Kvara only just managed to punch up with his good hand. His gauntlet closed over the incoming talons and he twisted, using his whole body to leverage the manoeuvre. The talons ripped free, and the creature roared in turn, sending pulsating shivers radiating through the water.

By then Kvara's armour had sealed off the severed vambrace. His blood had already started clotting, and his vision had cleared. Above him, the huge creature withdrew its tentative strikes and broke into a frenzy of pain-filled destruction. Its tail crashed round, demolishing the fragile peaks of the two pinnacles. Another pass, and the last of his protection would be ripped away. His sword-arm was useless, his armour was compromised, and his weapons were gone.

Kvara pulled two krak grenades from his belt and primed them. He clutched them both in his good hand and crouched down, coiled to spring.

Something like elation coursed through his heavily damaged body – the elation felt by a master swordsman having at last met his match in battle.

The beast had the measure of him. It was worthy.

I have found it.

Its tail crashed back across, demolishing the pinnacles on either side of the cleft, exposing him again to the full wrath of the wounded creature. When the debris cleared, Kvara just had time to see an enraged, bleeding face hurtling straight at him. It was obscenely stretched, utterly alien, devoid of anything but animal hatred and a primal lust for the coming kill.

Kvara pounced, propelling himself upward into the oncoming jaws, holding the twin grenades tightly in his one working gauntlet and thrusting them forward. The beast snapped its jaws closed out of instinct, ripping Kvara's arm off at the shoulder.

He bellowed with pain. Dark stars exploded before his eyes, quickly lost in a blur of shock and agony. He saw his own blood stream out in a long, viscous trail as he fell back, hanging in the water like a slick of promethium. He felt more water rushing into the breaches in his battleplate, cracking open the ravaged protection and sending him tumbling back down into the shadow of the rock-cleft.

Above it all was the face of the beast, grinning with alien malice, triumphant and malevolent. It came in close, its teeth stained with his blood, ready to finish him.

Then the grenades went off.

Kvara was hurled down against the rock as the twin booms rocked the sea floor. The creature spasmed and bulged as the explosions tore through its innards. A shockwave swept out from the epicentre of the blast carrying scraps of flesh and carapace with it and carpeting the stark rock needles. The swirling mass of tentacles seemed to implode, shrinking back in toward the bony ridge of the creature's spine before going suddenly limp. A long, echoing scream resonated through the water, hanging there until the beast, flailing for a moment longer in a desperate attempt to climb on to life, slumped immobile.

It still hung, buoyant and huge, drifting a little on the cold, dark currents, before beginning to tilt away, trailing lines of gore from its punctured torso.

With what little awareness that remained to him, Kvara gazed up at it. Though wracked by pain and feeling the frigid clutch of unconscious rush up to grasp him, he could still marvel at the beast's size.

My kill.

Kvara's head fell back on to the rock. Water had got into his helm, which was slowly filling up. Pain throbbed throughout his whole body, acute and blinding. He felt heady with stimms and adrenaline. Before they did their work, dragging him into the oblivion of the Red Dream, he only had one more thought – a correction – recognising the nature of the beast he had killed and the significance it possessed. The voices no longer echoed in his mind, and he could no longer see them as they had been. Death, next to that, seemed of little consequence.

Our kill.

The wound in his head never healed. He became sick, then dizzy, falling over the deck as the *drekkar* pitched with the winter sea. They laughed at him right until the time he couldn't get up.

Kvara saw the world through a mist of confusion, nauseous and slurring. The sea went flat, and the wind came hurling down from the heavens in a blaze of fire and smoke.

He cried out for Thenge, looking for the big man through the rushing noise. Thenge wasn't there. In his place stood a giant wearing a black metal skin and the mask of a wolf. His dried pelt cloak shook in the downdraught and he carried a skull-topped staff.

I am dead. This is the spectre of Morkai.

He felt hands reach out for him – human hands. He was pulled on to some kind of stretcher. He recognised the smell of those hands. Preja Eim, perhaps, the human female who had stood outside the interrogation chamber. Where was her superior, the man called Oen? There were others there, clad in environment suits and talking in low voices.

This is not real. I am not on Fenris.

The *drekkar* reeled, nearly sending him into the sea. He managed to lift his head, and saw the shaky outline of a huge metal casket in the sky. It was as grey as the clouds, and hung above the ship in defiance of all law. Gigantic rings of bronze thundered with flame, breaking through the storm and making the air shake with heat.

The giant with the black metal skin made a gesture, and more metal-clad warriors leapt down from the hovering casket. They wore snow-grey armour with runes hammered into it and none of their faces were visible. They lumbered up to Kvara, walking smoothly even as the ship plunged through the swell.

I have killed the krakken, and it has killed me. Now they come to take me to Halls of the Slain.

Kvara felt the water drain from his helm. In the distance, sounding as if still underwater, drills rang out, removing the surviving sections of battle-plate. Lights flashed painfully in his eyes, surgical and piercing. He heard voices with the accent of Lyses Gothic coming in and out of hearing. A man came to the forefront, his forehead creased with concern.

That is Oen. He fears me still. What is he doing here?

They took him up into the hovering casket of fire. The pain in his head grew worse. Kvara looked down from his impossible position for a final time, seeing his own blood on the decks below. Then, at last, he saw Thenge and the others, huddled at the far end of the ship, gazing up, open-mouthed.

They were afraid. He had never seen them afraid of anything before.

Huge doors closed with an echoing clang, sealing him in. The lights dimmed. He heard the sound of medicae equipment being dragged closer.

Someone leaned over him. It might have been the black wolf-mask. It might have been the man Oen.

It didn't matter. They both said the same thing.

'You will not die, warrior.'

'Could you not have got here quicker?'

'Throne, Preja, I do have other things to worry about.'

'He's scaring the hell out of everybody.'

'I don't doubt it. Is he up and walking?'

'No, he can't get up. But he's still scary, procurator.'

Oen walked as fast as he could down the corridors of the medicae unit, ignoring the nervous glances from the apothecary's staff as he went. Eim trotted along at his side, irritable and tense.

'What has he said?'

'He wants his armour. He wants to know what we've done with his ship.'

'And you told him?'

'That he can have it, and that we left it the hell alone.'

'Good.'

The pair of them reached the secure ward. Two sentries in full assault armour stood guard outside. They saluted briskly before opening the metal-banded doors.

The ward was spacious enough, but its lone occupant made it seem cramped. He lay on his back, his huge limbs barely fitting onto the reinforced slab of plasteel that served as a bed. Wires ran from his chest, his face and his limbs. One arm had been severed just below the shoulder and the stump was crowned with a metal cap.

As they entered, Kvara lifted his head. Even after so long, his face was still swollen with bruises. He looked at Oen and Eim with those strange, luminous gold eyes.

'I came as soon as I could, lord,' said Oen, bowing.

Eim stood to one side, chewing her lip nervously.

The Space Wolf took a long time to speak. When he did, his thick, growling voice had gone. His throat shook, and the sound that emerged was little more than a pale whisper.

'How long?' he rasped.

'Two standard months,' said Oen. 'I'm told you've been in some kind of deep coma. We've done what we can, so I'm glad to see you awake again.'

Kvara ran his eyes over the wires jutting from his body, and grunted.

Oen watched him carefully. Kvara looked even more ravaged than he had done on arrival. His long hair and beard hung in grey straggles over the edge of the cot. His massive barrel chest, covered in scars and tattoos, rose and fell under a thin coverlet. His skin was studded with metal devices, none of which the surgeons had made any attempt to investigate. They'd been terrified of doing anything invasive to him and had been half-appalled, half-fascinated by his outlandish physiology. As far as Oen could tell from their reports, the Space Marine had essentially cured himself.

'You recovered the creature?' Kvara asked. His eyes met Oen's blearily. Even with Kvara in such a state, the procurator found it hard to meet that gaze.

'What was left of it, lord. The remains are preserved.'

'The head?'

'I… er, the what?'

'Did you retrieve the head?'

'We did.'

Kvara let his head fall back. His breath was ragged and shallow.

Oen looked at Eim, who shrugged. He had no idea what to say.

'My armour,' said Kvara. His voice had slurred, as if he were fighting against sleep. 'Where is it?'

'Here, lord,' said Eim, motioning over to the far corner of the room. 'We brought it here, just as you asked, when you were sleeping.'

Kvara lifted his head again with difficulty, screwing his eyes up and peering out as if through a thick fog.

The armour had been hung on a reinforced metal scaffold. Even the broken pieces had been mounted on the rig, each one carefully hoisted into place by a team of engineers who'd been every bit as reverent and afraid as the surgeons.

The breastplate hung in the centre. Where once the surface had been covered in eight lines of runes, it was now almost bare. A series of huge impacts had scoured the surface clear, wearing away the grey paint and boring deep into whatever material it had been constructed out of. The curved surface glinted sharply in the light of the medicae chamber, as raw as newly-tempered steel.

'The names,' whispered Kvara, looking at it intently.

'Your pardon?'

Then the Space Wolf issued a dry, cracking chuckle. It seemed to pain him, and he looked away from the armour and back at Oen.

'Come here, mortal,' he ordered.

His throat dry, Oen shuffled closer. Kvara winced as he turned his head, exposing a pair of fangs between chapped lips.

'How did you locate me?' he asked.

Oen swallowed.

'I disobeyed your instruction, and your movements were tracked. By the time our flyers arrived, you'd destroyed the creature.'

Kvara nodded.

'I should add,' said Oen haltingly, remembering how he'd felt when Kvara's body had been retrieved, 'that we're sorry. We came too late. But, you should know, we did what we could for you. You were never alone. We couldn't keep up with you, but you were never alone.'

Kvara smiled at that. Unlike the weary, sardonic smile he'd worn on arrival at Lyses, the gesture was natural, almost human.

'Never alone,' he echoed thoughtfully.

Oen swallowed again, uncertain of what to say to that. An uneasy silence fell over the chamber.

'I don't expect you to understand the ways of my kind, human,' said

Kvara at last, his voice low. 'I don't expect you to understand why I came here, nor why I must take the head of that beast back to Fenris, nor what that will mean for the blood-debt of my pack.'

His bestial eyes shone wetly as he spoke.

'Their names have been erased, and it eases the torment of my soul. But we'll remember them in the sagas for as long as such songs are remembered. And among them, in the position of honour, will be yours, human. Take that as you will, but there are those in the galaxy who would see it as a compliment.'

Out of the corner of his eye, Oen saw Eim raise her eyebrows and give a little shrug. He tried to think of something suitably polite to respond with.

It was difficult. For all the reputation of the Adeptus Astartes, the reality of them was hard to come to terms with. Perhaps the Space Wolves were a minor Chapter, a fringe example of the species with more eccentricities than the others. Maybe the other ones he'd seen on the devotional holos with their gleaming cobalt armour and gold-lined pauldrons looked down on them as quaint or inferior.

By the time Oen had thought of something, though, Kvara seemed to have drifted back into an exhausted sleep, and to say anything further felt rather superfluous. For the sake of form, though, Oen bowed courteously and gave his reply.

'That's very kind, lord,' he said. 'What a nice tradition.'

He had learned to use his new body out in the wilds of Asaheim, and it gave him the strength and poise of a demigod. Even out of his armour he could withstand the biting air of the Fang with barely a flicker of discomfort. He had been changed, dragged beyond himself and into the realm of legend.

For all that, the first time he met them his tongue felt thick and useless. He'd never been much of a talker, and they already knew one another as well as mortal brothers. He envied the way they were with each other – easy, casual, close.

'So they've sent us a whelp,' said the one they called Mór, scowling at him as he entered the hearth chamber with his false-confident strut.

The one they called Lek laughed at that, grinding the edge of his axe with a whetstone. He stopped the wheel and pushed a loose strand of blond hair back behind his ear.

'So they have.'

Vrakk, Aerjak and Rann looked up from their game of bones. Vrakk shook his head wearily and went back to it. Aerjak and Rann exchanged a knowing smile, but said nothing.

'Can you use a blade, whelp?' asked Frorl, walking up to him and whirling a practice-sword expertly in his left hand.

'Of course he can't,' snorted Svensson, wrinkling his ruined nose sceptically. 'He's just been pulled off the ice.'

He felt his anger rising at that. Since the changes in his blood, he could be made angry so quickly. The Rune Priest had warned him of that, but still he struggled to control it. Perhaps he would never control it. Perhaps, having been shown the realm of the gods and his place within it, he would still stumble at the final hurdle.

'He'll learn,' said the big one, the one they called Beorth.

Of all of them, he was first to clap his hand on his shoulder. His rough palm fell heavily, like a blow, and he staggered.

'You'll learn, won't you, whelp?'

He looked into Beorth's eyes, and saw the calm, effortless strength there.

'Don't call me whelp,' he said, holding Beorth's gaze.

'Oh?' Beorth looked amused. 'What do you want to be called?'

'Brother.'

Vrakk snorted, still engrossed in his game.

'You have to earn that,' he said.

Aj Kvara didn't look at him. He looked at Beorth, whose hand still rested on his shoulder.

The big warrior seemed like he was going to say something, then paused. He looked down at Kvara, who was still bristling with youth and anger and uncertainty.

'Perhaps you will,' he said. 'For now, though, you need to learn to fight.'

Beorth grinned, and pulled out his blade. It was a short, stabbing sword, notched and serrated along one of the cutting edges and with inset runes lodged under the bronze-lined hilt.

'Let me show you,' he said.

THE IRON WITHOUT

Graham McNeill

NOW

His name was Soltarn Vull Bronn and ten of his vertebrae were mangled beyond the power of even the most mechanically adept Apothecary to save. His legs had been crushed to paste and his left arm jutted from the misshapen ruin of his chevroned shoulder guard like a broken girder. No amount of will could force it to move, but he was able to free his right arm from beneath his breastplate.

The circumvallations at the cave mouth were gone, buried beneath the collapsed ceiling of the enormous cavern. Through dust-smeared eyes, he saw that the wall and his command staff were a crushed ruin of flames and smoke. That meant Teth Dassadra was likely dead as well. Bronn had no feelings towards the man save apathy and an Iron Warrior's natural mistrust, but at least he had been a vaguely competent siege-smith.

His collapsing lungs heaved to sift enough oxygen from the smoke- and dust-clogged air as his ears rang from the apocalyptic detonation that had triggered the collapse. He coughed a wad of bloody phlegm, knowing the position was lost and that any of his warriors who had survived the cave-in he had caused were as good as dead. The Ultramarines' guns would see to that.

Had that been the plan all along?

Try as he might, Bronn could see no other conclusion.

He had followed the Warsmith's orders to the letter, with diligence and dogged loyalty.

In retrospect, perhaps that was the problem.

The Warsmith was a warrior like no other, a killer of men whose mind functioned in a radically different way to the Legion in whose name he once fought. To some, that had marked him for greatness, but to others it was a vile stain on their honour that he should bear the visored skull of the Iron Warriors.

Half-breed, they called him.

Mongrel upstart.

Honsou.

He had left them to die, and though Bronn suspected that defeat would be the inevitable outcome of so risky a war, he found he was still surprised. A lifetime of betrayals; from the dawn of the Imperium, when gods walked among their disciples, and all through the Long War to this latest spasm of rebellion. Ever was it the lot of the Iron Warriors to taste perfidy, but this latest treachery was the bitterest Bronn had ever swallowed.

He had *believed* in Honsou.

Despite his squalid inception, the half-breed had risen through the ranks with the persistence of a monotasked servitor digging an approach trench, displaying just the right balance of initiative and blind obedience to his betters until those less skilled had fallen by the wayside.

It had been on Hydra Cordatus his chance to excel had finally come. Bronn remembered the thundering violence of that siege, the brittle regolith that collapsed at every turn, the hot sun that baked slaves alive and bleached their bones before they were buried in the foundations of the redoubts. Most of all, he remembered the deep yellow rock that resisted every pick and shovel.

It had been a masterfully wrought approach, each sap pitched at a precise angle and every battery thrown up with a speed that would have made the artisan masters of lost Olympia proud. Bronn had fought in the Grand Company of Forrix, and he could still remember the pain of seeing his master gunned down by the Imperial battle engine at the moment of final victory. Standing triumphant in the ruins of the fortress, Forrix had been killed in the moment of regaining his lost fire.

At battle's end, Honsou was named the Warsmith's successor and he had given Forrix and Kroeger's warriors a stark choice: accept him as their new Warsmith and live, or deny him and be destroyed. It was no choice at all, and every warrior had dropped to one knee and sworn fealty to their new master. From Hydra Cordatus, they had battered a path through Van Daal's Black Legion whelps at Perdictor and returned to Medrengard. Honsou had claimed the timeless fortress of Khalan-Ghol for himself, as was his right, but brooding in a crooked spire was not to be the half-breed's destiny.

Jealous eyes had fallen upon Khalan-Ghol, and the grand armies of Lord Toramino had joined forces with the berserk horde of Lord Berossus to attack Honsou in his mountain lair.

Though pain was eating away at his formidable powers of endurance, Bronn grinned wryly at how the two lords of Medrengard had been humbled by the upstart half-breed, their armies broken and scattered to ashes beneath the cruel light of the daemon world's black sun.

Whisperers railed at being commanded by a warrior without lineage, a half-breed with no memory of the Great Betrayal, who had not known the pain of the thousand indignities heaped upon the Legion by the Emperor, and who had not earned his bitterness on the fire-blackened rock of Terra. Honsou's warriors were now fighters without a fortress, rootless wanderers little better than sell-swords, and that was hard to stomach for men who had stood at the side of a living god.

Even after the destruction of Tarsis Ultra, they called Honsou unworthy, and not even the release of the daemon lord M'kar from his imprisonment on the *Indomitable* had appeased his doubters. They hated him, called him impure, and plotted his downfall. Heritage and purity of genetics was all that mattered to these schemers, and no matter how many victories Honsou won, they would never accept him.

Bronn had hunted those who spread dissent and ended them, for he had always known that a warrior's worth was measured in the blood he shed, the soil he dug, the walls he raised and the citadels he split asunder.

By that measure, Honsou was a true Iron Warrior.

But now this...

Bronn could stomach betrayal, it was the Iron Warriors' lot, but to have it come from within on so grand a scale was galling.

What could be so important beneath the surface of Calth that was worth *this*?

THEN

Leaving Soltarn Vull Bronn to oversee the last preparations for the assault, Honsou made his way back through the cavern, relishing the sudden sense of excitement that filled him. It had been a spur of the moment decision to lead the assault into the great underground cavern, but it felt right. It felt good. Every word he had said to Bronn was true, but there was more to it than that.

Honsou cared little for the esteem of his fellow Iron Warriors, but the voices that harped at him from the darkest recesses of his mind demanded he prove his worth every moment of every day.

They are right to hate you...
The Clonelord should never have wrought you...
You are nothing but an aborted experiment that escaped the furnace...

Most of these voices made no sense to Honsou, for he remembered nothing but disjointed scraps of his birth as an Iron Warrior. Nor could he recall the life he had lived before being transformed into a thing reviled by those he had been crafted from and those he had been created for. No, the drive – the *obsession* – he had to place himself in harm's way came from the need to prove those voices wrong.

He *was* as good as any Iron Warrior.

He could fight as hard and with as much cunning and dogged determination as any of those crafted from Perturabo's gene-seed. And if he had to set the galaxy afire from one spiral arm to the other to prove it, then so be it.

Honsou had long ago come to this realisation, but had never voiced it to another soul. Let them think he wanted to be like them. Let them think he wanted to *be* one of them. Their hate only spurred him on, and their sneering condescension only made him stronger.

His fists clenched and he unsheathed the monstrous, night-bladed axe from its leather harness at his shoulder. The weapon had belonged to a warrior of the Black Legion, but like most of the accoutrements of war Honsou now sported, it had been taken as a trophy of murder. His augmetic eye had been plucked from the ruined skull of a Savage Mortician, and the impervious, silver-steel arm had been sawn from the body of a captive Ultramarine.

Further back in the long tunnel that led to the irradiated surface of Calth, a series of armoured blockhouses had been built in staggered chevrons. The Iron Warriors never paused on the march without constructing solid walls to protect their fighters. M'kar might have an inexhaustible army of daemons to call upon, but Honsou needed to husband his resources.

Warriors in burnished plate ran mock assaults with tiny clockwork armies thrown against miniature fortresses, cleaned weapons that had been cleaned a thousand times already or simply stood like ageless statues and waited for the order to attack. Honsou saw Cadaras Grendel and the Newborn working through a series of combat drills before a blockhouse at the centre of the ugly constructions of steel and stone.

Grendel had taken over the Newborn's training since Ardaric Vaanes' capture, but his methods were far from subtle, and he did not have the fluid panache of the former Raven Guard. Where Vaanes had sought to teach the Newborn from a standpoint of making it a better warrior, all Grendel wanted was to make it a better killer.

A subtle difference, and one that mattered little in the crucible of combat, but a difference nonetheless. Honsou had often watched the Newborn train with Vaanes, grudgingly enjoying the ballet of limbs and blades, the lethal choreography of death and the bouts that were more like dances than brutal combats. The Newborn had tried to learn more than just battle skills from Vaanes; it wanted to learn of its soul and how it could rise above its nature to become something more. No such teachings were to be found in Grendel's sparring, only bloody, bruising lessons in killing. If the Newborn sought any higher truths to its existence in Grendel's tutelage, it was having those desires beaten out of it.

Honsou found it hard to look upon the creature, seeing the face of his nemesis in its lopsided features and dead skin mask.

Hot-housed in the nightmarish Daemonculaba womb-slaves, the Newborn was a dark mirror of Uriel Ventris, a hybrid by-blow of warp spawned genetics. No one had expected it to survive, but it had lived and become stronger than anyone could have foreseen. Better to harness and mould such a creature in the ways of its masters before allowing it to become something of its own.

Honsou paused to watch Grendel and the Newborn fight.

It wasn't pretty, a brawl of superhumans who fought without the drag of honour, rules or the need to play fair. Knowing the skill of Grendel and the Newborn, it was likely the bout had been going on for quite some time. Elbows, knees and heads were weapons, a moment of weakness an opening. Their fight was not about who was the best, but about who was left standing. Grendel sent a vicious right cross at the Newborn's jaw, the fist driving with enough force to pulp rock. The Newborn swayed aside, but Grendel's elbow jabbed, cracking it in the jaw and hurling it from its feet.

Grendel followed up with a crushing knee to the groin and a thundering series of rabbit punches to the Newborn's throat. Honsou grimaced as he heard bone break and flesh rupture. The bout was over, but Grendel kept up his furious assault without pause.

'I think you beat him,' called Honsou, and Grendel turned to look at him with a grin of triumph. The mohawked warrior's chest heaved with the adrenaline of battle as the Newborn spat a geyser of brackish fluid and rolled onto its side.

'Remind me never to get into a fight with you, Grendel,' said Honsou, holding a hand out to his lieutenant. Grendel looked up, his malignantly scarred features a clenched fist of venomous anger.

Honsou saw the look and said, 'Don't even think about it.'

Grendel shrugged and took Honsou's silver hand. His fists were coated in blood that vanished into the depths of the alien limb as Honsou pulled him to his feet.

'After we're done here, you and I need to get in the ring,' said Grendel. 'Ever since Khalan-Ghol I've wanted to beat you bloody.'

'Trust me,' said Honsou. 'The feeling's mutual, but I need you alive.'

Grendel twisted his neck and spat a mouthful of crimson spittle as the Newborn climbed to its feet. A faint luminosity shimmered beneath its skin, as though its heart were a lumen globe buried beneath its armour instead of a beating organ. The bones Grendel had broken were already healing, and the cuts his mailed fists had opened on the Newborn's face were sealing even as Honsou watched. He'd long been aware of the Newborn's ability to undo the most horrific damage, but it never failed to unsettle him.

'Is it time to launch the attack?' it asked.

Honsou nodded, but kept his eyes on Grendel.

Though its skin hung loosely on the bone beneath with a mannequin's artificiality, there was no mistaking the patrician cast of its inherited features. He didn't know what the creature had looked like before its transformation in the Daemonculaba, but it bore the unmistakable gene-cast of Uriel Ventris.

'Bronn has everything in place, and we're ready to move,' said Honsou.

'I don't like Bronn,' said Grendel.

'You don't like anyone,' pointed out Honsou.

'True,' admitted Grendel. 'But he *really* gets under my skin.'

'Why?' asked the Newborn. 'From what I have seen, Soltarn Vull Bronn is a highly competent warrior. His geophysical knowledge is second to none. Better even than yours, Warsmith.'

Honsou wanted to feel slighted, but he knew the Newborn was right.

'There's a trace of the witch to him,' said Grendel, swinging his shoulders to loosen the muscles and twisting his neck from side to side. 'I don't care how many sieges a man's fought, you can't know the heart of a planet's rock just by touching it and looking at it.'

'I don't care how he does it,' said Honsou. 'He's never wrong.'

'There's truth in that,' nodded Grendel with customary capriciousness. 'How long before he gets a practicable wall up?'

'It won't be long, no more than a day,' said Honsou.

'We will lose a great deal of men to complete a wall in so short a time,' said the Newborn.

'We stand to lose a lot more than just men if we don't get this done quickly.'

The Newborn nodded, accepting Honsou's logic, but its head cocked to one side as it read a hidden truth behind his expression.

'What are you not telling us?' it asked.

The attack began, as all Iron Warrior attacks began, with a punishing artillery barrage. The guns at the tunnel mouth boomed and roared, filling the cavern with choking banks of acrid propellant smoke. Vast, ceiling-mounted extraction units sucked great lungfuls of the smoke and pumped it back through the rock to the surface of Calth, though no amount of machinery could totally eliminate the chemical reek of explosives fashioned in the heart of a daemon world. No sooner had the first barrage been launched than the second was away. Mutants and adrenal-boosted mecha-slaves fed the voracious appetite of the guns, hauling heavy flatbeds of shells to the artillery line.

Bronn watched the thundering power of the artillery and knew the field of fire was woefully narrow for the task at hand, but with the restricted frontage allowed by the cave mouth, there was little that could be done to widen it. The vibration of the shellfire was titanic, and the cavern shook with the violence of it. Dust and fragments of stone fell from the ceiling, and Dassadra looked up with a critical eye.

'Don't waste your energy worrying about the cavern,' said Bronn over the helm vox. 'The rock above will hold.'

'You're sure?'

'Positive.'

Dassadra looked unconvinced, but Bronn had little time to waste in reassuring him. Any Iron Warrior who couldn't read the structural strength of a cavern like this wasn't worthy of the name. Bronn heard the sound of distant explosions, a subtle change in the pitch of the unending pounding that filled the cavern.

'Earth and deep rock,' he said, angrily. 'We're hitting their earthworks.'

'You want the guns realigned?'

Bronn considered Dassadra's request. It was not a suggestion without merit, for the shellfire was killing nothing of note; maybe a few units of the Ultramar soldiery, but certainly none of the Space Marines sure to be in the valley beyond.

'Yes,' he said at last, 'but remember that these volleys aren't about killing, they're about keeping the bastards' heads down. Move the guns forward and increase the tempo as the flanking artillery widens its fields of fire.'

Dassadra passed the word to the gun crews, and moments later the rapid tempo of the guns stepped up as yet more shells arced into the valley. Dust and pulverised rock hung in the air like heavy fog as the artillery line moved forward with mathematical precision. Bronn felt the vibration of footsteps behind him, and knew from the weight and length of them that his Warsmith was approaching.

Bronn turned to see Honsou hefting a short-handled entrenching tool. Like *Earthbreaker*, it was as much a weapon as a tool of siege.

'Yours?' asked Bronn.

Honsou nodded, and hefted the tool up for him to see. The haft was scored steel and its blade was notched with repeated impacts on hard earth and brittle bones. Flaking brown stains coated its edges, the residue of a thousand or more deaths, and the dirt of myriad worlds encrusted its ragged edge.

'I crafted it myself,' said Honsou proudly, offering it to Bronn.

'As any proper Iron Warrior should,' agreed Bronn, feeling the heft of the entrenching tool. 'It's shorter than most I've seen.'

'All the entrenching tools made in the weapon forges of Warsmith Tarasios were short. Made them better weapons for fighting in a trench.'

Bronn's eyes widened in respect for the lost Warsmith.

'The Warsmith who broke open the Jade Bastion,' said Bronn with an admiring nod. 'I forgot he trained you. That explains why it's weighted towards the digging end.'

'You know as well as I do that battles fought in the trenches are bloody toe-to-toe affairs,' said Honsou, taking back his entrenching tool. 'Brute strength, ferocity and a short swing are more important than skill.'

'And you lack for none of these qualities,' laughed Bronn. 'You are a scrapper and a brawler.'

'Is that a compliment or an insult?' asked Honsou.

'You decide,' replied Bronn. 'Now are you ready to use that thing?'

Honsou grinned and tucked it in tight to his chest. 'Give the word, Soltarn Vull Bronn.'

Bronn lifted *Earthbreaker* and held it aloft for long moments before ramming it down into the hard rock of the cavern floor. The vitrified stone split apart and as the cracks spread out from his feet, a mighty roar went up from the thousands of workers gathered behind him.

As the guns fired once more, Bronn jogged with heavy, mile-eating footfalls towards the mouth of the cave. The rocky floor shook with the force of the heavy digging machines moving through the gaps between the artillery pieces, and trumpeting, honking, screaming war horns blared in unison as the Iron Warriors advanced into the teeth of the Ultramarines defences.

Bronn ran at a relentless pace, stolid and inexorable, with Honsou on one side and Teth Dassadra on the other. They moved without haste, but with a terrible inevitability that had seen even the mightiest citadels humbled. Howitzers spoke with thunderous booms, and the roar of engines echoed from the cavern sides like the howling of an army of daemons.

The light at the cavern mouth swelled before them. The noise was deafening, a titanic hammerblow of shockwaves that made a mockery of any attempt of their armour's auto-senses to attenuate the crescendo of destruction. Bronn felt the percussive body-slam of artillery fire as they ran past the forward line of emplaced Basilisk guns. Spewing clouds of ejected smoke billowed in chaotic vortices, hauled and yanked by the extractors and subterranean atmospherics.

'Iron Within!' shouted Honsou.

'Iron Without!' answered Bronn.

Honsou had seen Four Valleys Gorge before through the eyes of remote drone servitors, each time a fleeting glance before a lethally accurate artillery round atomised it, but this was the first time he had seen it with his own eyes. In times of peace, it would have been place of bucolic splendour that led deeper into the caverns beneath Calth, but now it was like a page from Perturabo's great *Castellum Arcanicus*, with entrenchments spread across the landscape like the sutures on the Newborn's face.

Earthen redoubts and permacrete strongpoints occupied the high ground, while firing trenches, automated pillboxes and armoured brochs covered the dead ground where landscape did not conform to the needs of defence. By any estimation, it was a fearsome array of textbook defences, but what was textbook to the Ultramarines was predictable to an Iron Warrior. Three fortresses of green marble barred further passage downwards at the cardinal points of the enormous cavern, and though each was a powerful bastion, with overlapping fields of enfilading fire, none offered serious impediment to the Iron Warriors.

Honsou saw this in an instant, spotting where the defences were weakest, where an approach might be made – though he would not be making it himself – and where the Ultramarines were hoping to lure them into attack. His view was obliterated a second later as a thundering series of hammerblow detonations marched across the landscape, booming mushroom clouds of geysering earth and fire and smoke.

The sound rolled over Honsou and he grinned at the visceral thrill of fighting at the sharp end of a charge. The plateau before him was empty and shaped like a flat oval, a place for visitors to Calth's underground to marvel in the sheer technical bravura that had shaped so vast a space for human habitation from the rock of a lethal world and rendered it as hospitable and welcoming as any heavenly paradise.

In a heartbeat that vision changed from a place of wonder to a place of death.

The first enemy artillery shells screamed down and exploded above the plateau in a storm of deafening horror. Air-bursting warheads flensed the ground with a hellstorm of red-hot steel fragments; some no larger than a fingernail, others like scything axe-heads, and the carnage wreaked amongst the slave workers was horrendous. Honsou saw a man shredded to the bone, his skeleton pulped to a rubbery mass a second later by the pounding shockwave of detonation.

A group of near-naked slaves with heavy picks slung over their shoulders vanished in a fiery mass of swirling fragments, their remains no longer recognisable as human. Hundreds died in the first instants of the barrage, and a hundred more in the rippling firestorm that followed. Honsou heard their screams, but paid them no mind. Mortal flesh was of no consequence to him. He would sacrifice a million lives on the altar of his ambition, and then a million more.

Shredded carcasses littered the ground, dancing bloody jigs as the ground shook and the air buckled with the bludgeoning force of the blasts. Black streaks of burned smoke and the sucking heaves of pressure drops, sudden vacuums and bangs of displaced air made all sense of direction meaningless. Any sense of up or down, left and right was obliterated in the terrifying disorientation of overloading sound and light and pressure.

Honsou's armour saved him from the worst of the hellish thunder, but it could not fully mask the cataclysmic hammering. His every plate rang with impacts, as though someone was unloading shotgun shells against the back of his helmet with every step. The ground heaved as though in the grip of a powerful earthquake, and fires erupted sporadically from the ignited clothing of the dead.

He could see little before him save banks of shrapnel-twitched smoke and sheeting knives of fire from above that lit fresh scenes of suffering and bloodshed with every strobing flash. Black gashes torn in the ground filled with boiling blood and severed limbs, headless trunks and bones shorn of their flesh. He lost sight of Bronn and the few other Iron Warriors who had made this charge with him. It was impossible to tell if they were still alive or were unrecognisable chunks of gouged meat and metal.

Adrenaline surged around Honsou's body, driving him on through the nightmarish blitzing hurricane of pounding blast waves and fizzing shrapnel. He knew it was foolish to expose himself like this, that he was risking the success of the invasion of Calth with his reckless theatrics, but there was little choice but to show the warriors who followed him that he was willing to risk his own life and that he could fight like an Iron Warrior.

Something struck the side of Honsou's helmet like the thunder hammer of a Dreadnought and he was sent flying. A body flashed past him, and he braced for impact as the clashing, intersecting waves of force flung him about like a leaf in a storm.

He hit the ground hard and skidded across the cratered rubble of the plateau. After a quick check to make sure he still had all his limbs, Honsou pushed himself to his knees with his entrenching tool. The sky rippled with orange and red streamers of arcing shells and fiery detonations, but it felt distant and somehow unreal.

The smell of cooking meat came to him, and Honsou looked down to see a long shard of shell casing jutting from the centre of his breastplate. The metal sizzled, and it was still possible to make out a white eagle and read the stencilled lettering on its side. He grunted and pulled the fragment from his body. Its tip was sharpened to a dagger point, the last ten centimetres coated in blood.

'You don't get me that easy,' he snarled, standing calmly in the midst of the barrage.

Along the length of the plateau, Bronn's earth-moving machines were advancing through the constant rain of artillery shells. The air-bursting shells were having little effect on their up-armoured topsides, and they were driving ever-increasing heaps of rubble and pulverised rock towards the edge of the plateau. A waist-high berm of Calth's earth was being pushed out before the machines, and would swiftly give the mortal slaves a measure of protection while they built up the more permanent defences.

Dozens of machines had been crippled with lucky strikes to vital components, while others had been comprehensively wrecked by enemy gun crews who'd realised the futility of air-bursting man-killers and switched their weapons to high-explosive shells. He saw Teth Dassadra waving more diggers forwards, allocating them work space in lieu of wrecked machines. Honsou remembered Dassadra from the final days of Khalan-Ghol, a warrior who had only too readily switched his allegiance from one master to another. Honsou couldn't fault him for that, where was the sense in staying with a master whose star had been eclipsed?

Honsou would have done the same, but it meant keeping such a man appeased with victory and enough scope for his own ambition to prevent him from turning to bite the hand that fed. Honsou remembered Huron Blackheart's last words to him, and decided that when the time came to abandon this front, he would leave Teth Dassadra behind.

'Are you just going to stand there or are you going to use that damn tool?' demanded Soltarn Vull Bronn, emerging from the smoke and hanging fog of dust particles. Honsou grinned and took a two-handed grip on its short haft.

'Show me where to dig,' he said, and Bronn gestured towards the forward edge of the plateau. Honsou and Bronn ran past a blazing digger, its cab a mass of fused metal and molten rubber pouring from its conduits and exposed pipework. Something writhed within the operator's cabin, something still alive and unable to die in the killing fires. Thick black smoke obscured the horror, and it was behind them before Honsou could make out more than a blackened skull twisting on a serpentine neck, screaming in pain that would never end.

'That trench needs to be another metre deep, and at least half a metre wider if the foundations are going to hold up to a barrage!' shouted Bronn. 'See it done.'

Honsou felt no anger towards Bronn at his brusque tone. This part of the campaign was Bronn's to run as he saw fit, and if that meant dragging the Warsmith towards a trench then so be it.

'Consider it done,' said Honsou, dropping into the trench. A hundred or more mortals in shredded work wear hacked at the earth, picks battering the bedrock of Calth in a staccato rhythm. Some looked up as he landed among them, but most kept their heads to the earth, terrified that if they looked up and acknowledged the carnage going on around them it might reach out and pluck them from their illusory safety.

'Dig together!' shouted Honsou, though he had no idea how many heard him over the constant pummelling of artillery. 'With me!'

Honsou bent his back and drove his entrenching tool into the earth, the blade biting deep and parting the soil of Calth like the softest flesh. He twisted and tossed the earth backwards without breaking the rhythm of his swing, and even before it landed, his shovel blade was embedded in the earth once again.

'Together!' bellowed Honsou, his digging like the regular piston strokes of a battle engine. Dig, lift, twist, thrust. The motion never changed, and Honsou grinned as the memory of his early days in the Legion returned to him. He remembered days spent digging on his belly, pushing approach trenches forward, filling sandbags and gabions with turned earth. Instinctive muscle memory drove his arms, his strength working his body like a perpetual motion machine. There was purity in this work, a singular purpose that allowed for none of the infighting between warbands or any rancour of past betrayals to interfere.

All that mattered was the man and the soil, and the powerful strokes to shift it.

Honsou glanced to his left, and saw the men around him were attempting to mimic his pattern of dig, lift, twist and thrust. They couldn't match his speed or apparently effortless rhythm, but they were at least working together. The trench was already widened and getting deeper with every passing minute.

He heard a screaming whine, louder than the others that blended together in a banshee's chorus, and looked up. Through the billowing, dancing clouds of smoke and dust, Honsou saw a bright streamer of a shell's contrail as it arced over with agonising slowness and aimed its warhead down towards his trench. It should have been moving too fast to see. There should have been little more than a split second's warning, but Honsou saw the gently spinning shell as though upon a slow-motion pict-capture. Its wide body was tapered at both ends, spinning slowly and painted sky blue. Its tip was gold, which struck him as needlessly ornate for a weapon of war, and he had time to wonder whether it would be better to be killed by a precious metal or a base one.

'Incoming!' he shouted, though few would hear his warning or be able to respond to it in time. Honsou threw himself into the forward wall of the trench he had just dug, pressing his body into the earthen rampart and hoping the shell wouldn't be one of the lucky ones to score a direct hit. He clutched his entrenching tool tight to his chest as the scream of the shell's terminal approach battered through the endless thunder of impacts and detonations.

Honsou knew artillery sounds, and this was the sound of a shell coming right at him.

He closed his eyes and exhaled as the shell struck.

The high-explosive shell slashed down and struck the centre of the trench, as though a mathematician had plotted its trajectory. Confined by the high walls, the blast roared out along the trench, incinerating those closest to its point of impact, and shredding those beyond in tightly packed storms of tumbling metal. The shockwave blew men out of their overalls, leaving them naked and twisted into grotesque knots of liquefied bone and shattered limbs.

Honsou was plucked from the trench and hurled into the air. Dozens of red icons flashed to life on his visor as the reflecting blast waves pulled his body in a hundred different directions. Seams split, plates cracked and pressurised coils beneath his breastplate ruptured, venting corrosive gases and precious oxygen. He lost all perception of spatial awareness, and only knew which way was down when he slammed into a line of prefabricated, mesh-wrapped blocks of wall being driven forwards by the second wave of diggers.

Gathered up in the tumbling debris before the blocks, Honsou had no control over his movement. His body was still paralysed by the numbing force of the explosion, and he roared in frustration as he was pushed back towards the trench line. Earth and rock gathered around him, pinning his arms in place, but every nerve in his body was still reverberating in the aftermath of the blast, and he couldn't move.

The yawning black line approached, and Honsou knew there was nothing he could do to prevent his being buried in the trench. A fitting end to his short-lived reign as Warsmith or a bitter irony to be buried in the foundations of a siegework? He kept struggling, though there was nothing he could do to prevent being buried alive. To the last breath he would fight, even as hundreds of tonnes of rubble crushed him to death in the depths of an invaded world.

The harsh rumble of the digger's engine changed pitch, changing from the throaty roar of a corpulent dragon to a squealing wail of a denied hedonist. Honsou teetered on the brink of the abyss, a rain of pebbles, soil and permacrete drooling into the trench in front of him. He let out the breath he hadn't realised he was holding and felt sensation return to his limbs. A hand reached out to him. He grabbed it unquestioningly and hauled himself upright, steadying himself with his entrenching tool.

'Getting buried in the foundations of a fortress wall is one way to prove you are a true Iron Warrior,' said Soltarn Vull Bronn. 'But I wouldn't recommend it.'

Honsou gasped, his body now his to control again, but his racing senses too stupefied to reply. He nodded his thanks as Bronn pulled him away from the front of the earth-moving machine as its engine revved up again, vomiting a petulant blast of exhaust fumes in his face.

'Brother Lacuna does not like to be stopped in his tracks,' explained Bronn, as the machine's horns emitted a series of angry honks and squirts of binary static.

Honsou saw a hostile pair of cybernetic eyes glaring at him from the thin slit cut into the armour of the operator's compartment, and moved away from the machine as its tracked wheels spun and bit. Its feed pipes retched as they poured sludgy grey permacrete into the trench. The oozing mixture set almost instantaneously to form a foundation bed for the blocks coming in on the mass-loaders.

'Won't happen again,' promised Honsou. 'He's bigger than me.'

'When has *that* ever stopped you getting in a fight?'

'Never,' grinned Honsou, taking stock of the work around him.

Despite the continuous bombardment, the shape of the fortification was taking shape all along the plateau. The trench line was filled with rubble and rapid-setting permacrete, onto which hundreds of rectangular, mesh-wrapped blocks of debris were being fixed. Already they formed a waist-high wall embedded with iron spikes and the beginnings of gun ports. The artillery duel was still ongoing, with the Ultramarines having the better of the exchange in terms of lives taken.

But this first sortie had never been about taking lives.

Booming reports exploded overhead, and hammering detonations shook the plateau, but kinetic mantlets were now in place, sheltering the slave workers from the worst of the barrage. As the ground level smoke began to thin, Honsou saw the plateau was a cratered no-man's-land of torn up rock, craters filled with steaming blood and bobbing body parts. A vision of desolation, ruin and death.

'You have your bridgehead, Warsmith,' said Bronn proudly.

'What's the cost?'

'Negligible,' replied Bronn, picking his way over the broken ground to stand in the outline of a gun tower yet to be built. 'Perhaps two thousand slave workers, but there are plenty more on the surface yet to be brought down.'

'Machines?'

Here, Bronn looked concerned. 'At least fifty out of action, and maybe half of those will never raise earthworks again.'

'Fifty? So many?'

Bronn shrugged. 'As I told Dassadra, this is not a normal foe we face. These are warriors of Ultramar. They fight hard, just like us.'

'You're wrong,' said Honsou. 'They don't fight like me.'

'Maybe not, but it's going to be a hard bloody slog to reach those fortresses, no matter how you fight. *That* I can promise.'

Honsou unsnapped the ruptured seals at his gorget and pulled off his helmet. Dried blood streaked his face and he felt a fragment of green glass embedded in his cheek. He had long ago become inured to pain and tore it clear without even noticing.

'The fortresses are unimportant, Bronn,' said Honsou, marching back through the mass of rumbling machines. Milling warriors and bustling slaves jostled in the smouldering ruins as they dragged more and more blocks forwards to raise the fortifications still higher. Much remained to be done on the wall before it could be called practicable, but the hard work had been done. The foundations had been laid and mortared with blood. All that remained was simply a matter of arithmetic and the cold hard logic of war.

'Unimportant?' repeated Bronn. 'That doesn't make any sense.'

Iron Warriors stood tall as Honsou passed, and he knew he had, if not won their unquestioning loyalty, at least earned a measure of temporary respect for his willingness to fight at the lethal edge of battle. The weapons of war may change, knew Honsou, but every war needed a powerful will of bone and muscle and living flesh to win it. No matter how big the guns, or towering the war machines, every siege came down to men putting themselves in harm's way and breaking open the soil of an enemy world. Since the first wooden palisade walls had been raised on hilltops by savages in a forgotten, lightless age it had ever been thus, and always would be.

'It will make sense all in good time, Bronn,' promised Honsou.

'Speak plainly,' demanded Bronn, taking hold of his arm. 'How can the fortresses be unimportant? How else are we going to get below the surface except by breaking them open?'

'*We* aren't getting below the surface,' said Honsou. 'I am.'

'Have you gone mad?' stormed Bronn. 'Ardaric Vaanes was your master of stealth and even he failed to insert himself behind the enemy lines.'

'I'm not planning on doing it stealthily, it'll be in plain sight, but they'll not see me coming,' said Honsou, shrugging off Bronn's hand. 'But this is where I need you to trust me like you have never trusted anyone. Can you do that?'

Bronn stopped to remove his helm, and tucked it under his arm. He looked at Honsou with a resigned expression that spoke of a lifetime of bitter disappointments.

'I would rather not,' he said.

'Honest, at least,' laughed Honsou.

'What did you expect? You didn't get to become Warsmith by being a model of trust and honour.'

'True,' admitted Honsou. 'But I need you to fight in a way you've never fought before.'

'What way is that?'

'I want you to attack this cavern like you're looking to win, but fight simply to hold.'

'What is the point of that? If I attack, it will be to win.'

'I don't need that,' said Honsou.

'Why? There is no purpose to war if not to crush the enemy.'

'Listen well, Bronn,' said Honsou. 'There is something beneath this world the daemon lord requires me to destroy, and I can't do that if I have a host of Ultramarines in pursuit. They need to be kept here, pinned in place for as long as I'm gone. I need them to think this is our true purpose in coming here.'

'Then what is our purpose if not to conquer this world?'

'Better you don't know,' said Honsou. 'We're here for one thing, and it's something I can only do without an army at my back.'

'You're leaving the army?' asked Bronn in disbelief. 'Who will command? The Grand Company won't accept Grendel as their leader; the man's a brute. And that... *creature* from Medrengard you keep around. It's an abomination and it insults every son of Perturabo that you allow it to wear our Legion's colours.'

'Don't worry,' said Honsou with the grin of a man who knows the punchline of a joke no-one even knew he was telling. 'Grendel and the Newborn are coming with me.'

'So who will command?'

'You will,' said Honsou.

It took another fifteen hours for the wall to rise to its prescribed height, twenty metres of hard-packed blocks sheathed in molten metal, strengthened with adamantium reinforcement, and built upon bloody permacrete footings hacked deep into the flesh of Calth. Circular towers with angled abutments, deflector hoardings and numerous loopholes where heavy guns could launch explosive warheads into the valley punctuated its length. Deep artillery pits were dug in the shadow of the banner-topped wall, and into them masked slaves dragged wide-barrelled howitzers on bloody chains. Shaven headed madmen attended these guns, iron-visored priests of the Dark Mechanicus and corrupted calculus-logi with eyes that saw not in hues of mortality, but in angles, trajectories and degrees of deflection.

The Bloodborn army was now ready for battle, thousands of soldiers clad in combat fatigues, gore-smeared armour, fright masks and ragged semblances of uniforms stitched with the daemon lord's rune. Entire regiments were poised in the shadow of the wall, eager to spill the blood of their enemies. Scattered through the host, impatient squadrons of battle tanks, hulking daemon engines and weaponised servitor-things blared their hatred from saw-toothed augmitters. Ten thousand Bloodborn swords clattered on spiked shields, and a rhythmic chanting of meaningless doggerel filled the air beneath the rumble of gunfire.

While the Bloodborn waited for the order to attack and the Iron Warriors busied themselves with the mortal mechanics of their craft, other beings made their way to the centre of the wall. Clad in flesh-sewn robes, they were an incongruous sight amid such industrial activity and mechanistic surroundings. They moved with the lurching, awkward gait of cripples, broken clockwork automatons or things that were unsuited to using mortal bodies for locomotion.

An unnaturally tall being in a fuliginous robe of crimson led them, skeletally thin and hunched over as though made from twisted wire. Its hood flapped loose, as though draped over the long skull of a crocodylus. Wheezing breath escaped from beneath the hood, cold as the grave and just as lifeless.

Bronn and Teth Dassadra watched the approaching warlocks from the centre of the wall with more than a measure of distaste.

'It offends the rites of advance that we use such unnatural means to fight the enemy,' said Dassadra. His hand rested on the butt of his boltgun, as though he was considering turning it upon the witches.

Bronn shrugged. 'We are at war, and we use what weapons are made available to us.' But he too was irked at the appearance of these lurching, wiry figures. Though they were ready to storm the valley, Honsou had postponed the attack until these daemonic sorcerers had done their work.

'What can warpcraft do that our guns cannot achieve?' pressed Dassadra.

'Wait and find out.'

'Where did they even come from? They weren't on any of the ships that came to Calth.'

'You know that for sure, do you?' said Bronn, growing tired of Dassadra's constant harping. 'You searched every scrap of darkness aboard our warships and know they were not among us?'

'I didn't see them when we took Ultimus Prime,' said Dassadra more warily. 'Where were they when we had to fight through an army of skitarii and battle-servitors?'

'Perhaps you should ask M'kar himself,' said Bronn. 'I'm sure the daemon lord would welcome your questions.'

Dassadra fell silent at the mention of M'kar's name, and watched as the figures formed a circle, into which was led a group of slaves who walked with the sluggish, dragging footsteps of sleepwalkers. Their flesh was excoriated and raw, cut with symbols that meant nothing to Bronn, but which he presumed were of significance to the warlocks. The slaves dropped to their knees, idiot grins plastered across their willing faces as they bared their necks.

The leader of the skin-robed witches stepped into the circle of sacrifices and a long blade of a finger unfurled from his ragged sleeve. Part organic, part sharpened wire, it flicked out like a scorpion's stinger, and a throat was opened with a whip-crack of metal on flesh.

'*M'kar tothyar magas tarani uthar!*' screamed the warlock as blood squirted from the slave's ruined artery. Before the first drop hit the ground, the pack of thrall-warlocks fell upon the slaves in a jagged, jerky frenzy of stabbing blades and shrieking wire-claws.

Like a shoal of ripper fish, they tore the slaves to gory tatters, letting their blood fill them like water pumped into empty bladders. The bodies of the warlocks, once so skeletal and thin, now swelled with black life as they gorged themselves on the slaves' life force. They howled with perverse satisfaction, but their joy was short-lived as the master of the sorcerers supped greedily from their newfound well of power.

The blood was drawn from them like dark mist, pulled towards the master of the warlocks like spiralling ribbons of oil in an ocean maelstrom. His hunched form gradually straightened until he stood taller than a Dreadnought, his once frail-looking frame now made monstrous. He raised his curling arms to the cavern's roof and loosed a piercing scream that split the air like the sonic boom of a Hell Talon.

The beat of a thousand Bloodborn drums echoed from the cavern walls in answer as roiling thunderheads formed just below the rocky ceiling. Bronn had quickly adjusted to the changeable weather patterns of the cave, but this was something else entirely.

Arcing bolts of lightning leapt from cloud to cloud, gathering strength and frequency with every passing second. The temperature in the cave dropped sharply, and a cold wind blew from the mouth of the tunnel that led back to the surface.

'Blood of Iron,' cursed Dassadra. 'Lightning? With this much metal? They'll kill us all!'

Bronn said nothing, knowing that this was no ordinary lightning to be drawn to iron as metal is drawn to a magnet. This was warp lightning, brought into being and directed by the towering figure at the heart of the sorcerers. A booming peal of thunder eclipsed the maddened drumming, and a sheet of dazzling lightning blazed from the clouds. The atmosphere in the cavern *twisted* as though some fundamental aspect of it had changed, and blinding traceries spat from the unnatural clouds. Black rain fell in torrents, turning much of the cavern floor to quagmire and slicking the armour of the Iron Warriors with an oily, rainbow sheen.

Instead of striking amid the Bloodborn as Dassadra had feared, the lightning slammed down again and again over the upland ridges where the enemy artillery pieces were sited. Mushrooming flares of explosions curled into the air, followed moments later by the crack of detonating munitions. Fire raced over the high ground as weapon after weapon went up, vanishing in a spreading bloom of electrical fire. Explosions lit the underside of the clouds, and Bronn blinked away dazzling afterimages of darting, invisible forms; all black wings, reptilian bodies and screaming fangs.

'Now do you see the worth of these warlocks?' asked Bronn.

Dassadra nodded curtly. 'They are effective, I'll give them that.'

That was as much as Dassadra would allow, and Bronn grinned as the ridges between the three fortresses burned in the fires of the warp.

'Order the advance,' said Bronn. 'Tanks and infantry only.'

Dassadra looked up, puzzled. 'Only tanks and infantry? Why not the daemon engines?'

'Because that is the order,' said Bronn.

'We should attack with everything we have,' protested Dassadra. 'First Wave doctrine requires overwhelming force to break the will of the defenders.'

'I know Perturabo's doctrines, Dassadra, I need no lessons from you.'

'Then why–'

'Carry out your orders!' snapped Bronn.

The sounds of battle were muted by the rain and distance, but even from behind the high wall he had built, Bronn could hear sharp exchanges of gunfire, explosions and screams. Dassadra remained on the wall, and though the man had balked at Bronn's seemingly inexplicable orders, Bronn had given him no choice but to obey.

Bronn marched through the screaming, stamping mass of cyborg battle engines Votheer Tark had contributed to the invasion of Calth, knowing better than to stare too long at the binding symbols hacked into the meat and iron of their bodies. Some were restrained by chains of cold iron, others by more esoteric means, but every one was a lethal engine of bloody death that could fight for an eternity without tiring of the carnage.

Had these machines been sent into the fight, the enemy might already be broken, but Honsou did not want the enemy broken. It seemed like folly of the highest order, but Bronn forced himself to stop second-guessing Honsou's plans. The Warsmith had the favour of the daemon lord, and the workings of such a mind were not for mortals to know.

Bronn entered the vast arch that led back towards the surface, following the sound of shrieking hydraulics, low-grade melta cutters and clattering armour. Arc lights riveted to the cavern walls illuminated ammunition and explosives gathered in towering stacks, and the light reflected dazzlingly from vast iron plates being bolted to the rock of the cavern. The metal roadway was being laid in readiness for the arrival of the Black Basilica, the hulking leviathan that was part mobile cathedral to the great gods of the warp, part awesomely destructive war engine with the power to level cities.

The Iron Warriors and the Bloodborn had reached the valley through tunnels dug by subterranean Hellbore diggers, but the Black Basilica needed the rubble blocking the full girth of the tunnel cleared before it could take part in the battle. Its overwhelming firepower would be decisive, and Bronn wondered how he could possibly maintain the stalemate Honsou desired with so powerful a weapon at his disposal.

He paused in his journey to place a hand on the cavern wall, letting the soul of the planet come to him through his gauntlet. The rock glistened in the glow of the arc lights, the quartz and nephrite shimmering like specks of sickly gold. Bronn pressed his cheek to the stone, feeling every tiny vibration, every imperfection and every teasing ripple from afar. The Black Basilica was close; he could feel the tremors of its monstrous weight and the core-deep rumble of its engines.

'Two hours perhaps,' he said quietly. 'No more than three.'

This world was hurting, and every pick, shovel and drill that pierced its skin was a wound that would never heal. Though Calth was a planet honeycombed by tunnels burrowed through its mantle, they were passages opened by people that had once called its surface home before Lorgar's spite had poisoned its sun. Calth had not resented those intrusions, but the Iron Warriors were unwelcome visitors, and every grain of soil they dug was begrudged.

Bronn pushed himself away from the wall and continued deeper into the cavern until he came to a row of five tubular machines shaped like enormous torpedoes with rock-drilling conical snouts. Each Hellbore was as long as a Stormbird, but wider in beam and more heavily armoured. Their flanks were bare, scraped iron and all five had their crew ramps splayed wide as the assault forces boarded.

Only the nearest of the Hellbores would be carrying Iron Warriors, the others transporting Bloodborn shock-troops or Astartes warriors from the renegade Legions spawned in the aftermath of the Great Betrayal. None of these latter warriors were closer than six foundings to the first Legions, and yet they called themselves Space Marines. Mixed in with these inferior copies were a bastard mix of xenos species, some bipedal and birdlike, crested with spines of many colours, others arachnid, quadruped or unclassifiable in form.

Bronn shook his head at such a mongrel mix of killers.

'I know what you're thinking,' said Honsou, approaching from the nearest Hellbore. 'It's an ugly looking army.'

'Ugly doesn't even begin to cover it,' said Bronn. 'I can accept a great many things, but to know that we have fallen so far is… galling. We once fought alongside the primarchs, gods of the battlefield, and now we draft sub-par warriors who call themselves Space Marines and unclean species from who knows where in the galaxy to fight our battles.'

'These are cannon fodder,' said Honsou. 'And if it makes you feel any better, they're all going to die.'

'Yet you are going with them into the valley.'

Honsou shook his head. 'No, these are just a distraction, something to keep the Ultramarines looking straight ahead while I go beneath them.'

'Hiding in plain sight,' said Bronn with a slow smile of understanding.

'Just so,' agreed Honsou.

Bronn's hand unconsciously moved towards his pistol as Cadaras Grendel and the creature Honsou called the Newborn approached. Both saw the gesture and their posture changed immediately. Grendel grinned in anticipation of a fight, while the Newborn looked at him curiously, as though trying to decide which limb to remove first. It took an effort of will, but Bronn removed his hand from his weapon.

Grendel laughed and jerked his thumb in the direction of the Newborn. 'Very wise, this one would have ripped your head off before that gun could clear its holster.'

Bronn ignored Grendel, watching as the sinuous forms of the blade dancers climbed into the last Hellbore. Each was a swordmaster of sublime skill that had followed their champion, Notha Etassay, to New Badab in search of enemies worthy of their blades. Bound to Honsou after he had defeated Etassay during the final duel of the Skull Harvest, they were devotees of the Dark Prince and therefore not to be trusted.

Honsou followed his gaze and said, 'This is war; and I'll make use of such weapons or warriors as I have without care or regret.'

'I said the same thing to Dassadra,' replied Bronn. 'But I was lying.'

Honsou shrugged. 'You still believe in the old ways, Bronn. That's always been your problem.'

'The old ways were good enough for Lord Perturabo,' said Bronn.

'And look where that got him,' said Honsou with sudden anger. 'Stuck in a dead city on Medrengard, imprisoned by his own bitterness and resentment. If he cared so much about the wrongs done to him, why isn't he out bringing every Imperial stronghold to ruin? There isn't one fortress wall left standing that he couldn't put to rubble in a day.'

Honsou's vehemence surprised Bronn. He hadn't thought the Warsmith cared anything for the Long War or Perturabo's notable absence from its battles. Had Bronn misjudged him or was this yet another piece of theatre designed to achieve an end that could not yet be seen?

'The ways of our master are not for us to judge,' he said, though words sounded hollow even to him.

'You're wrong,' said Honsou. 'They *are* ours to judge. And one day someone will take Perturabo to task for his lack of action.'

That made Bronn laugh. 'Really? And who will that be? You?'

Honsou's anger vanished, and Bronn was reminded how unpredictable Honsou could be, as violent as a berserker or as capricious as a pleasure-seeker of the Dark Prince.

'Who knows?' said Honsou with a broken-toothed grin. 'Maybe I will one day. Wouldn't that be delicious? A half-breed mongrel bastard sat atop the Ivory Throne. What I wouldn't give to see old Forrix's face if he could have lived to see that!'

'You're insane,' said Bronn, as sure of that fact as he was about the composition of Calth's bedrock.

'You might be right,' said Honsou, turning away and making his way towards the assault ramp of the Hellbore. 'But I have a shrine to find and you have a battle to prolong.'

A group of perhaps forty Iron Warriors marched ahead of Honsou, filing into the Hellbore with unquestioning discipline. Bronn knew a great many of these warriors; they were among the finest killers left to the Legion. All had fought on Terra, and each had sworn personal oaths of moment before the Ivory Throne. A pang of bitter and solemn regret touched Bronn to see such warriors engaged in such an ignoble war.

Honsou climbed to the top of the ramp and turned as Grendel and the Newborn went inside. He raised a fist to Bronn and slammed it hard against his breastplate.

'Give me a day,' said Honsou. 'Give me a day, and I'll give you a victory that will make you forget there ever were any "old ways".'

Bronn nodded as the assault ramp folded up into the body of the Hellbore, but his heart sank as he heard the lie in the Warsmith's voice.

Honsou was leaving them to die.

* * *

NOW

The pain was getting worse.

His armour was non-functional, and he could barely move. His strength, once so formidable, was deserting him. Plates that had once protected him from harm were now a burden his weakening body could no longer endure. He remembered being presented with his armour in the columned majesty of the Gallery of Stone, kneeling with thousands of his fellow warriors before the burnished form of the primarch.

Bronn remembered the unbreakable pride he had felt, the sense of belonging to something greater that had sustained him all through the darkest days of the Great Betrayal. The Long War and the decline of the Legion had shown him there was no such thing as unbreakable. Even the greatest pride could be humbled, even the mightiest fortress could be breached, and even the staunchest faith could be shattered in the face of betrayal.

How had he failed…?

The attack of the Bloodborn had been defeated, broken and hurled back by the combined might of the Ultramarines and their mortal armies. The savage warriors of the Mechanicus had fallen upon their dark brothers, fighting with a ferocious hatred born of the knowledge that their foes had once been like them. Yet even as the battle turned in the favour of the Imperial forces, the Black Basilica had joined the fight, and its vast array of guns had wrought fearful carnage upon the defenders, bringing them to the verge of destruction.

But even that mighty weapon had been lost…

Pieces of the dark leviathan lay scattered around the cavern, its priceless debris left to rust in the moist atmosphere, for no adepts of the Dark Mechanicus remained alive to gather them. Bronn should have anticipated a stealthy insertion, after all the Raven Guard had always been the masters of the shadow strike and the infiltration of the most heavily defended citadels.

Bronn remembered fighting alongside Corax and his warriors many years ago, in battles that had been forgotten by that primarch's sons, but which were still fresh in his mind. For all that the Space Marines of this stagnant Imperium were pale shadows of the great Legions of old, the man who had led his team into the heart of the Black Basilica was a warrior worthy of the title. Professional admiration gave way to pain as he coughed a wad of blood onto his chest.

With the destruction of the Black Basilica, the fight had gone out of the Bloodborn, and Bronn cursed Honsou for allying what little strength remained to their fragment of the Legion to such dross. Dassadra had slaughtered scores as they fell back over the wall, bloodied and broken against the ceramite and blue lines of the cavern's defenders.

A gloomy status quo had fallen between the two armies as Bronn and Dassadra sought to re-establish control over the shattered mortals of the Bloodborn. Threats, promises of plunder and a number of strategic executions had brought order back to the host, and Bronn had drawn up plans for a second assault when yet another disaster had struck.

With the Bloodborn drawn up in readiness to assault the valley once again, word came of an attack from the rear. Sporadic explosions and gunfire drifted from the tunnel they had fought to clear for the Black Basilica, the rattle of small-arms fire and the heavier blasts of wide-bore guns belonging to battle tanks. It should have been impossible. Hadn't the Ultramarines been broken on the surface? But as more contact reports screamed over the vox, it became impossible to deny the reality of the catastrophe.

A ragtag host of scavenged armoured vehicles, ad-hoc battalions and Ultramarines surged from the tunnel mouth and fell upon the Bloodborn with the fury of berserkers. Bronn knew some form of communication must have passed between these Ultramarines and the defenders of the valley when an answering battle cry went up from the three fortresses.

Their gates had opened and thousands of blue-armoured soldiers had charged out with squads of Ultramarines at their head. Despite the best efforts of Bronn and Dassadra, the sight of two forces closing on them had shattered the last courage of the Bloodborn and they had scattered into disparate warbands, striking out for their own survival, little realising that by doing so they had doomed themselves.

Hammer and anvil, both forces of Ultramarines had smashed together, crushing the Bloodborn between them, and they had not been merciful. Yet for all that the battle was lost, the Iron Warriors were not about to lay down their weapons and go quietly into defeat. Knowing that Honsou had left them to die, Bronn had prepared for such a moment and waited until the time was right to vent his last breath of hatred.

The traitor Warsmith Dantioch had called it the final solution to any siege, and in that at least he had been right.

A vast array of explosives rigged along the length of the tunnel awaited his trigger signal, and as Bronn saw an Ultramarines sergeant coming for him with murder in his stride, he had known that time had come. With one last look at the fortifications he had fought and bled to build, Bronn mashed the firing trigger and the world ended in fire, falling rock and thunder. He expected to die in the collapse, but he had lived, though it was to be only a brief respite.

Bronn blinked away afterimages of crackling detonations, strobing flashes of secondary explosions and crackling ammo fires.

He knew he was dying, but to die for this?

To be nothing more than... what, a distraction for a mission that had clearly failed?

That was galling for a warrior of his heritage.

He felt the earth shake again, and his eyes flicked towards the roof of the cavern. Dust fell in a dry rain, and spalling flakes of glassy stone sounded like sand trickling through an hourglass as it slowly coated the battlefield. Though the cavern's structure was sound, Bronn wished for the cave to collapse, to bury this moment of infamy beneath millions of tonnes of rock and deny his foes any succour in triumph.

The ground shook again, but this was no aftershock of his final solution, this was a tremor of something moving beneath the earth. Bronn knew rock well enough to know the difference, and he pressed his palm to the ground, letting it speak to him as it had on countless occasions before. He felt the seismic communication, the echoes and the gnawing bite of melta-bladed cutters as they clove the rock like a pack of subterranean borer-ambulls.

Beyond the mangled remains of a trio of Basilisk artillery pieces, the earth heaved upwards, and a geyser of spraying stone and mud exploded into the air as something iron and yellow heaved its bulk into the cavern. Bronn instantly recognised the conical snout and flared rock scoops of a Hellbore drilling rig.

'Careful, you idiot...' he hissed. 'The soil is always thinner nearer the surface.'

Whoever was driving the Hellbore was unskilled in the finer points of its operation, handling it like a runaway Land Raider instead of a precision tunnelling device. Sparks flew as its drill cogs tore through a wrecked chassis of a smouldering battle tank. Metal shavings flew like glittering decoy chaff ejected from the defence pod of a Thunderhawk.

The Hellbore vanished from sight as it lurched past its centre of gravity and crashed down onto its side. An explosion ripped up from the mangled tank as an ammo cache exploded. More than likely, the occupants of the Hellbore were now trapped within. If the Ultramarines didn't kill them, the lack of oxygen would eventually see them dead.

Whoever had brought the machine back to Four Valleys Gorge had returned to defeat and death, and Bronn dismissed the tunneller as he heard the voices of Ultramarines, curt orders barked in a battle cant that had not changed in ten thousand years.

Such a span of time was almost incomprehensible. To Bronn, those days of gods and heroes were a past he had lived in the span of a single lifetime, but these warriors had only half-remembered myths to tell them of such long ago days. They could not remember what was a recent memory for him...

I was there when the walls of the Imperial Palace fell.

Bronn turned his head, searching for a weapon to hold as he died. A bolter lay within easy reach, but beyond it he caught sight of *Earthbreaker*, the weapon that had cast unnumbered fortresses down and raised myriad others to the skies. His gauntlet closed on the T-shaped pommel, and he dragged it over the broken ground with his fingertips. The blade scraped over the black stone brought down from the cavern's ceiling, high-density igneous rock laid down in volcanic eruptions before men had set foot on this world.

'Fused metamorphic stone from close to the surface,' he said with a wheezing, frothed breath that told him his lungs had finally collapsed. With only his secondary organ dragging oxygen to his broken body, it was only a matter of time until hypoxia killed him.

'Aurelian's sons were thorough in their spite,' he noted, seeing fragments of irradiated flakes mixed in with the rock.

'Yet still they were defeated,' said a cultured, perfectly enunciated voice above him.

A foot stamped down on *Earthbreaker*'s haft, snapping the weapon in two. Anger engulfed Bronn, and he rolled onto his back, ignoring the shooting spikes of searing pain that engulfed his chest, yet left his body below untouched. He looked up at a broad-shouldered warrior in the azure battle plate of the Ultramarines. A golden eagle glittered at his chest and star-bleached emerald trim lined the notched edges of his shoulder guards.

'Things might have been different had the Iron Warriors been with them,' hissed Bronn, clutching the broken handle of *Earthbreaker* to his chest. The warrior shook his head and removed his laurel-wreathed helm, revealing a face of classic patrician proportions, symmetrical and with high cheekbones, a strong chin and close-cropped blond hair that framed eyes of milky blue. Every inch an Ultramarine.

'You are defeated here,' said the warrior, sliding a fresh magazine into his pistol. 'I do not think the outcome then would have been much different had a wretch like you been there.'

'You are wrong, whelp, iron is forever,' said Bronn, letting his head loll to one side. 'From iron cometh strength. From strength cometh will. From will cometh faith. From faith cometh honour. From honour cometh iron.'

'What is that?' asked the warrior, his voice dripping with contempt. 'A prayer?'

'It is the Unbreakable Litany,' said Bronn, his strength fading. 'And may it forever be so.'

Through the dancing flames of defeat, Bronn saw a darting figure slip through the wreckage of the Basilisks crushed by the Hellbore, a half-glimpsed shadow with a limb that threw the firelight queerly from its mercurial surface. Though it should have been impossible, Bronn thought he saw a pale blue glow of an augmetic eye through the sheeting dust and ash.

Your mission is complete, the eye seemed to say. *But mine goes on...*

'Why did you come here?' demanded the Ultramarine. 'You must have know you could not defeat the true sons of Guilliman.'

'Why did we come here?' smiled Bronn, shaking his head as a weight lifted from his broken body. 'Better you don't know.'

He loosened his grip on the iron will that held his life anchored to his flesh, staring up at the Ultramarines warrior with a last breath of defiance.

'You think you have won a victory here?' he said.

'I know we have,' said the warrior. 'Your force is destroyed, and Calth is ours again. All across Ultramar, your master's armies are being pushed from our worlds. Yes, I would say this is a victory.'

'The years have not been kind to the Ultramarines,' said Bronn. 'Once they were the Battle Kings of Macragge, but you are just poor shadows of those giants.'

The warrior levelled his pistol at Bronn.

'I should leave you to suffer your pain, but it insults me to let you sully this world with your life a moment longer.'

'Who are you?' asked Bronn. 'Tell me the name of the man who is going to kill me.'

The warrior considered his request for a moment before nodding.

'I am Learchus Abantes, sergeant of the Ultramarines Fourth Company.'

Bronn smiled. 'The Fourth, yes. Of course it would be one of you.'

Learchus pulled the trigger, and Bronn died knowing yet more blood would be spilled before the Iron Warriors were done with Calth.

DEUS EX MECHANICUS

Andy Chambers

The scream of the engines fought against the howling winds in a terrifying crescendo of doom. Hypervelocity mica particles skittered across the hull of the ship like skeletal fingers as it wallowed in the storm, shuddering and dropping by steps as the pilot struggled for control. In the midst of the tumult, Lakius Danzager, tech-priest engineer, Votaris Laudare, illuminant of Mars, adept of the Cult Mechanicus was struggling to open up the skull of that failing pilot, and cursing in a distinctly un-priestly fashion as he struggled to find the right tools for the job.

'Dammit! Osil, find me a hydro coupling, my boy. We'll need one if I can free these accursed fasteners. Look in the vestibule.' He tried to keep his voice calm so as not to frighten his acolyte, but Osil's face was pallid in his cowl as he nodded and hurried out through the rusty bulkhead hatch.

The ship's rattling, brassbound altimeter showed them at a height of nearly seven kilometres above the planet. They had already been dropping out of control for twelve. As Lakius turned back to the rune-etched panel enclosing the ship's pilot, another violent lurch smashed his shaven skull against it, triggering an emgram patch he had only recently divined from his auto-shrine. It was about their too-rapidly approaching destination, and ran in confusing counterpoint through his right optic viewer as he tried to focus on repairing the nav-spirit.

NAOGEDDON IS A DEAD WORLD.

The ringing impact of Lakius's metal-shod head had partially freed the rusting key-bolts. With a whispered prayer for forgiveness from the already distraught machine-spirit, he bent to the task. He carefully unscrewed the panel, murmuring the rite of unbinding and ensuring that he removed the keys in the correct cardinal directions. The ghostly image of a dun-coloured sphere hovered in his right eye. Red text scrolled past it.

Orbital distance: 0.78 AU.
Equatorial Diameter: 9,749 km.
Rotation: 34.6 hours.
Axial Tilt: 0.00.

As he'd feared, the coupling between the augur spike and the pilot-stone had ruptured, blinding the pilot to its landing beacon. He checked the altimeter as he began the ritual of dislocation to remove the charred remnants. Less than two kilometres of howling winds now lay beneath their rocking hull.

Weather: See storms*.

'Osil! Where's that coupling, boy?'

'Here, father. The first one was faulty and I had to go back for another.'

0% Precipitation. Wind speed: Constant 24 kts, Variance 76 kts.

Lakius took the twist of hydro-plastic without comment but silently gave praise to the Omnissiah that the lad had been attentive enough to spot the difference. Under current circumstances, a normally forgivable sin of oversight could prove fatal. Lakius took a breath to steady himself before beginning the ritual of insertion.

Lifeforms: Autochthonic: None.
Introduced: None.

Less than a league of free air remained before they would hurtle into solid rock. His servo-hand shook as he tried to apply the proscribed number of half-turns to the coupling mounts. He yearned to simply call the rite finished and resurrect the pilot. But years of discipline and doctrine drove him on as he completed the benediction against failure, applied the sacred unguents and retrieved the panel so he could begin the final rites of protection and sealing.

Archaeotech Resource: Limited/Xeno artefacts*/@ 600,000,000 yrs (pre. GA) Class: Omega.

'Father, I can see dust dunes below us. I think we're going to crash.'

Notes:
First Catalogued: 7/243.751.M32. Rogue trader Xiatal Parnevue. Orbital Augury Only*. Annexus Imperialus.

'Mechanism, I restore thy spirit! Let the God-Machine breathe half-life unto thy veins and render thee functional.' Lakius firmly depressed the activation rune on the pilot's casing and prayed.

Landed: 6/832.021.M35. Explorator Magos Dural Lavank. Expedition Lost.
Landed: 7/362.238.M37. Explorator Magos Prime Holisen Zi. Expedition Lost.

The ship's engines rose in a triumphant scream to drown out the rushing winds and skittering dust. Lakius and Osil felt the heavy weight of high-G deceleration as the ungainly craft steadied itself and slowed. Lakius could see dust dunes too now, through the curving port in the ship's prow, but the dunes with their trailing streamers of blowing dust were dwarfed by the serried ranks of sharp-angled black monoliths which rose up around the ship as it dipped between them. Osil let out an involuntary gasp as the scale of the structures became apparent. The monoliths were mountain-sized edifices of harsh, alien rock cutting the horizon into sawtooth edge, or a predator's maw.

Landed: 6/839.641.M41. Explorator Magos Prime Reston Egal. Surface Survey*. Xeno Structures Catalogued*.

The ship changed course, angling towards a vast dark triangle which blotted out half the sky. The pilot-spirit was faithfully following the beacon, bringing them in towards a tiny ring of light in the shadows below it. There lay the explorators' camp.

Gritty sand crunched underfoot and a cold, stinging wind blew more of it into their faces as they stepped down to the landing ground. Patchwork figures of steel and flesh were rolling towards them on armoured treads; Lakius and Osil waited by the ship and made no sudden moves.

'See there, Osil: the explorators have invoked a laser mesh for the protection of the camp. How powerful would you say it is?'

'I see three transformation engines on this side of camp. Assuming the same number on the far side I would estimate 10 to 20 gigawatts, father.'

The figures came closer. They were Praetorians, bionically reconstructed warrior-servitors of the Machine-God. Their cadaverous faces gazed stonily from a nest of targeting scopes and data-wires, gun barrels and energy tubes tracked Lakius and Osil until they halted. A chest-mounted speaker on one crackled into life.

'Two lifeforms identified. Classified non-hostile. Please follow, Father Lakius, Acolyte Osil.'

They followed a pair of the heavy servitors between low buildings of pre-fabricated armourplas panelling towards a central command sphere. Osil pointed to one of the smaller structures which had its panels folded back to create a workshop lit from within by welding arcs and showers of sparks.

'What works are being undertaken here, father?'

Lakius repressed a chill sensation of foreboding 'They are reinitiating servitors, Osil. Evidently there has been some accident or mishap which has rendered the units non-functional.' He forbore to comment on the row of ready caskets outside the workshop, containers for tech-priests whose biological components were fit only for incorporation into new servitors. Several priests must have died here already.

The Praetorians motioned them into the command-sphere and remained on guard outside. Inside was a scene of barely organised chaos. Wiring cascaded from panels and conduits, devices of a hundred types thrummed, buzzed and sparked, screenplates flickered and scrolled through endless lines of scripture. A robed priest detached himself from a group clustering around the central dais and addressed Lakius.

'Adept Danzager, your arrival has been greatly anticipated. I am Adept Noam, Lexmechanic Magos Tertius. I have the honour of analysing and compiling data on this expedition.' Noam was gaunt and emotionless, only his lack of bionic enhancement and priestly robes marking him apart from the servitors. Two other priests gathered behind him. Noam pointed to each in turn and pronounced their roles with toneless efficiency.

'Adept Santos, artisan, responsible for camp construction and maintenance.' A rotund man nodded. He was heavily rebuilt with a subsidiary lifting arm at his shoulder and a mass of diagnostic probes in place of his left hand and eye.

'Adept Borr, rune priest, extrapolation and theory.' Borr was slight and nervous-looking, and seemed to be on the edge of speaking when Noam cut him off. Noam and Borr evidently didn't get along. Noam gestured to the other robed figures within the chamber.

'Adepts Renallaird, Kostas and Adso are engineers like yourself, their areas of expertise covering the mysteries of generation, augury and metriculation. Adept Virtinnian is absentia, attending to the servitors at present.' Renaillard, Kostas and Adso looked up briefly as their names were mentioned and gave a perfunctory nod before bending back to their work.

'Blessings of the Omnissiah be upon you all,' Lakius said. 'Am I to assume that you are the leader of this expedition, Adept Noam?'

'No, Explorator Magos Prime Reston Egal has that blessing. He will be joining us shortly.'

'Can you tell me why I have been summoned here then? I know that this is an important undertaking; after all, it has already made me late for my own funeral.'

If Noam understood the joke he made no sign, but Borr grinned behind his hand. Noam replied, 'Yes, you were scheduled for dissemination at the termination of your last assignment. A post with the Officio Assassinorum, I understand. You must be disappointed that your emgrams cannot yet be joined with the Machine-God.'

'In truth, it is my belief that I serve better as a living being than a collection of memories and servitor wetware.'

'Understandable, and very biological.' Something close to disdain passed across Noam's features when he said biological. 'I see that you have never considered undertaking the unction of clear thought.'

'The unction of clear thought? What is that, father?' blurted Osil, forgetting that he should be seen and not heard amongst such adepts.

Noam replied smoothly, apparently not troubled by the acolyte's gaucheness. 'The full utilisation of cerebral mass is a simple matter of isolating our thoughts from the rigours and distractions of emotion – hunger, fear, joy, boredom and so forth. This we know as the unction of clear thought.'

'A common surgical practice among lexmechanics,' Lakius told Osil, 'whose renowned cognitive abilities are enhanced thereby.' At the price of becoming an emotionless automaton he thought to himself, before adding more diplomatically, 'In my own role as engineer I have always found crude emotions such as "fear" and "pain" to be useful motivators under the right circumstances.'

'Indeed?' Noam said, warming to his subject matter. 'Studies of stress–'

'Splendid! This must be our new expert in cryo-stasis!'

Noam was cut off by a newcomer who had lurched into the chamber like an animated scarecrow, all gangling arms and legs. His narrow, vulpine head, scrawny neck and thin body conspired to complete the illusion. He grinned voraciously at Lakius. 'Now you're finally here, we can get on with it! Splendid!'

Lakius bowed deeply. 'Magos Egal, I presume.'

'That's right. I see you've met the others and Noam's about to treat you to a sermon!' Magos Egal winked conspiratorially at Lakius, bouncing up and down on his heels as if he couldn't contain his delight. Lakius was astonished. He was used to a certain amount of... eccentricity among senior members of the Mechanicus, explorators in particular, but Egal seemed to be verging on the edge of lunacy. 'You come highly commended, you know! Highly commended! Two centuries of experience!'

'Almost fifty years aboard a single craft, servicing a single sarcophagus, magos. Admittedly, that was of alien design and its failure would have brought about my immediate dissemination – but I cannot imagine how I may be of service here.' In truth, Lakius had a strong and unpleasant suspicion exactly why cryo-stasis was of interest to this famed explorator, but he wished to hear it said out loud.

'You can't guess? I bet you can, but you want to hear it anyway! You're a sharp one! I like that.' Egal grinned lopsidedly, 'Do you know what this place is?' Egal thrust his arms outwards to encompass the whole world.

'Naogeddon... a dead world.'

'No!' Egal thrust up a finger to make his point. 'Not dead, sleeping! Sleeping these six hundred million years!' Lakius's stomach underwent a queasy lurch.

Egal composed himself a little and went on. 'Let me begin at the beginning. Over six hundred million years ago, a race we know as the necrontyr arose and spread across the galaxy. What little we know of these giants of prehistory has been learned from a handful of so-called dead worlds, like this one, scattered at the very fringes of the galaxy. On each world stand vast, monolithic structures which have remained all but impenetrable to every device at the hand of man. The level of technology evident in their construction is almost incomprehensible to us and many explorers have been lost winning the fragmentary knowledge we do have.

'On my first expedition to Naogeddon, we gained certain measurements and calibrations which are singular to the dead worlds of the outer rim, these ancient seats of the necrontyr. These have enabled myself and Adept Borr to fashion a device... a key, if you will, which can unlock these structures without awakening their occupants.'

Adept Borr had grown increasingly agitated as Magos Egal spoke and now he interjected, 'Magos, the last attempt caused an exponential jump in attacks–'

Noam cut him off smoothly. 'Adept Borr, those projections have not been verified. Adept Santos has confirmed the current threat is well within the capacity of our defences to contain.'

'The current threat, yes, but if things go wrong–'

Adept Santos seemed affronted by Borr's implied criticism. 'We have a fifteen gigawatt laser mesh, twenty armed servitors and storm bunkers built out of cubit thick, Titan-grade armourplas panels. What could possibly go wrong?'

Egal had passively watched the exchange with fatherly humour and a slight grin, but now he became animated again. 'Ah yes! Speaking of which, I believe they're due to attack any time now. Stations, everyone!'

Lakius's queasy stomach lurched up towards his mouth. Sirens wailed a second later.

'You mean they attack at the same time every day?'

'Well, every dusk. Strictly speaking.'

Lakius, Osil and Borr were in an observation gallery at the top of the command sphere. As a rune priest adept, Borr was trained to piece together fragmentary information and make a speculative theorem, something akin to black magic to most tech-priests. As such, Borr had explained, he was detailed to make observations of their attackers, try to understand their tactics, strengths and weaknesses and then feed effective protocols to the Praetorians.

'I thought it was already night,' Osil said.

'No, Osil, it's always this dark because of the dust in the atmosphere, most of the suns' light is reflected back into the void,' Lakius replied. 'Adept Borr, what are these attackers? Despite Adept Santos's reassurances, I note a number of casualties have already been incurred.'

'They appear to be mechanisms: humanoid, skeletal, most assuredly armed. We have not been able to secure one for study, despite strenuous efforts.'

'And I did not note an astropath adept among those spoken of so far.'

Hesitantly, Borr looked up at Lakius. His tattooed face was underlit by the greenly glowing glass of the augurs before him, but to Lakius the sickly pallor was underwritten by a deeper fear. 'Adept Arraius... disappeared prior to the very first attack. I–I fear Magos Egal has not fully thought through the implications of this site. There are machine spirits here which have functioned continuously for six hundred million years.'

Borr would have continued but an alarm began chiming, quietly but insistently.

The augur screen flashed and displayed a grid with moving icons, Borr glanced down and said, 'The Praetorians have spotted something. We should have it at any moment. There, eight energy sources, six hundred metres out on the west side. We'll have visual soon.' Another glass flashed and displayed icons. Borr was all business now, his fears forgotten in his devotion to his work. 'Eight more, at six hundred and closing from the south-east. They're tempting us to split our fire, I expect... yes here it is, a third group at six hundred metres north waiting to see which way we go.'

Outside, the dark skies had deepened to an impenetrable, inky blackness which the powerful arc lights of the camp barely kept at bay. Borr fed attack vectors and coordinates to the Praetorians while Lakius and Osil clustered around an augur glass. The laser mesh was shown as a ragged line of X's representing the ground based refraction spines. Red triangles approached in serried lines from two directions and held back on another angle. The Praetorians were represented by cog-shapes, in respect for their selfless devotion to the Machine-God. The Praetorians were moving southwest and an exchange of fire soon took place across the laser mesh. The tiny bolts flying back and forth on the glass were eerily echoed by the flashes visible through the observation ports. More frightening were the snaps and booms like distant lightning that came rolling across the compound.

The massed fire of the Praetorians was overwhelming the south-west group, the red triangles dimmed in quick succession, some disappearing altogether. Only two of the Praetorian-cogs showed the solid black of non-function, but even as Lakius watched one of the red triangles brightened momentarily and its shot turned another icon solid black. On the west the enemy was at the laser mesh, advancing through it in a tight wedge and destroying the spines with tightly controlled salvoes. Red lines flickered across the interloper's progress as detection beams were broken and the continuous energy flow of the mesh jumped to full output, searing through the ranks. Time and again the icons dimmed but recovered, they would soon break through. The northern group began to move.

'The north group are coming,' Lakius said.

'I see them.'

Most of the Praetorians turned west, leaving a small group to finish off the tattered southern group.

The artificial lightning storm was getting closer. Osil was not paying attention to the glass any more. The scenes unfolding outside in plain sight froze him. Stray shots flashed into the camp, exploding in sparks or gouging glittering welts in Santos's storm bunkers. Several Praetorians were in view, driving parallel with the laser mesh and firing at something out of view. More came into view from the camp, closing in around the spectral alien cohort forcing its way in from the west. The foe was terrible to see, their shining metal skulls and skeletons too symbolic to be missed. Here is Death, they had been built to communicate, in any language, across any gulf of time and to any race.

That was not the worst of them. These harbingers seemed in some horrible sense to live. Each was a mechanism, to be sure, but one with a fierce anime, like the idol of some ferocious, primitive god. Not only were they death, but they manifested a horrible sense of passion, even joy in their work. As machine spirits they were the most obscene perversions Lakius had ever seen, and inwardly part of him wept to see such things could still exist.

'Father,' Osil said, 'the northern group…'

Lakius couldn't tear his eyes away from the battle between the Praetorians and death machines below. The energy weapons of the aliens were frightening in their potency, their actinic bolts visibly flaying through whatever they struck layer by layer like some obscene medical scan compressed into a heart beat. The warrior-servitors fought back with plasma fire and armour piercing missiles, cutting down the skeletal apparitions one by one, but four more servitors had been cut down by the enemies' deadly accurate fire.

Borr used the same tactic again, the bulk of Praetorians broke off and wheeled north. A small group was left to finish off the alien machines which kept stubbornly rising after hits that would have stopped a Dreadnought. Lakius was grateful for Borr's obvious tactical skill. If either the western or southern groups were not completely eliminated the foe would undoubtedly get a foothold inside the camp. The trouble was the Praetorians moving north to parry the third thrust numbered only six; for the first time they would not outnumber the enemy.

'Borr, set the northern face of the mesh to maximum sensitivity,' Lakius said.

'But the spines will fire continuously, dissipate into the windblown dust!'

'Mica dust,' Lakius corrected.

Borr grinned and began a rite of supplication.

The Praetorians fought well on the northern side. They used a storm bunker to narrow the angles so they only fought part of the enemy at once. Clattering forward on armoured treads, a salvo of missiles scorched across the void-black sky and cut down two enemy machines as they emerged from the las-mesh. Lightning-crack discharges of plasma burned another, but a critical overheat damaged one of the servitors as his shoulder-mounted plasma cannon suffered meltdown. Five faced five. The storm bunker was being torn to pieces, its adamantium sheath impossibly burning with metal-fires. With a groan it collapsed in on itself, revealing more of the foe at the inner edge of the mesh. The Praetorians lost two of their number for only one of the enemy. Three armoured servitors were left against four skull-faced killers. The aliens grinned their hideous, fixed grins as they stepped forward.

Without warning the laser mesh crackled into a frenzy of discharges. Gigawatts of energy were dissipated into the swirling dust particles, pointlessly scattering their power in flashes of heat and light.

The flashes were harmless, but powerful enough to temporarily blind the optics of the nearby skeleto-machines. Their fire slackened momentarily and the Praetorians used the opportunity to halt and let rip with every weapon in their arsenals; bolter shells, missiles and plasma carved through the silhouetted enemy.

Osil gaped at the scopes. A moment ago he had thought he was going to be killed, but instead they had won.

They had won.

Lakius stood looking at Magos Egal's 'key', a fifteen metre-long phase field generator, poised like some giant, complex syringe of steel and brass over the unyielding black stone of the alien structure. The smooth, blank wall sloped away to giddying heights, making an artificial horizon of solid black against the grey sky. Adept Renaillard was connecting power couplings at the nether region of the key-machine, quietly reciting catechisms as he anointed each socket and clamped the cables in place. Noam stood nearby, arguing with Borr about something. Four paces further along the key the magos himself was making fine adjustments to the its controls. Four Praetorians were arrayed nearby, their torsos swivelling back and forth as they scanned for danger.

Lakius had just completed a long shift restoring what Praetorians and servitors they could from the casualties sustained in the attack. The unseen Adept Virtinnian, whose duty it was to undertake such blessings, had been crushed to death along with Adept Adso and six servitors in one of Santos's Titan grade storm bunkers. Adept Santos himself had lost an arm when he attempted to secure an alien machine which had reactivated.

If the alien machine-spirits kept to their rigid timetable the next attack was due in six hours. The thought of it crawled at the back of Lakius's mind constantly, a nagging fear which grew minute by minute, hour by hour. He wished he could find some reason to dissuade the magos, stop him pursuing this patently dangerous study, but his authority was beyond question on an expedition like this. The doctrine of the Mechanicus was clear – entire planetary populations of tech-priests could be sacrificed in pursuit of sacred knowledge; the individual weighed nothing against the Cult Mechanicus. But was this sacred knowledge or something ancient and tainted?

'All set?' Magos Egal trilled to Renaillard, who nodded his assent. 'Places everyone! Lakius, you stand with me and we can all chant the liturgy of activation together.'

Chanting in choral tones, Egal made a series of connections and static started to jump from the generator, accompanied by a rising humming noise and the reek of ozone. The black stone shimmered, glittering like quicksilver as it started to deform away from the spiralled needle of the generator. An arch was appearing, tall and tapering, of perfect dimensions and straightness. Within its angles the stone writhed and coiled like a living thing before fading away like mist to reveal the mouth of a corridor. The perfect alien symmetry of it was marred only by the head and shoulder of a Praetorian which appeared to be sunk into the wall on the left hand side – mute testimony to the previously failed attempt to penetrate the structure.

Unperturbed by its silent brother, the first Praetorian moved into the corridor, its powerful floodlights piercing the darkness within. Osil gasped, the outer shell of the structure had made him imagine the inside to be the same, unadorned stone. But the lights picked out complex traceries of silvery metal set into every surface; walls, floor and ceiling twinkled with captured starlight. A murmur of wonder rose from the gathered tech-priests. Magos Egal grinned with delight.

'You see! A simple adjustment of three degrees was all it took! Quite, quite fascinating! I haven't seen anything quite like this since the moons of Proxima Hydratica!' he chuckled. Lakius felt relieved; the magos was evidently more accomplished than he appeared. One by one, trailing sensor cables and power threads behind, the techno-magi entered the alien structure.

The corridor with its rich silver filigrees sloped down and away. After a dozen metres it dropped down in knee-high steps for another hundred. The Praetorians struggled to negotiate the giant steps, laboriously lowering themselves over each one. The slow progress gave Lakius ample time to examine the silver-traced corridor walls. They were undoubtedly depicting script in a language of some form. Spines and whorls marched in lines apparently formed from continuous individual strands. The lines and strands of script crossed and re-crossed up and down the walls, across the floor and on high in frozen sine waves, creating the sensation that the alien language was somehow conveyed by the totality of what was before him, rather than its individual elements.

Adept Noam was taking input from a cadaverous-looking scanning servitor, a long umbilical connecting its oversized eye-lenses to a socket in the lexmechanic's chest. Borr was nearby, puzzling over a hand-held auspex.

'Can you make anything of it, Adept Borr?' Lakius whispered to the rune priest. The sepulchral quiet of the necrontyr monolith seemed to demand silence, as if noise would manifest all of its invisible, crushing weight to punish the impudent interlopers.

By unspoken agreement none of the party had broken that brooding silence with more than a harsh whisper since they had entered.

'No, I'm not sure that it's supposed to be read in the human optic range. Set your view-piece to read magnetic resonance and you'll see what I mean.'

Lakius fumbled with the focusing knob on the rim of his artificial eye, tuning it to scan electromagnetic frequencies. The corridor was bathed in it, every whorl and spine was a tiny energy source which glowed with magnetic force. The overall effect was dizzying, like walking through a glass corridor over an infinite gulf full of stars. After a time Lakius had to reset his vision to blank it out.

After an hour of descent the corridor flattened out and then twisted sharply to the right before being blocked by a portal of black metal. The two lead Praetorians halted before it, their floodlights darkly reflected in the glossy metal of the obstacle. Three geometric symbols were marked on it at knee, waist and shoulder height.

'Should we use weapons fire, magos?' asked one of the Praetorians, its plasma cannon eagerly swivelling into the ready position. Magos Egal shook his head, stepping up to the door with Noam faithfully shadowing him with his trailing servitor.

'No, no,' Egal muttered 'I'm sure it's a simple matter of–' He touched the metal of the portal. Lakius flinched slightly, fearing some ancient necrontyr death trap. Nothing happened. 'Understanding how to trigger these symbols.'

A pregnant silence fell behind Egal's words. Noam began analysing the symbols, cross-referencing with all the data he stored in his machine-enhanced brain.

Lakius softly let out a breath he'd been holding until he heard a new sound, a low buzz which rose quickly to a high pitched whine. It sounded horribly like a weapon charging up, its capacitors being filled to maximum before it unleashed an atomising blast. Hairs rose on Lakius's neck. The sigils were flickering with their own light now; their ghostly fingers of energy could be felt tangibly. The Praetorians sensed it too and went to a threat response, readying and charging their own weapons with a hiss of servos and whine of capacitors.

Lakius felt a surge of panic, as if he stood beneath a giant hammer which would smash down at any second. He wanted to run back up the corridor but his way was blocked by the two rearmost Praetorians. They were swivelling back and forth with their baleful targeting eyes lit as they searched for enemies. One of them turned far enough to spot its companion and its ruby eye irised down into a pinpoint as it locked on target. The Praetorian's plasma cannon crackled up to a full charge, a compressed lightning bolt which would annihilate anything within metres of its impact point.

Osil was gibbering with fear.

Lakius was shouting out command dogma: 'Praetorians! Audio primus command! Deus ex Terminus est.'

The cannon fired, a searing flash and thunderclap which tore through the other Praetorian and sent white-hot shrapnel scything down the corridor. Osil bravely shouldered Lakius to one side, saving the old engineer from a fiery demise. Shouts and another roar echoed from near the portal, as a wave front of scorching heat washed back up the corridor. The nearby Praetorian swivelled round and trained its plasma cannon on Lakius and Osil, its eye glowed with single-minded determination to destroy as it narrowed at them.

'Ergos Veriat excommen!' Lakius shouted hoarsely. 'Shut down!'

The Praetorian sagged down on its chassis like a puppet with its strings cut and the crisis was over as suddenly as it had begun. The eerie silence fell like a curtain which was broken by the crackle of tiny fires, the plink of cooling metal and the groans of Osil as he writhed on the blood slick slabs. Metal splinters had struck him in his side when he saved Lakius. By the blessings of the Omnissiah, the wounds were not too deep and Adept Borr shrived them with a somatic welder.

Adept Renaillard had not been so lucky and a shard of smouldering casing had struck him in the throat, almost shearing his head off. Smoke rose from the smouldering remains of the two Praetorians nearest the portal. Noam's servitor had been destroyed in the exchange of fire as the two destroyed each other, but Magos Egal and the lexmechanic were unharmed.

'A sophisticated form of faeran field,' Noam explained dispassionately. 'It was cut off when I completed decryption of the portal locks.' A faeran field interfered with brain functions, inducing, among other things, extreme fear responses and seizures. Lakius couldn't help but think the lexmechanic sounded a little smug. Clear thought indeed.

Beyond the portal the corridor appeared to continue as before. Osil was sorely hurt in spite of Borr's ministration, and Lakius undertook the rituals to reboot the solitary remaining Praetorian so that it could carry him back to the surface. Osil protested weakly, but Lakius spoke a few quiet words to him before sending him on his way. The young acolyte looked very much like a child clinging to the Praetorian's wide back and Lakius prayed that nothing was waiting back there in the darkness for them. With only four tech-priests left in the expedition it seemed dangerous to Lakius to push on, but the magos insisted, convinced they were at the verge of a breakthrough.

Egal's breakthrough proved to be a labyrinth. The corridor split and then split again and again to become many. The different ways sloped sharply up and down, some narrowing to slits too small for even a servomat to enter. Within three turns Lakius felt thoroughly disorientated. The marching hieroglyphs on the walls seemed to hint at other corridors lying just out of sight, showing outlines of other labyrinths, turnings, dead ends which were just out of phase with themselves. In the Mechanicus doctrine the faeran portal alone would have been the subject of months of careful study before further advance was made. The twistings of this alien maze would constitute a lifetime's work with studies of geometry and numerology.

Magos Egal was in no mood to linger, though, and he set Noam and Borr to calculating a path through. Adept Noam's vast analytic power was directed entirely onto building an accurate map of the interweaving passages they moved through using direct observation, phasic scanning, micropressure evaluation and tactile interrogation. Adept Borr used his carefully learned arts conjecture and intuition to understand the underlying structure of the maze, and to determine what kind of xenomorphic logic would guide them through it.

Lakius was reduced to doing the work of a servitor, spooling out power thread and invoking marker-points at each junction so that Noam could tick them off on his mental plan.

The spool's metriculator showed less than a thousand metres left of its five kilometre length when they found another portal, though the term seemed inappropriate for the gargantuan metal slabs confronting them.

The gleaming, baroquely etched metal stretched up into the darkness further than their hand lights could reach. The corridor angled away in either direction, following some inner wall but leaving a sizeable vestibule that the four explorators now occupied. They were dwarfed by the new barrier, rendered so insignificant that the opening of those titanic gates could only foretell their doom at the hand of something ancient and monstrous. Adept Noam did not even flinch as he stepped forward to begin deciphering the locking-glyphs.

Lakius's mouth was dry with fear as the adept began tracing the first glyph. He looked back along the corridor, sure he had heard some scuttling noise. The twinkling silver traceries hurt his eyes, mechanical and organic. It took him a moment to realise that shapes were moving across them. Silvery, glittering shapes.

'Watch the rear!' Lakius shouted and hefted his personal weapon, an ancient and beautifully crafted laser made by Ortisian of Arkeness, whose spirit he had long tended to. Its angry red lash was sharp and true: it caught a shape, which blew apart in a blinding flash that spoke of minor atomics. The others crouched on their spindly legs and then leapt forward, buzzing down the corridor like a swarm of metallic insects.

Each was the size of a man's torso, flattened at the edges like scarabs and fringed with vicious looking hooks and claws. They were fast but so aggressive that they impeded each other's progress as they rattled and bounced over one another. Borr's bolt launcher joined its roaring song to the hiss of Lakius's laser. Their combined fire clawed down three more of the steely scarabs. Nonetheless, Lakius and Borr had to back towards the doors to keep their distance as more swarmed forward.

'Keep them back!' shouted Egal. 'Noam almost has it!'

Their backs were almost against the doors already. Lakius focused all his attention on tracking and eliminating the machine-scarabs, his laser flickering from one to another in a deadly dance of destruction. But they were still getting closer. One scarab ducked between two of its fellows at the point of their destruction, and surged forward while the tech-priests were half-blinded by the explosions. The machine's scrabbling claws ripped Borr's bolter from his hands before its momentum carried it over Lakius's head. It bounced off a wall and arrowed down amongst the priests. Lakius flinched away and saw it clamp on to Adept Noam's back even as he completed the last sigil. Surgical-sharp hooks ripped into the lexmechanic as the twin portals began to slowly separate.

'Could someone remove this?' Noam asked calmly, like a man being troubled by a wasp on a summer's day. 'I–'

The scarab exploded like a miniature nova and Adept Noam was gone, consumed in an actinic fireball which knocked Lakius flat. He rolled desperately, purple after-images flashing in his vision, ears filled with the roar of detonation. He expected to feel the dread weight of one of the machines landing on him at any second.

Osil lay gripped to an operating table by steel bands, the arms of an auto chirurgeon delicately sliced at his skin, pulling forth steel splinters and suturing his torn flesh together. Pain blockers numbed his body but his mind was racing. Father Lakius had told him to prepare their sacred cargo for release. Such a dangerous undertaking was normally only made in response to a signal from the Adeptus Terra on distant Earth.

To begin the investiture of the living weapon the ship carried in cryo-stasis without the initiation code was tantamount to suicide. If the assassin's crypt was opened without receiving the preparatory mnemonics and engrams specifying its target it would kill everything it found until it was destroyed.

Father Lakius, he concluded, must privately believe things had gone very, very wrong indeed.

Lakius flinched as something gripped his shoulder and started dragging him backwards. He realised someone was trying to pull him to safety and kicked his legs to scramble across the floor.

Moments later, Lakius's vision cleared enough to see that he was beyond the doors and that they were closing. The dark slit of the corridor outside narrowed rapidly as they smoothly swept together. He pointed the laser still gripped in his shaking hand but no scarab-machines came through the gap before it sealed.

'Splendid! They are without and we are within,' Magos Egal's voice said, close to Lakius's ear.

He scrambled to his feet as quickly as he could, fearfully looking around. Egal stood nearby and beyond him the chamber they had entered could be seen in its full majesty. Huge, angular buttresses marched away down either wall, and the floor sloped gently downward. Frosty pillars of greenish light shone down from an unseen roof to reveal row upon row of tall blocks covered in angular alien script. The air held a chill and the silence of the labyrinth outside had given way to a gentle susurration like waves against a distant shore.

'Where's Adept Borr?' Lakius demanded. Egal turned away from his accusing gaze, looking off down the cyclopean chamber.

'I'm sorry, I had to shut the portal or the scarabs would have killed all of us,' Egal seemed genuinely repentant. He could not even meet Lakius's gaze.

'You just left him outside!' Lakius's angry words rang hollow even to him. The young rune priest was dead and recriminations would not bring him back. They were trapped at the centre of the monolith now, the heart of the ancient structure. The Mechanicus-trained academic in him was already studying the chamber, too awed by the storehouse of alien archaeotech to give thought to the cost already incurred. The rows of man-high blocks seemed familiar, something about them... understanding blossomed with a now-familiar tang of fear.

'These are cryo-stasis machines,' he whispered. Metriculation memochips in his optic viewer calmly extrapolated that the chamber held over a million of them.

'It's what I brought you to see. They resemble the cryo-crypt of the Assassinorum vessel you arrived in, do they not? The best is at the centre, these are just... servants. Come and we may look upon a sight no living thing has seen in six hundred million years.'

Egal moved off down the slope and Lakius numbly followed. They passed block after block, each glittering with a rime of ancient frost. The floor got steeper until they had to crawl on hands and knees, gripping the blocks to lower themselves down to a flat circular section dominated by an immense stasis crypt. It was a sarcophagus in form, its top moulded into a representation of what lay within. Lakius expected to see a mask of death like the machine warriors, but instead found vivid life rendered in polished metal, beautiful but inhuman and cruel. Rows of sigils around the lid shone with an inner light, and it felt warm to the touch.

'Its already been opened,' said Lakius. 'Help me move the lid. I need to see inside.'

Between them they managed to turn the huge, heavy lid, swivelling it to reveal the interior. The sarcophagus was empty.

Egal seemed unsurprised; in fact, he was delighted. 'Splendid! Just as I had hoped.' He reached a gangling arm into the sarcophagus and brought out a silvery, metallic staff.

'Lakonius described an artefact like this in the Apocrypha of Skarros. He spoke of a symbol of mastery born by the lords of the necrontyr, called the "staff of light".' He hefted the ornate device in both hands. As he did so, an intense blue-white light flared in the symbol at the top of the staff. 'With this, we need fear no denizen of this edifice; with time they can even be tamed and made to serve.'

'But what of the occupant of the crypt?' Lakius asked, nervously noting the maniacal gleam in Egal's eye. 'The lord and master of this place that we're plundering from? I fear in our current circumstances we could scarcely fend off any kind of attack and that artefact is more likely to draw one to us. We should go while we still can.'

'Very well, but the staff of light could be our salvation. It would be madness to leave it behind.'

Osil limped towards the landing field where their ship lay. He had agonised greatly about whether to accede to his mentor's request. By Imperial and Mechanicus law, the activation of one of the lethal members of the Officio Assassinorum without proper authorisation was treason of the highest order. Death of the flesh would be a secondary consideration beside the terrible punishments that would entail.

But Osil had spent almost twenty Terran years in the company of Lakius Danzager, studying the tasks he would one day continue when the father was gathered to the Librarium Omnissiah. He had imagined he would spend the rest of his life aboard the ageing cutter, maintaining its systems and preparing its cargo of Imperial vengeance when it was required. That was not going to be the case now. Osil had learned enough of Lakius's clarity to understand that the explorator's expedition was woefully inadequate in the face of the alien terrors of Naogeddon. Father Lakius feared the worst, that they were about to unwittingly unleash something so terrible that he believed only an adept of the Eversor temple would have a chance of stopping it. And so the assassin must be prepared.

Magos Egal strode ahead confidently through the labyrinth, thrusting out the staff like a torch, its fierce light burning back the shadows and setting the hieroglyphs aflame with blue-white flashes. Lakius scuttled along behind him, jumping at each new scraping, slithering noise, jabbing his pistol towards each new vagrant glitter of steel as it flicked out of sight behind a corner. The denizens of the labyrinth were dogging their heels, giving back before the circle of light from the staff and closing in behind.

After what seemed like an eternity they reached the first portal where they had fallen foul of the faeran field. The melted wreckage of the

Praetorians and Renaillard's body were gone, the corridor clear except for the power threads trailing off into the darkness. Magos Egal wanted to stop and investigate but Lakius feared some assault would take place if they lingered, and urged him to press on. The soft scrapes and scratches of movement were behind them now, but following closely all the time. As they started to climb the steps Lakius looked back and caught sight of dozens of tiny lights floating in the gloom. They looked like blue fires, seemingly cold and distant, but drifting forward in pairs, the twin eye-lights of murder-machines on their trail.

The cool grey light of the outside seemed blinding after the blackness within. The edges of the phasic rift in the structure's outer sheath were wavering alarmingly and they ran past the entombed Praetorian to stumble out onto the gritty dust of the surface. It took Lakius a moment to gain his breath and he looked up to see Egal making adjustments to the phase generator.

'You're shutting it down, I trust,' said Lakius.

'Quite the contrary; I'm stabilising it so we can use the same entryway to go back in.'

'That's what I thought,' Lakius said, and fired his laser.

Osil's knees almost failed him when he saw their ship. A living sheath of machines covered it, their silvery bodies shifting over one another as they sought a way inside. The ship carried a great many devices to prevent tampering, as Osil knew all too well. If the machines found a way in, or worse still tried to breach the hull, the results could be devastating. He turned and forced his torn legs to start back to the command sphere.

Egal darted away from Lakius's laser with inhuman quickness. But Lakius had been aiming at the phase generator's power couplings, and the hit was more spectacular than he had imagined. The key-machine detonated and then imploded, a halo of white-hot flame flashing outwards for a moment before it was dragged back. A ragged distortion-veil skated erratically over the machine, crushing it smaller and smaller as it tried to suck everything nearby into it. Egal had been blown clear, but was left wrestling to hold onto the alien staff of light as it was drawn inexorably towards the rift.

'Help me, Lakius. I can't hold it!' Egal shouted over the piercing shriek of air being annihilated in the void. Lakius levelled his laser at the magos and shot him in the head without replying. Egal fell back clutching his face. The staff plunged into the rift and exploded with a crack like lightning. Ozone hung heavy in the air as Lakius backed away through the laser mesh spines towards the camp. He spared a glance for his treasured weapon's indicator jewel, and saw it was dim. His last shot had been at full strength, enough to punch through plasteel. Magos Egal was still moving, standing up.

'Have you any idea how hard it was to get this texture right?' he demanded indignantly, indicating the side of his face that had been caressed by a steel-burning laser. Charred welts revealed glittering metal beneath, quicksilver curves that betrayed an inhuman, yet familiar, anatomy. Lakius kept moving back, the figure of the thing that had pretended to be Egal was getting reassuringly distant, dwarfed by the solid black base of the alien structure. A pair of Praetorians came rattling forward from amidst the stormbunkers, balefully scanning Lakius with their targeters.

'One life form identified. Classified non-hostile,' one concluded.

The magos-thing was at the laser mesh. It leapt suddenly, astoundingly covering the hundred metres to Lakius and the Praetorians in a single somersaulting bound.

'One life form identified. Classified non-hostile,' the other Praetorian stated.

'Surely you didn't believe these clattering toys would be able to identify me?' the Egal-thing smiled. 'I had thought you one of the more intelligent specimens.'

Lakius's mouth was dry with fear, but he managed a curt nod of acceptance before crying out 'Praetorians! Audio primus command! Overwatch!' The Praetorians locked their weapons onto the alien with eye-blurring speed, their simple brains entirely devoted to obliterating the first rapid movement they sensed.

'You forget that I spent time repairing servitors after the last battle. I took the liberty of updating their command protocols at the same time,' Lakius said with more courage than he felt.

The thing smiled more broadly still, and slowly cocked its head to one side. The Praetorians' weapons tracked the minute movement faithfully.

'Good for you, Lakius Danzager. You really are a clever one. How did you know I wasn't human?'

Lakius hesitated for a moment. The thing before him exuded an almost primal sense of power. It was at his mercy for the present, but his instincts told him it could pounce on him at any moment. The Mechanicus in him yearned to learn what he could about it while his humanity screamed out to destroy it. His curiosity overpowered his instincts for a moment.

'I wasn't sure, but either you were the thing from the crypt or an insane explorer who was bent on unleashing something unspeakable upon the world. When I understood that, my choices became clear. How did you replace Egal? Did he wake you in there?' Icy daggers caressed Lakius's back as he talked to the thing. Its silver and flesh smile widened even further.

'What makes you think I replaced him at all? I have travelled a great distance since my first waking, walked in many places that have changed so very much since I saw them last.'

'What were you seeking?' whispered Lakius.

The thing's ferocious smile was spread almost ear to ear. 'Knowledge, mostly. I wanted to know how the galaxy had fared; who was left after the plague. You can't imagine my surprise on finding your kind and the krork scattered everywhere. I've seen you humans trying to forge an empire in the name of a corpse; I have seen your churches to the machine. Racially, your fear and superstition are most gratifying. You make excellent subjects.'

'You are necrontyr, then. You went into stasis to escape a disease.'

'No, your language is inefficient. The plague was not a disease and it couldn't harm us, but...' The necrontyr tilted its head back as if dreaming of long lost times. 'It was killing everything else.' It looked back at Lakius. 'And no, I am not a necron. You mistake the slave for the master. You'll understand better when I take you back inside.'

It leapt. The Praetorians blazed into it with lasers and plasma, their bolts lashing at the thin form. Lakius was momentarily blinded by the orgy of destruction, and he fled towards the command centre in the hope of finding reinforcements. He looked back to see a silvery figure ripping pieces out of one the Praetorians. The other battle-servitor was smouldering nearby. The figure waved a piece of carapace jauntily at Lakius.

'Sorry, Lakius, I couldn't resist it,' the thing called. 'My race raised what you call "melodrama" to a high art form before you were even evolved.' It chuckled and returned to eviscerating the Praetorian.

Lakius was spinning the locks shut on the command centre hatch when he sensed a presence behind him. He turned, too terrified and weary to fight but wanting to see his nemesis. He almost died of relief when he saw it was Osil.

'Osil, it's–'

'I know, father, I was watching on the monitor.'

'The assassin?' Lakius gasped as he sagged to the ground.

'I couldn't reach the ship, it was covered by a swarm of insect machines. I'm afraid they'll trigger its anti-tampering protocols sooner or later. I searched for something we could use to protect ourselves but there are only components, nothing complete.'

'I fear the thing out there may survive the blast anyway. If so it would be better to–'

A ringing blow sounded against the hatch, making both Osil and Lakius jump. Then another blow slammed into it, then a third. At the third blow a bulge appeared in the Titan-grade adamantium plate. Silence fell.

'I think we'd better look at those components, Osil.' Lakius said, struggling to his feet. Osil fussed around him, his fears assuaged by having someone else to think about. He showed Lakius the ready-caskets and crates he had brought.

'I've performed the rites of preparation on these pieces, and anointed the calibrators,' Osil said hopefully. A hissing, popping noise came from the hatch, and a bright heat-spot formed at its centre.

Lakius looked at the mass of unconnected components and despaired.

The heat spot had made a complete orbit of the door, leaving a trail of molten fire behind it. As the circle was closed the metal fell inward of its own weight, clanging to the ground and sending up a cloud of reeking fumes. A tall, inhuman figure stepped through the gap.

'Mechanism, I restore thy spirit. Let the God-Machine breathe half-life unto thy veins and render thee functional,' muttered Lakius, scarcely looking up. Osil gaped at the apparition, sure that his life was over.

'Ah, splendid, both of you,' it grinned. 'Don't tell me you've been trying to make something to stop me? With all your chanting and bone-rattling it would take days, years!'

There was a flash outside, and seconds later a titanic roar. The blast wave from the Assassinorum vessel's plasma reactor going critical was a second behind that.

'Don't worry, I can save you.' The thing grinned again.

'No need,' grated Lakius and closed the last connection.

A dome of shimmering, bluish light sprang into being. It filled the hatchway with the necron-master frozen at its centre. It was a charcoal-black silhouette in the glare of the plasma-flash beyond the field. The rest of the armoured command centre shook and rattled alarmingly but held, its vulnerable hatch protected by Lakius's improvised stasis bubble.

After the blast wave had passed there was a long moment of silence before Osil asked. 'Father, won't the Omnissiah be angry that you mistreated all those Machine Spirits making the field?'

'Let it be our secret, Osil. Deus Ex Mechanicus. The Emperor watches over us.'

PESTILENCE

Dan Abnett

The Archenemy infects this universe. If we do not pause to fight that infection here, within our own selves, what purpose is there in taking our fight to the stars?

– Apothecary Engane,
from his Treatise on Imperial Medicine

I

It is my belief that memory is the finest faculty we as a species own. Through the function of memory, we are able to gather, hone and transmit all manner of knowledge for the benefit of mankind, and the endless glory of our God-Emperor, may the Golden Throne endure for ever more!

To forget a mistake is to be defeated a second time, so we are taught in the sermons of Thor. How may a great leader plan his campaign without memory of those battles won and lost before? How may his soldiers absorb his teaching and improve without that gift? How may the Ecclesiarchy disseminate its enervating message to the universal populace without that populace holding the teachings in memory? What are scholars, clerks, historians or chroniclers but agencies of memory?

And what is forgetfulness but the overthrow of memory, the ruination of precious knowledge, and an abhorrence?

I have, in the service of His Exalted Majesty the Emperor of Terra, waged war upon that abhorrence all my life. I strive to locate and recover things forgotten and return them to the custody of memory. I am a scrabbler in dark places, an illuminator of shadows, a turner of long un-turned pages, an asker of questions that have lapsed, forever hunting for answers that would otherwise have remained unvoiced. I am a recollector, prising lost secrets from the taciturn universe and returning them to the safe fold of memory, where they might again improve our lot amongst the out-flung stars.

My particular discipline is that of materia medica, for human medicine was my original calling. Our understanding of our own vital mechanisms is vast and admirable, but we can never know too much about our own biology and how to protect, repair and improve it. It is our burden as a species to exist in a galaxy riven by war, and where war goes, so flourish its hand-servants injury and disease. It may be said that as each war front advances, so medical knowledge advances too. And where armies fall back in defeat or are destroyed, so medical knowledge retreats or is forgotten. Such are the lapses I seek to redress.

Upon that very purpose, I came to Symbal Iota late in my forty-eighth year, looking for Ebhoe. To provide context, let me say that this would be the third year of the Genovingian campaign in the Obscura Segmentum, and about nine sidereal months after the first outbreak of Uhlren's Pox amongst the Guard legions stationed on Genovingia itself. Also known, colloquially, as blood-froth, Uhlren's Pox was named after the first victim it took, a colour-sergeant called Gustaf Uhlren, of the Fifteenth Mordian, if memory serves me. And I pride myself it does.

As a student of Imperial history, and materia medica too, you will have Uhlren's Pox in your memory. A canker of body and vitality, virulently contagious, it corrupts from within, thickening circulatory fluids and wasting marrow, while embellishing the victim's skin with foul cysts and buboes. The cycle between infection and death is at most four days. In the later stages, organs rupture, blood emulsifies and bubbles through the pores of the skin, and the victim becomes violently delusional. Some have even conjectured that by this phase, the soul itself has been corroded away. Death is inescapable in almost every case.

It appeared without warning on Genovingia, and within a month, the Medicae Regimentalis were recording twenty death notices a day. No drug or procedure could be found that began to even slow its effects. No origin for the infection could be located. Worst of all, despite increasingly vigorous programs of quarantine and cleansing, no method could be found to prevent wholesale contagion. No plague carriers, or means of transmission, were identifiable.

As an individual man weakens and sickens, so the Imperial Guard forces as a whole began to fail and falter as their best were taken by the pestilence. Within two months, Warmaster Rhyngold's staff were doubting the continued viability of the entire campaign. By the third month, Uhlren's Pox had also broken out (apparently miraculously and spontaneously, given its unknown process of dispersal) on Genovingia Minor, Lorches and Adamanaxer Delta. Four separate centres of infection, right along the leading edge of the Imperial advance through the sector. At that point, the contagion had spread to the civilian population of Genovingia itself, and the Administratum had issued a Proclamation of Pandemic. It was said the skies above the cities of that mighty world were black with carrion flies and the stench of biological pollution permeated every last acre of the planet.

I had a bureaucratic posting on Lorches at that time, and became part of the emergency body charged with researching a solution. It was weary work. I personally spent over a week in the archive without seeing daylight as I oversaw the systematic interrogation of that vast, dusty body of knowledge.

It was my friend and colleague Administrator Medica Lenid Vammel who first called our attention to Pirody and the Torment. It was an admirable piece of work on his part, a feat of study, cross-reference and memory. Vammel always had a good memory.

Under the instruction of Senior Administrator Medica Junas Malter, we diverted over sixty per cent of our staff to further research into the records of Pirody, and requests were sent out to other Genovingian worlds to look to their own archives. Vammel and I compiled the accumulating data ourselves, increasingly certain we had shone a light into the right shadow and found a useful truth.

Surviving records of the Torment incident on Pirody were painfully thin, though consistent. It was, after all, thirty-four years in the past. Survivors had been few, but we were able to trace one hundred and ninety-one possibles who might yet be alive. They were scattered to the four cosmic winds.

Reviewing our findings, Senior Malter authorised personal recollection, such was the gravity of the situation, and forty of us, all with rank higher administrator or better, were dispatched immediately. Vammel, rest his soul, was sent to Gandian Saturnalia, and was caught up in a local civil war and thereafter killed. I do not know if he ever found the man he was looking for. Memory is unkind there.

And I, I was sent to Symbal Iota.

II

Symbal Iota, where it is not covered in oceans that are the most profound mauve in colour (a consequence, so I understand, of algae growth), is a hot, verdant place. Rainforest islands ring the equatorial region in a wide belt.

I made 'fall at Symbalopolis, a flat-topped volcanic outcrop around whose slopes hive structures cluster like barnacles, and there transferred to a trimaran which conveyed me, over a period of five days, down the length of the local island group to Saint Bastian.

I cursed the slowness of the craft, though in truth it skated across the mauve seas at better than thirty knots, and on several occasions tried to procure an ornithopter or air conveyance. But the Symbali are a nautical breed who place no faith in air travel. It was tortuous and I was impatient. It had taken ten days to cross the empyrean from Lorches to Symbal Iota aboard a Navy frigate. Now it took half that time again to cross a distance infinitesimally smaller.

It was hot, and I spent my time below decks, reading data-slates. The sun and seawind of Symbal burned my skin, used as it was to years of lamp-lit libraries. I took to wearing a wide-brimmed straw hat above my Administratus robes whenever I ventured out on deck, a detail my servitor Kalibane found relentlessly humorous.

On the fifth morning, Saint Bastian rose before us out of the violet waters, a pyramidal tower of volcanic flue dressed in jungle greenery. Even as we crossed the inlet from the trimaran to the shore by electric launch, turquoise seabirds mobbing over our heads, I could see no discernible sign of habitation. The thick coat of forestation came right down to the shore itself, revealing only a thin line of white beach at its hem.

The launch pulled into a cove where an ancient stone jetty jutted out from under the trees like an unfinished bridge. Kalibane, his bionic limbs whirring, carried my luggage onto the jetty and then helped me over. I stood there, sweating in my robes, leaning against my staff of office, batting away the beetles that circled in the stifling humidity of the cove.

There was no one there to greet me, though I had voxed word of my approach ahead several times en route. I glanced back at the launch pilot, a dour Symbali, but he seemed not to know anything. Kalibane shambled down to the shore-end of the jetty, and called my attention to a copper bell, verdigrised by time and the oceans, that hung from a hook on the end of the pier.

'Ring it,' I told him, and he did, cautiously, rapping his simian fingers against the metal dome. Then he glanced back at me, nervously, his optical implants clicking under his low brow-ridge as they refocused.

Two sisters of the Ecclesiarchy shortly appeared, their pure white robes as stiff and starched as the bicorn wimples they wore on their heads. They seemed to regard me with some amusement, and wordlessly ushered me to follow them.

I fell in step behind them and Kalibane followed, carrying the luggage.

We took a dirt path up through the jungle which rose sharply and eventually became stepped. Sunlight flickered spears of light through the canopy above and the steaming air was full of exotic bird-song and the fidget of insects.

At a turn in the path, the Hospice of Saint Bastian Apostate suddenly stood before me. A great, stone-built edifice typical of the early Imperial naïve, its ancient flying buttresses and lower walls were clogged with vines and creepers. I could discern a main building of five storeys, an adjacent chapel, which looked the oldest part of the place, as well as outbuildings, kitchens and a walled garden. Above the wrought iron lych-gate stood a weathered statue of our beloved God-Emperor smiting the Archenemy. Inside the rusty gate, a well-tended path led through a trimmed lawn punctured by tomb-stones and crypts. Stone angels and graven images of the Adeptus Astartes regarded me as I followed the sisters to the main door of the hospice.

I noticed then, fleetingly, that the windows of the two uppermost storeys were rigidly barred with iron grilles.

I left Kalibane outside with my possessions and entered the door behind the sisters. The main atrium of the hospice was a dark and deliciously cool oasis of marble, with limestone pillars that rose up into the dim spaces of the high vault. My eyes lighted on the most marvellous triptych at the altar end, beneath a stained glass oriole window, which I made observance to at once. In breadth, it was wider than a man's spread arms, and showed three aspects of the saint. On the left, he roamed the wilderness, in apostasy, renouncing the daemons of the air and fire; on the right, he performed the miracle of the maimed souls. In the centre panel, his martyred body, draped in blue cloth, the nine bolter wounds clearly countable on his pallid flesh, he lay in the arms of a luminous and suitably mournful Emperor.

I looked up from my devotions to find the sisters gone. I could feel the subliminal chorus of a psychic choir mind-singing nearby. The cool air pulsed.

A figure stood behind me. Tall, sculptural, his starched robes as white as his smooth skin was black, he seemed to regard me with the same amusement that the sisters had shown.

I realised I was still wearing my straw hat. I removed it quickly, dropping it onto a pew, and took out the pict-slate of introduction Senior Malter had given me before I left Lorches.

'I am Baptrice,' he said, his voice low and genial. 'Welcome to the saint's hospice.'

'Higher Administrator Medica Lemual Sark,' I replied. 'My dedicated function is as a recollector, posted lately to Lorches, Genovingia general group 4577 decimal, as part of the campaign auxiliary clerical archive.'

'Welcome, Lemual,' he said. 'A recollector. Indeed. We've not had one of your breed here before.'

I was uncertain quite what he meant, though in hindsight, the detail of his misunderstanding still chills me. I said 'You were expecting me? I voxed messages ahead.'

'We have no vox-caster here at the hospice,' Baptrice replied. 'What is outside does not concern us. Our work is focused on what is inside... inside this building, inside ourselves. But do not be alarmed. You are not intruding. We welcome all who come here. We do not need notice of an arrival.'

I smiled politely at this enigmatic response and tapped my fingers on my staff. I had hoped they would be ready for me, and have everything in place so that I could begin my work immediately. Once again, the leisurely pace of Symbal Iota was weighing me down.

'I must, Brother Baptrice, proceed with all haste. I wish to begin my efforts at once.'

He nodded. 'Of course. Almost all who come to Saint Bastian are eager to begin. Let me take you through and provide you with food and a place to bathe.'

'I would rather just see Ebhoe. As soon as it is possible.'

He paused, as if mystified.

'Ebhoe?'

'Colonel Fege Ebhoe, late of the 23rd Lammark Lancers. Please tell me he is still here! That he is still alive!'

'He... is.' Baptrice faltered, and looked over my pict-slate properly for the first time. Some sort of realisation crossed his noble face.

'My apologies, Higher Sark. I misconstrued your purpose. I see now that you are an acting recollector, sent here on official business.'

'Of course!' I snapped. 'What else would I be?'

'A supplicant, coming here to find solace. An inmate. Those that arrive on the jetty and sound the bell are always that. We get no other visitors except those who come to us for help.'

'An... inmate?' I repeated.

'Don't you know where you are?' he asked. 'This is the Hospice of Saint Bastian, a refuge for the insane.'

III

An asylum! Here was an inauspicious start to my mission! I had understood, from my research, that the Hospice of Saint Bastian was home to a holy order who offered sanctuary and comfort for those brave warriors of the Emperor's legions who were too gravely wounded or disabled by war to continue in service. I knew the place took in the damaged and the lost from warzones all across the sector. But I truly had no notion that the damage they specialised in was wounds to the psyche and sanity! It was a hospice for the deranged, individuals who presented themselves at its gates voluntarily in hope of redemption.

Worst of all, Baptrice and the sisters had presumed me to be a supplicant! That damned straw hat had given me just the air of madness they were expecting! I was lucky not to have been unceremoniously strapped into a harness and placed in isolation.

On reflection, I realised I should have known. Bastian, that hallowed saint, was a madman who found sanity in the love of the Emperor, and who later cured, through miracles, the mentally infirm.

Baptrice rang a bell cord, and novitiates appeared. Kalibane was escorted inside with my luggage. We were left alone in the atrium as Baptrice went to make preparations. As we waited, a grizzled man with an old tangle of scar-tissue where his left arm had been crossed the hall. He was naked save for a weathered, empty ammunition belt strung around his torso. He looked at us dimly, his head nodding slightly, then he padded on his way and was lost from view.

Somewhere, distantly, I could hear sobbing, and an urgent voice repeating something over and over again. Hunched down at my side, his knuckles resting on the flagstones, Kalibane glanced up at me anxiously and I put a reassuring hand on his broad, hairy shoulder.

Figures appeared around us: haggard, tonsured men in long black Ecclesiarch vestments, more phantom sisters in their ice-white robes and horned cowls. They grouped in the shadows on either side of the atrium and watched us silently. One of the men rehearsed silently from long ribbons of parchment that a boy-child played out for him from a studded casket. Another scribbled in a little chapbook with his quill. Another swung a brass censer around his feet, filling the air with dry, pungent incense.

Baptrice reappeared. 'Brethren, bid welcome to Higher Administrator Sark, who has come to us on official business. You will show him every courtesy and cooperation.'

'What official business?' asked the old priest with the chapbook, looking up with gimlet eyes. Magnifying half-moon lenses were built into his nasal bone, and rosary beads hung around his dewlapped neck like a floral victory wreath.

'A matter of recollection,' I replied.

'Pertaining to what?' he pressed.

'Brother Jardone is our archivist, Higher Sark. You will forgive his persistence.' I nodded to Baptrice and smiled at the elderly Jardone, though no smile was returned.

'I see we are kindred, Brother Jardone. Both of us devote ourselves to remembrance.'

He half-shrugged.

'I am here to interview one of your... inmates. It may be that he holds within some facts that even now may save the lives of millions in the Genovingian group.'

Jardone closed his book and gazed at me, as if waiting for more. Senior Malter had charged me to say as little as I could of the pandemic, for news of such a calamity may spread unrest. But I felt I had to give them more.

'Warmaster Rhyngold is commanding a major military excursion through the Genovingian group. A sickness, which has been named Uhlren's Pox, is afflicting his garrisons. Study has shown it may bear comparison with a plague known as the Torment, which wasted Pirody some three decades past. One survivor of that epidemic resides here. If he can furnish me with any details of the incident, it may be productive in securing a cure.'

'How bad is it, back on Genovingia?' asked another old priest, the one with the censer.

'It is... contained,' I lied.

Jardone snorted. 'Of course it is contained. That is why a higher administrator has come all this way. You ask the most foolish things, Brother Giraud.'

Another man now spoke. He was older than all, crooked and half-blind, his wrinkled pate dotted with liver spots. A flared ear-trumpet clung to the robes of his left shoulder with delicate mechanical legs. 'I am concerned that questioning and a change to routine may disturb the serenity of the hospice. I do not want our residents upset in any way.'

'Your comment is noted, Brother Niro,' said Baptrice. 'I'm sure Higher Sark will be discreet.'

'Of course,' I assured them.

It was late afternoon when Baptrice finally led me upstairs into the heart of the hospice. Kalibane followed us, lugging a few boxed items from my luggage. Ghostly, bicorned sisters watched us from every arch and shadow.

We proceeded from the stairs into a large chamber on the third floor. The air was close. Dozens of inmates lurked here, though none glanced at us. Some were clad in dingy, loose-fitting overalls, while others still wore ancient fatigues and Imperial Guard dress. All rank pins, insignia and patches had been removed, and no one had belts or bootlaces. Two were intently playing regicide on an old tin board by the window. Another sat on the bare floor planks, rolling dice. Others mumbled to themselves or gazed into the distance blankly. The naked man we had seen in the atrium was crouched in a corner, loading spent shellcases into his ammunition belt. Many of the residents had old war wounds and scars, unsightly and grotesque.

'Are they... safe?' I whispered to Baptrice.

'We allow the most stable freedom to move and use this common area. Of course, their medication is carefully monitored. But all who come here are "safe", as all who come here come voluntarily. Some, of course, come here to escape the episodes that have made regular life impractical.'

None of this reassured me.

On the far side of the chamber, we entered a long corridor flanked by cell rooms. Some doors were shut, bolted from outside. Some had cage-bars locked over them. All had sliding spy-slits. There was a smell of disinfectant and ordure.

Someone, or something, was knocking quietly and repeatedly against one locked door we passed. From another we heard singing.

Some doors were open. I saw two novitiates sponge-bathing an ancient man who was strapped to his metal cot with fabric restraints. The old man was weeping piteously. In another room, where the door was open but the outer cage locked in place, we saw a large, heavily muscled man sitting in a ladderback chair, gazing out through the bars. He was covered in tattoos: regimental emblems, mottoes, kill-scores. His eyes glowed with the most maniacal light. He had the tusks of some feral animal implanted in his lower jaw, so they hooked up over his upper lip.

As we passed, he leaped up and tried to reach through the bars at us. His powerful arm flexed and clenched. He issued a soft growl.

'Behave, Ioq!' Baptrice told him.

The cell next door to Ioq's was our destination. The door was open, and a sister and a novitiate waited for us. The room beyond them was pitch black.

Baptrice spoke for a moment with the novitiate and the sister. He turned to me. 'Ebhoe is reluctant, but the sister has convinced him it is right that he speaks with you. You may not go in. Please sit at the door.'

The novitiate brought up a stool, and I sat in the doorway, throwing out my robes over my knees. Kalibane dutifully opened my boxes and set up the transcribing artificer on its tripod stand.

I gazed into the blackness of the room, trying to make out shapes. I could see nothing.

'Why is it dark in there?'

'Ebhoe's malady, his mental condition, is exacerbated by light. He demands darkness.' Baptrice shrugged.

I nodded glumly and cleared my throat. 'By the grace of the God-Emperor of Terra, I come here on His holy work. I identify myself as Lemual Sark, Higher Administrator Medica, assigned to Lorches Administratum.'

I glanced over at the artificer. It chattered quietly and extruded the start of a parchment transcription tape that I hoped would soon be long and informative. 'I seek Fege Ebhoe, once a colonel with the 23rd Lammark Lancers.'

Silence.

'Colonel Ebhoe?'

A voice, thin as a knife, cold as a corpse, whispered out of the dark room. 'I am he. What is your business?'

I leaned forward. 'I wish to discuss Pirody with you. The Torment you endured.'

'I have nothing to say. I won't remember anything.'

'Come now, colonel. I'm sure you will if you try.'

'You misunderstand. I didn't say I "can't". I said I "won't".'

'Deliberately?'

'Just so. I refuse to.'

I wiped my mouth, and realised I was dry-tongued. 'Why not, colonel?'

'Pirody is why I'm here. Thirty-four years, trying to forget. I don't want to start remembering now.'

Baptrice looked at me with a slight helpless gesture. He seemed to be suggesting that it was done, and I should give up.

'Men are dying on Genovingia from a plague we know as Uhlren's Pox. This pestilence bears all the hallmarks of the Torment. Anything you can tell me may help save lives.'

'I couldn't then. Fifty-nine thousand men died on Pirody. I couldn't save them though I tried with every shred of my being. Why should that be different now?'

I gazed at the invisible source of the cold voice. 'I cannot say for sure. But I believe it is worth trying.'

There was a long pause. The artificer whirred on idle. Kalibane coughed, and the machine recorded the sound with a little chatter of keys.

'How many men?'

'I'm sorry, colonel? What did you ask me?'

'How many men are dying?'

I took a deep breath. 'When I left Lorches, nine hundred were dead and another fifteen hundred infected. On Genovingia Minor, six thousand and twice that number ailing. On Adamanaxer Delta, two hundred, but it had barely begun there. On Genovingia itself... two and a half million.'

I heard Baptrice gasp in shock. I trusted he would keep this to himself.

'Colonel?'

Nothing.

'Colonel, please...'

Cold and cutting, the voice came again, sharper than before. 'Pirody was a wasted place...'

IV

Pirody was a wasted place. We didn't want to go there. But the Archenemy had taken the eastern continent and razed the hives, and the northern cities were imperilled.

Warmaster Getus sent us in. Forty thousand Lammark Lancers, virtually the full strength of the Lammark regiments. Twenty thousand Fancho armour men and their machines, and a full company of Astartes, the Doom Eagles, shining grey and red.

The place we were at was Pirody Polar. It was god knows how old. Cyclopean towers and columns of green marble, hewn in antique times by hands I'm not convinced were human. There was a strangeness to the geometry there, the angles never seemed quite right.

It was as cold as a bastard. We had winter dress, thick white flak coats with fur hoods, but the ice got in the lasguns and dulled their charges and the damned Fancho tanks were forever refusing to start. It was day, too. Day all the time. There was no night, it was the wrong season. We were so far north. The darkest it got was dusk, when one of the two suns set briefly and the sky went flesh pink. Then it would be daylight again.

We'd been fighting on and off for two months. Mainly long range artillery duels, pounding the ice-drifts. No one could sleep because of the perpetual daylight. I know two men, one a Lammarkine, I'm not proud to say, who gouged out his eyes. The other was a Fancho.

Then they came. Black dots on the ice-floes, thousands of them, waving banners so obscene, they...

Whatever. We were in no mood to fight. Driven mad by the light, driven to distraction by the lack of sleep, unnerved by the curious geometry of the place we were defending, we were easy meat. The forces of Chaos slaughtered us, and pushed us back into the city itself. The civilians, about two million strong, were worse than useless. They were pallid, idle things, with no drive or appetite. When doom came upon them, they simply gave up.

We were besieged for five months, despite six attempts by the Doom Eagles to break the deadlock. Faith, but they were terrifying! Giants, clashing their bolters together before each fight, screaming at the foe, killing fifty for every one we picked off.

But it was like fighting the tide, and for all their power, there were only sixty of them.

We called for reinforcements. Getus had promised us, but now he was long gone aboard his warship, drawn back behind the fleet picket in case things got nasty.

The first man I saw fall to the Torment was a captain in my seventh platoon. He just collapsed one day, feverish. We took him to the Pirody Polar infirmium, where Subjunctus Valis, the Apothecary of the Doom Eagles company, was running the show. An hour later, the captain was dead. His skin had blistered and bubbled. His eyes had burst. He had tried to kill Valis with a piece of the metal cot he had torn from the wall brace. Then he bled out.

You know what that means? His entire body spewed blood from every orifice, every pore. He was a husk by the time it was over.

In the day after the captain's death, sixty fell victim. Another day, two hundred. Another day, a thousand. Most died within two hours. Others lingered... for days, pustular, agonised.

Men I had known all my life turned into gristly sacks of bone before my eyes. Damn you, Sark, for making me remember this!

On the seventh day it spread to the Fancho as well. On the ninth, it reached the civilian population. Valis ordered all measure of quarantine, but it was no good. He worked all hours of the endless day, trying to find a vaccine, trying to alleviate the relentless infection.

On the tenth day, a Doom Eagle fell victim. In his Torment, blood gouting from his visor grilles, he slew two of his comrades and nineteen of my men. The disease had overcome even the Astartes purity seals.

I went to Valis, craving good news. He had set up a laboratory in the infirmium, where blood samples and tissue-scrapes boiled in alembics and separated in oil flasks. He assured me the Torment would be stopped. He explained how unlikely it was for a pestilence to be transmitted in such a cold clime, where there is no heat to incubate and spread decay. And he also believed it would not flourish in light. So he had every stretch of the city wired with lamps so that there would be no darkness.

No darkness. In a place where none came naturally, even the shadows of closed rooms were banished. Everything was bright. Perhaps you can see now why I abhor the light and cling to darkness.

The stench of blood-filth was appalling. Valis did his work, but still we fell. By the twenty-first day, I'd lost thirty-seven per cent of my force. The Fancho were all but gone. Twelve thousand Pirodian citizens were dead or dying. Nineteen Doom Eagles had succumbed.

Here are your facts if you want them. The plague persisted in a climate that should have killed it. It showed no common process of transmission. It brooked no attempt to contain or control it, despite efforts to enforce quarantine and cleanse infected areas with flamers. It was ferociously contagious. Even Space Marine purity seals were no protection. Its victims died in agony.

Then one of the Doom Eagles deciphered the obscene script of one of the Chaos banners displayed outside the walls.

It said...

It said one word. One filthy word. One damned, abominable word that I have spent my life trying to forget.

V

I craned in at the dark doorway. 'What word? What word was it, colonel?'

With great reluctance, he spoke it. It wasn't a word at all. It was an obscene gurgle dignified by consonants. The glyph-name of the plague-daemon itself, one of the ninety-seven Blasphemies that May Not Be Written Down.

At its utterance, I fell back off my stool, nausea writhing in my belly and throat. Kalibane shrieked. The sister collapsed in a faint and the novitiate fled.

Baptrice took four steps back from the doorway, turned, and vomited spectacularly.

The temperature in the corridor dropped by fifteen degrees.

Unsteady, I attempted to straighten my overturned stool and pick up the artificer that the novitiate had knocked over. Where it had recorded the word, I saw, the machine's parchment tape had begun to smoulder.

Screaming and wailing echoed down the hall from various cells.

And then, Ioq was out.

Just next door, he had heard it all, his scarred head pressed to the cage bars. Now that cage door splintered off its mount and crashed to the corridor floor. Berserk, the huge ex-Guardsman thrashed out and turned towards us.

He was going to kill me, I'm certain, but I was slumped and my legs wouldn't work. Then Kalibane, bless his brave heart, flew at him. My devoted servitor rose up on his stunted hind limbs, the bionics augmenting his vast forelimbs throwing them up in a warning display. From splayed foot to reaching hand, Kalibane was eleven feet tall. He peeled back his lips and screeched through bared steel canines.

Froth dribbling from his tusked mouth, Ioq smashed Kalibane aside. My servitor made a considerable dent in the wall.

Ioq was on me.

I swept my staff of office around and thumbed the recessed switch below the head.

Electric crackles blasted from the staff's tip. Ioq convulsed and fell. Twitching, he lay on the floorboards, and evacuated involuntarily. Baptrice was on his feet now. Alarms were ringing and novitiates were rushing frantically into the corridor with harness jackets and clench poles.

I rose and looked back at the dark doorway.

'Colonel Ebhoe?'

The door slammed shut.

VI

There would be no further interview that afternoon, Brother Baptrice made plain, despite my protests. Novitiates escorted me to a guest chamber on the second floor. It was white-washed and plain, with a hard, wooden bed and small scriptorium table. A leaded window looked out onto the graveyard and the jungles beyond.

I felt a great perturbation of spirit, and paced the room as Kalibane unpacked my belongings. I had come so close, and had begun to draw the reluctant Ebhoe out. Now to be denied the chance to continue when the truly dark secrets were being revealed!

I paused by the window. The glaring, crimson sun was sinking into the mauve oceans, throwing the thick jungles into black, wild relief. Seabirds reeled over the bay in the dying light. Stars were coming out in the dark blue edges of the sky.

Calmer now, I reflected that whatever my internal uproar, the uproar in the place itself was greater.

From the window, I could hear all manner of screams, wails, shouts, banging doors, thundering footsteps, rattled keys. The word of blasphemy that Ebhoe had spoken had thrown all the fragile minds in this house of insanity into disarray, like red-hot metal plunged into quenching cold water. Great efforts were being made to quieten the inmates.

I sat at the teak scriptorium for a while, reviewing the transcripts while Kalibane dozed on a settle by the door. Ebhoe had made particular mention of Subjunctus Valis, the Doom Eagles' Apothecary. I looked over copies of the old Pirody debriefings I had brought with me, but Valis's name only appeared in the muster listings. Had he survived? Only a direct request to the Doom Eagles Chapter house could provide an answer, and that might take months.

The Astartes are notoriously secretive, sometimes downright blatant in their uncooperative relationship with the Administratum. At best, it might involve a series of formal approaches, delaying tactics, bargaining.

Even so, I wanted to alert my brethren on Lorches to the possible lead. I damned Saint Bastian when I remembered the place had no vox-caster! I couldn't even forward a message to the Astropathic enclave at Symbalopolis for transmission off world.

A sister brought me supper on a tray. Just as I was finishing, and Kalibane was lighting the lamps, Niro and Jardone came to my chamber.

'Brothers?'

Jardone got right to it, staring at me through his half-moon lenses. 'The brotherhood of the hospice have met, and they decided that you must leave. Tomorrow. No further audiences will be granted. We have a vessel that will take you to the fishing port at Math Island. You can obtain passage to Symbalopolis from there.'

'I am disappointed, Jardone. I do not wish to leave. My recollection is not complete.'

'It is as complete as it's going to be!' he snapped.

'The hospice has never been so troubled,' Niro said quietly. 'There have been brawls. Two novitiates have been injured. Three inmates have attempted suicide. Years of work have been undone in a few moments.'

I nodded. 'I regret the disturbance, but–'

'No buts!' barked Jardone.

'I'm sorry, Higher Sark,' said Niro. 'That is how it is.'

I slept badly in the cramped cot. My mind, my memory, played games, going over the details of the interview. There was shock and injury in Ebhoe, that was certain, for the event had been traumatic. But there was something else. A secret beyond anything he had told me, some profound memory. I could taste it.

I would not be deterred. Too many lives depended on it.

Kalibane was slumbering heavily when I crept from the chamber. In the darkness, I felt my way to the stairs, and up to the third floor. There was a restlessness in the close air. I moved past locked cells where men moaned in their sleep or muttered in their insomnia.

At intervals, I hugged the shadows as novitiate wardens with lamps made their patrols. It took perhaps three quarters of an hour to reach the cell block where Ebhoe resided. I stalked nervously past the bolted door of Ioq's room.

The spy-slit opened at my touch. 'Ebhoe? Colonel Ebhoe?' I called softly into the darkness.

'Who?' his cold voice replied.

'It is Sark. We weren't finished.'

'Go away.'

'I will not, until you tell me the rest.'

'Go away.'

I thought desperately, and eagerness made me cruel. 'I have a torch, Ebhoe. A powerful lamp. Do you want me to shine it in through the spy-hole?'

When he spoke again, there was terror in his voice. Emperor forgive me for my manipulation.

'What more is there?' he asked. 'The Torment spread. We died by the thousand. I cannot help with your cause, though I pity those men on Genovingia.'

'You never told me how it ended.'

'Did you not read the reports?'

I glanced up and down the dark cell-block to make sure we were still alone. 'I read them. They were... sparse. They said Warmaster Gatus incinerated the enemy from orbit, and ships were sent to relieve you at Pirody Polar. They expressed horror at the extent of the plague-loss. Fifty-nine thousand men dead. No count was made of the civilian losses. They said that by the time the relief ships arrived, the Torment had been expunged. Four hundred men were evacuated. Of them, only one hundred and ninety-one are still alive according to the records.'

'There's your answer then.'

'No, colonel. That's no answer! How was it expunged?'

'We located the source of infection, cleansed it. That was how.'

'How, Ebhoe? How, in the God-Emperor's name?'

'It was the height of the Torment. Thousands dead...'

VII

It was the height of the Torment. Thousands dead, corpses everywhere, pus and blood running in those damnably bright halls.

I went to Valis again, begging for news. He was in his infirmium, working still. Another batch of vaccines to try, he told me. The last six had failed, and had even seemed to aggravate the contagion.

The men were fighting themselves by then, killing each other in fear and loathing. I told Valis this, and he was silent, working at a flame burner on the steel workbench. He was huge being, of course... Astartes, a head and a half taller than me, wearing a cowled red robe over his Doom Eagles armour. He lifted specimen bottles from his narthecium, and held them up to the ever-present light.

I was tired, tired like you wouldn't believe. I hadn't slept in days. I put down the flamer I had been using for cleansing work, and sat on a stool.

'Are we all going to perish?' I asked the great Apothecary.

'Dear, valiant Ebhoe,' he said with a laugh. 'You poor little man. Of course not. I will not allow it.'

He turned to face me, filling a long syringe from a stoppered bottle. I was in awe of him, even after the time we had spent together.

'You are one of the lucky ones, Ebhoe. Clean so far. I'd hate to see you contract this pestilence. You have been a faithful ally to me through this dark time, helping to distribute my vaccines. I will mention you to your commanders.'

'Thank you, Apothecary.'

'Ebhoe,' he said, 'I think it is fair to say we cannot save any who have been infected now. We can only hope to vaccinate the healthy against infection. I have prepared a serum for that purpose, and I will inoculate all healthy men with it. You will help me. And you will be first. So I can be sure not to lose you.'

I hesitated. He came forward with the syringe, and I started to pull up my sleeve.

'Open your jacket and tunic. It must go through the stomach wall.' I reached for my tunic clasps.

And saw it. The tiniest thing. Just a tiny, tiny thing.

A greenish-yellow blister just below Valis's right ear.

VIII

Ebhoe fell silent. The air seemed electrically charged. Inmates in neighbouring cells were thrashing restless, and some were crying out. At any moment, the novitiate wardens would come.

'Ebhoe?' I called through the slit.

His voice had fallen to a terrified whisper, the whisper of a man who simply cannot bear to put the things haunting his mind into words.

'Ebhoe?'

Keys clattered nearby. Lamplight flickered under a hall door. Ioq was banging at his cell door and growling. Someone was crying, someone else was wailing in a made-up language. The air was ripe with the smell of faeces, sweat and agitated fear.

'Ebhoe!'

There was no time left. 'Ebhoe, please!'

'Valis had the Torment! He'd had it all along, right from the start!' Ebhoe's voice was strident and anguished. The words came out of the slit as hard and lethal as las-fire. 'He had spread it! He! Through his work, his vaccines, his treatments! He had spread the plague! His mind had been corrupted by it, he didn't know what he was doing! His many, many vaccines had failed because they weren't vaccines! They were new strains of the Torment bred in his infirmium! He was the carrier: a malevolent, hungry pestilence clothed in the form of a noble man, killing thousands upon thousands upon thousands!'

I went cold. Colder than I'd ever been before. The idea was monstrous. The Torment had been more than a waster of lives, it had been sentient, alive, deliberate... planning and moving through the instrument it had corrupted.

The door of Ioq's cell was bulging and shattering. Screams welled all around, panic and fear in equal measure. The entire hospice was shaking with unleashed psychoses.

Lamps flashed at the end of the block. Novitiates yelled out and ran forward as they saw me. They would have reached me had not Ioq broken out again, rabid and slavering, throwing his hideous bulk into them, ripping at them in a frenzy.

'Ebhoe!' I yelled through the slit. 'What did you do?'

He was crying, his voice ragged with gut-heaving sobs. 'I grabbed my flamer! Emperor have mercy, I snatched it up and bathed Valis with flame! I killed him! I killed him! I slew the pride of the Doom Eagles! I burned him apart! I expunged the source of the Torment!'

A novitiate flew past me, his throat ripped out by animal tusks. His colleagues were locked in a desperate struggle with Ioq.

'You burned him.'

'Yes. The flames touched off the chemicals in the infirmium, the sample bottles, the flasks of seething plague water. They exploded. A fireball... Oh gods... brighter than the daylight that had never gone away. Brighter than... fire everywhere... liquid fire... flames around me... all around... oh... oh...'

Bright flashes filled the hall, the loud discharge of a las-weapon.

I stepped back from Ebhoe's cell door, shaking. Ioq lay dead amid the mangled corpses of three novitiates. Several others, wounded, whimpered on the floor.

Brother Jardone, a laspistol in his bony hand, pushed through the orderlies and ecclesiarchs gathering in the hall, and pointed the weapon at me.

'I should kill you for this, Sark. How dare you!'

Baptrice stepped forward and took the gun from Jardone. Niro gazed at me in weary disappointment.

'See to Ebhoe,' Baptrice told the sisters nearby. They unlocked the cell door and went in.

'You will leave tomorrow, Sark,' Baptrice said. 'I will file a complaint to your superiors.'

'Do so,' I said. 'I never wanted this, but I had to reach the truth. It may be, from what Ebhoe has told me, that a way to fight Uhlren's Pox is in our reach.'

'I hope so,' said Baptrice, gazing bitterly at the carnage in the hall. 'It has cost enough.'

The novitiates were escorting me back to my room when the sisters brought Ebhoe out. The ordeal of recollection had killed him. I will never forgive myself for that, no matter how many lives on Genovingia we saved.

And I will never forget the sight of him, revealed at last in the light.

IX

I left the next day by launch with Kalibane. No one from the hospice saw me off or even spoke to me. From Math Island, I transmitted my report to Symbalopolis, and from there, astropathically, it lanced through the warp to Lorches.

Was Uhlren's Pox expunged? Yes, eventually. My work assisted in that. The blood-froth was like the Torment, engineered by the Archenemy, just as sentient. Fifty-two medical officers, sources just like Valis, were executed and incinerated.

I forget how many we lost altogether in the Genovingia group. I forget a lot, these days. My memory is not what it was, and I am thankful for that, at times.

I never forget Ebhoe. I never forget his corpse, wheeled out by the sisters. He had been caught in the infirmium flames on Pirody Polar. Limbless, wizened like a seed-case, he hung in a suspensor chair, kept alive by intravenous drains and sterile sprays. A ragged, revolting remnant of a man.

He had no eyes. I remember that most clearly of all. The flames had scorched them out.

He had no eyes, and yet he was terrified of the light.

I still believe that memory is the finest faculty we as a species own. But by the Golden Throne, there are things I wish I could never remember again.

TORMENT

Anthony Reynolds

Death was nothing to be feared. Death he would have welcomed. It was the in-between place that that filled him with dread.
To some it was the Undercroft, Tartarus, or Limbo; to others it was Sheyole, the Shadowlands, or Despair. On old Colchis it was known as Bharzek. Translated literally, its meaning was simple and direct – Torment.

Those condemned to wander its ashen fields were said to be cursed above all others. They lingered there, haunted, confused and lost, suffused with impotent rage, longing and regret. Unable to move on, yet equally unable to move back to the lives they had left behind, they were trapped in that empty, grey wasteland, doomed to an eternity of emptiness.

He knew now that the old stories were wrong, however.

It *was* possible to come back...

'*Burias.*' That voice was not welcome here. It was an intrusion. He tried to ignore it, but it was insistent.

'*Burias-Drak'shal.*'

He awoke to pain. It blossomed within him, building, compounding, multiplying, until every inch of his body was awash with fire. He was blinded by agony, yet he grinned, bloodied lips drawn back in a leering grimace.

Pain was good. Pain he could endure. He was alive, and not yet confined to the hell that the Dark Apostle had promised him. Burias embraced his pain, letting it draw him back from the brink of oblivion.

He knew where he was – deep within the Basilica of Torment, on Sicarus, adopted homeworld of the XVII Legion. He'd been dragged here in chains by his former brothers, but he had no concept of how long ago that had been. It felt like an eternity.

Gradually his senses returned.

The smell hit him first. Hot, cloying and repellent, it was the stink of a dying animal. It hung in the unbearably humid air like a fog, something that could be felt on the skin, oily, clinging and foul. He could taste it. Sickly stale sweat, charred meat and burnt hair; none of it could quite mask the stench of bile and necrotising flesh.

But more than anything else, he could smell blood. The room reeked of it.

He discerned low whispers and chanting, and the hushed shuffle of feet on a hard stone floor as his hearing returned. He heard the clank of chains, the hiss of venting steam, and the mechanical grind of gears and pistons.

This is not your fate.

The words were spoken with the confidence of one who does not need to raise its voice in order to make itself heard. It was familiar, but he could not place it. He tried to answer, but his lips were dry, cracked and bleeding, his throat raw and painful. He swallowed, tasting blood, and tried again.

'Who are you?' he managed.

I am the Word and the Truth.

'Your voice... is inside my head,' said Burias, wondering if his torture had driven him to insanity. 'Are you real? Are you a spirit? A daemon?'

I am your saviour, Burias.

The haze of his surroundings was slowly coming into focus. He was staring straight up at an octagonal, vaulted ceiling. It was shrouded in darkness, lit only by a handful of low-burning sconces mounted upon the eight pillars surrounding him. Oily smoke coiled from these fittings, rising languorously.

He lay spread-eagled upon a low stone slab, bound in heavy chains bolted to the floor. The links that bound him were each the size of a Space Marine's fist and heavy manacles were clamped around his ankles, wrists, and neck. The flesh around these bindings was blackened, raw and weeping, burnt almost to the bone.

The manacles were inscribed with ancient Colchisian cuneiform. Painstakingly replicated from the *Book of Lorgar*, the potent runic script glowed like molten rock, and the infernal heat radiating from them made the air shimmer. Yet more of the angular ideograms were carved directly into Burias's tortured flesh, and these too smouldered with burning heat.

His body was a ruin of raw scar tissue, burns, cuts, abrasions and welts. His sacred warplate had been torn away piece by piece, with all the eagerness and hunger of feeding vultures. Where over the years it had become fused to his superhuman frame, it had been crudely hacked off with cleavers and blades that he suspected had been purposefully dulled to make the work longer and bloodier.

Every conceivable torture had been inflicted on him. But he had not been broken.

You are already broken, yet your mind refuses to accept it.

'You lie,' Burias gasped.

I do not. I am here to help you.

'Then help me!'

Look to your left. That is your way out.

With some difficulty, his movement painfully restricted, Burias turned his head. Before him was the reinforced door of his cell. It was closed and bolted, and rust and corrosion was sloughing off its surface like dead skin. The door was massive, thick and solid, and the stonework around the lintel was carved with runic wards.

A pair of hulking executors were slumped in shadowed niches to either side of the door. Huge even compared to a Space Marine and vaguely simian in appearance, these mecha-daemon sentinels appeared completely lifeless except for their eye-sensors which blinked unceasingly in the darkness. They were behemoths of armour and barely-checked fury, mechanical constructs built around a brain and nervous system that had once been human, though daemonic entities had long since been bound within their steel bodies.

When roused, they were easily capable of ripping him in half with their immense powered mitts. Even in his weakened state, chained, tortured and stripped of his armour, Burias stared at them with eyes narrowed; an apex predator sizing up its rivals.

His muscles tensed as his body responded to his desire to fight, yet he was bound securely and he knew that any attempt to break his bonds was futile. There was no hope of escape.

All that imprisons you is your own perception, Burias, and nothing more. You believe that there is no escape, and so there is none.

'You can hear my thoughts,' said Burias.

Yes. You are not speaking aloud now, you realise?

'Who are you?'

Burias's question was met with silence.

'Are you Drak'shal?'

Again, silence.

His view of the dormant executors was abruptly blocked as a dark figure shuffled in front of him, chattering incoherently. More of these robed figures moved around him, attentive and whispering, their faces hidden in the shadow of deep cowls. They were loathsome creatures, emaciated and hunched, the definition of their ribs and vertebrae clearly visible through their black robes. Their arms were corpse-thin and grey. Rusting cables and tubes that leaked milky fluids protruded from their flesh, and their bony fingers were tipped with a plethora of needles, hooks, blades and callipers. All were stained with blood. *His* blood.

Lobotomised cantors were hard-wired into hooded alcoves positioned half way up the chamber's eight pillars. They chanted litanies of binding and containment in long, monotonous streams, their entire existence focused solely on this duty. Their eyes were wired open, and their grossly obese bodies were the pallid shade of a creature that had never seen daylight. Reams of parchment unfolded endlessly before them, and their mouths bled from the potency of the words they read aloud.

Everything about the cell, from the runic chains to the inscriptions upon the cell door and the drone of the cantors, had been designed with a singular purpose – to ensure that the daemon Drak'shal remained tightly bound, suppressed and quiescent.

With the daemon dormant within him, Burias was as any other warrior-brother within the Host; a demigod of war in comparison to lesser, unaugmented beings, yes, but nothing more than a shadow of his former self. He could hardly feel the daemon's presence at all, and this cut him more deeply than any physical torture. It felt like he was missing a part of himself, something so integral to his being that he felt like he had been hacked in two.

The daemon had been bound to his flesh in the early days of his induction into the Legion. He had been one of the special few, chosen for this path with great ceremony and care. Few warrior-brothers were able to survive the rituals of possession. Fewer still were able to master the daemon once joined.

There had been a period of struggle when Drak'shal had fought to gain ascendency, of course, but Burias had won out, asserting his dominance. He had been reborn. Everything of his former life was forgotten.

Drak'shal had given him strength – great strength – as well as speed, cunning, and rapidly accelerated healing that had seem him walk away from injuries that would have killed any other Space Marine. He'd fought in wars across a thousand battlefronts, and yet he bore not a single scar to show for all the countless wounds he had sustained – until now.

Fused with the daemon, his every sense had been heightened beyond anything he could ever have imagined. He could see in total darkness without the aid of his helmet's optic augmentations. He could taste a drop of blood in the air at a hundred metres. He could run as fast as a Rhino APC and maintain his pace for days on end. His strength was easily that of five of his Word Bearer brothers.

'You are nothing without Drak'shal,' Marduk had said, standing over him as the manacles that now held him had been welded shut. Burias and Drak'shal had roared as one, knowing what was to come, but powerless to prevent it. The Dark Apostle had smiled as the runes had burst into

flame, pushing the daemon back into enforced dormancy. *'This is the punishment for your treachery, Burias.'*

His muscles tensed at the memory, his lips curling back in a snarl.

It is your choice what path you take, Burias. To your left lies freedom; to your right, slavery.

Somehow Burias knew what he would see to his right, but he was still compelled to look.

For a moment the horror of the sight carried him somewhere else entirely; drowning, blinded, screaming.

The moment passed as quickly as it had come, and he was staring into a cavernous alcove, like the lair of some great beast. Slumped motionless in the shadow was the mechanical prison that would be Burias's tomb for all eternity.

A Dreadnought.

War machines of colossal power, with a chassis of heavy ablative armour and toting weaponry comparable to that of a front line battle tank, the Dreadnoughts had been conceived early in the Great Crusade. Every time a Legion lost a battle-brother, particularly a captain or veteran, a wealth of hard-won knowledge and wisdom was lost along with them. The Dreadnought was designed to ensure that the greatest warriors and heroes of a Legion might live on even after suffering fatal wounds.

It had been a noble aim, one that seemed to hold great merit, but the machine's creators on Mars had not foreseen the terrible, tortured existence that those interred within were forced to endure. Denied physical sensation, their existence was hollow, empty, and without end. They were cursed never again to experience physical sensation, and were cut off from everything and everyone.

To these poor unfortunates, the one thing that they had been gene-bred and trained for – war – was now a soulless and dissatisfying experience. They had become living war machines capable of laying waste to entire battlefields, and yet cruelly they were not able to elicit any satisfaction from doing so. Never again would they experience the rush of adrenaline that came from combat, nor feel the kick of a bolter in their hands, or watch the life leave a worthy enemy's eyes as the shuddering kill thrust was administered.

As years turned to decades, decades rolled into centuries, and centuries became millennia, those pitiful souls condemned to that horrid half-life were driven slowly and inexorably to madness, filled with longing for all that they had lost, and bitterness towards those who had imprisoned them.

It was therefore in an act of pure malice and barbarity that Marduk intended to take Burias, a healthy, living warrior of the Host, and forcibly inter him. It spoke of the Dark Apostle's vindictiveness that he would rather see Burias suffer for all eternity than have a fatally wounded warrior-brother saved from death's grasp.

Burias stared at the immense, motionless machine with rising terror.

It stood upon squat, armoured legs, and its massive torso was almost as wide as the machine was tall. Both of its arms ended in immense power talons that hung dormant at its sides. A helmet – one of the early Mark II helms, brutal and archaic – was half-hidden behind a gorget of reinforced adamantium. The lenses of the Dreadnought were dark.

The machine was an ancient relic, a shrine to the Dark Gods, and its armour plating was a work of peerless artifice. Every centimetre of its deep crimson hide was covered in intricately carved scripture, and barbed metal bands edged each individual plate. Strips of vellum hung from wax seals, each covered in long tracts of illuminated text.

The chest of the Dreadnought was a gaping cavity. That was where the sarcophagus would be secured. That was where Burias would be entombed, and not as a glorious martyr of the Legion – the only injuries he bore were the result of his torture at the hands of the Host's chirumeks. No, he was being interred within the Dreadnought as punishment for having dared turn against his sworn master Marduk.

Located behind his own was a second altar, mirroring the slab to which he was chained. Upon it rested a sarcophagus. *His* sarcophagus.

It was filled to the brim with liquid and ribbed pipes, cables and tubes spilled over its edges. Some of them connected into tall glass cylinders filled with murky amniotic fluid; others hung limp and lifeless, like parasites waiting to be affixed to a host.

The casket was not large – his arms and legs would be amputated in order for him to fit within. Cables and wires would be rammed into his nervous system, impulse-needles pushed into his cortex. Feed-tubes, ribbed-pipes and cables would be inserted into him, and oxygen-rich liquid would fill his lungs. Once sealed, his tomb could never be re-opened.

In times of war he would be interred within the Dreadnought and unleashed upon the foe, but at all other times his sarcophagus would lie dormant, collecting dust in the undercroft of the *Infidus Diabolus*. Denied outside stimuli, he would yet remain conscious, trapped in Torment...

Nothing is real but what you've chosen to accept.

'You speak nothing but riddles!' Burias snapped. 'You said you were here to help me.'

I am.

'Then tell me how to be free of his prison.'

Break your bonds.

Burias paused. 'What?'

Break your bonds, and you will be free.

As simple as that, thought Burias, mockingly.

As simple as that.

Burias smirked, and shook his head slightly. Humouring the disembodied voice, he pulled against the chains binding him. He gritted his teeth and groaned with the effort, but there was no give in the metal links at all. He gave up. They were too strong.

They are not too strong, Burias. Belief is the path to freedom. Believe that you can break them, and you will.

Burias breathed in deeply, gathering himself. *'Break, you bastards,'* he whispered, then hauled on the chains with all his prodigious, gene-enhanced strength. His abused, flayed musculature strained, veins protruding monstrously, like bloodworm parasites burrowing beneath the skin. He roared, pulling against his chains with reserves of strength that he did not know he had left.

He felt something stir within him.

The cuneiform runes carved upon his manacles burst into flame, their smouldering power surging. The droning intonation of the cantors lifted a pitch, becoming more strained, and the pair of slumbering mecha-daemon executors set to guard over him were roused, leaning forward on immense metal knuckles, emitting snuffling clicks from their vox-registers.

Burias's vision was red, and the sound of his blood pumping in his ears drowned out all else. He could not hear himself roaring, though he knew that he still was. The runic wards turned white hot, and Burias dimly registered the smell of burning flesh – his skin around the manacles being seared anew by the heat of the metal. He barely felt it.

The executors were advancing, the rotary-barrelled autocannons mounted in their forearms clicking and ratcheting as they moved towards him. He lifted himself up off the slab, his back arching with the strain.

The first weakening in the wards came when one of the cantors began to spasm, its words faltering as it began to convulse. Blood burst from its nostrils and ears.

Whatever affliction had struck the cantor down was evidently contagious, as those adjacent to it began to shake and stammer. The chant lost all coherence and was suddenly a confused mess of conflicting, stuttering voices. The burning runes that bound Burias flared erratically, and the executor's rotator cannons began to whine and spin.

With a scream that made reality shimmer, the daemon within Burias surged to the surface, rising like a monster from the deep. The warding runes exploded into blinding, glittering shards, and the chanting cantors' brains burst in one mass collective haemorrhage.

Drak'shal was unleashed.

The change came over him quickly. Burias's form shimmered and distorted like the display of a faulty pict-viewer, flicking back and forth between two incompatible images. It was as if two beings of vastly differing physiology were fighting to share the same location and the laws of reality did not know which to give precedence. Instead of a decision being made, the two images blurred together to become one.

Curving horns rose from Burias-Drak'shal's brow, and his shoulders were suddenly bulging with additional musculature, flesh remoulding like wax. Barbed spines pushed from his elbows and down his spine, and ridges of bone sprouted down the blade of his forearms. His fingers fused to form thick talons, each as long as a mortal man's thigh. Crimson hellfire burnt in eyes which were suddenly elongated slashes carved into a bestial visage, and thin lips drew back to expose the serrated teeth of a predator.

The whole change occurred within the space of a millisecond, faster than the time it took the guardian mecha-daemons to register the danger and open fire.

With a brutal surge of warp-spawned power, Burias-Drak'shal hauled himself upright. His arms and neck ripped free of the chains binding him, tearing the thick links effortlessly. One of the chain lengths held, and the heavy bracket securing it was instead ripped from the floor, bringing with it a torso-sized chunk of rockcrete.

With his legs still shackled, Burias-Drak'shal swung the chain around like a flail as the executors fired. The swinging rockcrete lump took the first in the side of the head, splattering blood and cancer-ridden brain matter as its armoured cranium crumpled.

The sheer brutal force of the blow almost tore the construct's head from its servo-thick neck. Knocked off balance, its autocannon sprayed a burst of heavy-bore shells across the room, ripping through the bodies of black-robed attendants and tearing gouges along the far wall. A rain of expelled shell cartridges fell to the floor.

The second executor was spraying wild gunfire at Burias-Drak'shal, but the possessed Word Bearer was already moving, too fast for mortal eyes to follow. He used his momentum to wheel himself off the blood-stained stone slab, ripping the chains that bound his legs free. Detonations chased him as he spun away from the shots.

With a casual shove Burias-Drak'shal sent one of his craven, black-cowled tormentors flying backwards, hurling it ten metres through the air to strike one of the pillars with a sickening wet crack. With the same movement, he brought the weighted chain swinging around towards the executor that still stood.

The mecha-daemon ceased firing and reached up to grab the chain early in its swing. The heavy links encircled the armoured gauntlet of its fist three times, and the rockcrete lump crashed against its armoured forearm and shattered. With a savage yank, the executor snapped the chain, and Burias-Drak'shal stumbled to his knees.

The bestial construct bellowed in triumph and surged forward on all fours, moving with surprising swiftness. It lifted one immense fist high and brought it down hard, intending to pound Burias-Drak'shal into the floor.

The possessed warrior rolled, and the executor's blow struck the flagstones, sending cracks rippling out from the impact and making the whole room shudder. Burias-Drak'shal scrambled to get away, but the executor managed to grab the short length of chain still attached to his left leg. With a triumphant roar that reverberated deafeningly in the confined space of the chamber, it hoisted him off the ground and swung him first into one of the stone pillars, then into the opposite wall.

Rock crumbled and dust fell as Burias-Drak'shal was pounded from side to side. One of the black-robed attendants cowering in a corner was crushed, brittle bones pulverised under the possessed warrior's weight as it was caught up in the executor's wild fury.

Then the Word Bearer was hurled violently across the chamber. He slammed against the far wall, which cracked under the impact, and fell to the floor. He spat blood as he pushed himself to one knee, momentarily blinded by pain.

The executor bellowed and came at him again.

Move. Leap to the right.

Burias-Drak'shal hurled himself aside as the voice commanded, and the executor thundered into the wall with tremendous force. Masonry dust fell from the ceiling, and cracks spread across the wall like veins. The monstrous executor's shoulder was embedded half a metre into the stonework, and it appeared momentarily stunned by the colossal force of impact.

Kill it.

With a snarl, Burias-Drak'shal scrambled up the executor's armoured body, climbing onto its hunched shoulders as it struggled to pull itself free of the crumbling wall. An outraged growl of scrap-code burst from its vox-grille and it whirled around, seeking to dislodge him, but Burias-Drak'shal clung on, holding tight to the edge of its armoured shell with one hand, claws digging deep into ceramite.

The executor's armoured hide was as thick as the frontal glacis of a Predator battle tank, but its joints were comparatively vulnerable. Its design compensated for this deficiency with overlapping, sheathed plating and a high gorget to shield its neck, but while this was powerful defence against an enemy facing it, there was little to protect against an enemy standing upon its shoulders.

With his free hand, Burias-Drak'shal began punching his talons into the executor's exposed neck, hacking into the thickly bunched mass of fibre-bundles, servos and ribbed cables. Oil, milky fluid and stinking synth-blood sprayed outwards, splattering across Burias-Drak'shal's face. Sparking electrical discharge arced from the wounds, and the executor went wild.

Spinning dementedly, roaring and bellowing, it sought desperately to throw off its smaller foe. It tried to slam him into one of the pillars, driving itself backwards at full force, but he clung on, hacking into its neck, ripping away cables and synthetic muscle-fibres, digging towards the vulnerable neural wiring deeper within.

The mecha-daemon's data-roars become a pitiful, crackling whine, and it stumbled as its nervous system began to fail. It collapsed to the floor, twitching as its life-fluid pooled beneath it, running freely from its savaged neck. It clung to life, trying vainly to push itself upright, but it had lost all coordination and was unable to rise.

Burias-Drak'shal finished it off by driving one of his talons through the back of its armoured cranium, then turned his feral gaze towards the cluster of lesser creatures cowering in the corners of the chamber, determined to vent his fury on their flesh.

Go now. The others are coming for you.

Snarling, he advanced towards the terrified acolytes.

The immense cell door exploded outwards, wrenched out of shape and torn from its hinges. It slammed against the opposite wall, and Burias-Drak'shal sprang through the gaping doorway into a wide shadowed corridor. Gore caked his arms from talon to elbow, and bright blood was splashed across his chin.

There were four sentinels on guard outside his cell. Burias-Drak'shal did not stop to think why they had not entered his cell at the cacophony of mayhem that had been unleashed within, though if he had he might have guessed that in this place such sounds were not unusual. They came at him with falchion blades that hummed with power, and they died with those weapons still in their hands.

When his flesh was his own, Burias was a consummate and graceful warrior, elegant and poised. When he was one with the daemon, he was pure bestial rage.

He tore the head from one of the sentinels and ripped the throat out of the next with his teeth. The third died with the daemon-talons of his fist through its armoured chest, and the last was hurled away with a backhand blow, its spine shattered by the force of it.

Without pausing, Burias-Drak'shal swung his heavy head from side to side, tasting the air.

The ceiling was high and arched. Katharte daemons crouched high up along spiked buttresses like gargoyles, watching over him indifferently. The darkness hid their skinless forms from mortal eyes, though Burias-Drak'shal saw them clearly, and acknowledged them with a snarl.

Clusters of robed curators and indentured servants fled before him, wailing and falling over themselves in their haste. Penitents, their flesh criss-crossed with self-inflicted wounds, dropped to their knees in worship, crying out to him, skeletally thin arms raised in supplication. He ignored them, cocking his head to one side and listening intently.

Mournful bells of alarm were echoing up through the halls. He could hear raised voices barking orders in the war-cant of Colchis, and the stamp of heavy nailed boots on stone, coming in his direction. The sound reached him of weapons powering up – he discerned the unmistakeable hum of plasma weaponry; the electric crackle of submission whips.

With a snarl Burias-Drak'shal launched into motion, bounding down the hall towards the sounds. Each leap tore up the stonework as his talons dug deep, propelling him onwards, urgency and rage lending him speed. He rounded a corridor at full tilt, his momentum forcing him up onto the wall. Rather than slowing, his pace increased.

He hit the approaching warriors with all the elemental force of a thunder strike, leaping in amongst them and starting to kill before they had even registered his presence or thought to raise a weapon.

They were indentured Sicarus warrior-clan, enhanced post-humans bred by the XVII Legion for devotional combat. Their faces were obscured by clockwork rebreather masks and external optical targeting arrays, and hyper-stimms flooded their nervous systems. Though they could never have matched one of the Legion, they were a highly trained, elite force that was worthy of respect.

Nevertheless, there were children next to the fury of Burias-Drak'shal. Three of them were dead without even raising a hand in defence.

Burias-Drak'shal towered head and shoulders over them and ploughed through their ranks, ripping and killing. He smashed gun barrels aside as they were swung up towards him, and warrior-clansmen inadvertently slew their own brethren with high-powered hellguns and plasma blasts in the frenzied mayhem. He punched heads from shoulders, and ripped arms from sockets. He crushed skulls against the passage walls, and slashed throats with his blood-slick talons.

Writhing submission whips sought to ensnare him, but he was too fast for their touch, and those wielding them died, their hot blood splattering up the walls.

All the while, Burias-Drak'shal kept focussed on one figure at the back of the regiment, the hulking warrior whom he had heard barking orders in the language of dead Colchis. He was one of the Host, a brother Word Bearer that Burias had fought alongside for countless years. His name was Eshmun, and he was of the 16th Cohort.

A respected veteran, Eshmun was a stoic and capable warrior who, Burias-Drak'shal recalled, had been marked out for greater things after butchering three White Consuls, bastard gene-descendants of the Ultramarines Primarch Guilliman, in close combat on the Imperial world of Boros Prime. In a hundred wars they had been comrades, fighting across innumerable worlds against all manner of foes. But here in these dark, sweltering corridors those bonds of brotherhood were forgotten.

Eshmun unslung his chainsword as Burias-Drak'shal leapt through the crush towards him, holding the weapon in a two-handed grasp. The blade's engines roared, adamantium teeth a blur of motion as they spun in combat readiness. 'Time to die, whoreson,' growled Eshmun, his voice wet and throaty.

Eshmun was fully armoured in battle plate, yet even it proved unable to withstand Buras-Drak'shal's fury. The possessed warrior took the swing of Eshmun's chainsword in his forearm, allowing the whirring blades to rip into his flesh. It bit deep, screaming and spraying gobbets of blood and shards of bone, and then stuck fast.

With his weapon effectively disabled, the warrior was unable to deflect Burias-Drak'shal's return strike, which punched straight through the front of his horned helmet and drove a half-metre long talon through his skull.

Eshmun died instantly but remained standing until Burias-Drak'shal withdrew, at which point the Word Bearer collapsed to the floor like a puppet with its strings cut.

Burias thought that killing one of his own Legion would have resonated powerfully within him... but it did not. It was merely another kill.

More of his kinsmen were closing in. He could taste their scent on the air.

It is the Anointed.

A part of him wanted to fight, but it was not a battle that he could win, and he knew that oblivion would not be granted to him; the Dark Apostle was too spiteful for that. He would fight, and a good number of them would die at his hands – Kol Badar included, if the Coryphaus dared face him – but Burias-Drak'shal would eventually fall.

Bloodied and broken, he would be dragged back to the cell, and once again he would be bound and shackled with wards and runes. The cantors would be replaced, their droning intonation would begin anew. Once Marduk grew bored, he would be torn limb from limb and sealed within the armoured sarcophagus that had been chosen for him.

Eternity in a box, going slowly and inexorably mad, was not a fate that he would welcome.

You must move quickly.

He stepped over the corpse of Eshmun and slaughtered a path free of the remaining clan warriors without a second thought.

Then he ran, the voice in his head guiding his every step.

Countless side corridors, hallways and tunnels branched off the main thoroughfares, like so many capillaries, veins and arteries. Each turn revealed ever more; thousands of passages spreading out in a bewildering, interconnected maze like an intricate spider-web.

Always, the voice guided him on.

It was impossible to fathom how many individuals were locked away down here, suffering, tortured and brutalised for all eternity. Still, he gave the matter just the barest moment of thought. What did he care? He was free – everything else was an irrelevance.

He passed by hundreds of heavy doors and cells, most of which were locked and barred. Agonised screams, wails and cries echoed from many. The curators of this hellish place knew their art well.

The corridors seemed to stretch out forever. It would have been possible to wander lost for a dozen lifetimes on any one level and never see the same corridor twice, and there were many hundreds of levels below ground, dug deep into the stifling, burning core of the daemon planet, and yet more were being excavated all the time.

Chained bondsmen, their eyes and mouths sutured shut, paused and raised their pallid heads blindly as he surged past them. Black-clad cenobites whipped them back into subservience, their faces obscured by masks of dead flesh.

Malforms with braziers surgically sculpted into their fleshy backs wandered the darkest corridors, existing merely to bring light where shadow lingered. In hidden alcoves, grinning chasteners scourged the bodies of proselytes, lashing them with barbed whips that grew from their wrist-stumps.

Tens of thousands of penitents shuffled along in endless lines, patiently and willingly awaiting ritual sacrifice, their minds turned to palsied mush by the blaring incoherence of floating Discords. Many of them had been standing in line for weeks on end. Flesh-eating cherubs circled around the weak and the sick, waiting for them to fall.

Burias-Drak'shal met his captors in battle once again at the foot of a majestic, sweeping staircase that spiralled up into pure darkness. Strobing lasfire puckered the air, and autocannons wielded by mono-tasked guardian-slaves tore apart the ornate, frescoed walls as they tried to lock onto his rapidly moving shadow.

He slaughtered everything that stood in his path, and bounded up the great stairs, taking them eight at a time. Up into the higher levels of the Basilica of Torment, Burias-Drak'shal climbed.

The scent-traces of the Anointed pursued him always.

He didn't know how long he'd been running. Drak'shal had departed for now, receding back within, leaving him drained and aching.

Time was always difficult to judge on Sicarus. It was not a reliable measure here, its flow dictated by the tidal flow of the ether. It ran slower within the basilica than elsewhere on the daemon-world, the winds eddying around its buttressed flanks becoming torpid and slothful. This was no accident – the edifice's location had been carefully chosen so as to maximise and extend the torment of those within.

Nevertheless, Burias had never been as disoriented as he was now. He might have been running for minutes, or it may have been weeks. Everything that had occurred since his escape from his cell had melded together into one confusing blur.

He vaguely recalled a restless urgency that had driven him up through the basilica. Sometimes he had ascended narrow, spiralling staircases echoing with ethereal wails and screams. At other times he hauled himself up yawning elevator shafts, climbing hand over hand up chains slick with grease and oily grime; he crawled through pipes gushing with liquid foulness, and shimmied up vertical chimneys where corpses were routinely dumped, broken bodies tumbling down into the bowels of the planet. He had fought and killed everything that sought to halt his progress.

Was any of that real? It seemed like a dream.

He tried to focus on his elusive, deceptive memories, but they were as insubstantial as smoke, dissipating like ghosts as he sought to grasp them. It felt like knives were twisting in his mind as he struggled to comprehend what was going on.

He rubbed his shoulders, feeling a ghost-ache there – residual pain from his torture, he guessed – along with a disconcerting recurring numbness in his arms and legs.

There was a heavy, wet feeling in his lungs, making his breathing painful and laboured. He could hear a dull repetitive thumping sound from somewhere nearby, as of metal striking stone. He dropped to his knees, an intense nausea threatening to overwhelm him.

Shaking his head, he struggled to focus on what was real – what he could see, hear, touch and feel. He could not allow himself to slip. Not now.

'Are you still there, spirit?' he growled.

I am no spirit. But I am here.

'What is going on?' he breathed. 'What is happening to me?'

You teeter on the edge of Torment. You must keep moving, lest you succumb.

'I cannot bear this,' Burias said. 'How can I know-'

Focus on what you feel. The stone beneath your hands, the ache of your muscles. The blood in your mouth.

Burias did as the voice bade him, and the nausea and throbbing pain in his head receded, along with the metallic pounding.

His strength slowly returning, he rose back to his feet.

Your pursuers are closing in on you once more.

'Then guide me away from here,' Burias replied.

After what seemed a lifetime he emerged, blinking, from the darkness.

He found himself upon a section of spiked battlement, high up on the basilica. Immense spires, turrets, towers, and domes soared above him, kilometres high, reaching up into the burning sky. Twin obsidian moons wreathed in hellfire stared down like the unblinking eyes of gods. Kathartes rode the heat-currents and swirling updrafts, circling lazily, descending occasionally to feast upon the twitching bodies of sacrifices.

He'd been guided up into the giant cathedral, driven ever higher by his relentless pursuers. The exits on the lower levels had been heavily guarded by warrior clans, sentry guns, and battle-brothers of the 34th Host. There had been no chance of escape there.

He allowed himself a moment, gazing across the surface of Sicarus, the adopted homewold of the Word Bearers. Vast cathedrals, temples, fanes, and gehemahnet towers stretched out across the scorched world, tightly clustered as far as the eye could see. Many of these grand structures were a dozen kilometres or more in height, yet the Basilica of Torment reared up over them all.

The surface of Sicarus was always changing, climbing ever higher into the heavens and the realms of the gods. Larger and more extravagant temples of worship were constantly being raised, constructed on top of the older, crumbling structures like the trees of a forest straining up to the sun and strangling out their rivals.

Ancient battleships, many of which had served the Legion since the Great Crusade, hung in low orbit like circling void sharks. Beyond them, the maddening heavens whirled.

The warp was alive with burning incandescence and surging, ethereal power. Semi-divine entities that defied description could be half-seen in the roiling fire out there, immense forms coiling and writhing, dwarfing the battleships below them. Their grasping tentacles reached down low in places, stretching toward the rising structures of Sicarus.

Burias leaned out over the battlements, gazing down. Cloying yellow cloud hugged the towers and flying buttresses below, obscuring the firmament and lower structures completely. Immense daemonic faces materialised within the fog, snarling and roaring in soundless fury. They seemed to be straining to rise and devour him, but they could not break free of the cloud bank. He found himself mesmerised by their languid, malevolent shapes.

The Anointed are upon you.

A whickering bolter shot whipped past Burias's head, and he hurled himself to one side, ducking for cover. The concussive thump of impact reached him a fraction of a second after the self-propelled shell had passed him by.

He cursed himself for not having sensed how close his pursuers had come.

Stealing a glance around the edge of the archway, he saw the Anointed – hulking Terminator armoured Word Bearers looming out of the gloom, striding belligerently toward his position with weapons raised. The lenses of their helms shone red as their auto-targeters locked onto him.

He ducked back behind the corner of the balcony, cursing. A crackling melta blast struck, liquefying the rockcrete and making it drip like syrup.

'You've led me to a dead end, spirit,' he snapped.

Death is no end for us, Burias.

More gunfire struck the corner at his back, ripping at the stonework.

'Where now, then?'

Up.

Drak'shal returned in an instant and Burias sprang vertically, talons latching onto a jutting ledge six metres above the balcony. The ledge began to crumble beneath his talons, and he scrabbled for purchase, feeling the dizzying pull of the void below...

Finding a foothold, he leapt powerfully upwards again, and latched onto the underside of a horned statue with one hand. As he hung there, he glimpsed the Anointed emerging onto the balcony below. He hauled himself up the daemonic stone figure as they raised their weapons and unleashed a torrent of fire towards him.

The statue fractured beneath the withering fusillade. Bolter rounds and splinters of rock sliced the thin air around him. He snarled as his blood was drawn.

Burias-Drak'shal pushed off from the head of the statue as it shattered, grabbing onto a jutting plinth and continuing his rapid ascent, bounding up the exterior of the basilica, leaping from handhold to handhold.

He swung out over a deep overhang, climbing hand over hand along stone ribs that formed arches supporting the underside of a protruding wing of the basilica. He could no longer see the Anointed or the balcony he had left below – both had been inexplicably swallowed up by the thick cloudbank that hung beneath him.

With a grunt of effort, he hauled himself up onto a ledge, disturbing a roosting katharte. The daemon beared its teeth at him and dived off the ledge, drawing its skinless wings tightly in to its body.

Moving swiftly and silently, Burias-Drak'shal slid in through an arched window and found himself in a long shadowed corridor. There was no living soul to be seen, though flayed human flesh was pinned to the walls, hair and fingernails still attached.

As he drew near, fresh ruinous symbols carved by unseen hands were cut into these skins. Blood ran from the wounds, dripping down the walls. The flesh began to ripple and twitch, and a large milky eye slid open to regard him impassively. Mouths tore open, and the dead flesh began to wail and gibber, flapping and twitching spasmodically.

Burias-Drak'shal picked up his pace, loping quickly along the corridor as more mouths opened, adding to the toneless wail.

Outside, a floating Discord descended, drawn to the sound, and hovered several metres beyond the portico's windows. It turned its brazen vox-grille toward him, a tangle of mechanised tendrils trailing behind it. A deafening blare of sound burst from the thing, a cacophonous wall of sound that made his eardrums vibrate painfully. It was the sound of Chaos itself, filled with ungodly screams, wailing children, pounding industry, and the beating of the Dark Gods' hearts.

Amongst the din, a familiar voice spoke his name. *'Burias.'*

In confusion, Burias-Drak'shal stared at the hovering Discord.

'Marduk?' he said.

Do not listen. It will speak only lies and falsehoods. The deceiver seeks to draw you back to Torment.

A second blast of noise rolled over him, and he reeled as if struck a physical blow. Blood dripped from his ears. Again he heard the voice of his former lord and master, coaxing him back to... where...?

The choking, drowning sensation rose within his throat once more, threatening to engulf him.

Focus, Burias. All that is real is here.

Stumbling blindly away from the aural assault, Burias staggered through an archway into shadow. It was cooler here in the cloistered darkness, and a rasping wind seemed to pull him eagerly along. Within moments, the blare of the Discord faded away.

He paused in his flight, breathing heavily, until he was back in control of his senses. His ears were ringing from the din.

A familiar scent reached his nostrils, and his lips pulled back in a snarl, exposing his serrated teeth. He spun, lashing out... but too late.

His strike was knocked aside contemptuously, and powered talons clamped around his neck.

'Hello, Burias,' snarled Kol Badar.

Burias-Drak'shal was hoisted half a metre off the ground to match Kol Badar's height, and his feet kicked futilely beneath him. The Coryphaus was wearing his quad-tusked Terminator helm, and his voice was a low, mechanised growl.

'It is time to go back, Burias,' said Kol Badar. 'You cannot keep running forever.'

Burias's windpipe was being crushed and his arteries compressed, stemming the flow of blood to his brain. Dimly he saw a distorted reflection in the elliptical lenses of Kol Badar's helmet, but it was not his own face that stared back at him – what he saw was a wasted, grimacing cadaver. Tubes and ribbed pipes emerged from its nostrils and mouth, and its hairless scalp was pitted with plugs, cables and wires. Blood, oil and dark mucus leaked from the crudely drilled holes in its skull.

Burias-Drak'shal cried out, thrashing and striking out wildly, but he could not break the Coryphaus's crushing grip. Kol Badar laughed at his frantic struggle.

His vision grew hazy and indistinct, his brain starved of blood and oxygen. Whispering shadows danced around the periphery of his vision, like grim spectres awaiting his death. His surroundings faded, the walls melting away, and flames erupted all around him. He gripped the Coryphaus's talons, straining to loosen them, but his strength was fading, along with his consciousness.

With a sickly crack, a vertical slit opened Kol Badar's helmet from chin to crown, yawning into a gaping, daemonic maw filled with rows of ceramite teeth. The jaws of this mouth distended impossibly, and Burias was dragged in towards it. Wriggling black worms emerged from deep in the monster's throat, straining toward his face.

If you surrender now, you will be lost to Torment forever.

'No!' roared Burias, straining to turn away. Surging with a last burst of desperate strength, he managed to wrench apart the daemon's talons, and he fell to the ground at its feet.

He rose fast, lashing out, but he hit nothing. He was alone.

The corridor was empty.

Still gasping for breath, Burias staggered down a narrow side tunnel and into an antechamber crowded with robed proselytes. Their heads were bowed as they hurried on their way, paying him no attention at all. The air was thick and cloying with smoke and incense, and the walls seemed to be closing in on him.

At the far end of the chamber, he could see the hellfire glow of the open sky, and he pushed his way towards it. He was battling against the flow of proselytes, and he roughly barged his way through the stinking press of bodies. Still they paid him no mind, not even complaining as he shoved them out of his path. Several fell to the ground and were instantly lost beneath the living tide.

Burias realised he was getting no closer to his goal, and he began to lay around him more forcefully, battering aside those in his path, breaking bones and limbs with sickening cracks. He trampled over those that fell and crushed them with his heavy steps.

At last he emerged into the light to find himself upon a wide bridge spanning the gap between two cathedral spires of the basilica. Statues of Word Bearers, each more than five metres tall, lined the bridge, each with hundreds of prayer papers fixed to their armour. Doleful bells sounded, reverberating across the maddening cityscape of Sicarus.

The flow of the faithful broke upon him, streaming around him like liquid. He was an island, a lone motionless figure in the midst of a migration as the bells called the faithful to worship.

'Burias.'

Again he heard someone speaking his name and he turned, scanning the sea of downcast faces for its source.

His legs gave way beneath him. They were completely numb, and the same loss of sensation was tingling up his arms. He felt suddenly confined, claustrophobic and trapped in the midst of the crowd.

'Burias-Drak'shal.'

Shut it out.

Burias clutched his head, confused and disoriented. 'What is happening to me?' Bodies pressed in around him, bustling past.

You are being called back.

'Back to where?'

Torment.

The immense Word Bearer statues began to move, stepping off their plinths with stonework crumbling away from their forms to reveal blood-red armour beneath. They strode through the crowd, moving toward Burias in step with the pealing of the distant bells, giant bolters clasped across their chests.

'This cannot be real,' he whispered, dragging himself to his feet.

The crowd turned, as if seeing him for the first time. In a rush they surged forwards, babbling and speaking in tongues. They crowded around him, their eyes burning hot with faith and fever, reaching out to touch him.

'Bless us, great one,' a scrawny proselyte begged, clutching at his leg. Burias kicked the wretch away, snapping the man's bones.

'This cannot be real!' he said again, pushing away from the crowd, making his way to the edge of the bridge.

This is all that is real, Burias. Everything else is Torment.

The giant Word Bearers were closing, making the bridge shudder with every footfall, crushing any who did not get out of their way quick enough.

Run. Fight. Kill. Do this, and you can live on here, forever.

Burias laughed at the absurdity of it all, and climbed up onto the edge of the soaring bridge's low wall and glanced down. The sickly cloud bank below was impenetrable even to his daemon-sight.

'To hell with this,' snarled Burias.

'Burias-Drak'shal,' said every proselyte in unison, speaking with the Dark Apostle Marduk's voice. 'Come to me.'

The immense statues hefted their bolters, closing in all around him. The voice cut through Burias's mind, tinged with desperation.

Do not do this!

'And to hell with both of you,' said Burias, speaking to both the spirit-voice and the voice of his master. He turned away from the crowd of believers.

With his head held high, he extended his arms out to either side. He closed his eyes, and breathed in deeply.

The thunderous fire of gigantic bolters echoed all around, but Burias had already let himself topple forwards.

The proselytes screamed as one. 'No!'

No!

Burias pushed off hard, and holding his cruciform pose, he plummeted down into the fog. The air rushed past him, yet he kept his eyes shut, giving himself over to the Ruinous Powers.

It felt as though he were flying, soaring the ether with the Kathartes. Not the foul, skinless harpies that filled the skies of Sicarus and frequented the *Infidus Diabolus*, but the beauteous angelic beings of pure light that those daemons became in the deep flow of the warp.

He was drowning.

Thick, viscous fluid filled his lungs, lukewarm and repulsive. He coughed and spluttered, crying out in shock and anger. The sound was muffled by the thick bundles of tubes and pipes that filled his throat and nostrils. All he achieved was to expel what little air he-

'No!' roared Burias, kicking and thrashing against his confinement, and then he was falling through the void once more.

Abruptly, the cloud bank parted and he smashed through a great dome of coloured glass. Coming down fast, he rolled and skidded along the length of a flying buttress to rob the fall of its impact, tumbling to the floor and ending the movement on one knee. Shards of coloured glass studded his flesh, and more showered down around him, filling the air with its tinkling music.

He found himself in a tiny chapel. It was a humble, ascetic space, a simple shrine to the Dark Gods that lacked the grandeur and ceremony that infested the rest of Sicarus. A plain altar was carved into one wall, atop which sat a skull with a simple eight-pointed star of Chaos burnt into its forehead.

Beneath a shadowed arch stood the lifeless, immense form of the Warmonger. Burias's skin began to itch as he looked upon the Dreadnought, his arms and legs tingling.

'You should not be here,' said a woman's voice, and Burias-Drak'shal snarled, turning sharply. He had not sensed a presence in the room.

He could tell by her manner of garb and bearing that she was a seer. She stood in the shadows, bedecked in robes the colour of congealed blood. Her hood was down, revealing an angular, pale face. Gaping, empty hollows were located where her eyes should have been, yet she seemed to stare at him unerringly. 'You have gone too deep.'

Drak'shal was raging within him, urging him to attack, to brutalise this witch and be away, but he resisted. He forced the daemon back. It struggled, attempting to gain ascendancy, but it was an old battle, and one that Burias had won long ago. Resentfully, Drak'shal receded, sinking within.

The daemon's presence had ensured that the wounds of his torture had now healed. All that remained was his dried blood upon his skin. No scars marred his flesh.

For a moment he thought he heard a distant voice speaking his name. He shook his head, clearing it of these errant distractions.

'There is someone waiting here for me,' he said. 'Who is it?'

'You do not need me to answer that question,' said the seer. 'You already know the answer.'

'I do not have time for riddles,' muttered Burias, turning to leave.

'Time is meaningless here,' she replied. 'You know this.'

'Speak plainly, witch, or do not speak at all.'

'It was he who released you from your bondage,' she said, her words giving him pause. 'It was he who brought you here.'

'Released me?' Burias snarled over his shoulder. 'I released myself!'

'No,' said the seer, shaking her head. 'He burnt away the wards holding you, opening the door for you to come here, to come to him. But I see that your mind refuses to accept what your heart already knows is true. You need to *see* in order to believe.'

The seer stepped away from a simple wooden door, and gestured towards it.

Burias frowned, his anger piquing, but he stepped past her and placed a hand upon the door's rough hewn panels. It swung inwards easily, revealing a narrow passage. Lowering his head, he stepped within.

He moved up the narrow passage until he came to a circular, windowless prayer-room lit by a single candle in an arched alcove. It was small, the kind of room used by fasting penitents or hermetic recluses. The walls were covered in tiny neat script-work. He recognised the handwriting. He had seen its like before.

'*Burias. Burias-Drak'shal.*' That voice again...

Burias's twin hearts began to pound. He could not breathe. He heard metallic pounding in the distance, beating in time to his hearts.

His gaze fell upon a figure kneeling in the centre of the room. Its back was turned to him, and it wore a plain robe of undyed, coarse fabric. Its head was smooth and hairless, the bare scalp glinting like gold in the candlelight.

The figure rose to its feet. It seemed to expand to fill the circular room, as if it were magnifying in volume to gigantic proportions. Then the illusion passed, and Burias realised that the figure stood no taller than he.

As the figure turned, Burias looked upon the golden face of a demigod.

His eyes began to bleed and his mind rebelled. His soul lurched, and he was driven to his knees, breathless and suffocating.

A veil seemed to be ripped aside, and the walls of the shrine disappeared, replaced with roaring flames and darkness. A maddening cacophony of screams and roars assaulted him from all sides.

'Urizen? Lord?' he breathed.

The flames seared his lungs, but he did not care. His mind was reeling. He did not understand. The primarch of the XVIIth had been locked in self-imposed isolation within the Templum Inficio since long before Burias's creation. How could he be here? Where, in fact, were they?

Burias's hearts were thundering, beating erratically and dangerously fast. He couldn't breathe. He was drowning. He was blind.

Look.

The voice was velveteen and smooth, once again calm and measured. It was the same voice that had guided him to freedom, yet it seemed more potent, more vital. There was a controlled intensity to it that was almost painful.

LOOK.

He opened his eyes. The figure that stood before him was not the holy primarch of the XVII Legion. He was staring at himself.

He jolted, and the vision was gone. He was alone in the cold darkness.

'Burias.'

That voice was not welcome here. It was an intrusion. He tried to ignore it, but its power was impossible to resist. He rebelled against it, but it dragged him back towards consciousness.

'Burias-Drak'shal.'

He was drowning.

Thick, viscous fluid filled his lungs, lukewarm and repulsive. He coughed and spluttered, crying out in shock and anger. The sound was muffled by the thick bundles of tubes and pipes that filled his throat and nostrils. All he achieved was to expel what little air he had left.

In panic, he registered that he was completely submerged, and as he struggled to rise he struck a hard, unyielding metal surface. He thrashed wildly, smashing against the sides of his containment, desperately seeking escape. There was none to be had. He was sealed in and drowning.

His hands refused to respond to his commands, and he could not move his arms. He could see nothing but darkness. He tasted oil and blood, battery acid and bile. He vomited violently, but the acidic foulness had nowhere to go.

His strength was fading, along with his consciousness. Metallic clangs, hammering and the whine of engines echoed loudly around him. Behind it, he heard the muffled murmur of voices, but could make no sense of the words.

The end was close now, and his struggles weakened. His lungs rebelled against him, causing him to reflexively suck in a deep breath of liquid and his own vomit. He began to convulse, shuddering and jerking violently.

Oblivion came for him then. But it was not to last.

He awoke to darkness. There was no pain. There was nothing at all, and he knew then that he was in hell.

He roared in a voice that was not his voice. He heard that mechanical, grinding, anguished bellow with ears that were not his ears; external sensors translated what they heard into electrical impulses and were transmitted directly into his cortex.

He clenched a hand that was not his hand into a fist, and an immense, blade-fingered power talon clenched. He pounded this great fist into the stone walls of his prison once again. It made a dull sound, metal on stone. *That sound...*

'Burias,' said a voice. 'Burias-Drak'shal.'

It was the voice that had called him back. It was the voice that had brought him into this hell. He swung towards it, servos whining.

'Back in the land of the living, finally. In a manner of speaking, at least.'

Optic sensors interpreted what they saw. A figure stood nearby, one that he recognised.

'You were in deep this time,' said the figure. 'I was not sure you were coming out. You resisted my call for the longest time yet. I am impressed.'

Burias lunged at the figure, pneumatic piston-driven legs driving him forward and giant claws reaching out to crush it, but immense chains bound with burning runes held him fast, restraining his mechanical strength.

Dark Apostle Marduk laughed. 'Now, now, Burias. Mind that temper.'

Hatred surged through what was left of Burias's body – amputated, rotten and curled foetus-like in the amniotic fluid sloshing within the sarcophagus implanted at the heart of the machine.

Hatred. *That* was something he was still capable of feeling. His mighty fists were clenching and unclenching unconsciously. With every last remaining fibre of his being he wanted to smash the author of his torment to paste.

'How long this time?' Burias managed, his voice deep and sepulchral, the sound of immense rocks grinding together.

'Not long. Ninety-seven years, unadjusted.'

To Burias it had felt like an eternity. He wondered how he could possibly endure.

'Why do you rouse me now?' he growled. 'There is no torment that you can unleash upon me that would make my suffering any more complete.'

'Torment, old friend? No, you mistake my purpose,' said Marduk. 'I come to you because the Host marshals for war. I am, for now, *releasing* you from torment. It is time you killed again for the Legion.'

Death was nothing to be feared. Death he would have welcomed. But denied that, the next best thing was the chance to kill once more. Burias ceased his struggles.

'War?' he boomed, unable to keep the eagerness from his grating, mechanical voice.

'War,' agreed the Dark Apostle.

A silken voice spoke in Burias's mind.

None of this is real.

COLD TRADE

Andy Hoare

The Adeptus Astra Cartographica listed the world by the short form designator SK0402/78, but the locals called it 'Quag.' It was an unpleasant little name for an unpleasant little world, but Brielle Gerrit, daughter of the infamous rogue trader Lucien Gerrit and next in line to inherit the Arcadius Warrant of Trade, had good reason to visit it. The corner of her mouth curling into a covetous grin, Brielle's hand was subconsciously drawn to the hidden pocket in her uniform jacket and the small object nestled within. Her costume was similar to that worn by the highest ranked officers of the Imperial Navy fleet of a sector very, very far away, and she most certainly did not bear the commission that granted her the right to wear it. But that just made the wearing of the deep blue frock coat with its shining gold epaulettes and fancy braiding all the more fun.

'Commencing final approach, mistress,' the pilot announced from the cockpit, snapping Brielle's attentions back to the here and now. She was seated in the astrodome of her Aquila-class shuttle, a small vessel configured as her personal transport and clad in the red and gold livery of the Arcadius clan of rogue traders. Really, she should have been strapped safely into her grav couch in the shuttle's passenger compartment, but she had always preferred to witness atmospheric interface first hand rather than relayed through a pict-slate. Her pilot, Ganna, was a trusted retainer of the clan and he had given up objecting to his mistress's habits years ago.

'How long?' Brielle said into her vox pick-up, the sound of Quag's atmosphere fusion-blasting the shuttle's outer skin making normal conversation impossible.

'We'll be through the upper cloud layer momentarily, mistress,' Ganna replied, the faintly mechanical edge to his voice betraying the latest of the machine augments he had recently been fitted with, at his own instigation. 'Stand by…'

Brielle gripped the handles beneath the armoured glass dome and raised herself upwards to look out. As she did so, the flames licking the shuttle's outer skin wisped away, and the scene opened up before her. The surface of the world below lurched upwards as Ganna brought the shuttle onto a new heading, the landscape resolving itself from the swirling mists.

'What a dump,' Brielle sneered, flicking her head back sharply as a stray plait fell across her face. 'Where's the settlement?'

'Just over the horizon, mistress,' Ganna replied. 'And if I might say so, I agree. It *is* a dump.'

'Hmm,' Brielle replied, settling in to watch the final approach, even if it was the final approach to an absolute festering boil of planet. As the shuttle gradually shed velocity and altitude, the landscape came into focus, not that Brielle paid it much attention. The surface of Quag was, as its name suggested, dominated by endless tracts of swamps, bogs, marshes and pretty much every variation on the theme of stinking, bubbling foulness. The planet's shallow seas were only distinguishable from its landmasses by the relative lack of trees, and even on the so-called land, these were twisted, stunted things that resembled skeletal limbs grasping for the wan skies. It wasn't pretty, and the humidity made her hair curl.

As the shuttle descended still lower, bucking sharply as it ploughed through the occasional pocket of atmospheric disturbance, Brielle caught sight of several small clusters of lights, out in the swamps and none closer to its neighbour than a hundred kilometres. The grin returned to Brielle's lips as she regarded the lonely, twinkling pinpricks. She knew exactly what they represented, though she would save that information for later.

At the exact moment that a burst of machine chatter spewed through the vox-net, Brielle located the shuttle's destination. Quagtown, some of the locals called it, while other preferred *the settlement*. Brielle's word for it wasn't fit to be expressed near those locals, though most would secretly agree with her general view of the badland town that even now was hoving into view. If the planet of Quag was a dump, then its only major settlement was the sump below it.

'Three minutes, mistress,' Ganna announced. 'Transmitting key now.'

As machine code blurted harshly in the background, Brielle watched Quagtown grow nearer. The first thing she saw was the towering rock column on which it was perched, a natural formation that looked anything but. The column was the only feature of its type on the entire world, resembling a flat-topped stalagmite rearing a kilometre into the air. At the summit was clustered the settlement itself, its oldest quarters built on the cap and the later ones clinging precariously to its sides. From this distance, the town looked like so many layers of festering metallic junk piled randomly on top of one another, and to be honest, it didn't look much different close up.

Both Brielle and Ganna remained silent as the machine chatter burbled away, and Brielle fancied she could discern the to and fro of electronic conversation in the atonal stream. After a minute or so, during which the shuttle continued its approach on the ramshackle town, the chatter ceased, to be replaced by a solid, grating tone.

'Did they go for it?' said Brielle, her gaze fixed on the command terminal before her. A small data relay slate showed a line of text, but while Brielle was relatively conversant in such things, the code was unknown to her.

'I believe they did, mistress,' Ganna replied, his cranial feed allowing him to read the data faster than it could be deciphered and relayed through a command terminal. 'Stand by… confirmed. Sector three nine zero high,' he said, and Brielle saw him nod towards the rapidly closing settlement.

Following his directions and gesture, Brielle saw what her pilot was indicating, for the shuttle was now only a kilometre or so out from the top of the column and Ganna was bringing it around on a wide, lazy turn. A guttering fire had been lit at the summit of a thin, precarious looking tower constructed from a jumble of metal stanchions from which protruded numerous aerials and revolving scanner dishes. As the distance closed still further, she could make out numerous small figures clinging to the framework, many of which had scanning devices raised to their eyes. They were all clearly heavily armed.

As the shuttle banked, Brielle saw movement at the base of the tower, and just for a moment, the breath caught in her throat. What looked like a multi-launch missile system was tracking the shuttle as it approached, at least a dozen snub-nosed projectiles nestled in an oversized hopper just ready to shoot her down and really ruin her day.

But, Brielle realised, that was Ganna's point. If the missile launcher was going to fire it would have done so by now. Letting out the breath she had been holding, she scanned the bulk of the ugly settlement as the shuttle completed its turn and fired its manoeuvring jets for landing. Close in, the details of its construction were revealed, and it was a miracle that had nothing to do with the God-Emperor of Mankind that the place stayed together at all. Quagtown was constructed from a bizarre mix of junk, much of it evidently scavenged from small space craft and surface vehicles by the haphazard surface detail. These disparate elements were supported and conjoined by a twisted mass of wood harvested from the trees in the swamps far below, and the whole lot was lashed together by what must have been hundreds of thousands of metres of vine, again, gathered from the lands all around.

And atop this confused, impossible mess of uncivil engineering was a vaguely circular landing platform roughly fifty metres in diameter. The pitted, blast-scorched surface was made from hundreds of deck plates welded crudely together and held up by a forest of wood and metal struts. It was crossed by dozens of snaking feed conduits and fuel lines, and numerous cargo crates were piled haphazardly at its edges. Guidance lumens set into the surface flashed a seemingly random pattern, no two of them the same colour, and Ganna fine-tuned the shuttle's approach, firing its landing jets as the vessel slowed to a halt above what Brielle assumed was its assigned berth.

From her vantage point in the astrodome Brielle was afforded a view of the entire landing platform, and she could see that three other vessels were already docked. One was a battered old Arvus lighter, and it was clear to Brielle's practised eye that it had once belonged to the defence fleet of a system spinward of Quag. Its new owner had made a very amateur attempt at painting over the livery of the vessel he had no doubt acquired via less than legitimate channels, and the spectacle brought a wry grin to Brielle's lips.

A second vessel was of a pattern Brielle had never actually seen in the flesh, though she had certainly seen it depicted in the Arcadius clan's archives held at the Zealandia Hab. In form it resembled some massively oversized insect, its domed, multi-faceted eyes forming its cockpit. Its wings were currently swept back into a stowed position, but Brielle knew they were fitted with an anti-grav array that granted the small ship such agility and grace it was no wonder its type was highly sought after by all manner of unusual or downright dangerous characters. Whether this was owned by an underworld lord, a powerful bounty hunter or even another rogue trader like herself Brielle could not say, though she silently resolved to be watchful.

The third vessel sat upon the uneven surface of the landing deck was a squat, armoured brick of a shuttle, and it was being tended by an indentured service crew, who were themselves being closely watched by a gang of heavily augmented, and no doubt combat-glanded thugs. This was evidence of two primary facts. The first was that it had only recently arrived at Quagtown, its owner having paid for an immediate, quick turnaround service to ensure it was ready for an expeditious departure. The second fact that presented itself to Brielle was that the individual who she had come to this festering dump of a town to meet with had arrived ahead of her, exactly as she had anticipated he would.

'Set us down, Ganna,' Brielle ordered, a thrill of danger and expectation fluttering through her belly. 'Let's do what we came here to do...'

* * *

The instant Brielle and Ganna climbed out of the Aquila shuttle and took a breath of the air she halted.

'Damn it,' she cursed as the stale air filled her lungs. 'Forgot my filtration plugs, this place stinks like an ork's...'

'Take my rebreather, mistress,' Ganna interrupted her unladylike outburst, unhooking his breathing mask from about his neck and passing to Brielle.

But Brielle was already walking away from the shuttle, waving the offer away dismissively. 'Make sure the cargo's unloaded,' she called back as she stalked away across the deck.

Caught between his concern for his mistress and the need to fulfil her order, Ganna muttered beneath his breath as he turned hurriedly towards the open passenger compartment. At the head of the short ramp stood two burly figures, each as much metallic machine as biological flesh. The biomechanical, mind-scrubbed servitors carried between them a heavy, armoured chest, the expressions on their hybrid metal/flesh faces dead-eyed and blank.

'Imperative meta-nine,' Ganna barked at the servitors, the code phrase causing them to stir as they recognised and acknowledged the words of a duly authorised superior. 'Heeding signal zero zero actual,' he ordered, and stood aside as the mindless automatons marched down the short ramp in perfect lock step and headed off after Brielle. With a final glance at the shuttle, Ganna punched a glowing rune plate mounted by the hatch, cycling the passenger bay to its sealed state, and followed after his mistress.

The metallic surface rang beneath the tread of Brielle's heavy, knee-high boots, and it took Ganna only seconds to catch up with her. The air was hot in the vicinity of the idling shuttles and scented by a nauseous mixture of fuel, filth and sin. Knowing that if anything untoward happened to Brielle, her father would hunt him down and feed him to the sump-rats in his cruiser's sub-decks, he determined to stay as close to her as it was possible to do, though he knew from experience that would really get on her nerves.

'Hey there!' Brielle called out to a cluster of ground crew struggling to affix a large feed-line to the intake on the armoured shuttle sharing the landing pad with her own Aquilla. When the men seemed to ignore her, choosing instead to concentrate on their duty, she raised an eyebrow and planted her fists firmly on her hips.

Just as Ganna stepped up beside her, Brielle started forward towards the ground crew, and at that very moment a pair of towering guards stepped in from nearby to bar her path. Obviously brothers, the pair were clearly in the employ of the local underworld, for they were heavily augmented as well as covered in the tattooed sigils that proclaimed the complex web of patronage commanding their loyalty. Brielle read it in a glance, and knew instantly that the pair belonged to one of the lowlife flesh brokers that dealt out of Quagtown.

Casting a seemingly casual glance over the bulk of the armoured shuttle the men were tending, Brielle craned her neck to look up into the face of the nearest thug. By the saints, they breed them homely around these parts, she thought to herself.

'Listen, boys,' she said sweetly, drawing a look of scepticism from both men. 'I need my lander overwatched while I'm doing business in town. What's the local scrip?'

Brielle knew full well what form of currency the locals would prefer, and how much of it they would demand, but she didn't want to play that card, not yet at least. After a moment of thinking hard on the matter, one thug replied, 'How much overwatch you need?'

'All of it,' Brielle replied on a whim, drawing a raised eyebrow from Ganna. In truth, it didn't matter what and how much she laid out for local security, not in the big picture, but she needed to make an impression in the right quarters.

'Half the crew're busy on *this* job,' the more talkative of the brothers replied, jerking the thumb of a mechanical hand towards the armoured shuttle.

'I'll pay double whatever they're on,' Brielle replied mischievously. 'In clan-bonded deaths-heads.'

The two thugs glanced at one another with eyes alight with greed, seeming to reach an unspoken agreement within seconds.

'Half now,' she interjected before either could reply, producing a single coin worth more than both men would normally earn in a month and holding it up where both could see. 'Half later, *if* you make me happy.'

'Done,' they said as one, clearly believing that Brielle had been.

'Then I'll leave it to you,' Brielle said, dropping the coin into the open hand of the nearest of the pair. She watched the two heavies pull their fellows off of the duty they were on and muster them to guard her own vessel. As the pair walked away, the two servitors close behind, the landing deck rang to the sound of the local hired muscle spreading the word that a sweet job was in the offing. Knowing it was unseemly to mock the hard of thinking, Brielle suppressed a sly grin and set off into Quagtown.

'Holy Terra,' Brielle muttered as the four turned into what passed as the town's main thoroughfare. 'It actually looks *more* of a dump than they say…'

The thoroughfare couldn't really be called a street, because it was more a valley between ramshackle buildings and travel along it was not in a straight, flat line, but up, down and across the numerous gantries, platforms, ledges and walkways that connected each building to the next. The buildings themselves were a tumbledown mess of sheet metals and unidentifiable machine components, with all manner of shipping containers providing the most desirable real estate. The numerous walkways were in many cases little more than parallel lengths of spar or rotted timber, with tread plate or mesh lashed crudely between with great lengths of dried vine.

But worst of all was the population. Every available space along the walkways and gantries was filled by the scum of Quagtown. Rag-clad beggars panhandled from the gutters while those afflicted by a variety of chemical addictions shivered and sweated in the shadows. Thieves and blaggers eyed Brielle and her party lasciviously, while meat-headed bullies and scarred mercs looked them over for hidden threats. The wealthy, a relative term in such frontier hell holes for the truly rich would pay to be anywhere else, promenaded along the gantries displaying what portable wealth their guards could be trusted to protect, while painted doxies fluttered their lashes from half-open doorways.

Brielle's eyes narrowed as she saw a number of mutants in amongst the press, individuals whose bodies were twisted and malformed and whose faces were more akin to those of beasts. Several of them sported skin and hair of garish hues; though it was possible the effect was artificial as numerous subcultures across the Imperium pursued the most outlandish of fashions. Several had additional limbs, an effect which only the wealthiest could, or indeed would, pay for, for it required the services of the most skilled of flesh-crafters to carry out well. Clearly, these were true mutants, born into their genetic heresy.

On many of the million and more worlds of the Imperium, such debased individuals would be ruthlessly controlled or even culled. They might be allowed to repent their sin of impurity by toiling their short, bitter lives away in the lathes and foundries of some brutal labour-prison, but rarely were they allowed to show their malformed faces in such a public manner. Only on or beyond the frontier was it possible for such creatures to walk about openly, unchallenged by the authorities.

If the presence of the mutants was a rare sight on a human world, that of the creature stalking along the uppermost gantry was an outright spectacle. A spindly being, its body vaguely humanoid but its overlong, stilt-like arms employed as an additional pair of legs, was progressing with something akin to grace from one building to the next. Its skin was dusty grey with mottled, darker patches down its back, and instead of clothing it wore what could only be a combat rig, a form of webbing with numerous pouches and packs attached all over. Its head was long and aquiline, sporting three pairs of eyes along its sides, while its mouth was a tiny, leechlike opening at the end of its proboscis snout. Brielle was fascinated, for she had never before encountered its species nor read of it in all of her education.

A crude, grunting shout from another walkway made Brielle instantly aware of another type or alien, and one that she had encountered on numerous worlds. Indeed, the barbarous, green-skinned orks plagued the known galaxy, their anarchic empires forming great lesions of war and disturbance that meant that no Imperial sector was ever safe from their incessant invasions and migrations. A group of the hulking xenos was making its way along a walkway clinging precariously to the side of a building constructed from a huge, cylindrical fuel transport, shouldering people aside and growling at passers-by. Brielle's lip curled in disgust, for these beasts truly were the scum of the universe, and it was rare for them to be tolerated even in such recidivist sumps as Quagtown. The place got even lower in her estimation.

Brielle halted at a relatively open gallery, standing aside as a party of drunken lay-techs staggered by, and scanned the buildings and walkways before her. Reaching into a pocket, she drew out a small data-slate, aware of the numerous eyes amongst the passers by that followed the motion while trying to look as if they weren't. With a flick of an activation rune, she awoke the slumbering machine, a rough schematic of the town appearing on its green-glowing surface.

As she studied the map, Brielle's brow furrowed. She'd paid a lot for it yet now, in the field, it seemed suddenly to bare scant resemblance to reality. The data had been purchased from an indentured sprint-skipper who supposedly knew the local wilderness zones better than any in the region, and the man had staked his reputation it was as accurate and up to date as it was possible to be. Brielle had made sure she had dirt on the skipper though, and knew exactly which interzone scum-ports he liked to haunt when off duty. If anything happened, he would be tracked down and shown the error of his ways in terminal fashion, she had made the arrangements before leaving.

But, despite the schematics' inconsistencies, Brielle was finally able to make some sense of it, and it soon became evident that part of the cause of the inaccuracies was the constant rebuilding of the ramshackle junk town. With nothing more sturdy than flotsam and jetsam to build their town from, the locals were forced to replace sections as they fell apart or came away from their precarious perch. A form of pattern gradually formed, and Brielle was able to get her bearings. Yes, the building she was looking for was less than fifty metres distant though it was not yet visible in the confused jumble of structures. To reach it she would have to wend her way up, down and across a crazy mess of walkways and galleries, passing through the mass of scrofulous locals. With a sense of cold dread, she saw that the path would almost certainly cause her to intersect the group of orks, and with a weary resignation, she just knew they were going to be trouble...

Having climbed the winding stairs and walkways, the locals muttering with surly bitterness at the need to stand aside as the lumbering servitors marched through the crowd without any hint of concern for those forced to clear the way, Brielle's small party came face to face with the orks as both stepped on to a narrow gantry high above the thoroughfare.

Brielle halted as she stepped on to the walkway and looking downwards realised that she could see through the mesh under her feet to the crowded thoroughfare twenty metres or so below. Looking back up, she saw that the lead ork had also stopped, and was grunting some orky quip to its three mates, who laughed uproariously at the unheard comment.

'Something funny?' Brielle called out, knowing from experience that orks were a demonstrative species that respected action and attitude far more than words and thought. The biggest ork looked her over dismissively, and Brielle took the opportunity to appraise it in turn.

Like most of its species, the ork was massive, taller than an average human and at least three times the bulk. Its short legs were bowed and muscular, its torso hunchbacked and top heavy. Its burly arms were almost long enough to touch the ground and its impressively ugly head sat so low between its shoulders it appeared to have no neck. It was carrying an array of weaponry, from pistols to cleavers, all stowed, for now, inside the bright red cummerbund wrapped about its middle. The barbarous creature's attire was a bizarre mixture of crudely stitched scraps and elements clearly intended to ape human modes of fashion. It wore a long, ragged frock coat, its hem frayed and dirty. On its head was perched a bicorn hat, and one of its beady, pig-like eyes was covered a patch.

Brielle grinned ever so slightly as she saw the details of the row of medals and other adornments crudely attached to its chest. Each was a roughly stamped icon that served to identify the bearer, to one who knew how to read them.

'Move,' the creature growled, its voice a low, threatening rumble. Ganna cast a wary glance at his mistress, but Brielle remained exactly where she was, folding her arms across her chest and nodding smugly to herself.

'You speak well,' she said, and she meant it. The fact that the ork had used even a single word in the Gothic of the Imperium marked it out as a uniquely gifted individual. 'For one of Skarkill's boys, anyway.'

From the ork's reaction to her statement, Brielle saw that she had read its glyph-medals correctly. It was indeed a member of the same clan as the ork warlord she had named. The ork folded its arms in apparent imitation of Brielle's posture, the simple act serving to corroborate Brielle's suspicions. By aping human modes of dress and language, by copying her stance, and by its very presence in a human-dominated settlement, the ork revealed itself to be a member of the Blood Axe clan. That meant it was almost certainly an associate of the warlord Skarkill, a being that Brielle's family had encountered several times in this region of space.

'Who you?' it grunted, its single, leering red eye looking Brielle up and down. 'You Admiral wossname? Vonigut the turd?'

'No,' Brielle said dryly. 'I am not Lord Admiral Alasandre Vonicurt the *Third*.' The officer in question was a man of two centuries service, Brielle knew, and well known for his exceptional girth and prodigious facial hair. Orks weren't the most observant of aliens, but still…

'I am Brielle Gerrit,' she said archly, suppressing her annoyance with an effort of will. 'Of the rogue trader Clan Arcadius.'

The ork seemed to think hard on that, for it evidently recognised the name despite its inability to tell one human from another. Brielle's fingers tapped against her arm and she flicked Ganna a glance that spoke volumes of her opinion of the greenskins' mental skills. She became aware that much of the noise and general hubbub of the thoroughfare had quietened down and that scores of upturned faces were watching the confrontation eagerly. What happened here might affect her entire visit to Quag, she realised. At length, the beast rumbled deep in its barrel chest, and it squinted its eye at Brielle.

'Hired Skarkill's mob?' the ork said. 'Big fight on church planet?'

'There we go,' said Brielle, relieved that the ork was indeed of the clan she thought it was, and an underling of the warlord Skarkill. 'The Arcadius had need of your clan's services on Briganta Regis. Skarkill's army took the city and hardly looted it at all. Everyone came away with a profit, and Skarkill said some nice words to my father. You remember those words?'

Now the entire thoroughfare went quiet as hundreds of the locals waited to see how things would play out. Brielle had no doubt that the greenskin mercenary would have terrorised many of these people, and that a fair few of them would be eager to see it put in its place. Others might have a vested interest in *her* being the one to come off the worse though...

'He said,' the ork slurred, the effort to recall his lord's words clearly taxing its tiny mind. 'Ever you need something done, you just got to ask.'

'That he did,' said Brielle, moving towards the make or break point of the conversation. 'Now, I need something done, understood?'

'You want something killed?' the alien mercenary said, suddenly animated as it believed itself back on more familiar territory.

'No,' said Brielle, eliciting visible disappointment from the ork. Lowering her voice so that only those on the walkway could hear her, she said, 'I need you to step aside and let me pass.'

The crowds below had not heard Brielle's demand, perceiving only a protracted silence during which the woman in the frock coat with the elaborate eye makeup and outlandishly plaited hair seemed to face down an alien warrior several times her bulk, and which had refused to give way to a single of *them* all time it had been in Quagtown. A ripple of excitement passed through the crowd and someone started issuing odds. Soon, bets were being placed and money was furtively changing hands, and then, the confrontation reached its conclusion.

The massive, green-skinned brute nodded at the woman and grunted at its companions. Now utterly silent, the crowd was clearly expecting an explosive and highly entertaining outburst of violence.

But then, the ork stepped aside so that the walkway was clear for

Brielle and her party to proceed across. The crowd exclaimed in shock and outrage, while several ruined bookkeepers made a sudden dash for the nearest side alley.

'Thank you,' Brielle said to the ork quietly and not without relief as she walked past, fighting hard to keep her voice steady so wildly was her heart pounding. 'Skarkill and my father will both be very pleased with your service, and I'm sure you'll be paid well.'

A moment later Brielle and Ganna were across, the two servitors stomping along after them and the orks had continued on their way. 'Mistress,' Ganna hissed once he was sure that no one would overhear. 'If your father ever hears that I allowed you to do what you just did, he'd…'

'I know,' said Brielle, dismissing her pilot's complaint with a wave of a hand. 'He'd be furious at you. He'd be even more furious at me though…'

Realising that his mistress was talking about more than he had knowledge of, Ganna slowed his pace and fixed Brielle with a dark stare. 'Might I ask why, mistress?'

'Because it wasn't him that hired the Blood Axes at Briganta Regis,' she said. 'It was the rebels. We were on the *other side*.'

Now Ganna halted entirely and rounded on Brielle as the colour drained from his face. 'What if he'd…'

'Remembered that little detail?' Brielle interjected. 'I was counting on him not being able to tell one human from another, as he proved when he mistook me for that pig Admiral Vonicurt. He had a choice between risking his warlord's wrath or losing face in front a few humans. Luckily, he decided he cared more what his boss thought of him than us.'

Brielle's audacity was too blatant for Ganna to reply, so she fished the data-slate from her pocket and looked around for the building that was their destination. 'There it is,' she said, setting off again. 'Are you coming?'

'I think I'd better, mistress,' Ganna mumbled towards Brielle's retreating back. 'I think I'd better…'

'Hold it right there, miss,' demanded the stubjack guarding the door to the nondescript building. 'What's in the crate?'

Brielle looked the man up and down, determining in less than two seconds that he was wearing armour concealed beneath his scruffy overalls and padded jacket, and armed with at least one hidden pistol weapon. She could take him if she needed, she judged, but there were three others of his type loitering nearby, thinking they were acting casual but clearly in on the action.

'Nothing that should worry you,' she said, not feeling a tenth of the cockiness she put into her voice. 'Let me pass and we'll all have a far nicer day, is that clear?'

The stubjack cast what he obviously thought was a furtive glance at the nearby group, and Brielle knew for sure that they were guarding the place as well. 'I said, what's in the crate?' the man repeated as his fellows ambled over, his voice lower and more threatening than the first time.

'And I said, *nothing that should worry you*,' Brielle replied. 'Looks like we're stuck, doesn't it.'

'Not really,' the stubjack said as his four fellow, equally heavily armed and armoured guards appeared at Brielle and Ganna's back. The pair were instantly surrounded by men much bigger than them, but still she refused to be cowed.

'Listen,' said Brielle, lowering her voice so that the guards were forced to lean in and concentrate to hear her clearly. It was a trick she'd learned from a particularly sadistic tutor growing up on Chogoris, and it forced the listener to concentrate on the speaker. 'I've already faced down a bunch of orks today, and they were far bigger than you. Let, me, pass,' she growled.

The man blinked as he held Brielle's gaze. Word had clearly spread quickly throughout the small town; hardly surprising, she thought, given the nature of its inhabitants. He glanced towards the crate held securely between the two servitors, evidently weighing up his desire to know what was inside it with his sense of self-preservation. Though he might try to hide behind the need to ensure that nothing dangerous was permitted inside the building he was employed to protect, Brielle knew that in reality, he was hoping it contained something he could take a cut of. Well, it most certainly didn't.

Swallowing hard, the man reached a decision. He nodded to his fellows and, with far more reluctance than the ork on the walkway, stepped aside to allow Brielle and her companions to pass. Grinning with theatrical sweetness, Brielle moved past him, allowing Ganna to push open the battered door, which appeared to be made from the rear hatch of a Chimera armoured carrier, for her to enter the darkness waiting inside.

Beyond the hatch, Brielle was plunged into shadow, which became pitch blackness the moment the guard slammed the portal shut after the servitors had passed through. Her heart pounding, she took a deep breath and straightened her back, before stepping forward into the unknown with one hand held lightly out before her. She soon found the floor to be littered with small fragments of debris, though she couldn't tell, and didn't really want to know, exactly what she was treading on.

A moment later, she became aware of a muted, but rowdy noise from somewhere up ahead, and stepped forward until her hand brushed against what felt like a metallic surface. The sound was definitely coming from the other side of what she guessed to be a second hatchway, and even as she listened she became aware of voices and wild strains of half-heard melody.

'Ready?' she said, as much to herself as to her loyal retainer. Without waiting for an answer, she pushed on the hatchway, and saw for the first time the interior of the place where she had come to earn herself a small fortune.

The space was far larger than seemed possible from the outside, for what seemed like a random jumble of shipping containers and tumble-down shanties was in fact a cunningly wrought building, housing an establishment known, amongst certain circles, across the entire region. It had no official name, though those in the know often called it 'Quagtown Palace' and a variety of similar titles, all of them deliberately and sarcastically investing the place with an entirely undeserved grandiloquence.

The crowded interior was in essence a huge, shabby theatre, dominated by a stage at the far end that was framed by great swirls of crudely but ambitiously made baroque detailing. The stage blazed with light made hazy by the banks of acrid smoke drifting through the air, and as she stepped through Brielle found she could make out very little of whatever spectacle was being enacted on that stage, though it was clear that the crowd seated before it most certainly could. Row upon row of tattered, mismatched velvet and leather seating, much of it scavenged from a wide variety of vehicles, accommodated an audience of several hundred. Every one of them was shrieking, whooping and clapping at whatever was happening on the distant, smoke-obscured stage.

The sounds Brielle had dimly heard through the hatch were suddenly so loud they made her wince. An anarchic cacophony of raucous crowd noise and skirling, wild cadences produced by some unseen band competing with the hubbub of conversation, merriment and clinking drinking vessels.

Moving forward to afford Ganna space to pass through the inner hatch, Brielle took in more of her surroundings. The walls were lined with shadowed nooks and by counters that sold all manner of wares, most of them alcoholic and probably decidedly unhealthy to imbibe without a large dose of counter-tox taken beforehand.

Seated around the bar area, Brielle saw a variety of underworld scum. She recognised the types from a hundred frontier star ports and way stations: out of work crew, surly press gangers, harried looking lay-techs and in amongst them all, the dark-eyed, tight-lipped ship's masters and other higher-ranked crew. Serving staff shimmied through the smoky scene carrying trays of refreshments and soliciting the richer looking patrons for whatever further services they might desire. The sight made Brielle's lip curl in disgust, but a part of her found the whole, sordid spectacle somehow alluring, despite her upbringing in the tenets of the Imperial Creed.

'Is this the right place?' said Ganna as he appeared at Brielle's side, the two servitors still waiting in the passageway. 'It looks kind of...'

'Fun,' Brielle interrupted. 'And yes, it *is* the right place. Shall we find a table?'

* * *

'Drink, ma'am?' said the waitress, who appeared at the table several minutes after Brielle and Ganna had found themselves somewhere to sit. It was far from ideal, Brielle knew, but if things played out right she'd be moving on pretty soon anyway. The servitors were stood immediately behind her, eliciting numerous furtive glances from those nearby. The glances told Brielle who was who and what they were here for. Many *really* wanted to know what was in the crate, while plenty more were keen to look anywhere else, deliberate in their efforts to blend into the crowd and not to draw attention to themselves. They were the dangerous ones, Brielle thought with a small, wry smile.

'Hmm?' Brielle replied, leaning back against the scruffy, padded seat and propping her elbows on its back as she looked around at the crowd one last time before addressing the waitress's question. 'I don't suppose you stock *Erisian Hors d'age*?' she said, knowing full well they didn't.

The waitress looked blankly back at Brielle, and just for a moment she suspected the girl might have undergone some form of pre-frontal neurosurgery, though her forehead bore no obvious scars.

'*Ganymedian Marc*?' she pressed mischievously, her curiosity piqued by the waitress's continued silence. Maybe she was under some form of xenos dominance, Brielle thought, like those priests on Briganta Regis...

'*Asuave*?' she said finally, realising she wasn't going to get an entertaining reaction.

'Certainly, ma'am,' the waitress replied. 'Terran vintage is it? Void-sealed to give that complex flavour...?'

Brielle's eyes narrowed and Ganna coughed uncomfortably. 'Two shots of whatever you've got,' she said finally, slightly put out by the sudden feeling that it was *she* who had been made sport of. Before she could say anything more, the waitress had disappeared into the crowd, leaving Brielle and Ganna with a view of the large stage dominating the establishment.

'Mistress,' said Ganna. It was obvious he was about to chastise her as only a retainer as valued as he would ever dare. 'Do we really want to draw so much attention to ourselves?'

Brielle grinned widely as she settled in for the wait for the drinks. 'Yes, Ganna. That's exactly what we want. Now will you relax?'

With that, Brielle set her feet upon the low table, crossing her heavy boots as she tried to work out what was happening on the gilded stage. Entertainment varied so wildly across the Imperium it was often damn near impossible to decipher what was going on, each depending on so many different cultural idioms they made little or no sense to outsiders. Even amongst those cultures that weren't rooted in a single location, the galaxy was such a huge place that what entertained one audience was utterly impenetrable to another. Nevertheless, Brielle had been raised in the uniquely free, wide-roaming culture of a rogue trader clan, and certainly considered herself open minded when it came to such things.

What she saw unfolding on the stage before her however was quite some way from anything she had seen before.

The stage was obscured by banks of drifting smoke illuminated red, violet and purple by the array of lumen-bulbs mounted at its head, but as Brielle watched, the smoke drifted past, turning what was a hazy, half-seen blur into something shockingly solid. At the centre of the stage stood an impossibly tall, almost skeletally thin man wearing a bizarre costume that seemed to be made from a hundred different items of clothing thrown randomly together. On his head he wore a tall stove-pipe hat and his eyes were made bug-like and bulging by a pair of heavy duty goggles inset with magnifying glass. He held in one hand an ancient brass vox-horn, while the other gesticulated towards the other dozen or so figure sharing the stage with him.

The stage show was clearly some form of exhibition, and the spectacle on display was a group of mutants whose bodies were so malformed by genetic deviation they would have been shot on sight on any civilised world, and most frontier or badland ones too. Brielle's first reaction was to reach for the laspistol holstered in her belt, but she caught herself before her hand could close around the grip. Clearly, if the mutants were dangerous they wouldn't be on show in such a way, she told herself, though in truth she was far from convinced that was the case.

The largest of the mutants was a hulking brute, and Brielle was only slightly relieved to see its ankles were clapped in heavy irons, a long, heavy chain snaking off behind the striped curtain behind. It was at least as massive as an ogryn, one of the stable, largely tolerated mutant strains recognised by most of the Imperium as a sanctioned branch of the human family tree. But its size was the only thing the beast had in common with the ogryns. Its skin looked like pockmarked bark and its hands, which were clad in heavy metal straps, were long, serrated claws. Its face was barely visible off centre in its chest, and consisted of a huge lower jaw, a massive brow and a pair of beady black eyes nestled in the folds between.

As if this hulking brute wasn't unusual enough, the rest of the mutants clustered on the stage were just as extreme, though thankfully none were anywhere near so large. One had multiple-jointed arms three times the normal length, while another had three heads, none of which had any visible mouth. One mutant was little more than a head mounted in a bizarre mechanical ambulatory contraption, while another had no head at all, its facial features set instead in the centre of a grossly distended belly.

With a flourish that brought forth another wave of applause from the audience, the scarecrow like impresario introduced the next act. The lights dimmed to be replaced by a single, harsh sodium beam, and as the applause died away a stir of movement from overhead drew Brielle's attention.

To a flurry of wheezing, atonal music emanating from a pit out of sight in front of the stage, a garishly painted hoop descended from the rafters over the stage, and seated daintily upon it was a female figure that sent the crowd truly wild. Its legs were fused together into a shape resembling the body of a fish, but that was far from its strangest feature. Upon its shoulders sat two heads, each of which dominated by hugely pouting, bright red lips. Neither face had any other features, yet the crowd clearly viewed the figure as the very pinnacle of female beauty. Even as Brielle watched, the figure stirred into motion, her hips writhing suggestively until the hoop in which she was perched began to swing back and forth, each pass taking her further out over the whooping crowd, who reached upwards with groping hands to get just a touch of the object of their devotion.

'Enjoying the show?' a voice said from behind Brielle, and she froze, determined not to betray the fact that she hadn't heard the figure approach. She had been entranced by the figure swinging in the hoop, hypnotised by the truly bizarre spectacle, but her attention, if not her gaze, was now entirely fixed on the man who had spoken.

'Seen better,' she said casually as Ganna turned around to look at the speaker directly. Brielle herself waited a few seconds more, then turned her head languidly to face him, praying as she did so that the front would work.

The speaker was, as she had guessed it would be, the man she had come to Quag to meet. His name was Baron Gussy, though Brielle had been unable to discover if either or both were titles, affectations or nicknames. While at first glance he appeared a tall, slender man of indeterminate age, that effect was only short lived. He wore the outfit of some ancient princeling, consisting of a jerkin made of brightly shimmering material, puffed sleeves, garish hose and an improbably large codpiece that brought a dirty smirk to Brielle's lips. But again, as outlandish as it was, it wasn't his attire that made his appearance unusual, it was his features.

Baron Gussy was a patchwork man, in every sense of the word. Every one of his features had been bought, or more often simply taken, from someone else, and recombined into the form standing over Brielle right now. His face was a jigsaw puzzle, each small section grafted to the next. Brielle had no idea how he thought the effect looked anything like natural, for no two parts were exactly matched. Perhaps that was the point, she realised. Perhaps he sought to deliberately project an air of macabre eccentricity, the better to put those he dealt with at a disadvantage.

Brielle's source had told her that the effect was not limited to the Baron's face however, and that every organ in his body had been sourced from someone else's, to create, so he told the loose-lipped doxies that kept him warm each night, the perfect example of mankind. Brielle couldn't see it herself.

His mismatched lips twisted into an unctuous grin, the baron bowed slightly at the waste and with a flourish indicated a shadowed alcove guarded by several more stubjacks of the type she had confronted outside. As she stood, she couldn't help but notice the covetous glance he cast towards the crate held between the two servitors.

'Shall we retire to somewhere more private, Madam Gerrit?' he said. Making her way past the baron, Brielle could not help but notice the furtive glances cast her way by many amongst the crowd. Many were appeared unhealthily curious, but the acid glares of a pair of richly dressed women nearby made her scowl with irritation, for clearly they thought her some morsel picked up for the baron's entertainment.

'Come on, Ganna,' she snapped as the waitress returned with their Asuave, a nasty little glimmer in her otherwise blank eyes.

Accompanied by a trio of obviously glanded house stubjacks, Baron Gussy led Brielle and her party through the crowded establishment, the masses parting without complaint as they advanced. Brielle fought the urge to pat the pocket hidden in the breast of her frock coat, and forced herself to be calm. She knew what she was doing, she told herself. She was walking right into the jaws of a trap, that was what she was doing, but that was the entire point of this little expedition...

At length, the lead stubjack reached an archway decorated with some mad artisan's ideal of baroque finery, and turned to wait as the rest caught up. Brielle took the brief opportunity to study the scene, acutely aware that she might have need to exit it very quickly indeed if this all went wrong. The low arch led off to a private seating area, a low table set between plush, cushioned sofas. A low hanging chandelier, its guttering flames blue from the gas that fed them, provided just enough light for clandestine business to be conducted comfortably in the shadowy nook.

'Please,' Baron Gussy demurred as he took position beside the arch, the stubjack looming behind him. 'Make yourself comfortable. But first, Madam Gerrit, you will understand if take a few... precautions.'

Brielle's eyes narrowed in suspicion, but she remained silent until she had some idea what the baron was intimating. Eyes open, mouth shut, that was what her father had taught her, and he'd done alright for himself, she mused.

At a nod from the baron, the stubjack following on behind the group reached into the inside of his jacket, Brielle's breath catching in her throat as she and Ganna exchanged a silent look. But she doubted Gussy intended harm, not quite yet at least, yet she was still relieved when the stubjack pulled nothing more dangerous than a portable scanning device from his pocket.

Brielle swallowed hard, but kept her expression as uncaring as she could as the stubjack ambled up to her, the scanner's main unit in one hand, and its detectrix-wand in the other. She raised one eyebrow in mild surprise that the lump had the skills to operate the device. But then, she'd once seen a ptera-squirrel trained to serve drinks to the worthies of a minor Navigator House, only for the creature to enter the second stage of its life cycle, morph into a ravening beast of teeth and claws, and butcher half the family before the dessert course had even been fully served.

''scuse me, ma'am,' the man slurred as he approached, gesturing with the wand for Brielle to raise her arms. She felt a flush of irritation and the intense desire to knee the meathead in the groin, and the feeling only got more intense as he wafted the wand up and down, tracing the contours of her body as the control unit bleeped and burbled. Even when the machine chimed to indicate no hidden weapons had been detected, the stubjack continued to play the wand over Brielle's body, until a cough from his master caused him to step back, a sneer on his grox-ugly face.

'She's clear,' the leering goon announced, and ambled up to Ganna with less enthusiasm than he had Brielle. 'Up,' he ordered, but before the pilot could raise his arms, Brielle interjected.

'He's heavily augmented. He'll set that thing off even on its lowest threshold.'

The stubjack hesitated and looked to the baron for guidance.

'Then he can wait out here,' said Gussy, his tone sending a quiver of silent revulsion up Brielle's spine. 'He'll be well looked after; you have my word on that. Now, Madam Gerrit, shall we?'

Brielle met Ganna's eye, the pilot nodding slightly to ensure her that he was fine with waiting outside, though he was obviously less than happy to allow her to enter the baron's lair on her own. Telling herself it would all work out to plan, Brielle waved the two servitors forward towards the arch.

'That won't be necessary, madam,' Baron Gussy said, the faintest hint of triumph in his voice.

Brielle's heart thundered in her chest, but she managed to keep her voice level as she replied, 'Baron, the exchange?'

'Has nothing to do with that crate, Brielle. I've been in this business for a while, you know, and can spot a decoy easily enough. I assume the item is secreted about your person, in some shielded pocket perhaps?'

Brielle afforded the smug bastard a shallow tip of the head and flashed him an ego-quenching smile. 'Fair enough,' she said, and gestured for the servitors to set the crate down out of the way, before stepping beneath the low archway and into the private alcove.

Without waiting to be invited, Brielle seated herself amongst the plush cushions, leaning back in an effort to appear entirely at ease with the situation despite what she felt inside. The air was sweet with incense, and not the sacred type burned in the shrines of the Ecclesiarchy. Despite its veneer of luxury, the place was cheap and dirty, soiled with a heady mix of sin and ennui.

'Ah,' said the baron, his voice dripping with what he evidently thought was sophistication and charm. Brielle had been patronised by far better men than he and she only ever tolerated it when there was a profit to be made. Now, sadly, was one of those times. 'Make yourself comfortable, my dear, and we'll begin.'

With a curt gesture, the baron despatched one of the stubjacks standing in the archway, before seating himself opposite the low table from Brielle. The flickering gaslight cast by the low chandelier seemed to exaggerate the patchwork effect of his skin and highlight the fact that each of his eyes was a different colour and size. In fact, the way he was sitting, it appeared almost as if his legs were a different length, the joints somehow wrong.

'I'm afraid we're all out of *Erisian Hors d'age*,' he said, a sly glint in his eye, the smaller, dark brown one. 'Though I was once offered an early first century M.37 amasec from the equatorial foothills of San Leor.'

Always the amasec, Brielle thought to herself. With a million worlds in the Imperium you'd think these people would try something different…

'I'm fine,' Brielle replied, not actually wanting to risk drinking whatever might be set before her.

'Quite sensible,' said the baron. 'Perhaps later, after we've done business, eh?'

Not on your life, Brielle thought sharply. 'That would be nice,' she said sweetly. 'Speaking of which…?'

'Indeed,' said the baron, reclining back into the cushioned seating as he spoke. It was clear from the predatory glint in his eye that he was about to play all of his hand at once, as Brielle had been counting on him doing. 'You have the item on your person. Please place it on the table where I can see it.'

Hesitating slightly for effect, Brielle smiled coyly. She reached up and slid her hand into the lining of her frock coat's left breast, watching him follow the movement with his mismatched eyes. With a deft motion, she unsealed the hidden, null-weave lined pocket and withdrew an object the size and shape of a simple, unadorned ring.

Reaching forward slowly, she placed the ring in the centre of the table, before leaning back to watch the baron's reaction. By the gleam in his eye, the larger, blue one this time, she knew he was hooked.

'What is its pedigree?' he said, his gazed fixed with unwavering intensity on the small item.

'It was retrieved from one of the rediscovered fane worlds spinward of the Ring of Fire,' said Brielle, and as far as she knew it had been.

'By who?' he demanded, his voice tinged with something akin to lust.

'By a flesh-wright clan out of the fourth quadrant,' she said, though that part of the tale was far from certain too.

'And you came into possession of it how?' he leered, his mask of sophistication and charm now almost entirely slipped. 'Tell me how you found this… *wonder*.'

'The flesh-wrights were contracted by a... competitor of the Arcadius,' she said, more certain of this part of the story, for she had been present throughout much of it. 'But they came off worse in a small war over trade rights with the Ultima Centaur annex. This,' she waved languidly towards the ring, 'Was part of the settlement.'

'Have you... tested it?' the baron all but whispered.

You must be mad, Brielle thought. She knew full well what it was said to be capable of. The ring was said to be imbued with the power of some impossibly ancient and thankfully extinct xenos race, that when worn, reshaped the flesh of the bearer into new and extreme forms. It was said that it took a mind of great power to control the drastic process, but that the results were spectacular, or hideous, depending on the willpower of the wearer. Though Brielle herself was undecided on the veracity of the claims, she had little doubt that Baron Gussy was mad enough to believe them and to try to utilise the artefact's power, hence the exchange.

Speaking of which, Brielle thought. 'And you have the icon ready?' she asked, making every effort to sound casual and relaxed despite her fluttering belly. If he'd just produce the icon and let her get on her way, she knew an eldar corsair prince who was prepared to cede a paradise world for possession of it.

But she knew it wasn't going to be that simple.

Tearing his eyes from the small ring in the centre of the table, Baron Gussy leaned back in the sofa and as he did so, he reached up to his own collar, just as Brielle had minutes before. Undoing the first few buttons of his jerkin and the shirt beneath, he revealed far more than the patchwork skin of his chest. About his neck, secured by a simple leather thong was a gleaming, bone white pendant, a sacred icon a mad alien was prepared to pay an entire world to possess.

'How much is this worth to you?' said Gussy.

Here we go, thought Brielle. She knew he wouldn't be able to resist it, though a small part of her had dared hope he might be reasonable.

'How much are *you* worth?' he continued.

'Baron,' she said, interrupting him in the hope that he might allow himself to be diverted, and to avoid the otherwise inevitable unpleasantness. 'I'd far rather...'

'*I'd* far rather you listen, my dear,' he interjected. 'Rather than interrupt. It's so rude.'

Brielle nodded sullenly, allowing the fool his moment of valediction.

'I've decided I want to expand my operations. I think a spot of extortion is in order.'

Brielle sighed and cast her eyes to the ceiling in what she hoped was a display of nonchalant dismissal. 'Go on then,' she breathed. 'Name it.'

The little display had the effect Brielle had hoped for, the baron's expression changing instantly from haughty pseudo-sophistication to flushed annoyance. Strange, she thought, how each section of the flesh on his patchwork face went a slightly different colour.

'You shall remain here,' he said coldly, all pretence of civility gone. 'Your father shall receive my demand when I've considered just what you might be worth.'

'You can't even *pronounce* how much I'm worth,' Brielle replied, her voice low and dangerous. This idiot was really starting to annoy her now.

'Oh, I wouldn't be so sure,' said Gussy. 'I'm told the trade routes on the far Eastern Fringe have been drying up for a few years now. They say there's a shadow out there, and that worlds are just falling silent, one system at a time.'

Brielle said nothing. Eyes open, mouth shut.

'Remind me,' said Gussy. 'Where does the Arcadius derive most of its wealth…?'

'You don't know half what you think you do, baron,' Brielle all but growled, though in truth it surprised her just how much knowledge of her family's business he had. It was true that something was stirring out beyond the Eastern Fringe and that it was affecting the trade routes the Clan Arcadius had relied upon for generations, but that was far from the whole picture.

'I know enough,' he snapped. 'Enough to know that your father might be keen shed certain, peripheral assets to have you returned safely to him.'

'Peripheral assets?' said Brielle. 'What are you…'

'I know the Arcadius owns half of Zealandia. How about that for an opening offer, hmm?'

Brielle was stunned. How this petty underworld crimelord thought he could get away with wresting ownership of a significant Terran conurbation was beyond her. Clearly, the man's ego outmatched his ability by some degree.

'Enough,' she said, waving a hand dismissively and leaning back once more. With a sudden motion, she swung her legs up and planted her booted feet on the low table, sending the priceless xenos ring pattering across the stained carpet. Gussy tried as hard as he could to look unconcerned, but his mismatched eyes tracked the ring as it rolled to a halt, then they switched back to Brielle. 'I'm offering you this one chance to play nice, Baron Gussy, then things get messy. Understood?'

The baron's lips twisted into a mocking sneer. Messy it is then.

Flicking her head back in a gesture that some might have taken for arrogance, Brielle caused one of her intricately plaited braids of dark hair to drop down across her face. She made to reach up and hook the errant strand away, but as finger and thumb closed about the braid, she squeezed, triggering the small, jokaero-built device secreted within.

'This,' she said to the baron, 'is a ground to orbit transmitter.'

'Nonsense,' he replied, though he licked his lips with evident nervousness. 'There's no way you'd have got it through the scanner.'

'Perhaps I wouldn't have, if your goon had had his mind on his duty, and not my...'

'You're bluffing.'

'My light cruiser is, right now, holding geosynchronous orbit overhead. My spies have passed on the locations of a number of your holdings out in the swamps, and even as we speak, several macro-scale bombardment batteries are trained in each. If I'm not back soon, *with* the icon, those holdings are getting bombed right back to the Dark Age.'

'Got it?'

'You're bluffing,' he repeated, before standing as if to intimidate her.

Her gaze fixed unblinkingly on his, Brielle brought the lock of hair to her mouth, squeezed, and said, '*Fairlight*, target alpha, now.'

A bead of sweat appeared on one of the sections of flesh on Baron Gussy's forehead and he flexed his velvet-gloved hands as he stood over the reclining Brielle. The moment stretched on for what seemed an age, and then a ghost of a smirk appeared at the baron's lips as he evidently decided that Brielle was, as he had hoped, bluffing.

But she wasn't. His smile vanished as a sound like distant thunder rolled over Quagtown, a low, growling tremor passing up trough the rock, transmitted through the metal and timber construction and causing the flickering chandelier to shake ever so slightly, yet ominously.

Gussy was the first to break the impasse, and he turned sharply to the house stubjack standing in the archway. 'Find out what that was, now!'

'That was your safe house twenty kilometres due south taking a direct hit from an orbital bombardment,' she said, not trying particularly hard not to smirk.

'What...? he stammered. 'How did you...?'

'And that,' she said as a second, far stronger rumble brought a wave of panicked shouts from the crowd in the main part of the palace, 'was your *secret* clearing house on the ridgeline seventy east.'

'You spoiled little harpy!' the baron spat, his rage exploding as several of his guards pressed into the archway with concern and confusion writ large on their faces. Brielle simply smiled and remained outwardly nonchalant, though she knew the moment of truth was at hand.

'Give me the icon,' she said flatly, and your little pleasure lodge on the coast doesn't get flattened.'

His eyes wide with dumb horror, the baron reached up to the icon at this throat and grasped it in a fist. 'You're mad! I'm not giving you a...'

In the blink of an eye, Brielle was up off of the cushioned sofa, propelling herself through the air in a cat-like leap that brought her into contact with the stunned baron. The two went down in a confused tangle, and when they came up again, the guards pressing in with pistols raised, Brielle had Gussy by the neck. One hand was twisted about the thong on which the eldar icon hung, constricting his neck and cutting off his breathing. Even now, each segment of his patchwork face was going a different shade of purple. The other hand was reaching under the upturned table, retrieving something mislaid but a moment before.

'Back, meatheads!' Brielle shouted, putting as much authority as she could into the order. 'Ganna! Are you there, Ganna?' she shouted as the guards took a step back, clearly not knowing what the hell to do.

'Here, mistress!' the pilot's strained voice sounded from somewhere behind the wall of hired muscle. 'I'm a little…'

'Let him go or your boss gets it,' Brielle demanded, one had twisting the thong still more and causing the baron to squeal in sudden panic while the other deposited a small object in voluminous coat pocket.

'Do it!' he managed, his voice high-pitched and breathless. 'Do as she says!'

There was a moment of tense, uncertain silence, before the guards lowered their pistols and started backing out of the alcove, though they moved slowly and were obviously ready to react to any sudden movement.

Brielle jerked on the thong and shoved Gussy forward, using his stumbling body as a shield should any of the goons open fire. It was a somewhat hollow threat, she knew, and one that relied on them being more concerned that their boss lived than that she died, but it seemed to be having the desired effect. Within seconds, the goons had all backed out of the alcove, revealing Ganna and the servitors, the formers concern etched across his face, the latter as blank-eyed and vacant as ever.

'Time we were leaving,' said Brielle, moving backwards towards the entrance. Ganna voiced a word of command and he and the two servitors set off after her, the already spooked crowd scattering at the sight of so many drawn weapons.

Just then, one of the guards made the worst move of his career. Raising a knock-off Arbites-issue stubber, he shouted, 'Let him go or I'll shoot your damn head clean off your…'

The idiot never got to complete his sentence, a shockingly loud blast filling the air and turning his entire chest cavity into a smoking, ragged mess even as he looked down with incomprehension. A moment later, the guard crashed backwards to the deck, revealing Ganna, his concealed, forearm mounted bolt pistol ready to fire at anyone else that fancied early retirement.

'*Now* its time we were leaving…' said Brielle, dragging the squirming Baron Gussy by the neck as she reached the hatch.

The flight back to the landing pad took far longer than Brielle had planned, for the entire town was in uproar. It wasn't the panic at the Quagtown Palace that Brielle had unleashed that had got the population so stirred up, but the continuous stream of fire lancing down through the murky clouds to strike death and destruction at seemingly random points out in the swamplands surrounding the settlement. Though the target of every bombardment was in fact one of Baron Gussy's holdings, the rest of the criminal fraternity weren't to know that. Every petty crime lord in the town thought he was the target of the attacks, and that they were being mounted by some bitter rival suddenly possessed of an overwhelming weight of orbital firepower.

At length however, Brielle and her prisoner, who was by now being carried between the two servitors, and Ganna, reached the head of the ramshackle iron stairway leading up to the landing pad. The deck was a riot of activity as the ground crew fought to get craft ready for a hasty departure, but Brielle's shuttle was, fortunately, still present, and intact. The guards she had employed to watch over the shuttle, largely as a means of announcing her presence to the local crime scene, were milling nearby, more interested in the distant, blossoming explosions than doing their job.

Knowing her small party had but seconds before they were noticed, Brielle rounded on the baron and gripped the alien icon hung about his neck. 'Mine, I think,' she said, before tearing it free with a savage twist.

'The shuttle!' Brielle yelled to her pilot. 'Run!'

Ganna and Brielle powered forward, but the servitors were left behind, the struggling Baron Gussy still held firmly between them in their vice like, biomechanical grip. In seconds, the pair had reached the shuttle and the access ramp was lowering on screaming hydraulics. The baron started screaming at the guards to apprehend Brielle and her pilot.

In a moment the pair were at the shuttle and Ganna had activated the ramp, which seemed to Brielle to be lowering far slower than it ever had. The roar of a handgun split the air and a hard round *spanged* off the hull right by Brielle's head, forcing her to duck down as Ganna tracked the firer with his concealed weapon.

A burst of stubber fire from off to the left told the pair that a stand up fight wasn't a great proposition, and an instant later the hull where Brielle had been standing just a moment before was peppered with rounds, sending up a riot of angry sparks.

Fortunately, the ramp was now lowered enough for Brielle to throw herself inside, and within seconds Ganna was in too, scrambling for the cockpit even as Brielle threw the hatch into reverse and hard rounds continued to ricochet from the hull.

At the sound of the engines powering up to full output, Brielle collapsed onto the deck, her head spinning with a potent mix of adrenaline and relief. Those, and something more, she thought as she collapsed in a fit of dirty giggles.

It took Baron Gussy's minions almost an hour to prise the mind-locked servitors's grip off of his arms, and by the time they had, he was beyond furious. Stalking back to the Quagtown Palace, his guards barging the panicked locals out of his path, he raged at this turn of events. He had sought to take advantage of a rumour that the fortunes of the Arcadius were on the wane thanks to a decline in trade from the Eastern Fringe, but he was lucky to have come away with his life. Lucien Gerrit's daughter was a she-devil, he saw, but she had made one crucial mistake. She had left him alive, an enemy at her back. That thought fired him with a curious mix of dread and desire. How he longed to break the Arcadius, he thought, and how he'd like to...

Before he realised it, the baron was back at the palace, its main hall now empty of patrons and the floors strewn with the detritus of panic. Drinking vessels were scattered or smashed across the ground and tables and chairs were upturned. His mouth twisting into a nasty sneer, Gussy made for his alcove, determined at least to recover the ring Brielle had offered in exchange for the eldar icon.

It wasn't there. Of course it wasn't, he thought. That harpy must have snatched it up in the confusion of her escape, and left him with nothing at all to show for his attempted double cross.

He could really use a drink, but it looked like the serving staff had all fled, along with the stampeding patrons. Resolving to fetch his own, he looked about for a discarded bottle, but instead, his eyes settled on the stasis crate Brielle's two servitors had carried into the palace. They had set it down by the alcove, he realised as his eyes narrowed in suspicion, at her word...

'No...' he breathed as his eyes darted nervously about the dark, empty hall. Several of the stitched-together segments of skin on his forehead began to sweat, and one of his mismatched eyes started to twitch involuntarily. 'No, no, no,' he stammered as he closed on the box, his gaze fixating on the status panel on its side, a red tell-tale indicating that the stasis field had just deactivated. 'There's no way you...'

But she had. Three seconds after the blinking light turned solid, the overloaded core of the plasma charge that had been placed in stasis an instant before it went critical, detonated. Baron Gussy saw his fate an instant before it overtook him, the second to last thing to enter his mind a curse on the Arcadius and all their daughters. The very last thing to enter his mind was the ravening nucleonic fires of the plasma charge as its core went into melt down, the discreet blast wave expanding to neatly and utterly destroy the shabby interior of the Quagtown Palace whilst leaving its exterior with barely a scratch. To the denizens of Quagtown, the bass roar was yet more evidence of their impending doom, touching off a stampede as hundreds fled to be anywhere but in the centre of their tumbledown settlement.

For many months after, only the toughest of mutants would be able to survive the radiation within that ramshackle shell. By that time, Brielle Gerrit would be light years away, perhaps visiting the golden shores of a paradise world that had recently come into her possession...

THE RELIC

Jonathan Green

The horde spread across the unsullied blue-white wilderness of the ice fields like an oily black stain. Filthy clouds of greasy smoke rose from the exhausts of fossil fuel-guzzling machines, sending sooty trails into the frozen air to mark their passing. Every warbike and cobbled-together trukk left a petrochemical smear across both land and sky behind it, marking the horde's progress across the polar wilderness as another region of the planet fell to the furious predations of the alien invaders.

An unstoppable tide of savage, growling machinery poured out across the riven glacier. Before it, still a league or more away, the stalwart line of armour that the Emperor's chosen had decreed would not be breached approached. Today – at this time and in this place, amidst the desolate ice fields of the Dead Lands of Armageddon – the Astartes would make their stand against the green tide.

Warbike outriders gunned their throttles excitedly, while those boyz clinging to the sides of guntrukks, wartrakks and battlewagons cannibalised from captured vehicles of Imperial design fired off round after round from their heavy calibre shootas in their overeagerness to engage with the enemy.

The drop pod fell from heaven like the wrath of the Emperor Himself. The force of its landing sent shuddering tremors through the iron-hard ice sheet, a network of treacherous crevasses fracturing outwards from the point of impact.

The echoing gunshot retort of the pod's landing still rumbling across the fractured face of the glacier, the armoured landing craft opened and from it emerged the instrument of the Emperor's holy vengeance.

Autoloaders clattered into operation as the barrels of an assault cannon noisily cycled up to speed. The four blunt digits of a huge robotic fist, easily large enough to crush an ork's skull, flexed and whirred, servo-motors in each finger giving it a crushing force equal to that exerted by a crawling glacier.

With heavy, pistoning steps, the revered Dreadnought emerged from the cocoon of its drop pod, some monstrous metal beetle birthing from its adamantium shell, roused and ready for war.

Bio-linked sensors scanned the rapidly-advancing line of greenskin vehicles, the Dreadnought's machine-spirit-merged sentience processing the constant stream of information – everything from average velocities to weapon capabilities to wind shear – and waited. Experience won on a thousand battlefields across a hundred worlds – including this Emperor-forsaken rock in particular – came into play, recalled from the depths of mind-linked implants. The orks weren't going anywhere. He could afford to be patient. Revenge was a dish served best cold, after all.

Heavy munitions fire chewed the frozen ground in front of him. The foul xenos had seen him fall from the heavens on wings of fire like some avenging angel and now that he was in their sights they were directing everything in their crude arsenal directly at him.

Shells threw chips of ice the size of Predator shells from the bullet-pitted surface of the glacier, many raining back down to strike against the Dreadnought's ancient adamantium armour. It had stood up to much worse over the centuries. The ice shards shattered harmlessly against its hull, some exploding into powder.

As the orks drew closer still and their haphazard targeting devices found their range at last, the greenskins let fly with rockets, high calibre shells and even smoky flamethrowers in their eagerness to engage with the ancient.

The Dreadnought disappeared amidst clouds of sooty smoke and roiling flames, the glacier reverberating now to the explosions and impacts of the orks' weapons which were, in general, noisy and heavy on the pyrotechnics, but not all that accurate or effective.

And all the time the ork line surged forwards, steadily closing on the Dreadnought's position.

Preceded by a torrent of cannon and bolter fire, the Dreadnought stepped from the smoke of its supposed destruction, swivelling about its waist axis, raking the hurtling ork vehicles with its arm-mounted weapons. The standard that hung from its banner-pole was scorched black and still smouldering at the edges, the halo of iron spikes surmounting its armoured body glowing orange in the oily flames lapping at its pockmarked hull.

Three times the height of a man, larger than many of the ork machines and as heavy as a warbuggy, armoured with adamantium plates and carrying an arsenal that rivalled the firepower of a battlewagon, it would take more than that to halt this juggernaut's advance.

It took the Dreadnought's symbiotic machine-spirit mere nanoseconds to divine the ancient's position relative to the speeding ork vehicles and select a succession of suitable targets. The Dreadnought opened up with its assault cannon and storm bolter again, a hail of hard shells reaping their own whirlwind of death and destruction.

'Death to the invaders!' Brother Jarold of the Black Templars Solemnus Crusade bellowed, his augmented voice booming from vox-casters built into his Dreadnought body-shell. What little of him that was still flesh and blood spasmed in fury, thrashing and sloshing within the amniotic fluids of his sarcophagus-tank. 'Cleanse this place of the xenos taint, in the name of the primarch and the Emperor. Death to the defilers of Armageddon!'

The squadron of warbikes leading the Kult of Speed in its attack was the first to taste his wrath. Burning rubber shredded under the attention of the Dreadnought's assault cannon, sending several bikes and their riders cart-wheeling over the ice, as sheared axles and wheel-less spokes stabbed into the ice, flipping the screaming machines through the air to land in broken piles upon the iron-hard glacier.

Those orks unfortunate enough to land at Jarold's feet had limbs and skulls crushed beneath his relentless, pounding footfalls.

A burst of storm bolter fire found a promethium barrel lashed to the side of wartrakk. The fuel inside touched off, blowing the vehicle apart, spreading pieces of wartrakk up to twenty-five metres away across the ice field.

With a series of hollow pops, the rocket launchers arrayed across the Dreadnought's broad shoulders sent a fusillade of mortar shells arcing into the pack of vehicles behind the disintegrating line of warbikes.

Unable to stop in time, some of the ork bikes skidded past the Dreadnought, and having already missed one target chose instead to rev their engines and plough on towards the advancing line of Astartes armour.

Three bikes crashed and burned as Brother Jarold's weapons-fire took them down, and just as many again collided with the wrecked vehicles.

Many of the ork drivers were horrified to discover that the Dreadnought still stood after their concerted bombardment of it, and swerved at the last moment to avoid the immovable hulk. But one wasn't quick enough and cleared the choking exhaust trail of another bike to find itself directly on top of the Dreadnought.

The warbike hit Brother Jarold with the force of an ork rokkit. Even as the bike hit him, Jarold grabbed hold of it with his huge power fist, the vehicle swinging up into the air in his grasp as its momentum spun them both around. The ork rider was still clinging to the wide handlebars when a direct hit from Brother Jarold's storm bolter ignited the contents of the bike's fuel tank, as he released the vehicle at the height of its rising arc. The bike spun through the air above him and became a fiery comet, annihilating another ork rider that was rounding on the Dreadnought as the bike crashed back down to earth.

The Dreadnought's deep strike insertion and deadly combination of cannon and bolter fire had decimated the front line of the ork Speed Freeks. And all the while, unheard over the roar of bike and trukk, assault cannon and bolter, as well as the concussive booms of fuel-tank explosions, Brother Jarold called down the wrath of the Emperor and His primarchs on the heads of the xenos filth.

The promethium roar of crude ork engines was joined by the well-tuned growl of the superior Astartes armour as the bikes of the Black Templars' rapid deployment force and its supporting Land Speeder squadron closed on the drop-pod's homing beacon.

If the orks had been surprised by the fury of the Dreadnought's initial attack, it proved to be only a foretaste of what was to come as Ansgar's Avengers – the strike force mustered in memory of the fallen Emperor's Champion – engaged the enemy.

Clouds of bittersweet incense swirled and ascended into the vault of the battle-chapel, filling the cathedral space with a sparkling aromatic mist. Shapes swam in and out of the constantly shifting vapours, giving glimpses of fluted columns a hundred metres tall, skull and cross adorned buttresses and statues commemorating the fallen of the Chapter.

The skull-set glow-globes had been dimmed and the forests of candles were in the process of being snuffed out by a trundling cenobyte servitor while its partner, following on behind, proceeded to trim their wicks and clear away the crusted wax that coated the black iron candelabra, like a series of frozen cataracts.

The sound of the pitted oak doors opening – the doors so old now the wood was black – resounded throughout the battle-chapel like the boom of distant gunfire. Chaplain Wolfram opened his eyes, finishing the prayer that was on his lips. He rose to standing from where he had been kneeling before the Solemnus Shrine, his eyes falling once again upon the empty indentations where the Black Sword, the Champion's laurel-wreathed helm and the lovingly ornamented Armour of Faith should have lain.

Wolfram turned, one armoured hand – every knuckle of the gauntlet embossed with the Templars' black cross and white skull insignia, a permanent memento mori to the one charged with watching over the souls of the crusaders – closing around the haft of his crozius arcanum. The ancient artefact was both a Chaplain's badge of office and a potent weapon in its own right. A disruptor generator was concealed within the wooden shaft of the relic, that one simple addition turning the flared blades of the Templar cross that surmounted it into a lethal power axe.

The sound of echoing footfalls on the stone-flagged floor of the cathedral space carried to the Chaplain through the muffling clouds rising from the glowing nuggets of flame-flecked incense smouldering within their braziers. Chaplain Wolfram relaxed his grip on his crozius.

The booming footsteps came closer, the incense smoke parting as a colossal shape, that was neither man nor machine but something of both, something greater than either, stepped into the light of the candles that guttered in the breeze of its advance.

Wolfram noted the battle-damaged banner pole and the deeply etched gothic lettering upon the Dreadnought's hull and bowed.

'In the name of Him Enthroned on Holy Terra, well met, Brother Jarold,' he said. 'And what brings you to this place of sanctuary, still an hour from matins?'

'May the Emperor's blessings be upon you, Brother-Chaplain,' *the machine-tempered voice of the ancient responded.*

'You are not slumbering with your brother Dreadnoughts aboard Forgeship Goliath?'

'Now is not the time for rest.'

'But our recent endeavours on Armageddon have cost us dear,' *the Chaplain warned.* 'Rest is what is needed now.'

'I cannot sleep, brother, not when there is still so much of His holy work left undone. And besides, I have slept for long enough already.'

'Then what can I do for you, brother?' *the Chaplain asked.*

'I would seek your counsel,' *the Dreadnought said in a voice like the slamming of sepulchre doors.*

'From me, brother?' *Wolfram asked, caught off guard for a moment by Brother Jarold's honesty. Ancients were usually the ones who shared their hard-won wisdom with the rest of the Chapter; they were not the ones who came seeking it from others.* 'You are troubled?'

'Yes, I am troubled, Brother-Chaplain.' *The Dreadnought broke off.*

'Speak, brother. You have nothing to feel ashamed of.'

'But I do.'

'I see. You speak of the loss of Brother Ansgar.'

'I do, brother. When the Emperor's chosen one needed me most, I was found wanting.'

'You have prayed about this?'

'I have sat in penitent vigil ever since my return to the fleet. I have thought on Brother Ansgar's fate and nothing else.'

'I too have spent time in prayer and contemplation on the same matter,' *Wolfram admitted.*

'You have, brother?'

'I have. You cannot blame yourself for what happened. Blame the beast, the heretic xenos that blight the world below still. Purge yourself of your guilt in the crucible of war. Smite the xenos with bolter and fist and cannon, all in the name of vengeance. Use the rage that the Emperor has placed within your soul to bring down His wrath upon the greenskin. Show no remorse. Show the alien no pity and you will have nothing to fear.'

Silence descended between Chaplain and Dreadnought as the latter considered the former's words.

'So you believe that this is all part of some greater plan? His divine plan for Armageddon? For our crusade? For me?'

'I do not know, Brother Jarold,' Wolfram admitted with a shake of his head, 'but what I do know is that no one has come forward since to take on the mantle of champion, having received His divine inspiration, and there are plenty who would be ready for such a role.'

'So you believe Brother Ansgar is still alive.' The Dreadnought's augmented voice suddenly sounded strangely like that of a young petitioner, yet to be admitted to the brotherhood, desperate for reassurance.

'That is what I know. Somewhere, and perhaps only barely, but the Emperor would not leave us without a source of inspiration to lead us at a time such as this, with the conflict to decide the fate of this world still raging around us. And Brother Ansgar does not have to fight alongside us to inspire we of the Solemnus Crusade to great deeds.'

Incense-smoke coiled about the motionless form of the monolithic Dreadnought. When Brother Jarold spoke again, the vibrations of his vox-casters sent ripples through the curling smoke, creating new eddying patterns within it.

'Then my course is plain,' he said.

Chaplain Wolfram looked up at the scrollwork decorations of Jarold's Dreadnought-locked sarcophagus.

'This day I vow that I shall not rest until Brother Ansgar has been found and we bear him back in triumph, or that we might lay his body to rest and reclaim the relics of our Chapter – the sanctified weapons that are the most potent symbols of his office.

'I shall petition Marshal Brant to muster an army that we might avenge Brother Ansgar and our Chapter against the orks of the Blood Scar Tribe,' the Dreadnought said. 'And then we shall return to Armageddon.'

Brother Jarold surveyed the wreckage that was all that remained of the Speed Freeks expeditionary force. The kult's predilection for speed had proved their undoing. Stronger armour and better armament would have perhaps given them a better fighting chance against the inviolable armour of the Black Templars battleforce.

Sensors that saw in wavelengths ranging from infra-red to ultraviolet scanned the devastation searching for life-signs. If any greenskin had survived the Black Templars' rout they would not remain alive for long.

The once pristine white wilderness was now befouled with the gouged ruts of tyre tracks, blackened mounds of snow and ice thrown up by the artillery shells of both sides, promethium spills and fossil-fuel slicks turning the ice desert black. Some puddles still burned, the oily smoke rising from them adding their own acrid pollution to the devastated wilderness. Impact craters pockmarked the glacier where some heavy shells had missed their targets; where others had hit, debris from large ork vehicles lay strewn across the snow.

The kult's battlewagon had met its end when the machine-spirit of Techmarine Isendur's personal Razorback transport targeted the battlewagon's primary weapon power cell. A single, directed pulse from the Razorback's twin-linked lascannon and the resulting detonation had not only taken out the gun-bristling battlewagon itself, but also a guntrukk, a warbuggy and three assorted warbikes.

This had also been the turning point in the battle, a devastating blow from which the orks never recovered. All that was left of them now were piles of burning debris, blackened craters in the ice and piles of crushed and eviscerated carcasses.

Brother Jarold stood at the centre of the devastation, amidst the splintered axle-shafts, buckled wheel-housings and twisted chassis of the orks' ramshackle vehicles.

Behind the imposing presence of the watchful Dreadnought massed the Black Templars of the Solemnus Crusade. That same crusade had set out twelve years before to avenge the atrocity perpetrated against the Templars' Chapter Keep on the world of Solemnus by the greenskins that fought under the banner of the Scarred Ork.

There were injuries among the crusaders, the most severe being the loss of a limb sustained by Brother Baldulf under the wheels of an ork warbike, although it wouldn't stop him from marching to battle alongside his brethren, his chainsword held high. But there were no brothers to mourn that day, to be marked on the roll of the fallen, maintained within the battle-chapel at the heart of the Solemnus fleet's flagship battle barge, the *Divine Fury*.

The Emperor was truly smiling upon their endeavours that day; for sixty-three verified enemy kills not one Black Templar had fallen to the Kult of Speed. It was all the proof Brother Jarold needed to feel vindicated that their search for their lost champion was the will of Him Enthroned on Holy Terra.

Brother Jarold gave thanks to the Emperor, the Primarch Dorn and Lord Sigismund, their Chapter-founder, that their sanctified boltguns had functioned fully during their battle with the greenskins and that not one of their war machines had been damaged beyond repair during the conflict.

The Black Templars land speeder squadron had decimated the ork bikes and trukks, the Rhinos and Razorbacks finishing off what Typhoon and Tornado had started, while the Space Marines bike squadron and two-manned attack bikes had harried those orks that attempted to flee the battlefield.

The bark of a storm bolter firing echoed across the ice field like the retort of a heavy artillery piece. It had a number of the Black Templars raking the mounds of debris and bodies with boltgun and flamer, seeking the source of the sound, ready to bring the fight to the enemy once again. Instead they found Brother Jarold, blue smoke coiling from the muzzles of his heavy storm bolter – a weapon so large it would not look out of place mounted on one of the fleet's precious Predators or Vindicators. The body of a greenskin Jarold had targeted spasmed as it was blown in two by the mass-reactive rounds.

Techmarine Isendur approached Jarold. The Dreadnought dwarfed even the crimson-armoured Techmarine, whose twitching servo-arm – which seemed to move with a life all of its own – made him appear even taller than the average superhuman Space Marine. Behind him, Isendur's servitor team were making repairs to superficial damage sustained by the Razorback in the battle, or keeping an unstinting watch over those working on the machine, depending on their designation and degree of sentient programming.

Sensing the Techmarine's presence before he had a chance to speak Jarold asked, 'Are our brothers ready to move on the objective again?'

'Affirmative, brother,' the other replied in that familiar emotionless way of his, that was so out of character when compared with the passion and zeal exhibited by the rest of the crusade's fanatical warriors. 'At your command.'

'How far do you judge us to be from our target?

'Twelve point zero-seven-six kilometres,' the Techmarine intoned. It had been remarked upon on more than one occasion that Isendur was more akin to the machines to which he ministered than his brother Space Marines.

'And the nature of the signal,' Jarold said. 'Is it still as it appeared from orbit?'

'More so,' Isendur said. 'As hypothesised, the anomalous readings detected from orbit are indicative of some form of primitive teleportation technology.'

Grim satisfaction warred with Jarold's overriding sense of guilt and barely-supressed rage. The memory of the moment Jarold witnessed the mech-enhanced greenskin warboss teleport out of the devastated mekboy's lab blazed within his mind as hot and red as the moment when he had been cut down by a rusting cybernetic claw, that had earned him the privilege of being encased within the Dreadnought shell that had formerly been the living tomb of Ancient Brother Dedric.

The moment Emperor's Champion Ansgar had been taken from right in front of him replayed itself through his mind for what seemed like the thousandth time…

He saw himself closing on the alien tyrant again, a sphere of crackling emerald light surrounding the ork and his unconscious prisoner. He watched again as the green glare of the crackling shield intensified.

And then, just as his crashing steps brought him within reach of the xenos brute, with a sub-sonic boom the sphere of light imploded, plunging the ruins of the laboratory into sudden darkness. Only a retina-searing after-image remained, trapped within the sensor-linked optic nerves of Jarold's physical body, but of Emperor's Champion Ansgar and the alien warboss Morkrull Grimskar there was no sign...

'Then the command is given,' Jarold said simply.

Wherever the orks were using their wildly unpredictable teleportation technology, there was the possibility that the reconstructed Grimskar, nemesis of the Solemnus Crusade, would be there too. And if the greenskin warboss *was* there, there was also the possibility that they would find Ansgar too.

Isendur made an adjustment to the signum he held out before him in one crimson gauntlet. Servo-motors whined as the Dreadnought turned to observe the Techmarine with its faceless sarcophagus front. 'Brother Isendur? Is there something else?'

'I am picking up another signal,' the Techmarine said.

'Another teleport signal?' Jarold asked.

'No. It is weak, like a resting pulse.'

'What is its source?'

'Bearing zero six-seven point three.'

'And what would you hazard is the nature of this signal?'

'There is a fifty-two per cent probability that it is electromagnetic interference caused by isotopes buried in the bedrock beneath the glacier,' the Techmarine explained. 'But there is also a twenty-three per cent probability that it is interference caused by the disruption of the planet's magnetic field by the teleportation matrix. One way or the other, probability tells us that it probably is not worth pursuing.'

'But what of the other twenty-five per cent?' Jarold enquired.

'There is a possibility that it is a signal from a dormant power source. But it is unlikely.'

'What sort of power source?' Jarold pressed.

'Like that of a dying power cell.'

'As might be found inside a Deathwind automated weapons system. Or a Dreadnought.'

'It is increasingly unlikely but still a slim possibility,' Isendur persisted, not prepared to have his logic refuted. 'If our mission is to find the source of the teleport signal I would recommend that we move on that target forthwith and ignore this weaker signum reading.'

The knowledge that there was a possibility – no matter how slim – that the signal was the last sign of a lost brother Dreadnought, whether Templar or otherwise, played on Jarold's mind. Dreadnoughts were potent weapons of the Astartes Chapters and revered relics. An entire battleforce would willingly fight to reclaim a fallen Dreadnought brother. Only in the direst circumstances would a Space Marine commander abandon such a sacred relic to the field of battle.

To recover such a potent treasure, whatever Chapter it might belong to, would be of incalculable value to the war effort. Just one Dreadnought could help bolster the Astartes forces on one of Armageddon's numerous war-fronts, and who knew what impact that could have in the long term on the struggle for the contested planet.

'I respect your opinion, Brother-Techmarine, you know that. You and your brethren of the Forge have tended to me on numerous occasions, but you see only the logic of variables and algorithms. I have the benefit of experience and the wisdom of years and I disagree. We shall investigate the source of this other signal and then, when we have resolved what it is, we will press on towards our primary objective.'

'Very well, brother,' Isendur conceded. 'As you wish.'

The Dreadnought turned to survey the re-ordered ranks of the Black Templars' strike force.

'Brothers,' he declaimed, his voice booming over the burning battlefield, flurries of snow hissing as they melted in the licking flames of the promethium fires. 'The word is given. In the name of the Emperor, Primarch Dorn and Lord Sigismund, move out.'

'Is this the place?' Jarold asked, scanning the blizzard-scoured ice valley. The ice sheet rose up before them to meet the frozen slopes of a ridge of razor-edged peaks beyond which curious green corposant flickered and danced across the sky.

'Affirmative,' Techmarine Isendur replied, consulting the signum in his hand once more.

The hulking black Dreadnought and the crimson-armoured Techmarine stood before a wall of blue ice as solid and as impenetrable as rockcrete.

'So where, precisely, is the source of the signal?'

'Six point eight-nine metres downwards. If we are to discover the source of the signal we are going to have to dig.'

'Then we dig,' Jarold stated bluntly.

'Leave it to me, brother,' Isendur said. The Techmarine signalled the waiting column. 'Brothers Larce and Nyle,' he said, summoning those two crusaders. Jarold understood what it was he had in mind.

Larce, flamer in hand, and Nyle, bearing his thrice-blessed meltagun, joined them before the wall of blue ice.

'Brothers,' Jarold said, 'let the Emperor's holy fire cleanse these xenos-blighted lands.'

Techmarine Isendur directing their fire, Larce and Nyle hit the glacier with everything their weapons could muster.

Initiate Tobrecan brought his bike up to join them and directed a series of searing blasts from the plasma gun mounted on the front of his machine at the glacier. When the steam and mist cleared, Brothers Larce and Nyle stepped up again, while Initiate Isen drove his attack bike forwards, Gunner Leax turning his multi-melta on the metres thick ice.

The Space Marines' flamers and plasma weapons swiftly melted a shaft through the ice to the source of the signal Isendur had located via his signum. Steaming geysers of cloud rose from the hole in the glacier as the boiling water bubbling at the bottom of the pit re-condensed as it came into contact with the cold air.

'Now then, Brother-Techmarine,' Jarold said, standing at the edge of the cone-shaped shaft, 'let us see what lies buried here.'

Using his servo-arm to assist him in his descent, Techmarine Isendur clambered into the steaming shadows of the ice pit. The rest of the strike force waited in tense anticipation to see which would be proved right; the Techmarine or the Dreadnought.

Bracing himself within the shaft Isendur looked down at the shadow still locked beneath one last remaining layer of ice.

'You were right,' his voice rose from the bottom of the pit. There was no hint of annoyance or praise in its tone.

'I was right,' the Dreadnought rumbled with righteous satisfaction.

'Do we wake him?' the Techmarine asked, something like awe tingeing his words, as he stared down at the statuesque creation of frost-rimed adamantium beneath him. A faint red glow pulsed weakly behind the ice, and yet as regular as a heartbeat.

'He is a brother Space Marine.'

'He is a Crimson Fist,' the Techmarine testified.

'But our brother nonetheless. So we wake him.'

He remembered...

Thunder rumbled over the ice fields and frozen, broken peaks of the Dead Lands. It was the crack and boom of heavy artillery fire. The iron-hard ground shook with the force of an earthquake, more so than it did at his own wrathful steps.

He remembered...

Rank upon rank of Space Marines, squad after squad of his fellow battle-brothers, marching against the enemy, their Chapter banners flying proudly above them. Magnificent in their regal blue power armour, their left hands blood-red – recalling the ceremony conducted at the initiation of new Chapter Masters in the former Imperial Fists Legion – their battle-consecrated boltguns cinched tight to their chest plates ready to deliver the Emperor's ultimate justice to the enemy.

And he remembered...

The war machine. A stompa, the rank and file troops of the Armageddon PDF had called it. A mobile war-altar dedicated to the hated greenskins' brutal heathen gods. An icon to thoughtless bloodshed and mindless destruction.

He remembered...

Marching to war across the bitter wastes, shoulder to shoulder with his battle-brothers, the ork host charging to meet them, the glacier's surface fracturing beneath the greenskins' advance, the freezing wind as sharp and as cold as a blade of ice slicing the air between them.

He remembered...

Faced with insurmountable odds, a new strategy had to be formed, shaped within the heat of battle.

He remembered volunteering, proud that he should be the one to bring an end to this conflict. He remembered sound and heat and light. He remembered dying a second time.

And then, amidst the clamour of battle and the cataclysmic roar of destruction, he heard a voice.

'Brother,' it said. 'Awake.'

The dull red glow behind the visor of the Dreadnought's sarcophagus helm pulsed more brightly with every word the Dreadnought spoke. Its voice was phlegmy and cracked from age and lack of use.

'I am sorry, brother, but what did you say?'

A sound like vox-distorted coughing crackled from the ancient. Then the Dreadnought tried again.

'You are on Armageddon, brother,' Jarold replied. 'You are here, within the Dead Lands.'

The coughing resumed, rose to a crescendo and then subsided at last.

'No. When is it?' the venerable asked. 'My internal chronograph appears to be malfunctioning.'

Techmarine Isendur answered in terms precise to three decimal places.

The Crimson Fist was silent for several long moments.

'How long have you been here, brother?' Jarold dared to ask at last. 'Since the conflict began?'

'You mean to tell me that Armageddon has been a contested world all this time?' the venerable said with something like disbelieving incomprehension.

'Yes, since the abomination Ghazghkull Mag Uruk Thraka fell upon this world for a second time.'

'A second time?'

Jarold regarded the ancient suspiciously.

'Tell me, brother, how long have you been trapped here, entombed within the ice?'

Several moments more passed before the venerable was able to speak again. 'Fifty years, brother Templar. I have been trapped here, lost, for fifty years.'

The vehicles had been parked up and the massed force of Brother Jarold's avenging angels had formed a circle of unbreakable armour. All were included, from the newest neophyte to the oldest initiate. The formation of the praying Space Marines served as a barricade against the biting winds that swept across the Dead Lands, stabbing at any exposed flesh with knives of ice. It affected the neophytes – Gervais, Feran, Eadig and Galan – worst, for they were yet to earn the right to wear the full power armour as worn by their brethren and their heads were exposed. But if the freezing wind caused them any discomfort they didn't show it. Weakness of the flesh was not permitted of a Space Marine.

Brother Jarold stood on one side of the circle and opposite him loomed the Venerable Rhodomanus of the Crimson Fists.

The latter's crimson and regal blue paintwork was in stark contrast to the predominantly black and white power armour of the Templars – although some of the older, more ornamented suits worn by those veterans among the battleforce were traced with gold and red as well.

The moaning wind whirled flurries of snow around them but over the voice of the blizzard, Brother Jarold's booming prayers could be heard quite plainly.

'We shall bring down His almighty wrath and fury upon the xenos and drive the greenskin from the face of this planet!' Jarold bellowed. 'For the Emperor and the primarch!'

'For the Emperor and the primarch!' his battle-brothers responded with fervent zeal.

'For the Emperor and the primarch,' Venerable Rhodomanus echoed.

Brother Jarold had not needed to ask the ancient whether he would deign to join the Templars on the continuation of their mission. To awaken to a world fifty years into his future and so unchanged despite the passage of time, and yet finding his brother Crimson Fists with whom he had fought shoulder to shoulder against the greenskins gone, the prospect of fighting alongside the Templars had given him a noble purpose. Here was a chance to finish what he and his brothers had started.

For what purpose could there be for a Space Marine, other than eternal service? If he were denied the right to serve Him Enthroned on Holy Terra, a Space Marine's long life, and all the battles he had fought, everything he had achieved in His holy name would count as naught.

The Black Templars and Crimson Fists – two Chapters formed in the aftermath of the Heresy ten thousand years before – were both successor Chapters of the original Imperial Fists Legion, created from the very genetic material of the Primarch Rogal Dorn. Templar and Fist owed their very existence to the lauded Rogal Dorn, so there had never been any question as to whether Rhodomanus would join the Black Templars of the Solemnus Crusade. They were brothers-in-arms; that was all that mattered.

Brother Jarold surveyed the assembled Templars, the ancient Fist and the ice-clad vista beyond.

'It is time,' he said, scanning the ridge of sickle-shaped peaks on the horizon. 'Whatever the source of the anomalous signals detected by the fleet, it lies beyond that ridge.

'Today we show the greenskins why they should fear us. We let them see why we are fear incarnate. Today we take the fight to the enemy. Today we purge the Dead Lands of the xenos plague that blights this world.

'Move out!'

Their act of worship concluded, with renewed steel in their hearts, shielded by the armour of their faith as much as by the ceramite of their power armour, the circle broke up as the Space Marines returned to their vehicles. With a roar of mighty engines, like the wrathful prayers of Brother Jarold himself, Ansgar's Avengers moved out.

The force progressed slowly, so as to never leave the Dreadnoughts far behind. Brother Jarold had deployed into the heart of the Dead Lands by drop pod and the Templars had not anticipated having another ancient join them in their quest to find the source of the anomalous readings. There was no means of transporting them, other than for them to continue under their own propulsion.

But it still did not take them long to climb the icy slopes of a pass between the jagged obsidian-black peaks. Initiate-pilot Egeslic took his Land Speeder on ahead, to scout out what lay in wait for them on the other side of the ridge. He returned presently, guiding his speeder deftly over the ice, compensating for wind shear as he descended from the crest of the pass, and brought the vehicle to a hovering halt beside the clumping Dreadnought.

'Brother Jarold,' Egeslic said, 'you should see this for yourself.'

'That,' said Techmarine Isendur, pointing into the heart of the crater that had been dug into the ice, 'is the source of the anomalous readings.'

From the Space Marines' position at the mouth of the pass, sheltered by the shadows of the looming wind-scoured ice sculptures that surmounted the ridge in impossible overhangs, Brother Jarold surveyed the rift in the ice below them.

The ork-dug crevasse was a hive of seemingly disorganised industry. Everywhere he looked he saw orks. The foul xenos covered the glacier in a thick, dense green carpet as they swarmed over the dig site, the clamour of their mining machines ringing from the ice walls around them. There were customised digging machines, and other ork vehicles had been pressed into strange service here too. Some of these machines bore banner poles, bearing the iconography that demonstrated the ork tribe's loyalty. The sight of the Scarred Ork again – the ugly steel-cut tribal glyph bearing a rust red lightning bolt scar that bisected its crude simulacra features – filled Brother Jarold with both righteous satisfaction and indignation in equal measure.

They had found the one tribe that Jarold had hoped they would. The orks labouring within the ice pit were of the Blood Scar tribe. Truly the

Emperor was smiling upon their endeavours that day.

But focusing again upon the coarse alien totem Jarold felt rage burn within him like he had not known since the moment the reconstructed warboss Morkrull Grimskar had made his cowardly escape, taking the body of the Emperor's Champion Ansgar with him as he teleported out of the mekboy's crumbling lab smothered within the foetid green depths of the equatorial jungle.

'Is there a teleportation device somewhere here?' Jarold demanded of the Techmarine, watching the waves of green corposant rolling across the underside of the thick clouds that covered the arctic valley. He had to be certain.

'I have recalibrated the signum and fine-tuned the signal, brother,' the Techmarine said. 'And there is.'

Excitement pulsed through the husk of Jarold's mortal remains locked within the life-preserving amniotic tank of the Dreadnought's sarcophagus.

Had they really tracked down their long-sought-for quarry at last? Was the warboss here? And if he was, was Brother Ansgar with him?

Jarold gazed down into the crater again and treacherous doubt began to creep between his thoughts of righteousness revenge. But it was not the size of the ork horde that filled Brother Jarold's mind with appalled awe and wonder but the effigy that they had virtually finished digging out of the solid ice of the glacier that had spilled between the frost-chiselled peaks into this valley like some great frozen and fractured river.

Venerable Rhodomanus saw it too. And remembered.

The war machine. An appalling amalgamation of scavenged weapons and armour, the product of unholy alien engineering and genetically pre-programmed habit, the living embodiment of ork savagery and the relentless desire for war.

The monster – for it was a monster – crashed across the glacier, decimating the Crimson Fists' frontline. The Space Marines brought their armour and heavy weapons to bear but it was too little compared to the might of the monstrous god-machine that now marched to war before them.

Desperate times called for desperate measures and Rhodomanus had never known them more desperate. Something had to be done to bring about the destruction of this angry god.

And so, supported by his noble brethren Fists, he had strode forth to conquer the beast in one final act of self-sacrifice. His battle-brothers falling one by one at his side, giving their lives – all of them – that he might complete his final mission, weathering shoota, kannon, gatler and a storm of rokkits, the ancient was able to breach the stompa's shields and place the thermal charges at its very feet.

'The Emperor protects,' he intoned, quietly resigned to his fate.

Then all was white noise, heat and light.

For one brief moment the ice of millennia became a torrent of liquid water again and the blazing stompa sank beneath the sudden waves. The force of the blast hurled Rhodomanus across the sky like a blazing comet and he thought he heard the Emperor calling him to serve at his side in the next world...

'The idol lives,' Rhodomanus breathed.

It was clear to all – and not just Techmarine Isendur's practised eye – that the orks had finished carving the remains of the war machine from the body of the glacier and were now busy attempting to reactivate it; re-fuelling it, testing its growling motive systems and firing off bursts of random weapons-fire from its many and varied weapon emplacements.

There was a hungry roar of pistons firing and thick billows of greasy black smoke gouted from the proliferation of smoke-stacks and exhaust flues that rose from the back of the alien war idol.

'That, I take it, is not the source of the signal we have been tracking, is it?' Jarold quizzed the Techmarine standing beside him.

'No, brother. That is.' Isendur pointed with his power axe.

'I see it,' Rhodomanus said.

Jarold looked again, refocusing his optical sensors, and then he saw it too.

It was a vast assemblage of iron beams and girders, crackling brass orbs and endless spools of cabling. It was supported by an immense scaffold and yet the whole massive structure had been hidden by the blizzard and the bulk of the ork effigy standing before it.

The device culminated in a huge gun-barrelled probe that Jarold imagined to be a beam transmitter, supported on strong gantry arms.

'By Sigismund's sword!' Jarold gasped.

'Its designation in this warzone is an ork teleporter, I believe,' Isendur said.

'We should warn the fleet,' Jarold said. 'We cannot allow the xenos filth continued access to such weaponry or technology,' he added as he pondered the matter in hand. It was clear to Jarold now that the orks intended to teleport their scavenged stompa out of the ice-locked Dead Lands to be used on another war front and bolster their forces there. Such a reinforcement could turn the tide of battle in the orks' favour. Such a thing could not be allowed to happen.

'Yes, brother,' Isendur replied.

Tense moments later, with Jarold watching the heavens as if he expected the *Divine Fury* to deliver a thunderbolt directly from heaven against the stompa, the Techmarine made his report. 'The interference being generated by the teleporter that we detected from orbit is now preventing my signal from getting through to the crusade fleet,' he said, delivering his bad tidings without any obvious emotion.

They were alone down there.

'We are going to have to deal with the stompa and the teleporter ourselves,' Rhodomanus declared. 'We cannot allow the greenskins to make it away from here with their idol intact. It is against the will of the Emperor.'

'Then we shall face the enemy in battle once again; fight them hand to hand if that is what it takes,' Jarold said, his assault cannon whining as it began to run up to speed. 'Just the way we like it.'

With the roar of bike engines and heavy armour running at maximum speed, the Black Templars poured through the ridge pass and into the carved crevasse in the ice before the orks had any warning as to what was happening.

'No pity! No remorse! No fear!' Brother Jarold boomed as he tramped down the glacial slopes towards the great ork-gouged hole, the toe-hooks of his Dreadnought feet locking him securely in place on the treacherous ice.

'There is only the Emperor!' Rhodomanus joined, urging the crusading Space Marines on. 'He is our shield and our protector!'

First came the bikes and attack bikes, pouring over the lip of the ridge, past the clumping Dreadnought. Then came the Razorbacks and the Rhinos, the heavy armour grinding over the ice of the glacier, pounding it to shards beneath their tracks, heavy bolter fire riddling both the ice sheet and those orks that had mustered enough awareness to try to do something about the approaching Space Marines.

The Land Speeder squadron hurtled over the ridge after the rest of the Templar armour past the advancing battleforce, the *whub-whub-whub* of their engines thrumming through the ice, the Tornado's assault cannon rattling off hard rounds into the milling orks as they hurried to respond to this new threat.

With a whooshing roar, the Typhoon fired off a barrage of missiles. The rockets corkscrewed through the air and impacted in a series of scathing detonations amidst the moving ork armour. Bodies, armour plating and wheels were thrown into the air to land in broken burning piles.

With a searing scream, the lascannon mounted on Techmarine Isendur's Razorback fired, a blinding spear of light burning through the constant snow flurries and illuminating the crevasse like an incendiary shell-burst. A moment later the crater was illuminated again as an ork halftrakk exploded in a sheet of flame, the las-blast having hit both its fuel tank and the rokkits loaded into the back of it.

There was the *crack* and *crump* of frag grenades detonating amidst the greenskin horde, and orks fell in their dozens.

Some of the orks had climbed aboard their trukks and bikes again. They revved their engines as they turned their vehicles to face the oncoming Black Templars armour.

The orks were rallying. Jarold's crusaders had made the most of the advantage that stealth and the blessings of the Emperor had brought them but now the enemy were starting to organise a cohesive defence.

As war trukks and heavy orkish bikes began to converge on the advancing Templar armour, those battle-brothers piloting the fleet's venerated vehicles urged them forwards, Techmarine Isendur making supplication to the Omnissiah in the same unmodulated tone, over and over.

At the bottom of the crater, in the shadow of the dug-out idol, the two sides met with a roar of over-revving engines and the scream of shearing metal. Sparks flew, armour plating buckled, axles sheared and fuel tanks ruptured. Orks were thrown over the hulls of Rhinos and Land Speeders. Milling grots were crushed under the tracks of Rhinos and ork bikes alike. Others among the horde were gunned down by the blazing, blessed bolters of the Templars, the ork guns unable to match the reliability or accuracy of the Space Marines' arsenal.

But despite their primitive design there was one thing that the ork guns had over the Templars' weapons; there were more of them. Far more. It was becoming painfully apparent that the Templars were drastically outnumbered, at least twenty to one. Although the Emperor's chosen were renowned for their fighting prowess, those were odds that tested even a Space Marine. There was a very real danger that sheer weight of numbers would see them overwhelmed, if the orks were able to unify their attack.

But Brother Jarold – now part of the rearguard, finishing off those greenskins that had evaded the Templars' guns – had realised this would be the case before he had committed his fighting force to this action.

It was clear that the Blood Scar orks were planning on teleporting the stompa from this location, to deploy elsewhere on Armageddon. Jarold's plan had always been to infiltrate the dig site and bring down the war-effigy or, failing that, seize and hold the colossal ork teleporter until Isendur found a way to destroy it.

With a scream of failing engines, Initiate-Pilot Egeslic's Land Speeder ploughed into the surface of the glacier: an ork shokk attack gun had made a lucky hit. A gaggle of snarling boyz piled onto the downed speeder, burying Egeslic and Initiate-gunner Fraomar beneath a flurry of thumping axes and stabbing serrated knives.

The two Rhinos slewed to a halt in the middle of the crater, dropped their hatches and the troops they were carrying poured out in a tide of funereal black and gleaming white. Boltguns barking and chainswords screaming, they met the milling rabble head on. They might be outnumbered, but they were in the thick of battle, which was the only place where a Templar might hope to win his honour-badges.

Venerable Rhodomanus's multi-melta pulsed, and a swarm of orks died as their blood boiled and their own bodily fluids broiled their internal organs.

The ice field was lit up again, this time as a sphere of actinic light exploded into life like a miniature sun at the periphery of the Templar lines. The explosion pushed a great wave of concussive force before it as the Land Speeder Typhoon and its remaining payload of missiles were obliterated by a direct hit from the stompa's now active deth kannon.

Brother Jarold stood firm, as ork bikes tumbled end over end past him, carried before the bow-wave of explosive force. He then turned his assault cannon on the surviving greenskins now running from the epicentre of destruction, holy wrath pounding through what little remained of him that was still flesh and blood.

'Brother Jarold,' Techmarine Isendur's voice crackled over the commnet, the interference caused by the orks' unstable teleporter technology affecting even close range communications.

'What is it, brother? Report.'

'We have our objective.' Isendur declared with something dangerously like emotion tingeing his words. 'The teleporter is ours.'

'Your objective is the teleporter; reconvene there,' Jarold commanded, his battle-brothers hearing him through the comm in their helmets, his words also carrying to them over the bestial roars and bolter fire of the battlefield. 'Repeat, rally at the teleporter.'

The device was huge, on a monumental scale that even an ancient such as Venerable Rhodomanus had never witnessed before. It was too big a target to miss. The Templars had teleport technology themselves, of course, hidden within the bowels of the Forgeship *Goliath* where it was carefully tended and operated by the Techmarine Masters of the Forge and their servitors, but they had nothing approaching the size of this brutal piece of esoteric machinery.

Techmarine Isendur felt something approaching heretical awe on seeing the monstrous device arrayed before him in all its terrible, alien glory.

The Templars were brutally outnumbered by the thuggish orks, but by launching a surprise attack, the vengeful Space Marines had been able to penetrate far into the dig site; the either arrogant or idiotic orks having failed to post anything like enough sentries to create an effective defensive perimeter. They had probably not thought to be interrupted out here in the trackless frozen wastes of the Dead Lands for little could survive in these bitter wastes other than the alien orks. But then, from what Jarold had witnessed first-hand, it seemed that orks could survive pretty much anywhere.

The Templars' fast-moving, heavy armour had been able to penetrate the ork crater that held the ice-locked stompa with ease, the Razorbacks and Rhinos ploughing into the aliens and their scratch-built vehicles as if sainted Sigismund himself were smiting the foul xenos from beyond the stars, where he now stood at Primarch Dorn's right hand.

But now the initially bewildered orks had rallied and were mounting an effective counter-attack against the Black Templars' lightning assault.

Despite the crusading Chapter's prowess in hand-to-hand combat, even hardened fighters such as Brother Jarold's avenging warriors would be hard-pressed to overcome when facing such impossibly overwhelming odds.

The best they could hope for was to sell themselves dear. They might not have found their lost Brother Ansgar or their nemesis the warlord Morkrull Grimskar, but they could end their crusade here, denying the ork host the war machine that the greenskins had fought so hard to win again.

Bikes – in both the black and white livery of the Templars and the scruffy red kustom paint jobs of the orks – roared past Brother Jarold as he stomped across the battlefield. He took aim and fired. The front wheel of a warbike that was pursuing a Space Marine attack bike – its gunner whooping wildly as it took pot-shots at the noble Templars – disintegrated in a hail of cannon fire. The wheel struts dug into the ice, halting the bike's forward motion. The vehicle flipped over, hurling the ork gunner into the path of a hurtling Land Speeder – the surprised-looking greenskin bouncing off the hull with the unmistakable sound of breaking bone – while the bike's driver was crushed beneath the great weight of the bike landing on top of it and crushing its spine.

Jarold turned his bolter on a gaggle of greenskins that charged him, large-calibre shootas and clumsy chain-bladed weapons in their meaty paws. A burst of flesh-shredding gunfire and then he was through. Nothing now stood between him and the ork teleporter.

And he wasn't the only one to have made it to the objective. Sergeant Bellangere had led the men under his command by example – bolt pistol in one hand, chainsword in the other dripping with alien gore – and hadn't lost a single member of his squad in the process. He and his troops were even now finishing off the last of the resistance being put up by the orks that crawled all over the vast gantries of the teleporter, an augmented mekboy falling to Bellangere's gutting chainblade.

Jarold turned to survey the smoking craters and tight knots of fighting that characterised the battlefield dig-site. The crumpled wreckage of a devastated Rhino lay nearby, as did the smouldering remains of a bike. Most of the Templar armour had made it through to the objective, but not all. Jarold caught glimpses of scratched black and blistered white amidst the bodies of the slain between billows of smoke from burning wrecks strewn across the combat zone.

On seeing his fallen battle-brothers Jarold felt his blood boil. The machine-spirit that resided with him inside his Dreadnought body informed him of the names of each and every one of the fallen – Initiate Garr and Gunner Heolstor, Brother Derian, Brother Eghan and Brother Clust of Squad Garrond, Clust's heavy bolter lying useless on the ice under his eviscerated body.

Brother Jarold was shaken from his enraged reverie by what felt like an earthquake.

The ground shook, splinters of ice twenty metres tall breaking free of the glacier as the stompa began to move. The orks had finally coaxed their idol into unnatural life once more.

Like Brother Rhodomanus it had lain locked in the ice for the last fifty years. Like Brother Rhodomanus it now had a second chance to finish what Ghazghkull Mag Uruk Thraka's hordes had started half a century ago.

At the growl of the effigy's engines, filthy smoke poured from its chimney-exhausts, filling the cerulean blue sky with stinking black clouds.

The stompa's wrecking ball attachment – the krusher itself looking like a huge rusted boulder – came whirling around over the top of its pintle arm mount, crashing down on top of a Rhino with all the force of a meteorite impact. The tank's adamantium plates buckled under the force of the wrecking ball blow, sending the troop transport bouncing off the uneven ice-gouged bedrock that had lain buried beneath the glacier until the orks had dug it up.

As Jarold watched, what was left of Neophyte Feran rocketed skyward as an ork skorcha engulfed his body in flame, detonating the krak grenades he carried at his waist.

Raging to the heavens at the death of another battle-brother, and one who had not yet had the chance to prove himself in glorious battle to his brethren's satisfaction, the Dreadnought turned his blazing weapons on the ork responsible.

The barrels of his assault cannon glowing red hot, his mind-linked machine-spirit informed him that his auto-loaders would soon be out of ammunition. But if today was his day to die a second death then he would make it his vow to take as many of the Blood Scar orks with him as possible.

Jarold surveyed the scorched glacier around him. The remaining Black Templar armour had formed a cordon around the teleporter, every vehicle's guns pointing outwards towards the enemy now pouring over the ground towards their position. The aliens' fury at the audacity of the Templars in taking the teleporter spurred them on, the savage brutes giving voice to harsh barks and hoots of wild abandon.

'Brothers!' Jarold declared, his voice echoing strangely from the derricks and hoists of the corposant-sheathed structure. 'This day we show the xenos filth that Armageddon is not theirs for the taking. This day we show the orks that we will leave no wrong unavenged, no slight unchallenged. This day we will deliver the Emperor's divine retribution upon the heads of the greenskin defilers of this world in the name of Primarch Dorn and his servant Lord Sigismund.'

Jarold turned his storm bolter on another charging ork and took its head off with one mass-reactive round.

'Brothers! Today we sell ourselves dear in the name of the Emperor that we might deny the orks another victory upon the shores of Armageddon. We have a new mission. We will not depart this world until we have ensured that they may never make use of their teleporter or their war-idol again. Today is a good day to die!'

With a scream of rending metal, lightning-drenched claws tore through the chugging engine of an ork wartrakk as its armour plating melted under the intense heat-blast of a multi-melta.

As the smoke and flames died back again, the Black Templar Dreadnought watched with grim satisfaction as the still more imposing and ornamented form of Venerable Rhodomanus strode through the devastation to reach the protection of the cordon of crusader armour, crushing a flailing ork beneath one colossal foot whilst snatching the mangled body of another from the wrecked wartrakk and quartering its head between the crimson talons of his colossal power fist.

'No, brother,' the ancient boomed. 'I am sorry to contradict you, but today is not your day to die.'

As he reached the Templar line, Rhodomanus turned his multi-melta on an ork bike, igniting its fuel tank; the vehicle and its rider disappeared in a sheet of incandescent flame.

'It is not your destiny that you give your lives in sacrifice to stop this blasphemy,' the venerable went on, as if making his decree. 'Your mission is not yet done. You must live to fight another day.'

Jarold did not interrupt, but listened, considering Rhodomanus's words as he targeted the ork manning the flamethrower mounted on the back of a rumbling halftrakk.

'This is my battle, brother,' Rhodomanus continued. 'It is up to me to accomplish what I and my brother Fists tried to fifty years ago.'

The ancient was right. This was not the Templars' battle. The destruction of the ork war machine had never been their objective. Brother Ansgar still awaited them, somewhere. And it was up to Jarold and the others to find him. It was as they had sworn it.

But none of that changed the fact that they were severely outnumbered and completely surrounded, with little hope of being able to turn the tide of battle in their favour now, unable to even call for extraction by the fleet.

The superstructure of the incomparable ork device in whose shadow they now sheltered hummed and twanged as orkish hard rounds and crackling energy beams spanged off its pylons and girders.

'Do you think you can fathom the workings of this teleporter?' Jarold asked his Techmarine.

'All ork machines are primitive and alien,' Isendur replied, 'but I would predict a seventy per cent chance of success.'

'Then set to work,' Jarold instructed. 'By the Emperor, I want this thing operational and locked onto the fleet in orbit as soon as is humanly possible.'

* * *

With a dull crump the speeding guntrukk exploded, obliterated by the massed barrage of heavy weapons that pounded it.

Standing side by side against the horde, the Dreadnoughts Jarold and Rhodomanus locked onto a new target and a warbike disintegrated into shrapnel.

Only a matter of metres away, Brother Huarwar died as he was decapitated at close quarters by a heavily mekanised ork. Roaring in grief-stricken pain, Jarold broke from the circle, advancing on the creature responsible, litanies of hate spouting from his vox-casters like bile as he shredded the alien's augmented body with raking bolter and cannon fire.

'Brother Isendur!' he bellowed over the howls of the orks and the savage chatter of their guns, ignoring the succession of hard rounds that rattled off his own adamantium body-shell as if they were no more than the stings of rad-midges. 'Give me some good news!'

'I have subjugated what passes for the device's machine-spirit, patching a link via one of my servitors and dominating it with a liturgical sub-routine, and, through its transmitter array, have located the fleet in orbit and Forgeship *Goliath*–'

'Brother!' Jarold boomed, bisecting an ork from midriff to neck with a barrage of bolter fire. 'Is it ready?'

'Aye, brother,' Isendur replied. 'It is ready.'

'Then begin the evacuation.'

As the two Dreadnoughts held back the press of the ork horde with bolter and fist, cannon and melta, at Jarold's command the strike force moved back beneath the beam emitter of the huge gantry, never once turning their backs on the enemy, claiming a dozen ork lives for every step they took in retreat.

It was not the Templars' way to retreat in the face of greater numbers of the enemy. But for the brethren of the Solemnus Crusade, this was their last action. They could not afford to sacrifice their lives so freely, not when their holy work remained undone. They were yet to recover Brother Ansgar's body and repay the warboss Morkrull Grimskar for all the monster had taken from them when the orks of the Blood Scar tribe razed the Chapter Keep on Solemnus.

They had all sworn it – every crusading battle-brother, from neophyte to initiate, Techmarine to Apothecary, Dreadnought to Marshal, Chaplain to Champion – and they could not relinquish the fight until their vow had been fulfilled, not when a way out of this impossible situation had presented itself.

So large was the ork teleporter – it having been intended to beam something as gargantuan as the stompa to another arena of battle – that the entirety of the survivors of Jarold's battleforce could fit within the circumference of the projection plate beneath the enormous beam emitter.

They would go together. That was how Brother Jarold wanted it. Whether their plan worked, and the teleporter returned them to the

Forgeship *Goliath*, or scattered their component atoms to the stars, they would go together. The only ones they would leave behind were one tech-servitor to initiate the firing sequence of the teleporter's beam-gun, and Venerable Brother Rhodomanus of the Crimson Fists.

'Brother Jarold,' came Techmarine Isendur's voice with something almost like urgency in his usually unexcitable tone. 'Our departure now waits only on your presence upon the plate.'

Jarold turned to Rhodomanus, swivelling about the pivot of his waist bearing, as if he were about to address the venerable, blasting a leaping axe-wielding ork out of the air with a single, well-placed shot.

'Go, brother,' Rhodomanus said, before the other could speak. 'Go to meet your destiny and leave me to face mine.'

'It has been an honour,' Jarold stated stoically.

'Aye, it has been that,' the ancient agreed.

'Die well, brother. For the primarch.'

'For Dorn. Now go.'

Rhodomanus directed another blast from his multi-melta into the press of the ork pack, the heat blast clearing ten metres around him in every direction.

Taking his leave, Brother Jarold defiantly turned his back on the orks and marched to join his battle-brothers at the heart of the humming teleporter, the venerable laying down covering fire behind him, like some colossal avatar of the Emperor's retribution.

And as he did so, he began to intone Dorn's litany of service.

'What is your life?' he began. 'My honour is my life.'

An ork fell to scything fire from his storm bolter.

'What is your fate? My duty is my fate.'

Another was impaled on the crackling blades of his power fist.

'What is your fear? My fear is to fail.'

As he retreated behind Rhodomanus, Brother Jarold gave voice to the defiant battle cry in one last act of defiance directed at the alien orks.

'No pity!' Brother Jarold boomed.

'No remorse!' his battle-brothers responded, taking up his battle cry.

'No fear!' they bellowed in unison, clashing their weapons against their holy armour in a clattering cacophony of defiance.

Corposant crawled over and around the superstructure of the ork teleporter in writhing serpents of sick green light. With an apocalyptic scream like the sundering of the heavens, the beam-emitter fired.

Rhodomanus did not look back. He knew the Templars were gone.

'And what is your reward?' he asked, his voice rising like a challenge against the ravening greenskins. 'My salvation is my reward!'

Three orks fell to a withering hail of bolter fire.

'What is your craft? My craft is death!'

The multi-melta put an end to another ork bike.

'What is your pledge?'

The venerable hesitated. He could see the stompa advancing on him now, and him alone, belching smoke into the air from its exhaust-stacks, its colossal mass shaking the ground with its every step.

'My pledge is eternal service!'

As the stompa closed on the teleporter at last, with heavy, purposeful steps that sent tremors skittering through the bedrock that lay beneath the glacier, an inescapable fact wormed its way into the spirit-linked mind of the ancient. This was to be his last stand, but even the glorious sacrifice of a venerable Dreadnought might not be enough to stop the stompa.

Rhodomanus and his brother Fists had been unable to destroy it fifty years before, during the Second War for Armageddon, only managing to delay the inevitable by trapping it within the glacier. And now, fifty years on, what hope was there for him as he stood before the devastatingly powerful war machine?

But still he kept firing, directing blast after blast of his multi-melta at the gun emplacements that bristled from the effigy's carapace, at the stompa's armour itself, and its crew, when his spirit-linked targeter could lock onto them.

The stompa loomed before him, blocking his view of the crater and the rest of the horde, the macabre god-machine filling his world. Nothing else mattered now. There was only the ancient and the idol, two relics from another battle for Armageddon, ready to make the final moves of a power play begun five decades before.

Sparkling emerald flame consumed the ork teleporter once more, power relays humming as the device came online again. Rhodomanus's optical sensors homed in on the roasted remains of the tech-servitor fused to the esoteric device by its last firing. The servitor was dead, so how was it that the teleporter was powering up to fire at all?

It was only then that Rhodomanus realised that in his face-off with the stompa he had backed himself onto the empty platform and now stood directly beneath the beam emitter.

A nimbus of actinic light formed at the centre of the teleporter, also directly beneath the focusing beam of the vast construction, surrounding him with its suffused essence. Something was being beamed back to the teleporter.

He felt the tingle of it at his very core, in every fibre of his body that was still flesh and blood. And the machine-spirit of his Dreadnought body felt the exhilarating rush of a trillion calculations as the impossible machine read and recorded the position of every atom within his body, the connection of every synapse, the binary pattern of every recollection-code stored within his memory implants. He was beaming out.

Framed by the skeletal structure of the alien device, the stompa seemed to peer down at him with the telescoping sights of its cannon-barrel eyes.

Through his one remaining mortal eye Rhodomanus saw adamantium, steel, ceramite and flesh become first translucent and then transparent. At the same time he saw something else taking shape within the sphere of light with him, becomingly steadily more opaque as it solidified around his departing form.

For the briefest nano-second he and the object shared the same space – his machine-spirit merging with its primitive programmed consciousness. Fifty metres long and weighing a hundred tonnes – the energy build-up already taking place within its plasma reactor perilously close to the point of critical mass and detonation – the torpedo was capable of blowing a hole in the side of an ork kill kroozer with armour plating several metres thick. The venerable's own machine-spirit continued the countdown to destruction.

Five.
Four.
Three.
Two.

Suffer not the alien to live, he thought.

And then actinic light blinded his optical sensors and the bleak white wastes of the Dead Lands, the collapsing structure of the teleporter and the impotently raging stompa. Everything vanished, melting into black oblivion, and Brother Rhodomanus was gone.

The battle-barge *Pride of Polux* hung in high orbit above Armageddon's second largest landmass.

All was still within the reclusiam. Captain Obiareus, Commander of the Crimson Fists Third Company, was alone with his thoughts and his strategium. There were not many minutes in the day when he could say that, and he savoured those times when it was the case. But such precious moments made all the difference to his command. They were those times when he could step back, reflect, consider and plan.

He sat, the elbows of his power armour resting on the cuisses of his armoured legs, gauntlets locked together before his face. His lips touched the reliquary that hung from his neck on its golden chain and which he held within his hands as reverentially as he might a newborn. He stared out of the roof-high windows of the reclusiam at the silent void beyond, pondering again his Chapter's gains and losses on the planet below, alone with his thoughts and the stars.

Footsteps disturbed the captain's contemplations, the sound of ceramite ringing from the stone-flagged floor shattering the silence of the reclusiam. Obiareus looked up in annoyance.

Brother Julio approached the strategium, head bowed respectfully.

'What is it?'

'My lord,' Julio began. 'We have received a hail from Marshal Brant of the Black Templars Solemnus Crusade. He wishes to speak with you, my lord.'

'The Templars wish to speak with us?'

'Yes, my lord.'

'Regarding what matter?' Obiareus probed further.

'They have news, my lord.' Brother Julio faltered, as if hardly able to believe what he himself was saying.

'Yes? What news?'

'News of Venerable Rhodomanus,' Brother Julio said hesitantly.

'Brother Rhodomanus?' Now it was Obiareus's turn to express his disbelief. 'Brother Rhodomanus lost to us these fifty years past since the Second War fought against the xenos for this world?'

'Yes, my lord,' Julio confirmed, 'but lost no longer. Venerable Rhodomanus has returned.'

FACES

Matthew Farrer

In the end Jann couldn't stay away, and so here she came again creeping back into the tower's red-blurred shadow, hunched over with a rusted torque-stave in her hand. The shouting, drumming storm was two days gone now, and no matter how hard Jann listened all she could hear was the soft crackle of her footsteps in the sandflake drift and her own breathing, dry and frightened. At this hour, at this angle, the depot tower was a lightless block of black against the blood of the sky behind it. No movement, no voices. Even the great metal bulk of the pipeline was inert.

The storm's trailing winds had smoothed out the ground, and the only footprints in front of the south door were Jann's own. They staggered and lurched out from the little storm-hatch and disappeared behind one of the giant pipeline buttresses, the spot where she had crouched and shivered all through the night at the mercy of strange, taunting dreams. Now the slower, softer prints stalked back out of hiding and up behind her, padding steps, trying for a stealth that she knew would make no difference. She would have to go in there and find them, all of them. She would have to show her...

...face.

She took light steps towards the hatch, holding the stave this way and that, trying to think how she could best swing it if one of them were waiting just inside. It would be dark. The only parts of the tower that were ever properly lit were the control room at the top and the living deck. For a moment that thought almost soothed her. She thought of the dark rooms and halls, dark country she had never seen, riding high and quiet over it, and strange mountains kissed with silver light, but that image split and twisted her thoughts and her strength fled her for a moment. She moaned, softly, and craned up to the sky, but there was no white moon there to help her. There should have been a white moon. Jann had never seen a moon, not of any colour, but there should have been a white moon.

She dropped her eyes from the sky and stood swaying in the doorway for a moment. It seemed as though she were about to break through to some understanding of what was happening to her, but a blink and a breath and it was all gone like

(*moonlight*)

smoke through her fingers and she found herself stepping through the storm-hatch, breathing hard, trying to force her eyes to dilate, gripping the stave so hard that the corroded texture of its haft bit into her palms. She held it closer to her, like a walking-staff, and found a little comfort in that. No moon-gems, but it would do.

The engines embedded in the tower's thick foundations sent their rumbling beat through the walls. A deep beat, a walking-beat, for a slow promenade before the dance began. The implications of that thought gave her chills but her steps, already in time to the engines, began to quicken. The emergency lights shone in their little cages high on the rockcrete walls, red like blood that washed from the sky, yellow like the sparks flying up from an anvil. Jann didn't know whose thoughts these were any more.

Staring into the light, she thought she heard a movement somewhere in the dimness, but the accessway behind her was empty. Jann turned her

(*or was it really her*)

face inwards towards the red-lit corridors, and pressed on.

She found Gallardi in the machine-shrine, as she had expected to. He had broken the bright blue-white floodlamps that Tokuin had always kept bathing the hall, and now worked only in the same dim red emergency light that Jann had walked through. He had thrown open the maintenance shutters to the enginarium crypt below them and the machine-noise was louder here, a furnace roar. Conduits and energy sinks glowed cherry-red and added their light and heat. The air was clear, but Jann's senses brought her the faint touch of smoke.

'Brother?' she whispered. Gallardi was standing with his back to her, his slabs of shoulders working, his thick body swaying and folding where the fat overhung his belt. From the other side of him came the ring of metal on metal.

'Brother?'

In the racket of the shrine, the engines below and half a dozen of Tokuin's workshop machines running, there was no way the sound of her whisper could have reached him. But his body shivered at the murmur of her voice and he turned. Good Gallardi with his callused hands and soft voice, who'd liked to watch the sunset with her from the tower's roof. He'd sung songs with her (but what songs? Why couldn't she remember them?) and... and danced... under six white moons...

There was no white moon. Jann had never seen a moon. She sobbed and took a half-step forwards. She wanted her friend, so blessedly familiar. His thin legs, of which he was so self-conscious. His belly, with the old runnelled scar from the solder-splash accident years before they had met. His grizzled, shaven head and his, his...

...face.

There was a hammer in his hand, and he raised it.

'I can't greet you the way I want to, my beautiful little sister,' he said. Was his mouth moving? One moment Jann thought so, and then thought not. 'You're welcome and safe in my home, always, you know that. But I must work.' There was a shrieking hiss from behind him. The steelcutting press, left to run unsupervised, had overheated and was trying to shut itself down.

'We aren't safe, brother, either of us!' Now she found proper voice, although her words sounded strange to her own ears, high and singsong, almost not her own. 'It's happening again. I heard them fighting up on the operational deck.' Her memories seemed to float and split. The brawl between her crewmates splayed out and overlapped itself like a pict-screen trying to show half a dozen images at once. But every image horrified her. There was nothing she wanted to see. 'He knows! He...' She stumbled over the name. Crussman. He reared up through every one of her memories, stinking of lho-smoke and of the blood that slicked the front of his coveralls and dripped from his hand. The simple picture of him sent a killing scream through her thoughts, and still she stumbled over his name, because couldn't she also remember...

(Crussman twisted around the edge of the driver's seat in the high, cramped little cabin of the crane-rigger, looking down at them. 'Lifts like a dream!' he shouted over the engine and the winches. 'Easy to see how beat-up it got. Who knows how far the storm threw it to get to here?' There was a huge, cheerful grin on his face. This was the best bit of storm-scrap they'd ever...)

'Crussman,' she managed to say, although somehow she thought she had mangled the word again, made it something shorter, guttural. 'He knows about... about you. He knows you're here. He knows...'

Knows what you did. Knows where we are. Knows what he has to do. Knows what has to happen. None of the answers that sprang to her mind made any sense. From somewhere around them she thought she heard footsteps, light as rushing air, and faint laughter. If Gallardi heard it too, he didn't show it. The red light shone steady from the emergency lamps but seemed to flicker on the man's

(that's not his real)

face as he hefted his hammer again and turned away. Jann followed him around the machine-shrine, stepping over Tokuin's corpse without looking down at it.

'He was too strong for me,' Gallardi said in a voice gruff with sadness, and let one hand drop to point to his leg. 'Too strong. I forged my very breath into my steel, and what did it aid me? No, no. It's done now. I've given the last one to Sabila, but that path is not mine. Bloodletting is his. His soul is there. And mine is here. Bound here.' Jann looked where his hand pointed. Her vision swam and doubled. She saw Gallardi's bare, pale foot beneath the cuff of a standard-issue rust-brown crewman's legging, and she saw a leg thick like a pillar, muscle-packed, anvil-heavy, riven and bent under the scars of the terrible wounds that Crussman had dealt when he had dragged Gallardi back here, mutilated and bereft, and picked up his chains.

Crussman had never been down here. This place had been Tokuin's. It had been sacred to him. A place where he came to work as a supplicant, a priest, where Gallardi had come as a master. Jann understood why they had fought, but she couldn't understand what she was seeing now. The dark-skinned man with the big scarred belly was as true as all her memories, but yet she knew the limping master of the anvil as truly as she did the shining features of her own

(but is this really my)

face. She cradled her stave in one hand and reached the other out to him.

'I ran and hid,' she said. 'I... I think I slept. I think I dreamed. I dreamed about us. I don't know if I dreamed about you and... him...' she pointed back to the body behind her, unable to think of the name of the engineer with whom she'd lived and worked for two years, '...or if I remembered. I saw you fighting him...'

('Gallardi!' Tokuin had screamed. Augmetics covered the adept's eyes and nose but his mouth was flesh, not a vocoder, and there was ugly organic fear in his voice. 'Stop it! Stop what you're doing!' He had coughed and doubled over as a fist had found his belly, then arched the copper-inlaid utility-arm that sprouted from the base of his spine, arched it like a scorpion's tail to block the downwards swing of the pneumatic clamp that Gallardi had loaded his other fist with. The clamp bounced away with a clang and the arm shot forwards snake-fast into Gallardi's chin, but it was only a push, not a blow. Tokuin didn't really understand what was happening, he had not done the thing that the rest of them had done that Jann's memory couldn't quite piece together. Tokuin didn't understand the wrongness of this, didn't understand that Gallardi had to take mastery of the forge or everything was false, in a way even she struggled to understand. Tokuin pushed Gallardi and held him, and Gallardi thrashed for a moment in the eight-fingered mechanical grips as they held him by the jaw before he battered the slender end-joints of the arm with the clamp and shook it loose.

'You're deranged, Gallardi!' Tokuin was a man of the machine-cloisters, no brawler, and he had staggered back through the workshop jerking with feedback as his battered arm malfunctioned. 'You're damaged! Jann! All of you! Where's Merelock? Make her take command again! You're all damaged!' He was retreating deeper into the forge and Jann wanted to call to him to stop, to explain how much more wrong he was making it, with his alien voice and his strange half-and-half face, but Gallardi was closing in again. 'It's those things, they've driven you mad! Gallardi! Jann, talk sense to him!' One of the mechanised pallet-jacks came to life and rolled forwards, Tokuin trying to manoeuvre its drive-block in front of Gallardi's body, its tines under his feet, but he spun and danced around it, lurched, caromed off the pipe-lathe and closed in. 'Take it off, Gallardi, it's wrecking your mind, Gallardi, listen–' And she had run away, then, because her friend was about to beat the engineer to death and she had already watched Crussman snarling as he hacked at Crewman Heng's arm while Heng grinned and giggled and looked on, and she knew Sabila was going to try to make everything right and she already knew what would happen, even though beneath that she didn't know what was happening at all. She had covered her eyes with her hands and staggered away as behind her Gallardi began the murder.)

'There are two of us,' Jann said. She padded around Gallardi, walking a slow circle around him as he leaned against the welding cage, his head hanging. Jann could see the sweat and grime coating his skin, and the way his shoulders sagged. He must have been labouring all night, unsleeping. She couldn't imagine how exhausted he must be – but he couldn't be exhausted from working here, could he? This was his place, he and his forge were part of each other. How could he tire from this labour?

'We are at war within ourselves,' she went on. Gallardi didn't move. It had been a stupid thing to say. He knew they were at war. Had he not forged that war's weapons with his own hands here? But that didn't make sense either, she could remember that Gallardi had only taken possession of the forge a day, two days ago. Every answer was wrong, every question was wrong. She continued in her circle, her steps careful and rhythmic. It soothed her, seemed to move things towards familiarity again. 'Not between us but within us. Can you feel it? Two things in you? Have you dreamed it? Do you feel yourself to be... not your own?' She was three-quarters of the way around her circle, and movement seemed to be helping the words come, as her thoughts drifted into alignment like moons in the sky. She thought back to how Gallardi had spasmed and struggled as the half-forgotten other had put out a metal hand and seemed to push his

(but it didn't look like his)

face, push it almost loose from his skull. That meant something. She was sure of it. She let her eyes drift half-closed, started to turn in circles as she finished her orbit of Gallardi. Even as she was thinking how ludicrous the movements were, the circles within circles quieted her, helped her thoughts ride soft and quiet in courses that felt familiar.

She opened her eyes and saw clearly. Only for a moment, but enough. Gallardi was standing in the middle of an idiot chorus of rattling, over-revved workshop machines, all Tokuin's engines with their controls jammed into working positions with crudely glued or soldered fragments of metal or plastek trash. One had already overheated and failed, two more were rattling ominously. Tools and debris littered the floor. Panniers and slider shelves where Tokuin had reverently arrayed his tools and spare components were tipped and smashed, their contents piled up at their feet. And in the middle of it all, here stood Gallardi, half-naked, dull-eyed, animal-filthy, standing at a work plinth and crashing his hammer down as though he were an old smith from the hive-fringe shanties working an iron blade. But instead of a hammer he swung one of the heavy subsonic solid-reader wands they used to test the strength of pipeline segments, the gauge in the tip (which could look like a hammer to a blurred eye in dim light) already with its casing split and the smashed internal components visible, and on the plinth no glowing-hot metal bar but the shattered remains of a running-light assembly from the crane rig.

Gallardi brought his improvised smithy hammer down again, sending plastek chips scattering. He had always been too big, too heavy for grace but Jann had always admired the powerful, confident economy with which he moved. Now his movements were empty, jerky, like nothing living. She tried to read his expression in his eyes but when she cast her gaze up to his

(no please what's happened to his)

face she cried out, spun through a circle, looked again but couldn't unsee what she'd seen, and ran from the forge. If he had called after her, even her name, even just a wordless cry, perhaps she could have found the courage to stay, but here came that slippery, kaleidoscopic haze again, splitting and doubling her thoughts, and although she resisted it, somewhere in that haze came a knowledge that this was ordained, this was right. Gallardi was bound to his place. Her dreams would not change that.

('Can we winch it?' Gallardi asked in her memory as they stood looking at this thing they had found. It was hard not to stare. The thing's shape had a way of pleasing the eye, leading it softly along curves and through gentle turns. Jann thought of the strange, scalloped lines of the fungi that grew in the coolways under the hive-sprawls where they took their leave rotations, and then she thought of the lines of the muscled arms and shoulders of the boy she'd stepped out with when last she'd been there. That made her redden, but none of the others had noticed. Crussman and Heng were talking in quiet voices, Gallardi was simply looking at it. It was a made thing, but all the made things Jann had ever seen had the sledgehammer-heavy arrogance of Imperial design, all

blocky angles and hard surfaces. Here Jann couldn't see a single straight line or flat plane. She didn't quite dare walk closer to it, none of them did until they'd told Merelock what they'd found, but she hunkered down and leaned forwards to stare at it. If those were control grips, then that had to be a seat, and if that were a seat then those things behind it were running-boards like their crane-buggy had, for them all to hitch and ride on? And along the back, under a tangle of shimmering cloth whose colours seemed to ripple and shiver in the corner of her eye... an engine? A mechanism? Or a container? A saddle-pannier? Jann wondered if there were cargo in there, what this thing had been carrying, and how bitter it was to her now that they had not smashed the thing, burned it with their torches, driven the crane-buggy back and forth and back and forth over the cargo panniers, treading them to splinters without any of them ever opening them and looking inside.)

Her eyes blurred with tears as she ran up the stairs and she misjudged the width of the exit. The ends of the torque-stave clanged into the doorframe and it bent her over at the midriff, unhurt but groaning with shock. The stave fell from her hands and she folded and dropped through the doorway, crawling clumsily onward without thinking to pick it up.

When she remembered it, she pushed herself against a dry, slick wall, and clambered half-upright. This was the storage level, a maze of tiny paths winding between the dark stacks of bales and drums and pallets. She leaned against the heavy plastic wrap around a stack of filter-blocks and looked around.

High, clear laughter drifted up through the red-lit door down into the forge, and her stave was gone.

Jann's breath caught in her throat but she made herself move. Her hands grasped air. This place was cramped, smothering whatever marginal use the stave would have had as a weapon, but it still felt like too much of a loss. She told herself it was a rusted, useless torque-stave only fit for Tokuin's scrap-furnace, but the feeling that she had lost a part of herself clung to her as she shuffled away from the forge door. The stacked pallets and drums were all edges and angles, no soothing circles, and she could feel her chest hitching and jerking, wanting to echo the laughter she had heard.

'He must fight on his own,' Merelock's voice murmured at her shoulder, and although Jann made to jerk and scream with the shock, all that she gave was a gentle shudder and gasp. As Jann half-turned Merelock placed the torque-stave in her hands.

'A staff should no more be left in the grass than a spear, little cousin,' Merelock whispered. Her voice doubled on itself, acquired an echo. "Twould be good to have you running at my flank, little one, if you'll stay with me. Green and white above the trees.' The sentence made no sense to Jann but the words had an odd power over her, and she tilted her head back as though she could look up through the thick walls and roof and see a night sky where the green and the white…

But Merelock was away, darting through the narrow spaces between the stacks. Jann smiled as she glided along behind, picturing Merelock as a night-hunting raptor, beak sharp as a spear, talons slitting the air, eyes as keen as its talons staring into the green-tinged darkness. But that laughter from the forge door would not leave her head now, and she found herself wanting to laugh, too, softly sing as she ran to and fro.

'On and ahead, cousin!' came the gruff hunter's whisper down the trail, and Jann quickened her pace even though she knew it was only Merelock's reedy voice from the other side of a pallet of hygiene packs. 'On and ahead to the Great Caern! We'll touch the stone for luck and turn about to hunt them!'

The geography of this place unfolded in Jann's mind with the quiet certainty of dream-knowledge, but as she ran up and down the aisles between the stores, her stave clanging awkwardly against crates and fittings, she was more and more aware that the place she was running through seemed phantom-like. Her mind kept dancing away through some great forest (she was sure that was the word; the last supervisor, Merelock's predecessor, had read books and had described forests to them), gliding between the boles of trees, up into the rich canopy, slipping along through the underbrush, airy as a moonbeam, following her fierce hawk.

All the places of the forest were known to her, their names talismanic weights in her mind. The Great Caern, the Tree of Hands, the Crying River, the Sky Hearth. Glorious places, wild places, and Jann cried out because *now* she was singing her dreams in the sky over the forest to a chorus of wind-chimes, and *now* she was tottering back and forth in a cramped and grubby storeroom, watching her portly little supervisor trotting ahead brandishing a splintered piece of pallet like some sort of spear, exulting at a mad beauty that she couldn't convince herself she was really seeing, laughing in the dark while her friend shuffled around in the forge with Tokuin's blood on his hands, crippled and beaten and… chained?

There was that strange ghost-certainty again. Chained? She had seen no chains. Gallardi had killed Tokuin and taken the forge as his own. Why did her mind cling to the memory of him defeated and bound?

Pad-pad-pad came Merelock's feet around the end of the aisle. The supervisor had kicked off her workboots and was running barefoot, leaving bloody prints from where something had cut into her left heel. She had plastered engine grease across the rank swatches on her jacket and crude garlands of torn fabric flopped around her brow and her biceps. She shook the spear in one hand. Her other, Jann realised, was dangling at the end of a broken arm.

'This isn't the path,' said Jann, propping her stave across the aisle to block Merelock's way. 'Ma'am? Merelock, do you even know where you are? Do you recognise this place? Do you recognise me?'

The other woman stopped with her belly up against the pitted metal of Jann's torque-stave, then stepped back and hefted her spear. Jann suppressed a wince as Merelock's broken arm banged against a crate corner, but the supervisor didn't even seem to notice. In the dimness her

(how could I have ever thought that was her real)

face was impassive, perhaps a little watchful. The designs around her eyes and across her cheekbones curled like rich summer leaves, like falcon-wings.

'What strange questions you ask, little cousin! Have you been dreaming again? You should have asked me before you came down to sleep. There are places where it's not safe to sleep, and your dreams are too precious for any of us to risk. Enemies make their way into the wild places, cousin. Stay close to my side.'

'Merelock, listen to me! Where are you? Can you tell me where you are? Can you describe where you are? Do you know what happened to Gallardi and Tokuin?'

'I...' Merelock began, and then straightened. Her broken arm still hung but the other lifted her makeshift spear in a pose that brought back to Jann that maddening deja vu. 'I run the trail like the moon and the wind, little cousin. I am the sound of my horn and the flight of my spear. When the nights chill and the green moon walks silent and alone, so there do I walk under it.'

Other voices, other sounds. Something danced in Jann's vision like the ghost of a hololith display in the instant after it was shut down. Merelock seemed to stand in the centre of a larger form, something tall and mantled in beast-pelts, lifting a lean arm, her/his words wrapped around by the dim sounds of wild horns and quick breathing. Merelock's voice struggled for power and melody but Jann could feel the words coming from that other silhouette too. Their rhythm made her want to chorus along, dance in a circle with her stave lifted high before she could laugh and sing, leap and hang in the air, shine high and bright above...

The sensation was like jolting awake just before the final release into sleep: Jann broke the reverie, pulled back from the brink, immediately felt guilty at disbelieving that beautiful voice. Before the guilt could lull her and draw her under again she gritted her teeth, squeezed her eyes almost shut and hit Merelock's broken arm with a clumsy, looping blow.

The supervisor wailed in pain, but although she lurched she did not fall and the chunk of pallet stayed gripped in her fist the way the stave stayed gripped in Jann's. For a moment, behind the sound, something in the darkness that might have been a sigh or a chuckle, but when Jann cocked her head to listen it was gone.

'I am wounded, but not beyond fighting or mending,' said Merelock, bent halfway to one knee before Jann and cradling her arm. 'But see, Jann?' Jann shook her head, not understanding, and for a moment not recognising the name Merelock had used. Her name, she was sure, should be longer, softer, more like a breathy lullaby on the tongue.

'See, now?' Merelock went on. 'See how wrong it all is? My own domain, my hunting-paths. I climbed to spy and wait for my enemies and the bough cast me down. Wouldn't bear my weight.' Her head swimming, Jann got a hand under Merelock's good shoulder and helped her to her feet, craning over her shoulder to follow the woman's gaze. Her first thought was that of course it wouldn't have borne weight: she was looking at a ripped stretch of tarpaulin over stacked drums of distilled water, and who would ever think that Merelock's stout, stiff-limbed little frame would let her clamber up there without something going wrong? And yet it made perfect sense to her when Merelock talked of the stack as though it were a great tree, and one that had done her a personal wrong by breaking its branch and letting her fall. Falling. Falling and hurting. Jann breathed hard, shook her head, reminded herself of her purpose.

'Look at it again, Merelock. Please, ma'am. Is it what you think it is? Look at me, do you see your cousin? I think I almost have what it is that's happening to us, ma'am, almost in my mind, but will you help me to try and understand it?' She could hear herself cracking and begging, near tears, but she seemed to have broken the trail of Merelock's delusion. Hope bloomed warm in her. She met the other woman's gaze, held it. Let her be jarred by the pain, Jann thought. Let her think! Let her see it in my

(but it isn't even my)

face.

For a long moment there was no sound, and then Merelock began making a low noise in her throat. Jann leaned in, listening for words, but there was just a soft moan of breath. Jann kept her eyes on Merelock's, trying to ignore what her senses were telling her about the woman's features, trying to pull insight out of the air by simple concentration.

'Jann?' The doubling of Merelock's voice was gone. It was a simple voice now, the voice Jann was familiar with, but it was faint and confused. 'Jann, is that you? I can't recognise you. What happened to us? What happened? I hurt, Jann. I hurt. I can hear the forge engines. Where's Tokuin? Jann?'

'We're going up from the forge,' Jann told her. 'Up to the top level, where that thing is. I know we... weren't always like this. I dream how we were before we found it. I think if we all go and find it we might understand about those people in my dreams.'

'Up,' said Merelock, still in that small, childlike voice. 'We'll go up.' She tried to hold out her broken arm but it wouldn't quite extend. 'You and I. Together.' Merelock wouldn't release her grip on her spear, so Jann held her as best she could under the broken arm and tried to help her along. 'We'll walk together. You and I. Together in the dark.' Grunting, Jann got Merelock to the end of the aisle and into a broader space where they could more comfortably walk abreast. 'You and I, walking in the dark,' Merelock said, 'and not our first such journey, no,' with an almost-chuckle that chilled Jann's blood. The sound seemed to be picked up and echoed in the gloom around them. Jann thought she heard soft, rapid footsteps counterpointing the echoes, but who could tell any more what was happening around her and what was the ghost-pantomime in her own head?

(*'Gallardi, Klaide, fetch a pair of piston-grips,' Merelock said. Her voice, never very powerful, was fighting against the stiff wind on the tower roof but there was still enough snap in it to cut through the arguments. 'Tokuin knows we've had a find, but he has some sort of ministration to attend to below before he'll come up and look at this thing. We'll make a start ourselves.'*

'Ma'am, Jann thinks there's definitely tech in there,' said Crussman, 'and I agree with her. Look, that long curve has the line of an engine cowl, and if you look under it you'll see, well, I'm sure it's machinery.'

'I'm sure you're right,' Merelock said as Klaide, Gallardi and Heng came past pushing the big piston-grip pedestals on their rumbling wheels. 'But the tech is the only thing I'm having him look at. If that stuff you think is machinery is part of the Mechanicus mysteries then we're best served by keeping them sweet from the start, but whatever there is here that's not machinery is legal salvage of the Filiate Guilds. There's no lack of piety in doing things by the letter and sorting out what's ours.'

That was what Crussman had wanted to hear, and he and Sabila had actually clapped as the pedestals halted next to this thing they had found, the thing like a long iridescent arrowhead that looked so heavy and lifted so light, with its strange controls and its riding-rails. None of them had openly discussed the bright gemlike crystals embedded in its sleek curves: most of the deep-desert pipeline crews held the same half-formed superstitions about gloating over salvage before the bonus warrants had been signed. But Jann had found herself studying them, counting them, and wondering about the shapes she was sure now were cargo panniers. As Klaide shooed the others away and started working the controls, the arms extended with a piston-hiss and the three-fingered grips slowly positioned themselves over the pannier lids...)

Jann didn't want to think about it any more. Didn't want to dream, didn't want to remember. Wasn't it her dream that had begun all this strife? She had dreamed of uprising (although that didn't fit), she had dreamed of war between them all (but was that really what had happened?), she had dreamed of a bloodshed that the telling of her dreams had brought to pass, prophecy and fulfilment in one closed and shining circle like the edge of a full white moon. But she had never told anyone. She hadn't even been the one to see the thing wedged in under the pipeline by the winds. Who had seen it first? They had been out checking that the new fixtures at pylon 171 had survived the hypervelocity sandblasting of the previous day and Tokuin's drone had spotted something his image catalogues couldn't quite identify. They had gone to hunt it out. But Merelock hadn't gone with them. And wasn't Merelock the one who hunted?

The thought of her companion dragged Jann's consciousness back to the moment. Merelock was still muttering to herself.

'Oh, we ran together when the ghosts sang in the waterfalls, do you remember? And the quarrels, when I had rancour with my black-haired love, and you were always the quiet voice. You called to me when there was burning iron in the... the smoke... and you were the star by which my... my stave, my hunting, my friends...' That throaty, guttural note was creeping back into Merelock's voice like a hunting-cat slinking forwards through a thicket, but at the same time she was faltering, reaching for words as though each path of thought had run into darkness. That was wrong twice over. Merelock was the station supervisor, the order-giver, she should be the certain one. Merelock was one with her home, swift like running feet in the wild night, sure like the strike of a hunting spear or the lunge of the falcon. She should be the sure one, no indecision behind the features she wore.

Jann was still trying to work out what that thought meant when she looked up and saw the figure watching them. It held itself in the light from the stairwell up to the living deck, and where that light fell on it it seemed to fray into crisscrossing sparks and threads. The thing moved a dancing half-step towards them and its whole skin cracked, shivered and crawled with glowing colour. For a moment the display calmed, and then it bent an elegant leg, cocked its head just so and somersaulted lazily backwards into the gloom.

Jann stood and gasped, her mind thrumming like a plucked string but empty of thought. Her heart wanted to leap at the sight of the thing, but her bones wanted to chill. On her arm, Merelock was still sagging and murmuring, and up from the forge level came a burst of laughter and an echoing, grinding crash.

Jann moved. She forgot about supporting Merelock along, simply dragged the other woman into a shambling half-run through the twisting, giggling shadows. Merelock stumbled at the foot of the stairs but pushed herself up with her spear and managed to keep pace. Climbing, Jann shot a look over her shoulder to see the supervisor panting hard two steps behind her, leaning forwards to run so she was bent almost double. Merelock's cap was long gone and her braid had disintegrated, her black curls hanging in her face, and Jann jerked around to face up the stairs again, glad that she hadn't seen Merelock's

(I can't even remember her real)

face in the brighter lights of the stairwell. None of the minds rioting in her head seemed able to predict what they'd see without the merciful blurring of the shadowy lower floors.

The light grew brighter as they rounded the hairpin and clambered up the second flight. The glow-loop over the door to the living deck was defective, Merelock never quite having managed to bully Tokuin into making time to fix it, and so they came into the ransacked dormitory and into flickering light and weeping.

The weeping voice was Klaide's, and peering past the clinking and winking of the light just above her Jann could make him out. He was slumped across a twisted nest of bedclothes and curtains, torn from the sleeping-booth partitions and now choking the dormitory aisle. In the middle of it all Klaide knelt tilted against one of the stripped curtain frames with one hand cupped against his face. It was a pose of grief so classic as to look contrived, as though Klaide was the centre of one of the bright-lit tableaux that enactors performed in front of the temples on holy nights.

At that thought Jann's scattered thoughts seemed to interlock and move in unison. Insight was as brief as a bright moonbeam spearing down through clouds, but as powerful. She shook her arm free from Merelock and ran down the aisle, so fleetfooted she almost seemed to glide over the debris and litter, and knelt at Klaide's feet.

'Klaide? It's me, Klaide,' although if he had asked her who 'me' was she'd have struggled to answer. 'Klaide, it's okay. You don't need to grieve. We're not... like this. We're not...' It had seemed so clear in that brilliant moonlit moment but now she was grasping for the words. 'We're not who we are, Klaide. I think I understand. I've dreamed us as...' and her voice choked in her throat because she wanted to say *ourselves* and she wanted to say *others*, and both of those and neither were true.

'You don't understand,' Klaide told her, his voice a travesty: rumbling and chesty as Jann had known it in the years they had been crewmates, not the clear contralto she knew it should really be. 'He's gone, he's...' and Klaide's body began to shudder, not with weeping now but with some more profound convulsion. He began shouting, spitting out words in a half-shriek.

'Dying-dead-he's-dead-he-will-yet-die-he-dies!' and while Jann tried to hold the man's hands down and murmur soft moon-songs to soothe him, still she understood. He had gone away to die. Who had? Jann couldn't fix on a name, two separate sounds slid into and out of her mind, but she knew he was Klaide's (champion-child-student-subject-follower), and she knew that whoever he was he had gone to die. He had gone to fight. He was already dead and they mourned. He lay dying, his wound mortal and his blood bright red as a moon whose light waxed upon his death and drenched the green and white moons and drowned their beauty.

He was all these things, all these states, always walking out to his doom, always lying stricken, lying dead. In all these states he was timeless as the tableau they made up now: Klaide grieving, Merelock poised over them with her spear high, Jann kneeling and placating, speaking of dreams. Even as she fought back tears of grief and fear, the form the three of them made felt so right, felt like she was falling into the steps of a dance she had been singled out for while even her own mother was yet waiting to be born.

She thought she heard a soft sigh of recognition from somewhere around them, but could see nobody but the three of them.

She looked at Klaide again. He had wrapped himself in a green curtain-cloth, and torn the front of his tunic so that the edges now echoed the crude garlands of torn fabric Merelock had adorned herself with. He had yanked off his metal collar of rank, and the electoo that ringed his bull-like neck, the badge of a Mechanicus-ordained lay artisan, stood out in the brightness. Its hard geometry made a cruel counterpoint to the tapering lines of Klaide's own features, elegant even in the depths of grief. It was not Klaide's own

(any more than this is my real)

face, but finally, finally Jann was coming to understand how that could be.

She found herself talking then, not even sure if Klaide or Merelock had mind enough left behind their

(I can almost remember their)

faces to understand, but letting the words pour out of her like moonlight. She talked about Gallardi taking the machine-shrine from Tokuin because of the steps and the songs that called him to the forge. She talked about her moonlit dreams flowered into prophecies as she spoke them, as her fingers traced the delicate intersecting circles worked into her strange, brittle skin. She talked about the memories she had dreamed and the dreams she couldn't quite remember, the strange, clumsy creatures they had all once been, with their brutish names (Gallardi, Klaide, Merelock, Jann, surely just the grunts and honks of beasts?) and the reeking, lumpen tower they called home. She talked about the temple tableaux and the passion-plays and the mythic dances, the pageant of Alicia Dominica where the Saint stood before a king with a face like the sun, sometimes to draw her sword on a traitor or sometimes to plead for her doomed children; the *Life of Macharius*, that her brothers had learned word for word, the general waging war across the heavens, the lay of the ninety-nine swords, the great strife of an aeon past when a murderous hand crushed the martyr-hero and spread his blood, so scarlet-red, the tales of the six magnificent warriors who had walked alive from the end of that great tribulation, ready to hand on the light of their learning.

They were good stories, powerful stories, and they sang in her blood, danced the way she thought she remembered dancing in moonlight to the drum and the cymbal, even as she remembered them all crying and howling and jerkily trying to dance on the roof of the tower when they had found the

(I don't want to think about the)

faces, broken the locks and found them and…

Now it was Jann sobbing, oblivious to the surprised looks from the other two – this was not her part, these were not her steps. But she staggered to her feet, cast the torque-stave away from her. She had no staff, she had no moonstone necklace, barely had a self. As the stories and the dances solidified in her mind she could feel Jann fragmenting and slipping away. She wanted to tell them, wanted to shout it at them, but the weight of understanding was too great and all she could do was cry for what was happening to them. She struggled to her feet and leapt over Klaide, a broken leap for the broken thing that she had become, and ran for the next stairwell, still sobbing. Behind her, Klaide and Merelock took each other in a clumsy embrace, but Jann didn't see or care. She understood now. There was no hope.

The lights were out on the operations deck, and only the glows of the instrument and monitor banks shone back at her. She felt the scraps of her mind twist and reach in two different directions to try and make sense of them, and for a moment she paused in her stumbling run to stare at the clear plastek desk where she had pored over the meteorological charts and dune maps. The edges of memories brushed at her again. Sitting at that table hot-eyed and yawning when Merelock had insisted on having the route for a maintenance round ready by the morning shift. Sitting on the table at Quarter Relief, a cup of rough alcohol in her hand, helpless with laughter as Gallardi and Crussman did one of their little songs mocking the guild controllers. Looking at the weather auguries and telling Merelock that yes, they could head out now, it was safe to move, and plotting a route to where the alerts showed that something had been carried up against the pipeline by the storm.

She couldn't bear that thought, that any action of hers might have helped along what had happened. Jann slumped against the doorframe, lifting her hands to her eyes to blot out the table and its memories, and when she lowered them it was on the table watching her. The shock of terror rhymed and meshed with the shock of familiarity so that she couldn't tell them apart. She gulped and found herself stepping forwards, reaching out a placating hand that her fear then made into a fist. The tall thing on the table, fringed and crested in colours that swirled and mixed with the air around it, posed and mocked her movements, and then it went from wearing all colours to no colours, fading from her eyes as it stepped back off the table, leaving her just the ghost of laughter.

It wasn't a mirage, she thought dully to herself, and it wasn't a memory. Something really had been in here with her, perhaps was in here still. Something that had– but she found herself pushing that idea away before it had managed to get any traction in her thoughts. They were being watched, nothing more. Nobody had done this to them. They had done it themselves.

(They were hushed as they came in procession down from the roof deck, each

carrying one of their strange new trophies. Their chatter had broken off after Crussman's shout, but now their silence was reverent instead of startled. Jann thought of the weighted silences that came over the throngs watching the grey and white banners unfurl from the sides of the hive spires the day after Tithing Day. Thinking of grey and white and silence, she felt empty eyes watching her from the thing she carried, which she knew was stupid. Crussman's words – 'It's full of faces!' *must have unnerved her more than she'd realised.*

And yes, once broken open the panniers had been full of faces. They had been mounted like artworks on the pannier's inner wall, each one veiled in a cloth of shifting, rippling colours the like of which Jann had never seen before. Some of the cloths had fallen away with the jolting of the craft and the cracking of the panniers, exposing the piece beneath it. Without realising it Jann had taken a pace towards one of them, a mask made to slip tightly over a head longer and slenderer than hers. Its features were odd and stylised, tilted so that the mask's wearer would always seem to have their face tilted slightly skywards. Stylised silvery-grey curls lined the porcelain-white face, and the alien features still carried a sweet and wise serenity that made Jann want to sigh.

She had caught herself and pulled herself back, and then looked around her and realised they had all reacted similarly.

'All right then, salvage divides equally,' said Merelock from behind them, trying to be brisk. 'We all know the rules.' And because it was the rules, Merelock took first pick. She reached out and unhooked a dark green mask, stern and masculine, with designs that might have been leaves curling about the cheekbones and the edge flaring with a design that seemed to evoke a tousled mane. Klaide pushed past her as she stepped away. One of these toys would be all right for his brother's little one, he muttered as though needing an excuse, and paused for a moment before he plucked up a mask that was as pale and delicate a green as Merelock's was dark, one that dusted to gold around the edges and on which a single deep-blue crystal tear glittered below one eye. Jann, equal in rank to Klaide, had darted in next for the face in white and silver-grey. It didn't seem to be warming from her hands, and in spite of how light it was she couldn't force it to bend or flex. Gallardi had picked a mask in a stunning orange-red which seemed to glow with its own light and pulse with yellow sparks when he turned it this way and that. The colour faded to an iron-black around the border, and Gallardi pronounced himself well pleased. 'I might even wear this back down there,' he had beamed, 'and see what Tokuin makes of it.'

Heng had complained about being left to last so Crussman had laughed and clapped him on the shoulder and sent him in next. Heng came away looking unhappy with a mask pinched in his fingers, a fierce and glowering one whose features struck Jann as somehow still feminine. Sabila, thoughtful, was carrying a golden mask, the set to its eyes and thin mouth speaking to Jann of youth and determination.

Crussman had been the daring one. There had been three compartments at the back of the pannier, three that were sealed tighter than the grips could easily break loose. Crussman had peered this way and that through the crumpled hull over them and seen a way to draw out what was inside. It was a mask the colour of old, rusted pig-iron, worked with rough designs that could have been streaks of corrosion or dried blood, worked into a snarl of such savage malevolence that when Crussman had held it up the very air around it seemed to darken and the rest of them had flinched back as though struck. Whatever little joke he'd been about to make died and slid back down his throat.

The expression on that mask had haunted them all, and when the wind had picked up and Merelock had suggested they go below they had all unconsciously given Crussman a wide berth. He was still smiling and waggling the thing in front of him, but Jann could tell he was forcing it. She had gone to sit beside Sabila in the control deck as they worked to raise a link to the depot, sitting beside the vox terminal turning the white mask over and over in her hands.

When the screaming started, Jann never had a moment's doubt what had begun it. Crussman had succumbed. He had put on his mask.)

And Jann was running again, pushing herself up the stairs to the roof-deck where the craft still sat in the holding gantry, lashed down against the wind. Both of the splintered lines of thought racing in her head were now revolving around that memory. The thing they had found, the crashed craft and the two containers they hadn't opened. Sunlight, kingship, a golden sword. Surely there was help there?

She had forgotten about her last three crewmates, but not for long. On the roof of the tower, on the landing pad under the cranes and gantries, Crussman and Sabila were at war.

Jann found herself empty of surprise. This was just another piece of mad whimsy, even while it had the inevitability of night falling. Jann nodded to herself as she slunk into hiding beneath a crane gantry. It was all so obvious. Everything had led to this.

Crussman's right hand gripped a cable-cutter from which he had stripped the safety cage. Whether by purpose or chance (*purpose*, Jann's mind whispered, *it's all on purpose*) he had cut his left hand with it: the palm glistened red and a steady stream of blood dripped from it as he moved. She gasped at the sight, couldn't take her eyes off the bleeding hand as the skinny pilot brandished it, thrust it forwards like a threat, held it theatrically high to counterbalance the roundhouse swings of his cutter. She had known she was going to see it, should have been prepared: every time she had thought about Crussman now it felt like that bleeding hand was gripping her heart. But surely the hand was bleeding for Sabila, and surely Sabila was still alive?

And so he was, alive and fighting although he must have known as soon as he left Klaide crying below that he was good as dead. Creeping from cover to cover, Jann watched the cycles of their battle, circling back and forth across the wide circle of the landing pad, Crussman's cutter arcing and smashing against the length of ceramite rod Sabila had taken from Gallardi's machine forge, and which he swung at Crussman like a sword. The cutter rang off the rod, and though the impact sounded light Sabila was driven down on one knee. Crussman flung back his head and screamed, holding the cutter two-handed over his head, and the sound of it wrenched Jann down to her very core.

She crawled between the tanks of ornithopter fuel and then darted behind a crane stanchion, peering around it. Sabila was on his feet, squaring off against Crussman, holding his makeshift sword high in challenge as Crussman held out his bloody hand and howled. The challenge, the defeat, the one sword, the bleeding hand, timeless and ever-renewing, a cycle as unbreakable as summer's decay into winter.

They closed and battled again as Jann ran around the lip of the landing pad, Sabila's movements swooping and elegant even as his slender arms shook with exhaustion, Crussman fighting back with a wild predator's savage purity of motion. And now Jann could see another form creeping and stooping behind Crussman as he roared and fought. Heng was shadowing Crussman in a bouncing stoop, clutching at the air and jabbing his fist and stump back and forth in manic counterpoint to the clash of weapons. Each time Sabila was knocked sprawling Heng would give a shrill, reedy cackle that made Jann flinch down deeper into cover. She knew what would happen if Heng turned his

(but now I know who really owns that)

face towards her and set eyes on her. He would know her name, he would recognise her, cackle and call, and from then on every path she walked would lead downwards and every day the shadows would lean a little closer to her, and night would come slithering on velvet-soft scales. In the last moments before she managed to tear her gaze away and start crawling again, Jann saw that Heng too had wounded himself. His thick bare forearms were mottled with bruises and gouges from where he had clawed at his own skin, and bitten at the flesh of his wrist beneath the stump where Crussman had hacked away his hand. That struck a chord of familiarity with her, a ripple of understanding like silver wind-chimes in her mind, but some of the wounds were bleeding and that was wrong, as wrong as the endlessly-renewed battle between Crussman and Sabila was right. Shuddering, Jann crawled towards the crane.

It was in there. A face they hadn't seen yet. She was sure it was the answer. The half-memory of it was in her mind now, like warm sunlight and her grandfather's voice, soft, meaningless comforting words to the tearful little girl who'd scraped her shin. She knew it had to be there. She could feel it.

Crussman howled again behind her, and mixed with it were two other cries: genuine pain from Sabila, and angry dismay from Heng. All Crussman wanted was to end Sabila, because all Crussman's nature understood was the ending, but somehow all three of them knew that ending it was wrong, something that would cast them adrift. Jann knew the reason, but she could barely have told them even if they had had mind enough left to listen. The wisdom was hers, not theirs, and that was part of the cycle too. The gritty bars of the gantry were under her hands now, and she grunted as she hauled herself up. Her reflexes seemed to belong to someone older than her but yet lighter, moonbeam-light.

She groaned as she closed on the craft and put her hands on it. Seeing it brought low like this grieved her, like seeing a beautiful dawn-bird cowering on the earth with a crippled wing, and she mourned for it with her heart even as the strange feel of its hull repulsed her skin. She stroked her fingers down the high spinal ledge, along the compartments ripped by the ugly metal arms, and found the final two, the ones they hadn't been able to breach.

Her fingers touched it and her thoughts seemed to touch it as well. She couldn't tell if she were remembering opening it, or thinking of opening it, or imagining opening it, or dreaming she had opened it. Behind her on the landing pad Sabila gave another cry, a choking, dying cry. Crussman's voice was ragged, his vocal cords worn to tatters; Heng's voice was the yowl of a cat in the dark. Jann barely heard them. This was salvation. Her senses were already reaching out for the voice she needed to hear. The sun-voice. The father-voice. The king-voice.

The compartment opened under her fingers. Jann retched, screamed, knew she was not dead but damned, poisoned, eaten, violated. Everything that was left of herself rotted in an instant. Her body seemed to go strengthless, boneless. She sagged, and would have fallen but for her torso wedging itself between two crossed struts.

Jann felt infinite desire and infinite contempt. She was paralysed, body and mind, except for the all-drenching cascade of fear. The face at the bottom of the compartment held her, ran her through as though she were a damsel-fly run through with a sleek stinger. She could not even sense an effort in it, or a will: it was something in herself that made her helpless to it, held her fast. Tears stung her eyes and her vision doubled and blurred. That didn't help. That face's grip on her mind remained, iron-cold and silk-strong. Only when her balance finally gave way and she sagged and fell to the metal decking at the gantry base did the extra distance stretch and lessen the hold.

Still in a half-sprawl, Jann reached for a strut to try and pull herself up. She didn't know what to do, couldn't think of words or a plan. The thought of that wonderful voice and the touch of the sun on her shoulders, that was gone, dropped without a trace into the abyss that had opened under her mind. Trying to increase the distance between herself and the terrible, devouring silence that seemed to be welling out from under the open lid, she forced herself onto her knees and began to shuffle back towards the landing pad. Whatever Crussman did to her, she would almost welcome it now. Anything to dislodge the memory of that face.

She stopped dead when she saw them come out of the shadows.

Six of them made a half-circle that closed smoothly on Crussman. As fatigue took the pilot and he started to sway and then stagger a step this way and then a step that, the six moved with sinuous ease, step and counter-step, the formation never breaking. Crussman's murder-scream was now not much more than a rasping moan, but still he had enough fury to drive his muscles: he lifted up the cutter, ready to drive it through the dying Sabila's skull at his feet. Maybe he hadn't seen the figures, maybe he didn't care.

Either way, there was nothing he could have done. The semi-circle parted, three scintillating figures darting one way and three darting the other in graceful unison, and through the centre of the gap they opened up came another figure, leaping and turning in the air, wrapped in shades of red and flashing gold that sparkled and dripped in the early evening gloaming. It landed on the balls of its feet and pirouetted, wheeling and spinning around Crussman's sagging, grubby form. The tails of a long coat whirled around it, now a rich blue, purple, silver, green, scattering shards and coins of light. A high crest of silver – hair or feathers, it was hard to know – ran up its hood and down between its shoulder blades, and Jann could hear the soft *shh-shh* as it whipped from side to side.

The bright shape froze in a deep fencer's pose over Sabila, and after a moment the dazzling sparks that had swirled around it coalesced onto it. Jann could see its lithe limbs, the crested hood, the outline of its coat and mask. One slender arm was up, staying the cutter's death-stroke. Dimly, she became aware that the six other strangers were echoing its stance in perfect, precise unison.

The newest stranger held its pose for a moment, and then suddenly its face and then its whole body flashed golden, pouring out a deep and beautiful light like sunlight that set Jann's heart leaping for a moment with a hope she couldn't quite understand or describe. But then its colours sank into black, shot through with coiling veins of red like cracks in the crust of a lava flow, and its upraised arm flicked through three curt, precise motions. For the first time since the faces had broken them all Crussman seemed to be speaking, or trying to, but now with his throat so delicately open he could not make the words. He crumpled, his legs folding and his arms falling into segments where the shining figure had cut them apart.

Heng, groaning and crooning, tried to scrabble away from Crussman's killer, and the figure straightened to its full, frightening height and watched him go. Its companions closed in, now moving in low crouches that put them almost on all fours, keeping their colours muted so that lined up on each side of their master they looked almost like shadowy wings. As Jann watched, their colours shifted from smoke-grey to the dirty white of old bones, and their faces blurred and arranged themselves into screaming harridan masks bursting from shocks of scarlet hair. Wailing, they scrabbled forwards hard on Heng's heels, caught his ankles and pinned them, caught his wrists and pinned them, held him writhing and gasping until the master stranger, still a shape of coal-black and smoulder-red, shot an arm out again. This time, instead of sparks of light, the arm was surrounded by dancing specks of blackness, swarming like cinders borne up from a great fire, and with each twitch of the arm Heng's body shuddered, bled, died, bled more and finally came apart.

The masks, the grief, the madness, the deaths: Jann had little left to her now, but somewhere in the ruins there was still the survival urge, and the capacity for fear. She found her feet, turned, made to flee and hide before they could turn their attention to her.

It was standing behind her. Staring up, her gaze met the darkness of its hood.

This was not the horror that the simple mask had been. The darkness beneath the deep fold of cloth was a space. A neutrality. Her eye and mind could find no purchase in it.

Jann stood perfectly still. Her muscles seemed to relax, as though they understood that all this was finally ending.

The hooded figure's cloak whispered as it took a step towards her. Its arms were held demurely in front of it, the hands folded below the cloak-folds of its chest. The hands were five-fingered, slender, longer than a human's, and now they rose up to push back the hood.

'No', Jann wanted to say. Nothing more than 'no'. It was all she could think of. But the hood fell back.

It was Jann's own face she was looking at, and it made her weep. The beautiful maiden-face, upturned to watch the white moon, the sacred circles shining on its skin. One of Jann's own hands crept up and wonderingly traced the lines of her own features.

Then the face opposite her began to change. It stretched, deformed. It became a caricature of itself, an exaggerated travesty of grotesque eyes, canted cheekbones, a tapered chin and high forehead that mocked the lines of Jann's own... her own...

...face.

Her hands pressed in on the side of her head. The figure opposite her did not move, except that now its features changed again. Now it became a bestial face, a vermin face. Crude and gawping, the features lumpy, meaty, the eyes muddy, the mouth slack. A repulsive face. An alien face. The face she had carried all her life.

Jann's fingers began to work. She dug them into herself, drawing blood with her broken and dirty nails. She found sweaty, gritty skin on which her fingers skidded, and smooth and cool skin with a firmness that her touch did not recognise. She dug and gouged and a bright bolt of madness sheared through her. Her fingers seemed to slide into her very flesh and she could feel her skull soundlessly parting. Her thoughts whirled and swarmed out of her into the cooling air like moths. She felt herself split and part. There was a sensation of bone cracking, tissue tearing, but no sound, no blood, no physical pain.

The white mask landed softly at her feet.

And now there was no kinship left with any of these strangers, no familiarity. There was the stink of blood and offal where poor sweet slow-talking Heng lay dead, and the butchered body of twinkle-eyed Crussman, and here she stood, and what was her name now? What was her name?

She jerked and fell backwards, rolled, got her feet under her by nothing more than blind chance, and ran, shrieking and wailing, not a scrap of mind left in her any more. She ran with nothing more than a merciful roaring void inside her, a perfect hollow, and her course took her away from the strangers, away from the gantry, towards the edge of the roof-deck. The rail was not high, and she hit it at a flat run.

Jann was still thrashing her limbs as she fell, trying to flee, but it was only a moment before the packed earth at the tower's foot ended it.

Quietly, without haste, they assembled on the roof. They made their way up through the stunted, squalid spaces where the animals had lived. They moved in soft procession, angular and high-stepping like bright wading birds, moving through precise sequences of poses both careful and utterly relaxed. Their colours and masks flickered gently in the dusk. None of them spoke.

They made a circle around the roof, then the circle became a spiral, leading them inwards, until they broke the spiral and spread into a pattern that made the fire-rune, the rune of lost glory and the dream of rekindling, with Ehallech at its crux.

Ehallech carried a bright mask in his hands, the Fire Mask, the visage of Vaul. Ehallech was learning the craft of the weaponwright and the myths of the crippled god of the forge had great meaning for him. It was only right that he be the one to take the mask from Gallardi, whose corpse now lay next to Tokuin's amid silenced machines below them.

The troupe broke after a moment and then silently formed around Lhusael, who carried the dark-green mask she had taken after her blades had killed Merelock. Lhusael was a devotee of her people's most primal, heartfelt stories, the stories of their parents and progenitors. Already she had mastered the spirit of Isha, danced that role, sang the grieving-songs, learned the intricate blade katas that represented the harvest-mother's tears. Now she was completing her grasp of those story-cycles by learning the role of Isha's husband, silent Kurnous, the god of the hunt, whose face was in the Hunter's Mask that had driven Merelock to prowl the dark paths with a spear in her hand. Behind her, moving in beautiful synchronicity, came Melechu, who had spent so long behind a bone mask dancing in the retinue of Nysshea the troupe's death-jester. Now was the time to balance the role of death with the role of a life-giver:

Melechu's bridge into that role was Isha's sacred grief, and so she had taken the Mourning Mask from Klaide, the visage of Isha of the harvest, weeping for her dead champion and her lost children.

When Nysshea had danced in the jester's train, her brother Edreach had danced with her. Before that, when she had danced the role of the fire-ghosts in Vaul's train, he had mirrored her by dancing a water-sprite in the footsteps of Isha. Now that they had both been chosen for greater roles, he was balancing her again: as she took on the role of Isha, he became Eldanesh, the greatest hero of the mortal eldar, the champion upon whom Isha smiled, who went forth to do battle with bloody-handed Khaine and met his fated death. Deftly, elegantly, never falling out of the overarching rhythm, Edreach dipped low and plucked the Hero Mask from Sabila's corpse, holding it high and proud. Others before him had interpreted Eldanesh as a doomed victim, even a fool, but Edreach revered him as one whose courage was exalted by the manner of his death.

Sheagoresh kept his vigil over the two mon-keigh corpses as the others broke the circle and reformed around him, coalescing around those in the troupe who held the ceremonial masks aloft, each Harlequin selecting a mask and shifting the colours of their *dathedi* to match it. In moments the Fire Mask was surrounded by flickering orange; the Mourning Mask by the gentle golden-green of sunrise over an orchard; the Hunter's Mask by the dusk-dark shades of the green moon that was Kurnous's totem; the Hero Mask by bright silver and gold.

And still more came, running swift-footed up the stairs or alighting from the shrouded air-sleds that took silent position at the building's edges. When Dheresh'mel walked down the curved prow of her air-sled and stepped smoothly onto the roof, Sheagoresh rose and stepped back, muting his colours to yield to her. For many journeys Dheresh'mel had danced in the footsteps of Eldanesh, finding ways in every pageant they played, every war they fought, to interpret another telling of his story. But she had learned Eldanesh's sagas from Ytheommel, the Great Harlequin of her old troupe whom the green beasts had laid low under the forest-spires of Toiryll, and whose name-element she had taken to carry his story on. Since that war her spirit had darkened. Her performances had become rougher, tinctured with anger. It had only been at their last resting that she had come to Sheagoresh and formally relinquished the Hero's Mask. Now it was time to step into a new role, and cast her life-story through a new perspective.

Sheagoresh bowed as she walked forwards, silently, already moving as though she were in armour, and reached down to Crussman's corpse. She straightened again holding the Blood Mask, the snarling face of Kaela Mensha Khaine, the Bloody-Handed God, lord of murder, whose wars had raged across heaven, slaying Eldanesh and binding the crippled and beaten Vaul to his anvil. There was silence and stillness as she carried the mask away. The mythic roles would pass around the troupe at every performance, but always there was one to lead and define them, and a new heart in the portrayal of Khaine would mean changes.

Sheagoresh looked over to the gantry base, to where Jann had been standing, at the one who was closer to him than any lover or sister could be. Ythoelle did not pick up the mask for herself: as the troupe's Shadow Seer she wore the Mirror Mask, and would until her dying moments. But as he walked to her and past her he saw that she had taken up the Moon Mask from where the last of the thieving vermin had dropped it, the face of Lileath, the maiden-goddess, dreamer and prophetess, whose symbols were the white moon, the staff, the closed circle, the wind-chime. Her hood was forwards again; as he walked past he could see the Mirror Mask fading into and out of many faces. At least one of them, he knew, would be his own.

There was no one to wear the Moon Mask, not yet. Abhoraan, who had danced the part since she had first joined the troupe so many years ago on the dragon-steppes, had been one of the ones who had died when their air-sled could not outrun the storm.

Soon they would perform the elegy for Abhoraan and her companions, and it would fall to Sheagoresh to decide what form that would take, what performance, what elements of the great myths they would draw on to take this tragedy and weave into the fabric of their living stories, to give it meaning and closure. It was a task he did not expect to enjoy, but every tale had its songs of mourning as well as its dances of triumph, and the tale that was his life was no exception.

Shapes moved around him. His Harlequins bounded and swung up through the scaffold to the wreck of the air-sled, ready to free it so it could be carried with them when he gave the signal. Their colours and faces danced, each reflecting a role that the Harlequin felt it right to play at this task and at this stage in their own life narratives. He lifted his arm for silence and their forms stilled, their colours muted.

The last sealed compartment flowered open at his touch and he gave voice to a low, resonant song, a single sustained note from deep in his chest. Those around him took up the song and flared their colours in salute as he took out the Sun Mask, the face of Asuryan, the Phoenix King, Monarch of Heaven, the teacher of the six great Phoenix Lords. Sheagoresh took it, held it in both hands, stepped slowly back off the gantry. His flip belt engaged with a thought and he felt the shift as his weight all but vanished: he stretched out and turned as he fell, always keeping the mask above him, and touched down feather-light on the rockcrete pad, one knee bent, head bowed but shoulders square and proud, both paying fealty to the mask and claiming ownership of it.

He stayed there, muted his colours down and made his own face blank. There was only one mask left to collect.

All around him, the others knelt. Colours shut off into black and greys and faces became featureless. A jetbike, the bare off-grey of wraithbone given form but no colour, adorned only with a black swathe wrapping its tail vane, coasted to a silent halt in the middle of the landing pad and Sheyl'emmen stepped down from it.

Her face was in shadow, like Ythoelle's, but unlike Ythoelle she made no move to shift her stiff, flaring hood. Hair cascaded from it, void-black and marble-white, and white silver chains twined around her hands and hung jingling from each fingertip. Vanes of wraithbone jutting from her shoulders caught the wind; at the sound of that moaning whistle every Harlequin shuddered and closed their eyes.

Sheyl'emmen did not look at any of them. Her step was steady and her sombre expression did not change. She walked with the careful stillness of a prisoner walking towards the scaffold. At the gantry she lengthened her step into a bound, and with her belt taking her weight away she sailed smoothly to stand on a crossbar before the ripped-open pannier. The other Harlequins turned in place to present their backs to her as she reached in and plucked out the mask that the last mon'keigh had glimpsed.

The mask did not glower or snarl, it had no artful changes to its scale or features. It was the face of an eldar, classic, genderless. There was no expression in the eyes, no set to the mouth. It was a blank face, blanker than the featureless grey hoods the Harlequins had taken on around it. It was a face that could place itself over any nightmare the beholding eye could imagine.

Sheyl'emmen the Solitaire picked up the Hell Mask and, like Sheagoresh before her, leapt off the platform, spreading her cloak out to cast its dread shadow into the heart of every eldar on the platform. She landed opposite the Great Harlequin and the two of them stepped and danced and spun together, neither visibly acknowledging the other. When a half-circle was complete and each stood where the other had a moment ago, they raised their masks in precise unison and donned them. Sun Mask, Hell Mask, Asuryan and Slaanesh, the two faces that the grubbing vermin had not soiled with their touch.

Then, shadow-fleet, Sheyl'emmen was gone: astride her jetbike with a single leap, then arrowing across the platform and away through the night, the vanes on her back shrieking in the slipstream. Sheagoresh leapt into the air then, head back, throwing his arms wide. Light came, a beautiful blaze from the Sun Mask driving back the night, bringing the Harlequins' colours to joyous life as they capered and danced.

In that moment, each feature-shifting holographic face became the mask they all wore beneath every other, the Harlequin Mask, Cegorach the Laughing God, trickster and knower of secrets. Every face was different, as every Harlequin's imagining of the leader of their great dance was different, but as Cegorach's features burst onto each of their faces every Harlequin burst into laughter. Some gave the coarse guffaws of an oaf who has seen a clumsy joke, some the elegant trill of a princess admiring the tumbling of her jester. There was the joyous laughter of tragedy from which a traveller has returned, and the wrenching laughter that casts a cloak of merriment over direst grief. Air-sleds and jetbikes left their holding positions and made interweaving circles, bright and laughing figures leaping up to catch hold and ride them, their colours leaving bright and shimmering mosaic-trails.

The laughter pealed out from the top of the tower like bells, and hung in the air behind the line of jetbikes and air-sleds like the wake of a boat. Deep in the wasteland beyond where the mon-keigh travelled they would slip into the webway, and soon they would be breathing the fragrant air of a maiden world, rich with spices and flower-perfumes, dancing in warm water across delicate coral sand while the waves chuckled in amongst the roots of the mangrove towers and the moons danced and pinwheeled overhead.

They would mourn their dead, and re-enact the greatest of their myths: the Dream of Lileath, the Veil of Isha, the War in Heaven, the Doom of Eldanesh, the Fall. With the tale-telling they would reconsecrate their precious ritual masks, the heart of the troupe, and then they would roam again, roam up from the coral oceans to the great sighing seas of grass. They would find the camps of their cousins and steal in amongst their tents and tethered dragons, dazzling and bemusing them with shadow and laughter, and then they would make themselves known, step into the light, and dance for them. Perhaps they would tell one of the great stories, perhaps they would tell one of the lesser, perhaps one of the younger stories of the Devourer or the bestial wars about the great Gate.

Or perhaps they would dance a newer story still. A story of strays and travellers, forced by the decay of their old paths to leave the safety of their webway and make quick and secret passage across a world of crackling dunes and bloody, moonless skies. A story of a monstrous storm that not even these swift travellers could outrun. A story of the search for what the storm had taken from them, something more precious to them than the features of their own faces. A story of ugly, upstart animals who had meddled with something they should never have seen, a story of insolence punished, thievery justly rewarded, desecration turned back on itself. A story of how the great tales would try to play themselves out even through such lumpen mockeries of minds.

That was the power of the tales. That was the power of the masks. It was a story Sheagoresh had never imagined when he left his old troupe and wrought a new cast of great masks to form the core of a new one, but now they had lived it, the story was part of theirs, to tell and reinterpret and dance for themselves and for others all down the coming years.

The wind picked up, dust-cloud and nightfall drew curtains across the desert. Dull emergency lights glowed in the tower corridors, control telltales sparkled on the operations deck, a vox-alarm squawked unanswered. Nothing moved, and Pipeline Maintenance Depot 347-South-East was swallowed by the desert night.

BENEATH THE FLESH

Andy Smillie

'I am His vengeance as He is my shield. I will deliver death to His enemies as He brings deliverance to my soul.'

Noise filled his world. An incessant thrum reverberated under his feet. The metal and ceramite around him squealed as angry thrusters were pushed to their tolerance. Bolts and arc-welded plates rattled as their construction was tested. A thunderous staccato of impacts rang like bolter fire against the hull around him. Yet in his mind, there was only silence: a sanctifying stillness, in preparation for battle. He would not be distracted from the consecration, his weapons would be ready.

'Brother Maion, ready yourself.'

Maion lifted his head at his sergeant's command and touched the blade of his chainsword to his temple, finishing the rite. He sheathed his weapon, and pulled the combat harness over his head, activating the mag-lock. 'Ready, brother-sergeant.'

The Stormraven gunship powered through the void, its crimson hull charred and pitted from hundreds of recent atmospheric entries. The serrated black symbol on the gunship's wing was almost indistinguishable from the scorch marks emblazoned on its flanks, eroded by the vengeful impacts of dense minerals and debris clusters. Flames licked the Stormraven's surface, tracing a searing thread along its squat outline. It dived lower, pushing into Arere's embrace.

The planet's twin arid continents were turning from the system's single sun. Had any of Arere's citizens still been alive to gaze skyward, they would have marvelled at the descending gunship. The brightest light in the sky, Arere's dead populace would have mistaken the Stormraven for yet another meteor, destined to crash into the desert-earth and forever change the maze of ravines punctuating the landscape.

++Entry achieved++ The pilot-serf's mechanical voice crackled across the vox-link.

Maion juddered in his harness as the gunship knifed downwards, turbulent crosswinds breaking against the hull. Next to him, Harahel sat immobile, a massive eviscerator held across his lap. Maion smiled; it was a fitting weapon. Harahel was from Taci, a province of their homeworld Cretacia. The region was well known for the broad, well muscled and aggressive individuals it bred, traits further amplified when they underwent the physiological enhancements required to transform them into Space Marines. Brother Amaru had replaced Harahel's harness with one normally used to secure warriors in Terminator armour, in order to accommodate the Assault Marine's bulk.

'Bring up the tactical hololith.' Sergeant Barbelo was on his feet, clasping an overhead assault-rail with a gauntleted hand. His face and shaven head were a mess of re-grafted skin and thick, serpentine scars.

'A moment, brother.' Amaru extended a bundle of data cables from his armoured-forearm and plugged them into a control slot in his seat. The Techmarine muttered something to the gunship's machine-spirit and closed his left eye. The glowing bionic that replaced his right continued to shine like a targeting reticule.

The compartment's luminators dimmed as a three-dimensional overview of Arere's primary continent appeared in the middle of the deck, the blue-hued landscape hololithically projected by an optical lens mounted in the ceiling. With a thought, Amaru narrowed the focus on a line of canyons towards the north-east. A series of fortified buildings resolved out of the map.

'Substation 12BX sits between the two walls of this canyon.' The area changed colour to a deep crimson as Amaru continued, 'The approach to the main entrance is overshadowed by a narrow gorge and high spires, landing improbable.' The Techmarine paused as he calculated an approach. 'We can land here.' Amaru manipulated the image again and an octagonal courtyard sprang into view.

'What of the enemy?' Barbelo's brow furrowed as his thoughts turned to battle, turning the deep lines of his forehead into shadowy ravines.

The image oscillated and zoomed out, the substation receding into the distance to glow faintly among the canyons. 'We do not have real-time data but estimates would place enemy forces here.' Amaru indicated the black mass surrounding the substation, representing the disposition of the Archenemy army on Arere.

Maion stared at the display, his muscles tensing instinctively at the mention of the Archenemy. Their forces had dispersed from their landing zones like an aggressive cancer, brutalising their way across the globe. The outpost was the last bastion of sanctity.

'We have less than two hours until they reach the substation,' Amaru stated plainly.

'And if the worse has happened and our brothers are as we fear?' Maion voiced what he knew the others were thinking.

'That should be time enough to retrieve their gene-seed,' Nisroc touched his narthecium in emphasis. The Sanguinary Priest's gleaming white armour was in stark contrast to the deep crimson and black worn by Maion and the others.

Barbelo scowled. 'That is not our primary mission Apothecary. We must understand what happened on Arere, we must retrieve the compound's data files.'

Nisroc felt his jaw tighten. 'The Chapter is on the brink of extinction, recovering the gene-seed is paramount. I am bound by duty–'

'Brothers...' Amaru paused as one of the gunship's many auspexes drew his attention. 'We are closing on their augur range,' the Techmarine looked expectantly at Barbelo. 'We need to do it now.'

Barbelo glared at Nisroc. He knew as well as the Apothecary that the Chapter's supply of gene-seed was critical. But the data files held vital information. Without them, they risked losing the entire Itan sector to the Archenemy. 'They are our orders, and you will follow them.'

The Apothecary said nothing.

The sergeant took his seat and turned to Amaru. 'You are sure this will work, Techmarine?'

Amaru nodded, 'I sanctified this vessel myself. Its spirit is strong. It will not fail us.'

'Very well, relieve the pilot.'

The hololith stuttered and dissolved as Amaru disengaged his cables and assumed the cockpit.

'Prepare yourselves,' Barbelo activated the mag-lock on his harness and clamped his helmet down over his head.

'Emperor's strength be with us,' to his right, Nisroc locked his own helm in place.

'Emperor's strength,' Maion joined the rest of the squad as they repeated the Apothecary's words and donned their helmets. He felt his pulse quicken as hissing pressure seals locked his helmet to his armour, readying him for war.

'It is done,' Amaru moved at pace, taking his seat next to Barbelo. 'The machine-spirit has us now.'

The gunship fell.

Amber warning lights lit up across the craft's interior as the gunship surrendered to gravity. Maion was driven into his harness by the force of the descent, the metal bars gouging into the ceramite of his battle-plate as the gunship plummeted towards the earth. The reassuring rumble of the gunship's engines was replaced by the frantic chiming of the altitude counter that counted down to their doom. 'Ave Emperor, stand with me and I shall not fail in your sight,' Maion mouthed the prayer, banishing the thought that he was about to be crushed to death inside an armoured coffin. By the Emperor's grace, he would meet his end on the field of battle.

'Ten seconds,' Amaru's voice cut over the vox-link.

The Stormraven bucked violently as it fell. Even with the benefit of his Lyman's Ear and the myriad of other implants that were working to relieve the stress on his body, Maion struggled to stay conscious.

'Five.'

Maion redoubled his grip on the harness.

'Brace!'

The Stormraven's thrusters fired on full burn, exploding downwards in a hail of fury as they fought to arrest the gunship's descent. Their tumultuous roar drowned out the angry hum of warning runes and the whining collision siren. For the briefest of instants the world was silent and Maion was no longer falling.

A heartbeat later and the world was enveloped in noise. The Stormraven slammed into the earth, and Maion winced as he was driven up into his harness. The hull squealed in protest as fractures stabbed across its outer armour. The landing supports shattered, their metal struts fracturing on impact. Armoured glass broke from the cockpit and flooded into the compartment as dislodged rock hammered it. The gunship ploughed forwards, tearing a dark trench in the earth until its momentum was spent.

'Egress!' Barbelo was on his feet and out of his harness before the hull had stopped shaking, slamming his fist into the door release and motioning for the others to disembark.

The assault ramp lowered part of the way and stalled, its hydraulics spitting oleaginous fluid. Harahel barrelled forward, throwing himself at the stricken ramp. It slammed down into the earth with a dull thud, tossing powdered dirt into the air as the giant Space Marine rolled to his feet.

Maion pushed the catch on his harness. Nothing happened. The locking mechanism was broken.

'Sit back, brother.' Micos flicked the activation switch on his chainaxe and the weapon roared into life. He freed Maion with a casual downward stroke, his weapon's adamantium teeth making light work of the harness.

'You have my thanks, brother.' Maion unsheathed his blade and followed Micos down the ramp.

Outside, beneath Arere's starless sky, it was pitch dark and the elements conspired to impair visibility. Howling winds tossed grit and earth into a storm. Torrential rain fell in near vertical sheets. Neither fact mattered to Maion. His helmet's ocular sensors filtered and illuminated the darkness, allowing him to see as clear as day.

Reams of tactical and situational data scrolled across his right eye, assimilated by his eidetic memory. The atmosphere was breathable. The Stormraven's engines were cooling and unlikely to combust. His left pauldron had sustained mild damage during the landing but the servos were working within normal ranges. The squad had formed a perimeter around the stricken Stormraven. Their ident-tags and vitals hovered on the peripheral of Maion's retinal display.

'Stay alert! We may not be alone.' Barbelo's voice crackled over the vox-link.

Maion panned his bolt pistol around, scanning for targets. The outpost's walls towered over them from all sides. He glanced at them briefly and a new set of data drifted over his helmet's display. The base was designate Arere Primus. Its walls were an adamantium and ceramite compound, capable of withstanding a full-scale bombardment.

'Stay in close formation, the storm is restricting comms,' Barbelo's annoyance was evident in his tone. 'Amaru, can we extract in the Stormraven?'

'Undetermined. I'll need time to assess,' the Techmarine's reply rasped in Maion's ear.

'Atoc, secure the Stormraven while Amaru works.'

'Harahel,' Barbelo abandoned the hissing comm-feed. 'Lead us into the strategium.'

The towering warrior grunted in affirmation and sprinted towards the metres-thick blast door that sealed off the compound's command and control centre.

Harahel ran a gauntlet hand over the access panel, wiping away the dirt.

++Internal Protocol Active++

A command rubric blinked through a veneer of rapidly settling dust.

++Terminal Sealed++

The words blinked at Harahel. Harahel snarled and smashed his fist into the screen. 'Brother-sergeant, the door has been locked from the inside.'

'There are melta-charges and cutting equipment in the armoury,' Maion recalled the information he'd assimilated during the briefing.

'Apothecary, you and Micos cover our rear,' Barbelo thumbed the power slide on his plasma pistol. 'No one comes out of those doors. Maion, Harahel, follow me.'

The doors to the armoury unlocked with a hiss of pressurised gas. The toothed slabs slid apart and disappeared into the recess of the armoured frame. Maion followed Barbelo in, sweeping left as Harahel moved right. Maion grimaced as his helmet worked to filter out the putrid air. Evidence of battle was everywhere. Broken luminators stuttered in the ceiling, throwing jagged patches of light around the entrance chamber.

Fist-sized holes studded the walls. Sparks cascaded from exposed cabling that hung in thick bunches. The metal of the floor was scorched and charred. Webs of blood and viscera clung to everything.

'No bodies.' Harahel voiced what Maion had been thinking.

'The dead are not our concern. Keep your eyes open for the living.' Barbelo aimed his plasma pistol towards the adjoining corridor and advanced to the rear of the room.

Maion nodded. According to the schematics, the passageway extended half a kilometre before a set of stairs would lead them down to the armoury proper. 'Ideal place for an ambush,' Maion said as he stared into the darkness of the passageway. 'Luminators are out.'

'Harahel, maintain position and assume overwatch.'

'As you wish,' Harahel hid his displeasure poorly. Though he knew the sergeant was right – they'd be forced to advance down the corridor shoulder to shoulder; there'd be no room to wield his eviscerator.

Maion advanced into the darkness.

Harahel stood immobile, panning his gaze around the chamber. He could hear Maion's footsteps as he moved down the corridor; the other Flesh Tearer was halfway to the stairs, the fizz of the electrical cables as they spat in their death throes… and the shifting of metal – Harahel pivoted left as a grenade hit the ground. His ocular sensors dimmed, shielding his eyes from the piercing flash that flooded the chamber. With a dense clatter, a half-dozen of the ceiling grilles fell to the ground. A cluster of figures in sodden fatigues dropped down after them and opened fire.

'Contact!' Harahel shouted into the vox even as a hail of las-fire pattered off his armour.

'How many?' Barbelo turned his head as the sporadic flash of weapons fire lit up the corridor behind him.

'Contact front,' Maion swung his bolt pistol up, advancing and firing as las-fire erupted from further along the corridor.

'Micos,' Barbelo summoned the other Flesh Tearer as he opened fire, following Maion into the enemy ahead, 'Assist Harahel.' The sergeant didn't wait for affirmation, deactivating his comm-link. He wanted no distractions; he wanted to be in the moment, to relish the kill.

Harahel's attackers bore the Imperial eagle on their filth-encrusted chests. Traitors, he growled, grinding his teeth as a las-round struck his helm. Harahel clasped his eviscerator with both hands, twisting the handle to activate the power core. The weapon's giant blade snarled into life, a physical manifestation of the rage churning through his veins. He ran at the traitors, heedless of the beads of las-fire that stung his armour.

Harahel grinned; the traitors were holding their ground. He tore the first of them apart with a savage upward swing that cut the man in half from groin to shoulder. Pivoting as the two halves of the man's torso hit the ground, Harahel bisected another from hip bone to ribcage. A third died as he finished the move, chopping the eviscerator down through the man's head and dragging it out through his ribs.

Maion counted fifteen muzzle flashes. The traitors had ambushed them with woefully inadequate numbers. The cowards were nestled behind some overturned supply crates and sheets of metal they'd dragged up from the floor. Maion stitched a line across the barricade with his bolt pistol. His enhanced hearing registered the changing sound as the mass reactive rounds hammered into metal and blew apart flesh. Twelve muzzle flashes. To his left, Barbelo's pistol hissed as it discharged, sending a flickering plasma round down the corridor. The barricade exploded in a blue flash as Barbelo's shot struck home. Men screamed as superheated shrapnel perforated their bodies. Others were luckier, dying instantly as the round liquefied them. Maion knew that underneath his helmet, Barbelo was smiling. A dishevelled traitor stumbled over the corpse of his comrade, toppling onto the wrong side of the cordon. He struggled on all fours, scrabbling for a weapon. Maion shot him in the head.

Bathed in blood-spatter and faced with an opponent whose armour bore their comrade's eviscerated innards, the traitors fell back. One held his ground, staring wide-eyed at Harahel as he pulled a clutch of grenades from a harness. Harahel decapitated the man as he advanced on the others. The grenades fell from the headless corpse's fingers. A cloud of flame and shrapnel washed over Harahel's battleplate as they detonated. A slew of warnings lit up on the Flesh Tearer's retinal display. Harahel blinked them away; his armour's integrity was intact.

Ahead of him, the traitors had rallied behind a pillar. He could see the fear on their gaunt faces as he emerged unscathed from the billowing fire. Harahel heard the distinctive click of las power packs locking into place. It was insulting they thought the pillar offered any protection from his wrath. The huge Flesh Tearer growled, the metallic resonance of his helmet's audio amplifier lending the sound a bestial quality. The stench of ammonia wafted on the air. He smiled, one of the traitors had pissed himself.

Harahel rushed them. He leapt the last few yards, swinging his eviscerator through the pillar as he landed. The blade showered him in sparks and pulped organs as it chewed through the metal of the column and into the bodies of the two traitors closest to it. The men died screaming, flesh ripped from their bones and tossed into the air by the churning, adamantium teeth. Harahel ripped the weapon free, maiming another traitor as he drew the blade back to the guard position.

A scarred traitor screamed at him, lunging at him with a bayonet. Harahel sidestepped the attack and backhanded the man across his face, smashing his skull and sending chunks of his teeth spearing into the face of a heavy-set warrior who was fumbling with the activation stud of a shock maul. The man cried out in pain, dropping his weapon and clutching his ragged face. Harahel clamped his hand over the man's head and squeezed, crushing his skull.

'Cowards,' he snarled, throwing the twitching body into the press of traitors as they scrambled away.

Five muzzle flashes winked at Maion from behind the barricade. The disorientated traitors' shots flew wide. He sighted on the nearest of them.

'Save your ammo,' Barbelo held his arm out blocking the shot. 'We are almost upon them,' he growled as a las-round ricocheted off of his rerebrace. 'Sanguinius!' Barbelo broke into a run, enraged by the pitiful attempts to kill him.

Maion stopped firing. Barbelo was lost for the moment, lost to a part of the rage they all shared. Chainsword roaring, he followed the sergeant into the press of traitors.

Barbelo dived over the barricade to land on top of a blood-caked traitor. Ribs broke under the impact, splintering into internal organs with a crunch. Barbelo drove his knee into the man's face as he rose, crushing the traitor's skull into the deck.

Maion went straight through the barricade, chopping his chainsword down through a scorched supply crate before reversing the motion and eviscerating the traitor that was using it for cover. Blood and viscera splashed across his helmet. His ocular sensors adjusted, allowing him to see through the flesh-mire. To his right, a stick-thin traitor turned to run. Maion threw his combat knife. The blade shot pierced the traitor's back and went through his chest. The man pitched forward as the blade clattered to the floor. Maion grinned ferally. He turned, searching for someone to kill but Barbelo had beaten him to it. The sergeant punched his fist through a screaming man's chest before stamping his boot down on the head of another, pulping it. Maion retrieved his knife as Barbelo stalked past him towards the armoury chamber, vines of intestine and bloody matter hanging from his gauntlet.

Nisroc listened to the exchange of weapons fire over the open vox-channel. With each broken retort he became more envious of his brothers. To be a Flesh Tearers was to be at the vanguard of the assault, to be elbow-deep in the enemy's bloody remains, not holding the rear like some Imperial Fist strategist. His muscles swelled with blood and adrenaline as his body willed him to engage the enemy. Targeting reticules swam over his display as his helmet translated his mind's unconscious need to fight. 'Reclothe my mind, that it may temper the needs of my soul,' Nisroc took a calming breath. Ascertain why Brother-Sergeant Paschar had not answered the summons to exfiltrate Arere. Locate and secure the squad or retrieve their gene-seed. Rendezvous with the fleet. Nisroc ran through the mission objectives, focussing his thoughts. He could not afford to lose control, too many had been lost to The Rage persecuting the campaign already. He cast a fleeting glance up towards the barren sky; there was something about this sector of space that left him ill at ease, something malevolent that hung in the darkness where the stars should be. Nisroc bit down another burst of adrenaline, he would not allow himself to succumb to The Thirst. He was a Sanguinary Priest, duty demanded he control his rage. Too be lost in the throes of battle was to lose sight of the future. He lived to maintain the gene-seed and through it the Chapter. For without that precious link to their progenitor father, the Flesh Tearers had no future. 'For the Chapter,' Nisroc exhaled, emptying the last of the tension from his body – battle would find him soon enough.

Barbelo entered the armoury. Maion was about to follow but stopped as weapons fire erupted from within.

A noise like the birth of thunder filled the corridor as a heavy weapon roared. The sergeant jerked backwards as high-calibre rounds slammed into his armour, pitting the ceramite. His own shot went wide as a round clipped his gauntlet, the plasma blast scorching the ceiling. Barbelo dropped his chin and raised his shoulder as another torrent of rounds hammered him. Even as his pauldron cracked, the icon of the Chapter blasted from his shoulder in a shower of splintered ceramite, the sergeant took a step forward.

Maion recognised the harsh bark of an autocannon as the traitors poured fire onto Barbelo – the sergeant's armour would not hold. Maion lunged forward, tossed a frag grenade into the room, grabbed Barbelo's gorget, and pulled him back into the corridor.

'You dare!' The sergeant snarled at Maion, back-fisting him across the helm.

Maion staggered cursing. With disciplined restraint he quashed the rage boiling up inside him. 'Calm yourself brother. To proceed would have been folly.' Maion kept his voice level, but lifted his gaze to stare Barbelo in the eyes. He steeled his jaw, ready to receive another blow. But Barbelo's posture shifted, and Maion relaxed as the sergeant regained control of his emotions. The traitors continued to fire, their shots spitting into the corridor to impact on the wall opposite.

'You waste your time, brother,' Barbelo motioned towards the doorway as more rounds zipped into the corridor. 'They are entrenched behind a barrier. Your grenade will have done little more than chip the–'

Maion held up his hand, the firing had stopped. His enhanced hearing had heard the bark of every round as they tore from the autcannon's barrel. His eidetic memory had catalogued every shell casing that struck the ground. The weapon's magazine was still half full. The traitors weren't reloading, they were baiting them.

Barbelo knew it, too. Incensed by their obvious ploy, the sergeant took a step towards the doorway. Maion grabbed his vambrace.

'Brother...' Maion knew that behind the red lenses of his helmet, the sergeant's eyes were redder still, his pupils alight with rage. 'You will die.'

Harahel knelt among the corpses, blood dripping from his armour, his weapon humming on idle, and watched the last of the traitors run for the doorway. The cowards would not make it. Micos's ident-tag flashed on Harahel's helmet display as the other Flesh Tearer approached the entrance from outside. Harahel saw the pilot light of Micos's flamer as it shone in the gloom. Some of the traitors caught sight of the other Flesh Tearer and stopped running; they slumped to the ground in abject defeat. The others kept running, too lost in panic for rational thought. Harahel smelt their fear as Micos fired, blanketing the traitors in a sheet of burning promethium that washed away flesh and dissolved bone to ash. He watched them burn, frail wicks eaten up by a ravenous flame. The meek and the brave, they all died.

'Are you injured?' Micos asked Harahel over a closed channel. He knew his friend would not have wanted his condition shared with anyone save perhaps the Apothecary.

Harahel didn't respond, his gaze remained fixed on the dying embers of the traitors. His twin hearts hammered in his chest like the pistons of a giant engine, fuelled by the tang of spilt blood that filled his senses. A boiling darkness cloyed at his mind, threatening to overwhelm his restraint. He tore his helmet off and roared, driving his eviscerator into the armoured floor. Gripping the hilt with both hands, he rested his head on the blade and prayed, 'Emperor bless me with your temperament. Fill me with a righteousness inferno that I may burn away my bloodlust. Emperor keep me from the darkness of my soul.'

'Outer room pacified, proceeding to your position,' Micos's voice came through the comm-feed in Maion's helmet.

'The corridor is clear. Move to our position and assist,' Maion voxed Micos and turned to Barbelo, 'Micos is on his way.' The sergeant nodded, his comm-link still powered off.

The traitors' weapons had fallen silent as the two Flesh Tearers waited out of sight, their backs pressed against the wall of the corridor. But there was no peace for Maion. His pulse filled his head like the tribal drum his villagers used to attract the roaming karcasaur at High Feast. His hands trembled like the ground beneath the giant reptile as it loped through the jungle. Every genetically-enhanced cell in Maion's body wanted to rush into the room and tear the traitors limb from limb, to bask in their death throes and drink deep of their blood. Maion clenched his fist and struck the aquila sigil on his breast plate. 'What nourishes you also destroys you. Either conquer your gift or die,' Chaplain Appollus had spoken those words to Maion when he was but a noviciate. He focused on his battle gear as the Chaplain had taught him, testing the weight of his bolt pistol, the balance of his blade. Maion needed to be as they were: furious and unyielding in battle, cold and impassive in respite. He glanced at Barbelo. The sergeant would be struggling with his own blood-rage. Over his centuries of service, Barbelo had slain more enemies of the Throne than Maion and the rest of the squad had tallied between them. For Barbelo, the call to violence would be stronger, harder to deny. Maion considered what he would do if the sergeant gave in to his desires, if he–

'I stand ready brothers.' Micos's voice drew Maion's attention. The other Flesh Tearer glanced at Barbelo's smashed shoulder guard but knew better than to ask after his sergeant's wellbeing.

Barbelo nodded towards the doorway.

Maion thumbed the selector on his bolt pistol, switching it to full auto. He stuck the barrel of the weapon into the room and opened fire. A man cried out as the explosive rounds tore across the chamber.

Micos swung low, sending a stream of fire into the chamber. The burning promethium swarmed over the barricade to feast on the cowards behind it. The traitors screamed.

Barbelo dived into the room. Maion heard him snap off three shots and the hungry growl of his chainsword as it cut into bone.

'Armoury secure,' Barbelo's voice came over the comm-link a heartbeat later. 'Apothecary, join us at once.'

Nisroc bent over the Flesh Tearer's corpse. A gaping hole dominated the fallen Space Marine's scorched breastplate. The flesh around it was fused with armour, a dark stain billowing out from the wound like a web. 'Melta weapon or fusion-based explosive,' Nisroc spoke for the benefit of his helmet's data recorder, documenting his findings. 'The high level of penetration suggests close range detonation.' Nisroc extended a needle-like probe from his narthecium and stabbed it into the wound. Brother Haamiah, Second Company. Lines of biometric and biological data scrolled across Nisroc's helmet display as the probe analysed the Flesh Tearer's blood. There were traces of human flesh too, melded to Haamiah's; a traitor had given their life to plant the charge.

'Maion, if you would,' Nisroc stood to give the other Flesh Tearer space.

'My honour, brother,' Maion nodded and knelt next to Haamiah's body. Maion was the closest thing the squad had to a Chaplain. He had studied under the revered Appollus. Most of the Chapter had expected Maion to follow in the High Chaplain's footsteps. But he could not, not yet. He wasn't ready to accept that the Flesh Tearers were beyond saving. Maion bowed his head, 'Emperor, your servant's duty is at an end. Grant him peace.' Maion made the sign of the aquila over his breastplate and rose. 'I'll wait for you in the corridor.'

Nisroc paused a moment. Of all the duties that were his to complete, this was the most important, the heaviest burden to bear. Only in death does duty end, the axiom may have been true for the soldiers of the Imperial Guard or the Sisters of the Adeptus Sororitas but not for a son of Sanguinius. In death, a Space Marine had one more thing to give. The transformative Progenoids implanted in his body had to be returned to the Chapter, ready to be received by the next generation of aspirants. Only through the harvesting of the glands would the Flesh Tearers continue to survive. Without the precious gene-seed they would be unable to stand against the Emperor's foes.

The Apothecary extended his reductor and punched the bladed tube into Haamiah's neck. A jolt of energy rippled along the blade's length as the moulded end closed around the first progenoid gland. With a wet hiss, the gland was sucked up through the blade into the narthecium. A green icon blinked in the corner of Nisroc's helmet display. The gland had been recovered safely, and was being frozen for transport to the gene-banks on the Flesh Tearers home world. Nisroc activated his bone-drill; the second gland was harder to reach.

It had taken over thirty minutes to cut through the mag-seals on the strategium's door and a further ten to fasten melta-charges to the piston hinges. Amaru had abandoned repairs on the Stormraven to oversee the work, directing Harahel as he wielded the industrial laser-cutter with the same ease the others handled their bolters.

'Ready to detonate, brother-sergeant.' Amaru turned his back on the huge door and paced back towards the Stormraven. The Chaos forces were under an hour away and he still had much work to do.

'Prepare yourselves,' Barbelo's order hissed in Maion's ear as the storm continued to hamper vox communication. He checked the ammo-counter on his bolt pistol and activated his chainsword, its roar inaudible over the wind. To his left and right, his brothers were preparing their own wargear. Micos's flamer hung by his side, its pilot flame would remain extinguished until they were inside. Maion shifted his weight to the balls of his feet, moving his weight forward.

'Go!' On Barbelo's command Amaru blew the charges.

The hinges detonated in rapid succession, like the quickening heartbeat of a colossal beast. The door fell from its housing, slamming into the earth an inch from Barbelo and his squad. Under his helmet, Amaru's mouth twitched in an approximation of a smile. His calculations had been perfect.

Maion was in motion before the doors had settled in the dirt. Adrenaline flooded his system as he powered into the strategium's entrance chamber. A warning rune filled his helmet display. 'Defence turrets.'

Maion's warning came too late. Two automated weapons burst into life, pumping a stream of high-explosive rounds towards the Flesh Tearers.

'Cover!' Barbelo shouted the order even as he realised there was none. Whoever was cowering in the strategium had been waiting for them.

Maion winced, dropping to one knee as a round clipped his thigh. Barbelo threw himself into a roll as the weapons stitched a line towards him. Nisroc spun on the spot, turning his back to shield the gene-seed stored in his narthecium. Explosive rounds slammed into his backpack, knocking him to the floor. Micos's world went dark as a round tore through his pauldron and broke against his helmet. Atoc bucked, dropping his bolter as his breastplate was pulverised by a fusillade of explosions.

Harahel ground his teeth as Atoc's ident-tag disappeared from his peripheral display. 'Forgive me, brother,' He swung his eviscerator over his shoulder, mag-locking it to his back, and picked up Atoc's body. 'For the Chapter!' Harahel raised the corpse-shield in front of him and ran flat out toward the guns. Anger drove him on as merciless shells hammered into Atoc's corpse, the weapons ignoring the other Flesh Tearers to focus on the immediate threat of Harahel. Atoc's armour broke like glass under the relentless assault, the dead Flesh Tearer's head spinning from his body as his legs and arms were pulped.

Harahel roared as he closed inside both turrets' sensor range. Dropping the stump of Atoc's corpse, he swung his eviscerator round to shear the barrel off the nearest weapon. The gun exploded as the round in its chamber detonated. Harahel ignored the hail of shrapnel that cascaded over his armour, oblivious to the pain warnings blinking over his left eye. Cursing, he brought his blade down on the other gun, cutting through its ammo feed. The weapon continued to fire, making a tortured grinding noise as it cried out for ammunition. Harahel kicked it over, stamping on it until he'd flattened the firing chamber. 'Weapons neutralised.'

Maion was on his feet, advancing with Barbelo towards Harahel and the stairwell that led to the inner sanctum.

Nisroc pushed himself up off the deck. A damage alert scrolled across his display. The shots to his backpack had damaged his armour's power source. He checked the output. It would last an hour, two at best. 'Micos?' Nisroc's vox went unanswered. He turned to the other Flesh Tearer.

'I am fine, Apothecary,' Micos snarled, throwing his ruined helmet across the chamber. 'A flesh wound.'

The Apothecary cast his gaze over Micos. A blackened hole sat where his right eye should have been and his face was a mess of dark scabs. 'As you say, brother.' Nisroc switched to his vox, 'Orders, brother-sergeant?'

'We advance on the inner sanctum. Secure the level beneath.'

Lasgun fire stabbed at Maion as he crossed the threshold into the command sanctum and peeled left. He raised his bolt pistol and shot two traitors in the chest. Their bodies snapped backwards, covering diode-encrusted consoles in blood and viscera. A third traitor opened fire, a bolter bucking in his hands and destroying a bank of data-screens as he struggled to adjust for the recoil. 'The Emperor's tools serve only his servants,' Maion pumped two rounds into the man, plastering his innards across the wall.

Harahel entered behind Maion and moved right. Three men blocked his path. He shouldered them aside, decapitating two with a single stroke of his blade, and killing the third with a thunderous head-butt. Ahead, a panicked traitor struggled with a grenade launcher. Harahel tore the skull from the nearest corpse and threw it at the man. The macabre projectile shot into the traitor's chest, cracked his sternum and stopped his heart.

Barbelo was the last to advance into the chamber. He moved straight forwards, sighting a traitor in a heavy overcoat wielding a plasma pistol. The man fired. The sergeant dropped his shoulder to avoid the shot. The plasma round burnt through the air to melt the wall where his head had been an instant before.

The man fired again. 'In the name of–'

Barbelo, dodged left and fired, his round vaporising the man's head and shoulders before the traitor could finish his sentence. 'We will not hear the name of your heathen god, heretic,' Barbelo fired again; his plasma round obliterating what remained of the treacherous commissar's corpse in a crackle of blue energy. 'Sanctum secure. Nisroc, status?'

'They were keeping their wounded down here,' Maion heard Nisroc's report as it came over the comm-feed. 'Resistance was minimal. Lower chambers cleansed.'

Nisroc entered the inner sanctum to find Amaru poring over the main data console. The Techmarine had nano-wires and connective fibres plugged into every available data jack.

'Brother Atoc?' Barbelo had his back to the door and spoke without turning around, his gaze fixed on a wall-mounted viewer.

'His duty is at an end.' Nisroc touched a hand to his narthecium. 'His gene-seed survives. His death served its purpose.'

Barbelo turned to face the Apothecary, pausing before he spoke. 'And his body?'

'His–' Nisroc faltered. Bodies, where were the bodies?

'Micos,' the other Flesh Tearer snapped his shoulders back at the sergeant's summons. 'Return Atoc's corpse to the Stormraven, his weapon too.'

'Bodies,' the word tumbled from Nisroc's lips.

'What is it, Apothecary?' the grille mouthpiece of Barbelo's helmet did little to filter his annoyance.

Nisroc cast his gaze around the chamber. Harahel's armour was pitted and scared. Maion's cuisse was fractured. The dismembered bodies of traitors were strewn around the floor, a madman's mosaic. 'Where are the other bodies?' Nisroc repeated the question straining at his mind.

'What?'

'There were ten of our brothers stationed here. We have found only one, Brother Haamiah. Where are the others? There was no trace of them on the lower levels or here in the sanctum. They must be somewhere.'

'I agree with you brother, it is an oddity. But we do not have the time,' Barbelo turned back to the monitor, 'the enemy advances from all sides. Their vanguard will contact us in thirty-eight minutes.'

'Then we must make the time. We must find them. We must retrieve their gene-seed and honour their deaths.'

'And what if they are not here? What if they are as ash, carried from here by the blasted storm?'

Barbelo's tone brooked no discussion but Nisroc persisted. 'Then we shall mourn their loss and the loss of their gift. But we must first check everywhere. We must be sure.'

Barbelo turned to face Nisroc, his poise threatening. 'The enemy outnumbers us thousands to one.'

Nisroc moved towards Barbelo. 'Death means nothing as long as the gene-seed survives.'

'And who will collect our gene-seed when we lie dead beneath the starless sky of this world?'

'We must–'

'No!' Barbelo pressed his forehead against Nisroc's. 'Amaru has affected repairs on the Stormraven. Once we acquire the data from the base's cogitators we are leaving. You have until then.'

'Very well,' Nisroc took a step back and made to turn away. 'But know that I shall take no pleasure in reporting our mission as a failure to the High Priests.'

Barbelo snarled. Never had he failed his Chapter. His grip tightened on his chainsword. He should gut Nisroc. Stain the Apothecary's white breastplate crimson with his own sanctimonious blood. Out of his peripheral vision he saw Maion and Harahel edge closer. The other Flesh Tearers had remained silent but Barbelo doubted they would stand by and watch him kill the Apothecary. A warning shone on his display as he threatened to crush the chainsword's handle. He fought to bring his rage under control. Now was not the time. 'Go then. Look for the others. We will do what we must.'

Nisroc dipped his head, 'Thank you, brother.'

Barbelo growled, 'Do not push me, Apothecary.' His voice was void cold. 'Harahel...' The sergeant drew his gaze from Nisroc in an effort to calm himself. 'Go with him.'

Harahel walked silently beside Nisroc as they approached the chapel annex. It was the only spine of the compound the Flesh Tearers had yet to explore. If any evidence of Haamiah's squad remained then it had to be there. The chrono display in Harahel's helmet clicked down to thirty. He turned it off, uncaring as to whether they made it off Arere before the Chaos advance struck. It didn't matter if he fought here or redeployed to another world, as long as he fought, as long as he killed. Blood, the thought rolled into his mind like an invading army. Saliva began to build in his mouth, his nostrils flaring as they searched for arterial juices. Blood, Harahel hungered for blood.

'We are here,' Nisroc's voice crackled in Harahel's ear breaking his stupor.

Harahel blinked hard, clearing the fog from his senses.

'Is something the matter?'

'No, I am fine,' Harahel unlatched the eviscerator from his back.

'Wait,' Nisroc held up his hand. Stepping ahead of Harahel, he moved to the chapel door's access panel and removed one of his gauntlets. He wiped the grime from the console and pressed his palm onto the biometric scanner. The ancient machine chimed green as it recognised Nisroc's genetic code as that of a Space Marine. With a pressurised hiss, the arched doors to the annex swung inwards.

Harahel grunted and followed the Apothecary inside.

'The enemy will contact us here first,' Barbelo spoke as a hololithic representation of the compound rotated in the air between him and Maion.

'I would have thought here a more likely target,' Maion gestured to the curving walls that formed the east side of the central courtyard.

'No, they will expect that area to be mined; more than a handful of detonations would bring the rock face down on top of them.' Barbelo pointed to the compound's main entrance way. 'They will attack from here.'

Maion studied the hololith, the sergeant was right. Had the base been fully manned, then attacking down the wide avenues of the main corridors would have been suicide. Under current circumstances the wide avenues would allow them to enter in force and overwhelm the Flesh Tearers. 'What is this area here?' He pointed to a dark spot on the display behind the armoury. 'It wasn't on the briefing schematics.'

'That area…' Amaru paused as his implants sifted through the compound's memory banks for an answer. 'It's a missile silo. Surface-to-orbit ordnance. No use against ground targets.'

'We cannot hope to defend the entire complex, we will make a stand here,' Barbelo indicated a group of passageways that sprung from the main corridors and ran to the courtyard. 'We'll collapse these four and split ourselves into pairs to defend the remaining two.'

'Four against–' Maion paused, turning to Amaru.

'Four thousand and seventy-eight separate contacts.'

Maion grinned, 'Seems there'll be blood enough even for Harahel.'

'I think I can help even the odds,' the hololith changed to show the

Stormraven as Amaru spoke. 'The Stormraven's hurricane-bolters and missile launcher can be removed,' the gunship's weapon systems floated away from its hull, illustrating the Techmarine's point. 'It wouldn't take much to reconfigure them as defensive turrets.'

'What about the Stormraven?' Maion's face hardened. 'The courtyard is uncovered, even a glancing hit from a siege gun and– '

'We needn't worry about artillery,' Barbelo interrupted. 'I have fought this enemy before. They are like us.'

Maion glared at the sergeant, 'You would liken us to the Archenemy?'

'You have fought beside our Chapter's Death Company?'

Maion nodded, his unease growing at the mention of the Chapter's damned warriors. The Black Rage was a genetic curse that threatened to overwhelm all of the sons of Sanguinius. Once afflicted, a Flesh Tearer would be lost to battle lust, his sanity replaced by a desperate need for violence. Those that succumbed to the madness where inducted into the ranks of the black-armoured Death Company where they'd soon find redemption in death.

'Like our coal-armoured brethren, the enemy we face is lost to bloodlust. They are fuelled by an insatiable rage, ever hungry for battle. They will want to taste our blood when they kill us,' Barbelo tested the weight of his chainsword. 'They will not attack from range.'

With the storm's howl locked outside, silence permeated the chapel. Harahel moved ahead of Nisroc, his eyes adjusting to the change in light as a string of angular luminators hummed into life along the ceiling, filling the corridor with the hushed yellow glow the Imperial church reserved for religious buildings and the homes of cardinals.

Harahel smelt blood. He touched his thumb to the activation stud on his eviscerator, 'Stand ready.'

Nisroc raised his bolt pistol, letting its scope feed targeting data to his helmet display. He knew better than to question Harahel's instincts.

From the reception chamber, they entered the Hall of Solace, a long corridor with single-occupant prayer cells joining it every few metres. The two Space Marines stopped. Dried blood and fleshy matter coated the metal floor ahead of them, paving the way like the regal carpet of some warp-spawned fiend.

Nisroc knelt and extended a probe from his narthecium, using it to scrape away a fragment of gore. A line of genetic sequence flashed across his display as the probe finished its analysis. 'Sanguinius gut them,' the Apothecary slammed his fist into the ground, cracking the metal panelling. 'This blood belongs to the Chapter.'

Harahel tightened his grip on his weapon as his pulse began to quicken. He swallowed hard in an attempt to stop salivating. 'Blood calls out to blood,' Harahel recited the battle mantra as he fought down the urge to tear apart the walls.

'The main chapel lies at the far end,' Nisroc spoke as the chrono display flashed a warning in his display. 'Time is–'

'Advance behind me,' Harahel activated his eviscerator, the weapon's barbed blades impatiently churning the air as they search for something to rend. 'If anyone emerges, shoot them.' Harahel spat the words through a pool of saliva. He dropped his weight and flexed his knees.

Nisroc nodded and slammed a fresh clip into his bolt pistol.

'For the Chapter!' Harahel broke into a run, the servos in his armour whirring as he picked up pace. The enhanced musculature of his thighs powered him forward at a speed that belied his bulk, an engine of ceramite and fury. 'One, clear. Two, clear,' Harahel looked left and right as he ran, updating Nisroc as his armour's optical and audio sensors checked and recorded the disposition of each of the prayer cells in a heartbeat. 'Three–'

Las-rounds stabbed at Harahel from either side.

'Contacts, five through nine,' Harahel kept running, ignoring the smattering of fire coming from the cells. Most shots went wide, his powerful strides carrying him past the cell openings before his attackers could take aim. A handful of rounds grazed his armour, picking the paint from his war plate. Harahel growled. The combination of his helmet's vox amplifier and the hall's acoustics amplifying his annoyance until it filled the corridor like the roar of some terrible beast.

'Keep moving,' Nisroc opened fire. His bolt pistol bucked in his hand as he sent three traitors sprawling to the floor, their heads blasted from their malnourished shoulders. 'Your rear is secure.'

Harahel blinked an acknowledgement to Nisroc and pushed onwards. He was nearing the last cluster of prayer cells. His targeting overlay lit up with data, tracking the trajectory of the three fist-sized globes that rolled onto the corridor in front of him. 'Grenades!' Harahel bellowed a warning to the Apothecary, and threw himself into the nearest prayer cell as the devices exploded, avoiding the wash of flame and shrapnel that billowed out from them. He heard a muffled cry and a wrenching snap as the cell's occupant's bones broke under his immense bulk. Harahel snorted and picked the dead man up by his skull.

'Harahel?' Nisroc's voice crackled in Harahel's ear.

'I am unharmed,' Harahel emerged from the cell carrying the head of the dead traitor by the spinal cord, his gauntlet slick with blood.

'The way is clear brother.'

'No, there is one left, there,' Harahel tossed the dismembered head into the cell opposite. A man screamed, firing on reflex as the head landed with a wet mulch.

Nisroc stepped into the cell, allowing his armour to filter out the smell of excrement. The man had the nose of his lasgun pressed inside his mouth. His eyes trembled as they looked up at the Flesh Tearer. The Apothecary growled. The man juddered, reflexively pulling the trigger.

The single las-round blew apart his skull, painting the wall behind him with superheated brain matter. Nisroc turned from the corpse to find Harahel on bended knee, his helmet discarded at his side. The veins in the other Flesh Tearer's forehead were threatening to push through his skin, his brow ran with sweat. Nisroc took a tentative step towards Harahel, his finger resting on the trigger of his bolt pistol.

'Stay back!' Harahel held a hand out to the Apothecary.

Nisroc resisted the urge to fire, 'Control yourself! Now is not the time. The Archenemy has taken the lives of our brothers.' Nisroc gestured to the arched doors of the chapel, 'We must know what lies behind those doors.'

Harahel said nothing, saliva dripped from his mouth to burn away at the floor.

'On your feet, Flesh Tearer! You can report to Appollus as soon as we return to the Victus, I'm sure he'll welcome you into the Death Company. But right now, you need to get to your feet or, Emperor help me, I'll put a bolt-round through that thick skull of yours.'

Harahel titled his head to look up at the Apothecary, his eyes bloodshot.

'On your feet.' Nisroc proffered Harahel his helmet. 'Use your rage for something useful, like getting through that door.'

Harahel took the helmet and locked it in place. 'Never threaten me again, brother.' He regarded the fusion marks on the chapel doors. Someone had welded them shut from the outside. He took a step back and then drove forwards, slamming his armoured shoulder into the weld-line. The metal buckled. Harahel brought his knee up and kicked out, the doors snapped inwards. A bank of suspended luminators stuttered into life as he stepped into the chamber.

'Emperor save us…'

The mutilated corpses of eight Flesh Tearers decorated the curved walls of the chapel. Fixed in place by the blades of their chainswords, they hung like nightmare visages of the saints that decorated Cretacia's Reclusiasms. Their armour was pitted and dented from numerous impacts and lacerations; their helms had been torn from their locking mounts, mangling their gorgets; all that remained of their faces were sunken husks, matted with bloodied hair.

'Blood of Sanguinius,' Nisroc fell to one knee, the desecration of his brother's flesh staggering him.

'Blood will bring blood,' with a grunt of effort, Harahel pulled the blade from the nearest of corpses. The dead Flesh Tearer's remains made a dull thud as they dropped to the ground. Harahel stared at the deep hole in the chapel wall; the blade had been driven through the outer rock into the metal support behind. 'It took great strength to do this.'

Nisroc nodded, and cast his gaze around the chamber. The plaster finish and faux-brickwork of the walls was undamaged. The flagstones that paved the way to the raised, wooden alter were unblemished save for a single dark spot left behind by an errant blood droplet. 'They weren't killed here,' Nisroc pushed himself to his feet. 'There's no sign of battle. Someone brought them here.' The Apothecary struggled to talk, grinding his teeth in rage 'After.'

Harahel snarled. 'Brother-sergeant,' he summoned Barbelo over the vox. Static filled his ear as he waited for a response. 'Emperor damn this storm,' the Flesh Tearer punched the wall, cracking it in a cloud of plaster-dust.

'Report,' Barbelo's voice crackled back.

'We have cleared the chapel annex.' Harahel paused as another burst of static shot across the vox-link, 'Eight of our brothers lie here.'

'Status?'

'Dead. All of them.' Harahel turned his eyes from the corpses, his fists bunching in restrained fury as he glared at the aquila etched on the floor.

'Show me.'

Harahel closed his eyes. He had no wish to look upon the massacre a second time. Activating his helmet's visual feed, he panned his head around the room, streaming what his optics registered to the others.

For a long moment, the vox-link fell silent.

'Nisroc, get what you came for. Harahel, meet us at the Stormraven.' Barbelo's voice rasped through another bout of static.

Six minutes. Time continued to count down at the edge of Maion's peripheral display. The Archenemy's army was almost at their door. 'Let them come,' he snarled, affixing the last of the melta-charges to the crossbeam that supported the ceiling. The charge was directional, and he'd taken care to make sure that the blast would travel down the corridor away from where he and Micos would be positioned.

'Brother,' Harahel's voice rasped over a secure channel, 'Back in the armoury, we gutted the traitors without incident. The ones in the command centre put up no more of a fight.'

Maion knew where Harahel was headed. 'Yes, I had the same thought.'

'How could such, such filth,' Harahel spat the word, 'have overcome our brethren? Those weaklings could scarcely have lifted a chainsword, let alone driven it into solid rock.'

Maion brought the percentile counter that recorded the progress of the data-stack download to the forefront of his helmet's display. It ticked down slow and deliberate, like a dying man's laboured breath. 'Emperor willing, we'll live long enough to find out.' Maion sighed and blinked the counter away.

'Jetpack assault troops. Bearing down on the courtyard,' Amaru's voice cut across on the main channel, interrupting Harahel's reply. The Techmarine was still jacked into the compound's data banks in the inner sanctum and was observing the Archenemy's advance through a remote-link with the Stormraven's sensors. The Archenemy's jetpack squad appeared as solid red blips that drifted over the landscape and grew in size as they neared. 'I count six of them...' Amaru's voice trailed off as he worked a calculation. 'Harahel, you will not clear the courtyard before they descend.'

Harahel emerged from the chapel annex and growled up into the blackness of Arere's starless sky, his enhanced eyes searching for the tell-tale flares of jetpacks. 'I see no enemy.'

'I assure you brother, they are coming.'

'They're a vanguard, nothing more.' Barbelo growled over the vox-feed, his impatience evident in every syllable. 'Harahel, ignore them and get to my position. The main force will hit us in less than five minutes. Amaru, cover his advance.'

The Techmarine blinked an acknowledgment icon to Barbelo and concentrated on communicating with the Stormraven's machine-spirit. The gunship's sentient mind was silent, almost dormant. It resisted Amaru's gentle interrogation, blocking his attempts to rouse it.

'My skin for yours.' The Techmarine invited the machine-spirit into his armour as he probed deeper into the gunship. The connection sent a spasm through his muscles as he gained access to the Stormraven's weapon systems. Amaru teased power into the gunship's turret-mounted assault cannons.

'*Battle*,' the machine-spirit whispered in the Techmarine's head as it stirred to readiness.

The red-blips pulsed on Amaru's display as the enemy neared weapons range. He cycled the twin-assault cannons to firing speed, their multiple barrels whirring with a metallic hiss as the autoloader fed them rounds.

'*Enemy*.' The word growled from within the Stormraven's machine soul, washing through Amaru's mind like the strained rumble of thruster backwash. It was awake now, wearing the Stormraven like a suit of ceramite war plate, wielding its turret-mounted weapon with the same ease and precision that a Flesh Tearer hefted a blade.

A sound wave spiked across Amaru's display as the Stormraven's auditory sensors detected the roar of enemy jetpacks. The Chaos Space Marines were gunning their thrusters, slowing their descent.

'Purge the heretics.' the Techmarine urged the gunship to open fire.

The enraged machine-spirit obliged. The twin-assault cannon's twelve barrels flared into life, lighting up the sky like miniature starbursts as they fired. Caught unaware, the Chaos Space Marines dived straight into the fusillade. The first three died in a heartbeat, their armour and flesh torn asunder by the unceasing hail of armour piercing rounds.

Harahel was two-thirds of the way across the courtyard when the assault cannons opened fire. He risked a glance skyward and saw the visceral red power armour of the Archenemy's warriors. Their breastplates were shaped like cruel gargoyles and snarled at him from the darkness. A burst of rounds clipped the nearest of the Traitor Marines, blowing apart his thrusters in a shower of flame. The enemy warrior veered downwards towards Harahel, carried by what remained of his earlier momentum. The Flesh Tearer smiled and swung his eviscerator up through the stricken Chaos Space Marine's ribcage, ripping him in two. Harahel kept moving, tearing his giant weapon through the body of another foe that slammed into the earth in front of him a moment later. The Flesh Tearer bit into his lip, relishing the taste of his own blood as he pounded towards Barbelo and the slaughter to come.

Amaru watched as the Stormraven continued to track and fire. He felt his pulse quicken to the hoarse wheeze of the assault cannon's barrels as they spun. Several more of the red blips disappeared from his display, shredded by the gunships' unerring fire. The Techmarine could feel the machine-spirit's cold rage, its lust for violence and the gleeful abandon with which it massacred the enemy. He gasped, clutching the cables that linked him to the compound's datastacks, and fought the urge to sever the link. He needed to be outside with the Stormraven, fighting, killing. His body began to tremble as he tried to restrain his urges. The download sequence was in its final stage, any interruption now would corrupt the data. Amaru dropped to one knee, screaming in rage as the machine-spirit's emotions threatened to overcome him. 'My work is iron, my will steel.' The Techmarine held his clenched fist against the machine-cog on his left pauldron as he growled his way through the devotion, 'I shall not falter, I shall not heel.' Defend, he forced the order onto the machine spirit and drew his mind away, severing the link to the gunship and the violence outside.

Panting hard, Amaru focused on finishing the protocol. 'There is no truth beyond the data, it is the muniment of the future. Guard it well.' Download complete, Amaru unplugged from the datastacks and completed the rites of remembrance, secreting the data-keeper within his armour. The Techmarine let out a slow breath as the after-shadow of the Raven and the compound fell away, and the confines of his world reasserted themselves.

Alone in his armour, he took reassurance from the cold, impassive touch of the bionics and augmetics that punctuated his body. Perfect where he was flawed, the machine components of the Techmarine would continue to function long after The Rage drove his flesh to destruction. 'Download complete,' Amaru voxed the update to the rest of the squad and pushed himself to his feet.

'Nisroc, status?' Barbelo's voice crackled over the vox.

'I need three minutes,' Maion listened to the Apothecary's reply as the chrono-counter on his display blinked down to one.

He stood immobile in the darkness. His gaze fixed on the heavy blast doors at the far end of the corridor, as the chrono display floating at the edge of his peripheral vision blinked down to zero. The attack had begun. If Barbelo was right and this enemy did indeed wage war like the Flesh Tearers, then they would have fallen upon the outer walls with all the fury of a scorned god. Maion imagined the scene outside, picturing the Archenemy's forces as they descended on the compound. Vindicator siege tanks would have led an armoured charge, unleashing a devastating bombardment as accompanying Rhinos and Razorbacks disgorged frothing assault squads. With the siege shells exploding overhead, the assault troops would use melta weapons and crackling thunder hammers to finish the job, smashing an entry hole into the compound. Right now, the Archenemy would be tearing towards him and the others like a swarm of berserker locusts.

Yet the scene ahead remained unchanged, the blast door intact. The only sound Maion could hear was the gentle purr of his armour and the wash of his rebreather. His muscles twitched. The urge to break from his defensive posture and meet the enemy head on was almost overwhelming.

'The longer you stand, the more blood you can spill,' Micos placed a calming hand on Maion's shoulder guard, reading the other Flesh Tearer's mood. 'Save your fury, we'll be steeped in their entrails soon enough.' Micos thrust his chainaxe towards the blast door as a trio of sparks dripped to the floor.

Maion nodded, allowing Micos's words to soften the call to violence that rang in his mind like the summoning gong of an ancient arena. The other Flesh Tearer looked odd in Atoc's helm. Atoc, Maion's anger returned in force as he thought of his brother's death. His knuckles turning bone white inside his gauntlets as he squeezed his weapons, desperate for something to rend. Another burst of super-heated metal flared in the gloom. He blinked away a myriad of tactical icons from his display; he was going to kill whatever came through the blast doors, nothing else mattered.

The drizzle of sparks tumbled into a downpour as the Archenemy intensified their assault on the door. A pulsing, amber line resolved into focus, bisecting the door from floor to ceiling.

'Here they come,' Maion crouched down, motioning for Micos to do the same.

The cutting stopped. The weld-line hung in the gloom, glowing and raw like a fresh scar. Silence filled the corridor, threatening to steal the last of Maion's restraint.

An immense, metallic hand punched through the centre of the blast door. Pneumatic pistons hissed and spat as elongated fingers flexed in search of something to rend. The audio dampeners in Maion's helmet worked to filter out the torturous screech of metal as the hand reached backwards, gripped the door, tore it from its hinges and dragged it backwards into the darkness. An instant later, the hand and the lumbering body it was attached to, bolted into view.

'Dreadnought, corridor one,' Maion warned, resisting the urge to open fire with his boltgun. He couldn't afford to waste the ammo and even the weapon's mass-reactive rounds would do little more than scratch the paint from the armoured behemoth bearing down on him. A dread fusion of Space Marine and technology, the Dreadnought was more foe than he and Micos could stop unaided. The towering walker stomped over the wreckage of the door, emerging into the corridor proper, and opened fire.

Maion threw himself flat. 'For the Chapter!' he roared, thumbing the control stick Amaru had fashioned for him. On the ceiling above him, one of the missile tubes stripped from the Stormraven's wings screamed into life, sending its payload burning on a plume of fire towards the walker.

The first of the missiles slammed into the Dreadnought's sarcophagus and exploded, splintering its armoured hide. The missile's secondary booster ignited a moment later, driving a tertiary charge in through the weakened armour plating to detonate in the Dreadnought's core. Flame engulfed the walker, wreathing it like a burial wrap. Autocannon rounds tore across the walls and ceiling as the Dreadnought continued to fire.

Maion fired again, sending another missile towards the metallic beast. A shrill cry resounded from the Dreadnought's vox-casters as it raised its clawed arm in defence. The second missile's primary warhead broke against the arm, blowing it apart in a shower of silver shrapnel. The remaining warhead burrowed into the Dreadnought's flank, detonating with enough force to finish the job, destroying the Archenemy walker.

A blood-curdling roar filled the corridor as a tide of blood-armoured warriors swarmed over the Dreadnought's corpse towards the Flesh Tearers. Micos roared back, pushing himself to his feet and striding forward to bathe the enemy in a jet of liquid fire. The Archenemy's warriors ran through the flame, heedless of their bubbling armour and the flesh that ran from it like water.

Maion advanced to Micos's right, his boltgun flashing in the darkness as he pumped a stream of rounds into the press of enemy. Each time Maion caught sight of a foe it forced a curse from his lips. Their red armour seemed in direct mockery of the sons of Sanguinius. Where Maion's breastplate was adorned with the holy aquila and his shoulder guard carried the mark of his Chapter, the foe's armour was inlaid with brass skulls and blasphemous runes.

'We can't hold here,' Micos's flamer stuttered and died, its fuel tank exhausted. Letting it hang on its sling, he drew his bolt pistol and continued to fire. In the close confines of the corridor he couldn't miss, each round found its mark. He shot an enemy point-blank in the chest, then two more. At such close range, even power armour offered little protection, his bolt rounds punching out through their backs in a hail of gore.

Maion stood level to Micos's right, firing his boltgun on full-auto until the round counter flashed zero. There was no time to reload the next enemy only ever a breath away. 'Micos, down!'

Micos grabbed the nearest corpse as it fell to the ground and pulled it down on top of himself. Maion did likewise. Behind them, the hurricane bolter emplacement they'd fashioned from the Stormraven's sponson weaponry opened fire. The noise was deafening as the three pairs of linked boltguns pumped a storm of shells into the corridor. Funnelled by the walls of the corridor, and pushed onwards by the press of warriors at their backs, the Archenemy were driven heedlessly into the salvo. They died in droves, their torsos pulped and limbs severed by the vicious onslaught.

Maion lay under the twitching corpses of half a dozen enemy. His pulse was racing, his twin-hearts echoing to the call of the hurricane bolters. The smell of blood and burnt flesh was choking. He was lying in an expanding pool of blood that dripped from all around him, congealing into a puddle of thick, viscous fluid that threatened to swallow him.

'Emperor, fashion my thirst to your unbending will.' Maion focused on the data overlaid on his helmet display, turning his thoughts to the tactical challenges that an endless horde of berserker foe presented, and away from the bloodlust burning in his veins. The weapon emplacement's ammo counter was racing towards zero. 'Two seconds.' Maion subvocalised the warning to Micos and slammed his last clip into his boltgun.

With a final thrum, the hurricane bolters racked empty. Maion shot upwards from beneath the corpse-cover. The Archenemy dead were heaped upon one-another like red-armoured sandbags. Yet still they came. He opened fire, sending two more abominations to join the pile of dead that choked the corridor. The smell of promethium and burnt flesh flooded towards Maion as the enemy turned their flamers on their dead, burning a path towards the Flesh Tearers. The damning clack of an empty firing chamber drew a curse from Maion's lips as his boltgun spat its last round. He discarded the spent weapon and gripped his chainsword with both hands. 'I am His vengeance!'

'Harahel!' Barbelo tore his chainsword from an enemy's ribcage as he shouted for the giant Flesh Tearer.

Harahel wasn't listening, his attention fixed on the dismembered bodies of the three Chaos Space Marines he'd just slain.

'Harahel, fall back!'

Harahel ignored the sergeant, launching himself back into the press of enemy. Ducking a whirring chainaxe, he shouldered an enemy warrior into the wall, pulping his skull between rockcrete bulkhead and ceramite pauldron. Harahel smiled and swung his eviscerator around in a tight arc, hacking into the onrushing press of red armour with a cold fury.

'Emperor damn you.' The other Flesh Tearer's disobedience drew a curse from Barbelo's lips as a roaring chainblade flashed out towards his neck. He leaned back as far as his balance allowed. The weapon's teeth sparked as they grazed his gorget. Growling, he fired a plasma round into his attacker's leering helm, vaporising the Chaos Space Marine's head and torso. The headless body twitched backwards and disappeared in the press of red armour. 'Harahel! When they cross the line, I will detonate.' Barbelo let his smoking pistol drop to the floor, its power pack exhausted, and drew his combat knife. 'Harahel!'

Harahel snapped his head around, sighting the sergeant. Barbelo was embroiled with two Chaos Space Marines, a blade in each of his hands as he fought his way clear of the melee. A bolt round stung off Harahel's shoulder guard. He ignored it, snapping the neck of a charging foe with a thunderous backhand and delivering a low kick that broke the leg of another. It went against his every instinct to move backwards. Faced with the immediate need to kill, duty was a secondary consideration. The rage that burned in Harahel's veins was insatiable. Roaring like a mad-man, he continued into the enemy. Behind him, Barbelo went down under a flurry of blows.

Distressed bio-data filled Barbelo's display. A stray round had clipped his helmet, dazing him long enough for one of the enemy to rake his midsection with a whirring blade and batter him to the ground. He tried to focus but his head was ringing. Pain lanced through him as a blade dug into his back. Gritting his teeth, he pulled a bolt pistol from beneath a corpse. Twisting, he fired it on full-auto, sending half a clip into his would-be executioner. The Traitor Marine juddered and fell as the rounds slammed into him. Surrounded and badly wounded, Barbelo knew he had little chance of regaining his footing. *I am redeemed.* Proud that he had remained master of his rage, that his armour had not been daubed in the black of madness, the sergeant clasped his hand tightly around the detonator. The Cretacian symbol for caution flashed across his display, warning him that he was within the blast radius.

'In His name.'

Barbelo released the device's pressure-clasp.

The melta-charges ignited, blasting apart the corridor's support studs in a hail of shrapnel and filling the passageway with an expanding ball of flame. Harahel was tossed like a leaf in a hurricane as the explosion slammed him into the walls and ground. Strobing runes filled his retinal display, as fire washed across his armour, testing the limits of its ceramite plating. The screed of warnings were in vain, Harahel unable to process them before the ceiling collapsed and his world went dark.

'The gene-seed is secure. Moving to the Stormraven.'

Maion struggled to hear Nisroc's voice over the pumping of his hearts and the roar of his chainsword as its teeth tore through another enemy. 'Understood,' he growled, turning aside an enemy chainaxe. He parried the weapon down to expose his attacker's neck, driving his combat knife into the Chaos Space Marine's windpipe. Maion immediately withdrew the blade and buried it in the face of another of the Dark Gods' minions. 'If we're not there in two minutes, leave.'

'Sanguinius guide you.'

Maion was in no doubt that the Apothecary would be leaving without him. The Archenemy had him surrounded. His armour had been struck clean of paint and insignia. Deep lacerations covered his arms and torso. His muscles ached with exhaustion. It would not be long before even his indomitable constitution gave out, and the enemy killed him. Only his rage kept him on his feet, allowing him to fight on. The insatiable need to rend powering his blows and staying death's probing touch. In death's sight, you are fury. In his colours you are reborn a reaper. None shall evade your wrath, Maion recalled the mantra Chaplain Appollus used to rouse the Death Company for war. Until now, he'd embraced only the edges of the beast growling inside of him. Never daring to fully embrace the whispering voices that scratched at his mind. But here, on starless Arere, in the darkness of the corridor, Maion stopped resisting. He invited the red mist to descend to light up his world in a whirlwind of gore. He felt his rage swallowing him, the shadow in his mind–

A staccato of miniature explosions snapped Maion from his morbidity. He felt the press of enemy ease off behind, allowing him to take a step backwards. Risking a glance over his shoulder, he saw Amaru. The Techmarine stood in the centre of the corridor like a vengeful daemon, the quad arms of his servo-harness spitting death from an array of laser cutters and plasma burners. In his gauntleted hands, Amaru carried his power axe, Blood Cog. The Techmarine had forged the weapon himself upon his return from Mars. The axe's sparking head was shaped like the gearwheel from a giant machine. A weapon of exquisite beauty and terrible power, it was imbued with all Amaru's artisanship. Blood Cog rose and fell like the levers of an antiquated stenogram, as the Techmarine hacked down the Archenemy in brutal swipes that crackled on impact.

'Quickly brother, fall back,' Amaru called out to Maion as he chopped Blood Cog through another Chaos Space Marine, bisecting the unfortunate from shoulder to hipbone. 'Fall back now.'

'Micos.' Maion cast his gaze around. He had long since lost sight of the other Flesh Tearer but his ident-tag still shone. He was alive, for the moment at least. 'We can't leave him.'

'They will rally soon.'

Maion ignored the Techmarine's caution, and bludgeoned his way past another assailant to where his retinal display indicated Micos should be. With a huge effort, Maion began tossing back the bodies of the Archenemy, until he spotted the familiar ashen helm of a Flesh Tearer. 'I have him,' knifing his chainsword into the thigh of an onrushing foe,

Maion grabbed Micos' vambrace and dragged him from under a heap of corpses.

'Can you carry him?' Amaru's question bore no insult.

Maion growled, tearing his blade free and beheading the wounded Traitor Marine. 'To Cretacia and back.' With a grunt of exertion, he hoisted Micos over his shoulders.

The Techmarine nodded and hacked the weapon arm from one of the Archenemy, before beheading him. Amaru's fury was methodical, the aggression of his flesh tempered by the cold efficiency of his machine parts. Maion envied his calm. Though he knew that someday, the Techmarine's rage would no longer be held in check. On that day, Maion would know pity for the enemies of his Chapter.

Pulling his axe from the chest plate of another Chaos Space Marine, Amaru tossed a glowing canister over Maion's head. 'Run.'

Harahel pushed himself off the ground, shrugging a pile of debris and a limbless body from his back. He felt his twin-hearts quicken as they worked with his armour to pump pain suppressors through his bloodstream. Angry runes flashed on his display as his helm's optics tried and failed to focus. The lenses were cracked. Stumbling to his feet, Harahel spat a curse and unclasped his ruined helmet. The Chapter's armourers had their work cut out for them. He mag-locked it to his thigh and paused while his eyes adjusted to the darkness. Thick silence hung in the air. It was in almost painful contrast to the cacophonous din of battle that preceded the explosion. Harahel listen for signs of the enemy but could hear nothing beyond his own shallow breathing. The blast had levelled the corridor, chocking it with collapsed rockcrete and the dead. The Flesh Tearer searched for his weapon, picking through the rubble and bodies nearest him. 'The mists rot you', he said. Cursing in tired frustration, Harahel kicked a fallen Chaos Space Marine in the chest. The ceramite skull adorning the fallen warrior's breastplate cracked under the blow. There was no trace of the eviscerator. His weapon was gone. Harahel staggered forwards, steadying himself on a dislodged support beam. There was movement up ahead. Two figures, one crouched over the other. He stepped towards them, unsteady on his feet as he fought to remain conscious.

'Nisroc?' Harahel cried out, delirious from the chemicals keeping him alive while his body healed itself. 'Brother?'

He moved closer, stopping as the crouched figure's armour resolved into focus. It was not the white of the Apothecary or the deep crimson of Barbelo's garb, but a vibrant, arterial red. Harahel took a step forwards, and saw Barbelo slumped underneath the figure. The sergeant's breastplate was peeled open, his organs scattered on the ground. Harahel bared his teeth and snarled.

The hunched figured turned and rose. Fresh blood stained his baroque armour, tracing the outlines of the ruinous brass symbols that adorned it. Skulls rattled on rusted chains as the Chaos Space Marine stood. He was a walking effigy of death. A vicious chainaxe barked to life in his hand.

Harahel gripped his helmet and strode towards his enemy, all thoughts of injury gone as rage invigorated him. He would avenge the sergeant. The traitor would pay in blood.

'Skulls for His throne,' the Archenemy warrior roared through the skull-shaped vox-grille of his helmet, and charged at the Flesh Tearer.

Harahel caught his opponent's arm as he slashed down with the chainaxe, pivoting and smashing his helm into the side of the Chaos Space Marine's head. He followed with his elbow, folding it into his opponent's left ocular lens. The Traitor Marine roared as the shattered armourglass dug into his eye, and threw a panicked hook with his free hand. Harahel felt his jaw break as the gauntleted blow struck his unarmoured face. He struggled to keep a hold of the Chaos Space Marine's weapon arm, spitting a glob of bloody mucous and teeth as he slammed his head into his opponent's other lens. Pain shot through Harahel's skull as his toughened skeleton protested at the cruel misuse. The Archenemy's head snapped backwards under the blow, unbalancing him.

'Die!' Harahel roared and smashed his helmet into the Chaos Space Marine's head. The enemy warrior's grip on the chainaxe loosened. The Flesh Tearer struck him again, and again, using his helmet as a hammer, bludgeoning the Chaos Space Marine to his knees. The chainaxe clattered to the ground as Harahel battered his foe into unconsciousness. 'Die!' The Traitor Marine's body went slack but the Flesh Tearer held him upright and continued to batter him. 'Die! Die! Die!'

Only when his helmet was mangled beyond recognition, and his opponent's head was nothing but bloody spatter on the wall, did Harahel let the body drop to the ground. The giant Flesh Tearer stood panting, the Archenemy's blood dripping from his face. He growled, bunching his fists as he fought the urge to smash down the wall. 'Strengthen me to the demands of blood. Armour my soul against the Thirst.' Harahel looked down at Barbelo's corpse. 'Let me kill those who blaspheme against your sons.' Calmer, Harahel knelt and unfastened Barbelo's helm. 'Forgive me,' Harahel said as he locked it in place over his head. Both retinal displays lit up with sigils of bonding as the sergeant's helmet synchronised with his armour. Harahel called up the squad's ident-tags, thankful that his brothers were still fighting. Slinging Barbelo's body over his shoulder and picking up the fallen chainaxe, Harahel made for the Stormraven. 'Come, brother, there's more blood to spill yet.'

The Stormraven was a burning wreck of charred metal and crumpled ceramite. The courtyard compromised. Enemy assault troops sat perched on the upper gantries like sentry-carrion, their weapons searching for targets. Half a dozen more sat crouched on their haunches, nursing wounds the Stormraven had dealt them before its demise.

'Wretches! Sanguinius drink you dry,' Nisroc opened fire, pulverising the nearest enemy with a hail of explosive rounds. There was no place in a Flesh Tearer's mind for dismay. If he were trapped on Arere, then he would kill his enemies until death came to stop him. The Apothecary dived into cover, throwing himself against a metal container as a slew of bolt-rounds and melta-blasts tore towards him in retort. 'I'm in the courtyard. The Stormraven's gone.' Nisroc's voice was punctuated with rage as he voxed the update. Movement to the left drew his attention. He opened fire, suppressing a pair of Chaos Space Marines that were trying to encircle him.

'Sanguinius's blood. What now?' Harahel snarled over the vox.

Another torrent of rounds smashed into Nisroc's cover, forcing him to crouch low as he reloaded his bolter. 'We fight, we–'

'I know a way,' Amaru interrupted.

'Explain…' Nisroc trailed off. The enemy had stopped firing. On instinct, he subvocalised the Cretacian rune for haste to the rest of the squad.

'Apothecary!' The word rang out in a garbled roar, its syllables tortured by a voice unaccustomed to speech. 'I will feast on your hearts and savour the seed of your brothers.'

At the corner of his peripheral vision, Nisroc saw four more Chaos Space Marines, their weapons trained on him. He ground his teeth in frustration. His only option was to face the challenger.

'Not while I draw breath!' Nisroc drew his chainsword and stood to face his opponent. The Chaos Space Marine was a giant, taller even than Harahel, his bronzed armour covered in egg-shell cracks where it struggled to contain his warped bulk. 'Tell me,' Nisroc said in a low growl. 'Whose blood shall my blade taste?' The Apothecary activated his visual feed as he spoke, transmitting the locations of the Chaos Space Marines in the courtyard to the rest of the squad.

'Krykhan, Fist of Khorne,' the traitor growled as he launched himself at Nisroc.

Amaru sprinted from the corridor firing, Maion close behind him. 'Fall back to the missile silo.' The Techmarine dropped to one knee to avoid a plasma round, the arms of his servo-harness whirring as they turned to return fire. The Chaos plasma gunner died in a heartbeat, dissected by the merciless cutting lasers.

Maion ran past the Techmarine, Micos draped over his shoulders. It irked him to be unarmed, but he hadn't the time to find a weapon. Bolt-rounds barked at his heels and churned up the dirt as he moved. He spat a curse, desperate for a chance to return fire. Angry runes flashed on his display as shell fragments spattered off of his legs. 'Where?'

'Back through the armoury.' Amaru was forced to shout over the din of bolter fire. 'The rearmost corridor.'

Harahel felt Barbelo's body jerk as bolt-rounds hammered into it. Growling, he took cover behind a shorn off section of the Stormraven's wing. The orphaned appendage stood in the ground like a piece of industrial sculpture. A grenade exploded, showering Harahel in shrapnel. The noise reminded him of a Cretacian thunderstorm. Ahead, he saw Nisroc. The Apothecary was about to die. A massive warrior stood over the prone Flesh Tearer, his murderous intent obvious. Harahel growled, standing to throw his chainaxe into the Chaos Space Marine's back. The towering warrior roared, pitching forwards under the force of the impact. 'Get up and kill him,' Harahel snarled at Nisroc.

The Chaos Space Marine turned away from Nisroc, reaching for the axe in his back. The Apothecary summoned the last of his strength, shooting upwards to thrust his combat knife through his opponent's neck. The Archenemy warrior's body shuddered as his brain died. Nisroc caught the body before it could fall, pulling it around as a shield against the two Chaos Space Marines who immediately opened fire on him. He drew the dead warrior's boltgun and put down his attackers with pinpoint shots. 'Harahel, move! I'll cover you.'

Too late, Amaru realised a Chaos Space Marine had landed behind him. His servo-harness sparked violently, its arms falling limp as the Archenemy warrior sliced through its control fibres. Amaru hit the release clasp and rolled away, pivoting as he rose to face his enemy. He spun forwards, tearing Blood Cog down through his foe's shoulder and ripping it from his ribcage.

A round struck Maion's pauldron as he cleared the threshold of the armoury. Another hit his abdomen. He fell, Micos toppling with him. He pushed himself onto all fours and tried to focus. Everything was faint, murky, as though he were a long way underwater. Pain forced a growl from his throat. His injuries were severe.

'On your feet.' Harahel grabbed Maion by his backpack and hoisted him up.

'Micos…'

'I have him.' Harahel pushed Maion further into the armoury, stooping to gather up Micos.

'Amaru, where now?' Nisroc backed into the chamber, a boltgun barking in each hand.

'Enter the third launch annex.' Amaru pointed to the passageway leading from the rear of the armoury. 'Go!'

Debris dust drifted into the missile silo, bathing the Flesh Tearers in powdered rockcrete. Amaru had used the last of the melta-charges to bring the corridor down behind them, creating a barricade between them and the Archenemy. He hoped it would give them enough time.

In the centre of the chamber stood a single, towering missile, its base disappearing down into the earth, its tip several stories above the control deck. A laddered gantry snaked around the missile, weaving between vines of cabling and fuel hoses to connect the deck with its upper reaches.

'We don't have long.' Amaru pointed up towards the missile. 'Quickly, into the nose.'

'What?' Maion stopped, unsure if he'd misheard the Techmarine.

'It is a Mark-XV defence missile, the nose space is relatively empty.' Amaru detached a plasma cutter from his pack and passed it to Maion. 'Make entry with this and seal it once you're inside.'

'And you?'

'I will remain here to ensure your withdrawal.'

Maion made to speak, but the Techmarine held up a hand, 'The missile will not launch itself.'

The other Flesh Tearer nodded grimly and took the plasma cutter.

Amaru grabbed Nisroc's vambrace as he walked past. 'Wait.' He held his axe out to the Apothecary. 'The Chapter has lost enough this day.'

Silently, Nisroc clasped his hand to Amaru's vambrace and took the proffered weapon.

The nosecone was cramped, only just accommodating the four Flesh Tearers. Nisroc had removed the gene-seed from Barbelo's body while Maion had cut them an access hatch. They'd left what remained of the sergeant on the gantry. Maion bent the armoured panelling back into shape, heat-sealed it with the plasma cutter and squeezed his bulk between Harahel and Nisroc. Micos was still unconscious, and was only on his feet because there was no room to fall over.

'We're in.' Nisroc opened a private channel to Amaru.

'Ensure Tabbris sanctifies Blood Cog. Its spirit is strong; it will serve him well.'

'It will taste flesh again,' Nisroc answered. Tabbris was Amaru's pupil, a novitiate Techmarine. That Amaru would cede him his weapon signified his faith in the novitiate's abilities. Nisroc would see to it that the Master Artificer knew of Amaru's wishes. 'Death find you well, brother.'

Amaru said nothing. Extending a cable from his armour, he plugged into the firing console. Behind him, the forces of the Archenemy had already blasted through the rubble. He could hear them striding along the corridor. There was no time to perform the correct consecration or rites of firing. The missile's machine-spirit was ancient. He hoped it would not be offended. *Launch*. Amaru sent the command to the missile. A tremor passed underfoot, rattling a canteen pack off a nearby workstation. Shrill klaxons screamed through the corridor as the warhead powered up. The Techmarine deactivated them. Sensors and bundles of thick cabling detached and fell away from the rocket as pressurised hydraulics moved it into the firing position. More rumbling. Fuel pipes retracted. Exhaust vents ground open beneath the floor of the silo. Amaru interrupted them, closing the grilles. The engines gurgled into life. More alarms rang out as the compound's safety systems detected the block in the ventilation, Amaru overrode them, silencing the alarms and pushing the missile up thorough the shaft into the final position.

'For the Chapter.'

A wash of flame erupted from the missile's booster like the breath of an angry dragon, propelling it upwards on an expanding pillar of fire. Amaru's world burned away in an instant, the temperature gauge on his retinal display flashing red as the thruster backwash broiled him. A second warning blinked across his vision for the briefest of instants before he, and everything else in the compound, was incinerated.

The maglift whispered to a stop. He stepped off into the corridor, his armoured boots making a dull thud as they contacted the deck plating. He paused for a moment while his enhanced eyes strained to adjust to the gloom. They could not. The walkway floated in complete, impenetrable darkness, shrouded by a long-forgotten technology that defied even the keenest of auspexes. To walk the passageways of this level was to know exactly where to tread or to fall to your doom amid the ancient bowels of the ship. He continued along the corridor, making the turns instinctively, following the pattern imprinted in his eidetic memory. His pace quickened as he felt his ire rise, his warrior blood drumming in his veins at the frustrating tediousness of the journey. He stopped and drew a breath, calming his mind. He did not have the luxury of indulging his baser nature. Such things were his burden to bear and some secrets were not meant for the light.

A door slid open into a darkened chamber. He stepped inside and the door closed behind him. The faint glow of an idling pict-screen cast the face of the room's single occupant into half-shadow.

'Where did you find them?' As always, his voice was dangerous, his pensive demeanour only ever a heartbeat removed from the violent rage that made him such an implacable warrior.

'The strike cruiser *Jagged Blade* intercepted them just beyond the Arere system.' Captain Araton stepped closer, the light from the pict-screen illuminating the crimson of his breastplate. The serrated blade emblazoned on his armour was thrown into menacing relief.

'Survivors?'

'Only three, lord. The fourth...' Araton paused, unsure how to continue. 'The fourth, Brother Micos, was killed in transit.'

'Explain.'

'He succumbed to... a rage. The others were left with little choice.'

'The curse?'

'Perhaps, but Nisroc believed it to be something more, something worse.' Araton turned to a console and activated the playback on the pict-screen. 'These feeds were extracted from the datastacks the squad recovered from the outpost.' The captain stepped away from the screen, retreating into the darkness.

++Recorder 3: Sanctum: I808++

The sanctum was alive with motion. Men clambered behind consoles and data stacks as explosions wracked the chamber. A straggler was hit in the back, the force of the blow spinning him through the air, his torso a bloodied mess. The Guardsmens' fatigues marked them out as the Angorian Rifles, the garrison regiment of Arere. A figure burst into the room, too quick for the pict-recorder to capture fully. It barrelled into a huddle of Guardsmen. They tried to run. A vicious chain-weapon struck out and sent a bodiless head spinning past the pict-recorder lens.

An officer stood up and screamed, motioning for his men to fall back. His battleplate was blackened and pitted, his creased face caked with mire. Shrapnel danced around him as mass-reactive rounds slammed into the console he was using for cover. He shouted again, dragging the man nearest him to his feet.

A jet of super-heated flame blew over the console, incinerating both men in a wash of burning promethium.

++Recording Interrupted++
++Recorder 7: Barracks: I827++

Two squads of Angorian Rifles were taking cover behind a row of overturned kit-lockers. The barrels of their lasguns glowed hot as the troopers poured an endless stream of fire towards the doorway. Two objects flew in from off camera and exploded in front of the lockers. Ashen smoke filled the viewer.

It cleared to reveal a twisted mass of metal, the Angorians' makeshift barricade in ruins. The corpses of half their number lay slumped lifelessly over the shredded lockers, shards of metal embedded in their flesh. A figure advanced from the doorway, his armoured back filling the viewer. The Guardsmen opened fire. Untroubled, the attacker fired back. The unmistakable muzzle flash of a boltgun illuminated the Angorians as they flipped backwards, torn apart by the mass-reactive rounds.

The attacker turned his crimson breast plate–

++Recording Interrupted++
++Recorder 19: Armoury: I901++

A crimson armoured warrior was sprinting down the corridor into a hail of las-fire, his breastplate scorched clean of insignia by their attentions. A bright muzzle-flash blazed into life up ahead. Heavy calibre, solid-state rounds began churning up the floor and walls as they stitched a line towards him. One struck his right pauldron. Splintered armour fragments struck the pict-recorder as he spun to the ground. The warrior rolled to his feet and continued into the gunfire, his weapon forgotten on the ground behind him as he disappeared from view.

The ruined corridor lay empty, battered ceramite flaking to the ground. The intensity of the gunfire lessened, sporadic rounds zipping down to the corridor. Then it died altogether. Within moments, the armoured warrior emerged from the end of the corridor. Blood pooled in the recesses of his damaged armour, which was pitted and cracked like the surface of a moon. His hands and forearms were thick with gore. Blood dripped from his fingertips, leaving a macabre trail behind him as he strode back towards his weapon.

++I901: Segment Ends++
++Recorder 12: Courtyard: I873++

A Flesh Tearer lay slumped against the wall, one of his brothers bent over him. The brother turned, withdrawing the blade he'd driven into the other's heart. His helmet was gone, his face contorted into a bestial snarl. He made to rise when a searing plasma round struck his chest.

A shadow fell over the Flesh Tearer's prone form. He pushed his hands into the dirt and tried to stand when a second plasma round obliterated his head in a stream of sparking gore.

The shadow grew larger until the Flesh Tearer's executioner was right beneath the pict-recorder. The man looked up, straight into the lens.

The image froze as the viewer's recog-system analysed the man's face. The image blinked once as data began to scroll down the screen.

First Commissar Morvant, attached to the Angorian Rifles. Awarded Iron Faith honours for the Ivstyan Cleansing. Last posting Arere, Substation 12BX. Current status: Unknown.

The image blinked again and playback continued.

The man's passive stare didn't change as he raised his pistol towards the pict-recorder.

++Recording Interrupted++

The viewer clicked off, emitting a faint buzz of static as it returned to idle.

Silence persisted.

'Destroy it.'

'And Arere?'

'Exterminatus.' Gabriel Seth, Chapter Master of the Flesh Tearers, turned on his heel and headed back into the darkness.

He had a world to kill.

EVEN UNTO DEATH

Mike Lee

The Wolf Scouts flew like spectres down the dark, tangled paths of the forest, their heightened senses keen as a razor's edge. Red moonlight shone along the edges of their blades, and death followed in their wake.

Guttural howls and roaring bursts of gunfire rent the night air all around them, echoing off the boles of the huge trees. The orks were everywhere, boiling up from hidden tunnels like a swarm of ants and crashing through the undergrowth in search of the Space Wolves. With every passing moment the cacophony of noise seemed to draw more tightly around the small pack of Space Marines, like a shrinking noose. Skaflock Sightblinder tightened his grip on his power sword and led the Wolf Scouts onward, racing for the landing zone some fifteen kilometres to the east.

Ork raiders had been terrorizing the worlds of the Volturna sector since the end of the Second Battle of Armageddon, slaughtering tens of thousands of the Emperor's faithful and putting entire continents to the torch. Their leader, a warlord known as Skargutz the Render, was as cunning as he was cruel. He never lingered too long on any world, pulling back his forces and retreating into the void before help could arrive. The Imperial Navy was left to chase shadows, and with every successful raid the warlord's reputation – and his warband – grew in stature. When the orks struck three systems in as many years, the sector governor appealed to the Space Wolves for aid. A rapid strike team was assembled and slipped stealthily into the sector. Fast escorts patrolled likely targets, waiting for the call to action. Skaflock and his men had been on one such frigate, the *Blood Eagle*, when astropaths on the forge world of Cambion reported that they were under attack. They and nearly a dozen other small packs of Scouts had been unleashed onto the world via drop pods, to pinpoint enemy positions for the lightning assault to come. The Scouts had slipped close to scores of landing sites and ork firebases, leaving behind remote-activated designator beacons that would allow the fleet to unleash a devastating initial bombardment within moments of arrival.

The operation had gone according to plan, right up to the point the fleet reached orbit and the initial assault wave began its drop. Then everything went to hell.

The night air trembled beneath the roar of huge turbojets as a Thunderhawk gunship made a low-altitude pass over the forest, but the assault craft held its fire, unable to tell friend from foe in the darkness below. Skaflock bit back a savage curse and tried his vox-caster again, but every channel was blanketed in a searing screech of manufactured noise. He had little doubt that the fleet couldn't pick up the designator beacons through the intense vox jamming, it was even possible that their surveyors were blind as well. He couldn't reach the fleet, much less the assault force his team was supposed to link up with; everyone had been cut off. Instead of catching the ork raiders unawares, they had stepped into a trap.

How, Skaflock's thoughts raged. How could we have been so blind?

The game trail the Wolf Scouts were following angled downwards into a narrow, twisting gully split by a shallow stream. With the wind at their backs and the thunder of the gunship passing overhead, the Space Wolves had no warning as they leapt into the gully and found themselves in the midst of an ork hunting party.

For a moment the orks didn't realize who had fallen in amongst them in the darkness. The hesitation was fatal. Skaflock's nerves sang with bloodlust and adrenaline – to him and the rest of the Wolves it was as though the greenskin raiders were moving in slow motion. Without breaking his stride the Space Wolf decapitated two orks with a single sweep of his blade and buried his armoured shoulder into the chest of a third with bone-crushing force. The air was filled with startled cries and shrieks of pain as the rest of the pack joined the fray, and suddenly the panicked orks were shooting and chopping at anything that moved.

Two heavy ork rounds flattened against Skaflock's power armour. As a member of the great company's Wolf Guard he was better protected than the Scouts under his command, and the impacts barely fazed him. Blood sizzled off the power sword's energy field as he leapt at a cluster of orks further down the gully. The first of the greenskins raised a crude axe, aiming a blow at Skaflock's head, but the Space Marine ducked beneath the swing and cut the raider in two. Before the body had hit the ground Skaflock was upon the second ork, smashing his bolt pistol across the raider's knobbly skull and stabbing it through the chest. The ork pitched forward with a moan – doubling up on the searing blade and trapping it with its death throes.

Skaflock leant against the ork, trying to push it off the blade and narrowly avoided the third greenskin's swing. The crude axe glanced off his right shoulder plate and opened a long, ragged cut on the back of his unprotected neck. A second blow bit into his side, driving the axe's chisel point through the breastplate and into the flesh beneath. Baring his teeth at the pain, Skaflock spun on his heel, tearing his sword free and bringing the blade around in a glowing arc that separated the ork's head from its shoulders. For a few heartbeats the body remained upright, steam rising from the cauterized stump of its neck, then the axe tumbled from nerveless fingers and the corpse pitched over onto the ground.

Within moments, the battle was over. The six Wolf Scouts under Skaflock's command were veterans of more than a dozen campaigns, as skilled with sword and axe as they were with stealth and guile. Nearly two dozen orks lay dead or dying in the gully, staining the stream with their blood. As Skaflock watched, Gunnar Dragonbane, a giant of a man even by Space Marine standards, sent the last of the orks sprawling with a mighty sweep of his axe.

The greenskin landed in a heap, then rolled over onto its back, a grenade clenched in each bloodstained hand. Without thinking, Gunnar brought up his bolt pistol and shot the ork through the head.

Skaflock snarled as the distinctive *crack* of the bolt pistol echoed through the trees. 'I said no shooting!' he cried. As if in answer, the forest erupted in eager cries as the orks sought out the source of the gunshot.

Gunnar let out a rumbling growl, spitting a pair of shiny black pits into the crimson-tinged stream. The huge Scout had a habit of chewing lich-berries; how he kept himself supplied on the long missions off Fenris was a mystery to everyone in the pack. A single berry was poisonous enough to kill a normal human in ten agony-filled seconds. Gunnar claimed the taste improved his disposition. 'Let them come,' he snarled, hefting his axe. 'We've plenty of cover and darkness on our side. We should be hunting *them*, not the other way around.'

'We're not here to hunt orks, Gunnar!' Skaflock snapped. 'We've got to link up with the assault team and guide them off the landing zone to a more defensible position – provided we aren't overrun by ork patrols in the meantime. Now, move out.' Without waiting for an answer, the Wolf Guard leader broke into a run, leaving the Scouts to fall in as he sped on.

The orks were right on their heels. Skaflock heard the greenskins stumble into the gully moments behind them, and then the chase was on. Bursts of wild gunfire tore through the forest around them, kicking up plumes of dirt or blowing branches apart in showers of splinters. The

Wolf Guard increased his speed, pushing his augmented muscles to the limit. Only his enhanced eyesight and agility allowed him to dodge the treacherous roots and low-hanging branches that lay in his path. Slowly but surely, the Wolf Scouts began to pull away from their pursuers, melting into the darkness like shadows.

The sounds of battle called to the Space Wolves like a siren song, growing in intensity. Every few moments Skaflock closed his eyes and focused all of his concentration on the maelstrom of noise, picking out the distinctive notes of different weapons with a practiced ear: storm bolters, boltguns, plasma weapons and the distinctive hammering of crude ork guns.

After fifteen minutes the sounds of the Imperial weapons began to falter; Skaflock bared his fangs in a soundless snarl and drove himself on. Two minutes later he could no longer hear any plasma weapons being fired. Four minutes after that all he could hear were bolters pounding in rapid-fire mode. Then slowly, minute by minute, the bolter fire dwindled away to nothing.

Not long afterwards the wind shifted, blowing from the north-east, and they could smell the blood on the air. The woods had grown silent. Skaflock abandoned all pretence of stealth for the last two kilometres, breaking into a sprint and praying to Russ that his senses had somehow deceived him.

The Wolf Scouts charged headlong into the broad meadow they'd designated as the assault team's drop zone. The gently sloping, grassy field was now a wasteland of mud, ravaged flesh and spilled blood. The black silhouettes of the drop pods reared like tilted gravestones in the crimson moonlight, wreathed in plumes of greasy smoke from the blazing hulls of ork battlewagons.

The dead lay everywhere. Skaflock's mind reeled at the slaughter. The orks had struck from three sides, charging right into the exhaust flames of the drop pods as they settled to the ground. The Space Wolf packs had been cut off from one another even before the drop ramps opened.

The rest of the pack gathered around their leader, staring bleakly at the scene of carnage. Hogun stepped forward, shaking his head mournfully. 'It's a disaster,' he whispered, his voice bleak.

'It's a defeat,' Skaflock said flatly. 'The orks have turned the tables on us for now, but that's the way of war. We've seen worse, Hogun. All of us have.'

'Skaflock's right,' Gunnar said. The expression on his face was bitter, but he nodded solemnly. 'We've been through harder scrapes than this one and won out in the end. We'll just fade back to the mountains and wait for the rest of the company–'

Before the Wolf Guard could finish, the night air trembled with a distant howl of rage and pain that echoed among the derelict drop pods.

As one, the Veteran Scouts looked to their leader. Skaflock flashed a rapid set of hand signals and the pack fanned out into skirmish order, sweeping silently towards the source of the noise.

The howl came from the far side of the drop zone. As the Scouts crept closer, Skaflock caught sight of a dozen Space Wolves – Blood Claws, judging by their youthful features and the markings on their blood-stained armour. They stumbled and staggered through the piled corpses, flinging green-skinned bodies left and right as they searched frantically among the dead. Many of the young Space Marines had removed their helmets, and their faces were twisted with grief.

Skaflock waved the Scouts to a halt and stepped forward. 'Well met, wolf brothers,' he called out. 'We feared there were no survivors.'

Heads darted in Skaflock's direction. Several growled, showing their teeth. One Blood Claw in particular, who had been crouched beside a pile of corpses, rose to his feet. He was tall, and pale with rage, a still-healing gash running from high on his right temple diagonally down into his blood-matted beard. His bolt pistol was holstered, but the deactivated power fist covering his right hand clenched threateningly as he glared at Skaflock and his pack.

The Blood Claw took a step towards the Wolf Scouts. 'All too few,' he snarled, 'thanks to the likes of *you*!' The words dissolved into a bestial roar as the Space Wolf lunged at Skaflock, his eyes burning with hate. The sudden attack caught the Scout leader unawares. Before he could react the Blood Claw closed the distance between them and smote Skaflock on the breastplate of his armour with a sound like a hammer against a bell. The Wolf Scout went sprawling, stunned by the impact. Had the power fist's field been active his chest would have been crushed like an egg.

The red-haired Space Wolf pounced on Skaflock in an instant, knocking him back against the ground. 'Cowards!' he roared, nearly berserk with fury.

Pinned beneath the Blood Claw's bulk, Skaflock barely rolled aside as the Marine's huge fist smashed into the mud mere centimetres from his head. 'Did you slink out of the woods to view your handiwork, or to pick over the bodies of the dead like carrion crows?'

Skaflock felt the Blood Claw's left hand close around his throat. Surprise gave way to a killing rage, rising like a black tide in his chest. Unbidden, his hand tightened on the hilt of his power sword, thumb reaching for the activation switch.

'Remember your oaths, men of Fenris! Russ cannot abide a kinslayer, and the Emperor's eyes are upon you!'

The shout came from the shadow of one of the drop pods, ringed with the bodies of huge, armoured orks. Recognition struck Skaflock like a hammer blow, but it was the Blood Claw who spoke the name first.

'Rothgar!' The young Marine scrambled to his feet, heedless of the power sword pointed at his chest.

The great company's wolf priest stepped slowly into the moonlight. At once, Skaflock could see that the priest was very gravely injured. Rothgar's Terminator suit was rent in half a dozen places, and the jagged tip of a dead ork's power claw jutted from his chest. His face was deathly white, and drops of red glistened in his grey beard. It was a testament to the wolf priest's legendary prowess that he lived at all.

'Well met, Sightblinder,' Rothgar said, showing blood-slicked teeth. 'Late to the battlefield, thank the primarch. What is your report?'

'We've been lured into a trap,' he said simply. 'Once the assault teams began their descent the damned orks started jamming all the vox frequencies somehow.' The Wolf Scout bit back a curse. 'You and these Blood Claws look to be all that's left from the team that landed here.'

'Our pod suffered a malfunction on the way down and we landed some ten kilometres north of the drop zone,' the red-haired Blood Claw said. 'The woods were crawling with ork patrols. We had to fight every step of the way to make it here. Two of our brothers and our Wolf Guard leader were slain.'

'The orks had more time to scout the area than we did. If we could find the best drop zones in each sector, so could they,' Skaflock said. 'But I've never known a greenskin to show such patience and forethought. There's more at work here than meets the eye.'

Rothgar's eyes narrowed conspiratorially. 'This Skargutz has ambitions, I think. He's no Ghazghkull, but he's no mere warboss, either. I think he's got his sights set on uniting the ork warbands in this sector under his banner. If he can prove to them that he can strike anywhere he wants *and* get the best of any force the Imperium can throw at him, they'll join his mob without hesitation.'

'And now that he's bloodied us, he'll pull out of Cambion with whatever plunder he's gathered and start rousing the other warbands.' It was a clever move, as much as it galled Skaflock to admit it.

Skaflock forced his anger and guilt aside and tried to find a way to salvage the situation. 'All right,' he said, addressing the wolf priest. 'The orks have us cut off for now, but our fleet isn't going to sit idle. With every pass they make over the planet their surveyors will have a clearer picture of where the ork landing sites are hidden. The orks can't keep this jamming up forever – they need the vox channels to coordinate themselves almost as much as we do. Most likely they will wait until they think the power cells on our designator beacons have run dry, then they'll begin their pullout. In the meantime, Kjarl here can watch over you at one of our campsites while my pack and I locate the main ork camp. When the jamming lifts, we can contact Lord Haldane and coordinate a counter strike before Skargutz can escape.'

Kjarl shook his head in disgust. 'Have you no idea what's happened?'

'How could he?' Rothgar said darkly. When he turned to Skaflock, his expression was even more pained than before. 'Have you ever known

Haldane Ironhammer to let another lead an assault in his place? He dropped with us in the first wave, lad. Your lord lies somewhere among the fallen.'

Lord Haldane and his Wolf Guard had made their stand on a low hillock just to the side of their drop pod. They'd fought like wolves at bay, like heroes of old, but one by one they had been overcome.

Haldane's Terminator armour hadn't been hacked apart, as Skaflock had expected. It had been hacked *open*. The body of the wolf lord was nowhere to be seen.

Tears of rage coursed freely down Kjarl's face. 'What have they done with our lord?'

The Space Wolves parted as Rothgar moved slowly and painfully among them. The pain in his eyes as he surveyed the scene had nothing to do with his injuries. 'They have taken him,' he said hoarsely.

'Why?' Kjarl said.

'The orks must mean to give him as a trophy to their leader,' Skaflock replied, biting back his rage. 'A wolf lord's head would be a tremendous prize for an ambitious warboss like Skargutz.'

'Then it's a blood feud, by Russ!' Kjarl raised his fist and howled a challenge to the sky. The rest of the Blood Claws followed suit, the intensity of their cries raising the hairs on the back of Skaflock's neck.

'The filthy greenskins have defiled our lord.' Kjarl roared. He turned to Rothgar. 'Hear me, priest, I swear that I and my pack will find Lord Haldane and reclaim the honour of our company, and woe to any ork that steps in our way.'

'Don't be a fool,' Skaflock said coldly. 'You won't get more than a kilometre before the orks kill you.'

The Blood Claws snarled in wordless anger. Kjarl turned on the Scout leader, his power fist raised. 'Keep your gutless bleating to yourself,' he snarled. 'This is a matter of honour – something you clearly know little about.'

Skaflock advanced on the Blood Claw. 'I know that you've been on this planet less than an hour, and I've been here for three months. I know approximately how many orks there are in this sector. I know their tactics, their equipment, the location of their bases and the routes they're likely to take. I know *exactly* what your chances are, charging about on an ork-held world and lashing out at every foe that presents itself.'

The vehemence in Skaflock's voice took Kjarl aback for a moment. 'What would you have us do then? Cower in the bushes and let them get away with this? What about your duty to Haldane?'

'Don't lecture me about my duty, whelp,' Skaflock said darkly. Meeting Rothgar's eye, he knelt by Haldane's armour and solemnly took up the wolf lord's axe. 'If we hope to reclaim Haldane's body we will have to swallow our anger and put our lord's honour before our own.' He raised the axe before the wolf priest. 'I swear on this axe that I will find Haldane and do what must be done.'

The wolf priest held Skaflock's gaze for a long moment, and then Rothgar nodded slowly. 'I hear you, Skaflock Sightblinder,' he said, 'and I hold you to your oath.'

'And *I* swear,' Kjarl hissed, 'to tear your head from your shoulders if you fail.'

Skaflock grinned mirthlessly. 'If I fail, I doubt you'll have the chance, but so be it,' he said. 'For now, you and your men gather weapons and ammunition from the dead: flamers, grenades and spare bolt pistol rounds.'

Kjarl glared at the Wolf Scout, but beneath the forbidding gaze of the wolf priest he swallowed his pride. 'We will not be long,' he growled, and issued orders to his pack.

Skaflock turned to Rothgar, but the wolf priest raised a gauntleted hand. 'I will abide here, Sightblinder. Do not concern yourself about me. Russ knows I've survived worse than this.' With his other hand he drew the Fang of Morkai from his belt. 'Whatever else, I still have my duty to the dead.'

'As do we, Rothgar. As do we.'

Haldane's blood made his scent easy to follow. Even where countless ork feet had trampled across the wolf lord's trail, Hogun's sharp eyes picked out dark spots of crimson to mark where their fallen leader had gone.

Skaflock had assigned a pair of Blood Claws to each Scout, taking Kjarl and another young Blood Claw for himself. After several kilometres the trail led out of the woods and down into a narrow, twisting valley dominated by isolated stands of stunted, twisted trees. Here the ork trail was easy to follow, and Skaflock knew at once where they were headed.

'There's a firebase up ahead,' he said to Kjarl as they loped stealthily along the valley floor. 'A small one. We scouted it out a couple of weeks ago. It's probably where they're staging all of the patrols in this sector, so there will likely be a lot of traffic. I expect the orks carrying Haldane will commandeer a vehicle there to carry their trophy to Skargutz.'

Kjarl glared resentfully at Skaflock. 'We'll see,' he said darkly.

Half a kilometre from the firebase Skaflock waved the Scouts off the trail, following a path that led to higher ground and offered a commanding view of the ork encampment. Hogun and Kjarl lay to either side of Skaflock as he scanned the firebase from a stony ledge using his magnoculars.

'No sign of Haldane. If he was still there the orks would be showing off the body,' Skaflock said, passing the magnoculars to Hogun. 'There is something interesting though, a convoy of large trucks unloading fresh troops. And I don't recognize their clan markings.'

'What does this have to do with Haldane?' Kjarl hissed impatiently.

'This sector has the largest number of major ork landing sites on the planet,' Skaflock explained, 'so we always suspected that Skargutz himself was somewhere nearby. We never could find him, though. At the time, we thought that was pretty strange, but now it's clear they must have set up a hidden base to conceal the vox jammers and shelter the bulk of their reserve troops from the initial bombardment.' The Wolf Guard studied the ork trucks thoughtfully. 'I'll bet he's still there, waiting for word that the ambush was successful, and those trucks will lead us right to him.'

Kjarl let out a snort. 'And how do you expect the trucks to get us anywhere once we've killed the drivers?'

Skaflock frowned. 'Killed the drivers?'

'You don't expect they'll survive once we've stormed the base, do you?'

'We aren't storming the base, Kjarl. We're sneaking onto those vehicles as they head back to their base.'

'*Sneaking.*' Kjarl's lip curled in distaste. 'Cowering like a craven is more like. This is not the way the sons of Russ are meant to behave.'

'I won't speak for you, Blood Claw, but I'll behave any way I must if it gets me one step closer to my goal. And so will you, so long as I'm in command.' Skaflock's stare was hard as adamantine. 'Tell your men we're going to *sneak* down to the firebase's northern gate. Pistols will be holstered and flamers doused. Combat will be avoided at all costs. Understood?'

'Understood,' Kjarl said contemptuously, and slid down the slope to where the rest of the group waited.

Hogun watched the young Space Wolf go. 'A good thumping would knock sense into that lad,' he muttered.

'No time for that now. I want you to round up our melta bombs and set up a diversion on the southern end of that base.'

'Good as done,' Hogun said, handing back the magnoculars and heading down the slope.

Skaflock gathered the Space Marines and made for the road north of the firebase in a single, widely spaced group. The Space Wolves reached the dirt road almost a kilometre north of the base, then began working south until they were within less than a hundred metres of the base's crude gate. There they separated into their three-man teams and settled into cover near the road's edge.

The firebase itself was simple and rugged. An irregular perimeter of packed earthen ramparts five metres high was topped with razor wire and littered with small mines. Rough, uneven watchtowers composed of scrap metal and cannibalized shipping containers rose behind the ramparts, sprouting a lethal assortment of heavy guns and wandering searchlights. The noise within the earthen walls was tremendous, a discordant roar of shouting voices, revving engines, machine tools and occasional bursts of gunfire.

Barely a few minutes after the Space Wolves had settled into place, Hogun seemed to materialize out of the darkness at Skaflock's elbow. 'Three minutes,' he reported, then went to take his place along the line.

Kjarl eyed the ork base expectantly. 'What now?'

'When the bombs go off, the orks will think they're under attack. I expect that whoever is running that mob in there is going to send the trucks back to Skargutz for more troops.'

Before Kjarl could reply a string of blue-white flashes ran along the base's southern perimeter, followed by the sharp *crack* of the melta charges. Streams of wild tracer fire fanned and corkscrewed into the air. 'Get ready,' Skaflock called to the Space Marines.

Within minutes, the scrap metal gate at the northern entrance was pulled back with a tortured shriek of twisted metal, and eight huge ork trucks lumbered onto the road in a billowing cloud of blue-black exhaust.

Skaflock turned to Kjarl. 'We'll wait for the last three trucks, then I'll give the signal–'

The Wolf Scout's instructions were cut short as a stream of heavy ork rounds whipsawed through the air over his head. Skaflock's heart clenched as he ducked his head and stole a look at the firebase to his left.

The watchtowers had somehow spotted the three Space Marines at the far end of the line. Searchlights transfixed the Space Wolves from three separate directions, and the orks in the towers opened fire with every weapon they had. Skaflock watched as one of the Wolf Scouts rose to a crouch and drew his bolt pistol in a single, fluid motion. He snapped off two quick shots, destroying two of the searchlights in a shower of sparks, but as he pivoted to fire at the third a burst from an ork gun blew his head apart in a shower of blood and bone. The two Blood Claws leapt to their feet as one, drawing their weapons and charging at the enemy encampment.

'No,' Kjarl roared, surging to his feet. Skaflock tackled him before he was fully upright.

'Stand your ground,' Skaflock cried, shouting into the maelstrom.

'My men–'

'Your men are already dead, Kjarl,' Skaflock said. At the firebase the Blood Claws had made it into cover beneath the reach of the guns, but a mob of orks was already charging from the gates, their crude axes held high. 'You can either die alongside them or remember your obligation to your lord. Which will it be?'

With a wordless snarl Kjarl shoved Skaflock away and readied himself to move.

The last three ork trucks were coming up fast. Skaflock gauged speed and distance, then shouted 'Now,' and bolted for the road.

The Space Wolves rose in a ragged line and rushed at the ork transports, leaping for struts and flanges on their armoured flanks. Kjarl landed easily to Skaflock's right, both men glaring balefully back at the firebase dwindling in the distance.

The ork trucks roared along dirt roads and broken trails for nearly two hours, then abruptly turned onto an old, sharply sloping roadway littered with rocks and debris. The small convoy climbed steadily up the side of a mountain for several minutes, then turned suddenly into the mountainside itself. The trucks' huge engines thundered in the tight confines of the tunnel as the convoy descended deep into the bowels of the mountain. The vehicles finally came to a stop in a cavernous, dimly lit chamber reeking of exhaust fumes and echoing with the bedlam of an ork warband at work.

Skaflock slowly eased himself from the truck's undercarriage and lowered himself to the ground. Peering left and right, he could see that the ork trucks had been driven into an enormous staging area crowded with other vehicles, piles of crates and gangs of grease-stained gretchin mechanics. Illumination in the cavernous space was poor, creating dark alleys between stacked crates and pools of shadow cast by the looming vehicles. Skaflock rolled out from under the truck to the right and dashed into cover between two stacks of looted shipping containers. The Wolf Guard kept moving, trusting that his brothers would track his scent as he worked his way towards the edge of the broad cavern.

Dark shapes emerged from the shadows, weapons held ready. Kjarl was the first to reach Skaflock, his eyes searching the shadows. 'Where are we?'

'We're in an old mine, somewhere south of the landing zone,' Skaflock said. 'There's scores of them honeycombing the mountains in this region. The orks are probably tapping the mine's abandoned reactors to power their jamming system.' The Wolf Guard sought out Hogun. 'Do you have the scent?'

The Scout nodded. 'His blood's like a beacon. Not much further to go, I think.'

'All right.' To the assembled Marines, Skaflock said, 'Stick to your teams. No shooting until I give the signal. Hogun, you're on point. Gunnar, cover the rear. Move out.'

Moving quickly and quietly the Space Wolves made their way around the perimeter of the cavern and down a rough-hewn passage running deeper into the side of the mountain. Few of the mine's lamps still functioned, and the darkness served them well in the wide tunnels. They passed numerous side passages, abandoned lifts and galleries; on several occasions the Space Marines had to find an alternative route to avoid mobs of orks along their path. Each time Hogun led them unerringly back on track.

This sector of the mine had been given over to offices and dormitories for the indentured miners who once laboured in the tunnels below. Up ahead, the Space Wolves began to hear the raucous sounds of a celebration, and Skaflock felt a cold, black rage welling up in his heart.

The passageway ahead ended in a broad double doorway, opening onto a huge rectangular space carved from the living rock. Once it had served as a dining hall for the miners, but now it was packed with orks feasting on the plunder of Cambion. Several hundred greenskins tore at haunches of bloody meat and drank from steel casks of ale, roaring drunken boasts of their fighting skill.

The far end of the chamber was given over to a raised dais, where priests of the Ecclesiarchy once exhorted the faithful as they took their meals. Now it supported a crude throne of black iron, where an enormous, armoured ork sat, surrounded by his bodyguard.

A man's bloody body lay at the foot of the throne, wearing only the black undergarment of a Space Marine. As the Space Wolves watched, Skargutz the Render laid an armoured boot on Haldane's dead chest, like a hunter posing with his prize.

The Marines made not a single sound, but Skaflock could feel the fury seething from them like heat from a forge. Kjarl's eyes were fixed on Skargutz, his fangs bared. 'Here it ends,' he said, his power fist crackling into life.

Skaflock nodded solemnly. 'The time for stealth is done at last,' he said, slipping into the tongue of their homeland. 'Now is the time for broken swords and splintered shields, for red ruin and the woeful song of steel. Haldane's eyes are upon us; his honour lies in our hands. Let no man falter until the deed is done.'

Raising Haldane's frost axe high, Skaflock charged through the doorway, and suddenly the hall was filled with the howl of Space Wolves.

The orks nearest the doorway stared in shock at the sudden appearance of the Space Marines. Skaflock leapt forward, swinging the frost axe in a wide arc and carving through the torsos of the three greenskins before him. Grenades flew overhead and bolt pistol shells tore through the packed ranks of orks. With an angry hiss, a half-dozen streams of liquid fire immolated scores of shrieking greenskins; their grenades and ammunition detonated in the heat, adding to the carnage.

An ork clambered over a table wielding an axe and Skaflock shot it in the face. The range was so close the mass-reactive shell had no time to arm, blowing the greenskin's head apart and bursting in the chest of the ork behind. Another of the foul creatures charged him from the right; the Wolf Scout ducked under the greenskin's wild swing and cut the ork's legs out from under it with a backhanded stroke of the axe.

Pandemonium swept the hall. The greenskin mob recoiled from the fire and slaughter around the doorway, many shooting wildly into the backs of those who tried to put up a fight. A heavy bullet smashed into Skaflock's shoulder, cannoning off his armour and half-spinning him around, but the impact barely halted his headlong charge. The orks gave way before him, those that did not move fast enough were shot point-blank or split like a melon by a stroke of the axe. Dimly, Skaflock was aware of Kjarl close by his side, protecting his flanks and firing bolt pistol shells into the retreating mob.

Suddenly the ork retreat stopped, surged backwards, then parted like a wave, and Skaflock found himself face-to-face with Skargutz's bodyguard.

With a roar, the armoured orks opened fire at the oncoming Space Wolves. Two more rounds smashed into Skaflock's chest, flattening against his breastplate, and men screamed behind him as more bullets found their mark. Skaflock raised his bolt pistol and fired at an approaching bodyguard, but the shells bounced harmlessly off the ork's armoured skull. Then the two sides crashed into one another and all semblance of order dissolved into a chaotic melee.

Skaflock leapt at the bodyguard before him, swinging the frost axe at the ork's claw-tipped arm. The keen blade sheared through the metal joint and the flesh beneath, severing the arm at the elbow in a fountain of blood. The ork bellowed in pain and the Wolf Scout put a bolt pistol shell into its gaping maw, blowing out the back of its skull. He ducked around the armoured form as it toppled to the ground, only to be struck in the chest by a blow that drove the air from his lungs and racked him with searing waves of agony. Skaflock fell to the ground, convulsing in pain as a lithe, black-armoured form stepped over him, levelling a long-barrelled pistol at his head. The alien's face was hidden behind a helmet shaped like a leering skull. Its black, chitinous armour was painted with runes of clotted gore, and squares of expertly flensed skin flapped like parchment from fine hooks hung about its waist. A detached part of Skaflock's mind recognized the scraps of flesh as the skinned faces of human children.

The Wolf Guard's mind reeled. A dark eldar? Here? He'd heard tales of exiles from the hidden world of Commorragh offering their skills to warlords in exchange for plunder – usually paid in living flesh for the sadistic xenos to sate their lusts upon. Skaflock realised now where Skargutz had got his powerful jamming devices from, and was horrified to think of how many innocent lives the foul xenos would claim in return.

'You offer me such poor sport,' the dark eldar said. The words came out as a liquid rasp, bubbling wetly from mutilated lungs. The xenos lashed the air with a long, barbed whip of darkly glimmering steel. 'But fear not. You shall have many opportunities to entertain me in the months to come.'

Suddenly the air around the dark eldar shimmered as a flurry of bolt pistol shells streaked at his head and chest – and vanished as if swallowed by the void. From out of the raging melee Hogun and six Blood Claws rushed at the xenos warrior, bloodied chainswords held high.

The alien slipped among the Space Wolves like quicksilver, lashing with his barbed whip. One viper-like blow was enough to paralyze a Space Marine with waves of pain, a second strike shredded the nerves and brought agonizing death. Three Blood Claws died without landing a single blow, the rest hurled themselves at the dark eldar, aiming a flurry of blows at the alien that would have ripped a mere human into tatters. Yet for all their speed and skill, the dark eldar dodged their blows with ease, or absorbed them with his powerful force field. Hogun emptied his bolt pistol at the alien's head, each shell swallowed up by the warrior's eldritch defences. The dark eldar casually pointed his pistol at the Wolf Scout's head and shot him through the eye. One of the Blood Claws leapt at the dark eldar with a roar and the alien spun effortlessly away from the attack. Faster than the eye could follow, the alien's whip struck once, twice, and the Space Wolf died in mid-swing.

With an effort of will, Skaflock forced his traumatized muscles to work, raising his own pistol and squeezing off shot after shot as the dark eldar's whip took another Blood Claw in the throat. Each round disappeared like all the rest – until suddenly an actinic flash obscured the alien and a sound like a thunderclap rang out as his force field finally overloaded. The dark eldar staggered, and the Wolf Scout saw a ragged hole in the breastplate of his armour.

The dark eldar let out a shriek of fury and a bubbling stream of curses – and then Kjarl seemed to materialize behind the alien, seizing its helmet in his power fist and tearing the alien's head from his armoured shoulders.

Skaflock rolled onto his side and tried to push himself to his feet. His muscles twitched and spasmed from the effects of the whip, and bursts of intense pain rippled through his chest. Then a huge fist closed on his arm and pulled him upright. 'No... faltering... yet,' Kjarl said breathlessly, flashing a wolfish grin. His armour was pierced in a dozen places and streaked with blood and gore, but his eyes were fierce and bright.

The Wolf Scout forced his eyes to focus and take in the scene around him. Over half the hall was ablaze, and the dead lay in heaps from the doorway to the dais. At the foot of his throne, Skargutz and a handful of orks fought the battered remnant of Skaflock's band. As he watched, Gunnar decapitated an ork with a stroke of his chainsword then darted in to strike at Skargutz's knee. Sparks flew as the sword's razor-edged teeth glanced off the armoured joint. The Scout leapt back for another strike, but not quite fast enough. The warboss's power claw caught Gunnar in mid-leap, slicing the Space Marine in two.

Skaflock roared in rage and anguish, pushing away from Kjarl and staggering towards Skargutz, gaining speed with each painful step. His bolt pistol thundered and bucked in his hand; two orks fell with gaping holes in their chests and a third round punched a bloody hole through the warboss's leg before the ammunition ran out. He tossed the empty pistol aside and gripped the frost axe with both hands. 'Skargutz the

Render, your end is upon you,' he cried. 'You have dared the righteous wrath of the Allfather, and now there will be a reckoning.'

The warboss spun with surprising speed, scattering two Marines with a sweep of his claw. Skaflock leapt forward, rolling between the ork's massive legs, then rose to a crouch and sliced across the back of the warboss's knees. Pistons and hydraulic lines burst; joints and muscles failed, and Skargutz toppled with a crash. The huge ork tried to twist onto his side and lash backwards with his claw, but Kjarl caught its bloodied blades in his power fist. For a moment both warriors struggled, neither gaining ground on the other until, with a shriek of tortured metal, the power claw gave way in a shower of sparks.

Skaflock leapt forward, raising the frost axe high in a two-handed grip. 'When Morkai's kin drag your soul past the Hall of Heroes, tell them it was Haldane Ironhammer's axe that slew you!' The ork's snarl was cut short as the frost axe fell and the warboss's head bounced across the dais to stop at the dead wolf lord's feet.

Kjarl looked down at the dead warboss, his shoulders heaving with exertion. 'It is done.'

'Not quite yet,' Skaflock said. He gestured to the surviving Space Wolves, a single Scout and two Blood Claws. 'Go and stand watch at the door.' Then, to Kjarl: 'Let us clear a table to place our lord upon, and lay the bodies of his foes at his feet.'

They pulled a table onto the dais and laid Haldane upon it, and piled his dead foes around him. As Kjarl laid the body of the dark eldar on the pile, he suddenly frowned. 'What's this?'

Skaflock watched the Blood Claw pull a small, silvery object from the alien's belt. A pale cobalt light gleamed on its surface. 'Some kind of control box?' he suggested.

'Perhaps,' Kjarl said, and crushed it in his fist. Suddenly the Blood Claw tensed, his hand going to his ear. 'Static!' he said. 'I can hear static on my vox-bead! That box must have controlled the vox jammers.'

One of the Blood Claws called from the doorway. 'The greenskins are massing at the end of the corridor. They'll be on us in minutes.'

Thinking quickly, Skaflock started digging through his carry-bags. He still had three designator beacons that the Scouts hadn't found time to deploy. 'A few minutes are all we need,' he said, laying out the beacons and pressing their activation runes. 'Soon this whole base will be a pyre for our lord, and the end of the ork invasion of Cambion.'

As he worked, a shadow fell over the Wolf Guard. Skaflock glanced up to see Kjarl watching him appraisingly. After a moment the Blood Claw steeled himself and said, 'It appears I misjudged you, Skaflock. You're a braver man than I gave you credit for, and a true son of Russ.'

Skaflock grinned and raised his hand in a weary salute. 'And you fought well, Kjarl Grimblood. I owe you my life. I expect the skalds will sing of your deeds for years to come.'

'So do I, by Russ.' Kjarl said with a smile. 'Speaking of which – I don't suppose you've got a plan for getting us out of here?' Nearly the entire chamber was ablaze, the rock walls running with streams of jellied fire. The heat and smoke was beginning to affect even the Space Wolves' enhanced endurance.

Skaflock grinned. 'Listen.' Beyond the high ceiling came distant, heavy beats, like the pounding of a massive drum. Each one was louder than the one before. 'Bombardment rounds,' the Wolf Guard said.

From the doorway, one of the Space Wolves let out a yell. 'The orks are retreating.'

'I doubt they want to get buried alive any more than we do,' Skaflock said. He glanced at Kjarl. 'Ready?'

Kjarl's eyes widened. 'You want to fight your way through a horde of panicked orks and out into the middle of an *orbital bombardment*?'

'Of course.' Skaflock raised the frost axe. 'I'd rather take my chances with the bombardment than risk Rothgar's fury if I failed to return this. He'd curse my soul until the end of time!'

Kjarl Grimblood threw back his head and roared with laughter. 'Lead on, brother,' he said, clapping Skaflock on the shoulder. And with a last salute to their fallen lord the Space Wolves charged after the fleeing orks, filling the air with their bone-chilling howls.

ORPHANS OF THE KRAKEN

Richard Williams

I am not yet dead.

I am only on the brink. I cannot tell anymore how long I have been here. My first heart begins its beat. I count the minutes until it finishes and begins again. I clutch at the sound as long as I can. It is my only reminder that I am still alive.

It is not fear that holds me from the edge. I see what is ahead and it welcomes me. But I have made an oath. Until I have held to my word, I cannot allow myself to fall.

The tyranid hive ship drifted silently in space. I watched it through my window. It was vast and it was an abomination, ugly beyond description, organic but no creation of any natural god. It was also, as best as we could determine, very, very dead.

My name is Brother Sergeant Tiresias of the Astartes Chapter Scythes of the Emperor, and I came here searching for legends.

I command the 21st Salvation Team, and if that sounds like a grand title then let me correct you now. It is not. There were eight of us at the beginning, myself and seven neophytes. Battle-brothers in training, youths, juveniles, children. I am told that they are our future. I know better; we do not have a future.

By that day I had been in their company, and they in mine, for over two years. Our time together had not been easy, nor without loss. The three empty seats beside me were testimony to that. But the three we had left behind had not disappointed me nearly as greatly as the four who remained. They had slunk to the far end of the assault boat, gathered around one of their number who was making some small adjustment to the squad's heavy bolter. They spoke softly, thinking they would not be heard.

'There… I think it'll work better that way.'

'Are you sure, Brother Narro? It is not Codex.'

'Of course he's sure, Hwygir. Who're you going to trust? Your brother here who's been slicing up these vermin as long as you have, or a book written by some hoary old creaker? These bugs weren't even around back then so the codex is as much use as a–'

'Show some respect, Vitellios,' the fourth of them interrupted. 'The sergeant can hear you.'

'Pasan. I tell you, after all he's put us through, I don't give a scrag if he does.'

It had not always been like this. At the start, in our first few insertions, their voices had been full of hope and they had spoken of what we might find. They had repeated the stories they had heard during their training: rumours of Space Marines wearing the insignia of the Scythes still alive inside the tyranid bio-ships; stories of Navy boarding parties surrounded, nearly destroyed, before being saved by such warriors who then disappeared back into the depths; stories of bio-ships convulsing and crumpling in the midst of battle, though untouched by any external force. Stories. Legends. Myths.

They believed, though. They fantasised that, in every dead bio-ship we sought, whole companies of Astartes waited. That they had not been annihilated in the onslaught of Hive Fleet Kraken at all. That Hive Fleet Kraken, that almighty judgement upon us which had destroyed fleets and consumed worlds, might have simply overlooked them. And so they had survived, forgotten, until these seven brave neophytes arrived to rescue them and become heroes to the Chapter, and become legends themselves.

Myths. Fantasies. Lies. As I already knew and they, once they stepped aboard a bio-ship for the first time, quickly discovered.

'Ten seconds!' the pilot's voice crackled over the intravox. 'Brace! Brace! Brace!'

I braced. Here we went again. Another legend to chase, another myth to find, another lie to unmask. How many more before we finally accept it? How many more until we finally decide to end it all?

My wards advanced cautiously from our insertion point into the ship. They fell into their formation positions with the ease of long experience. The hivers, the up-spire Narro and the trash Vitellios, took turns on point and edge. The trog savage Hwygir carried the heavy bolter on his shoulder further back as snath. Pasan, one of the few of the neophytes to have been born, as I, on noble Sotha, walked in the tang position to allow him to command.

If our auspexes and scanners had not already told us that the hive ship was dead, we would have known the instant we stepped aboard. The corridors were dark; the only light our own torches. As they illuminated our path ahead we could see the skin of the walls sagging limply from its ribs, its surface discoloured and shrivelling. The door-valves gaped open, the muscles that controlled them wasted.

We waded through a putrid sludge. Though it moved like a sewer it was no waste product, it was alive. It was billions of microscopic tyranid organisms, released by the bio-ship at the moment of its death and designed solely to consume the flesh of their dead parent, consume and multiply. More creatures, gigantic to the microbes, tiny to us, floated amongst them, eating their fill, then were speared and devoured by larger cousins who hunted them.

The hive ship was dead, and in death it became filled with new life. Each creature, from the sludge-microbe up, was created to feed and to be fed upon in turn, concentrating the bio-matter of the ship into apex predators that would bound gleefully aboard the next bio-ship they encountered to be re-absorbed and recycled. In this way, the tyranid xenoforms transformed the useless carcass of their parent into another legion of monsters to take to the void. The carcass of their parent, and any other bio-matter foolish enough to have stepped onboard.

'Biters! To the right!' Vitellios called. The lights on the gun barrels swung around in response. I heard the double shot as Vitellios and Pasan fired and then the screech of their target.

'Step back! Step back!' Pasan ordered automatically. 'Narro!'

Scout Narro had his bolter ready and triggered a burst of fire at the creatures. The shells exploded in their midst, bursting their fat little bodies and tossing them to the side.

The shots would alert every active tyranid nearby. Pasan swivelled his shotgun with its torch across the leathery walls of the chamber, searching for more. Vitellios simply blasted every dark corner. There was another screech for his trouble. The Scouts swung their weapons towards the noise, illuminating the target with blazing light.

There was nothing there. The corner was empty. The sludge rippled slightly around the base of the armoured buttress supporting the wall, but that was all.

I waited for Pasan to order Vitellios to investigate. I saw the acolyte's helmet turn to the hiver, his face shining gold from his suit lights. I waited for him to give the order, but he did not. He turned his head back and started to move out of position himself.

'Scout Pasan, hold!' I ordered angrily. 'Scout Vitellios, assess that area.'

Vitellios, expecting the order, stepped forward with a confidence no one in his situation should have. He enjoyed it, though, defying the others' expectations, claiming that places like this reminded him of home.

Though having seen myself the lower hive levels on the planet where he was born, I would not disagree.

Vitellios prodded the floor beneath the sludge to ensure it was solid and then stepped right into the corner. He shone his torch up to where the armoured buttress ended just short of the roof.

'Vitellios!' Narro whispered urgently. 'It's moving!'

Vitellios had an underhiver's instincts. He did not question. He did not waste even a split-second to look at the buttress that had suddenly started shifting towards him; he simply ran.

'Hwygir!' he called as he sprinted clear, kicking up a spray of sludge behind him.

Hwygir pulled the trigger on the big gun. The hellfire shell sped across the chamber and smashed into the buttress even as it launched itself at the Scout fleeing away. The sharp needles within the shell plunged into the creature's body, pumping acid, and it spasmed. It tore itself from the wall, revealing the tendrils and sucker-tubes on its underside and collapsed into the sludge, there to be recycled once more.

What it revealed, what it had slowly been consuming, was even more horrific. Three metres high, even collapsed against the wall, was a tyranid monster the size of a Dreadnought. Its skin was armoured like a carapace, its limbs ended in claws like tusks, its face was all the more dreadful for having been half-eaten away.

'Fire!' Vitellios shouted, and he, Pasan and Narro poured a half dozen rounds into the juddering, foetid corpse.

'It is dead already, neophytes. Do not waste your ammunition.' Shaking my head, I rechecked the auspex for the beacon's signal. 'This way.'

I had begun with seven neophytes under my command. On the hive ship identified as #34732 *Halisa*, we stumbled across a colony of dormant genestealers and Neophyte Metellian was killed. On #10998 *Archelon*, Neophyte Quintos lost an arm and part of his face to a tyranid warrior corpse that had more life in it than he had assumed. It almost bested me before I caught it with my falx and finally put an end to it. On #51191 *Notho*, Neophyte Varos slipped through an orifice in the floor. When we finally located him in the depths of the ship, he had been crushed to death.

We have inserted into over a dozen dead hive ships now. We Salvation Teams have probably stepped aboard more bio-ships than any other human warrior. Perhaps more than any alien as well. When I speak, it is with that experience. For all the vaunted diversity of the tyranid fleet, for all that Imperial adepts struggle to catalogue them into thousands of ship classes; the truth is that once you are in their guts they are all the same: the same walls of flesh, the same valve portals; the same cell-chambers leading to the major arteries leading to the vital organs at the ship's heart.

But for all the now routine horrors I have witnessed within these ships, on occasion they can still surprise me.

'God-Emperor...' Narro whispered as he looked out across the expanse.

The beacon had taken us up, but the tubule we followed did not lead into another cell-chamber, nor even into an artery. Instead it dropped away into a cavity so vast that our torches could not reach the opposite wall. At our feet, the sludge slovenly poured over the ledge in an oozing waterfall into the darkness on the floor. To our left, one side of the cavity was filled with a row of giant ovoids; each one as big as, bigger even, than our mighty Thunderhawks. They glistened with a sickly purple sheen as we shone a light upon them. Several of them were split open. One was cracked. Inside, emerging from it, still clenched tight upon itself in a rigor of death, I saw the creature these birthing sacs contained.

Bio-titans.

Bio-titans. Massive war-engines that, even hunched like spiders, towered over our heaviest tanks on the battlefield. Screaming, hideous, living machines bristling with limbs, each one a weapon, which had carved apart so many Imperial lines of defence.

'There... there's another one,' Pasan said and I shone my torch after his. It wasn't just one. The cavity was filled with these monsters, every one collapsed, knocked aside, dead. Their bloated bodies and scything limbs were barely distinguishable from the flesh of the hive ship beneath them.

It was Narro who finally broke the silence.

'Hierophants,' he concluded as he peered at them. 'Immature, judging from their size.'

'You mean these are runts?' Vitellios exclaimed, his usual cocksure manner jolted from him.

'Oh, indeed,' Narro replied. 'Certain reports from defence troopers quite clearly–'

'Of course they are, Scout Vitellios,' I interrupted. 'Do not underestimate our foe in the future. Acolyte Pasan, the beacon leads us forwards, organise our descent.'

Pasan stepped along the cliff-face, examining the floor far beneath. The other neophytes watched the path or checked their weapons.

'Honoured sergeant... could you... could you look at this?' Pasan asked me quietly.

Throne! Could this boy not even command as simple a task as this by himself?

'What is it, acolyte?' I said, biting down on my irritation as I went over to him.

'The floor...' He lay down flat and angled his torch to the base of the cavity directly beneath us. 'They look... they're biters, aren't they? It's covered with them.'

I looked; he was right. What appeared to be solid ground was indeed the segmented backs of a thousand biters packed together as though they were crammed in a rations can.

'And what will you do about it, acolyte?'

Pasan hesitated. Vitellios did not.

'We should head back, we can find a way around–'

I cut him off. 'An Astartes does not retreat in the face of common insects, neophyte. He finds a way through.'

I turned back to Pasan and watched the youth think. He finally produced an answer and looked at me for approval. His plan was sound, but still I was unimpressed by his need for my validation.

'What are you waiting for, acolyte? That is your plan, issue your orders.'

'Yes, sergeant. Culmonios, load a hellfire shell and deploy here.'

Hwygir nodded with all the eagerness of one who knows his inferiority and only wishes to be accepted. He had been birthed Hwygir, most certainly on some dirt rock floor on Miral. He had chosen the name Culmonios when he became an Astartes, I found it distasteful to address a stunted savage such as he with such a noble appellation. I used it in speech at first, but I could never bring myself to think it. Only Pasan still used it now.

The trog hefted the bulky heavy bolter to the lip of the ledge.

'He'll need bracing,' Vitellios muttered.

'I was just coming to that,' Pasan replied. 'Vitellios, dig in and brace him. Narro too. Have the next shell ready as soon as he fires.'

Finally I saw something of command coming to Pasan. He organised the squad into a firing team slowly and methodically. He even carved into the tubule wall itself to provide a steadier base to shoot directly down at the floor and strapped the heavy weapon to Hwygir tightly to ensure the recoil at such an awkward angle did not tear it from his hand.

'Fire!' Pasan ordered finally. The squad braced and Hwygir pulled the trigger. 'Reload. Adjust aim. Fire. Reload. Adjust aim. Fire. Reload.' Pasan continued, the squad following along. 'Halt!'

He and I looked over the edge. The flesh scouring acid of the hellfire had eaten into the biters and, without a foe close by, they had scattered away from the wall and started to feed instead on the corpses of the bio-titans, leaving a path clear across the cavity. It was as I had expected.

What I had not expected was what had now been revealed, the food on which the biters had been feasting. I looked down, my throat tight in horror, at the field of damaged and pockmarked power armour now on display, black and yellow like my own. The feast had been my brothers.

I had only ever seen such a sight before in my dreams, my nightmares of Sotha's destruction. I was there at the fall, but I did not witness the worst of it. By the time our last lines were being overrun, I was already aboard a Thunderhawk, unconscious, my chest and legs a mess of cuts and bio-plasma burns. A sergeant had pulled me from the barricade as I fell, thrown me upon an exhausted ammo-cart returning for fresh supplies and then stepped back into the battle. None who survived knew my rescuer's name.

I do not know how I made it from the ammo-cart onto one of the escaping Thunderhawks. I do remember how the Thunderhawk spiralled and dropped as it desperately sought to dodge through the rain of landing spores still pouring down, now unopposed, upon my home. I was awake in time to feel the last tug of Sotha's gravity upon me as we left it to be consumed by our foe, and to know that we had failed our holy duty.

We cleared the bio-titan birthing cavity of the biters and lesser xenoforms. It took nearly a full day, with the mysterious beacon still a steady pulse upon our auspex, but it had to be done. This place was no longer a simple obstacle to be surmounted in our larger search; it was sacred ground. We called back to the boat and ordered our retainer workers despatched to join us. When they arrived they added their firepower to our own in the final clearance of the cavity. My wards stayed on watch while our retainers began their work to recover our fallen brothers. We counted, as best we could, the armour of thirty-seven battle-brothers. Over a third of a company had died in this place, battling the fledgling bio-titans as they burst from their sacs. What a fight it must have been.

The armour bore the markings of the Fifth Company. They had not been on Sotha when Kraken came. They had fought and died months before. Chapter Master Thorcyra had despatched them to the very edges of the sectors the Scythes protected, responding to reports of rebellion and xenos incursion, while he himself led a force to counter an uprising to the galactic north. He did not know then that those incursions were the mere tip of the emerging Hive Fleet Kraken. We received a few routine reports back from the Fifth, garbled by psychic interference, and then they were swallowed by the shadow in the warp.

By the time another company was free to go after them the truth of the Kraken had emerged, as had the threat it posed to Sotha itself. A general recall was ordered, every battle-brother was called back in defence of our home. And so the Fifth became just another mystery, a hundred warriors amongst the millions who had already died at the talons of the Kraken and the billions more who were to follow.

'So it's true,' Senior Retainer Gricole said as he approached me in the birthing cavity. 'Another mystery solved.'

'Get your men working with all speed, Gricole. Secure the area so I can lead my wards on. We are here for the living more than the dead.'

Gricole ordered his men to their tasks, as I did my wards. But then he returned to my side and regarded me sceptically.

'You have something you wish to say?' I asked.

A Chapter retainer, a servant, would never consider questioning a full battle-brother. But not Gricole. I had found him on Graia, a hydropon-sprayer turned militia captain in the face of the hive fleet. His woman was long dead, spared the sight of the tyranid assault, his children died fighting under his command. He had seen the worst that the galaxy held; he was not going to be intimidated by me. He spoke his mind when it pleased him. I respected him for that.

'You can't think there's any chance they're still kicking,' Gricole said in his broad Graian accent. 'That they've been living, battling, inside one of these monsters all this time?'

I looked down at him. 'You are human, Gricole. I know it is hard for you to understand. The human soldier needs regular supply: food, ammunition, shelter, sleep, even fresh orders from those of a higher rank to reassure him that he has not been forgotten. Without any one of those the human soldier cannot function. He weakens and breaks. We are Astartes; we are not the same as you. We can eat what you cannot, sleep yet still be on our guard, and to give an Astartes a mission is to give him a purpose which he will seek to fulfil until ordered to stop or until the Emperor claims him.'

Gricole listened to me closely, nodding in thought, then he spoke again. 'So d'ya think there is a chance?' he repeated.

Gricole was being wilful. 'Consider for whom we are searching here.' I assented. 'This is the Fifth Company: Captain Theodosios, Commander Cassios, Lieutenant Enero, Ancient Valtioch. If anyone could survive it would be warriors such as these.'

'I understand.' Gricole nodded. 'And so... do you think there is a chance?' he asked a third time. He smiled, bearing his stained brown teeth. Such stubborn impertinence, if it had been from a neophyte I would not have stood it for a moment, but unlike them Gricole had earned such familiarity with blood.

'The truth then?' I drew breath and looked away. 'Of course not. Death is all we will find in this ship. It is all we will ever find on these missions. You have seen the same as I. Even dead, these ships consume all within them. How can there be survivors? Master Thracian's Salvation Teams are a fool's errand.'

I had let my bitterness against the new Chapter Master show again. It did not matter in front of Gricole, however; I trusted his discretion.

'He told me he called us Salvation Teams for we will be the salvation of the Chapter,' I continued, still angry at the far distant commander. 'Do you know what the brothers of the Battle Company call us?'

Gricole shook his head gently.

'Salvage squads,' I said.

'Hmph,' he muttered. 'Catchy.'

Salvage squads. It was meant as an insult, but I found the name more fitting with each new insertion. Despite our efforts, we had found none of our missing. None living, at least. What we did find was salvage. The tyranid xeno-species can plunder every last atom of use, but their booty of choice is biological material. Our flesh. This they choose over any other.

The fruit of our own labours then were those items a hive ship, especially if crippled by an assault party's attack, might overlook. Weapons, armour; our tools of destruction. It did not come only from fellow Scythes; the Astartes equipment we found came in an array of colours: yellow and red, blue, silver, black and green. Irrespective of whether those Chapters might consider it sacrilegious, we took it. Our orders were precise: salvage it all.

Gricole's men worked quickly and with determination. Like Gricole himself, they were born on worlds that had fallen to Kraken: Miral, Graia, and others, worlds that we had tried to defend in our long retreat from Sotha. The Chapter's original retainers all died defending Sotha; no matter how young, how old, how injured or frail, they had picked up a weapon and given their lives to buy a few more seconds for their masters, for we Astartes, to escape.

We did escape, but at that time our flight appeared only to delay our destruction. The survivors of Sotha stumbled back to the Miral system, there to report the loss of our home to our returning Chapter Master. Thorcyra was stunned, near-shattered by the news. Some advised further retreat against such overwhelming odds, but he rejected the notion and led us all in oaths of defiance. The Kraken was approaching and we would stand and die in the jungles of Miral.

The Kraken came, and we made our stand on the rocky crags of a place named the Giant's Coffin. We fought hard, and we died once again. I do not know if Thorcyra believed some miracle would save us, that perhaps his faith alone might bring the blessing of the Emperor upon us and grant us some astounding victory. It was not to be. Thorcyra fell, torn apart by his foes, and Captain Thracian ordered the retreat. And, once more, I survived.

If you think I was grateful for my life, you would be mistaken. To leave behind so many brothers once was a tragedy that cut deep into my soul. To have to do so again was more than any man could endure. My body survived Miral, but my spirit did not. As I watched Captain Thracian swear the oaths of a Chapter Master on the bridge of the *Heart of Cronus*, I was certain that my next battle would be my last.

But after Miral, I am ashamed to say, we grew more cautious. Thracian did not believe any other world worth the extinction of our Chapter, short of Holy Terra itself. We were told no longer to contemplate the possibility of victory, only of what damage we could cause before we would retreat again. Thracian planned our withdrawals to the last detail and demanded their precise execution. Brothers died, but none without reason. But I felt the dishonour burn inside me each time the order was given to abandon another world to the Kraken, to retreat while others fought on. I obeyed, but I rejected Thracian's orders to leave all other defenders to their fate and I brought back with me those I could who had proven themselves worth saving. I was not alone in such actions and those brothers and I shamed Thracian into allowing such noble men as Gricole to remain with us.

The signal from the beacon led us deeper into the ship. We located one of the major arterial tubes, but we found it packed with biters. They were not feeding, rather they had fed themselves to bursting and were dragging their distended bodies along the ground, all heading into the ship. A few hellfire shells here would not have made a dent in their number, and so reluctantly I ordered the Scouts to find another route. The hard muscle wall of the artery cut across all the chambers on our level, barring any further progress, until Pasan noticed the sludge draining in a corner. There was a valve in the floor, kept from closing by the thick sludge's flow. It was too small for us, but we wedged it open wider. I should have sent one of the Scouts first, but I did not wish to be trapped above a panicking neophyte who had lost his nerve. I stowed my pistol, drew my falx, and plunged headfirst straight down into the tight shaft.

At once, I felt that the sludge might suffocate me as I forced myself down. I had only my helmet light to shine ahead of me, but there was nothing to see except the sludge seeping ahead. I moved slowly, leading with my falx and levering the shaft open, then deliberately pressing the wall back and widening the area as I went. My only comfort was the thought that any tyranid xenoform who might have lurked in such a place would have been dissolved by the sludge long before.

The line about my waist pulled tight and then went slack as my wards climbed down after me.

World after world fell to the Kraken, but under Thracian we small remnant of the once proud, once brave, once honourable Scythes of the Emperor survived. But then, against such odds, I told myself still that it was solely a matter of time. The absolution of a violent death would still be mine. Then came Ichar IV.

The tendrils of the Kraken had concentrated against that world and there, ranged against them, amidst a great gathering of Imperial forces stood the Ultramarines. Together, they smashed the body of the Kraken. The planet was nearly destroyed, its defenders were decimated, but the tyranids were scattered.

It was the victory for which we Scythes had prayed so fervently, the victory that Thracian had told us we could no longer achieve.

And we were not there.

Word of the victory at Ichar IV filtered through to the latest planet on which we had taken refuge. Bosphor, I think its name was. Still, even then we did not know the extent to which the Kraken had been cast back. We continued to prepare the planet's defences, trained their wide-eyed troops in the combat doctrines we had learned at bitter cost. We waited for the Kraken to come and turn the skies red with their spores. But the bio-ships never came.

It was only then that I realised that I had survived. That I would survive, not just a few more days, a few more weeks, until the next battle, but decades more. It was only then that we counted the cost and the truth of our plight struck home. Of all my battle-brothers, only one in ten survived. One in ten.

Our officers, who had stood and fought even as they ordered others to retreat, were wiped out nearly to a man. Our vehicles, our machines of war, had been abandoned; our own blessed ancestors in their Dreadnought tombs had been torn to pieces by the Kraken's claws. Their voices and memories, our connection to our legacy and that of the Chapter before us, were lost to us forever.

Thracian told us that it was not the end. That the dead would be honoured, but that their ranks would be filled, that we would rise once more and be as we once were.

I knew, even as I stood listening to his words, how wrong he was. More youths might be recruited, more Astartes might wear the colours, more mouths might shout our battle cries and recite our oaths. But it would not be us. Everything that had made us a Chapter of Space Marines, everything beyond the ceramite of our armour, the metal of our weapons, the cloth of our banners, was gone.

The termagants scuttled across the slope. The tendrils that covered the area, the curved floor, the walls, even hanging from the roof, would normally have reached out at any movement and grasped at it, but instead they lay flaccid. One of the termagants paused and lowered its head, sniffing; it turned quickly to the rest of its brood and they changed direction. They moved with purpose, they sensed an intruder. They saw a light ahead of them and closed in around it. The leader reached down with one of its mid-claws to pick up the torch, while the others sniffed closer, discerning that the scent-trails had divided. It was then that the trap was sprung.

The half-dozen tendrils closest to the torch suddenly burst as the frag grenades tied to them detonated. The termagants howled as the shrapnel tore into their bodies. Narro, Pasan and Vitellios rose up from their hiding places on to one knee and targeted those few creatures still standing. When the last of them fell, hissing and jerking, I ordered ceasefire and had the Scouts cover me as I approached the carnage. The termagants appeared dead: their weapon-symbiotes hung limply from their claws, limbs were severed and all were covered in their own tainted ichor. I took no chances and raised my falx and cut the head off each one. It was little victory. I felt no more revenged for having done so. I never did. Soon the biters would move in and begin to eat, and through them the dead flesh of these 'gaunts would be reformed into the next generation.

'These freaks wouldn't last a minute in the underhive,' Vitellios said as he lit his helmet light and swaggered over to admire his handiwork. 'Even a yowler would scope a dome before picking up a piece of trash. These 'gaunts are not too smart.'

I looked down at the torch. In the midst of the violence it was still shining. I picked it up and switched it off.

'Extinguish your helm-light, neophyte,' I ordered. 'Pasan, form a watch. Don't assume that these were alone. Narro, come here.'

The Scouts followed my orders instantly, even Vitellios. He was an arrogant upstart, but not when his own neck was on the line. He had been picked out from amongst the scum pressed into service as militia in the defence of the hive-world Radnar. Barely into his teens, he was already the leader of several gangs of juves who had run rampage through a few underhive sectors. The Scythe Apothecaries had removed his gang markings, tattoos and the kill-tags of the dozen men he claimed to have bested, but they could not extract the smug superiority he carried with him. His training record identified him as a natural leader. I disagreed. To lead, one must first learn how to follow, a task he continually failed. He may have been born to lead a gang of hive-trash, but never command Astartes.

'What do you think, Narro?' I asked, indicating the tyranid bodies. Unlike Pasan, Scout Narro always grasped instantly whatever task I had for him. He had been recruited from Radnar as well and he, at least, had come from one of the noble families. He had already been marked for additional training that would lead him to become a Techmarine when he became a full battle-brother. He picked up one of the severed heads and peered fascinated at its sharp and vicious features.

"Gaunt genus, obviously. Termagant species.'

'Correct,' I replied. 'Go on.'

'Strange, though, to see them here…'

'Within a hive ship? Yes, truly bizarre, neophyte,' I directed him back. 'Are they fresh? Have they just been birthed?'

We had learned the hard way that newborn xenoforms were one of the danger signs. Even within a dead ship, certain vestigial reflexes might induce fresh tyranid fiends from their sacs if an interloper triggered them. Yet another defence against grave robbers such as us. If these termagants were freshly hatched then more of them might descend upon us at any moment.

'It is…' Narro murmured. 'It is not easy to say conclusively.'

'Then give me your best guess,' I replied curtly. 'Show me that Forge Master Sebastion's efforts with you were not wasted.'

Narro put the head down and ran a gloved hand down the flank of the slug-body, examining the texture of the flesh. I grimaced in disgust at such contact.

'No. They are not,' he said finally, and I let a fraction of the breath I had held escape. 'You see this scarring, and the skin, and this one here has lost part of its...' he began to explain.

'Thank you, neophyte,' I dismissed him before he could digress.

'But what Sebastion said was...' he began with fervour, then faltered when he saw my expression. But then I relented and nodded for him to continue.

'Master Sebastion, in his teachings, speaks of how in the assault upon Sotha and Miral and the rest, the ships of the Kraken released millions of such creatures and expended them as... as a company of Marines would the shells of their boltguns. Yet we Salvation Teams have rarely encountered them. He believed that, because they must be so simple to produce and had so little purpose once their ship was dead, that they were the first to be reabsorbed...'

Beneath my gaze, his voice trailed away.

'Thank you, neophyte,' I told him clearly. 'That is all.'

I looked towards our path ahead. If the auspex could be trusted then the beacon was close. Once it was recovered I could quit this insertion and leave the ship to rot. I did not want to delay any further, but then, out of the corner of my eye, I saw Narro reach down and grasp something. He had picked up the 'gaunt head again and was about to stow it in his pack.

'Drop it,' I told him.

He fumbled to explain: 'But if it is rare I only thought it might provide insight, if I could study–'

'Drop it, neophyte,' I ordered again. It had been Narro's affinity with the holy ways of the machine that had first brought him to Sebastion's attention, but his curiosity had bled from the proper realm of the Imperial engineer into the living xenotech of the tyranid. I had overheard him speak to his brothers of his fanciful ideas of where such study could lead; to a weapon, some ultimate means to destroy the Kraken and its ilk and drive them back into the void. He did not understand the danger. The young never did.

'And consider in future to what infection or taint such trophies may expose you and your brothers. Save your thoughts of study until you are assigned to Mars. Until then, do not forget that you are here to fight.'

Shamed, Narro released it and the snarling, glassy-eyed trophy rolled a metre down the slope until it was lost in a knot of tendrils.

'There is an explanation for why these 'gaunts may have survived,' he said.

'And that is?'

'This ship... It is not dead.'

* * *

It was a ridiculous idea, but even so I felt the briefest chill at the thought. Every scan we had done of the hive ship before insertion told us that it was exactly as it appeared to be: a lifeless husk. But what if…? Could it still…?

No, I told myself as we continued on. I was no whelp neophyte. I would not fall prey to such paranoia. Every instinct I had, instincts honed from two long years of such expeditions, told me that this ship was dead. If it had been alive, we would never have made it this far. We would have been surrounded and destroyed within the first hundred steps. We certainly would not have been able to ambush those 'gaunts; some creature, some tiny insect would have been watching us and through it, the ship would have seen through our design.

We went deeper, the atmosphere thickening as we went. We climbed ridges of flesh and traversed the crevices between, squeezed our way through tiny capillaries and valves, and down passages ribbed with chitinous plates or covered with polyps crusted with mucus. We passed over caverns crammed with bulbs on stalks so that they resembled fields of flowers, and under roofs criss-crossed with lattices of tiny threads like spiders' webs. And everywhere we saw the same decay, the slow deconstruction of this grotesque, complex organism back into raw bio-matter by the biters and the smaller creatures they fed upon.

'There it is!' the cry finally went up. Vitellios shone his torch into a wall-cavity and there it was indeed, driven into the flesh-wall like a service stud. A piece of human technology, bound in brass and steel, as alien in this place as any tyranid xenoform would be aboard a human craft.

Excited, my wards crowded in to see. I batted them back, telling them to set watch. I did not wish to be taken unawares now of all times. Narro scraped away the translucent skin that had grown over the metal. I saw him instinctively reach to deactivate the signal and I grabbed his hand away. He looked at me askance and I slowly shook my head. He nodded in understanding and levered open the beacon's cover, exposing its innards. He groaned in dismay.

'What is it?' Pasan backed towards us, shotgun up, and glanced at the beacon.

'The data-slate,' Narro explained. 'Acid. It's been burned through.'

There was something more though. I looked closer. There were markings on the interior of the casing, distorted by the acid-damage, but still recognisable. They had been scratched by human hand and not tyranid claw.

'But it doesn't make sense…' Narro thought out loud.

'What doesn't make sense?' Pasan replied, the concern clear in his voice.

VIDE SUB, it read. Vide Sub. It was not code. It was High Gothic. An order. A command.

'Why would they destroy the message and leave the beacon transmitting?'

Look down.

The floor burst into a mass of scythes and talons as the monster exploded from its hiding place. The force of its eruption launched me into the air and threw me to the side. I smashed headfirst into a flesh-wall and slumped down to my knees.

'God-Emperor! Get back!' I heard someone cry as I slipped to the ground.

I forced myself onto my back. The gun-torches danced across the chamber as the Scouts moved. Pasan's was stationary, skewed at an angle, far to the other side. Vitellios's jumped as he sprinted away. One still remained in the centre; Hwygir was turning, bringing his heavy weapon to bear. His light caught the monster for an instant; it reared, jaws and mandibles gaping wide, as it swept two scything claws above its head to cut down the diminutive figure standing in its way. The Scout pulled the trigger and the monster's black eyes sparked orange with the ignition of the shells.

The first bolt clipped the bone of the claw even as it cut down towards him and ricocheted away. The second passed straight through the fleshy arm before detonating on the other side. But the third struck hard between two ribs of its exoskeleton. The explosion jolted the monster from its attack even as its blowback blinded Hwygir for a critical moment. The injured claw retracted early, the other was forced off its line and carved a bloody streak down the side of the Scout's leg instead of chopping his head in two.

Both Hwygir and the monster stumbled back for a moment. The savage dropped the sights of the heavy bolter, trying to blink his eyes clear, and his torch swivelled away from the monster just as it sprang and flipped over, digging back underground. Its thick snake-tail shot from the darkness, puncturing the casing of the heavy weapon on Hwygir's shoulder with such force as to knock it into the side of his head and leave him stunned.

'Burrower! Get clear!' It was Vitellios, shouting from cover.

Vitellios on one side and Pasan on the other desperately flashed their torches in every direction, hoping to catch a glimpse of the creature before it struck again.

'There!' Vitellios shouted.

'There!' Pasan cried.

They were facing in different directions. Vitellios had already fired; the hollow bark of a shotgun blast hitting nothing but the empty air echoed back to us. I pulled the torch from my pistol and twisted it in my hand. It blossomed with light in every direction.

'Quiet, you fools!' I hissed at them, drawing my falx as well. 'It's a ravener. It goes after the vibrations!'

They both stopped talking at that. I looked about the cavern in the dim, grey light. There was nothing on the surface to suggest any movement beneath. Hwygir was moving slightly beside the hole from which the ravener had burst. I saw Narro as well; he was lying beneath the beacon, smashed between it and the ravener's first attack. Hwygir saw him too and started slowly to crawl over to him, leaving the heavy bolter where it had fallen.

'No, you…' I cursed, but the trog did not hear me. Pasan did though. He suddenly stepped forwards, then picked up his feet and started to run. Great, booming, heavy steps. Not towards the heavy weapon, but away from it. I sensed, rather than saw, the ravener below us twist within the ship's flesh to go after him.

'Pasan! I order you–' I called after him, but I knew he was not going to stop.

I jerked my head around to Vitellios. 'Get the bolter. I'll get him.' I snapped, and powered after the running Scout.

Pasan knew both I and the ravener were after him now and quickened his pace over the leathery surface. In a shower of flesh and fluid, the ravener burst not from the floor, but from the wall. Pasan leapt and rolled, but the tyranid beast caught his leg in one of its grasping hands, flicked him around and hammered him against a chitinous strut. The shotgun flew from Pasan's hands as his body went limp, and it drew a claw back to slice him in two.

I bellowed at the beast as I ran and fired my pistol as fast as it allowed. My snap-shots blew the flesh from the walls and the beast indiscriminately and it twisted in pain. It coiled, ready to burrow again, and I dropped my pistol and raised my falx with both hands. The ravener leapt. I swung. The falx's tip pierced its carapace and hooked inside. I was yanked off my feet as the ravener dug down at an extraordinary rate. It dragged me on and I braced as I sped towards the hole it had created. My body hit the ground splayed across the hole and went no further. The ravener threatened to pull my weapon from my hands, but my grip was like steel. It thrashed beneath me, churning up the ship-flesh around it. Its tail, still in the air, whipped back and forth, battering at my side. I held on. It strained even harder against the hook of the falx and I felt it begin to tear itself clear. The next time the tail struck, I seized it with one arm, then released the falx and grasped it with my other.

'Vitellios!' I called. He was already running towards me, the heavy bolter cradled in his arms.

Beneath me, the ravener spiralled in my grip to try and escape; its scythes lashed up and punctured my armour, but I was too close for it to cut deep. Vitellios, only a few steps away, brought the bolter up, ready to fire. With a heave, I wrenched it out of the ground to give Vitellios a clear shot and, as I did so, it coiled into the air. Part of its thorax came free and I saw it grow an ugly pyramid-like cyst. It was a weapon, and it was pointed straight at me.

Vitellios and the ravener fired at exactly the same instant. The hive-trash pumped the beast full of bolt-shells that burrowed down along the length of its body and exploded. The bio-weapon shot a burst of slugs into me that burrowed up into my body and did nothing more.

I collapsed over the tyranid's remains. I did not know then what had hit me, only that my armour had been pierced. There was pain, but it was not incapacitating. I had seen brothers hit by tyranid weapons go mad or be burnt from the inside out, but as my hearts beat all the harder to race my blood around my veins I felt neither come upon me.

'How do, sergeant? You okay?' Vitellios had fallen to his knees beside me, his tone even more self-satisfied in victory. 'Caught ourselves a big one today.'

'Coward,' I replied coldly.

'What?' He looked shocked. 'Coward? I just saved your–'

'After you ran. After you fled.'

'I… That wasn't…' He was incensed. Almost ready to reload that bolter and use it on me. I did not care. 'That was doctrine! You're ambushed, you break free! Then you look to strike back!'

'Leaving your brothers to fend for themselves? Do not use doctrine to try to excuse that.'

Pasan had come round and was struggling upright. I heaved myself to my feet; my blessed body was raging, fighting to repair the damage done to it, but I would not show these neophytes even a hint of my weakness.

'You're pathetic. Both of you,' I told them. 'Pasan, get yourself up. Vitellios, go back. Check on the others.'

Vitellios stomped away and called after his brothers.

'Narro! Hwygir! If you're dead, raise your hands…' After a moment's pause, he turned back to me: 'They're good.'

Then he made a gesture in my direction that I am certain would have meant something to me had I been born amongst hive-trash like him, and continued away. Pasan was on his feet now, his helmet facing shattered, his face cut, bruised and crumpled.

'Honoured sergeant–' he began.

'Later,' I said. 'You will explain your actions later. Let us just get ourselves off this piece of thrice-damned filth.'

We hobbled back to where Narro and Hwygir had fallen. In spite of Vitellios's ignoble sense of humour, both still lived. I caught sight of the beacon again and the order scrawled there: VIDESUB. Look down. Another joke.

But it wasn't. For Vitellios spoke up again, and this time his voice was neither smug nor bitter. It was in awe.

'Sergeant Tiresias.' He shone his torch down into the hole below the beacon where the ravener had hibernated. In the violence of its awakening, however, it had scratched open a cavity even further beneath. Down there, glinting back in the light, shone the shoulder armour of a Space Marine. And upon that armour was inscribed the legend:

CASSIOS

The Space Marine's vital signs barely registered on our auspex. His metabolism was as slow as a glacier. He might easily have been mistaken for dead, but we knew better. Even in suspended animation, he was an impressive figure. His chest was the size of a barrel, his armour was crafted and worked with a pattern of lamellar, festooned with images of victories and great feats through the owner's life. The neophytes stood, slack-jawed, gaping at him. For once, I shared their sense of wonder.

We dug him from his cradle and commenced the ritual to rouse him there. It was not worthy of a survivor, a hero such as he, to be borne back to his home as though he were an infant. I would not have the retainers see him in such a state. I would give him the chance to stand alone, if he willed it, and return as a hero should.

We waited on guard, expectant, for an hour or more. Tending our own wounds, but staying silent aside from checking the auspex readings. Then, finally, his chest heaved. His eyes opened.

Commander Cassios stepped from the darkness of the tunnel and into the beams of the powerful floodlights set up by the retainer crews working within the cavern of the bio-titans.

Gricole saw him at once and called his workers to order. They stood, hushed, as Commander Cassios walked amongst them. He, in turn, acknowledged them, and appeared about to speak, and then he saw what their work was. He dropped to his knees, resting his hands upon the armour of his men. His head was bowed, he was praying. Gricole ordered his men away and I did the same with my wards. A warrior such as Cassios deserved to be allowed to keep such a moment private.

After they had cleared away from the cavity, he stood and moved through the rest of the armour and possessions that Gricole's men had been carefully storing.

'Valens. Nikos. Leo. Abas. Tiberios. Messinus. Herakleios.' Names; he could name each one just from what little remained.

'Theodosios. He was my captain.' I realised that Cassios was addressing me. 'It was so hard for him to ask me to lead the diversionary attack. I volunteered. I insisted! I knew that our company only stood a chance of escape if he was leading the way...' his voice trailed off.

I brought Cassios out with me and took him back to the boat. Only Gricole was waiting for us there. He looked at me, concerned. He tried to see to my wounds, but I waved him away. My Astartes physiology had started healing me from the moment I was wounded; whatever poison the ravener had pumped into me, my body would defeat that just as I had overcome the beast. In any case, I had a more pressing task to address, though it was one I would have given my life not to have to fulfil.

The 5th Company had fought and died against the Kraken before the rest of us had even known it had emerged from the void. Cassios had been here ever since. He believed he had lost his men. He did not know he had lost so much more.

The days and weeks after Ichar IV were ones of celebration for the militia defenders of Bosphor, who had never fought the Kraken and now never would. My brother Astartes and I were in no mood to join them and we retreated to our ships.

Some of us immersed ourselves in prayer, others in rage. A few, gripped by madness at what they had seen and what they had lost, rampaged around the ship until they were forcibly restrained. There were accidents. At least, we called them accidents. We Astartes have no word for the act where a brother chooses to end his service in such a manner. It is not spoken of, but his gene-seed is sequestered, marked as potentially deviant, as though it was a disease of the body and not of the soul.

I thought I had seen every reaction there was to the tragedy of our Chapter. I was wrong. When I told Cassios of the battles, of the losses, of what we had been reduced to, he showed me something different. He showed me the response of a hero.

Cassios had had his eyes closed, standing perfectly still, for nearly a minute. Then his face screwed up in rage, but he did not shout, he breathed. He took great heaving breaths as though he could blow the emotion out from his body and into the air. Then his eyes opened.

'And what is being done?' he asked.

'About what?'

'What is being done to revenge ourselves against this abomination? What is being done to strike back? What is being done to rid our space of this bastard xenos curse for good?'

I placed my hand upon his shoulder.

'As soon as we return to the *Heart of Cronus* they will tell you all. We will leave at once. Your brothers will be most eager to see you again.'

I smiled at him, but he did not return it.

'We cannot leave before we are finished here.'

'Before we are finished?' I asked. 'You are here with us. What more is there?'

Cassios tilted his head a fraction, indicating out the window. 'This ship, nearly half my company, it killed them, feasted on them.'

'And it is dead now,' I reassured him.

'We did not kill it.'

'No, but perhaps our brother-Chapters did on Ichar IV or perhaps it was the servants of the Navy. I understand you want satisfaction, commander. Believe me, I want that for every brother we lost. But our service is done. You cannot kill it again.'

'You misunderstand me, brother-sergeant. It was never killed. The ship still lives.'

Thracian disappeared from our midst then; for several days we were told he had secluded himself to meditate upon the Emperor's will for our Chapter, but then we discovered he had left us entirely on some secret task. He had told us before that we would take the time to rebuild, restore ourselves, and there were many who disagreed with that intention.

I do not expect you to understand. We are Astartes. We are not like you. We do not wake in the morning and muse upon what our purpose may be that day. We know. From the day we are chosen to the day that we die we know what our purpose is. We fight in the name of the Emperor. If we are ordered, then we go. If we are struck, we strike back. If we fall, then we do so knowing that others will take our place. We do not pause, we do not hold back, we do not relent.

We fight. That is our service to the Emperor. That is what we are. If we do not fight, then we do not serve Him. If we do not serve Him, we are lost. One might as soon as tell a mechanicus not to build, a missionary not to preach, a telepath not to think, a ship not to sail. How can they? What use are they without it? And yet that was what Thracian was asking us to do because if we were to suffer the casualties of even the most minor of campaigns, it would be enough to finish us for good. If we wanted to survive, we could not lose anymore. We could not lose anymore, so we could no longer fight. And for how long?

Our armoury, our training grounds, a whole world of our recruits that had been lost with Sotha, perhaps those could be restored. But what of the gene-seed? Both in our living brothers and in our stores lost with Sotha, both now devoured by the Kraken. Without gene-seed there could be no more Astartes, and gene-seed can only be grown within an Astartes, from the progenoid glands implanted in us as youths. There were barely more than a hundred of us left. Most had already had their glands taken when they had matured, to be kept safe in the gene-banks of Sotha. Those few of us in whom they had still not matured... how many new generations would it take to recover our numbers? How many years would the Chapter be leashed, unable to put more than a bare company into the field? Fifty? A hundred? Could we ever recover or would we just fade into ghosts of what we had been? A cautionary tale: the Chapter that feared its own end so greatly they placed themselves above their oaths, their service to Him.

No, better to end it all with a final crusade. That is what my commander, Brother-Sergeant Angeloi, said to me, and I agreed as many others did in the corridors of the *Heart of Cronus*. When Thracian returned to us we would tell him what his men had decided and we would require his acceptance. This was not for glory, this was for our souls. We had been great once, let our story end well in a great crusade that would end only when the last of us fell. Other Chapters would then stand forward to take up our duty and our spirits would join His light as His proud warriors and our names would be spoken with glory as long as mankind endured.

'Trust me, commander–' I raised my voice higher, trying to make him see sense.

'You may trust me, sergeant. I have been aboard that monster for nearly three years. Do not doubt what I say.'

'The auspex–'

'The auspex is wrong. Our technology, blessed be His works, has been wrong as often as it has been right. We are not some dependent xenos like the tau, we rely on human flesh and blood, and there is a spark of life there, I know it.'

'Even so,' I declared, 'it does not matter.'

Cassios blinked. That had surprised him.

'It does not matter?' Cassios raised his eyebrow. 'Explain yourself, sergeant.'

'So it lives, despite the auspex, despite what we saw aboard, the ship lives. It does not matter. We will still leave. We will send a despatch to the battlefleet, they will send a warship and destroy it for good.'

'You said yourself, sergeant, the battlefleet is fully engaged with the hive fleets splintered from Ichar IV. There will be no warship, and this abomination will heal and be the death of further worlds. It is not befitting an Astartes to pass his duty on to lesser men.'

'Then we will return with all our brothers. With *our* warships. We shall destroy this beast ourselves.'

'We are here now. We shall finish it now. Make your preparations for reinsertion. That is my last word on the matter.'

'But it is not mine...' I told him.

'Are you challenging my authority, sergeant?'

'No,' I replied calmly. 'You are challenging mine, commander. This team is mine. This mission is mine. And you... are not permitted to command.'

'What?'

'You have been aboard that ship three years, brother,' I spoke softly. 'Surrounded by the xenos, one of them just centimetres from you. We do not know what has happened to you. *You* do not even know. Doctrine is clear. Until you return with us, until you are examined by the Apothecary and purified, you have no authority to hold.'

To that, Cassios had no answer.

* * *

I left Cassios to himself and started walking back along the narrow corridors of the assault boat. I headed for the Apothecarion. I was sick. I did not know if it was the other injuries or the infection of the ship, but whatever war was being waged inside me against the ravener's venom, I was losing. My guts burned, my head felt as though it was floating above my body. I stumbled on a step and, at that noise, the neophytes appeared from the next cabin. Concerned, they rushed to my side, but I waved them away. No weakness. No weakness in front of them.

'Get away... get away...' I tried to push them off, and stagger on. I saw them back away as my vision dimmed. I did not feel the deck hit me.

Even in my poison-fever, I could not escape my wards. They plagued my mind as the toxin did my body. In my dreams I saw them clearly. I saw how each would add to the slow disintegration of my Chapter; to its reduction to a shadow of its former self. Hwygir was unable to step beyond the feral thinking of the savage world on which he had been born. Was that the purpose for which the Astartes were created? To be unthinking barbarians? No.

Narro was the reverse, his mind too open. His young fascination with the xenos was a danger he did not comprehend. He thought to save humanity by studying the technology of its enemies, using such xenotech against them, integrating it within our own forces, within ourselves. His path would lead us to create our own monsters, corrupt our blessed forms and thereby our spirits. We Astartes may have bodies enhanced to be greater than any normal human, but our souls remain those of men. The only knowledge an Astartes needs of a xenos is how it may be destroyed. Anything more is heresy.

Vitellios, I could see however, was destined for a different kind of heresy. Years of training, hypno-conditioning in the ways of the Chapter, and still he clung to his old identity. His arrogant presumption of self-importance. That he might be right and the Chapter might be wrong. Our history lists those Astartes who doubted the Emperor, and each of their names is blackened: Huron, Malai, Horus, and the rest.

Pasan, though, was my greatest disappointment. Every advantage that could be offered, a destiny nigh pre-ordained, and this lacklustre boy was the result. Insipid, full of self-doubt, unable to grasp the mantle of leadership even when presented to him. If half-men like him were to be the future of the Scythes then, Emperor help me, I would rather the Chapter had stood and died at Sotha.

'Gricole,' I croaked when next I awoke. 'How am I?'

Gricole raised the dim light a fraction and bent to study the readings from the medicae tablet.

'Your temperature is down. Your hearts are beating slower. And your urine... is no longer purple. I would guess you are through the worst.'

I coughed. It cleared my throat. 'Good,' I said, my voice stronger. 'Too much time has been wasted already.'

I levered myself up and off the tablet. I felt a touch of weakness in my legs.

'The time has not been completely wasted,' Gricole began. 'We have been making some progress–'

'We have set out for home?' They should have waited until I was conscious again, but in this instance I would forgive them. 'How far have we gone?'

I looked into Gricole's stout, troubled face. I pushed past him, out of the Apothecarion, and to a porthole. The hive ship filled my view.

I turned back to my retainer, my thoughts gripped with suspicion. 'They have not gone onto the ship without me?' I strode across the room, my weakness vanishing before my anger. 'I expressly forbade it!'

I stalked out into the antechamber. My four wards were there. Startled, they stumbled to attention.

'Who was it?' I demanded. 'One of you? All of you? Who here did not understand my orders?'

I looked pointedly at Vitellios, but he stared straight ahead, not moving a muscle.

'You will find your tongues or I will find them for you,' I said sternly.

'Honoured sergeant.' It was Pasan. 'Your orders were understood and followed. We have not left this craft.'

His words were bold, but the slightest quiver in his voice betrayed his nervousness. I stepped close to him and studied him carefully.

'Then explain to me, Neophyte Pasan, what is this progress that you have made?'

I saw his eyes flick for an instant behind me, to Gricole, and then away. He blinked with a moment's indecision.

'We found a–' Narro started.

'Quiet,' I overruled. 'Neophyte Pasan can speak for himself.'

'We have... we have been mapping the surface,' he spoke, gaining confidence with each word. 'We found an aperture that we believe will lead us straight to our target.'

'Is this impertinence, Pasan? We recovered the beacon. What target is this?'

'My men,' Cassios said from the entrance hatch. He stepped into the antechamber. 'My apologies, brother-sergeant, we could not make you aware during your indisposition. These Scouts were fulfilling my instructions.'

'It is a second beacon, honoured sergeant.'

I looked from Cassios to Pasan. 'Another beacon? Our auspex read only the one.'

Vitellios chipped in. 'It signalled only once, at the exact time we discovered the commander's beacon.'

'It makes sense, sergeant,' now Narro spoke again. 'If some of the xenoforms can detect the beacon's signal you would not wish to lead them to all your hiding places. You would wait until a rescue party might be close, close enough to reach a primary beacon. Then once we accessed that, it must have sent a signal to all the secondary beacons to begin transmitting.'

'And one replied. Once.' I looked back at Cassios, but he was concentrated upon the neophytes' explanation. 'Our auspex did not detect a second signal at that time.'

'Not our squad auspex, no,' Narro continued, 'but the one on the boat did. It is noted within the data-log. It is at the far end of the ship, so deep inside we would not have detected it.'

'Very well. Commander?' I fixed my gaze upon Cassios. 'Do you know what we may find?'

'Our boarding parties struck all across the ship. There are several for whom I have not accounted.' He shook his head sadly. 'I only pray they were as lucky as I and that we may reach them in time.'

My wards appeared convinced, but I was not. Yet if more of our brothers were still sent aboard that abomination, I could not leave them behind.

'So, Scout Pasan, tell me. What is this aperture that you have discovered?'

'Arse!' Vitellios swore as he took another grudging step along the dim tunnel. 'I can't believe I have to climb up this bio-ship's arse.'

His overblown irritation elicited a smattering of laughter from the other neophytes.

'Keep the chatter off the vox!' I snapped at them all, my patience worn thin. There was no atmosphere in this part of the ship so we were fully encased within our armour with only the squad-vox to keep in contact. I was still not recovered, I felt weak, uncomfortable, and my discomfort frustrated me even further. Such petty inconveniences should be nothing to an Astartes. My body should be healed fully, not still ailing. I pushed on, the temperature rising and my temper shortening with each step.

How had I come to this? Reduced to a haemorrhoid on a hive ship's backside! Was this what heroes of the Astartes did? Would, one day, a new generation of battle-brothers listen in hushed tones to the tale of this adventure?

'Brother-sergeant?' Cassios's voice came through to me. He had set it to a private channel. Cassios, though, would be my salvation. When we returned home after this insertion, we would not be met by a Tech-marine adept to catalogue our salvage. No, we would have an honour guard fitting for the hero we would restore.

'Commander?'

'I asked the neophytes, during the days you were inconvenienced, of the circumstances of my rescue.'

'With what purpose?' I had intended my query to be polite, but as I heard it back through the vox it had the tinge of accusation.

'No more than to further my understanding of them. It struck me that Scout Pasan in particular showed considerable courage in leading the ravener away, allowing the heavy bolter to be retrieved.'

'It would have shown considerable courage had I ordered him to do it,' I said, my voice sounding testy, 'but in the midst of battle, you must act as one. You cannot have a single person deciding to act alone, expecting everyone else to understand his meaning.'

'And yet at other times you have remarked on his failure to use initiative. That he has waited for orders.'

'He must learn to judge between the two. That is also part of leadership; when to act and when to listen to others.'

'You truly believe he is the right one to groom as acolyte?'

I knew to whom Cassios was referring, but I held firm in my opinion. 'Pasan is Sothan. Like you and I. One of the last. He has it within him. He merely needs to discover it.'

The conversation ended shortly after that. Cassios did not understand; he had spent two days with the neophytes. I had fought alongside them for over two years. My mind dwelt on Cassios's behaviour. It had been the neophytes who had pushed for this second insertion yet I knew it was exactly what he wished. There are reasons why any Space Marine discovered still living aboard a hive ship must be examined by the Apothecarion before returning to duty. It is not the constant danger and warfare, our minds are enhanced so that we may fight without rest, but it is the unknown influence of the greater tyranid consciousness that bears down on each and every living thing within its grasp. No one yet knows what effect that may have.

There is another reason as well. Not all tyranid xenoforms are created simply to destroy their enemies. Many are designed to infiltrate their minds, turn them against their friends and lead them into traps to be devoured. Cassios's behaviour seemed normal, but then perhaps that was a sign. How normal should a man be after such an experience?

I led them on in silence. The torches on our suits illuminated only a fraction of the gloom ahead of us. In truth, we did not know what function this part of the hive ship performed. Pasan had found the entrance at the stern of the vessel; it had been small, shrivelled, but the tunnel had widened out considerably after we had penetrated the initial portal. The bio-titan birthing cavity was nothing to the size of this cavern. Walking along the middle, the lowest point, we could see neither wall nor ceiling. We might as well have been walking upon the surface of a planet, the only difference being that the ground sloped upwards rather than down as it disappeared into the darkness on either side. It was desolate; there were no remains here of any of the lesser tyranid creatures that we had waded through in our earlier expeditions. The floor was bare, a series of shallow crests as though we were on the inside of a giant spring, and the footing was firm. It appeared as though we had found the one part of the vessel where nothing had ever lived.

Or I may have spoken too soon. I noticed to my right Cassios stop suddenly, he kneeled and held his gauntleted hand on the ground.

'Something's coming. Take cover,' his commanding voice coming through the vox crackled around the inside of my helmet. What cover? I asked myself, but Cassios was already breaking to one side.

'To the right,' I ordered my wards after him. They responded instantly, ready to follow him. We ran for a minute until the rising wall hove up into view, soaring above our heads into the shadow. Cassios climbed the slope until it was as steep as we could manage and then stopped there, looking further ahead.

'What is it?' I asked him. The auspex showed nothing.

'Do you not see them?'

I peered into the gloom. 'No,' I said.

He bade us wait, however, and within a few moments I saw what he had seen. A ridge emerged ahead of us, stretching across the horizon, as though a mighty hand had gripped the ship from the outside and was squeezing it up towards us. I heard my wards gasp as they saw it too.

'Holy Throne…'

'God-Emperor…'

'Sotha preserve us…'

'What in the name of a hive-toad's spawn-baubles are those?'

The ridge was no muscle contraction: it was a phalanx of huge tyranid creatures of a sort I had never seen before. Each as big as a tank, as big as a Baneblade, packed tightly together so there was not a centimetre between them, and moving as a line slowly towards us. Their armoured eyeless heads were down, so low as to be ploughing over the surface in front of them, dragging their bulbous bodies behind. Their limbs had atrophied so they oozed their way forward like snails. I did not know what their slime would do, but their weight alone would crush us. I looked to the left, to the right, there was no way around; they ringed the circumference of the cavern, somehow sticking to the walls even as they arched round and became the ceiling. I doubted whether all the weaponry we had to hand would be enough to stop one of these brutes in its tracks.

I looked down the line, searching for a tank-beast that appeared smaller or weaker. If we targeted one with concentrated fire there might be a chance, but my attention was dragged away when my wards suddenly let out a great cheer. Cassios was advancing, climbing the curving slope as he went. He had gone mad, I realised, the sight of his foe had driven his wits from him.

'After him!' I ordered the Scouts. I would be damned if I would let him die now, after all he had survived, before he could be welcomed back home. We chased him as quickly as we could, struggling at the steep angle this close to the wall. He charged ahead of us, not even drawing his weapon. Scrabbling higher, he leapt from the cavern wall onto the top of the nearest tank-beast's head. Then, balanced precariously as the beast chomped forward, his power sword appeared in his hand and he stabbed down.

The tank-beast did not seem to notice.

'Back!' I shouted, appalled, to the others. 'Back! Firing positions!'

The beasts' pace had appeared slow from a distance, but up close they ground forwards with surprising speed. On such a slope, it was as if a Land Raider was barrelling towards us, teetering on a single tread.

'Stay on the curve! Stay high!' Cassios's voice blasted into our helmets as we fell back and he stabbed down again. I glanced behind, this time the beast acknowledged the strike with a flicker of its head that nearly threw Cassios off, but then it returned to its path and he regained his grip.

The Scouts stood ready to fire, but I hesitated, fearing the volley would hit the commander.

'Fire above me!' Cassios ordered, and we fired a battery of shells and shot over Cassios's head as he ducked and swung again. He cut to the right side of the beast's head, on the underside of where he was crouching. This time the beast shied slightly away from the barrage, but again returned to its course.

'Again!' He cut. We fired, the beast looming before us as though we were insects.

'Again!' he cried one last time before the beast steamrollered over us. We fired and he jammed the sword in as deep as it would go. The beast reacted. It squirmed away from our shot and lazily snapped towards the pinprick causing it pain. Its weight shifted and the upper edge of its body detached from the wall. For the first time we glimpsed the immense pores and suckers that had held it fast. As those came away from the surface, its weight shifted even further and more suckers came loose. With the inertia of a battleship ramming another, it slowly toppled down upon the tank-beast to its side and both monstrous creatures halted for a moment in confusion. Above them, their collision had left a gap. None of us needed to be told what to do.

We raced forwards to pass through before the tank-beast recovered. As we crossed into the valley we had created in the advancing ridge, it regained its grip and lumbered back. The valley's wall closed in upon us and I willed every last jolt of energy to my legs. The walls slammed shut as we shot from them and skidded upon the deep coating of mucus the tank-beasts left behind. I gained purchase for an instant before Hwygir, out of control, knocked me flying. We slid down the curved wall of the cavern right back into the centre until we finally stuck where the mucus was pooling.

I cut through the groans on the vox, demanding my squad to report. Haltingly, they did so. Slowly, trying not to fall again, I picked myself up from the laden ground and then checked the others. Cassios was rising as well. Hwygir was holding the heavy bolter high in the air, keeping it dry. Narro and Pasan were scraping the fluid off themselves as Vitellios just stood there, a look of horror on his face as he stared down at the mucus dripping off from every part of him.

'I've been slimed,' he said.

I forwent commenting that such dross reminded me of the grime-swamp where he'd been birthed; I had more pressing concerns.

'Neophytes, get yourselves up. Check your weapons, check your weapons!' I chivvied Vitellios. 'Straighten yourselves and get ready to move.'

I stepped away a little to check my own pistol and could not help but reflect once more on the new depths to which my command had sunk. I saw Cassios stepping around the neophytes, congratulating them individually. It did not matter, as soon as I returned him to the *Heart of Cronus* I would request transfer to the Battle Company and no one would be able to deny me.

'What is this place anyway?' I overheard Vitellios ask the rest.

'A no good place,' Hwygir concluded.

Narro was already working on hypotheses. 'Maybe some kind of alimentary canal, maybe a funnel or blow-hole.'

'Maybe the barrel of a bio-cannon?' Pasan queried.

'One big cannon,' Vitellios said.

'Either way, I just hope there's nothing bigger coming up out the pipe.'

I allowed them their inane chatter this once. I had checked my pistol and by His grace it still functioned. Our weapons last hundreds of years for a reason. I holstered it and then punched the auspex back to life to check the path ahead. I looked at its readings and then punched it again. The readings did not change. My body still moved, taking a few steps forward, but my brain, for this moment, had frozen. There *was* something bigger coming up the pipe. It wasn't a tank-beast or a carnifex or even a bio-titan. It was the spark of life that Cassios had claimed to sense. Ahead of us, growing, feeding, ready to be born, was a creature far larger than any we had encountered. It was the Kraken's offspring. It was another hive ship.

'Brother Tiresias?' The lieutenant stopped me as I walked the corridors of the *Heart of Cronus*.

'Brother Hadrios,' I responded, surprised. 'I thought you were away with Master Thracian?'

'We have just returned,' the lieutenant said flatly, his eyes heavy. 'He wishes to see you. You will come with me.'

He turned away, expecting me to follow. After a moment's hesitation, I did. The lieutenant offered no further conversation and so we walked in silence. He led me to the Master's chambers and left me there. The chambers were still dark, the mosaics along its walls unlit, unprepared for their master's return, much as the rest of us. This was not how I expected matters to unfold. We imagined we would have forewarning when Thracian reappeared, to gather our strength so that we might confront him together and demonstrate our collective will. Instead, he had stolen back like a thief in the night and taken us off-guard.

A line split down the panelling on one side and the chamber filled with light. Hidden in the light, Master Thracian stood. I imagine that I have already created in your mind's eye a character for Master Thracian. A careful man, a smaller man; lesser than those who came before him. Desperate, perhaps. Petty. Failing. Let me dispel that character from your mind now. No man can become an Astartes without the potential for greatness, and no Astartes can become the master of a Chapter without a part of that greatness realised. Thracian was no exception and he was to achieve even more over those next few years. He was big, big even for one of our kind, but his face had stayed thin. His long hair was still black where Chapter Master Thorcyra's had turned grey, and he wore his beard shorter. He was wearing a simple robe in the Chapter's colours and beneath it a vest of ceremonial scale armour, fastened loosely across his chest. I knew him to be a fierce warrior, a master tactician, and brave without question, but at that moment I saw him only as the obstacle to our Chapter finding the destiny it deserved.

I bowed; he bid me stand.

'Brother Tiresias, welcome. I regret that my absence had to be of such great duration,' he spoke. 'I understand that Brother-Captain Romonos has kept the Battle Company busy.'

Busy, yes, with small raids, petty battles and hasty withdrawals.

'I am told that you brought honour upon the Chapter by your actions during the campaign upon Tan.'

'My thanks, Master.' I nodded without emotion, but I relaxed a little. So this was merely to be a little perfunctory commendation. I would humour him and then find Sergeant Angeloi and tell him that our opportunity had come.

'What did you think of that campaign?' he asked.

'It was a great success. A significant victory,' I spouted what I knew I should say and bit my tongue on the rest.

The Chapter Master regarded me. 'I have read the reports, Tiresias, I asked what you thought.'

'Master, I have said already what I think. I do not know what you require from me.'

'That is an order,' he said calmly.

Well, if that was what he wished, that is what he would have. 'The campaign on Tan...' I snorted. 'The campaign on Tan was a joke. No, worse, it was a travesty. A few skirmishes, and standing guard throughout an evacuation. Providing support to others instead of leading from the front, where an Astartes should be. It does not even deserve to be called a campaign, let alone a victory.'

I stopped then. I had said too much, far too much. I had breached protocol, discipline, even simple good judgement. I looked at the Master, but his face was without expression.

'Did we lose any of our brothers?' he asked quietly.

I knew he knew already, but he wanted me to say it. 'No, no brothers lost. A few injured. Most minor. One more serious.'

'Brother Domitios, yes, but he will recover. I know also, Tiresias, that when he fell it was you who went to his defence. It was you who skewered the xenos beast that threatened him. It was you who saved his life.'

I nodded again. It was true, but I did not think it remarkable. Astartes are trained to do nothing less.

'You acquitted yourself well, brother. Very well,' the Master continued. 'You have always done so, even when you have had misgivings about the orders you have been given. That is why I wished you to speak your mind. Why I am talking to you now.'

'Do not mistake my words, Master.' I countered. 'I understand the value of restraint, of retreat when circumstances dictate. We defended the orbital stations, but we did not even try to save that planet. We did not even step foot upon the surface. Before we even entered the system we were defeated in our hearts.'

I paused. Thracian let the silence hang in the air between us for a long moment. 'You wish for it to be as it was.' he said.

'Yes!' I gasped. 'Kraken is broken, its fleets are scattered. We do not need to sell our lives merely to delay their advance. If we commit ourselves in force we can win a victory, a true victory. As Calgar did on Ichar IV, as we did at Dal'yth Tertius, and Translock. Yes, I wish to fight as we did, with every weapon, every muscle, every sinew at our command. Come victory or death, to fight as an Astartes should.'

I had not expected to burst out with such sentiments now, to anticipate the statement that Sergeant Angeloi was readying to give him. I expected Thracian to roar back at me, but his reply was very quick.

'One day, Tiresias, we shall fight like that again. But for now it cannot be. For now, any action where no brother is lost must be victory enough,' he said simply. 'I know that it is far easier to say than it is to accept in one's heart. That is my challenge, one of them at least, to help us understand what has happened to us. How we must change. So many brothers dead; Sotha gone, mere rubble in space. The noble Scythes of the Emperor, loyal reapers of mankind's foes, cut down ourselves by the Great Devourer. It is not a fate we deserved.'

He stepped away from me, his robe brushing lightly over the polished floor.

'I understand your frustration, but you must have hope in our future. And that is what I left you to acquire. Here.'

He keyed a sequence into a control and the mosaics along the walls rose smoothly, revealing pict-screens behind. They all displayed images of one of the ship's hangar bays. It had changed greatly. The fighters had gone; the machinery had all been stripped away. In their place, a bizarre maze had been constructed. Plasteel walls covered and painted to resemble the corridors of a tyranid bio-ship. Inside the maze I could see Space Marines advancing in their squads; not Space Marines, no, they were too small. They were neophytes.

As I watched, one of them trod upon a pressure-switch. A trapdoor in the floor opened and he vanished before even catching his breath to shout.

'Traps, creatures, combat servitors programmed with tyranid attack patterns. It is as real as we can make it. We have paid close attention to the data we gathered fighting these monstrosities, after all, it came to us dear.'

'How many?' I asked, my voice a whisper.

'Three hundred in total, and more to come. Young, untested, but keen. All orphans of the Kraken like ourselves. All ready to be baptised with tyranid blood.' Thracian placed his hand upon my shoulder then. 'They only need leadership, guidance, from brothers like you. Sergeant Angeloi recommended you specifically, Tiresias. Promotion and this, your first command.'

I opened my mouth, but found for once no words were waiting there. Thracian continued:

'You see, Tiresias, one day it shall be as it was. And it shall not take a hundred years, or even fifty. When the next hive fleet comes to plague these sectors we will be ready to answer the Emperor's call.'

I stepped back a little, and Thracian's hand fell from me.

'I will... thank you, Master. I will be sure to thank my sergeant when I–'

And then I saw a look in Thracian's golden eyes.

'I will ensure you will have the chance to send a message after him,' he interrupted. 'Brother-Sergeant Angeloi has already departed to join the xenos hunters of the Inquisition, the fabled Deathwatch. Given our experiences, they requested as many brothers as we could spare to help spread the knowledge of the forms of the tyranid blight and how each may best be destroyed. I granted him, and a few others, the honour of carrying our name and our teachings to the galaxy.'

A few others, Thracian said, but in truth over forty brothers had gone already, reassigned to the Deathwatch. They were nearly a third of our strength and each one of them was one of Angeloi's crusaders. And the chance to compel Thracian to order one last, glorious campaign had gone with them.

'Now rest a moment, brother,' Thracian directed me to sit, 'and allow me to share with you how your new command will aid our Chapter's salvation.'

I never discovered the truth behind the creation of the neophyte companies. The recruits themselves I knew were, just like Gricole and our retainers, from the worlds of the long retreat. Even before the hive fleet arrived in the Sotha system, even while my squad-brothers prepared the planet's defences, plans were being made so that the Scythes might rise again.

The best of the youngsters of Sotha had already been secretly evacuated. Each place we turned to make our stand, Miral, Graia, and the rest; while my brothers fought and died, the most promising youths were recruited and rescued. Harvested by us, I suppose, while those left behind were harvested by the xenos.

But the gene-seed, that was the question. Three whole companies of neophytes and more to come, Thracian had promised. How was it possible? There were many theories. A few were sensible; that Thorcyra had been forewarned of the attack on Sotha and ordered the gene-seed to be removed in secret, or that the old Chapter Master had struck an agreement with the Inquisition to return our gene-tithe and whether the Deathwatch Marines were the only price he had had to pay. Other theories were darker, that Thracian had found or purchased arcane or alien tech that allowed progenoids to develop artificially far faster than in a Space Marine, or that most of the neophytes did not receive true gene-seed, they were merely bio-engineered and would never mature into true Astartes. I even heard a whisper that the gene-seed was not ours; that before the Salvation Teams there were squads designated Reaper Teams. I do not credit such thoughts, however; no Astartes would stoop to such measures even if the future of the Chapter depended upon it.

But then, I have had cause to wonder, can you ever be sure what lengths a creature will go in order to ensure the survival of its children?

'A kilometre and a half long, millions of tonnes, and a face only a hormagaunt could love...' Vitellios murmured, watching the muscles of the hive ship's offspring ripple beneath its hull-skin.

'And it's trying to get out,' Pasan said.

This was it then, the source of the 'gaunts we had encountered, the spark of life that Cassios had sworn existed. The bloated biters we had seen were not venturing inwards to wait; they were coming here to feed this offspring on the bio-matter of the corpse of its parent.

'Very well,' I decided. 'As soon as we return to the boat, we will send a despatch to the closest battlegroup, Ultima priority. They will respond to that.'

'No,' Cassios said.

I scoffed. 'I assure you, commander, they will!' But then, through the visor of his faceplate, I saw the expression in his eyes.

'They will still be too late. We are the only ones who are close enough and we are here to kill that creature.'

I had had enough of him. He had challenged my command once already and I was not going to waste my breath diverting him from such vainglorious stupidity.

'As you wish, commander,' I told him and gave the signal for the Scouts to gather and follow. 'I will ensure your final action is recorded with the proper honour.' I had walked several steps before I realised my wards were not with me.

'Ensure it is recorded for all of us,' Vitellios spoke up.

I should have seen it. I should have seen it as soon as I saw them standing with Cassios as he convinced me there were others within the ship that may be saved. They were not looking at me to lead them; they were looking at me to see whether I believed their lie.

'A second beacon?' I did not look at Cassios, but rather at Narro. He knew I would have trusted him to double-check the auspex readings.

'It was not his idea,' Pasan said. 'Nor was it the commander's. It was mine.'

'Yours?' I shot back at my acolyte.

It was Cassios who replied. 'I would have left you back there. It is clear to me that you have failed as their teacher and you have failed even as their leader. But Brother Pasan wanted you here.'

I looked away from him; there was nothing he could say to me. Two days it had taken him, two days to take the loyalties of the wards I had cared for for two years. I looked back at Pasan. 'Why did you want me here? So that you may see my face as you disgrace me?'

'No,' Pasan said. 'So that you may have the chance to join us.'

'Join you?' I exclaimed. 'For what purpose would I do that? What do you offer but the futile waste of your lives?'

Pasan replied, but the four of them may as well have spoken as one.

'To know what it is to fight as an Astartes.'

I could not credit this from such youths. 'You do not know,' I told them. 'You have never seen the full Chapter deployed in battle. Squad after squad standing proud in their armour, bolters raised. Reciting your battle-oaths with one voice and then marching forwards, knowing your brothers are there for you as you are there for them. You draw such strength from them, being not one warrior fighting alone, but one of a thousand fighting together. Ten hundred bodies forming a single weapon. Until you have experienced that... you do not really know what it is to fight as an Astartes.'

The neophytes were silent. I felt my words had reached them at last.

'You are right, honoured sergeant,' Pasan said. 'We do not know. We have never experienced that. But then, when will we?'

'When you are full battle-brothers,' I said.

'Will we? Even if we do as you say. We leave here now, with you; we survive to take a place in the Battle Company,' Pasan glanced at his brother-Scouts for support. 'When will we ever march into battle a full Chapter strong? How long will it take us to recover before we do anything more than nip and pinch at our enemies? A hundred years, two hundred? How much more will be lost to the devourer by then?'

Pasan stood forwards and Vitellios stepped with him.

'I know you think little of me,' the hive-trash said. 'That I don't take being a high and mighty Astartes seriously. But there's one thing I am serious about. My life. I joined to scour our galaxy of the alien bastards that slaughtered my world. I didn't raise myself up from hive-trash, put myself through all the trials to be chosen as a Scythe so I could dig through the dead and grow old training the next generation. I didn't do all I've done just to become an antiquated relic…'

'As I am, you mean?' I snapped back. I was beyond anger, I was furious. I raised my hand and Vitellios braced himself for the blow, but Pasan stepped in front of him.

'Why are you against us?' he cried. 'We all know that this is what you truly want. We've heard you rail to Gricole often enough.'

'Now you are spying upon me as well?' I said, incredulous.

Hwygir grunted in the corner, 'A small craft, our transport.'

'You are not the only one with an Astartes' senses,' Vitellios chipped in, but Pasan cut him off.

'No excuses, honoured sergeant. You wanted us to hear. You wanted us to know how much you resented this mission, resented us for what we took you from. Now here is your chance. There is the enemy. We can reach it. We can kill it. Yes, some of us, all of us may die. But is this not the chance for glory you want?'

All four of them were standing now, united against me, yet united in favour of everything I believed. The anger that had flared inside me vanished.

'Yes, it is,' I agreed with them. 'More than you know. Every sinew and muscle in my body craves to carry the fight to the xenos without caution, without restraint. To serve as an Astartes should serve.'

'Then you are with us!' Pasan shouted.

'But then…' I continued. 'I look deeper than my muscle, I look into my bones. And there, inscribed a thousand times, is the oath I took to the master of this Chapter to obey his orders and the Emperor's word therein. It is an oath that I have never broken, and never will. As for the rest… I give it up.'

I swept my arm up and pointed at them. 'You are my witness! You hear me now! I give up my glory, I give up my revenge, I give up my hope of what I could have been,' I shouted even though they were close, but I knew I was not addressing them. 'I accept it cannot be as it was! A battle where no brother falls is glory enough!'

I saw their faces, they thought me mad, but in truth I was healed. The weight of the loss of my brothers, the weight of my rage that I had survived when they had not was lifted. I took a breath and breathed free for the first time since Sotha.

'No glory,' I finished quietly, 'is greater than the future of our Chapter. We are not greater than it, none of us. Any Astartes who thinks they are... there is a word for those...'

'Renegades,' Cassios said from behind me. 'But which of us is the renegade, brother? You, who defend our Chapter's crippled body or I, who defend its soul?'

'It's starting to move...' Narro reported.

'Then we shall as well,' Cassios gestured to the Scouts, once my wards, now his men, then turned back to me. 'I offer you the chance to fight as a Scythe should, with his hand, his oath on his lips and his brothers by his side. If you do not come, let it be upon you.'

'It shall be upon me,' I stated, 'but I shall come. I take this oath now: you may take these children to their deaths but I shall bring them back again.'

It was to be the final insertion of the 21st Salvation Team. The ship, the offspring, was grinding itself forward down the lifeless channel. We blew a hole through the young, unhardened skin as close to our target as we could manage. If the offspring noticed our pinprick at all its reaction was lost amidst the wild throes of its agonising birth. The chambers inside could not be more different than the dead, dark halls of its parent. Luminescent algae lit our path, the ground was springy beneath our boots, the wall-skin taut, the door valves firm, and the noise... each chamber and tunnel vibrated with the screeching noise as the offspring pulsed and squirmed out into space, but below that you could hear the hum, the pulse, the beat of its life all around you. The life the Scythes were here to take.

We moved quickly. Cassios led the way, allowing his warrior instincts to draw him towards the creature's heart. The Scouts followed a step behind; their excitement did not dull their skill, and nor did their fear. They moved easily, not in a single formation, but always shifting from one to another, running, covering. First Vitellios would run, as Pasan protected him, then Narro as Vitellios did the same, then Hwygir would charge up, bursting as ever with pride at being entrusted with the vital heavy weapon. They protected one another. For two years I had tried to find one amongst them suited to be their leader; at that moment I realised that they did not need one. They fought as one: as Hwygir reloaded, Narro shot into the tyranids to keep them from recovering; as Narro was caught by a tendril, Pasan forced his gun down into its maw and blew its brain out; as Pasan forced open a door-valve, Vitellios destroyed the creature lurking above it; as Vitellios ran quickly back from a new rush of 'gaunts, I lent my fire to his to halt them where they stood.

Our foes were not the fearsome monsters of Macragge and Ichar IV. The ship had grown only its most basic defenders: termagants, other 'gaunts and the like; and it itself was focused on its struggle towards freedom. However, its plight, its vulnerable state, triggered a response from the creatures barring our path that was all the more visceral. Cassios did not care, he simply battered them aside. These tyranids, who had overwhelmed countless star systems with force of numbers, now found themselves overwhelmed in turn by Cassios's simple force. Every chamber we encountered he stormed, every 'gaunt in his way fell to the shells of his pistol or the curved edge of his power sword. He gave them no chance to gather, but charged into the thick of them, relying on his speed to spoil their aim and his thick armour to protect his flesh. That it did for him, but it did not for the rest of us and we suffered our first loss.

'Brother!' Hwygir shouted after Narro as he stumbled. One of the shots of bio-acid aimed too quickly at Cassios had flown past the commander and struck Narro. Across the vox, I heard him clamp down on his scream. Hwygir had already raised the heavy bolter and was struggling across to check on him.

'Keep us covered!' I yelled at him and shoved his weapon around to face the closing enemy. I heard his frustrated roar as he fired, but my focus was on the stricken Narro. He was still breathing. I rolled him and saw his arm clutching his side. Without ceremony I pulled the arm away to see the wound and discovered that the arm ended at the wrist. His hand had been eaten away.

His eyes snapped open, he looked down in shock at his stump and breathed in to holler in pain. I punched him sharply in the chest and he gasped instead, winded.

'Overcome it!' I shouted into his ear. 'You shall build yourself a new one.'

He struggled to nod as his Astartes metabolism kicked in and dampened the shock and the pain. I took his weapon and handed him my pistol.

'Sergeant!' Hwygir called back as he released the trigger for a moment. 'How is–'

I looked up as Hwygir turned his head to ask after his brother. I saw the shot hit the back of his helmet and the blood splatter on the inside of his face-plate as the tiny beetles of the bio-weapon bored through his skull and ate the flesh of his face from the inside. The savage fell and, in that instant, I felt the loss of a brother.

I dived towards his body firing wildly to force his killers to scuttle back. I cannot claim any sentimentality – I had fought too long to allow such feelings cloud my reactions – it was solely his weapon I was after.

I rose and aimed the heavy bolter. I had not fired one in battle since the long retreat from Sotha. I pulled the trigger, felt the reassuring recoil and watched as its shells blew a line of bloody death across the 'gaunts' first ranks.

The offspring lurched suddenly to one side and all of us, tyranid and Space Marine alike, were knocked from our feet. Hwygir and the 'gaunt bodies rolled away. I hefted the cumbersome gun and scrambled back where Cassios and the rest of the squad had regrouped.

'It's accelerating,' Cassios said without a glance back towards where Hwygir had fallen. 'We have to move faster.'

'Does it matter?' Vitellios asked. 'We're inside it now, it's not getting away!'

'Every second we delay gives it time to call in more beasts.'

'Then what are we waiting for?' he jumped up, ever the fearless one, and smashed the butt of his shotgun against the next door-valve. The valve shrank back and he led us through. He made it a single step before a set of jaws within the valve snapped shut, razor-sharp teeth puncturing the length of Vitellios's body from his ankle to his head. I grabbed his arm, wedged the barrel under his shoulder and fired into the darkness, into whatever monster lay beyond. The door-mouth rippled in pain and slid back into the walls. It was too late, though, for Vitellios. His face was fixed in an expression of surprise, no last witticism to give. The hive-trash fell and I felt the loss of a brother.

It was then that we truly understood that it was not just these 'gaunts: every single piece of flesh around us wished us dead. The wall algae blazed brightly as we came near to draw the beasts, bulbed stalks burst and covered us in spores that sought to burrow into our armour, cysts showered us with bio-acid, even the muscles of the floor rippled as we fired, to disrupt our aim. It would have been enough to stop any human warriors, but we are Astartes. The Angels of Death. And all the offspring's efforts could not keep us from our quest's end.

'We are close,' Cassios declared, as another 'gaunt lay in pieces at his feet.

'How close?' I shouted as I delivered another volley of fire against the creatures pursuing us.

'Can't you hear it?'

I could hear nothing over the explosions of the bolt shells and the roar of the offspring's progress. It must be close to birthing now, but I did not care. Gricole would see it as soon as it emerged, he would know to carry a message back to the fleet. Others would know, they just would not know what had happened to us.

'I hear it!' Pasan cried, and then I heard it too: a deep throbbing sound.

'Brothers!' Cassios announced. 'I give you the heart of the beast!'

The single organ, if it was just one, filled the chamber beyond. It was a giant column, surrounded by red bloated chambers. From the top of each chamber split massive leeches that surmounted the top of the pillar and descended into the centre. It looked as though eight great Sothan phantine beasts were drinking from a pool. The entire structure constantly pulsed and shifted as gallons of fluid pumped through it each second. It was the energy cortex, and it was covered by tyranids. Smaller 'gaunts with bio-weapons, larger ones with great scything claws, a few at the top even had wings.

'It's a trap,' Pasan gasped. 'It let us get this far...'

'It's not a trap if we know it's coming,' Cassios told him.

No, it's insanity. I glanced at Cassios again; his eyes were at peace. Perhaps he really had been tainted, perhaps all he had done was in service of some xenos impulse inserted into his brain. Perhaps all the while we had been inside the offspring, the offspring had been inside him.

'Why don't they attack?' Pasan whispered.

'Maybe... maybe...' Narro's mind raced, he was feeling the disorientation worst of all. 'Maybe they did not wish to risk fighting here, risk damaging the cortex.'

But then the great thundering of the offspring as it climbed out the channel of its parent reached a crescendo and went silent. It was out. It was into space. My faith was with Gricole. He would do what needed to be done. It just remained for me to do the same, call this assault off, to save the lives I could. But Cassios was already advancing, a brace of mining charges in his hand. I stopped him and held one of the charges up.

'It's set to instant detonation,' I told him.

'Of course,' he replied and we locked gazes for the last time.

'Then we stay here. They deserve the chance, Cassios. Give them that.'

He shrugged, uncaring. This was to be the epic of his death; whether others were with him did not matter. I looked at my last two wards – Narro quickly nodded agreement with me, and so too, slowly, did Pasan.

'Cover him,' I told them, as Cassios raised his power sword high and cried:

'For Sotha! For the Emperor! Death! Death! Death!'

My wards and I fired in unison: heavy bolter, boltgun and pistol together, blowing holes in the ranks of the tyranid. The tyranids responded in kind, releasing a volley of borer-beetles, bio-acid and toxin-spines against Cassios as he charged.

Cassios slammed to a halt and flinched, drawing his cloak around him. I saw his mighty frame collapse under the onslaught.

'No!' Pasan shouted and sprinted after him, spraying fire wildly as he went. The hormagaunts had already leapt from the energy cortex and were surging towards the downed commander. I did not call to bring Pasan back, I saved my breath, he would not come. I had lost him long before. Instead I trained the heavy bolter to clear his path. The first of the hormagaunt wave exploded as my shell hit home, the one behind stumbled and was knocked down by those behind it, pushing forwards, the third leapt and my next shell caught its leg and its body cart-wheeled away in pieces. The fourth reached Cassios and took the brunt of Pasan's fire. The next rank sprang, arcing high to clear the bodies before them. Two fell to my shells, one to Narro's, but three fell upon the son of Sotha. One sliced through his gun and then his arm, the second caught his knee and cut deep into his side and the third split his head straight down the middle. The son of Sotha fell and I felt the loss of a part of myself.

Then, in a crackling arc of light, the three 'gaunts were carved apart themselves. Cassios rose, his cloak dissolved, his armour cracked and scarred. Blood streamed from the split in his armour at the neck. He spun to face the approaching horde and threw himself into their midst.

He was beyond our help now. I might have only seconds to fulfil my oath and save who I could. I turned to Narro, the last of my wards, and told him:

'I never thought it would be you. But it is best that it is.'

He looked at me, confused. I shook my head and pointed to our escape. This one at least I would save, I thought, the most brilliant of them. Perhaps, I thought, that would be enough. But I was not to be allowed even that. Above us, I heard a familiar bestial scream, first one, then a second. Without thinking, I brought the heavy bolter up straight into the ravener's face.

The brutal claw carved through the heavy bolter even as I pulled the trigger. The round rocketing down the barrel suddenly struck bone and exploded. Shrapnel burst through the barrel-cover and flew at me. I stumbled back, dropping the useless heavy weapon and clutching my face. I pulled the ruined helmet off, blinking to catch the ravener's next attack. I looked and saw it collapsed on the ground, its claw blown off, its face a mass of blood and bone. The second still held Narro's body impaled upon its scythe-claws as it twisted towards me. I drew my falx. This was to be the end.

The second ravener leapt, its two scythe-claws high. I dove forwards. The scythes came down but I was inside their reach and they glanced off my shoulders. My falx was already embedded through its chestbone. Its mid-limbs plunged through my armour and unloaded its venom as I twisted and pushed it off my blade. I staggered back, holding my guts inside my body, I was still not dead. Neither was it. It flew at me in one last attack, my falx came up and caught its scythes as they came down and pushed them to one side. As its blades went down mine cut back across its gaping mouth and sliced its head open.

I felt its ichor splatter my face, I tasted it as my mouth opened to roar my defiance. At that moment, somewhere behind me, a dying hand released its grip upon the mining charges and the chamber was filled with the Emperor's wrath.

* * *

I woke aboard a dead ship, a ravener my bedside companion. I rolled the corpse away. I dragged myself to my feet and began to search about the dark and lifeless chamber. Whether the tyranids had fled or died on the spot from the psychic shock I did not know. I was searching for something else. I found it. I thought it impossible for any one, any Astartes, to live through that. I was right. The body of Commander Cassios was a shell. But I was not there for sentiment, I did not do that. I was there in the hope that something inside him survived. I grimaced in pain as I felt the bite of the ravener poison. A stronger dose this time, from a young beast, rather than a stale relic. I took the reductor from my pack and placed it first against Cassios's throat and then against his chest, and took from him the Chapter's due.

My second heart finishes its beat. My recollection concludes, as it always does, with the memory of dragging myself into this hole and, even as the bio-poison burned its way around my body, focusing on my training, slowing my mind, suspending my system and halting the poison's spread. It was too late for me; I know that. I will die when I wake. Pasan, Vitellios, Narro, Hwygir; Cassios had taken them in, but I will carry them out again. I know they are dead, their bodies lost, perhaps more bio-matter for the devourer, but their spirits live on. Two of them in the reductor in my hand, in the progenoid glands of Commander Cassios from which new gene-seed and two new Astartes would arise. And two of them my own shell. The glands in my throat and in my chest that would bear two more. Cassios and I are lost, as we should have been long ago. These four are the future of the Scythes now, and I will live and bear the pain of poison until I deliver them back home.

'Sergeant! Over here!' the neophyte called.

Sergeant Quintos, commanding the 121st Salvation Team, strode over to his ward. The neophyte gestured down with his torch into a crevice in the floor of the dead bio-ship. Sergeant Quintos activated the light built into his bionic arm. He had lost the original years before when he himself had been a scout in a Salvation Team. Down there, glinting back in the light, shone the shoulder armour of a Space Marine. And upon that armour was inscribed the legend: **TIRESIAS**

BLACK DAWN

C L Werner

Labourers bustled about the busy star port of Izo Primaris, capital city of Vulscus. Soldiers of the Merchant Guild observed the workers with a wary eye and a ready grip on the lasguns they carried. Hungry men from across Vulscus were drawn to the walled city of Izo Primaris seeking a better life. What they discovered was a cadre of guilds and cartels who maintained an iron fist upon all commerce in the city. There was work to be had, but only at the wages set by the cadre. The Merchant Guild went to draconian extremes to ensure none of their workers tried to augment their miserable earnings by prying into the crates offloaded from off-world ships.

As a heavy loading servitor trundled away from the steel crates it had unloaded, a different sort of violation of the star port's custom was unfolding. Only minutes before the steel boxes had rested inside the hold of a sleek galiot. The sinister-looking black-hulled freighter had landed upon Vulscus hours before, its master, the rogue trader Zweig Barcelo, having quickly departed the star port to seek an audience with the planetary governor.

Behind him, Zweig had left his cargo, admonishing the Conservator of the port to take special care unloading the crates and keeping people away from them. He had made it clear that the Guilders would be most unhappy if they were denied the chance to bid upon the goods he had brought into the Vulscus system.

Most of the crates the servitors offloaded from the galiot indeed held an exotic menagerie of off-world goods. One, however, held an entirely different cargo.

A small flash of light, a thin wisp of smoke and a round section of the steel crate fell from the side of the metal box. Only a few centimetres in size, the piece of steel struck the tarmac with little more noise than a coin falling from the pocket of a careless labourer. The little hole in the side of the crate was not empty for long. A slender stick-like length of bronze emerged from the opening, bending in half upon a tiny pivot as it cleared the edges of the hole. From the tip of the instrument, an iris slid open, exposing a multifaceted crystalline optic sensor. Held upright against the side of the box, the stick-like instrument slowly pivoted, searching the area for any observers.

Its inspection completed, the compact view scope was withdrawn back into the hole as quickly as it had materialised. Soon the opposite side of the steel crate began to spit sparks and thin streams of smoke. Molten lines of superheated metal disfigured the face of the box as the cargo within cut through the heavy steel. Each precise cut converged upon the others, forming a door-like pattern. Unlike the small round spy hole, the square carved from the opposite side of the crate was not allowed to crash to the ground. Instead, powerful hands gripped the cut section at each corner, fingers encased in ceramite immune to the glowing heat of the burned metal. The section was withdrawn into the crate, vanishing without trace into the shadowy interior.

Almost as soon as the opening was finished, a burly figure stalked away from the crate, his outline obscured by the shifting hues of the camo-cloak draped about his body. The man moved with unsettling grace and military precision despite the heavy carapace armour he wore beneath his cloak. In his hands, he held a thin, narrow-muzzled rifle devoid of either stock or magazine. He kept one finger coiled about the trigger of his rifle as he swept across the tarmac, shifting between the shadows.

Brother-Sergeant Carius paused as a team of labourers and their Guild wardens passed near the stack of crates he had concealed himself behind. The single organic eye remaining in his scarred face locked upon the leader of the wardens, watching him carefully. If any of the workers or their guards spotted him, they would get their orders from this man. Therefore the warden would be the first to die if it came to a fight.

A soft hiss rose from Carius's rifle, long wires projecting outwards from the back of the gun's scope. The Scout-sergeant shifted his head slightly so that the wires could connect with the mechanical optic that had replaced his missing eye. As the wires inserted themselves into his head, Carius found his mind racing with the feed from his rifle's scope, a constantly updating sequence indicating potential targets, distance, obstructions and estimated velocity.

Carius ignored the feed from his rifle and concentrated upon his own senses instead. The rifle could tell him how to shoot, but it couldn't calculate when. The Scout-sergeant would need to watch for that moment when stealth would give way to violence. There were ten targets in all. He estimated he could put them down in three seconds. He didn't want it to come to that. There was just a chance one of them might be able to scream before death silenced him.

The work crew rounded a corner and Carius shook his head to one side, ending the feed from his rifle and inducing the wires to retract back into the scope. He rose from the crouch he had assumed and gestured with his fingers to the shadows around him. Other Scouts rushed from the darkness, following the unspoken commands their sergeant had given them. Three of them formed a defensive perimeter, watching for any other workers who might stray into this quadrant of the star port. The other six assaulted the ferrocrete wall of the storage facility, employing the lowest setting of the melta-axes they had used to silently cut through the side of the cargo crate.

Carius watched his men work. The ferrocrete would take longer to cut through than the steel crate, but the knife-like melta-blades would eventually open the wall as easily as the box. The Scout Marines would then be loosed upon Izo Primaris proper.

Then their real work would begin.

Mattias held a gloved hand to his chin and watched through lidded eyes as the flamboyant off-worlder was led into the conference hall. The governor of Vulscus and the satellite settlements scattered throughout the Boras system adopted a manner of aloof disdain mixed with amused tolerance. He felt it was the proper display of emotion for a man entrusted with the stewardship of seven billion souls and the industry of an entire world.

Governor Mattias didn't feel either aloof or amused, however. The off-worlder wasn't some simple tramp merchant looking to establish trade on Vulscus or a wealthy pilgrim come to pay homage to the relic enshrined within the chapel of the governor's palace.

Zweig, the man called himself, a rogue trader with a charter going back almost to the days of the Heresy itself. The man's charter put him above all authority short of the Inquisition and the High Lords of Terra themselves. For most of his adult life, Mattias had been absolute ruler of Vulscus and her outlying satellites. It upset him greatly to know a man whose execution he couldn't order was at large upon his world.

The rogue trader made a garish sight in the dark, gothic atmosphere of the conference hall. Zweig's tunic was fashioned from a bolt of cloth so vibrant it seemed to glow with an inner light of its own, like the radioactive grin of a mutant sump-ghoul. His vest was a gaudy swirl of crimson velvet, vented by crosswise slashes in a seemingly random pattern. The hologlobes levitating beneath the hall's vaulted ceiling reflected wildly from the synthetic diamonds that marched along the breast of the trader's vest. Zweig's breeches were of chuff-silk, of nearly transparent thinness and clinging to his body more tightly than the gloves Mattias wore. Rough, grox-hide boots completed the gauche exhibition, looking like something that might have been confiscated from an ork pirate. The governor winced every time the ugly boots stepped upon the rich ihl-rugs which covered the marble floors of his hall. He could almost see the psycho-reactive cloth sickening from the crude footwear grinding into its fibres.

Zweig strode boldly between the polished obsidian columns and the hanging nests of niktiro birds that flanked the conference hall, ignoring the crimson-clad Vulscun excubitors who glowered at him as he passed. Mattias was tempted to have one of his soldiers put a shaft of las-light through the pompous off-worlder's knee, but the very air of arrogance the rogue trader displayed made him reconsider the wisdom of such action. It would be best to learn the reason for Zweig's bravado. A rogue trader didn't live long trusting that his charter would shield him from harm on every backwater world he visited. The Imperium was a big place and it might take a long time for news of his demise to reach anyone with the authority to do anything about it.

The rogue trader bowed deeply before Mattias's table, the blue mohawk into which his hair had been waxed nearly brushing across the ihl-rugs. When he rose from his bow, the vacuous grin was back on his face, pearly teeth gleaming behind his dusky lips.

'The Emperor's holy blessing upon the House of Mattias and all his fortune, may his herds be fruitful and his children prodigious. May his enterprise flourish and his fields never fall before the waning star,' Zweig said, continuing the stilted, antiquated form of address that was still practised in only the most remote and forgotten corners of the segmentum. The governor bristled under the formal salutation, unable to decide if Zweig was using the archaic greeting because he thought Vulscus was such an isolated backwater as to still employ it or because he wanted to subtly insult Mattias.

'You may dispense with the formality,' Mattias cut off Zweig's address with an annoyed flick of his hand. 'I know who you are, and you know who I am. More importantly, we each know what the other is.' Mattias's sharp, mask-like face pulled back in a thin smile. 'I am a busy man, with little time for idle chatter. Your charter ensures you an audience with the governor of any world upon which your custom takes you.' He spat the words from his tongue as though each had the taste of sour-glass upon them. 'I, however, will decide how long that audience will be.'

Zweig bowed again, a bit more shallowly than his first obeisance before the governor. 'I shall ensure that I do not waste his lordship's time,' he said. He glanced about the conference hall, his eyes lingering on the twin ranks of excubitors. He stared more closely at the fat-faced ministers seated around Mattias at the table. 'However, I do wonder if what I have to say should be shared with other ears.'

Mattias's face turned a little pale when he heard Zweig speak. Of course the rogue trader had been scanned for weapons before being allowed into the governor's palace, but there was always the chance of something too exotic for the scanners to recognise. He had heard stories about jokaero digi-weapons that were small enough to be concealed in a synthetic finger and deadly enough to burn through armaplas in the blink of an eye.

'I run an impeccable administration,' Mattias said, trying to keep any hint of suspicion out of his tone. 'I have no secrets from my ministers, or my people.'

Zweig shrugged as he heard the outrageous claim, but didn't challenge Mattias's claim of transparency. 'News of the recent... fortunes... of Vulscus has travelled far. Perhaps farther than even you intended, your lordship.'

An excited murmur spread among the ministers, but a gesture from Mattias silenced his functionaries.

'Both the Adeptus Mechanicus and the Ecclesiarchy have examined the relic,' Mattias told Zweig. 'They are convinced of its authenticity. Not that their word was needed. You only have to be in the relic's presence to feel the aura of power that surrounds it.'

'The bolt pistol of Roboute Guilliman himself,' Zweig said, a trace of awe slipping past his pompous demeanour. 'A weapon wielded by one of the holy primarchs, son of the God-Emperor Himself!'

'Vulscus is blessed to have such a relic entrusted to her care,' Mattias said. 'The relic was unearthed by labourers laying the foundation for a new promethium refinery in the Hizzak quarter of Izo Secundus, our oldest city. All Vulscuns proudly remember that it was there the primarch led his Adeptus Astartes in the final battle against the heretical Baron Unfirth during the Great Crusade, ending generations of tyranny and bringing our world into the light of the Imperium.'

Zweig nodded his head in sombre acknowledgement of Mattias's statement. 'My... benefactors... are aware of the relic and the prosperity it will surely bestow upon Vulscus. It is for that reason they... contracted me... to serve as their agent.'

The rogue trader reached to his vest, hesitating as some of the excubitors raised their weapons. A nod of the governor's head gave Zweig permission to continue. Carefully he removed a flat disc of adamantium from a pocket inside his vest. Wax seals affixed a riotous array of orisons, declarations and endowments to the disc, but it was the sigil embossed upon the metal itself that instantly arrested the attention of Mattias and his ministers. It was the heraldic symbol of House Heraclius, one of the most powerful of the Navis Nobilite families in the segmentum.

'I am here on behalf of Novator Priskos,' Zweig announced. 'House Heraclius is anxious to strengthen its dominance over the other Great Families sanctioned to transport custom in this sector. The novator has empowered me to treat with the governor of Vulscus to secure exclusive rights to the transportation of pilgrims to view your sacred relic. The agreement would preclude allowing any vessel without a Navigator from House Heraclius to land on your world.'

There was no need for Mattias to silence his ministers this time. The very magnitude of Zweig's announcement had already done that. Every man in the conference hall knew the traffic of pilgrims to their world would be tremendous. Other worlds had built entire cathedral cities to house lesser relics from the Great Crusade and to accommodate the vast numbers of pilgrims who journeyed across the stars to pay homage to such trifles as a cast-off boot worn by the first ecclesiarch and a dented copper flagon once used by the primarch Leman Russ. The multitudes that would descend upon Vulscus to see a relic of such import as the actual weapon of Roboute Guilliman himself would be staggering. To give a single Navigator House a monopoly on that traffic went beyond a simple concession. The phrase 'kingmaker' flashed through the governor's mind.

'I will need to confer with the full Vulscun planetary council,' Mattias said when he was able to find his voice. House Heraclius would be a dangerous enemy to make, but conceding to its request would not sit well with the other Navigators. The governor knew there was no good choice to make, so he would prefer to allow the planetary council to consider the matter – and take blame for the consequences when they came.

Zweig reached into his pocket again, removing an ancient chronometer. He made a show of sliding its cover away and studying the phased crystal display. Slowly, he nodded his head. 'Assemble the leaders of your world, governor. I can allow you time to discuss your decision. Novator Priskos is a patient... man. He would, however, expect me to be present for your deliberations to ensure that a strong case is made for House Heraclius being granted this concession.'

Mattias scowled as Zweig fixed him with that ingratiating smile of his. The governor didn't appreciate people who could make him squirm.

'That which serves the glory of the God-Emperor is just and will endure. That which harms the Imperium built by His children is false and shall be purged by flame and sword. With burning hearts and cool heads, we shall overcome that which has offended the Emperor's will. Our victory is ordained. Our victory is ensured by our faith in the Emperor.'

The words rang out through the ancient, ornate chapel, broadcast from the vox-casters built into the skull-like helm of Chaplain Valac, repeated by the speakers built into the stone cherubs and gargoyles that leaned down from the immense basalt columns that supported the stained plexiglass ceiling far overhead. Stars shone through the vibrant roof, casting celestial shadows across the throng gathered within the massive temple.

Each of the men who listened to Valac's words was a giant, even the smallest of their number over two metres in height. Every one of the giants was encased in a heavy suit of ceramite armour. The bulky armour was painted a dull green, dappled with blacks and browns to form a camouflaged pattern. Only the right pauldron was not covered in the patchwork series of splotches or concealed by fabric strips of scrim. The thick plate of armour above the right shoulder of each giant bore a simple field of olive green broken by a pair of crossed swords in black. It was a symbol that had announced doom upon a thousand worlds. It was the mark of the Adeptus Astartes, the heraldry of the Chapter of Space Marines called the Emperor's Warbringers.

'This day I remind the Fifth Company of its duty,' Valac continued, his armoured bulk pacing before the golden aquila looming above the chapel's altar. Unlike the rest of the Warbringers, who had removed their helms when they entered the holy shrine, the Chaplain kept his visage locked behind his skull-like mask of ceramite. He alone had not covered his armour in camouflage, his power armour retaining its grim black colouration.

'The Emperor expects us to do that which will bring honour upon His name. All we have accomplished in the past is dust and shadow. It is the moment before us that is of consequence. We do not want to fail Him. Through our victory, we shall show that we are proud to serve Him and to know that He has chosen us to be His mighty servants.

'The Fifth Company is ready for anything and we shall not be found lacking. Let no doubt enter your mind. We have no right to decide innocence or guilt. We are only the sword. The Emperor will know His own. The Emperor has commanded and we will follow His holy words before all others. In this hour of reflection and contemplation, we see victory before us. We need only deny the temptations of doubt and seize it. That is the duty of this hour!'

At the rear of the chapel, Inquisitor Korm listened to Chaplain Valac preach to his fellow Warbringers. A guest upon the Warbringers' battle-barge, the inquisitor had decided to keep himself as inconspicuous as possible. Even Korm felt a trickle of fear in his heart as he heard Valac's fiery words, as he watched the Chaplain instil upon the armoured giants kneeling before him a cold, vicious determination to descend upon their enemies without mercy or quarter. Korm knew he was hearing the death of an entire city echoing through the vaulted hall of the chapel. A twinge of guilt flickered through his mind as he considered how many innocent people were going to die in a few hours.

Korm quickly suppressed the annoying emotion. He'd done too many things over his life to listen to his conscience now. Ten thousand, even a million hapless citizens of the Imperium were a small price to pay for the knowledge he sought. Knowledge he alone would possess because only he knew the secret of the relic that Governor Mattias had unearthed.

Unleashing the Warbringers upon Vulscus was a brutal solution to Korm's problem, but the inquisitor had learned long ago that the surest way to victory was through excessive force.

If there was one thing the Warbringers did better than anyone, it was excessive force. Korm smiled grimly as he listened to the Chaplain's closing words.

'Now, brothers, rise up and let the Emperor's enemies discover the price of heresy! Let the storm of judgement be set loose!'

The factory worker crumpled into a lifeless heap as the vibro-knife punctured his neck and slashed the carotid artery. Carius lowered the grimy corpse to the peeling linoleum tiles that covered the floor. The Scout-sergeant pressed his armoured body against the filthy wall of the hallway and brought the tip of his boot against the clapboard door the worker had unlocked only a few seconds before. Slowly, Carius nudged the door open. Like a shadow, he slid into the opening, closing the portal behind him.

Scout-Sergeant Carius had been lurking in the dusty archway that marked a long-forgotten garbage chute, biding his time as he waited for the factories of Izo Primaris to disgorge their human inmates. He had watched as workers trudged down the hall, shuffling down the corridor half-dead with fatigue. He had let them all pass, maintaining his vigil until he saw the man he wanted. Carius's victim was just another nameless cog in the economy of the Imperium, a man of no importance or consequence. The only thing that made him remarkable was the room he called home. That minor detail had caused fifteen centimetres of gyrating steel to sink into the back of the man's neck.

Carius paused when he crossed the threshold, his ears trained upon the sounds of the dingy apartment he had invaded. He could hear the mineral-tainted water rumbling through the pipes, could fix the lairs of sump-rats in the plaster walls, could discern the pebbly groan of air rattling through vents. The Scout-sergeant ignored these sounds. It was the slight noise of footsteps that had his attention.

The apartment was a miserable hovel, ramshackle factory-pressed furnishings slowly decaying into their constituent components. A threadbare rug was thrown across the peeling floor in some vain effort to lend a touch of dignity to the place. A narrow bed was crushed against one wall, a scarred wardrobe lodged in a corner. Table, chairs, a mouldering couch, a lopsided shelf supporting a sorry collection of crystal miniatures, these were the contents of the apartment. These, and a wide window looking out upon the boulevard.

Carius followed the sound of footsteps. The main room of the apartment had two lesser ancillary chambers – a pail closet and a galley. It was from the galley that the sounds arose.

The Scout-sergeant edged along the wall until he stood just at the edge of the archway leading into the galley. The pungent smell of boiling vegetables struck his heightened olfactory senses, along with a suggestion of sweat and feminine odour. Carius dug his armoured thumb into the wall, effortlessly ripping a clump of crumbly grey plaster free. Without turning from the archway, he threw the clump of plaster against the apartment door. The impact sounded remarkably like a door slamming shut; the fragments of plaster tumbling across the floor as they exploded away from the impact resembled the sound of footsteps.

'Andreas!' a woman's voice called. 'Dinner is–'

The worker's wife didn't have time to do more than blink as Carius's armoured bulk swung out from the wall and filled the archway as she emerged from the galley to welcome her husband. The vibro-knife stabbed into her throat, stifling any cry she might have made.

Carius depressed the vibro-knife's activation stud, ending the shivering motion of the blade and slid the weapon back into its sheath. Walking away from the body, he shoved furniture out of his way, advancing to the window. The sergeant stared through the glazed glass and admired the view of the boulevard outside. From the instant he had inspected the building from the street below, he had expected this room to offer such a vantage point.

The apartment door opened behind him, but Carius did not look away from the window. He knew the men moving into the room were his own.

'Report,' Carius ordered.

'Melta bombs placed at power plant,' one of the Scouts stated, his voice carrying no inflection, only the precise acknowledgement of a job completed.

'Melta bombs in position at defence turrets nine and seven,' the other Scout said.

Carius nodded his head. The two Scouts had been charged with targets closest to their current position. It would take time for the others to reach their targets and filter back. The sergeant studied the chronometer fixed to the underside of his gauntlet. The attack would not begin for some hours yet. His squad was still ahead of schedule. By the time they were finished, all of Izo Primaris's defence turrets would be sabotaged, leaving the city unable to strike any aerial attackers until it could scramble its own aircraft. Carius shook his head as he considered what value the antiquated PDF fighters would have against a Thunderhawk. The defence turrets had been the only real menace the Space Marines could expect as they made their descent from the orbiting battle-barge, the deadly *Deathmonger*.

Other melta bombs would destroy the city's central communications hub and disable the energy grid. Izo Primaris would be plunged into confusion and despair even before the first Warbringers descended upon the city.

The local planetary defence force was of little concern to the Warbringers. Unable to contact their central command, they would be forced to operate in a disjointed, fragmented fashion, a type of combat for which they were unprepared. There was only one factor within Izo Primaris that might prove resilient enough to react to the havoc preceding the Warbringers' assault.

Carius motioned with his hand, gesturing for the two Scout Marines to occupy rooms to either side of the apartment he had secured. The Scouts slipped back into the hall with the same silence with which they had entered. Carius unslung the needle rifle looped over his shoulder. The back of the scope opened, sending wires slithering into his artificial eye.

Through the prism of the rifle's scope, Carius studied the massive, fortress-like structure of plasteel and ferrocrete that rose from the squalor of the district like an iron castle. A gigantic Imperial aquila was etched in bronze upon each side of the imposing structure, the precinct courthouse of the city's contingent of the Adeptus Arbites.

Brutal enforcers of the *Lex Imperialis*, the Imperial Law every world within the Imperium was bound by, the Arbites had the training, the weapons and the skill to prove a troublesome obstacle if allowed the chance. Carius and his Scouts would ensure the arbitrators did not get that chance. Their mission of sabotage completed, the Scouts would fan out across the perimeter of the courthouse. Sniper fire would keep the arbitrators pinned down inside their fortress. In time, the arbitrators would find a way around the lethal fire of Carius and his men. By then, however, the Warbringers should have accomplished their purpose in Izo Primaris.

Carius watched as armoured arbitrators paced about the perimeter fence separating the courthouse from the slums around it. His finger rested lightly against the trigger of his rifle, the weapon shifting ever so slightly as he maintained contact with the target he had chosen.

When the signal came, Carius and his Scouts would be ready.

It wasn't really surprising that the planetary council of Vulscus met in a section of the governor's palace. Mattias was a ruler who believed in allowing his subjects the illusion of representation, but wasn't foolish enough to allow the council to actually conduct its business outside his own supervision. Even so, there were times when the representatives of the various merchant guilds and industrial combines could be exceedingly opinionated. Occasionally, Mattias had found it necessary to summon his excubitors to maintain order in the council chamber.

The debate over the proposal Zweig had brought to Vulscus was proving to be just such a divisive subject. Lavishly appointed guilders roared at fat promethium barons, the semi-mechanical tech-priests lashing out against the zealous oratory of the robed ecclesiarch. Even the handful of wiry rogues representing the trade unions felt they had to bare their teeth and demand a few concessions to compensate the unwashed masses of workers they supposedly championed. As soon as one of the industrialists or guilders tossed a bribe their way, the union men would shut up. The others would be more difficult to silence.

Arguments arose over the wisdom of defying the other Great Families by honouring the request of House Heraclius. Some felt that the pilgrims should be able to reach Vulscus by whatever means they could, others claimed that by having a single family of Navigators controlling the traffic there would be less confusion and more order. Those guilders and industrialists who already had exclusive contracts with House Heraclius to ship goods through the warp sparred with those who had dealings with other Navigators and worried about how the current situation would impact their own shipping agreements.

Throughout it all, Mattias watched the planetary council shout itself hoarse and wondered if perhaps he should have bypassed them and just made the decision himself. If anyone had been too upset with his decision, he could have always sent the PDF to re-educate them.

He glanced across the tiers of the council chamber to the ornate visitors' gallery. No expense had been spared to make the gallery as opulent and impressive as possible. Visiting dignitaries were surrounded by vivid holo-picts of assorted scenes of Vulscun history and culture, the walls behind them covered in rich tapestries depicting the wonders of Vulscun industry and the extensive resources of the planet and her satellites. If the vicious debates of the planetary council failed to interest a visiting ambassador, the exotic sculptures of Vulscun beauties would usually suffice to keep him entertained.

Zweig, however, didn't even glance at the expensive art all around him in the gallery. He stubbornly kept watching the debate raging below him, despite the tedium of such a vigil. Mattias could tell the rogue trader was bored by the whole affair. He kept looking at his antique chronometer.

The governor chuckled at Zweig's discomfort. The man had asked for this, after all. He'd kept pestering Mattias about when the council could be gathered and if all the leaders of Vulscus would be present to hear him make his case for Novator Priskos. Despite repeated assurances from the governor, Zweig had been most insistent that all of the men who controlled Vulscus should be in attendance when he introduced the Navigator's proposal.

Well, the rogue trader had gotten his wish. He had presented his proposal to the planetary council. Now he could just sit back and wait a few weeks for their answer.

Mattias chuckled again when he saw Zweig fussing about with his chronometer again. The governor wondered if the rogue trader might consider selling the thing. Mattias had never seen a chronometer quite like it. He was sure it would make an interesting addition to his private collection of off-world jewellery and bric-a-brac.

The governor's amusement ended when there was a bright flash from Zweig's chronometer. At first Mattias thought perhaps Zweig's incessant toying with the device had caused some internal relay to explode. It was on his lips to order attendants to see if the rogue trader had been injured, but the words never left his mouth.

Shapes were appearing on the gallery beside Zweig, blurry outlines that somehow seemed far more real than the holo-picts playing around them. With each second, the shapes became more distinct, more solid. They were huge, monstrous figures, twice the height of a man and incredibly broad. Though their outlines were humanoid, they looked more machine than man, great bulky brutes of tempered plasteel and adamantium.

Mattias stared in shock as the strange manifestations began to move, lumbering across the gallery. The giants were painted in a dull olive drab, mottled with splashes of black and brown to help break up their outlines. If not for the confusing blur of colour, the governor might have recognised them for what they were sooner. It was only when one of the giants shifted its arm, raising a hideous rotary autocannon over the railing of the gallery, that the governor saw the ancient stone cruciform bolted to the armoured shoulder. It was then that he knew the armoured giants surrounding Zweig were Space Marines.

The chronometer Zweig had been toying with was actually a homing beacon. The Space Marines had fixed the beacon's location and teleported down into the council chamber. There could be no doubt as to why. For some reason, the rogue trader had brought death to the leaders of Vulscus.

A hush fell upon the chamber as the councillors took notice of the five giants looming above them from the gallery. Arguments and feuds were forgotten in that moment as each man stared up into the waiting jaws of destruction. Some cried out in terror; some fell to their knees and pleaded innocence; others made the sign of the aquila and called upon the Emperor of Mankind.

Whatever their reaction, their end was already decided. In unison, the Warbringers in their heavy Terminator armour opened fire upon the cowering councillors. Five assault cannons tore into the screaming men, bursting their bodies as though they were rotten fruit.

In a matter of seconds, the ornate council chamber became a charnel house.

Sirens blared throughout Izo Primaris. Smoke curled skywards from every quarter, turning the purplish twilight black with soot. Crisis control tractors trundled into the streets, smashing their way through the evening traffic, oblivious to any concern save that of reaching the stricken sections of the city. No industrial accident, no casual arson in a block of filthy tenements, not even the tragic conflagration of the opulent residence of a guilder could have provoked such frantic, brutal reaction. The explosions had engulfed the defence batteries, all five of the massive forts crippled in the blink of an eye by melta bombs.

Even as the crisis tractors smashed a path through the crowded streets, tossing freight trucks and commuter sedans like chaff before a plough, more explosions ripped through the city. Lights winked out, a malignant darkness spreading through the capital. A pillar of fire rising from the heart of the metropolitan sprawl was the only monument to the site of Izo Primaris's central power plant. It would be hours before tech-priests at the substations would be able to redirect the city's energy needs through the battery of back-up plants. They wouldn't even try. To do that, the tech-priests required absolution from their superiors.

The destruction of the communications hub made the earlier explosions seem tame by comparison. Plasteel windows cracked a kilometre and a half away from the cloud of noxious smoke that heralded the silencing of a planet. A skyscraper of ferrocrete and reinforced armaplas, the communications tower had bristled with satellite relays and frequency transmitters, its highest chambers, five hundred metres above the ground, devoted to the psychic exertions of the planet's astropaths. Governor Mattias, always mindful of his own security and power, had caused all communications on Vulscus to be routed through the tower, where his private police could check every message for hints of sedition and discontent.

Now the giant tower had fallen, brought to ruin by the timed blast of seven melta bombs planted in its sub-cellars. With the death of the hub, every vox-caster on Vulscus went silent.

All except those trained upon a different frequency. A frequency being relayed from a sinister vessel in orbit around the world.

Izo Primaris maintained three PDF garrisons within its walled confines. Two infantry barracks and a brigade of armour. Despite the silence of the vox-casters and their inability to raise anyone in central command, the soldiers of the Vulscun Planetary Defence Forces were not idle. Lasguns and flak armour were brought from stores, companies and regiments were quickly mustered into formation.

There was nothing to disturb the hasty muster of soldiers at the two infantry barracks. The tank brigade was not so fortunate. The Scout Marine who had visited them had not placed melta bombs about their headquarters or tried to sabotage the fifty Leman Russ-pattern tanks housed in the base's motor pool. What he had done instead was even more deadly.

A bright flash burst into life at the centre of the courtyard where the PDF tankmen were scrambling to their vehicles. A survivor of the massacre in the council chamber would have recognised that flash, would have shouted a warning as hulking armoured shapes suddenly appeared. From the orbiting battle-barge, five more Terminators had followed a homing beacon and been teleported with unerring precision to their target.

The olive-drab giants opened fire upon the tankmen, tearing their bodies to pieces with concentrated fire from their storm bolters. One of the Space Marines, his bulky armour further broadened by the box-like weapon system fastened to his shoulders, targeted the tanks themselves. Shrieking as they shot upwards from the cyclone missile launcher, a dozen armour-busting krak missiles streamed towards the PDF tanks. The effect upon the armoured vehicles was much like that of the storm bolters upon the stunned tankmen. Reinforced armour plate crumpled like tinfoil as the missiles slammed home, their shaped warheads punching deep into the tanks' hulls before detonating. The effect was like igniting a plasma grenade inside a steel can. The tanks burst apart from within as the explosives gutted their innards.

In a few minutes, the surviving tankmen retreated back into their barracks, seeking shelter behind the thick ferrocrete walls. The Terminators ignored the sporadic lasgun fire directed on them, knowing there was no chance such small arms fire could penetrate their armoured shells. They turned away from the barracks, maintaining a vigil on the gated entryway to the motor pool.

Despite the carnage they had wrought, the mission the Terminators had been given was not one of slaughter. It was to keep the tanks from mobilising and spreading out into the city where they might interfere with the Warbringers' other operations.

Carius followed the read from his scope and opened fire. He aimed thirteen centimetres above the arbitrator he had chosen for his victim, allowing for the pull of gravity upon his shot. The slender sliver-like needle struck home, slicing through the arbitrator's jaw just beneath the brim of his visor. The enforcer didn't even have time to register pain before the deadly poison upon the needle dropped him. His body twitched and spasmed upon the cobblestones outside the courthouse, drawing in other arbitrators, rushing to investigate their comrade's plight. Three more of the enforcers were dropped as the other snipers staged around the courthouse opened fire.

The arbitrators fell back into their fortress, employing riot shields to protect themselves as they withdrew. Carius kept his rifle aimed upon the entrance of the courthouse. Experience and the mem-training he had undergone when a neophyte told Carius what to expect next. These arbitrators were especially well trained, the sergeant conceded. They beat his estimate by a full minute when they emerged from the courthouse in a phalanx, employing their riot shields to form a bulwark against the sniper fire.

Emotionlessly, Carius scanned the crude defensive line. He nodded his head slightly when he saw the man he wanted. The judge wore a stormcloak over his carapace armour and a golden eagle adorned his helmet. Carius aimed at that bit of ostentation, sending a poisoned needle sizzling through one of the riot shields to embed itself in the beak of the eagle. The judge felt the impact of the shot, ducking his head and reaching to his helmet. The Scout-sergeant wasn't disappointed when he saw the judge's face go white when his fingers felt the slivers of Carius's bullet embedded in his helmet.

The judge rose and shouted at the arbitrators. It was again to the credit of the enforcers that they did not allow the judge's panic to infect them and their second retreat into the courthouse was made in perfect order, the phalanx never disintegrating into a panicked mob.

Carius leaned back, resting his elbows against the sill of the window. The next thing the arbitrators would try would be to use one of their Rhino armoured transports to affect a breakout. Brother Domitian would be in position with his heavy bolter to thwart that attempt. After that, the enforcers would have to think about their next move.

Carius was content to let them think. While the arbitrators were thinking they would be safely contained inside the courthouse where they couldn't interfere with the Warbringers.

With the defence batteries destroyed and communications down, there was no warning for the people of Izo Primaris when five gun-laden assault craft descended upon the city. Two of the powerful Thunderhawk gunships hurtled into the ferrocrete canyons of the city, guided through the black maze of the darkened metropolis by holo-maps taken by the battle-barge from orbit. As the Thunderhawks progressed only a dozen metres above the streets, their speed gradually slowed. Intermittent bursts of lascannon fire slammed into the sides of buildings or gouged craters from the tarmac. Screams of terror rose from civilians as they streamed from their wounded homes, filling the streets with a mass of frightened humanity.

Coldly, with a callous precision, the Warbringers employed the heavy bolters mounted upon their Thunderhawks to herd the frantic mob through the streets. The objective of this brutal tactic soon showed itself. The infantry regiments were finally marching from their garrisons, trying to restore order to the stricken city. The desperate mob rushed into the face of their marching columns.

The PDF commanders hesitated to give the order to open fire on their own people. The delay could not be recovered. Even as the belated command was given, the civilians were crashing into the soldiers, confusing their ranks, breaking the cohesion of their units.

The Thunderhawks dropped still lower, the ramps set into the rear of their hulls opening. Green-armoured giants jumped from the moving gunships, rolling across the tarmac as they landed. Each of the Warbringers was soon on his feet again, the lethal bulk of a boltgun clenched in his steel gauntlets. While the PDF still fought to free themselves of the civilian herd, the Space Marines moved into position, establishing a strongpoint at the intersection nearest their enemies.

Both Thunderhawks surged forwards with a burst of speed, sweeping over the embattled PDF troops. One soldier managed to send a rocket screaming up at one of the gunships, the warhead impacting against the hull and blackening the armour plate. Any jubilation over the attack was quickly extinguished as the Thunderhawks reached the rear of the PDF columns. Spinning full around, the gunships came back, their lascannons blazing. The withering fire slammed into the PDF regiments, forcing them forwards. It was their turn to be herded through the streets, herded straight into the waiting guns of the Warbringers on the ground.

Of the remaining Thunderhawks, one sped across Izo Primaris to disgorge its cargo of power-armoured giants at the armour base so that they might support the action entrusted to the Terminators. The other two made straight for the governor's palace.

The compound was in a state of siege, frightened citizens hammering at its gates, demanding answers from their leaders. The red-uniformed excubitors held the mob back, employing shock mauls to break the arms of anyone trying to climb over the walls, using laspistols on those few who actually made it over the barrier.

The gunships unleashed the fury of their heavy bolters into both mob and guards, the explosive rounds shearing through the crimson armour of the excubitors as though it were paper. Citizens fled back into the darkened streets, wailing like damned souls as terror pounded through their hearts. The excubitors attempted to fall back to defensive positions, but the punishment being visited on them by the heavy bolters soon caused the guards to abandon that plan and retreat back into the palace itself.

In short order, a landing zone had been cleared. The Thunderhawks descended into the lush gardens fronting Governor Mattias's palace, the backwash of their powerful engines crushing priceless blooms imported from Terra into a mess of mangled vegetation. Armoured ramps dropped open at the rear of each gunship, ceramite-encased giants rushing to assume a perimeter around the garden. Two gigantic machines, lumbering monstrosities twice as tall as even the gigantic Space Marines, emerged from the Thunderhawks behind the Warbringers. Vaguely cast in a humanoid form, the torso of each machine encased the armoured sarcophagus of a crippled Warbringer, his mind fused to the adamantium body which now housed it. The Dreadnoughts were revered battle-brothers of the Warbringers, ancient warriors who fought on through the millennia in their ageless metal tombs.

The two Dreadnoughts fanned out across the gardens, one training its deadly weapons on the wall at the front of the compound, the other facing towards the palace itself. Almost immediately the huge machine was spurred into action as solid shot from a heavy stubber mounted in an ornate cupola began firing upon it. The bullets glanced off the Dreadnought's thick hull, barely scratching the olive drab paint that coated it. Power hissed through the oversized energy coils of the immense weapon that was fitted to the machine's left arm. When the coils began to glow with the intensity of a supernova, the Dreadnought pivoted at its waist and raised the arm towards the cupola.

A blinding burst of light erupted from the nozzle that fronted the Dreadnought's cumbersome weapon. The blazing ball of gas sizzled across the gardens, striking the cupola at its centre. Instantly the structure vanished in a great cloud of boiling nuclear malignance as the charged plasma reacted with the solid composition of the cupola. The plasma gun immolated the excubitors who had fired upon the Dreadnought, reduced their heavy stubber to a molten smear and fused the cupola into something resembling a charred brick.

After that, an eerie silence fell across the compound. The governor's guards were not about to provoke the wrath of the Dreadnoughts a second time.

With the Dreadnoughts in command of the exterior, the twenty Warbringers left the defence of the perimeter to their ancient brethren and rushed the palace itself. Gilded doors designed to withstand the impact of a freight tractor were quickly shattered by the chainswords of the Space Marines, the diamond-edged blades tearing through the heavy oorl-wood panels and the plasteel supports.

As the first Warbringers breeched the doors and entered the palace itself, Inquisitor Korm emerged from one of the Thunderhawks, his imposing figure dwarfed by the huge armoured warriors who flanked him. Captain Phazas held his helmet in the crook of his arm, exposing a leathery face and a forehead bristling with steel service studs. Chaplain Valac, as ever, kept his countenance locked behind the death's head mask of his helm.

Phazas pressed a finger against his ear, closing one eye as he digested the vox-cast being relayed to him. 'Squad Boethius has secured the council building,' he told Korm. The captain's grim face twisted in a scowl. 'Zweig reports that Governor Mattias escaped before the operation was complete. Some kind of personal force field.'

'We will track down the heretic,' Korm assured the fearsome Phazas. 'There is no escape for him. With his regime broken, he will try to flee Vulscus.' The inquisitor's eyes burned with a fanatical light, his lip curling in disgust. 'First he will try to secure his most precious treasure.'

'The obscene shall be cast low in the midst of their obscenity,' Chaplain Valac's stern voice intoned. 'For them, death is but the doorway to damnation.'

Korm turned away from Valac and directed his attention back to

Phazas. 'Have your men search the palace, sweep through it room by room. Mattias must not leave the compound with the relic.'

'The Warbringers know their duty,' Phazas answered, annoyance in his tone. 'The heretic will be found. The relic will be recovered.' He spoke as though both tasks had already been accomplished, statement rather than speculation. Korm knew better than to question the captain's belief in his men.

A man didn't live long enough to become an inquisitor if he were a fool.

Governor Mattias had retreated to a fortified bunker deep beneath his palace. The Warbringers had intercepted the governor before he could reach his escape route: a private tunnel connecting the complex to the underrail network beneath Izo Primaris. Twenty excubitors had been killed in the ensuing firefight. Mattias and his ten surviving guards had fallen back to the bunker.

Designed to be proof against rebellion and civil unrest, the governor's bunker proved no obstacle to the Warbringers, warriors used to breaching the bulkheads of renegade starships and assaulting the citadels of xenos armies. The huge steel doors that blocked the entrance to the bunker were quickly reduced to slag by a concentrated blast from a plasma cannon. The Warbringers rushed through the opening while molten metal still dripped from the frame.

One of the power-armoured giants vanished in a burst of light, flesh and ceramite liquefied by the searing energy that smashed into him. Instantly the other Warbringers flattened against the walls, voxing warnings to their comrades. Mattias only had a few guards left to him, but these last excubitors had something the others didn't. They had a multi-melta.

The crimson-armoured excubitors swung the heavy weapon around on its tripod. Nestled behind a ferrocrete pillbox, the guards tried to bring their deadly weapon to bear on the Warbringers already in the corridor. The armoured giants could see the barrels of the multi-melta pivoting within the narrow loophole. One of the Warbringers racked his boltgun and emptied a clip into the pillbox, the explosive rounds digging little craters in the thick surface, drawing the attention of the gun crew.

As the multi-melta swung around to fire on the shooter, he threw himself flat to the floor. The superheated beam of light flashed through the air above him, melting the stabiliser jets and air purification intakes on the Warbringer's backpack, but doing no harm to the Space Marine himself.

Instantly, the other Warbringers in the corridor charged the pillbox. It would take three seconds for the multi-melta to cool down enough to be fired again. The Space Marines intended to have the strongpoint disabled before then. The foremost of the armoured giants reached to his belt, removing a narrow disc of metal. He flung this against the face of the pillbox, black smoke filling the corridor as the blind grenade exploded. The optical sensors built into the Warbringers' helmets allowed them to pierce the dense cloud of inky smoke. The excubitors inside the pillbox were not so fortunate. Frantically they tried to fire the multi-melta into the darkness, the blazing beam of light striking only the ferrocrete wall of the bunker.

Pressed against the face of the pillbox, two of the Warbringers pushed tiny discs through the loophole, then turned away as the frag grenades detonated inside the strongpoint. The menace of the multi-melta was over.

The Warbringers swept around the now silent pillbox, pressing on down the corridor. Las-bolts cracked against their power armour as they converged upon an armaplas barricade thrown across the middle of the hallway, the governor and the last of his guards mounting a hopeless last-ditch effort to defy the oncoming Space Marines.

'This is an unjust act!' Mattias shrieked. 'I have paid the Imperial tithe, I have exceeded the conscription levels for the Imperial Guard! You have no right here! Vulscus is loyal!'

The governor's desperate plea went unanswered by the Space Marines sweeping down the hall. Precise shots from the huge boltguns the Warbringers bore brought death to two of the remaining excubitors. A third threw down his weapon, climbing over the barricade in an effort to surrender. A bolt-round tore through his chest, splattering his organs across the armaplas fortification. The orders the Warbringers were under had been explicit: no prisoners.

'Surrender the relic,' the sepulchral voice of Chaplain Valac boomed through the bunker, magnified by the vox-amplifiers built into his skull-faced helm. The black-armoured Warbringer marched down the corridor, the winged crozius clenched in his fist glowing with power as he approached the barricade. 'Atone for your faithlessness and be returned to the Emperor's grace in death.'

The governor cringed as he heard Valac's words, but quickly recovered. His face pulled back in a sneer of contempt. 'The relic? That is why you have destroyed my city?' Bitter laughter choked Mattias's voice. 'The noble Adeptus Astartes, sons of the Emperor! Common thieves!'

Perhaps the governor might have said more, but his tirade had focussed every bolter in the corridor upon him. Mattias was thrown back as the concentrated fusillade struck him, tossing his body back from the edge of the barricade. The last two excubitors, their reason broken by the hopelessness of their situation, broke from cover and charged straight towards the Warbringers, their lasguns firing harmlessly at the power-armoured giants.

Chaplain Valac pressed forwards, climbing over the barricade and walking towards the crumpled body of Governor Mattias. The governor's reductor field had prevented the fusillade from ripping apart his body, but hadn't been equal to the momentum of the shots. The impact had hurled him across the corridor to crash against the unyielding ferrocrete wall.

There was no sympathy as Valac stared down at the broken governor. Even with half his bones shattered, Mattias tried to defend the object cradled against his chest. Wrapped tightly in a prayer rug soaked in sacred unguents and adorned with waxen purity seals and parchment benedictions, even now the governor could feel the supernatural power of the relic giving him strength.

'You have no right,' Mattias snarled at Valac. 'Roboute Guilliman left it here, left it for Vulscus!'

'No,' Valac's pitiless voice growled. He raised the heavy crozius he carried, energy bristling about the club-like baton. 'He didn't leave it.' The Chaplain brought his staff smashing down, its power field easily bypassing the reductor field that protected the governor. Mattias's head was reduced to pulp beneath Valac's blow.

Grimly, Valac removed the relic from the bloodied corpse. Turning away from Mattias's body, the Chaplain began stripping away the pious adornments that surrounded the relic, flinging them aside as though they were unclean filth. Soon he exposed a bolt pistol of ancient pattern, its surface encrusted by millennia of decay and corrosion.

'You have secured the relic,' Inquisitor Korm beamed as he marched down the corridor, Captain Phazas beside him. A triumphant smile was on Korm's lean face. 'We must get it to the fortress on Titan so that the Ordo Malleus may study it.'

Valac shook his head. 'No,' he intoned. His fist clenched tighter about the bolt pistol, the pressure causing some of the corrosion to flake away, exposing the symbol of an eye engraved into the grip of the gun. 'It is an abomination and must be purged. You have brought us here to do the Emperor's work, and it shall be done.'

Korm stared in disbelief at the grim Warbringer Chaplain. The inquisitor had been the one who had uncovered the truth about the relic so recently discovered on Vulscus, a truth locked away in the archives on Titan. Roboute Guilliman had indeed been on Vulscus, but it had not been the Ultramarines or their primarch who had brought the planet into the Imperium, though such was the official version preached by the Ecclesiarchy and taught in sanctioned histories of the world. The real liberators had been the Luna Wolves. If a primarch had left a relic upon a Vulscun battlefield, it had been left by that of the Luna Wolves. It had been left by the arch-traitor, Warmaster Horus.

The fearsome Chaplain marched across the bunker to the shambles that had been left of the pillbox. Clenching the relic in one hand, Valac ripped the damaged multi-melta from the emplacement. Korm gasped in alarm as he understood the Chaplain's purpose. The relic was tainted, a thing of heresy and evil to be sure, corrupting even the innocent by pretending to be something holy. But it was more important that it be studied, not destroyed!

Phazas laid a restraining hand upon Korm's shoulder before the inquisitor could interfere. 'Two fates present themselves,' the captain told him. 'You can return to Titan a hero who has brought about the destruction of an unholy thing. Or you can be denounced as a Horusian radical and perish with the relic. Make your choice, inquisitor.'

Sweat beaded Korm's brow as he watched Chaplain Valac throw the relic onto the ground and aim the heavy multi-melta at it. At such range, the bolt pistol would be reduced to vapour, annihilated more completely than if it had been cast into the centre of a sun.

Korm knew he would share the same annihilation if he broke faith with the Warbringers. The Adeptus Astartes had a very narrow definition of duty and honour. Anything tainted by contact with heresy was a thing to be destroyed.

As he watched Valac obliterate the relic, Korm decided to keep quiet. He'd been an inquisitor for a long time. A man didn't last that long if he were a fool.

UNFORGIVEN

Graham McNeill

The midnight dark closed on Brother-Sergeant Kaelen of the Dark Angels like a fist. The emission-reduced engines of the rapidly disappearing Thunderhawk were the only points of light he could see. His visor swum into a ghostly green hue and the outlines of the star shaped city below became clear as his auto-senses kicked in.

The altimeter reading on his visor was unravelling like a lunatic countdown, the shapes below him resolving into clearer, oblong forms. The speed of his descent was difficult to judge, the powered armour insulating Kaelen from the sensations of icy rushing air and roaring noise as he plummeted downwards.

With a pulse of thought, Kaelen overlaid the tactical schematics of the city onto his visor, noting with professional pride that the outline of the buildings below almost perfectly matched the image projected before him.

The altimeter rune flashed red and Kaelen pulled out of his drop position, smoothly bringing his legs around so that he was falling feet first. Glancing left and right he saw the same manoeuvre being repeated by his men and slammed the firing mechanism on his chest. He felt the huge deceleration as the powerful rocket motors ignited, slowing his headlong plunge into a controlled descent.

Kaelen's boots slammed into the marble flagged plaza, his jump pack flaring a wash of heated air around him as he landed. Streams of bright light licked up from the city, flak waving like undersea fronds as the rebels sought to down the departing Thunderhawk. But the heretic gunners were too late to prevent the gunship from completing its mission; its deadly cargo had already arrived.

Kaelen whispered a prayer for the transport's crew and transferred his gaze back to the landing zone. Their drop was perfect, the Thunderhawk's jumpmaster had delivered them dead on target. A target that was thronged with screaming, masked cultists.

Kaelen ducked a clumsy swing of a cultist's power maul and punched his power fist through his enemy's chest, the man shrieking and convulsing as the energised gauntlet smashed though his flesh and bone. He kicked the corpse off his fist and smashed his pistol butt into the throat of another. The man fell, clutching his shattered larynx and Kaelen spared a hurried glance to check the rest of his squad had dropped safely with him.

Stuttering blasts of heat and light flared in the darkness as the remaining nine men in Squad Leuctra landed within five metres of him, firing their bolters and making short dashes for cover.

A cultist ran towards him swinging a giant axe, his features twisted in hatred. Kaelen shot him in the head. By the Lion, these fools just didn't stop coming! He ducked behind a giant marble statue of some nameless cardinal as a heavy burst of gunfire stitched its way towards him from the gigantic cathedral at the end the plaza. Muzzle flashes came through smashed stained glass windows, the bullets tearing up the marble in jagged splinters and cutting down cultists indiscriminately. Kaelen knew that advancing into the teeth of those guns would be bloody work indeed.

Another body ducked into cover with him, the dark green of his armour partially obscured by his Chaplain's robes. Interrogator-Chaplain Bareus raised his bolt pistol. The weapon's barrel was intricately tooled and its muzzle smoked with recent firing.

'Squad form on me!' ordered Kaelen, 'Prepare to assault! Evens advance, odds covering fire!'

A prophet had risen on the cathedral world of Valedor and with him came the planet's doom. Within a year of his first oration, the temples of the divine Emperor had been cast down and his faithful servants, from the highest cardinal to the lowliest scribes, were cast into the charnel fire-pits. Millions were purged and choking clouds of human ash fell as grotesque snow for months after.

The nearest Imperial Guard regiment, the 43rd Carpathian Rifles, had fought through the temple precincts for nine months since the planet's secession, battling in vicious close combat with the fanatical servants of the Prophet. The pacification had progressed well, but now ground to a halt before the walls of the planet's capital city, Angellicus. The heavily fortified cathedral city had withstood every assault, but now it was the turn of the Adeptus Astartes to bring the rebellion to an end. For the Space Marines of the Dark Angels Chapter, more than just Imperial honour and retribution was at stake. Many centuries ago, Valedor had provided a clutch of fresh recruits for the Chapter and the planet's heresy was a personal affront to the Dark Angels. Honour must be satisfied. The Prophet must die.

Dozens of cultists were pitched backwards by the Space Marines' first volley, blood bright on their robes. More died as the bolters fired again. Kaelen exploded from cover, a laser blast scoring a groove in his shoulder plate. The first cultist to bar his path died without even seeing the blow that killed him. The next saw Kaelen bearing down on him and the Space Marine sergeant relished the look of terror on his face. His power fist took his head off.

Gunfire sounded, louder than before, as more covering fire raked the robed cultists. Kaelen fought and killed his way towards the temple doors, gore spattering his armour bright red. All around him, Squad Leuctra killed with a grim efficiency. Short dashes for cover combined with deadly accurate bolter fire had brought them to within eighty metres of the temple doors with no casualties. In their wake, more than two hundred cultists lay dead or dying.

Powerful blasts of gunfire spat from the smashed windows. Too heavy to charge through, even for power armour, Kaelen knew. He activated his vox-com.

'Brother Lucius.'

'Yes, brother-sergeant?'

'You have a good throwing arm on you. You think you can get a couple of grenades through those windows?'

Lucius risked a quick glance over the rim of the fountain he was using for cover and nodded curtly. 'Yes, brother-sergeant. I believe I can, the Lion willing.'

'Then do so,' ordered Kaelen. 'The Emperor guide your aim.'

Kaelen shifted position and spoke to the rest of his squad. 'Be ready. We move on the grenade's detonation.'

Each tiny rune on his visor that represented one of his men blinked once as they acknowledged receipt of the order. Kaelen glanced round to check that Chaplain Bareus was ready too. The hulking figure of the Chaplain was methodically examining the dead cultists, pulling back their robes like a common looter. Kaelen's lip curled in distaste before he quickly reprimanded himself for such disloyalty. But what was the Chaplain doing?

'Brother-Chaplain?' called Kaelen.

Bareus looked up, his helmeted face betraying nothing of his intent.

'We are ready,' Kaelen finished.

'Brother-sergeant,' began Bareus, moving to squat beside Kaelen. 'When we find this Prophet, we must not kill him. I wish him taken alive.'

'Alive? But our orders are to kill him.'

'Your orders have been changed, sergeant,' hissed the Chaplain, his voice like cold flint. 'I want him alive. You understand?'

'Yes, Brother-Chaplain. I shall relay your orders.'

'We must expect heavy resistance within the temple. I will tell you now that I do not expect many, if any, of your men to survive,' advised Bareus, his voice laden with the promise of death.

'Why did you not brief me on this earlier?' snapped Kaelen. 'If the forces we are to face are so strong then we should hold here for now and call in support.'

'No,' stated Bareus. 'We do this alone or we die in the attempt.' His voice brooked no disagreement and Kaelen suddenly understood that there was more at stake with this mission than simple assassination. Regardless of the Chaplain's true agenda, Kaelen was duty bound to obey.

He nodded, 'As you wish, Chaplain.' He opened the vox-com to Lucius again. 'Now, Brother Lucius!'

Lucius stood, lithe as a jungle cat and powered a frag grenade through each of the windows either side of the cathedral doors. No sooner had the last grenade left his hand than the heavy blast of a lascannon disintegrated his torso. The heat of the laser blast flashed his super-oxygenated blood to a stinking red steam.

Twin thumps of detonation and screams. Flashing light and smoke poured from the cathedral windows like black tears.

'Now!' yelled Kaelen and the Space Marines rose from cover and sprinted towards the giant bronze doors. Scattered small arms fire impacted on their armour, but the Space Marines paid it no heed. To get inside was the only imperative.

Kaelen saw Brother Marius falter, a lucky shot blasting a chunk of armour and flesh from his upper thigh, staining the dark green of his armour bright red. Chaplain Bareus grabbed Marius as he staggered and dragged him on. Kaelen's powerful legs covered the distance to the temple in seconds and he flattened his back into the marble of the cathedral wall. Automatically, he snapped off a pair of grenades from his belt and hurled them through the smoking windows. The shockwave of detonation shook the cathedral doors and he vaulted through the shattered window frame, snapping shots left and right from his bolt pistol.

Inside was a blackened hell of smoke, blood and cooked flesh. Bodies lay sprawled, limbs torn off, skeletons pulverised and organs melted. The wounded gunners shrieked horribly.

Kaelen felt no pity for them. They were heretics and had betrayed the Emperor. They deserved a death a hundred times worse. The Dark Angels poured inside, moving into defensive positions, clearing the room and despatching the wounded. The vestibule was secure, but Kaelen's instincts told him that it wouldn't remain that way for long. Marius propped himself up against the walls. The bleeding had already stopped, the wound already sealed. He would fight on, Kaelen knew. It took more than a shattered pelvis to stop a Dark Angel.

'We have to keep moving,' he snapped. Movement meant life.

Chaplain Bareus nodded, reloading his pistol and turned to face Kaelen's squad.

'Brothers,' he began, 'we are now in the fight of our lives. Within this desecrated temple you shall see such sights as you have never witnessed in your darkest nightmares. Degradation and heresy now make their home in our beloved Emperor's vastness and you must shield your souls against it.'

Bareus lifted his Chaplain's symbol of office, the crozius arcanum, high. The blood-red gem at its centre sparkled like a miniature ruby sun. 'Remember our primarch and the Lion shall watch over you!'

Kaelen muttered a brief prayer to the Emperor and they pressed on.

'They are within your sanctuary, my lord!' said Casta, worry plain in every syllable. 'What would you have us do to destroy them?'

'Nothing more than you are already, Casta.'

'Are you sure, lord? I do not doubt your wisdom, but they are the Adeptus Astartes. They will not give up easily.'

'I know. I am counting on it. Do you trust me, Casta?'

'Absolutely, lord. Without question.'

'Then trust me now. I shall permit the Angel of Blades to kill all the Space Marines, but I want their Chaplain.'

'It will be as you say, lord,' replied Casta turning to leave.

The Prophet nodded and rose from his prayers to his full, towering height. He turned quickly, exposing a sliver of dark green beneath his voluminous robes.

'And Casta...' he hissed. 'I want him alive.'

Chaplain Bareus swung the crozius in a brutal arc, crushing bone and brain. Fighting their way along a reliquary studded cloister, the Space Marines battled against more followers of the Prophet.

The Dark Angels fought in pairs, each warrior protecting the other's back. Kaelen fought alongside Bareus, chopping and firing. The slide on the bolt pistol racked back empty. He slammed the butt of the pistol across his opponent's neck, shattering his spine.

Bareus slew his foes with a deadly grace, ducking, kicking and stabbing. The true genius of a warrior was to create space, to flow between the blades where skill and instinct merged in lethal harmony. Enemy weapons sailed past him and Kaelen knew that Bareus was a warrior born. Kaelen felt as clumsy as a new recruit next to the exquisite skill of the Interrogator-Chaplain.

Brother Marius fell, a power maul smashing into his injured hip. Hands held him down and an axe split his skull in two. Yet even though his head had been destroyed, he shot his killer dead.

Then it was over. The last heretic fell, his blood spilt across the tiled floor. As Kaelen slammed a new magazine into his pistol, Bareus knelt beside the corpse of Brother Marius and intoned the Prayer for the Fallen.

'You will be avenged, brother. Your sacrifice has brought us closer to expunging the darkness of the past. I thank you for it.'

Kaelen frowned. What did the Chaplain mean by that? Bareus stood and pulled out a data slate, displaying the floor plans of the cathedral. While the Chaplain confirmed their location, Kaelen surveyed his surroundings in more detail.

The walls were dressed stone, the fine carvings hacked off and replaced with crude etchings depicting worlds destroyed, angels on fire and a recurring motif of a broken sword. And a dying lion. The rendering was crude, but the origins of the imagery was unmistakable.

'What is this place?' he asked aloud. 'This is our Chapter's history on these walls. Lion El'Jonson, dead Caliban. The heretics daub their halls with mockeries of our past.'

He turned to Bareus. 'Why?'

Bareus looked up from the data-slate. Before he could answer, roaring gunfire hammered through the cloisters. Brother Caiyne and Brother Guias fell, heavy calibre shells tearing through their breastplates and exploding within their chest cavities. Brother Septimus staggered, most of his shoulder torn away by a glancing hit, his arm hanging by gory threads of bone and sinew. He fired back with his good arm until another shot took his head off.

Kaelen snapped off a flurry of shots, diving into the cover of a fluted pillar. The concealed guns were pinning them in position and it would only be a matter of time until more cultists were sent against them. As if in answer to his thoughts, a studded timber door at the end of the cloister burst open and a mob of screaming warriors charged towards them. Kaelen's jaw hung open in disgust at the sight of the enemy.

They were clad in dark green mockeries of power armour, an abominable mirror of the Space Marines' glory. Crude copies of the Dark Angels' Chapter symbol, spread wings with a dagger through the centre, adorned their shoulder plates and Kaelen felt a terrible rage build in him at this heresy.

The Space Marines of Squad Leuctra screamed their battle cry and surged forward to tear these blasphemers apart and punish them for such effrontery. To mock the Dark Angels was to invite savage and terrible retribution. Fuelled by righteous anger, Squad Leuctra fought with savage skill. Blood, death and screams filled the air.

As the foes met in the centre of the cloister, the hidden guns opened fire again.

A storm of bullets and ricochets, cracked armour and smoke engulfed the combatants, striking Space Marines and their foes indiscriminately.

A shell tore downwards through the side of Kaelen's helmet. Redness, pain and metallic stink filled his senses, driving him to his knees. He gasped and hit the release catch of his ruined helmet, wrenching it clear. The bullet had torn a bloody furrow in the side of his head and blasted the back of the helmet clear. But he was alive. The Emperor and the Lion had spared him.

A booted foot thundered into the side of his head. He rolled, lashing out with his power fist and a cultist fell screaming, his leg destroyed below the knee. He pushed himself to his feet and lashed out again, blood splashing his face as another foe died. Kaelen sprinted for the cover of the cloister, realising they had been lured out of cover by the fraudulent Dark Angels. He cursed his lack of detachment, angrily wiping sticky redness from his eyes.

The tactical situation was clear, they could not go back the way they had come. To reach the main vestibule was not an option; the gunfire would shred them before they got halfway. The only option was onwards and Kaelen had a gnawing suspicion that their enemies knew this and were channelling them towards something even more fearsome.

Bareus shouted his name over the stuttering blasts of shooting, indicating the timber door the armoured cultists had emerged from.

'I believe we have only one way out of this. Forwards, sergeant!'

Kaelen nodded, his face grim as the icon representing Brother Christos winked out. Another Space Marine dead for this mission. But Kaelen knew that they would all lay down their lives for the mission, no matter what it was. Chaplain Bareus had decided that it was worth all of them dying to achieve it and that was good enough for him.

Under cover of the cloisters, Bareus and the remaining five members of Squad Leuctra sprinted through the studded door that led out of this firetrap. Sergeant Kaelen just hoped that they weren't running into something worse.

'Is the Angel ready to administer the Evisceral Blessing, Casta?' inquired the Prophet.

'It is my lord,' said Casta, his voice trembling with fear. The Prophet smiled, understanding the cause of his underling's unease.

'The Angel of Blades makes you uncomfortable, Casta?'

Casta fidgeted nervously, his bald head beaded with sweat. 'It frightens me, my lord. I fear that we count such a thing as our ally. It slaughtered ten of my acolytes as we released it from the crypts. It was horrible.'

'Horrible, Casta?' soothed the Prophet, placing both hands on the priest's shoulders, his gauntlets large enough to crush Casta's head. 'Was it any more horrible than what we did to take this world? Was it bloodier than the things we did when we stormed this temple? There is already blood on your hands, Casta, what matters a little more? Is what we do here not worthy of some spilt blood?'

'I know, but to actually see it, to taste and smell it... it was terrible!' The priest was shaking. The memory of the Angel had unmanned him completely.

'I know, Casta, I know,' acknowledged the Prophet. 'But all great things must first wear terrible masks in order that they may inscribe themselves on the mind of the common man.'

The Prophet shook his head sadly. 'It is the way of things.'

Casta nodded slowly, 'Yes, my lord. I understand.'

The Prophet said, 'We bring a new age of reason to this galaxy. The fire we begin here will ignite a thousand others that will engulf the False Emperor's realm in the flames of revolution. We shall be remembered as heroes, Casta. Do not forget that. Your name shall shine amongst men as the brightest star in the firmament.'

Casta smiled, his vanity and ego overcoming his momentary squeamishness. Fresh determination shone in his zealous eyes.

The Prophet turned away.

It was almost too easy.

Sergeant Kaelen stalked the darkened corridors of the cathedral like a feral world predator, eyes constantly on the move, hunting his prey. Flickering electro-flambeaux cast a dim glow that threw the carved walls into stark relief and he deliberately averted his gaze from them. Looking too carefully at the images carved into the walls left his eyes stinging and a nauseous rolling sensation in the pit of his stomach.

Since leaving the death trap of the cloisters they had snaked deeper into the cathedral and Kaelen couldn't help but feel that they were in terrible danger. Not the danger of dying, Kaelen had stared death in the face too many times to fear extinction.

But the dangers of temptation and blasphemy... they were another matter entirely. The paths to damnation were many and varied, and Kaelen knew that evil did not always wear horns and breathe fire. For if it did, all men would surely turn from it in disgust. No, evil came subtly in the night, as pride, as lust, as envy.

In his youth, Kaelen had known such feelings, had fought against all the whispered seductions that flesh and the dark could offer in the dead of night, but he had prayed and fasted, secure in his faith in the Divine Emperor of Mankind. He had achieved a balance in his soul, a tempering of the beast within him.

He understood that there were those who gave into their base desires and turned their faces from the Emperor's light. For them there could be no mercy. They were deviants of the worst kind. They were an infection, spreading their lies and abomination to others, whose weakened faith was an open doorway to them. If such forces were at work within these walls, then Kaelen would fight till the last drop of blood had been squeezed from his body to root it out and destroy it.

Bareus led the way, his strides long and sure. The passageway they followed dipped slightly and Kaelen could feel a cool breath of night air caress his skin. The stone walls gave way to a smooth, blackened glass, opaque and blemish free, widening to nearly ten metres across. The walls curved up into a rounded arch above them and were totally non-reflective. Doors constructed of the same material barred the way forward, the susurration of air coming from where the glass had been cracked near the top of the frame. An ominous stain dripped down the inside face of the door from where a torn fragment of white cloth was caught, flapping in the breeze on a jagged shard of broken glass.

'Blood,' said Bareus.

Kaelen nodded. He had smelt it before seeing it. An odd whickering mechanical sound came from the other side of the doors and Kaelen felt an instinctive dread send a hot jolt of fear into his system. Bareus stepped forwards and thundered his boot into the door, smashing it completely from the frame. Black glass flew outwards and Kaelen swept through the portal, bolter and power fist at the ready.

Kaelen entered a domed arena, its stone floor awash with blood and sliced chunks of flesh. The stink of the charnel house filled the air. The same non-reflective black substance that had formed the door enclosed the arena. He pounded down some steps and skidded to a halt, his blood thundering in horror at the sight before him.

A mad screaming echoed around the enclosed arena. A dome of utter darkness rose above them as the horrifying bulk of the creature before the Space Marines turned to face them with giant, slashing strides. Perhaps it had once been a Dreadnought. Perhaps it had evolved or mutated in some vile parody of a Dreadnought. But whatever it was, it was clearly a beast of pure evil. Even Bareus, who had fought monstrous abominations before, was shocked at the terrifying appearance of the bio-mechanical killing machine. Fully six metres high, the creature stood on four splayed, spider-like legs of scything blades, that cut the air with a deadly grace. A massive, mechanically muscled torso rose from the centre of the bladed legs and clawed arms, lightning sheathed, swung insanely from its shoulders, upon which was mounted an ornately carved heavy bolter. At its back, a pair of glittering, bladed wings flapped noisily, their lethal edges promising death to any who came near.

The bio-machine's head was a pulped mass of horribly disfigured flesh. Multiple eyes, milky and distended, protruded from enlarged and warped sockets. Its vicious gash of a slobbering mouth was filled with hundreds of serrated, chisel-like teeth and its skin was a grotesque, oily texture – the colour of rotten meat.

It was impossible to tell where the man ended and the machine began.

Its entire body was soaked in blood, gobbets of torn flesh still hanging from its claws and teeth. But the final horror, the most sickening thing of all was that where the metal of the Dreadnought's hide was still visible, it was coloured an all too familiar shade of dark green.

And upon its shoulder was the symbol of the Dark Angels.

Whatever this creature was, it had once been a brother Space Marine.

Now it was the Angel of Blades and as the Space Marines recoiled in horror, the monster howled in mad triumph and stamped forwards on its scythe legs.

The speed of the Angel of Blades was astonishing for such a huge creature. Blood burst from its face as the Space Marines overcame their shock and began firing their bolters. Every shell found its mark, detonating wetly within the Angel's dead skin mask, but its lunatic screams continued unabated.

A silver blur lashed from the monster. A casual flick of its bladed leg licked out and eviscerated Brother Mellius quicker than the eye could follow. His shorn halves collapsed in a flood of red, but his bellows of pain were drowned by the Angel's hateful shrieks. The baroque heavy bolter mounted on the beast's shoulder roared and blasted the remains of Mellius apart.

Kaelen knew it had to die. Now.

He sprinted across the courtyard as the rest of his squad spread out and leapt in front of the rampaging machine, a brilliant burst of blue-white lightning arcing from his power fist as he struck at the beast's face. A coruscating corona of burning fire enveloped its huge frame as the lethal power of Kaelen's gauntlet smashed home. Its deformed flesh blistered and sloughed from its face, exposing a twisted metallic bone structure beneath. The Angel struck back, unheeding of the terrible hurt done to it.

Kaelen dodged a swipe meant to remove his head and rolled beneath its flailing arms. He powered his crackling fist into its groin and ripped upwards.

The power fist scored deep grooves in the Angel's exterior, but Kaelen's strike failed to penetrate its armoured shell. The beast side-stepped and another leg slashed out at him. He ducked back, not quick enough, and the armoured knee joint thundered into his chest, hurling him backwards.

Kaelen's breastplate cracked wide open, crushing his ribs and shattering the Imperial eagle on his chest into a million fragments. Bright lights exploded before his eyes as he fought for breath and struggled to rise, reeling from the massive impact. Even as he fell, he knew he had been lucky. Had the cutting edge struck him, he would now be as dead as Mellius. Heavy bolter shells spat from the shoulder-mounted gun, hammering into his legs and belly, driving him to his knees.

One shell managed to penetrate the cracks in his armour and he screamed, white hot fire bathing his nerves as the shell blasted a fist-sized hole in his hip, blood washing in a river down his thigh. He fell to the ground as the Angel loomed above him, its bloody claws poised to deliver the death blow and tear Kaelen in two.

With a howling battle cry, Chaplain Bareus and the surviving members of Squad Leuctra rushed to attack the monstrosity from the flanks and rear. Brother Janus died instantly, decapitated by a huge sweep of the creature's claws. Another leg whipped out, impaling his corpse and lifting him high into the air. Brother Temion leapt upon the thing from behind, holding his sword in a reverse grip and driving it into the Angel's back with a yell of triumph. The monster screamed and bucked madly, casting the brave Space Marine from its back. Its wings glittered in the torchlight and powered wide with a ringing clash of metal. A discordant shriek of steel on steel sounded as the Angel's wings slashed the air and a storm of razor-edged feathers flew from the beast's back and engulfed Temion as he raised his bolter. He had no time to scream as the whirlwind of blades slashed through him and tore his body to shreds. The bloody chunks of flesh and armour that fell to the ground were no longer recognisable as human.

Bareus smashed his crozius arcanum against the back of one of the Angel's knee joints, ducking a swipe of the beast's razor wings. Brother Urient and Brother Persus hammered the huge machine from the front while Kaelen pushed himself unsteadily to his feet.

Urient died as the Angel caught him with both sets of claws, ripping his body apart and tossing the pieces aside in contempt. The beast staggered as Bareus finally chopped through the silver steel of its leg. It tried to turn and slash at its diminutive assailant, but staggered as the severed leg joint collapsed under its weight. The huge arms spun as it fought for balance. Kaelen and Bareus were quick to press home their advantage.

Kaelen smashed his power fist into the monstrosity's mutated face, the huge gauntlet obliterating its features and tearing through its armoured sarcophagus. Kaelen kept pushing deeper and deeper inside the heart of the monster's body. The stench gusting from the rotted interior was the odour of a week old corpse. His fist closed around something greasy and horribly organic and the Angel shuddered in agony, lifting Kaelen from the ground. He grasped onto the beast's shell with his free hand, still struggling to tear the beast's heart out. Agony coursed through his body as the Angel's limbs spasmed on his wounded hip and chest. Kaelen's grip slid inside the Angel's body, glistening amniotic fluids pouring over his arm and preventing him from slaying the vile creature that lurked within its body. His grip finally found purchase. A writhing, pulsing thing with a grotesque peristaltic motion. He closed his fist on the fleshy substance of the monstrosity's heart and screamed as he released a burst of power within the bio-machine's shell.

The monster convulsed as the deadly energies of the power fist whiplashed inside its shell, blue fire geysering from its exhausts. Its legs wobbled and the massive beast collapsed, sliding slowly to its knees. A stinking black gore gushed from every joint and its daemonic wailing dimmed and at last fell silent. Kaelen wrenched clear his gauntlet, a grimace of pain and revulsion contorting his features as the lifeless Angel of Blades toppled forwards, a mangled heap of foetid meat and metal.

Kaelen slid down the Angel's shell and collapsed next to the foul creature, blood loss, shock and pain robbing him of his prodigious strength. Breathless, Chaplain Bareus grabbed Kaelen's arm and helped him to his feet. Brother Persus joined him, his dark green armour stained black with the monster's death fluids.

The three Dark Angels stood by the rotted corpse and tried to imagine how such a thing could possibly exist. Kaelen limped towards the remains of the beast and stared at the shattered carapace of the Angel's shell. The iconography on the sarcophagus was of a winged figure in a green robe carrying a scythe, its face shrouded in the darkness of its hood. Fluted scrollwork below the image on its chest bore a single word, partially obscured by black, oily blood. Kaelen reached down, wiping his hand across the carapace and felt as though his heart had been plucked from his chest. He sank to his knees as he stared at the word, willing it not to be true. But it remained the same, etched with an awful finality.

Caliban.

The Dark Angels lost home world. Destroyed in the Great Heresy thousands of years ago. How this thing could have come from such a holy place, Kaelen did not know. He rose and turned to Bareus.

'You knew about this, didn't you?' he asked.

The Chaplain shook his head. 'About that abomination, no. That we would face one of our brothers turned to the Dark Powers... yes. I did.'

Kaelen's face twisted in a mixture of anger and disbelief, 'The Dark Powers? How can that be possible? It cannot be true!'

A voice from the shadows, silky and seductive said, 'I'm afraid that it is, sergeant.'

Kaelen, Bareus and Persus spun to see a tall, hugely built figure in flowing white robes emerge from the shadows accompanied by a stoop shouldered man with a shaven head. The tall figure wore his black hair short, close cropped into his skull and three gold studs glittered on his forehead. His handsome features were smiling wryly. Bareus swiftly drew his bolt pistol and fired off the entire clip at the robed figure. As each shot struck, a burst of light flared around the man, but he remained unharmed. Kaelen could see the faint outline of a rosarius beneath his robes. The small amulet would protect the Prophet from their weapons and Kaelen knew that such protection would be almost impossible to defeat. All around the arena the opaque glass walls began to sink into the ground and a score of armed men stepped through, their weapons aimed at the three Space Marines. Bareus dropped the empty bolt pistol and reluctantly Kaelen and Persus did likewise.

'How can it be true?' asked Kaelen again. 'And who are you?'

'It is very simple, sergeant. My name was Cephesus and once I was a Dark Angel like you. When your dead husk of an Emperor still walked amongst you, we were betrayed by Lion El'Jonson. He abandoned our Chapter's true master, Luther, and left with the Emperor to conquer the galaxy. The primarch left him to rot on a backwater planet while he vaingloriously took the honour of battle that should have been ours! How could he have expected us not to fight him on his return?'

Bareus stepped forwards and removed his helm, tossing it aside as he stared at the tall figure with undisguised hatred. He raised his crozius arcanum to point at the other's chest.

'I know you, Cephesus. I have read of you and I will add your name to the Book of Salvation. It was necessary for Luther to remain behind on Caliban. His was a position of great responsibility!'

'Necessity, Chaplain, is the plea for every act of ignorance your Imperium perpetrates. It is the argument of tyrants and the creed of slaves,' snapped the Prophet. 'Wipe the virtue from your eyes, we were cast aside! Scattered throughout time and space to become the Fallen. And for that I will kill you.'

He nodded towards the dead monstrosity, his earlier composure reasserting itself and said, 'You killed the Angel of Blades. I am impressed.'

The Prophet smiled and parted his robes, allowing them to fall at his feet. Beneath them, he wore a suit of powered armour, ancient and painted unmistakably in the colours and icons of the Dark Angels. The ornate form of a rosarius, similar to the one worn by Bareus, hung on a chain, nestling against the eagle on his breastplate. 'I was Cephesus, but that name no longer has any meaning for me. I foreswore it the day Lion El'Jonson betrayed us.'

'The primarch saved us!' roared Bareus, his face contorted in fury. 'You dare to blaspheme against his blessed name?'

Cephesus shook his head slowly. 'You are deluded, Chaplain. I think that it is time you start looking at yourself and judge the lie you live. You can project it back at me, but I am only what lives inside each and every one of you. I am a reflection of you all.'

Sneering, he descended the steps to stand before the Interrogator-Chaplain, pulling a thin chain from a pouch around his waist. Attached along its length were several small polished blades, each inlaid with a fine tracery of gold wire. Bareus's eyes widened in shock and he reached for his hip scabbard, drawing an identical blade.

'You call these weapons Blades of Reason. Such an irony. It is as much a badge of office to you as your crozius, is it not? I have eleven here, each taken from the corpse of a Dark Angels Chaplain. I will take yours and make it an even dozen.'

Without warning he snapped a blade from the chain and spun on his heel, slashing it across Persus's throat. The Space Marine sank to the ground, arterial blood bathing his breastplate crimson.

Kaelen screamed and launched himself forwards, swinging his power fist at the Prophet's head. Cephesus swayed aside and smashed his bladed fist into Kaelen's ribs.

The neural wires inscribed in the blades shrieked fiery electric agony along Kaelen's nerves, and he howled as raw pain flooded every fibre in his body. His vision swam and he fell to the ground screaming, the blades still lodged in his side.

Bareus howled in fury and slashed with his crozius arcanum. Cephesus ducked and lunged in close, tearing the rosarius from around Bareus's neck. Silver and gold flashed; blood spurted. The Chaplain fell to his knees, mouth open in mute horror as he felt his life blood pump from his ruined throat. He fell beside Kaelen and dropped his weapons beside the fallen sergeant.

Cephesus reached down and knelt beside the dying Chaplain. He smiled indulgently and scooped up Bareus's intricate blade, threading the thin chain through its hilt.

'An even dozen. Thank you, Chaplain,' hissed Cephesus.

Sergeant Kaelen gritted his teeth and fought to open his eyes. The Prophet's blades were lodged deep in his flesh. With a supreme effort of will, each tiny movement bringing a fresh spasm of agony, he reached down and dragged the weapon from his body. His vision cleared in time for him to see the Prophet leaning over Chaplain Bareus. He growled in anger and with strength born of desperation lunged forwards, throwing himself at the heretic.

Both hands outstretched, he slashed with the blades and tried to crush the Prophet's head with his power fist. But Cephesus was too quick and dodged back, but not before Kaelen's hand closed about an ornate chain around his neck and tore it free. He rolled forwards, falling at the Prophet's feet and gasped in pain.

Cephesus laughed and addressed the men around the arena. 'You see? The might of the Adeptus Astartes lies broken at my feet! What can we not achieve when we can humble their might with such ease?'

Kaelen could feel the pain ebbing from his body and glanced down to see what lay in his hand and smiled viciously. He lifted his gaze to look up into the shining, mad face of the Prophet and with a roar of primal hatred, struck out at the traitor Dark Angel, his power fist crackling with lethal energies.

He felt as though time slowed. He could see everything in exquisite detail. Every face in the arena was trained on him, every gun. But none of that mattered now. All he could focus on was killing his foe. His vision tunnelled until all he could see was Cephesus's face, smugly contemptuous. His power fist connected squarely on the Prophet's chest and Kaelen had a fleeting instant of pure pleasure when he saw the heretic's expression suddenly change as he saw what the sergeant held aloft in his other hand.

Cephesus's chest disintegrated, his armour split wide open by the force of the powerful blow. Kaelen's power fist exploded from his back, shards of bone and blood spraying the arena's floor. Kaelen lifted the impaled Prophet high and shouted to the assembled cultists.

'Such is the fate of those who would defy the will of the immortal Emperor!'

He hurled the body of Cephesus, no more than blood soaked rags, to the ground and bellowed in painful triumph. Kaelen was a terrifying figure, drenched in blood and howling with battle lust. As he stood in the centre of the arena, the black glass walls rapidly began to rise and the armed men vanished from sight, their fragile courage broken by the death of their leader.

Kaelen slumped to the ground and opened his other fist, letting the rosarius he had inadvertently torn from around the Prophet's neck fall to the ground. A hand brushed his shoulder and he turned to see the gasping face of Chaplain Bareus. The man struggled to speak, but could only wheeze breathlessly. His hand scrabbled around his body, searching.

Guessing Bareus's intention, Kaelen picked up the fallen crozius arcanum and placed it gently into the Chaplain's hand. Bareus coughed a mouthful of blood and shook his head. He opened Kaelen's fist, pressed the crozius into the sergeant's hand and pointed towards the corpse of the Fallen Dark Angel.

'Deathwing...' hissed Bareus with his last breath and closed his eyes as death claimed him.

Kaelen understood. The burden of responsibility had been passed to him now. He held the symbol of office of a Dark Angels Chaplain and though he knew that there was much for him yet to learn, he had taken the first step along a dark path.

News of the Prophet's death spread rapidly throughout Angellicus and within the hour, the rebel forces broadcast their unconditional surrender. Kaelen slowly retraced his steps through the cathedral precincts, using the vox-comm to call in the gunship that had delivered their assault. He limped into the main square, squinting against the bright light of the breaking morning. The Thunderhawk sat in the centre of the plaza, engines whining and the forward ramp lowered. As he approached the gunship, a lone Terminator in bone white armour descended the ramp to meet him.

Kaelen stopped before the Terminator and offered him the crozius and a thin chain of twelve blades.

Kaelen said, 'The name of Cephesus can now be added to the Book of Salvation.'

The Terminator took the proffered items and said, 'Who are you?'

Kaelen considered the question for a moment before replying.

'I am Deathwing,' he answered.

SHADOW KNIGHT

Aaron Dembski-Bowden

The sins of the father, they say.
  Maybe. Maybe not. But we were always different. My brothers and I, we were never truly kin with the others – the Angels, the Wolves, the Ravens...
  Perhaps our difference was our father's sin, and perhaps it was his triumph. I am not empowered by anyone to cast a critical eye over the history of the VIII Legion.
  These words stick with me, though. The sins of the father. These words have shaped my life.
  The sins of my father echo throughout eternity as heresy. Yet the sins of my father's father are worshipped as the first acts of godhood. I do not ask myself if this is fair. Nothing is fair. The word is a myth. I do not care what is fair, and what is right, and what's unfair and wrong. These concepts do not exist outside the skulls of those who waste their life in contemplation.
  I ask myself, night after night, if I deserve vengeance.
  I devote each beat of my heart to tearing down everything I once raised. Remember this, remember it always: my blade and bolter helped forge the Imperium. I and those like me – we hold greater rights than any to destroy mankind's sickened empire, for it was our blood, our bones, and our sweat that built it.
  Look to your shining champions now. The Adeptus Astartes that scour the dark places of your galaxy. The hordes of fragile mortals enslaved to the Imperial Guard and shackled in service to the Throne of Lies. Not a soul among them was even born when my brothers and I built this empire.
  Do I deserve vengeance? Let me tell you something about vengeance, little

scion of the Imperium. My brothers and I swore to our dying father that we would atone for the great sins of the past. We would bleed the unworthy empire that we had built, and cleanse the stars of the False Emperor's taint.

This is not mere vengeance. This is redemption.

My right to destroy is greater than your right to live.

Remember that, when we come for you.

He is a child standing over a dying man.

The boy is more surprised than scared. His friend, who has not yet taken a life, pulls him away. He will not move. Not yet. He cannot escape the look in the bleeding man's eyes.

The shopkeeper dies.

The boy runs.

He is a child being cut open by machines.

Although he sleeps, his body twitches, betraying painful dreams and sleepless nerves firing as they register pain from the surgery. Two hearts, fleshy and glistening, beat in his cracked-open chest. A second new organ, smaller than the new heart, will alter the growth of his bones, encouraging his skeleton to absorb unnatural minerals over the course of his lifetime.

Untrembling hands, some human, some augmetic, work over the child's body, slicing and sealing, implanting and flesh-bonding. The boy trembles again, his eyes opening for a moment.

A god with a white mask shakes his head at the boy.

'Sleep.'

The boy tries to resist, but slumber grips him with comforting claws. He feels, just for a moment, as though he is sinking into the black seas of his home world.

Sleep, the god had said.

He obeys, because the chemicals within his blood force him to obey.

A third organ is placed within his chest, not far from the new heart. As the ossmodula warps his bones to grow on new minerals, the biscopea generates a flood of hormones to feed his muscles.

Surgeons seal the boy's medical wounds.

Already, the child is no longer human. Tonight's work has seen to that. Time will reveal just how different the boy will become.

He is a teenage boy, standing over another dead body.

This corpse is not like the first. This corpse is the same age as the boy, and in its last moments of life it had struggled with all its strength, desperate not to die.

The boy drops his weapon. The serrated knife falls to the ground.

Legion masters come to him. Their eyes are red, their dark armour immense. Skulls hang from their pauldrons and plastrons on chains of blackened bronze.

He draws breath to speak, to tell them it was an accident. They silence him.

'Well done,' they say.

And they call him *brother*.

He is a teenage boy, and the rifle is heavy in his hands.

He watches for a long, long time. He has trained for this. He knows how to slow his hearts, how to regulate his breathing and the biological beats of his body until his entire form remains as still as a statue.

Predator. Prey. His mind goes cold, his focus absolute. The mantra chanted internally becomes the only way to see the world. *Predator. Prey. Hunter. Hunted.* Nothing else matters.

He squeezes the trigger. One thousand metres away, a man dies.

'Target eliminated,' he says.

He is a young man, sleeping on the same surgery table as before.

In a slumber demanded by the chemicals flowing through his veins, he dreams once again of his first murder. In the waking world, needles and medical probes bore into the flesh of his back, injecting fluids directly into his spinal column.

His slumbering body reacts to the invasion, coughing once. Acidic spit leaves his lips, hissing on the ground where it lands, eating into the tiled floor.

When he wakes, hours later, he feels the sockets running down his spine. The scars, the metallic nodules…

In a universe where no gods exist, he knows this is the closest mortality can come to divinity.

He is a young man, staring into his own eyes.

He stands naked in a dark chamber, in a lined rank with a dozen other souls. Other initiates standing with him, also stripped of clothing, the marks of their surgeries fresh upon their pale skin. He barely notices them. Sexuality is a forgotten concept, alien to his mind, merely one of ten thousand humanities his consciousness has discarded. He no longer recalls the face of his mother and father. He only recalls his own name because his Legion masters never changed it.

He looks into the eyes that are now his. They stare back, slanted and murder-red, set in a helmet with its facial plate painted white. The blood-eyed, bone-pale skull watches him as he watches it.

This is his face now. Through these eyes, he will see the galaxy. Through this skulled helm he will cry his wrath at those who dare defy the Emperor's vision for mankind.

'You are Talos,' a Legion master says, 'of First Claw, Tenth Company.'

He is a young man, utterly inhuman, immortal and undying.

He sees the surface of this world through crimson vision, with data streaming in sharp, clear white runic language across his retinas. He sees the life forces of his brothers in the numbers displayed. He feels the temperature outside his sealed war armour. He sees targeting sights flicker as they follow the movements of his eyes, and feels his hand, the hand clutching his bolter, tense as it tries to follow each target lock. Ammunition counters display how many have died this day.

Around him, aliens die. Ten, a hundred, a thousand. His brothers butcher their way through a city of violet crystal, bolters roaring and chainswords howling. Here and there in the opera of battle-noise, a brother screams his rage through helm-amplifiers.

The sound is always the same. Bolters always roar. Chainblades always howl. Space Marines always cry their fury. When the VIII Legion wages war, the sound is that of lions and wolves slaying each other while vultures shriek above.

He cries words that he will one day never shout again – words that will soon become ash on his tongue. Already he cries the words without thinking about them, without *feeling* them.

For the Emperor.

He is a young man, awash in the blood of humans.

He shouts words without the heart to feel them, declaring concepts of Imperial justice and deserved vengeance. A man claws at his armour, begging and pleading.

'We are loyal! We have surrendered!'

The young man breaks the human's face with the butt of his bolter. Surrendering so late was a meaningless gesture. Their blood must run as an example, and the rest of the system's worlds would fall into line.

Around him, the riot continues unabated. Soon, his bolter is silenced, voiceless with no shells to fire. Soon after that, his chainsword dies, clogged with meat.

The Night Lords resort to killing the humans with their bare hands, dark gauntlets punching and strangling and crushing.

At a timeless point in the melee, the voice of an ally comes over the vox. It is an Imperial Fist. Their Legion watches from the bored security of their landing site.

'What are you doing?' the Imperial Fist demands. 'Brothers, are you insane?'

Talos does not answer. They do not deserve an answer. If the Fists had brought this world into compliance themselves, the Night Lords would never have needed to come here.

He is a young man, watching his home world burn.

He is a young man, mourning a father soon to die.

He is a traitor to everything he once held sacred.

Stabbing lights lanced through the gloom.

The salvage team moved slowly, neither patient nor impatient, but with the confident care of men with an arduous job to do and no deadline to meet. The team spread out across the chamber, overturning debris, examining the markings of weapons fire on the walls, their internal vox clicking as they spoke to one another.

With the ship open to the void, each of the salvage team wore atmosphere suits against the airless cold. They communicated as often by sign language as they did by words.

This interested the hunter that watched them, because he too was fluent in Adeptus Astartes battle sign. Curious, to see his enemies betray themselves so easily.

The hunter watched in silence as the spears of illumination cut this way and that, revealing the wreckage of the battles that had taken place on this deck of the abandoned vessel. The salvage team – who were clearly genhanced, but too small and unarmoured to be full Space Marines – were crippled by the atmosphere suits they wore. Such confinement limited their senses, while the hunter's ancient Mark IV war plate only enhanced his. They could not hear as he heard, nor see as he saw. That reduced their chances of survival from incredibly unlikely to absolutely none.

Smiling at the thought, the hunter whispered to the machine-spirit of his armour, a single word that enticed the war plate's soul with the knowledge that the hunt was beginning in earnest.

'Preysight.'

His vision blurred to the blue of the deepest oceans, decorated by supernova heat smears of moving, living beings. The hunter watched the team move on, separating into two teams, each of two men.

This was going to be entertaining.

Talos followed the first team, shadowing them through the corridors, knowing the grating purr of his power armour and the snarling of its servo-joints were unheard by the sense-dimmed salvagers.

Salvagers was perhaps the wrong word, of course. Disrespectful to the foe.

While they were not full Space Marines, their gene-enhancement was obvious in the bulk of their bodies and the lethal grace of their motions. They, too, were hunters – just weaker examples of the breed.

Initiates.

Their icon, mounted on each shoulder plate, displayed a drop of ruby blood framed by proud angelic wings.

The hunter's pale lips curled into another crooked smile. This was unexpected. The Blood Angels had sent in a team of Scouts...

The Night Lord had little time for notions of coincidence. If the Angels were here, then they were here on the hunt. Perhaps the *Covenant of Blood* had been detected on the long-range sensors of a Blood Angel battlefleet. Such a discovery would certainly have been enough to bring them here.

Hunting for their precious sword, no doubt. And not for the first time. Perhaps this was their initiation ceremony? A test of prowess? Bring back the blade and earn passage into the Chapter...

Oh, how unfortunate.

The stolen blade hung at the hunter's hip, as it had for years now. Tonight would not be the night it found its way back into the desperate reach of the Angels. But, as always, they were welcome to sell their lives in the attempt at reclamation.

Talos monitored the readout of his retinal displays. The temptation to blink-click certain runes was strong, but he resisted the urge. This hunt would be easy enough without combat narcotics flooding his blood. Purity lay in abstaining from such things until they became necessary.

The location runes of his brothers in First Claw flickered on his visor display. Taking note of their positions elsewhere in the ship, the hunter moved forward to shed the blood of those enslaved to the Throne of Lies.

A true hunter did not avoid being seen by his prey. Such stalking was the act of cowards and carrion-eaters, revealing themselves only when the prey was slain. Where was the skill in that? Where was the thrill?

A Night Lord was raised to hunt by other, truer principles.

Talos ghosted through the shadows, judging the strength of the Scouts' suits' audio-receptors. Just how much could they hear...

He followed them down a corridor, his gauntleted knuckles scraping along the metal walls.

The Blood Angels turned instantly, stabbing his face with their beam-lighting.

That almost worked, the hunter had to give it to them. These lesser hunters knew their prey – they knew they hunted Night Lords. For half a heartbeat, sunfire would have blazed across his vision, blinding him.

Talos ignored the beams completely. He tracked by preysight. Their tactics were meaningless.

He was already gone when they opened fire, melting into the shadows of a side corridor.

He caught them again nine minutes later.

This time, he lay in wait after baiting a beautiful trap. The sword they came for was right in their path.

It was called *Aurum*. Words barely did its craftsmanship justice. Forged when the Emperor's Great Crusade took its first steps into the stars, the blade was forged for one of the Blood Angel Legion's first heroes. It had come into Talos's possession centuries later, when he'd murdered *Aurum*'s heir.

It was almost amusing, how often the sons of Sanguinius tried to reclaim the sword from him. It was much less amusing how often he had to kill his own brothers when they sought to take the blade from his dead hands. Avarice shattered all unity, even among Legion brothers.

The Scouts saw their Chapter relic now, so long denied their grasp. The golden blade was embedded into the dark metal decking, its angel-winged crosspiece turned to ivory under the harsh glare of their stabbing lights.

An invitation to simply advance into the chamber and take it, but it was so obviously a trap. Yet... how could they resist?

They did not resist.

The initiates were alert, bolters high and panning fast, senses keen. The hunter saw their mouths moving as they voxed continuous updates to each other.

Talos let go of the ceiling.

He thudded to the deck behind one of the initiates, gauntlets snapping forward to clutch the Scout.

The other Angel turned and fired. Talos laughed at the zeal in his eyes, at the tightness of his clenched teeth, as the initiate fired three bolts into the body of his brother.

The Night Lord gripped the convulsing human shield against him, seeing the temperature gauge on his retinal display flicker as the dying initiate's blood hit sections of his war plate. In his grip, the shuddering Angel was little more than a burst sack of freezing meat. The bolt shells had detonated, coming close to killing him and opening the suit to the void.

'Good shooting, Angel,' Talos spoke through his helm's crackling vox-speakers. He threw his bleeding shield aside and leapt for the other initiate, fingers splayed like talons.

The fight was mercilessly brief. The Night Lord's full gene-enhancements coupled with the heightened strength of his armour's engineered muscle fibre-cables meant there was only one possible outcome. Talos backhanded the bolter from the Angel's grip and clawed at the initiate.

As the weaker warrior writhed, Talos stroked his gauntleted fingertips across the clear face-visor of the initiate's atmosphere suit.

'This looks fragile,' he said.

The Scout shouted something unheard. Hate burned in his eyes. Talos wasted several seconds just enjoying that expression. That passion.

He crashed his fist against the visor, smashing it to shards.

As one corpse froze and another swelled and ruptured on its way to asphyxiation, the Night Lord retrieved his blade, the sword he claimed by right of conquest, and moved back into the darkest parts of the ship.

* * *

'Talos,' the voice came over the vox in a sibilant hiss.

'Speak, Uzas.'

'They have sent initiates to hunt us, brother. I had to cancel my prey-sight to make sure my eyes were seeing clearly. *Initiates*. Against *us*.'

'Spare me your indignation. What do you want?'

Uzas's reply was a low growl and a crackle of dead vox. Talos put it from his mind. He had long grown bored of Uzas forever lamenting each time they met with insignificant prey.

'Cyrion,' he voxed.

'Aye. Talos?'

'Of course.'

'Forgive me. I thought it would be Uzas with another rant. I hear your decks are crawling with Angels. Epic glories to be earned in slaughtering their infants, eh?'

Talos didn't quite sigh. 'Are you almost done?'

'This hulk is as hollow as Uzas's head, brother. Negative on anything of worth. Not even a servitor to steal. I'm returning to the boarding pod now. Unless you need help shooting the Angels' children?'

Talos killed the vox-link as he stalked through the black corridor. This was fruitless. Time to leave – empty-handed and still desperately short on supplies. This… this *piracy* offended him now, as it always did, and as it always had since they'd been cut off from the Legion decades ago. A plague upon the long-dead Warmaster and his failures which still echoed today. A curse upon the night the VIII Legion was shattered and scattered across the stars.

Diminished. Reduced. Surviving as disparate warbands – broken echoes of the unity within loyalist Chapters.

Sins of the father.

This curious ambush by the Angels who had tracked them here was nothing more than a minor diversion. Talos was about to vox a general withdrawal after the last initiates were hunted down and slain, when his vox went live again.

'Brother,' said Xarl. 'I've found the Angels.'

'As have Uzas and I. Kill them quickly and let's get back to the *Covenant*.'

'No, Talos.' Xarl's voice was edged with anger. 'Not initiates. The real Angels.'

The Night Lords of First Claw, Tenth Company, came together like wolves in the wild. Stalking through the darkened chambers of the ship, the four hunters met in the shadows, speaking over their vox-link, crouching with their weapons at the ready.

In Talos's hands, the relic blade *Aurum* caught what little light remained, glinting as he moved.

'Five of them,' Xarl spoke low, his voice edged with his suppressed eagerness. 'We can take five. They stand bright and proud in a control chamber not far from our boarding pod.' He racked his bolter. 'We can take five,' he repeated.

'They're just waiting?' Cyrion said. 'They must be expecting an honest fight.'

Uzas snorted at that.

'This is your fault, you know,' Cyrion said with a chuckle, nodding at Talos. 'You and that damn sword.'

'It keeps things interesting,' Talos replied. 'And I cherish every curse that their Chapter screams at me.'

He stopped speaking, narrowing his eyes for a moment. Cyrion's skulled helm blurred before him. As did Xarl's. The sound of distant bolter fire echoed in his ears, not distorted by the faint crackle of helm-filtered noise. Not a true sound. Not a real memory. Something akin to both.

'I... have a...' Talos blinked to clear his fading vision. Shadows of vast things darkened his sight. '...have a plan...'

'Brother?' Cyrion asked.

Talos shivered once, his servo-joints snarling at the shaking movement. Magnetically clasped to his thigh, his bolter didn't fall to the decking, but the golden blade did. It clattered to the steel floor with a clang.

'Talos?' Xarl asked.

'No,' Uzas growled, 'not *now.*'

Talos's head jerked once, as if his armour had sent an electrical pulse through his spine, and he crashed to the ground in a clash of war plate on metal.

'The god-machines of Crythe...' he murmured. 'They have killed the sun.'

A moment later, he started screaming.

The others had to cut Talos out of the squad's internal vox-link. His screams drowned out all other speech.

'We can take five of them,' Xarl said. 'Three of us remain. We can take five Angels.'

'Almost certainly,' Cyrion agreed. 'And if they summon squads of their initiates?'

'Then we slaughter five of them *and* their initiates.'

Uzas cut in. 'We were slaying our way across the stars ten thousand years before they were even born.'

'Yes, while that's a wonderful parable, I don't need rousing rhetoric,' Cyrion said. 'I need a plan.'

'We hunt,' Uzas and Xarl said at once.

'We kill them,' Xarl added.

'We feast on their gene-seed,' Uzas finished.

'If this was an award ceremony for fervency and zeal, once again, you'd both be collapsing under the weight of medals. But you want to launch an assault on their position while we drag Talos with us? I think the scraping of his armour over the floor will rather kill the element of stealth, brothers.'

'Guard him, Cyrion,' Xarl said. 'Uzas and I will take the Angels.'

'Two against five.' Cyrion's red eye lenses didn't quite fix upon his brother's. 'Those are poor odds, Xarl.'

'Then we will finally be rid of each other,' Xarl grunted. 'Besides, we've had worse.'

That was true, at least.

'Ave Dominus Nox,' Cyrion said. 'Hunt well and hunt fast.'

'Ave Dominus Nox,' the other two replied.

Cyrion listened for a while to his brother's screams. It was difficult to make any sense from the stream of shouted words.

This came as no surprise. Cyrion had heard Talos suffering in the grip of this affliction many times before. As gene-gifts went, it was barely a blessing.

Sins of the father, he thought, watching Talos's inert armour, listening to the cries of death to come. *How they are reflected within the son.*

According to Cyrion's retinal chrono display, one hour and sixteen minutes had passed when he heard the explosion.

The decking shuddered under his boots.

'Xarl? Uzas?'

Static was the only answer.

Great.

When Uzas's voice finally broke over the vox after two hours, it was weak and coloured by his characteristic bitterness.

'Hnngh. Cyrion. It's done. Drag the prophet.'

'You sound like you got shot,' Cyrion resisted the urge to smile in case they heard it in his words.

'He did,' Xarl said. 'We're on our way back.'

'What was that detonation?'

'Plasma cannon.'

'You're... you're joking.'

'Not even for a second. I have no idea why they brought one of those to a fight in a ship's innards, but the coolant feeds made for a ripe target.'

Cyrion blink-clicked a rune by Xarl's identification symbol. It opened a private channel between the two of them.

'Who hit Uzas?'

'An initiate. From behind, with a sniper rifle.'

Cyrion immediately closed the link so no one would hear him laughing.

* * *

The *Covenant of Blood* was a blade of cobalt darkness, bronze-edged and scarred by centuries of battle. It drifted through the void, sailing close to its prey like a shark gliding through black waters.

The *Encarmine Soul* was a Gladius-class frigate with a long and proud history of victories in the name of the Blood Angels Chapter – and before it, the IX Legion. It opened fire on the *Covenant of Blood* with an admirable array of weapons batteries.

Briefly, beautifully, the void shields around the Night Lords strike cruiser shimmered in a display reminiscent of oil on water.

The *Covenant of Blood* returned fire. Within a minute, the blade-like ship was sailing through void debris, its lances cooling from their momentary fury. The *Encarmine Soul*, what little chunks were left of it, clanked and sparked off the larger cruiser's void shields as it passed through the expanding cloud of wreckage.

Another ship, this one stricken and dead in space, soon fell under the *Covenant*'s shadow. The strike cruiser obscured the sun, pulling in close, ready to receive its boarding pod once again.

First Claw had been away for seven hours investigating the hulk. Their mothership had come hunting for them.

Bulkhead seals hissed as the reinforced doors opened on loud, grinding hinges.

Xarl and Cyrion carried Talos into the *Covenant*'s deployment bay. Uzas walked behind them, a staggering limp marring his gait. His spine was on fire from the sniper's solid slug that still lodged there. Worse, his genhanced healing had sealed and clotted the wound. He'd need surgery – or more likely a knife and a mirror – to tear the damn thing out.

One of the Atramentar, elite guard of the Exalted, stood in its hulking Terminator war plate. His skull-painted, tusked helm stared impassively. Trophy racks adorned his back, each one impaled with several helms from a number of loyalist Chapters: a history of bloodshed and betrayal, proudly displayed for his brothers to see.

It nodded to Talos's prone form.

'The Soul Hunter is wounded?' the Terminator asked, its voice a deep, rumbling growl.

'No,' Cyrion said. 'Inform the Exalted at once. His prophet is suffering another vision.'

SURVIVOR

Steve Parker

Bas was up and running full tilt before he even knew why. Part of his brain reacted the moment the cry went out, then his legs were moving, pounding the dusty alleyways as he flew from his pursuers.

The first rule was simple: *don't be seen*. He'd broken it only a few times since the monsters had come, and never by choice. This time, as before, it wasn't through clumsiness. It wasn't carelessness. It was just raw bad luck, plain and simple. He had taken all the usual precautions. He'd stuck to the shadows. He'd moved low and fast. He'd been patient and silent and constantly aware. But the monsters chasing him now, yapping and chittering joyously at the prospect of spilling his blood, had come from below. They had emerged from a sewer grate just a few metres behind him and the day's quest for clean water was suddenly forgotten in favour of a far more pressing need.

Bullets smacked into the alley walls on either side of him as he fled, blowing out little clouds of dust and stone chips. Some came near to ending his life, their passage close enough to whip at his filth-caked hair. That lent him an extra burst of speed, extra adrenaline to further numb the agony of his aching joints and muscles.

Up ahead, he saw the twisted remains of a fire escape and bolted towards it. The rooftops – those were his domain. In the months since their coming, he had spent hours laying boards and planks between what was left of the town's roofs. Up there, he moved where he pleased and saw all. He had the advantage. The big ones never went up there, and the smaller ones didn't know the terrain like he did. The rooftops were his – control your environment and you would always be one step ahead.

The crooked metal stairs shook and groaned as he thundered up them, heart hammering in his ears, skull pounding with accelerated blood flow. He chanced a look down and saw his pursuers, four scrawny green figures with red eyes and needle teeth. They reached the bottom of the fire escape and leapt onto it, clambering up after him.

Bas kept on and made the roof in a few more seconds. For the briefest moment, he took stock of where he was. Here in the town's south-west quarter, he had a few established hiding places, two of which were close by. But he couldn't risk leading his enemies to one of his sanctuaries. He had to put some distance between them first. He could go north across the makeshift bridges he had laid weeks ago, or he could head east where the gaps between the tenements were narrow enough to leap.

North, then. The monsters behind him could leap as far as he could. East was a bad gamble.

He sped on across the roof, avoiding the gaps where alien artillery shells had bitten great gaping holes. He was at the far side when the first of the wiry green killers topped the fire escape and resumed shooting wildly at him. The others appeared beside it and, seeing that their guns were missing the mark, they rushed towards him.

Eyes front, Bas told himself as he took his first hurried step out onto the twin planks. Don't look down.

The gap between the buildings was five metres wide. As he neared the middle, the wood sagged under him, but he knew it would hold. He had tested the strength of the wood before he laid it.

A couple of bullets sang past his ears. He half-ran the last few steps across and leapt the final one. Behind him, his pursuers were halfway across the previous rooftop.

Bas turned to face them. There wasn't time to pull the planks in like he wanted to, not with his enemies wielding those scrappy, fat barrelled pistols. Instead, he kicked out at the planks and watched them tumble end-over-end to the dark alley below.

His pursuers howled and spat in rage and opened fire. One, perhaps more reckless than the others, or perhaps with a greater bloodlust, refused to be beaten. The creature took a run up to the edge of the roof and leapt out into space. Bas was already sprinting towards the next rooftop. He didn't see the creature plunge to its death, but he heard the chilling scream. Soon, he had left his hunters far behind, their alien cries of frustration and outrage ringing in his ears.

He was dying.

Maybe. Probably. He couldn't be sure. Bas was only ten years old, and all the dying he had seen so far in this short life had been the violent, messy kind – and all of that in the last few months.

This was different. This was a loosening of his back teeth. This was a burning in his gut on those increasingly rare occasions when he ate something solid. This was blood in his phlegm when he spat and in his stool when he made his toilet. Pounding headaches came and went, like the sharp cramps that sometimes wracked his weakening muscles.

After his flight across the rooftops, all these symptoms came on him at once. He fought them off until he reached relative safety. Then he lay down, and the pain rolled over him like a landslide.

Had he known any better, he would have recognised the signs of dehydration and malnourishment. As his scavenged supplies dwindled, he was forced to spread them ever thinner. But Bas didn't know. He could only guess.

How long had he lived like this now? Was it months? It felt like months. What date was it? He couldn't be sure of anything. Time passed for him not in hours and minutes, but in periods of hiding and running, of light, tormented sleep and the daily business of surviving on a knife edge. He felt like the last rodent in a tower of ravenous felines.

If the green horrors ever caught him, his end would come quickly enough. It would be painful and horrific, but it would be short. Shorter than disease or hunger, anyway. He wondered if a slow, quiet death was any better. Something instinctual made him back away from that train of thought before he formed an answer. For now, he was alive, and here, in one of his many boltholes, he was safe.

He chided himself. No, not safe. Not truly. He was never that.

He heard the old man's voice in his head, berating him from memory, as sharp and harsh as a rifle's report.

Safety is an illusion, boy. Never forget that.

Aye, an illusion. How could Bas forget? The words had been beaten into him until he learned to sleep only lightly and wake to a readiness any frontline Guardsman would have envied. While living with the old man, if he wasn't up and at attention three seconds after first call, that heavy cane would whistle through the air and wake him up the hard way. Now, if a blow ever caught him in his sleep, it wouldn't be for the sake of a lesson. It would be the bite of a greenskin blade, and his sleep would be the eternal sleep of the dead.

His traps and snares, he knew, wouldn't protect him forever. One day, maybe soon, one of the savages would get all the way in. Not one of the tusked giants. Bas was careful to bed down only in small, tight spaces where they couldn't go. But the scrawny, hook-nosed ones could slip into all the places he could, and they were wicked, murderous things, gleeful in their bloodletting. He trusted his defences only as much as he trusted himself, so he was diligent to a fault. He triple-checked every last point of entry before he ever allowed his eyes to close. Simple though they were, his traps had already saved him a dozen times over. The old sod had drilled him relentlessly, and Bas had despised him for it. But those lessons, hard-learned and hated, were the thin line between life and death now, the reason one last ten-year-old boy survived in the remnants of this rotting town where eighteen thousand Imperial citizens had died screaming, crying out to the Emperor for salvation.

Bas lived, and that in itself was spit in the eye of the greenskin nightmare.

He had never thanked the old man. There had been a moment, back when they had parted company for good, in which Bas had almost said the words, but the memories of all the fractured bones and cuts and bruises were still too sharp back then. They had stilled his tongue. The moment had passed, never to come again, and the old man was surely dead. For what it was worth, Bas hoped the old bastard's soul would take some satisfaction in his grandson's survival.

Time to rest now. He needed it more than ever. It was blackest night outside. The wind screamed in the shell-holes that pocked the walls of this four-storey tenement. A hard cold rain beat on the remains of the crumbling roof and the cracked skylight above.

Good, thought Bas. The greenskins wouldn't be abroad tonight. They kept to their cookfires when it rained this hard.

At the thought of cookfires, his stomach growled a protest at long hours of emptiness, but he couldn't afford to eat again today. Tomorrow, he'd have something from one of the tins, processed grox meat perhaps. He needed protein badly.

Hidden deep at the back of a cramped metal air-vent, the boy drew a filthy, ragged sheet up over his head, closed his eyes, and let a fragile, temporary peace embrace him.

When Bas was just seven years old, his parents died and what he was told of it was a lie. Two officers brought the news. His father's major-domo, Geddian Arnaust, asked for details, at which point the officers exchanged uncomfortable looks. The taller of the two said something about a bombing at the planetary governor's summer mansion – an attack by elements of an anti-Imperial cult. But Bas knew half-truth when he heard it. Whatever had really happened, the grim, darkly-uniformed duo in the mansion's foyer would say no more about it. Bas never found out the real story.

What they did say, however, was that, on behalf of the Imperium of Man and the Almighty God-Emperor Himself, the noble Administratum was taking full possession of the Vaarden estate and all assets attached to it. War raged across the segmentum. Money was needed for the raising of new troops. Imperial Law was clear on the matter. The mansion staff would be kept on, the tall officer assured Arnaust. The new tenant – an Administratum man, cousin of the planetary governor, no less – would engage their services.

'What will happen to the young master?' Arnaust had asked with only the mildest concern, less for the boy than for the simple practicality of dispensing with an unwanted duty. He had never held any particular affection for his master's son.

'Maternal grandfather,' said the officer on the left. 'His last living relative, according to records. Out east, by New Caedon Hive. The boy will be sent there.'

'There's a cargo train taking slaves that way this afternoon,' said the taller. 'It's a twenty-hour trip. No stops.'

Arnaust nodded and asked how soon the boy might embark.

'We're to take him to Hevas Terminal as soon as he's ready,' said the shorter officer. 'He can bring one bag, enough for a change of clothes. Whatever else he needs, the grandfather will have to provide.'

It was as simple as that. One moment, Bas had been the son of a wealthy investor with mining concerns on a dozen mineral-rich moons, the next he was a seven-year-old orphan stuffed into the smallest, filthiest compartment of a rusting train car with nothing but a tide of cream-coloured lice for company and a bag of clothes for a pillow.

At least he wasn't put with the others. Among the slaves all chained together in the larger compartments, there were several hunched, scowling men who had eyed him in the strangest manner as he'd walked up the carriage ramp. Their predatory stares, unreadable to one so naive, had nevertheless chilled Bas to the marrow.

Father and mother gone, and him suddenly wrenched from the security and stability of the wealth and comfort they had provided! Curled up in his grimy, closet-sized space, Bas had wept without pause, his body trembling with sobs, until exhaustion finally took over. Asleep at last, he didn't feel the lice crawling over his arms and legs to feed. When he awoke much later, he was covered in raw, itching bumps. He took vengeance then, the first he had ever known, and crushed all the blood-fat lice he could find. It took only moments, but the satisfaction of killing them for their transgressions lasted well beyond the act itself. When the pleasure of revenge finally subsided, he curled up into a ball and wept once more.

A scream ripped Bas from a dream immediately forgotten, and he came awake at once, throwing off his filthy sheet and rolling to a crouch. His hand went to the hilt of the knife roped around his waist. It sounded again. Not human. Close by.

The traps in the hall! One of the snares!

Bas scrambled to the opening of the air-vent. There, he paused for a dozen thunderous heartbeats while he scanned the room below him.

No movement. They hadn't gotten this far in, thank the Throne.

He jumped down. Crouching low, he scooted towards the door in the far wall. Beyond the grimy windows to his left, the sky was a dull, murky green. Morning. The sun would rise soon, not that it would be visible.

The rain had ceased, but the clouds hung thick and heavy and low.

Bas stopped by the room's only door just long enough to deactivate the hinged spike trap above it. He stretched up on tip-toes to fix the simple safety lock in place. Then, cautiously, quietly, he opened the door and peered through, eyes wide against the liquid darkness of the hallway beyond.

A mewling sound guided his gaze towards the intruder. There, barely visible among the mounds of fallen concrete and shattered glass that littered the floor, was one of them, distinguishable from the rubble only by the sound it made and the panicked scrabbling of its long-fingered hands as it struggled with the wire that bit into its flesh.

Bas could smell its blood on the dusty air – salty and metallic like human blood, but with strong overtones of something else, something like mould.

He checked for any sign of movement in the shadows beyond the intruder. If the creature wasn't alone, he would have to flee. There could be no fighting toe-to-toe. Much as he valued the little sanctuary he had worked so hard to create here, he wasn't fool enough to die for it. He had abandoned other boltholes for less.

Though Bas matched most of the hook-noses in size, they had the physical edge. The hideous creatures were far stronger than they looked. Their long powerful hands and razor-lined mouths made them deadly. Even one so hopelessly entangled in his sharp wire snares could still do him lethal damage if he got careless.

But Bas hadn't lived this long by being careless.

The old man's voice rose again in his mind.

No slips, boy. A survivor minds his details. Always.

Satisfied that the monster was alone, Bas acted quickly. He dashed from the doorway, low and silent as ever, and closed on his scrabbling prey. Before the alien knew it had company, Bas was on it, stamping viciously down on its face. Bones snapped. Teeth broke. The vile, misshapen head hammered again and again against the stone floor. With the creature stunned, Bas straddled it, drew his knife and pressed the long blade up under the creature's breastbone. He threw his whole weight behind the thrust, leaning into it with both hands. The creature's body heaved under him. It began flailing and bucking wildly, but Bas held on, gripping its skinny torso between his knees. Then, with his knife buried up to the hilt, Bas began to lever the blade roughly back and forward, cleaving the creature's heart in two.

A wheezing gasp. A wet gurgle. A last violent tremor, and the creature went limp.

Bas rolled off the body, leaving the knife buried in his foe. Withdrawing it now would only mean spillage and he wanted to avoid that as much as he could. Lying in the gloom, catching his breath, he watched his hands for the moment they would stop shaking.

Don't be afraid, he told himself. This is nothing new. We've done this before.

That gravelly voice rasped again from the past.

Adrenaline is your ally, boy. Don't mistake it for fear. They're not the same thing.

The shaking subsided far faster than when he'd made his first kill, but Bas knew from experience that the hard work would start in earnest now. He had a body to deal with. If the other savages smelled blood – and they always did – they would come. He had to move the corpse.

Hissing a curse, he kicked out at the thing's ugly, dead face.

Being abroad in daylight was a constant gamble, much more so with a burden like this one, but he knew he could still save this precious bolthole from discovery if he moved fast. The more time he gave the greenskins to rouse, the more danger he'd be in.

With a grunt, he forced his aching, exhausted body to its feet and set about his grisly business.

The cargo train ground to a slow halt at noon on the day after its journey had begun. The iron walls of Bas's tiny cabin shuddered so much as the brakes were applied that Bas was sure the train would come apart. Instead, after what seemed an eternity, the screeching of metal against metal ended and the vehicle gave one final lurch.

Bas, unprepared for this, cried out as he was flung against the wall, bumping his head. He sat rubbing his injury, fighting to hold back tears.

A scruffy teenaged boy in the orange overalls of a loader came looking for him a few minutes after the massive vehicle's engines had powered down.

'Arco Station,' he rasped around the thick brown lho-stick he was smoking. 'It's yer stop, grub. Up an' out.'

Bas stood shakily and lifted his bag, then followed the young loader and his trail of choking yellow smoke to the nearest exit ramp. As they walked, he asked meekly, 'Why did you call me *grub*?'

Bas wasn't offended per se. He was unused to insult, sheltered as his life had been until now. He was simply confused. No one had ever called him names before. He had always been *the young master*.

The loader snorted. Over his left shoulder, he said, 'Lookit yerself, grub. Small an' pale an' fat. Soft an' squirmy. You got rich written all over you. I 'eard about you. Serves you right, the likes o' you. Serves you right, all what happened.'

Bas didn't understand that. He wasn't rich. That was his father. He hadn't done anything wrong. Suddenly, he felt fresh tears rising and a tightness in his throat. This boy hated him, he realised. Why? What had he done? Before he could ask, they reached the train car's portside personnel ramp. The loader stepped aside and shoved Bas forward. The light outside was blinding in contrast to the dank interior of the huge train. Bas felt the harsh radiance stabbing at his eyes. The sun was glaring, the sky a blue so intense it seemed to throb.

As his eyes adjusted, he squinted down the long ramp, taking in the rockcrete expanse of the loading platform. Beyond it, shimmering in the heat haze way off to the north, stood the shining steel towers of a great city.

New Caedon Hive.

His new home, surely, for one of the Civitas officers had mentioned the place by name. From here, it looked glorious. He had read all about the great hive cities of the Imperium in one of his father's databooks. Their streets teemed with all manner of people, living and working together in unity to fuel the glorious machine that was the Imperium of Man. He felt a momentary thrill despite his fears. What would it be like to live in such a place, so different from the quiet isolation of the estate? What grand role would he come to play there?

Already, indentured workers and mindless servitors were unloading crates from the other cars on to the sun-baked surface of the platform. Armed men, their faces hidden beneath black visors, pushed and kicked the newly arrived slaves into orderly lines. Someone Bas couldn't see beyond the rows of slaves was barking out a list of rules which, if broken, would apparently be met with the direst physical punishment.

'Go on, then,' spat the loader from behind Bas. 'Get on about yer business, grub. Someone's waiting for you, they are.'

Bas scanned the platform again. He had never met his maternal grandfather. His mother, distant at the best of times, had never once mentioned the man. Bas could see no one who stood out from those he had already noted.

A hand on his back started him down the ramp, forcing that first step. Numbly, he let his legs carry him further, step after step, clutching his bag tight, eyes still searching for his grandfather with a growing sense of panic and confusion.

'Emprah 'elp you, grub. Thassa mean-lookin' bastard you got waiting for you.'

Bas turned, but the loader was already tramping back into the carriage's shadowy interior. Returning his gaze to the platform, he saw it at last, a single figure marked out because it wasn't moving, wasn't hefting crates or bags or boxes or bundles. It was a man, and he stood in the shadow of a rusting green cargo container, his back resting against its pitted surface.

Bas couldn't see him well, not cloaked in such thick, black shadow, but his skin turned to gooseflesh all the same. The cold hand of dread gripped his heart. He slowed. He wanted to turn back, but to what? To a dark metal cabin crawling with lice? He kept moving.

When his feet touched level ground, he gave a start and looked down, surprised that he had descended the whole ramp. There was nothing else to do now. He had to keep on. His numb legs drove him reluctantly towards the green container. When he was five metres from it, a voice as rough as grinding rocks said, 'Took your blasted time, boy. What are you, soft in the head as well as the body?'

There was no introduction beyond this, no courtesies.

'Don't fall behind,' said the man as he pushed himself upright from the side of the container. 'And don't speak.'

As the man stepped into the glaring sunshine, Bas saw him properly for the first time and failed to stifle a whimper. A sudden hot wetness spread from his crotch, soaking his trousers. The old man turned at the lack of following footsteps. He took in the pathetic sight, a scowl of disgust twisting his awful features.

'Blasted Throne,' he hissed. 'If you've got any of my blood in you, it's not much!'

Bas stared back, frozen in place, lip quivering, hands trembling. This man couldn't be his mother's sire. There had to be some mistake. His mother had been beautiful and refined. Cold, if he were being honest, but nonetheless a woman he had loved and admired above all others. He searched the stranger in front of him for any sign of his mother's bloodline.

If it was there at all, it was buried deep beneath leathery skin and scar tissue.

The man before him was old, over seventy standard years if he was a day, but impressively muscled for his age. He carried barely an ounce of fat. Veins stood out on his hard shoulders and arms and snaked up his neck to the temples on either side of his shaved head. He wore a beard of middle length, untidy and uneven, and some kind of silver chain with two small metal plates hanging from it. His clothes were olive green, both the sweat-stained vest and the tattered old pants, and his boots, which could hardly be called black anymore, were scuffed and covered with dirt.

The worst thing about the old man by far, however – the thing that held the boy's eyes for the longest time – was the huge crater of missing flesh where his right cheek should rightly have been. It was monstrous. The tissue that remained was so thin Bas could make out individual teeth clenched in anger beneath it.

The old man noted where the boy's eyes had settled.

'Think I'm a horror, boy?' he said. 'One day, I'll tell you about horrors.'

At this, a strange, far-away look came over him. In that instant, the old man seemed suddenly human, almost vulnerable somehow, a man with his own very real fears. But it was just a moment. It passed, and the hard, cold glare of contempt returned as fierce as before.

'The sun will dry your trousers,' said the old man as he turned away, 'but not your shame, if you've any left.' He started walking again, off towards the southwestern edge of the platform where another broad ramp descended to ground level. It was now that Bas noticed the pronounced limp in the old man's right leg and the muffled sound of grinding metal that came from it with every step.

'Keep up, boy,' the old man shouted back. 'Keep up or I'll leave you here, Emperor damn you.'

Bas hurried after him and was just close enough to hear him mumble, 'I'm all you've got, you poor little bastard. Throne help the both of us.'

The alien's body was heavy despite its size, and Bas laboured hard as he carried it across the roofs to a place he felt was far enough from any of his boltholes. He was glad for the clouds now. The assault of a blazing sun would have made the task that much harder. It might even have finished him off.

Dizziness threatened to topple him twice as he crossed his plank-bridges, but both times he managed to recover, just. There hadn't been time to eat. Once the body had cooled and the blood inside had congealed, he had withdrawn his knife from the beast's chest and stuffed the wound with rags. There was almost no spillage at all. He had bound the wrists and ankles with lengths of wire, to make carrying it more manageable, and had wrapped it in an old curtain he had torn from a third-floor window. Even so, as careful as he was, every moment he remained with the corpse was a moment closer to death. Hunger raged like a fire in the pit of his empty stomach and his legs and shoulders burned with lactic acid. As soon as he was done dumping the body, he promised himself, he would eat a whole can of something. Part of him balked at the thought of such excess. Eating well now meant running out of food that much sooner. But it couldn't be helped. He had felt it yesterday running for his life. He felt it now. He was getting weaker, putting himself at a disadvantage, and he had to sustain himself. One day soon, he would no longer be able to dump the ones he killed. He would be forced to cook their flesh and eat it just to survive. He knew it would come to that. It was inevitable. He'd have cooked and eaten sewer rats first, but they seemed to have disappeared, perhaps eaten by the strange ovoid carnivores the invaders had brought with them. Bas didn't care about taste, but he suspected alien flesh, cooked or otherwise, would fatally poison him. No matter what he did, one way or another, they would kill him in the end.

But not today. Not while he still had power enough to defy them.

Up ahead he could see the shattered chimney pots of the last standing tenement on the town's southern edge. There, on that rooftop, he would leave the body. The smell of its decay wouldn't reach the ground. The winds from the wastelands would carry it off.

He left the carcass near the centre of the roof, burying it in rubble so that any hook-noses that did come up here wouldn't see anything to get curious about. At least, not from a distance.

With his labours done, Bas was about to turn back and retrace his steps when he heard a great rumble from the plains south of the town. He flattened himself and crawled to the rooftop's edge. A vast cloud of dust had risen up, at least a mile wide. At first he thought it was a sandstorm, but it was closing on Three Rivers and the wind was blowing against it.

Insistent as it was, Bas forgot his hunger then. This was something new, something unexpected. He had to stay and watch. He had to know what it was and how it would affect his survival. A spark of hope almost lit in his heart. Could it be humans? Could it be Imperial forces come to take back the town? Throne above, let it be so.

But it was just a spark. The darkness inside him swallowed it quickly. He had lived too many days and nights without succour to believe things would change now. For all he knew, he was the last living human on Taos III. Given the unstoppable strength and violent nature of the alien invaders, that didn't seem unlikely at all.

Thus, he wasn't disappointed so much as unsurprised when the cloud of dust turned out to be a massive greenskin convoy. The air filled with engine noise that would have rivalled a summer thunderstorm. Vehicles of every possible description raced across the plains towards the town. There were hundreds of them with wheels and treads in every possible configuration. Bas's eyes could hardly take them all in, such was the variety of strange shapes. Monstrous weapons sprouted at all angles from heavily plated turrets. Radiator grills and glacis plates had been modified to look like grotesque faces. Gaudy banners of red and yellow snapped in the windblown dust, painted with crude skulls and axes rendered with childish simplicity.

There was nothing childlike about the riders, though. They were hulking brutes, all green muscle, yellow tusks and thick metal armour. They revelled in the noise of their machines, raising their bestial voices to roar along with them. They cavorted on the backs of bastardised trucks and troop transports. Those that fell off were crushed to red smears beneath the wheels and treads of the vehicles behind, drawing cackles of laughter from all that noticed.

They were terrible to behold and Bas felt his bladder clench. If they had come to stay, to reinforce the greenskins that already controlled Three Rivers, his time was surely up. The odds of evading numbers like these were slim at best. He still had to scavenge for old cans of food each day, still had to fill his water-bottles from any source he could find. He still had to venture out from the safety of his boltholes. When he did, he would face a town swarming with savage nightmares. Why had they come? What had driven them here?

It was then, as this question formed in his mind, and as the first of the vehicles roared along the street below him into the town proper, shaking the foundations of the building atop which he rested, that he saw them:

Humans!

At first, he couldn't believe his eyes. He stopped breathing and his heart beat a frantic tattoo on his ribs. He wasn't the last after all. He wasn't alone on this world. There were dozens of them, chained and caged in the back of slaver trucks. Bas ignored the warbikes and heavy armour that rumbled past now. He had eyes only for the cages.

They looked a weak lot, these people. Beaten down, tortured. It wasn't a criticism. Bas pitied them. He knew what they must have endured. He alone had lived to witness the deaths of the people of Three Rivers. So many deaths. He had seen what the invaders were capable of. Theirs was a brutality wholly reflected in their terrible appearance.

The slaves in the cages wore soiled rags or nothing at all, men and women both. At one time, Bas might have been curious to look on the women, naked as they were. What ten-year old boy wouldn't be? Not so now. Not like this. Now, he noticed only the wasted muscles, the clotted blood on their faces and scalps, the ribs that protruded from their bruised torsos.

Most of them looked dead already, like they had given up. Perhaps they didn't have it in them to end their own lives, but from the looks of them, they would welcome the end when it came.

They are not like me, Bas found himself thinking. They are not survivors. And there are no children.

In that last regard, he was wrong. A moment later, as the last slaver truck passed beneath Bas's rooftop perch and off up the street towards the town centre, he looked at the rear wall of its cage and saw a boy roughly his own age and height. A boy! Unlike the others, the child was standing upright gripping the bars of the cage, his knuckles white.

There was fire in his eyes. Even from this distance, Bas saw it, felt it. Defiance and the will to live burned bright in this one.

A brother, thought Bas. A friend. And suddenly he knew that his months of loneliness and torment had had a purpose after all, a purpose beyond just spitting in the red eye of the foe. He had survived to see this day. He had survived to find this boy, and he would rescue him so that he would never be alone again. Together, they could bring meaning to each other's lives. They could look out for each other, depend on each other. Between them, the burden of caution could be shared. Life would be better. Bas was certain of it.

His grandfather's voice snapped at him from the past.

Weigh everything against your survival. Live to fight. Don't throw everything away on lost causes.

No, Bas argued back. I can't go on alone. I will save him for my own sake.

If the old man had been alive, he'd have beaten Bas black and blue for that. Not out of anger – never that – but because each man gets only one life, and some mistakes, once made, cannot be undone.

The streets were still trembling with the roar and passage of the convoy as Bas got to his feet. He suppressed his hunger once again and followed the slaver trucks towards the town centre. There, he would stay low, observe, and draw his plans.

It quickly became clear, as his grandfather drove them away from Arco Station, that Bas was not to live in the great hive city to the north as he had imagined. The road they followed ran south and the rail terminal's blocky buildings soon fell away behind them, obscured by dust, heat haze and distance. The land on either side of the wide, empty road was flat and largely dry, populated by little else but hardy grasses and shrubs and the tall, strange cattle which plucked at them. Bas was too scared to ask his grandfather where they were going, or anything else for that matter. The old man smelled of sweat, earth and strong alcohol, and he drove his rickety autocar with his jaw clenched, neither looking at nor speaking to his terrified young charge.

After two or three hours in the vehicle's hot, stuffy interior, Bas saw a town materialise from the wavering line of the horizon. As the old man drove nearer, Bas became depressingly certain that this was his new home. The buildings at the settlement's north edge were lop-sided, patchwork affairs with rusting, corrugated walls. It was the first slum-housing Bas had ever seen. Beyond them, the structures got taller and more dense, though little more appealing. An oily pall hung over everything. Towering smoke stacks belched thick, dirty smoke into the sky. As they drove deeper into the town, Bas peered through the windows at the scowling, hard-eyed people on the streets. Tenements dominated. The inky alleys between them spilled tides of refuse onto the main thoroughfares.

Who would live like this? Bas asked himself. Who would stay here?

For the second time that day, he felt the desperate urge to turn around, to run to anywhere but here. But there was simply nowhere to go. He was a seven-year old boy, alone in the Imperium but for the man next to him, linked by blood and nothing else.

'Welcome to Three Rivers,' grunted his grandfather.

Bas didn't feel welcome at all.

Ironically, Three Rivers boasted only one. The other two rivers had dried up as the result of a Munitorum hydropower project some two hundred kilometres to the west, and the town, once prosperous, had gone into economic collapse. The agriculture on which it depended struggled to survive. The workhouses began to fill with children whose parents could no longer sustain them. Many turned to alcohol, others to crime. The streets became unsafe, and not just at night.

In this environment, a man like Bas's grandfather, former Imperial Guard, hardened and honed by decades of war, found work where others could not, despite his age. As Bas would later learn from snippets of hushed conversation on the streets, the old man worked as an occasional fixer, solving problems with violence for those willing to pay the right price. The local public house also paid him to keep troublemakers out, though, if word was to be believed, he caused at least as much trouble as he solved. But on that first night, Bas knew none of this. All he knew was that his former life was over and he had been cast into absolute darkness, a living hell. He had no idea then of just how bad things would get.

The old man's home was a dingy basement at the bottom of a black tenement in which every window was shielded by wire mesh. The steps down to its entrance were slick with urine and wet garbage. The smell made Bas feel sick for at least the first week. It was better inside, but not by much. A single glowglobe did its best to light a room with no natural illumination whatsoever.

Bas was shown where he would sleep – an old mattress stuffed into a corner near a heater that, in the three years he would live there, would never once be switched on. He was shown the tiny kitchen and told that, in return for food and lodgings, he would be expected to prepare meals for both of them, among a score of other chores. Bas couldn't even imagine where to start with cooking. His father had employed two private chefs back on the estate. He had never once thought about the effort that went into preparing food.

The lavatory was another shock – little more than a thirty-centimetre hole in the tiled floor with a water pump above it that had to be worked by hand. A steel basin could be filled for washing one's body, but the water was always ice cold. That first day, Bas held his waste in for hours rather than use that horrid little room, until finally, he thought he would burst. Necessity took him beyond his initial reluctance. He adapted.

They had dinner together an hour after arriving, if it could even be called dinner. His grandfather made that meal. It was a tasteless stew of tinned grox meat and potatoes and, though it smelled awful, Bas was desperately hungry by then and cleared his bowl. His grandfather nodded approvingly, though the hard look never left his eyes. When they had finished, the old man ordered Bas to clear the table. Another first. And so it went, day after day, until Bas learned how to do all the things that were expected of him. When he made mistakes or dared complain, he was punished – a hand as fast as a striking snake would flash out and clip him on the ear. Weeping brought him no sympathy, only contempt.

As hours became days, and days became weeks, Bas discovered he was learning something else he had never known.

He learned to hate.

Salvation Square hadn't seen this much noise since its construction. Maybe not even then. The ruined buildings shuddered with the ruckus of the greenskin horde and the throaty rumbling of their war engines.

Bas crouched low behind the only intact statue left on the black-tiled roof of the Imperial church that dominated the square's west side.

The sky above was clearing of clouds, beams of bright sunlight slicing through like a hundred burning swords.

He had arrived in time to see the slaver trucks emptied and their occupants whipped and kicked towards the broken double-doors of the Administratum building, carrying barrels and sacks. The boy from the last truck had trudged in line with the others, keeping his head down, never meeting the glare of the living nightmares that herded him, but Bas could still feel the boy's defiant hate radiating from him until he moved out of sight.

The greenskin newcomers began mixing with those that already occupied the town, sizing them up, eyeing their buggies and bikes and tanks. A few fights broke out, bringing hoots of laughter and encouragement that rose to compete with the rumble and stutter of their machines. Losers were butchered without mercy or remorse, to the delight of both groups. Despite the appeal of these fights, however, the alien crowds parted fast when a great red truck roared into the square, cutting down a dozen greenskins with the jagged blades fixed to its radiator grill. There it halted, the arms and legs of the slain sticking out from beneath its dirty red chassis.

From the back of this truck leapt a group of bellowing brutes, each bigger than the last. They glared at all those around them in unspoken challenge, but none dared answer. Their size and bearing made the others step back, creating a circle of open space around the truck. From the vehicle's rear, their leader stepped down. Bas was sure the statue to which he clung trembled as the huge creature's iron boots added fresh cracks to the square's ruined paving.

There could be no doubt that this was an ork of particular status. Size aside, his armour was bright with fresh paint and bore more iconography than any of the others. A pole jutted from the iron plate on his back, rising two metres above his head, seeming to give him even more height than his already daunting three metres. It was strung with helmets and human skulls, some still carrying dry, desiccated flesh. A banner with two crossed hatchets painted in red hung from it, rippling in the warm breeze.

The warboss stomped forwards to the centre of the square where the fountain of St. Ethiope had once stood, roaring and bellowing in what passed for its brutish language. Bas glanced across at the dome of the Administratum complex. It had taken a lot of damage in the greenskin invasion. Most of its cobalt-blue tiles had been blasted off, revealing the fractured bare stone beneath. Great gaps had been blown in its surface, making it look like the detritus of a massive cracked egg from which some unimaginable animal had already emerged.

Bas had to see inside. He had to find the boy. He had to find a way to save him.

With a veritable army of orks filling the streets below, he knew he had never been at greater risk than he was now. It was broad daylight. If he moved, one of the beasts might spot him, and it would take only one to alert the others. More than ever, he felt himself balanced on a knife's edge. But there was no way he could turn back now. His mind was filled with thoughts of companionship. For the first time since he had emerged from hiding into a town held by horrors from another world, he knew purpose and, more importantly, and perhaps more dangerously, he remembered what it was to hope.

He needed to wait. He needed the horde below to become preoccupied with something.

He didn't have to wait long.

From the doorway of the Administratum building, the previously entrenched greenskin leader emerged, roaring and swiping at his subordinates to get them out of his way. In his own right, he was a monster of terrifying proportions, but to Bas's eye, the newcomer looked bigger and better armoured.

The two bosses locked eyes, both refusing to look down in submission. The horde parted between them, sensing the violence that was about to erupt. The newcomer threw his head back and gave a battle cry, a deafening, blood-freezing challenge. The other howled and foamed with rage, hefted a double-handed chainaxe over his head, and raced down the steps to meet his rival. The greenskin mob roared with delight and bloodlust.

Bas had his opening.

He didn't hesitate. Crouching low, he slid away from the statue and set off for the gaping wound in the side of the dome, moving roof to roof, careful to keep his distance from the edges lest his silhouette give him away.

He needn't have worried. Every beady red eye in the area was locked on the battle between the greenskin leaders.

At the end of his first week in Three Rivers, Bas's grandfather enrolled him in a small scholam owned and operated by the Ecclesiarchy, and the nightmare Bas was living became much, much worse. The other boys who attended were merciless from the start. Bas was a stranger, a newcomer, the easiest and most natural of targets. Furthermore, he had gotten this far in life without ever needing to defend himself, either verbally or physically, and they could smell his weakness like a pack of wild canids smell might smell a wounded beast. It drew them down on him from the first day.

The leader of the pack – the tallest, strongest and most vindictive – was called Kraevin and, at first, he feigned friendship.

'What's your name, then?' he asked Bas in the minutes before the day's long hours of work, prayer and study began.

Other boys drifting through the wrought iron gates noticed the newcomer and gathered round.

Bas was suddenly uncomfortable with all the attention. It didn't feel very benign.

'I'm Bas,' he answered meekly.

Kraevin laughed at that. 'Bas the bastard!' he told the others.

'Bas the maggot,' said another.

'Bas the cave toad!'

The boys laughed. Kraevin folded his arms and squinted down at Bas. 'I've seen you on Lymman Street. You're livin' with Old Ironfoot?'

Bas gaped at the other boy, confused. He didn't know who 'Ironfoot' was. His grandfather insisted on being called 'Sarge', never grandfather or any variation thereof. Bas had heard others call him the Sarge when they spoke of him, rather than to him. Then it dawned on him and he nodded.

Kraevin grinned. 'You like that? You know, because of his leg.'

He started walking around Bas with an exaggerated limp, making sounds like a machine. The other boys broke into fits of laughter.

Bas didn't. He had never asked the Sarge about his leg. He didn't dare. He knew it caused the old man frequent pain. He had seen that pain scored deep in his face often enough. He knew, too, that the leg made a grinding noise on some days and not on others, though there seemed no particular pattern to it. It didn't sound anything like the noise Kraevin was making, but that didn't seem to stop the boys enjoying the joke.

Kraevin stopped in front of Bas. 'So, what are you to him, eh? You his new boyfriend?'

Again, great fits of laughter from all sides.

'I… I'm his grandson,' Bas stuttered. It suddenly dawned on him that every moment spent talking to this boy was a moment spent digging a deeper hole for himself. He needed an escape… and he got it, for all the good it did.

A bronze bell rang out and a portly, stern-looking man with thick spectacles and a hooded robe of rough brown canvas appeared at the broad double doors of the main building. He bellowed at them to get inside.

'We'll talk later, maggot,' said Kraevin as he turned and led the rest of the boys in.

Bas barely made it back to the Sarge's home that evening. He had stopped screaming by then, but the tears continued to stream down his cheeks. His clothes had been cut with knives. His lip was ragged and bloody. One eye was so swollen he couldn't see out of it, and two of his fingers would no longer flex.

The Sarge was waiting for him at the rickety dining table in the centre of the room, bandages and salves already laid out.

'How many hits did you land?' he asked simply.

Bas couldn't speak for sobbing.

'I said how many hits,' the old man snapped.

'None,' Bas wailed. 'None, alright? I couldn't do anything!'

The old man cursed angrily, then gestured to the empty chair opposite him at the table. 'Sit down. Let's see if I can't patch you up.'

For half an hour, the Sarge tended his injured grandson. He was not gentle. He didn't even try to be. Bas cried out in pain a dozen times or more. But, rough as he was, the old man was good with bandages, splints and a needle and thread.

When he was done, he stood up to put away the medical kit. Looking down at Bas, he said, 'You're going back tomorrow. They won't touch you again until you're healed.'

Bas shook his head. 'I don't want to go back. Don't make me go. I'd rather die!'

The Sarge launched himself forward, getting right in Bas's face.

'Never say that!' he hissed. 'Don't you ever back down! Don't you ever let them win! Do you hear me, boy?'

Bas was frozen in absolute terror, certain the old man was about to rip him apart, such was the vehemence in his voice and on that terrible face.

His grandfather stood up straight again.

'The hard lessons are the ones that count,' he said in more subdued tones. 'You understand? Hard lessons make hard people.'

He turned and walked to a cupboard on the left to put the kit away.

'When you get sick of being an easy target, you let me know, boy. I mean it.'

He threw on a heavy groxskin coat and made for the door.

'Rest,' he said as he opened it. 'I have to go to work.'

The door slammed behind him.

Bas rested, but he could not sleep. His wounds throbbed, but that was not the worst of it.

Abject fear had settled over him like a wet shroud, clinging to him, smothering him.

Closing his eyes brought back stark memories of fists and feet pummelling him, of the wicked, joyous laughter that had mocked his cries for mercy.

No, there would be no sleep for him that night, nor for many others to come.

Bas found the human slaves already locked in a broad cage of black iron, the bars of which were crudely cast and cruelly barbed. As before, all but one of the slaves – and Bas judged there were over twenty of them – sat or lay like lifeless dolls. There was no talking between them, no sobbing or whimpering. They had no tears left. Bas wondered how long they had endured. As long as he had? Longer?

He saw the boy standing at the bars, hands clenched tight around them. What was he thinking? Did he always stand like this? Did he ever sleep?

The interior of the building had once been a grand place, even in the years of the town's decline. Now, though, each corner of the great lobby was heaped with mountains of ork excrement and rotting bodies. The walls were splattered with warlike icons in the same childishly simple style as the greenskin vehicles and banners. The air in here was foul, almost overpowering, even for Bas. Part of his success in remaining undetected for so long had depended on rubbing dried greenskin faeces onto his skin. At first, he had gagged so much he thought he might die. But after that first time, he had adjusted quickly, and the regrettable practice had masked his human scent well. Had it not, he would have been found and slaughtered long ago. Even so, the miasma of filth and decay in the wide lobby was sickening.

Much of the marble cladding which had graced the interior walls here had shattered and fallen to the floor, revealing rough brick and, in many places, twisted steel bars, making a descent fast and easy. Bas did a last visual scan to make sure all the greenskins were outside watching the fight, then dropped quickly to the lobby floor. The falls of his bare feet were silent as he moved around the west wall and closed on the black iron cage. None of the human captives saw or heard him until he was almost standing right in front of the boy. Even then, it seemed that they were too exhausted to register his presence. The boy continued staring straight ahead, eyes still intense, unblinking, and Bas felt a moment of panic. Perhaps the boy was brain-addled.

He took an instant to study him at close range. Like the others, he was skinny to the point of ill health, clearly malnourished, and bore the marks of cuts and bruises that had not healed properly. In the centre of his forehead was a black tattoo about three centimetres across. Bas noted it, but he had never seen its like before. He had no idea what it meant – a single stylised eye set within a triangle. Bas looked down at the boy's arms and noticed another tattoo on the inside right forearm. It was a barcode with numbers beneath it. The greenskins had not done this to him. It was far too cleanly rendered for that. Bas couldn't imagine what these tattoos meant, and right here, right now, he didn't care.

He reached out and touched the boy's left hand where it gripped the bar.

Human contact must have pierced the veil over the boy's senses, because he gave a start and his eyes locked with Bas's for the first time.

Joy exploded in Bas's heart. Human contact! A connection! He hadn't dared hope to experience it ever again, and yet here it was. Damn the bars that stood between them. He might have embraced the boy otherwise for all the joy he felt at that moment.

He opened his mouth and tried to greet the boy, but the sound that emerged was a dry croak. Had he forgotten how to speak already? With concerted effort, he tried again, shaping his lips to form a word so simple and yet so difficult after his long months alone.

'Hello,' he grated, then said it again, his second attempt much better.

The boy blinked in surprise and whipped his hands from the bars. He retreated a step into the cage.

Bas couldn't understand this reaction. Had he done something wrong?

In his head, words formed, and he knew they were not his own. They had a strange quality to them, a sort of accent he did not recognise.

Who are you?

Bas shook his head, unsure of what was happening.

Seeing his confusion, the tattooed boy gingerly returned to the bars.

Who are you? the voice asked again.

'Is that you?' Bas returned hoarsely. 'It that you in my head?'

The boy opened his mouth and pointed inside. Most of his teeth were gone. Those that remained where little more than sharp, broken stubs. But this was not the reason the boy couldn't vocalise. Where his tongue should have been, only a dark nub of flesh remained. His tongue had been cut from his mouth.

Sounds of movement came suddenly from either side of the boy. Bas looked to left and right and saw that the other captives had roused at last. Barging each other aside, they surged to the walls of the cage, shoving the tattooed, tongueless boy backwards in order to get closer to Bas.

Bas stepped away immediately, warily. He didn't like the look in their eyes. Such desperation. He felt the sudden burden of their hopes and expectations before anyone gave voice to them.

It was an ugly, shabby, middle-aged woman who did so first. 'Get us out, child! Free us, quickly!'

Others echoed her urgently. 'Open the cage, lad! Save us!'

Bas looked for the cage door and found it easily enough. It was to his right, locked and chained with links as thick as his wrist.

A tall, thin man with deeply sunken eyes and cheeks hissed at the others. 'Shut up, damn you. They'll hear!'

When he was ignored, he struck the loudest of the prisoners in the jaw, and Bas saw her sink to the cage floor. Another quickly took her place, stepping on the shoulder and arm of the first in her need to get closer to her potential saviour. Bas shrank further from them all. This was not right. He did not want to be responsible for these people. He just needed the boy.

Despite the logic in the words of the gaunt man, the others would not be quiet. They thrust their hands out between the bars, tearing their weak, papery skin on the iron barbs. Pools of blood began forming on the tiled floor, filling cracks there. Bas took another step back, searching the crowd in front of him for sign of the tattooed boy, but he had been pushed entirely from view.

'Don't you leave us, son,' begged a bald man, his right arm docked at the elbow.

'Emperor curse you if you leave us,' screeched a filthy woman with only a dark scab where her nose should have been. 'He will, boy. He'll curse you if you don't save us.'

Had the monsters outside not been making such a din of their own, they would surely have heard this commotion. Bas knew he had to go. He couldn't stay here. But it was hard to leave the boy. How could he open the cage? He had no way of cutting through that chain. Had he found this boy only to be frustrated by his inability to save him? Was the universe truly so cruel?

A mighty roar sounded from Salvation Square, so loud it drowned out even the wailing humans. The fight between the warbosses was over. The entertainment had ended. Three Bridges belonged either to the new leader or the old, it didn't matter to Bas. What mattered was that, any second now, massive green bodies would pour into the building through the shattered oak doors.

Go, said the tattooed boy's projected voice. *You have to go now*.

Bas still couldn't see him, but he called out, 'I'll come back for you!'

Don't, replied the boy. *Don't come back. You cannot help us. Just run*.

Bas scrambled back up the lobby wall like a spider. At the top, crouching on the lip of the great jagged wound in the dome, he paused and turned to look down at the cage one more time. The prisoners were still reaching out towards him despite being twenty metres away. They were still calling to him, howling at him.

Bas frowned.

'There's nowhere to run to,' Bas said quietly, wondering if the boy would pick up his thoughts. 'I only have you. I have to come back.'

Jabbering greenskins poured into the building then, laughing and grunting and snorting like wild boar.

Bas slid from view and made for the nearest of his boltholes to prepare for his return tonight. He didn't know how he would set the boy free, but something told him he would find a way. It was all that mattered to him now.

There are two ways to deal with fear, as Bas found out in his first few months in Three Rivers. You can let it corrode you, eat away at your freedom and sanity like a cancer, or you can fight it head on, maybe even overcome it. He didn't have much choice in the approach he was to take. His grandfather had already decided for him.

Kraevin and his gang of scum did indeed wait until Bas recovered before they brutalised him again. When it came, it was as vicious as the first time. They kicked him repeatedly, savagely, as he lay curled into a ball on the ground, and Bas thought they might never stop. Maybe they would kill him. Part of him wished they would. At least it would be an end.

When no more kicks came, it felt like a blessing from the God Emperor Himself. He opened his eyes to see the gang strolling off down the street, the boys laughing and punching each other playfully on the arm. Two local women walked past and looked down at Bas where he bled on the pavement, but they didn't stop. There was no sign of pity in their eyes. They looked at him in passing as they might notice a dead rat on their path.

The next passerby did stop, however. Bas didn't know him. He was a big fat man with skull and sword tattoos on both forearms. 'Having a bad day, son?' he asked as he helped Bas to his feet. 'Let's get you home, eh? The Sarge will fix you up.'

Bas hobbled along at the man's side, doing a fair job of stifling his sobs for once.

'D... do you know the Sarge?' he stammered.

The man laughed. 'You could say that,' he replied. 'I employ him.'

Bas looked up at him.

'I'm Sheriddan,' said the fat man. 'I own the public house on Megrum Street. You know, where your grandfather works at night.'

It turned out that Sheriddan liked to talk. In the twenty-two minutes Bas spent with him that day, he learned more about his grandfather than he had in the weeks since he had come to this accursed place. And what he learned, he could never have guessed.

According to Sheriddan, the sour old bastard was an Imperial hero.

As he had promised himself, Bas ate a full can of processed grox meat, knowing he would need the strength and energy it would give him. Sitting in the bolthole closest to Salvation Square, he thought hard about how he would get the boy out of the cage. One of the orks had to be carrying a key. Which one? How would Bas get it?

He thought, too, about what to do once the cage door was open. The others... he couldn't look after them. They'd have to fend for themselves. They were adults. They couldn't expect him to take the burden of their lives onto his shoulders. Such a thing was well beyond his power. It was too much to ask of him. They'd have to make their own way. He would lead the boy out at speed, climbing up to the rooftops before the orks realised what was going on. Together, they could return to this bolthole without drawing attention.

Bas looked at the few cans of food remaining in the metal box at his feet. There were no labels on them, but he didn't suppose it mattered. Like himself, the tattooed boy would be glad of whatever food he could get. Together, they would eat well in celebration of their new friendship. Tomorrow, they could search out new supplies as a team.

With these thoughts buoying his spirit, Bas bedded down and tried to sleep, knowing he would need to be well rested for the dangers of the night ahead.

Darkness fell fast in Three Rivers, and this night the sky was clear and bright. Overhead, the planet's three small moons glowed like spotlit pearls. The stars shone in all their glory. Had Bas deigned to look up, he might have noticed some of them moving inexplicably northwards, but he did not. His eyes were fixed on the scene below.

In the ruined plaza, ork cookfires burned by the dozen, surrounded by massive bodies turned orange by the flames. The majority of the brutes were drinking some kind of stinking, fermented liquid from barrels they had unloaded from their trucks. Others ripped hunks of roasted meat from bodies that turned on their spits. Bas didn't know what kind of meat the greenskins were cooking, but he could hear the fat pop and sizzle as the baking skin cracked and burned. Others still were barking at each other in their coarse tongue. Fights broke out sporadically, each ending in a fatality as the stronger hacked or bludgeoned the weaker to death.

Bas's stomach groaned, demanding he act on the savoury smell that wafted up towards his perch, but he ignored it. He needed all his focus, all his attention, to recognise the moment he could slip back inside the dome of the Administratum building.

It seemed that a great many hours passed as he hunched there atop the ruins of the old church once more, clinging to the statue that broke up his silhouette. In fact, only two hours had gone by when, with their fill of meat and drink and fighting, most of the orks settled down to sleep. Their communal snoring soon rivalled the noise of their engines from earlier in the day.

It was time to move.

With all his concentration centred on avoiding detection, Bas made his way across his plank-bridges and soon reached the gaping crack in the dome. There, pressing himself close to the exposed stone, he peered inside and scanned the hallway below.

There were fires in here, too, though smaller than the ones outside. Around them slept the biggest of the greenskins, those with the heaviest armour, the largest weapons, the most decoration. There were a few hook-noses, too, sleeping in groups near the fly-covered dung piles. They had not been allowed to bed down near the fires of their giant masters.

Bas watched and waited and decided that the orks within were as sound asleep as those without. He steeled himself for what had to be done, then stepped out from behind the cover of the dome and began his descent. The stars cast his shadow on the tile floor below, but nothing stirred, nothing noticed.

With all the stealth he could muster, Bas descended, his toes and fingers seeking and finding the same holds he had used earlier in the day. But while the daytime descent had taken only moments, this one took minutes. There was too much at stake to rush, and nothing to be gained.

Finally, his bare feet reached the cold tiles and he turned from the wall. He realised that, even had he slipped and made a noise, none of the orks would likely have heard him. Up close, their snoring was preposterously loud. Good. That would work in his favour.

Bas avoided looking directly at any of the fires. His eyes had adjusted well to the shadows over the last few hours of patient observation. He didn't want to lose that. He had to be able to see into the dark places, for the cage with the human prisoners was flush against the far wall and the marble staircase next to it cast a black cloak over it.

He moved, keeping to pools of deep shadow wherever he could, at the same time careful to steer clear of the huddled hook-noses. Had he not masked his scent with ork filth so often and so diligently, their sensitive noses might well have detected him. But they did not awaken. Bas reached the cage and stood exactly where he had earlier that day.

Gentler sounds of sleep issued from behind the black iron bars.

Good, thought Bas. *Most of them are sleeping, too.*

He hoped they would stay that way. *But where was the boy?*

A figure moved to the cage wall. Bas squinted, and was relieved to see the boy standing there before him. Bas smiled and nodded by way of greeting.

The boy did not smile back.

I told you not to come back. Don't take this risk. Escape with your life.

Bas shook his head and spoke in low tones, unsure if the boy could read thoughts as well as he transmitted his own. 'How do I open the door? How do I unlock this thing?'

He pointed to the heavy chain and crude cast-iron padlock where they lay at the foot of the cage door. The chain's coils wrapped around the bars twice.

I ask you one more time, said the boy. *Will you not leave me and save yourself?*

'No!' hissed Bas. 'I will not go on alone. I'm sick of it. Don't you understand?'

The boy's voice was silent in Bas's mind for a while. Then, it said, *There is a key. The head slaver wears it on his belt, tied to it by a piece of thick rope. If you can cut the rope and get the key without waking him…*

'Which one is he?' Bas whispered.

He lies by the fire closest to your left. His right ear is missing.

Bas stalked off towards the fire, still careful to avoid looking directly at its heart. There were seven orks around it and, as Bas drew close to them – closer than he had ever physically been to one of the tusked giants before – the sheer size of them truly dawned on him for the first time. He had always known they were huge, these savage horrors. But it was only this close, their wide, powerful backs heaving with each breath, that he realised how small he truly was and how fragile. There was nothing he could do against even one of them. If everything went wrong here tonight, he knew it would be the end.

Bas quickly found the slave master and moved around him to find the monster's key.

The slaver's barrel chest expanded like some huge bellows each time he took a deep, rumbling breathe and, when he exhaled, strands of thick saliva quivered on his long, curving tusks. The smell of his breath in Bas's face was foul, like a carcass rotting in the sun.

Against his better judgement, Bas moved between the slave master and the fire. It was the only way to reach the key on the beast's belt. But, as his shadow passed over the closed eyes of the monster, its huge shoulders twitched.

It stopped snoring.

Bas's adrenaline, already high, rocketed. He stood rooted to the spot, his hands and knees shaking. If the beast came awake now, he didn't know what he would do. He simply stood there, and the seconds seemed to stretch out like hours.

But seconds they were, and only a few, before the monster settled again and began to snore even louder than before. Bas's relief was palpable, but he didn't want to be near the damned thing any longer than necessary, so he crouched down by the monster's thickly-muscled belly and, with slow precision, drew his grandfather's knife from the sheath at his waist.

The rope was thick and the key itself was heavy, but the Sarge's old knife was razor sharp. It had never lost its edge, despite all the use it had seen. It parted the rope fibres with ease. Bas lifted the key, re-sheathed the knife and made his way back over to the barbed cage.

'I have it,' he whispered as he crouched down by the massive padlock.

'It turns clockwise,' said a voice from the deep shadows within the cage.

Bas looked up with a start and saw the tall, gaunt man from before standing in front of him on the other side of the cage door.

'I'll help you, son,' said the man, lowering himself into a crouch. 'You turn the key. I'll keep the chain and lock from rattling.'

Bas looked for the boy he had come to save and saw him come to crouch silently by the gaunt man's side.

'You'll need both hands to turn it,' said the man.

Bas fitted the head of the key into the hole and tried to turn it until his fingers hurt.

Nothing.

An act of no effort whatsoever for the aliens was near impossible for Bas. The torque in his wrists just wasn't enough.

'Here,' said the man, handing Bas a smelly rag that had once been clothing. 'Wrap this around the handle and try again.'

Bas did. With his teeth gritted and the effort raising the veins on his arms and neck, he wrestled with the lock. There was a screech of metal. The lock slid open. Bas turned, certain that he had achieved this feat only to bring death on himself. Every sound seemed so much louder when stealth was paramount. He scanned the hall behind him, not daring to breathe. He sensed the tension on the other side of the cage, too. The orks, however, slumbered on. Perhaps there was little to fear after all. Perhaps the beasts slept so soundly he could have run through here clapping and yelling and not have roused a single one.

Overconfidence kills more men that bullets do, snapped the remembered voice of his grandfather. *Stay grounded!*

'This will be tricky,' said the man in the cage. 'Lift the lock away from the chains and put it to the side. I'll try to uncoil this thing without too much racket.'

That made sense to Bas. The chain looked particularly heavy, and so it was. In the end, it took all three of them – the gaunt man, Bas and the tattooed boy together – to remove it quietly. Remove it they did, but before the gaunt man could try to open the door, Bas raised a hand. 'Wait,' he whispered. 'We should spit on the hinges.'

The man cocked an eyebrow, his face just visible in the gloom. 'Good thinking, boy.'

Bas was surprised by the compliment. His grandfather would never have handed one out so easily.

Regardless of how good the idea was, it proved difficult for the man and the tattooed boy to generate enough saliva for the task. Too long without adequate food and water had made their throats itchy, their mouths bone dry. After a few failed attempts, however, the man had an idea. Instructing the tattooed boy to do the same, he put a corner of his ragged clothing in his mouth and began to chew it.

Soon enough, the door's two large iron hinges gleamed wetly with fresh lubrication. Awakened by the sound of spitting, other prisoners rose and shuffled forward to see what was going on. That made Bas uncomfortable. He was sure they would give him away and bring the whole rescue down about his head. He was wrong. They had learned early in their captivity not to awaken their captors if they didn't want to be tortured and beaten, or worse.

'Stay quiet, everyone,' the gaunt man told them. 'The lad has freed us, but getting out will be no easy matter. You must stay quiet. Exercise patience or we'll all die here tonight.'

'We're with you, Klein,' whispered someone at the back. Others nodded assent.

Assured of their compliance, the gaunt man, Klein, turned back to the cage door and gently eased it open. The hinges grated in complaint, but only a little. At last, the cage stood open.

Bas stepped back.

Klein put a hand on the tattooed boy's shoulder and ushered him through first. He stopped just in front of Bas, who couldn't prevent himself from reaching out and embracing the boy.

'I told you I'd get you out,' Bas whispered, then stepped back, abruptly self-conscious.

Klein led the others out now, until they stood together outside the cage, a silent, terrified gaggle of wretches, all looking at Bas expectantly.

'What's your plan for getting us away from here, son?' Klein asked now. 'How will you get us to safety?'

Bas almost blurted, 'I only came for him,' but he stopped himself. Looking at these people, each hanging on to life and hope by the thinnest of threads, he knew he couldn't just turn his back on them. He had come into their lives, a light in the dark, and he could no more extinguish it now than he could abandon the boy who would give new meaning to his survival.

He turned and pointed to the broad crack in the dome up above. The closest of Taos III's moons, Amaral, was just peaking from the eastern edge of the gap, casting its silver light down into the hall, revealing just how many of the huge greenskin brutes lay sleeping there.

Bas's gut clenched. It could still go so wrong. One slip would bring slaughter down on them, and yet he was so close, so close to getting himself and the tattooed boy away from here.

Klein followed Bas's finger, his eyes roving from the gap in the dome, down the rough wall to the cold marble floor. He frowned, perhaps doubtful that some of his group would manage the climb. Nevertheless, he nodded and told Bas, 'Lead us out, son. We will follow.'

Thus, with the utmost care, the group picked its way between the ork fires, freezing in terror every time one of the beasts shifted or grunted loudly in its sleep. Crossing the hall seemed to Bas to take forever. This was foolish. Even if these people did get out, how slowly would they have to cross the bridges he had laid between the rooftops? It would take forever for them to...

To get where? Where was he going to lead them?

He couldn't take them to any of his boltholes. Those had been chosen for the difficulty of their access, for their small size. They were meant to be inconspicuous, but there was nothing inconspicuous about a group of clumsy adults struggling to pack their bodies into such a tiny space. And the smell of these people! They smelled so human. Bas hadn't realised until now, standing there among them, just how strong people smelled. The greenskins would track them like hounds when they awoke. No doubt these people thought Bas smelled foul, standing there with dried ork faeces rubbed into his skin, clothes and hair. But they would learn to do the same or they would die.

At the wall, the group huddled together and Klein spoke to them again.

'The boy will go first,' he said. 'All of you, watch him carefully. Watch how he ascends and try to remember the handholds he uses. We have to do this quickly, but not so quick as to cause any mishaps. Syrric,' he said, addressing the tattooed boy, 'you will go second. Once you and – I'm sorry, son, I don't know your name.'

'Bas,' said Bas.

Klein put a fatherly hand on Bas's head. 'Bas. And now we know the name of our saviour.' He smiled, and Bas saw that he, too, had had his teeth broken, no doubt by a blow from one of the greenskins. 'Bas, when you reach the top, you and Syrric will help the rest climb up, okay?'

For an instant, Bas imagined just taking Syrric and running. The duo would have far better odds alone. But no sooner had the thought come to him than he felt the beginnings of a sickening guilt. What would his grandfather have done? There had been no lessons about this. No tests. How he wished there had been. Had the Sarge ever made such a decision? Had Bas's education simply never gotten that far?

What should I do, grandfather? Bas silently asked the old man in his memories.

No sharp voice rose from the past to answer him.

He looked over at Syrric, and the boy nodded back at him in support. 'Right,' whispered the Klein. 'Up you go, son. Show us the way.'

Bas started climbing, not looking down, letting his hands and feet find the holds he knew were there. He scaled the wall without noise or incident and, at the top, turned to find Syrric only a few metres below him. As the boy neared the top of the wall where the dome opened to the air, Bas reached down and helped him up.

Below, Klein was helping the first of the adults, a woman with short hair, to begin her climb.

How frail they all looked. How shaky. Could they really manage it?

Bas heard a shout in his head.

No! Dara, no!

It was Syrric. He had seen or sensed something about to happen. From the desperate tone of his thoughts, Bas knew it was bad.

Surging from the back of the group, a woman began shouldering others roughly out of her way, screeching hysterically, 'I have to get out! I have to get out of here! Me first! Let me up first!'

Her mad cries echoed in the great hall, bouncing from the domed ceiling back down to the ears of the sleeping greenskins. With grunts and snarls, they started to wake.

Klein tried to stop her as she surged forward, but panic had given her strength and he reeled backwards as she barged him aside. Then, from the bottom, she reached up and tore the short-haired woman from the wall, flinging her backwards to land with a sickening crack on the marble floor.

The short-haired woman didn't rise. Her eyes didn't open.

Bas saw the orks rising now, vast furious shapes given a doubly hellish appearance by the light of their fires. The first to stand scanned the hall for the source of the noise that had awoken it. Baleful red eyes soon picked out the pitiful human escapees.

Roars filled the air. Blades were drawn. Guns were raised.

Bas loosed a string of curses. There on the lip of the crack in the dome, he and Syrric could see it all play out below them. It would have been wise to flee then, and deep down, Bas knew that. But there was something about the inevitable horror to come that kept him there, kept him watching. He had to bear witness to this.

Was this his fault? Were they all to die so he could assuage his loneliness?

Dara scrabbled at the wall, desperately trying to ascend at speed, ignorant of the imminent slaughter her foolishness had initiated. Though she hadn't been composed enough to map Bas's path in her head, she made progress by virtue of the frantic nature with which she attacked the task.

She was halfway up when the others began to scream. The first orks had reached them. Heavy blades rose and fell, hacking their victims to quivering pieces. Fountains of blood, black in the moonlight, geysered into the air, drenching the greenskins' leering faces. Deep, booming cries of savage joy sounded from a dozen tusk-filled maws. Bestial laughter ricocheted from the walls.

Bas saw Klein looking straight up at him, the last of the escapees still standing, hemmed in on all sides, nowhere to run. The orks closed on him, red eyes mad with the joy of killing. Klein didn't scream like the others. He seemed resigned to his fate. Bas saw him mouth some words, but he never knew what they were. They might have been good luck. They might have been something else.

A dozen ork blades fell at once. Wet pieces hit the floor. Klein was gone.

Outside Government Hall, the commotion spread to the rest of the horde. Those asleep in Salvation Square came awake, confused at first, then eager to join whatever fracas was taking place within the building. They began streaming inside, fighting with each other to be first. Perhaps they could smell human blood. It was thick and salty on the air. Bas could smell it, too.

Dara was almost at the gap in the dome now, still scrabbling manically for every protruding stone or steel bar that might get her closer to freedom. She was within reach. Bas looked down at her. He could have reached out then, could have gripped her arms and helped her up the last metre, but he hesitated. This madwoman had sealed the fate of the others. She had killed them as surely as the orks had. If he tried to bring her with him, she would get him killed, too. He was sure of it, and the darkest part of him considered kicking her from the wall to plunge backwards, joining those she had condemned. It would be justice, he thought. A fitting revenge for the others.

But he didn't kick her. Instead, without conscious decision, he found himself reaching out for her, committed to helping her up.

Even as he did, he became aware of a strange whistling noise in the sky.

He didn't have time to wonder what it was. The stone beneath him bucked violently and he grabbed at the wall for support. There was a blinding flash of light that turned the world red behind his eyelids. Blazing heat flooded over him, burning away his filth-caked hair.

Dara's scream filled his ears, merging now with more strange sounds from the sky. Bas opened his eyes in time to watch her plunge towards the bellowing greenskins below. He didn't see her hacked to pieces. Syrric grabbed his shoulder and spun him around.

Look at the square, he told Bas.

From the stone ledge around the dome, the two boys could see everything. The night had been turned to sudden day by great pillars of fire that burst upwards. Buildings on all sides, half-shattered in the original invasion, were toppled now as massive artillery shells slammed into them, blowing chunks of stone and cement out in great flaming clouds.

Bas watched with wide eyes. Again and again, high-explosive death fell screaming from the sky.

The orks were arming themselves and racing for their machines. Bas saw half a dozen armoured fuel trucks blown apart like cheap toys when a shell struck the ground between them. Burning, screaming greenskins scattered in every direction, their arms pinwheeling as the flames gorged on their flesh.

The whistling stopped to be replaced by a roar of turbine engines. Black shapes ripped through the sky above Bas's head, fast and low. They were too fast to see properly, but the stutter and flare of their guns tore up the square, churning ork bodies into chunks of wet meat. Greenskin vehicles returned fire, filling the air with a fusillade of solid slugs and bright las-blasts. Missiles screamed into the air on smoky trails as the aliens brought their vehicle-mounted launchers to bear. One of the black shapes in the sky was struck hard in the tail and began a mad spiral towards the ground. It struck an old municipal building not two hundred metres from Bas and Syrric. Both the building and the aircraft tumbled into the square in a cloud of smoke, flame and spinning shrapnel.

Bas grabbed Syrric's hand. 'We have to go!' he yelled over the noise.

He didn't wait for an answer. He pulled Syrric to the planks connecting the dome of their perch to the nearest roof and they crossed quickly, Bas first, then Syrric. Screeches from behind made Bas turn. Some of the hook-noses had scaled the wall inside the dome. They spotted the boys and gave chase, firing their oversized pistols as they came.

As soon as Syrric was over the first gap, Bas kicked the planks away. Then, grabbing Syrric's hand again, he ran.

Anti-aircraft fire poured into the sky, lighting their way across the rooftops. The shadowy shapes assaulting the orks from above were forced to pull out. Moments after they did, the artillery strikes started again. Bas was halfway across one of his makeshift bridges when a shell plunged into the building he was crossing towards. It punched through the tenement roof and a number of upper floors before it exploded somewhere deep within the structure. Bas watched in horror as the building in front of him began to disintegrate, turning to little more than loose stone. He turned and leapt back towards the edge of the roof where Syrric stared in horror, just as the planks beneath his feet fell away.

His fingers missed the lip of the roof. He felt his dizzying plunge begin. But small hands reached for him just as he fell, gripping his wrists and hauling him in towards the building. Bas struck the stone wall hard, winding himself, but the small hands didn't let go. He looked up and saw Syrric stretching over the edge, face twisted in pain, grunting and sweating with the effort of keeping Bas from plummeting to his death.

Bas scrabbled for a foothold and found a thin ledge, not enough to support his full weight, but enough to take some of the strain off Syrric.

Can you climb up?

Bas stretched and gripped the lip of the roof. Then, with Syrric pulling, he heaved himself up and rolled over the edge. There, with death averted once more, he lay panting, adrenaline racing through his veins. Syrric crouched over him.

We can't stay up here. Isn't there some other way?

The ground shook. More explosions rocked the town, striking just to the north of their position. Bas didn't have time to wait for the shaking to stop. As soon as he had his breath, he got up.

'The greenskins will be everywhere at ground level,' he said miserably, but, looking at the empty space where the next building had been only moments ago, he knew that staying high would be just as dangerous. Besides, that building had been the only one linked to this. It looked like there was little choice. If they couldn't travel above ground, and they couldn't travel on the ground...

'There's one more way,' said Bas. 'Let's go.'

Bas began training under his grandfather after the fourth time Kraevin's gang beat him up. It was the worst beating yet. One of the smaller boys – an ugly, rat-faced lad called Sarkam – had actually stabbed Bas in the belly with a box-cutter. It was the sight of so much blood that brought the beating to an early end this time. Instead of strolling off in casual satisfaction, Kraevin and his gang ran, knowing this level of violence would mean serious trouble for them if they were caught.

Bas staggered home, both hands pressed to his abdomen, drawing sharp looks from everyone he passed. A rough-looking woman in a filthy apron called out, 'You need help, boy?'

Bas ignored her and kept on. He knew the Sarge would be waiting at the table with the medical kit laid out. He had warned Bas that the other boys might attack him today. He had just about healed from the last beating, after all.

But this time was different, in more ways than one.

Bas wasn't crying.

More important than that, he had actually fought back.

True, his unpractised attempts to retaliate had met with dismal failure, but they had caught the other boys off guard. For the first time, Bas saw an instant of doubt in their eyes. They knew fear, too, he realised. They loved to dish out pain, but they didn't want any coming their way.

That was when he knew his grandfather was the answer.

This time, while the old man stitched the wound in Bas's belly, Bas glared at him.

'Something you want to say to me, boy?' said the Sarge.

Bas's words came out as a growl that surprised even him.

'I know who you are,' he told the old man. 'I know what you did, how you fought. Sherridan told me. He called you an Imperial hero!'

A sudden scowl twisted those terrifying features. 'You think Imperial heroes live like this, you fool?' the Sarge snapped back. He gestured at the dank, water-stained walls of their home. 'Sherridan had no business saying anything. I'll bet he didn't tell you I was stripped of my medals. I'll bet he didn't mention that I was dishonourably discharged after forty bloody lashes! Sherridan sees what he wants to see. You hear me?'

'I don't care about that,' Bas shot back. He would not be denied. Not this time. 'You could teach me. You could help me, make me stronger. Make it so I could kill them if I wanted to.'

His grandfather held his gaze. For what seemed an eternity, neither blinked.

'I can teach you,' the old man said at last with a solemn nod. 'But it'll hurt more than everything you've endured so far. And there's no going back once we start, so you'd better be damned sure.'

'It will be worth it,' hissed Bas, 'to smash those bastards even just once.'

The old man's eyes bored into his. Again, he nodded. 'We'll begin when you're able,' he told Bas.

And so they did.

It started simply enough. Bas drilled footwork for hours around the old dead tree at the back of the tenement. Slowly, the number of push-ups, chin-ups and sit-ups he could do increased from single digits to double. Within a month and a half, the old man had him into triple digits. Then they began training with weights, anything they could find whether it be rocks or old tyres or bags of cement.

Bas learned to wield sticks, knives, broken bottles, anything that could be used as a weapon. He became lean and hard like the grox meat they ate at every meal. He became faster, stronger, better than he had ever believed possible, and every bit of it was bought with sweat and blood, but never tears.

Tears were forbidden.

His grandfather was a brutal, relentless instructor. Every day was harder, more painful, more severe than the last. But Bas endured, his hatred burning within him, spurring him on. It wasn't just hatred for Kraevin and his schoolhouse thugs. It was hatred against all the wrongs he had known. Even as his grandfather forged him into something new, something tough and independent, Bas learned a fresher, deeper hate for the old man. His mistakes, fewer and fewer as time went by, were exploited with merciless brutality, until Bas wondered who was worse: Kraevin, or the Sarge himself.

It hardly mattered. He saw the results. And others saw them, too.

Kraevin's gang spent less time taunting him as the days passed. Sometimes, he saw them glancing nervously in his direction from the corner of his eye. He recognised that doubt he had seen before. The weeks since they had attacked him stretched into months. Bas started to wonder if they had given up for good.

Then, as he was walking home three days before Emperor's Day, Kraevin and his gang ambushed him from an alley and dragged him in.

Bas lashed out immediately without pausing for thought and smashed one boy's nose to a pulp.

The boy yowled and broke from the fight, hands held up to his crimson-smeared face.

Kraevin shouted something and the whole gang backed off, forming a semi-circle around their target. Bas watched as they all drew knives. If they expected him to piss his pants, however, they were gravely mistaken.

'Let's have it!' Bas hissed at them. 'All of you!'

Reaching into the waistband of his trousers, he pulled his own blade free.

The Sarge didn't know about this. Bas hadn't told him he was now carrying a weapon. He had found it on the tenement stairwell one morning, a small kitchen knife stained with a stranger's blood. After washing it and sharpening it while the Sarge was at work, Bas had started to carry it with him. Now he was glad of that. It was his equalizer, though the odds he faced here were still far from equal.

Kraevin didn't look so smug right then, but he motioned and the boys lunged in.

Bas read their movements, just as the old man had taught him. The closest boy was going for a thrust to his midsection. Bas slipped it. His hand flashed out and cut the tendons in the boy's wrist.

Screaming filled the alley and the boy dropped to his knees, clutching his bleeding arm.

Bas kicked him hard in the face. 'Come on, bastards!' he roared at the others. Again, he kicked the wounded boy.

This display was unlike anything the others were prepared for. They didn't want any of it.

The gang broke, boys bolting from the alley in both directions, knives abandoned, thrown to the ground. Only Kraevin remained. He had never run from anything. If he ran now, he'd be giving up all his status, all his power, and he knew it. Even so, Bas could see it in his eyes: the terroriser had become the terrified.

Bas rounded on him, knife up, stance loose, light on his feet.

'Bas the bastard,' said Bas, mimicking Kraevin's voice. 'You've no idea how right you were, you piece of filth.'

He closed in, angling himself for a lightning slash to the other boy's face. Something in Kraevin snapped. He dropped his knife and backed up against the alley wall, hands raised in desperate placation.

'Bas, please,' he begged. 'It wasn't me. It was never me. Honestly.'

Bas drew closer, ready to deliver a flurry of nasty cuts.

'He said never to tell you,' cried Kraevin. 'Said he'd see us right for money and lho-sticks. I swear it!'

'Groxshit!' snarled Bas. 'Who? Who said that?'

He didn't believe Kraevin for a moment. The boy was just buying time, spinning desperate lies.

'The Sarge,' Kraevin gasped. 'Old Ironfoot. He came to us after the first time we beat you. Honest, I thought he was going to murder us, but he didn't. He said he wanted us to keep on you, keep beating you down. Told us to wait until you were healed each time.'

Bas halted his advance. That couldn't be true. No.

But... could it? Was the old man that twisted? Why would he do such a thing?

'Talk,' he ordered Kraevin, urging him on with a mock thrust of his knife.

'Th... that's it,' stammered the boy. 'Two days ago, he found us and told us to ambush you. Said to use knives this time. I told him he was crazy. No way. But he tripled the money he was offering. My old man's got lung-rot. Can't work no more. I need the money, Bas. I didn't want to, but I had to. But it's over now, okay? Throne above, it's over.'

Bas thought about that for a second, then he rammed his right boot up between Kraevin's legs. As the bully doubled over, Bas kicked him again, a blistering shot straight to the jaw. Teeth and blood flew from Kraevin's mouth. He dropped to the ground, unconscious.

Bas sheathed his little knife in his waistband and looked down at the boy who had taught him the meaning of fear.

'Yes,' he told the crumpled figure, 'it is over.'

At home, he found the Sarge at the back of the tenement, leaning against the old dead tree, smoking a lho-stick in the sunlight.

'No medical kit this time?' Bas asked as he stopped a few metres from the old man.

The Sarge grinned at him. 'Knew you wouldn't need it.'

'You paid them to do it, didn't you?' said Bas.

The old man exhaled a thick cloud of yellow smoke.

'You've done well,' he told his grandson. It was all the confirmation needed.

Bas said nothing. He felt numb.

'Stay grounded, boy,' rumbled the Sarge. 'Stay focused. We're just getting started, you and I. You think you've bested your daemons, and maybe you have, for now. But there are worse things than childhood bullies out there. Never forget the fear and anger that brought you this far.'

Bas didn't answer. He stared at the dirt between his feet, feeling utterly hollow, consumed by a raw emptiness he hadn't known was possible.

'There's more to learn, boy,' the Sarge told him. 'We're not done here. Remember the chubby runt you used to be. Think of how you've changed, what you've achieved. I gave you that. Keep training, boy. Keep learning. Don't stop now. As much as you hate me, you know I'm right. Let's see how far you can take it.'

The old man paused, his brows drawing down, and added in a voice suddenly harsh and hateful, 'If you want to stop, you know where the damned door is. I won't give bed and board to an Emperor-damned quitter.'

Bas looked at his hands. They were clenched into fists. His forearms rippled with taut muscle. He wanted to lash out at the Sarge, to bloody him, maybe even kill him for what he'd done. But, for all he'd changed, all he'd learned, his hands were still a child's hands. He was still only seven years old, and he had nowhere else to go. Besting other boys was one thing, but the old man was right about greater foes. Bas had seen big, barrel-chested men from the refineries beating their wives and children in the street. No one ever stopped them. No one dared, despite how sick it made them to turn away. Bas always wished he was big enough and tough enough to intervene. The impotence inherent in his age and stature angered him. More than any daydreams of dispensing justice, however, he knew that training had brought focus and purpose to his life. His newfound strength, speed and skill had burned away that clinging shroud of fear he'd lived with for so long. Every technique he mastered brought him a fresh confidence his former weakness had always denied. He saw it, saw that he needed to keep growing, keep developing, to master every skill the old man offered and more. No. He didn't just need it. He wanted it. Right then and there, it was all he wanted.

There was nothing else.

He locked eyes with his grandfather, his gaze boring into him with cold fire.

'All right,' he spat. 'Show me. Teach me. I want all of it.'

A grin twisted the Sarge's scarred face. 'Good,' he said. 'Good.'

He ground his lho-stick out in the dirt at the base of the tree.

'Go change your clothes and warm up. We'll work on nerve destructions today.'

Two and a half years later, in the shadow of that same dead tree, a slightly taller, harder Bas – now ten years old – was working through a series of double-knife patterns while his grandfather barked out orders from a wooden bench on the right.

The sun was high and bright, baking the dusty earth under Bas's feet.

'Work the left blade harder!' the Sarge snapped. 'Watch your timing. Don't make me come over there!'

A deep rumble sounded over the tenement rooftops, throaty and rhythmic. It must have meant something to the old man, because the Sarge stood bolt upright and stared up at the azure sky, muscles tensed, veins throbbing in his neck.

Bas, surprised by the intensity of the old man's reaction, stopped mid-pattern and followed the Sarge's gaze.

Seven black shapes crossed directly overhead.

'Marauder bombers,' said the old man. 'And a Lightning escort out of Red Sands. Something's wrong.'

Despite their altitude, the noise of the aircraft engines made the air vibrate. Bas had never seen craft like these before. They had the air of huge predatory birds about them. They had barely disappeared below the line of tenement roofs on the far side before another similar formation appeared, then another and another.

The old man cursed.

'It was just a matter of time,' he said to himself. 'This planet was always going to get hit sooner or later.'

He limped past Bas, iron leg grinding, heading towards the tenement's back door. But he stopped halfway and turned.

'They'll be coming for me,' he said, and there was something in his eye Bas had never seen before. It was the closest thing to fondness the old man had ever managed, though it still fell far short. 'They always call on the veterans first,' he told Bas. 'No one ever truly retires from the Guard. I've done the best I could with you, boy. You hate me, and that's only proper, but I did what I had to do. The Imperium is not what you think. I've seen it, by the Throne. Terrors by the billion, all clamouring to slaughter or enslave us. And now it looks like they're here. Only the strongest survive, boy. And you're my blood, mark you. My last living blood! I've done my best to make sure you're one of the survivors.'

He paused to look up as more bombers crossed the sky.

'Come on inside,' he told Bas. 'There's something I want to give you before I go. May it serve you well in what's to come.'

They went inside.

A few days later, just as the old man had predicted, the Imperium came to call on him, and he answered.

It was the last time Bas ever saw him.

The shelling from the sky had opened great craters in the streets below. Through choking clouds of smoke and dust, over hills of flaming debris, the boys searched for a way into the sewers. Many of the massive holes were filled with rubble and alien bodies, but Bas quickly found one which offered access to the dark, round tunnels that laced the town's foundations. He had mostly avoided these tunnels during his time alone. Those times he had come down here looking for sources of potable water, he had encountered bands of scavenging hook-noses. Each time, he had barely escaped with his life.

There didn't seem to be any of the disgusting creatures here now, however. In the utter darkness, he and Syrric held hands tightly, using their free hands to guide themselves along the tunnel walls. They couldn't see a damned thing. Bas had no idea how or when they would find a way out, but he couldn't let that stop him. The tunnel ceiling rumbled with the sound of war machines on the move and explosive detonations. If he and Syrric were to survive the journey to one of his boltholes, they would have to travel down here in the dark.

As they moved, Bas became sharply aware of the comfort he was drawing from Syrric's hand. He wondered if that made him weak. His grandfather had used that word like a curse, as if weakness was the worst thing in the universe, and perhaps it was. Bas hadn't lived this long by being weak. He knew that. But he wasn't so sure it was weak to want the company of your own kind. Syrric's presence made him feel stronger. His body seemed to ache less. The other boy was following his lead, depending on him. Here was the sense of purpose Bas had so desperately missed. Alone, his survival had been nothing more than an act of waiting, waiting for a time in which he'd find something to live for, to fight for. Now he had it: someone to share the darkness with, to watch his back. He had gotten Syrric out, just as he had intended. Despite the deaths of the others, it still felt like the greatest victory of his young life, better even than beating Kraevin.

Kraevin!

Bas hadn't thought of the former bully in quite a while. What kind of death had he suffered the day the orks came? Had he been hacked to pieces like Klein and the prisoners? Had he been shot? Eaten?

As Bas was wondering this, he spotted light up ahead.

'There,' he whispered, and together he and Syrric made for the distant glow.

It was moonlight, and it poured through a gap in the tunnel ceiling. An explosive shell had caused the rockcrete road above to collapse, forming a steep ramp. The boys waited and listened until Bas decided that the sound of alien battle cries and gunfire was far enough away that they could risk the surface again. He and Syrric scrambled up the slope to stand on a street shrouded in thick grey smoke.

Which way? Syrric asked.

Bas wasn't sure. He had to have a bolthole somewhere near here, but with all the smoke, he couldn't find a landmark to navigate by. It seemed prudent to move in the opposite direction from the noise of battle.

'Let's keep on this way,' said Bas, 'at least for now.' But, just as they started walking, a hoarse shout sounded from up ahead.

'Contact front!'

The veils of smoke were suddenly pierced by a score of blinding, pencil thin beams, all aimed straight at the two boys.

'Down!' yelled Bas.

He and Syrric dropped to the ground hard and stayed there while the las-beams carved the air just above their heads. The barrage lasted a second before a different voice, sharp with authority, called out, 'Cease fire!'

That voice made Bas shiver. It sounded so much like the Sarge. Could it be the old man? Had he survived? Had he come back for his grandson after all this time?

Shadowy shapes emerged from the smoke. Human shapes.

Nervously, Bas got to his knees. He was still holding Syrric's hand. Looking down, he tugged the other boy's arm. 'They're human!'

Syrric didn't move.

Bas tugged again. 'Syrric, get up. Come on.'

Then he saw it. Syrric was leaking thick fluid onto the surface of the road. Arterial blood.

Bas felt cold panic race through his veins, spinning him, sickening him. His stomach lurched. He squeezed Syrric's hand, but it was limp. There was no pressure in the boy's grip. There was no reassuring voice in Bas's head. There was only emptiness, an aching gap where, moments before, the joy of companionship had filled him.

Bas stood frozen. His mind reeled, unable to accept what his senses told him.

Boots ground to a halt on the rockcrete a metre away.

'Children!' growled a man's voice. 'Two boys. Looks like we hit one o' them.'

A black boot extended, slid under Syrric's right shoulder, and turned him over.

Bas saw Syrric's lifeless eyes staring at the sky, that defiant glimmer gone forever.

'Aye,' continued the rough voice. 'We hit one all right. Fatality.' The trooper must have seen the tattoo on Syrric's head, because he added, 'He was a witch, though,' and he snorted like there was something humorous about it.

Bas sprung. Before he realised what he'd done, his grandfather's knife was buried in the belly of the trooper standing over him.

'You killed him,' Bas screamed into the man's shocked face. 'He was mine, you bastard! He was my friend and you killed him!'

Bas yanked his knife out of the trooper's belly and was about to stab again when something hit him in the side of the head. He saw the stars wheeling above him and collapsed, landing on Syrric's cooling body.

'Little bastard stabbed me!' snarled the wounded trooper as he fell back onto his arse, hands pressed tight to his wound to stem the flow of blood.

'Medic,' said the commanding voice from before. 'Man down, here.'

A shadow cast by the bright moonlight fell over Bas, and he looked up into a pair of twinkling black eyes. 'Tough one, aren't you?' said the figure.

Bas's heart sank. It wasn't his grandfather. Of course it wasn't. The Sarge was surely dead. Bas had never really believed otherwise. But this man was cast from the same steel. He had the same aura, as hard, as cold. Razor sharp like a living blade. He wore a black greatcoat and a peaked cap, and on that peak, a golden skull with eagle's wings gleamed. A gloved hand extended towards Bas.

Bas looked at it.

'Up,' the man ordered.

Bas found himself obeying automatically. The hand was strong. As soon as he took it, it hauled him to his feet. The man looked down at him and sniffed the air.

'Ork shit,' he said. 'So you're smart as well as tough.'

Other figures wearing combat helmets and carapace armour came to stand beside the tall, greatcoated man. They looked at Bas with a mix of anger, curiosity and surprise. Their wounded comrade was already being attended by another soldier with a white field-kit.

'Gentlemen,' said the tall man. 'Unexpected as it may be, we have a survivor here. Child or not, I'll need to debrief him. You, however, will press on into the town as planned. Sergeant Hemlund, keep channel six open. I'll want regular updates.'

'You'll have 'em, commissar,' grunted a particularly broad-shouldered trooper.

Bas didn't know what a commissar was, but he guessed that it was a military rank. The soldiers fanned out, leaving him and the tall man standing beside Syrric's body.

'Regrettable,' said the man, gesturing at the dead boy. 'Psyker or not. Were you two alone here? Any other survivors?'

Bas didn't know what a psyker was. He said nothing. The commissar took silence as an affirmation.

'What's your name?'

Bas found it hard to talk. His throat hurt so much from fighting back his sorrow. With an effort, he managed to croak, 'Bas.'

The commissar raised an eyebrow, unsure he had heard correctly. 'Bas?'

'Short for Sebastian... sir,' Bas added. He almost gave his family name then – Vaarden, his father's name – but something made him stop. He looked down at the blood-slick knife in his right hand. His grandfather's knife. The old man's name was acid-etched on the blade, and he knew at that moment that it was right. It felt right. The old man had made him everything he was, and he would carry that name for the rest of his life.

'Sebastian Yarrick,' he said.

The commissar nodded.

'Well, Yarrick. Let's get you back to base. We have a lot to cover, you and I.'

He turned and began walking back down the street the way he had come, boots clicking sharply on the cobbles, knowing the boy would follow. In the other direction, fresh sounds of battle echoed from the dark tenement walls.

Bas sheathed the knife, bent over Syrric's body and closed the boy's eyelids.

He whispered a promise in the dead boy's ear, a promise he would spend his whole life trying to keep.

Then, solemnly, he rose and followed the commissar, taking his first steps on a path that would one day become legend.

EMPEROR'S DELIVERANCE

Nick Kyme

Blood. There was too much blood.

Athena's hands were slick with it, right up to the elbows. The crimson morass where she buried her fingers was a man's chest, the ribs splintered and the organs exposed. She was searching for an artery. It was hard to find in all the viscera and vital fluid. Flickering lumenstrips overhead were weak and ineffective. Athena could barely see the novitiate beside her, handing over surgical tools. Betheniel was almost apologetic – the blades and saws were crude, woefully inadequate, but it was all they had at Emperor's Deliverance. It was all anyone had in the shadow of Devil's Ridge on the war-torn world of Armageddon.

Athena held out a steady, blood-soaked hand. She'd tried to wipe it on her smock but the nails were red-rimed, the gore so deeply ingrained it was like her skin was swathed in a patina of rust. With her other hand, she pinched the spewing artery.

'Clamps, sister. Quickly now.'

An explosion overhead shook the roof of the infirmary, making the novitiate fumble. Some of the tools clattered noisily into the gloom, but she found the clamps.

Athena staunched the bleeding, muttering as she tied off the vein. 'Fortunate that we don't require the rib spreaders.' Most of the man's chest cavity was gone, torn out by a greenskin bomb. Part of his jaw was missing too.

She addressed Betheniel directly. 'When a life is at stake we must show resolve, even in the face of danger. Those were Marauders overhead, our

Imperial Navy bombers, heading for what's left of Hades Hive.'

The novitiate nodded, contrite. She recoiled a moment later when Athena threw down a ragged piece of cloth she'd been using to clean her instruments.

'Throne and Eye!'

'What is it, sister? Have I done something wrong?'

'Grant me the fortitude of Saint Katherine...' she whispered, making the sign of the aquila for the blasphemous outburst. 'No...' Athena wiped a hand across her brow, smearing an incarnadine line in the sweat. 'There's nothing more we could've done.' She deactivated the medi-cogitator next to the man's bunk. Cardiac response was negative, blood pressure flat-lined. 'He's dead.'

A grey-haired orderly, cheeks peppered with stubble, emerged from the shadows and caught Athena's attention. Sanson used to be a hiver, a low-labourer in the 'sinks' who'd made machine parts all the way into his middle years until Hades was sacked. Calm-headed and meticulous, he made a reliable orderly. He'd made his way quietly through the numerous groaning bodies, the blood and sweat-stained beds, the thousands of wounded that were pouring into the camp's infirmary every single harrowing day.

'They have arrived, sister.'

'At the perimeter?' Athena was removing her smock as she made for a small basin with its sub-standard sanitising spray and dermal-scrubbers. Two acolytes approached her from either side as she stooped to wash her grubby hands, and took off her medical fatigues. For a few moments, she was naked in the half-light – Athena had long since foregone modesty – until her handmaidens dressed her in white robes and gilded iconography.

When she faced Sanson she was a Sister Hospitaller again, officious and noble in the trappings of the Adepta Sororitas. She clutched a string of rosarius beads to her breast, the sigil of a burning candle swinging from the end. Ornamental armour clad her body, a slim silver breastplate and vambraces. Lastly, she drew a hood over her jet-black hair which was scraped back by scalp locks.

'Across from the Eumenidies River, yes,' replied the orderly. Sanson had kept his eyes low and his integrity intact.

A vox-radio was playing somewhere in the shadows. A trooper hunched over, listening to the propaganda messages with the volume turned low.

++...innocence does not exist, only degrees of guilt. Freedom must be earned, it must be fought for. Cowards, the weak and the impure do not deserve to live. Hades was lost on the backs of the craven. Armageddon will only be won by the strong. We of the Marines Malevolent will stand before this menace and we will–++

'Turn that tripe off,' Athena scowled at the trooper, a private called

Kolber who was wise to do as she asked. 'I'd rather listen to Yarrick espousing the virtues of resistance that listen to *him.*' Captain Vinyar's rhetoric was fleeting on the vox-band but his propaganda was always directed at the disparagement of the weak and their worthlessness to war.

Angry, she summoned Betheniel, who was attired in the less ostentatious garments of a novitiate. Head bowed, she followed her superior.

'Shouldn't this be brought to the attention of Colonel Hauptman?' Sanson inquired of Athena's back.

She paused momentarily. The colonel had been responsible for the protection of the camp. He was an officer of the Cadian Fifth, a good soldier and an honourable man who understood the plight of those who couldn't fight for themselves.

'Tell him yourself,' she replied, disappearing into the dark. 'He's lying on that slab in front of you.'

With Elias Hauptman dead, it would fall to others to protect Emperor's Deliverance. Athena saw them at the crest of a muddy rise, waiting at the perimeter of the camp. She tried not to think about the thousands of refugees from Hades Hive housed below her, the wounded and the inadequate block houses, the unsanitary conditions of her infirmary, the dead and the pits where she and the servitor units she was afforded had buried them. Disease and vermin were becoming a problem. She'd taken to carrying a shock maul with her when not in surgery and had a tally of bludgeoned sump rats to rival any hiver.

She felt Betheniel trembling beside her and briefly clutched her hand.

'Have courage, sister. They are here to keep us safe.'

But as she regarded the towering knights in front of them, their weapons low-slung and ready, the kill-markings and the battered armour, Athena felt doubt... and fear.

There were two of them, both wearing the same gritty yellow and black battle-plate, a winged lightning-strike on their left shoulder guards. Both wore their battle-helms. One was beak-shaped and had been made to look like a shark's mouth with teeth painted on either side of the cone; the other was plainer, stub-nosed with a vox-grille.

As she bowed, Athena felt their baleful stare and fought to keep the tremor from her voice.

'I am Sister Superior Athena and this is my novitiate, Betheniel. I am pleased that such august warriors have deemed Emperor's Deliverance worthy of their protection.'

'We have not,' the shark-faced one replied. He spoke flatly, but with an edge like that of the serrated blade scabbarded at his hip. He stepped forward, looking down on the woman at a sharper angle. The pectoral on his plastron read *Nemiok* in archaic script.

'I don't understand.' There was steel in Athena's eyes and a defiance that suggested she wouldn't be cowed by these warriors.

The other spoke. His voice was grating but not as harsh as his comrade's. 'Our mission is to take and hold this river, the camp too. Nothing further.' According to his battle-plate, his name was Varik.

'So who is charged with defending the camp? I have over twelve thousand refugees, many of whom are wounded, not to mention another thousand Ministorum staff.'

Brother Nemiok leaned in, using all of his bulk and height to intimidate.

'Look to yourselves, if you're able.' He glowered into the distance, unwilling to speak further on the matter.

Athena was shaking her head. Betheniel desperately wanted to leave and even risked pulling at her superior's arm. She snatched her hand away again at the sister's scathing glance, which was then turned on the Space Marines.

'This is unacceptable. I will speak to Colonel Destrier about this–'

Nemiok swung his head around, the gears in his armour plate growling, 'Begone! And pray the orks do not come.'

Despite herself, Athena backed away. Her heart was pounding. She could barely breathe. 'I will at least know whom you serve.'

Varik replied before Nemiok decided to do something more than threaten.

'Captain Vinyar of the Marines Malevolent. Now return to your camp and consider this a warning.'

The discussion was over. If she lingered, there would be violence. It practically exuded from the Space Marines. Betheniel was sobbing, scared to lift her eyes from their boots.

Athena had to help her novitiate back down the muddy slope. Even when they'd reached the relative safety of the camp, the sister superior was still shaking.

While Betheniel sipped from Private Kolber's flask of grain liquor to steady her nerves, Athena listened to the vox-radio.

++*...will not lie to you. We are experiencing Imperial losses in the Eumenidies region of the Diablo Mountains. But though we must surrender ground now, stand fast good citizens, for we shall gather our forces and reclaim it. Be vigilant. Greenskins are at the edge of the Diablo Mountains, but are unlikely to forge a crossing. Resist, fight and we shall win this war together.*++

Yarrick's bombast meant more refugees would be coming in. Athena looked at the ranks of beds and the already overcrowded conditions. Their 'protectors' were monsters, masquerading as heroes. She prayed to the Emperor for his mercy.

Nemiok was scouring the mountains for any sign of the orks, one hand on the stock of his combi-bolter as it hung by a strap from his shoulder.

'Do not do that again, brother.'

Varik was cleaning the dirt from his chainblade and looked up. 'Do what?'

'Pander to that woman. She must be made to know her place. Remember your Chapter and duty...' Nemiok paused to turn and meet his battle-brother's fierce gaze, '...or I shall remind you of it.'

Chastened, Varik only nodded.

Nemiok went to the comm-feed in his ear and listened.

'Mobile artillery is being moved in on the opposite side of the camp,' he said a minute later. 'It seems Captain Vinyar is planning on starting that push a little early.'

He smiled when he saw the tank column emerging from the cloud of dust opposite their sentry position, missile points glistening in the pale sun, but there was no mirth in it, no humour at all.

Rain at Emperor's Deliverance was only good for washing away the blood. Even then it coalesced in the sink holes and basins of the camp, making the ground muddy and hard to traverse on foot or track. Ravines of the grisly matter ran thick and red, gumming up boots and thickening the air with a metallic smell.

Athena was out in the downpour wearing medical fatigues, having abandoned ceremony in favour of pragmatism. Betheniel was lagging behind on the slope, a storm cloak clutched tight around her tiny frame.

'I need your help,' she said to the Space Marine sentries, hoping her directness would get their attention.

Nemiok deigned to look at her. 'Go on.'

'The *Salvation*, it's a medical transport, has broken down. They're mired in the earth and have over five hundred wounded aboard. I need to get them to the infirmary as soon as possible. You are stronger than anyone in camp and could get us back on the road quickly. Not protection,' she explained, showing her palms, 'just saving lives.'

Nemiok waited. The rain drizzled down Athena's face, saturating her clothes. She was shivering; so too was her half-drowned novitiate.

'Please... I know I spoke out of turn yesterday, but it would not take long. I'm begging you. Help us.'

Slowly and deliberately, the Marines Malevolent removed his battle-helm and attached it to his belt by the neck strap. His eyes were pitiless, his mouth sneering. The rain lashed his horrible, scarred face and he did not move, he did not *feel*. It was like speaking to a slab of granite.

'No. You can manage without us.'

'Over five hundred wounded!' she pleaded. 'You can save them by doing this, at least give them a chance.'

The sneer turned into a scowl on Nemiok's face. He drew his spatha. The jagged blade was almost black. No amount of scrubbing would remove the murder stains.

His voice lowered with implicit threat. 'I abhor weakness.'

Beside him, Varik kept his helmet on and his eyes forwards.

'What about you?' Athena asked, 'Won't you help us, either?'

Nemiok snapped, snarling, 'Don't look to him! I speak for the Marines Malevolent. Go back and pray my mood stays this sanguine.'

Athena stormed off into the rain, catching up to Betheniel several metres farther down the slope.

She returned alone several hours later, bloodied and ragged with fatigue, but kept her distance. It was still raining, though the deluge had lessened.

'You were right,' Athena said, without emotion. 'I dug out the *Salvation*. It took six labour servitors four hours to do it. We also lost over half the wounded by the time it reached the infirmary.' Her eyes were like chips of ice, dark as coal in the gloom. 'I wanted you to know that, to know that a mindless flesh-mech slave showed greater compassion for humanity than the Emperor's Angels.'

Nemiok said nothing. He didn't even acknowledge her presence.

Only Varik betrayed his shame with a slight awkward shift in his posture. He was about to tell her to leave, but Athena had already gone.

A blurt of comm-static got Nemiok checking the feed in his ears.

His tone with Varik was like stone. 'We're moving.'

Smoke from distant fires smudged the sky above the Diablo Mountains a dirty orange. Burning resolved on the breeze, the stench of munitions, wood and human flesh. There was another odour too, something stagnant, earthy and fungal.

Betheniel huddled her legs close to her body, relieved that her sister superior had returned unharmed.

'And they said nothing?'

'Like statues, sister.' Athena was weary, bone and spirit. 'I've never felt coldness like that before.'

They were sitting outside the infirmary, getting some air. The vox-radio hummed in the background.

++*Efforts to repel the orks at the Diablo Mountains have failed. Imperial Guard regiments are already in place on Devil's Ridge and will halt the greenskins there. Solely as a precaution, civilians south of the River Eumenidies are advised to head away from the mountains and seek shelter. Trust in the Emperor.*++

A grim silence fell for a few moments.

A fearful Betheniel, staring up at the crags, interrupted it.

'That's close to camp.' She bit her lip as the years drained off her, leaving behind a little girl afraid of the darkness. 'Shouldn't we try to move the injured?'

Athena was resigned. 'There are too many. We'll have to make a stand and hope the Guard blockades stop them.'

'And if they don't?'

Echoing from the mountains, there emitted such a roar that it swallowed Athena's response with its fury.

'WAAAAAAGGH!'

Athena was up on her feet. Her tone was urgent.

'Back inside.'

After their sojourn outside, the heady stink of sweat, blood and piss hit them like a hammer when they rushed into the infirmary.

Sanson looked up from a tray of bandages and medical gauze.

'What's happening?'

Private Kolber was hobbling over to where his sidearm hung from a wall hook.

'The greenskins are here, aren't they? The blockade didn't stop them.' Only a young man, the trooper had aged a decade in the week he'd been in the infirmary.

Athena had no time for explanations. 'Lock all doors and shutters,' she told Sanson. 'No one goes outside.'

A pair of her fellow Hospitallers began to pray at a small shrine.

Overhead, a piercing whine made them all look up; nearly three thousand heads turned to the sky, pleading for salvation.

'More bombers?' asked Betheniel. She was watching the juddering lumen-strips, the dust motes cascading from the ceiling picked out in their flickering light.

The sound was decreasing in pitch.

Athena was slowly shaking her head. 'Hide! Get to cover!' she cried, just as the first shells fell.

The ceiling crashed down with an awesome, terrifying din. The praying Hospitallers disappeared under a mountain of debris, rewarded for their piety. Those who were able pressed their hands over their ears. A massive explosion blew out the walls and sent bodies flailing. A second later, the lights went out and panic rushed in along with the dark.

Having survived the initial blast, Athena was staggering through the carnage. Poor Sanson was dead, riddled with shrapnel. It had almost cut him in two. She clung to Betheniel, the only person she could realistically still save, and tried to find a way out.

Another incendiary burst tore across the sister superior, forcing her to the ground as it swept away a host of screaming silhouettes. Something hot splashed across her face. It stank of copper. There was grit too from the churned up earth, some of it too hard and sharp to be mud. She hauled her body up, dragging Betheniel.

Belatedly, she noticed her ears were bleeding. A perpetual monotone deafened her, so she failed to hear the piercing shriek presaging another blast.

It landed further out, throwing up corpses like flesh-rain. Bodies hit the ground bent and broken, entangled with their bunks.

Somewhere, a fire had started. Athena saw the ruddy glow that suggested the twisted remains of men and women strewn about the infirmary floor; she could smell the smoke. It mixed with the reek of cordite from the heavy mortars.

The orks in the mountains don't use mortars.

Horrified, she realised what was happening. They were in the midst of an Imperial barrage.

Blundering in the darkness, clambering over the dead and dying, her fingers found the edge of a hatch to the outside.

Athena was about to yank on the handle when a thunderous boom filled her senses and she was lofted into the air.

Betheniel was screaming.

Nemiok watched the shells fall with immense satisfaction. As they poured down from Devil's Ridge, the greenskins were blasted apart. Behind him, the Whirlwinds kept up a relentless barrage, but it was indiscriminate. Structures in the refugee camp were flattened. Some of the humans had taken to running outside as soon as the shelling began.

'Fools,' he muttered.

Those not sundered in the bombardment were picked off by the orks that made it through the gauntlet. A horde of the beasts was gathering, returning fire, attempting to mass for a counterattack.

Nemiok racked the slide of his combi-bolter to full auto.

'Ready, brother?'

'There are people down there,' said Varik.

Nemiok was dismissive. 'There are greenskins too.'

Varik nodded, thumbing the activation stud of his chainblade. They'd been joined by a Marines Malevolent vanguard attached to the armoured column.

Together with their battle-brothers, they descended into the camp.

Athena woke, coughing up blood. Pain sent hot knives down her right side where she'd fractured her ribs. Internal bleeding explained the ruddy sputum. She was groggy as if just punched. Light was filtering in from above. It took her a few seconds to realise it was because the infirmary roof was gone, shredded to nothing. It revealed a grisly scene of prostrate bodies and dismembered limbs. Some were still moving and groaning. Most were still and silent.

She'd been blown several metres from the hatch, which now hung open like a torn scab. Betheniel was nearby, alive but in shock. Her soot-smeared face was fixed in a catatonic grimace of terror.

'Come on,' Athena said, soothing. 'Follow me, sister. Here...' She held out her hand but had to grasp Betheniel and pull her up. The novitiate staggered, moving warily as if blind.

Together they made it through the ragged hatch, stumbling outside.

Smoke wreathed the camp. A fog thickened it, rolling down from the mountainside and across the river, creating a murky pall that rested over Emperor's Deliverance like a shroud. Gunfire and screaming raked the breeze, so loud that it made Athena cower at first. There were more of the dead in the muddied, blood-drenched streets. She saw a mother and daughter slumped cold and lifeless, their fingers barely touching. Inside a shattered blockhouse a Guardsman hung over a window-lip trying to get out. A broken helmet sat on the ground just below him and a lasgun dangled from his grasp. Dozens of her fellow sisters, pious women she had known for many years, lay red and open; she had to avert her gaze.

Monsters emerged through the smog with leathern, gnarled green skin. Huge and brutal, they stank of cloying earth and spoiled meat. One with a fat-bladed cleaver, its left arm missing from elbow down and carrying a gash to its forehead, saw them through the carnage. Violence radiated off it so powerfully that it made Athena dizzy.

'God-Emperor...' she breathed. The beast roared, tasting prey, and stumbled into a loping run. Armour plates clanked against its muscular body, as did the bones and flesh-trophies it had taken.

Private Kolber was lying in the street too. Athena saw his corpse resolve through a passing belt of smoke.

'Stay here,' she said to Betheniel, who nodded dumbly, and rushed towards the dead trooper. It brought her closer to the ork, but also to a gun. She wrenched Kolber's sidearm from its holster. Backing off until she reached Betheniel, she took aim.

'Stop,' she yelled at the beast, more to charge her courage than in any real attempt to stall it. As predicted, the ork kept coming.

Athena fired. The first shot went wide; the second struck the greenskin's torso. It grunted but didn't slow. She fired again and again, venting the laspistol's power pack and praying to hit something vital.

The ork was bleeding and burned, but not dead. The gun whirred, temporarily drained. Athena threw it down and drew her shock maul. Now in killing range, the ork lunged, its cleaver swinging down to cut off her head. Desperately, she threw herself clear and smashed a blow against its knee.

The beast was laughing, about to slay them both when a shadow loomed out of the smog behind it. Athena saw the muzzle flare in slow motion, realising that the bolter's salvo would hit them too.

'Throne, no!' she screamed, diving to the ground and praying her novitiate would do the same.

She heard a cry just after the bolter's retort and knew it was Betheniel.

'Engaging left.' A bark of fire erupted from Nemiok's bolter, chewing up an ork crawling from a crater. He followed up with a grenade from an under-slung tube launcher, slinging a charging truck tailgate over axle and cooking the driver in the fiery aftermath.

Another, running out of the incendiary smoke, went down missing half of its skull.

'Threat eliminated,' uttered Varik, swinging his weapon around as he sought a fresh target.

They were advancing through the camp, methodically gunning down any greenskins in their path. After the bombardment, Emperor's Deliverance was to be cleansed. No restraint. The order came from Captain Vinyar.

From the left, a burst of heavy bolter fire ripped up a mob of stunted greenskin scavengers, turning them into a visceral mist. Brother Drago was heedless of the humans scurrying into his firing line as he opened up on an ork vehicle wreck and the greenskins trying to liberate a heavy stubber from the rig's flatbed. Everything disappeared in a massive explosion and the angry flare of the belt-fed cannon.

Out of the smoke clouds a Land Speeder descended. It hovered in low, engine wash kicking up dirt, aiming its nose-mounted heavy flamer at a ruined blockhouse.

A female refugee, cut up and hobbling, shouted at it to turn around.

'There are people trapped inside!'

'Step aside,' growled the pilot, unleashing a jet of super-heated promethium into the ruin. Burning orks and humans staggered out as the structure burned. Any last resistance was dealt with when the gunner swung around his rail-mounted assault cannon and thumbed the triggers. A salvo of high velocity shells spat from the rotating barrel that blew out the blockhouse's windows in a glassy storm, killing everything left inside. Then he turned their wrath on the flaming survivors.

Laughter made an ugly sound through Nemiok's battle-helm as he hailed the gunner's kills.

'Wipe them from existence!' he roared, sighting a group of orks that had escaped the fusillade. He unclipped a grenade and tossed it towards them.

As the greenskins were engulfed by explosion, he called to Varik. 'Brother, I wish to anoint my blade with their xenos blood!'

Varik nodded, his drawn chainsword burring in his iron grip.

Though battered, the orks charged, cleavers and cutters swinging. Varik sliced the head off one as his battle-brother impaled another. Nemiok then eviscerated a third before Varik finished the last, bifurcating the beast from groin to sternum.

Sheathing his chainsword, Nemiok headed down a narrow street that led into a larger plaza.

'Hold!' Varik's cry fell on deaf ears as he rushed to catch his brother.

Emerging from between a pair of smouldering blockhouses, Nemiok drew a bead on a greenskin's back. It was already wounded, missing half an arm and badly shot up. It was rushing at a kill the Marines Malevolent couldn't see and didn't care about. He scythed the ork down, opening up its back and spine as the mass reactive bolter shells exploded. As it fell, Nemiok saw two females he recognised through his blood-flecked crosshairs. He pulled his finger from the trigger, but it was too late.

* * *

Betheniel was dead. Her eyes were open as she lay on her back in a growing pool of blood. The shell shrapnel had only clipped her, but it was enough for a killing blow. Athena held the novitiate in her arms, muttering a prayer.

'Saint Katherine, I beseech you, bring this faithful soldier to the side of the Emperor. Protect her soul for the journey to the Golden Throne...'

She did not weep. Her resolve was hard as marble. Athena tightened her grip around Private Kolber's sidearm and stood up. She wasn't unsteady, nor did she feel any fear or doubt as she approached the armoured giant in yellow and black.

'You are a disgrace to the aquila,' she spat, bringing up the laspistol.

The shot was almost point-blank. It made Nemiok grunt and stagger but otherwise left him unscathed. He tore off his helm, uncaring of the battle around them. Underneath, he wore a mask of pure hatred.

'For that show of strength, I will let you see my face before I execute you,' he snarled, letting the bolter drop to its strap and drawing his spatha. 'This will *really* hurt,' he promised.

The punch to his unarmoured jaw sent Nemiok reeling and the spatha spiralling from his grasp to land blade down in the earth.

'You've shamed yourself enough.'

Nemiok looked like he was about to reach for another weapon but stopped when Varik shook his head.

'Killing innocents in cold blood, there is no honour in that.' Varik turned to Athena.

'Get out of here. A warzone is no place for a sister of mercy,' he told her. 'Stay alive and do some good at least.' He took the pistol, crushed it. 'Draw on my brothers a second time and I won't stay my hand.'

She nodded, realising what Varik had sacrificed so that she could live.

Athena rushed to Betheniel's side. Another group of refugees had found them and helped lift the body onto an Imperial Guard half-track. They drove off south, away from Devil's Ridge and the orks. There were still more greenskins thronging the edge of the camp, coming down from the mountains.

She didn't know what had made Varik intercede. Perhaps there was more compassion in the Space Marines than she realised. It didn't matter. Compassion wouldn't win this war. Only Yarrick could do that.

Overhead the barrage began anew, stealing away her thoughts and keeping the orks pinned. It would be several hours before the battle was done. Many more civilians would die. Only a few would know the Emperor's deliverance.

Varik kept his brother in his sights until he was sure his ire had cooled.

'You'll regret that,' Nemiok told him.

'You go too far.'

The dense throb of heavy engines interrupted and they looked up to see a squadron of gunships coming down to land in the distance.

'Now there'll be trouble,' Varik muttered.

The gunships were forest green, emblazoned with the snarling head of a firedrake. They belonged to the Salamanders.

Vinyar yanked off a gauntlet as he reclined on his throne in the Marines Malevolent barrack house. It was gloomy within the boxy ferrocrete structure, furnished with all the austerity expected of his puritanical Chapter. The captain kept banners and trophies close at hand. It was the only ornamentation he allowed in the stark chamber, except for a broad strategium table where a host of maps and data-slates were strewn.

He reviewed one, a report of the bombing at Emperor's Deliverance, not deigning to look at the two warriors standing silently in his presence.

'How many human casualties?'

'Around four thousand, sire.'

'And the orks?'

'Total annihilation.'

Vinyar set down the slate, smiled at the two warriors.

'Acceptable losses.'

'There was also significant structural damage.'

'Negligible,' Vinyar waved away any concerns. 'The greenskins are in retreat, the Marines Malevolent are victorious.'

'What of Armageddon Command? I have heard talk of sanctions against us.'

Vinyar's laugh was derisive. 'Destrier has been *reminded* of his place and purpose in this war, Brother Varik. There'll be no further repercussions from him.'

The warriors lingered, prompting the captain to ask, 'Was there something more?'

Varik awaited Nemiok's damning account of what had happened with Sister Athena, but his response was surprising.

'No, sire,' he rasped, jaw tight.

'Then you're dismissed.'

Both warriors saluted, turned on their heel and left.

Vinyar was poring over the maps on his strategium table, planning the next assault, when he heard the barrack house door opening again.

'Changed your mind, Nemiok?' he asked, looking up but finding someone else in his chambers. Vinyar sneered. 'You.'

An onyx-skinned warrior was standing before him, armoured in forest green. A scaled cloak hung from his broad shoulders, attached beneath gilded pauldrons. Iconography of drakes and fire, hammers and anvils emblazoned his battle-plate. His voice was abyssal deep.

'I have spoken with Colonel Destrier,' he said. 'I have also witnessed the excessive force used at Emperor's Deliverance and been told of the civilian casualties.'

'There is collateral damage in any war,' protested Vinyar. 'If I had not acted as punitively as I did, there would still be orks roaming that camp. Besides, cowards are unworthy of being spared.'

The green-armoured warrior had unhitched a thunder hammer from his back and slammed it on the strategium table, cracking data-slates and tearing maps. He was unbuckling a holstered pistol when he said, 'You misunderstand the purpose of my visit, Vinyar.' He looked up and his eyes flashed fire-red. 'This isn't a discussion.' He glanced at the gauntlets the Marines Malevolent captain had discarded. 'Put those back on. I want this to be even.'

Vinyar was belligerent, but reached for his gauntlets anyway. 'What are you talking about, Tu'Shan?'

'Penance and restitution,' said the Chapter Master of the Salamanders. Bones cracked in his neck as he loosened them.

'I'll give you one piece of advice,' he added, clenching and unclenching his fists to work the knuckles. 'Don't go for a weapon.'

Then he closed the barrack room door.

THE LAST DETAIL

Paul Kearney

The monsoon rains came early that year, as if the planet itself were tugging down a veil to hide its broken face. Even cowering in the bunker, the boy and his father could hear them, thunderous, massive, a roar of noise. But the rainstorm was nothing to that which had gone before – in fact even the bellowing of the monsoon seemed almost like a kind of silence.

'It stopped,' the boy said. 'All the noise. Perhaps they went away.'

The man squeezed his son's shoulder but said nothing. He had the wiry, etched face of a farmer, old before his time, but as hard as steel wire. Both he and his son had the sunken, hollow look of folk who have not eaten or drunk in days. He passed a dry tongue over his cracked lips at the sound of the rain, then looked at the flickering digits of the comms bench.

'It'll be dawn soon. When it comes, I'm going to look outside.'

The boy clenched him tighter. 'Pa!'

'It'll be all right. We need water, or we won't make it. I think they've gone, son.' He ruffled his boy's hair. 'I think it's over, whatever it was.'

'They might be waiting.'

'We need the water. It'll be all right, you'll see.'

'I'm coming with you.'

The man hesitated a second, and then nodded. 'All right then – whatever we find out there, we'll meet it together.'

A summer dawn came early in the planet's northern hemisphere. When the man set his shoulder to the bunker door only a few hours had passed. The heavy steel and plascrete door usually swung light and noiseless on its hinges, but now he had to throw himself at it to grind it open centimetre by centimetre. When the opening was wide enough for a man's bicep, he stopped, and sniffed the air.

'Get the respirators,' he snapped to his son. 'Now!'

They tugged on the cumbersome masks, and immediately their already enclosed world became tinier and darker still. They breathed heavily. The man coughed, took deep breaths.

'Some kind of gas out there, a chemical agent – but it's heavy. It's seeped down the stairs and pooled there. We've got to go up.' He looked round himself at the interior of the bunker with its discarded blankets, the dying battery-fed lights and useless comms unit. A pale mist was pouring in through the opened door almost like a kind of liquid, and with it, the gurgling rainwater of the passing monsoon.

'This place is compromised,' he said. 'We have to get out now, or we'll die here.'

They pushed together at the door. It squealed open angrily, until at last there was a kind of light filtering down on them from above. The man looked up. 'Well, the house is gone,' he said calmly.

They clambered over wet piles of debris which choked the stone stairs, until at last they stood at the top.

Inside a ruin. Two walls still stood, constructed out of the sturdy local stone, but that was all. The rest was blasted rubble. The clay tiles of the roof lay everywhere, and the boy saw his favourite toy, a wooden rifle his father had carved for him, lying splintered by what had been their front door. The rain was easing now, but he still had to rub the eyepieces of his respirator clear every few seconds.

'Stay here,' the man said. He walked forward, out of the shadows of their ruined home, his boots crunching and clinking on broken glass and plastic, splashing through puddles. Around them, the pale mist was receding. A wind was blowing, and on it the rain came down, washing everything clean. The man hesitated, then pulled off his respirator. He raised his face to the sky and opened his mouth, feeling the rain on his tongue.

'It's all right,' he said to his son. 'The air is clean now. Take it off, boy, but don't touch anything. We don't know what's contaminated.'

All around them for as far as the eye could see, the countryside which had once been their farm, a green and pleasant place, was now a stinking marsh of shell-holes. The trunks of trees stood up like black sword-blades, their branches stripped away, the bark burnt from their boles. Here and there, one of their cattle, or a piece of one, lay bloated and green and putrid. Smoke rose in black pillars along the horizon.

Such was their thirst that they had nothing to say, but stood with their tongues out trying to soak up the rain. It streamed into the boy's mouth, reinvigorating him. Nothing in his life had ever felt so good as that cold water sinking into his parched mouth. He opened his eyes at last, and frowned, then pointed skywards, at the broken wrack of clouds which the wind was lashing across the sky.

'Pa, look,' he said, eyes wide with wonder. 'Look at that– it's like a cathedral up-ended in the clouds.'

His father looked skywards, narrowed his eyes, and curled a protective arm about the boy's shoulders. Many kilometres away, but still dominating the heavens, a vast angular shape hung shining above the earth, all jagged with steeples and adornments and improbable spikes. It broke out in a white flash as the sun caught it turning, and then began to recede, in a bright flare of afterburners. After a few seconds they caught the distant roar of its massive engines. As the sun rose higher, so they lost sight of it in the gathering brightness of the morning.

'It's moving out of orbit,' the man said.

'What is it – is the God-Emperor inside it, Pa?'

'No, son.' The father's arm curled tighter about his son's shoulders. 'It is the vessel of those who know His face. It is the Emperor's Angels, here in our sky.'

The man looked around him. At the reeking desolation, the craters, the puddled steaming meres of chemicals.

'We were their battleground,' he said.

They ranged over what was left of the farm during the next few days, setting out containers to catch rainwater, gathering up what remained of their canned goods, and throwing away anything which the man's rad-counter began creaking at. At night they made camp in the ruins of the farmhouse and coaxed fire out of the soaked timbers which had once upheld its roof.

'Is the whole world like this?' the boy asked, gazing into the firelight one night, huddled under an old canvas tarp that the rain beat upon.

'Could be,' his father said. 'Perreken is a small place, not much more than a moon. Wouldn't take much to trash the whole thing.'

'Why would the Emperor's Angels do this to us?' the boy asked.

'They do things for reasons we can't fathom,' his father told him. 'They are the Wrath of the Emperor made real, and when their anger sweeps a world, no-one escapes it, not even those they are sworn to save. They are our protectors, boy, but also, they are the Angels of Death.'

'What are they like – have you ever seen one, Pa?'

The man shook his head. 'Not I. I did my spell in the militia same as most, and that's as far as my knowledge of things warlike goes. I don't think they ever even came close to this system before. But that was a big Imperial ship in the sky the other morning, I'm sure of it – I seen pictures when I was your age. Only they ride in ships like that – the *Astartes* – the Angels of the God-Emperor.'

* * *

Three days later the boy and his father were trudging through the black shattered crag north of their farm which had once been a wooded hillside, looking to see if any of their stock had by some chance survived the holocaust. Here, there had been a rocky knoll some two hundred metres in height, which gave a good view down the valley beyond to the city and its spaceport. It seemed the hill had been bombed heavily, its conical head now flattened. Smoke still hissed out of cracks in the hillside, as molten rocks cooled underground. Out towards the horizon, the city smoked and flickered with pinpoints of flame.

'Pa! Pa!' the boy shouted, running and tumbling among the rocks – 'Look here!'

'Don't touch it!'

'It's – it's – I don't know what it is.'

Looming over them was a hulk of massive, shattered metal, a box of steel and ceramite broken open and still sparking and glowing in places. It had legs like those of a crab, great pincers, and the barrels of autocannon on its shoulders. Atop it was what might once have been a man's head, grotesquely attached, snarling in death. It was a machine which was almost an animal, or an animal which had become a machine. Carved onto the bullet-pocked carcass of the thing were unspeakable scenes of slaughter and perversity, and it was hung with rotting skulls, festooned with spikes and chains.

'Come away,' the man told his son hoarsely. 'Get away from it.'

They backed away, and were suddenly aware that all down the slope below them were other remnants of battle. Bodies, everywhere, most of them shaven-headed, snarling, mutilated men, many with a pointed star cut into their foreheads. Here and there a bulkier figure in heavy armour, horned helmets, dismembered limbs, entrails underfoot about which the flies buzzed in black clouds.

'They fought here,' the man said. 'They fought here for the high ground.'

The boy, with the curiosity of youth, seemed less afraid than his father. He had found a large firearm, almost as long as himself, and was trying to lift it out of its glutinous glue of mud and blood.

'Leave that alone!'

'But Pa!'

'That's an Astartes weapon.' The man knelt and peered at it, wiping the metal gingerly with one gloved hand. 'Look – see the double-headed eagle on the barrel – that's the badge of the Imperium. The Space Marines fought here, on this hill. These are the dead of the great enemy lying around us, heretics cursed by the Emperor. The Astartes saved us from them.'

'Saved us,' the boy repeated grumpily. He pointed at the burning city down in the valley. 'Look at Dendrekken. It's all burnt and blown up.'

'Better that than under the fist of the Dark Powers, believe me,' the man said, straightening. 'It's getting dark. We've come far enough for one day. Tomorrow we'll try and get down to the city, and see who else is left.'

That night, shivering beside their campfire amid the bodies of the dead, the boy lay awake staring at the night sky. The clouds had cleared, and he was able to see the familiar constellations overhead. Now and again he saw a shooting star, and now and again he was sure he saw other things gliding in the dark between the stars. New constellations glittered, moving in formation. He found himself wondering about those who lived out there in that blackness, travelling in their city-sized ships from system to system, bearing the eagle of the Imperium, carrying weapons like the massive bolter he had found upon the battlefield. What must it be like, to live like that?

He got up in the middle hours of the night, too restless and hungry for sleep. Stepping away from the fire, he clicked on his little battered torch, an old wind-up contraption he had had since he was a toddler. He walked out upon the rocky, blasted slope upon which the bodies of the dead lay contorted and rotting, and felt no fear, only a sense of wonder, and a profound restlessness. He picked his way down the slope and apart from his yellow band of torchlight there was no other radiance in the world save for the stars.

And one other thing. Off to his left he caught sight of something which came and went, an infinitesimal red glow. Intrigued, he made his way towards it, sliding his knife out of the sheath at his waist. He crouched and padded forwards, as quiet as when hunting in these same hills with his father's old lasgun. Several times the light died altogether, but he was patient, and waited until he could see it again. It was at the foot of a looming, broken crag which stood up black against the stars.

Something half-buried in rubble, but still with a shine to it that reflected back the torchlight. It was a helmet, huge, fit for a giant. It looked almost like a massive skull. In the eye-sockets were two lenses, one cracked and broken, and the other with that flickering scarlet light oozing out of it. The boy knelt down and gently tapped the helmet with the butt of his knife. There was a hiss of static, and the thing moved slightly, making him spring backwards in fright. He saw then that it was not just a helmet. Buried in the fallen stone there was a body attached to the helm. Off to one side lay a massive hemispherical shape – the boy could have sat in it – and painted upon it in white was the symbol of a double-headed axe. A shoulder-guard made for a giant.

The boy scraped and scratched frantically at the stones, levering away the looser ones, uncovering more and more of the buried figure. There was a gleam of silver below the helm, and he saw that he had unearthed shining wings engraved upon a mighty breastplate, and in the centre of the wings, a skull emblem. He stared, open-mouthed. This was no

Chaos fiend, no armoured heretic. He had found one of *them*, one of the Astartes his father talked about.

A fallen angel, he thought.

'Pa!' he shouted. 'Pa, come here quick and see this!'

It took them most of the remainder of the night to uncover the buried giant. As dawn broke, and the relentless rain began again, so the water washed the mud and caked filth and blood from its armour, making it gleam in the sunrise. Dark blue metal, as dark as an evening sky, save for the white silver wings on the chest. The boy and his father knelt, panting before it. The armour was dented and broken in places, and loose wiring sprang out of gashes in the metal. There were bullet-holes in the thigh, and here and there plates had been buckled out of shape by some inconceivable force, bent out of place; the heavy dark paint scraped off them so they could see the bare alloy underneath.

The boy's father wiped his brow, streaking it with mud. 'Help me with the helmet, boy – let's see if we can get a look at him.'

They felt around the helmet seal with their fingertips, that savage visage staring up at them, immobile. The boy's quicker fingers found the two pressure points first. There were two clicks, and a hiss, then a loud crack. Between the two of them they levered up the mass of metal, and eased it off. It rolled to one side, clinking on the stones, and they found themselves staring at the face of an Astartes.

The skin was pale, as though it seldom saw the sun, stretched tight across a huge-boned skull, long and somehow horse-like. It was recognisably human, but out of scale, like the face of a great statue. A metal stud was embedded above one colourless eyebrow. The head was shaved, criss-crossed with old scars, though a bristle of dark hair had begun to regrow on it. The right eye was gone – he had been shot through the lens of his helmet – but the hole was already healed, a ragged whorl of red tissue.

Then the left eye opened.

The boy and his father tumbled backwards, away from the glare of the eye. The giant stirred, his arm coming up and then falling back again. A rasping growl came up from somewhere deep in the barrel-wide chest, and the legs quivered. Then the giant groaned, and was still again, but now his teeth were bared and clenched – white, strong teeth which looked as though they could snap off a hand. He spoke, a slur of pain-filled words.

The boy's father approached the giant on hands and knees. 'You're among friends here. We're trying to help you, lord. The fighting is over. The enemy is gone. Can you hear me?'

The eye, bloodshot and as blue as midwinter ice, came to rest on the boy's father. 'My brothers,' the giant said. 'Where are they?' His voice was deep, the accent so strange that the boy could barely understand him.

'They've gone. I saw the great ship leave orbit myself, six days ago.'

A deep snarl, a cross between rage and grief. Again, the helpless movement of the massive limbs.

'Help me. I must stand.'

They tried, tugging at the cold metal armour. They managed to get him sitting upright. His gauntleted hand scrabbled at the rubble.

'My bolter.'

'It's not here – it must be buried, as you were. We had to dig you out.'

He could not raise himself. The single eye blinked. The Astartes spat, and his spittle spattered against the rocks, bright with blood.

'My armour is dead. We must get it off. Help me. I will show you what to do.'

The rain came lashing down. They struggled in the muck and gravel around the giant, clicking off one piece after another of the armour which enclosed him. The boy could not lift any of them, strong though he was. His father grunted and sweated, corded muscles standing out along his arms and chest, as he set each piece of the dark blue carapace to one side. The massive breastplate almost defeated them all, and when it came free the giant snarled with pain. As it fell away, slick, mucus-covered cables slid out of his torso along with it, and when they sucked free, the boy saw that his chest was pocked with metal sockets embedded in his very flesh. The armour had been part of him.

He had been shot through the thigh, but the wound was almost closed. It was a raised, angry lump, in the midst of which was a suppurating hole. The Astartes looked at it, frowning. 'Something's in there. My system should have fixed it by now.' He probed the hole with one finger, teeth bared against the pain, and raised his bloody pus-covered digit to his face and sniffed at it. 'Something bad.' He put a knuckle to his empty eye-socket. 'It feels hot. I have infection in me.' His voice held a note of incredulity. 'This should not be.' He thought for a moment. 'They used chemical agents in the fighting. Maybe biological too. It would seem my system has been compromised.'

The Astartes looked at the man who knelt by him. 'I must rejoin my brethren. I need a deep space comms link. Do you know where there would be such a thing?'

The boy's father tugged at his lower lip. 'In the city, at the spaceport I suppose. But the city is pretty much destroyed. There may be nothing left.'

The Astartes nodded again. Something like humanity came into his surviving eye. 'I remember. Our deep strike teams made planetfall not far from the landing fields. The Thunderhawks took out positions all up and down the pads. They had drop-ships there, three of them. We got them all.'

'Who were they, lord, if I might ask?'

The Astartes smiled, though the effect was less humorous than ferocious on that massive, brutal face. 'Those who brought us here were the enemies of Man – a Chaos faction my Chapter has been charged with eradicating for decades now. They call themselves the *Punishers*. They meant to take over your world and use it as a bridgehead to conquer the rest of the system. My brothers and I saved you from that fate.'

'You destroyed my world,' the boy said, high and shrill with anger. 'You didn't save anything – you burnt us to ash!'

The giant regarded him gravely. 'Yes, we did. But I promise you that the Punishers would have done worse, had they been allowed. Your people would have been cattle to them, mere sport for the vilest appetites imaginable. Those who died quickly would have been the lucky ones. You will rebuild your world – it may take twenty years, but you can do it. Had it been tainted by Chaos, there would have been nothing for it but to scald it down to the very guts of the planet, and leave it an airless cinder.'

The man grasped his son's arm. 'He's young – he knows nothing.'

'Well, consider this part of his education,' the Astartes snapped. 'Now find me something we can use to splint my leg – and something to lean on that will take my weight. I must get mobile – and I need a weapon.'

Their search took much of the day, until finally they hit upon dismantling one of the discarded weapons lying on the battlefield and using the recoil rod within the firing mechanism to splint the Astartes's thigh. As he tied it tight about his lacerated flesh with lengths of wire, the giant ground his teeth, and pus popped out of the hot red wound in his leg. The boy's father retrieved the Imperium weapon his son had found the day before. The Astartes's eyes lit up as he saw it, then narrowed again as he popped the magazine and checked the seat of the rounds within. 'Maybe thirty, if we're lucky. Well, a working bolter is worth something. Now hand me that pole.'

The pole was part of the innards of one of the great biomechanical carcasses which littered the field. The Astartes regarded it with disgust, wiping it clean with wet soil and sand. He used it as a staff, and was finally able to lever himself upright. In his free fist he held the bolter. He found its weight hard to manage in his weakened state however, and so fashioned a sling from more gleaned wire so that he might let it swing at his side. The wire of the sling cut into his shoulder, slicing the skin, but he seemed not to feel the pain.

'It'll be dark soon,' the boy's father said. 'We should perhaps stay here another night and then set off at dawn.'

'No time,' the Astartes said. Now that he was upright he seemed even huger, half as tall again as the man in front of him, his hands as big as shovels, his chest as wide as a dining table. 'I see in the dark. You can follow me.' With that, he set off, hobbling down the slopes of the shattered hillside to the valley below, where the sun was setting in a maelstrom of black cloud and toiling pillars of even blacker smoke, still rising from the stricken city that was their destination.

* * *

They walked half the night. The ground they traversed was broken by great bombardments and littered with the wreckage of war machines, some tracked, some wheeled, and some it seemed fashioned with arms and legs. They stopped once beside a great burnt-out carcass which squatted as tall as a building. So shot to pieces was it that its original shape could hardly be made out, but the Astartes limped up to it and carefully, reverently clicked off a metal seal with a tattered remnant of parchment still clinging to it. He bowed his head over this relic. 'Ah, brother,' he whispered.

'What is it?' the boy asked, even as his father tried to hush him.

'One of my battle-brothers; a spirit so bold, so fine, he chose to be encased in this mighty Dreadnought after his own body was destroyed, to carry on the fight, to stay with us, his brethren. His friends. His name was Geherran. He was with my company, and saved us from these–' Here the Astartes gestured at the other wrecks which stood round about, evil, crab-like structures adorned with all manner of ordnance, emblazoned with sickening symbols, '–these defilers. Abominations of Chaos. He broke them, took their heaviest fire upon himself so we might bring them down one by one.'

The Astartes blinked his one eye, then straightened, and limped on without another word.

The boy and his father followed him through a graveyard of the great machines, awed by their size, and the way in which they had been blasted to pieces where they stood. As the planet's two moons began to rise, it seemed they were in the midst of some ancient arena, where the dead had been left forgotten in mounds about them. But the dead were all twisted, snarling, white-faced and putrid. In the moons' light, it did not do to look at them too closely.

They entered the suburbs of the city and began to encounter signs of life. Rats flickered and squealed amid avalanches of rubble, and here and there a dog growled at them from the deepest shadows, eyes alight with madness, luminous foam dripping from its jaws. Once, a stream of cockroaches, each as big as a man's fist, went chittering across their path, dragging some unidentifiable chunk of carrion with them as they went. The Astartes watched them go thoughtfully, hefting the bolter.

'Such creatures are not native to this world, am I right?'

The boy's father was wide-eyed. 'Not that I have heard.'

'Something has been happening here. My brothers would not have left this world again so quickly unless there was a good reason. My guess is something called them out of orbit. A secondary threat of some kind.'

'You think they destroyed all the enemy down here on the surface?'

'We do not leave jobs half done.'

'How do you know?' the boy piped up. 'You were buried under a ton of stone, dead to the world. They left you behind.'

The Astartes turned, and in his eye they could see a light not unlike that in the dog's caught by lamplight. But he said nothing. The boy was cuffed across the back of his head by his father.

They moved on, more slowly now, for the Astartes was straining to keep his massive firearm at the ready. An ordinary man would struggle to lift, let alone fire it. His metal staff clicked against the plascrete underfoot, and stones skittered aside as his feet found their way. Watching him, the boy realised that the giant was near the end of his strength, and now he noticed also that the Astartes was leaving a thickly stippled trail of dark liquid in his wake. He was bleeding to death. He pointed this out to his father, who grasped up at the giant's arm.

'Your leg – you must let me look at it.'

'My systems should have taken care of it. I am infected. Some kind of bio-agent. I can feel it in my skull, like red-hot worms writhing behind my eyes. I need an Apothecary.' The Astartes was panting heavily. 'How far to the spaceport?'

'Another four or five kilometres.'

'Then I will rest, for now. We must find somewhere to lay up until daylight. I don't like this place, these ruins. There is something here.'

'No bodies,' the boy said, making his companions stare at him. He shrugged. 'Where are all the dead people? There's nothing but vermin left.'

'Lean on me,' the boy's father said to the ailing giant. 'There are houses on our right, up ahead, and they look more intact. We'll find one with a roof.'

By they time they bedded down for what remained of the darkness the Astartes was shivering uncontrollably, though his skin was almost too hot to touch. They gathered rainwater out of puddles and broken crockery and sipped enough of the black, disgusting liquid to moisten their mouths. The air was full of smoke and soot which left a gritty taste on the tongue and there were sparks flying in the midst of the reek.

'The fires are up north, towards the spaceport,' the boy's father said, rubbing his aching shoulder.

The Astartes nodded. He stroked the bolter in his lap as though it comforted him. 'It may be best if I go on alone,' he said.

'My other shoulder is still good enough to lean on.'

The giant smiled. 'What are you, a farmer?'

'I was. I had cattle. Now I have rocks and ash.'

'And a son, who still lives.'

'For now,' the man said, and he looked at the filthy, pinched face of his son, who lay sleeping like an abandoned orphan, wrapped in the charred rags of a blanket on the floor.

'Think of him, then – you have accompanied me far enough.'

'Yes,' the boy's father said dryly. 'And you are in such tremendous shape. You want rid of us because you think something bad is up ahead, at the spaceport, and you want to spare us.'

The giant inclined his head. 'Fighting is my life, not yours.'

'Something tells me this thing is not over. Your brothers overlooked something when they left. This is my world we are on – I will help you fight for it. There is nothing behind me but burnt earth, anyway.'

'So be it,' the Astartes said. 'At daybreak we will walk out together.'

Daybreak did not come. Instead there was only a slight lightening of the darkness, and in the sky ahead, a glow which had nothing to do with the colour of flame. The two moons were setting amid oceans of smoke, and the smoke itself was tinted on its underside, a colour like the underbelly of a maggot.

The Astartes rose unaided. His remaining eye seemed to have sunk into his skull, so that it was but a single gimlet gleam in his soot-blackened face. He cast aside his iron staff and stood upright as the pus ran yellow and pink from his swollen leg. The agony of it brought the sweat running down his forehead, but his face was impassive, at peace.

'The Emperor watch over us,' he said quietly as the boy and his father rose in turn, rubbing their smarting eyes. 'We must be quick and quiet now, like hunters.'

The three set off.

The scream burst ahead of them like a fire in the night, a tearing shriek which rose to the limits of human capacity, and then was cut off. There was a murmur, as of a distant engine, heavy machinery moving. And when it stopped they heard another sound, murmuring through the heavy smoke and the preternatural darkness. Voices, many voices chanting in unison.

The three of them went to ground in a burning house as the gledes and coals of the rafters spat and showered them. Some hissed as they landed on the sweat of the Astartes's back, but he did not so much as twitch.

'Cultists,' he said, listening. 'They're at the work of the warp, some ceremony or sorcery.'

His two companions stared at him, uncomprehending.

'Followers of the Dark Powers,' he explained, 'gulled or tortured into subservience. They are fodder for our guns.' Carefully, he unloaded the magazine from his bolter, eyed the rounds, and then kissed the cold metal before reloading. He eased back the cocking handle with a double click, like the lock of a door going back and forth.

'How far to the spaceport now?'

'We're almost on it,' the man told him. He was gripping his son's shoulder until his knuckles showed white. 'Up ahead the road turns to the right, and there's a gate, and walls – the spaceport is within.'

'I doubt the walls still stand,' the Astartes said with grim humour.

'There's a guardpost and a small barracks for the militia just within the gate – and an armoury out back, by the control tower. Ammunition, lasguns.'

'Lasguns,' the Astartes said with a kind of contempt. 'I am used to heavier metal, my friend. But it may be worth checking out. We need something to up our killing power. From here in, you stay close to me, both of you.'

He sprang up, and was off with barely a limp. With astonishing speed he sprinted to the end of the street and disappeared into the shell of the last house on the right. After a moment's hesitation, the man and his son got up and followed him.

He was right – the walls had been blasted away. In fact most of the buildings on this side of the spaceport lay in ruins, and the landing pads themselves were cratered with massive shell-holes and littered with the debris of all sorts of orbital craft. At the western end, three tall towers of twisted wreckage stood out, the smoke wreathing them, fires still burning deep in their tangled hulls.

'Punisher drop pods' the Astartes said. 'We got all three.'

'There's another one,' the boy spoke up, pointing.

They peered together, squinting in the smoke. The boy was right. A fourth, undamaged drop pod was squatting to the east, where the damage to the landing pads was less severe. Infantry was marching down its ramps.

The Astartes's face creased with hatred. 'It would seem my brothers and I were not as thorough as we thought. We must get word to my company, or your planet will fall to the enemy after all. We must have comms!'

'It'll be in the control tower, out yonder – if it's still intact,' the man said, jerking his head to the north. Dimly through the smoke they could make out a pale white pillar with a cluster of grey plascrete buildings around its foot. There seemed to be no enemy activity out in that direction, but with the smoke and gathering darkness it was hard to be sure.

'Then that is where we go,' the Astartes said simply. 'My brothers must be brought back to this world to cleanse it – or else they will have to extinguish it from space – get down!' This last was in a hiss. A troop of enemy infantry marched past. Strange, angular bald-headed men with heavily tattooed faces. They wore long leather coats adorned with studs and chains and what seemed to be human body parts. They bore lasguns, and chattered and snarled incessantly as they passed by.

'Their talk hurts my ears,' the boy said, rubbing his head.

'The warp infects them,' the Astartes told him. 'If we cannot cleanse this place, then it will begin to infect the remainder of your people.' He lifted a hand to the wound where his eye had been, then dropped it again. 'To the tower, then.'

They ran, right into the heart of the foul-smelling smoke. The boy became dizzy, and found it hard to breathe, and the distant chanting of the cultists seemed to cloud over his thinking. He faltered, and found himself standing still, staring vacantly, aware that he was missing something.

Then he found himself lifted into the air and crushed against an enormous, fever-hot body. The Astartes had picked him up and tucked him under his free arm, still running.

Out of nowhere a cluster of pale faces appeared in the smoke. Before they could even raise their weapons the Astartes was upon them. A kick broke the ribcage of one and sent him hurtling off into the darkness. The heavy bolter was swung like a club and smashed the heads of two more into red ruin, almost decapitating them. The fourth got off a red burst of lasgun fire that spiked out harmlessly into the air, before the Astartes, dropping the boy, had him by the throat. He crushed the man's windpipe with one quick clench of his fist, and tossed him aside.

'Get with the weapons,' he said to the man and the boy, panting. 'Grenades, anything.' He bent over and coughed, and a gout of dark liquid sprayed out of his mouth to splatter all over the plascrete landing strip. He swayed for a second, then straightened. When his companions had retrieved two lasguns and a sling of grenades from the bodies he nodded. 'Someone may have seen that las-fire. If we run into more of them, do not stop – keep running.'

They set off again. The giant was hobbling now, and left a trail of blood behind him, but he still set a fearsome pace, and it was all the man and his son could do to keep up with him, as they fought for air in the reeking hell that surrounded them.

At last the white pillar of the control tower appeared out of the smoke – and a band of cultists at its foot. They saw the shapes come running out of the darkness at them and set up a kind of shriek and began firing wildly. Las-fire came arcing through the air.

In return the Astartes halted, set the bolter in his shoulder, and began firing.

Short bursts, no more, two or three rounds at a time. But when the heavy ordnance hit the cultists it blew them apart. He took down eight of them before the first las-burst hit him, in the stomach. He staggered, and the bolter-muzzle dropped, but a second later he had raised it again and blew to pieces the cultist who had shot him.

The boy and his father lay on the ground and started firing also, but the heavy Chaos lasguns were unwieldy and hard to handle – their shots went wild. The boy fumbled with the sling of grenades and popped out one thumb-sized bomb. There was a tiny red button at the top of the little cylinder. He pressed it, and then tossed the thing at the cultists. It clinked on the base of the tower and lay at their feet. One looked at it with dawning horror on his face, and then the grenade exploded, and splattered him in scarlet fragments across the white painted wall of the control tower, along with three of his comrades.

The rest broke and ran, quickly disappearing into the toiling darkness. The Astartes sank to one knee, leaning on his bolter. His other hand was bunched in a fist where the lasgun had burnt a black hole through his torso from front to back.

'You need my shoulder again, I think,' the man said, helping up the maimed giant. 'Not far to go now. Lean on me, my friend. I will get you there.'

The Astartes managed a strangled laugh, but said no more.

They found the door ajar, a tall steel affair whose command-box had been blown out. The man made as if to enter but the Astartes held him back. 'Grenade first,' he rasped.

The boy tossed another of the little explosives inside. He was smiling as he did so, and when the thing went off, he laughed.

'I am glad everyone finds this so amusing,' his father said, as he stepped inside.

Two dead bodies, blown to pieces in the confined chamber at the base of the tower. There was an elevator, but the boy punched its buttons in vain.

'No power, Pa,' he said. 'The whole place is dead.'

'Stairs,' the Astartes gasped.

'Listen,' the man said. 'Outside – can you hear it?'

A confused babel, a roaring, bellowing sound of voices, some shrill, some deep. Even as they listened, it grew louder.

'Get the door closed,' the Astartes snapped. 'Block it, jam it – use anything you can.'

They slammed the heavy steel door shut, and piled up whatever they could find in the way of wreckage and furniture against it. The Astartes, with an agonised cry, wrenched a stretch of iron piping free of the wall and wedged it against the steel. Seconds later, the cacophony of voices was right outside, and they were hammering on the door. Gunfire sounded, and shells rang loudly against the metal.

'That won't hold them,' the man said. He and his son were white-faced, and sweat was cutting stripes down the grime on their faces.

'Up,' the Astartes said impatiently. 'We must go up. You first, then your boy. I will hold the rear. Any sounds ahead of you, start firing and keep firing.'

'We're trapped here,' the man said unsteadily.

'Move!' the giant barked.

The stairs wound round the inside of the tower like the thread of a screw. They laboured up them in almost pitch darkness, the sound of their own harsh breathing magnified by the plascrete to left and right, their feet sounding hollow on the metal steps. Several times the Astartes paused to listen as they ascended, and once he ordered them to halt.

'Anyone got a light?' he asked.

'I have,' the boy said. There was a whirring sound, and then a feeble glow began, yellow and flickering. It strengthened as the boy kept winding up his torch.

'Good for you,' the Astartes said. 'Give me those grenades.' He popped one out of the sling and peered at it.

'They copy us in everything – these are just like Imperium charges. They have three settings: instant, delay and proximity. The most obvious one is delay, the red button on top – give thanks to the Emperor you picked that one back outside. You twist the top of the cylinder for the other settings.' He did so. 'Move up the stairs.' He set down the little cylinder upright, pressed the red button on its top, and then followed them. Behind him there were three tiny clicks, and then silence.

'The next thing to approach that is going to have a surprise. I just hope there are no rats in here. Move out.'

Round the tower they went by the flickering glow of the boy's clockwork torch. Finally they came to another steel door. It was very slightly ajar, and there were voices on the far side. The boy reached for the grenades, but the Astartes stopped him. 'We need this place intact. Get behind me.'

He kicked open the door and there was a roar of bolter fire, a stuttering series of flashes, and then a click as the bolter's magazine came up empty. The Astartes roared and lunged forward.

Behind him, the boy and his father burst through the doorway, coughing on the cordite stink that filled the space beyond. They were in a large circular room filled with consoles and monitors, with huge windows that overlooked the entire spaceport. A trio of cultists lay dead, their innards scattered like red streamers across the electronic wall-consoles of the tower. On the far side of the room, a titanic battle was raging, smashing back and forth, sending chairs flying, filling the air with broken glass. The Astartes was struggling with a dark, armoured figure almost as massive as himself, and the two were grappling with each other, bellowing like two bulls intent on mayhem. The boy and his father stood staring, lasguns almost forgotten in their hands.

The Astartes was knocked clear across the room. He crashed into the heavy blast-proof glass of the tower and the impact spidered it out in a web of cracks. His adversary straightened, and there was the sound of horrible, unhinged laughter.

'Brother Marine!' the voice gargled, 'You have not come dressed for the occasion! Where is your blue livery now, Dark Hunter? Can't you see you are on the wrong world? This place is ours now!'

The speaker was clad in power armour similar to that they had found the Astartes wearing, but it was bone-white in colour, and a black skeleton had been picked out upon it with ebony inlays. Its bearer wore a helm adorned with two great horns, and the light from his eye sockets glowed sickening green. The many-arrowed star of Chaos had been engraved on his breastplate, and in his hand he held a cruel monomolecular blade which shone with blood.

'How many of you are left now, heretic?' the Adeptus Astartes spat. 'My brothers will wipe you from this system as a man wipes shit from the sole of his boot.'

'Big words, from the mouth of a cripple,' the Chaos warrior snarled. He drew a bolt pistol from its holster and aimed it at the Astartes's head.

The boy and his father both raised their lasguns and fired in the same moment. The man missed, but his son's burst caught the enemy warrior just under the armpit. The fearsome figure cried out in pain and anger, and dropped the knife. The pistol swung round.

'What are these, brother – pets of yours? They need chastising.'

He opened fire. The pistol bucked in his hand and the impact of the heavy rounds sent the boy's father smashing back against the wall behind, ripping open his chest and filling the air with gore. The Chaos warrior stepped forward, still firing, and the bolter shells blew open the wall in a line of explosions as he followed the flight of the boy, who had dropped his lasgun and was scrabbling on hands and knees for the shelter of the consoles. The magazine clicked dry, and the warrior flicked it free, reaching in his belt for another one. 'Such vermin on this world – they must be exterminated to the last squealing morsel.'

'I agree,' the Astartes said.

The Chaos warrior spun round, and was staggered backwards by the force of the blow. He fell full length on his back. Dropping his pistol, his hands came up to his chest to find the hilt of his knife buried in his own breastplate. There was a thin, almost inaudible whine as the filament blade continued to vibrate deep in his body cavity.

The Astartes, his face a swollen mask of blood, dropped to his knees beside his prone enemy.

'We have two hearts each, you and me,' he said. 'That is how we are made. We were created for the betterment of man, to make this galaxy a place of order and peace.' He gripped the knife blade, slapping his struggling adversary's hands aside, and pulled the weapon free. A thin jet of blood sprang out, and the Chaos warrior grunted in agony.

'Let me see if I can find that second heart,' the Astartes said, and he plunged the knife downwards again.

The boy crept out of his hiding place and crouched by the mangled remains of his father. His face was blank, wide eyes in a filthy blood-spattered mask. He closed his father's staring eyes and clenched his own teeth on a sob. The he stood up and retrieved his lasgun.

The Astartes was lying by the wall in a pool of his own blood, his dead enemy sprawled beside him. His body was white as ivory, and the blood leaking from his wounds had slowed to a trickle. He looked up at the boy with his remaining eye. They stared at one another for a moment.

'Help me up,' the Astartes said at last, and the boy somehow climbed behind him and pushed his immense torso upright.

'Your father–' the Astartes began, and then there was a dull boom from below them.

'The grenade,' the boy said dully. 'They're on the stairs.'

'Toss another one down there and then lock the door,' the Astartes said. 'Bring me over that bolt pistol when you're done.'

'What's the point?' the boy asked, sullen. His eyes were red and bloodshot. He looked like a little old man, shrunken and defeated.

'Do as I say,' the Astartes cracked out, glaring. 'It's not over while we live, not for us, not for your world. Now toss the grenade!'

The boy looked round the door.

'There's movement on the stairs,' he said, calm now. He pressed the red button on the explosive and threw it down the stairs. It bounced and clinked and clicked as it went down the steps. He shut the heavy metal door and slid the bar-lock in place. Another boom, closer than the first. There were screams below them, and the floor quivered. The boy handed the Astartes the bolt pistol, and the giant ripped the ammo belt off the fallen Chaos Marine, clicking in a fresh magazine and cocking the weapon.

'I've found the comms,' the boy said, across the room. He flicked several switches up and down. 'At least I think so – it looks like a comms unit anyway. But it's dead. There's no power.'

The Astartes laboured over to the boy on his hands and knees. Blood dripped out of his mouth and nose and ears. He sounded as though he were breathing through water.

'Yes, that's it. Old-fashioned. But it still needs power.' He sighed deeply. 'Well, that's that then.'

The boy stared at the dead lights on the console. He was frowning. He did not even start when the first battering began on the door to the control room, and a slavering and snarling on the other side of it, as though a herd of beasts milled there.

'Power,' he said. 'I have power – I have power here.' His face quickened. 'My torch!'

He drew it out of the bag of oddments at his waist. 'I can attach it – I can plug it in and get it running!'

The Astartes drew himself up and sat on the creaking chair before the console. 'A fine idea, but you'll never crank up enough power with that little hand-held dynamo.'

'There must be something!'

They stared at the dead array of lights and switches before them. The comms unit was a relic, a patched up antique for use on a far-flung border world. The Astartes's good eye narrowed.

'Plug in your torch and start winding,' he said.

'But–'

'Just do it!' He scrabbled open the wooden drawer below the console, while behind them both, blow after heavy blow was rained down on the door to the chamber. The lock-bar bent inwards. A chorus of cackles and growls sounded on the other side, like the memory of a fevered nightmare.

'Sometimes they hang on to the most obsolete of technologies on worlds like yours,' the Astartes said. He smiled. 'Because they still work.' From a tangle of junk in the drawer, he produced a contraption of wires and a small knobbed device. He stared at it, considering a moment, and then set it up on the bench, plugging it into the adaptor socket. Immediately, a small green light came on within it.

'Built to last,' he muttered. He closed his eye, and then began tapping down on the device. A high series of clicks and tones was audible. He adjusted the frequency with an ancient circular dial, and there was a faint crackle.

The two of them were so intent, the boy turning the handle on his creaking torch, the giant tapping away on the strange device, that they were almost oblivious to the grinding and banging at the room's door.

'Is it working?' the boy asked.

'The signal is going out. The code is ancient; a relic of old Earth, but we still use it in my Chapter, for its simplicity. It is elegant, older even than the Imperium itself. But like many simple, elegant things in this universe, it has endured.'

The Space Marine stopped his tapping. 'Enough. We must see if we can get you out of here.'

'There's no way out,' the boy said.

'There's always a way out,' the Astartes told him. He turned and fired at the plexi-glass of the control tower. It shattered and cascaded in an avalanche of jagged shards. Then he reached into the console drawer with a fist and produced a long coil of dull coppery wire.

'It will slice your hands as you go down,' he said to the boy, 'but you must hold on. When you get to the bottom, start running.'

'What about you?'

The Space Marine smiled. 'I will be on the other end. Now do it.'

The door burst open, and was flung back against the wall with a clang. A huge figure loomed out of the darkness, and more were behind it.

The Astartes was slumped by the huge broken maw of the plexiglass window, a glint of wire wrapped round one arm, disappearing into the smoky vacancy beyond. He bared his teeth in a rictus.

'What kept you?' he asked the hulking shapes as they advanced on him. Then he raised his free arm and fired a full magazine from the bolt pistol into the intruders. Screams and yowls rent the air, and the foremost two shapes were blasted off their feet.

But more were behind them. The howling mob in the doorway poured into the room, firing bolters as they came, the heavy rounds blasting everything to pieces.

* * *

Away from the tortured little world, the vastness of hanging space was utterly silent, peaceful, but in the midst of that peace tiny flowers of light bloomed, white and yellow, lasting only an instant before lack of oxygen snuffed them out. From a distance – a great distance – they seemed minute and beautiful, brief jewels in the blackness. Closer to, the story was different.

There were craft floating in the blackness, immense structures of steel and ceramite and titanium and a thousand other alloys, constructed with an eye to utility, to endurance. Made for destruction. They looked like vast airborne temples created for the worship of a deranged god, kilometres long, their flanks bristling with turrets and batteries. About them, smaller craft wheeled and dove like flycatchers on the hide of a rhino.

Within the largest of these craft an assemblage of giants stood clad in shining dark blue armour, unhelmed, their pale faces reflecting back the distant infernos that were on the viewscreens to their front. All around them, travesties of man and machine worked silently, murmuring into their stations, hands of flesh working in harmony with limbs of steel and muti-hued wiring. Incense hung in the air, mixed with the unmistakable fragrance of gun-oil.

'You're sure of this, brother?' one of the giant figures said, not turning his head from the scenes of kinetic mayhem on the screens about him.

'Yes, captain. The signal lasted only some forty-five seconds, but there was no doubting its content. Several of my comms-techs know the old code, as do the Adeptus Mechanicus. It is a survival from ancient days.'

'And the content of the message?'

'One phrase, repeated again and again. Captain, the phrase was *Umbra Sumus*.'

At this, all the standing figures started and turned towards the speaker. They were all two and a half metres high, clad in midnight-blue armour. All had the white symbol of the double-headed axe on one of their shoulderguards. They carried their helms in the crook of their arms, and bolt-pistols were holstered on their thighs.

'Mardius, are you sure – that is what it said?'

'Yes, captain. I have triple checked. The signal was logged and recorded.'

The captain drew in a sharp breath. 'The motto of our order.'

'*We are shadows*. Yes, captain. No Punisher would ever utter those words – the hatred they feel for the Dark Hunters is too great. It is my belief one or more of our brethren sent it from the surface of the planet; he was contacting us in the only way he could. Or warning us.'

'The signal cut off, you say?'

'It was very faint. It may have been cut off or it may merely have passed out of our range-width. We are too far away to scan the planet. The signal itself took the better part of ten days to reach us.'

'Brother Avriel,' the captain snapped. 'Who was unaccounted for after we left the surface?'

Another of the giants stepped forward. 'Brother Pieter. No trace was found of him. We would have searched longer, but–'

'But the Punishers had to be pursued. Quite right, Avriel. No blame is attached to my query. It was the priority at the time.' The captain stared up at one of the giant screens again. Within the massive nave of the starship, there was almost silence, except for the clicks and muttering of the adepts at their posts.

'No other communications from planetside?'

'None whatsoever, captain. Their infrastructure was comprehensively destroyed during our assault, and it was a backwater to begin with. One spaceport, and nothing but suborbital craft across the whole planet.'

'Yes, yes, I am aware of the facts of the campaign, Avriel.' The captain frowned, the studs on his brow almost disappearing in the folds of scarred flesh there. At last he looked up.

'This engagement here is almost concluded. The Punisher flotilla has been crippled and well nigh destroyed. As soon as we have finished off the last of their strike craft we will turn about, and set a course for Perreken.'

'Go back?' one of the Astartes said. 'But it's been weeks. If it was Pieter–'

'Avriel,' the captain snapped, 'What is our estimated journey time to the planet?'

'At best speed, some thirty-six days, captain.'

'Emperor guide us, that's a long time to leave a Brother Marine alone,' one of the others said.

'We do this not just for our brother,' the captain told them. 'If any taint of Chaos has remained on the planet then it must be burnt out, or our mission in this system will have utterly failed. We return to Perreken, brothers – in force.'

The ceremony was almost complete. For weeks the cultists and their champions had danced and prayed and chanted and wept. Now their mission was close to its fruition. Across the plascrete of the landing pads, a dark stain had grown. This was no burn mark, no sear of energy weapon or bombardment crater. Within its shadow the ground bubbled like soup left too long on a stove. It steamed and groaned, cracking upwards, segments of plascrete floating on the unquiet surface. The screaming chant of the cultists reached a new level, one that human ears could barely comprehend. Hundreds of them were gathered around the unquiet, desecrated stain of earth.

'Hold your fire until I give the word,' the boy said, and up and down the line the order was passed along. In a series of impact craters to the east of the spaceport scores of men and women lay hidden by the broken rubble. They were a tatterdemalion band of ragged figures weighed down by bandoliers of ammunition and a bewildering assortment of weaponry, some modern and well-kept, some ancient and worn-out. Once, a long time ago it seemed now, they had been civilians, non-combatants. But now that distinction had ceased to exist on Perreken.

A black-bearded man who lay beside the boy was chewing on his thumbnail nervously. 'If we've got this wrong, then all of us will die here today,' he said.

'That is why I didn't get it wrong,' the boy said. He turned to stare at his companion and the black-bearded man looked away, unable to meet those eyes.

Almost three months had passed since the boy had slid down a piece of wire held by a dead Space Marine. In that time he had broadened, grown taller, and yet more gaunt. The flesh of his face had been stripped back to the bone by hunger and exhaustion, and his eyes were blank with the look of a man who has seen too much. Despite his youth, no one questioned his leadership. It was as if his fellow fighters recognised something unique in him, something none of the rest of them possessed.

The boy held an Astartes bolt pistol in his hands, and as he lay there in the crater with the rank sweat of fear filling the air around him, he bent his head and kissed the double-headed eagle on the barrel. Then he fumbled in the canvas satchel at his side and produced a mess of wires and a little control panel. A green light burned on the heavy battery still in the satchel.

'Send it,' he said to the black-bearded man. 'It's time.'

His companion began tapping clicks out on the elderly wired contraption. 'May the Emperor smile on us today,' he muttered. 'And may His Angels arrive on time.'

'When the Astartes say they will do something, they do it,' the boy said. 'They gave their word. They will be here.'

Across the landing fields, the cultists were dancing and stamping and screaming their way into a frenzy. Some of the madly cavorting figures had once been smallholders and blacksmiths and businessmen, friends and neighbours of the ragged guerrillas who lay in wait among the craters to the east. Now they had been turned into chattels of the Dark Gods, worshippers of that which drew its strength from the warp. And now the warp had stirred them into a kind of ecstasy, and it fed off their worship, their blood-sacrifices. The patch of ground which they circled darkened further, popping and undulating as though cooked on some great invisible flame.

And inside that roiling cauldron, something stirred. There was a momentary glimpse of something breaking the surface, like the fin of a great whale at sea. The earth spat upwards, as though trying to escape whatever writhed beneath it. The cultists went into paroxysms, prostrating themselves, shrieking until the blood vessels in their throats burst and sprayed the air with their life fluids. Farther back from the edge, the armour-clad champions of their kind stood and stamped and clashed power swords against their breastplates. The darkness thickened over them all like a shroud.

The boy lay and watched them with his face disfigured by hatred and fear. Up and down the line there was a murmur as his fellow fighters brought their weapons into their shoulders. Some were priming homemade bombs, others were checking magazines. They were an underfed, rancid, ill-equipped band, but they held their position with real discipline, waiting for their young leader's word.

I did that, the boy thought. I made them like this. I am good at it.

He could barely remember a time now when he had been a mere farm boy, living on a green planet where the skies were blue and there was fresh food to be had, clean water to drink. He could barely even remember his father. That boy who had known a father was someone else, from another time. All he could remember now was the endless smoke-shrouded landscape, the constant fear, the explosions of bloody violence, the carnage. And the face of the Astartes who had died while helping him to live. That, he could not forget.

Nor could he forget the moment of sheer bubbling joy and relief when the ancient comms device he had found in the city had proved to work as well as that which they had found in the control tower. One of the older men knew the ancient code by heart and taught it to him. When the first message had come clicking back at them from a far-flung starship on the other side of the system it had seemed like a benediction from the God-Emperor Himself. It was enough to engender hope, to help him recruit fighters from the shattered survivors of the population. They had lived like rats, scavenging, scurrying for weeks and then months in the ruins of their world. Until today. Today they would stand up and take it back.

That was the plan.

The boy clambered to his feet just as the battery-fed contraption in the satchel clicked by itself in a sharp staccato final message.

An incoming message.

The boy smiled. 'Open fire!' he shouted.

And all around him hell erupted.

The chanting of the cultists faltered. They looked up, distracted, angry, shocked. The first volley cut down almost a hundred. Then the ragged guerrillas followed the boy's lead and charged forward across the broken plascrete of the landing field, firing as they came and yelling at the top of their voices.

The ring of cultists opened up, fraying under the shock of the assault.

But there were many hundreds more of them further west by their drop pods. These now set up a cacophony of fury, and began running eastwards to meet the attack.

The boy went to one knee, picking his targets calmly, firing two or three rounds into each. The enemy formation had splintered – they were confused, scattered, but in their midst their champions were restoring discipline quickly, shooting the more panicked of their underlings, roaring at the rest to stand fast.

Now, the boy thought. *It must be now.*

In the sky above the spaceport, eye-blinding lights appeared, lancing even through the heavy smoke and the preternatural night. With them came a sullen, earth-trembling roar.

In an explosion of concrete and soil, a behemoth thundered to earth. It was dozens of metres tall, painted midnight blue, and on its multifaceted sides was painted the sigil of the double-headed axe. It scattered the cultists through the air with the force of its impact, and in its wake came another, and another, and then two more. It was as if a series of great metal castles had suddenly been hurled to earth.

With a scream of straining metal, long hatches fell down from the sides of these monstrous apparitions, as though they were the petals opening on a flower. These hatches hit the ground and buried themselves in earth and shattered stone and the bodies of the screaming cultists, becoming ramps. And down the ramps came an army, a host of armour-clad warriors blazing a bloody path with the automatic fire of bolters, meltaguns, plasma rifles and rocket launchers. In their midst hulking Dreadnoughts strode, picking up the cultist champions in their clawed fists and tossing them away like discarded rags. They belched flame as they came, incinerating the cultists, boiling their flesh within their armour, making of them black desiccated statues.

And overhead the engines of destruction swooped down to unloose cargoes of bombs on the unholy stain which the Chaos minions had inflicted upon the tortured planet. As they went off, so in their brilliant light something bestial and immense could be seen twisting and thrashing in its last agonies. It sank down below the level of the plascrete launch pad as though below the surface of a lake, bellowing, and as the missiles rained down on it, so the blackened earth became solid again, and the stain became that of normal charred earth and stone, the desecration lifted before it could be consummated.

The boy stood with his bolt pistol forgotten in his hands, staring at that great storm of fire, a scene like the ending of a world. He felt the concussion of the shells beat at the air in his very lungs, and the heat of them crackled the hair on his head, but he stood oblivious. Tears shone in his eyes as he watched the obliteration of those who had destroyed his home, and in that moment there was only a single thought in his mind.

He stared at the massive, fearsome ranks of the advancing Space Marines, and thought: this is me – this is what I want to be.

Thus did the Dark Hunters Chapter of the Adeptus Astartes return to the planet of Perreken, to save a world, and to retrieve the remains of one of their own.

MASTER IMUS'S TRANSGRESSION

Dan Abnett

'I suppose,' he sniffed, 'you get a lot of cases like mine.'

The officer did not reply. In the ten minutes since Master Imus had been received, the officer had made very few remarks, except to announce his credentials and ask a few general questions.

Master Imus had presented himself, of his own free volition, at the portico of the dark, unfriendly building late that afternoon. He had been invited to wait in an anteroom off the inner yard.

The anteroom was cold and forlorn. The fretful fingers of individuals previously invited to wait there had marked the white plaster with a greasy patina, and pacing feet had worn the wooden floor. There were no windows, but light poked in through a trio of dingy filters. From outside, faraway, Master Imus could hear the street noises of workers flooding home to their habs and their evening meals.

Master Imus sat in one of the old wooden chairs provided.

A clerk attended him first. The clerk led Master Imus through to a side office panelled in dark wood, and sat him at a small desk. The clerk was hunched over with the weight of the stenogram built into his chest. He sat on a stool, handed Master Imus a form, and told him to read out the questions printed on it and answer them in his own words. As Master Imus spoke, haltingly at first, the clerk's bird-foot hands pecked over the keys of the stenogram and recorded his comments. The stenogram clattered like an adding machine, a sound that made Master Imus feel exceptionally sad.

When the form was completed, the clerk left the office, and was replaced, after a few minutes, by a second clerk. The second clerk led Master Imus into a chamber that smelled of machine heat, and was cluttered with banks of whirring cogitators.

The second clerk examined Master Imus's papers, and copied them on one of the cogitators. Several versions of Master Imus's biographical particulars flashed up on the multiple screens for a moment and then faded into a dull, green glow. This slow, silent dissolution of all he was seemed unpleasantly symbolic to Master Imus.

He was taken back to the anteroom, and left alone again. The daylight was ebbing. A small lamp had been lit in his absence. Master Imus waited for twenty minutes, and then the officer arrived.

'Johan Imus?' the officer asked as he entered the room, reading from a dataslate.

Master Imus stood up. 'That's me, sir,' he said.

The officer was a tall, well-made man with dark hair. He was dressed, and this came as no surprise to Johan Imus, in black clothes and a black leather coat. The officer looked Master Imus up and down with unforthcoming eyes, and announced his credentials with a cursory wave of his rosette.

'You have been received for inspection. Follow me, please,' he said.

Master Imus followed him obediently. He followed him across the twilit yard, in through an archway, and up an endless flight of varnished stairs. The officer opened a door, and ushered Master Imus into a small room. The room had a large, ornamental fireplace that looked as if it had not seen a fire in centuries. A guilt clock ticked on the mantle. There was a rug on the wooden floor, and two plain chairs on either side of a desk. An armchair stood in one corner, a comfortable and friendly item of furniture that Master Imus never got to sit in.

They took their seats on either side of the desk.

'What is the nature of the crime you are confessing?' the officer asked, after studying the data-slate for a few minutes.

'Not a crime, as such,' Master Imus replied hastily.

'No?'

'A transgression. Yes, transgression, that is a better word altogether.'

'The nature of the transgression, then?'

'I have already explained this,' Master Imus offered, 'to the clerk.'

The officer scrolled back through the slate's files. 'Have you born false witness to this statement as I read it?'

'No, sir.'

'Were you coerced, invited or urged to make this report?'

'No, sir,' Master Imus said. 'I have come here of my own free volition. I... I said as much.'

'That is noted here, strenuously. You made that point several times during the preliminary examinations.'

'I simply wanted it to be clear,' said Master Imus. 'I was persuaded to come here by my own conscience, nothing else.'

The officer was silent for a moment. 'You say you have been suborned by the Ruinous Powers, drawn into their evil, and set upon an unholy task?'

Master Imus nodded. 'I suppose,' he sniffed, 'you get a lot of cases like mine.'

Everything must be held carefully to account, stated Johan Imus. I am an indentured book-keeper and a citizen of Imperial Hesperus, the latter an honour I hold even more dear than my work at Slocha and Daviov et Cie. My father was keeper of books for Slocha and Daviov, and his before him. My work, like theirs, involves the ennumeration of company accounts, the allocation of funds, the scrutiny of audits, and the day to day upkeep of financial income and outgoings. I have held my post for sixty two years, and run a department of eighteen under-keepers. No, I have no wife. No kin to speak of. My work is my life.

Slocha and Daviov? An illustrious auction house, surely you've heard of it? Well, it maintains offices in the Garcel Commercia, just off the Place 14th Jaumier. In the main, we deal with antique furnishings, silks, Sameterware, Brashin monaquins, and fine arts. The sale rooms are on Varsensson's Street, beside the lifter depot. There are open fare sales every Mainsday, and specialist auctions every other Solday. Occasionally, we hold irregular fetes for particular customers or particular treasures. Last Gorgonsday, we offered a list that included eight small ouslite busts by Sambriano Kelchi and a series of humaniques from the jokaero ruins on Tornish.

No sir, I am no connoisseur. My salary does not provide me with the funds to collect or speculate. But funds are my business. I am painstaking and exact in my work. I would never wish to cause Master Slocha or Master Daviov professional embarrasment by misplacing a decimal point or wrongly adding a column of figures.

This is why I have come. I do not make mistakes.

Ah, well, now you ask, we come to the meat of it, I suppose. Last Solday I set out to review the quarterly accounts. The year end looms, and the Imperial tithe statements must be returned correctly. I found an error. Well, not an error so much as an abberation. Something that could not be accounted for. It was an idle annoyance at first, but the more I studied the pages of the ledger, the more peculiar it became.

There was a void, you see. A void: a gap or empty place in the flow of the accounts that defied explanation. It was as if a page or two was missing from my ledger.

No, not at all. This was the master ledger. Only I had access to it.

Sir, you belittle my craft with such a question. I keep books, and I have kept books my whole life. I am a creature of accuracy. It was not simply a matter of a creeping error, a stray sub-total. There were figures missing. Simply missing. And yet, a page or two on, the books balanced, seamlessly, as if there had been no hole.

This is what I mean by the word 'void'. Numbers are my language, my life. I know when they are lying. There was a void in the accounts, and the more I struggled to identify it, the more the figures hid it from me. It was as if they were closing ranks to conceal the truth.

Why have I come to you with a book-keeping error? Sir, again you mock me. It was no error. I reviewed and recalculated. I redid the accounts eight times. As I added to this column and subtracted from that, the numbers began to betray me. They became numbers that I did not understand.

Sir, I believe I have calculated something that should not be. I believe I have found the Number of Ruin.

He regarded Master Johan Imus for a moment. Such a small man, shrivelled by age, his sparrow bones lost in heavy robes that had evidently been cut to fit his father or his grandfather. The guilt clock ticked on the mantle. Its face had no hands, a simple ordo trick. The constant, measured ticking was all that mattered. Tock, tock, tock, flicking time away without a trace of its passage on the enammelled face. Guilt got them all in the end.

Imus possessed a small, neat face with a wide, slit mouth that might have revealed a toothy grin had the circumstances been different. His hair was straggly and white, and he wore half moon eye glasses. His knuckles bulged with arthritis.

'The Number of Ruin?' asked the officer.

Imus nodded. 'That is my transgression. Will it be painless?'

'Will what be painless?'

Imus struggled. 'My punishment. I presume... well, censure is inadequate. Will it be burning? Poison?'

The officer had been making notes in a small copy book. He dipped his pen into the desk's power well.

'Do you believe you have committed a crime, sir?' he asked.

'No, no not at all. But I believe I have become a crime. I am a criminal thing.'

'I see.'

Master Imus sat forward and adjusted his eye-glasses. 'I see you are quite a young man, sir. Will this have to go to a superior?'

'My superior?'

'Yes, sir. I imagine something this grave-'

'My master's name is Hapshant. He is indisposed, an old ailment. I hold the rank of interrogator, as I told you. I can deal with this matter.'

'Oh, good. That's good. Very good. So, how will you proceed?'

The officer stared at Master Imus. 'Forgive me, Imus, you don't seem alarmed at all by this process.'

'Alarmed?' Imus echoed. 'Of course I'm alarmed. I'm terrified. I've been terrified of this day all my life.'

'Why?'

'Because it happens to us all, sooner or later, doesn't it? Every day of my working life, I have walked to work up Sarum Street, and come by this place, so dark and unfriendly. I never pass it without a shudder. It is mortality. It is the fate that awaits us all should we cross the line. Do you think it was easy coming here today? No, sir. It has taken me a week to find the confidence. This afternoon, as I raised my hand to rap at the door, my courage almost fled. But I am a true citizen of Imperial Hesperus. I am a true son of the Emperor. It was my duty to report this, no matter what fate awaits me.'

The officer nodded. The clock ticked.

'Tell me what you understand by "the Number of Ruin",' said the officer.

Master Imus sat back and shrugged. 'It is an impossible number, an abomination. It is a notation of filthy power. Numbers own power, you see. My father raised me to respect three and seven, thirteen and the triple sixes, the primes, the constants. But the Number of Ruin, that is the number of-'

'Of?'

'Of the warp,' Imus whispered, looking to one side and then the other as if in fear of being overheard.

The officer nodded his head. 'So Hapshant has taught me. Can you show me the number? Can you write it down?'

'Are you mad?'

'This room is warded and I am armed. Can you show me the number?' Master Imus took a dataslate from his robe pocket. It was battered and worn from use. He activated it and entered a series of digits into the display.

'There are the accounts,' he said, pausing before handing the slate over. 'I have selected the key section. Please be careful.'

The officer held out his hand. 'Show it to me, please, sir.'

Master Imus hesitated. 'What did you say your name was, young man?'

'Eisenhorn,' the officer replied. 'Interrogator Eisenhorn of the Emperor's Holy Ordos. Why?'

'Please, please be careful with this, Interrogator Eisenhorn.'

Master Imus handed the old data-slate to the officer. The officer looked at the screen with a slight frown.

The guilt clock stopped ticking. A strange silence filled the room.

'I-' the officer began to say, and caught fire. Blue flames, as hot as a burner torch, consumed his skin and roasted the flesh off his bones until nothing remained except dripping, blackened meat and a charred skull wrenched into a rictus by heat-tightened sinews. The data-slate dropped onto the desk from a smoking, skeletal hand with a thump. The officer's clothing was untouched.

The flames guttered out and the scorched corpse slumped forward with a crack of dry ligaments. Imus got up and backed away. His eyes were wide. He fought back a terrible desire to urinate.

'Someone,' he murmured, 'someone, anyone... help me!' He reached the door, and tried to open it, but it was locked. He knocked on it, gingerly, as if hoping someone on the other side might open it without being put to too much trouble.

A hand took his arm. 'Please sit down, Master Imus,' the officer said.

Master Imus started rather badly and recoiled with such surprise he banged his elbows and the back of his head against the door. The officer, who was not burned in any way, was standing in front of him.

'Master Imus?'

Master Imus began to shake. Then he started to hiccup. He continued to stare at the officer.

'What did you see?' the officer asked.

'You were on fire,' replied Master Imus. 'You caught fire. The fire burned you until you were dead!'

'Master Imus?'

Johan Imus repeated his previous commentary, this time forcing his voice to actually make some sounds.

'Ah,' said the officer, 'an illusion, that's all, necessary to the work.'

'Necessary?' asked Master Imus. 'Necessary how? To what work?'

'To my work.' The officer gestured towards the chair Imus had vacated. He paused. His tone became more sympathetic. 'I apologise. I have shaken you, haven't I?'

Master Imus shrugged and managed a small, dry laugh. 'Indeed. I have never seen a man combust before. I have never even seen a man die. How was the illusion done? What was the point of frightening me?'

The officer's sympathetic air melted. 'I'm not about to answer any questions, sir. All the questions will be mine.'

There were a great many of them. They came at Master Imus so rapidly, he became rather flustered. The officer asked him the names of his parents, and his votation numeral, and inquired of his political leanings. He asked Master Imus to account for his whereabouts on certains dates stretching back two years. He asked if Master Imus could operate a cogitator, if he held keys to the auction house premises, if he had ever been off-world, and where his family orignated from.

Master Imus attempted to answer as best he could. Sometimes a new question came at him before the last answer had been completely recited.

Is there a record of public misdemeanors in your family? How long have you resided at your current address? Can you detail your diet in general terms? Are you receiving medicae treatment for any ailment? Have you ever been to Ausolberg? How many languages do you speak? How many languages do you read? Do you dream? What do you dream about? How often do you attend templum services? Have you ever taken the Standard Psykana Test? Have you ever been in trouble before?'

'Am I in trouble now?' asked Master Imus.

He was made to wait in the anteroom again. Night had fallen. The lamp, almost out of prometheum, fluttered valiantly.

The officer came to get him, and led him out into the street. The evening was warm and humid. Master Imus could smell the roasting and poaching and frying underway in the kitchens of the local eating houses. A few pedestrians passed by along the pavement under the street lamps.

'Where are we going?' Master Imus asked.

'What did I tell you about questions?' the officer asked.

Master Imus pursed his lips and shrugged.

Two men joined them from the dark building. One was an old, shuffling being in long, dark robes. The other was a young man, of an age and mode of dress that matched the officer's. This man was more handsome, however, more genial in his countenance.

'Is this the fellow?' he asked.

The officer nodded.

'Let's process this, Gregor,' the man requested. 'I had plans for tonight.'

They walked off down the street. The officer and the other young man walked on either side of Master Imus, like an escort of gaolers walking a convict to the scaffold. The old, hunched man followed them.

'We will inspect your hab,' the officer said.

'Of course,' said Master Imus. 'It's not far.'

Master Imus took out his keys and opened the deadbolts of his door one by one. A baby was crying loudly on the floor below, and the stairwell was pungent with the odour of steamed cabbage. Mistress Elver, from down the landing, came out and made a point of sweeping her front step so she could get a good look at the dark men Master Imus had brought home with him.

As Master Imus finished the business of unlocking, the officer's companion turned to look at Mistress Elver.

'Are these your eyes, goodwife?' he called. 'I found them in the back of my head.'

Mistress Elver bridled and went inside. The young man laughed.

'Don't start, Titus,' the officer said.

The other man leaned against the wall. 'Nosey old bitch,' he remarked.

'Forty-eight,' said the old man lurking behind them.

'Forty-eight what?' asked the officer, turning.

'Steps. Two flights of twenty-four. Asquar spruce, not local. Vitrian glass in the lamp housings, though some of them have been replaced by cheaper alternatives.'

'And this is pertinent how?' inquired the young man called Titus.

The old man shrugged with a bionic hiss. 'Oh, it's not.'

Master Imus opened the door. He felt rather ashamed of the musty smell that breathed out of the doorway.

The officer produced a docket. 'Sign this,' he told Master Imus.

'What is it?':

'A waiver. Interrogator Endor and I are about to search your residence.'

Master Imus initialled the docket.

The two interrogators entered the hab. Master Imus followed them, and the old man shuffled in behind him.

The old man sniffed. 'Sec vinegar,' he said.

'What?' asked Master Imus.

'Sec vinegar, and kayleaf.'

'I use the vinegar to clean my fingers,' said Master Imus. 'It's the only thing that gets the ink out.'

'The only thing that gets the ink out,' the old man repeated.

'And I use kayleaf, in a paste, to re-grind my quills.'

'You don't smoke it then?' asked the old man.

'Smoke it? Why?'

'As a balm against rheumatic inflammation?'

'No.'

'Ah,' the old man said. He shuffled fowards into the living room, his legs creaking like a servitor's. He was terribly hunched, and his augmetic eyewear clicked as it hunted. 'You should. It's very medicinal. It would help your hip.'

'My hip?' asked Master Imus.

'You walk with a slight counter rotation. Two centimetres short on each right step. You shuffle, sir. I presume it is rheumatism.'

Master Imus felt quite dismayed. These three men had intruded into his home. The officer was in his bedroom, overturning the mattress. The other man, Endor, was in the little side kitchen, sniffing the contents of various jars. No one new had been inside Master Imus's hab for years. It felt like a violation.

'Are you the inquisitor?' Master Imus asked.

'Me? Bless you, no,' replied the old man. 'Why would you think that?'

'I just assumed...'

The old man shuffled over to the sideboard. 'Fuse-fit sampwood. No maker's mark. A vase.'

He picked the vase up.

'Please be careful,' Master Imus said.

The old man ignored him. He held the vase in his spindly fingers. 'Sameterware. Third Dynasty.' He looked inside it. 'Oh, paper clips.'

The officer came back from the bedroom holding several books. 'You have books,' he said.

'Is there something wrong with that?' asked Master Imus.

'You like poetry?'

'The Early Imperials. The Tacits. Is that a crime?'

'This is,' said Endor. He walked in from the side kitchen with something in his hand. There was an ugly, almost triumphant grin on his face. Master Imus realised that what he first registered as handsome in the features of the officer's companion was in fact a cruel arrogance. Interrogator Endor was accustomed to winning.

'What is it?' asked the officer.

'Buried at the bottom of a jar of caffiene,' Endor replied. He held out his hand. Six little pills lay in his palm.

'Yellodes,' he said.

'Most perturbatory,' said the old man.

'They're not mine,' said Master Imus.

Master Imus sat on the threadbare couch tugging at his robe.

'They're not mine. Not mine, not at all. I don't use that sort of thing. I wouldn't even know how to get that sort of thing.'

'Zespair Street, or the dealers that frequent the depot,' said the old man.

'Be quiet, Aemos,' said the officer. He stared down at Master Imus. 'This is a bad turn of events for you. It compounds things.'

'They're not mine. How many times do I have to say it?'

'They were in your kitchen,' said Endor, who seemed to be relishing Master Imus's discomfort.

'I didn't put them there.'

'Oh, so someone just came in and hid them in your caffiene, did they?'

'That must be it. I can think of no other explanation.'

'I've had enough. Let's process him.'

'Slow down, Titus,' said the officer.

'He's up to his ears in it.'

'Slow down, I said.'

'I had plans for tonight,' Titus Endor scowled.

'Fantastic for you. Give me the tablets.'

Endor tipped the yellodes into the officer's hand. The offcer sat down on the couch next to Master Imus.

'Get lost,' he told his companions. Endor went out onto the landing to smoke a lho-stick. The old man shuffled away to examine the books in the bedroom.

'I'll be frank. This is going badly for you, sir,' the officer explained to Master Imus.

'I realise that.'

'The matter of the accounts is the main thing. But the yellodes. They complicate the matter.'

'I understand.'

'They are a prohibited substance. That's the first thing. The second thing is, they're yellodes.'

'I don't know what you mean,' said Master Imus.

'This isn't the first time I've inspected an individual's hab and found evidence of drug use. Obscura, gladstones, that sort of business. But yellodes... they're mind expanders. We typically find them in circumstances connected to cult activity.'

'Cult?'

'We often find them used in association with prohibited texts and deviant knowledge. A man who has the Number of Ruin might use yellodes to help him fathom it and master its use.'

Master Imus put his head in his hands.

'They're not mine.'

'Is the *Ur-Saker* yours?'

'The what?'

'I found it between the Frobisher and the early Tacits in your bedroom.'

'I don't know what an *Ur-Saker* is. I don't know it's significance.'

'It's a proscribed text. It defines the methodological use of psychotropic drugs in gnomic enlightenment. So that was just placed there too, was it? Someone just put it there?'

'They must have done!'

The officer sighed. 'Master Imus, you brought a matter to our attention, a serious matter. The numbers you showed me in the ledger are quite pernicious.'

'And I came of my own free volition! Remember that!'

'I do, and that leaves me with two possibilities. You are a practising heretic with a pathological desire to be caught and condemned.'

'Or?'

'Or, Master Imus, you have been set up to take the fall for someone. There's one last thing I would like to do. It's necessary, for my work.'

'What is it, sir?' asked Master Imus.

The officer turned to look at him. His face was no longer human. It was a snout of rancid, gnashing teeth, spatulate and broad, with sharp edges. The snout opened, drooling spit, and seemed about to bite Master Imus's face clean off. Master Johan Imus smelled the pit-stink of the warp, and the shadows of dark places where no human ever willingly walked. He saw a monstrous horror lunging at him, pallid tentacles whipping up out of the distended throat. He cried out in fear and wet himself.

'I'm sorry I had to do that, Master Imus,' said the officer, wiping his mouth.

Titus Endor came in from the stairhead. 'Throne, Gregor. I felt that.'

'Sorry. Would you and Aemos please stay here and tidy the place? And help Master Imus to get cleaned up?'

'I had plans for tonight,' replied Endor.

'And now I have plans of my own,' said the officer.

* * *

Titus Endor stayed until midnight, and then made some vague excuse and left. The old man remained with Master Imus until dawn. They played regicide, and talked of antiques.

The officer returned at first light. 'The matter is settled,' he said. 'Thank you for your cooperation.'

When Master Imus went to work the next day, he found that Slocha and Daviov et Cie had been closed down. *With immediate effect and until further notice*, the seal on the door said.

Most of the staff had gathered in the street, bewildered and dispondent.

'Master Slocha was shot,' muttered one of the underkeepers.

'He was shot last night by the Inquisition,' another confirmed.

'Oh dear!' said Master Imus.

Three days later, the officer called on Master Imus at his hab.

'Sit down, please,' said Master Imus.

'I've come to tell you that you've been formally cleared of all charges.'

'Even my transgression?'

'Even that.'

'I'm very relieved,' said Master Imus.

'Your employer was conducting bad business, heretical business, in fact. He was engaged in the importation of illicit texts under the cover of the auction house's primary dealings. We'd been after him for a year. We had no proof of his activities.'

'I see.'

'Your employer knew we were on to him, of course. He set you up to act as a distraction. He wanted us to concentrate on you instead of him. And we would have, if you hadn't been so honest as to bring the matter to our attention.'

'Did you kill Master Slocha?' asked Johan Imus.

'I'm afraid I did.' The officer rose. 'Well, I must be on my way.'

'What happens now?' asked Master Imus.

'What do you mean?'

'I have no job to go to. The auction house is finished. What will become of me?'

'I'm sorry, sir. That's not my problem.'

The officer turned to leave.

'I think I might be allowed to ask one question, in all fairness,' said Master Imus.

'Ask it.'

'Why was it necessary?'

'Why was what necesary?' asked the officer.

'Why was it necessary to scare me?'

'Fear simplifies the mind, Master Imus. It is so strong and pure, it quite empties the head and removes all barriers and falsehoods. I scared you so I could read the truth inside you, the honest part of you that you could not dissemble. I'm sorry about that.'

'You're a psyker, then?' Master Imus asked.

Yes.

'Ah. I see. If you can read into the future, tell me... I have no job, and no references. I am too old and set in my ways to retrain. I have no means of support. I came forward of my own free volition, helped you hunt out a heretic, and proved my innocence, and I am left the poorer for it. What do I do now?'

I'm a mind-reader, not a clairvoyant.

'Right. Thank you for your candour anyway.'

'Goodbye, Master Imus.'

Interrogator Eisenhorn closed the door behind him.

Master Imus sat on the threadbare couch. From the floor below, he could hear a baby crying. He could hear the knock of the landlord, going from hab to hab for the week's rent. Master Imus's rent dues were in the sideboard drawer. This week's, and the next's, but nothing more.

Master Imus was glad he had come forward, and glad he had spoken out. Duty was duty, after all. He tried to inflate some sense of civic pride in his heart.

But he wished, more than anything, he had just kept himself to himself.

THE LONG GAMES AT CARCHARIAS

Rob Sanders

The end began with the *Revenant Rex*.

An interstellar beast. Bad omen of omens. A wanderer: she was a regular visitor to this part of the segmentum. The hulk was a drifting gravity well of twisted rock and metal. Vessels from disparate and distant races nestled, broken-backed amongst mineral deposits from beyond the galaxy's borders and ice frozen from before the beginning of time. A demented logic engine at the heart of the hulk – like a tormented dreamer – guided the nightmare path of the beast through the dark void of Imperial sectors, alien empires of the Eastern Fringe and the riftspace of erupting maelstroms. Then, as if suddenly awoken from a fevered sleep, the daemon cogitator would initiate the countdown sequence of an ancient and weary warp drive. The planetkiller would disappear with the expediency of an answered prayer, destined to drift up upon the shores of some other bedevilled sector, hundreds of light years away.

The *Revenant Rex* beat the Aurora Chapter at Schindelgheist, the Angels Eradicant over at Theta Reticuli and the White Scars at the Martyrpeake. Unfortunately the hulk was too colossal and the timeframes too erratic for the cleanse-and-burn efforts of the Adeptus Astartes to succeed: but Chapter pride and zealotry ensured their superhuman efforts regardless. The behemoth was infested with greenskins of the Iron Klaw Clan – that had spent the past millennia visiting hit-and-run mayhem on systems across the segmentum, with abandoned warbands colonising planetary badlands like a green, galactic plague. The Warfleet Ultima, where it could gather craft in sufficient time and numbers, had twice attempted to destroy the gargantuan hulk. The combined firepower of hundreds of Navy vessels had also failed to destroy the beast, simply serving to enhance its hideous melange further.

All these things and more had preyed upon Elias Artegall's conscience when the *Revenant Rex* tumbled into the Gilead Sector. Arch-Deacon Urbanto. Rear Admiral Darracq. Overlord Gordius. Zimner, the High Magos Retroenginericus. Grand Master Karmyne of the Angels Eradicant. Artegall had either received them or received astrotelepathic messages from them all.

'Chapter Master, the xenos threat cannot be tolerated…'

'The Mercantile Gilead have reported the loss of thirty bulk freighters…'

'Master Artegall, the greenskins are already out of control in the Despot Stars…'

'That vessel could harbour ancient technological secrets that could benefit the future of mankind…'

'You must avenge us, brother…'

The spirehalls of the Slaughterhorn had echoed with their demands and insistence. But to war was a Space Marine's prerogative. Did not Lord Guilliman state on the steps of the Plaza Ptolemy: 'There is but one of the Emperor's Angels for every world in the Imperium; but one drop of Adeptus Astartes blood for every Imperial citizen. Judge the necessity to spill such a precious commodity with care and if it must be spilt, spill it wisely, my battle-brothers.'

Unlike the Scars or the Auroras, Artegall's Crimson Consuls were not given to competitive rivalry. Artegall did not desire success because others had failed. Serving at the pleasure of the primarch was not a tournament spectacle and the *Revenant Rex* was not an opportunistic arena. In the end, Artegall let his battered copy of the Codex Astartes decide. In those much-thumbed pages lay the wisdom of greater men than he: as ever, Artegall put his trust in their skill and experience. He chose a passage that reflected his final judgement and included it in both his correspondence to his far-flung petitioners and his address to the Crimson Consuls, First Company on board the battle-barge *Incarnadine Ecliptic*.

'From *Codicil CC-LXXX-IV.ii: The Coda of Balthus Dardanus, 17th Lord of Macragge* – entitled *Staunch Supremacies.* "For our enemies will bring us to battle on the caprice of chance. The alien and the renegade are the vagaries of the galaxy incarnate. What can we truly know or would want to of their ways or motivations? They are to us as the rabid wolf at the closed door that knows not even its own mind. Be that door. Be the simplicity of the steadfast and unchanging: the barrier between what is known and the unknowable. Let the Imperium of Man realise its manifold destiny within while without its mindless foes dash themselves against the constancy of our adamantium. In such uniformity of practice and purpose lies the perpetuity of mankind." May Guilliman be with you.'

'And with you,' Captain Bolinvar and his crimson-clad First Company Terminator Marines had returned. But the primarch had not been with them and Bolinvar and one hundred veteran sons of Carcharias had been forsaken.

Artegall sat alone in his private Tactical Chancelorium, among the cold ivory of his throne. The Chancelorium formed the very pinnacle of the Slaughterhorn – the Crimson Consuls fortress-monastery – which in turn formed the spirepeak of Hive Niveous, the Carcharian capital city. The throne was constructed from the colossal bones of shaggy, shovel-tusk Stegodonts, hunted by Carcharian ancestors, out on the Dry-blind. Without his armour the Chapter Master felt small and vulnerable in the huge throne – a sensation usually alien to an Adeptus Astartes' very being. The chamber was comfortably gelid and Artegall sat in his woollen robes, elbow to knee and fist to chin, like some crumbling statue from Terran antiquity.

The Chancelorium began to rumble and this startled the troubled Chapter Master. The crimson-darkness swirl of the marble floor began to part in front of him and the trapdoor admitted a rising platform upon which juddered two Chapter serfs in their own zoster robes. They flanked a huge brass pict-caster that squatted dormant between them. The serfs were purebred Carcharians with their fat, projecting noses, wide nostrils and thick brows. These on top of stocky, muscular frames, barrel torsos and thick arms decorated with crude tattoos and scar-markings. Perfectly adapted for life in the frozen underhive.

'Where is your master, the Chamber Castellan?' Artegall demanded of the bondsmen. The first hailed his Chapter Master with a fist to the aquila represented on the Crimson Consuls crest of his robes.

'Returned presently from the underhive, my lord – at your request – with the Lord Apothecary,' the serf answered solemnly. The second activated the pict-caster, bringing forth the crystal screen's grainy picture.

'We have word from the Master of the Fleet, Master Artegall,' the serf informed him.

Standing before Artegall was an image of Hecton Lambert, Master of the Crimson Consuls fleet. The Space Marine commander was on the bridge of the strike cruiser *Anno Tenebris*, high above the gleaming, glacial world of Carcharias.

'Hecton, what news?' Artegall put to him without the usual formality of a greeting.

'My master: nothing but the gravest news,' the Crimson Consul told him. 'As you know, we have been out of contact with Captain Bolinvar and the *Incarnadine Ecliptic* for days. A brief flash on one of our scopes prompted me to despatch the frigate *Herald Angel* with orders to locate the *Ecliptic* and report back. Twelve hours into their search they intercepted the following pict-cast, which they transmitted to the *Anno Tenebris*, and which I now dutifully transmit to you. My lord, with this every man on board sends his deepest sympathies. May Guilliman be with you.'

'And with you,' Artegall mouthed absently, rising out of the throne. He took a disbelieving step towards the broad screen of the pict-caster. Brother Lambert disappeared and was replaced by a static-laced image, harsh light and excruciating noise. The vague outline of a Crimson Consuls Space Marine could be made out. There were sparks and fires in the background, as well as the silhouettes of injured Space Marines and Chapter serfs stumbling blind and injured through the smoke and bedlam. The Astartes identified himself but his name and rank were garbled in the intruding static of the transmission.

'...this is the battle-barge *Incarnadine Ecliptic*, two days out of Morriga. I am now ranking battle-brother. We have sustained critical damage...' The screen erupted with light and interference.

Then: 'Captain Bolinvar went in with the first wave. Xenos resistance was heavy. Primitive booby traps. Explosives. Wall-to-wall green flesh and small arms. By the primarch, losses were minimal; my injuries, though, necessitated my return to the *Ecliptic*. The captain was brave and through the use of squad rotations, heavy flamers and teleporters our Consul Terminators managed to punch through to an enginarium with a power signature. We could all hear the countdown, even over the vox. Fearing that the *Revenant Rex* was about to make a warp jump I begged the captain to return. I begged him, but he transmitted that the only way to end the hulk and stop the madness was to sabotage the warp drive.'

Once again the lone Space Marine became enveloped in an ominous, growing brightness. 'His final transmission identified the warp engine as active but already sabotaged. He said the logic engine wasn't counting down to a jump... Then, the *Revenant Rex*, it – it just, exploded. The sentry ships were caught in the blast wave and the *Ecliptic* wrecked.'

A serf clutching some heinous wound to his face staggered into the reporting Space Marine. 'Go! To the pods,' he roared at him. Then he returned his attention to the transmission. 'We saw it all. Detonation of the warp engines must have caused some kind of immaterium anomaly. Moments after the hulk blew apart, fragments and debris from the explosion – including our sentry ships – were sucked back through a collapsing empyrean vortex before disappearing altogether. We managed to haul off but are losing power and have been caught in the gravitational pull of a nearby star. Techmarine Hereward has declared the battle-barge unsalvageable. With our orbit decaying I have ordered all surviving Adeptus Astartes and Chapter serfs to the saviour pods. Perhaps some may break free. I fear our chances are slim... May Guilliman be with us...'

As the screen glared with light from the damning star and clouded over with static, Artegall felt like he'd been speared through the gut. He could taste blood in his mouth: the copper tang of lives lost. One hundred Crimson Consuls. The Emperor's Angels under his command. The

Chapter's best fighting supermen, gone with the irreplaceable seed of their genetic heritage. Thousands of years of combined battle experience lost to the Imperium. The Chapter's entire inheritance of Tactical Dreadnought Armour: every suit a priceless relic in its own right. The venerable *Ecliptic*. A veteran battle-barge of countless engagements and a piece of Caracharias among the stars. All gone. All claimed by the oblivion of the warp or cremated across the blazing surface of a nearby sun.

'You must avenge us, brother–'

Artegall reached back for his throne but missed and staggered. Someone caught him, slipping their shoulders underneath one of his huge arms. It was Baldwin. He'd been standing behind Artegall, soaking up the tragedy like his Chapter Master. The Space Marine's weight alone should have crushed the Chamber Castellan, but Baldwin was little more than a mind and a grafted, grizzled face on a robe-swathed brass chassis. The serf's hydraulics sighed as he took his master's bulk.

'My lord,' Baldwin began in his metallic burr.

'Baldwin, I lost them...' Artegall managed, his face a mask of stricken denial. With a clockwork clunk of gears and pistons the Chamber Castellan turned on the two serfs flanking the pict-caster.

'Begone!' he told them, his savage command echoing around the bronze walls of the Chancelorium. As the bondsmen thumped their fists into their aquilas and left, Baldwin helped his master to the cool bone of his throne. Artegall stared at the serf with unseeing eyes. They had been recruited together as savage underhivers and netted, kicking and pounding, from the fighting pits and tribal stomping grounds of the abhuman-haunted catacombs of Hive Niveous. But whereas Artegall had passed tissue compatibility and become a Neophyte, Baldwin had fallen at the first hurdle. Deemed unsuitable for surgical enhancement, the young hiver was inducted as a Chapter serf and had served the Crimson Consuls ever since. As personal servant, Baldwin had travelled the galaxy with his superhuman master.

As the decades passed, Artegall's engineered immortality and fighting prowess brought him promotion, while Baldwin's all-too-human body brought him the pain and limitation of old age. When Elias Artegall became the Crimson Consuls' Chapter Master, Baldwin wanted to serve on as his Chamber Castellan. As one century became the next, the underhiver exchanged his wasted frame for an engineered immortality of his own: the brass bulk of cylinders, hydraulics and exo-skeletal appendages that whirred and droned before the throne. Only the serf's kindly face and sharp mind remained.

Baldwin stood by as Artegall's body sagged against the cathedra arm and his face contorted with silent rage. It fell with futility before screwing up again with the bottomless fury only an Adeptus Astartes could feel for his foes and himself. Before him the Crimson Consul could see the faces of men with whom he'd served. Battle-brothers who had been his parrying arm when his own had been employed in death-dealing; Space Marines who had shared with him the small eternities of deep space patrol and deathworld ambush; friends and loyal brethren.

'I sent them,' he hissed through the perfection of his gritted teeth.

'It is as you said to them, my lord. As the Codex commanded.'

'Condemned them…'

'They were the door that kept the rabid wolf at bay. The adamantium upon which our enemies must be dashed.'

Artegall didn't seem to hear him: 'I walked them into a trap.'

'What is a space hulk if it not be such a thing? The sector is safe. The Imperium lives on. Such an honour is not without cost. Even Guilliman recognises that. Let me bring you the comfort of his words, my master. Let the primarch show us his way.'

Artegall nodded and Baldwin hydraulically stomped across the chamber to where a lectern waited on a gravitic base. The top of the lectern formed a crystal case that the Castellan opened, allowing the preservative poison of argon gas to escape. Inside, Artegall's tattered copy of the Codex Astartes lay open as it had done since the Chapter Master had selected his reading for the First Company's departure. Baldwin drifted the lectern across the crimson marble of the Chancelorium floor to the throne's side. Artegall was on his feet. Recovered. A Space Marine again. A Chapter Master with the weight of history and the burden of future expectation on his mighty Astartes' shoulders.

'Baldwin,' he rumbled with a steely-eyed determination. 'Were your recruitment forays into the underhive with the Lord Apothecary fruitful?'

'I believe so, my lord.'

'Good. The Chapter will need Carcharias to offer up its finest flesh, on this dark day. You will need to organise further recruitment sweeps. Go deep. We need the finest savages the hive can offer. Inform Lord Fabian that I have authorised cultivation of our remaining seed. Tell him I need one hundred Crimson sons. Demigods all, to honour the sacrifice of their fallen brethren.'

'Yes, Chapter Master.'

'And Baldwin.'

'My master?'

'Send for the Reclusiarch.'

'High Chaplain Enobarbus is attached to the Tenth Company,' Baldwin informed Artegall with gentle, metallic inflection. 'On training manoeuvres in the Dry-blind.'

'I don't care if he's visiting Holy Terra. Get him here. Now. There are services to organise. Commemorations. Obsequies. The like this Chapter has never known. See to it.'

'Yes, my master,' Baldwin answered and left his lord to his feverish guilt and the cold words of Guilliman.

* * *

'By now your lids are probably frozen to your eyeballs,' growled High Chaplain Enobarbus over the vox-link. 'Your body no longer feels like your own.'

The Crimson Consuls Chaplain leant against the crumbling architecture of the Archaphrael Hive and drank in the spectacular bleakness of his home world. The Dry-blind extended forever in all directions: the white swirl, like a smazeous blanket of white, moulded from the ice pack. By day, with the planet's equally bleak stars turning their attentions on Carcharias, the dry ice that caked everything in a rime of frozen carbon dioxide bled a ghostly vapour. The Dry-blind, as it was called, hid the true lethality of the Carcharian surface, however. A maze of bottomless crevasses, fissures and fractures that riddled the ice beneath and could only be witnessed during the short, temperature-plummeting nights, when the nebulous thunderhead of dry ice sank and re-froze.

'Your fingers are back in your cells, because they sure as Balthus Dardanus aren't part of your hands any more. Hopes of pulling the trigger on your weapon are a distant memory,' the High Chaplain voxed across the open channel.

The Chaplain ran a gauntlet across the top of his head, clearing the settled frost from his tight dreadlocks and flicking the slush at the floor. With a ceramite knuckle, he rubbed at the socket of the eye he'd lost on New Davalos. Now stapled shut, a livid scar ran down one side of his brutal face, from the eyelid to his jaw, where tears constantly trickled in the cold air and froze to his face.

'Skin is raw: like radiation burns – agony both inside and out.'

From his position in the twisted, frost-shattered shell that had been the Archaphrael Hive, Enobarbus could hear fang-face shredders. He fancied he could even spot the tell-tale vapour wakes of the shredders' dorsal fins cutting through the Dry-blind. Archaphrael Hive made up a triumvirate of cities called the Pale Maidens that stood like ancient monuments to the fickle nature of Carcharian meteorology. A thousand years before the three cities had been devastated by a freak polar cyclone colloquially referred to as 'The Big One' by the hivers. Now the ghost hives were used by the Crimson Consuls as an impromptu training ground.

'And those are the benefits,' Enobarbus continued, the High Chaplain's oratory sailing out across the vox waves. 'It's the bits you can't feel that you should worry about. Limbs that died hours ago. Dead meat that you're dragging around. Organs choking on the slush you're barely beating around your numb bodies.'

He had brought the Tenth Company's Second and Seventh Scout sniper squads out to the Pale Maidens for stealth training and spiritual instruction. As a test of their worth and spirit, Enobarbus had had the Space Marine Scouts establish and hold ambush positions with their sniper rifles in the deep Carcharian freeze for three days. He had bombarded them endlessly with remembered readings from the Codex

Astartes, faith instruction and training rhetoric across the open channels of the vox.

Behind him Scout-Sergeant Caradoc was adjusting his snow cloak over the giveaway crimson of his carapace armour plating and priming his shotgun. Enobarbus nodded and the Scout-sergeant melted into the misty, frost-shattered archways of the Archaphrael Hive.

While the Scouts held their agonising positions, caked and swathed in dry ice, Enobarbus and the Scout-sergeants had amused themselves by trapping fang-face shredders. Packs of the beasts roamed the Dry-blind, making the environment an ever more perilous prospect for travellers. The shredders had flat, shovel-shaped maws spilling over with needle-like fangs. They carried their bodies close to the ground and were flat but for the razored dorsal fin protruding from their knobbly spines. They used their long tails for balance and changing direction on the ice. Like their dorsals, the tails were the razor-edged whiplash that gave them their name. Their sharp bones were wrapped in an elastic skin-sheen that felt almost amphibious and gave the beasts the ability to slide downhill and toboggan their prey. Then they would turn their crystal-tip talons on their unfortunate victims: shredding grapnels that the creatures used to climb up and along the labyrinthine crevasses that fractured the ice shelf.

'This is nothing. Lips are sealed with rime. Thought is slow. It's painful. It's agony. Even listening to this feels like more than you can bear.'

Enobarbus pulled his own cape tight about his power armour. Like many of his calling the High Chaplain's plate was ancient and distinct, befitting an Adeptus Astartes of his status, experience and wisdom. Beyond the heraldry and honorifica decorating his midnight adamantium shell and the skull face helmet hanging from his belt, Enobarbus sported the trappings of his home world. The shredder-skin cape hung over his pack, with its razor dorsal and flaps that extended down his arms and terminated in the skinned creature's bestial claws: one decorating each of the High Chaplain's gauntlets.

'But bear it you must, you worthless souls. This is the moment your Emperor will need you. When you feel you have the least to give: that's when your primarch demands the most from you. When your battle-brother is under the knife or in another's sights – this is when you must be able to act,' the High Chaplain grizzled down the vox with gravity. Switching to a secure channel Enobarbus added, 'Sergeant Notus: now, if you will.'

Storeys and storeys below, down in the Dry-blind where Enobarbus and the Scout-sergeants had penned their captured prey, Notus would be waiting for the signal. A signal the Chaplain knew he'd received because of the high-pitched screeches of the released pack of shredders echoing up the shattered chambers and frost-bored ruins of the hive interior. The Codex Astartes taught of the nobility of aeon-honoured combat tactics and battle manoeuvres perfectly realised. It was Guilliman's way. The Rules of Engagement. The way in which Enobarbus was instructing his Scouts. But in their war games about the Pale Maidens, Enobarbus wasn't playing the role of the noble Space Marine. He was everything else the galaxy might throw at them: and the enemies of the Astartes did not play by the rules.

With the Space Marines Scouts undoubtedly making excellent use of the hive's elevation and dilapidated exterior – as scores of previous Neophytes had – Enobarbus decided to engage them on multiple fronts at once. While the starving shredders clawed their way up through the ruined hive, intent on ripping the frozen Scouts to pieces, Scout-Sergeant Caradoc was working his way silently down through the derelict stairwells and halls of the hive interior with his shotgun. The High Chaplain decided to come at his Scouts from an entirely different angle.

Slipping his crozius arcanum – the High Chaplain's sacred staff of office – from his belt and extending the shredder talons on the backs of his gauntlets, Enobarbus swung out onto the crumbling hive wall exterior and began a perilous climb skywards. The shell of the hive wall had long been undermined by the daily freeze-thaw action of Caracharian night and day. Using the sharpened point of the aquila's wings at the end of his crozius like an ice pick and the crystal-tip claws of the shredder, the High Chaplain made swift work of the frozen cliff-face of the dilapidated hive.

'There is nothing convenient about your enemy's desires. He will come for you precisely in the moment you have set aside for some corporal indulgence,' Enobarbus told the Scouts, trying hard not to let his exertions betray him over the vox. 'Exhaustion, fear, pain, sickness, injury, necessities of the body and as an extension of your bodies, the necessities of your weapons. Keep your blade keen and your sidearm clean. Guilliman protect you on the reload: the most necessary of indulgences – a mechanical funeral rite.'

Heaving himself up through the shattered floor of a gargoyle-encrusted overhang, the High Chaplain drew his bolt pistol and crept through to a balcony. The tier-terrace was barely stable but commanded an excellent view: too much temptation for a sniper Scout. But as Enobarbus stalked out across the fragile space he found it deserted. The first time in years of such training exercises he'd discovered it as such.

The High Chaplain nodded to himself. Perhaps this cohort of Neophytes was better. Perhaps they were learning faster: soaking up the wisdom of Guilliman and growing into their role. Perhaps they were ready for their Black Carapace and hallowed suits of power armour. Emperor knows they were needed. Chapter Master Artegall had insisted that Enobarbus concentrate his efforts on the Tenth Company. The Crimson Consuls had had their share of past tragedies.

The Chapter had inherited the terrible misfortune of a garrison rotation on the industrial world of Phaethon IV when the Celebrant Chapter could not meet their commitments. Word was sent that the Celebrants were required to remain on Nedicta Secundus and protect the priceless holy relics of the cardinal world from the ravages of Hive Fleet Kraken and its splintered tyranid forces. Phaethon IV, on the other hand, bordered the Despot Stars and had long been coveted by Dregz Wuzghal, Arch-Mogul of Gunza Major. The Crimson Consuls fought bravely on Phaethon IV, and would have halted the beginnings of Waaagh! Wuzghal in its tracks: something stirred under the factories and power plants of the planet, however. Something awoken by the nightly bombing raids of the Arch-Mogul's 'Green Wing'. Something twice as alien as the degenerate greenskins: unfeeling, unbound and unstoppable. An ancient enemy, long forgotten by the galaxy and entombed below the assembly lines and Imperial manufacturing works of Phaethon, skeletal nightmares of living silver: the necrons. Between greenskin death from above and tomb warriors crawling out of their stasis chambers below, the industrial worlders and their Crimson Consuls guardians hadn't stood a chance and the Chapter lost two highly-decorated companies. As far as Enobarbus knew, the necron and the Arch-Mogul fought for Phaethon still.

The High Chaplain held his position. The still air seared the architecture around him with its caustic frigidity. Enobarbus closed his eyes and allowed his ears to do the work. He filtered out the freeze-thaw expansion of the masonry under his boots, the spiritual hum of the sacred armour about his body and the creak of his own aged bones. There it was. The tell-tale scrape of movement, the tiniest displacement of weight on the balcony expanse above. Back-tracking, the High Chaplain found a craterous hole in the ceiling. Hooking his crozius into the ruined stone and corroded metal, the Crimson Consul heaved himself noiselessly up through the floor of the level above.

Patient, like a rogue shredder on ambush in the Dry-blind – masked by the mist and hidden in some ice floor fissure – Enobarbus advanced with agonising care across the dilapidated balcony. There he was. One of the Tenth Company Scouts. Flat to the steaming floor, form buried in his snow cloak, helmet down at the scope of his sniper rifle: a position the Neophyte had undoubtedly held for days. The balcony was an excellent spot. Despite some obstructive masonry, it commanded a view of the Dry-blind with almost the same breathtaking grandeur of the platform below. Without a sound, Enobarbus was above the sniper Scout, the aquila-wing blade-edge of his crozius resting on the back of the Scout's neck, between the helmet and the snow cloak.

'The cold is not the enemy,' the High Chaplain voxed across the open channel. 'The enemy is not even the enemy. You are the enemy. Ultimately you will betray yourself.'

When the Scout didn't move, the Chaplain's lip curled with annoyance.

He locked his suit vox-channels and hooked the Scout's shoulder with the wing-tip of the crozius.

'It's over, Consul,' Enobarbus told the prone form. 'The enemy has you.'

Flipping the Scout over, Enobarbus stood there in silent shock. Cloak, helmet and rifle were there but the Scout was not. Instead, the butchered body of a Shredder lay beneath, with the hilt of a gladius buried in its fang-faced maw. Enobarbus shook his head. Anger turned to admiration. These Scouts would truly test him.

Enobarbus switched to the private channel he shared with Scout-Sergeant Notus to offer him brief congratulations on his Scouts and to direct him up into the ruined hive.

'What in Guilliman's name are–' Enobarbus heard upon the transferring frequency. Then the unmistakable *whoosh* of las-fire. The High Chaplain heard the Scout-sergeant roar defiance over the vox and looking out over the Dry-blind, Enobarbus saw the light show, diffused in the swirling miasma, like sheet lightning across a stormy sky. Something cold took hold of the High Chaplain's heart. Enobarbus had heard thousands of men die. Notus was dead.

Transferring channels, Enobarbus hissed, 'Override Obsidian: we are under attack. This is not a drill. Second and Seventh, you are cleared to fire. Sergeant Caradoc, meet me at the–'

Shotgun blasts. Rapid and rushed. Caradoc pressed by multiple targets. The crash of the weapon bounced around the maze of masonry and worm-holed architecture.

'Somebody get me a visual,' the High Chaplain growled over the vox before slipping the crozius into his belt. Leading with his bolt pistol, Enobarbus raced for the fading echo of the sergeant's weapon. Short sprints punctuated with skips and drops through holes and stairwells.

'Caradoc, where are you?' Enobarbus voxed as he threaded his way through the crumbling hive. The shotgun fire had died away but the Scout-sergeant wasn't replying. 'Second squad, Seventh squad, I want a visual on Sergeant Caradoc, now!'

But there was nothing: only an eerie static across the channel. Rotating through the frequencies, Enobarbus vaulted cracks and chasms and thundered across frost-hazed chambers.

'Ritter, Lennox, Beade…' the High Chaplain cycled but the channels were dead. Sliding down into a skid, the shredder-skin cape and the greave plates of his armour carrying him across the chamber floor, Enobarbus dropped down through a hole and landed in a crouch. His pistol was everywhere, pivoting around and taking in the chamber below. An Astartes shotgun lay spent and smoking nearby and a large body swung from a creaking strut in the exposed ceiling. Caradoc.

The Scout-sergeant was hanging from his own snow cloak, framed in a gaping hole in the exterior hive wall, swinging amongst the brilliance of the Dry-blind beyond. The cloak, wrapped around his neck as it was, had been tied off around the strut like a noose. This wouldn't have been enough to kill the Space Marine. The dozen gladius blades stabbed through his butchered body up to their hilts had done that. The sickening curiosity of such a vision would have been enough to stun most battle-brothers but Enobarbus took immediate comfort and instruction from his memorised Codex. There was protocol to follow. Counsel to heed.

Snatching his skull-face helmet from his belt, Enobarbus slapped it on and secured the seals. With pistol still outstretched in one gauntlet, the High Chaplain felt for the rosarius hanging around his neck. He would have activated the powerful force field generator but an enemy was already upon him. The haze of the chamber was suddenly whipped up in a rush of movement. Shredders. Lots of them. They came out of the floor. Out of the roof. Up the exterior wall, as the High Chaplain had. Snapping at him with crystal claws and maws of needle-tip teeth. Enobarbus felt their razored tails slash against his adamantium shell and the vice-like grip of their crushing, shovel-head jaws on his knees, his shoulder, at his elbows and on his helmet.

Bellowing shock and frustration, Enobarbus threw his arm around, dislodging two of the monsters. As they scrambled about on the floor, ready to pounce straight back at him, the High Chaplain ended them with his bolt pistol. Another death-dealer tore at him from behind and swallowed his pistol and gauntlet whole. Again, Enobarbus fired, his bolt-rounds riddling the creature from within. The thing died with ease but its dagger-fang jaws locked around his hand and weapon, refusing to release. The darkness of holes and fractured doorways continued to give birth to the Carcharian predators. They bounded at him with their merciless, ice-hook talons, vaulting off the walls, floor and ceiling, even off Caradoc's dangling corpse.

Snatching the crozius arcanum from his belt the High Chaplain thumbed the power weapon to life. Swinging it about him in cold fury, Enobarbus cleaved shredders in two, slicing the monsters through the head and chopping limbs and tails from the beasts.

The floor erupted in front of the Space Marine and a hideously emaciated shredder – big, even for its kind – came up through the frost-shattered masonry. It leapt at Enobarbus, jaws snapping shut around his neck and wicked talons hooking themselves around the edges of his chest plate. The force of the impact sent the High Chaplain flailing backwards, off balance and with shredders hanging from every appendage.

Enobarbus roared as his armoured form smashed through part of a ruined wall and out through the gap in the hive exterior. The Crimson Consul felt himself falling. Survival instinct causing his fist to open, allowing the crozius to be torn from him by a savage little shredder. Snatching at the rapidly disappearing masonry, Enobarbus elongated his own shredder claw and buried the crystal-tip talon in the ancient rockcrete. The High Chaplain hung from two monstrous digits, shredders in turn hanging from his armour. With the dead-weight and locked jaw of the pistol-swallowing shredder on the other arm and the huge beast now hanging down his back from a jaw-hold on his neck, Enobarbus had little hope of improving his prospects. Below lay thousands of metres of open drop, a ragged cliff-face of hive masonry to bounce off and shredder-infested, bottomless chasms of ice waiting below the white blanket of the Dry-blind. Even the superhuman frame of the High Chaplain could not hope to survive such a fall.

Above the shrieking and gnawing of the beasts and his own exertions, Enobarbus heard the hammer of disciplined sniper fire. Shredder bodies cascaded over the edge past the High Chaplain, either blasted apart by the accurate las-fire or leaping wildly out of its path. Enobarbus looked up. The two talons from which he hung scraped through the rockcrete with every purchase-snapping swing of the monsters hanging from the Crimson Consul. There were figures looking down at him from the edge. Figures in helmets and crimson carapace, swathed in snow cloaks and clutching sniper rifles. On the level above was a further collection looking down at him and the same on the storey after that.

Enobarbus recognised the Scout standing above him.

'Beade...' the High Chaplain managed, but there was nothing in the blank stare or soulless eyes of the Neophyte to lead Enobarbus to believe that he was going to live. As the barrel of Beade's rifle came down in unison with his Space Marine Scout compatriots, the High Chaplain's thoughts raced through a lifetime of combat experience and the primarch's teaching. But Roboute Guilliman and his Codex had nothing for him and, with synchronous trigger-pulls that would have been worthy of a firing squad, High Chaplain Enobarbus's las-slashed corpse tumbled into the whiteness below.

The Oratorium was crowded with hulking forms, their shadows cutting through the hololithic graphics of the chamber. Each Crimson Consul was a sculpture in muscle, wrapped in zoster robes and the colour of their calling. Only the two Astartes on the Oratorium door stood in full cream and crimson ceremonial armour, Sergeants Ravenscar and Bohemond watching silently over their brothers at the circular runeslab that dominated the chamber. The doors parted and Baldwin stomped in with the hiss of hydraulic urgency, accompanied by a serf attendant of his own. The supermen turned.

'The Reclusiarch has not returned as ordered, master,' Baldwin reported. 'Neither have two full Scout squads of the Tenth Company and their sergeants.'

'It's the time of year I tell you,' the Master of the Forge maintained through his conical faceplate. Without his armour and colossal servo-claw, Maximagne Ferro cut a very different figure. Ferro wheezed a further intake of breath through his grilles before insisting: 'Our relay stations on De Vere and Thusa Minor experience communication disruption from starquakes every year around the Antilochal Feast day.'

The Slaughterhorn's Master of Ordnance, Talbot Faulks, gave Artegall the intensity of his magnobionic eyes, their telescrew mountings whirring to projection. 'Elias. It's highly irregular: and you know it.'

'Perhaps the High Chaplain and his men have been beset by difficulties of a very natural kind,' Lord Apothecary Fabian suggested. 'Reports suggest carbonic cyclones sweeping in on the Pale Maidens from the east. They could just be waiting out the poor conditions.'

'Enjoying them, more like,' Chaplain Mercimund told the Apothecary. 'The Reclusiarch would loathe missing an opportunity to test his pupils to their limits. I remember once, out on the–'

'Forgive me, Brother-Chaplain. After the Chapter Master's recall?' the Master of Ordnance put to him. 'Not exactly in keeping with the Codex.'

'Brothers, please,' Artegall said, leaning thoughtfully against the runeslab on his fingertips. Hololithics danced across his grim face, glinting off the neat rows of service studs running above each eyebrow. He looked at Baldwin. 'Send the Tenth's Thunderhawks for them with two further squads for a search, if one is required.'

Baldwin nodded and despatched his attendant. 'Chaplain,' Artegall added, turning on Mercimund. 'If you would be so good as to start organising the commemorations, in the High Chaplain's absence.'

'It would be an honour, Chapter Master,' Mercimund acknowledged, thumping his fist into the Chapter signature on his robes earnestly before following the Chamber Castellan's serf out of the Oratorium. Baldwin remained.

'Yes?' Artegall asked.

Baldwin looked uncomfortably at Lord Fabian, prompting him to clear his throat. Artegall changed his focus to the Apothecary. 'Speak.'

'The recruitment party is long returned from the underhive. Your Chamber Castellan and I returned together – at your request – with the other party members and the potential aspirants. Since they were not requested, Navarre and his novice remained on some matter of significance: the Chief Librarian did not share it with me. I had the Chamber Castellan check with the Librarium...'

'They are as yet to return, Master Artegall,' Baldwin inserted.

'Communications?'

'We're having some difficulty reaching them,' Baldwin admitted.

Faulks's telescopic eyes retracted. 'Enobarbus, the *Crimson Tithe*, the Chief Librarian...'

'Communication difficulties, all caused by seasonal starquakes, I tell you,' Maximagne Ferro maintained, his conical faceplate swinging around to each of them with exasperation. 'The entire hive is probably experiencing the same.'

'And yet we can reach Lambert,' Faulks argued.

Artegall pursed his lips: 'I want confirmation of the nature of the communication difficulties,' he put to the Master of the Forge, prompting the Techmarine to nod slowly. 'How long have Captain Baptista and the *Crimson Tithe* been out of contact?'

'Six hours,' Faulks reported.

Artegall looked down at the runeslab. With the loss of the Chapter's only other battle-barge, Artegall wasn't comfortable with static from the *Crimson Tithe*.

'Where is she? Precisely.'

'Over the moon of Rubessa: quadrant four-gamma, equatorial west.'

Artegall fixed his Chamber Castellan with cold, certain eyes.

'Baldwin, arrange a pict-link with Master Lambert. I wish to speak with him again.'

'You're going to send Lambert over to investigate?' Faulks enquired.

'Calm yourself, brother,' Artegall instructed the Master of Ordnance. 'I'm sure it is as Ferro indicates. I'll have the Master of the Fleet take the *Anno Tenebris* to rendezvous with the battle-barge over Rubessa. There Lambert and Baptista can have their engineseers and the Sixth Reserve Company's Techmarines work on the problem from their end.'

Baldwin bowed his head. The sigh of hydraulics announced his intention to leave. 'Baldwin,' Artegall called, his eyes still on Faulks. 'On your way, return to the Librarium. Have our astropaths and Navarre's senior Epistolary attempt to reach the Chief Librarian and the *Crimson Tithe* by psychic means.'

'My lord,' Baldwin confirmed and left the Oratorium with the Master of the Forge.

'Elias,' Faulks insisted as he had done earlier. 'You must let me take the Slaughterhorn to Status Vermillion.'

'That seems unnecessary,' the Lord Apothecary shook his head.

'We have two of our most senior leaders unaccounted for and a Chapter battle-barge in a communications black-out,' Faulks listed with emphasis. 'All following the loss of one hundred of our most experienced and decorated battle-brothers? I believe that we must face the possibility that we are under some kind of attack.'

'Attack?' Fabian carped incredulously. 'From whom? Sector greenskins? Elias, you're not entertaining this?'

Artegall remained silent, his eyes following the path of hololithic representations tracking their way across the still air of the chamber.

'You have started preparing the Chapter's remaining gene-seed?' Artegall put to the Lord Apothecary.

'As you ordered, my master,' Fabian replied coolly. 'Further recruiting sweeps will need to be made. I know the loss of the First Company was a shock and this on top of the tragedies of Phaethon IV. But, this is our Chapter's entire stored genetic heritage we are talking about here. You have heard my entreaties for caution with this course of action.'

'Caution,' Artegall nodded.

'Elias,' Faulks pressed.

'As in all things,' Artegall put to his Master of Ordnance and the Apothecary, 'we shall be guided by Guilliman. The Codex advises caution in the face of the unknown – *Codicil MX-VII-IX.i: The Wisdoms of Hera*, "Gather your wits, as the traveller gauges the depth of the river crossing with the fallen branch, before wading into waters wary." Master Faulks, what would you advise?'

'I would order all Crimson Consuls to arms and armour,' the Master of Ordnance reeled off. 'Thunderhawks fuelled and prepped in the hangers. Penitorium secured. Vox-checks doubled and the defence lasers charged for ground to orbit assault. I would also recall Roderick and the Seventh Company from urban pacification and double the fortress-monastery garrison.'

'Anything else?'

'I would advise Master Lambert to move all Crimson Consuls vessels to a similarly high alert status.'

'That is a matter for Master of the Fleet. I will apprise him of your recommendations.'

'So?'

Artegall gave his grim consent, 'Slaughterhorn so ordered to Status Vermillion.'

'I can't raise the Slaughterhorn,' Lexicanum Raughan Stellan complained to his Librarian Master.

'We are far below the hive, my novice,' the Chief Librarian replied, his power armour boots crunching through the darkness. 'There are a billion tonnes of plasteel and rockcrete between us and the spire monastery. You would expect even our equipment to have some problems negotiating that. Besides, it's the season for starquakes.'

'Still...' the Lexicanum mused.

The psykers had entered the catacombs: the lightless labyrinth of tunnels, cave systems and caverns that threaded their torturous way through the pulverised rock and rust of the original hive. Thousands of storeys had since been erected on top of the ancient structures, crushing them into the bottomless network of grottos from which the Crimson Consuls procured their most savage potential recruits. The sub-zero stillness was routinely shattered by murderous screams of tribal barbarism.

Far below the aristocratic indifference of the spire and the slavish poverty of the habs and industrial districts lay the gang savagery of the underhive. Collections of killers and their Carcharian kin, gathered for security or mass slaughter, blasting across the subterranean badlands for scraps and criminal honour. Below this kingdom of desperados and petty despots extended the catacombs, where tribes of barbaric brutes ruled almost as they had at the planet's feral dawn. Here, young Carcharian bodies were crafted by necessity: shaped by circumstance into small mountains of muscle and sinew. Minds were sharpened to keenness by animal instinct and souls remained empty and pure. Perfect for cult indoctrination and the teachings of Guilliman.

Navarre held up his force sword, *Chrysaor*, the unnatural blade bleeding immaterial illumination into the darkness. It was short, like the traditional gladius of his Chapter and its twin, *Chrysaen*, sat in the inverse criss-cross of scabbards that decorated the Chief Librarian's blue and gold chest plate. The denizens of the catacombs retreated into the alcoves and shadows at the abnormal glare of the blade and the towering presence of the armoured Adeptus Astartes.

'Stellan, keep up,' Navarre instructed. They had both been recruited from this tribal underworld – although hundreds of years apart. This familiarity should have filled the Carcharians with ease and acquaintance. Their Astartes instruction and training had realised in both supermen, however, an understanding of the untamed dangers of the place.

Not only would their kith and kin dash out their brains for the rich marrow in their bones, their degenerate brothers shared their dark kingdom with abhumans, mutants and wyrds, driven from the upper levels of the hive for the unsightly danger they posed. Navarre and Stellan had already despatched a shaggy, cyclopean monstrosity that had come at them on its knuckles with brute fury and bloodhunger.

Navarre and Stellan, however, were Adeptus Astartes: the Emperor's Angels of Death and demigods among men. They came with dangers of their own. This alone would be enough to ensure their survival in such a lethal place. The Crimson Consuls were also powerful psykers: wielders of powers unnatural and warp-tapped. Without the technospectacle of their arms, the magnificence of their blue and gold plating, their superhuman forms and murderous training, Navarre and Stellan would still be the deadliest presence in the catacombs for kilometres in any direction.

The tight tunnels opened out into a cavernous space. Lifting *Chrysaor* higher, the Chief Librarian allowed more of his potential to flood the unnatural blade of the weapon, throwing light up at the cave ceiling. Something colossal and twisted through with corrosion and stalactitular icicles formed the top of the cavern: some huge structure that had descended through the hive interior during some forgotten, cataclysmic collapse. Irregular columns of resistant-gauge rockcrete and strata structural supports held up the roof at precarious angles. This accidental architecture had allowed the abnormality of the open space to exist below and during the daily thaw had created, drop by drop, the frozen chemical lake that steamed beneath it.

A primitive walkway of scavenged plasteel, rock-ice and girders crossed the vast space and, as the Space Marines made their tentative crossing, Navarre's warplight spooked a flock of gliding netherworms. Uncoiling themselves from their icicle bases they flattened their bodies and slithered through the air, angling the drag of their serpentine descent down past the Space Marines and at the crags and ledges of the cavern where they would make a fresh ascent. As the flock of black worms spiralled by, one crossed Stellan's path. The novice struck out with his gauntlet in disgust but the thing latched onto him with its unparalleled prehensility. It weaved its way up through his armoured digits and corkscrewed up his thrashing arm at his helmetless face.

Light flashed before the Lexicanum's eyes. Just as the netherworm retracted its fleshy collar and prepared to sink its venomous beak hooks into the Astartes' young face, Navarre clipped the horror in half with the blazing tip of *Chrysaor*. As the worm fell down the side of the walkway in two writhing pieces, Stellan mumbled his thanks.

'Why didn't you use your powers?' the Chief Librarian boomed around the cavern.

'It surprised me,' was all the Lexicanum could manage.

'You've been out of the depths mere moments and you've already forgotten its dangers,' Navarre remonstrated gently. 'What of the galaxy's dangers? There's a myriad of lethality waiting for you out there. Be mindful, my novice.'

'Yes, master.'

'Did it come to you again?' Navarre asked pointedly.

'Why do you ask, master?'

'You seem, distracted: not yourself. Was your sleep disturbed?'

'Yes, master.'

'Your dreams?'

'Yes, master.'

'The empyreal realm seems a dark and distant place,' Navarre told his apprentice sagely. 'But it is everywhere. How do you think we can draw on it so? Its rawness feeds our power: the blessings our God-Emperor gave us and through which we give back in His name. We are not the only ones to draw from this wellspring of power and we need our faith and constant vigilance to shield us from the predations of these immaterial others.'

'Yes, master.'

'Behind a wall of mirrored-plas the warp hides, reflecting back to us our realities. In some places it's thick; in others a mere wafer of truth separates us from its unnatural influence. Your dreams are one such window: a place where one may submerge one's head in the Sea of Souls.'

'Yes, master.'

'Tell me, then.'

Stellan seemed uncomfortable, but as the two Space Marines continued their careful trudge across the cavern walkway, the novice unburdened himself.

'It called itself Ghidorquiel.'

'You conversed with this thing of confusion and darkness?'

'No, my master. It spoke only to me: in my cell.'

'You said you were dreaming,' Navarre reminded the novice.

'Of being awake,' Stellan informed him, 'in my cell. It spoke. What I took to be lips moved but the voice was in my head.'

'And what lies did this living lie tell you?'

'A host of obscenities, my lord,' Stellan confirmed. 'It spoke in languages unknown to me. Hissed and spat its impatience. It claimed my soul as its own. It said my weakness was the light in its darkness.'

'This disturbed you.'

'Of course,' the Lexicanum admitted. 'Its attentions disgust me. But this creature called out to me across the expanse of time and space. Am I marked? Am I afflicted?'

'No more than you ever were,' Navarre reassured the novice. 'Stellan, all those who bear the burden of powers manifest – the Emperor's sacred gift – of which he was gifted himself – dream themselves face to face with the daemonscape from time to time. Entities trawl the warp for souls to torment for their wretched entertainment. Our years of training and the mental fortitude that comes of being the Emperor's chosen protects us from their direct influence. The unbound, the warp-rampant and the witch are all easy prey for such beasts and through them the daemon worms its way into our world. Thank the primarch we need face such things for real with blessed infrequency.'

'Yes, my lord,' Stellan agreed.

'The warp sometimes calls to us: demands our attention. It's why we did not return to the Slaughterhorn with the others. Such a demand led me beyond the scope of the Lord Apothecary's recruitment party and down into the frozen bowels of Carcharias. Here.'

Reaching the other side of the cavern, Navarre and Stellan stood on the far end of the walkway, where it led back into the rock face of pulverised masonry. Over the top of the tunnel opening was a single phrase in slap-dash white paint. It was all glyph symbols and runic consonants of ancient Carcharian.

'It's recent,' Navarre said half to himself. Stellan simply stared at the oddness of the lettering. 'Yet its meaning is very old. A phrase that predates the hives, at least. It means, "From the single flake of snow – the avalanche".'

Venturing into the tunnel with force sword held high, Navarre was struck by the patterns on the walls. Graffiti was endemic to the underhive: it was not mere defacement or criminal damage. In the ganglands above it advertised the presence of dangerous individuals and marked the jealously guarded territories of House-sponsored outfits, organisations and posses. It covered every empty space: the walls, the floor and ceiling, and was simply part of the underworld's texture. Below that, the graffiti was no less pervasive or lacking in purpose. Tribal totems and primitive paintings performed much the same purpose for the barbarians of the catacombs. Handprints in blood; primordial representations of subterranean mega-vermin in campfire charcoal; symbolic warnings splashed across walls in the phosphorescent, radioactive chemicals that leaked down from the industrial sectors above. The Carcharian savages that haunted the catacombs had little use for words, yet this was all Navarre could see.

The Chief Librarian had been drawn to this place, deep under Hive Niveous, by the stink of psychic intrusion. Emanations. Something large and invasive: something that had wormed its way through the very core of the Carcharian capital. The ghostly glow of *Chrysaor* revealed it to Navarre in all its mesmerising glory. Graffiti upon graffiti, primitive paintings upon symbols upon markings upon blood splatter. Words. The same words, over and over again, in all orientations, spelt out in letters created in the layered spaces of the hive cacography. Repetitions that ran for kilometres through the arterial maze of tunnels. Like a chant or incantation in ancient Carcharian: they blazed with psychic significance to the Chief Librarian, where to the eyes of the ordinary and untouched, among the background scrawl of the hive underworld, they would not appear to be there at all.

'Stellan! You must see this,' Navarre murmured as he advanced down the winding passage. The Librarian continued: 'Psycho-sensitive words, spelt out on the walls, a conditioned instruction of some kind, imprinting itself on the minds of the underhivers. Stellan: we must get word back to the Slaughterhorn – to Fabian – to the Chapter Master. The recruits could be compromised...'

The Chief Librarian turned to find that his novice wasn't there. Marching back up the passage in the halo of his shimmering force weapon, Navarre found the Lexicanum still standing on the cavern walkway, staring up at the wall above the tunnel entrance with a terrible blankness. 'Stellan? Stellan, talk to me.'

At first Navarre thought that one of the deadly gliding worms had got him, infecting the young Space Marine with its toxin. The reality was much worse. Following the novice's line of sight, Navarre settled on the white painted scrawl above the tunnel. The ancient insistence, 'From the single flake of snow – the avalanche' in fresh paint. Looking back at the Lexicanum, Navarre came to realise that his own novice had succumbed to the psycho-sensitive indoctrination of his recruiting grounds. All the wordsmith had needed was to introduce his subjects to the trigger. A phrase they were unlikely to come across anywhere else. The timing intentional; the brainwashing complete.

Stellan dribbled. He tried to mumble the words on the wall. Then he tried to get his palsied mouth around his master's name. He failed. The young Space Marine's mind was no longer his own. He belonged to someone else: to the will of the wordsmith – whoever they were. And not only the novice: countless other recruits over the years, for whom indoctrination hid in the very fabric of their worlds and now in the backs of their afflicted minds. All ready to be activated at a single phrase.

Navarre readied himself. Opened his being to the warp's dark promise. Allowed its fire to burn within. Slipping *Chrysaen* from its chest scabbard, the Chief Librarian held both force blades out in front of him. Each master-crafted gladius smoked with immaterial vengeance.

For Stellan, the dangers were much more immediate than brainwashing. Stripped of his years of training and the mental fortitude that shielded an Astartes Librarian from the dangers of the warp, Stellan succumbed to the monster stalking his soul.

Something like shock took the Crimson Consul's face hostage. The novice looked like he had been seized from below. Somehow, horribly, he had. The Librarian's head suddenly disappeared down into the trunk of his blue and gold power armour. An oily, green ichor erupted from the neck of the suit.

'Ghidorquiel…' Navarre spat. The Chief Librarian thrust himself at the quivering suit of armour, spearing his Lexicanum through the chest with *Chrysaor*. The stink of warp-corruption poured from the adamantium shell and stung the psyker's nostrils. Spinning and kicking the body back along the treacherous walkway, Navarre's blades trailed ethereal afterglow as they arced and cleaved through the sacred suit.

Howling fury at the materialising beast within the armour, the Chief Librarian unleashed a blast wave of raw warp energy from his chest that lit up the cavern interior and hit the suit like the God-Emperor's own fist.

The suit tumbled backwards, wrenching and cracking along the walkway until it came to rest, a broken-backed heap. Even then, the armour continued to quiver and snap, rearranging the splintered ceramite plating and moulding itself into something new. On the walkway, Navarre came to behold an adamantium shell, like that of a mollusc, from which slithered an explosion of tentacles. Navarre ran full speed at the daemon while appendages shot for him like guided missiles. Twisting this way and that, but without sacrificing any of his rage-fuelled speed, the Chief Librarian slashed at the beast, his blinding blades shearing off tentacular length and the warp-dribbling tips of the monster feelers.

As the psyker closed with the daemon nautiloid, the warp beast shot its appendages into the fragile walkway's architecture. Hugging the snapping struts and supports to it, the creature demolished the structure beneath the Crimson Consul's feet.

Navarre plummeted through the cavern space before smashing down through the frozen surface of the chemical lake below. The industrial waste plunge immediately went to work on the blue and gold of the Librarian's armour and blistered the psyker's exposed and freezing flesh. Navarre's force blades glowed spectroscopic eeriness under the surface and it took precious moments for the Space Marine to orientate himself and kick for the surface. As his steaming head broke from the frozen acid depths of the lake, Navarre's burn-blurry eyes saw the rest of the walkway collapsing towards him. Ghidorquiel had reached for the cavern wall and, pulling with its unnatural might, had toppled the remainder of the structure.

Again Navarre was hammered to the darkness of the lake bottom, sinking wreckage raining all about the dazed psyker. Somewhere in the chaos *Chrysaen* slipped from Navarre's grip. Vaulting upwards, the Space Marine hit the thick ice of the lake surface further across. Clawing uselessly with his gauntlet, skin aflame and armour freezing up, Navarre stared through the ice and saw something slither overhead. Roaring pain and frustration into the chemical darkness, the Chief Librarian thrust *Chrysaor* through the frozen effluence. Warpflame bled from the blade and across the ice, rapidly melting the crust of the acid bath and allowing the Crimson Consul a moment to suck in a foetid breath and drag himself up the shoreline of shattered masonry.

Ghidorquiel was there, launching tentacles at the psyker. Hairless and with flesh melting from his skull the Librarian mindlessly slashed the appendages to pieces. All the Space Marine wanted was the daemon. The thing dragged its obscene adamantium shell sluggishly away from the lake and the enraged Astartes. Navarre bounded up and off a heap of walkway wreckage, dodging the creature's remaining tentacles and landing on ceramite. Drawing on everything he had, the Chief Librarian became a conduit of the warp. The raw, scalding essence of immaterial energy poured from his being and down through the descending tip of his force sword. *Chrysaor* slammed through the twisted shell of Stellan's armour and buried itself in the daemon's core. Like a lightning rod, the gladius roasted the beast from the inside out.

Armour steamed. Tentacles dropped and trembled to stillness. The daemon caught light. Leaving the force blade in the monstrous body, Navarre stumbled down from the creature and crashed to the cavern floor himself. The psyker was spent: in every way conceivable. He could do little more than lie there in his own palsy, staring at the daemon corpse lit by *Chrysaor*'s still gleaming blade. The slack, horrible face of the creature had slipped down out of the malformed armour shell: the same horrific face that the novice Stellan had confronted in his dreams.

Looking up into the inky, cavern blackness, Navarre wrangled with the reality that somehow he had to get out of the catacombs and warn the Slaughterhorn of impending disaster. A *slurp* drew his face back to the creature; sickeningly it began to rumble with daemonic life and throttled laughter. Fresh tentacles erupted from its flaming sides and wrapped themselves around two of the crooked pillars of rockcrete and metal that were supporting the chamber ceiling and the underhive levels above.

All Navarre could do was watch the monster pull the columns towards its warp-scorched body and roar his frustration as the cavern ceiling quaked and thundered down towards him, with the weight of Hive Niveous behind it.

The Oratorium swarmed with armoured command staff and their attendants. Clarifications and communications shot back and forth across the chamber amongst a hololithic representation of the Slaughterhorn fortress-monastery that crackled disturbance every time an officer or Crimson Consuls serf walked through it.

'They discovered nothing, my lord,' Baldwin informed Artegall in mid-report. 'No High Chaplain; no Scout squads; nothing. They've scoured the Dry-blind around the Pale Maidens. They're requesting permission to bring the Thunderhawks back to base.'

'What about Chief Librarian Navarre?' Artegall called across the Oratorium.

'Nothing, sir,' Lord Apothecary Fabian confirmed. 'On the vox or from the Librarium.'

'Planetary Defence Force channels and on-scene enforcers report seismic shift and hive tremors in the capital lower levels,' the Master of the Forge reported, his huge servo-claw swinging about over the heads of the gathering.

'What about the *Crimson Tithe*?'

'Patching you through to Master Lambert now,' Maximagne Ferro added, giving directions to a communications servitor. The hololithic representation of the Slaughterhorn disappeared and was replaced with the phantasmal static of a dead pict-feed that danced around the assembled Crimson Consuls.

'What the hell is happening up there, Maximagne?' Artegall demanded, but the Master of the Forge was working furiously on the servitor and the brass control station of the runeslab. The static disappeared before briefly being replaced by the Slaughterhorn and then a three-dimensional hololith of the Carcharian system. Artegall immediately picked out their system star and their icebound home world: numerous defence monitors and small frigates were stationed in high orbit. Circling Carcharias were the moons of De Vere, Thusa Major and Thusa Minor between which two strike cruisers sat at anchor. Most distant was Rubessa; the Oratorium could see the battle-barge *Crimson Tithe* beneath it. Approaching was Hecton Lambert's strike cruiser, *Anno Tenebris*. The hololithic image of the Adeptus Astartes strike cruiser suddenly crackled and then disappeared.

The Oratorium fell to a deathly silence.

'Master Maximagne...' Artegall began. The Master of the Forge had a vox-headset to one ear.

'Confirmed, my lord. The *Anno Tenebris* has been destroyed with all on board.' The silence prevailed. 'Sir, the *Crimson Tithe* fired upon her.'

The gathered Adeptus Astartes looked to their Chapter Master, who, like his compatriots, could not believe what he was hearing.

'Master Faulks,' Artegall began. 'It seems you were correct. We are under attack. Status report: fortress-monastery.'

'In lockdown as ordered, sir,' the Master of Ordnance reported with grim pride. 'All Crimson Consuls are prepped for combat. All sentry guns manned. Thunderhawks ready for launch on your order. Defence lasers powered to full.'

Captain Roderick presented himself to his Chapter Master: 'My lord, the Seventh Company has fortified the Slaughterhorn at the Master of Ordnance's instruction. Nothing will get through – you can be sure of that.'

'Sir,' Master Maximagne alerted the chamber: '*Crimson Tithe* is on the move, Carcharias bound, my lord.'

Artegall's lip curled into a snarl. 'Who the hell are they?' he muttered to himself. 'What about our remaining cruisers?'

Faulks stepped forwards indicating the cruisers at anchor between the hololithic moons of Thusa Major and Thusa Minor. 'At full alert as I advised. The *Caliburn* and *Honour of Hera* could plot an intercept course and attempt an ambush...'

'Out of the question,' Artegall stopped Faulks. 'Bring the strike cruisers in above the Slaughterhorn at low orbit. I want our defence lasers to have their backs.'

'Yes, my master,' Faulks obeyed.

'Baldwin...'

'Lord?'

'Ready my weapons and armour.'

The Chamber Castellan nodded slowly, 'It would be my honour, master.' The Crimson Consuls watched the serf exit, knowing what this meant. Artegall was already standing at the head of the runeslab in a functional suit of crimson and cream power armour and his mantle. He was asking for the hallowed suit of artificer armour and master-crafted bolter that resided in the Chapter Master's private armoury. The gleaming suit of crimson and gold upon which the honourable history of the Crimson Consuls Chapter was inscribed and inlaid in gemstone ripped from the frozen earth of Carcharias itself. The armour that past Masters had worn when leading the Chapter to war in its entirety: Aldebaran; the Fall of Volsungard; the Termagant Wars.

'Narke.'

'Master Artegall,' the Slaughterhorn's chief astropath replied from near the Oratorium doors.

'Have you been successful in contacting the Third, Fifth or Eighth Companies?'

'Captain Neath has not responded, lord,' the blind Narke reported, clutching his staff.

Artegall and Talbot Faulks exchanged grim glances. Neath and the Eighth Company were only two systems away hunting Black Legion Traitor Marine degenerates in the Sarcus Reaches.

'And Captain Borachio?'

Artegall had received monthly astrotelepathic reports from Captain Albrecht Borachio stationed in the Damocles Gulf. Borachio had overseen the Crimson Consuls contribution to the Damocles Crusade in the form of the Third and Fifth Companies and had present responsibility for bringing the Tau commander, O'Shovah, to battle in the Farsight Enclaves. Artegall and Borachio had served together in the same squad as battle-brothers and Borachio beyond Baldwin, was what the Chapter Master might have counted as the closest thing he had to a friend.

'Three days ago, my lord,' Narke returned. 'You returned in kind, Master Artegall.'

'Read back the message.'

The astropath's knuckles whitened around his staff as he recalled the message: '...encountered a convoy of heavy cruisers out of Fi'Rios – a lesser sept, the Xenobiologis assure me, attempting to contact Commander Farsight. We took a trailing vessel with little difficulty but at the loss of one Carcharian son: Crimson Consul Battle-Brother Theodoric of the First Squad: Fifth Company. I commend Brother Theodoric's service to you and recommend his name be added to the Shrine of Hera in the Company Chapel as a posthumous recipient of the Iron Laurel...'

'And the end?' Artegall pushed.

'An algebraic notation in three dimensions, my lord: Kn Ω iii – π iX (Z-) – v.R (!?) 0-1.'

'Coordinates? Battle manoeuvres?' Talbot Faulks hypothesised.

'Regicide notations,' Artegall informed him, his mind elsewhere. For years, the Chapter Master and Albrecht Borachio had maintained a game of regicide across the stars, moves detailed back and forth with their astropathic communiqués. Each had a board and pieces upon which the same game had been played out; Artegall's was an ancient set carved from lacquered megafelis sabres on a burnished bronze board. Artegall moved the pieces in his mind, recalling the board as it was set up on a rostra by his throne in the Chancelorium. Borachio had beaten him: 'Blind Man's Mate...' the Chapter Master mouthed.

'Excuse me, my lord?' Narke asked.

'No disrespect intended,' Artegall told the astropath. 'It's a form of victory in regicide, so called because you do not see it coming.'

The corridor outside the Oratorium suddenly echoed with the sharp crack of bolter fire. Shocked glances between Artegall and his Astartes officers were swiftly replaced by the assumption of cover positions. The armoured forms took advantage of the runeslab and the walls either side of the Oratorium door.

'That's inside the perimeter,' Faulks called in disbelief, slapping on his helmet.

'Well inside,' Artegall agreed grimly. Many of the Space Marines had drawn either their bolt pistols or their gladius swords. Only Captain Roderick and the Oratorium sentry sergeants, Bohemond and Ravenscar, were equipped for full combat with bolters, spare ammunition and grenades.

With the muzzle of his squat Fornax-pattern bolt pistol resting on the slab, the Master of Ordnance brought up the hololithic representation of the Slaughterhorn once more. The fortress-monastery was a tessellation of flashing wings, towers, hangars and sections.

'Impossible...' Faulks mumbled.

'The fortress-monastery is completely compromised,' Master Maximagne informed the chamber, cycling through the vox-channels.

Bolt shells pounded the thick doors of the Oratorium. The Seventh Company captain held a gauntleted finger to the vox-bead in his ear.

'Roderick,' Artegall called. 'What's happening?'

'My men are being fired upon from the inside of the Slaughterhorn, my lord,' the captain reported bleakly. 'By fellow Astartes – by Crimson Consuls, Master Artegall!'

'What has happened to us?' the Chapter Master bawled in dire amazement.

'Later, sir. We have to get you out of here,' Faulks insisted.

'What sections do we hold?' Artegall demanded.

'Elias, we have to go, now!'

'Master Faulks, what do we hold?'

'Sir, small groups of my men hold the apothecarion and the north-east hangar,' Roderick reported. 'The Barbican, some Foundry sections and Cell Block Sigma.'

'The Apothecarion?' Fabian clarified.

'The gene-seed,' Artegall heard himself mutter.

'The Command Tower is clear,' Faulks announced, reading details off the hololith schematic of the monastery. Bolt-rounds tore through the metal of the Oratorium door and drummed into the runeslab column. The hololith promptly died. Ravenscar pushed Narke, the blind astropath, out of his way and poked the muzzle of his weapon through the rent in the door. He started plugging the corridor with ammunition-conserving boltfire.

'We must get the Chapter Master to the Tactical Chancelorium,' Faulks put to Roderick, Maximagne and the sentry sergeants.

'No,' Artegall barked back. 'We must take back the Slaughterhorn.'

'Which we can do best from your Tactical Chancelorium, my lord,' Faulks insisted with strategic logic. 'From there we have our own vox-relays, tactical feeds and your private armoury: it's elevated for a Thunderhawk evacuation – it's simply the most secure location in the fortress-monastery,' Faulks told his master. 'The best place from which to coordinate and rally our forces.'

'When we determine who they are,' Fabian added miserably. Artegall and the Master of Ordnance stared at one another.

'Sir!' Ravenscar called from the door. 'Coming up on a reload.'

'Agreed,' Artegall told Faulks. 'Captain Roderick shall accompany Master Maximagne and Lord Fabian to secure the apothecarion; the gene-seed must be saved. Serfs with your masters. Sergeants Ravenscar and Bohemond, escort the Master of Ordnance and myself to the Tactical Chancelorium. Narke, you will accompany us. All understood?'

'Yes, Chapter Master,' the chorus came back.

'Sergeant, on three,' Artegall instructed. 'One.' Bohemond nodded and primed a pair of grenades from his belt. 'Two.' Faulks took position by the door stud. 'Three'. Roderick nestled his bolter snug into his shoulder as Faulks activated the door mechanism.

As the door rolled open, Ravenscar pulled away and went about reloading his boltgun. Bohemond's grenades were then followed by replacement suppression fire from Captain Roderick's bolter.

The brief impression of crimson and cream armour working up the corridor was suddenly replaced with the thunder and flash of grenades. Roderick was swiftly joined by Bohemond and then Ravenscar, the three Space Marines maintaining a withering arc of fire. The command group filed out of the Oratorium with their Chapter serf attendants, the singular crash of their Fornax-pattern pistols joining in the cacophony.

With Roderick's precision fire leading the Lord Apothecary and the Master of the Forge down a side passage, Bohemond slammed his shoulder through a stairwell door to lead the other group up onto the next level. The Crimson Consuls soon fell into the surgical-style battle rotation so beloved of Guilliman: battle-brother covering battle-brother; arc-pivoting and rapid advance suppression fire. Ravenscar and Bohemond orchestrated the tactical dance from the front, with Artegall's pistol crashing support from behind and the Master of Ordnance covering the rear with his own, while half dragging the blind Narke behind him.

Advancing up through the stairwell, spiralling up through the storeys, the Astartes walked up into a storm of iron: armoured, renegade Crimson Consuls funnelled their firepower down at them from a gauntlet above. Unclipping a grenade, Ravenscar tossed it to his brother-sergeant. Bohemond then held the explosive, counting away the precious seconds before launching the thing directly up through the space between the spiral stair rails. The grenade detonated above, silencing the gunfire. A cream and crimson body fell down past the group in a shower of grit. The sergeants didn't wait, however, bounding up the stairs and into the maelstrom above.

Dead Crimson Consuls lay mangled amongst the rail and rockcrete. One young Space Marine lay without his legs, his helmet half blasted from his face. As blood frothed between the Adeptus Astartes' gritted teeth the Space Marine stared at the passing group. For Artegall it was too much. Crimson Consuls spilling each other's sacred blood. Guilliman's dream in tatters. He seized the grievously wounded Space Marine by his shattered breastplate and shook him violently.

'What the hell are you doing, boy?' Artegall roared, but there was no time. Scouts in light carapace armour were spilling from a doorway above, bouncing down one storey to the next on their boot tips, bathing the landings with scattershot from their shotguns. Bolt-rounds sailed past Faulks from below, where renegade Crimson Consuls had followed in the footsteps of their escape. The shells thudded into the wall above the kneeling Artegall and punched through the stumbling astropath, causing the Master of Ordnance to abandon his handicap and force back their assailants with blasts from a recovered bolter.

'Through there!' Faulks bawled above the bolt chatter, indicating the nearest door on the stairwell. Again Bohemond led with his shoulder, blasting through the door into a dormitory hall. The space was plain and provided living quarters for some of the Slaughterhorn's Chapter serfs. Bright, white light was admitted from the icescape outside through towering arches of plain glass, each depicting a bleached scene from the Chapter's illustrious history, picked out in lead strips.

Ravenscar handed Artegall his bolter and took a blood-splattered replacement from the stairwell for himself.

'There's a bondsman's entrance to the Chancelorium through the dormitories,' Artegall pointed, priming the bolter. Their advance along the window-lined hall had already been ensured by the bolt-riddled door being blasted off its hinges behind them.

'Go!' Faulks roared. The four Space Marines stormed along the open space towards the far end of the hall. The searing light from the windows was suddenly eclipsed, causing the Adeptus Astartes to turn as they ran. Drifting up alongside the wall, directed in on their position by the renegade Astartes, was the sinister outline of a Crimson Consuls Thunderhawk. As the monstrous aircraft hovered immediately outside, the heavy bolters adorning its carrier compartment unleashed their fury.

All the Space Marines could do was run as the great accomplishments of the Chapter shattered behind them. One by one the windows imploded with anti-personnel fire and fragmentation shells, the Thunderhawk gently gliding along the wall. The rampage caught up with Ravenscar who, lost in the maelstrom of smashed glass and lead, soaked up the heavy bolter's punishment and in turn became a metal storm of pulped flesh and fragmented armour. At the next window, Artegall felt the whoosh of the heavy bolter rounds streak across his back. Detonating about him like tiny frag grenades, the rounds shredded through his pack and tore up the ceramite plating of his armoured suit. Falling through the shrapnel hurricane, Artegall tumbled to the floor before hitting the far wall.

Gauntlets were suddenly all over him, hauling the Chapter Master in through an open security bulkhead, before slamming the door on the chaos beyond.

By comparison the command tower was silent. Artegall squinted, dazed, through the darkness of the Chancelorium dungeon-antechamber, his power armour steaming and slick with blood, lubricant and hydraulic fluid.

As Artegall came back to his senses, he realised that he'd never seen this part of his fortress-monastery before; traditionally it only admitted Chapter serfs. Getting unsteadily to his feet he joined his battle-brothers in stepping up on the crimson swirl of the marble trapdoor platform. With Sergeant Bohemond and Master Faulks flanking him, the Chapter Master activated the rising floor section and the three Crimson Consuls ascended up through the floor of Artegall's own Tactical Chancelorium.

'Chapter Master, I'll begin–'

Light and sound: simultaneous.

Bohemond and Faulks dropped as the backs of their heads came level with the yawning barrels of waiting bolters and their skulls were blasted through the front of their faceplates. Artegall span around but found that the bolters, all black paint and spiked barrels, were now pressed up against the crimson of his chest.

His assailants were Space Marines: Traitor Astartes. The galaxy's archtraitors: the Warmaster's own – the Black Legion. Their cracked and filthy power armour was a dusty black, edged with gargoylesque details of dull bronze. Their helmets were barbed and leering and their torsos a tangle of chains and skulls. With the smoking muzzle of the first still resting against him, the second disarmed the grim Chapter Master, removing his bolter and slipping the bolt pistol and gladius from his belt. Weaponless, he was motioned round.

Before him stood two Black Legion officers. The senior was a wild-eyed captain with teeth filed to sharp points and a flea-infested wolf pelt hanging from his spiked armour. The other was an Apothecary whose once-white armour was now streaked with blood and rust and whose face was shrunken and soulless like a zombie.

'At least do me the honour of knowing who I am addressing, traitor filth,' the Chapter Master rumbled.

This, the Black Legion captain seemed to find amusing.

'This is Lord Vladivoss of the Black Legion and his Apothecary Szekle,' a voice bounced around the vaulted roof of the Chancelorium, but it came from neither Chaos Marine. The Black Legion Space Marines parted to reveal the voice's owner, sitting in Artegall's own bone command throne. His armour gleamed a sickening mazarine, embossed with the necks of green serpents that entwined his limbs and whose heads clustered on his chest plate in the fashion of a hydra. The unmistakable iconography of the Alpha Legion. The Space Marine sat thumbing casually through the pages of the Codex Astartes on the Chapter Master's lectern.

'I don't reason that there's any point in asking you that question, renegade,' Artegall snarled.

The copper-skinned giant pushed the anti-gravitic lectern to one side, stood and smiled: 'I am Alpharius.'

A grim chuckle surfaced in Artegall. He hawked and spat blood at the Alpha Legionnaire's feet.

'That's what I think of that, Alpha,' the Chapter Master told him. 'Come on, I want to congratulate you on your trademark planning and perfect execution: Alpharius is but a ghost. My Lord Guilliman ended the scourge – as I will end you, monster.'

The Legionnaire's smile never faltered, even in the face of Artegall's threats and insults. It grew as the Space Marine came to a private decision.

'I am Captain Quetzal Carthach, Crimson Consul,' the Alpha Legion Space Marine told him, 'and I have come to accept your unconditional surrender.'

'The only unconditional thing you'll get from me, Captain Carthach, is my unending revulsion and hatred.'

'You talk of ends, Chapter Master,' the Legionnaire said calmly. 'Has Guilliman blinded you so that you cannot see your own. The end of your Chapter. The end of your living custodianship, your shred of that sanctimonious bastard's seed. I wanted to come here and meet you. So you could go to your grave knowing that it was the Alpha Legion that had beaten you; the Alpha Legion who are eradicating Guilliman's legacy one thousand of his sons at a time; the Alpha Legion who are not only superior strategists but also superior Space Marines.'

Artegall's lips curled with cold fury.

'Never...'

'Perhaps, Chapter Master, you think there's a chance for your seed to survive: for future sons of Carcharias to avenge you?' The Alpha Legion giant sat back down in Artegall's throne. 'The Tenth was mine before you even recruited them – as was the Ninth Company before them: you must know that now. I lent you their minds but not their true allegiance: a simple phrase was all that was needed to bring them back to the Alpha Legion fold. The Second and Fourth were easy: that was a mere administrative error, holding the Celebrants over at Nedicta Secundus and drawing the Crimson Consuls to the waiting xenos deathtrap that was Phaethon IV.'

Artegall listened to the Alpha Legionnaire honour himself with the deaths of his Crimson Consul brothers. Listened, while the Black Legion

Space Marine looked down the spiked muzzle of his bolter at the back of the Chapter Master's head.

'The Seventh fell fittingly at the hands of their brothers, foolishly defending your colourfully-named fortress-monastery from a threat that was within rather than without. The Eighth, well, Captain Vladivoss took care of those in the Sarcus Reaches – and now the good captain has earned his prize. Szekle,' the Alpha Legion Space Marine addressed the zombified Chaos Space Marine. 'The apothecarion is now in our hands. You may help yourself to the Crimson Consuls' remaining stocks of gene-seed. Feel free to extract progenoids from loyalists who fought in our name. Fear not, they will not obstruct you. In fact, the completion of the procedure is their signal to turn their weapons on themselves. Captain Vladivoss, you may then return to Lord Abaddon with my respects and your prize – to help replenish the Black Legion's depleted numbers in the Eye of Terror.'

Vladivoss bowed, while Szekle fidgeted with dead-eyed anticipation.

'Oh, and captain,' Carthach instructed as Artegall was pushed forwards towards the throne, 'leave one Legionnaire, please.'

With Captain Vladivoss, his depraved Apothecary and their Chaos Space Marine sentry descending through the trapdoor on the marble platform with Bohemond and Faulk's bodies, Carthach came to regard the Chapter Master once again.

'The *Revenant Rex* was pure genius. That I even admit to myself. What I couldn't have hoped for was the deployment of your First Company Terminator veterans. That made matters considerably easier down the line. You should receive some credit for that, Chapter Master Artegall,' Carthach grinned nastily.

A rumble like distant thunder rolled through the floor beneath Artegall's feet. Carthach seemed suddenly excited. 'Do you know what that is?' he asked. The monster didn't wait for an answer. Instead he activated the controls in the bone armrest of Artegall's throne. The vaulted ceiling of the Tactical Chancelorium – which formed the pinnacle of the Command Tower – began to turn and unscrew, revealing a circular aperture in the roof that grew with the corkscrew motion of the Tower top.

The Alpha Legionnaire shook his head in what could have been mock disappointment.

'Missed it: that was your Slaughterhorn's defence lasers destroying the strike cruisers you ordered back under their protection. Poetic. Or perhaps just tactically predictable. Ah, now look at this.'

Carthach pointed at the sky and with the Chaos Space Marine's bolter muzzle still buried in the back of his skull, Artegall felt compelled to look up also. To savour the reassuring bleakness of his home world's sky for what might be the last time.

'There they are, see?'

Artegall watched a meteorite shower in the sky above: a lightshow of tiny flashes. 'I brought the *Crimson Tithe* back to finish off any remaining frigates or destroyers. Don't want surviving Crimson Consuls running to the Aurora Chapter with my strategies and secrets; the Auroras and their share of Guilliman's seed may be my next target. Anyway, the beautiful spectacle you see before you is no ordinary celestial phenomenon. This is the Crimson Consuls Sixth Company coming home, expelled from the *Crimson Tithe*'s airlocks and falling to Carcharias. The battle-barge I need – another gift for the Warmaster. It has the facilities on board to safely transport your seed to the Eye of Terror, where it is sorely needed for future Black Crusades. Who knows, perhaps one of your line will have the honour of being the first to bring the Warmaster's justice to Terra itself? In Black Legion armour and under a traitor's banner, of course.'

Artegall quaked silent rage, the Chapter Master's eyes dropping and fixing on a spot on the wall behind the throne.

'I know what you're thinking,' Carthach informed him. 'As I have all along, Crimson Consul. You're pinning your hopes on Captain Borachio. Stationed in the Damocles Gulf with the Third and Fifth Companies... Did you find my reports convincing?'

Artegall's eyes widened.

'Captain Borachio and his men have been dead for two years, Elias.'

Artegall shook his head.

'The Crimson Consuls are ended. I am Borachio,' the Alpha revealed, soaking up the Chapter Master's doom, 'and Carthach ... and Alpharius.' The captain bent down to execute the final, astrotelepathically communicated move on Artegall's beautifully carved regicide board. Blind Man's Mate.

Artegall's legs faltered. As the Crimson Consul fell to his knees before Quetzal Carthach and the throne, Artegall mouthed a disbelieving, 'Why?'

'Because we play the Long Game, Elias...' the Alpha Legionnaire told him.

Artegall hoped that the Black Legion's attention span didn't extend half as far as their Alpha Legion compatriots. The Space Marine threw his head back, cutting his scalp against the bolter's muzzle. The weapon smacked the Chaos Space Marine in the throat – the Black Legion savage still staring up into the sky, watching the Crimson Consuls burn in the upper atmosphere.

Artegall surged away from the stunned Chaos Space Marine and directly at Carthach. The Alpha Legion Space Marine snarled at the sudden, suicidal surprise of it all, snatching for his pistol.

Artegall awkwardly changed direction, throwing himself around the other side of the throne. The Black Legion Space Marine's bolter fire followed him, mauling the throne and driving the alarmed Carthach even further back. Artegall sprinted for the wall, stopping and feeling for the featureless trigger that activated the door of the Chapter Master's private armoury. As the Chaos Space Marine's bolter chewed up the Chancelorium wall, Artegall activated the trigger and slid the hidden door to one side. He felt hot agony as the Chaos Space Marine's bolter found its mark and two rounds crashed through his ruined armour.

Returned to his knees, the Chapter Master fell in through the darkness of the private armoury and slid the reinforced door shut from the inside. In the disappearing crack of light between the door and wall, Artegall caught sight of Quetzal Carthach's face once more dissolve into a wolfish grin.

Throwing himself across the darkness of the armoury floor, the felled Crimson Consul heaved himself arm over agonising arm through the presentation racks of artificer armour: racks from which serfs would ordinarily select the individual plates and adornments and dress the Chapter Master at his bequest. Artegall didn't have time for such extravagance. Crawling for the rear of the armoury, he searched for the only item that could bring him peace. The only item seemingly designed for the single purpose of ending Quetzal Carthach, the deadliest in the Chapter's long history of deadly enemies. Artegall's master-crafted boltgun.

Reaching for the exquisite weapon, its crimson-painted adamantium finished in gold and decorated with gemstones from Carcharias's rich depths, Artegall faltered. The bolt-rounds had done their worst and the Chapter Master's fingers failed to reach the boltgun in its cradle. Suddenly there was sound and movement in the darkness. The hydraulic sigh of bionic appendages thumping into the cold marble with every step.

'Baldwin!' Artegall cried out. 'My weapon, Baldwin… the boltgun.'

The Chamber Castellan slipped the beautiful bolter from its cradle and stomped around to his master. 'Thank the primarch you're here,' Artegall blurted.

In the oily blackness of the private armoury, the Chapter Master heard the thunk of the priming mechanism. Artegall tensed and then fell limp. He wasn't being handed the weapon: it was being pointed at him through the gloom. Whatever had possessed the minds of his Neophyte recruits in the Carcharian underhive had also had time to worm its way into the Chamber Castellan, whose responsibility it was to accompany the recruitment parties on their expeditions. Without the training or spiritual fortitude of an Astartes, Baldwin's mind had been vulnerable. He had become a regicide piece on a galactic board, making his small but significant move, guided by an unknown hand. Artegall was suddenly glad of the darkness. Glad that he couldn't see the mask of Baldwin's kindly face frozen in murderous blankness.

Closing his eyes, Elias Artegall, Chapter Master and last of the Crimson Consuls, wished the game to end.

HELION RAIN

George Mann

Amongst the ruination of the ancient scriptorium, a statue of white marble was stirring. Slowly, tentatively, the figure came to life, shifting its position to better observe the courtyard on the other side of the broken balustrade. It moved with a practised silence, resting the nose of its bolt pistol on a fragment of the shattered stairwell, its jaw set firm with grim determination.

High above, through the canopy of shattered beams and broken roof tiles, birds wheeled in an empty sky, punctuated only by the distant heat trails of drop pods bombarding the grassy savannahs to the east. The place was shrouded in an eerie cloak of stillness, as if the building itself was somehow holding its breath, waiting for something inevitable to happen.

Veteran Sergeant Grayvus of the Raven Guard peered around the debris with eyes of pure obsidian, his pale skin stark against the surrounding stonework. The alien was barely visible, even with his augmented senses. Only the occasional alteration in the quality of light or the ghost of movement betrayed its presence in the courtyard at all. He wasn't yet sure if the creature had noticed him, or whether it was toying with him, waiting for him to make his move.

Grayvus turned his head, slowly, searching for any sign of his Scouts.
Nothing.
He smiled. They were learning.
Grayvus returned his attention to the courtyard. His finger tensed on the trigger of his weapon. Just a second longer...

It moved again. He depressed the trigger, spraying a round of hot bolt-fire across the flank of the concealed beast.

What followed happened in a blur of movement so swift and so precise that Grayvus was almost caught off guard.

The tyranid creature emitted an angered howl, spinning around with surprising agility and leaping over a ruined wall towards its attacker. Grayvus could see now that his instincts had been correct – the thing was a lictor: three metres tall, with a hard, pink chitinous shell and a festering mouth filled with wriggling, writhing proboscises. Its eyes gleamed an angry red and two immense, bony blades scythed the air above it, the ferocious tips of extra limbs that jutted up and out from its shoulders. Its ribcage was covered in a series of angular barbs that Grayvus knew, from experience, were to be avoided at all costs. And it smelled like death. Like the very essence of death itself. It was a scent that Grayvus would never forget. Althion IV would be burned in his memory forever.

The creature raised its head towards the sky and howled once again before stalking forwards with menacing intent.

The scriptorium erupted into a cacophony of sound and a blur of movement: the roar of a chainsword, the bark of shotguns, the sound of boots crunching gravel. The ominous clacking of the lictor's claws against the broken flagstones. Where previously the only sounds had been the distant cawing of the birds, now the ruined building was filled with the riot of battle.

The Scouts materialised from the shadows like ghosts stepping between the fabric of worlds, grey camo cloaks billowing around their shoulders, weapons charged and ready; prepared, as always, for the battle to come. Grayvus backed away from the lictor as the others swarmed around it, encircling it, trapping it between them with an ease and discipline that made Grayvus's heart sing.

Grayvus squeezed the trigger of his bolt pistol again, loosing a hail of shots. The lictor thrashed around, unsure of which direction to focus its attack. Grayvus offered suppressing fire as Tyrus leapt forwards, his chainsword growling as he swung it around in a wide arc, lopping off one of the lictor's bony limbs with a single, easy movement. Green ichor gushed from the wound as the arm fell twitching to the ground. Tyrus fell back to avoid the slashing talon that threatened to decapitate him in retaliation.

'Concentrate your fire on its head,' bellowed Grayvus as he strode forwards, raising his weapon and firing directly into the nest of tentacles that swarmed around the monster's gaping mouth. The lictor screeched in defiance. It lashed out to the left, catching Corbis hard with a flick of its remaining clawed arm, sending him sprawling to the floor, his shotgun spitting wildly into the sky as his aim was knocked violently askew. He rolled across the flagstones and remained there on the ground, still, his face hidden from view. Grayvus wondered if the Scout's neck had been snapped by the ferocity of the blow. He had little time to worry about it now.

A second chainsword roared to life and Grayvus heard it biting into the thick chitin plates that covered the creature's back, whining as it cut through layers of bone and gristle. Another of the Scouts was assaulting the lictor from behind. Tyrus, meanwhile, had pulled his bolt pistol from his belt and was showering the lictor's head with a volley of hot slugs, taking Grayvus's lead. The creature buckled, one of its legs folding beneath it, as the Scouts continued their onslaught.

'Bring it down before it can call for more of its kind!' Grayvus called as he moved to the left, trying to close the gap left in the circle by the prone Corbis, all the while keeping his black eyes fixed on the beast, his weapon trained on its head. It wouldn't do to offer the monster an escape route. Lictors hunted alone, but their kind were never far behind; if they didn't bring it down swiftly, its pheromones would bring swarms of the things down on them

There was a cry from behind the lictor. Avyn or Shyal – Grayvus couldn't see which. But he could see the creature's barbed tail flick up over its shoulder, blood dripping from the bony protrusions that crested its tip.

Grayvus felt something *thunk* into his chest plate and cursed that he'd allowed himself to be distracted. He looked down in horror to see one of the lictor's flesh-barbs had embedded itself in his armour. Extruded from the alien's chest, the barb was attached to a glistening tendril of thick, ropey flesh. The lictor jerked and Grayvus lurched forwards, only just managing to retain his footing. The creature was drawing him in, pulling the tendril back inside itself and dragging him closer in the process. Its slavering proboscises – or, at least, those that still remained after the rounds of bolt-fire that Grayvus had shot into its face – quivered with anticipation. This was what he had seen on Althion IV. The horror of what those tendrils could do. He *wouldn't* let it happen to him.

Grayvus dropped his bolt pistol and kicked backwards, allowing his feet to come up off the ground and throwing all of his weight against the pull of the lictor's tendril. The barb held, and although the xenos staggered, it remained firm, continuing to drag Grayvus closer.

Grayvus took a deep breath. His next move was all about timing. Around him, the other Scouts were still pounding the lictor with bolt-fire and swipes from their chainswords, and he could see it was close to death. Syrupy ichor ran from numerous wounds in its torso and the air was filled with the stench of scorched bone and seared flesh. But the creature's eyes still burned with fury and he knew that it would not stop, not until it had burrowed its unholy, bone-tipped probes inside his head and stolen his memories, absorbed all of his thoughts. Death was one thing – a thing he would welcome when the time came and he knew that he had proved himself to the Emperor – but this alien, this *monster*, it represented something else. The loss of everything he was. He would not allow this creature inside his head.

Grayvus's feet skittered across the shattered floor of the scriptorium. The creature was close now, so close he could feel the heat of its foetid breath. He flexed his shoulders, readying himself. Then, in one swift movement, he reached up and clasped the grip of his chainsword, tearing it free from its holster and thumbing the power. He swung it round before him, at the same time allowing his body to go limp, forgoing all resistance so that he was pulled sharply forwards towards the straining lictor. He collided with it, caught for a moment in its bony embrace.

For a moment he thought he saw a flicker of triumph in the alien's eyes as it readied itself to feast on his mind, before it realised the chainsword was buried to the hilt in its chest, thrumming with power, wedged there by the force of its own trap.

The lictor screamed as Grayvus forced the chainsword up and out of its torso, ripping through organs and muscles and bones until, at last, the roaring blade burst free, slicing unceremoniously through its neck and finally silencing it forever. The alien wavered for a moment before toppling to one side, Grayvus still tangled in a heap of limbs beneath it.

'Get me out of here,' he barked at the others, who still stood in a circle around the dead beast, looking on with something approaching awe.

Sometimes, in the stillness, the quiet moments of anticipation before a battle, he thought of Deliverance. He remembered the clusters of smouldering venting towers, erupting from the moon's surface like bristling spines, puncturing the grey regolith to belch oily fumes into the midnight sky. He recalled the constant rumbling beneath his feet: the reverberations of subterranean mining engines, coring out the centre of the tiny world, harvesting minerals to feed the scores of ever-hungry forges and manufactories. He saw the dark, towering monolith of the Ravenspire, silhouetted against the planet-light of distant Kiavahr, and thought of home.

He hadn't returned to Deliverance for nearly a century, drawn instead by the constant need to protect these outer worlds on the fringes of the Imperium. Or – he smiled grimly – to protect the local human forces from their own incompetence.

Perhaps, in truth, there was more to it than that. Perhaps something else was keeping him away. He buried the thought.

Idos was a backwater, a long way from that half-remembered home. A world infested with the stink of xenos, fodder for the enemy spawning pools. Yet Idos had been granted the Emperor's protection, and the Raven Guard were there to ensure it was enforced. And besides, any opportunity to halt the advance of a tyranid hive fleet was an opportunity worth taking. He'd fought tyranids before, back on Althion IV, and he knew them for the abominations they were. A plague, a virus

– a scourge that needed to be purged; they had infested the galaxy and obliterated innumerable worlds with their insatiable appetite for the raw materials from which they procreated. Yet the tyranids were an enemy that he could understand. Their motives were simple, their strategy pure. They wished only to feast on the biomass of a world, to conquer it and consume it completely, and they would take it through weight of numbers alone. Single-minded and devastating.

Captain Aremis Koryn surveyed the ruined landscape before him, the grassy plains covered in straw-like grass, the undulating hills and ridges that formed from the shattered wreckage of Proxima City in the distance.

It was too late for this place. He knew that already, an indisputable truth. His Raven Guard would halt the flow of the xenos, but the planet itself would never recover. Too much had been lost, and the world was too far out on the rim of the Imperium for it to be worthy of rebuilding. The native warriors knew that, too. It was what had driven them to such desperate measures, to using inferior weapons in an attempt to destroy the hive ship that hung in planetary orbit: a moon-sized abomination. Their targeting had been off, however, and instead they had inadvertently destroyed their own moon, Helion, splintering the worldlet into a billion fragments that now wracked Idos below with fierce meteor storms and gravitational instability. And all the while, the xenos kept coming, an insatiable maw devouring the planet.

Koryn looked down upon the serried ranks of Space Marines, their black armour gleaming in the morning sunlight. To his left, bike squadrons formed a protective flank, covering the line of trees in case anything emerged unexpectedly from the forest. To his right, assault squads readied themselves for the coming onslaught, their talons glinting. And between them stood the main bulk of the Fourth Company, bolters at the ready.

The Raven Guard were few, but they would hold firm. This, to Koryn, was another indisputable truth.

Koryn himself stood upon the crest of a hill, resplendent in his ancient armour. It was an antique, worn for millennia by the captains of the Fourth Company, created in the Martian forges before the time of the great Heresy. It was engraved with the names of all those who had worn it before him and given their lives in service to the Emperor. A litany for his dead brethren, covering every centimetre of its pitted black surface. Koryn felt the burden of their memory, but also the honour of their company, the pedigree from which he had come. Today he would make his forebears proud. He would honour their memory. And one day his name would be added to theirs, etched onto a pauldron or leg plate or arm brace. One day he would give his life in the service of his Emperor, and it would be glorious. The thought gave him much comfort.

Koryn flexed his shoulders. On the horizon he could see the alien swarm approaching, a hazy cloud of buzzing wings, slashing limbs and putrid, slavering jaws. Behind the flared respirator of his helmet, he smiled. Soon his talons would taste alien blood.

Grayvus kneeled beside Corbis, rolling the young Scout over onto his back to check for any signs of life. Behind him, the corpse of the lictor still quivered nervously in its final death throes.

Corbis was tall but stocky, with a square jaw and a long, puckered scar running across his cheek from his left eye to his ear. His flesh was already beginning to lose its pinkish hue, becoming pale and translucent, and his hair had darkened to the colour of dusk: a sign that his melanchromic organ was flawed. He had the mark of the Raven.

Grayvus's flesh had long since been bleached by time and experience. His eyes, too, had lost their colourful hue, becoming orbs of the purest black, glossy pools of impenetrable darkness. He was older than the others and had seen combat in all its multifarious facets, had fought xenos and traitors alike on myriad worlds throughout the Imperium. It was his role to train the fresh-faced Scouts, to shape them into fully-fledged battle-brothers... *if* they managed to survive their training. And Idos was no simple exercise. The enemy was lurking around every corner.

Grayvus stood, his boots crunching on the splintered flagstones. 'He's breathing,' he announced, without ceremony. He walked over to where Tyrus and Avyn were standing over the prone form of Shyal, stooping to reclaim his bolt pistol from where he'd dropped it during the fight. His exposed arms were covered in lacerations and scars, as well as ichor and bodily fluids spilled from the chest of the lictor when he had brought it down.

'He's dead, sergeant,' said Tyrus, without turning his head away from the body of his fallen brother.

Grayvus glanced at the corpse. He most certainly was. Half of his face was missing from where the lictor's whip-like tail had caught him beneath the chin, crushing his jaw and pulping his right eye socket at the same time. His other eye remained open, as if staring expectantly at Tyrus, willing him to do something more. Dark blood was seeping out over the grey stone floor, forming glossy pools in the midday sun. 'He was probably dead before he hit the ground,' Grayvus said, his voice a low growl. He dropped to his haunches beside the body. Shyal's camo cloak was wrapped around his ruined form like some sort of funerary shroud. Grayvus pulled it back to reveal the black armour beneath. The Scout's belt was adorned with the skulls of Kiavahrian ravens: tiny, yellowing heads with long, curved beaks, tied in a little cluster to a thin silver chain.

These totems, these *corvia*, were tokens of honour and skill. They were a representation of the raven spirit and a symbol of their home world. They were a measure of the Scout's aptitude and stealth, a part of the initiation rites through which the man Shyal had given himself over to the

Emperor to become an Adeptus Astartes. Each initiate would prove his cunning by catching these birds in the great woodlands of Kiavahr, moving so silently amidst the lush flora that he could grab the avians where they perched, taking them with his bare hands and gently breaking their necks. It took months of practice and great skill for a Scout to be light enough on his feet and swift enough in his movements to grab the birds before they fluttered away.

Grayvus cupped the bundle of tiny skulls in his fist and pulled them free of the dead Space Marine's belt. He looked up at the others. 'Who will carry his *corvia*?'

Tyrus stepped forwards. 'I would be honoured, sergeant.'

Grayvus gave a swift, sharp nod and handed the totems over to the other Scout. 'Then remember that you carry with you his honour, also. He will rest when you return them to the soil from whence they came.'

The others waited in silence while Tyrus affixed the skulls to his belt beside his own. Grayvus turned to see Corbis climbing to his feet, rubbing his neck. 'You took your time,' he said gruffly, before gesturing down a ruined side street with the nose of his bolt pistol. 'Move out.'

The Scouts moved like shadows through the wreckage of Proxima City, silent wraiths picking their way amongst the dead. The city had yielded entirely to the invading alien horde. As Grayvus and his squad clambered over the debris of a toppled Administratum building, they realised the extent of the devastation. As far as they could see, in all directions, the city was in ruins. The jagged spires of fractured buildings were like misshapen teeth, clustered in a broken grin. Dead civilians lay in rotting heaps, ready for the ripper swarms that would soon devour them, processing their flesh and blood and bones, feeding their raw biomass back into the tyranid gestalt. Within hours their constituent parts would be remoulded, formed into new alien paradigms. It was this that made Grayvus's skin crawl, this that appalled him most about the nature of the enemy: not only would they annihilate an Imperial settlement, but they would inextricably absorb it too, twist it and corrupt it and reform it in their own image.

Grayvus ground his teeth. The city had been decimated, shattered by the onslaught of the rampaging xenos and pummelled by the near-constant meteor storms as the remnants of the moon, Helion, rained down upon the planet below. There was nothing he could do to change that now. But he could halt the tide of stinking xenos. He could keep them away from the dead. The Raven Guard would have their revenge upon the tyranid filth. He would be sure of it.

Grayvus scrambled down the fractured remains of a colossal statue, swinging his bolt pistol in a wide arc, alert for any signs of danger. He heard Corbis drop down beside him.

'Sergeant, over here.' He glanced over at where Tyrus had slid down the other side of the ruined statue. Here, the head and shoulders of the monument lay half submerged in the dirt, the eyes of an ancient, unknown warrior staring up at them in silent vigil.

He crossed to where Tyrus and Avyn were standing. 'What is it?'

Tyrus pointed at the ground near his feet. 'Spawning pools. They've already started work.'

Grayvus nodded. 'They'll be coming for the dead. Be on your guard.'

The Scouts edged around the glistening pools, pushing their way further through the wreckage.

As they neared the boundary of the fallen Administratum complex, Grayvus felt the hairs on the back of his neck prickle with warning. Something was close. He stopped, and the others followed suit, turning as one to regard him. The sergeant gestured for them to remain silent.

Creeping forwards, his bolt pistol tight in his fist, Grayvus approached the half-collapsed entranceway to the building, using what was left of the wall as cover. He peered out at the street on the other side.

Two enormous tyranid creatures were hovering amongst the wreckage, about thirty metres from the Scout's current position. They were unlike anything Grayvus had seen before: fat, bloated bodies crested by an array of chitinous plates and spines, each atop a long, curling tail that floated a metre above the ground. Their heads resembled that of the lictor, but bigger, their mouths ringed with squirming tendrils. Two small arms ended in vicious-looking talons. They were the colour of rotting flesh, pink and lurid, and towered at least three or four times the height of the Scout sergeant.

Grayvus watched as one of the creatures used its talons to skewer the corpse of a Guardsman from a nearby heap of shattered rockcrete, lifting it hungrily towards its tentacled maw. He turned away as the beast chewed noisily into its carrion meal. The sound of crunching bones made his skin crawl. His finger twitched on the trigger of his bolt pistol, but he held himself in check. He turned and made his way back to where the others were waiting in silence.

'We find another way around,' he said.

Tyrus offered him a quizzical expression. 'Is the way impassable, sergeant?'

Grayvus nodded. 'Enemy hostiles block our path.'

Tyrus reached for his chainsword. 'Then we cut our way through.'

Grayvus put a hand on the Scout's arm, preventing him from drawing his blade. 'Sometimes, Brother Tyrus, winning the battle means losing the fight. Remember your training. Our mission is to survey the situation behind enemy lines and report on our findings. We will not needlessly engage the enemy and put that mission in jeopardy.'

Tyrus relaxed his grip on his weapon, but Grayvus could see the fire burning behind his eyes. 'Yes, sergeant. Forgive me.'

Grayvus smiled. He recognised that same impulse himself, that burning desire to purge the enemy, to seek revenge for his fallen brothers. But he knew nothing of the strange creatures out there amidst the rubble, and would not put his squad and his mission at risk – not for his own, or for Tyrus's, satisfaction.

Grayvus glanced around the ruined building, looking for another route. Without warning, the vox-bead in his ear sputtered to life with a hissing burst of static.

'Sergeant Grayvus?' The voice sounded tinny and distant.

'Captain Koryn.' Grayvus moved further into the shattered building so that his voice would not draw the attention of the feasting xenos outside.

'State your position, sergeant.'

'We're on the eastern fringe of the city, captain. Approximately ten kilometres from the main engagement, just inside the Administratum complex.'

The vox went silent for a while. 'Captain?' Grayvus prompted after a minute had passed.

When he spoke again, Koryn sounded distracted. 'Grayvus. There's a power station three kilometres north of your position. I need you to destroy it.'

Grayvus frowned. 'Destroy it?'

'Yes. And don't leave anything standing. Cause the biggest explosion you can.'

'But we don't have any explosives, captain.'

'Then be creative, Brother Grayvus.' The voice was firm, unyielding.

'Yes, captain.'

'And sergeant?'

'Captain?'

'Be swift, too.' The link went dead.

Grayvus pulled his auspex from his belt and consulted the readout. Three kilometres of rubble and wreckage stood between them and the power station, not to mention the risk of lurking enemy combatants and the ripper swarms feasting upon the dead. And he had no idea how they were going to destroy a power station with only bolt pistols and chainswords. It would be a test of their mettle, and a test of his training.

Grayvus glanced up at the expectant faces of his Scouts. 'Our mission parameters have changed,' he said, unable to contain the wide grin that was now splitting his face.

The enemy swarm was more substantial than even the reports of his own Scouts had led him to believe. There were thousands of them, a great, shifting ocean of flesh and bone. Koryn watched from his place on the hillside as the oncoming tide of xenos swarmed in towards his Raven Guard and the Space Marines came to life; immoveable, holding firm in the face of untenable opposition. The noise was incredible: the chatter of bolter-fire, the pounding of taloned limbs, the rending of plasteel and metal, the screeching of the xenos as they fell in waves.

Heavy bolters punched the air somewhere behind Koryn, sending hellfire rounds whistling into the conflict below, splashing searing mutagenic acid over the howling aliens, burning their unclean flesh. The bike squads roared to life, churning the earth as they shot into the melee, bolter rounds spitting from their forward-facing emplacements, mowing down scores of tyranids as they ploughed through the chaotic ranks of the enemy army. To the right, talons flashed as the assault squads pinned the enemy's left flank, slicing through the mass of darting hormagaunts and termagants that clambered over one another to get at the Space Marines.

And in the distance, like an eye at the centre of a vast storm, the hive tyrant. It was immense: an abomination rendered in flesh and blood. Its great, crested head towered high above the rest of its kin, swaying from left to right, taking in the enemy positions. Its huge cannon belched fat gobbets of venom that scorched the earth where they fell. Its limbs terminated in long, scything blades that cleaved the air around it, hungry for the blood of its enemies. It carried itself with an air of intelligence uncommon to the other, more animalistic creatures that surrounded it.

The captain knew that this creature – this monster – was the node that held the aliens together, the conduit by which the orbiting hive ship organised its troops, ensured the mindless individuals of the swarm were not, in their multitudes, mindless at all. They were a gestalt – one organism formed out of many. But if Koryn could sever that link between them, if he could interrupt that flow of information from the central intelligence above… then they became nothing. They would lose their cohesion. They would lose their purpose. And an enemy without purpose was no enemy at all.

Koryn turned to see one of his veterans approaching, his ebon armour scarred by the marks of a thousand prior battles. 'Argis. It is time for us to join our brothers in the fray.'

Koryn could not read Argis's expression behind his faceplate, but there was hesitation in his voice when he spoke. 'Captain. We are few. The enemy are legion. We cannot withstand a full engagement with the xenos. If the battle becomes protracted…' He let his words hang for a moment. 'As keen as I am to spill their foul blood, this is not our way.'

Koryn nodded. 'I hear your concerns, brother. But we must have faith. The Raven Guard will triumph this day.' Koryn knew he was taking an enormous gamble, playing a dangerous game. But that *was* their way. They would not defeat this enemy through brute force alone. They would out-think it. They would lead it into a trap. It was up to Grayvus now.

'Watch the skies, brother-captain!' Koryn turned at Argis's cry to see two winged gargoyles sweeping out of the sky towards him, their fangs chattering insanely, their jaws dripping with venom. Their heads and backs were plated with the same pink armour as their larger, flightless kin. But their exposed bellies were soft and fleshy; the perfect target.

Koryn tested his lightning claws. They fizzed and crackled with energy. He held his ground, waiting as the creatures swooped closer. He became aware of the sputter of bolter-fire as others around him began firing indiscriminately into the gargoyle flock, which suddenly filled the sky in all directions. He heard the beating of a hundred leathery wings as the hillside was cast in deep shadow, the density of the baying flock momentarily blotting out the sun. Swathes of the creatures tumbled from the air like fleshy missiles, shredded by bolter-fire, colliding noisily with the ground by the Space Marines' feet. But the onslaught continued unabated.

Koryn kept his eyes trained on the two gargoyles approaching him from above. The beast on the left squeezed the trigger of its strange, bone-coloured weapon, spitting a fine spray of acid across the captain's chest plate and pauldrons. He ignored it, remaining perfectly motionless as the venom chewed tiny holes in his armour. He dismissed the warning sigils that flared up angrily inside his helmet.

Waiting... Waiting...

The gargoyles manoeuvred themselves in for the kill, swinging around to offer their viciously barbed tails to the Space Marine, aiming their poison-spewing weapons at his faceplate.

Still waiting...
Still waiting...

Koryn pounced. He sprang into the air, twisting his body and uncoiling like a tightly wound spring. He extended his talons skywards to skewer the gargoyles through their exposed bellies, impaling one on each of his sparking fists. His manoeuvre was timed to perfection. The gargoyles had no time to react, screeching in pain and fury, twisting on the hissing metal claws that now punctured their pink, alien flesh. Pungent ichors coursed down Koryn's arms.

He landed neatly, his fists still held aloft as if brandishing the splayed gargoyles as obscene trophies. They thrashed for a few seconds more, their wings beating his arms and his face, their claws scrabbling at his power armour, before falling still, nothing but dead weights. Koryn roared in triumph and lowered his arms, casting the twin corpses to the ground. His ire was up.

He glanced around him, seeing only the spatter of xenos blood as his brothers tore through the gargoyle swarm, bolters chattering away at the sky, lightning claws and chainswords flashing in the stuttering light of the battle.

Below, his sergeants were holding the line, keeping the aliens back, refusing to buckle. But Koryn could see them straining against the sheer numbers and unrelenting ferocity of the tyranid assault. It was time. There was nothing more he could do from his vantage point on the hillside. He had committed the Raven Guard to this course of action and if he failed, then it would be a glorious death. All that was left was to hold the line. All that was left was the fight.

Koryn charged down the hillside, his boots pounding the earth as he ran. He leapt into the fray, his weapons ready. The blood sang in his veins. This was why he had been created, what he was made for. This: the glory of battle. This: the smiting of the Emperor's foes. This: the great war against the enemies of man. This was his purpose, his entire reason for being.

Koryn allowed the hunger for battle to consume him, gave himself utterly to the fight. He became one with his flashing talons. He danced and parried, transforming himself into a whirling dervish of death amidst a sea of pink flesh and chitin. Xenos fell in his wake. He carved through them like a spirit passing through walls of solid rock, his lightning claws spitting and humming as they cleaved skulls and separated limbs from torsos. His ancient, ebon armour glistened with alien blood. He dragged air into his lungs and bellowed as he fought: 'Victorus aut Mortis!' The aliens came at him in a relentless tide, but he cut them down. He would hold the line. Grayvus would prevail.

Behind Koryn, the Raven Guard pressed forwards anew.

Grayvus studied the hololithic readout of his auspex and glanced warily up at the sky. It had taken the Scouts over half an hour to pick their way through the rubble of the Administratum building and now a fresh meteor storm was threatening the horizon, and also their progress. He could see fragments of planetary debris beginning to burn up in the upper atmosphere, leaving long, fiery streaks across the sky in their wake.

The storms had plagued the Raven Guard's campaign ever since their arrival on Idos, rocks and boulders hurtling indiscriminately out of the sky at incredible velocities; a terrible, deadly rain. Helion rain.

Grayvus shook his head at the thought of it. An entire moon destroyed, a planet now ravaged by meteoric storms and tidal instability. A planet plagued by the stink of xenos. Idos had once been an idyllic world on the fringes of the Imperium. Now it was a living hell.

A high-pitched whistling pierced the air. Grayvus tracked the trajectory of a fist-sized rock as it smashed into the outcropping of a nearby building. The masonry exploded with the deafening echo of stone striking stone. This was followed by another, then another, fragments of the former moon clattering amongst the ruins with the explosive force of successive heavy bolter rounds.

'Incoming, sergeant!' bellowed Tyrus, and Grayvus turned to see a hail of debris showering out of the fire-streaked sky all around them. Tiny stones pinged off his carapace; a larger piece struck his right arm brace, nearly knocking him from his feet. Another tore a deep gash in his exposed forearm. The blood looked startlingly bright against the wintery paleness of his flesh.

'Take cover!' he called to the others, scrambling for the nearest building. The others scattered. Corbis fell in behind Grayvus, running over to share the shelter of an immense, arched doorway. Much of the building had been destroyed and Grayvus knew that what remained of it would be little help when faced with a major impact, but it would offer some protection from the accompanying hail of debris. If they were lucky, the larger strikes would occur further afield.

Grayvus heaved a frustrated sigh. They would have to wait for the storm to pass. This was one enemy that neither their bolt pistols nor their cunning could defeat.

The meteor storm swept in, bombarding the city, pummelling what remained of the buildings into heaps of rockcrete and stone. Grayvus dropped to his haunches, listening to the rhythmic drumming of the impacts, the bellowing echoes of the distant explosions that signalled the larger impacts elsewhere in the city. The sounds sparked memories of Haldor and the battle for Exyrian, all those years ago, trapped inside the city boundaries, besieged by the traitorous Iron Warriors. If he closed his eyes and concentrated he could still hear the screams of the dying, echoing in the darkness of the ruins. The siege had lasted for innumerable days, and it was only due to the unrelenting campaign of Captain Koryn – hitting the Iron Warriors with a series of swift, surgical strikes, then melting away again before the traitors could muster – that the Imperial forces had broken the enemy and brought the siege to an end. By then it was already too late for the civilians, of course. They were all dead, killed by the constant bombardments, the lack of food and the raging fever, this latter a result of the sheer volume and proximity of the putrefying corpses trapped in the ruins.

A voice cut through Grayvus's memories, snapping his attention back to the present. 'You've fought them before, sergeant?'

Grayvus tore his eyes away from the hailstorm ravaging the city, glancing back at Corbis, who was regarding him with interest, leaning against a fragment of broken pillar, his shotgun clutched in his hands. Grayvus nodded. 'Althion IV. We were ambushed. Most of my squad were killed. We were inside the hive when they came out of the darkness and hit us, attacking with all the fury of the warp itself. Terrible, deadly things with four arms. Until then I'd assumed the tyranids were nothing but beasts, animals that lacked any real intelligence, a pestilence that infested human worlds because it didn't know any different. But those things – those genestealers – there was darkness behind their eyes, a keen intelligence that spoke of something else.'

Corbis was watching him intently. 'How did you survive when so many others fell?'

Grayvus stiffened. He heard no accusation in Corbis's gruff tone, but the questions, and the memories, stirred feelings of guilt within him. He could not explain why he had lived when so many of his brothers had died. 'I cannot say. I was blinded by rage. I killed five, six of the creatures, tearing them apart with my bolter and my fist. My brothers had wounded many of them before they had fallen, but my hatred spurred me on. I covered my armour with their blood. Then one of them caught me in the shoulder with its claws, splitting my armour like a tin can. I was on my back. The thing was on top of me, its sickening jaws dripping toxins, its hot breath fogging my helm. I prepared myself. I was ready to die alongside my brothers. I had fought well and made my peace with the Emperor. And then a sudden burst of bolter-fire, and the creature was dead, shredded by explosive rounds. Erynis had saved my life.

'He was dead when I got to him, disembowelled and lying in a pool of his own blood. One other – Argis – was injured but alive. I carried him back to our base outside the hive.'

Corbis nodded gravely. 'What happened?'

Grayvus studied the Scout's face. He was young and had not yet witnessed a campaign on the scale of Althion IV. He did not know of the necessary lengths they would go to, to protect the Imperium from its enemies. 'We destroyed the hive. It was lost. We were too late, and too few.'

'The entire hive?'

Grayvus nodded. 'And now we are here,' he said, turning his head to watch the hailstorm showering the street outside, 'and so are those stinking xenos. This time, the Raven Guard will have their revenge.'

Grayvus jerked suddenly and let off a series of short, sharp shots with his bolt pistol. There was a soft *thump* amongst the clatter of meteors as something fell dead to the ground nearby.

Grayvus rose slowly from his crouching position, tracking his weapon back and forth across the street. 'Be ready, Corbis. Those things don't hunt alone.'

'What wa–' Corbis fell silent as a small tyranid creature – about the size of a large dog – hopped up onto a slab of fallen masonry just in front of him. Tiny meteor-rocks were pinging off its armoured plating, but the creature seemed unaffected by the constant pummelling from above. It turned and hissed at the Scout, baring its fangs and its long, curling tongue. It held a bone-coloured gun of some sort in its bony claws. It cocked its head and moved as if about to strike. Corbis squeezed the trigger of his shotgun and took the creature's head clean off. The stench of burning meat filled the air around them as the body slumped soundlessly to the ground.

Grayvus stepped out into the street and released a volley of bolt-rounds into the storm. He could see a pack of termagants swarming through the wreckage towards him, their heads bobbing as they ran, twitching as the debris from the shattered moon continued to stream down around them. He knew that they would not be alone: if there were termagants here, experience told him that there would be bigger and more ferocious tyranid warriors just behind them.

Grayvus waved for the Scouts to join him as he unleashed another round of bolts into the oncoming mass of aliens. Bodies shuddered and fell, but more swarmed over the top of their dead kin, drawing closer. Grayvus felt the sting of tiny stones puncturing his flesh, burying themselves in his exposed arms and cheeks. Bright, red blood began to course freely over his pale flesh. Behind him, Corbis was crouching with his shotgun balanced on some fallen masonry, picking off termagants, one at a time. The other Scouts emerged from their shelter too, following suit, dropping aliens with every shot.

A lucky blast of return fire from one of the termagants caught Avyl full in the chest, bowling him backwards. Grayvus heard him cry out as he fought at whatever it was that had struck him and was now attempting to burrow its way through his carapace armour. There was no time to help him. The sergeant raised his bolt pistol again, searching for another target.

And then he was being pitched forwards, the sound of a massive impact ringing loudly in his ears. The ground shook violently beneath him. Darkness swam at the edges of his vision. His last thought before the black cowl of unconsciousness swallowed him entirely was that they needed to get out of there as quickly as possible.

The battle raged with a fierce intensity. Koryn was surrounded by a sea of flashing claws, creatures scrabbling to climb over his power armour, striking him as they tried to get at the Space Marine inside. He fought them off with ease, carried along by his fury, swept up in a storm of death. His talons hummed and spat with electrical energy as he cut a swathe through the mass of pink flesh and bone.

He heard more than felt the meteor storm as the hail of tiny stones rained down on his armour, scoring the black ceramite where it fell.

Further afield, boulders hurtled out of the sky, decimating the clashing armies, tearing great furrows and ridges in the landscape. Impact craters formed huge pockmarks across the battlefield and chaotic piles of the dead lay all around them, xenos and Raven Guard alike swallowed indiscriminately in the waves of earth that rushed out from the site of each strike. Above, the sky looked as if it were on fire.

Koryn twisted sharply to the right, swinging his talons up to spear a hormagaunt through the head. He gave his wrist a quick jerk and the creature's face came away in a spray of sickly ichor. Its twitching body fell to the ground, but Koryn had no time to savour the moment: for every alien he killed another two took its place.

The vox-bead buzzed suddenly to life in his ear. 'Captain?'

Koryn grunted. The sound of another voice pulling him momentarily from the trance of the battle. 'Go ahead, Fabis.'

'We're ready, captain. The alien force is in position.'

Koryn grinned inside his helm, striking down another hormagaunt with a swipe of a lightning claw. 'Your timing couldn't be better, brother. Mount your attack. And may the Emperor ride with you.'

The vox crackled and went dead. Koryn spun, arcing around to catch another of the beasts that had managed to get behind him. He jabbed his fists through the hormagaunt's torso, pulling them apart to splay the creature open, spilling its organs in a bloody heap.

The ground shook as another massive meteor struck from above, gouging the landscape, ripping an immense furrow across the battlefield. Scores of aliens died in its wake, buried in the accompanying deluge of mud and loam. Koryn glanced up. The Raven Guard were still showering the tyranid army with bolter shells and frag grenades, but many of them were being thrown off course as they collided with the meteors that filled the sky, or worse, exploding in mid-air before reaching their targets.

He looked to the left. It was difficult to see through the tangle of grappling limbs, but the bike squads had now closed on the left flank of the tyranid army, closing off their escape route through the trees. Koryn laughed as he turned his attention back to the swarm of aliens, freeing his arm from the grip of a hormagaunt that was trying to scrabble up and over his leg. He crushed its skull in his fist.

His plan was working. With Fabis closing in on the xenos army from behind, flanking them with a Raven Guard force comparable in size to that under Koryn's direct command, they had the xenos pinned. To the right, like a great dam, were the walls of the ruined city. The tyranids were completely surrounded. Now it was a waiting game. All they had to do was hold the line. Koryn willed Grayvus to hurry.

Light bloomed before his eyes. Light, and the sound of raindrops striking the ground, a relentless pitter-patter, pitter-patter. Grayvus coughed and heaved himself up off the ground. He shook his head to clear the wooliness. The sound wasn't rain. It was tiny stones. It was Helion.

The memories flooded back into his consciousness. The meteor storm was still pounding the city. He couldn't have been out for long. He cast around, looking for his bolt pistol. He found it jutting out from beneath a pile of rubble and retrieved it, dusting it off. He stretched and felt a long gash on his left cheek tug uncomfortably. The flesh had already begun to knit itself back together, but his face was crusted with dry blood. Smaller wounds covered his arms like a spider's web, or a chaotic street map.

The scene all around Grayvus was one of utter devastation. Behind him, a large meteor had slammed into the street, toppling a basilica. The building's metal substructure had buckled and warped, and it now described a twisted skeleton against the sky, having shed its rockcrete skin. The ground itself had risen in a vast wave from the impact point, ruffling the earth like a rug pulled out from somewhere deep beneath the city. Steam rose from the impact crater like so many ethereal spirits, desperate to return to the warp. And all the while, the meteors continued to fall, stinging Grayvus's already battered flesh.

Grayvus realised he had been flung out over the lip of the crater during the impact. He began searching the immediate area for the other Scouts but found only dead termagants, their weak bodies crushed by the wreckage of the building or shattered by the force of the impact. One of them was still squirming, its back legs clawing pathetically at the exposed soil. It made a high-pitched mewling sound as he approached, and then hissed viciously as he stood over it, turning its lolling head with the edge of his boot. He put a bolt through its skull, not out of any sense of mercy, but simply to ensure it was dead.

'Sergeant?' He heard the call from over the other side of the crater and ran over to find Corbis crouched over the dead figure of Avyl. The fallen Scout's body was covered in a fine layer of grit and stone, and Corbis was brushing it away with his hand, searching for Avyl's *corvia*. He located the tiny bird skulls and Grayvus watched him tug them free, fixing them carefully to his own belt, a tribute to his dead brother.

'Was it the blast?'

Corbis shook his head. 'It was the xenos.' He indicated a hole in Avyl's chest carapace where the living ammunition that the termagant had fired from its weapon had bored a hole through to the Scout's chest, devouring his hearts.

'Where's Tyrus?'

'Down there.' Corbis nodded behind him. Grayvus started over, increasing his pace to a run when he heard bolt-fire coming from that same direction, assuming that the Scout had engaged the enemy. He crested a large mound of earth to discover Tyrus was in fact following his lead, quickly and effectively terminating any remaining aliens he found amidst the wreckage. He looked up when he noticed Grayvus watching.

'Avyl is dead. We have a mission to complete.' The statement was matter-of-fact, pointed. The authority behind it was implicit.

Tyrus nodded. Grayvus could see the Scout's knuckles were white where he clenched his bolt pistol hard. He was feeling the loss of his brothers keenly. Grayvus smiled grimly. Tyrus would have his chance to avenge the dead. And so would he. He would be sure of it.

The power station loomed out of the hailstorm like a jagged tooth, a towering edifice of pipework and fuel vats that spewed a constant stream of oily smoke into the sky for miles in every direction. This was the generatorium, until recently the power hub for an entire quadrant of the city. Amidst the destruction wrought around it, this leviathan was somehow still operational. Or at least, Grayvus considered as they approached through the wide, ruined street, *something* was keeping it running.

Grayvus and the two remaining Scouts ran through the pummelling rain towards their goal. Time was running out. It had been hours since their last communication from the captain, many of those hours lost to the meteor storm and their encounter with the termagants. Now was the time to act.

Grayvus scanned the approach to the generatorium before ushering the others forwards. He clipped his auspex to his belt and reached for his chainsword. He didn't know what to expect inside the building, but he wasn't about to be caught unawares.

Tyrus was first to approach the large, arched doorway. He stepped cautiously through the entrance, his bolt pistol braced and ready. A moment later he reappeared, indicating that the others should follow. Grayvus and Corbis kept their backs to the wall as they moved slowly around the doorway to join Tyrus inside.

The corridor beyond the door was dank and industrial, with bare metal plating covering the walls and floor, and exposed pipes worming their way through the passageways like a network of arteries and veins. It was dimly lit, with only flickering emergency beacons to guide them. The stench of oil and burning coal was almost palpable.

Grayvus motioned for the others to be silent. He listened for a moment, trying to discern any sounds of movement. There was nothing but the noise of a dripping pipe, echoing throughout the empty corridor. That and the continuous background sounds of the meteor storm, striking the building outside.

He looked up, meeting the eyes of the others. They were injured and bedraggled, but their eyes shone with a burning intensity. 'We need to find the reactor. That's the only way we can destroy this place without any explosives. We set it to overload, and we get out of here as quickly as possible.'

Corbis straightened his back and flexed the fibrous muscles in his neck. 'May the Emperor protect us.'

'We will do our duty,' was Grayvus's only reply.

They set off down the passageway, their boots ringing loudly on the metal floor plates. They passed along a series of almost identical corridors as they wound their way towards the heart of the structure. The low, red lighting cast long shadows, and the occasional clank of a pipe or the thrum of a power line kept Grayvus alert and ready.

'The place seems deserted, sergeant,' said Corbis, but as they turned a dogleg in the passageway it became instantly clear that it was not. A large, bulbous sphere hung in the air just ahead of them, a fleshy ball of pink and grey. A long tail hung from the base of it, which quivered like a twitching snake as they approached. The xenos had been here, and they had left this behind.

Tyrus hefted his bolt pistol and took aim.

'No!' Grayvus bellowed, foregoing all sense of stealth. But it was already too late. The bolt-fire lanced the spore mine, which exploded in a spray of searing acid, splashing across Grayvus's face and arms and raising instant welts in his pale flesh. His skin burned for a moment and he gritted his teeth and waited for the pain to subside. But Tyrus had taken the brunt of the explosion and he fell to his knees, clutching ineffectually at his face. His bolt pistol clattered to the floor.

Grayvus rushed to his side. 'Tyrus?'

'Forgive me, sergeant.' The voice was a stuttering lisp.

Grayvus prised the Scout's fingers away from his ruined face. The bio-acid had done its work. Tyrus's right eye was nothing but a puddle of jelly in its socket, and where his cheek had been there was now only stringy remnants of flesh and muscle, exposing his hind teeth.

'You're alive, brother, and that's enough. Get up.' There was a hard edge to Grayvus's voice. 'We have a job to do.'

Corbis helped the wounded Scout to his feet. 'Can you see?'

Tyrus nodded but didn't speak. He stooped to reclaim his bolt pistol, and they moved on.

The corridors and passageways of the generatorium continued to wind into the dank depths of the earth. They were drawing closer to their target now, closer to the throbbing heart of the power station, closer to their mission objective.

They'd passed another three of the spore mines, but had crawled beneath them on their bellies, an undignified but necessary means of avoiding detection, ensuring the biological triggers did not detonate in the confined space of the corridors.

Now, they had come upon a bulkhead door that had been dropped across the corridor, blocking their way: one of the safety barriers that locked into place during a shutdown. Grayvus had considered turning back, finding an alternative route, but that meant doubling back and passing the spore mines again, and worse, it meant wasting time. He consulted his auspex. Going through the bulkhead was the quickest way to the reactor. They were only a matter of metres away. Once they were through they could set the reactor to overload and get out of there. They would have to break through with bolters and chainswords.

He was about to outline this plan to the others when he heard a distinctive *tap-tap* ringing out against the metal floor plates. He glanced at the others inquisitively but was met with only blank stares. He hesitated, a cold sensation spreading across his chest. There it was again, *tap-tap*, like the clicking of a claw. Grayvus stiffened. His finely tuned hearing had detected breathing now, a ragged, rasping breath. A hissing. Something drew a claw across a wall plate, scratching a loud warning. It was toying with them. He knew what it was. They'd been herded into a trap.

Grayvus turned to see not one but two genestealers appear at the far end of the corridor, their heads bobbing, their multiple, viciously clawed arms tapping the walls menacingly as they approached. Wriggling proboscises surrounded their mouths and their eyes were blood-red and shone with a startling intelligence. They crept forwards, taking their time with their cornered prey.

The Scouts formed a line, keeping their backs to the bulkhead.

'Don't let them get close!' Grayvus barked. 'Don't let them get anywhere near you.' He knew first-hand what this genus was capable of.

Grayvus squeezed the trigger of his bolt pistol, spraying the genestealers with shells. But the creatures were too fast. They pounced, launching themselves into the air, springing off the walls to land only centimetres away from the Grayvus and the others. Grayvus's bolt pistol went spinning away down the corridor, wrenched from his grip by a glistening talon.

Corbis squeezed off a series of shots with his shotgun, catching one of the genestealers across its left flank, slowing it for only a second. It whipped out a claw and pinned the Scout by the throat, dragging him closer, its proboscises writhing with anticipation.

'No!' Grayvus's chainsword roared to life. He would not let this happen again. And he would not fail his captain.

He charged the nearest alien, swinging his chainsword in a wide arc, aiming to take off its head. The creature swiped at him with a claw, battering his blade to one side and sending Grayvus sprawling to the ground. He wasn't staying down, however, and twisted quickly up onto one knee, forcing the chainsword up. The genestealer's claw came down, centimetres from his head, but clattered uselessly to the floor as Grayvus's blade tore through the alien's carapace, chewing out its belly. It squirmed and thrashed, but Grayvus pressed the blade home even harder, twisting it round to maximise the damage. He stood, grabbing a fistful of the quivering mouth tentacles, yanking the creature's head to one side. The alien's claws raked his chest plate as it tried to pull itself free, but Grayvus was lost to his rage. He left the chainsword buried in its innards and reached for his combat knife. He looked deep into the creature's eyes as he buried the knife to the hilt in its exposed throat. 'That's for Erynis,' he whispered, as he saw the life flee its body. The genestealer squirmed once in his grasp and then fell still. Grayvus dropped the corpse to the floor.

Beside him, the other genestealer still had Corbis pinned by the throat but was also grappling with Tyrus, who had managed to draw his chainsword and was busy sawing his way through the creature's chitinous armour plating. He was bleeding freely from a long wound in his arm. Grayvus calmly pulled his own chainsword free of the corpse at his feet, stepped across the corridor and wordlessly lopped off the head of the occupied genestealer. It fell to the metal floor with a dull *thunk* and the body went limp. Corbis and Tyrus both disentangled themselves from the mass of limbs. Tyrus was breathing heavily. What with the acid burns and the fresh injuries caused by the genestealer, he was in a bad way.

'I told you not to let it get close to you,' Grayvus said, without a hint of irony in his voice.

Corbis laughed grimly. 'What now?'

Grayvus motioned to the bulkhead. 'Through there. The reactor is on the other side of this barricade. Corbis – see if you can breach it with your shotgun.' He stepped back to make room for the other Scout. 'And be quick. I don't want to be cornered by any more of these *things*.' He kicked at the dead remains of the nearest genestealer and moved off in search of his bolt pistol.

The shotgun soon punched a series of irregular holes in the thick metal plating causing the steel to splinter like rotten wood. Grayvus kept watch, keen to avoid another encounter with the genestealers that were likely haunting the corridors around them, drawn in by the sounds of the battle. Presently, however, the bulkhead issued a long groan and a large section of plating dropped inwards, clanging loudly where it fell.

Corbis called him over.

Grayvus approached the makeshift door, his bolt pistol clutched in his fist. He could see little through the hatch but a bank of winking diodes and controls: the reactor room. He dipped his head and pulled himself through the opening.

And that's when he saw it: the biggest tyranid biomorph he had ever seen, squatting inside the reactor room, its enormous, dripping maw bared in what he could only imagine was a wicked smile.

Koryn thrust and cut, parried and spun: a riotous dance of destruction. He could barely see for the blood spray hanging in the air all around him. He was injured, but was choosing to ignore the warning sigils that flashed up inside his helm, alerting him to the deep gash in his thigh. Analgesics had already flooded the area and his body would have time to repair itself later. If he survived.

Many of his brothers were dead. He knew that instinctively. He had no need to witness the sorry ranks of the lost, the discarded bodies, ripped apart by uncompromising alien jaws. He knew it, and it filled his heart with sadness. The Raven Guard were few and they could ill afford to sacrifice themselves. But his brothers had died with purpose. They had died in the glory of battle, holding the tyranid army at bay while their brethren engineered the means of their victory. He only hoped that Grayvus was close to achieving his goal. They could not hold out for much longer. Koryn could see the hive tyrant was growing restless. The end was in sight, one way or another.

Grayvus eyed the creature warily. It was huge, towering at least three times his height, with a flared crest of blood-red chitin atop its massive head. Its lower jaw was wide and pink, splayed like a shovel and connected to two mandibles that twitched ominously from side to side as it regarded him. Its fangs were as big as his forearms and coated in dripping venom. Its body was long and snake-like and – Grayvus realised – disappeared into the ground, from where the monster had evidently burrowed its way into the generatorium, digging its way in from beneath the city. Three huge pairs of limbs terminated in scything talons, with two sets of smaller, more human arms bursting out from its chest. It filled the reactor room utterly.

The creature emitted a shrill chirp and shifted its bulk, lowering its head to show them its fangs. Its foetid breath smelled of moist earth and decay. It couldn't twist itself around enough to reach them with its talons.

Once again, Grayvus was taken aback by the intelligence displayed by the xenos. Had they known the Scouts were coming? Was that why the biomorph had burrowed its way here? Or worse, had they planned to use the same trick? Were the tyranids actually intending to use the power station for the same purpose as the captain, to detonate it at a time when it would prove most devastating to the Imperial forces? Either way, they had been out manoeuvred.

'What is it?' Corbis was standing beside him, staring up at the monstrous thing.

'It's between us and the reactor,' was Grayvus's only response.

Tyrus stepped forwards, brandishing his chainsword. 'This time, sergeant, I think we're going to have to cut our way through,' His slurred voice was barely recognisable.

The Scout was right. There was little else they could do. 'Corbis. Get to that reactor. Tyrus and I will keep it occupied.' Grayvus raised his bolt pistol. 'We don't have to kill it, Tyrus, just keep it busy. The reactor will do our job for us if we can get to it.'

Tyrus nodded, but Grayvus wasn't clear whether it was in understanding or something else entirely. The injured Scout seemed distant, distracted.

Corbis approached the creature tentatively, trying to search out the best route to the reactor. He moved left and it howled like a baying wolf, slamming its talons down into the churned earth, trying its best to reach him. The bony blades scratched the walls in frustration. Corbis fell back, raising his shotgun and loosing a handful of shots. They pierced its flesh but did little more than anger it.

Tyrus fired up his chainsword. He extended his arm and placed something in Grayvus's hand. It was a tiny bundle of bird skulls. 'Honour me, sergeant, in the fields of Kiavahr.'

'Tyrus!'

The Scout charged forwards towards the beast, his bolt pistol flaring as he fired round after round into the creature's open maw. It screeched in fury and lashed out with its scything talons, one of them catching him full in the chest, bursting out of his back and spattering Adeptus Astartes blood across the room.

Tyrus growled in agony as he was lifted fully from the ground. His chain-sword roared, biting deep into the monster's flesh, as it pulled him closer to its slavering jaws.

'Corbis. Get to that reactor, now!' Grayvus swung his bolt pistol around and fired into the alien's wide mouth, satisfied to see the bolt-rounds flashing inside its head as they exploded brightly, cracking its teeth. The creature reared its head and thrashed alarmingly, swinging Tyrus violently from side to side. Tyrus was still alive, barely, speared on an outstretched claw. With one hand he was firing his bolt pistol into its face, with the other he was driving his chainsword repeatedly into the thick hide of its torso, searching for any vital organs.

Grayvus moved back and forth in a wide semi-circle, keeping his weapon trained on the monster, firing clip after clip at its head, desperate to keep it from realising that Corbis had now passed it and was working on the reactor controls behind it. He reappeared a moment later, scrambling over the mound of earth and rushing towards Grayvus.

Too late, Grayvus saw the arcing talon as it swung down from above, catching Corbis square between the shoulders and pitching him forwards. The Scout stumbled and dropped. The talon raised again, ready to finish the prone Corbis.

Grayvus dived forwards, grabbing at his brother and flinging him across the reactor room. The talon sliced down, puncturing his shoulder and opening his chest, bursting a lung. Grayvus slumped to the floor. The world was spinning. The creature pulled Tyrus's now unconscious body towards its mouth and chewed off his head.

Behind it, the reactor was reaching critical levels, warning sirens blaring.

Grayvus saw only darkness.

Koryn heard the explosion from almost four kilometres away, even above the clamour of the raging battle, even above the screams of the dying aliens and the screeching of their claws across his power armour. He heard it, and he knew they were victorious.

The ground rumbled and groaned, knocking him from his feet. He heard the vox-bead buzz in his ear but made no sense of the words as, all of a sudden, the planet seemed to lurch violently to one side. He heard a sound like rending stone and scrambled to his knees in time to see the city walls give way, crumbling to the ground as titanic forces rent the earth apart. All around him, the tyranids were scrabbling for solid ground, their animal minds unable to comprehend what was happening.

Koryn caught sight of the hive tyrant, its head thrust back, bellowing insanely at the sky. He watched as the ground cracked open beneath it, sucking the creature down into its rocky depths, pulling it into the canyon opened by Grayvus's destruction of the power station. It was as if the planet itself was enacting its revenge against these insidious invaders, swallowing them whole, crushing them with its immense power. The Raven Guard had executed their plan to precision: the fault line had opened right beneath the heart of the tyranid army, exactly where the Space Marines had pinned it in place.

Scores of aliens spilled into the newly opened crevasse like a tide, unable to prevent themselves from falling. Their screams were a violent cacophony, a tortured howl that Koryn would never forget. That was the sound of triumph. That was the sound of the Emperor's might.

Those aliens that still swarmed around Koryn himself seemed suddenly to lose direction, their psychic link with the hive mind interrupted by the death of their tyrant. They pressed on with their attack, but they had lost their cohesion, their underlying purpose, and were now fighting on instinct alone. It would be a simple matter for the remaining Raven Guard forces to mop up what was left of the alien brood.

Koryn sliced another alien in two with his talons. He was covered in xenos blood and his leg wound was still causing warning sigils to flare incessantly inside his helm. He watched as a group of hormagaunts turned and fled from an approaching assault squad, who showed no mercy, mowing down the retreating aliens with their bolt pistols.

He turned to see Argis approaching from behind, striding across the battlefield towards him, his power armour rent open across the chest in a wide gash, his bolter hanging by his side. Clusters of *corvia* hung from his belt, signifying the losses his squad had sustained during the thick of the battle. The veteran stopped beside Koryn, surveying the scene across the battlefield. After a moment, he spoke. 'Faith, you said, captain.'

Koryn nodded. His voice was subdued. 'Faith.'

Argis put his hand on Koryn's pauldron. 'That is most definitely our way.'

Grayvus sucked noisily at the air and winced at the lancing pain it caused in his chest. He peeled open his eyes. He was outside, slumped against a wall. The meteor storm had abated and the sun was perforating the clouds. His mouth was full of gritty blood and he was gripping something tightly in his fist. He glanced down. It was Tyrus's *corvia*. He allowed his hand to drop to his lap. He would take them back to Kiavahr, bury them in the soil from whence they came.

Corbis was standing over him. When he saw Grayvus was awake, his pale face cracked into a wide grin. 'Sergeant.'

Grayvus spat blood. 'Corbis. You should have left me.'

Corbis didn't answer.

Grayvus stared over at the enormous cavity that had opened in the ground behind them. The power station had been completely subsumed. What remained of it after the explosion had slid noisily into the hungry earth, tumbling down into the depths of the fractured landmass. Its destruction had opened a canyon across the face of Idos like a long, puckered scar, a fault line stemming from the site of the explosion and stretching for kilometres in both directions. Much of the city had been swallowed in the ensuing devastation. And the biomorph, too, along with most of the tyranid brood.

Corbis dropped to his haunches beside the wounded sergeant. 'What now, sergeant?'

Grayvus put his hand on Corbis's shoulder pauldron. 'Now, brother? Now you may call yourself Adeptus Astartes.'

ECHOES OF THE TOMB

Sandy Mitchell

If there's one basic principle I've learned in over a century of rattling around the galaxy fighting the Emperor's enemies (whenever I couldn't avoid it), it's 'leave well alone'. Three simple words which have stood me in good stead over the years; judiciously applied they've made my commissarial duties a great deal easier than they might have been. Unfortunately it's a phrase the Adeptus Mechanicus seems incapable of grasping, a failing which almost cost me my life.

I suppose I'd better explain. By the end of 928 my undeserved reputation for heroism had grown to such a ridiculous level that I'd finally attracted the attention of the upper echelons of the Commissariat, who had decided that a man of my obvious talents was wasted in the posting to an obscure artillery unit I had so carefully aranged for myself in the hope of being able to sit out my lifetime of service to the Emperor a long way away from any actual fighting. As it turned out, by sheer bad luck I'd managed to put myself in harm's way an inordinate number of times, emerging on every occasion trailing clouds of undeserved glory, so that to the sector at large I seemed to be the very epitome of the swashbuckling hero that commissars are generally considered not to be. (Most regiments regard us as something akin to the engineseers in the transport pool; sometimes necessary, occasionally useful, generally best avoided.)

Accordingly I found myself transferred to a desk job at brigade headquarters, which at first seemed like a gift from the Emperor himself. I had a nice comfortable office, with an anteroom in which Jurgen, my aide, was able to lurk, deterring all but the most determined of visitors with his single-minded devotion to following orders as literally as possible and his paint-blistering body odour. For a while it seemed that my days of fleeing in terror from genestealers, Chaos cultists, and blood-maddened orks were over. But of course it was all too good to be true. The staff officers were delighted to discover that they had a bona fide hero among them (at least, so they believed), which meant every time they needed an independent commissar to accompany some particularly dangerous or foolhardy mission, they sent for me.

Thanks to my finely-honed instinct for self-preservation I managed to make it back every time, though this which only encouraged them to think I was the greatest thing since Macharius, and just the man to send out on an even more dangerous assignment just as soon as they could think of something sufficiently lethal.

Enough was enough, I decided, and hearing that someone was needed to liaise with an Astartes company which was campaigning alongside the Guard in a routine action to clear some heretics off an agriworld on the spinward fringes of our sector decided to volunteer for the job. After my last little jaunt, rescuing some hostages from an eldar pirate base, I thought a bit of quiet diplomacy would be just the change of pace I needed.

'You don't think you'll find this sort of thing a little... tame?' General Lokris, a genial old buffer I'd probably quite like if he didn't keep trying to get me killed, asked, raising a shaggy white eyebrow in my direction. We were dining together in his private chambers, the skill of his chef more than making up for the tedium of his company, and I had a shrewd suspicion that this demonstration of his regard was intended to sway me into changing my mind. I took another mouthful of the salma, which was poached to perfection, to give myself time to formulate an acceptable answer.

'Well it's got to be more interesting than shuffling datafiles,' I said, smiling ruefully. That fitted his mental image of Cain the Man of Action quite nicely, and he nodded sympathetically. 'Besides,' I went on, seeing no harm in laying it on with a trowel, 'how often am I going to get the chance to go into battle alongside the Astartes?' Never, if I had anything to do with it, but Lokris didn't need to know that. He nodded eagerly at the prospect, quite enthused on my behalf, and took an extravagant pull at his wineglass to restore his composure.

'Quite right, my boy. What an experience that would be.' He sipped at his drink again, growing quietly contemplative. 'By the Emperor, if I were a hundred years younger I'd volunteer myself.'

'It's not as though there's anything urgent I need to do here,' I went on. 'Jurgen can take care of the routine stuff while I'm gone.' I would have preferred to take him with me, of course, but I was uncomfortably aware of the impression he was bound to make on the genetically-enhanced supermen of the Astartes, and had no wish to undermine my credibility before the assignment had even begun. Besides, while he was here he could watch my back, making sure I wasn't earmarked for any more suicide missions. I knew something was in the wind, which was why I'd seized on this diplomatic assignment so eagerly. For once, whatever Lokris and his cronies were planning they could leave me out of it.

'You should reach the Viridian system in about a month,' the general said. 'I don't suppose the heretics will be able to hold out for much longer than that, but even if they do you ought to be back here by around two hundred next year at the latest.'

'Emperor willing,' I said, making a mental note to spin the assignment out for longer than that if I could. He might not have a specific reason for wanting me back by then, but you never know.

My first surprise was the transport ship I'd been assigned to. Instead of a troopship or a supply vessel, both of which I was intimately acquainted with after all my years of shuffling from one warzone to the next, I found my shuttle docking at a light freighter bearing the unmistakable sigil of the Adeptus Mechanicus. They seemed to be expecting me. There was an honour guard of their augmetically enhanced troopers lining the walls of the hanger bay, and a tech-priest with a wide smile and a couple of mechadendrites waving lazily over his shoulders was waiting at the bottom of the shuttle's exit ramp. He stuck out a hand for me to shake as I descended, and on taking it I was surprised to find it was still unaugmented flesh.

'Commissar Cain,' he said. 'Welcome aboard. I'm Magos Killian, leader of the expedition, and this really is a tremendous honour. We've heard all about you, of course, and I must say we're thrilled to have you travelling with us.'

'Expedition?' I said, trying to ignore the sudden lurching sensation in the pit of my stomach. 'I was under the impression I've been assigned to liaise between the guard units and the Reclaimers task force in the Viridia system.'

'Didn't they tell you?' Confusion, exasperation and amusement chased themselves across Killian's face. 'Well, that's the Munitorum for you, I suppose. We're making a rendezvous with a Reclaimers battle-barge in the Interitus system, so some clerical drone obviously thought it would save you a bit of time to hitch a lift with us and transfer across when we meet them.' He fished a data-slate from some recess of his immaculate white robes, and fiddled with it for a moment. 'The next scheduled departure for Viridia is in another three weeks. Allowing for the wait before the barge arrives in orbit around Interitus Prime, you should be there about...' he consulted the slate again, making a couple of quick calculations as he did so, 'about thirty-six hours ahead of them. If the warp currents are favourable, of course.'

'Of course,' I said. I wasn't sure whether to be relieved or angry. On the one hand I'd be spending an extra three weeks on a roundabout voyage to Emperor-knew-where, but on the other that was three weeks I wouldn't have to worry about Lokris and his friends trying to find some new and inventive way of getting me killed. On balance that was an acceptable trade-off, I felt. I smiled, and nodded with every appearance of polite interest I could summon up. 'I'm looking forward to hearing all about this expedition of yours.'

A servitor scuttled past me and up the ramp of the shuttle to retrieve my kitbag, which from habit I'd left lying where it was on the subconscious assumption that Jurgen would deal with it. Killian nodded with every indication of eagerness as we strolled past the line of tech-guards, every one of them immaculate, hellguns at the port. They looked formidable enough on parade, I found myself thinking, but I was by no means sure their fighting prowess would be a match for real Guardsmen.

As it turned out I was to see for myself how effective they were before very long, and if I'd realised that at the time, and against how terrible a foe, I would certainly have thanked the tech-priest politely for his offer and bolted for the shuttle without a second thought. But of course I didn't, so I simply strolled along beside him, blithely unaware that we were all on a voyage to perdition.

Despite my forebodings the trip itself turned out to be remarkably pleasant. In striking contrast to the basic conditions aboard the troopships I was used to, the *Omnissiah's Blessing* felt more like a luxury liner. I had a well-appointed stateroom assigned to me, with a couple of hovering cyber-skulls humming quietly in the corner with nothing better to do than scoot off to find anything I required, and the cuisine was first rate. A real surprise this, as in my experience tech-priests tend not to worry about that sort of thing, looking on the necessity of taking in regular nourishment as a distasteful reminder of their fleshly origins or some such nonsense. I'd been steeling myself to face a plateful of soylens viridiens or something equally unappetising the first time I wandered down to the mess hall, only to find a pleasantly appointed dining room which wouldn't have looked out of place in a smart hotel, and was immediately assailed by the mouth-watering odour of sautéed grox.

I was still enjoying my first meal aboard when Killian ambled over, a plate of grox and fresh vegetables in one hand, a large bowl of ackenberry sorbet in the other, and a steaming mug of recaf waving precariously from a mechadendrite. I gestured for him to join me, and after a few preliminary pleasantries he began to chat about their voyage.

'No reason you shouldn't at least know where we're going,' he said cheerfully, the unoccupied mechadendrite diving into the recesses of his robe for the data-slate. He placed it on the table and continued to manipulate the controls with the mechanical limb, while his real ones plied knife and fork with evident enthusiasm. A star chart appeared, the Viridian system just at the fringes of the display, and a small, sullen stellar revenant centred in the screen.

'Looks inviting,' I said, with heavy irony. To my surprise Killian chuckled.

'Does rather, doesn't it?' he said, zooming the display so that the target system filled the screen. A handful of dark and airless worlds orbited the decaying star, seared to cinders when it went nova millions of years before, taking whatever life had existed there into oblivion before sinking back into the sullen, cooling ember about which the few surviving rocks still drifted.

'This is the Interitus system,' he said. 'Well named, I'm sure you'll agree.' I nodded.

'I can't for the life of me see what you'd want there,' I admitted. 'Let alone why an Astartes Chapter would divert a battle-barge from a warzone to meet you.'

Killian positively beamed, and pointed to the largest chunk of rock in the system.

'This is Interitus Prime. The whole system was surveyed by explorators back in the twenty-eighth millennium. In the most cursory fashion I may add, if the surviving records are anything to go by.'

'Your records go back that far?' I couldn't keep an edge of incredulity from my voice. That was the all but unimaginable golden age when the Emperor still walked among men and the Imperium was young and vigourous, its domination of the galaxy uncontested, instead of being riven by heresy and threatened on all sides by malevolent powers. Killian nodded.

'Only in the most fragmentary form, of course. But there are still tantilising hints for those prepared to meditate for long enough upon them, and put their trust in the benevolence of the Omnissiah.'

'And you think there's something there worth going after,' I said. There wasn't much which would drag a ship full of cogboys halfway across the sector, and it wasn't hard to guess which item on that very short list was the attraction here. 'Some significant stash of archeotech perhaps?'

'Perhaps,' Killian nodded, evidently pleased at my perspicacity. 'We won't know for sure until we get there, will we?'

'I suppose not,' I conceded, turning my attention to the desserts.

The rest of the voyage passed pleasantly enough, although apart from Killian I had little to do with the tech-priests on board. For company I gravitated naturally to the tech-guards, with whom I had a little more in common, finding that despite their augmetic enhancements and a devotion to the Cult of the Machine which I found a trifle disconcerting (I've little enough patience with Emperor-botherers at the best of times, let alone ones who seem to think he runs on clockwork), they were as disciplined and professional in their way as any of the warriors I'd served with. Moreover they'd heard of me, and believed every word of my reputation. Their only drawback from my point of view was that they didn't seem to have any currency, being some sort of vassals of the Adeptus Mechanicus, so there wasn't much point in getting my tarot deck out. Their commanding officer, a Lieutenant Tarkus, was a keen regicide player however, and a hard opponent to beat, so I was able to keep my brain ticking over while the ship scuttled nervously through the warp towards whatever might be lurking at our destination.

It was Tarkus who finally put my mind at rest about the battle barge; it seemed that, despite my obvious concerns, its formidable firepower wasn't to be deployed in our defence.

'Omnissiah no!' he said, casually dispatching one of my lancers with a sudden flanking movement I should have seen coming. 'It's on its way to clean out the rebel base on Viridia Secundus.' I nodded gravely, pretending I'd read the briefing slate about the tactical situation in the Viridia system. It seemed the heretics had taken control of more than just the main world, then. 'They're only hooking up with us long enough to transfer a squad of Space Marines over. And to pick you up, of course.'

Well that was something, although a potential threat potent enough to require an Astartes squad to contain wasn't to be taken all that lightly. I consoled myself with the reflection that it wasn't my problem anyway, I'd be safe aboard one of the most powerful vessels in space and a long way away from Interitus Prime before anyone started to meddle with whatever chunk of archeotech the cogboys were after. I nodded judiciously, playing for time, and made a feint with a trooper hoping to draw his ecclesiarch out of position.

'I'm sure you'll feel safer having them around,' I said blandly. 'Can't be too careful, after all.' As I'd hoped, the half of his face which wasn't made of metal coloured visibly as he considered the implied slur on his command, and he moved a little too hastily, creating an opening I should be able to exploit a couple of moves further on in the game.

'I don't see why that'd make a difference,' he said, a little too levelly. 'My boys can cope with anything the galaxy might throw at us.'

'I don't doubt it,' I said. 'From what I've seen we could do with a few more like them in the Guard.' Tarkus nodded as I moved my portside citadel, setting up what I hoped would be a chance to win in another three turns. I waited until he was considering his response before adding: 'But Magos Killian obviously doesn't share my confidence.'

Tarkus almost knocked his ecclesiarch over as he picked it up and moved it, blowing his only chance of blocking my next attack. His jaw clenched.

'It's not a question of confidence,' he said. 'There are... longstanding obligations.'

I perked up at that, as you can imagine, although what sort of pact there might be between an Astartes Chapter and the Adeptus Mechanicus I was at a loss to understand. I don't doubt that I would have been able to worm a little more out of Tarkus given time, but I decided not to press him any further that evening (having just set myself up for a comfortable win despite his superior skill at the game, and wanting to savour it), and by the time we'd agreed on for our next joust across the board he was already dead.

'Well, there it is.' Killian waved an expansive hand at the armourcrys window which dominated the far end of the ship's lounge. Beyond it the dying star guttered fitfully, casting a dim blue glow over us which reminded me of autumn twilight. A slice of darkness distorted the glowing sphere, the bulk of the planet we'd come so far to reach rising up to take a bite out of it.

The landscape below us was in darkness, but enough of the wan glow of the system's primary leaked across the horizon for me to make out a blasted wasteland, cracked by heat almost impossible to imagine, and riven with impact craters. That alone was a testament to how old this place was, as it must have been left almost smooth by its fiery transformation; the pockmarking of its face would have been the work of aeons. Despite the awful bleakness of the prospect I couldn't deny that it had a desolate grandeur to it, and a faint chill akin to awe touched my soul as I took it all in.

'It's certainly... impressive,' I agreed. Nonetheless a vague sense of unease took hold of me, and I found myself grateful for the thought that I'd be transferring to the Reclaimers' battle-barge and leaving this system forever within a day or two.

'We've already begun to establish our base camp,' Killian continued. I strained my eyes in the direction he'd pointed, failing to see anything for a moment, then picked out a faint flash of light as one of our shuttles ignited its engine many kilometres below. 'I think you'd be impressed.'

'No doubt I would,' I agreed, grateful for the secrecy he'd displayed up to now, which almost certainly meant I wouldn't have to leave the security of the ship. 'But I'm sure you don't want me getting underfoot.'

'Well...' Killian hesitated, clearly torn between conflicting impulses, and not entirely sure whether he was doing the right thing. 'Obviously we're on a mission from the Omnissiah. Normally we wouldn't dream of involving an outsider...' Here it comes, I thought, with an ominous sinking feeling in the pit of my stomach. That reputation for heroism is about to hit me over the back of the head again. The tech-priest cleared his throat. 'But given your extensive experience as a military man, do you think Lieutenant Tarkus would listen to your opinions at all?'

'Lieutenant Tarkus strikes me as a man who doesn't need much advice from anyone,' I said smoothly, cursing myself for undermining his confidence the previous evening. 'And if he does, I'm sure the Astartes contingent will have far more pertinent comments to make when they get here than anything I might have to say.'

'Well, that's the thing.' Killian coughed delicately again. 'Technically, they'll be led by a sergeant, won't they?'

Of course. And Tarkus would be too stubborn to ask the opinion of a lower ranking squad leader now his pride had been hurt. Notwithstanding the fact that the Space Marine sergeant would probably have decades of combat experience, and refuse to take orders from anyone outside his Chapter in any case. I had a sudden premonition of the administrative problems which would be awaiting me on Viridia, and wondered for a moment if I'd done the right thing in volunteering.

Oh well. I might as well get a little practice in now. I had nothing better to do until the barge arrived after all.

'I'll do my best to help, of course,' I said. 'Perhaps if I had a little chat with him?'

'Would you?' Killian snagged a plate of canapés from a passing servitor, and offered me one. 'We'd be very grateful. He's an admirable young man, of course, but rather headstrong.'

'Where is he?' I asked, biting into the delicacy. 'Still in his quarters?'

'Omnissiah no.' Killian smiled, and gestured towards the planet below. 'He's down there.'

As it happened that was a stroke of luck which was to save my life, but I had no idea of that at the time, so spent the shuttle ride down to the surface of Interitus Prime feeling resentful at being dragged off on a pointless errand. Technically I had no authority over Tarkus in any case, since he wasn't a member of the Imperial Guard, but Killian didn't seem to think that would matter, sure that the young officer would be sufficiently impressed with my fraudulent reputation to listen to whatever advice I might have to offer. He was also very grateful for my assistance, as he kept telling me from the adjacent seat as we descended, and in the end I found myself feigning interest in the desolate landscape below just to shut him up for a minute or two.

Truth to tell, after a while my interest was becoming genuine, even if it remained somewhat muted. The closer we got to landing, the more forbidding that airless landscape became, smaller craters becoming visible as we got closer to them, and faint spiderwebs of shadow swelling into chasms deep beyond measure and wide enough to swallow a hive block. The shuttle continued to descend, and I began to wonder whether the pilot was paying attention to the altitude, despite knowing it to be a servitor which could by its very nature be nothing but vigilant. There was still the faint possibility of malfunction, of course, and I began to tense subconsciously, waiting for the retros to kick in, but they never did.

'Aren't we getting a little close to the ground now?' I ventured after a while, and Killian smiled lazily.

'I suppose we are,' he said, showing no sign of concern. Well I wasn't going to make a fool of myself in front of the magos, so I simply shrugged with the best expression of casual indifference I could summon up.

'Thought so,' I said. A few moments later the reason for his lack of concern became evident even to me. A grey haze in the distance, which I'd taken for the horizon, began to close in on us, looming over the slowly descending shuttle like a thunderhead, and I nodded in sudden understanding. We were sinking gently into one of those titanic rifts in the planet's surface, already at least a couple of hundred metres below ground level. 'How far down does this go?'

'About eight hundred kilometres,' Killian said casually. 'It's the deepest chasm on the planet.' He produced a flask of something from the depths of his robe with his right hand, the mechadendrites pulling out a cup apiece. 'So we've got time for a recaf before we land if you like.' I did like; under the circumstances I thought I deserved one.

The dim illumination of the dying star above had dwindled to nothing by now, but the running lights of the shuttle were enough to let me pick out a few of the details of that incredible fissure. Layer after layer of different strata slipped past the porthole, subtle graduations of hue marking the ticks of some long wound-down geological clock, and a couple of times I thought I caught a glimpse of something white, fossils perhaps, of creatures already extinct for millions of years before their planet died in its turn. The thought was a morbid one, and I tried to turn my mind away from the contemplation of death and eternity with casual conversation.

'I can see why you think this place is so special,' I ventured after a while. 'It's quite...' I tried in vain to think of a suitable adjective, before concluding somewhat lamely with 'impressive.' Killian chuckled throatily. I have to say that of all the tech-priests I've ever met he was by far the most likable, as well as the most untypical of his kind. Factors which were probably not unconnected, come to think of it.

'I think we can still surprise you, commissar.' At that point I rather doubted it, to be honest, although I have to concede that he was right.

My first presentiment that there was even more to this chasm than at first met the eye was a faint glow from below us, which soon resolved itself into the actinic glare of several gigantic luminators set on pylons around a makeshift landing pad. Our shuttle settled gently in what seemed to be the exact centre of the flattened area, and Killian bounced from his seat with every sign of eagerness to get outside; it was only as he hit the rune to lower the exit ramp that I remembered the world was airless.

'Wait a minute!' I called, struggling up from the deeply-padded seat which suddenly seemed a lot less comfortable now that I needed to stand in a hurry. He might have some augmetic enhancements that let him manage without air, but I most certainly didn't. Killian smiled at me.

'I told you you'd be surprised,' he said as the seals broke with an audible hiss. But it was the sound of equalising pressure, I realised with a sudden surge of relief, having become all too familiar with the sound of explosive decompression when the *Hand of Vengeance* took a torpedo volley amidships at the seige of Perlia. Thin, cold air began to seep into the shuttle, leeching the warmth away with tendrils of mist. Having spent most of my career with Valhallan units, who like their air conditioning turned up to the maximum, I found the chill bearable, but oddly dispiriting.

'I am,' I admitted. 'I didn't think you'd been here long enough to create an atmosphere.' I followed him down the ramp, my boots crunching gently on the gravel beneath, which had something of the texture of ash.

'We haven't.' Killian was rubbing his hands together, although whether for warmth or from enthusiasm I couldn't tell. Probably both. 'So the survey reports were right about that at least.'

'So why haven't the gasses frozen?' I asked. Even if the feeble sun were warm enough to prevent them turning to ice it never penetrated this deep below the surface, and the world was too long dead to have any residual heat left in its core. My breath puffed the words into little clouds as I spoke, although Killian's, I noticed absently, did not.

'Exactly!' Killian said, as though I were his favourite pupil, and led the way between the two nearest luminator gantries, following a clearly-defined trail in the brittle ground. Once we were beyond the glare my eyes adjusted, and I could make out a cluster of dimmer lights on the walls of the chasm. 'There has to be something else down here emitting energy. It's the only explanation.'

I was intrigued in spite of myself, I don't mind admitting it. As we approached the lights I could see they were suspended in the mouth of a vast cavern, with servitors scuttling about reinforcing the makeshift ramp of broken shale leading up to it. I'll never know if Killian's enthusiasm would have led him to expound further on what he was after, or if he would have realised he was revealing adeptus secrets to an outsider and clammed up again, because at that point a young tech-priest appeared in the cave mouth gesticulating wildly.

'Magos!' he called, practically jigging up and down on the spot with excitement. 'We've found something!' Without even pausing to ask what it was, Killian picked up the pace and practically ran inside the gaping hole in the cliff face, which was large enough to have taken our shuttle with room to spare. Not wanting to lose my guide I trotted after him, more than a little intrigued.

Killian barely slowed at any of this, hurrying on into the darkness which surrounded that scene of activity. Red-uniformed tech-guards were hovering deferentially at the fringes of the illuminated area, and I made a mental note to suggest to Tarkus that they be redeployed a little further out, where their eyes would be adjusted to the surrounding gloom and better able to distinguish any infiltrators moving in on the bustling researchers. Of course there didn't seem the remotest chance of anyone else being here, and for all I knew they had augmetic eyes which could see perfectly well in the dark anyway, but by that stage in my career I was already beginning to acquire the healthy sense of paranoia which has probably done more than anything else to ensure my survival long enough to reach an honourable retirement.

Plunging into the gloom after him I found the way easy enough to negotiate despite the lack of illumination, as he was making more noise than an ork in a distillery. Another patch of light was visible in the distance and I hastened towards it, picking out a cluster of white robes and red uniforms without difficulty. More of the peculiar circle-and-stick markings were embossed on the far wall, and as I moved closer it became obvious that the surface here was worked to a glossy smoothness which somehow seemed to swallow the light falling on it.

'These sigils are undoubtedly of necrontyr origin,' a tall, cadaverous tech-priest was saying as I entered the circle of brightness. He broke off to glare at me, until Killian gestured to him to continue. The name meant nothing to me at the time, of course, although when I finally reported back to Lokris he showed me some highly classified files which did nothing at all to make me feel better. I suppose he thought if something was going to try that hard to kill me without him instigating it, the least he could do was let me know what it was.

'This is all very interesting, Brother Stadler,' Killian said, with every sign of impatience. 'But what about the artifact?'

'It's over here,' Stadler said after a moment, during which I'd made it abundantly clear that I wasn't moving. The circle of light surrounding us shifted a little, moved by some technosorcery I wasn't privy to, revealing the mouth of a tunnel. Like the wall it penetrated the archway was perfectly smooth, composed of stone blocks of an eerie glossy blackness which only served to intensify the darkness beyond. 'We started down the tunnel hoping to find more heiroglyphs, and stumbled over this.' He permitted himself a wintery smile. 'Quite literally, in the case of our escort.'

A couple of red-uniformed figures emerged from the gloom, the scowl on Tarkus's face enough to tell me who the tech-priest was referring to. The trooper with him was walking backwards, his hellgun aimed at something still in the darkness beyond, and a moment later a couple of tech-priests appeared leading something metallic between them. It was big, I could tell that even before it came into the light, supported by a dozen cyber-skulls which had managed to wedge themselves into the interstices of its body. A small, detached part of my mind noted that the cogboys at least must be able to see in the dark, as there was no sign of illumination further back.

'Remarkable!' Killian looked like a juvie on Emperor's Day morning who's just seen the toy soldiers he always wanted at the top of his bowl. I could have thought of a number of other adjectives to describe the thing, starting with 'hideous' and growing steadily more pejorative.

It resembled nothing so much as a metallic sump spider, although even one of those would have seemed cuddly by comparison. Mechanisms protruded from its head, and six limbs dangled from its bloated body. Even inert it exuded a palpable malevolence which wrapped itself around me like a suffocating blanket.

'What have we here?' Killian bent over it, probing with the mechadendrites. 'Looks like a power core. Completely inert, of course.' He shrugged. 'Pity, but there you go. It would have been interesting to see what it does.' *Interesting* wasn't quite the word I would have used, needless to say. The other tech-priest nodded in agreement.

'I dare say we could rig something up. Possibly a fusion bottle...' He seemed to remember my presence all of a sudden, and subsided, glaring at me again.

'Are you sure that's wise?' I asked. Everyone looked at me, and I shrugged, determined not to seem too concerned at their evident hostility. 'I'm no expert, but –'

'Quite right, you're not,' Stadler snapped. 'So kindly leave theological matters to those who are.'

'Fine.' I tried to look as reasonable as I could. 'But might I suggest you at least delay the attempt until the Astartes arrive?' And I was a long way away from any potential danger, of course. 'That should at least minimise any risk to the security of the expedition.'

'The expedition is perfectly secure,' Tarkus cut in, his voice tight, and I cursed myself for wounding his pride all over again. 'I see no reason to delay the furtherance of the Omnissiah's work.'

At that point it all became academic anyway. Killian muttered something under his breath, and a faint click came from somewhere in the bowels of the machine.

'Ah,' he said. 'That looks like a power coupling...'

Without any warning at all, a thin metal probe shot from the depths of the arachnoid automaton and buried itself in one of the hovering cyberskulls. A blue arc of energy sparked between them and the servitor fell lifeless to the ground, bouncing off into a corner somewhere.

'Remarkable!' Killian said again, and stepped forward for a closer look. I did exactly the opposite, you can be sure, retreating just far enough to ensure that Tarkus and his trooper stood between me and the sinister device.

'Stay back!' I warned, drawing my laspistol. Tarkus seemed to remember my reputation at that point, and clearly reasoning that if I was concerned he ought to be too, began to follow suit. The trooper raised his hellgun again.

'Put those down!' Killian was outraged. 'Have you any idea of the importance of this artifact?' Tarkus and the trooper began to obey, although I wasn't about to holster my weapon under any circumstances. Before we could debate the point, however, a loud crack echoed through the cavern. The spider thing had teleported away, leaving air to rush into the void it had occupied like a miniature thunderclap.

We stared at one another in mutual incomprehension for a moment.

'Where did it go?' the trooper asked, an expression of bafflement on his face which was almost comic. I shook my head.

'Emperor alone knows,' I said.

'It must be somewhere nearby,' Killian said. 'How far do these tunnels extend?' Stadler shrugged.

'Kilometres. We've barely begun to map them.' Killian began to look as though his new soldiers had been trodden on by an adult before he got the chance to play with them.

'We'll establish a search pattern,' he said. 'We're bound to find it eventually.'

'If it doesn't find you first,' I added, before I could prevent the words from slipping out. Tarkus, to his credit, took my meaning at once.

'You think it's a guardian of some kind?'

'I don't know,' I admitted. 'But it's a reasonable guess. Whatever it's for it was built to last.'

'I'll double the sentries around the base camp,' Tarkus said. But I already had an uncomfortable feeling that wasn't going to be enough.

My first instinct, I might as well admit it, was to find some excuse to get back on the shuttle and return to the safety of the orbiting starship. This wasn't as easy as it sounds, though; despite the fact that I was clearly unwelcome so far as the majority of the tech-priests were concerned, and Tarkus remained as prickly as ever, he was sensible enough to realise that someone who'd survived as many clashes with the enemy as I had was someone whose advice he should listen to. So despite my impatience I spent most of the day reviewing his plans for the defence of the camp (which were pretty sound, I'm bound to admit, although I was able to plug a couple of holes that would only have been obvious to someone with field experience), and it was several hours before I had the chance to contact the *Omnissiah's Blessing* and let them know I was on my way back.

I'd just finished talking to the officer of the watch, whose image was floating in the hololith display, when his expression changed.

'Just a moment, commissar.' He turned to confer with someone out of the hololith's field of vision. When he turned back his expression was one of mild surprise. 'We're picking up a discharge of warp energy. It looks like the Astartes are here already.' That was the best news I'd heard since boarding the freighter. I had no doubt they'd make short work of the metal spider, and anything else that might be lurking down here with us.

'Good,' I said. 'If you can arrange to transfer my kit I'll report aboard the barge directly from here.' No point in taking any chances, after all, and I'd certainly be safer scrounging a ride in a Thunderhawk than an unarmed shuttle. The officer just had time to look mildly surprised before his expression turned to one of alarm.

'Unknown contact, closing fast. They're making an attack run!'

'Download your sensor data!' Killian ordered at my elbow. Someone on the bridge must have complied because the image in the hololith changed suddenly, showing us the pin-sharp starfield you only ever see from above an atmosphere. Something was moving across it, a crescent of darkness visible against the blackness of space only because of the flickering of the stars it briefly occulted.

'What the hell...' I began, then found myself stunned into silence. A burst of light blazed from somewhere within that sinister silhouette, branching and spreading as it came, until an instant later it enveloped our point of view. The hololith went blank.

'They've gone!' Stadler was standing at a nearby lectern, his face lined with shock.

'They can't be,' I said, already feeling the truth of his words in the pit of my stomach. Killian nodded in confirmation.

'I'm afraid he's right. All we're picking up is a cloud of debris.'

'Then we're just going to have to sit tight,' I said, fighting to keep my voice calm. 'The Astartes ship will be here soon, and it ought to be more than a match for these raiders.' I wished I was as confident as I sounded. 'So long as nobody panics we'll be fine.'

But of course we weren't.

The first attack came an hour or so later, while I was talking to Tarkus about the possibility of barricading the tunnel mouth we'd found. It would only have been a token gesture, of course, but one of the first things they teach you at the schola is that anything you can do to make the troops feel they're taking the initiative is good for morale. And, needless to say, after the casual destruction of our ship, morale was pretty low. We'd been reviewing the available supplies, hoping to find something we could use, when Tarkus broke off in mid-conversation.

'Can you hear that?' he asked. I nodded. A faint scuttling sound had been tickling my eardrums for the last few moments, but until he mentioned it my subconscious had been editing it out. It was a sound I was so familiar with I could identify it without thinking.

'It's just vermin,' I said. In my extensive experience of underground passageways it had been a constant background noise. Then I remembered how desolate this world was, and that we'd seen no sign of life since we got here. I drew my laspistol slowly. Tarkus followed suit, picking up a nearby luminator with his other hand and pointing it into the surrounding darkness.

My first impression was that the floor was moving, the beam shining back from a rippling surface which reminded me of sunlight on ocean waves, and then with a cry of revulsion I began shooting. The metallic carpet which surged towards us was composed of miniature duplicates of the spider machine, thousands of them, and the las-bolts detonated in the middle of the swarm with about as much effect as if I'd been throwing stones. True, every shot was rewarded with a satisfying impact and a spray of metal, but there were so many that even with Tarkus's help I couldn't even hope to slow them down.

'First squad to me!' the lieutenant ordered, and within seconds we'd been joined by half a score of his redshirts, who directed a withering volley of hellgun fire at the scuttling swarm. They began to break, to my momentary relief, but only to part like the tide around a rock before rushing on towards the main bulk of the camp.

They hit it like a tsunami, swarming over the precious equipment and ripping it to pieces with their metallic mandibles. Guards and tech-priests alike scattered in panic, but many were too slow, being pulled down and engulfed by that hideous carpet of scuttling death. Within seconds a few muffled screams, quickly silenced, were the only traces of their presence left.

'Pull back!' I ordered, taking command by reflex as I'd been trained to do. A few scattered survivors regrouped around us, Killian and Stadler among them. The cadaverous tech-priest's eyes were wide as he watched the swarm of automata demolishing the camp.

'Merciful Omnissiah!' he gasped. 'What are those things?'

'Beats me,' I said. 'I'm not qualified to comment on theological matters.' It was a cheap shot, and I suppose I ought to be ashamed of myself, but I must admit to taking some quiet satisfaction in his venomous expression. I began edging the ragged group back towards the wall, hoping that with our backs to it at least the machines couldn't get behind us.

'Good thinking,' Tarkus agreed, fanning his remaining subordinates out to form a skirmishing screen between us and the scuttling horrors. Stadler reached that obsidian surface first, and pressed his back against it as though hoping he could squeeze an extra couple of millimetres of space out of the cavern.

All at once his expression changed to one of astonishment, blood and lubricants fountaining from his augmented body as something invisible slashed him to pieces from behind. I whirled, seeking a target, and suddenly saw it looming over his shattered corpse. A ghastly skeletal visage hovered in the air on gently humming grav units, the razor-edged blades of its fingers stained crimson, its torso ending in a long, curved tail which looked like vertebrae. To add to the horror the apparition was constructed of the same gleaming metal as the spider and its miniature offspring.

'It came through the wall!' One of the troopers was gibbering in shock, his face white, at least the parts of it which were still composed of flesh. 'It came through the wall!' He raised his hellgun and ripped off a burst on full auto. The entity drifted forwards unhurriedly, the flurry of las-bolts detonating against the wall behind it, defacing the enigmatic symbols etched there. With a deepening sense of horror I realised that the volley had been on target, but the las-bolts had simply passed through the apparition, whatever it was. The trooper was still firing, his finger clamped on the trigger in a rictus of panic, as the drifting horror reached out casually and tore his face off. The man's screams were abruptly terminated as the thing's tail lashed up to transfix him; his spasming corpse hung there for a moment before dropping to the floor again.

The group disintegrated immediately, troopers and tech-priests alike fleeing in panic whichever way their feet took them. I laid a restraining hand on Killian's arm as the metallic ghoul accelerated after them, casually slashing down a couple of victims as it passed.

'Stay put!' I snapped. 'These things are trying to panic you!' The strategy was obvious: split everyone up and hunt us down one by one. If we stayed together we could watch one another's backs, and greatly increase our chances of survival.

Tarkus had clearly realised this too.

'Regroup!' he was bellowing, despite the obvious disinclination of any of his men to follow orders. Hellguns spat almost at random, a few of the las-bolts actually managing to hit the hovering ghoul as it solidified for long enough to eviscerate another unfortunate cogboy, but the vast majority of shots passed through it or missed altogether. 'Reform at once, you sons of–'

His voice broke off abruptly, rising to a suddenly terminated scream, as a bolt of vivid green light enveloped him. For a moment I could see a bloody mess of internal organs as he seemed to fade away from the outside in, dwindling like candle wax, and then he was gone as though he'd never existed.

'Emperor on Earth!' I turned to see what fresh horrors this place had disgorged, and a sudden rush of terror hit me in the gut. Thin, skeletal automata were advancing across the cavern, casually blasting everything that still lived with those hideous beams. Wherever those messengers of death walked people died, dwindled to nothing by their hellish guns, or sliced apart by the combat blades attached to the barrels.

To give them their due the tech-guards gave a good account of themselves in the main, their hellguns felling two or three of their assailants, but it seemed to take a lot of fire to down one. I even saw one with its chest blown open stir and rise to its feet again, the eldritch metal of which it was composed flowing like liquid to heal its wounds.

'Frak this!' I said, dragging the magos towards the mouth of the tunnel. If we stayed where we were we'd be killed with the others, but there was a remote chance that we might find some kind of refuge if we slipped away while these ghastly automata were slaughtering our companions. All we had to do, I kept telling myself, was hold on until the Astartes arrived. How we'd know they were here, or let them know we'd survived, was a problem for later which I resolutely refused to consider right now.

To my astonishment we made it to the tunnels without further mishap, and I hurried Killian along as rapidly as I could, the sounds of carnage diminishing in our ears. The slick black stone seemed to absorb sound as well as light, silence descending around us like a shroud. My old hive boy's senses were sufficently acute for me to be able to tell from the subtle change in the echoes around us when we passed the openings of cross corridors, but on several occasions I was grateful for my companion's apparent ability to see in the dark.

At least the metallic warriors were easy to evade, their hellish weapons giving off an eerie green glow which forewarned us of their presence in plenty of time to dive for cover.

It was after we'd been wandering for some time that I noticed the darkness around me was beginning to attenuate, a diffuse green refulgence becoming visible from up ahead. At first I thought it was merely another patrol but after lurking cautiously for a moment and finding that it remained unchanged in its intensity, we pressed on. Killian was curious to discover the source, still hoping to bag a piece of archeotech probably, and if I was going to have to fight again I preferred to do it where I could see what was trying to kill me.

As the glow grew brighter I began to hear something too, a faint buzzing sound which resonated in my skull and set my teeth on edge. The palms of my hands began to tingle as we reached a chamber bathed in that sick, green glow, and a faint sense of nausea rose within me.

Killian, on the other hand, seemed enraptured. The cavern was vast, even larger, if that were possible, than the one we'd first discovered, but rather than being empty was stuffed with strange devices beyond my ability to comprehend. Most were emitting that strange, necrotic light, however, and I began to apprehend that it was somehow connected to their power source.

'Fascinating.' The tech-priest wandered into the centre of the room, his eyes darting everywhere, trying to take in every detail of his surroundings. Mine, on the other hand, were concerned only with making sure we were alone. At least we appeared to be safe in that assumption...

Abruptly the light flared, and a sudden thundercrack of displaced air echoed across that unholy room. A dozen of the skeletal warriors were suddenly standing on a raised dais before a curtain of rippling green light, and turning their expressionless heads towards us.

'A warp portal!' Killian seemed transfixed. 'We've known it's a theoretical possibility of course, but...'

'Fight now, talk later!' I screamed, certain we were staring death in the face and determined to defy it for as long as possible. As I unleashed a flurry of las-bolts at the nearest figure I could see that its torso was already damaged, a couple of holes punched through it by what looked like armour piercing rounds. I hadn't noticed any bolters among the tech-guards' armoury, but I was glad of somebody's foresight as one of my rounds entered the gap and blew the automaton apart from the inside. The others all lifted their greenly-glowing weapons as one, and aimed them at me; for an instant the conviction of my own immanent death left me paralysed.

'Get down!' Killian cannoned into me the instant they fired, knocking me to one side, and taking the full force of the barrage himself. He flashed into vapour in an instant, leaving me rolling across the floor towards those murderous statues. I raised my right hand to aim the las-pistol and found it was gone, along with two of my fingers, but there was no time to worry about that now. My survival instinct had kicked in like never before and I lunged desperately past the dreadful automata, a direction they never expected me to take, diving headfirst into the curtain of energy behind them.

You might be wondering how anyone could be so foolish, but consider: remaining where I was would be certain death, there was absolutely no doubt about that, whereas taking my chances with the portal meant death was only virtually assured. And it was that narrow difference which preserved me for long enough to record this account.

The actual passage was a timeless instant: one moment I was in the chamber below the bowels of Interitus Prime, the next I found myself surrounded by the noise of combat. The light, wherever I was, was the same bilious hue, but the chamber I was now in was far smaller, and, as I was subsequently to discover, my immediate guess that I was aboard the starship which had attacked our freighter was an accurate one.

Staccato explosions echoed from the sloping walls surrounding me and I rolled to my feet, dazed, as another of the metal warriors came at me. I tried to draw my chainsword, but stumbled, weak from the loss of blood, and would surely have fallen had not a vast forearm encased in ceramite swung out of nowhere to bear me up. A storm bolter barked about a metre away, deafening me for a moment, and tearing the gleaming assassin to shreds.

'Brother-captain. I've found a survivor,' a voice louder than any I'd previously heard boomed, and I turned to find myself in the grasp of a giant, encased in a suit of Terminator armour.

'Bring him,' a second giant said, looming into view from behind another of the incomprehensible alien devices. 'The demolition charges are set.'

Despite everything, I found a smile beginning to force its way onto my face.

VOIDSONG

Henry Zou

The evening chill comes quickly to the mountains of Sirene Primal. Already, the twilight made shadow puppets of the rumbling vehicle column, transforming them into boxy silhouettes against an ochre backdrop.

Captain Gonan of the Eighth Amartine Scout Cavalry heaved himself above the roll cage of his half-track, panning the pintle-mounted stubber across the deep shadows of dusk. His convoy was rolling through yet another orchard village. Another ruptured settlement of paperbark pagodas, the walls of straw rotting with mildew and the roof tiles bearded with moss. In some places curtains of overgrown tea orchard clung to the frames of empty buildings, hiding any sign of settlement before the Secessionist Wars.

It was the tenth village that the captain's column had passed that day. Through the smoky haze of dusk, boredom and weariness dulled his senses. It was little wonder that Gonan did not see the armoured figure lurking within a rough bank of myrtle reed.

He never saw the shot that killed his driver. The snapping hiss of a lasrifle was followed by a blossom of arterial blood that misted the windshield. The driver, an inexperienced young corporal, began to screech in shock and hysteria, ramming down hard on the brakes of his half-track. Immediately, the slithering file of a dozen vehicles collapsed into an awkward accordion as treads fought for purchase on the mountainous shale.

Above the shriek of brakes and throbbing engines Gonan began to yell. 'Contact! Enemy at left axis of advance!'

By then, the ambush was well and truly sprung. A scattering of lasrifles released their shots into the scout cavalry half-tracks. The AM-10 Hammer Goats indigenous to the Amartine Eighth were two-ton buggies with rear caterpillar tracks and pintle-mounted heavy stubbers. Also dubbed AM-10 Scapegoats by virtue of soldierly cynicism, they were regarded as death traps for the two-man reconnaissance teams that operated them. Immediately, six Guardsmen were killed and two vehicles disabled before they could even react.

The second salvo of las-shots was followed by the thrumming war cry of fifty warriors erupting from ambush. Cold panic seized Gonan and for a moment he was paralysed by neural overload. In their full regalia of war, the secessionist fighters of Sirene Primal were an awesome sight to behold. Three score were Khan-Scholars, tall, fierce-looking men, clad in hauberks of mosaic jade and armed with all manner of lance and flak-musket. Another dozen were pounding through the undergrowth in the tectonic armour of Symbolists, their salvaged lasrifles already discarded for spine sabres. Others still were Blade Artisans, charging with their robes of embroidered tapestry flared, like the wings of some great hunting bird.

Pandemonium followed. When the line of baying warriors collided against the left flank of the vehicle column, it did not in any way resemble the heroic battle murals so vividly brocaded on Symbolist robes. Instead, what unfolded before Gonan was the messy, ugly affair of men killing each other at close quarters.

An Amartine Guardsman was screaming and babbling as a Khan-Scholar beat him to death with the broken halves of his lance. A Guard sergeant grappled with a Blade Artisan for control of his halberd before sinking his teeth into the warrior's neck.

Captain Gonan had barely freed his bayonet from the AM-10's gun rack when a Khan-Scholar surged over the cowling of his vehicle. Gonan had never seen a more vicious predator. The warrior's mane of thick black dreadlocks flowed down to his calves and silver quills were threaded through his cheekbones. Around his torso was a hauberk of interlocking jade scales, worn brown-green in its antiquity, and that was where Gonan aimed his fighting knife.

He thrust thirty centimetres of steel just below the ribs, but the Khan simply stepped into the blow with a carnivorous grace and hooked with an open palm. The first strike smeared Gonan's nose across his right cheek in a burst of blood and mucous. Reflexively the Guard officer stabbed his bayonet into his opponent's kidney, steel puncturing through the ancient jade. If the Khan felt anything, he did not show it. The next punch fractured Gonan's sternum and slammed him against the roll cage of his AM-10.

Gonan had no doubt that in a straight melee, the secessionist would dismantle him piece by piece. The martial sects of Sirene embraced close combat as an art form. He understood now, why the Sirenese culture, so reverent of art and literature, would consider these fighters the greatest artists of all. From glaive dancing to the way of the mauling hand, these men were brutally beautiful to watch. It was suicide to fight them.

Instead the Guard officer drew the laspistol from his chest holster and emptied half a clip to his front. Gonan didn't know what happened next. He may have blacked out temporarily, but for how long he did not know. When the fog of concussion ebbed away, Gonan found himself on the mesh flatbed of his vehicle with a dead secessionist sprawled over him. He felt as if someone had just run a battle tank over his skull and for a moment was content to slip into the velvet black of unconsciousness.

But the sounds of hacking and stabbing soon roused his pain-hazed mind. All around was the killing. Loud and brutal. Gonan heaved the corpse off before pulling himself up behind the mounted heavy stubber. Legs still teetering, he collapsed to his knees before pulling himself upright again and racking the weapon.

'Firing now!' Gonan screamed, voice hoarse.

It was as if a secessionist chose that very moment to rival Gonan's warning with the thick avalanche of his own war cry. Thundering over the AM-10's windshield, the secessionist brandished his spine sabre. Tracking to meet his approach, Gonan thumbed the firing stud on the stubber's butterfly trigger. The stream of high velocity rounds hit his target so hard that the warrior snapped backwards and his sabre spun the other way.

Without pause, Gonan re-sighted the heavy stubber down the column of his convoy and fired again. A long enfilade burst this time. Mosaic armour exploded into chips and splinters as Gonan hosed lambent tracer into a dense maul of Khan-Scholars not more than ten metres to his vehicle's rear.

Despite the devastation wrought by a heavy weapon at point blank range, it was too late to turn the assault. Eight of the AM-10 Hammer Goats were wrecks, their occupants dragged out and butchered by the roadside. By his estimate, Gonan didn't have more than six men left, too few to mount any meaningful resistance. So he did what any Imperial officer should have done, he juiced out the last rounds of his pintle weapon, drew his laspistol and staggered off his vehicle toward the killing.

By the time Imperial patrols came across Gonan's waylaid convoy, it was well into midnight. They found the body of Captain Saul Gonan horribly desecrated and staked upright on a lance, his men laid out in a neat row before him. They had been stripped of their boots and rifles, yet Captain Gonan still gripped an emptied laspistol in his fist. His eyes were still open.

It was a scene all too common across the wounded landscape of Selene Primal. Imperial and Secessionist forces alike were guilty of inflicting an almost theatrical barbarity towards one another. Entire Guard battalions were crucified while villages and refugee camps would be shelled in reprisal, fuelling a cycle of bitter conflict. Despite this, Imperial historians later argued that events which unfolded toward the latter stages of the war would render the atrocities of the Secessionist Campaign utterly inconsequential.

The mountains were treacherous at this time of year.

The polar equinox was at an end, and the ice caps were melting, sluicing great sheets of water and ice down the mountain paths. Thousands of people were migrating that day. The narrow defiles were swollen with caravans, baggage mules and the crush of toiling bodies. Hordes of refugees, the remnants of haemorrhaged villages and cities, and bands of weary secessionists were toiling over the icy spines of those mountains.

It was here that Inquisitor Obodiah Roth found himself, well into the fourth year of the guerrilla war. He had come here on dispatch from the Ordo Hereticus. The case itself was no matter of significance. The original briefing from the ordo had read – *mild psychic disturbances emanating from Sirene Primal, priority – minor*. It had never seemed like much to begin with.

Initial disturbances had first occurred eight months ago. Sanctioned psykers of the Imperial war fleet had sensed a strong psychic flux from the planet itself. Then reports from the neighbouring Omei Subsector began to surface. Astropaths of a missionary outpost on the tundras of Alipsia Secundus had slashed their throats, writing the name of the planet in blood, and silently mouthing *Sirene Primal* until death claimed them.

The phenomena had initially been dismissed as the psychic backlash of Sirene Primal's war. It was uncommon but not unheard of, for the anguish of billions in suffering to cause to coalesce into psychic disturbance. Scholars had named it a *planetary swansong*. Regardless, senior members of the ordo had deemed the matter worthy of further investigation, an open and shut affair perfect for wetting the noses of virgin inquisitors. Or so it had seemed.

Sirene Primal had not always been like this. Set adrift on the Eastern Fringe of the Imperium, it floated like a muted pearl within the oceanic darkness of the universe. The last of the ancients had died aeons ago, their ossified remains forming mountains of colossal spines and plates. Upon them, Sirenese architects had raised the colonnades and flower-draped monoliths of their ziggurat-gardens.

It was a very different world now. Standing on a jagged tusk of rock, Roth watched the menacing shapes of Vulture gunships, prowling across the Sephardi Peaks as they hunted for targets. Higher up amongst the cloud vaults, Imperial Marauder destroyers hurtled like knife points through the sky.

Beneath him, the mountainous slopes swept into a rocky spur. Among the scree and rubble could be seen the glint of shell casings, and even the odd helmet. Further down the pass, the rusted carcass of a battle tank could be seen, submerged in a glacial melt. The cold air was cut with the smell of fuel.

Despite the icy chill, Roth had suited up in Spathean fighting plate. The form-fitting chrome was coated with a hoar of frost that bled vaporous curls into the air. Over this he framed a tabard of tessellating obsidian. The tiny panes of psi-reactive glass, although a potent psy-dampener, did little to insulate him against the temperature. He was cold and thoroughly miserable.

Yet his shivering condition was just another irritation on his long list of simmering anxieties. He had been on-world for close to a month now and no amount of investigation, research or cross-referencing had yielded any clue as to the cause of the psychic disturbances. While millions suffered, he was mousing about with the nuisances of some psychic irregularity that no one in the ordo really cared about. He felt tired, drained and hopeless. It was, he thought with dry rumination, not a good start to his career.

'They're at it again, sire.' A voice, stern and patrician, jostled Roth out of his brooding.

The man who had spoken was Bastiel Silverstein. One of Roth's best, a xenos game hunter from the arboreous forests of Veskepine, Silverstein was right of course. A huntsman with augmented bioscope lenses was seldom wrong about such things. Already the target reticles oscillating on the pupils of his eyes had locked on the Marauder destroyers swooping in the distance.

Beneath the banking aircraft, spherical eruptions of fire and ash were accompanied by the unmistakeable rumble of explosives, deep and distant. Even without Silverstein's optic enhancements, he could see that the Imperial Navy was bombing south-west of them.

Roth swore terribly.

There would be more killing today. Not the flattening of Chaos Legions, or the epic banishment of daemon princes that Roth had read about in the Scholam-Libraries of the Progenium. No. It would be the killing of more desperate, scared and malnourished refugees. The bombs would fall, people would die, and by sunset, the war would be no closer to finishing and Roth would be no closer to clearing his damn case.

As if to emphasis his thoughts, the keening hum of distant engines began to build sonic pressure. Looking up Roth spotted a Vulture gunship roaring down from a bar of clouds, two kilometres up and diving steeply. Roth's blood ran colder. He could almost anticipate what was about to occur.

From the surge of panic amongst the refugees down slope, they did too. No more than one hundred paces away from him the mountain defile was congested with a sea of malnourished faces looking skyward in mute fear. Most of the native Sirenese did not know what a Vulture gunship was, but they knew that the ominous shape in the distance was shrieking towards them.

His man Silverstein however, scoped it clearly, complete with a statistical read-out that scrolled down in the upper left corner of his vision.

+++ *Obex-Pattern Vulture gunship, VTOL sub-atmospheric combat aircraft. Organic weapon systems: Nose-mounted heavy bolter – Optional wing-mounted autocannons – Pod-racked double missile systems.* +++

Silverstein looked to Roth, clearly concerned.

The inquisitor turned to his companion and mouthed the word 'wait'.

The gunship blurred past their jutting fist of rock, snorting jet exhaust. It sharply arrested its descent forty metres above the exodus, pivoting on the fulcrum of its tail. There it hovered on the monstrous turbines of vector thrust engines.

From his vantage point up the slope, Roth was almost at eye-level with the gunship. He watched with growing trepidation as half a dozen tendrils of rope uncoiled from the belly of its hold, reaching out like the tentacles of a waiting beast. Troops, bulky with combat gear, began to rappel down the steel cables.

Roth recognized them immediately as men of the 45th Montaigh Assault Pioneers. Great shaggy men, broad and bearded, descending with shoulder-slung lascarbines. Their insulated winter fatigues lined with mantine fur and coloured in the distinctive grey and green jigsaw pattern were unmistakeable.

He had been impressed, years before, when he had first studied the elite mountain troops in the Schola Progenium. Their engineering of trenches, field fortifications and bridges was renowned. Amongst the death marshes of Cetshwayo in M609.M41, Assault Pioneers had spearheaded their advance through supposedly impenetrable terrain with a system of drainage dams and mobile pontoons. Their ingenuity resulted in a single division of Assault Pioneers overwhelming an estimated eighty thousand orks. Where all battles are won by manoeuvre, the men of Montaigh paved the way.

Roth was not so impressed now, as he watched nine Assault Pioneers hit the ground and immediately form supporting fire positions. Fanning out into a loose arrowhead, they took a knee on the steep slope overlooking the refugees, lascarbines sitting firmly against the shoulder. By his side, Silverstein placed a gloved hand to his mouth in disbelief. Surely they wouldn't. But they did.

When they first opened fire, it was aimed above the heads of the people. Warning shots. Hemmed in between the ledge of the defile and the firers, people began to hurl themselves down the almost vertical slope in desperation. White-hot beams lacerated the air, fizzing and snapping.

'Do something!' Silverstein yelled.

In his shock, it took Roth a moment to realize the huntsman was talking to him. He was caught up watching the catastrophe unfold before him. The panic was total. A caravan was almost scuttled off the edge; a pack mule went over tumbling. The press of frightened refugees was pushing their own people down the pass, gathering momentum like a rolling landslide.

'I know! I know! Just let me consider my options–' he began.

'There aren't any options! Just do something!'

Silverstein was right. He would have to improvise. Of course, making it up on the run was one of the rudimentary lessons taught to all Inquisitorial acolytes. His masters had called it *aptitudinal adroitness*, but it amounted to much of the same thing.

Brandishing his Inquisitorial signet in an upthrust hand, Roth broke into a run. The mountain sediment slipped and slid beneath him, pitching his run into a violent descent. He slid half of the distance and slammed his knees and elbows into the shale several times for good measure. Roth ended his skittering plummet with a flying leap over the scree bank, flailing briefly in the air before landing with a shuddering impact. He was right in the thick of it now.

'Cease fire! Cease fire!' he roared.

To the credit of the Guardsmen, their well-drilled fire discipline showed through. The whickering fusillade died out, but they didn't lower their steaming muzzles. Roth was suddenly very aware of nine lascarbines trained on him.

'Lower your weapons, I am Obodiah Roth of the *Inquisition*.' Roth stressed the significance of his last word, thrusting his badge of office towards the troops.

As all soldiers would have done, they looked to their sergeant, a grizzly beast with the well-nourished build of a lumberjack. The sergeant, levelling his gaze on Roth, didn't move.

'Don't listen to him lads,' snarled Grizzly.

Roth breathed deeply. The still air was now heavy with the smell of burnt ozone. The gaping maws of nine las-weapons filled his vision. He didn't realise when exactly the Sirenese behind him had stopped screaming, but they didn't utter a sound now. He could tell the sergeant was staring at the stout chrome-plated plasma pistol in his shoulder rig, daring him to make a move.

Roth drew it.

'Lower. Your. Weapons.' Roth repeated.

'Don't be stupid now. We wouldn't want there to be any accidents between us,' replied Grizzly, his tone cold and even.

'I have the authority.'

'And I have my orders, inquisitor. This isn't your war.'

Roth's pulse felt like a war drum. He could tell they were not going to see reason. They were forcing him to play his final hand and Roth had hoped it wouldn't come to this. The inquisitor clenched his jaw and pointed up the mountain slope.

'Sergeant. Up there, three hundred paces behind you, is a huntsman with a Vindicare-class Exitus rifle. Don't bother looking, he's well hidden. What I can tell you, is that he was trained by the lodge-masters of Veskepine and I've seen him shoot the eyes off an aero-raptor in mid flight. Give him four seconds, he'll put down half your squad. It's your call sergeant.'

'You're bluffing,' said Grizzly, but his voice wasn't so calm. This wasn't his game anymore.

'If you say so.'

There was a pause. Then the sergeant looked to his men and nodded reluctantly. Nine lascarbines were lowered to the ground. Far up the slope, a crop of slate rock and gorse weed juddered then moved. Bastiel Silverstein, in a fitted coat of dark green piranhagator hide unfurled himself from concealment. In his hands was a rifle, long and lean. Roth flashed his man the hand signal for *stay alert* and turned his attention back on the sergeant.

'Sergeant…'

'Sergeant Clais Jedda, Second battalion Airborne Sappers of the 45th Montaigh Assault Pioneers.'

'Sergeant Jedda.' Roth repeated, letting the name hang heavily in the air before continuing. 'What the hell are you and your men doing?'

'Clearing a path, until you got in the way,' he replied, still defiant.

'A path to where?'

'Urgent priority mission. On orders from my battalion colonel. It's none of your concern, inquisitor.'

'You made it my concern, sergeant. If you tell me nothing, I will charge both you and your colonel for collusion of criminal activity. He would be very displeased, don't you think?' Roth had cornered him. He knew Jedda was the type of soldier who would rather risk ire from the Inquisition than the wrath of his commanding officer.

'There's nothing criminal here. These people are all potential threats. Two days ago we lost a patrol of Pioneers on their way to an AOI. Gone. Wiped out. I'm not taking any chances with my boys.'

AOI. Guard terminology for *area of interest*. Roth raised an eyebrow, 'What area of interest, sergeant?'

'An off-world landing craft. A four-man patrol picked up signs of a large metallic object in an ice cavern two kilometres west of here. Their last transmission confirmed it was a lander, frozen solid with snow. Must have been right under our noses since before the winter months.'

Roth was definitely interested now. The snow entombment meant it must have slipped past the planetary blockade at least six or seven months ago. Perhaps it was linked to the psychic disturbances, perhaps not, either way he would need to know more.

'Sergeant Jedda. You will cease terrorising these people immediately. Furthermore, you will not fire at all, unless permission is granted.'

'Permission…' he was really caught off guard now.

'Yes sergeant. Permission from me. I'm coming with you.'

The ship was a merchant runner, entombed under a tongue of glacial ice. The burnt sepia of its painted hull appeared incandescent under the striated ice, almost aglow with lambent energy. A cavern formed its cradle, where it slumbered in the throat of a frosty maw, framed by fangs of icicles.

The ship itself was a blunt-nosed cruiser about two hundred paces long, the hammerhead of its prow pockmarked with the scars of asteroid collision. Roth surmised by its squat boxy frame that it was a blockade runner, similar to the type favoured by illicit smugglers and errant rogue traders.

Roth and his team approached the ice cave down a narrow gorge, advancing slowly down the rock seam. The inquisitor led the way, auspex purring in his grip. Behind him, Silverstein and the Montaigh Guardsmen formed a staggered file with weapons covering every angle of approach. They reached no further than the shadow of the cave entrance when the auspex chimed three warning tones. A solitary target flashed on the display, half a kilometre from their position, almost right on top of the beached cruiser.

Roth signalled for a halt and lower. Sinking to a wary crouch, he squinted into the cavern with his plasma pistol primed. He took in the vastness of the cave, its immensity dwarfing the colossal docking hangars of Imperial battleships. Before him, towering colonnades of ice buttressed a vault ceiling of shimmering white-blue. Arroyos of melt water reached like veins across the cavern floor and forked through the grooves of snow dunes. Roth couldn't see a damn thing.

'Bastiel,' he hissed, almost at a whisper. The huntsman hurried to him, keeping low to the ground.

'Sire, what did you find?'

'Nothing. That's the problem. See what you can make of this.' Roth showed the huntsman his chiming auspex.

Silverstein lowered his Exitus rifle and scanned the cave, optiscopic eyes whirring and feeding data. He achieved a lock-on almost instantly.

+++*Solitary target, stationary. Height 1.5 metres. Mass density approx. 40–50kg. Target identification: Female, human 98% – Female, xenos 57% – Humanoid, other 36%. Target distance: 298.33 metres. Status temperature – ALIVE*+++

'Sire, I'm reading what appears to be a lady sitting on a snow dune, about three hundred metres to our front. What would you like me to do?' Silverstein asked.

'Nothing yet. Good job Bastiel.' Roth then turned around to face

Sergeant Clais Jedda and clicked once for his attention. 'Sergeant, were there any women in the patrol which was lost here?'

The sergeant shook his head. 'There aren't any women in the Assault Pioneers, sah.'

Roth chewed his lip, a nervous habit he had never quite shaken off. Finally, he stood up and gave the hand signal for his team to do likewise. 'Bastiel, we're going to press on as before, but I want you to cover that target with your rifle. Make sure it never leaves your sights and tell me what you see. Clear?'

'Clear, sire.'

With that, the team resumed its cautious advance, prodding through the snow. The ship's ice mesa loomed closer and so did the lone figure at its base.

'Sire, it's definitely a woman. She's seen us too and she has stood up.' They were less than two hundred and fifty metres away now.

'What do you see Bastiel? Tell me what you see.'

'She's young; I'd say no more than thirty standard. She has a weapon too. Some sort of polearm. Could be a secessionist, sire.'

Two hundred metres and closing. Roth's eyes darted across the ice-scape, seeing a possible ambush behind every crest, every ridge. Despite the relentless cold, Roth was suddenly very glad for the frictionless trauma-plates that hugged his body.

'She's looking straight at me sire,' reported Silverstein.

They were within one hundred metres now and Roth no longer needed Silverstein's relay to see the young woman on the snow dune. He could tell she was slim, made slimmer by the brocaded sapphire silks that cascaded down her frame. Where the broad painted sleeves ended, her forearms were tattooed with verse after verse of war-litanies. She was unmistakably a Blade Artisan.

'Kill her!' urged Sergeant Jedda.

'No! Stand down!' Roth turned and snapped ferociously at the Guard squad.

Ahead, on the crest of the dune, the Blade Artisan had anchored her weapon in the snow: if not a sign of peace, then at least a gesture of armistice. The weapon was as exactly long as she was tall. It was a thin glaive, half of it leather-bound staff, half of it straight blade.

'Come forth and announce yourself,' she commanded firmly.

Roth was wary but recognized diplomacy as the greatest faculty at his disposal. He emulated her gesture by inserting his plasma pistol back onto its shoulder rig.

'I am Inquisitor Obodiah Roth of the Ordo Hereticus, and these–,' he said, gesturing to the men behind him, '–are servants of the God-Emperor.'

'Tread lightly, inquisitor. I am Bekaela of the Blade and this ship is mine to guard.'

'Was it you who slew the soldiers, who came here two days past?'

'Nül. The ship killed them.'

At this reply, Roth heard the thrum of lascarbines as the Guardsmen racked their weapons off safety. Their blood was up and unless Roth could extract some straight answers soon, the situation would be out of his hands.

'Blade Artisan, these men will shoot you soon, unless you tell us what happened.'

Bekaela did not seem at all daunted by his warning. 'Shoot then, if you wish. But I have foresworn my oath to the Sirene Monarch. I have no quarrel with your soldiers.'

'Very well then. What lies in that ship?'

'Nothing. Everything. Sixteen moons ago, they came here to Sirene and claimed to be the Monarch's children – his scions.'

It was not an answer he had been expecting. The Sirene Monarch, Roth knew, had been a cultural figurehead of Sirene, a tradition that harked back to the pre-Imperial history of the planet. It had been the Sirene Monarch who had renounced Imperial dominion and ousted Lord Planetary Governor Vandt. Pre-war records had shown that when the isolated Imperial outposts and missions had been overrun, the natives certainly had no access to interplanetary travel and there had never been mention of the Monarch's offspring.

'Scions?' Roth asked.

Bekaela nodded. 'Yes, his children came in this ship, sixteen moons ago. The Monarch embraced his children and welcomed them home. It had been a grand ceremony; many clan-fighters had feasted there. I know because I was there too.'

'The Sirene Monarch has been in hiding ever since the war began, if not dead,' Roth countered. He could sense something poisonous was at work on this planet and part of him did not want to believe it.

'He is not dead. I know where he hides,' Bekaela said.

That was almost too much information to digest at once. Since the beginning of the campaign, Imperial forces had been driven in relentless pursuit of the fugitive Monarch, slated as the spiritual leadership of the guerrilla insurgency. Hundreds of aerial bombing runs, thousands of infantry patrols had all amounted to nothing. But now this.

'Why would you give us this information?' Roth pressed.

'Because, I've seen what lies in that ship and if they are the Monarch's bloodline, then he is no Monarch of mine!' she proclaimed.

It only dawned on Roth then, that Bekaela was not guarding the ship from intruders. She was guarding against whatever lay within from getting out.

Sergeant Jedda, however, was not one to be convinced. 'It's a trap. That witch probably gave my boys the same speech before they got off'd,' he growled. His men chorused in assent.

Roth was not so quick to make his conclusion. The significance of her story, if true, was far too monumental to dismiss. His duty as an inquisitor compelled him to investigate deeper. Stepping forward, slightly away from his team, Roth summoned a subtle wisp of mind force and gently probed her mind. Bekaela tensed visibly from the intrusion.

'What did you just do?!' she hissed.

'I was testing your intentions.'

'Don't do that again, or I'll kill you and make it painful.'

Roth nodded sincerely. He would not. Besides, he already knew all that he needed to know. She was telling the truth, on both accounts.

'My team and I, we must explore this ship.'

'Then I will come with you,' she said. Her tone brokered no argument.

'So you are willing to aid us?' Roth mused. 'As an ally?'

'No. I hate you. But I will help my people. They do not know what I know. I've been in that ship.'

'What's in there?' Roth asked.

'You will see,' was the answer.

The ship was alive.

Or at least that was what Roth first thought. Wet ropes of muscle and pulsing arteries groped and twisted along the walls and mesh decking of the dormant ship. The air was nauseatingly warm and humid. It was as if something infinitely virulent and shapeless was incubating within the cruiser's metal chassis.

Roth's team had entered via a breach in the ship's hull and found themselves in a disused maintenance bay. Banks of workbenches lined the walls where raw tendrils of flesh had begun to creep over them. In the upper-left corner of the ceiling, an enormous balloon of puffy flesh expanded and contracted rhythmically like a monstrous lung.

Further exploration of the ship's corridors, deck and compartment revealed only more of its pulsating innards. The deeper into the heart of the cruiser they progressed, the thicker the infestation. The walkway that led to the ship's bridge funnelled into an orifice of ridged cartilage. They could see no further, as a pink membrane of tissue expanded over the entrance.

'Do you know where we are?' Roth asked Bekaela.

'Nül. I have never been beyond the first compartment. This place is cursed, it's all bad following.'

Roth was not sure the Blade Artisan's prognosis was the correct one, but it was apt enough. He moved toward the membrane, careful not to step in the pools of semi-viscous liquid that collected on the deck plating. He holstered his pistol and was in the act of gingerly reaching out to touch the organic membrane when all three auspexes in his team chimed simultaneously. Roth froze.

'What's the reading?' he asked.

'I'm getting multiple rapid movements converging on this corridor intersection,' one of the assault pioneers reported.

'Yes sir, I'm getting the same readings,' another trooper echoed.

Roth about turned, drew his pistol and trained it on the inflamed flesh cavity that was once a T-junction.

'Readings are too fast. I suspect we're just picking up latent electrical currents from the ship's circuitry,' a third trooper added. They waited in tense silence.

'Trooper Wessel, double time ten paces back and get me a new reading. We could be standing under an electrical hub,' Sergeant Jedda barked.

With his eyes on the auspex and carbine hard against the shoulder, Trooper Wessel approached the intersection. He peered into the gloom, sweeping his auspex about to get a better reading.

The thing slashed out of the darkness so fast it severed Wessel's spine and bounded off his corpse. Streaking through the air in a shower of blood, it landed on another trooper crouched within the corridor and eviscerated him too. An eruption of wild las-fire crazed the spot where the thing had been, but it was moving again.

'What the hell is that?' Roth shouted at Silverstein as his plasma pistol unleashed a mini-nova of energy down the corridor.

The huntsman tried to get a lock on the creature as it slammed into its third victim. He barely registered the profile of its blurring outline.

+++*Target analysis: Xenos, Hormagaunt. Subspecies: Unknown. Origin: Unknown. Hivefleet: Unknown – Data Source: Ultramar (745.M41)*+++

'Tyranid,' Silverstein replied. With a spectacular shot that anticipated the creature's next running leap, he blew out its skull carapace with an Exitus round.

Another two shapes shrieked into the corridor, straight into the storm of fire laid down by Roth's team. The inquisitor aimed his pistol, ready to fire when it seemed like the world exploded behind him. The membrane plugging the ship's command bridge burst, and from the darkness surged a monster so tall it was almost bent double in the corridor. From its segmented torso, four bone scythes connected to hawser cables of muscle slashed like threshing sickles. As an inquisitor, Roth was privy to knowledge otherwise deemed heretical for others. Yet knowing the enemy and its power sometimes replaced ignorance with fear. Roth recognised the thorny frame of sinew and plate hurtling towards him and froze in shocked awe.

It was a genestealer broodlord and it was on him so fast he had no time to react. The only thing that saved him was Bekaela's glaive singing through the air to intercept the beast. The Blade Artisan pirouetted with a twirling downward stroke that severed one of the monstrosity's upper limbs. In reply, the tyranid speared her into the wall with a battering ram of psychic force.

Roth wasted no time in engaging the broodlord. He activated his Tang

War-pattern power gauntlet and moved inside the broodlord's guard with a thunderous right-hook. The creature snaked back its torso with serpentine grace, evading the blow and swept in with its three remaining hook-scythes. Roth ducked, feeling an organic blade skip against the frictionless shoulder plate of his armour.

They fought on two separate planes. While their bodies raged, so too were their minds locked in a psychic duel. The tyranid was much stronger, its mind a tidal wave of raw, seething force. Roth was not a potent psyker, but what ability he had, he utilised well, sharpening and tightening his will into a poignard of deliverance. Although the broodlord's mind was like the staggering force of a blind avalanche, Roth's was the clean mind-spikes and mental ripostes of a Progenium-trained psychic duellist. It was like a death struggle between the kraken and the swordfish.

On the physical plane, Bekaela struck again. She was barely conscious and fought purely from muscle memory. Spinning her glaive like a lariat she hoped she was aiming for the right target. The paper-thin blade sliced deep into the broodlord's flank, snapping through the corded muscle. The creature shrieked at a decibel so high, the ship quavered in empathy.

It was exactly the distraction Roth needed. Sensing the sudden gap in the genestealer's mental defences, Roth tightened his will into an atom of focus and surged through the slip in its psychic barrier. Once through, he exploded into a billion slivered needles, expanding infinitesimally outwards.

The broodlord died quickly. With it, the last of the hormagaunts in the corridor lost all synaptic control and were literally disassembled by gunfire. Yet as it expired, the broodlord's mental shell collapsed, plunging Roth into its mind, like a spearman breaking through a shield wall headlong through the other side. Roth was utterly unprepared for what happened next.

He saw a hive fleet, at the furthest edges of his mind's eye. He saw it looming larger, so ravenous and hungry. He felt, no, heard the psychic song that was drawing it closer, like a pulse, like droplets of blood rippling outwards in the ocean. The song was coming from Sirene Primal, a poisonous ugly sound that drove spikes into his psyker mind. A swan-song. All at once, it fell into place like a crystal fragmenting in rewind. He saw the ship, and its genestealer brood, the children of the Sirene Monarch. He saw their minds pulsing in unison, calling to their hive, calling for salvation. The psychic vacuum shut down his nervous system and Roth's heart stopped beating.

'Sire! Can you hear me?!'

The voice wrenched Roth back into consciousness, wrenching him to the surface like a drowning man. The first thing he saw was Silverstein, the yellow pupils of his bioscope implants wide with concern. Had it not been for the huntsman's voice, he would have died standing up.

'Sire? You look bloodless,' said the huntsman reaching forward to steady Roth. The inquisitor, in a daze, brushed Silverstein off and fell against the cartilage tunnel, sliding down to his knees.

'Kill it... kill him. Find him. Kill him,' he murmured weakly.

'Kill who?'

'Kill the Monarch,' Roth called, a little louder as he pulled himself up. 'The Monarch. Father of the brood.'

Beyond the Sephardi ranges, Imperial artillery was pounding the mountains to rubble and the rubble to dust. The steady *krang krang krang* of the batteries sounded like thousand tonne slabs of rockrete in collision. In the tomb-vaults below the mountains, deep within the arterial labyrinth, billions of ancestral caskets tremored under the brutal bombardment. Finally, down amongst their dead, the Sirene Monarch's hidden legions would make ready for their last battle.

The assault on the Sirene tomb-vaults had started before dawn. To their credit, Imperial high command had been quick to react, with Lord Marshal Cambria personally overseeing the mobilization of a quick reaction force within six hours. Inquisitor Roth's discovery had hammered a shockwave through the campaign's war-planners and they were eager to seize the initiative. The stalemate, it seemed, was about to be broken.

By the time the Sirenese sunrise had tinged the night sky a bruised orange, Assault Pioneers of the Montaigh 45th had breached the tomb underworld. Combined elements of the Kurassian Lance-Commandoes and five squadrons of the Eighth Amartine Scout Cavalry, alongside three full battalions of Assault Pioneers had been committed to the operation.

It was all a decoy. The decisive strike of the assault had been the insertion of a kill-team directly into the Sirene Monarch's last refuge, once secessionist forces were pre-engaged. Led by Inquisitor Roth and guided by Bekaela of the Blade, a platoon of Montaigh 45th and a squad of bull-necked Kurassian Lance-Commandoes had penetrated the cerebral core of the tomb complex. Precision breach charges rigged up by airborne sappers had seen to that.

The kill team now prowled beneath a monolithic vault of basalt. According to Bekaela's hand-sketched schematics, which Roth had committed to memory, it was the Monarch's atrium. The walls were so thick and black with age they seemed to absorb sound and light. Of the distant sounds of combat, Roth heard nothing. Even their long-range vox-sets were dead.

It was the oceanic silence that unsettled him most.

The atrium was so very still, dark and quiet. A white bar of sun lanced from the soaring heights of the ceiling, laying down a smeared ghostly light. But it wasn't just the silence that was unsettling, there were those damned pools of water too, Inquisitor Roth seethed to himself. There was water everywhere.

From enormous bowls to dishes, troughs and ponds, basins and urns, everywhere Roth looked he saw stagnant bodies of water stretching into the deepest shadows of that chamber. Most of the pools had developed a slick surface of green algae, and others were scattered with pale lotus blossoms; all of them sat stagnant and silent.

'When the Sirene Monarch meets the boys of the Montaigh 45th, I want it to be the most traumatic experience of his life!' Sergeant Jedda's call clapped through the still air. The Guardsmen all roared in unison.

Despite his failings, Jedda was a natural troop leader. As an inquisitor, Roth was glad the Imperium had men like Sergeant Clais Jedda to unleash upon its enemies. The kill-team broke into a run now, cutting for the throne chamber that lay beyond.

Falling in step behind Roth was Bastiel Silverstein. He toggled the target lock of his hunting crossbow to active and loaded a prey-seeker missile. The light polymer sleekness of a Veskepine *arcuballista* was ideal for tunnel assault. Running point was Bekaela, who was now dressed in the Sirenese regalia of vengeance. Her face was painted a leering mask of white and crimson, symbolising the witch-ghosts who claimed the dead. Her sapphire robes were cinched tight by a waist belt, woven from the hair of slain enemies and a flak-musket was slung over her shoulder.

Racing down the thousand-metre walkway, Roth's retinue finally emerged into the Sirene throne chamber. The room was vast, humbling even the impressive scale of the antechamber. Basalt walls and pillars of thickly veined marble soared up into the heavens, the ceiling completely lost from sight. A path of jade flowed down the centre of the throne room, flanked on either side by legions of water-bearing vessels. Once again, Roth noted there was water everywhere. He didn't have time to ask Bekaela why.

'The patient court of the Sirene Monarch bids you welcome,' a smooth androgynous voice announced. The source of the voice came from powerful vox-casters set into the arms of the Monarch's jade throne. Upon that throne sat the Monarch himself.

He wore a high-collared gown of ruby red silk, the hem and sleeves spilling out for several metres from his throne. His hands, folded demurely upon his lap, were capped with long needles of silver. None could look upon his face for a veil of pearls shimmered down his onion-domed crown. The Monarch's ten dozen scions were arrayed below his throne in seated tiers, a chilling calm instilled by their impassive stares.

The aura of ethereal dignity was so great, Roth noticed, that some of the troops lowered their guns and gazes involuntarily. Roth, on the other hand, raised his chin and stared deep into the pearl veil.

'The Ordo Hereticus is here to bury you,' he shouted in reply.

The choir of sons arrayed below the Monarch rippled with shrill chortling. They were exactly as Bekaela had described in the pre-op briefing. Eunuchs, all of them. Slim and effete, all were clad in ankle-length gowns of pastel silk, pinks and purples and creamy jades. They appeared human enough, but even at a distance Roth could see their coral pink skin, semi-opaque and laced with delicate red veins.

Curiously, all of their left hands had been amputated. The gold-capped stumps of their forearms were attached to thick tendrils of silk cord. The long braids forming a muscular rope of fabric over a metre long. Like some bizarre pendulum, at the end of each length interwoven knots formed a fist-sized sphere of silk.

Roth could not gauge the symbolic significance of these amputations. Dimly, he remembered archival files regarding the Tyrant of Quan, on the fringes of the Tuvalii Subsector. Such was his fear of assassination, the Tyrant had ordered all who entered his court to don fluted gauntlets of glass. The flutes of those fragile gloves had been chased with acid and shattered under the slightest force. So great was his paranoia the Tyrant had even forced his three thousand wives to wear them in his bedchambers. Alas, Roth remembered with a glimmer of dark humour, those gloves did not save him from the mouth dart of a Callidus assassin.

However, if the Monarch was offended by his brazen threat, his veiled visage offered no sign. Instead his soft sexless voice emitted through his throne-casters, emotionless and measured.

'I cannot allow that,' he stated, rising from his throne.

The air immediately grew brittle and cold. To Roth's right, Bekaela's glaive went slack in her grip and her eyes glazed over. To his left, Bastiel Silverstein moaned softly.

'Witchery!' Roth raised his plasma pistol a millisecond too late. A psychic bolt exploded from the Monarch, warping the air around it into an oscillating cone. It tore through Inquisitor Roth and threw him thirty feet down the ivory path in a spray of blood and black glass. The psychic aftershock rippled through the room like a stone in a pond, coating every surface in a thick rime of frost.

The mind blow would have liquefied any normal man. But Obodiah Roth had a trump card. The glinting hauberk of psy-reactive crystal had absorbed the brunt of the psyker's power. As shards of black glass scattered in a blizzard around him, Roth realised the armour would not survive another psychic attack. And neither would he. Blood and bile oozed from his mouth and nose in thick strings. His head swam and he could barely see.

Dimly, he could hear the chatter of gunfire, as if very far away in the distance. He could hear Silverstein yelling but he couldn't make out the words. The only coherent thought in his mind was that the Monarch psyker must be temporarily weakened from his tremendous mind blast. That gave Roth a few seconds to nullify him before he gathered the strength to finish them all off.

He looked up, fighting down the urge to vomit. The world appeared at a slant. The Monarch's scions had formed a phalanx around him. As one, they dipped their long silk pendulums into the many water vessels in the chamber, letting the water soak into the fabric. The innocuous silk spheres instantly become heavy flails.

'Sly bastards,' Roth hissed through a mouthful of broken teeth. To his flanks, the Guardsmen continued to rake a steady stream of las-rounds at the Monarch's scions. 'I'll bet my balls that they're wearing armour under those gowns too,' Roth laughed darkly to himself. Some of the scions were slammed off their feet by the kinetic force of the shots, only to get back up and continue charging the inquisitor's team.

'Fix bayonets!' someone, somewhere, shouted. The voice was washed with distortion to Roth's trauma-shocked ears.

Assault Pioneers did as commanded, forming a staggered rank of fighting blades. The Kurassian Lance-Commandoes drew their serrated short-swords, howling and clashing the weapons to armoured chests. Together they met the charge of the scions.

Roth staggered to his feet, fighting to regain his balance as a eunuch stormed down the ivory path toward him. Bastiel Silverstein's polished boots suddenly filled Roth's vision, as the old retainer stood over the dazed inquisitor. The xenos game hunter aimed his crossbow. He had swapped to a rapid-fire cartridge, designed to bring down swift moving game. On automatic, Silverstein could empty all twelve bolts into his assailant in three seconds. He needed only one. A salvo of bolts tore out the eunuch's face, the neural toxins causing the assailant to spasm so hard his spine broke. He dropped to the floor, his one hand locked into a flexing claw.

'Are you good? Are you good?' Silverstein screamed at the inquisitor.

Roth finally found his footing and nodded vaguely.

'Stop fussing over me and snipe that psyker bastard already,' Roth managed to gasp.

'Can't draw a bead. He's got some sort of force generator. The kill-team almost bled their ammunition dry trying to crack him open. We'll have to get in close,' said Silverstein.

Roth grimaced and ran a hand over his bloodied face. 'Well he's thought of everything then, hasn't he? Cover me.' The inquisitor shook his head once more to clear it. There was a dark spot in his left field of vision and he hoped his brain wasn't haemorrhaging. Casting all doubt aside, he lifted his right hand. The one clad in a slim-fitting gauntlet of blue steel. A Tang War-pattern power gauntlet. The weapon hummed with a deep magnetic throb, the disruption field sparking like a blue halo.

Breaking into a run, he made straight for the throne. Assailants appeared in the corners of his vision but Silverstein's covering fire was lethally efficient. The streaks of grey slashed over his shoulder and head, one passing so close to his face he could feel its passing and hear its viper-like hiss. The bolts intercepted the scions as Roth ran their deadly gauntlet, down the ivory path towards the throne.

The inquisitor kept a mental count of each bolt as they flew past until finally, he counted the full twelve. Silverstein would need to reload. He was only a scant ten paces away from the throne; the Monarch still slumped in his seat recovering when a eunuch threw himself at him.

Roth turned, his reflexes still sluggish from his mind thrashing. Howling, the eunuch whipped the silk flail into his lower ribs and Roth exhaled a painful jet of air. He tried to bring his plasma pistol to bear but the flail lashed in again, this time snapping into his hand. My hand's broken, Roth thought numbly, adding it to his long list of injuries as the pistol slipped from broken fingers.

Eager for the kill, the eunuch pressed his advantage. The silk flail's trajectory arced toward Roth's head. With more luck than timing, the inquisitor slipped under the blow and drove his power fist into the eunuch's chest. The gauntlet's disruption field flared into a bright corona of light as he drove his hand clean through the Eunuch's chest. His assailant simply dropped onto his rear and slumped over backwards.

Knowing he had no time to spare, Roth spun on his heels and turned on the Monarch. The psyker was almost at full strength. Already he had forced himself onto his feet, his eyes turning into milky orbs as he gathered his will for another psychic bolt. The temperature was dropping like a countdown timer. Roth had all of one second to react before he was dead.

'Now!' cried Inquisitor Roth as he launched himself at the psyker. Extending his power fist, he rammed the weapon into the Monarch's invisible force bubble. As disruption field met force field there was a static shriek and a blossoming wall of blinding light. Then the jade throne's force generator blew a fuse. The force field shattered, air filling its void with a low thunderclap. Roth flew himself flat before the throne.

Bastiel Silverstein emptied all twelve bolts into the Monarch in three seconds flat. At fifty paces, every bolt found its mark and pinned the psyker to his throne like a broken marionette. Almost as an afterthought, Bekaela's flak-musket spat a cone of flechette at the corpse, stitching it with smoking holes.

Then it was over, as quickly as it had begun. Except for the cordite hiss of gun smoke, and the baying of the Kurassian Lance-Commandoes as they took the eunuchs apart, the battle was over. The metallic scent of blood and gunfire filled the chamber.

Inquisitor Obodiah Roth picked himself up and brushed himself off. He coughed and spat a bloody tooth at what was left of the Monarch. Bending down, he slapped the Monarch's veiled crown with a backhand.

A face of sharp alien angles stared back at him with dead eyes. Dead dark xenos eyes. The ridged forehead was streaked with blood and his slack mouth was a nest of teeth, like translucent needles.

'Genestealers,' said the inquisitor.

Wearily, he turned to his team and the carnage before him. During his tenure as an interrogator, Roth had survived a clutch of firefights. His mentor, Liszt Vandevern, had been a prolific field inquisitor who believed a raid would always reap more answers than clinical investigation. Before his thirtieth year, Roth had skirmished with half a dozen heretic cults, and even besieged the compound of a narco-baron on the death world of Sans Gaviria. But none of that could compare to the brutality of a close-quarter firearms assault.

The throne room was a butcher's hall. Most of the bodies were dressed in gossamer silks, thrown in disarray like crushed butterflies. Dozens of immense water vessels had been upturned or shot through, flooding the chamber with a pane of rosy, blood-tinted water. Other bodies scattered about were in either Montaigh or Kurassian battledress. Nearest to Roth, a Kurassian commando had died sitting up, the fingers of his gauntlet locked around the throat of an enemy. The Guardsman had been shot over a dozen times, but he had not released the chokehold.

Around Roth, his kill-team moved quickly from body to body. It seemed to him that they were but going through the motions, high-powered weapons at close proximity rarely left survivors.

'Sire – we have a live one sire,' Silverstein said.

Roth snapped out of his post-conflict daze and realised Silverstein had been standing at the base of the throne for some time, calling repeatedly. He followed the huntsman, sloshing through the pink water towards a huddle of Guardsmen with their weapons raised. As the circle parted for the inquisitor, they revealed a scion sitting wounded on the chamber floor.

It was genetically more man than xenos, Roth recognized that immediately. Yet nestled within the brow of its orbed forehead, its eyes were like iridescent pools of black oil devoid of any human quality. Most startling of all was the creature's parody of symbiote weapons. Up close, the silk flail, damp and glistening was not unlike a muscled mace appendage. Its right sleeve was torn, unveiling a hand fused to an obsolete machine pistol, brown with well-worked grease. The flesh and fingers were smeared like wax into the heavy calibre pistol, whether by coincidence or design to resemble some organic biomorph.

'It can talk, sire,' said Silverstein, nodding towards the creature.

The scion had taken the stray round of a Kurassian shotgun. Its left leg was peppered with bleeding perforations and pockmarked with powder burns. It looked up, met Roth's gaze and smiled mockingly, revealing clusters of quill-like teeth.

Perhaps if Roth had been older, wiser and more patient he could have dealt with the matter by more tactful means. But as it was, Roth was none of those things. The inquisitor simply pounded forward and snagged the scion's collar in his fist.

'How long has this planet been infected?!' Roth screamed into the creature's face.

'Why does it matter?' the scion replied, his vocal cords cut with a coarse alien inflection.

'Because I asked you!' shouted Roth. He hauled down on the scion's embroidered collar, slamming its head into the marble floor. The creature came up snorting water out of its nostril slits and started to laugh, a thrilled harmonic peal that bounced around the chamber walls.

Bekaela appeared by Roth's side and laid a hand on his shoulder. 'Kill him. Just kill him and be done,' she said.

'Not until it answers me!' hissed Roth. Still tight in his clinch, he manhandled the creature, jerking the scion from its seated position and forcing it down on its wounded side. The action elicited a shuddering exhalation of agony. Satisfied, Roth repeated the question again. 'How did it start?'

'Three generations ago,' the scion snarled through its teeth. 'Our fathers came to Sirene as missionaries to spread the seed of the great family and his blessed children.'

In truth, the admission did not surprise Roth. It was almost elementary. Sirene was a frontier world and missionaries had been the only true Imperial outposts on the planet. Incidentally, those clerics and ecclesiarch were also the only ones to access warp-capable vessels.

'It was perfect,' crooned the scion. 'By seven winters of equinox, Sirene's firstborn prince was of blessed blood. He was the father of fathers. When He ascended the throne, this world was ours for the taking.'

'When did the taint spread to the rest of Sirene?' Roth asked through gritted teeth.

'Patience, patience. I'm getting to that,' chortled the creature. It was clearly enjoying the narrative, drawing itself up theatrically. 'We did not need to, you see. The martial sects had always chafed under Imperial occupation and when our Monarch declared rebellion, they were our herd and we their shepherd. With the sect warriors under our banner, the rest of the Sirenese followed quietly enough.

'We set about purging all Imperial influence from this realm. Sect-Chieftains who were resistant quickly became silent when their wives were poisoned and denounced as conspirators. There were a thousand public executions of Imperial loyalists each day for many years. The Sirene renaissance was endemic.

'The PDF did not even try to fight but we cleansed them anyway. Soft and idle, they were civic militia drawn from the ranks of poets, sculptors and merchants, for no sect fighter would ever debase himself by devotion to the Imperium. Any Sirenese in the PDF uniform of tan brocades and gilded tall-helm was a traitor. When the executions started, they barely knew how to operate their autorifles. Most of their weapons were still wrapped in the soft plastic covers they were delivered in.

'They died so quickly. On the Isles of Khyber the blessed children killed an entire division of them in one day. Can you believe it? Twelve thousand loyalists lined up and buried alive. Oh, it was a golden age.'

At this Bekeala interjected, her eyes red and watery with rage, 'Enough! We do not need to hear this. Let me kill him!'

'One more thing,' growled Roth as he pulled the scion's grinning visage close to his face. 'The psychic backlash, the planetary swansong. Your brood is responsible...'

'I am surprised you belittle yourself by asking,' it said smugly.

Roth released the scion and took a step back. He let the answer settle heavily on his chest and sink into the pit of his stomach. Like the final stroke of an oiled brush, the painting was complete. He had resolved the matter for the ordo, but it would be a pyrrhic victory. It was already too late for Sirene Primal.

'Absolutely correct psyker. It is far too late. Our choir has been singing to the family, calling out to the warp and the family answered our call.'

Looking down, Roth drew his sidearm in anger. He had slackened his guard and the xenos breed had gleaned his surface thoughts. 'How long do we have?' asked Roth, reasserting his question with an octave of psychic amplification.

The scion simply rolled back his head and laughed. His laughter came in great shrieking bursts, resonating with the thunderous acoustics of a cyclopean hall. It was all too much. Roth took aim with his pistol. His finger slipped inside the trigger. Yet before he applied pressure, the scion's face threw out a great crest of blood.

Roth lowered his weapon, breathing heavily. Bekaela was by his side, her silver glaive streaked with strings of crimson gore. She was terrifying. The paint on her face smeared with sweat and fury, a daemonic visage melting down her cheeks. At her feet the scion lay, a cloud of bright red hazing the water and forming a halo around its skull.

But the laughter did not abate. Long after the scion was dead, the laughter continued to toll through the chamber.

The annals of Imperial history would not be kind to Sirene Primal. It was recorded in M866.M41 that a xenos armada known collectively as a hive fleet entered the Orco-Pelica Subsector. On the most urgent warning of an Inquisitor Obodiah Roth, all senior officers and dignitaries were evacuated. The Imperial Navy was ordered to withdraw, regroup and re-engage. Sporadic reports from retreating Naval forces described the incursion as a *seething wave of oblivion*.

On Sirene Primal, seventy thousand Guardsmen of Montaigh, Kurass and Amartine dug in on the rugged Sephardi ranges to stall the xenos advance. It is said, that within three months the mountains had been transformed into a sprawling network of artillery palisades, tunnelled barbicans and interlocking firing nests. Once the xenos made landfall, the Guardsmen were expected to hold out for eight weeks. They lasted less than five hours.

The ensuing campaign to reclaim the subsector is itself a historic epic worthy of narrative, but of Sirene Primal there was no more. In the end, the lonely jewel on the Eastern Fringe became little more than a smudged ink record in the forgotten archives of Terra.

WE ARE ONE

John French

Victory and defeat are a matter of definition.
– from the *Axioms of War*, Tactica Imperialis

I have grown tired in this war. It has eaten me, consuming everything I might have done or been. I have chased my enemy across the stars and through the decades of my failing life. We are one, the enemy and I, the hunter and the hunted. The end is close now. My enemy will die, and at that moment I will become something less, a shadow fading in the brightness of the past. This is the price of victory.

My fist hits the iron door with a crack of thunder. The impact shatters the emerald scales of the hydra that rears across their width. Inside my Terminator armour, enfolded in adamantium and ceramite, I feel the blow jolt through my thin flesh. Lightning crackles around my fist as I pull it back, the armour giving me strength. I bring my fist down and the metre-thick doors fall in a shower of splintered metal. I walk through their shattered remains, my feet crushing the scattered ruby eyes of the hydra to red dust on the stone floor.

The light glints from my armour, staining its pearl-white surface with fire and glinting from eagle feathers and laurels. The chamber beyond the doors is silent and creeps with shifting shadows. Burning torches flicker from brackets on jade pillars, the domed ceiling above coiling with smoke. Targeting runes and threat augurs swarm across my vision, sniffing for threats, finding only one. The shackled power in my fist twitches like a thunderbolt grasped in a god's hand.

He sits at the centre of the chamber on a throne of beaten copper. Void-blue armour mottled with the ghost pattern of scales, swathed in spilling cloaks of shimmering silk; features hidden behind the blank faceplate and glowing green eyes of a horned helm. He sits still, one hand resting on the pommel of a silver-bladed sword, head turning slowly to follow me as I advance.

'Phocron of the Alpha Legion,' I shout, my voice echoing through the shadow-filled silence. 'I call you to justice at the hands of the Imperium you betrayed.' The formulaic phrase of accusation fades to silence as Phocron stands, his sword in his hand. This will be no simple duel. To fight the Alpha Legion is to fight on a shifting layer of deception and trickery, where every weakness can hide strength and every apparent advantage may be revealed as a trap. Lies are their weapons and they are their masters. I am old, but time has armoured me against those weapons.

He moves and cuts, his blow so quick and sudden that I have no chance to dodge. I raise my fist, feeling the armour synchronise with the movements of my ageing muscles, and meet the first strike of this last battle in a blaze of light.

Ninety-eight years ago –
The Year of the Ephisian Atrocity

Knowledge can make you blind, some say, but ignorance is simply an invitation to be deceived. I can still remember the times when I knew little of the Alpha Legion beside a few dry facts and half-understood fears. I look back at those times and I shudder at what was to come.

The death of my ignorance began on the mustering fields of Ephisia.

Millions of troops stood on the dust plains in the shadow of soot-covered hives, rank upon rank of men and women in uniforms from dozens of worlds. Battle tanks and ground transporters coughed exhaust fumes into the cold air. Munitorum officers moved through the throng shouting orders above the noise, their breath forming brief, white clouds. Above it all transport barges hung in the clear sky, their void-pitted hulls glinting in the sunlight, waiting to swallow the gathering mass of human flesh and war machines. It was the mustering of an army to break the cluster of renegade worlds that had declared their secession from the Imperium. It was a gathering of might intended to break that act of folly into splinters and return billions to the domain of the God-Emperor. That was the intention, though perhaps ours was the folly.

'Move!' I bellowed as I charged through the crowd, shoving aside men and women in newly issued battle gear. Helena came with me, pushing people out of our way with her will. Grunts and oaths followed us, dying to silence as they saw the tri-barred 'I' engraved on my breastplate and the hissing muzzle of the inferno pistol in my hand. My storm cloak flapped behind me as I ran, the burnished adamantium of my segmented armour bright under the sun. Anyone looking at me knew that they were looking at an inquisitor, the left hand of the God-Emperor, one who had the power to judge and execute any beneath the Golden Throne. The crowd parted before me like cattle scattering in front of a wolf.

'There!' shouted Helena from a metre to my left. I twisted my head to see the dun colour of our quarry's uniform vanish into a knot of troops. She was already moving before I had changed direction, confused-looking Guardsmen twitching out of her path as she ran through the parting crowd. I could feel the back eddies of the telepathic bow wave that she projected in front of her as she ran, hard muscles flowing under flexing armour plates, dark hair spilling behind.

I saw our quarry a second after Helena. A thin man in the ill-fitting uniform of an Ephisian trooper, his skin pale from poor nutrition and lack of daylight. He looked like so many of the rest gathered on that day, another coin of flesh for the Imperium to spend. But this man was no raw recruit for the Imperial Guard; he was an agent of rebellion sent to seed destruction at this gathering. We had been tracking him for days, knowing that there were more and that our only chance to stop them all was to let one run until he led us to the others. That had been the plan – my plan. But there was no more time. Whatever atrocity they intended was so close I could feel the cold fear of it in my guts.

'Take him down!' I shouted. Helena was raising her needle pistol when the man jerked to one side with the agility of a predator. He rolled and came up into a shooting crouch, lasgun at his shoulder. Helena dived to the ground as the lasgun spat bursts of energy in a wide arc across the space she had occupied. People dropped in the crowd around us, shouts of pain spreading like a tide. Dead and dying troops lay on the ground while their comrades formed a blind herd, scattering without direction or order.

Our man was already up and moving, weaving amongst the panicked troops, using the tide of confusion he had created as cover. I felt a twinge of admiration at the man's ingenuity. He was good, I had to give him that: determined, ruthless and well trained.

I came level with Helena as she pulled herself off the ground.

'Wait,' she said. 'We will not outrun him. I will handle this, master.' She bit off the last word. I looked at her. She had a face that was too thin and pale to be pretty, and a Scholastica Psykana brand surrounded her left eye with a blunt letter 'I' and a halo of wings. She gave me a humourless smile. Helena was my interrogator, my apprentice in the duties of the Inquisition. We did not like each other. In fact, I was sure she hated me on some level. But she was a fine interrogator and a devoted servant of the Imperium. She was also a psyker, and a lethally powerful one at that.

I nodded in reply. She looked away, closing her eyes, and I felt the air around us take on a heavy, burned-sugar texture as she drew power to her. Our quarry had already vanished into the shifting forest of human bodies around us. Hundreds of troops jostled like frightened cattle, and I heard officers shouting for order and situation reports in the distance. There was a frozen moment, a sliver of time that for an instant was quiet and still. I saw a young trooper no more than a pace from me, his face expressing puzzlement, his tan-coloured uniform still creased from storage. I whispered a prayer for forgiveness in that moment.

An invisible shockwave tore out from Helena, ripping bodies from the ground and tossing them into the air like debris in a cyclone's path. Bodies fell, broken, screaming as the telekinetic storm followed our quarry. It reached him, fifty paces from us, and flicked him off his feet. He hit the ground with a crack of bones. When I got to him he was sucking in air in wet gasps, his mashed fingers scrabbling at the lasgun just beyond his reach. I raised my inferno pistol and burned his reaching hand to a charred and blistered stump.

I did not bother to ask him how many other saboteurs were hidden in the mustering, or what their target was. I knew he would not give me an answer. It did not matter. He would tell me what I wanted to know anyway.

'Take it from him.' I flicked my pistol at the broken man on the ground. 'We need to know how many of them there are and what targets they are intending to bomb.' Helena took a deep breath, closing her eyes for a second before looking down at the man who twitched and gurgled at our feet. He went still, and I could feel the cold witch-touch on my skin. Helena's eyes were closed, but as I looked at her she spoke.

'I have him, but...' her voice quivered and I saw she was trembling. 'There is something wrong.'

'Get the information,' I snarled. 'We are running out of time. How many have infiltrated the muster? Where are the bombs?'

'They–' she began, but was cut off by a laugh that bubbled up from the man on the ground. I looked down. He was staring back at me with corpse-white eyes. In that moment I knew I had made a mistake. We are cautioned that assumptions are worse than ignorance, and looking at the man I knew that my assumptions would see me dead. This was no saboteur ring bent on a mundane atrocity. This was something more, something far more. Icy fear ran through me.

'We are many, inquisitor,' he said, his voice a racking gurgle of blood and shattered ribs. Beside me Helena began to spasm, blood running from her mouth and eyes. Her mouth was working, trying to form words.

'Witches. They are witches...' she gasped, her hand reaching to grip my arm, as the psychic storm built around us. 'I can feel their minds. There are more, many more.' I felt a greasy charge lick my skin and detected a stink of burned blood on the air. The broken man laughed again, his skin crawling with lurid warp light.

'We are many,' he screamed, and he was still screaming as I vaporised his head. The sound did not end, but filled my head, getting louder and louder. I looked up from the dead man and saw the extent of my mistake.

Across the plain, figures rose into the air on pillars of ghost light, their limbs pinned to the air, arcs of lightning whipping from one to another, connecting them in a growing web. Dark clouds the colour of bile and dried blood spilled into the sky. Across the mustering fields, hundreds of thousands fell to their knees, moaning, clawing at their skin, blood dribbling from their eyes. Some, with stronger will, had been able to arm their weapons and fire at the witch-chorus. Some found their mark and sent psykers to their death. But there were many, and the witch-storm rose in power with every heartbeat. I could feel the unclean power crawling over me like insects and the witches' voices pulling my thoughts apart. All I could hold on to was anger, anger that I had failed, that an enemy had fooled me. All the while their voices grew louder and louder, spiralling around each other as a single word emerged from the telepathic cacophony.

Phocron.

Dozens of minds screamed the name and the storm broke in an inferno that washed across the mustering fields. It turned flesh to ash and scattered it on a superheated wind. Hundreds of thousands died in a single instant, an army to conquer worlds reduced to twisted metal and dust. I watched the fire come for me, and felt something enfold me like a cloak of ice. I realised that Helena still gripped my arm as I fell into darkness.

I woke on a plain covered in ashes. Helena was next to me, her exposed skin burned and blistered, her breathing so shallow I thought she was dead until I saw her eyes twitch open. The energy needed to shield me still lingered on my skin as a cold shroud. I know now that she had saved us both, but at a price. The power she had channelled to shield us had almost burned her psychic talent out. She lived, but she was a shadow of what she had been and never became an inquisitor. Amongst an overwhelming tragedy, her sacrifice still lives in my memory like the ghost touch of a lost life.

Around us there was nothing but a landscape of desolation beneath a bruised sky. It was quiet, but in my mind echoed the name of he who had perpetrated this atrocity.

Eighty-four years ago

We came out of the iron-grey sky on streaks of blood-red fire. Staccato lines of flak and the bright blooms of defence lasers rose from the fallen city like the claws of a dying god raking the sky. Landing craft and assault carriers were punched from the air. Burning wreckage fell in oily cascades of smoke amongst the city's glittering domes and spires. The air rang with shells fired from orbit and the howl of attack craft engines.

The wrath and might of the Imperium fell on the city, and it screamed as it burned.

In the gloom of my Valkyrie's crew compartment, we felt the ferocity of the invasion as shuddering blows that shook the frame around us. It was close inside the assault carrier, the air tinted red by the compartment's tactical lights and spiced with the smell of sweat. Even in such a confined space, my storm trooper detail kept their distance, even if that distance was only centimetres. I knew each of them by name, had fought beside all of them and personally selected them as my guard during this invasion. We had bled and struggled side by side, but I stood apart from them. To feel the power of the Emperor in your hand is to know what it is to be alone. It is a fact that I had long ago accepted.

'Lord?' The voice was raised against the thunderous sound of the battle outside. I looked up from the holographic map to see Sergeant Draeg looking down at me, his face framed by oil-black armour. 'Theatre command wishes to know where you intend to make your landing.'

I smiled, letting careless humour wash over my face. 'Do they indeed?' I asked.

Draeg grinned back at me. 'Yes, lord. They say it is so that they can coordinate to properly support your operations.'

I nodded, pursing my lips in mock consideration. I am not given to humour, but to lead people to death, you must wear many masks. Something exploded close by and the Valkyrie bucked. I felt my back pressed against the hard metal of the flight bench as the pilot banked hard.

'Little late in the day for a coordinated strike, don't you think, Draeg?' I gave a small shake of my head. 'Tell them I will update them shortly.'

'Yes, lord,' nodded Draeg. 'And our actual target?'

I looked back to the holo-display, coloured runes winking in clusters over a plan view of the city, shifting with objectives and tactical intelligence. The city was called Hespacia, a glittering jewel that had fallen to greed and lies and pulled the rest of its planet with it. The ruling guilds had overthrown the Imperial government and given their souls, and those of their people, to the Dark Gods. This, though, was not why I had come to see it fall beneath the hammer of Imperial retribution. I had come not because of Hespacia's heresy but because of its cause.

'The Onyx Palace.' I handed the sergeant my holo-slate. 'Assault position marked.' I watched the thinnest cloud of fear pass over the sergeant's blunt features. We were heading into the heart of the corruption, and we were doing it alone, without support.

'Very good, my lord,' said Draeg and began to bark a briefing to the other storm troopers. I checked my own weapons: a blunt-nosed plasma pistol, holstered on the thigh of my burnished battle plate, and an eagle-headed hammer, which lay across my knees.

The Valkyrie bucked again, shaking from invisible blows. We were close. I did not need to see the tactical data to know it; I could feel it in the shuddering metal around me. In the decade after the burning of the Ephisian mustering I had changed much and learnt more. Suspicion is the armour of the Inquisition, and I had come to appreciate its value. Rebellion had spread, pulling a dozen worlds into heresy and corruption, and with it had come a name, a name I already knew: Phocron. Arch-heretic and puppet master of betrayal, his agents and traitors spread through our own forces like a contagion. Even with the might of a crusade at our backs, we bought every victory with blood. Ambushes, sabotage and assassination ate our strength even as we advanced step by bleeding step. So I came to this damned city to cut off the rebellion's head, to kill the enemy I had never seen. I came to kill Phocron.

The side doors of the Valkyrie peeled back, and the burning stink and howl of battle flooded over us. Beneath us buildings flicked past, aflame and so close that I could see the patternwork on the blue-green tiles that covered so many of their domed roofs. In the streets, figures moved from cover to cover, the sound of their small battles lost amongst the roar as fire fell from the sky in an unending rain.

Above the burning city sat a tiered mountain of pale stone the colour of dirty ice. A series of ascending domes and balconies, it glowed under the luminous haze of void shields, which flickered and sparked with the impact of munitions and energy blasts. This was the Onyx Palace, seat of governorship on this world and the heart of its betrayal. Phocron was there; it was his bastion. The layered shields sheltered him from the bombardment, but they would not deny us.

The Valkyrie hit the void shield envelope, sparks arcing across its fuselage and an electric tang filling the air. The tiered balconies of the palace rose before us, studded with dark weapon turrets that spat glowing lines of fire. We banked and tipped, rounds hammering into the armoured airframe. The engines howled as they thrust us towards the palace's summit. Others came behind us, delta-shaped wings of Vulture gunships and more assault craft. The air shuddered with the rolling scream of launching rockets and the bellow of explosions. Domes and statue-lined bridges flicked past. I could see figures, some crouched behind sandbags, others already running from the detonations that walked up the flank of the palace in our wake.

As we crested the highest dome I saw Phocron for the first time, a figure in dark armour with a single, black-clad companion and a cluster of cowering figures in billowing silk robes. He stood close to the edge of the balcony as if he had been watching the ruin that he had forced the Imperium to bring to this world.

The Valkyrie pivoted, its engines screaming as it skimmed the stone slabs of the platform. My storm troopers were already dropping out of the door, hitting the ground one after another. Draeg gave me a grin, hurled himself out, and then it was me tumbling the few metres to hit the tiled platform. The world spun for a second, then I was up on my feet, training and instincts doing the work of thought. My armour responded to my movements, thrusting me forwards faster than muscle could. Behind me, more storm troopers spilled onto the platform.

The robed figures clustered around Phocron died, hellgun blasts burning through their silk finery. A few ran, swathes of coloured fabric spilling behind them, their bare feet slapping on the marble. Phocron stood impassively, his hands empty, the sword at his waist undrawn. Behind him, a figure in a black storm coat and silver domino mask stood equally unmoved. I fired, plasma hissing from my pistol. Others were firing too. Bolts of energy converged on the two figures, but splashed against a shimmering dome of energy.

Draeg and his squad were in front of me, sprinting towards Phocron and his aide.

'Try and keep up in that armour, lord.' I heard the sergeant's grin over the vox. I spat back a very unlordly oath.

As the first shots hit Phocron's energy field, Draeg drew his sword. Lightning sheathed it with a crackle. 'Close assault, get inside the shield dome,' the sergeant spat over the vox. The hammer in my hand sprang to life, its generator making it vibrate with straining power.

Draeg was the first through the shield dome, raising his sword for a backhanded cut, muscles ready to unfold the momentum of his charge into an armour-cracking blow. But Phocron moved at the last instant before the blow struck.

I have fought a lifetime of wars and met many enemies blade to blade. I have studied the business of killing, the workmanlike cut, the parry and riposte of a duel, the nicety of a perfectly timed blow. I have watched men kill each other in countless ways. The art of death holds no mystery to me. Yet I swear, I never saw death dealt with more malign genius than at that moment.

Phocron's sword was in his hand. It was long, its double-edged blade damasked in a scale pattern. A saurian head snarled from its crossguard. It met Draeg's sword in a thunder crack of converging power fields. Draeg was fast and conditioned from years of war to react to such a counter, but in this moment those instincts killed him. He shifted his weight to let the Space Marine's blow flow past and open his enemy to another cut. He did not expect Phocron to drop his sword.

With no resistance, Draeg's sword sliced down and cut air. Phocron turned around the sergeant's sword, so close their armour brushed. The gauntleted hand slammed into Draeg's armour at the throat. I saw the sergeant's head snap back, his body rag-loose as he fell to the ground.

The rest of Draeg's squad had not been far behind him and they opened up as they came through the shield dome. Phocron was already moving towards them at a flat run. The first died as he squeezed his trigger. Phocron's hand closed over the hellgun, crushing the storm trooper's fingers into the trigger guard. The man screamed. Phocron pivoted, the gun still spewing a stitched line of energy. The hellgun's fire hit the next two storm troopers at point-blank range, burning through flesh and armour. With swift delicacy, the Space Marine looped an arm around the screaming man and gripped the webbing belt of grenades across his chest.

I was a pace from the edge of the shield dome when I realised what was about to happen. Phocron turned and threw the screaming man at the rest of the storm trooper squad. The force of the throw broke the man's back with a sharp crack. I could see the pins of the grenades glinting in Phocron's fingers. The dead man hit the platform in front of his comrades and exploded.

The blast sheared through the rest of the squad in an expanding sphere of shrapnel. Fragments of metal, flesh and bone pattered off my armour. I could see Phocron and his storm-coated henchman through the pall of smoke and dust. They were running.

'Target is moving,' I shouted across the vox. 'Close and eliminate.'

I fired, plasma burning ionised trails through the dust cloud. I ran after the two figures. Behind me, the rest of the strike force advanced. I reached the edge of the dust cloud. The fleeing pair were at the edge of the platform. Behind them, the city burned. They turned and looked back at the force running past the bloody remains of Draeg and his squad. They ran without looking at Phocron's sword, left forgotten on the ground.

The plasma charge concealed in the blade detonated, unfolding into a glowing sphere of sun-hot energy. I felt the heat through the skin of my armour as the blast tossed me into the air and slammed me into the paving. Warning chimes sounded in my ears as my armour's systems sensed damage. Something wet moved in my chest as I sucked in a breath and found I was alive. For a few seconds, I could see nothing. I tried to raise my head and found that my vision was smeared with blood. I blinked until I could see. Bright light shone from behind me where the sphere of plasma still burned. Phocron stood, his blue armour black in the glare of the plasma bloom.

I pulled myself to my feet with a flare of pain and a grind of servos from inside my armour. My hammer was gone, scattered across the platform by the explosion. Two storm troopers who had been close beside me began to haul themselves up. Phocron shot them before they could stand, the guttural bark of the bolt pistol almost lost in the sound of the battle raging in the city. I was standing, my plasma pistol whining in my hand as it focused its power. The muzzle of Phocron's pistol pointed directly at me, a dark circle ready to breathe fire.

A Valkyrie crested the edge of the platform with a wash of downdraft. Its hull was painted in the storm-grey of Battlefleet Hecuba. I could see the worn kill marks and unit tags under the cockpit. For an instant, I expected it to open up with its chin weapon, for it to rake Phocron and his companion with fire. Then it spun, drifting down until its open side doors were level with the platform. A crewman in an Imperial Navy uniform reached down to help the storm-coated figure into the side door. Phocron vaulted after and the Valkyrie swooped away. I fancied that the Alpha Legionnaire was looking at me with his emerald eyes until the craft was lost amongst the hundreds of others that swarmed above the dying city.

I breathed, letting pain and frustrated anger spill out. Something did not fit. It had seemed as if Phocron had anticipated our attack, that he had waited for it to come so that he could slaughter us. No, it was not just a slaughter. It was a demonstration of superiority. I can defeat you in a thousand ways, I can kill you as I choose, it had said. Then this sudden retreat. It did not fit. His forces were being overwhelmed, the city filling with thousands of Imperial troops – but then why not withdraw as soon as this became clear. Unless…

I suddenly felt cold, as if ice had formed inside my armour. I thumbed my vox-link, breaking through clearance ciphers until the voice of the invasion's commanding officer spoke into my ear. General Berrikade had a thick voice that spoke of his ample waist and heavy jowls. He was no fool, though.

'Lord inquisitor,' he said, his voice chopped by static.

'General, all troops are to be withdrawn from the city immediately.' There was a pause, and I could imagine Berrikade staring incredulously at the vox-speaker in the strategium aboard an orbiting battleship.

'Lord,' he began, speaking carefully. 'If I may ask…' He never finished because at that moment Phocron answered the unspoken question. As the words left Berrikade's lips, the city's plasma reactors, promethium stores and chemical refineries exploded.

Across the city, glowing clouds rose into the sky, their tops broadening and flattening as they met the upper air currents. The shockwaves broke buildings into razor-sharp fragments and clouds of dust. An instant later, concentric waves of fire and burning gas swept through the streets. The sound and shockwave reached me in seconds, flipping me through the air with a bellow of noise. I must have hit the ground, but I never felt it. The blast wave had already pulled me down into darkness.

Later, while I healed, I was told that tens of thousands of Imperial troops had been killed, and hundreds of thousands more renegades and millions of civilians burned to nothing or crushed under rubble. The rebellion died, but the Imperium had taken a great wound and nothing was left but charred ruins. Only the Onyx Palace had survived. Its plasma reactors had not been overloaded, and that had saved my life. When I was told this, my first thought was that Phocron had wanted someone to survive to witness him rip another bloody chunk from the flesh of the Imperium. Then I thought again of the dark mouth of Phocron's bolt pistol and the death that he had withheld. No, I thought, he did not want just anyone to witness his victory; he had chosen *me* to witness it. To this day I do not know why.

* * *

A year ago

The ship drifted closer. Through the polished armourglass of the viewport, I could see its crippled engines bleed glowing vapour into the vacuum. It was a small vessel, barely large enough to be warp-capable, and typical of the cutters used by traders and smugglers who existed on the fringes of the Imperium. The ship I stood on was massive by comparison, layered with armour and weapons bastions. It was a predator leviathan closing on a minnow. The *Unbreakable Might* was an Armageddon-class battle cruiser and mounted enough firepower to break other warships into glowing debris. Against the nameless clipper, it had barely needed to use a fraction of its might. A single, precise lance strike had burned the smaller ship's plasma engines to ruin and left it to coast on unpowered.

I turned from the view with a clicking purr of augmetics. My eyes focused on Admiral Velkarrin from beneath the cowl of my crimson robe. He was rake-thin, the metal flexes of command augmentation hanging from his grey-skinned skull in a tangled spill down the back of his gold-frogged uniform.

'Launch a boarding party, admiral,' I said. Velkarrin pursed his colourless lips but nodded.

'As you wish, my lord.' He turned to give an order to a hovering officer.

'And, admiral…' He turned back. 'They are to observe maximum caution.'

'Yes, my lord.' He gave a short bow. I could tell he resented my commandeering his command and his fleet. Hunting smuggler vessels and pirates while war washed across star systems must have galled him. Part of me was faintly amused by watching his pride war with fear of the Inquisition. The rest of me cared nothing for what he felt.

'I will meet the boarding team personally upon their return,' I told him.

Velkarrin gave another curt bow in acknowledgement and stalked away, hissing orders at subordinates.

I turned back to watch our latest prey draw closer, my eyes whirring as they focused. They had rebuilt me after Hespacia. My eyes and face were gone, replaced by blue-lensed augmetics and a mask of twisted scar tissue fused onto a ceramic woven skull. My left leg and a portion of my torso had been so mangled that they had been replaced. Ceramite plating, organ grafting and a leg of mechanised brass meant that I still lived and walked, even if it was with a bent back and the stutter of gears and pistons. For a while after the disaster of the Hespacia attack, I thought of my injuries as a penance for my lack of foresight, a price for ignorance written forever into my body.

Since that lesson I had done much to address my failing. The war against the rebel worlds had grown many times over, sucking in armies and resources from across many star systems. The Imperium was no longer fighting a war of containment but a crusade of retribution. Under my authority, and that of the Adeptus Terra, it was named the Ephisian Persecution. I had watched our forces struggle for decades as more and more worlds had fallen to rebellion and the influence of the Dark Gods. It was a war we were losing because we were fighting an enemy for whom lies were both a weapon and a shield. Understanding that enemy had been my work in the decades since Hespacia burned.

I had expended great energy in tracking down information on the Alpha Legion. From the sealed reports of Inquisitor Girreaux to half-understood accounts from the dawn of the Imperium, I had reviewed them all. I knew my enemy. I knew their nature, their preferred forms of warfare, and their weaknesses. Sometimes, I thought I knew them better than I knew myself.

Their symbol was the hydra, a many-headed beast from legends born in mankind's earliest days. It was both a mark of their warrior brotherhood and a statement of methodology. To fight the Alpha Legion was to fight a many-headed beast that would twist in your grasp. As soon as you thought you had a part pinned, another unseen part would strike. Should you cut off one head, two would grow to replace it. They wove secrets and lies about themselves, hoping to baffle and confuse their enemies. Subterfuge, espionage, ambush and the untameable tangle of guerrilla warfare were their specialities: wielded through networks of corrupted followers, infiltrators, spies and, on occasion, their own martial skill. They were wrapped in the corruption of Chaos, steeped in betrayal and bitterness ever since their primarch and Legion had betrayed mankind ten millennia before.

The enemy I faced now was but a single scion of that heretic brood, but no less formidable for that. Phocron was a name that had infiltrated every theatre of the Ephisian Persecution like a silent, coiling serpent. I knew that even before we had learnt his name he had seeded a dozen worlds with insurgent ideologies and built up control over witch-cults and heretic sects. Now he moved from warzone to warzone, plunging worlds into rebellion, corrupting our forces and punishing the Imperium for every victory. The Ephisian Atrocity and the Burning of Hespacia were just two amongst the subtle and devastating attacks he had made on the Imperium. Throughout his coiling dance of destruction, he had stayed out of my grasp, a shadow opponent locked in a dual with me across dozens of worlds.

Beyond the reflective layer of armourglass a shuttle boosted towards the crippled ship on trails of orange flame. Rather than follow Phocron's trail I had decided to attack him where he was most vulnerable: his transportation. He had no fleet of warships for he did not take planets by orbital invasion or the threat of bombardment. He took worlds from within, moving from one to another unseen. That implied that he moved using pirate and smuggler craft; small ships that could pass unnoticed and unremarked through the wild borderland of the subsector. A scattered task force of Imperial ships had tracked and boarded nineteen vessels so far with no result. The ship I watched would be the twentieth.

Two hours later, I stood amidst the promethium stink and the semi-ordered chaos of one of the *Unbreakable Might's* main landing bays. Bright light flooded the cathedral-like space, gleaming off the hulls of lighters, shuttles and landing craft. Figures moved over them, working on the mechanical guts exposed under servicing plates.

I stood with Velkarrin and a guard of twenty armsmen, their bronzed void armour reflecting the bright light. The admiral stood a few paces away, consulting with two of his attending officers. The away team had reported that the vessel appeared to be nothing but a smuggler, crewed by deserters and outlanders. They had found a cargo of illegal ore destined for some pirate haven out in the Halo Margins. The lexmechanic who had accompanied them had drained the smuggler ship's data reservoirs for later analysis. As on the nineteen previous occasions no connection with Phocron or his shadow network appeared to exist. Still, I wanted to meet the boarding party on their return, to search their accounts for details that they might have failed to report. Once that was done, the smuggler ship would be blasted into molten slag.

The armoured shuttle glided into the dock, its passive antigravity field filling the air with an ionised tang. It settled onto the deck with a hiss of hydraulics and a creak of ice-cold metal. The shuttle was a blunt block of grey armour the size of a mass ground hauler, its surface pitted and scored by atmospheric translation. Blast shields covered the armourglass of its cockpit. I heard the echoes of vox-chatter between the pilots and the deck crew as they moved in to attach power lines and data cables. The ramp under the chin of the shuttle hinged open, revealing a dark space inside. Velkarrin and the armsmen looked towards it, expecting the boarding team to appear from the gloom.

Something was wrong. I reached for the plasma pistol at my waist, my hand closing on the worn metal of the grip at the same moment that the docking bay went dark. Complete blackness enfolded us. For an instant, there was silence, and then voices rose in confusion. The pistol was in my hand, its charge coils glowing as it built power with a piercing whine. In the direction of the shuttle, two eyes glowed suddenly green. There was a motorised growl as a chain weapon gunned to life, and then the shooting started.

Our armsmen guard opened up, shotgun muzzles flaring as they fired into the dark. The noise was like a ragged, rolling bellow. In the jagged light of muzzle flare I saw my enemy standing on the ramp of the shuttle. His armour was dark, mottled by patterns of scales. In one hand he held a toothed axe, in the other a bolt pistol. He stood still for an instant as the shot rattled from his warplate, looking at us with glowing green eyes. Behind him stood a figure in a silver mask and storm coat. In that brief moment I thought that the empty eyes in the silver face were looking into mine.

The armsmen had closed ranks around Velkarrin and I, forming a deep circle of bronze armour. I aimed and fired, but Phocron was already gone, moving through muzzle flash, a whirlwind of slaughter caught through blinked instants.

He hit the first armsmen with a downward blow. I heard the scream of motorised teeth meeting metal and flesh.

He was two strides nearer, an arc of dismembered dead at his feet. I heard a yelp of fear close by, recognising the admiral's voice by its tone.

The bolt pistol flared and roared, three armsmen dying in an oily flash of light. He was three strides away. There was a smell of offal and meat in my nose. Beside me, I heard Velkarrin turn to run and thud to the deck as his feet slipped on something slick and soft. The plasma pistol whined in my hand.

I raised my pistol, lightning dancing across its charge coils. Phocron was above me, chainaxe raised, scale-patterned armour glistering with blood. He brought the axe down in a diagonal cut. I pulled the trigger and plasma flared from the barrel of my pistol.

I missed, but the shot saved my life. Jerking aside to avoid my shot, Phocron missed his target. The teeth of the chainaxe met my gun arm just below the elbow, the back-swing slicing through Velkarrin as he tried to stand.

The lights came on as shock hit me. Blood was spilling from the chewed stump of my arm. I staggered a step before my legs gave way, and I collapsed to the floor in a clicking whir of gears. People moved, shouting. I was aware of a lot of weapons surrounding me very quickly.

I looked around, trying to focus through a pale fog that seemed to be floating across my vision. Blood glistened under the bright lights. The ramp of the shuttle was still open. Later, I would find out that none of its crew or the boarding party had returned from the smuggler ship; the voices in the vox-chatter and reports had been perfect mimicry. Of Phocron and the man in the silver mask, there was no sign.

One month ago

The war council overseeing the Ephisian Persecution gathered on board the *Unbreakable Might*. Generals, war savants, vice-admirals, magi, bishops militant, palatines, commissar lords and captains of the Adeptus Astartes; all came to my call. The strategium of the battle cruiser was a two-hundred-paces-wide circular chamber of raked seats carved from granite. I waited at the centre, under the eyes of the gathering worthies, and watched.

They came in small groups, looking for faces they knew, judging where it was their right to sit, who they had to avoid and who they had to greet. It was like watching the shifting gears of Imperial politics and power play out in miniature. There a Sparcin war chief in burnished half-plate and white fur cloak, trailed by a clutch of tactical advisers. Here a psykana lord, a withered white face within a hood of cables, sat next to a spindle-limbed woman in carmine robes, the cog-skull of the Adeptus Mechanicus etched on the brass of her domino mask. Servo-skulls moved above the assembling throng, scanning, recording, sniffing the air for threats and spreading incense in thick breaths.

Amongst the crowd I saw some of my own kind, inquisitors or their representatives, moving amongst the rest like imperious masters, or remaining still and silent on the edges. I had invited none of them but they came anyway, my reputation enough to bring them. Some even called me 'lord inquisitor'. Rank within the Inquisition is a complex matter. No formal structure exists amongst this shadow hand of the Imperium that answers to none but the will of the Emperor. Lordship is a matter of respect, a title of acknowledgement granted by peers to one who has earned it by the power of their deeds. My war against Phocron had pulled respect and renown to me like a flame gathers insects. As the greatest masters of war in this volume of space gathered at my call, I could see why some might call me lord.

I sat on a high-backed chair at the centre of the chamber. A symbolic hammer rested beneath my left hand, my right on the black iron of the chair's arm, fingers of polished chrome clicking softly on the dark metal. It had been a year since I had lost my right arm in the ambush that had killed Admiral Velkarrin and nearly claimed my life. The bionic replacement still ached with phantom pain.

In that year, I had not been idle. Following his attempt on my life, Phocron had simply vanished. No trace of him could be found on the ship or on the smuggler vessel. This, and the sudden loss of light at the moment of attack, could only mean that his network of traitors extended deeper and higher in our forces than I had considered possible. Trusted acolytes and agents of my own had gone to work, and now I gathered together the leaders of the Persecution to share what I had found. A few knew what was about to happen, most did not.

I watched as black-visored troopers sealed the doors to the chamber and waited for the grumble of conversation to fade. When it had, I stood.

'There is much to speak of,' I said, my voice carrying up the tiered seats. I saw some shift at the lack of formal greeting or acknowledgement of the honour and position of those gathered here. I let myself smile at the thought. 'But first there is a matter that must be dealt with.' I gave a slight nod as if to emphasise the point, and those waiting for that signal acted as one.

Even though I was prepared for it, the psychic shockwave made me stagger. On the tiered seats, a dozen figures convulsed as the telepathic and telekinetic power enfolded them in a vice-like grip. I felt an oily static charge play over my skin. There was a sound like wind rustling through high grass. The needle slivers hit the convulsing men and women, and one by one they went still as the sedatives overrode nerve impulses. There was an instant of shocked silence.

'Do not move,' I shouted as the black-visored troopers moved through the crowd. They clustered around each of the stricken figures. Null collars and monowire bindings were slipped over necks and limbs, and the bound figures were dragged across the stone floor like sacks of grain. The shock in the rest of the crowd was palpable; they had just seen a dozen of their senior peers, men and women of power and distinction, overcome and dragged away. You could almost feel the thought forming in all their minds; *traitors in our midst*. The pale-faced psykana lord nodded to me and I favoured him with a low bow of thanks. A murmur of anger and fear began to build in the chamber.

'Our enemy is among us.' I raised my hammer up and brought its adamantine head down on the granite floor. Silence gathered in the wake of the fading blow. 'It walks amongst us, wearing faces of loyalty.' My voice was soft but it carried in the still air. 'Our enemy has used our strength against us, directed us into traps, mired us in blood and shackled our strength with lies. A year ago, on this ship, that enemy came close to ending my life with his own hand. That such a thing was possible is a testament to his ability and audacity.' I paused, looking around at the faces watching me, waiting to see what would come next. 'But I survived, and in that attempt he exposed the extent of the treachery within our forces.' I pointed to the dozen spaces on the tiered seats. 'Today I have removed the heads of the hydra from among us.' I paused as murmurs ran through the audience.

The traitors had been difficult to find without arousing their suspicion. It had been delicate work to find them, and more delicate still to prepare to remove them in a single instant. The twelve taken in the chamber had been the most senior, the most highly placed of Phocron's agents and puppets. Some, no doubt, had not known what end they served; others, I was sure, were willing traitors. There had been generals amongst them, senior Munitorum staff, an astropath, a confessor and even an interrogator. At the moment they had been taken, parallel operations had gone into action throughout the Persecution's forces, cutting the corruption out from among us. Most of the infiltrators would be killed, but many would be taken and broken until their secrets flowed from them like blood from a vein.

'The enemy has blinded us and led us by the hand like children. But at this moment he has also handed us weapons with which to destroy him. Knowledge is our weapon, and from the traitors who walked among us we will gain knowledge.' I stood and picked the hammer up, its head at my feet, the pommel resting under my hands. 'And with that knowledge, this Persecution will cut the ground from under the feet of our enemy. We will wound and hound him until he crawls to his last refuge. And when he is crippled and bleeding, I shall take the last head of this hydra.'

Twelve hours ago

A hundred warships came to bear witness to our victory. They ringed the jagged space fortress, their guns flaring as they hammered it with fire. The *Hydra's Eye* turned in its orbit around the dead world like a prize fighter too dazed to avoid the blows mashing his face to bloody pulp and splintered bone.

In the end, it had been the words of a traitor that had betrayed Phocron's refuge. One of those taken from the strategium of the *Unbreakable Might* had known of another agent in Naval command. That agent had been taken in turn, and his secrets ripped from his mind by a psyker. That information had been added to fragments gleaned from others, winding together to make a thread that had led to the system of dead planets in which the *Hydra's Eye* hid. That it was the current refuge for Phocron was implied and confirmed by many sources once we knew where to look. Once I had the location of Phocron's base, I ordered an immediate attack.

The *Hydra's Eye* was truly vast, an irregular star of fused void debris over fifteen kilometres across at its widest point. Its hull was a patchwork skin of metal that wept glowing fluid as macro shells and lance strikes reduced its defences to molten slag. There had been enemy ships clustering around the irregular mass of the space fortress like lesser fish beside a deep-sea leviathan. Most had been pirate vessels, wolf packs of small lightly armed craft. All died within minutes, their deaths scattering light across the jagged bulk of the *Hydra's Eye*. Our guns went silent as a cloud of assault boats and attack craft swarmed towards the wounded fortress. I had not watched as Phocron's last means of escape died in fire. This was the end of my war and I was ready to strike its last blow myself. When the first wave of attack craft swarmed towards the space fortress I was there, my old body wrapped in armour forged by the finest artisans of Mars.

An animal is at its most dangerous when wounded and cornered. Phocron's followers did not fail to hammer this lesson home. The forces on the *Hydra's Eye* were a mixture of piratical scum and renegades inducted into Phocron's inner circle. They spent their lives without thought, their only care being to make us pay many times over for each of them that we killed. I could see Phocron's vile genius in their every tactic. Some hid in ceiling ducting or side passages, waiting for our forces to pass before attacking from behind. Others pulled Guardsmen quietly into the dark, strangling them before taking their uniforms and equipment. Dressed as friends, the renegades would join our forces, waiting until the most advantageous moment to turn on the men beside them.

The structure of the fortress itself spoke of a twisted foresight. Dead ends and hidden passages riddled the structure. Passages and junctions seemed to split and channel us, portioning our forces so that they became divided. We had bodies enough to choke every passage. We would win, that was without doubt, but every inch cost blood. Those bloody steps had led me here to this chamber and this final battle.

Yes, every step had cost blood; every step for a hundred years, from the mustering fields of Ephisia, through the Burning of Hespacia to here, where I will face my enemy for the last time. I am alone, the rest of the Imperial force lost behind me in the bloody tangle of the *Hydra's Eye*. So I will face my enemy alone, but perhaps that is as it should be.

Phocron moves and cuts, his blow so quick and sudden that I have no chance to dodge. I raise my arm, feeling the armour synchronise with the movements of my ageing muscles. My fist meets his strike in a blaze of light. For a second, it is his strength against mine, the energies of weapons grinding against each other. I am looking into his face, so close that I can see the pattern of finer and finer scales on his faceplate. The deadlock lasts an eye blink. I fire my storm bolter a fraction of a second before he moves. The burst hits him in the chest at point-blank range and spins him onto the floor with the sound of cracking ceramite. I spray his struggling form with explosive rounds as he tries to rise.

I take a step closer – a mistake. He is on his feet faster than I can blink, spinning past me. The tip of his sword glides over my left elbow as he moves. The energy field sheathing my fist vanishes, the power feeds severed with surgical care. I turn to follow him. His sword flicks out again, low and snake-strike fast. The tip stabs through the back of my left knee. Pain shoots up my leg an instant before it collapses under me. Tiles shatter under the impact. He is gone, moving into blind space behind me. I try to twist around, my targeting systems searching. He is going to kill me, one cut at a time. Despite the pain, I smile to myself. The Alpha Legion do not simply kill, they bleed you bite by bite until you have no doubt of their superiority. But that pride is their weakness.

A cut splits the elbow of my right arm. I do not even see where it comes from. Blood is running down my alabaster-white armour and dribbling across the crushed tiles. My right arm is hanging loose at my side, but I hold on to my storm bolter through the pain.

He walks into my view. There is a casual slowness to his movements. He has stripped me of my strength, crippled me and now wants to look into my eyes as he kills me. He stops two paces from me and stares down at me with green eyes. The tip of the blade rises level with my face. His weight shifts as he prepares to ram the sword into my eye.

This is the death stroke, and it is the chance I have been waiting for.

I bring my left arm around in a swing that hits him behind the right knee. The fist has no power field, but it is still a gauntlet of armour propelled by a layer of artificial muscles. It hits with a dry crack of fractured armour and bone.

Phocron falls, the hand gripping the knife splayed out to the side. I pull myself to my feet, gripping my storm bolter with the last of my strength. It does not take much. All I need to do is squeeze the trigger. Fired at point-blank range, the explosive rounds shred his arm. Before he can react, I move and squeeze the remainder of the storm bolter's clip into his left arm.

He flounders in a pool of blood and armour fragments. I put my knee on his chest and grip the horns of his helmet with my left fist. Seals squeal and snap as I wrench the helmet from his head. For an instant, I expect to see the face of a monster, a monster that created me, that drove me to become what I am. But the face under the helm is that of a Space Marine; unscarred, dark eyes looking up at me from sharp features. He has a small tattoo of an eagle under his left eye, the ink faded to a dull green.

I reach up and take my own helmet off. The air smells of weapons-fire and blood.

'Phocron,' I say. 'For your crimes and heresies against the Imperium of Mankind, I sentence you to death.'

He smiles.

'Yes, you have won. Phocron will die this day.' There is movement at the edge of my vision.

I look up. There are figures watching me from the edges of the room. They wear blue armour, some blank and unadorned, some etched with serpentine symbols, others hung with the sigils of false gods. They look at me with green glowing eyes. Amongst them is a normal-sized man wrapped in a storm cloak, his face hidden by a silver mask. The image of a figure in a mask stood against the burning backdrop of Hespacia, and caught in muzzle flash on the *Unbreakable Might* flicks through my memory.

The man steps forwards. His right hand is augmetic and holds a slender-barrelled needle pistol. There is a clicking purr of gears and pneumatics as the masked man walks towards me. I start to rise. The masked man reaches up with his left hand and pulls the silver mask away. I look at him.

He has my face.

The needle dart hits the inquisitor in his left eye and the toxin kills him before he can gasp. He collapses slowly, the bulk of his armour hitting the tiled floor with a crash.

We move quickly. We have only a few moments to secure our objective, and we can make no mistakes. The inquisitor's armour is stripped from his body, piece by piece, the injuries he sustained noted as they are revealed. As the dead man is peeled from the armour I remove my own gear and equipment, stripping down until there are two near identical men, one dead and bleeding on the floor, the other standing while his half-brothers finish their work.

My augmetics and every detail of my re-sculpted flesh match the man who lies dead before me. Years of subtle flesh-craft and conditioning mean that my voice is his voice, my every habit and movement are his. There is only the matter of the wounds that were carefully inflicted to injure, but not kill. I do not cry out as my Legion brothers cut me, though the pain is nothing less than it was for him, the dead man whose face I wear. The wounds are the last details, and as the blood-slick Terminator armour covers my skin, all differences between the dead inquisitor and I end. We are one, he and I.

They take the inquisitor's body away. It will burn in a plasma furnace to erase the last trace of this victory. For it is a victory. They take away our crippled brother who was the last to play the role of Phocron. A corpse is brought to take his place, its blue armour chewed by bolter-rounds and crumpled by the blows of a power fist. A horned helmet hides his face and a shimmering cloak hangs from his shoulders. This corpse is the final proof that the Imperium will require to believe they have won this day: Phocron, dead, killed by his nemesis. Killed by me. The Imperium will see this day as their victory, but it is a lie.

Phocron never existed, his name and legend only extant in the mind of the Imperium and the obsession of the man whose place I take. Phocron existed only to create this last meeting. Many of the Legion were Phocron, playing the role to create a legend that was a falsehood. I will walk from this chamber in victory and my legend will grow; my influence and power will spread further. Decades of cultivation and provocation have led to this one moment of transformation, the moment we give the Imperium a victory and transform it into a lie. This is our truth, the core of our soul, the essence of our craft. We are warriors unbound by the constraints of truth, assumption, or dogma. We are the reflection in the eternal mirror of war, ever-changing, unfixed, and invincible. We serve lies and are their masters. We are their slaves and they are our weapons, weapons which can defeat any foe, break any fortress and grant one warrior victory against ten thousand. I am the one who stands against many. I am Alpha Legion, and we are one.

BITTER END

S P Cawkwell

For many years, he had made bargains, accords and dark pacts, both with powers he could name and several more that he dared not. He could not remember the last time he had merely requested something and the Imperium had provided it. In the days of his hated and enforced servitude to the Corpse-Emperor, he had but to requisition something and it was his.

Now, whenever he wanted something, Huron Blackheart simply reached out with the might of his loyal Red Corsairs and he took it. His greedy, grasping claws closed around objects, people and entire star systems and stole them away. He looted and plundered, he stole and he murdered. Occasionally, though, he would come upon a treasure that he could not simply claim.

When this happened, he would be roused from the shadows in which he now existed and he would hunt down his quarry in an entirely different manner. He would sit down with agents of the most powerful and most influential, and he would talk. He would barter and negotiate, bringing his considerable charisma and cunning to the fore, and he would make more deals.

His reputation preceded him wherever he went, and many wisely shied away from reaching any sort of arrangement with the Tyrant of Badab, fearing for their lives. But there were many more who boldly sealed their agreements with him in blood.

Sometimes, Huron Blackheart even kept his word.

* * *

It had been an agri-world once, before an Exterminatus had rendered it an uninhabitable wasteland. Its given name was lost to memory, leaving it only with the identifier bestowed upon it during the halcyon days of the Great Crusade: Eighty-Three Fourteen. Nothing grew here any more, and the only things that lived upon its surface were the most tenacious of bacteria. Its seas had boiled away, leaving vast expanses of arid ground that was cracked and blistered. The ferocity of the bombardment had broken open the crust and disturbed something deep in the planet's core. Now, volcanic lava bubbled up through the wounds in the earth and spilled across its ruined surface like blood. There was a constant smouldering heat haze that loaned everything a slightly distorted, unreal appearance.

It was a prime example of an inhospitable environment, but the gigantic figures making their steady way across its broken surface were not in the slightest bit bothered by the poisoned air or the excruciating heat. They walked without tiring, keeping up a pace they could sustain for many days if they so desired. They had marched to war in this way many times. But on this day, there was no war to be had. This was a deputation sent to accompany their lord and master to a summit.

Huron Blackheart walked in the midst of half a dozen of his Red Corsairs, his face alone exposed to the hostile environment. The countless implants and prosthetics that held his brain within what remained of his skull meant that wearing a helm caused him great discomfort, and it was such a laborious and time-consuming process to rewire his cranium to accept one that he viewed it more as a hindrance than a benefit. The complex, wheezing workings of his replacement lungs and respiratory system filtered the atmosphere in much the same way as a helmet anyway, and thus the choking, sulphuric air had no effect on him at all.

He could have made this journey alone but had elected to field a show of strength. He was wily and astute, blessed with cunning and guile like no other. But he did not trust the individual with whom he was dealing.

It had been a tedious process setting up this meeting. Dengesha had not been prepared to travel to Huron Blackheart's stronghold deep in the heart of the Maelstrom, and neither did the Blood Reaver care to board a ship almost entirely populated by warp-witches. (He had used sorcerers for his own ends before, of course. Indeed, it had been his own cabal that had suggested Dengesha as the best possible candidate for the task at hand.) Increasingly heated exchanges had taken place until an impasse had been reached. Neutral ground was the only solution.

Before a rocky outcrop overlooking the volcanic plains of a world that had once teemed with life, the Red Corsairs stopped. Above them, the shape of another giant could be made out. A baroque silhouette, picked out by the weak rays of the sickly yellow sun, stood alone. One of Huron's retinue pointed upwards with the muzzle of a bolter, indicating the other's presence.

'I see him,' Huron said, simply. 'I told you he would come.' A deep chuckle came from his ravaged throat. 'He could not help himself.'

Dengesha took no sobriquet in order to convey his greatness; it was not in his nature to embrace an honorific that extolled his deeds to the outside world. He was no Despoiler or Betrayer. He chose instead to let his actions speak for themselves. For centuries he had stood at the head of the Heterodox, a cabal of sorcerers who, it was rumoured, had splintered centuries earlier from the Word Bearers. Dengesha was said to have studied the heart of Chaos Undivided for more than five thousand years and, as a result, his well of knowledge ran deep.

There was nothing about Dengesha that suggested such great age. His visage was timeless and its individual features unimpressive. He bore several scars on his face, but more numerous were the countless runes and brands that had been seared into his skin. They writhed and twisted now under Huron's scrutiny, living things that spoke of a true disciple of the Dark Powers. He felt no discomfort in the sorcerer's presence. He was confident and fully at ease.

The two Space Marines, the warrior and the psyker, had moved to meet one another within a cave in the rock face. Neither's attendant retinues were with them as per the terms of their agreement.

The cave had once been a natural wonder, the source of a wellspring that had kept the local agricultural workers provided with water. As high as a refinery tower within, it was studded with broken, jagged stalagmites and stalactites that glittered with seams of semi-precious rock. Here, high above the shattered plains, was the only moisture remaining anywhere on the planet.

Now, the underground spring that had once nourished crops and quenched the thirst of thousands of Imperial workers was a toxic sinkhole, steaming and roiling gently. Periodically, air would escape from a fissure and expand with a rush, spraying boiling water in all directions. It spattered against the armour of the two giants, who stood face-to-face. Neither gave ground or spoke for some time, and then the psyker broke the stalemate with a bitter greeting.

'Blood Reaver.'

Huron greeted the sorcerer in kind and they considered each other in silence a while longer. As their eyes locked, the sorcerer's head tipped slightly to one side. The master of the Red Corsairs felt the faintest brush on his mind as the other attempted a psychic evaluation. Dengesha's resultant sharp intake of breath brought a smile to Huron's lips.

'Difficulties, Dengesha?'

'You are no psyker and yet you are warded... What is it that shields your mind from my sight?'

'Should you not be wary of admitting that you seek to invade my thoughts without permission?' Huron's voice was grating and harsh, dragged from replacement vocal cords and a vox-unit that had been tuned and retuned until it sounded as close to human as could be achieved. Which was not very close.

'You know my nature, Lord Huron. It is, after all, why you sought me out. Now answer my question.' Dengesha's words were demanding, yet his tone remained deferential. Huron approved of the approach. 'What is it that grants you this protection?'

'Perhaps you should tell me what you have heard?' The question was thrown back at the sorcerer, who folded his arms across his chest.

'I have heard,' he said, choosing his words carefully, 'in rumours whispered throughout the Eye, that the Four favour you. You carry a boon they have gifted you. I have heard that something walks at your side and grants you certain... benefits.'

'You are very well informed.' Dengesha took another sharp intake of breath and Huron continued. 'Does that surprise you, sorcerer? Do you taste envy? Are you curious as to why it is that the Dark Powers see fit to grant me such a gift? Look closely, Dengesha. Tell me what you see.'

The sorcerer considered the Red Corsair for a few moments. He looked the warrior up and down. A giant clad in desecrated red armour with so many augmetics and implants that he looked more like a blighted tech-priest or engineer than the scourge of the Imperium. The metal-plated head shook slightly and a quirk of amusement twitched the lipless mouth.

'No, Dengesha. Look *properly*. Use your witch-sight.'

The sorcerer *looked*. And he *saw*.

The word hamadrya had never been a part of Huron Blackheart's vocabulary until the day he had been reborn. There had been many deals made in those few days when he had hovered in the grey mists that lingered between life and death. His body had been left all but useless in the wake of the Star Phantoms' assault on the Palace of Thorns, and without the anchor of its corporeal weight, his soul had been free to wander at will.

Nobody knew who – or what – he had consorted with in those days. But if the thought was never expressed aloud, all of the Red Corsairs knew that their lord and master had made *some* pact. He could not have survived otherwise, despite the ceaseless labours of his most faithful Apothecaries. They could repair the physical damage to their Chapter Master's body, but that was all.

But no one ever asked of the events that had transpired, and Huron Blackheart never volunteered the information.

The hamadrya had begun its life as a *thought*. A potentiality. A tendril of insubstantial warp-stuff that draped itself invisibly across Huron's mantle. Over weeks, months and years it had become something more tangible. In its earliest stages, it was nothing more than a wisp. A curl of smoky air that lingered around the warrior's shoulder like a mist snake wrapping itself protectively around him. Huron himself seemed either oblivious or indifferent to its presence, but over time he began to notice that he was developing a sensitivity, and then a resistance, to psychic intrusions.

The more he realised this, the stronger the warding became, until eventually the ethereal presence at his shoulder took on a more corporeal form. Sometimes it was reptilian, sometimes avian, other times simian – but always animalistic and never larger than the breadth of the warrior's shoulder span. Others could see it, but never for long. Most of the time it could only be glimpsed briefly out of the corner of the eye, leaving the viewer wondering if they had seen it at all.

It granted Huron Blackheart an extra layer of power, one that boosted his already overinflated sense of ego. But it had limitations. It was a creature of the warp, after all.

The sorcerer looked. And he saw.

'I confess, my lord, that I did not believe the rumours to be true,' Dengesha confessed. He had considered the tale of the familiar to be nothing more than a figment of the mad Tyrant's overwrought imagination. Yet his witch-sight gave him a unique view. 'I have never seen its like before. Is this what they call the hamadrya?'

'Indeed it is. And you would do well not to concern yourself further with its origins, or its purpose. Consider instead the question my agent put to you.' Always quick to the point, Huron Blackheart did not care to linger on matters past.

'Yes, Lord Huron.' Dengesha bowed from the waist. 'I consider it a great honour that you seek my assistance in this matter. I understand that your... blessing loses power, that it becomes weaker the further from the heart of the Maelstrom you travel. In conjunction with your own *cabal*,' there was unmistakable superiority in Dengesha's tone as he said the word, 'I have determined what you need to overcome this limitation.'

'The hamadrya is a thing of the warp,' Huron said. He drummed his fingers idly against his armour-plated thigh. The noise reverberated through the cavernous chamber, the acoustics oddly distorted. 'It draws its strength from the powers therein. And the further from its source I travel...' He broke off and raised his head to study Dengesha. 'My cabal have told me what I need. A potent soul, shackled by arcane powers. The hamadrya can feed from its torment for all eternity. But my sorcerers, strong as they are, cannot do this one thing.'

Huron's red, artificial eye whirred softly as it focused upon the sorcerer. 'Give me my solution, Dengesha, and we will share the spoils of war.'

'You need a potent soul.'

'I have found such a thing. Sister Brigitta of the Order of the Iron Rose.'

'I have heard of this Order, and of this woman. The self-proclaimed saviour of her people. She who bears the sins of a generation upon her shoulders.'

'Aye. One of the faithful. A powerful symbol.'

'You need a suitable vessel. Such a thing will not be easy to locate, my lord. It could take many long months of searching…'

'You underestimate my resources, Dengesha.' Huron's twisted face distorted in a smile again and he twisted a loop on his belt, bringing an object slowly into view.

It was exquisite. Deep emerald green in colour, it was a fusion of bottle and vial, with a wide lip tapering to a long, slim neck that fed into a small oval bowl. It was encased within beautiful fretwork, wrought from copper or brass or some other burnished metal that snaked around its delicate surface.

'My cabal attached this vessel to my belt,' said Huron. 'They told me that only another sorcerer could remove it, that if I were to touch it myself the power would be tainted.' He shifted his hip slightly so that it was facing Dengesha, who snapped open the belt loop, taking the bottle in his hands. He could feel its imbued power; a thrum of psychic energy that made his hands vibrate gently as he held it. Huron studied him.

'On the understanding that you will give me what I ask for, I make a gift of this vessel to you so that you may work whatever fell deeds necessary. Do you accept?'

'Gladly, my lord. Such an arcane item… such a *relic* must have cost you dearly. Where did you locate it?'

'My sources are many and varied. Do not bother yourself with detail. Is it adequate for its purpose?'

'More than adequate.' Dengesha studied the bottle in admiration for a while, then with a series of hand movements, caused it to disappear. It was little more than cheap theatrics, and it did nothing to change the expression on Huron Blackheart's artificial face. 'This Sister Brigitta of yours will be heavily guarded, of course. I will need absolutely no distractions whilst I perform the binding.'

'Leave that side of the bargain to me, master sorcerer. My Red Corsairs will distract whatever pitiful forces guard her and you will take your coterie and perform your rituals. You will present me with what I want, and in return I shall give the Heterodox the world in her charge for your chapels, and its people for...' He gave a creaking shrug, 'whatever you see fit.' His augmetic eye darkened briefly as though he blinked – a slow, thoughtful thing that was somehow unsettling. 'Do we have an agreement?'

'A world and its subjects? My lord, that is… very generous of you.'

Huron shrugged again. 'My Corsairs and I will still take what spoils we desire, but it is not beyond me to show gratitude and generosity. Now tell me, Dengesha of the Heterodox, do we have an agreement?'

'We do.'

There were many who boldly sealed their agreements in blood. Dengesha of the Heterodox was one such individual.

Sometimes, Huron Blackheart even kept his word.

The temple burned.

Since time immemorial, the Order of the Iron Rose had been cloistered within their monument to the Emperor of Mankind. A building of dizzyingly beautiful aesthetics, the temple had stood proudly within well-guarded walls for countless generations. The Sisters of Battle lived their studious lives there quietly, only leaving at times of war when their fierce battle skills were most needed. Then, their comparative gentleness could easily be forgotten in the face of their roaring battle madness.

Sister Brigitta was the incumbent canoness, but had always eschewed the title, preferring to remain on the same level as her sisters. She was dearly beloved by all who knew her. Intelligent and insightful, her words of wisdom on any number of subjects were treated as precious jewels to be collected and admired.

She stood now, clad in her copper-coloured battle armour, her silver-flecked black hair streaming in the breeze. The armour forced her to stand upright with a grace and dignity that added weight to her command. Her jaw was tightened and her face bore an implacable expression as she stared down from the highest chamber of the steeple at the slaughter taking place far below.

Tears ran down her face – not of fear, but of rage and regret that the sanctity of the temple had been violated. At either side, her two most trusted lieutenants also wept at the wanton destruction that rampaged below.

They had come without warning. They had struck fast and without mercy. The loyal Palatine Guard who protected the sacred grounds had done an admirable job of holding the enemy at bay, but ultimately they were only human. What hope did they have against the Adeptus Astartes?

Sister Brigitta surveyed the carnage. Seemingly endless forces of the giant Space Marines pitted against a pitiable wall of humanity. Delicate mortal flesh was the only thing standing between the Chaos forces and the Sisters.

From here, she could not see the faces of the brave Guardsmen dying in their futile efforts to protect the Order, but she imagined that each shared the same look of zealous ferocity. The Order of the Iron Rose preached that fear made one weak and had no place on the battlefield.

The barking report of bolter-fire filled the air, and the murderous whine of chainblades was all-pervading. The screams of the dying were agony to listen to, and the ground below was already running scarlet with the blood of the fallen. Some of the Chaos warriors fell upon their victims, hacking and dismembering. The sight sickened Sister Brigitta. Beside her, Sister Anastasia murmured a soft litany, commending the souls of the departed to the Emperor.

'We must meet in the central chamber,' the canoness said finally, tearing her eyes from the slaughter. 'Gather the Order, Sister Anastasia.'

'Yes, sister.' Anastasia left immediately to carry out her superior's command. Brigitta stood for several moments longer, salt-tears running down her weather-tanned face.

'The Order of the Iron Rose will stand to the last, traitors,' she promised, raising her voice to be heard above the growing wind.

The Red Corsairs had dealt with the pathetic human threat in short order. Even as the last Guardsman died, pierced on the end of a chainblade, Huron Blackheart's warriors had turned their weapons on the temple walls and gates. They had been erected over the course of many years by master craftsmen and artisans, but what had taken humanity years to perfect and construct was levelled in minutes by four Traitor Marines and their multi-meltas. The irony of that equation amused Huron Blackheart enough that he laughed out loud.

He had accompanied his forces to the surface of this world but had taken no part in the battle. He stood to one side with Dengesha and his cabal of sorcerers, watching with displaced indifference as his Corsairs butchered their way forwards.

Another direct hit on the wall finally reduced it to molten slag, a huge cloud of pale steam billowing outwards from the destruction and coating the armour of the warriors in a fine film of grit. The Red Corsairs did not wait for their master's order to proceed. They crossed the threshold of the sacred temple and met the second wave of defensive forces with renewed vigour.

Dengesha walked forwards dispassionately, his cabal moving with him like a flock of birds flittering around their mother. Fighting independently, each warrior-psyker was capable of incalculable destruction; fighting as a unit, they were imbued with such power that no mortal man could look upon the forces of the warp flowing from them and hope to survive.

Dark lightning flickered from fingertips, fire burst from the palms of their hands and the very earth itself trembled where they trod. The sheer, raw power they exuded was tremendous, and Huron Blackheart watched their performance with something akin to hunger on his face.

Three Guardsmen were incinerated with a blast from Dengesha's fingers, their bodies catching fire as though they were nothing more than dead wood. They died in terrible agony, screaming and begging for mercy. Huron watched as their ravaged faces slowly melted, like candles burning down to the taper.

Another unfortunate soldier was caught in the mesmerising stare of one of the Heterodox and found himself unable to move. With a press of psychic power, the sorcerer burst the Guardsman's brain like a ripe fruit. The man fell to his knees, blood and grey matter dribbling from his ears before he pitched over, face first into the dust.

The wind had whipped up into a frenzy now, but this was no natural weather condition. This was the work of the Heterodox, and the gusts carried maddening whispers, half-heard promises and dire threats. They blew from the very heart of the warp itself and plucked at the souls of men with ethereal claws. Some who were caught in their path went mad in an instant, hacking and slashing at phantasms only they could see or hear. Others stood their ground more firmly, litanies of warding on their lips.

But each was slain. Each pitiful stalk was reaped, and the more death and destruction there was, the more powerful the cabal seemed to grow, until with a feverish cry to the Dark Gods of Chaos Undivided, the Heterodox unleashed the true horror of their collective.

From without, the sounds of battle echoed. From within, the Sisters of the Order radiated a calm composure. A small order, barely one hundred Sisters of Battle had gathered together in the central chamber. They were all clad in armour similar to Sister Brigitta's, although where hers was a burnished copper hue, theirs was a deep reddish bronze that glinted in the light cast by the candles on the walls.

'Our time here is short, sisters,' the canoness began when she had Anastasia's assurance that all were present. 'Our enemy has breached the gate and they will soon dare to desecrate the most sacred inner sanctum of our beloved Order.' Brigitta reached up as she spoke and braided her thick hair into a plait that hung like a rope down her back. None of the Order would go into battle with their hair loose. It was an affectation, but an important one. Brigitta's visual reminder of the very physical pre-battle preparation instilled focus amongst the gathered Sisters. In the ensemble, others mirrored her action.

'We will not stand by and allow that to happen. We will hold out against these intruders for as long as the Emperor gives us the strength to prevail. We will stand our ground until the bitter end. We fight the gravest of traitors, my sisters. We battle against fallen angels. Traitor Space Marines. And they bring witch-kin with them.'

A palpable ripple of dismay ran through the Sisters. They had stood proud against countless enemies. Aliens, cultists, even a preceptory of Sisters of Battle who had lost their way, and they had always triumphed. They had fought alongside Space Marines many times, too. But the Order of the Iron Rose had never fought *against* them.

Brigitta raised a hand for silence and she got it immediately. From outside the fortified walls of the temple, the muffled sounds of gunfire and terrible, bloody death could be heard, filling in the pauses in her impassioned speech.

'We are the beloved of the Emperor. We are the Sisters of the Iron Rose. We stand as a reminder that the flower of that name is protected by thorns. We will not allow these foul traitors to reach out and pluck us from existence without exacting our payment in blood first.'

She raised her bolter to her shoulder and cast her eyes around the assembled warriors. 'We will make our stand in the rear courtyard. If we draw the traitor filth out into the open, they may exact less damage on our temple.' It was likely a futile gesture, and most of the Order knew it, but they were words that encouraged her sisters. Brigitta was under no illusions; the battle that was coming towards them would likely be the last thing any of them saw. But they would die as they had lived, defending the Emperor's legacy.

The clouds above the temple boiled, swirling together in a dark mass of intangible horror. The wind was now a gale, screaming its unnatural, elemental fury across the surface of the planet and whipping up the detritus from the fallen walls into plumed, choking columns. Lightning coruscated within the cloud, and as it moved, it picked up dust and debris, including the corpses of the fallen.

The Chaos-driven maelstrom moved with almost agonising slowness across the battlefield. Beneath it, the earth split and wept streams of tar and sulphur. Those who still stood were either knocked from their feet by the quaking of the ground beneath them, or they were caught up in the storm's passage and sucked, screaming, into its abyssal depths.

From what remained of the temple walls, valiant surviving forces turned the defence guns on the cabal who stood as a pack, their hands raised, palms upwards, to the skies that bubbled overhead. Each of the twelve was a perfect mirror image of the others. All wore horned helms, and their stance was arrogance itself.

The armoured turrets around the temple roared defiance and one of the sorcerers was destroyed, his torso chewed apart by the stream of high-velocity shells. The cabal did not change position but, as one, their heads turned towards the weapons mounted on the wall.

Dengesha made a slicing motion with his hand, and the wind changed direction and increased speed, moving with impossible haste towards its new target.

Sister Brigitta stood defiant amidst her battle-sisters. She was a woman who had lived a life filled with devotion to the Emperor, who she loved every bit as much as she cared for every woman who stood around her. Their honour and courage now, in the face of overwhelming odds, was a reward unlike any other.

From the youngest novice to Sister Anastasia, with whom she had fought in many engagements, she knew each one of them. She knew their life histories. She knew their hopes and she knew their fears. She was no psyker, but you could not live your whole life within an order and not gain an insight into the souls of those around you.

She loved her sisters and though she knew she might die here today, she knew that love would strengthen her faith and her resolve to stand her ground.

Her thoughts were wrenched back to the present as she heard the echo of a crashing thump in the distance. The sound of weapons being brought to bear against the gate.

'They come,' she said, her voice low and soft, yet carrying such authority that every one of the Order stood straighter. There was the sound of weapons being readied, of magazines being slammed into place, of swords being drawn from sheaths. There were overlaying voices murmuring litanies and prayers.

Another sickening *crump* against the gate.

'We will stand defiant,' Brigitta said, raising her bolter above her head. '*Ave Imperator!*'

The battle-cry was echoed, but it was drowned out by the sound of an explosion that blew in the ancient, stained crystal windows as the enemy breached the gates.

'Be ready! Hold firm! Do not doubt in yourself for one moment. Trust to your sisters and trust to your blessed weapons. *A morte perpetua. Domine, libra nos!*'

Battle-cries were torn from their throats and one hundred Sisters of Battle took up arms and prepared to make their stand.

The maelstrom ripped the guns from their mountings as though they were plants placed in dry soil. The Guardsmen who had manned them were pulverised by the shrapnel from the destruction as the howling, unholy winds ripped the turrets into nothing more than scrap metal. Mangled pieces of weaponry tore through their bodies, cutting them to ribbons and, in one young soldier's case, decapitating them. The spiralling morass of metal and ruined flesh added its mass to the storm, and above the temple the skies began to rain droplets of blood.

At the final gate, Huron Blackheart's traitors had set melta-charges against the armoured portal. The blocky devices clamped to the towering hinges with a metallic *clang* and the Corsairs withdrew. The bombs detonated with a wash of heat and an earth-shattering explosion that rocked the ground.

Slowly, Dengesha's cabal ceased the link with their powers and the violent, raging winds began to subside. The first obstacle had been overcome. The second – and their objective – lay behind the devastated walls.

The Chaos sorcerer turned his helmeted head towards Huron. 'You must not kill her,' he said through the vox-bead in the Tyrant's ear. 'If she dies, her soul will be as good as useless to us. Do not let your barbarian horde rip the Order apart without first isolating the mark.'

A twitch of irritation showed on Huron's face. 'I am not completely without intellect, Dengesha.' The fingers that were wrapped around his massive battle-axe tightened visibly. The sorcerer's face could not be seen, but Huron could *sense* his smirk. 'I will be taking care of dear Sister Brigitta myself.'

'*My sincerest* apologies. I did not mean to imply you were anything but knowledgeable in the ways of warp, my lord.' Dengesha's sarcasm was biting, and Huron turned away from the sorcerer cursing the necessity of their temporary association. It would be over soon. The Order of the Iron Rose would be obliterated and he would take his prize.

He comforted himself with the thought. In due course, his familiar would feast from a soul most worthy of its hunger.

Striding across the courtyard, Huron surveyed the damage with an approving expression. What remained of the gate was barely recognisable as any sort of portal. Broken spurs of plasteel jutted in all directions, and the metal composite that had been mixed into the gate for reinforcement was little more than dust. Occasionally, more dust would fall in a pathetic clump from the walls either side of the entrance way.

The Red Corsairs strode forwards, warriors with a clear objective and purpose. In the eyes of the Imperium, they were renegades. But they were still Space Marines and the regimental mindset came easily to them. Until the fighting started, at least.

'Listen to me, my Corsairs,' said Huron across the vox. 'When we locate the Sisters, do not touch their leader. She belongs to me.' He addressed the entire group, but knew that not all of them would truly hear him. 'The toys we have despatched thus far have been an easy enemy and they will have sent out the word for aid. By the time that aid arrives, there will be nothing left but a smoking ruin.'

A few scattered roars of approval drew a nod from Huron. 'What we will come up against in there will be more challenging, but do not falter. We come to take a prize that will make us even greater than we are. The Imperium of Mankind and their pathetic Corpse-Emperor will rue the day they ever named us traitor.'

There were grunts of acknowledgement across the board, some coherent, others less so. Just as his band of renegades was drawn from a vast number of different Chapters, so their levels of sanity varied. Huron cared little for the butchers amongst his followers. They served a purpose in war, but when it came to more delicate matters they were an encumbrance.

Fortunately, he had enough sane followers to keep the borderline berserkers in check.

'Then we move with all haste to the final stage of our action here. Find the Sisters. Kill those you must, but leave the canoness alive.'

Without further hesitation, the Red Corsairs streamed into the sacred Temple of the Blessed Dawn.

They rampaged through the temple without thought for preservation. Marble floors cracked and split beneath their heavy tread. Chainblades chewed through statuary and carvings alike, making firewood of huge portraits of Sisters and saints. Some riches were left intact. Over the years, the Red Corsairs had all developed an eye for goods that would please their lord and master, for it was said his collection of Imperial relics was beyond compare. They would retrace their steps before they departed and gather up such treasures, along with the weapons of the fallen. For them, that was the most valuable reward.

Their plundering steps ultimately took them through the central chamber where the Sisters of the Order had recently gathered. Dengesha nodded approvingly.

'This will be a good place for the ritual,' he said.

'Then you remain here, sorcerer, and make whatever preparation is necessary. We will seek out Sister Brigitta and I will bring her to you personally.' Huron ran his tongue over his metal teeth in a parody of hunger. He swung his battle-axe easily and it chewed its way through a beautifully painted rendition of some long-ago battle at which the Sisters had been victorious. Its shredded remnants dangled to the ground and the memory of the great war was lost to no more than a single stroke.

The first two Red Corsairs to throw open the heavy door that led out to the courtyard were torn apart by incoming bolter-fire. The Sisters of Battle had kept their weapons trained on the exit and the moment it opened they had pulled their triggers. The explosive rounds buried themselves in the armoured hides of the traitors and burst them apart in a storm of gore and ceramite shards. The bodies disintegrated messily, but their sacrifice bought those who followed enough time to bring their weapons to bear and return fire. Four Sisters were thrown backwards, unbalancing several more. Before they were back on their feet, the Red Corsairs had flooded into the courtyard and the fight began in earnest.

The Sisters of Battle were greater in number than the Red Corsairs and their armour afforded them a degree of protection. But they were facing an undisciplined rabble whose tactics were unpredictable at best and unfathomable at worst. The Sisters held their position, clustered around the canoness like a sea of bronze with a copper island at their centre. They formed a circle around where she stood on the rim of a fountain, crying out orders to her warriors.

The initial firefight did not last long. At a word from the Tyrant, the Red Corsairs pressed forwards, chainblades whining, and began to cut their way through the serried ranks of women. The ring surrounding the canoness grew tighter and smaller.

The stink of ruined flesh and spent bolter-rounds was strong in the air, and so much smoke rose from the detonations that it choked the courtyard with a fog of bloody vapour and fyceline.

'Courage, sisters!' Brigitta's voice was clear, like a bell sounding through the uproar. 'Remember your teachings! You tread the path of righteousness. Though it be paved with broken glass, you will walk it barefoot...'

Brigitta paused in the recital as she watched Sister Anastasia's broken body fall to the ground. A grief unlike any she had ever known before passed through her with a shudder. She summoned up every ounce of her considerable inner strength and brought her bolter to bear on the hated enemy. Her voice rose through the noise once again.

'Though it crosses rivers of fire, we will pass over them…'

Her voice was strong and did not waver, but the strength of her armed guard was failing. Not through lack of zeal or fire – if she were to take any reward from this abysmal horror before her, it was that her beloved sisters died honourably and bravely – but through dwindling numbers. What had once been a ring several bodies deep now presented a barrier of barely a dozen of her Sisters.

A number of the traitor Red Corsairs had been felled, but their armour, stronger and more finely wrought than that of the Sisters of Battle, deflected more and protected them for longer. Brigitta realised with a sinking heart that they were probably not even dead; that their enhanced physiology would aid their recovery and that they might rise to fight another day. She *despised* them for it. She loathed their continued existence. To her mind, they represented the worst kind of faithless traitors the Imperium could have conceived.

She abhorred them for tearing apart the temple, her home, the place where she had grown from a teenage girl to womanhood.

She…

…was bleeding.

Brigitta tasted, for the first time in her life, a tremor of fear. It was seasoned with the coppery taste of her own blood as she bit her lip hard enough to put her teeth through the delicate skin. The flavour of her own mortality gave her enough strength to complete her fervent prayer.

'Though it wanders wide, the light of the Emperor guides my – our – step.' She slammed a fresh magazine into her bolter and, letting out a screaming roar of battle rage, unleashed her full fury at the encroaching enemy.

At her feet, dead and dying Sisters spilled blood and viscera across the courtyard stones. The image of their defeat burned itself onto her retinas and branded hatred on her heart. Tears of anger and terrible, terrible grief blurred her vision, but she did not – she *would* not – falter. Not now.

She continued to fire her bolter into the enemy no longer caring whether she hit them or not. It became an act of sheer venomous loathing.

After a few short moments, she became aware that outside her immediate sphere of awareness the sounds of battle had ceased. Only one weapon continued to fire and that was hers. It did not detract from her focus, however, and she poured ammunition at the enemy until the last bolter-shell clattered to the floor.

One of the enemy, bareheaded and terrible, moved from the pack to stand before her.

'You are Sister Brigitta of the Order of the Iron Rose,' he stated. It was not a question. She looked up into his inhuman face and drew in a rasping breath. She had seen unhelmed Space Marines before and was used to their exaggerated features. But this... *creature*... who stood before her was so far removed from anything even remotely human that she felt, against her will, the urge to scream in incoherent contempt. A poisonous air of evil came from him and she felt sick to her stomach.

She began to quietly recite litanies of faith to herself, never once taking her gaze from this augmetic monstrosity. She neither confirmed nor denied the accusation of her identity but instead ripped the combat blade from its sheath at her side and struck at the traitor's throat. Blackheart sighed wearily before catching her wild lunge on the back of his claw. Then, with excruciating care, not wanting to kill her outright, he backhanded her into unconsciousness.

She was like a rag doll in his arms, limp and lifeless, and as he carried Sister Brigitta into the chamber, Huron Blackheart marvelled as he always did at the papery inefficacy of the human body. He wondered how it was they had any resilience without the enhancements that he shared with all his gene-bred brothers. Brigitta's face where he had struck her was distorted. He had fractured her cheekbone at the very least, and purple bruising was swelling up around her jaw. Her braided hair had come loose and hung freely down.

Dengesha turned to study them. He had removed his helm, and Huron was struck once again by the wriggling sigils that marked the sorcerer's face. 'You did not kill her?'

'She is merely unconscious. Allow me a little credit.'

'Then lay her next to the vessel and I can begin the ritual.' Already Dengesha had made the preparations for the rite that would bind the potent soul to the cursed vial. The green bottle lay on its side, an innocuous and inanimate object. Around the chamber, Dengesha had marked out a number of unreadable symbols, each one drawn at the point of what formed the eight-pronged star of Chaos. Members of his cabal stood at seven of the points, the top-most remaining free and evidently awaiting Dengesha's leisure.

Huron moved forwards and dumped Brigitta's body without any ceremony on the ground where the sorcerer indicated. He noted as he did so that the sigils drawn on the floor were marked in blood, most likely that of the dead soldiers.

'You should step outside the borders of the mark, my lord. Once we channel the powers necessary to perform the binding, they will be potent.'

From beyond the broken walls of the temple, the distant sounds of shouting could be heard. The assistance that the temple guards had called for was finally arriving. Huron nodded to several of his warriors who moved wordlessly out of the chamber.

'They cannot be allowed to enter this place whilst I am working. The balance of this work is delicate.'

'My men will keep them away.' Huron took several steps back. 'Trust to their abilities to do that. I, however, will remain.'

'As you wish.'

Huron Blackheart had witnessed many rituals of this kind in his life, but he had never seen one driven with such determination and single-minded focus. He watched Dengesha closely as the sorcerer moved back to take his point at the tip of the star, and listened intently to the words that he recited. It did him little good, as the sorcerer spoke in some arcane tongue that Huron did not understand, though the inflection was clear.

The seven other members of the Heterodox echoed his words, one at a time until the chant was being repeated with a discordant, impossible to follow rhythm. The sound grew and swelled, and all the while there was the underscore of the battle taking place beyond the temple walls.

A thick black substance, like tar from a pit, began to bubble up in the space marked out by the points of the star. It rose upwards, never spilling over the edge of its limits, and coated first the bottle and then the unconscious Sister Brigitta in a film of inky blackness. Dengesha's chant became almost musical, as though he were singing. His eyes were fevered and his expression one of pure ecstasy.

As the thick, gelatinous substance became more and more viscous, Brigitta stirred from her unconsciousness. Realising that she was being smothered, she opened her mouth to cry out. The fluid rushed into her mouth and she began to choke on it, writhing desperately on the floor as she struggled to breathe.

Dengesha stepped forwards from his position and moved to stand above her. Huron watched, leaning forwards ever so slightly. This was it. This was the moment. He had made countless pacts and agreements to reach this point, and so had his followers. This was the point at which it would all pay off. Or the point at which it would fail.

Outside, the sounds of gunfire had stopped, but the Chaos sorcerer paid no heed.

Dengesha looked down at the wriggling human woman with a look of total contempt, then reached to take her arm firmly in his grip. He guided it to the glass vial and placed her hand upon it, wrapping his gauntlets around her tiny hands. He then spoke the only words that Huron could understand.

'Be forever bound.'

The oily liquid began to slowly ebb away, draining until all that remained was the faintest slick on the ground. Brigitta, who was in tremendous pain and almost frozen with terror, stared at the green vial, then up at the sorcerer.

Summoning every ounce of strength and fortitude she possessed, she spat in his face. Dengesha began to laugh, a hateful, booming sound that bounced around the walls of the chamber and resonated across the vox-network.

Then, abruptly, the laughter stopped. A look of utmost dread crept slowly over Dengesha's face. His fist, which had been ready to crush Brigitta's skull, suddenly opened out flat. His face slackened, his posture changed and he slouched suddenly as though wearied.

Huron smiled at him.

'What is this treachery?' The sorcerer spun around to face the Tyrant of Badab, who stood watching him with an air of amusement. 'What have you done, Blackheart?'

'Ah, Dengesha. Your fate was sealed the moment you took the vial from me. You were quite right. I needed a potent soul. And my sorcerers found me one. *Yours*, in fact. And now, with the ritual of binding complete, your soul and the vial are united. You quite literally belong to me.'

'This is not possible! There is no way you could have... Your sorcerers are nothing compared to the glory of the Heterodox!'

'Arrogance has been the downfall of many a warrior of the Adeptus Astartes over the millennia, brother. My sorcerers may not be as powerful as you and your former cabal, but they are far more cunning.'

Seemingly bored of the conversation, Huron began to move around the chamber, occasionally turning over the body of a fallen soldier with his booted foot. He picked up a boltgun, empty of ammunition and dropped it back down with a clang.

Dengesha's face was fury itself, and he reached out to the powers of the warp. But none of them answered him. His black, tainted soul was no longer his to command. He looked to each of his cabal in turn and for their part, they turned from him.

'You all *knew* of this,' he stated flatly. 'You betrayed me to this *cur*...'

'Come now, Dengesha. If you seek to wound my feelings, you will have to try a lot harder than that.' Huron stooped and picked up a meltagun. 'My agents have been dealing with your cabal for months. They agree that their prospects with me and my Corsairs are more interesting than a lifetime of servitude under your leadership. It has been vexing, true – but I think you will agree that the ultimate reward is well worth it.'

On the ground, Sister Brigitta was listening to the exchange without understanding it. All she knew was that these two traitors were speaking such heresy as was almost unbearable to be party to.

Dengesha stared at Huron's back with a look that could have killed and perhaps once, before his soul had been plucked from his body, could have done.

'So you see, Dengesha. In a way, my promise to you is truth. Now that your Heterodox are part of my Corsairs, they will help themselves to the spoils of this world. You, however...'

The Tyrant of Badab crossed the distance between them with uncanny speed and fired the meltagun at the sorcerer. His head was vaporised, and seconds later what remained of his body crashed to the ground. Brigitta gazed up at Huron and there was a look of serene understanding on her face. Her doom had come and it was clad in the desecrated armour of the Imperium of Man.

'My faith is my shield,' she said, softly. The words rang hollow in her ears.

'No,' said Huron, equally softly, as one of the claws of his hand tore through her breast and skewered her. He raised her to eye level. 'It is not. And it never was.'

She let out a sigh as she died and slid free from his claw to the floor below. Without looking at the two corpses at his feet, Huron reached up and plucked the vial from the ground, reattaching it to his belt.

Sometimes, Huron Blackheart kept his word. But this was not one of those times. He did not care who he betrayed to reach his goals. Loyal servants of the Imperium or those who served the Dark Gods of Chaos. It made little difference to him. The end *always* justified the means.

'Take what we need,' he said. 'And then we leave.'

'It worked perfectly.'

'Surely you did not doubt that it would, my lord?' Valthex turned the vial over in his hand before handing it back to Huron.

'The curse worked exactly as you said it would. Thanks to your efforts, my familiar now has the strength it needs to grant me the blessing of the Four beyond the Maelstrom. Well done, Armenneus.'

'I live to serve, Blood Reaver.' Valthex dropped a low, respectful bow and Huron stalked away. Straightening himself up, the Alchemancer absently rubbed at a sigil branded into the skin of his hand.

It was not just the Tyrant who made pacts. The Patriarch would have to wait to see when he would be called upon to deliver his side of the bargain.

APOSTLE'S CREED

Graham McNeill

The Thunderbolt cut through the frigid air like an ivory dagger, trailing white contrails from the leading edges of its wings. Following the manoeuvres of Apostle Seven, Larice Asche executed a perfect quarter roll before inverting and pulling into a shallow turn. She took her time, not pushing the aircraft. After three months strapped down in the hold of a Munitorum mass conveyer, it was never a good idea to ask too much of a plane until you'd given it some time to stretch its wings and get used to being in the air again.

She watched the crisp movements of Apostle Seven through the canopy, a cream-coloured Thunderbolt that hung in the air like an angel basking in the sunlight. Dario Quint was at its controls, his flawless stickwork apparently effortless. Larice knew that wasn't the case. Quint had logged thousands of hours and flown hundreds of sorties to hone his skill.

'Level flight, Apostle Five,' said Quint. 'There's murderous shear coming off the Breakers, so use vectors to compensate if you go in close.'

'Understood, Seven,' responded Larice. It was the longest single sentence Quint had said to her since Seekan had invited her to join the Apostles back on Enothis. She'd tried to engage him in conversation aboard the *Rosencranz*, en route to Amedeo, but he'd always ignored her. Not in a way she could get mad about, and not with any rudeness. More like he chose not to engage because he didn't know how to.

Despite Quint's warning, the air at nine thousand metres was calm, and it was a simple matter to stay on his wing. Larice scanned the auspex inbetween craning her neck to look around for the telltale glint of sunlight on metal that might indicate a hostile contact.

Nothing. The skies were clear. She was disappointed.

They'd already made kills today, an intercept with some Tormentors returning from a bombing raid on Coriana, foremost city of the Ice, but that tussle had been too easy to be properly interesting. The bombers had already shed their payloads, but that didn't matter. Bombers that didn't make it back to their base wouldn't return with fresh ordnance to crack the Ice.

Cordiale had always said it was bad luck to tangle with the enemy on a shakeout flight, but his luck had run out over the Zophonian Sea, so what did he know? In any case, a Thunderbolt was a weapon of war, a lethal sabre that, once drawn, needed to taste blood before being sheathed.

The Tormentors had been rushing through the valleys of the Breakers, hoping their speed, low flight and the lousy auspex bounces from the peaks would hide them from Imperial retribution.

No such luck.

Apostle Seven had found them, though she had no idea how, since they were running with their auspex silent, and had to rely on Operations to guide them to intercepts. Seekan once told her that Quint, the ace of aces, had an innate sense for where bats were hiding, and she hadn't questioned it.

The bombers had top cover, a trio of Hell Talons, enough to give most pilots pause, but they were the Apostles. Quint took a line on them before firing up his auspex.

'Turn and burn,' he said, his clipped, economical tones muffled by his mask.

His Thunderbolt stood on its wing and dived for the deck.

Coming in high from the east, she and Quint pounced on the Hell Talons, and Larice had relished the panic she'd seen in their desperate scatter. Quint had splashed two bats before they even realised the direction of the attack. He raked the Talons with las before punching through their formation and leaving the last for Larice.

The bat broke high and she turned into it, anticipating its next move and mashing the firing stud on her stick. She had a good angle of deflection, and her bolts tore the bat to burning wreckage. Hauling on the stick, she pulled into a shallow dive to engage the Tormenters themselves.

Quint had already gutted the first bomber and was lining up on his second, viffing and jinking to avoid the turret fire that seemed unable to pin him in place. Larice turned into the third bomber and raked it end to end with her quads. It dropped from the sky, almost cut in two. Pulling a high-g turn, she closed on the last bomber. The pilot was heading for the deck, trying to gain speed, but that was just stupid. There was no way he could outrun her.

It drifted into her firing reticule, and Larice gently lifted the nose of her plane. Quad fire hammered from her guns and the Tormentor obligingly flew into the lashing bolts. The pilot's canopy bloomed glass and fire, and the ponderous bird described a lazy arc towards the ground.

It slammed into the mountainside, leaving a blackened teardrop of fire on the snow.

She'd pulled up and they resumed their patrol circuit as though nothing had happened. Seven kills between them, not a bad outing for one day. It had been an easy intercept. The bats hadn't seen them until it was too late. The glaring white of the ever-present ice and snow made it hellishly difficult to spot incoming craft until they were right on top of you, a situation that had served them well here, but cut both ways.

Looking down past her port wing, Larice saw a dappled black line of giant ice floes detaching from the coastline where the frozen sea had loosened its grip on the land. To her right, the Breakers reared like gleaming white fangs, a jagged rampart of mountains keeping the worst of the razor-ice storms that swept down from the northern polar wastes from ravaging the southern cites.

Archenemy land forces were moving in on those cities from the west, but lately waves of bombers and ground attack fighters had opened up a new flank, striking from the heart of the northern ice wastes. Though it had been declared impossible, it seemed the enemy had managed to establish a base somewhere on the frozen surface of the ocean. Orbital auspex had been unable to locate this base, and the existence of a mass carrier on the ice had been ruled out as impossible.

After the war on Enothis, Larice knew that anything high command decided was impossible had an inversely proportional chance of being true.

'Apostle Five, hold my wing,' said Quint. 'You're drifting.'

Larice returned her focus to her instruments, making a visual check on her positioning.

Quint was right, she had drifted. By a metre.

At first she was irritated – a metre was nothing when you were flying in such an easy pattern – but she cut herself off. She was an Apostle now, and a metre *was* a big deal. Leave lazy flying to other pilots. The 101st Apostles were the elite flyers of the Navy, and she was better than that.

'Sorry, Apostle Five,' she said.

Quint didn't answer, but she didn't expect him to. Instead, he rolled and pulled his plane in a steep turn to the north. He was heading out over the frozen surface of the ocean. Larice followed automatically, matching Quint's turn and keeping tight to his wing.

'What's up, Seven?' she asked.

'Getting a vector from Operations,' said Quint. 'There's an intercept going on. Indigo Flight from the 235th. They need some help.'

'Where?'

'Fifty kilometres over the ocean ice, a thousand metres off the deck.'
'Auspex?'
'Yes, light them up,' voxed Quint.

Larice did so, but all she got was a hissing wash of backscatter from the mountains. The tech-seers had blessed her auspex before takeoff, but it looked like it was still sluggish from its time inactive. She cursed, heightening the gain, and immediately saw the engagement. It looked like a bad one. Four Navy machines, with at least nine bats swarming them.

'Got them?'

'Yeah, nine of them,' said Larice. 'You sure you want to tangle with that many?'

'There's two of us,' clarified Quint. 'And we are Apostles. *They* should be asking that question.'

'Good point.'

'Afterburners,' said Quint. 'Hit it.'

Larice flipped up the guard on the afterburner trigger, and braced herself for the enormous power of the Thunderbolt's turbofan in her back. She eased the stick forward, just enough down angle to take them into the upper reaches of the fight.

'Grip,' she said, and thumbed the trigger.

A sucking machine breath. A booming roar of jets. A monstrous hand pressed her hard against her seat. The airframe shuddered and the few clouds blurred as the plane leapt forwards like an unleashed colt. The sense of speed was intoxicating. She held the stick, keeping her body braced in the grip position as she felt the blood being forced from her extremities. She held course, feeling the plane straining at her control.

'Incoming contacts, twelve thousand metres,' said Quint. 'Cut burners and go subsonic.'

Larice cut the afterburners and immediately felt the blood return to her hands and feet with a painful prickling sensation. She glanced at the auspex, taking in the shape of the fight in a second. The four Navy flyers were in a dirty scrap, using all their skill to dance out of weapons locks and converging streams of las fire.

'Hell Blades,' said Larice, recognising the enemy flyers' flight profile. She felt a tremor of excitement. Fast-moving, highly manoeuvrable fighters that could easily match a Thunderbolt in a vector dance, Hell Blades were a far more fearsome prospect than Tormentors.

The vox crackled in her helmet, the voice of a controller in Operations.

'Apostle Flight, be advised we have nine hostiles north on your location,' said the controller. 'Speed and flight pattern indicates–'

'Hell Blades, yeah we know,' snapped Larice. 'Way to keep up, Ops.'

Even with the planes of the 235th, they were outnumbered two to one, but Quint was right. They were Apostles, the best flyers in the Navy. She flew with the ace of aces, and her own Thunderbolt boasted no shortage of kill markings on its cream-coloured nose. She checked her dials, noting her fuel and armament status. Aerial combat manoeuvres burned fuel at a terrifying rate, but there was enough in the tank for this one fight.

With Quint at her side, Larice was confident they'd turn the bats into dark smudges of wreckage on the sea ice. With relative closing speeds in excess of a thousand kph, the gap between the two forces was shrinking rapidly. It was going to get real ugly, real quick.

There! Nine lean darts with tapered wings like the fins on a seeker missile. The sky filled with light as the bats opened up. The Navy birds, painted a brusque camo-green, were twisting and diving with desperate turns and rolls, using every trick in the book to shake their pursuers. In an evenly matched fight, that might work, but not against so many bats.

One Thunderbolt exploded as a flurry of shots from a darting enemy fighter found its engines and blew it apart.

'Indigo Flight, Apostles inbound,' said Quint, and it was the only warning anyone got.

Larice and Quint slashed down into the fight, coming in high and fast. She slipped in behind a Hell Blade taking his sweet time in lining up a shot. Too confident of the kill, the enemy pilot was making the first and last mistake most rookies made.

She squeezed her trigger and the bat flew into her streaming las bolts, coming apart in a seething fireball. She slipped sideways and barrelled past the dead Hell Blade's wingman as Quint tore up the fuselage of another bat.

A wing flashed past her canopy and Larice yanked the stick right. She rolled, pushing out the throttle and inverting. She deployed the air brakes and viffed onto the tail of the aircraft that had nearly hit her. A crimson Hell Blade, its tapered nose spiralling as it slid back and forth through the air.

'Too easy,' she said, sending a hail of quad fire into its tail section. The wounded Hell Blade shuddered as though invisible hammers pounded its engine until it ruptured in a spewing blaze of fire.

'Five, break, break!' ordered Quint.

Larice sidestepped, viffing up to let the enemy fire paint the air beneath her. A Hell Blade had broken from attacking the Navy flyers and turned into her.

'He's good,' she said, dancing through the air in a dazzling series of rolls, banks and vectored slips. He stuck with her, firing bursts of las as he tried to anticipate her next move. She put her plane into a shallow climb, and slammed the throttle back as the air brakes flared. She was risking a stall, but her manoeuvre worked and the bat zipped past her port wing. She took a snap shot, jinking sideways and ripping her fire along its wing and hull.

Its wing snapped off and it rolled uncontrollably, spinning down towards the ice and leaving a plume of black smoke in its wake.

Five on five, suddenly the odds were evened.

Or they would have been if Quint hadn't already splashed another two bats.

Two more Navy birds were down, and Larice didn't see any chutes. Not that the odds of survival punching out over the ocean ice were much better than going down in flames. She'd hit the silk once before and it wasn't an experience she cared to repeat.

A las-round smacked her Thunderbolt. She jinked low, rolling to bring her guns back on target. She had a fraction of a second to act. Her quads barked, and booming thunder spat from her craft. The deflection was bad and her shots went over the bat. Correction, another burst. This time the bat blew apart in a shredding flicker of mauve and crimson.

She turned hard, pushing the envelope in the race to get behind the last bats. She grunted as heavy g-forces pressed on her, despite the grip position supposed to make it easier to bear. The rubber of her mask flattened against her face, and she tasted the metallic quality of her air mix.

She rolled and pulled hard, feathering her air brakes and flattening out as she caught a flash of a Hell Blade's vector flare.

'Got you,' she hissed, unleashing a brilliant salvo. The Hell Blade blew apart, its engine exploding as her bolts blasted it from the air. Her guns coughed dry, the battery drained, and she switched back to her quads.

'Apostle, break, break!' shouted a voice she didn't recognise.

Larice hauled on the stick and threw out her tail rudder, twisting her plane into a tight loop. A blitz of tracers flew past her port side, a single shell kissing the rear quarter of her canopy and crazing the toughened glass.

She snapped left and right, hunting the bat that had her.

'On your seven,' said the voice.

'I see it,' she said, pulling into the Hell Blade's turn and opening out the throttle as she viffed in a jagged sidestep. The bat matched her turn, pushing her outwards, and she knew there was more than likely another aircraft waiting to take the kill shot. Instead of playing that game, she threw her plane around, using the vectors to pull a near one-eighty and reverse her thrust. The pressure pulled the cracks in the canopy wider.

The pursuing Hell Blade filled her canopy and she mashed the trigger, feeling the percussive recoil from the heavy autocannons mounted in the nose. The Hell Blade viffed up over her burst. It had her and there was nothing she could do.

A camo-green shape zipped over her canopy, quad cannons blazing.

The bat ripped in two. Black smoke and a blooming fireball blew outwards. Larice threw her Thunderbolt into a screamingly tight turn and inverted to take the brunt of the explosion on her underside. Air was driven from her lungs, and her vision greyed at the force of the turn. Her fuselage lurched, and hammering blows of metal on metal thudded along its length as debris from the Hell Blade struck her bird.

Warning lights and buzzers filled the canopy. She flipped over, restoring level flight.

Larice loosened the throttle. Her breathing eased and she screwed her eyes shut for a second to throw off the greyness lurking at the edge of her vision. She tasted blood and pulled off her mask, spitting into the foot well.

A dark shape appeared off her starboard wing. She looked up to see the last surviving Navy flyer of Indigo Flight.

'You okay there?' said the pilot. 'Your bird's pretty banged up.'

'Yeah,' she said, though the stick felt sluggish and unresponsive in her hand. It galled her that she'd needed an assist, but it had been a hell of a move coming in over her to take out that bat. Only a pilot supremely sure of himself would try something that risky.

One wrong move from either pilot would have seen them both splashed.

Quint pulled in on her port wing, the ivory of his aircraft untouched and pristine.

'Indigo Flight, identify,' said Quint.

'Flight Lieutenant Erzyn Laquell, 235th Naval Attack Wing,' said the pilot with a thumbs-up. 'You're the Apostles. It's an honour to fly with you.'

'You're not flying with us,' said Quint. 'You just happen to be sharing my sky.'

'Of course I am,' returned Laquell. 'I'll be sure to tell my pilots to steer clear next time one of your high and mighty Apostles needs an assist.'

Though a glossy black visor and rubber air-mix mask covered Laquell's face, she just knew he was grinning a cocksure grin.

'Keep talking like that and I'll make sure you never fly again,' promised Quint.

Before Laquell could answer, a flurry of winking lights appeared on the auspex and Larice blinked away moisture to be sure she was seeing what it was telling her correctly.

'Seven, are you getting this?'

'Affirmative.'

The auspex was a mass of returns. From their speed and height they were clearly fighters. They weren't squawking on any Imperial frequency, and that made them bad news. Razors most likely. Or more Hell Blades.

'Ten more bats,' she said. 'High and coming in fast. Too many to fight.'

'Agreed,' answered Quint. His plane dipped below her wing before coming level once more. He chopped his hand down towards the belly of her Thunderbolt.

'Five, you're leaking fluid,' he said 'Check your fuel status.'

Larice scanned her gauges, watching with dismay as the numbers unspooled like an altimeter in a power dive. She tapped the dial with her finger, but the numbers kept going.

'Frig it! I'm losing fuel fast. Must've taken a hit to the feed lines.'

'Do you have enough to return to Coriana?'

'Negative, Seven,' said Larice. The airfield where the 101st were stationed was way beyond her range now. 'At the speed I'm losing fuel, I'll be lucky to get down in one piece, let alone back to Coriana. I'll need an alternate.'

'I'll get your wounded bird down,' said Laquell, doing a passable job at keeping the smugness from his tone. 'Rimfire is only a hundred and ten kilometres east.'

Rimfire was the designation for the airbase set up to face the Archenemy's newly opened flank. It was a rush job, hardened hangars cut into the ice and honeycomb landing strips laid out on the Ice by Munitorum pioneers. Its tower facilities were mobile command vehicles and its auspex coverage came from airborne surveyor craft originally designed to hunt for ground minerals. Flyers based at Coriana joked that the pilots based at Rimfire were either too dumb or too reckless to be based anywhere else.

'Will you make it that far?' asked Quint. 'That's a valuable piece of machinery you're flying and we need all the aircraft we have.'

'Thanks for your concern,' replied Larice. 'I'll be flying on fumes and the Emperor's mercy by then, but, yeah, I think I can make it.'

'Then head for Rimfire. I'll see you back at Coriana if you live. Seven out.'

Quint's plane peeled off, leaving a slick of vapour-white fumes in his wake. His plane surged back towards the Breakers and within seconds it was lost to sight.

'Friendly sort, isn't he?' said Laquell.

'He's earned the right to choose his friends with care,' said Larice.

'I guess he has.'

'Okay, Laquell. Lead on,' said Larice. 'In case you hadn't noticed I'm losing fuel.'

'Sure thing. Make your bearing one-six-five and start climbing.'

'I know how to extend,' she snapped, pulling around and aiming her Thunderbolt towards Rimfire. She pulled her stick back, putting her plane into a fuel-efficient climb. When her tanks ran dry she'd be able to glide some of the way in if she had enough altitude.

'Just trying to help,' said Laquell. 'Listen, you know my name, but what do I call you?'

'Apostle Five,' said Larice.

'Yeah, I got that, but what's your real name? You know, what your friends call you?'

'Asche,' she sighed. 'Call me Larice Asche.'

'Pleased to meet you Larice Asche,' said Laquell. 'Follow my wing and I'll get you down in one piece. I promise.'

* * *

Laquell was as good as his word, and they crossed the Breakers high and with a favourable tailwind that gifted Larice a thousand metres of altitude. There was a nasty squall of ice crystals swelling out over the ocean ice, a skin-shredding storm of frozen blades that would do no end of damage to an aircraft, but the luck of the Emperor was with them and it blew west before reaching the mountains.

Though she tried to keep her flight smooth and level, Larice watched her fuel reserves dwindle like she was in the midst of the most furious engagement imaginable, viffing, pulling high-g turns, escape climbs and power dives. The shear Quint had mentioned clawed up from the wind-sculpted cliffs, buffeting her plane as though an invisible leash tethered to her fuselage was being pulled and tugged.

Then they were over, and the landscape fell away from them, tumbling to the flatlands of Amedeo, bleak tundra of browns and muted greens. It wasn't the most welcoming world, but then what she'd seen of Enothis had been mostly desert and swamp, so at least it offered a different view from the canopy.

Located in the trailing arc of the crusade to liberate the Sabbat Worlds, Amedeo had been largely ignored by both the Imperium and the Archenemy, but then the forces of Magister Innokenti had fallen on Herodor. Though the tactical significance of Herodor was, at best, debatable, the soldiers' rumour mill had it that Innokenti himself had descended to that world's surface.

And that made Amedeo important. Perfectly positioned to allow a flanking thrust to hamstring the Imperial defence, the planners of the crusade were swift to recognise the danger to Herodor. Naval wings and Guard regiments were deployed with unaccustomed swiftness, alongside, so the rumour-spinners went on to claim, a detachment of Adeptus Astartes.

Larice had seen nothing of any Space Marines, but Amedeo was a big theatre of operations, and entire campaigns were being fought out of sight of the aerial duellists.

Her fuel warning light, which had been hypnotically blinking throughout the crossing of the Breakers, now assumed a more constant aspect. Her engines flamed out and the rpms of her twin turbofans spiralled south.

'I'm dry,' she voxed to Laquell. 'I'm flying fourteen tonnes of scrap metal unless we're close to Rimfire.'

'Yeah, we're not far,' replied Laquell, his voice calm and reassuring. 'Switch on your transponder and key it to this frequency or else the base defences will tag you as hostile and shoot you down.'

A data squirt appeared on her slate and she keyed in the corresponding frequency, thumbing the activation switch. An answering light appeared on her tactical plot, thirty kilometres out. Rimfire. But was it close enough? Her altimeter was unwinding fast, and she did a quick mental calculation. It was just within reach.

'Stay on my wing,' said Laquell. 'Keep the nose up and fly steady.'

Larice nodded to herself, holding the stick tight and trying to keep any unnecessary movement from her path. Every second she spent in the air was a few hundred metres closer to safety.

'You're doing great, Larice. That's it, steady and smooth. Gradually ease around to two-seven-seven.'

'I don't have time for manoeuvre,' she said.

'I know, but there's some crazy thermals that come up from the southern rift plains. They'll give you some extra lift. Trust me, I've used them before when I'm coming back with a tank of vapour.'

Larice adjusted her course, the stick feeling leaden in her grip and the plane responding like she imagined a tank would manoeuvre. They came down through a light dusting of clouds, and there it was, a down and dirty collection of air-defence vehicles, ad hoc runways, quick-fire launch racks and fuel bowsers clustered around a random scattering of landing mats strewn across the ice.

Rimfire was around three kilometres away, but at the rate she was shedding height it might as well have been three thousand. She wasn't going to make it.

'I'm short,' she said. 'I don't have enough–'

A slamming wind hoisted her higher, the spiralling tunnel of warm air Laquell had promised her. Her descent slowed and she saw it might be enough. Her Thunderbolt could transition to vertical landing, but without fuel that wasn't going to be possible.

'Rimfire Tower, this is Apostle Five, requesting emergency landing clearance.'

'Apostle Five, confirmed. You are clear to land on runway six-epsilon. Directing now,' said an echoing voice that sounded like it was coming from inside a small metal box. Looking at the haphazard collection of vehicles gathered beneath arctic camo-netting at the edge of the runway, Larice decided that was exactly where it was coming from.

'Emergency vehicles are standing by, Apostle Five,' said the controller.

'Thanks for the vote of confidence, Rimfire,' snapped Larice, wrestling with the stick as vicious crosswinds and random vector gusts bounced up from the ground. She lowered her claws at the last moment, and fought to bring the nose up before she ploughed straight into the runway.

Her wing claws bit and the nose slammed down a second later. Her speed bled off and the ice-crazed surface of the runway threw up a blinding flurry of ice and snow. She was pretty much blind. Larice threw up her arrestors and slammed on the brakes, feeling the Thunderbolt turn in a lazy skid. The plane slid around until it was pointed back the way it had come, and Larice let out a shuddering breath.

On a runway next to hers, she saw Laquell's plane touch down and make a point-perfect rollout, managing the slipperiness of the runway with the aplomb of a veteran flyer. He taxied over the ice and parked up ten metres from her starboard wing.

Fitters and emergency ground crew ran over to her plane. One drew a finger over his throat, and she nodded, shutting off her armaments panel and disconnecting her fuel lines – not that there was any fuel left to ignite. She popped the canopy and the cold hit her like a blow. Her breath caught in her throat, the raw ice of it like a full-body slap. Fitters propped a ladder against her plane and she unsnapped herself from the cockpit and climbed down. Someone wrapped her in a foil-lined thermal blanket and she took an unsteady step away from her cream-coloured Thunderbolt.

Long and heavily winged, the Thunderbolt wasn't an elegant flyer, but it had a robust beauty all of its own. The ivory paint scheme was scarred and smeared with oil and scorch marks where her fuel lines had ruptured. She waved away a medicae, watching as red and yellow-jacketed ground crew milled around her plane, eager to work on a plane belonging to one of the Apostles. She felt a stab of protectiveness towards her damaged bird as fitters began appraising the damage, wincing at the sound of whining power-wrenches and pneumo-hammers.

Armoured plating hung like scabbed skin from its underside, and dribbles of hydraulic fluid and lubricant spotted the ice beneath its belly. A tow rig rumbled towards the planes from a hangar buried beneath ten metres of snow and ice.

She heard footsteps and Laquell's voice said, 'Took a beating, but she'll fly again.'

'You talking about the plane or me?' she said without turning.

'The plane, of course,' said Laquell. 'You look just fine.'

She turned and saw him, like her, wrapped in a thermal blanket. He sipped a mug of something hot that steamed in the cold air. He was striking in an Imperial-recruiting-poster kind of way: angular chin, high cheekbones and eyes that radiated trust and courage. His dark hair was cut close to the skull, and he was smiling at her.

'You want one?'

'One what?' she said.

'Soup,' said Laquell, holding up his mug and making it sound like a joke. 'You don't want a caffeine, you'll get the jitters, even though the Munitorum actually make a pretty decent brew around here. Soup'll warm you up and won't have you bouncing off the flakboard.'

Larice nodded, feeling the strain of her sortie settle upon her. 'Sure, soup sounds good.'

He handed her his mug and she took a grateful sip. It tasted of hot vegetables and game.

It was the best thing she'd drunk in months.

'Come on,' said Laquell, leading her towards the buried hangar. 'The mess facilities here don't look like much, but you can get a halfway decent meal and a hot shower.'

'Now *that* sounds better,' said Larice, disarmed by his easy manner and winning smile.

They passed his plane, and Larice saw the kill markings painted on the nose.

'You have thirty-seven kills,' she said.

'Yeah, it's been a busy day.'

'You're a frigging ace,' she said.

'So they tell me,' said Laquell, as if it was nothing.

'How long have you been flying?'

'On Amedeo? Two weeks, but I bagged my first kill about six months ago.'

Larice found herself re-evaluating the cocky young flyer, now seeing a combination of skill and natural ability in his flying.

'And you've thirty-seven kills to your name? Confirmed?'

'Every one of them,' he said. 'One's even on pict-loop in the officer's quarters.'

'Nice work,' said Larice, impressed despite herself.

Laquell nodded, pleased with her compliment, but too much of an aviator to look too pleased. They stepped into the hangar. Out of the winds whipping across the isolated base, the temperature was at least bearable. Inside, a dozen Thunderbolts in the camo-green paint scheme of the 235th sat in a herringbone pattern, attended by an army of servitors and fitters in orange jumpsuits. Gurneys of missiles and heavy boxes of shells threaded their way between the planes, and a robed priest of the Mechanicus, together with his cybernetic entourage, attended to the guts of a partially disassembled aircraft. Its nose was wreathed in fragrant smoke and hot unguents dripped from an exposed turbofan.

As they walked between the aircraft towards the crew quarters, Larice knew she was attracting stares. Word that one of the Apostles had landed at Rimfire had circulated through the base with a speed normally reserved for the pox after a tour of shore leave. Her jet-black flight suit, compact form and girlish good looks didn't hurt either.

They looked at her and she looked back, counting no fewer than seven aircraft with kill markings indicating that their pilots were aces. And the rest weren't too far behind. None of them had thirty-seven kills, though. She saw Laquell notice her appraisal, but said nothing.

There was clear order and discipline to the work going on throughout the hangar, a sense of purpose that was common to most air wings, but which was even more focussed than usual. This far out from support, everyone's survival depended on keeping these aircraft ready to fly and fight at a moment's notice. Far from being the dumping ground for reckless or deficient pilots, Rimfire was a base where only the best survived.

'That was a hell of a piece of flying you did up there,' said Laquell. 'You and that other Apostle really pulled us out of it.'

'Quint's a hell of a flyer,' she said.

'That was Quint?' said Laquell. 'The ace of aces? Maybe I shouldn't have cheeked him.'

'Maybe not,' agreed Larice, already wondering what Seekan would make of this young, cocksure colt of a pilot. She looked at him and he returned her gaze with a frankness she found unsettling, like she was a target in the reticule of a quad gun sight.

I remember that look, she thought, and that made her mind up.

'So tell me about that kill, the one on pict-loop,' she said.

'Why?' he said, faintly embarrassed. 'It's not that good, and it's over too quick.'

'Sounds like a lot of lovers I've had,' said Larice.

'Seriously, why do you want to see it?'

She smiled and said, 'Because if I'm going to recommend you to Wing Leader Seekan, then I'll need to know I'm not going to be making a damn idiot out of myself.'

They always pick the places that used to be magnificent.

The Aquilian had once been the toast of Coriana's wealthy gadabouts apparently, a grand folly built in opposition to a rival's hotel further down the city's main thoroughfare. Which of the two had come out on top was a mystery now, for Archenemy shock troops had destroyed the other hotel in the opening stages of the war. High command had been using it as their lodgings and strategic planning centre, and only an accident of timing had seen them elsewhere when the blood-masked enemy troopers attacked.

Since then, the brass kept on the move.

Which meant the next grandest structure in Coriana was free for the taking.

Processional steps led up to its columned entrance, the space between each column draped with a gold and black flag of the Imperium. Larice led Laquell up the steps and through the cracked marble-floored vestibule, following the booming sounds of martial music. She recognised the tune, *Imperitas Invictus*, a rousing tune said to have been written for Lord Helican's triumphal march through the Spatian Gate. It wasn't a tune played much any more.

'I can't believe I'm going to meet the Apostles,' said Laquell, and Larice was amused at the star-struck quality to his voice. His eyes were bright and his features eager.

'Then be prepared to be disappointed,' she said. 'They're just pilots.'

'You don't see it because you're one of them,' said Laquell. 'They're more than "just pilots": they're legends, warriors of the air, killers of enemy aces. They're the best flyers in the Navy. And they want me. I think that's pretty damn fine.'

'Hold on there, pilot,' warned Larice. 'All I'm doing is putting you forward for consideration. It'll be Seekan's decision whether to take you or not.'

'Come on,' he said, puffing out his chest and tapping the service ribbons on his chest. 'Look at me. How could they not want me? I expect they'll offer me a place on the spot.'

'I wouldn't bet on it,' said Larice as the music swelled as a door opened and shut.

'Are we missing a party?' asked Laquell, straightening his dress uniform jacket, a deep russet colour with tasteful silver frogging over the shoulders and a stiffened collar of lacquered leather.

Larice didn't answer.

Her former commanding officer, Bree Jagdea, had told her about the habits of the Apostles, and she knew there was only one reason her new squadron mates would gather like this. She crossed the chequerboard floor and swept down a wide corridor towards a set of walnut-panelled doors. She pushed through them into what had once been a grand ballroom, but was now an echoing empty space hung with blast curtains. Almost every item of furniture was draped in dustsheets, cobwebs laced the spaces between the chandeliers and a faint smell of mildew lurked below the hot crackle of the fire and scent of burning sapwood.

A group of people clad in cream-coloured frock coats gathered around an enormous fireplace. Seven of them, the best and luckiest damn pilots in the Navy.

The Apostles.

They looked small; diminished and alone in a vast space that normally held grand revelries and magnificent dances. The ballroom echoed with unloved music and drunken debate.

Seekan was the first to notice them, turning and favouring her with a quizzical smile. His dark hair was swept back and oiled, his uniform crisp and gleaming with row upon row of medals.

'Larice,' he said, crisp like a cold morning. 'We weren't expecting you.'

'Why not?' she said, glaring at Quint, who perched on a stool opposite Jeric Suhr. A regicide board sat between them. 'Did you think I was dead?'

'Not at all,' said Seekan. 'We heard the chatter that an Apostle had landed at Rimfire. We knew you were alive.'

'So why the drink and the dress uniforms?'

'Because the *Rosencranz* is gone,' said Ziner Krone, pushing away from the fire surround and making his way to an isolated drinks cabinet. His dark-skinned cheeks were flushed with amasec and heat. The scar on his cheek twitched and he poured a drink, which he promptly downed. He poured another and thrust it towards Larice with a lascivious grin.

'Drink it,' he ordered. 'Drink to the lost souls of the *Rosencranz*.'

Larice didn't want the amasec, but took it anyway. Krone watched her sip it, making no attempt to hide his lingering glance at her chest and hips. He'd propositioned her in the crew barracks aboard the *Rosencranz*, but Larice had told him where to get off in no uncertain terms. Those days were behind her.

'The *Rosencranz* is gone?' said Laquell. 'How?'

Krone ignored his question and turned back to the drinks.

Larice had last seen the Munitorum mass carrier when she'd flown her Thunderbolt from its cavernous hold to the planet's surface. Kilometres long, the mass conveyer was a city adrift in space, a landmass capable of interstellar flight. Bulky and ungainly, it seemed inconceivable that anything so colossal could possibly be destroyed.

'Who gives a shit?' snapped Jeric Suhr. He waved his balloon of liquor, spilling some on the board. Quint scowled at Suhr as his wiry opponent rose unsteadily to his feet. Suhr's chest seemed too narrow to contain all the medals he'd won, and his sharp features were thrown into stark relief by the firelight. 'Warp core failure, a plasma meltdown, fifth columnists in the dock crews, infiltrators? Who cares, it's all the same in the end. We're one carrier and a shitting load of planes and pilots down.'

'And who the hell is this anyway?' said Krone, finally acknowledging Laquell's presence and pouring another drink. 'This is a private party. For Apostles only. Get out before I throw you out.'

Larice felt Laquell bristle and said, 'Krone, this is Flight Lieutenant Erzyn Laquell of the 235th Naval Attack Wing.'

'Ah, the Navy flyboy who hauled your backside out of the fire,' said Suhr, slumping back onto his stool, though he'd plainly abandoned interest in the regicide board.

'Shut your mouth, Jeric,' said Seekan.

'Well he did, didn't he?'

'Flight Lieutenant Laquell came to my assistance, yes,' said Larice. 'He has thirty-seven confirmed kills in less than six months of flying time.'

'Ah, I see,' noted Seekan, turning away towards the fire. Saul Cirksen, the pilot he'd recruited on Enothis, stood there, nursing his drink. He'd been an Apostle for only slightly longer than Larice, but had already adopted the disaffected mannerisms of his adopted wing. He didn't look at Laquell, as though he didn't want to acknowledge his presence, like he was someone who'd go away if only they pretended he wasn't there.

Likewise Owen Thule and Leena Sharto, the two pilots Seekan had recruited at the very end of the war on Enothis, ignored him. Thule was a big-boned flyer from the 43rd Angels, a pugnacious man with heavy jowls and bushy sideburns. Leena Sharto had been tagged from the 144th Typhoons, and affected an air of disinterest that she couldn't quite pull off. Larice had tried to get to know them, seeking solace in the solidarity of their shared newness to the Apostles, but none of her overtures had been returned, and she had eventually given up.

'Larice, am I given to understand that you have brought the Flight Lieutenant here as a potential candidate for elevation to the Apostles?'

'Yeah, take a look at his jacket and you'll see what I mean.'

'I am quite familiar with Flight Lieutenant Laquell's record.'

'You are?'

'Of course he is,' slurred Krone. 'You think he's not always on the lookout for flyers that've slipped beneath fate's gaze? Some lucky bastard who's fallen off death's auspex?'

'I don't understand,' said Larice. 'If you know his jacket, you must know that–'

'He has the highest flight to kill ratio on Amedeo, greater even that that of Quint here?' said Seekan. 'Yes, I am well aware of that.'

Quint looked up from the board at the mention of his name, but said nothing.

'Then why wouldn't you invite him to become an Apostle?' asked Larice.

'Because the Apostles are a unique group, Larice,' said Seekan. 'Even to those newly promoted to its ranks. And every new member dilutes that exclusivity, makes us less select. I know, I know, it makes no sense, of course.'

Seekan turned to his fellow flyers. 'After all, of the Apostles that went to Enothis, only four of us survive, and by the end of this crusade, I do not expect any of us to be alive. Death is, at heart, a tallyman, and all the books must balance eventually.'

'He's a hell of a flyer,' pressed Larice. 'I've seen captures from his gun-picters.'

'As have I, Larice, but I sense there is more to this than simply Flight Lieutenant Laquell's skill in the cockpit.'

'What's that supposed to mean?'

'He means you like him,' snapped Suhr. 'And we don't need anyone likeable in the Apostles. Only odious shits like me, lechers like Krone or misery magnets like Quint.'

Seekan sighed and said, 'I'm thankful I was left off that list, but for all his boorishness, Jeric is right. I told Commander Jagdea this, and I'll tell you too, Larice. It doesn't do to have friends when you've flown as long as us and seen as much death through your canopy as we have. It's a liability, a weakness that slows you down and clouds your judgement. And you know as well as I, that anything that keeps you from the top of your game in the air gets you killed.'

'It doesn't have to be like that,' insisted Larice. 'It wasn't like that in the Phantine XX, and they exceeded your combined kills on Enothis.'

'Then why don't you go back to them?' said Krone.

Larice hesitated, suddenly missing the easy back and forth of the crew dorms perched on the rock above the Scald or the card schools Milan Blansher used to run in the hold of whatever Munitorum transport they were travelling within.

'I don't know where they are,' she said, now realising how much that hurt to say.

'You're an Apostle now, Larice,' said Seekan. 'I know it's hard to adjust to our way of thinking, but if you want to survive, it's the best way.'

'It's the only way,' said Quint, surprising them all. 'It's the Apostles' Creed. Live by it or get the hell out.'

Laquell returned to Rimfire and Larice took her place in the rotation as the war on Amedeo continued at its brutal pace. The flyers at Rimfire found themselves under ever more pressure as the attacks over the Breakers increased in frequency and the cities of the Ice were hit by more and more bomber waves. The Apostles flew a dozen intercepts in three days, splashing sixty-eight craft between them.

As expected, Quint took the highest tally. Larice was a hair's breadth behind him.

Nothing more was said of the night Larice brought Laquell to the Aquilian, yet it festered like a splinter of rotten wood beneath her skin. In the short period between flights she checked the Operations logs for any mention of Laquell, and was gratified to see his kill count climb steadily.

Eight days passed before she saw him again, amid a furious intercept in the skies ten kilometres north of Coriana. A huge wave of bombers and fighter escorts, two hundred and ten aircraft in total, appeared without warning over the snow-lashed Breakers, and the Lightnings and Thunderbolts based at Rimfire had only moments to scramble.

Less than three-quarters of the planes managed to get airborne before the first bombs hit, flattening the makeshift runways and obliterating what little infrastructure there was. The Imperial aircraft immediately tangled with the bombers' escort planes, a mix of Razors, Talons and Hell Blades, and a furious engagement began.

The Thunderbolts danced with the escorts while the faster Lightnings powered through the low-flying formations to target the slow movers above. Like wolves in the fold, the Lightnings savaged the packs of bombers, sending twenty to the ice in palls of smoke and fire, before the Archenemy escorts could break from the fight below to come to their aid.

The Thunderbolts followed them up, but before the two groups of fighters locked horns, another forty enemy fighters screamed down from the north. Operations at Coriana screamed a warning to the pilots, unable to believe that so many bats had simply popped into existence on their auspex.

The arrival of so many enemy aircraft forced the flyers from Rimfire to disengage.

And with their base now a volcanic crater in the ice, they turned south for Coriana.

Larice yanked the stick hard right, viffing down and barely avoiding a drifting stream of cannon fire from a diving Hell Talon. The pilot had misjudged his deflection, and she rolled back and deployed her air brakes, coming in around behind the bat as it slashed through the formation. She pushed out the throttle, lining up her shot, when she heard the shrill warning tone of a weapons lock.

'Five, break left!' shouted Leena Sharto.

Her target forgotten, Larice pulled left and down, driving the engine to full military power and weaving in and out of the morass of duelling planes. A Razor flashed in front of her, a Navy bird in hot pursuit, and she squeezed off a short burst of las. The pilot's canopy disintegrated in a shower of diamond splinters as it spun away.

Larice didn't watch it die. She twisted left and right, trying to locate her pursuer. It was still locked on to her, but she couldn't see it. An eye-wateringly bright blizzard of las-fire flashed over her and she threw her aircraft down, finally catching the blaze of light from the enemy guns.

Larice flew like a flock of Killers were on her tail, jinking and viffing through the air like an aerial acrobat. Her pursuer stayed with her, but there were few who understood how a Thunderbolt danced as well as Larice Asche, and it couldn't match her turns.

'You're fixated,' she said, grunting as a high-g turn drove the breath from her. 'And that's gotten you killed.'

She hauled back on the stick and flexed her plane through a screaming hammerhead turn, pulling vertical before rolling her tail section over and aiming her aircraft straight down. It was a risky manoeuvre, bleeding speed and leaving her hanging in the air. The Razor was right below her, lining up its shot, but Larice fired first.

Her quads banged and thumped, and the Razor split open in a storming burst of debris. Larice dropped through the flaming wreckage, her canopy awash with fire and the fuselage thumping with impacts. Nothing flashed red and she pulled out of her dive, coming level and increasing speed in case any other enemy craft were waiting to pounce.

None were, and she rolled back into the fight. The sky was thick with bats, swarming, razor-winged darts that flew aggressively and protected the slower bombers with the tenacity of a mother grox defending her offspring.

They outnumbered the Imperial aircraft, but that advantage wasn't counting for much. Larice knew the Archenemy were careless with their craft, preferring overwhelming numbers to skill and talent in the air. With every passing minute, the bombers were getting closer to Coriana, but their numbers were thinning as they went. The Apostles and sixty other planes were dancing with them at low altitude, screaming over the ice and outlying industrial complexes surrounding the city.

Larice saw a stretched V of aircraft taking the low-level approach to Coriana and thumbed the vox.

'This is Five, seven plus heavy bombers with escort going in low over the refineries.'

'I see them, Five.' Seekan.

'Take the lead, Five. I'm right behind you.' Suhr.

'Lead us in, Larice,' said a familiar voice and she smiled as she recognised the laconic tones.

She smiled. 'Good to have you on board, Laquell.'

'I've got Schaw and Ysor from Indigo with me,' voxed Laquell. 'On your left wing.'

Larice looked over, seeing Laquell's trio of fighters, and pushed her stick forwards and surged power to the afterburners.

'Five on lead,' said Larice, switching to quads.

'Bear in mind that we're flying over incredibly volatile structures,' advised Seekan as though informing them of light cloud cover. 'Short, controlled bursts only.'

'Diving in now,' said Larice. 'Stoop and sting those escorts!'

Almost as soon as she'd armed her guns, the two groups of aircraft were tangled up in a madly spinning, close-range dogfight. Larice rolled hard left, catching sight of a Razor's tail section, and followed it down.

Every move the Razor made, Larice was with him, the planes spinning around the sky like insects in a bizarre mating ritual. The plane spun right, but Larice was waiting for it. It flashed across her gunsight and she pulled the cannon trigger.

'Got you,' she hissed as bright laser bolts tore into the enemy plane's fuselage and ripped the darting craft in two. The plane spewed smoke and flames, tumbling downwards, and Larice caught a glimpse of the blood-splattered pilot as he struggled weakly with his doomed aircraft.

She rolled out of her attack, turning back into the fight. Aircraft swooped and dived around her, and she watched Seekan saw the tail off a Tormentor with a precise burst of las-fire. Owen Thule peppered a Hell Blade with his quads and lit up a Razor seconds later as he viffed over the wreckage and stood his plane on its wing to shred a spinning Hell Talon.

A diving Razor slotted itself in on his six and gunfire punched holes in his right wing.

'Eight, break right!' yelled Larice as her threat board lit up. She slammed the stick right and feathered the engines as a white rocket contrail speared past her canopy.

Red metal suddenly filled her vision and she swore, pushing the plane down and left as the belly of a Hell Blade screamed over her canopy, so close she felt she could reach out and touch it. Its jetwash threw her around for a moment until she was able to bring herself level again and come back on Owen Thule. She breathed deeply, amazed at how close the near miss had been.

'He's stuck to my six!' shouted Thule.

'I'm on him,' shouted Laquell, spinning his Thunderbolt into a rolling S to come in on the bat's five. His deflection was perfect and the bat flew straight into his storm of shells, blowing apart as its engine detonated.

'Thanks,' voxed Thule, turning into another engagement.

'Laquell! Heads up!' called Larice, 'You got one on your high six!'

Cannon shells spat from a Hell Blade's guns, a couple raking the topside armour of the Thunderbolt. Larice saw it was armed with underslung rockets too.

'Damn! Bad guy on my tail! Schaw, get him off me!'

'I'm on it,' replied his wingman.

The rear of Laquell's Thunderbolt spat brightly burning flares in an attempt to prevent the enemy rocket from locking onto his engine emissions. He threw the plane into a series of wild manoeuvres to try and shake his pursuer.

'Damn, this guy's good!' swore Laquell as the bat matched him move for move.

'Rocket away!' shouted Schaw.

'Breaking left!' answered Laquell, rolling hard and down.

'Come on...' prayed Larice, kicking in the afterburner and diving hard. She felt her vision greying under the pressure of the increased G-forces. Her flight suit expanded and she felt the composition of her air-mix change as she pushed the craft to the edge of the envelope.

She mashed the cannon trigger and filled the air behind Laquell's plane with las-fire.

The missile detonated prematurely as one of Larice's shots clipped its warhead. She felt the shockwave of its detonation and laughed in relief.

Laquell spun his plane round in a screaming turn and chopped the throttle, almost stalling the craft. The pilot of the Hell Blade tried to stay with him, but the explosion had concealed Laquell's survival, and its pilot couldn't match the Thunderbolt's turn.

The cocky pilot of the 235th rolled inverted and pulled in behind the red aircraft, slotting it neatly between his gunsights. Quad fire banged from the nose guns, shredding the bat's tailpipe and blowing the aircraft apart in a spectacular orange fireball.

Laquell hollered his triumph over the vox and flew over the debris.

Larice checked the auspex and saw the remaining five bombers had broken through the fighter cordon and were heading towards the civilian areas of Coriana. A screen of twelve bats lingered in their wash, ready to turn on any pursuit.

'Apostle Five in pursuit,' said Larice. 'Who's with me?'

'Apostle Lead,' said Seekan.

'Indigo Lead,' replied Laquell.

'Apostle Nine,' said Ziner Krone.

'Apostle Six,' said Saul Cirksen.

'Indigo Two,' said Schaw.

'Rise to Angels minus five hundred and dive on burners,' ordered Seekan, asserting his natural authority over this ad hoc squadron. A flight's destination altitude was never given in the open, and 'Angels' was a set altitude that changed every day. In this case it had been set at a thousand metres.

The Thunderbolts, a mix of camo-green and cream, snapped up in a sharp climb before aiming their guns down upon the bats.

'Turn and burn,' ordered Seekan.

Larice hit her afterburners, closing the distance to the bombers and their escort in a matter of moments. The bats broke into a combat spread and the Thunderbolts slashed through their formation. Larice tagged one plane, shearing its left wing off with her quads. It tumbled end over end into the ground, and ploughed a fiery gouge through a maze of pipework extending from an aluminium-skinned structure.

Laquell splashed another and each of the Apostles claimed a kill before they vectored back into the fight. Now it was one on one, and Larice shot her quads at a crimson Hell Talon with bloody teeth painted on its swept wings. The Talon threw itself into a low dive, sweeping under an aqueduct of pipes, and Larice followed him down. The bat slashed through the air, jinking past flame-topped towers, around vast, portal-framed fabriks and between enormous cylindrical ore-silos.

Larice kept to her quads, loosing a sharp burst every time she got weapons lock, but the bat was good. He kept her at arm's length, always anticipating her deflections and viffing out of the way in time.

'Stand still, frig you,' she hissed, deploying air brakes and vectoring right to sidestep around the tall lifter derricks of a Leman Russ assembly yard. Swaying pallets of building materials flashed past her canopy and she caught the terrified 'O' of the derrick's crewman, passing within a metre of her wingtip. The bat spun around a blazing plume of venting gases from a promethium refinery and a host of las-bolts exploded around her. She felt the hammer blows on her fuselage and jinked down.

Whip aerials on the roof of a manufactory snapped off on her underside and she snagged a trailing cord from a Mechanicus banner. It burned up in her heat bloom, and Larice couldn't decide what kind of omen that was. The bat arced past her canopy, and she stood her plane on its end, rolling inverted and hitting the burners again to get on its tail.

The gases from the refinery surged in her jetwash and punched her after the bat like she'd been launched from the rails with her rocket assist. The acceleration slammed her back in her seat, but seconds later she was right on the bat's tail. Larice cut her burners and mashed the firing trigger. A stream of autocannon shells ripped into the bat's engines and sliced through its entire length. Literally sawn in two, the shorn halves of the bat fell out of the sky in flames.

Larice pulled up, hearing triumphant shouts from the other pilots as they splashed their targets. Only Schaw failed to take down his bat, misjudging a turn and ending up with a bat on his tail instead. Seekan shot down the bat, and the Imperial planes roared after the rising bombers as they started their attack runs.

Too slow to evade the Imperial pursuit, the Tormentors unloaded their bombs early and aimed their aircraft towards the ground. Each one ploughed into the tangle of pipes, bridges and construction yards of Coriana's industrial hinterland, leaving a trail of devastation hundreds of metres long. Fires raged in the swathes of burning jet fuel wreckage, and Larice pulled up through banks of shimmering thermals and buffeting winds of exploding ordnance.

It wasn't pretty, but looking towards the untouched hab-stacks, residential sprawls and commercia districts, she knew it could have been a lot worse.

Two more attacks came in over the mountains, again with little warning until they'd crossed the Breakers, and the Apostles flew round-the-clock sorties with the regrouped diaspora of aircraft from the forward airbases. It was brutal flying, the Archenemy planes battering at the gates of Coriana as though it were the ultimate prize in the war.

Larice supposed it was, looking up at the map pinned to the wall of the market hall. The air carried the taste of spoiled fruit and dairy products, of decay and abandonment. She sat on a camp chair with her booted feet resting on a packing crate that had once contained Mark V magazines for lasguns.

Pilots on the rotation hustled back and forth between mission briefings and Munitorum supply depots where cold caffeine and hot food were on offer. The abandoned market hall now served as a makeshift Operations centre. At the far end of the vaulted, echoing chamber, a heaving mass of cogitators and logic engines were hooked up to a series of coughing generators. A gaggle of uniformed officers and tech-priests surrounded an illuminated plotting table. It bathed their faces in a bleaching light, and a fug of incense hung over their deliberations. Runners sped back and forth, updating senior flight officers on developments over the Ice, and commands were barked into vox-horns to scramble this flight, divert that flight or assist another. One particular flight officer, a fat man in a voluminous robe, seemed to be the centre of attention, and Larice wondered how he'd ever managed to fit in the cockpit of an aircraft.

Seekan stood next to him, taking animatedly and using his hands a lot. He seemed to be demonstrating air combat manoeuvres and gesturing over to where the Apostles waited.

Larice had never thought much about the men and women who directed her in the air, assuming they were sitting in a calm, ordered command centre. Watching the chaos surrounding the plotter and hearing the barked flood of information gathered by the ground-based and aerial augurs, she found a new respect for their skill in juggling so many variables.

Ziner Krone lay sprawled in a cot bed, arms crossed over his chest like a body in a funerary parlour. Jeric Suhr and Quint played a bad-tempered game of regicide, and Larice wondered if it was a continuation of the one they'd been playing in the ballroom of the Aquilian. She looked over at the duty roster, confirming that she wasn't on the rotation for another two hours.

Larice knew she should rest, but she was too wired to sleep, and the noise from the freshly hammered-down runways and launch rails beyond the walls of the market hall made it too difficult to sleep. Some aviators found a natural rhythm in flight operations, snatching sleep when they could, eating on the run and flying in the spaces inbetween. Larice always found it took time to settle into any kind of routine, and they'd flown out of three different bases already.

In any case, she'd hooked up with Laquell, whose squadron was deployed in the same hangars and runways as the Apostles. They'd taken to spending their downtime playing cards and talking of particularly memorable intercepts, and Larice found herself warming to the handsome flyer. Seekan still hadn't offered him a place in the Apostles, which Larice found baffling. Laquell's kill count had climbed steadily, now standing at an impressive seventy-three, and he'd provided assists to no fewer than six of the Apostles.

Leena Sharto, Saul Cirksen and Owen Thule were in the sky, running air superiority missions over the Imperial Guard. Three regiments, two Mordian and one Vostroyan, were engaged in a bitter land war two hundred kilometres west of Coriana. Larice had flown on such missions before, finding it hard to imagine waging war without being strapped to the awesome power of a Thunderbolt. To face the guns of the enemy without its speed, armour and powerful guns seemed like a sure-fire way to get yourself killed.

The medicae convoys pouring into Coriana and the number of facilities converted to deal with the dead appeared to back this up.

'Busy I see,' said Laquell, returning with a pot of caffeine and two battered tin mugs.

'Just keeping an eye on things,' said Larice, accepting a mug and taking a sip. She grimaced.

'Yeah, I know,' he said, sitting next to her. 'I sure do miss the caffeine at Rimfire.'

'It was that good?'

'No, but it was better than this. So how's it going?' said Laquell, nodding towards the map. Junior flight officers moved coloured tacks around the board as intercepts developed and fresh intelligence became available.

'A map tacked to the wall isn't the most efficient way of hearing what's going on, but it's better than nothing,' said Larice. 'I think something big's on the way. All the runners got called back to the table and the tech-priests nearly had a frigging fit.'

'Any idea what's up?'

'Not a clue,' said Larice. 'You know we're always the last to know what's happening.'

'Looks like Seekan's in amongst it.'

'*Wing Leader* Seekan,' corrected Larice.

'Yeah, sorry.'

'You think he's putting you in harm's way?'

'Him or someone with more medals on their chest.'

Laquell nodded and looked over at the map. 'Looks like the Guard are getting hit hard.'

'Not as hard as they'd be without us watching over them from above.'

'True.'

'When are you up?' she asked.

Larice checked her wrist chron. Every pilot had one. They delivered a warning note and a mild electric shock when an alert came in, and were universally hated.

'Two hours,' he said. 'You?'

'The same.'

'Looks like the Apostles and Indigo will be flying together again.'

'Good to know,' she said, draining her caffeine as Seekan strode from the plotting table towards them. His crisp demeanour was animated and his face flushed with excitement, like a junior pilot after his first kill. Larice didn't know whether to be amused or scared.

Krone came awake as Seekan approached, but Suhr and Quint continued their game.

Larice took her feet down from the packing crate and said, 'We've got a mission?'

'That we have, Larice,' said Seekan. 'And it's rather a big one.'

As the Breakers passed beneath her Thunderbolt, Larice began to appreciate Wing Leader Seekan's gift for understatement. As part of Winter Spear, the name given to the attack force heading out over the ocean ice, the Apostles had been tasked with the toughest job of the sortie. Two hundred and sixty-six aircraft filled the air, a mix of vector jets, ground attack craft, air-superiority fighters, heavy bombers and a pair of converted Marauders equipped with souped-up auspex gear. Designated Orbis Flight, these last two planes would attempt to provide mobile command and control over the coming battle.

Forty Marauders, comprised of aircraft from the 22nd Ysysarians and the 323rd Vincamus, growled behind the fighter screen. Their bomb bays were fully laden with armour-penetrating warheads so heavy it seemed like the aircraft might not make it over the peaks. Together with the slower, prop-driven Laredo-class bombers, seventy-two slow movers shook the mountaintops clear of snow, wallowing in the jetwash of the racing fighters.

Ranging ahead of the bombers, the Apostles formed the tip of the spear, eight cream-coloured Thunderbolts flying at seven thousand metres. Fast-moving Lightnings from the 39th Buccaneers prowled the bombers' flanks, and squadrons from the 666th Devil Dogs and 42nd Prefects provided low and top cover for the formation. Two dozen locally-produced fighters, known as Y-ten-tens but which the Navy flyers had christened Die-ten-tens due to their lack of manoeuvrability and slow speed, flew alongside the bombers. Everyone knew that if it came to these planes defending the bombers, then the assault was as good as defeated.

The three pilots of Indigo Flight cruised behind and below the Apostles. Larice had given Laquell the traditional Navy send-off before a mission.

'Good hunting,' she'd said on the hardstands of Coriana.

'You too,' he'd replied, and she'd smacked his arse as he climbed the ladder.

'What was that for?' he said, climbing in and strapping himself down as the fitters pulled the arming pins on the hellstrike rockets mounted on the pylons beneath his wings.

'For luck.'

'Don't I get to give you one?'

'When we get back, Laquell,' she'd said, turning and jogging over to her own plane.

Seekan's voice crackled over the vox, pulling her back to the present, and she checked her spacing and gripped her stick with hands that were sweating inside her textured gloves.

'Coming up on Initial Point,' he said. 'Combat spread and drop to Angels minus five. The enemy will have been watching for us, and will undoubtedly have their bats airborne by now. Expect contact any minute.'

One by one, the Apostles acknowledged and Larice thumbed her auspex into active search mode, watching as the scope began filling with rapidly ascending contacts. High-speed interceptors, slower close-in defence craft, and heavy ground contacts.

But in the centre of the slate one contact overshadowed all the others, a monstrous return that was far too large to be a flyer. This was what they had come to destroy. This was how the Archenemy had launched their attacks over the Breakers without warning.

This was why their aerial armada was sweeping down over the mountains.

Though it was over ten kilometres away, Larice saw it clearly; its stark blackness a stain on the ocean ice. It was locked in the ice by the rapidly freezing water and huddled, though it seemed impossible that something so vast could huddle, in the midst of ice spires pushed up from the water by undersea volcanic activity.

Nearly two thousand metres long and glossy black with a flat topside bristling with crooked towers, sloped takeoff ramps and jet blast deflectors, the Archenemy mass carrier swarmed with bats.

And Larice saw how it had evaded detection for so long.

It was a *submersible* mass carrier.

'Apostle Lead, this is Orbis One. We are reading strong auspex bands low on the ice, five kilometres from your position,' said the monotone voice of one of the tech-priests. 'Identification: six outlying superheavies on the ice equipped with surface-to-air rockets between Winter Spear and its objective.'

'Understood, Orbis One,' said Seekan. 'The Apostles will clear the way.'

Seekan's plane dropped from the formation and the seven cream-coloured Thunderbolts followed him down towards the ocean ice. As the Apostles dived, the fighter element of Winter Spear surged forward, ready to engage and destroy the enemy screen of bats before they could splash the bombers.

Target information from Orbis inloaded onto Larice's armaments panel, the target of her Thunderbolt's wrath blinking a taunting red. Six multiple rocket launching batteries surrounded the mass carrier, each capable of throwing up a lethal screen of seeker rockets. They had to be taken out before any slow movers could reach the carrier.

'You all heard what I heard,' said Seekan over the vox to his pilots. 'Switch your targeting auspex to ground engagement. We will be going low and fast. Pair off. Odds will be on unmasking duty, Evens on termination.'

He spoke with crisp authority, and as Larice heard the confirmations coming over the vox she was again struck by the machine-like obedience of her fellow Apostles. There was no verbal roughhousing like you'd find in most Navy wings, no wishes of good hunting or benedictions to the Emperor. The Apostles were all about the task, anything else was a liability.

'You and me, Asche,' said Jeric Suhr, sliding into view on her port wing. 'Let's go.'

Larice nodded and pushed the stick straight down, diving for the ice. No point in giving the rocket batteries an easier target until it was time to kill them. The ice roared up to meet her, and she found herself relying on her altimeter to gauge her pull-out. The immensity of the glaring pack-ice filled her canopy, a blank vision of emptiness that made it next to impossible to judge exactly how high she was.

The numbers unspooled, and when they hit two hundred metres, she yanked back on the stick and feathered her engines, viffing her vectors hard and flaring out with a thunderous boom that split the ice. She shot off at ninety degrees to her dive, and a slashing V of ice crystals ripped up from the ice in her flashing wake.

She flew a mere twenty metres above the ocean ice with Suhr a hundred metres behind on her starboard wing. Such flying required the coolest of hands on the stick as the slightest miscalculation would send her plane ploughing into the ice.

Nap-of-the-ice flight was necessary if they were going to take out these rocket batteries. Thunderbolts and Lightnings could outrun missiles and outfly gunners, but the Marauders would have no chance against them.

Larice had trained in fire suppression missions, but had never actually flown one before.

In theory it was simple.

The aircraft worked in pairs. One pilot would fly their plane into the arc of anti-aircraft fire and allow the rocket battery to acquire him. Once the battery had 'unmasked' itself in this way, the second aircraft would swoop in to attack the gun battery and blow it to pieces.

In theory.

Flying fire suppression was one of the most testing and dangerous missions a pilot could undertake. Playing chicken with streams of shells and missiles was a task few had the stomach for, requiring the most fearless, skilful and, some would say, reckless flyers.

Truth be told, Larice was thrilled to be flying into harm's way.

As a native of Phantine, she was, literally, born to fly. Any moment she wasn't in the cockpit of an armed aircraft was a moment wasted.

'Apostle Six,' said Larice.

'Six here,' replied Suhr. 'Go ahead, Five.'

'You ready to do this?'

'Of course,' replied Suhr, sounding insulted she'd even asked.

The Thunderbolts were fast approaching the mass carrier and its ring of protection. Her low-level approach would make it difficult for the enemy gunners to achieve weapons lock. The auspex feed from Orbis showed the rocket battery, but Larice didn't need it to see the ugly construction of black metal, blades and the rearing templum-organ of its launch tubes fastened to the ice by extended clamps like a raptor's claws. A number of armoured vehicles and stalk tanks clustered around the battery, and red-armoured warriors with raised rifles spread out from it. Larice ignored them. Only the rocket battery mattered.

She thumbed the vox.

'Apostle Five inbound and ready.'

Larice armed her quads, pushing the throttle out and dropping her fighter suicidally close to the ice. Meltwater blasted from the pack-ice flashed by her canopy as she flew at high speed along her approach vector.

'Asche!' cried the normally unflappable Jeric Suhr. 'You're too low!'

'Shut up, and don't frigging miss,' snapped Larice, hauling violently on the stick, pulling the Thunderbolt into an almost vertical climb. Her ivory plane roared into view above the rocket battery, flashing its underside and largest surface area. She eased into an unforgivably lazy banking turn and waited on the *shoom, shoom, shoom* of smoke from the battery.

A bloom of yellow-stained propellant exploded from the battery's rear and a trio of seeker warheads leapt from the launch tubes. Slaved autocannons followed her passage, banging high explosive shells in a near-constant stream into the air.

She rolled over and dived for the ice as shots blasted around her. She twisted and looped the plane like a lunatic. The autocannon shells were well wide and Larice grinned as adrenaline dumped into her system, keeping the effects of her high-g turns at bay.

She pulled the Thunderbolt into a long, slow climb, allowing the rockets to close before throwing the aircraft into a dazzling pirouette, hammering the throttle and pumping out clouds of decoy flares. The Thunderbolt shot away at almost ninety degrees to its original course and two rockets overshot, exploding as their seeker warheads fell for the flares.

The third rocket twisted round and followed her down, the gap closing. Jeric Suhr's Thunderbolt overflew the battery and fired two of his hellstrike missiles. Even as the Archenemy crew realised that they were now the hunted, the missiles slammed into the rocket vehicle's topside.

The battery exploded in a searing white fireball, burning fuel and wreckage flying in all directions. Three other vehicles detonated, caught in the blast and veering across the ice to crush the soldiers gathered around them. Lumbering stalk-tanks fired their heavy guns, but the Thunderbolts were too quick for the gunners and every one of their shots missed.

The rockets in the battery's magazine cooked off explosively. Warheads blew in a string of roaring booms. Razor-sharp fragments sprayed out and enemy soldiers ran from the destruction, their grossly misshapen bodies twisting in agony as they burned.

Larice let out a yell of exultation as the explosions lit up the ice and flew through the expanding mushroom cloud of fire rising from the destroyed battery. Flames rippled over her canopy like liquid orange light and the last rocket followed her into the fire. It detonated in the midst of the explosion and Larice pulled her Thunderbolt into a looping, inverted climb.

'Good shooting, Suhr,' she said, feeling her heart rate climbing down from its rapid tattoo.

'What else did you expect?' replied Suhr, closing on her wing. Larice called up the auspex feed from Orbis and tallied off the destroyed rocket batteries.

One, two, three, four, five...

Before she could get to six, the live feed flickered and died.

'Orbis Flight is down!' shouted the voice of a panicked Marauder pilot. 'Orbis is down!'

Larice looked up, seeing a sky thick with swarming bats and Imperial craft. A major air battle was going on above their heads and it wasn't clear who had the upper hand. Slashing red Hell Talons and Razors filled the air with las and the dance of fighters above was a blazing free-fire zone.

Larice switched vox channel, and the cockpit was filled with the frantic chatter of pilots screaming at each other to break, dive, roll, cover and eject.

Seekan's voice cut through the babble.

'Apostles,' he said, 'take back the sky.'

Larice stood her plane on its tail and hit her burners, melting a ten-metre-wide crater in the ice as her Thunderbolt leapt skyward.

Larice picked her target, a spiralling Hell Talon flying an aggressive pursuit against one of the 42nd Prefects. The Lightning was dancing through the sky, but the Talon was stuck to it like glue. Larice waited until the Lightning rolled over on an escape turn and the Talon bled off speed to follow it round. A spurt of las tore a wing from its body and the madly spinning craft looped down towards the ice. She broke off and fanned her aircraft down after a flash of a crimson wing. A Hell Blade swished past her wing, its speed a match for hers, and she looked into the cockpit of the enemy pilot.

His helmet was a carved, daemonic leer and hellish red light lit his masked face. A long, reptilian tongue slid from his mouth, and Larice recoiled as she realised the pilot wasn't wearing a helmet. She punched her air brakes and cut her thrust, viffing in behind the enemy plane. He broke right and stepped down with a flutter of vector thrust. Larice angled her plane down, knowing he would surge forward.

Her quads banged, the recoil fierce and loud.

Shells streamed from the nose guns and tore up that damnable cockpit, erasing that monstrous visage from existence. Her breathing stoked shallow, spiking pulse rate high. A pilot never normally saw the face of the enemy, and to know the hideous things they were flying against had shaken her. It took her a moment to regain her calm, but in an aerial fight, a moment can be too long.

Heavy fire thumped her wings and fuselage, tearing over the armour behind her canopy. Red icons winked to life and she threw the Thunderbolt into a looping roll. A sidestepping viff put her back level and she twisted in her seat, hunting her hunter.

'Larice, break right!' shouted a voice over the vox. Laquell.

She hauled around, narrowly avoiding a collimated blaze of las-fire. Left, right, up, roll left. Her attacker was still with her. She saw it behind her, a gleam of purple and gold. Hell Blade. She saw a flicker of camo-green and the enemy plane lit up like a sunflare shell as Laquell's guns shredded it and its engine core went critical.

'Thanks, Laquell,' said Larice, rising up above the engagement and getting her breath back under control.

'You all right?' asked Laquell, pulling out alongside her.

'Fine.'

'Where's your wingman?'

'Suhr? I don't know. Where's yours?'

'Ysor got tagged. A bat tore up his wings and his missiles cooked off on the pylon.'

'Damn,' hissed Larice.

'Yeah,' agreed Laquell. 'I'll watch your wing if you watch mine.'

'Deal,' she said, turning her aircraft back down into the madly swirling engagement.

Their aircraft slashed down through a wedge of attacking Razors, splitting them and blowing two to fragments. Larice pulled wide and splashed a Hell Blade as it lined up a shot on Apostle Eight.

'You're welcome, Thule,' she said as his aircraft zoomed back into the fight.

The two mobs of fighters were well and truly enmeshed now, like starving hounds locked in a cage, the battle an impossible-to-follow tangle of explosions, missile contrails, air-bursting flak, las-fire and vector flare. Larice and Laquell danced through the battle with muscular turns and delicate spins, dancers in the midst of a stampede. They made a good team, instinctively understanding how the other flew, matching turns and viffs with the accuracy of flyers who'd fought together for years.

Larice lost count of how many kills she took, mashing the firing trigger on the stick until the battery of her las coughed dry. She switched to quads, claiming another three kills. This engagement alone would make every pilot an ace in a day.

Flashing wings, speeding tail sections and spirals of engine noise. Snap shots and desperate breaks. Larice was sweating and her body ached from gripping on hard turns. Every muscle burned and she was in for a hell of an adrenal comedown when she put her plane back on the deck.

A shadow shimmered over her canopy, and she saw a trailing formation of bombers coming in, diving and looking like a flock of migrating birds coming into nest.

Seekan's voice came over the vox. 'Apostles, this is Lead,' he said. 'The door is open, so while the Lightnings have the bats' attention, we'll escort the Marauders in.'

'Laquell,' she voxed, aiming her Thunderbolt towards the mass carrier. 'You want to fly with the Apostles?'

'Sure, Larice,' replied Laquell 'I could do with another heart attack today.'

Larice flipped her aircraft over and pushed its nose down. The two fighters spread out and increased power, diving for the deck at high speed. She saw the enormous carrier was wallowing in the ocean, industrial-grade meltas flaring around its edges to melt the ice and allow it to escape beneath the water. The bats in the air would have nowhere to land if it submerged, but that didn't seem to matter to the Archenemy commanders.

Autocannon shots burst around them and Larice grinned as she jinked the Thunderbolt up and down, avoiding the flak as though it was coming at her in slow motion. She flew instinctively, not even consciously aware of any decision-making process, just flying as though she knew, just *knew*, where the streams of tracers would be.

'There's too much fire!' shouted Laquell.

'You might be right,' agreed Larice, calmly lining up her cannon's gunsight on the command spire of the mass carrier. Her quads opened up, and drifting blooms of fire erupted across the surface of the black tower like orange-petalled flowers with every impact.

'We've got to pull up, Larice! We're too close!' screamed Laquell, hauling his plane away in a desperate climb that cost him valuable speed.

Three rockets leapt from the deck of the carrier as Larice pulled the trigger on her control column again. The quad-mounted autocannon thundered and blazed, the noise like a roaring chainsaw. The shells impacted ten metres in front of one of the carrier's launch batteries before tearing into it and ripping it messily in half.

She pushed out the throttle to full military power and executed a tight, rolling spin, flipping up and over the deck of the carrier. Masked warriors fired pistols and rifles at her, and the rockets streaked across the deck in pursuit of her furnace-hot turbofans. Booming waves of icy water surged up from the carrier's sides as it began to submerge.

Her auspex screamed warnings at her. She pulled a recklessly tight turn around the carrier's command spire, spitting a string of incandescent flares as she punched the engines.

The rockets couldn't match a vector turn and two of them slammed into the control spire of the carrier, gutting its upper levels with fire and high explosives. Its top section keeled over drunkenly, falling slowly, like the tallest tree in the forest. It slammed into the deck as Larice pulled higher and aimed her Thunderbolt towards the heavens as the Marauders swooped down like sharks with the scent of blood.

She saw the first bombs shedding from their bellies, falling like black raindrops towards the carrier. A few streams of close-in defence fire licked upwards. Some of the bombs would be caught in the flak storm, but nowhere near enough of them to make a difference.

Larice turned away from the doomed carrier, bleeding off airspeed in time to see the last rocket explode five metres from the engine of Erzyn Laquell's Thunderbolt.

The blast sheared off his aircraft's port wing and tail section, sending the aircraft into an uncontrolled downward spin.

'Punch out!' screamed Larice, 'Come on, damn you! Eject!'

But the Thunderbolt continued to fall. It smashed into a spire of ice, cartwheeling end over end in a brilliant fireball. It slammed into the ice in a blizzard of silvered shrapnel.

'Damn you, Laquell, I told you to punch out!' she yelled at the wreckage of the burning aircraft. She cut her speed as low as she dared, flying over the crash site even though she knew there was no way anyone could have survived so fierce an impact. Hot tears pricked her eyes and she pulled up and away from the carrier as thunderous detonations rocked the air with hammerblows of searing air and percussive shockwaves.

Behind her, the Archenemy mass carrier shuddered like a dying beast as the Marauders spilled their load of iron and fire upon it. Bombs punched through its decks and exploded in the hangars, the dark temples and the slave pens. They vaporised the engines, the ballast tanks, the supply halls and the torture cells.

Blazing columns of tar-black smoke coiled from its ruptured innards, hundred-metre flames roaring from its wounds like elemental blood. The air went phosphor white as a collection of incendiaries, dropped from a Marauder of the 22nd Yysarians named *Give 'em Hell*, sailed through the cratered deck of the sinking carrier and exploded in the midst of its ruptured engine core.

Larice didn't see it break in two and didn't watch as it came apart in cracking splits of unclean metal. She didn't watch it upend and spill its thousands-strong crew into the freezing water beneath the sea. She didn't watch the greatest victory any of the men and women on Amedeo had ever seen.

She flew with her wings dipped over the remains of Erzyn Laquell's Thunderbolt and felt her heart turn as cold as the ocean ice below.

'Get up,' said Seekan.

'Get out,' replied Larice.

'I said get up, Apostle Five,' said Seekan. 'And if it makes things clearer, that's an order.'

Larice rolled over, seeing Seekan silhouetted by the door of her room with a suit bag slung over his shoulder. Dressed in his heavily-medalled cream frock coat, dress blue trousers and polished boots, he looked every inch the Wing Leader of an elite squadron of Navy flyers. His hair was immaculately oiled and his thin features were almost expressionless.

Almost, but not quite.

Seekan came into the room and sat on the edge of the bed, laying the linen fabric of the suit bag across his lap. One of the advantages of taking the Aquilian as their billet meant there was plenty of space for each pilot to have their own room. What would once have housed wealthy off-world socialites now sheltered weary Naval aviators. In case of flash alerts, all their rooms were on the first floor, and Larice heard the booming strains of *Laude Beati Triumphia* coming from the ballroom. Clearly Krone was in charge of the music again: he favoured rousing marching tunes.

'Another carrier destroyed?' she asked, pulling the bed sheets around her naked body.

'No,' said Seekan. He didn't elaborate.

'Then what? None of the Apostles died.'

Winter Spear had been an unqualified success, with a combined tally of three hundred and ninety-six enemy bats accounted for in the air, together with however many were aboard the mass carrier when it sank. A total of one hundred and six Imperial craft were shot down, mostly the Die-ten-tens and Laredo bombers, but none of the attacking squadrons had come through without losses.

No squadron but the Apostles.

'None of the Apostles died, that's true,' agreed Seekan. 'But one of them learned a valuable lesson.'

'That's why you didn't offer Laquell a place, isn't it?'

Seekan nodded. 'I'm not as unfeeling as I appear, Larice. We don't have the camaraderie of other Naval wings, and now you know why. We can't afford to be friends with the people we fly alongside. Out of all the wings that fought in the attack on the carrier, we are the only ones to escape loss. Fate's wheel has turned, and once again we escape its notice. The galaxy isn't ready for us to die, and you need to show it that you don't care one way or another. You need to show it that you don't fear it, to spit into the darkness and say that nothing it can do will make the slightest bit of difference.'

Larice bunched the sheets in her fists. 'I don't know if I can.'

'You have to,' said Seekan. 'The minute you start to care, that's when they get you.'

'They?'

He shrugged. 'Fate, Death, whatever's out there in the darkness.'

'And that's what you do? Not care?'

'I do what I have to. I drink and I sing and I rage at the stars, whatever really. Each of us has his own way. You've seen that.'

'Does it help?'

'It makes it easier. I don't know if that's the same thing, but it means I can climb into the cockpit of a Thunderbolt and not care if I come back.'

Larice felt tears brimming on her eyelids, but forced them back with a swallow and grim nod. She reached for the suit bag draped across Seekan's lap.

'Give me it,' she said. 'I'll be down in ten minutes.'

Attired in her full dress uniform, Larice strode into the ballroom, her heels clicking on the hardwood floor in time with the clashing timpani of Krone's music. The Apostles gathered around the fire, drinking, arguing and behaving like naval ratings on their first shore leave in a year. Saul Cirksen had his pistol drawn and was taking potshots at the busts of forgotten notables of Amedeo.

Leena Sharto smoked a huge cigar and burned holes in the armrest of her chair, while Owen Thule knocked back shot after shot of hard liquor. Seekan gave her the briefest nod of acknowledgement as she approached. Jeric Suhr and Quint continued their endless game of regicide. Ziner Krone pressed a heavy balloon of amber-coloured liquor into her hand.

His skin gleamed dark, dangerous and powerful, and the scarring on the side of his face pulled tight in a grin as she downed the entire glass in one long swallow. It burned her, but it felt good. The heat and pain in her chest reminded her that she was alive. She looked at her fellow flyers and felt nothing for them. No emotions at all, not even contempt.

She threw the glass into the fire and it shattered with a brittle explosion.

Larice gripped Krone's jacket. She pulled his face to hers and kissed him hard on the mouth. He responded hungrily and pulled her to his wide chest.

'About time,' he said.

'Shut your mouth,' she snapped, turning and pulling him towards the stairs.

Crisp sunlight beat down on the hardstands of Coriana, heating the honeycombed landing mats, but leaving the day cold. Pilots, fitters and armourers milled back and forth between the planes, dodging speeding tow-rigs and flashing gurneys laden with missiles and ammo boxes. Peristaltic fuel lines snaked from juddering bowsers to feed the thirsty aircraft, and ground crew directed taxiing fighters and bombers to their designated runways.

Larice clambered over the upper fuselage of her cream Thunderbolt, checking the repair job the fitters had done and watching the controlled dance of military might as the Imperium took the fight to the Archenemy. With the defeat of the northern flanking thrust, all assets were being directed to aid the ground war in the west. Confidence was high that the newly established air superiority would soon result in victory.

She knelt beside an opened panel behind the canopy. The damaged armour plates had been replaced and a tangle of cables ran from the exposed mechanisms of the aircraft to a diagnostic calculus-logi servitor. One of the Martian priesthood studied the tickertape clattering from the brass-rimmed slate fitted to its chest, a soft burble of binary spilling from the shadows beneath his hood.

Larice slid over the wing to the crew ladder and swung her leg around to hook the top rung. She climbed down and dropped to the hardstand, slapping her palm on the warmed flank of her plane.

Seven Thunderbolts in the same pristine colour scheme as hers were parked in a neat row, just one of a dozen squadrons being prepped and made ready to fly. Three Lightnings surged from launch rails, powering skywards on blazing plumes of firelit smoke. She watched them go, shielding her eyes from the low sun as they rolled over their port wings to head west.

Her gaze lowered as she saw a young, good-looking pilot in a camo-green uniform approaching her. He cocked his head to one side as he drew near, like he wasn't sure he had the right person, but was going to ask anyway.

'Flight Lieutenant Asche?' he said. 'Larice Asche?'

'Yeah, who wants to know?' she said, walking down the line of her plane's fuselage.

The young man jogged after her and held out his hand.

'Flight Officer Layne Schaw,' he said with a beaming smile. 'It's an honour to meet you.'

Larice looked at the proffered hand and Schaw's earnest smile.

'Get the frig away from me,' she hissed. 'And don't tell me your name.'

MISTRESS BAEDA'S GIFT

Braden Campbell

Lord Malwrack was rich, powerful and emotionally dead inside. Even though his was a race renowned for their passions and lust for life, time had tempered him. With every passing century he became all the more desiccated, both physically and spiritually, until all that remained was a perpetually scowling, slightly hunched old man who treated each new day with a dismal contempt. It therefore came as a great surprise when he suddenly found himself in love.

Malwrack and his daughter, Sawor, had been attending one of Commorragh's endless gladiatorial games and their box seat, perched high along the curving wall of the arena, offered them a spectacular view. Sawor watched with rapt interest as below her the combatants slashed each other with razorsnares, eviscerated each other with hydraknives and turned one another into large cubes of bloody meat with the aid of a shardnet. She was young and vigorous, and her senses were sharp. Even from so far above the killing floor, Sawor could smell its erotic mixture of sweat and blood, could taste the fear and adrenaline steaming from the participants, could see the detail of sinew, flesh and bone in every severed limb.

Malwrack, on the other hand, had long ago lost most of his senses. It happened with eldar his age when they let themselves go. Taste, touch and smell were greatly diminished now, as if coming to him from behind a thick blanket. Even his sight was cloudy and, grunting in dissatisfaction and submission, he reached into the folds of his robes and withdrew an ornate pair of opera glasses. For a time he too watched the ballet of carnage below, but it didn't bring him the same exhilaration as it did Sawor. Malwrack had seen such wych-work hundreds of times before on worlds throughout the galaxy. At first he felt only a deep malaise, but as his daughter began to cheer more loudly, he felt something else: envy.

He felt that quite a lot these days, truth be told. Well aware of his own infirmity, he hated nearly everyone around him; hated them for their youth. The one exception was Sawor. She was the only person in his kabal to whom he might extend forgiveness for an attempted assassination or coup. The mere thought of her made the wrinkled corners of his mouth twitch; the faintest echo of a smile. Of all the things he owned, of all the people who served under him, she was his most favoured. There was a word, a single word, used by the other, lesser inhabitants of the galaxy to describe this feeling, but it escaped his aged brain at the moment.

Malwrack's attention drifted from the fighting, and he began to look around the stadium. His wandering gaze eventually turned to the other box seats where the Dark City's social elite sat. One came to the theatre to be seen after all, and he idly wondered who was here today. Suddenly, he stopped and sat upright. Halfway across the arena sat a woman. She was alone, flanked on either side by a pair of stalwart incubi bodyguards. Her black hair, shot through with grey, was piled high atop her head and spilled around her neck and shoulders in thick waves. Her skin was flawlessly pallid, stretched smooth and tight like a drumhead. Her eyes were dark and luminous, her lips painted obsidian. As she reclined into her throne-like chair, Malwrack saw that she wore a form-fitting suit of armour with leg greaves shaped like spike-heeled stiletto boots, and an upper section that was more like a bustier than a protective chest plate. Black evening gloves ran from her tapered fingertips to her elbows, and the train of a charcoal dress with multiple layers flowed around her. A large pendant, obviously a shadow field generator, nestled between her pale breasts.

'Who is that?' he breathed.

Sawor's head snapped around, and she raised an eyebrow. It was a rare event to see her father actually interested in something. Quickly, she followed his line of sight until she too was looking at the statuesque woman across the way. With her younger eyes, Sawor could make out the intricate spider-web pattern etched onto the woman's dress with silver thread. She rifled through her memory, comparing faces to names. As her father's most trusted aide, his sole hierarch, it was her job to know every one of Malwrack's enemies. After a few seconds, she drew a blank. 'I don't know her,' she said.

'Find out,' he muttered as he continued to stare through his glasses. 'Now.'

Sawor nodded and immediately gathered up her weapons. Grasping a glowing halberd in one hand, she checked her sidearm with the other.

'Just discover her name, Sawor,' he said. 'Nothing more.'

Disappointed that she wouldn't be killing anyone this afternoon, Sawor shrugged and left.

Malwrack watched intently as the mysterious woman sipped from a goblet. Everything about her seemed to crystallise for him: the sensual, languid way she swallowed, the colour of her fingernails as she brushed a lock of hair from her face, the slight pulsing of the drug injector tube that ran into her jugular. It was as if the longer he observed her, the younger he became. His body stirred, pulse flaring, muscles tensing. He licked his lips, salivating for the first time in a decade. Something was washing over him in a sudden wave, a feeling that had been absent from his life for so long that he shook as if electrified. He knew then, without question, that he had to have this woman, had to impress and then utterly dominate her. His sole purpose in life now was to make her his cherished yet personal property. He was head over heels in... what was that word the *mon-keigh* used?

The woman furrowed her brow suddenly, cocked her head to one side, then looked directly at Malwrack. The old archon gasped and dropped his glasses. He awkwardly gathered up his belongings, and hurried out into the hallway. His own incubi, silent as ever, followed behind him. 'Been so long,' he muttered, chastising himself for his lack of obfuscation. Within minutes he was outside, seated aboard his modified Raider, waiting for Sawor. When she arrived, she had barely enough time to grasp onto the handrail before Malwrack signalled to the pilot. The machine bobbed slightly, then rocketed off into the air.

'You're in a hurry,' Sawor said teasingly. The wind whipped her hair and skirt out behind her in fluttering purple waves.

'What did you find out?' Malwrack demanded. He leaned in closer to hear her reply.

'I couldn't get very close to her,' Sawor prefaced.

'Because of her bodyguards?'

'Because of her entourage. She might have been sitting alone in that box, but the hallway beyond was filled with people. Not just her own servants either. There were representatives from half a dozen different kabals, all apparently waiting to see or speak with her.'

'I did discover a few things though. Her name is Baeda, and she's only just moved to Commorragh from one of the outlying web cities. Shaa-Dom, I believe. She was apparently the consort of an archon there, and when he finally died, she inherited the entire kabal. Extensive resources at her disposal now, they say.'

Malwrack nodded and narrowed his eyes. That certainly explained why so many others were trying to gain access to her. A rich widow had come to town, and now the Dark City's most eligible bachelors were positioning themselves to claim her. He wondered just who his competition was.

As always, Sawor seemed to read his mind. 'I saw warriors there in several colours. The kabals of the All-seeing Eye, Poisoned Fang, and Rending Talon. That means Lord Ranisold, Lord Hoenlor and Lord Ziend.'

Malwrack knew them. Each one an up-and-comer who had managed to gain control of a kabal through exploitation and murder. They were as formidable as they were young and handsome.

'I need to get back into shape', he said.

It was some time later that Malwrack finally felt prepared enough to go and see the widow. He brought no bodyguards with him, no warriors. Only Sawor, who carried a large box and kept a respectable distance. To arrive at a woman's home with an army in tow not only betrayed fear and insecurity, he thought, but was quite rude. A deformed and mutilated servant answered the door, and ushered him through the cavernous house. As he passed an ornate mirror, Malwrack paused briefly to assess himself. His haemonculus surgeons had really outdone themselves, he thought. You could see the staples in the back of his skull that pulled his flaccid face tight. A half a dozen of his warriors had been scalped, and now his limp, greasy hair was replaced by a magnificent raven mane. A mixture of drugs and concoctions ran through his injection harness, toning his muscles and giving his eyes a healthy green glow. He curled his lips back, admiring his new stainless-steel teeth. He had dressed in his finest suit of combat armour, replete with a golden tabard, flowing purple cape and the largest shoulder pads that money could buy. This poor woman, he thought to himself, doesn't stand a chance.

He was brought into a grand sitting room filled with voluptuous, high-backed furniture. Arched windows looked out over the Commorragh cityscape. Baeda stood before them, drinking in the view. 'Lord Malwrack,' she muttered without so much as a turn of her proud head. Her voice was throaty and soft.

'Mistress Baeda,' he announced loudly. 'I welcome you to our fair city.'

At last she faced him, her eyes so black against her alabaster skin they looked like empty sockets. Her expression was that of an unreadable statue. Malwrack's pulse raced nonetheless, and his injector automatically compensated for the increased endorphin level.

'And?' she asked with some impatience.

Malwrack showed his new teeth. 'And, I come to proclaim my intentions.'

She did not swoon and fall on her knees before him as she had in Malwrack's fantasies, but instead blew out her cheeks, crossed the room and draped herself across a settee. 'Of course you do,' she said with a slight shake of her head.

Malwrack closed towards her and spread his arms wide. 'Lady, I am rich and powerful, and my kabal is composed not only of many fine warriors, but also of hireling wyches and Scourges. I command a fleet of war machines, and an armada of starships. Those who know me, fear me, and my combat prowess–'

'–is legend across the galaxy,' she finished. 'I've heard this speech.'

Malwrack was taken aback. 'You have?'

'From men more supple than you.' She looked past him then, towards Sawor and said coldly, 'At least you come with only one slave in attendance, though whether that speaks of respect or arrogance remains to be seen.'

Sawor's eyes flashed, incensed. 'I am no slave,' she hissed.

Malwrack raised a gloved hand to calm her. 'Sawor is my daughter,' he said calmly. 'She serves me willingly. Just as you must.'

Baeda's eyebrows arched. 'My, but the men in this city are bold! Do you suppose you are the first to come before me, making such overtures?'

'Not at all,' Malwrack replied. 'I know that Lord Ranisold, Lord Hoenlor and Lord Ziend covet you.'

'To name a few.'

'They pursue you no longer,' Malwrack said quietly. Sawor marched forwards, opening the box she carried. Inside, neatly arrayed, were a dozen faces, peeled away from the skulls of his competition. For the briefest of moments, an expression of shock crossed Baeda's face, but she instantly regained her composure. She stared at Malwrack.

'All that was theirs, is now mine,' he said. His gaze travelled hungrily up the length of her body. 'Just as you will be.'

With startling swiftness, Baeda was on her feet. Malwrack and Sawor were suddenly aware of incubi standing where there had been only shadows before. The tension in the air was palpable.

Baeda's voice was strained. 'You are... passionate, Lord Malwrack, but you do not impress.'

Sneering, Malwrack gave a curt nod, spun on his heel and walked towards the door. Sawor dropped the box. It clattered on the floor as she followed her father, spilling the remains of the archon's rivals like dried flowers across the parquet.

The planet Franchi was cold, its days rainy and its nights foggy. It was covered in sweeping mountain ranges, dense forests and churning oceans of grey foam. In short, it was a world that any dark eldar could appreciate, and Malwrack was determined to present it to Baeda as a gift. In fact, Franchi had only one flaw: there were humans living on it. So, the old archon got to work.

First, his air force lanced and bombed their paltry fortifications and bastions. Then, once they had only ruins in which to hide, he unleashed his main forces upon the surviving defenders. His Raiders glided silently over the smashed cityscape, indiscriminately firing grenades into bunker and building alike. The corrupted wraithbone spheres exploded into a chalky powder so fine that even the Imperium's best filtration system couldn't completely block it out. It made its way into eyes, ears, and lungs, and once there, created such terrifying hallucinations that those affected could do nothing but scream and wail. As they rolled on the ground, clawing at their faces and gouging out their own eyes, Malwrack's warriors shot the good people of Franchi with hails of poisoned crystal shards or ran them through with bayonets. Those who weren't killed outright were hauled to their feet and bound with lengths of barbed chain. They would be spared a quick and painless death, lingering instead for years or even decades as slaves, playthings and foodstuffs when the dark eldar returned to Commorragh.

All in all, it was a thrilling, glorious time and Malwrack's followers delighted in it. Yet, he himself was strangely uninterested. He knew he should have been right there in the thick of it, revelling in the murder and mayhem. Instead, he stood alone in a city square filled with toppled monuments and heaps of dead humans, watching everyone else have all the fun. His thoughts remained focussed on Baeda.

He waded ankle-deep through spilled intestines, as fragrant to him as the flowers of spring, but all he could see was her face. Nearby, a commissar was struggling to free himself from where he lay pinned beneath the remains of his men. One of Malwrack's sybarite lieutenants ran up gleefully and shot him square in the face, detonating the man's head like an overripe melon. There were squeals of delight from the other warriors who watched the brain and bone fragments fly outwards like ruby-coloured fireworks.

All Malwrack felt was a burning desire to throw the widow to the floor and suffocate her body beneath his. To him, the slaughter on Franchi was work, not play. He committed genocide as one might polish silver, because his gift to her must be unblemished. It was irrational he knew, but he had to impress her. After all, he was in... he was in.... the *monkeigh* word escaped him again.

His soldiers were now carving up the dead bodies with their knives, taking small trophies such as fingers, ears or teeth. He looked up at them from within his distracted thoughts and was about to say something, when there was an explosion. For a brief second, Malwrack saw his men engulfed in fire. Then, the ground beneath him heaved upwards and he was in freefall. Instincts taking over, he pulled his limbs in tight to his body and rode the shock wave. His personal force field flared to life, wrapping him tightly in a cocoon of black energy and utterly protecting him. Even when he hit the ground, the shadowy field absorbed the impact that would otherwise have shattered every bone in his willowy frame. Malwrack rolled up onto his feet, and sensing somehow that he was safe for the moment, the field became transparent.

Rumbling towards him out of the smoky haze was an Imperial tank, behind which he could make out several dozen human forms. He glanced behind him, but where his warriors had been a moment before, there was now only a smoking crater. Body parts were scattered everywhere, humans and dark eldar now indistinguishable from one another in death. Fury swept though Malwrack's mind; he had ordered all of Franchi's war machines to be neutralised before his main forces moved into the city, but obviously, something had been overlooked. As technologically underdeveloped as the *mon-keigh* were, he knew from painful experience that his forces stood little chance of survival unless this mechanical monstrosity was immediately destroyed.

The Guardsmen, who had been cowering behind the tank, were now fanning out around it. They were lightly armed, save for a trio who hastily began assembling a large cannon of some kind. Malwrack was alone, and out in the open. He snarled, disgusted with himself for letting this happen. He had not been focussed on the here and now, but had been distracted again by thoughts of how best to debase and titillate the widow Baeda. Then, as he often did, he redirected his loathing outwards, vomiting it upon the Guardsmen. There was a clunking sound from within the tank as it loaded another shell into place. Malwrack knew he had only one hope. He jerked his neck sharply, activating his drug injector, and charged.

The humans opened up with everything they had. They spat out a rain of lasgun fire and heavy bolter rounds. Autocannon shells flew wildly. The tank fired its main gun with a deafening roar, and the men who were huddled around its bulk winced and closed their eyes. The square exploded. For a moment, there was nothing to see but dust and smoke, but then a singular form leapt forwards, high into the air, and plunged down into their midst.

Malwrack's right hand was sheathed by an enormous glove with short swords in place of fingers. He flicked this now, activating its agony-inducing electrical properties, and killed three Guardsmen before the rest of the platoon could even blink. Their corpses twitched wildly and collapsed like discarded puppets. Then, they were all around him, punching, kicking, trying vainly to beat him with their rifles. Malwrack was calm and collected, his breathing controlled as he parried their blows. He found the humans almost comical in their ferocity; they did more frothing, cursing and grunting than they did actual damage. Still, they pressed in, refusing to break or flee. They pummelled away, hammering on his protective field as if trying to chisel rock with their bare hands.

It was mildly admirable, so Malwrack killed few, opting to maim instead. He swept another of them off his feet, removing the man's leg as he did so. Each time he slashed or stabbed, another Guardsman went down. They piled around his feet, wailing and screaming, whispering prayers to their God-Emperor or calling out for their mothers.

Suddenly, the telltales on Malwrack's forearm bracer lit up. His shadow field was a formidable piece of technology, but it was not infallible. There was only so much punishment it could take before it either overloaded or shut down to recharge itself. With a popping sound, it collapsed, and as it did, the butt of a lasgun slammed into his face. The old archon's head snapped around violently, and inky blood sprayed out from between his steel teeth. Malwrack glared back at the man who had actually managed to hurt him, and drove the agoniser through his face. Arcs of electricity hissed and sparked. The man's eyes liquefied and ran down his cheeks, while he wailed like a thing possessed. The remaining Guardsmen recoiled at the sight and, while they were momentarily stunned, Malwrack finished them off in a whirling flourish. He killed four of them outright. The rest he left lying on the ground, fodder for his slave takers.

Beside him, the tank was trying to reposition itself so that it could once again bring its weapons to bear on him. Malwrack's eyes grew wide in horror. For a moment, caught up in the rush of the melee, he had forgotten all about the thing. Now, he realised that without his protective shield, any one of the machine's weapons would tear him in half. Certain that he was about to die, his last thought was of Sawor. She would lead the kabal in his stead, and she would do it well. His only regret was that he would no longer be around to see her come into her own.

Miraculously, the turret rotated away from him to face back into the square. Malwrack glanced over to see a Ravager coming to his rescue, firing as it came. Beams of black energy burrowed into the armoured side of the tank, and with a tortured sound, its turret exploded into twisted metal ribbons. Gouts of flame burst from every seam and joint, and its sponson weapons sagged. Malwrack recovered his composure and strode towards the waiting gunboat. Already, the gunnery crew was leaping down from the running boards and rushing to meet him.

'My lord,' one of them panted, 'are you all right?'

The archon pointed to the destroyed remains of the tank. 'Who is responsible for this?' he asked.

'An oversight,' another of his soldiers replied as bat-like aircraft raced across the sky. 'A military base outside of the city that escaped our orbital survey. It's being dealt with as we speak.'

Malwrack watched the jets pass, trailing sonic booms behind them. 'Well then,' he said, 'let's make certain it's properly taken care of.'

When at last he arrived, there was little left of the Imperial base save for wreckage. Buildings burned out of control. Dead Guardsmen and destroyed vehicles lay scattered about. A single bunker remained; its solitary door had been wrenched free.

Within it, his warriors reported, a handful of scared refugees had holed up in the hope that they might be spared. Lord Malwrack descended a narrow set of concrete steps into a damp, square room littered with blankets and pre-packaged food wrappers. The only light came from a few dim panels set into the walls. Four dead bodies lay splashed across the floor, the handiwork of his sybarites. The last two survivors had been reserved for him.

Malwrack assessed them quickly: a male and female, dressed in soiled, khaki uniforms accentuated only by identification tags around his neck, and a diamond ring on one of her fingers. They sat in a corner with their arms wrapped tightly around one another. The female buried her face in the man's chest, muting her sobs. He in turn rocked her gently and tried to whisper soothing words of comfort.

'Well,' Malwrack said joylessly. 'Best get this over with.'

At the sound of his voice, the man looked up, his eyes wide. 'Please,' he spat in his ineloquent tongue. 'We know what you are. Please, don't take us away with you.'

'Not to worry, *mon-keigh*,' he said in clipped Low Gothic. 'It's not you I'm after. Just your planet.'

In the name of expedience, he pulled his pistol from its holster, intending to shoot the female. Then, quite unexpectedly, there was an explosion of movement as the man launched himself forwards. He grabbed Malwrack's left wrist, bending it upwards, and a cloud of splinters tore into the ceiling. In a single motion Malwrack slammed his forehead down onto the human's nose, jerked his knee into the man's stomach, and drove an elbow into his back when he doubled over. Malwrack effortlessly shifted his weight, and kicked him square in the chest. The man's body collapsed against a computer display screen. Glass shattered and sparks flew. Malwrack leapt and drove his bladed glove through flesh, bone and concrete flooring. He snorted loudly as he inhaled the man's escaping life essence.

This, it seemed, was finally enough to snap the female out of her paralysis. She ran over to her partner's body, howling, and draped herself across it.

He chambered another round into his pistol, and looked down at the female. 'He doesn't deserve so touching a tribute as your tears and wails,' he said to her. 'Why do you weep for such an insignificant man?'

She glared at him with her cornered animal eyes. 'He was my husband,' she roared. 'I loved him!'

Malwrack suddenly brightened. He snapped the fingers of his gloved hand, and pointed at her with one of its talons. 'That's it!' he said with glee. 'That's the word I've been trying to remember. Thank you.'

Seeing her bewilderment, he knelt down to be at eye level. 'You know, it just so happens that I am in love myself. Tell me, did it take much for him to dominate you?'

'Dominate me?' she asked dumbly.

'Yes. We say *inyon lama-quanon*: to make another person one's prized property or subservient. But I like your barbaric term, "love". It's concise, powerful, like a killing blow.'

The woman stifled a hysterical laugh. 'I always thought the xenos profiles were exaggerated, but you really believe it, don't you? That there's nothing more to life than degrees of enslavement.'

'I'm afraid I don't follow,' Malwrack said.

'Love is about being together,' she continued. 'It's a sharing experience, an equal partnership. No ownership. No control. Love is about caring for someone so much that you can't bear to be apart.' She looked down at the blood-soaked remains of her husband and began to weep again.

Malwrack thought about the things he owned: his collection of hell-masks, his agonisers, his spire in Commorragh, his followers. Certainly he had his favourites among these, people and possessions held in high esteem. Yet, he was still confused. Sharing? Partnership? Perhaps he had been trying to remember the wrong word.

'Now kill me,' the woman said with impertinence.

'Kill you,' the archon said slowly, 'so that you can be together again.'

The woman did not reply, and the warriors crowded in the doorway held their collective breath. Malwrack stood, his ancient knees popping, and holstered his gun. He glanced towards his lieutenants and with a curt nod, they filed up and out of the bunker. He turned to do likewise.

The woman gasped. 'What are you doing?'

'Leaving you to savour your agony, of course.'

He lingered in the doorway, waiting for her to say something courteous, but she simply stared at him, agape. Perhaps it was too much to expect proper manners from the *mon-keigh*. After a moment he sighed and said, 'You're welcome'. Then he left her to revel in her pain, if it were even possible. Poor, limited creature that she was, Malwrack doubted the woman could properly appreciate a decent bout of anguish.

However, it seemed ingratitude was a quality not limited to human females. Upon his return to the Dark City, Malwrack went to Baeda's home to present her with Franchi. Her servant informed him carefully that Baeda refused to see him. She relayed that she had no interest in the planet he had ransacked for her, for she had worlds and captives of her own. Frothing, Malwrack considered forcing his way inside, but thought better of it when confronted by a pair of Baeda's incubi. Attacking them would be an open declaration of war, and despite his growing frustration, he wanted to win the widow, not slay her.

Sawor was exercising when he returned home. Stripped down to the barest of coverings, skin glistening, she ducked and weaved her way around a half-dozen sparring partners wielding serrated knives. Shallow cuts adorned her arms, legs and abdomen, and her oily sweat made them sting gloriously. Part training, part foreplay, she loved these midday sessions almost as she did actual combat. All activity screeched to a halt however when Malwrack threw the doors wide.

'That woman!' he bellowed, spittle flying from his mouth. 'I'll make her choke on her arrogance.'

Sawor made a shooing motion with her hand and her companions backed away fearfully. She had seen her father angry many times, but this was something different. He reminded her of some caged monster that the wyches might fight in the arena, incoherent with frustration and rage.

'She defeated you in a fight?' she asked hopefully, thinking it to be the only logical explanation. 'Are our kabals now at war?'

'She wouldn't even see me,' he said breathlessly. 'I kill her suitors, but I do not impress. I go through all the effort of cleansing a planet for her, and she spurns it.'

Sawor bit her upper lip and said 'Father, you have my fear and respect, but you know nothing about women. Trophies? Planets? How could you expect her to be impressed by you when you gift her with such commonalities? She has standards, Father. If you want her, truly want her, you are going to have to give her something unique. Something that no one else has ever dared to.'

The old archon deflated a little. Had anyone else tried to quench his fury, he would have slain them in a stroke, but Sawor was different. As always, she was like a salve placed on a burn; thankfully the pain remained, but the ferocity of it was dimmed.

'You're right, of course,' he muttered. 'Something that takes her breath away. Makes her realise, instantly, that it's in her best interest to yield to me.'

He thought again of the married couple on Franchi. The woman had loved the man, but why? What had he given her in exchange for her submission? She had been the plainest creature in existence, practically rag-clad, except for–

Malwrack placed a hand on Sawor's shoulder. 'Gather the kabal,' he said. 'Our entire force. I know now what to give Mistress Baeda.'

Cthelmax was a desert world. Outside a baleful sun beat down, but here, in the vast interior of the tomb complex, it was so cool that Malwrack could see his breath when he spoke. He and Sawor stood bathed in an eerie green glow. In all other directions stretched an inky blackness, stabbed by beams of light as the warriors set up a defensive perimeter and studied how best to abscond with their prize.

'Do you know what human males customarily use to buy the loyalty of their women?' Malwrack asked his daughter. 'Stones. Lumps of compressed carbon, especially.'

'I've never understood your fascination with *mon-keigh* culture,' Sawor answered distractedly. There was something about this place, this city-sized mausoleum that genuinely frightened her. The sooner they left here, the better.

Malwrack was too enraptured to notice the slight. 'I have no idea what this thing is actually made of, but its size and rarity should finally stifle that damned widow.' He turned to Sawor and laughed.

The necrontyr power crystal towered above them. Its base fitted into some kind of circular pedestal from which arcane conduits ran off in all directions. It glowed from within, but dimly, like a lamp nearly out of oil. A sybarite approached and informed Malwrack that the men were ready to disconnect it. The archon nodded impatiently.

Sawor frowned. 'I think you misunderstood me. When I said you had to give her something no one else could, I didn't mean–'

The green light went out suddenly, as the crystal was separated from its base. It grew very dark, and very still.

Malwrack clapped his hands together. 'Right, let's get this back home.'

Sawor walked a few steps away. Her breath came in short spasms. There was something stirring here now, touching her latent senses. Then she heard it. Over the grunts of the men working, and of her father barking orders, there was a scraping sound from the blackness. Metal on stone. Tiny dots appeared in the distance, and for a moment Sawor thought that some kind of phosphorescent carpet was undulating towards them with fantastic speed.

Realisation splashed over her like cold water. 'Father!' she screamed.

Then the scarabs were on them, surging forwards like a wave. They swarmed around the disconnected crystal with hissing, chittering sounds. The warriors attempted to defend themselves with pistols and knives even as the tiny machines slashed at their leg armour.

Malwrack backed away and jerked his neck, feeling the drugs pour through him. He had time to see Sawor do likewise before his incubi formed a protective circle around him. From the darkness above, massive forms were descending with thick, pointed legs unfurling. Their faces were tightly packed clusters of camera lenses, glowing brightly. They made a churning noise, and from their abdomens more scarabs appeared, raining down. The archon's bodyguards began to slash out with their pole arms, their every motion fluid. Malwrack activated his shadow field, and shoved his way between two of his protectors. One of the tiny machines tried to amputate his foot. He impaled it on his bladed glove for its trouble.

He had an unobstructed view now. The power crystal, its base and everyone who had been standing on or around it were covered by hundreds of tiny insectoid robots. For each one his soldiers killed, the large spider-forms floating above made several more. Sawor was in full swing, surrounded by wyches and attacking anything that got too close to her. She was shouting something, but Malwrack couldn't make it out.

A moment later, there was a rush of hot wind and the sound of rocket engines. Sawor had called in reinforcements from their base camp outside, Malwrack surmised. More soldiers leapt from Raiders while behind them several slower-moving gunboats began to blow the scarabs apart with volleys from their energy cannons. The horde of machines began to thin. One of the large spiders crashed to the floor in a pool of slag.

As if in response to the shifting tide of battle, twisting streams of green fire stabbed forth from out of the darkness. Humanoid shapes were slouching towards them, skeletal and hunched; cumbersome weapons hung heavy in their hands. Every soldier they hit flew apart into piles of burned flesh and charred bones. The gunboats began to ignore the scarabs and turned their attention to this new threat.

There was a bright flash to Malwrack's left that cast twisted shadows across the broken floor. Another group of necrons, nearly two dozen in all, suddenly appeared. Above them floated a machine that looked like one of the scarab-making spiders with a skeletal torso fused to the top. In one hand, it raised a long stave. In the other was a glowing sphere. The ones on the ground immediately began firing their rifles. Two of the incubi were killed outright, but the armour of the others withstood the barrage. The archon's protective field turned opaque in several places, protecting his eyes from the blinding beams as it saved his body from vaporisation. Then it was his turn.

Malwrack leapt the distance and slashed out with his gauntleted hand. Five of the machines collapsed, heads severed and torsos ripped open. Wires spilled gut-like onto the ground. Behind him, his remaining retinue thrust forwards with their pole arms. Nine more of the things were destroyed. The floating machine brought its stave around in a sweeping arc, effortlessly decapitating two incubi, and the remaining necrons fell into the melee. There was a flurry of blows, all of which Malwrack easily parried. Then, responding to some command only they could hear, the machines began moving backwards, stunned perhaps at the ferocity of the dark eldar attack.

Malwrack let them retreat for the moment, and struggled to locate Sawor amidst the chaos. Despite the great strides he was making, the rest of his kabal was not faring half as well. Two of his gunboats were floating helplessly, abandoned by their crews and gutted by fire. The bodies of his soldiers were piling up everywhere, blackened and smoking. Amidst them, dead necrons were staggering back to their feet, reassembling themselves somehow until they again looked like gunmetal skeletons. Worse yet, two of the giant spiders were setting the crystal back into place. Newly minted scarabs swirled around them like a river of chrome. An archon came to power by knowing two things: when to fight, and when to run. For Malwrack, it was time to run.

'Back to the boats!' he yelled.

Those that could, began to fall back, weapons blazing and throats screaming. Malwrack and his remaining two guards ran to where Sawor stood alone again. Bodies, both flesh and bone and metallic, lay in pieces all around her. She herself was bleeding from a score of lacerations, none of which seemed to slow her down or lessen her fury. Malwrack grabbed her forearm, dragging her from atop the charnel pile, and together they sprinted towards a nearby Raider. Bolts of green energy flew around them. The last incubi staggered and fell, but Malwrack never so much as glanced back at his erstwhile defenders. If none but he and Sawor escaped this, he would consider the day a victory.

Underlings were clamouring around the transport. Malwrack shot one of them and impaled another, flinging the man into the encroaching necron phalanx. Sawor, following suit, lopped off the arm of one warrior who refused to give up his place for her. The machine lurched violently before it blasted up and out of the tomb. Dark walls sped past them as they raced towards the exit. Sawor held on tightly and craned her neck to look behind them. A squadron of necron vehicles was in pursuit, firing powerful beams at them, but their speed was no greater. The Raider would make it to surface first, where their base camp and a portal to Commorragh awaited. Despite all the carnage, it seemed that she and Malwrack would live to fight another day. Sawor looked over at her father. He met her gaze, and realising the same thing, he actually smiled.

They were almost to the exit when the Raider crashed. Without warning, serpentine enemies emerged from the walls and floor of the tomb. They lashed out with pointed tails and monstrously bladed hands, tearing through the hull and engine housing. The transport pitched downwards and cartwheeled through space with a terrible velocity. It careened through the exit, and impacted on the sand outside, crumpling and shearing. Malwrack's shadow field flared into protective mode, turning pitch-black as he was thrown free of the wreckage.

How long he lay there, Malwrack had no way of telling. His shadow field was clear, so any danger was apparently past. Slowly he sat up. While he waited for his vision to stop swimming, he registered a pile of flaming wreckage, a half-dozen bodies clad in purple armour and the silent entrance to the tomb. Presumably, the necrons within were under no instructions to pursue invaders out here into the desert. He looked around for Sawor, but didn't see her. He called her name, but there was no response from anyone. He called again, louder. Still no reply. With a twinge of panic, he limped to the bulk of the downed Raider.

He found her beneath one of the running boards, literally folded in half. Jagged pieces of the transport protruded from her in several places, the most gruesome of which exited through her gaping mouth. He made a mewling sound and dropped down to her side. He inhaled desperately, but there was nothing there. Her life essence, her soul, had dissipated. She was dead beyond any haemonculus's resuscitational skill.

'Get up,' he said.

He stood once more and looked down at her shattered form. 'Get up,' he repeated. 'I order you to get up.'

Malwrack realised with a start that he was powerless. No beating, no threat, no command would make her live again. This was not the way it was supposed to have happened, his kabal gutted, his successor gone.

He activated the portal back to Commorragh, and strode purposefully through the gate, oblivious to the fact that as he did so, he was crying.

When her servant refused him entry, he kicked down the door. When five of her incubi formed a wall across the foyer, he gutted two of them in a flash, and massacred the rest as they tried to fall back. On the grand staircase that led up to her personal chambers, an entire unit of warriors fired their weapons at him. He walked through the hail of splinters and, with shadow field blazing darkly, killed every last one of them. Then, he made his way upstairs. Throwing the doors wide, he found her in the room with arched windows where he and Sawor had first come to see her. She bolted off her settee, one hand flying up to her pendant, the other pulling an ornate handgun from the folds of her dress. Malwrack strode in, arms wide, eyes unblinking, head lowered. His tattered cape flowed behind him like a purple sea.

'What does a man have to do around here to get a little attention?' he roared.

Two more incubi, lying in ambush behind the door, lunged at his back. Malwrack spun low. His gauntleted hand tore out the throat of one assailant, then flashed back to impale the other before either one could even land a blow. When he rose and faced Baeda again, his forearm was dripping with gore.

She backed away, slowly, never taking her eyes off him. 'To what do I owe the pleasure?' she asked coldly.

'Don't you be coy,' he growled. 'Don't you even dare.'

'Is this about that planet you wanted to give me?'

He kicked a chair with such force that it sailed across the room. 'You know what this is about! It's about you. You've destroyed me.'

Baeda noticed then that something was terribly wrong with his face. Streams of water were gushing uncontrollably from his eyes. She'd never seen the like.

'I tried so hard to win you, and all you did was spurn me. I killed for you, and all you could say was that I did not impress. I should have stopped even then, just called the whole thing off and moved on, but I couldn't. It was like you'd infected me. You were all I could think about.

'I gave you a world, but you wouldn't even see me. Why wouldn't you see me? If you'd just let me in that day, she'd still be here, but no, you thought it would be more fun to refuse me. Was that your plan, mistress, to starve me? Like a dog? Deprive me of your presence until I just went rabid?'

He was babbling, Baeda saw, hyperventilating and lost in a dark train of thought. She could have shot him dead right then and there, he was so distracted, yet there was something about his behaviour that was fascinating.

'Who would still be here?' she asked him.

'Well, it worked,' he continued. 'I swore that I would have you, Baeda. *Inyon lama-quanon*. To the detriment of everything else. My followers, my armies, all gone. My kabal is finished because of you; because I became so enraptured, and thought I'd finally found the perfect gift with which to win you.'

He still had not answered her question, and so she asked again. 'Malwrack, who would still be here?'

The old archon appeared to deflate, shoulders stooping, his chest caving in. He gave a heart-wrenching sigh and said, 'Sawor.'

Outside the room, Baeda could hear running footsteps. More of her soldiers and protectors were rushing to her defence. They would surely kill the old man, by weight of numbers if not by martial skill. Yet, she had to hear him out first. His tears, his ragged breathing, his palpable aura of loss were entrancing.

When he spoke again, his voice was almost inaudible. 'I took her to Cthelmax. There are ruins there. Very well preserved. I looked over at her. I was so certain that we would be all right. Then she was gone.'

Weapons clicked into readiness behind him as Baeda's forces piled into the room. At the slightest signal from her, they would open fire, and that would be the end of Lord Malwrack. He seemed to take no notice, however. Instead, his whole being shuddered, and he collapsed at the widow's feet.

'She's gone!' he cried from a place so dark, it made Baeda gasp. Malwrack could see now that Sawor had been no mere hierarch. She had been his sounding board, his strong-arm, his partner in all things. She had been his most prized possession, and he had loved her. He would never be complete again, and thus, there was no point in his life continuing. Sobbing, he waited only for a volley of splinter fire or a killing blow from Baeda to end it all.

He felt her lift him up. Spent, he didn't resist. Baeda looked him square in the face, placed a hand on each of his cheeks, and clamped her mouth over his. Malwrack was certain she was giving him the kiss of death, but it just went on and on. Instead of stabbing or shooting him, he felt Baeda's body soften and press into his. Her tongue darted around his steel teeth. Her fingers dug into his cheeks. He kissed her back and wrapped his arms around her so tightly that her body armour creaked. When she finally pulled away, she had a dreamy expression on her face.

'*Lama-quanon*,' she said. 'I yield to you.'

'I don't understand,' Malwrack said. 'I have no kabal left to fight you with. You wouldn't take the planet, and I couldn't retrieve the crystal, so I have nothing with which to buy your obedience.'

'Of course you do,' she purred as her long fingers traced his wrinkled brow. 'You've given me the greatest gift imaginable: your suffering. There's a void in you now, a delicious emptiness that will never heal. Say you'll always give that to me, that you'll feed me with it the rest of our days, and all that I have will be yours.'

Malwrack looked over his shoulder at the horde of warriors behind him. Baeda began scratching at his armour as if she meant to undress him here, immediately, and in front of everyone, cement their new partnership in a torrent of public lovemaking.

A smirk slowly crept across Malwrack's face. He had squandered one kabal only to inherit another. These soldiers would live and die at his command, and he was not, after all, defeated. Malwrack pointed to the doorway, and after a moment, the soldiers lowered their heads and shuffled out. He threw his bladed gauntlet to the floor, increased the flow to his drug injector, and grabbing a fistful of her hair, wrenched Baeda's head back. She smiled at him. Soon he and the widow would ride out across the galaxy together, inflicting anguish on any who could bear it. With his experience and Baeda's resources, there would be no stopping them. He could avenge his daughter's death a thousandfold upon the whole of creation.

'It's going to be glorious,' Baeda said cryptically. She kissed Malwrack again, deep and long. Through the window behind them, the spires and lights of the Dark City watched without comment.

FLESH

Chris Wraight

Fifty years ago, they took my left hand.

I watched, conscious, heavy-headed with stimms and pain suppressants. I watched the knives go in, peeling back the skin, picking apart muscle and sinew.

They had trouble with the bones. I had changed by then and the ossmodula had turned my skeleton as hard as plasteel. They used a circular saw with glittering blades to cut through the radius and ulna. I can still hear its screaming whine.

They were simply following protocol. Indeed, they were further along the path than I was and there was something to be learned from the way they operated.

I kept it together. I am told that not everyone does.

It took three weeks for the new mechanism to bed down. The flesh chafed for a long time after that, red-raw against the metal of the implant.

I would wake and see it, an alien presence, bursting from the puffed and swollen stump of my left arm. I flexed iron fingers and watched micropistons and balance-nodes slide smoothly past one another. It looked delicate, though I knew it was stronger than the original had been.

Stronger, and better. Morvox spent a long time with me, explaining the benefits. He cast the issue in terms of pragmatism, of efficiency margins. Even back then I knew there was more to it than that.

This was an aesthetic matter. A matter of form. We were changing ourselves to comply with the dictates of taste.

Do not mistake this for regret. I do not regret what has been done to me. I cannot regret, not in any true sense.

My iron hand functions competently. It serves, just as I serve. It is an implement, just as I am an implement. No praise can be higher.

But my old flesh, the part of me that was immolated in the rite, overseen by those machine faces down in the forges, I do not forget it.

I will, one day. Like Morvox, I will not remember anything but the aesthetic imperative.

Not yet. For now, I still feel it.

I

From the Talex to Majoris, then over to the spine shafts and the turboclimbers. Levels swept by, all black, mottled with grime. Out of Station Lyris, and things got cleaner. Then up past the Ecclesiast Cordex, taking grav-bundles staffed by greyshirts, and into the Administratum quarter. That looked a lot like real grass on the lawns, baking under hololamps, before up again, through Securum and the plexiglass domes of the Excelsion.

Then things were really sparkling. Gleaming ceramics, floor-to-ceiling glass panels. You could forget the rest of the hive, the kilometres of squalid, close-pressed humanity, rammed into the angles between spires and manufactoria.

Right at the top, right where the tip of Ghorgonspire pierced the heavy orange fug of the sky, it felt like you'd never need a gland-deep dermoscrub again. You could imagine that everything on Helaj V was pristine and smooth as a Celestine's conscience.

Raef Khamed, being a man of the world, was not prone to think that. He stalked up to Governor Tralmo's offices, still in his Jenummari fatigues, still stinking from what had happened in 45/331/aX and from the journey up. His lasgun banged against his right thigh, loose in its waist-slung holster. It needed a recharge. He needed a recharge. He'd emptied himself out on those bastards, and they just kept coming.

The two greyshirts flanking the doors saw him coming and snapped their heels.

'Jen,' they said in rough unison, making the aquila.

'She's in there?' asked Khamed, pushing the door open.

'She is,' came a voice from inside the chamber. 'Shut the doors behind you.'

He went in, and did as he was told.

Khamed stood in a large circular chamber. The floor was veined stone, grey and pink. False windows lined the walls, looking out on to false meadows and false skies. A bonestone statue of Sanguinius Redemptor stood by the walls, pious and gloomy.

There was a desk at the far end, but it was empty. Set off to one side, three low couches had been set around a curved table.

In one of the couches sat Governor Planetary Anatova Tralmo, tight-skinned from a century of rejuvenat and with oil-shimmer hair. Next to her was Astropath Majoris Eridh, milk-eyed and staring.

'How goes it?' Tralmo asked as Khamed sat down. She winced a little as his grimy fatigues marked the cream surface of the couch.

'Awful,' said Khamed, not noticing. 'Bloody awful. I'm not even going to try to describe what I saw this time.'

The Governor nodded sympathetically.

'Then you'll like this, I hope. Eridh?'

'A response,' said the astropath, looking at Khamed in that eerie, sightless way of his. 'Two cycles back, just deciphered and verified.'

Khamed's weary face lit up. He'd begun to doubt there'd be one.

'Throne,' he said, letting his relief show. The time for bravado was long gone. 'At last. Regiment?'

'It's not a Guard signal, Jenummari.'

'Then what? Who?'

Eridh handed him a data-slate with a summary of the transmission, elucidated into verbose Helaj vernac.

Khamed looked at it, and his muscles tensed. He read it again, just to be sure. He discovered he was holding the slate rather too tightly.

If he'd been less tired, he might have hidden his response better. As it was, when he looked up, he knew he'd given everything away. For the first time, he noticed the air of tight expectation on Tralmo's face.

Khamed had always liked her. Tralmo was tough. She didn't shake easily and had been good during the difficulties.

Just then, she looked like she was going to throw up.

'How long have we got?' he asked, conscious of the sudden hoarseness in his voice.

'Less than a standard Terran,' replied Tralmo. 'I want you to meet them, Raef. It's protocol. We should keep this military to military.'

Khamed swallowed. He was still holding the slate too tightly.

'Got you.'

Bitch.

The docking bay doors were a metre thick. They dragged open, grinding along rust-weakened rails. Outside, the platform was open to the elements. On Helaj, the elements were always hateful.

Tracer lights winked in the orange gale. Further out, deeper into the sub-zero atmospheric bilge, more lights whirled. The storm roared, just as it always did, grumbling away like a maddened giant turning in its sleep.

There was another roar over the platform, closer to hand than the storm, and it came from the blurred outline of a ship. The thing was a brute, far larger than the shuttles that normally touched down at the spire summit.

Khamed couldn't make much out through the muck – his visor was already clouding up – but the engine backwash was huge. As he'd watched it come down on the local augurs he'd seen rows of squat gun barrels along its flanks, gigantic thruster housings and glimpses of a single infamous insignia.

That hadn't made him feel well. He was on edge. His hands were sweaty even in the thick gloves of his environment suit. His heart hadn't stopped thumping.

His men, twelve lostari lined up behind him, weren't any better. They stared into the raging clouds ahead, their weapons clutched tight, held diagonally across their body armour.

We're all soiling ourselves. Throne of Earth, trooper – get a handle on this.

The roar transmuted into a booming thunderclap, and the ship pulled away, back into the raging cloudscape. Its dark outline faded quickly, though the noise of those engines lingered for much longer.

New shapes emerged from the smog-filth, resolving into clarity like a carcharex out of the acid sea.

Five of them.

The Imperial Guard garrison in Ghorgonspire was over a hundred thousand strong. They'd made no progress against the incursion for six local lunars, which converted into a lot longer if you went with Terran.

Five of them. *Five.*

'Formal,' hissed Khamed over the vox.

His men snapped their ankles together and stared rigidly ahead.

The quintet approached. Khamed swallowed, and looked up.

Their armour was night-black and plainer than he'd expected. There were white markings on the shoulder-guards, but the finish was matt. Blunt, uncomplicated.

There was no getting away from the size of them. He'd been warned what to expect from Namogh, who'd witnessed a squad of Argent Sabres twenty years ago while on an exchange placement off-world.

'You never get used to it,' he'd said, his ugly face thoroughly disapproving. 'You think, *that's a machine. It has to be.* But in there, there's a man. And then it moves, all that plate, tonnes and tonnes of it, and you know it can move quicker than you can, it can kill you quicker than you can blink, and then you think: I was right the first time. It is a machine, a nightmare machine, and if we need to make a thing like this to keep us alive, then the universe is a scary place.'

Their armour hummed. It was barely audible over the roar of the storm, but you knew it was there. Just like the ship Khamed had seen, the power stored up in those black shells was obvious. They didn't need to hide it. They didn't want to hide it. They strode – *strutted* – up to him, every movement soaked in menace and confidence and contempt.

Khamed bowed.

'Welcome to Helaj V, lords,' he said, and was disgusted to hear how his voice carried a tremor even over the tinny transmission of his helm vox. 'We're grateful to have you.'

'I think that unlikely,' came the response. It was machine-clipped. 'But here we are. I am Iron Father Naim Morvox of the Iron Hands. Brief me as we descend, then the cleansing will begin.'

'They come up from the underhive. We isolate the spearheads and respond with contagion-pattern suppression.'

Khamed had to trot beside the stalking figure of Morvox as he tried to explain the situation. The Iron Hands Space Marine made no effort to slow down and kept up a punishing, metronomic stride. Behind him, the other four giants matched pace. Their heavy treads clunked on the polished surface of the transit corridor. Khamed's own men trailed in their wake.

'With little success,' observed Morvox. His voice. It was a strangely muted sound to come out of such a monstrous mouthpiece. Like all the Iron Hands squad, Morvox kept his helm on. The faceplate was a blank, dark mask.

'We've succeeded in keeping them from the upper hive,' replied Khamed, knowing how weak that sounded.

Morvox was approaching the honour guard: fifty lostari in greyshirt trim, ranked on either side of the corridor, guns hoisted.

'But you have not eliminated the source.'

'Not yet, no.'

From somewhere, Khamed heard Namogh's voice call the troops to attention, and their ankles slammed together. It wasn't done smoothly. The men were nervous.

'I need access to your hive schematics,' said Morvox, ignoring the troops and carrying on down the corridor. 'When did it happen?'

'8.2 Standard Terran lunars ago,' replied Khamed, shrugging an apology as he sailed past Namogh's position. His deputy looked even more irritated than usual. 'Insurgents control fifty-five per cent, all lower hive. We have no access to the levels below the base forge.'

'And I'll need full asset inventory. All troops are under my command. What is your name?'

Only now. Now you ask.

'Raef Khamed, Jenum–'

'You will remain with me. We will commence assault as soon as I have the data. Your men will be mobilised by then and I will order their deployment.'

'Very good. The men stand read–'

'Warn them they will need to be.'

They passed from the long corridor, through a pair of slide doors and into an octagonal command node. The walls were lined with picts. There were cogitator banks along the near flank, attended to by servitors bearing the cog-skull of the Mechanicus. Hololiths shimmered over projection pillars showing various cross-sections of the Ghorgonspire.

Morvox stopped walking. He said nothing, but his squad immediately fanned out and began to assimilate information from the picts. One of them pushed a servitor aside and extruded a dataclaw from a compartment in his gauntlet. None of them spoke out loud, though Khamed guessed that there was plenty of chat over closed channels.

'Leave us now,' ordered Morvox.

Khamed hesitated for a moment. Only minutes had passed since the docking bay doors had opened. This was all happening very quickly and he'd expected... well, he didn't know what he'd expected.

'Your will, lord,' he said, bowing.

He withdrew from the command node and blast doors slid closed behind him. He turned, and saw Namogh waiting for him.

'So?' the deputy asked. Orfen Namogh looked out of place in ceremonial armour, and it fitted him badly. Then again, the deputy only looked comfortable with dirt smeared on his face and a lasgun stock wedged against his shoulder.

'We asked for help,' said Khamed. He suddenly felt weary. He hadn't slept for twenty hours. 'We got it. Get everything together – we're going in again and they're in charge now.'

It took longer than he expected. The Iron Hands didn't emerge from the command node for over seven hours, during which time Khamed snatched some sleep, reviewed tactical readouts from the containment operation, and shared a meal of dried multimeat and tarec with Namogh.

'We're going to have to work with them, Orfen,' said Khamed, chewing through the gristle methodically.

'No,' said Namogh bluntly. 'No, we're not. You don't work with them. They order you into shitholes. You go down them. That's the way it works.'

'Fine. But stow your attitude. I don't want it getting down to the grunts.'

Namogh laughed, and took a swig of tarec. He had flecks of meat all over his big, yellow teeth.

'Don't worry. They're all crapping themselves already. And I haven't said a thing.'

A bead on Khamed's starched collar blinked red. Despite himself, he felt his stomach lurch.

'What are we afraid of?' he muttered, getting up and retrieving his helmet.

'You heard of Contqual?' asked Namogh, wiping his mouth and following Khamed out of the hab. 'You heard what they did there?'

Khamed brushed his uniform down and put his helmet on, twisting the seal as he walked.

'You shouldn't believe what you read, Orfen,' he said. 'There's a lot of crap on the grids.'

'One in three. That's how many they killed. Punitive measures, they called them. And those poor bastards were on our side.'

Khamed opened the blast doors from the officers' quarters and strode out into the antechamber of the command node. He kept his shoulders back, head straight. The little things were important.

'Like I said. There's a lot of crap out there.'

He opened the doors. Morvox was waiting on the far side of them, vast and mordant.

'We have what we need,' said the Iron Father. 'Now we go in.'

Out of the Excelsion, moving at a clip, and into the long bunkers of Securum, lit by gloomy strip-lumens. Administratum was amusing, with scholiasts looking terrified at the sight of the black giants striding through the lexchambers. Then down into the vaults of the Cordex. Some of the priests had tried to perform some kind of benediction on the Space Marines there, but had been simply brushed aside, just like everyone else.

After that, the dirt got bad. The air got hot. The floor got sticky, and the aircon wheezed like a phenexodrol junkie. There were men waiting at Station Lyris, arranged in ranks of a hundred. They looked pretty good, kitted out in full staff grey and assault armour. There wasn't much blood to be seen. The floors must have been swabbed.

'Will you address them?' asked Khamed, not really knowing whether that would be good or bad for morale.

'No,' said Morvox, and kept moving.

He never stopped moving. He just kept going.

Then you think: I was right the first time. It is a machine, a nightmare machine.

It was the implacability that was so unsettling. They looked almost invulnerable, to be sure, and their armour-hum was eerily threatening. But it was the sense you got, the sense that they would just keep on going, that got to you.

A mortal would know when to quit, even a dogged one like Namogh. They wouldn't. Ever.

'How do you want the Lostari deployed?'

'You have orders on the tac. For now, just try to keep up.'

Then down again, past the station bulwarks and along service runners towards the core hab clusters. The light got worse. The shafts got smaller and less well repaired. Loops of cables hung down from the roof, and moisture pooled in dark corners. Defective lumens guttered behind panels of iron mesh.

They were getting to the heart of it. Half a kilometre down in Ghorgonspire was like being a long way underground. The nearest patch of sky was buried under a lot of rockcrete. The air that coughed through the circulation systems was humid and smelled of human excreta. Major power grids had gone down early on in the difficulties, and battlefield gen-units struggled to keep the lumens in operation.

Khamed switched on vision-aug in his helmet. The men in his lead unit, twenty of them, did the same. They were all practically running in the wake of the Iron Hands, none of whom had broken their striding rhythm.

'This is Node 4R,' announced Morvox, coming up to a massive, closed siege gate at the end of the corridor. On either side of it, teams of greyshirt sentries waited warily, weapons hoisted. 'We will cleanse it. Consolidate in our wake. Are you prepared?'

Khamed was already out of breath. He shot a quick glance back down the crowded corridor. His lead unit was in readiness. Behind it, stretched out in the gloom of the long tunnel, were more squads coming into position. He could see some of them ramming energy packs into their lasguns and strapping helmets securely. They were as prepared as they would ever be.

'On your command,' he said, nodding to Morvox.

'We do not need your fire support. Do not join the assault. Secure the ground we clear. You will be given new orders on completion.'

Something was exchanged over a private channel, and the Space Marines unlocked their sidearms. Four of them, Morvox included, carried huge, boxy guns with blunt barrels and a chunky protruding magazine. They looked more like grenade launchers than regular firearms.

The fifth hoisted a truly massive weapon – an artillery piece with a core housing the size of a man's torso. It took both hands to hold it and there was a grip over the main carriage. A loop of ammunition hung underneath, stiff and chain-linked.

That wasn't all. They had blades. Some of them were like the short stabbing swords Khamed's own men used, albeit twice as big. Others weren't. Two of the giants carried massive rotary saws in their free hands, each one shaped like a gigantic broadsword.

Those weapons were ludicrous. Outsized, industrial-scale killing implements, dreamed up by some crazed enginseer and borne by superhumans. Khamed knew that he would have barely been able to lift one of those guns, and yet they hefted them lightly, one-handed.

He swallowed dryly. He also knew what was on the other side of the barrier.

'Open the gate,' he voxed.

And so the doors opened, grinding against metal, punishing old and arthritic gears, gradually exposing the chamber beyond and framing a window on to a nightmare.

II

Land Engine. Long for its class – a kilometre from sensorium fronds at the head to waste grinders at the arse. Vast, swaying, crowned with parapets of dusty smog that rolled down the side armour. Faint yellow lights studded weathered plate, tiny in the howling storm.

It rocked against the wind. Gigantic suspension coils flexed with the movement, supporting the thousands of tonnes of superstructure and its long, long train of drive mechanics, processing tracks, forges, crew habs and weapon banks.

All the time, the engines growled. On and on. They never stopped.

It was making good speed: 0.3 kilometres an hour, Medusan measures. The drives were operating noisily, making the floors tremble and shaking the black dust from the intakes.

Outside, it was blowing a gale, thick and black and grimy. There were voices on the wind, wailing.

On Medusa, it was always blowing a gale, thick and black and grimy. On Medusa, there were always voices on the wind.

Ahead of the Land Engine, the plain stretched away in a morass of cracks and sharp-stepped rock. On the far horizon, red lightning jumped down from the smogline.

Haak Rejn sat back in his metal lattice chair and rubbed his eyes. He felt the metal of his right optical implant snag on his skin.

There were picts around him in the sensorium chamber – a narrow control unit perched right out at the fore-left corner of the lead crawler unit. The screens were close-packed and flickering orange. Runes burned dimly, summarising feedback from the *Mordecai*'s seven thousand augur pinpoints. His implant helped him make sense of them.

It also gave him headaches. The implant burned the whole time, dull and hot. The damn thing was like a chunk of molten metal in his skull. But he didn't complain. It had never occurred to him to complain. Neither had it occurred to him to complain when they'd flank-wired him into the lattice chair, nor when the flesh of his thighs had withered away to straws from lack of movement, nor when he'd found he could no longer sleep except after a double shot of dousers and a course of binreflex exercises.

Very few people on Medusa saw the point in complaining. It wasn't that kind of place.

Something flickered on one of the picts. Rejn blinked blearily and reached over to it. He turned the gain up and calibrated his implant with it.

'Throne,' he swore, and ramped up the feed. 'Traak, you getting that?'

A thousand metres away, on the far side of the *Mordecai*'s lead unit, a commlink crackled into life.

'Yeah.' Traak's voice was sluggish, like he'd been trying to snatch a nap. 'I know what I'd like to think. Put a crawler down?'

'Good. I'm on it.'

Rejn's right hand, the one that could still move, worked the input vectors. His left, the one that terminated in a bunch of steel cables, twitched as his neural link communicated with the *Mordecai*'s Soul. It took a few moments for the protocols to clear.

Acknowledgement came back over the grid. From somewhere a long way down, he heard metal grind back against metal. There was a shuddering movement, and then a heavy crash. He switched to another pict, one that watched the port flank of the Land Engine's lead unit.

A hatch had opened near the base of the unit between two tread housings. A ramp extended from it, gouging a slow furrow in the rock below as it made contact.

A four-tracked crawler rolled down. Its angular, ugly frame rocked as it hit the plain. Exhaust columns belched black soot, and then it was off, lurching across the uneven surface.

Rejn switched to the crawler feed. Static rushed across the pict before clarifying. He saw the shape of a man resolve out of the blinding duststorm. The figure was still on his feet, leaning into the wind, limping badly. His ragged clothing was covered in plains-dust, making him look like so much charred meat.

The crawler reached his position and ground to a halt. The man staggered up to the back of it and hauled himself in. The crawler swung round and headed back to the ramp.

Rejn switched to an interior cam. The man was slumped in the corner of the crawler's load bay.

'Life signs,' ordered Rejn.

A series of indicators ran down his nearside pict. All low, all borderline viable.

Tough bastard. He'd make it, if they got him up to the medicae in time. Rejn punched the order into the grid and heard the click as the Soul registered.

'Any markings?' asked Traak, no doubt looking at the same feed.

'Not yet,' said Rejn, zooming in and scanning across the dirt-streaked face. Whatever the man had been doing, it had nearly killed him. Half his storm armour had been ripped away. 'He's not one of ours.'

'Can you patch an ident?'

'Yeah, just give me a second, dammit.'

Rejn watched as the crawler came back onboard. He ran a request and got clearance for a deep scan. The augurs calibrated, and a line of laser red ran down the man's body in a long sweep. The temple-stud got picked up and a fresh burst of data loaded on to the grid. Rejn looked at it carefully.

'Anything?'

Traak was getting annoying.

'Nothing to get excited about,' replied Rejn, preparing to shunt the data up to medicae and close the crawler hatch. 'Gramen clan, long way from home. Manus only knows what he's doing out here.'

'And a name?'

'Morvox. Doesn't mean much to me. You? Naim Kadaan Morvox.'

* * *

Land Engine. Smaller than the *Mordecai* but taller and more heavily armoured. It had no clan markings on the hull and its flanks were black. No lights blinked across the carapace, and the steep sided flanks were free of ore intake ramps.

As it inched its way across the desolate plain, the storm hammered uselessly against it. It didn't sway.

Deep within the core, far into the sarcophagus of metal and rockcrete and machinery, there was a half-lit chamber, perfectly square. The floor was black stone. The walls were lined with an organic mass of piping. The roof was vaulted, crowned with an iron boss and studded with weak downlights.

A man knelt in the centre of the chamber. He was naked, and the light glistened from the sweat on his skin. His shaven head was lowered in submission. Around him were robed figures, tall and broad-shouldered. They wore metal masks.

The grind of engines made the walls tremble.

One of the robed figures stepped out. He looked down at the kneeling figure for a long time, saying nothing.

When he spoke at last, the voice did not match his huge frame. It was thin and flat, as if run through overzealous audio filters.

'Of all the aspirants from Gramen, only you survived the trial of the plains. What lesson is there in this?'

The kneeling figure neither responded nor moved.

'Well?'

'I do not know, lord.'

'There is no lesson. You are not chosen. You are not unique. Some years, none come back. Some years, many do.'

The kneeling figure kept his head down. His muscles trembled slightly from holding position. His physique was impressive – tight, lean flesh over a tall frame. There were many scars on that flesh. Fresh wounds too.

'You may prosper in the trials to come. You may die from them. In all this, do not look for fate. Do not look for significance. There is only what functions and what does not.'

'Yes, lord.'

The robed giant withdrew a long steel blade. It was not a fighting blade – too clean, too fragile. It had a look of a surgical instrument, albeit one with a ceremonial purpose.

'You will learn this. You will learn that the path of your life is not unique. It has purpose only as part of a whole. You are an element within a system. You are a piece within a mechanism.'

The blade came closer. The kneeling man extended his left arm, holding it rigid before him, fist clenched. His head stayed bowed.

'As time passes, you will see the truth of this. You will wish to discard those things that remind you of how you are now. You will forget that you were the only survivor of the trial. You will only remember the trial itself. You will remember the process. You will be the process.'

The giant kneeled in front of the naked man, and placed the blade against the flesh of the forearm, halfway between wrist and elbow. The cutting edge rested on the sweat-sheened skin.

'This is the first mark of that process. Do you wish it to continue?'

The question was incongruous. The journey had already been started, and there were no choices left. Perhaps the question was a hangover from some older rite, a rite where personal determination had mattered more than it did now.

'I wish it,' came the response.

The blade pressed into the skin, carving deep. It slid to the right, leaving a clean cut in the muscle before slipping out. The man emitted the faintest intake of breath at the pain. Blood welled up quickly, thick and hot.

He was still mortal. His control was not yet perfect.

The giant stood up, letting the blood run down the blade, and withdrew.

'That is the mark,' he said. 'That is where the greater cut will be made.'

The blade passed from view.

'Rise, Aspirant Morvox. You are no longer what you were. From this point on, you will be a battle-brother of the Iron Hands Clan Raukaan, or you will be nothing.'

III

The siege gates opened.

They exposed a long, wide hall beyond. It was almost totally dark, lit only by flares of orange gas from a broken supply conduit. The ceiling was lost in a writhing morass of gloomy mechanics. Bracing pillars, heavy columns of black iron, studded the rust-streaked floor.

They came out of the shadows, as if released by some soundless command. Dozens of them, bloated and chattering. Some hauled their distended stomachs along the ground, leaving trails of glittering pus in their wake. Others were emaciated, nothing more than sacks of leathery skin and splintered bone. Some of the bodies had fused together, creating sickening amalgams of men with multiple limbs, suppurating flesh and weeping organs hanging in chains. Some had talons, or bone outgrowths, or dull black teeth, or wickedly spiked spine ridges.

Only the eyes were the same on all of them. They glowed in the dark, lime green and as bright as stars. No pupils studded those eyes, just blank screens of eerie witchlight. As the gates opened to the full, the eyes narrowed. Faces, marked with fangs and hanging jaws and long lines of clumsy sutures, contorted into a mix of hatred and joy.

They scuttled into combat like spiders. They wanted it. What debased existence they possessed hungered for it in a way that they would hunger for nothing else ever again.

Khamed, still in the relative safety of the corridor outside the hall, watched them come, a weary sickness in his stomach. He'd been fighting those monsters for months. Every week, he'd fallen back a little further. Every week, a few dozen more of his men hadn't got back to the rally points in time.

And back then he'd always known that the next time he saw them the shambling horde would have more tattered grey uniforms hanging from hunched shoulders, and there would be more remnants of faces he recognised.

He gripped his sidearm with sweaty hands, keeping it in position, ready to go in again when the order came.

Then the Iron Hands got to work.

They didn't move fast. Khamed had heard that the Emperor's Angels could fight like daemons, hacking and whirling and tearing their foe apart in an orgy of destruction. These ones didn't. They walked out calmly, spreading out in front of the siege gates, opening fire from their massive weapons in long, perfectly controlled torrents.

Khamed just watched. The more he watched, the more he appreciated the truth of the legends he'd heard. For the first time in months, he dared to hope that the Spire would be saved. It was then that he realised just how strange that emotion – hope – had become to him.

The giants' firearms were neither las-tech nor solid ammunition. Khamed realised what they were as soon as the first volley went off. The Iron Hands used explosive charges, primed to ignite on impact. The noise of their discharge was phenomenal. They maintained a withering wall of fire, tearing apart the oncoming ranks of walking dead in an orgy of slime and fluid. The muzzle flashes lit up the hall in a riot of sharp electric light, exposing the tortured faces of their victims in brief, snatched freeze-frames.

The heavy weapon that one giant carried two-handed thundered like nothing Khamed had heard before. Its operator, placed right in the centre of the squad formation, wielded it calmly, drawing the devastating column of destruction across the enemy in a slow, deliberate sweep.

The enemy were not just killed. They were obliterated, blasted apart, torn into tatters of flapping skin and powdered bone. Bitter experience had taught Khamed that you couldn't down them with a flesh wound – you had to take them out with a headshot or knock their torsos into pulp. That wasn't a concern for the giants. They walked into the hall, methodically firing the whole time, laying down a maelstrom of destruction, not letting a single mutant get out of the path of their awesome, silent vengeance.

Then, suddenly, the deluge stopped. The echo of the massed volley died away. The hall sunk back into gloom. The Iron Hands remained poised to fire, their weapons held ready. They had advanced halfway across the space. Everything in front of them had been killed.

Khamed stayed where he was for a moment, ears ringing, stunned by what he had just witnessed. Then, cursing himself, he remembered his orders.

'Follow them in,' he snapped over the comm to his men. 'And look like you know what you're doing.'

He stepped over the threshold, sweeping his lasgun warily up and around. His boot nearly slipped and he looked down. The floor was covered in a thick carpet of bubbling sludge. It was moving. Some of it was bloody; some looked like sewage. An eyeball, swollen and yellow, floated past him, carried down into foaming drainage ducts by the current.

They'd been rendered down into soup. Flesh soup.

Ahead of him, the Iron Hands were calmly reloading. One of them took out what looked like a handheld sensor and tapped on it with a blunt armoured finger.

'Raef Khamed,' said Morvox. There was no inflexion there, nothing to indicate the extreme violence the giant had just unleashed. 'The area is cleansed. We will progress to Nodes 34, 45, 47 and then assess. Immolate this chamber and secure it. Deployment patterns are on the tac.'

'As you command, lord,' said Khamed, his voice sounding very quiet after the wall of noise.

The Iron Hands hadn't waited for the acknowledgement. They pressed on, heading deeper into the dark reaches of the lower hive. Already, from far below, sounds of scratching and screaming were massing.

Namogh's voice crackled over the comm.

'You need backup, Jen?' he asked. His voice sounded worried. 'We've got a lot of static at your position.'

'No,' said Khamed, knowing that he sounded distracted and not really caring. 'No, maintain your position. I think we're good. Throne, I actually think we're good.'

It got harder. The lower levels had been dens of disease and corruption for years, and the mutants had had time to turn it into a paradise of pustulation.

The walls were alive with curtains of viscous slime. Growths burst out of air-con ducts, corpulent and luminous. Quasi-human mutants shambled up from the depths, heedless of their losses, jaws wide and ringed with filed-down teeth. They screamed like mockeries of children, stretching warped vocal cords beyond their tolerances. Khamed saw one grotesque long-necked mutant scream itself to a standstill, its throat overflowing with a bubbling cocktail of phlegm and clots. Morvox aimed a single shot and the creature's head exploded in a shower of sticky, whirling gobbets, silencing the shrill chorus from its owner.

As they descended, the layout of the tunnels changed. Ceilings closed in and walls narrowed. The slurry of excreta was ankle-deep at the best of times, knee-deep at the worst. There was no reliable light – just the sweeping lumen beams from helmets, exposing the breadth of the horror in fragmentary pools of surgical illumination.

Every mutant coming for them had once been a human inhabitant of the hive. Every contorted face had once run the full gamut of human laughs and tears. They had been technicians, lectors, machine operators, arbitrators.

No one knew exactly when it had started. The first signs had been small ones – increased workload at the medicae stations, reports of infection in the scholae, power-loss in the deep hive and rioting across the semi-policed hinterlands running out to the ore-plains.

The authorities hadn't been slow to act. Tralmo was sharp, and had never been negligent. There had been quarantines, shipments of antibiotics, blockades of crime-controlled sectors and curfews across the Ghorgonspire.

But by the time the 1324th Lostari 'Greyshirt' Imperial Guard had been mobilised to restore order, it was already out of hand. The situation had changed from a public health problem to a fight for survival, and so it had stayed for months.

They never got to the bottom of what had caused it. The originator was, presumably, buried far down in the depths, squatting in the dark places under Ghorgonspire that had long been lost to the contagion. The Holy Emperor alone knew what was down there, pumping bile and energy into the ruined bodies of those it had corrupted.

Such speculation was useless. The Iron Hands moved with purpose. They punched through the ragged columns of mutants like a blade through rusty armour, tearing and burning and hacking and blasting. They never sped up, never slowed down. Step by step, metre by metre, they reclaimed lost ground, operating like silent golems of myth.

In their wake came the mortal troops, reinvigorated by the example they had in front of them. Exhausted Lostari found the will to take the fight to the mutants. Volleys of lasfire suddenly found their marks more often. Objectives were isolated, taken and consolidated. With the indomitable example of the Space Marines in front of them, the 1324th Lostari of Helaj V stood up, and found they were stronger than their desperation had made them believe.

They descended from level to level in orderly bursts of activity, clearing out connecting chambers of filth and pressing on into the tunnels beyond. Flamers came next, boiling off the stinking layers of slime and acid and charring the metal beneath. Obscene sigils were scored from the walls. Power was restored. The mark of the Imperium was reinstated.

At the forefront, as ever, were the Iron Hands, the Emperor's holy Angels of Death.

And as they killed in those terrible, industrial quantities, never had a moniker seemed so apt.

* * *

The eyes came out of the darkness as if swimming up from the frigid abyss. They swarmed, flocking at the invaders, locked into snarls and yells of utter mindless hatred. As they neared, limbs became visible. Limbs with hooks run through them, or stitches running down them, or iron pins shoved up under the necrotic skin and bulging like parasites.

Khamed shrugged off his tiredness and shouldered his lasgun. He moved smoothly, aping the frictionless methods of the Iron Hands who fought ahead of him, and drew a bead on the lead mutant.

He fired, and his las-beam cracked off, impacting between a pair of staring green eyes and cracking the skull into hemispheres.

Another kill.

And then he was moving again, marshalling his squad and pushing them forward. He swept his muzzle round, looking for mutants crawling across the roof or punching their way through sewer outlets.

They were deep down and the air was hot and steamy. No light existed save for the mess of helmet lumen beams, and every trooper was now on full infrared. The chamber was just like a hundred they'd already cleansed – close, claustrophobic, stuffed with a crawling mass of suppurating terror.

It had ceased to matter. Khamed had begun to forget his life had ever involved anything different. The undead poured towards him, snapping fangs and loping on all fours into contact. He reacted passionlessly, efficiently, optimising his shots and taking time over the targeting. He could rely on the Iron Hands to take out the mass of them – he was there to mop up the stragglers and the outriders.

He swung round just as three skinny mutants, their bulbous heads bobbing on scrawny necks, bolted from cover and out toward the leftmost Space Marine of the Iron Hands squad. Each one was carrying heavy projectile weapons and let off a flurry of lead as they splashed through the ankle-deep lake of effluvium.

Khamed got his aim and fired, missing the lead mutant by a finger's width. In the time it took him to curse, wipe his eyes and re-aim, it was over.

The Iron Hand didn't seem to move fast. He seemed to move with the same unearthly, ponderous manner as his brothers. But, somehow, he got his weapon up and fired off a round before the mutants had taken another step. The bolt crashed through the neck of the first, tearing the muscles open and leaving the head lolling on stretched sinews like an amulet. It exploded in the chest of the second, blowing open a ravaged ribcage into splayed splinters.

Then the sword, the mad sword with its insane rotary blades, swept round in a heavy lash, whipping out sticky fluid from previous kills. The surviving mutant tried to dart under it, aiming to get close enough to use a rusty killing blade it held in its left hand.

The Iron Hand adjusted the weapon's descent and the sword whirred into the mutant's leading shoulder. It burrowed down, carving its way through diseased muscle bunches and flinging out gouts of boiling, frothing blood. The mutant screamed for a fraction of a second, locked in agony as the juddering blades ate through its bony frame and minced what was left of it into a marrow-flecked broth of body fluids.

The Space Marine hauled the sword free, breaking the ruined body of his prey into two pieces as it was withdrawn. Then he turned, implacable as ever, and kept on fighting.

He'd never said a word. He'd not changed a thing. No hurry, no fuss.

Nightmare machines.

Khamed laughed.

The Jenummari laughed as he brought his own weapon round and splashed through the filth, looking for new targets. It was a laugh of disbelief, a laugh of wonder that killers of such intensity existed in the universe. It was a laugh of fear, and of relief that they were on his side. He had last laughed six months ago, and the noise of it was unfamiliar in his parched throat.

'Keep up, you dogs!' he snapped over the comm.

He wasn't scared anymore. His body pumped with adrenaline. He was beginning to enjoy himself.

That, of course, was his first mistake.

It was fast as well as strong. Its hide was pale brown, like old leather. It had four heavy arms, perhaps grafted on to the torso by some demented chirurgeon. Its face was long, stretched by weights nailed to its distended chin. The skin of its cheeks was ripped and weeping and its clustered eyes bled witchlight.

As it crashed through the slurry, it howled like a dog. Its hands clenched pairs of gouges, each dripping with virulent, glistening fluid. Long, lank hair flailed around it as it came, and trails of livid saliva hung down from a bloodstained jaw.

It veered sharply, crashing its way through a knot of its own warped kin. They were crushed underfoot as it came, trampled into the mix of blood and mucus that bubbled underfoot.

For once, the Space Marines missed the main target. They were all occupied, pinning back the tide of raging, screaming fury that hammered against them. Their guns slammed back into their armoured fists, spitting the surge of reactive rounds that cracked and boomed into the oncoming wall of corrupted flesh.

Khamed saw the mutant come in his direction, and the laughter died in his mouth. One of his men got a shot, and a las-beam whipped across it.

It didn't drop. It launched itself into the close-packed press of Lostari, limbs whirling, roaring a strangled cry of ecstasy and fury.

Khamed tried to swivel round to get an angle, but slipped. He crashed back to the ground, bracing himself with his free arm, only to see three of his men taken out by the mutant. It went for their throats, biting through the neck armour and shaking their limp corpses. Las-beams seared into it, ripping away whole strips of skin, but that didn't slow it down much. It rampaged through the knot of men, shrugging off anything that hit it, scattering the survivors. Then it turned and saw Khamed.

It smiled.

The mutant leapt at him, all four arms extended. Khamed fired again, hitting it once in its massive chest. Then he was scrabbling back through the scummy fluid, desperately trying to clear some distance.

The mutant stumbled from the las-impact, then regained its feet. It lurched down and grabbed Khamed's trailing boot. Khamed felt the vice close around his ankle and thrashed to escape, kicking wildly.

He stood no chance. The mutant pulled him back savagely, gurgling, readying its blades for the plunge that would rip his stomach open. Khamed was wrenched back, dragged through the liquid and along the chamber floor. Frothy slime splashed across his helmet, running across the visor and clouding it in a film of brown.

Khamed fired again, blindly, and heard the snap of the las-beam as it shot harmlessly into the roof. Then the gun was knocked from his grasp. He tensed for the bite of the gouges, knowing that they would plunge low, right into his gut.

Then something huge exploded above him, throwing the slime up in waves. The grip on his ankle released. Khamed pulled himself out of the grime and shook the screen of filth from his visor.

The mutant was gone. Its lifeless body was crumpled up against the metal wall, pumping black blood solidly. In front of Khamed loomed an Iron Hand, filling his field of vision, vast, black and indomitable.

'Can you fight?' came the voice from behind the visor.

It wasn't Morvox. The tone wasn't as metallic, not as heavily filtered. It almost sounded human, albeit far more daunting and resonant than any human Khamed had ever encountered.

'Yes,' he said, shaking himself down and bending to retrieve his lasgun. 'Yes, I can.'

'Then do so,' replied the Space Marine, turning away from him and striding back to the main fighting. The chamber was still full of the sounds of combat. Fresh Lostari were piling in to replace those felled by the mutant, but there was no sign yet of the horde of bloated horrors relinquishing the chamber. The clamour of bolter detonations, howls and screams just kept on going.

Khamed watched the Iron Hand go, his heart thumping hard. He realised his hands were shaking, and clenched his fists to stop it.

Then do so.

He hefted his lasgun again, checking to see if the fluids had interfered with the mechanism. The simple things helped.

'Very well,' he muttered, still trembling. He braced himself and looked for a target. 'I will.'

The noise of the assault died away. The Iron Hands began to move on, wading their way toward a long access shaft. They maintained the same pace as before, never speeding up, never slowing down.

The same punishing pace wasn't possible for the mortal troops. They needed rotations, rest periods, resupply and medicae treatment. After hours of fighting, almost without respite, Khamed's turn had finally come.

Namogh's force-signal flashed across his helmet display, indicating that he was moving into position to relieve him. Khamed turned to the Space Marine who had rescued him, still the closest to hand of the quintet. For some reason, it felt more natural to address that one than Morvox, who in any case had already stalked off into the dark ahead.

'My deputy will provide fire support beyond this node,' Khamed announced. His voice gave away his extreme fatigue. The adrenaline from the last encounter had drained away, leaving him feeling empty. 'This detachment needs to rotate.'

The Space Marine turned to face him. His facemask was streaked with blood and bile, making him look even more grotesque than normal. There was a pause, possibly due to some internal comms between the squad.

'We will maintain the assault,' the Iron Hand replied. 'Order relief forces to follow us down when they get here.'

The Space Marine turned to move off, then stopped. He looked Khamed up and down.

'How long have you been on your feet?'

'Fifteen hours, lord. The same as you.'

The Space Marine nodded slowly.

'Fifteen hours.' There was a strange noise from the vox grille. On a human, it might have been a laugh – a strange, attenuated snort. From one of the giants, Khamed wasn't willing to assume anything.

'We forget where we come from, sometimes,' said the Iron Hand. The tone of voice was almost reflective. 'You fought well, human. Tell the others they fought well.'

Khamed didn't reply at once, stunned by the unexpected compliment. Then suddenly, from nowhere, encouraged by the unlikely candour from the Angel of Death, he dared to ask for more.

'I will, lord,' he said. 'But I have no name to give them.'

Again, the noise. Perhaps irritation. Perhaps amusement. Perhaps warning.

'Ralech,' came the reply, before the Space Marine strode off to join his brother warriors. 'Ralech Grond, Clan Raukaan, Medusa. Tell them that.'

* * *

'He said that?'

Khamed nodded between gulps of stimm-laced water. He was enjoying Namogh's expression – a cross between disbelief, horror and disapproval.

'I don't believe it.'

Khamed put the canteen down. He was sitting on an old iron crate, shoulders hunched and head low. He could already feel oncoming sleep crowding out his thoughts. The chamber was full of men, exhausted ones from his command being replaced with fresher ones under Namogh's.

'He was almost... normal.'

'Crap.'

'I'm telling you.'

Khamed watched the survivors of his platoon limp back up toward the transit shafts at the rear end of the chamber. Their armour was caked in filth and blood. Some couldn't walk unaided and hung like sides of meat from the shoulders of their comrades. He'd be joining them soon.

'I think they change,' said Khamed thoughtfully. 'The leader – Morvox – he's further down the road than the others. They forget.'

Namogh spat into the floor-slurry, and the spittle spun gently away toward the drain meshing.

'You've taken a hit, Jen,' he said, shaking his head. 'They don't feel nothing. They'd throw us into the grinder without a blink.'

'I'm not sure.'

'They ain't human.'

'Not now, no.'

'We're *nothing* to them. Just spare parts.'

Khamed looked up at his deputy. Namogh was as adamant as ever. His ugly face was twisted with distaste. There was anger there, to be sure, but also fear. Khamed couldn't blame him for that. The Iron Hands scared everyone, even the mutants.

'I don't want to believe that, Orfen,' said Khamed quietly. 'They are sons of the Emperor, just as we are. We fight together.'

'Crap. You're delusional.'

'But what changes them?' asked Khamed, ignoring Namogh. He remembered the way Grond's voice had sounded. 'Why do they change? I'd like to know that.'

IV

The knife went in, moving across the flesh of the arm, tracing a thin line of blood.

Morvox watched it. He had an almost uncontrollable urge to seize the nearest medicae servitor by its desiccated throat and slam it against the walls of the apothecarion.

That had been predicted. He fought the urge down. The hormones in his body, the ones introduced during the changes, made him belligerent in the face of injury.

The servitors carried on, heedless of the turmoil in their patient. They moved on tank tracks around the metal chair Morvox had been clamped into. Their faces were shiny curves of steel, dotted with sensoria. Their limbs were entirely augmetic and terminated in a dozen different surgical devices. They chattered to one another in a basic form of binaric. It was a soft, low clicking backdrop to their grisly work.

The skin was peeled back, exposing raw muscle. The ligatures below the bicep tensed. The knives went in again, parting the muscle mass.

Morvox watched it happen. He watched the rotary saw whine through the bone. It had only just finished growing into its new, improved form. Amputating it seemed wasteful.

They broke the bones. He watched his hand fall away, clutched in the claws of a metal servitor. He watched the blood run out of the wrist, steaming as it cooled in its steel bowl. He watched sutures run across his severed forearm, rebinding the muscles and stabilising them. He watched the drills go in and the pre-augmetic bindings lock on to his broken bones.

There was hours of work to come. Rods would be implanted, running nearly up to his elbow. Braces would encircle the pronator, studding through the skin of his forearm. Neural relays would be dropped into place, and nerve-sockets, and tendon housings. And then, finally, they would drill in the new hand, the mark of his Chapter, the sign of fealty to the primarch and to the ideals of Medusa.

He would watch it all. The procedure was the mark of passage, the signal of his transition from mortal to superhuman. When it was complete, it would make him stronger. He knew this. It was fact, as revealed by Iron Father Arven Rauth, and so could not be doubted.

But, even though he knew it to be true, even as he watched the rods go in, bisecting the muscles that had kept him alive out on the ash plains, he did not yet believe it.

One day, like the Iron Father who had retrieved him from the trials, Morvox would not remember anything but the aesthetic imperative, the desire to purge the machine of the flesh that impeded it. One day, Morvox would no doubt pass on the ways of Manus to another, believing it with both hearts, no longer regretting the loss of a part of himself.

But not yet.

For now, he still felt it.

There were more trials. Long years as a neophyte, learning the ways of the Adeptus Astartes. A hundred worlds, all different, all the same.

He saw them first as a Scout, learning to use his enhanced body without the full protection of power armour. He enjoyed feeling his augmented muscles flex. He revelled in the strength of his new sinews. He could run for hours without fatigue, or lay in wait for days without the need for sustenance. He was a miracle, a scion of demigods.

The disquiet grew slowly. He noticed during an engagement with the greenskin how quickly his iron hand functioned, how elegantly it curled into a punching fist, how efficiently it was able to turn the cutting blade. He moved his close combat weapon to his left hand after that, trusting in its ability more than the natural flesh of the right.

It was after the Valan Campaign when he was elevated into the ranks of the Clan proper. His carapace protection was returned to the foundry and, for the first time, he was bolted into the hallowed shell of power armour. He remembered the cool touch of the interface nodes against his carapace, how the ceramite skin worked in such perfect conjunction with his own.

He remembered the first time the helm was lowered over his face, sealing him off from the universe in a cocoon of dense protection. He remembered how it made him feel. He flexed the gauntlets, watching the ceramic plates move over one another, watching the artificial perfection of the curves.

'What do you feel?' came a familiar voice.

Morvox looked at Rauth. His vision was mediated by the datastream of the helm's lensfeed.

There were a number of answers to the question. He felt powerful. More powerful than he had ever been. He felt honoured, and unworthy, and impatient for the next engagement. He felt all of these things.

'I feel…' he began, looking for the right words.

The Iron Father waited patiently, locked behind his own mask.

'I feel… imperfect,' said Morvox, landing at last on what he wanted to say. He looked down at his left hand and his emotions clarified. 'I feel flawed.'

Rauth nodded.

'Good,' he said.

Medusa was a planet of scarcity, of wastes, of darkness. Mars was a planet of wonder, of abundance, of dull red light that bled from a horizon of a million foundries.

The translation took several months, during which time Morvox trained incessantly. He read the rites of the Machine over in his mind until the words cycled in his sleep, burning themselves on to his unconscious mind like a brand. He learned the lore given him by the Iron Father perfectly, making full use of the eidetic function he'd possessed since his mind had been transformed. By the time he'd arrived, he felt almost prepared for what awaited him. All that remained was anticipation.

As the drop-ship fell steadily through the thin atmosphere, Morvox watched the landscape resolve into detail beneath him. Every metre of surface was covered in an industrial landscape of dark iron, belching red smoke from soaring towers. Structures ran up against each other like jostling herd beasts, massive and obscure. He could see transit tubes run across the face of gigantic factories like arteries on a flayed corpse.

The drop-ship flew low on its approach vector. It passed huge trenches, alive with glittering light, glowing at their bases from the magma that pooled there. There were clusters of cyclopean refineries, dark and shrouded in boiling walls of smog. Huge areas looked semi-derelict. Fields of tarnished steel ran away toward the horizon, marked by trenches and studded with arcane citadels. There were cages, each the size of a hive spire, within which vast war machines – superheavy vehicles, Titans, even starships – were being slowly assembled.

As the drop-ship slowed its descent ready to be received by its iron docking cradle, Morvox had a final glimpse of the Martian landscape at close quarters. Every surface was covered in a layer of red dust. The metal beneath was near black with age and corrosion. Nothing living was visible. Everything was ostentatiously artificial.

Morvox thought it was beautiful.

The vessel came to rest, and the airlock doors hissed open. Beyond them was a cavernous hall lit by long red strips of subdued neon. The air was dry and tanged with rust. The sound of hammering echoed up from deep vaults.

A single figure waited for him. It was human – of a sort. Deep green robes covered what looked like a skeleton of plasteel. No face was visible under the cowl, just a long iron snout from which wheezing breath issued.

Morvox's helm feed added extra information. He knew that the figure's rank was Magos, and that her name had been Severina Mavola on accession to the priesthood in 421.M38. He knew that her body was now 67 per cent augmetic and that she hadn't communicated verbally for nearly a century.

He also knew that she had once written poetry in the manner of Hervel Jho, but doubted that she retained the capacity. Service to the Machine-God demanded nothing less than full commitment.

+Naim Morvox,+ she canted in Martian-accented binaric. +Be welcome to Mars. I trust your journey was efficient.+

Few non-Mechanicus personnel could communicate directly with a magos when they chose to speak natively, instead relying on intermediaries or translating cogitators.

The Iron Hands however, as in so many other ways, were different.

+Most efficient, magos,+ he replied. +I am eager to learn.+

Mavola motioned for him to join her.

+You wish to become Iron Father,+ she said, walking with him into the colossal hall. Her gait was smooth, giving no trace of the artificial nature of her musculature. +You know the process will be arduous.+

+If it were not, it would not be worth aspiring to.+

+You will be on Mars for ten years. In those years, many of your battle-brothers will lose their lives. When you return, Medusa will be a changed place.+

+I know this.+

The magos stopped walking. Behind her, a vast caldera boiled with molten metal. servitors, some as large as Sentinel walkers, laboriously tilted it over, ready for the casts below to be filled.

+We will show you mysteries that we show no other Chapter of the Adeptus Astartes. We extend this privilege in honour of Manus. Know now that the value of the instruction is almost without price.+

Morvox looked at her carefully.

+Almost?+

Mavola didn't elaborate. She turned on her heel, and resumed her fluid walk across the hall.

+Come now,+ she said. +To the forges.+

When he returned to Medusa, almost eleven years after he'd left, it was as the magos had warned him. Clan Raukaan had experienced a decade of near-constant action, and many faces he'd known well had been gathered into the Emperor's Rest. Iron Father Arven Rauth was now Clan Commander.

To replace losses in the ranks, new aspirants had been inducted from across the planet throughout the decade. Morvox was escorted to his appointment with Rauth by one of them, a raw recruit named Ralech Grond. The youth still had his natural hand intact and almost no sign of augmetics. Morvox couldn't decide whether he envied that or not.

Once Grond had left them, Morvox and Rauth stood alone in the inner sanctum of the Land Engine *Diomedes*. Both wore their armour, though the commander's skull was bare, revealing a pattern of steel markings across the synthetic skin like a circuit board.

'The training was successful?' he asked.

'As I judge it, lord. The Mechanicus reports are on the grid.'

'Much modification?'

Morvox raised his right arm. The ceramite of his vambrace slid back, exposing a deep well within. It looked like the entire forearm had been hollowed out and lined with nanotronics. Rauth examined it carefully.

'Unusual,' he said. 'What purpose did they have in this?'

Morvox withdrew the arm. As he did so, the covering clicked shut. From the outside, there was no indication that his right limb was anything other than normal.

'They did not tell me.'

'Nothing at all?'

'No. I assume it will become apparent.'

Rauth nodded.

'They do nothing randomly. Anything else?'

'No. I am ready to serve. It has been too long since I wielded weapons on the field. I'm eager to employ my new aptitudes.'

'You are not Iron Father yet,' warned Rauth.

'I know. On the day I left Mars, I asked for the magos's prediction of when that day would come. She gave me a definite answer.'

Rauth's eyebrow raised. It was a curiously human gesture on a generally expressionless face.

'She told me I had incurred a debt on Mars,' said Morvox. 'They do not give up their secrets for free. A time will come when that debt must repaid. Only then will I earn the rank – at least in their eyes.'

'Presumptive of them. What kind of debt?'

Morvox looked down at his hands. Both were metal now, as was much of the rest of his limb structure. That ongoing augmentation would only accelerate now. He was beginning to forget his life out on the plains, back when he'd been nothing more than human muscle and blood. All that remained was the process, the long march to perfection, just as he'd been warned.

'I do not know,' he said.

V

Time was measured by chrono in the lower hive. There was no daylight to announce the dawn and no nightfall to bring the days to a close – just the endless cycle of artificial light, delivered via grimy lumens and flickering pict screens.

Except that these were all smashed now. In their absence, the deep dark was oppressive and eternal. The troops measured time in shifts, in hours-long assaults on the enemy. Only the chronos, ticking away like heartbeats in the dark, recorded the time they'd been down there.

Four days, Helaj-medium, before they encountered the beast. Four days of back-breaking slog and grind. More men died during those four days than had died in the last month of attritional defence.

The assault was driven by the Iron Hands and there was no respite. They fought their way down the transit shafts, clearing them with flamers before sending grenades down into the squealing hordes. Then the boltguns would open fire, tearing the corroded flesh of the mutant into scraps and strips of bloody pulp. The Iron Hands waded through seas of grasping hands, carving through them with the chainswords. They went in close, using those massive armoured gauntlets to choke the half-life from their prey. They stayed long, using ranged fire to blow out kneecaps or crack open skulls. Whatever the tactic, the result was the same.

In their wake came the Lostari, the ragged, exhausted mortal defenders of Helaj, mopping up in the aftermath and killing whatever got around the spearhead. The rotations began to blur and timekeeping slipped, but they kept stumbling onward, deeper and deeper, down toward the heart of the sickness.

Khamed was rarely away from the heart of the action, despite the need for down-periods. The more he fought, the more he watched the Space Marines fight, the more he hated to be away from the front. He could see why myths built up around such warriors. For the first time, the panegyrics on the grid seemed less than ludicrous. All the fear, the terrible fear that he'd suffered since learning that it was to be the Iron Hands responsible for the purging of Ghorgonspire, had gone. It was replaced by a wary awe.

Sure, they looked grim and sounded worse. They fought without pause or pity, but those were the qualities demanded by the task. They spoke rarely and had little patience for mortal weakness, but Khamed couldn't blame them for that. If he'd been in their position, he'd have felt the same way.

He managed to stay close to Grond. They exchanged few words during the engagements – just enough to keep the linked forces in coordination. Morvox seemed to have delegated responsibility for mortal-liaison to the lower-ranked Space Marine, which suited Khamed fine. Though Grond's huge presence could never have been mistaken for merely human, at least he sounded slightly like one.

Perhaps that was an illusion. Perhaps what lay under that facemask was nothing but gears and diodes.

But Khamed didn't believe that. Not entirely.

The purging of a narrow hab-block had been completed and the flames were dying down. The empty doorways of the hab-units gaped like maws. As Khamed and Grond strode toward the far end of the main access corridor, their boots crunched through a floor of powdered bone.

'My deputy still resents your presence here,' Khamed said.

Grond didn't reply. His armour was covered in a thick layer of filth. In proper light, it would have been a dirty brown.

'He's heard... stories,' continued Khamed, knowing he was pushing his luck. 'He mentioned Contqual.'

Did the Space Marine break stride, just a fraction, then? Maybe not. Hard to tell.

'He said you killed one in three. After the fighting was over. Is that true?'

Grond kept walking for a while, then stopped. His massive armoured head turned slowly.

'Suppose it were true,' said Grond. 'Would you disapprove, human?'

Khamed looked up at the facemask, guessing he'd pushed things too far.

'I wasn't there.'

'No. You weren't. You are here. Do not concern yourself with other worlds. They are the Emperor's concern, and ours.'

The tone was cold. Khamed instantly regretted his question. He felt ashamed and foolish.

'I'm sorr–'

Grond held his hand up. For a moment, Khamed thought the gesture was something to do with him. Then he realised the Iron Hand was listening to something on his internal comm.

'Prepare your men,' ordered Grond, resuming his stride toward the hab-block access corridor.

Khamed scurried to catch up with the Space Marine.

'What is it?'

'Objective. Morvox has found it.'

Two levels down, and the air was hot and wet. Rebreathers wheezed against the filmy low-oxygen mix, struggling as particulates clogged the intakes. Slime was everywhere, coating the walls completely and obscuring whatever patterns had once been on the metal. The surface shone pale green where the lumen beams swept across the viscous matter, studded with bleeding sores.

They had to fight all the way down. Mutants had clustered tightly in the narrow access routes, and fought with a redoubled fervour. They hurled themselves on the blades of the Iron Hands, perhaps hoping to bring them down through weight of numbers.

The Space Marines maintained the pace as they always did, striding calmly into the onslaught, firing without pause. Bolters blazed, ripping holes in the torrent of diseased bodies. Screams echoed down the long corridors, throaty and gargled with phlegm. Khamed's men came in their wake, backing up the main advance and picking out anything that somehow escaped the rage of bolter rounds.

Smaller mutant breeds scampered and darted through the hail of fire, eyes alive with feral hatred and teeth bared. Khamed saw one spring from the bile-cloaked shadows and launch itself at one of his men. He took the shot and watched it slam into the far wall. There was a sickening squelch as the diminutive body plunged into the mucus layer and slid down into the bubbling miasma below.

Khamed tried not to notice the residual pigtails clinging to the otherwise clean-plucked skull, nor the tattered remnants of its dress flap weakly before it was swallowed by the filth.

They kept going. Step by step, they carved their way through the mob. And then, finally, they reached the heart of it.

A huge chamber opened up before them. Khamed knew what it was from the schematics – an old Mechanicus bunker, long disused even when the hive had been functioning normally. It was down in the heart of the underhive, one of the many forgotten relics of a distant past. Once, perhaps, there had been tech-priests there, doing whatever it was they did in their strange sanctums of industry.

Now it had all been changed. The high roof throbbed with pulsating veins of lurid bile-fluid. The expansive hexagonal floorspace swam with lapping slurry. Lines of what looked like saliva hung down in loops and the air drifted with tiny spinning spores.

Ranks of mutants splashed towards them, all distorted into lumpen, bloated bags of stretched-tight skin. They staggered into combat carrying rusted shards of metal or looted lasguns, howling in a mix of lust and agony, stumbling over one another in their haste to reach their foes.

But that wasn't what held Khamed's gaze.

'Hold your nerve!' he roared over the comm.

Around him, his men lined up and picked their targets. Las-fire cracked across the chamber, prompting fresh screams and gurgling cries.

The mutants began to tumble into the slime as they were felled. But they weren't the primary target any more. They were so much chaff, so much fodder. The real reason they were there reared up behind them.

It was massive. It filled the far end of the chamber and its vast, blubbery body ran up against the walls. The skin was translucent. Growths were visible beneath it, pulsing in sacs of pus. It was shaped like some obscene grub, warped and malformed into a veritable mountain of trembling, glistening flesh.

A face, sore-encrusted and sloppily fat, perched atop slick folds of blubber. It was still vaguely human, though its features were distorted horribly – a single eye stared out from a muscle-white face, red-rimmed and weeping. The mouth opened far wider than it should have done, exposing concentric rings of teeth and a huge, lashing tongue.

Many limbs extended from the mass of that expanded torso, some shaped into tentacles with grasping suckers, others twisted into claws. As the Iron Hands advanced towards it, the limbs lashed out, grappling for purchase.

It stank. Even through his helmet's filters, Khamed nearly choked on the stench. With his eyes streaming, he did his best to direct his troops. The creature screamed like its progeny, though the sound was even more disturbing – high and unearthly in a bizarre mockery of a woman's voice.

Khamed saw Grond go in, flanked by his battle-brothers. There was no hesitation. The Iron Hands plunged in close, firing the whole time from their bolters, stabbing holes in the vast flank of the obese monster. The translucent skin shook and burst as the bolts went off. Yellow liquid shot out from the wounds, thick and steaming. It cascaded down the black armour of the Space Marines, washing off the patina of days like a deluge of acid.

'Follow them in!' bellowed Khamed, feeling his heart beating like a drum.

He was scared. He could feel his muscles tensing up, locked into stiffness. Panic welled up in his gullet, and he fought to keep it down. The monster in front of him radiated such a wave of sickness that it nearly dragged him down into it.

He gritted his teeth, knowing his men would all be feeling the same. This was what the Iron Hands had come to show them. The horror could be fought.

'For the Emperor!' he cried, swinging his lasgun round and cracking off another beam. It hit an oncoming mutant in the face and ripped its cheek away, exposing rotten sinews and bone. 'Fight, you dogs! Fight!'

The Iron Hands had closed in by then, and the swords came out. The blades shone in the darkness, lit up by disruptor fields. For the first time, the Space Marines' movements broke from uniformity. They span on their ankles, shifting to evade the lash of the tentacles, before chopping through the curtains of flab. They remained silent, working with cool expertise, moving their limbs with exactitude.

The beast was the first opponent capable of truly contesting their will. It raged against them, flailing and whipping. One of the Space Marines was slammed back on to its back by a lightning jab from the claws. It crashed to the floor, rolling across the slime before coming to a halt. The mutants were on it in a second, hacking and chopping.

The Iron Hand powered back to its feet, scattering the corrupted bodies around it as it rose. The bolter juddered as it was drawn around in a tight arc, blasting the mutants to slivers. Then he charged back into contact with the beast, just as silent as before, just as implacable. By then two more of the Iron Hands had been forced on to the defensive, rocked by the furious response from the bloated horror before them.

Khamed advanced cautiously, maintaining a steady rate of fire. His entire platoon was in the chamber, and the flicker of their las-beams lit the walls up. For the first time, it felt like his contribution might make a difference. The horde of lesser mutants began to thin out, exposing the monster at their heart.

'Aim for... that!' he roared, striding through the clinging fluid and feeling it slop over the lip of his boots.

The thicket of las-beams concentrated, cracking against the beast's hide and puncturing the wobbling epidermis. It wailed under the barrage. The las-beams alone would have done little to trouble it, but combined with the fury of the Iron Hands bolter fire and bladework, they had an effect.

The downed Space Marines cut themselves free. One of them – Morvox, perhaps – fought his way up to the folds of neck-flesh, slicing and plunging with his crackling energy weapon. Another took the killing claws off the end of a tentacle with a savage swipe from his sword.

Slowly, purposefully, they were killing it. Barbs snapped out, wrapping around necks and limbs, but they were snapped off. Bile streamed from the beast's mouth, acidic and searing. It splattered against the hard armour and cascaded to the floor in fizzing lumps. The heavy bolter kept up its drumming, thunderous roar, punctuated by staccato bursts from the sidearms.

The residual mob of lesser mutants was beginning to lose cohesion. They blundered around, no longer advancing with any purpose.

'Pick your targets!' shouted Khamed. 'Headshots! Maintain barrage on the beast! Do not give–'

Then it happened. The skirts of flesh shrunk back, withdrawing into a shivering kernel. The screaming reached a fresh crescendo of hate-laced desperation. The beast thrashed around in its death-agony, jaws splayed and bleeding, tentacles writhing. It bled from a thousand wounds, each of them pouring with jelly-like tumours. The bolts kept punching into it. The blades kept biting, crackling with disruptor energy.

Its face went white. Its eye stared wildly, straining from the single socket. Veins stood out from the white skin in a lattice of purple, throbbing and tight with incipient destruction.

For a second longer, it still burned in agony.

Just a second.

Then it exploded. The beast blew itself apart, rocking the structure above and around it to the core. A tide of rubbery flesh rolled out like a breaking wave, surging across the chamber and rushing up the walls. Greasy, fist-sized hunks of gristle peppered the chamber. Flaps of skin sailed into the air, trailing long lines of sputoid blood and plasma. Semi-formed organs sailed high, falling apart in mid-air and breaking into slabs of quivering muscle.

Khamed was knocked from his feet by the storm, just like the rest of his men. He crashed on his back, felled by a rain of slapping body parts. He hit the filth hard and body-hot fluid ran through the chinks in his armour.

Repelled, he staggered back to his feet, shaking himself down. He wiped his visor and dirty streaks of red ran across it.

Ahead of him was a crater of gelatinous meat, laced with sticky globules of nerve-endings and lymph nodes. It shivered as the fluid cascaded over it, running over the floor and swaying with the current.

And amid the ruin of the beast, the five Iron Hands stood. Their armour dripped with sludge. Their guns were silent. For the first time in days, the howls of the mutants were gone. The only sound was the echo of the explosion and the slap and gurgle of the gore-tide as it ran against the walls.

Khamed watched them, feeling the weakness in his overtired limbs.

'Throne,' he whispered, hardly daring to believe it. 'Throne of Earth.'

Khamed looked around him. His men – those that had survived – were dead on their feet. All were exhausted. A few had collapsed into the foul water and stayed there. Despite that, despite everything, most of the rest carried themselves with more pride that at any time over the past six months. They knew what they'd achieved.

Khamed let a smile crease across his grimy face.

'Namogh,' he voxed, hoisting his lasgun over his shoulder. 'Get your grunts down here.'

'Progress?' came the reply. He sounded worried.

'Pretty good. Fast as you can.'

Khamed killed the link and limped over to where the Iron Hands were congregating. All five of them were still standing in the centre of the beast's gigantic cadaver. Four of them, Grond included, were calmly reloading their weapons. The fifth, Morvox by the look of his armour, had waded deeper into the slough of burned flesh and was rummaging around in the heap of entrails and fluid.

'You have our thanks, lord,' said Khamed, coming up to Grond and smiling broadly. 'We could not have done this without you.'

Grond didn't turn to face him. He was looking intently at Morvox. They all were. Intrigued, Khamed followed their gaze.

After some more searching, the sergeant seemed to find what he was looking for. He straightened up, clutching something in his left hand.

It was a tube, formed from dark metal. Khamed couldn't make much out in the dim light – it was less than twenty centimetres long, blunt and rounded at the ends. There were markings on it, but nothing he could make out clearly.

Morvox turned back and strode toward them. As he did so, the armour of his right forearm opened. The vambrace panel came apart in two halves, exposing an empty space where the limb should have been. Morvox stowed the tube inside the receptacle and closed the shell of ceramite over it again.

Khamed frowned. For some reason, he felt suddenly worried. There had been no mention, at any time, of a mission to retrieve an object from the underhive.

'What is this, Grond?' he asked.

The Iron Hand didn't reply. Morvox spoke instead.

'Our task is complete, mortal,' came the metallic voice, as eerily thin as ever. 'Our ship has been summoned from orbit. The cleansing is over.'

For a moment, Khamed didn't believe what he was hearing. He stumbled over his response.

'But, with respect, lord–' he began. As the words left his mouth, his earlier euphoria was replaced with a cold dread. 'There are hundreds of mutants left alive. We have cleansed less than half of what we came for. There may be more such beasts. We need you.'

Morvox's dark facemask loomed over him. Khamed suddenly realised that the other Iron Hands were all facing him. They said nothing. They were like images in a cathedral, cold and dead.

'You make demands on us now, human?' Morvox asked. There was no emotion in the question, but somehow it conveyed a sense of absolute, utter menace.

Khamed swallowed, and felt his fists clench uselessly. He felt ridiculous, like a child stealing in on some adult affair and demanding attention. Stubbornly, from somewhere, he found the will to protest.

'No demands,' he said, disgusted at how timorous his voice sounded. 'But, lord, we cannot defeat the enemy that still remains. You cannot leave us now.'

'You speak as if your battle here is the only concern we have. You know nothing of the war that burns across the galaxy. You know nothing of the demands on us. If you wish to be worthy of preservation, then guard this ground. The Emperor protects those who resist.'

Then Morvox pushed past him and began to stalk back the way he'd come, back through the thousands of shafts and chambers and up into the inhabited zones. One by one, his squad turned to follow him.

Khamed watched them go in desperation. He knew, just as they surely did, that for them to leave now was little short of murder. The mutants would rally. Mortal troops alone were no match for the horrors that still squatted in the underhive – something that had been proved time and again over the past six months.

'Grond!' he cried, reaching out to clutch at the Iron Hand who had saved his life. 'You cannot mean this! The Spire can be cleansed! Do not leave us. Mercy of the Emperor, do not leave us!'

Grond looked at him just once. Khamed stared up into the softly reflective surface of the helm's lenses. He realised then that he had no idea what kind of creature existed behind that mask. No idea at all.

'Can you fight?' asked the Space Marine.

The question needed no answer. Khamed knew what the responses were. Perhaps Grond had tried to warn him of this the first time he'd asked it. The Iron Hands only cared about strength.

Namogh had been right. Old, cynical Namogh.

Khamed hung his head, and let his hand slip from the Space Marine's arm. He could already hear scrabbling from the levels below. The mutants were stirring again.

Grond strode off to join his battle brothers, not giving Khamed another glance. All five of them walked past the Lostari in the chamber, ignoring the looks of disbelief from the human troops. Their heavy footfalls gradually receded as they passed through the connecting chambers and headed on up.

Khamed only raised his head when Namogh's squad burst into the chamber.

'What the hell's going on?' demanded the deputy. 'We just marched past your beloved Space Marines, and they're all going the wrong–'

He stopped short. Perhaps something in Khamed's empty expression told him all he needed to know.

'We're on our own,' said Khamed, and his voice was hollow.

For a moment, Namogh was lost for words. He looked at Khamed, then back at where the Iron Hands had gone, then back at Khamed.

'Those… bastards,' he spat. 'Those damned… bastards.'

The troops in the chamber, all of whom had heard the exchanges with Morvox, began to disintegrate. Some collapsed, empty-eyed and limp. Others started weeping. None of them ran. They knew there was nowhere to go.

Namogh managed to get a lid on his fury, and fixed Khamed with an urgent glare. His indignation made him speak too fast.

'What are we going to do, Jen?' he blurted. 'What are we going to tell Tralmo? What the hell am I going to tell my men? Holy Terra, what are they thinking, running out now? Why the hell come here, if they didn't intend to finish this thing off? What're we going to do?'

Khamed only half listened. He had no answers. He could hear the first screams of fury and lust from the tunnels below. The mutants were coming already. Soon they would be in the chamber, rushing through the slime, eyes shining with hatred.

Khamed felt a deep, horrifying weariness suffuse his limbs. His whole body ached. He'd pushed himself to the limit, and there was nothing left to give.

We're nothing to them. Just spare parts.

'Gather your men,' he said, unhoisting his lasgun and checking the charge. 'We'll make a stand three levels up. Call in the reserves – if we can get the siege doors closed, we might hold some ground for a while.'

Namogh looked at him as if he were mad.

'You think we'll hold them? You really think we stand any kind of chance? What's different this time?'

Khamed shook his head grimly.

'Nothing's different, Orfen,' he said. 'Nothing. Except, perhaps, for one thing.'

He looked away, past the stinking morass of the beast's carcass and down the tunnels beyond. He could feel the tide of unreasoning madness building down there. He knew it would not respect defiance. It respected nothing. It would just keep on coming.

Can you fight?

'I now know how the universe operates, my friend,' he said bleakly. 'For a while, I had dared to hope otherwise. I believed that this place might have some significance for them. That we might.'

He laughed bitterly.

'Better to die knowing the truth, do you not think?'

VI

The probe made a 98-per cent efficient descent from orbital platform 785699 to the receiving station in sector 56-788-DE of Forge 34 Xanthe manufactorium-schola-astartes. The statistics were logged on the grid and interpreted by the usual team of lexmechanics, after which three anomalies were corrected and allowed for, resulting in a two percentage point increment, to the satisfaction of all involved.

From the docking claw, the contents of the probe were conveyed by servitor nineteen levels down, past the major foundry zones and into the dense ganglia of shrines known colloquially in the sector as 1EF54A.

The cargo was transferred to tech-priests after a soak-test for data contagion and wrapped in three layers of soft dust-repelling cloth. The mark of the Machine-God had been embroidered on the material in gold thread.

Thus clad, it went through six further pairs of hands, only two of which had any organic flesh left on the bones. More tests were performed, and ledgers filled out, and records made for the core lists.

Then, finally, the cargo reached its destination. It came to rest on an obsidian tabletop in a room lit by dark red tubes. For a long time, it lay there alone, untroubled and untouched.

Several local days later, Magos Technicus Yi-Me, once called Severina Mavola, entered the chamber and carefully unwrapped it. A tube lay at the centre of the cloth, its glossy surface reflecting the light of the lumens.

Yi-Me studied it for a long time. She use her basic optical replacements, as well as seventeen additional sensors built into her plasteel cranium.

Deep within her, in a part of her body that had remained relatively unchanged throughout all the years of biosurgery, a sensation of deep pleasure blossomed. If she'd still had lips, she would have smiled.

The artefact was powerful. Powerful, if the initial readings were confirmed, beyond even her expectations. It would certainly suffice for the task she had in mind, and perhaps for many more in the years ahead. Lucky, that it had been discovered. Lucky, also, that it had proved possible to retrieve.

She bowed her head, silently acknowledging the service rendered by the one who had once been her pupil.

+Debt paid,+ she canted, knowing he couldn't hear her, but enjoying the irony of addressing him nonetheless. Such tropes were a staple of the Jho school, something she still appreciated. +Naim Morvox, Iron Father: debt is paid in full.+

A hundred worlds. All different, all the same.

As I bring the light of the Emperor to each of them, knowing that every foe I face could be the one that ends me, a single encounter remains prominent in my thoughts.

Helaj V, the Ghorgonspire. I remember the mortal there, the one named Raef Khamed. Even in sleep, sometimes, I see his face.

He expected much of us, once he had forgotten to fear. We could never match that expectation, not if we had eternity to accomplish the task and infinite resources to bring to bear.

Even so, I left the planet troubled. I never discussed it with Morvox. He would not have tolerated dispute from me, and that was before he was Iron Father. It seemed to me that our task was not finished, even though the objective was secured and our goals satisfied.

I remember how the mortals fought. I remember how they rose up when we were with them. Back in the warp, where dreams are ever vivid, I heard them plead for us to return. Or perhaps I heard their screams.

We never went back. I do not know what fate befell them. Maybe they prevailed. Maybe they were lost.

For many years, that troubled me.

Now, it does not. I understand what Morvox was doing. He had been purged of sentiment by then, just as I will be. He saw the greater pattern, and followed it. Such is the galaxy we inhabit. Resolve will preserve us; sentiment will see the light of humanity extinguished.

And so we allow ourselves to become this thing. We allow ourselves to become the machine. We are the result of a necessity, of the process.

The alternative is weakness.

I see this now. I see the truth of what I have been told by Morvox. Perhaps Helaj was the last time that I doubted. I am stronger now. I feel the imperfection within me, and long to purge it. In time, Emperor willing, I will go to Mars and learn the mysteries, just as he did.

Not yet. For now, there is too much of my old self, my old corruption. The flesh remains, impeding the progress of the machine.

I still feel the ghost of my old hand, the one they took away to mark my ascension into Raukaan. Far less, it is true, but I feel it nonetheless.

I wish never to feel it again. I wish to forget the face of Raef Khamed, to forget that there is hope and disappointment in the universe.

This is my task, the reason for my existence, and nothing else will suffice. I will work at it. I will persevere. I will purge the weakness of the flesh.

I will be Ralech Grond, Iron Hand, or I will be nothing.

TWELVE WOLVES

Ben Counter

The sons of Fenris look not only to the future, but also to their noble past and so my task is a most arduous one. Think not that the saga I speak comes to this tongue easily, or that to bend the ear of a mead-soaked Blood Claw is a task any less worthy than bringing the bolter and chainsword to the Emperor's foes! No, indeed, to tell these tales of the past, and to have them listened to by the Brothers of the Wolf, is a task whose difficulty is matched only by the weight of the duty I bear in telling them.

I hear you now, throaty and raucous, demanding to hear a saga of some great battle or feat of arms that will fill your hearts with fire. Lord Russ fighting the One-Eyed traitor, you cry! The many crimes of the Dark Angels, you demand, so that we might feast and drink and remember our grudges! But my purpose here is not to serve this feasting throng with whatever bloody tale they desire. No, I have gathered you by this roaring fire, in the grand hall of the Fang where generations of Space Wolves have celebrated their victories and toasted their dead, because there is a lesson I have to impart.

I do not need an Astartes' augmented senses to hear your sighs. What use, you whisper to yourselves, is a saga not dripping with the blood of foes and thundering with the sound of chainblade on heretic flesh? Fear not! There will be blood. Could an old thrall like me, a broken, haggard thing kept in pity by the Chapter whose standards I failed to reach in my youth, hope to survive if he spoke of anything but battles and glory to a roomful of Astartes? It is from the Wolf Priests themselves, the guardians of your spirits, that I learned this tale, and they know better than to impart lessons that will not be heeded.

It is in a great battle of the past, then, that our tale takes place. Those attentive young wolves will know of the Age of Apostasy, one of the direst lessons that mankind has ever had to learn, during which the corrupt clergy of the Imperial Creed sought to seize power for themselves. It is a long and grim story in its own right that I will not tell here. Suffice it to say that it was a time of blindness, fear and chaos, when the Imperium of Man sought to crumble in a way not threatened since the dark times of Horus. Among the many tales of sorrow in this time, our story concerns that of the Plague of Unbelief, when a wicked man named Cardinal Bucharis carved out an empire of his own, throwing off Imperial authority to rule as a king!

Bucharis, while a cunning and fearless man, was a fool. For as his empire grew, conquered by renegades of the Imperial Guard and armies of mercenary cutthroats, he came to the threshold of Fenris. Arrogant in the extreme, Bucharis did not halt there and turn back, afeared of the Space Wolves who called it their home then as you do now. No, he sent his armies to Fenris, to conquer its savage peoples and force the Space Wolves to cede their world to him!

Ah, yes, you laugh. Who could have thought that an Apostate Cardinal and a host of mere men could defeat the Space Wolves on their home world? But it happened that at this time very few Space Wolves were at the Fang, with most of them having joined the Wolf Lord Kyrl Grimblood on a crusade elsewhere in the galaxy. The Space Wolves left there to face Bucharis's villains numbered little more than a single Great Company, along with the newly-blooded novices and the thralls who dwell within the Fang. Bucharis, meanwhile, bled the garrisons of his empire white to flood Fenris with soldiers and lay siege to the Fang. Do not think that the Fang was impregnable to them! Any fortress, even this ancient and formidable mountain hold, can fall.

In the third month of this siege two Space Wolves were abroad in the valleys and foothills around the Fang. They were patrolling to disrupt and observe the enemy forces, as the sons of Fenris were wont to do at that time in the battle. One of them, and his name was Daegalan, was a Long Fang such as those battered, leather-coloured Astartes who watch us even now from the back of the hall. They have heard this tale many times, but take note, young Blood Claws and novices, that they still listen, for they understand its lesson well. The other was much like you. His name was Hrothgar, and he was a Blood Claw. Daegalan was wise and stern, and had taken Hrothgar as a student to teach him the ways of war that, with the Fang and the Chapter in great peril, he had to learn very quickly.

Imagine a mountain ridge at night, bare flint as sharp as knives clad in ice that glinted under the many stars and moons of mother Fenris. It overlooked a wide, rocky valley, cleared of snow by tanks and shored up by engineers, like a black serpent winding between the flinty blades of the Fang's foothills. Now you are there, the story can begin.

Two Astartes made their way up to the lip of this ridge. One of them wore a wolf skin cloak about his shoulders, and across his back was slung a missile launcher. This was Daegalan. His face was like a mask of tanned leather, so deeply lined it might have been carved with a knife, his grey-streaked hair whipping around his head in the night's chill wind. He wore on his shoulder pad the symbol of Wolf Lord Hef Icenheart, who at that time was directing the defence of the Fang from its granite halls. The other, with the red slash marks painted on his shoulder pad, was Hrothgar. The scars, where the organs of an Astartes were implanted, were still red on his shaven scalp. His chainsword was in his hand, for it rarely left, and his armour was unadorned with markings of past campaigns.

'See, young cub,' said Daegalan. 'This is the place where our enemy creeps, like vermin, thinking he is hidden from our eyes. Look down, and tell me what you see.'

Hrothgar looked over the edge of the ridge into the valley. The night's darkness was no hindrance to the eyes of an Astartes. He saw a track laid along the bottom of the valley, along which could be wheeled the huge siege guns and war machines which Bucharis's armies hoped would shake the sides of the Fang and bring its defences down. Slave labour on the worlds the Cardinal had captured had created countless such machines and they filled the bellies of spacecraft supplying his war on Fenris. Indeed, it was the mission of the two Astartes to locate and disrupt the bringing of these war machines to a location where they could fire on the Fang.

Many Guardsmen, from the renegade Rigellian regiments who had thrown their lot in with Bucharis, guarded the tracks, knowing that soon the precious war machines would come trundling along it.

'I count twenty of the enemy,' said Hrothgar. 'Imperial Guard all, they are reasonably trained – not the equal of a Space Wolf, of course, but dangerous if they can fire upon us in great numbers. See, Long Fang, they have assembled defences of flak-weave and ammunition crates, and they seem ready for an attack by such as us. They know the importance of their mission.'

'Good,' said Daegalan, 'for a first glance. But our task here is to destroy these enemies. What can you see that will ensure they fall?'

'This one, 'said Hrothgar, 'is the officer that leads them. See the medals and badges of rank on his uniform? That silver skull on his chest is granted by the heretic Cardinal to followers who show great ruthlessness in leading the troops. Upon one sleeve are the marks of his rank. In his hand is a map case, surely marking out the route of these tracks. This man must die first, for with their leader dead, the others will fall into disarray.'

Daegalan smiled at this, and showed the grand canine teeth that are the mark of a true Long Fang. May you who listen to this one day sport such fangs as these, sharp and white, to tell the tale of your years spent fighting with the Sons of Russ! 'Young Blood Claw,' said Daegalan, 'can it be that even with the eyes of an Astartes you are so blind? You must learn the lessons of the Twelve Wolves of Fenris, those great beasts who even now hunt through the mountains and snowy plains of our world. Each wolf is taken as the totem of one of our Great Companies, and for good reason.' Daegalan here tapped the symbol of his Great Company on his shoulder pad. 'I wear the symbol of Wolf Lord Icenheart. He took as his totem Torvald the Far-Sighted, the wolf whose eyes miss nothing. This wolf of Fenris teaches us to observe our enemy, much as we would love to get our claws around his throat first, for it is in looking ahead that the victory can sometimes be won before a blow is struck.

'Look again. The man you see is indeed an officer, and no doubt a ruthless one at that. But there is another. There, seated on an ammunition crate, his lasgun propped up by his side. See him? He is reading from a book. Even these old eyes can read its title. It is the *Collected Visions*, a book written by the Apostate Cardinal himself, serving as a collection of his madness and heresies. Only the most devout of his followers, when the night is this cold and the mission is this crucial, would read it so earnestly. This man may not be the officer who leads these soldiers on paper, but he leads them in reality. He is their spiritual heart, the one to whom they turn for true leadership. This man must die first, for when it is shown that the most devout of them is no more than meat and bone beneath our claws, then all their hope shall flee them.'

Hrothgar thought upon this, and he saw the truth in the Long Fang's words.

'Then let us fight,' said the Blood Claw. 'The reader of books shall die first, beneath these very hands!'

'Alas, I have but two missiles left,' said Daegalan, 'otherwise I would sow fire and death among them from up here. I shall fight alongside you, then. When you tear the heart from them, I shall slay the rest, including that officer to whom you paid so much attention.'

With this Hrothgar vaulted down from the ridge and crashed with a snarl into the heart of the enemy. He charged for the spiritual leader, and was upon him before the other Guardsmen had even raised their lasguns! At that time the Space Wolves were sorely lacking of ammunition for their guns and power packs for their chainswords, and so it was with his hands that Hrothgar hauled the reader of books into the air and dashed his brains out against the rocks.

'He is dead!' came the cry from the Guardsmen. 'He who assured us that the divine Cardinal would deliver us, he whose survival proved to us the sureness of our victory! He is dead!' And they wailed in much terror.

Daegalan was among them now. He was not as fast as the Blood Claw, but he surpassed him in strength and cunning. He fought with his knife, and plunged it up to the hilt in the skull of the first Guardsman who faced him. Another died, head cracked open by the swinging of his fist, and then another, speared through the midriff. The officer, who was shouting and trying to steel the hearts of his men, fell next, knocked to the ground and crushed beneath Daegalan's armour-shod feet.

It was, but the space of a few heartbeats, as a non-Astartes might reckon it, that the enemy were torn asunder and scattered. Those that were not dead cursed their fates and fled into the snowy wilderness, eager to face the teeth and claws of Mother Fenris rather than spend another moment in that blood-spattered valley.

The hot breath of the two Astartes was white in the cold as they panted like predators sated from the hunt. But this hunt was not finished. For from down the tracks came the sound of steel feet on the rocks, and the roaring voice of an engine. And before the Astartes could ready themselves, from the frozen darkness lumbered a Sentinel walker.

Many of you have seen such a thing, and perhaps even fought alongside them, for they are commonly used by the armies of the Imperial Guard. This, however, was different. Its two legs were reinforced with sturdy armour plates and its cab, in which its traitor driver cowered, was as heavily plated as a tank. It had been made with techniques forgotten to the masters of the forge worlds today, and it bore as its weapon a pair of autocannon. This was no mere spindly scouting machine! This was an engine of destruction.

'Despair not!' shouted the headstrong Hrothgar as this monster came into view. 'You shall not have to face this machine, old man, wizened and decrepit as you are! I shall ensure this traitor's eyes are on me alone. All you need do, venerable one, is fire that missile launcher of yours!'

Daegalan had it in mind to scold the Blood Claw for his insolence, but it was not the time for such things.

Hrothgar ran into view of the Sentinel. He fired off shots from his bolt pistol, and the Sentinel turned to hunt him through the valley's shadows. But Hrothgar was fast and valiant, and even as the Sentinel's mighty guns opened fire he sprinted from rock to rock, from flinty fissure to deep shadow, and every shell spat by the Sentinel's guns was wasted against unyielding stone. At that time it happened a flurry of snow was blown up by Mother Fenris's icy breath and Hrothgar ventured closer still, diving between the metal feet of the Sentinel, knowing that he was too fast and his movements too unpredictable for the machine's pilot to fire upon him with accuracy.

So infuriated was the pilot of the Sentinel that he forgot, as lesser soldiers than Astartes are wont to do, the true threat he was facing. For

Daegalan the Long Fang had indeed taken aim with his missile launcher, the only weapon the Astartes had between them that might pierce the machine's armour. With a roar the missile fired, and with a vicious bark it exploded. The rear of the Sentinel was torn clear away, and the pilot mortally wounded. Exposed to the cold night, the blood from his many wounds froze. But he did not have long to suffer this fate, for Hrothgar the Blood Claw climbed up the legs of the Sentinel and tore out the traitor's spine with his bare hands.

'You may think,' said Daegalan, 'to have angered this old Long Fang with your insolence, but in truth you have expounded the lesson of another of Fenris's wolves – or rather, two of them, for they are Freki and Geri, the Twin Wolves who were companions of Leman Russ himself. See how this enemy, a match for both of us, was destroyed by the fruits of our brotherhood! When wolves fight as a pack, as one, they slay foes that would confound them if they merely attacked as individuals. You have learned well, though you did not know it, the lesson of the Twin Wolves!'

With that, the two Astartes set about destroying the tracks, and for many days as a result the walls of the Fang were spared the bombardment of Bucharis's war machines, and the lives of many Space Wolves were surely spared.

Now, it was about this time that the Apostate Cardinal, accursed Bucharis himself, was upon Fenris directing the siege of the Fang. You already know that he was a man possessed of great arrogance and blindness to the rage he inflamed in those who suffered under his conquest. He was also a wrathful man, much given to extravagant punishments and feats of cruelty when angered. Having heard from a subordinate that his war machines (which he expected to shatter the Fang and slay all those within) would be delayed by the actions of the Astartes, he flew into a rage. He supposed that a great host of Space Wolves had done this deed, and that with their destruction the defenders of the Fang would be greatly weakened in number. A foolish man, I hear you cry. Indeed he was, but he was also a very dangerous man, whose foolishness lay not in an inability to achieve his goals but in ignorance of the consequences his cruelty would have. You know, of course, that Bucharis was eventually to meet an end as befits a man like him, but that is a story for another time.

Many units of the Imperial Guard were sent to punish the host of Astartes that Bucharis believed to be abroad in the foothills of the Fang. They were men picked by Bucharis's warmaster, the renegade Colonel Gasto, from the regiments of Rigellians he commanded. They had been well versed in the beliefs of Bucharis, which were heretical in the extreme and shall not be spoken of by this humble tongue. They believed Bucharis's lies that the Imperium had fallen and that only by obeying Bucharis could they hope to survive its collapse. Gasto gave them tanks and heavy weapons, and the kind of murderous cutthroat mercenaries that Bucharis had swayed to his cause to lead them.

These men and machines left the great siege encampment of the Rigellian Guard and headed for the Fang, ordered on pain of death to destroy the Astartes.

Meanwhile, Daegalan the Long Fang and Hrothgar the Blood Claw were making their way back to the Fang, for their mission was completed. Though it was now daylight a storm had fallen over the area and Mother Fenris was breathing ice across the flinty hills. Terrible gales blew and showers of ice fell like daggers.

'Remember,' said Daegalan as he led Hrothgar up the slippery slope of a barren hill, 'that it is cruel weather such as this that makes every blasted and inhospitable place the domain of Haegr, the Mountain Wolf. For he endures all, indeed, he thrives in such inhospitable climes. It is to him that we must look, for is it not so that the physical endurance of an Astartes is a weapon in itself, and that by taking this hazardous path we make better time towards the Fang and further confound our enemies?'

Hrothgar did not answer this, for while he was young and vigorous, the Long Fang was so much inured to hardships and gnarled by Fenris's icy winds that the old Astartes did not feel the cold as much as the Blood Claw. But he did indeed recall the Mountain Wolf and, knowing that the sons of Fenris are made of stern stuff, he shrugged off his discomfort and the two made good speed over the hills.

It was at the pinnacle of the next hill that a break in the storm gave them a glimpse of the Fang. It was the first time they had seen it in many days. Daegalan bade his companion to stop, and look for a moment upon the Fang itself.

'This tooth of ice and stone, this spear piercing the white sky, does this not fill your heart with gladness, young Blood Claw?'

'Indeed,' said Hrothgar, 'I am now struck by the majesty of it. It gladdens me to think of the despair our foes must suffer when they see it, for those are the slopes they must climb! Those are the walls they must breach!' And all of you have seen the Fang and, I do not doubt, imagined how any foe might hope to silence the guns that stud its sides or climb the sheer slopes that guard its doors more surely than any army.

'Then you feel,' said Daegalan, 'the howl of Thengir in your veins! For he is the King Wolf, the monarch of Fenris, and everything under his domain is alight with glory and majesty. So you see, ignorant and insolent young cub, that another of Fenris's wolves has a lesson to teach us today.'

Hrothgar did indeed hear Thengir, like a distant howl, speaking of the kingly aspect of the Fang as it rules over all the mountains of Fenris.

'And mark also the Wolf Who Stalks Between Stars,' continued

Daegalan, 'as you look above the Fang to the moons that hang in the sky. The Stalker Between Stars was the totem of Leman Russ himself, and even now his symbol adorns the Great Wolf's own pack. Our pawprints may be found even on distant worlds and the farthest-flung corners of the Imperium. So long as we, like that wolf, hunt abroad among the stars, then Fenris is not merely the ground beneath our feet but also any place where the Sons of Fenris have trod, where the Space Wolves have brought fang and fire to their enemies!'

Hrothgar's hearts swelled with pride as he thought of the mark the Space Wolves had left upon the galaxy beyond Fenris. But the Astartes could not tarry for long, and quickly made their way on.

Soon Daegalan saw the white tongues of engine exhausts nearby, and knew that the traitor Guard were close. He led Hrothgar into a winding valley, deep and dark even when the sun broke through the blizzards. Many such valleys lead through the foothills of the Fang, chill and black, and within their depths lurk many of the most deadly things with which Mother Fenris has populated her world.

'I can tell,' said Daegalan after some time, 'your frustration, young Blood Claw. You wish to get to grips with the foe and cover your armour with their blood! But remember, if you will, that another wolf stalks beside us. Ranek, the Hidden Wolf, goes everywhere unseen, silent and cunning. In just such a way do we stalk unseen. Do not scorn the Hidden Wolf, young one! For his claws are as sharp as any other, and when he strikes from the shadows the wound is doubly deep!'

Hrothgar was a little consoled by this as he listened to the engines of the enemy's tanks and the voices of the soldiers raised as they called to one another. They could not traverse the foothills of the Fang as surely as a Space Wolf, and many of them were lost as they stumbled into gorges or fell through thin ice. Driven by their fear of Bucharis they made good time but paid for it in lives, and with every step the force became more and more ragged. Hrothgar imagined slaying them as he emerged from hiding, and he smiled.

'Now you think of killing them by the dozen,' continued Daegalan, for he never passed by the opportunity to instruct a younger Astartes. 'But ask yourself, in this butchery you imagine, is there any place for me, your battle-brother? You need not reply, for of course there is not. I do not admonish you this, Blood Claw. Quite the opposite, I commend you to the spirit of Lokyar, the Lone Wolf. While the Twin Wolves teach us of brotherhood, Lokyar reminds us that sometimes we must fight alone. He is the totem of our Wolf Scouts, those solitary killers, and now he may be your totem, too, for it is Lokyar whose path you tread as you imagine yourself diving into our enemy alone.'

Now our two Astartes came to the head of the valley, where it reached the surface. They espied before them fearsome barricades set up by the traitor Guard, the bayonets of the heretics glinting in the sun that now broke through the storm clouds. Dozens of them were waiting for the Astartes, and they were trembling for they believed that a host of Astartes would stream from the black valley.

'Ah, may we give thanks to Mother Fenris,' said Hrothgar the Blood Claw, 'for she has guided our friends to meet us! What a grand reunion this shall be! I shall embrace our friends with these bloody hands and I shall give them all gifts of a happy death!'

'Now I see the battle favours the youthful and the heedless of danger,' said Daegalan in reply, 'and is content to leave the old and cunning behind. Go, Brother Hrothgar! Bestow upon them the welcome your young wolf's heart lusts for! And remember the Iron Wolf, too, for he watches over the artificers of our Chapter forge wherein your armour was smelted. Trust in him that your battlegear will turn aside their laser fire and their bullets, and run with him into battle!'

Hrothgar recalled, indeed, the Iron Wolf, whose pelt can turn aside even the teeth of the kraken who haunt the oceans of Fenris. And he ran from the darkness of the valley. The soldiers opened fire as one and bolts of red laser fell around the Blood Claw like a rain of burning blood. But his armour held firm, the Iron Wolf's teachings having guided well the artificers of the Fang.

Ah, how I wish I had the words to describe Hrothgar in that bloody hour! His armour was red to the elbow and the screams of his enemies were like a blizzard gale howling through the mountains. He leapt the barriers the traitors had set up and even as he landed, men were dying around him. He drew his chainsword and its teeth chewed through muscle and bone. One heretic he spitted through the throat, throwing him off with a flick of a wrist, and a heartbeat later a skull was staved in by a strike from his gauntleted fist. He cut them apart and crushed them underfoot. He threw them aside and hurled them against the rocks. He took the lasgun from one and stabbed him through the stomach with his own bayonet. Some traitors even fell to their own laser fire as the men around them fired blindly, seeing in their terror Astartes charging from every shadow.

Daegalan followed Hrothgar into the fray. Some leader amongst the traitors called out for a counterattack and bullied a few men into charging at Hrothgar with their bayonets lowered. Daegalan fell amongst them, his combat knife reaping a terrible toll. He cut arms and heads from bodies, and when he was faced by the officer alone he grabbed the heretic fool with both arms. He crushed the life out of the man, holding him fast in a terrible embrace.

The Guardsmen fled, but Hrothgar was not done. Some he followed behind outcrops of rock where they sought to hide. He hauled them out, as a hunter's hounds might drag an unwilling prey from a burrow, and killed them there on the ground. When they tried to snipe at him from some high vantage point he trusted in his armour to scorn their fire and clambered to meet them, holding them above his head and throwing them down to be dashed to pieces against the rocks below.

When the traitors bled, their blood froze around their wounds, for Mother Fenris had granted the Astartes a day bright yet as cold as any that had ever passed around the Fang. Blood fell like a harvest of frozen rubies. Now Daegalan and Hrothgar rested in the centre of this field of bloody jewels, as bright and plentiful as if Mother Fenris herself was bleeding. They were exhausted by their killing and they panted like wolves after the kill, their breath white in the cold. They were covered in blood, their faces spattered with it, their pack emblems and Great Company totems almost hidden. Silently, each gave thanks to Fenris herself for the hunt, and even to Cardinal Bucharis for his foolishness and arrogance, for it was he who had sent them such prey.

Above them loomed the Fang, wherein their battle-brothers waited to receive the news of their success. Prey lay dead all around them, and the majesty of Fenris was all about. What more could a Space Wolf ask for? It was indeed a good day, and may you young pups have many such hunts ahead of you.

'Well fought, my brother,' said Daegalan. 'It is well that the Apostate Cardinal stumbled upon Fenris, for without his ill fortune we would not have such hunts upon our very doorstep!'

'He should have a statue in the Hall of Echoes,' agreed Hrothgar. 'Was there ever a man who did more for the glory of the Space Wolves? I think I shall toast him with a barrel of mead when we celebrate this hunt.'

They laughed at that, and it was to this sound that the rumble of engines grew closer and a shadow fell over them. For the mercenaries who led the Guardsmen were hard-bitten and foul-minded men, well versed in the low cunning of war, and they had prepared a trap for the Astartes.

The force the Space Wolves had slaughtered were just the vanguard of the army sent to punish them. Bucharis had sent in his fear ten times that number, sorely stretching the forces that besieged the Fang elsewhere. They had with them tanks: Reaper-class war machines such as can no longer be made by the forge worlds of the Mechanicus. Six of these machines had survived the journey, and they all rumbled into view now, their guns aiming at the place where the two Astartes stood.

The Guardsmen, though sorely pressed by the harsh journey through the foothills, numbered hundreds, and they had brought many heavy weapons with which to destroy the Astartes from afar – for they feared to face the claws and teeth of the Space Wolves up close, and rightly so. Their leaders, Bucharis's chosen mercenaries, were strong and brutal men who wore pieces of uniform and armour from a dozen places they had plundered, and all wore the scars of war like banners proclaiming their savagery. They, too, were afraid of the Astartes, but they turned their fear into brutality and so the men under them obeyed them out of terror.

One such man addressed the Astartes through the vox-caster of his tank. By the standards of such men, it was a bold thing to do indeed!

'Astartes!' he called to them. 'Noble sons of Fenris! The honoured Lord Bucharis, monarch of his galactic empire, has no quarrel with the Space Wolves. He seeks only to grant protection to those within the fold of his generosity. For the Imperium has fallen, and Terra lies aflame and ruined. Lord Bucharis promises safety and sanity for those who kneel to him!

'But we do not ask you to kneel. How could we, mere men, demand such of Astartes? No, we ask only that Lord Bucharis count Fenris among the worlds of his empire. What do you care for this grim and frozen place, its savage peoples and its bitter oceans? To the Space Wolves, of course, we shall leave the Fang, and the right to rule yourselves, excepting a few minor and quite necessary obeisances to Lord Bucharis's undoubted majesty. So you see, there is no need for you to fight any more. There is nothing left for you to prove. Stand down and place yourselves within our custody, and we shall deliver you safely unto the Fang where you can pass on word of Lord Bucharis's matchless generosity.'

The Astartes, of course, saw through these lies. They knew the Imperium was eternal, and had not fallen, and moreover they believed no more than you do that Bucharis meant to destroy the Space Wolves and take the Fang for himself. No doubt he wished to install himself in our great fortress, and to use as his throne room the hall wherein Leman Russ himself once held court! The only answer to such a speech lies at the tip of a wolf's claws, or in the gnashing of his fangs!

'Now, young wolf,' said Daegalan, 'we face our death. How blessed are we that we can look it in the face as it comes for us. And moreover, we die on Fenris, on the ground upon which we were born, and first ran with our packs in the snow. This is the world that forged us into the Astartes we are, that gave us the strength and ferocity to be accepted into the ranks of the Space Wolves. Now we shall repay that honour by choosing this very ground for our deaths! How blessed are we, Blood Claw, and how blessed am I that it is beside my brother that I die.

'And do not think that we shall die alone. For I hear the snarling of Lakkan, the Runed Wolf, upon the wind. Once Lakkan walked across Fenris, and wise men read the symbols he left in his footprints. These men were the first Rune Priests and those who still follow the path of Lakkan even now watch us from the Fang. They scry out our deeds, and they shall record them, and give thanks as we do that we die a death so fine.'

Daegalan now drew his bolt pistol. He had but a single magazine of bolt shells, for at that time the Astartes were sorely pressed for ammunition with their fortress besieged. Hrothgar, in turn, drew once more his chainsword. Its teeth were clotted with the frozen blood of traitors, but soon, he knew, he would plunge it into a warm body and thaw out that blood so its teeth could gnash again.

'I do not seek death,' said the Blood Claw, 'as easily as you do, old man.'

'Your saga shall be a fine one,' replied Daegalan, 'though it is short.'

'Perhaps you are right,' said Hrothgar, and in that moment the guns of the tanks were levelled at the place where they stood in the field of blood rubies. 'You are a Long Fang, after all, and wise. But I fear that in all you have taught me you have made a single error.'

'And what might that be, Blood Claw?' said Daegalan. 'What omission have I made that is so grave I must hear of it now, in the moment of my death?'

Now a strange countenance came upon Hrothgar the Blood Claw. His teeth flashed like fangs and his eyes turned into the flinty black orbs of the hunting wolf. 'You have spoken of the wolves of Fenris that follow us and impart to us their lessons. Twelve of them you have described to me, each one mirroring an aspect of Fenris or of the teachings the Wolf Priests have passed down to us. These lessons were well earned, and I thank you for them, Brother Daegalan. But I am wiser than you in but one aspect.'

'Speak of it, you cur!' demanded Daegalan with much impatience, for the guns of the traitor tanks were now aimed at them, awaiting the order to fire, as were the heavy weapons of the Guardsmen.

'I have counted twelve Fenrisian wolves in your teachings, each one taken as the totem of a Great Company of the Space Wolves. But here you are mistaken. For I know that in truth, there are not twelve wolves. There are thirteen.'

It is time, I fear, for this old tongue to lie still and for a draught of mead to warm this thrall's bones. You wish the story to continue? I have no doubt you foresee great bloodshed of the kind you love to hear. And there was bloodshed after that moment, it is true. Terrible it was, perhaps worse than any that fell upon the face of Mother Fenris during the besieging of the Fang. But it is not for me to speak of it. I hear you groan, and a few even flash your fangs in anger! But look to the Long Fangs who sit at the back of the hall. Do they growl their displeasure? No, for they know the truth. A thrall such as I has no place speaking of such things. Even the most ancient among the children of Russ, the mighty Dreadnoughts who have marched to war for a thousand years or more, would not speak of it.

There is, however, a legend told among the people of Gathalamor, the world where the Apostate Bucharis first came to prominence. They are a fearful and religious people, for upon them has fallen the burden of redeeming their world from the stain the Apostate left upon it. But sometimes they speak of legends forbidden by the cardinals of their world, and among them is this one, brought back, it is said, by the few survivors of the armies who fought on Fenris.

Once an army was sent by Bucharis to destroy the Astartes who had been sowing much death and confusion among the besieging forces. The army cornered the Astartes but found, much to their delight, that they faced not a Battle Company or even a single pack, but a single Space Wolf.

In some versions of the tale there was not one Space Wolf, but two. The difference matters not.

Now the soldiers drove their tanks into range and took aim at the Astartes. And they awaited only the order to open fire, which would surely have been given but a moment later. But then they were struck by a great and monstrous fear, such as rarely enters the hearts even of the most cowardly of men.

The Space Wolf was an Astartes no more. In fact, he appeared as nothing that could once have been a man. A bestial countenance overcame him, and the winds howled as if Fenris herself was recoiling in disgust. Talons grew from his fingers. His armour warped and split as his body deformed, shoulders broadening and spine hunching over in the aspect of a beast. The soldiers cried that a daemon had come into their midst, and men fled the sight of it. Even the gunners in their tanks did not think themselves safe from the horror unfolding in front of them.

And then there came the slaughter. The beast charged and butchered men with every stroke of its gory claws. It tore open the hulls of their tanks and ripped out the men inside. In its frenzy it feasted on them, and strips of bloody skin and meat hung from its inhuman fangs. Men went mad with the force of its onslaught. The leaders of that army fired on their own men to keep them from fleeing but the beast fell on them next and the last moments of their life were filled with terror and the agony of claws through their flesh.

The soldiers were thrown to the winds of Fenris and scattered. Some say that none survived, either torn down by the beast or frozen to death as they cowered from it. Others insist that a single man survived to tell the tale, but that he was driven hopelessly mad and the legend of the Beast of Fenris was all that ever escaped his quivering lips.

But this is a tale told by other men, far from the Fang and the proud sons of Fenris who dwell therein, and I shall dwell upon it no more.

Now it came that many days later, when the battle had waxed and waned as battles do, a pack of Grey Hunters ventured forth from the Fang to drive off the traitor Guardsmen who were thought to be encamped in the foothills. There they came across a place like a field of rubies, where frozen blood lay scattered across the snowy rocks with such great abandon that it seemed a great battle had been fought there, though the pack-mates knew of no such battle.

'Look!' cried one Space Wolf. 'Someone yet lives! He is clad in the armour of a Space Wolf and yet he is not one, for see, his bearing is that of an animal and his face bears no trace of the human we all were before becoming Astartes.'

The pack leader bade his battle-brothers to cover him with their boltguns as he went to see what they had found. As he approached he saw countless bodies torn asunder, many with the marks of teeth in their frozen flesh, and still others dead in the ruins of their tanks.

The figure in the centre of the battlefield indeed wore the power armour of an Astartes, but split apart and ruined as if rent from within. He crouched panting in the cold, as if fresh from a hunt. His form was not that of a human, but of a beast.

'He is touched by the Wulfen,' said the pack leader. 'The Thirteenth Wolf of Fenris has walked here, and its inhumanity has found a place to dwell inside this Blood Claw. Some flaw in his gene-seed went unnoticed during his novicehood, and now it has come to the fore in this place of bloodshed.'

Another Space Wolf cried out. 'There lies another of our battle-brothers, dead beside him! What appalling wounds he has suffered! What monstrous force must have torn his armour so, and what claws must have ripped at his flesh!'

'Indeed,' said the pack leader, 'this noble brother was a Long Fang, one of that wise and hardy breed, and he shall be borne by us to a proper place of resting within the Fang. Alas, I knew him – he is Brother Daegalan, I recognise him by his pack markings. But see, the claws of the survivor made these wounds! His teeth have gnashed at the fallen Astartes's armour, and even upon his bones.'

The pack was much dismayed at this. 'What Space Wolf could turn on his brother?' they asked.

'Mark well the path of the Wulfen,' said the pack leader sternly. 'His is the way of deviant and frenzied bloodshed. He cares not from whom the blood flows as long as the hunting is good. This ill-fated Long Fang is testament to that – when this Blood Claw ran out of foes to slay, under the Wulfen's influence he turned upon his brother.'

The pack spoke prayers to mighty Russ and to the ancestors of the Chapter, and all those interred in the Fang, to watch over them and protect them from such a fate as suffered by the two Astartes.

You might think that a beast such as they found should have been put down, but imagine for a moment you were confronted by such a sight. It would surely be impossible for you to kill one such as Hrothgar, for though a warped and pitiable thing he was still a Son of Fenris and to slay him was still to slay a brother. So the pack brought Daegalan's body and Hrothgar, still living, to the Fang. I have heard it said they led him by a chain like an animal, or that they called upon a Wolf Priest to administer a powerful concoction that sedated him long enough to be carried to the Fang.

And so it came to be that Daegalan the Long Fang was given his rightful place among the packmates who had fallen over the decades, and there he lies still. As for Hrothgar, well, he was interred in a similar way, this time in a cell hollowed out from the rock of the Fang's very heart where from the lightless cold none can hope to escape.

Hush! Cease the sound of clinking tankards. Ignore the crackling of the fire. Can you hear it? That scratching at the walls? That is Brother Hrothgar, scrabbling at the boundaries of his cell, for he is now but an animal and yearns to run in the snows of Fenris, hunting beast and brother alike. But sometimes he remembers who he once was, and the Long Fang who fought alongside him, and then he lets out a terrible mournful howl. You can hear it in the longest of Fenris's nights, echoing around the heart of the Fang.

Now, my tale has come to an end. Perhaps now you understand why it was to a lowly thrall that this saga has been given to tell, and not one of the venerable Wolf Priests or well-scarred Long Fangs who uttered its grim words. What true Space Wolf could bear to have such things pass his lips?

And perhaps a few of you have even understood the lesson that lies at its heart. The rest will have to listen for Hrothgar's claws, for Hrothgar's howl, and perhaps the truth will come to you.

Remember always, whether you hunt in the wilds that Mother Fenris tends, or you stalk between the stars, the thirteen wolves hunt beside you.

SUFFER NOT THE UNCLEAN TO LIVE

Gav Thorpe

Yakov caught himself dozing as his chin bowed to his chest, lulled by the soporific effect of the warm sun and the steady clatter of hooves on the cobbled street. Blinking himself awake, he gazed from the open carriage at the buildings going past him. Colonnaded fronts and tiers of balconies stretched above him for several storeys, separated by wide tree-lined streets. Thick-veined marble fascias swept past, followed by dark granite facades whose polished surfaces reflected the mid-afternoon light back at him.

Another kilometre and the first signs of decay began to show. Crumbling mosaics scattered their stones across the narrowing pavements, creeping plants twined around balustrades and cornices. Empty windows, some no longer glazed, stared back at him. With a yell to the horses, the carriage driver brought them to a stop and sat there waiting for the preacher to climb down to the worn cobbles.

'This is as far as I'm allowed,' the driver said without turning around, sounding half apologetic and half thankful.

Yakov walked around to the driver's seat and fished into the pocket of his robe for coins, but the coachman avoided his gaze and set off once more, turning the carriage down a sidestreet and out of sight. Yakov knew better – no honest man on Karis Cephalon would take payment from a member of the clergy – but he still hadn't broken the habit of paying for services and goods. He had tried to insist once on tipping a travel-rail porter, and the man had nearly broken down in tears, his eyes fearful. Yakov had been here four years now, and yet still he was adjusting to the local customs and beliefs.

Hoisting his embroidered canvas pack further onto his shoulder, Yakov continued his journey on foot. His long legs carried him briskly past the ruins of counting houses and ancient stores, apartments that once belonged to the fabulously wealthy and the old Royal treasury, abandoned now for over seven centuries. He had already walked for a kilometre when he topped the gradual rise and looked down upon his parish.

Squat, ugly shacks nestled in the roads and alleys between the once-mighty edifices of the royal quarter. He could smell the effluence of the near-homeless, the stench of unwashed bodies and the strangely exotic melange of cooking which swept to him on the smoke of thousands of fires. The sun was beginning to set as he made his way down the long hill, and soon the main boulevard was dropped into cool shadow, chilling after the earlier warmth.

Huts made from corrugated metal, rough planks, sheets of plasthene and other detritus butted up against the cut stones of the old city blocks. The babble of voices could now be heard, the screeching of children and the yapping and barking of dogs adding to the muted racket. The clatter of pans as meals were readied vied with the cries of babes and the clucking of hens. Few of the inhabitants were in sight. Most of them were indoors getting ready to eat, the rest still working out in the fields, or down the mines in the far hills.

A small girl, perhaps twelve Terran years old, came running out from behind a flapping sheet of coarsely woven hemp. Her laughter was high-pitched, almost a squeal, as a boy, slightly younger perhaps, chased her down and bundled her to the ground. They both seemed to notice Yakov at the same time, and instantly quelled their high spirits. Dusting themselves down they stood up and waited respectfully, heads slightly bowed.

'Katinia, isn't it?' Yakov asked as he stopped in front of the girl.

'Yes, preacher,' she replied meekly, looking up at him with her one good eye. The other was nothing more than a scabbed, red mass which seemed to spill from the socket and across her face, enveloping her left ear and leaving one half of her scalp bald. She smiled prettily at him, and he smiled back.

'Shouldn't you be helping your mother with the cooking?' he suggested, glancing back towards the ramshackle hovel that served as their home.

'Mam's at church,' the girl's younger brother, Pietor, butted in, earning himself a kick on the shin from his sibling. 'She said we was to wait here for her.'

Yakov looked at the boy. His shrivelled right arm and leg gave his otherwise perfectly human body a lopsided look. It was the children that always affected him the most, ever cheerful despite the bleakness of their future, the ghastliness of their surroundings. If all the Emperor's faithful had the same indomitable spirit, He and mankind would have overcome all evil and adversity millennia ago. Their crippled, mutated bodies may be vile, he thought to himself, but their souls were as human as any.

'Too early for church, isn't it?' he asked them both, wondering why anyone would be there at least two hours before mass was due to begin.

'She says she wants to speak to you, with some other people, Preacher Yakov,' Katinia told him, clasping her hands behind her back as she looked up at the tall clergyman.

'Well, get back inside and make sure everything's tidy for when your mother returns, you two,' he told them gently, hoping the sudden worry he felt hadn't shown.

As he hurried on his way, he tried to think what might be happening. He had heard disturbing rumours that in a few of the other shanties a debilitating plague had begun to spread amongst the mutant population. In those unhygienic close confines such diseases spread rapidly, and as slaves from all over the world congregated in the work teams, could leap from ghetto to ghetto with devastating rapidity.

Taking a right turn, Yakov made his way towards the chapel that was also his home. Raised five years ago by the mutants themselves, it was as ramshackle as the rest of the ghetto. The building leaked and was freezing in the winter, baking hot in the summer. Yet the effort put into its construction was admirable, even if the result was deplorable, if not a little insulting. Yakov suspected that Karis Cephalon's cardinal, Prelate Kodaczka, had felt a perverse sense of satisfaction when he had heard who would be sent to tend the mutant parish. Coming from the Armormants, Yakov strongly believed that the edifices raised to the Emperor should be highly ornamented, splendid and glittering works of art in praise of the Holy Father of Mankind. To be given charge of something he would previously have declared unfit for a privy was most demeaning, and even after all this time the thought still rankled. Of course, Kodaczka, like all the native clergy of Karis Cephalon and the surrounding systems, was of the Lucid tendency, preferring poverty and abstinence to ostentation and excessive decoration. It had been a sore point between the two of them during more than one theological discussion, and Yakov's obstinate refusal to accept the prevailing beliefs of his new world did his future prospects within the Ecclesiarchy no favours. Then again, he mused ruefully to himself, his chances of any kind of elevation within the hierarchy had all but died when he had been assigned the shanty as a parish.

As he walked, he saw the rough steeples of the chapel rising over the squat mutie dwellings. Its battered, twisted roofs were slicked with greying mould, despite the aggressive efforts of the voluntary work teams who maintained the shrine. As he picked his way through a labyrinth of drying lines and filth-strewn gutters, Yakov saw a large crowd gathered outside the chapel, as he expected he would. Nearly five hundred of his parishioners, each mutated to a greater or lesser degree, were stood waiting, an angry buzz emanating from the throng. As he approached, they noticed him and started flocking in his direction, and he held up his hands to halt them before they swept around him. Pious they might be, but kind on the nose they were not. They all started babbling at once, in everything from high-pitched squeaks down to guttural bass tones, and once more he raised his hands, silencing them.

'You speak, Gloran,' he said, pointing towards the large mining overseer whose muscled bulk was covered in a constantly flaking red skin and open sores.

'The plague, preacher, has come here,' Gloran told him, his voice as cracked as his flesh. 'Mather Horok died of it this morning, and a dozen others are falling ill already.'

Yakov groaned inwardly but kept his craggy, hawk-like face free of expression. So his suspicions were correct, the deadly scourge had arrived in the parish.

'And you are all here because...?' he asked, casting his dark gaze over the misshapen crowd.

'Come here to ask Emperor, in prayers,' replied Gloran, his large eyes looking expectantly at Yakov.

'I will compose a suitable mass for this evening. Return to your homes and eat; starving will not aid you against this plague,' he said firmly. Some of the assembly moved away but most remained. 'Go!' snapped Yakov waving them away with a thin hand, irritated at their reticence. 'I cannot recall suitable prayers with you taking up all my attention, can I?'

After a few more murmurs the crowd began to dissipate and Yakov turned and strode up the rough plank stairs to the chapel entrance, taking the shallow steps two at a time. He pulled aside the sagging roughspun curtain that served as a barrier to the outside world and stepped inside. The interior of the chapel was as dismal as the outside, with only a few narrow gaps in the planking and crudely bent sheets of metal of the walls to let in light. Motes of dust drifted from the rough-cut ceiling, dancing lightly in the narrow shafts of the ruddy sunlight. Without thought he turned and took a candle from the stand next to the entrance. Picking up a match from next to the pile of tallow lights, one of the few indulgences extracted from the miserly Kodaczka, he struck it on the emery stone and lit the candle. Rather than truly illuminating the chapel the flickering light created a circle of puny light around the preacher, emphasising the gloom beyond its wavering light.

As he walked towards the altar at the far end – an upturned crate covered with an altar spread and a few accoutrements he had brought with him – the candle flame flickered in the draughts wheezing through the ill-built walls, making his shadow dance behind him. Carefully placing the candle in its holder to the left of the altar he knelt, his bony knees protesting at the solidity of the cracked roadway that made up the shrine's floor. Cursing Kodaczka once more – he had taken away Yakov's prayer cushion, saying it was a sign of decadence and weakness – Yakov tried to clear his turbulent thoughts, attempting to find that place of calm that allowed him to bring forth his litanies to the Emperor. He was about to close his eyes when he noticed something on the floor in front of the altar. Looking closer, the preacher saw that it was a dead rat. Yakov sighed, it was not the first time. Despite his oratories against it, some of his parishioners still insisted on their old, barbaric ways, making such offerings to the Emperor in supplication or penance. Pushing these thoughts aside, Yakov closed his eyes, trying to settle himself.

As he stood by the entrance to the shrine, nodding reassuringly to his congregation as they filed out, Yakov felt a hand on his arm and he turned to see a girl. She was young, no older than sixteen standard years by her looks, and her pale face was pretty, framed by dark hair. Taking her hand off his robe, she smiled and it was then that Yakov looked into her eyes. Even in the gloom of the chapel they looked dark and after a moment he realised they were actually jet black, not a trace of iris or white could be seen. She blinked rapidly, meeting his gaze.

'Yes, my child?' Yakov asked softly, bowing slightly so that he could hear her without her needing to raise her voice.

'Thank you for your prayers, Yakov,' she replied and her smile faded. 'But it will take more than prayers to heal your faithful.'

'As the Emperor sees fit,' the preacher murmured in reply, keeping his gaze steady.

'You must ask for medical supplies, from the governor,' she said calmly, not asking him, but stating it as a fact.

'And who are you to tell me what I must and must not do, young lady?' Yakov responded smoothly, keeping the irritation from his voice.

'I am Lathesia,' was her short reply causing Yakov's heart to flutter slightly. The girl was a wanted terrorist. The governor's Special Security Agents had been hunting her for months following attacks on slave pens and the homes of the wealthy landowners. She had already been sentenced to death in absentia in a trial several weeks ago. And here she was talking to him!

'Are you threatening me?' he asked, trying to keep his voice level even though a knot of fear had begun to tighten in his stomach. Her blinking rapidly increased for a moment before she gave a short, childish laugh.

'Oh no!' she squealed, stifling another giggle by covering her mouth with a delicate hand, which Yakov noticed had rough skin peeling on each slender knuckle. Taking control of herself, her face became serious. 'You know what you must do for your parish. Your congregation has already started dying, and only treatment can help them. Go to the prelate, go to the governor, ask them for medicine.'

'I can already tell you what their answer will be,' Yakov said heavily, gesturing for her to follow him as he pulled the heavy curtain shut and started up the aisle.

'And what is that?' Lathesia asked, falling into step beside him, walking with quick strides to keep up with his long-legged gait.

'Medicine is in short supply; slaves are not,' he replied matter-of-factly, stopping and facing her. There was no point trying to make it easier. Every one of Karis Cephalon's ruling class could afford to lose a thousand slaves, but medical supplies, bought at great expense from off-world, could cost them half a year's profits.

Lathesia understood this, but had obviously railed against the fate the Emperor had laid down for her.

'You do realise you have put me in a very awkward position, don't you, child?' he added bitterly.

'Why so?' she answered back. 'Because a preacher should not be conversing with a wanted criminal?'

'No, that is easy to deal with,' Yakov replied after a moment's thought. 'Tomorrow when I see the prelate I will inform him that I saw you and he will tell the governor, who will in turn send the SSA to interrogate me. And I will tell them nearly everything.'

'Nearly everything?' she said with a raised eyebrow.

'Nearly,' he replied with a slight smile. 'After all, if I say that it was you who entreated me to ask for medical supplies, there is even less chance that I will be given them.'

'So you will do this for me?' Lathesia asked with a bright smile.

'No,' Yakov replied, making her smile disappear as quickly as it came.

He stooped to pick up a strip of rag littering the flagstones of the floor. 'But I will do it for my parishioners, as you say. I have no hope that the request will be granted, none at all. And my poor standing with the prelate will be worsened even more by the confrontation, but that is not to be helped. I must do as my duty dictates.'

'I understand, and you have my thanks,' Lathesia said softly before walking away, disappearing through the curtained doorway without a backward glance. Sighing, Yakov crumpled up the rag in his hand and moved to the altar to finish clearing up.

The plexiglass window of the mono-conveyor was scratched and scuffed, but beyond it Yakov could see the capital, Karis, stretched out beneath him. Under the spring sun the whitewashed buildings were stark against the fertile plains surrounding the city. Palaces, counting houses, SSA courthouses and governmental office towers reared from the streets towards him as the conveyor rumbled noisily over its single rail. He could see other conveyor carriages on different tracks, gliding like smoke-belching beetles over the city, their plexiglass-sided cabs reflecting the sun in brief dazzles as it moved in and out from the clouds overhead.

Turning his gaze ahead, he looked at the Amethyst Palace, seat of the governor and cathedral of Karis Cephalon. Its high walls surrounded the hilltop on which it was built, studded with towers from which fluttered massive pennants showing the symbol of the revolutionary council. Once each tower would have hung the standard of one of the old aristocratic families, but they had been burnt, along with those families, in the bloody coup that had overturned their rule seven hundred and thirty years ago.

The keep, punctured at its centre by the mysterious kilometre-high black Needle of Sennamis, rose above the walls, a conglomeration of millennia of additional wings, buttresses and towers obscuring its original architecture like successive layers of patina.

Under his feet, the conveyor's gears began to grind and whirr more loudly as the carriage pulled into the palace docking station. Yakov navigated his way through the terminus without thought, his mind directed towards the coming meeting with Prelate Kodaczka. He barely acknowledged the salutes of the guards at the entrance to the cardinal's chambers, only subconsciously registering that they carried heavy-looking autorifles in addition to their ceremonial spears.

'Ah, Constantine,' Kodaczka murmured as the doors swung closed behind the preacher, looking up at Yakov from behind his high desk. A single laserquill and autotablet adorned its dull black surface, reflecting the sparsity of the rest of the chamber. The walls were plainly whitewashed, like most of the Amethyst palace's interior, with a single Imperial eagle stencilled in black on the wall behind the cardinal. He was a handsome man in his middle ages, maturing with dignity and poise. Dressed in a plain black cassock, his only badge of office the small steel circlet holding back his lustrous blond hair, the cardinal was an elegant, if severe, figure. He wouldn't have looked out of place as a leading actor on the stage at the Revolutionary Theatre; with his active, bright blue eyes, chiselled cheekbones and strong chin he would have enthralled the ladies had he not had another calling.

'Good of you to see me, cardinal,' replied Yakov. At a gestured invitation from Kodaczka the preacher sat in one of the high-backed chairs that were arranged in a semi-circle in front of the desk.

'I must admit to a small amount of surprise at receiving your missive this morning,' Prelate Kodaczka told him, leaning back in his own chair.

'You understand why I felt it necessary to talk to you?' inquired Yakov, waiting for the customary verbal thrust and parry that accompanied all of his conversations with Kodaczka.

'Your parish and the plague? Of course I understand,' Kodaczka nodded as he spoke. He was about to continue when a knock at the door interrupted him. At Kodaczka's call they opened and a servant in the plain livery of an Ecclesiarchal servant entered with a carafe and glass on a small wooden tray.

'I suspect you are thirsty after journeying all this way,' Kodaczka indicated the drink with an open palm. Yakov nodded his thanks, pouring himself a glass of the crisp water and sipping it carefully. The servant left the tray on the desk and retired wordlessly.

'Where was I? Oh yes, the plague. It has struck many of the slave communities badly. Why have you waited until now before requesting aid?' Kodaczka's question was voiced lightly but Yakov suspected he was, as always, being tested somehow. He considered his reply for a moment, sipping more water as an excuse for not answering.

'The other slaves are not my parishioners. They are not my concern,' he said, setting the empty glass back on the tray and raising his eyes to return the gaze of the cardinal.

'Ah, your parish, of course,' agreed Kodaczka with a smile. 'Your duty to your parishioners. And why do you think I can entreat the governor and the committee to act now, when they have let so many others die already?'

'I am simply performing my duty, as you say,' replied Yakov smoothly, keeping his expression neutral. 'I have made no promises other than to raise this with yourself, and I do not expect any particular success on your part. As you say, there has been an abundance of time to act before now. But still, I must ask. Will you ask the governor and the committee to send medical aid and staff to my parish to help defend the faithful against infection by this epidemic?'

'I will not,' Kodaczka answered curtly. 'They have already made it clear to me that not only is the expense of such resources unjustified, but the lifting of the ban on full citizens entering slave areas may prove a difficult legal wrangle.'

'My congregation is dying!' barked Yakov, though in his heart he felt less vehement. 'Can you not do something to help them?'

'I will offer up prayers for them,' the cardinal responded, showing no sign of being perturbed by Yakov's outburst. Yakov caught himself before he said anything. This was one of Kodaczka's traps. The cardinal was desperate to find some reason to discredit Yakov, to disband his unique parish and send him on his way.

'As I already have,' Yakov said eventually. There was an uncomfortable silence for several seconds, both preacher and cardinal gazing at each other over the desk, weighing up the opposition. It was Kodaczka who broke the quiet.

'It irks you to preach to these slaves?' the cardinal asked suddenly.

'Slaves are entitled to spiritual guidance even by the laws of Karis Cephalon,' the preacher replied.

'That is not an answer,' Kodaczka told him gravely.

'I find the… situation on this world difficult to align with the teachings of my faith,' Yakov admitted finally.

'You find slavery against your religion?'

'Of course not!' Yakov snorted. 'It is these mutants, these creatures that I preach to. This world is built upon the exploitation of something unholy and abhorrent and I believe it denigrates everyone involved in it.'

'Ah, your Armormant upbringing,' the prelate's voice dripped with scorn. 'So harsh and pure in intent, and yet so soft and decadent in execution.'

'We are an accepted and recognised sect within the Ministorum,' Yakov said defensively.

'Accepted? Recognised, I agree, but acceptance... That is another matter entirely,' Kodaczka said bluntly. 'Your founder, Gracius of Armorm, was charged with heresy!'

'And found innocent...' countered Yakov. He couldn't stop himself from adding, 'After a fair trial in front of his peers.'

'Yes,' agreed Kodaczka slowly, his sly smile returning once more.

Yakov's audience with the cardinal had lasted most of the afternoon and once again the sun was beginning to set as he made his way back to the shanty town. As on the previous night there were many of the mutants gathered around the shrine. Rumour of his visit to the cardinal had spread and he was met by a crowd of eager faces. One look at his own expression quelled their anticipation and an angry murmur sprang up. It was Menevon who stepped forward, a troublemaker by nature in Yakov's opinion. He looked down at Menevon's bestial features and not for the first time wondered if he had been sired by unholy union with a dog or bear. Tufts of coarse hair sprung in patches all across his body, and his jaw was elongated and studded with tusk-like teeth stained yellow. Menevon looked back at him with small, beady eyes.

'He does nothing,' the mutant stated. 'We die and they all do nothing!'

'The Emperor's Will be done,' replied Yakov sternly, automatically echoed by some of the gathered mutants.

'The Emperor I trust and adore,' Menevon declared hotly, 'but the governor I wouldn't spit on if he were burning.'

'That is seditious talk, Menevon, and you would do well to curb your tongue,' warned Yakov, stooping to talk quietly to the rabble-rouser.

'I say we make him help us!' shouted Menevon, ignoring Yakov and turning towards the crowd. 'It's time we made ourselves heard!'

There were discontented growls of agreement from the others; some shouted out their approval.

'Too long have they lorded over us, too long we've been ignored!' continued Menevon. 'Enough is enough! No more!'

'No more!' repeated the crowd with a guttural roar.

'Silence!' bellowed Yakov, holding his arms up to silence them. The crowd fell quiet instantly at his commanding tone. 'This discord will serve for nothing. If the governor will not listen to me, your preacher, he will not listen to you. Your masters will not tolerate this outburst lightly. Go back to your homes and pray! Look not to the governor, but to yourselves and the master of us all, the Holy Emperor. Go now!'

Menevon shot the preacher a murderous look as the crowd heeded his words, dispersing with backward glances and muttered curses.

'Go back to your family, Menevon. You can do them no good dead on a scaffold,' Yakov told him quietly. The defiance in the mutant's eyes disappeared and he nodded sadly. He cast a long, despairing glance at the preacher and then he too turned away.

The touch of something cold woke Yakov and when he opened his eyes his gaze fell first upon the glittering knife blade held in front of his face. Tearing his eyes away from the sharpened steel, he followed the arm to the knife's wielder and his look was met by the whitened orbs of the mutant he knew to be called Byzanthus. Like Lathesia, he was a renegade, and hunted by the Special Security Agents. His face was solemn, his eyes intent upon the preacher. The ridged and wrinkled grey skin that covered his body was dull in the silvery light which occasionally broke through the curtain swaying in the glassless window of the small chamber.

'I had your promise,' Yakov heard Lathesia speak from the shadows. A moment later she stepped forwards, her hair catching the moonlight as she passed in front of the window.

'I asked. They said no,' Yakov replied, pushing Byzanthus's arm away and sitting up, the thin blanket falling to his waist to reveal the taut muscles of his stomach and chest.

'You keep in good shape,' she commented, noticing his lean physique.

'The daily walk to the capital keeps me fit,' Yakov replied, feeling no discomfort as her penetrating gaze swept over his body. 'I must stay physically as well as spiritually fit to serve the Emperor well.'

A flickering yellow light drew the preacher's attention to the window and he rose from the thin mattress to pace over and look. Lathesia smiled at his nakedness but he ignored her; fleshly matters such as his own nudity were beneath him. Pulling aside the ragged curtain, Yakov saw the light came from dozens of blazing torches and when he listened carefully he could hear voices raised in argument. One of them sounded like Menevon's, and as his eyes adjusted he could see the hairy mutant in the torchlight, gesticulating towards the city.

'Emperor damn him,' cursed Yakov, pushing past Lathesia to grab his robes from a chair behind her. Pulling on his vestments, he rounded on the mutant girl.

'You put him up to this?' he demanded.

'Menevon has been an associate of mine for quite some time,' she admitted, not meeting his gaze.

'Why?' Yakov asked simply. 'The governor will not stand for this discontent.'

'Too long we have allowed this tyranny to continue,' she said with feeling. 'Just as in the revolution, the slaves have tired of the lash. It is time to strike back.'

'The revolutionary council was backed by two-thirds of the old king's army,' spat Yakov, fumbling in the darkness for his boots. 'You will all die.'

'Menevon's brother is dead,' Byzanthus growled from behind Yakov. 'Murdered.'

Yakov rounded on the grey-skinned man. 'You know this? For sure?'

'Unless he slit his own throat, yes!' replied Lathesia. 'The masters did this, and no one will investigate because it is just one of the slaves who has died. Justice must be served.'

'The Emperor judges us all in time,' Yakov replied instinctively. He pointed out of the window. 'And He'll be judging some of them this evening if you let this foolishness continue. Damn your souls to Chaos. Don't you care that they'll die?'

'Better to die fighting,' Lathesia whispered back, 'than on our knees begging for scraps and offal.'

The preacher snarled wordlessly and hurried out through the chapel into the street. As he rounded the corner he was met by the mutant mob, their faces twisted in anger, their raucous, raging cries springing to life as they saw him. Menevon was at their head, holding a burning brand high in the air, the embodiment of the revolutionary ringleader. Only he wasn't, Yakov thought bitterly; that honour belonged to the manipulative, headstrong teenage girl back in his room.

'What in the name of the Emperor do you think you are doing?' demanded Yakov, his deep voice rising to a deafening shout over the din of the mob. They ignored him and Menevon pushed him aside as the crowd swept along the street. The preacher recognised many faces in the torchlight as the mob passed by, some of them children. He felt someone step up beside him, and he turned and saw Lathesia watching the mutants marching past, her face triumphant.

'How did one so young become so bloodthirsty?' muttered Yakov, directing a venomous glare at her before setting off after the mutants. They were moving at some speed and Yakov had to force his way through the crowd with long strides, pulling and elbowing aside mutants to get to the front. As they neared the edge of the ghetto the crowd began to slow and he broke through to the front of the mob, where he saw what had stalled their advance. Across the main thoroughfare stood a small detachment of the SSA, their grey and black uniforms dark against the glare of a troop transport's searchlamp behind them. Each cradled a shotgun in their hands, their visored helms reflecting the flames of the torches. Yakov stopped and let the mutants swirl around him, his mouth dry with fear. Next to him the pretty young girl, Katinia, was staring at the SSA officers. She seemed to notice Yakov suddenly and looked up at the preacher with a small, uncertain smile. He didn't smile back, but focused his attention on the law enforcers ahead.

'Turn back now! You are in violation of the Slave Encampment Laws,' screeched a voice over a loudhailer.

'No more!' shouted Menevon, hurling his torch at the security agents, his cry voiced by others. Stones and torches rattled off the cobbles and walls of the street and one of the officers went down to a thrown bottle that smashed across his darkened helmet.

'You were warned, mutant scum,' snarled the SSA officer's voice over the hailer. At some unheard command the agents raised their shotguns. Yakov hurled himself across Katinia just as gunfire exploded all around him. There were sudden screams and shouts; a wail of agony shrieked from his left as he and the girl rolled to the ground. He felt something pluck at his robes as another salvo roared out. The mutants were fleeing, disorder reigned as they scrabbled and tore at one another to fight their way clear. Bare and booted feet stamped on Yakov's fingers as he held himself over Katinia, who was mewling and sobbing beneath him. Biting back a yell of pain as a heel crushed his left thumb between two cobbles, Yakov forced himself upright. Within moments he and the girl were alone in the street.

The boulevard was littered with dead and wounded mutants. Limbs, bodies and pools of blood were scattered over the cobblestones, a few conscious mutants groaned or sobbed. To his right, a couple he had wed just after arriving were on their knees, hugging each other, wailing over the nearly unrecognisable corpse of their son. Wherever he looked, lifeless eyes stared back at him in the harsh glare of the searchlight. The SSA were picking their way through the mounds of bodies, kicking over corpses and peering at faces.

Yakov heard the girl give a ragged gasp and he looked down. Half her mother's face lay on the road almost within reach. He bent and gathered the girl up in his left arm, and she buried her face in his robes, weeping uncontrollably. It was then he noticed the silver helmet of a sergeant as he clambered down from the turret of the armoured car.

'You!' bellowed Yakov, pointing with his free hand at the SSA man, his anger welling up inside him. 'Come here now!'

The officer gave a start and hurried over. His face was hidden by the visor of his helmet, but he seemed to be trembling.

'Take off your helmet,' Yakov commanded, and he did so, letting it drop from quivering fingers. The man's eyes were wide with fear as he looked up at the tall preacher. Yakov felt himself getting even angrier and he grabbed the man by the throat, his long, strong fingers tightening on the sergeant's windpipe. The man gave a choked cough as Yakov used all of the leverage afforded by his height to push him down to his knees.

'You have fired on a member of the Ministorum, sergeant,' Yakov hissed. The man began to stammer something but a quick tightening of

Yakov's grip silenced him. Releasing his hold, Yakov moved his hand to the top of the sergeant's head, forcing him to bow forward.

'Pray for forgiveness,' whispered Yakov, his voice as sharp as razor. The other agents had stopped the search and helmets bobbed left and right as they exchanged glances. He heard someone swearing from the crackling intercom inside the sergeant's helmet on the floor.

'Pray to the Emperor to forgive this most grievous of sins,' Yakov repeated. The sergeant started praying, his voice spilling almost incoherently from his lips, his tears splashing down his cheeks into the blood slicking the cobbles.

'Forgive me, almighty Emperor, forgive me!' pleaded the man, looking up at Yakov as he released his hold, his cheeks streaked with tears, his face a mask of terror.

'One hour's prayer every sunrise for the rest of your life,' Yakov pronounced his judgement. As he looked again at the bloodied remnants of the massacred mutants and felt Katinia's tears soaking through his tattered priestly robes, he added, 'And one day's physical penance a week for the next five years.'

As he turned away from the horrific scene Yakov heard the sergeant retching and vomiting. Five years of self-flagellation would teach him not to fire on a preacher, Yakov thought grimly as he stepped numbly through the blood and gore.

Yakov was tired and even more irritable than normal when the sun rose the next day. He had taken Katinia back to her home, where her brother was in a fitful, nightmare-laden sleep, and then returned to the site of the cold-blooded execution to identify the dead. Some of the mutants he did not recognise from his congregation, and he assumed they were more of Lathesia's misguided freedom fighters.

When he finally returned to the shanty town, the preacher saw several dozen SSA standing guard throughout the ghetto, each carrying a heavy pistol and a charged shock maul. As he dragged himself wearily up the steps to the chapel, a familiar face was waiting for him. Just outside the curtained portal stood Sparcek, the oldest mutant he knew and informal mayor-cum-judge of the ghetto.

Yakov delved into his last reserves of energy as the old mutant met him halfway, his twisted, crippled body making hard work of the shallow steps.

'A grim night, preacher,' said Sparcek in his broken, hoarse voice. Yakov noticed the man's left arm was splinted and bound with bandages and he held it across his chest as much as his deformed shoulder and elbow allowed.

'You were up there?' Yakov asked, pointing limply at Sparcek's broken arm.

'This?' Sparcek glanced down and then shook his head sadly. 'No, the

SSA broke into my home just after, accused me of being the leader. I said they couldn't prove that and they did this, saying they needed no proof.'

'Your people need you now, before they...' Yakov's voice trailed off as his befuddled mind tried to tell him something. 'What did you just say?'

'I said they couldn't prove anything...' he started.

'That's it!' snapped Yakov, startling the old mutant.

'What? Talk sense, you're tired,' Sparcek snapped back, obviously annoyed at the preacher's outburst.'

'Nothing for you to worry about,' Yakov tried to calm him with a waved hand. 'Now, I am about to ask you something, and whether you answer me or not, I need your promise that you will never tell another living soul what it is.'

'You can trust me. Did I not help you when you first arrived, did I not tell you about your congregation, their secrets and traits?' Sparcek assured him.

'I need to speak to Lathesia, and quickly,' Yakov said, bending close so that he could whisper.

'The rebel leader?' Sparcek whispered back, clearly amazed. He thought for a moment before continuing. 'I cannot promise anything but I may be able to send her word that you wish to see her.'

'Do it, and do it quickly!' insisted Yakov, laying a gentle hand on the mutant's good arm. 'With all of these trigger happy agents around, she's bound to do something reckless and get more of your people killed. If I can speak to her, I may be able to avoid more bloodshed.'

'I will do as you ask, preacher,' Sparcek nodded as he spoke, almost to himself.

The dank sewers resounded with running water and constant dripping, punctuated by the odd splash as Yakov placed a booted foot in a puddle or a rat scurried past through the rivulets seeping through the worn brick walls. Ahead, the glowlamp of Byzanthus bobbed and weaved in the mutant's raised hand as he led the way to Lathesia's hidden lair. Though one of the larger drainage systems, the tunnel was still cramped for the tall preacher and his neck was sore from half an hour's constant stooping. His nose had become more accustomed to the noxious smell which had assaulted his nostrils when the grey-skinned mutant had first opened the storm drain cover, and his eyes were now used to the dim, blue glow of the lantern. He was thoroughly lost, he was sure of that, and he half-suspected this was the point of the drawn out journey. They must have been walking in circles, otherwise they would be beyond the boundaries of the mutant encampment in the city proper, or out in the fields.

After several more minutes of back-breaking walking, Byzanthus finally stopped beside an access door in the sewer wall. He banged four times, paused, then banged twice more. Rusted locks squealed and the door opened a moment later on shrieking hinges.

'You should loot some oil,' Yakov couldn't stop himself from saying, earning himself a cheerless smile from Byzanthus, who waved him inside with the lantern.

There was no sign of the doorkeeper, but as Yakov preceded Byzanthus up the wooden steps just inside the door he heard it noisily swinging shut again.

'Shy?' Yakov asked, looking at Byzanthus over his shoulder as he climbed the stairwell.

'Suspicious of you,' the mutant replied bluntly, giving him a hard stare.

The steps led them into a small hallway, decorated with flaking murals on the walls, they were obviously inside one of the abandoned buildings of the royal district.

'Second door on the left,' Byzanthus said curtly, indicating the room with a nod of his head as he extinguished the lamp.

Yakov strode down the corridor quickly, his hard-soled boots clacking on the cracked tiles. Just as he reached the door, it opened to reveal Lathesia, dressed in ill-fitting SSA combat fatigues.

'Come in, make yourself at home,' she said as she stepped back and took in the room with a wide sweep of her arm. The small chamber was bare except for a couple of straw pallets and a rickety table strewn with scatters of parchment and what looked like a schematic of the sewer system. The frescoes had been all but obliterated by crudely daubed black paint, which had puddled on the scuffed wooden floor. The remnants of a fire smouldered in one corner, the smoke drifting lazily out of a cracked window.

'We had to burn the carpet last winter,' Lathesia said apologetically, noting the direction of his gaze.

'And the walls?' Yakov asked, dropping his haversack onto the bare floor.

'Byzanthus in a fit of pique when he heard we'd been found guilty of treason,' she explained hurriedly, moving over to drop down on one of the mattresses.

'You share the same room?' Yakov asked, recoiling from her in disgust. 'Out of wedlock?'

'What of it?' she replied, genuinely perplexed.

'Is there no sin you are not guilty of?' he demanded hotly, regretting his decision to have anything to do with the wayward mutant. He fancied he could feel the fires of Chaos burning his soul as he stood there. It would take many weeks of repentance to atone for even coming here.

'Better that than freezing because we only have enough fuel to heat a few rooms,' she told him plainly before a smile broke over her pretty face. 'You think that Byzanthus and I... Oh, Yakov, please, allow me some standards.'

'I'm sure he doesn't see it that way,' Yakov pointed out to her with a meaningful look. 'I saw the way he looked at you in my bedchamber last night.'

'Enough of this!' Lathesia snapped back petulantly. 'I didn't ask you to come here to preach to me. You wanted to see me!'

'Yes, you are right, I did,' Yakov admitted, collecting his thoughts before continuing. 'Have you any other trouble planned for tonight?'

'What concern is it of yours, preacher?' she asked, her black eyes narrowing with suspicion.

'You must not do anything. The SSA will retaliate with even more brutal force than last time,' he warned her.

'Actually, we were thinking of killing some of them, strutting around with their bludgeons and pistols as if their laws apply here,' she replied venomously, her cracked hands balling into fists.

Yakov went over and sat down beside her slowly, meeting her gaze firmly.

'Do you trust me?' he asked gently.

'No, why should I?' she asked, surprised.

'Why did you come to me before, to ask the cardinal for help?' he countered, leaning back on one hand but keeping his eyes on hers.

'Because... It was... I was desperate, it was foolish of me, I shouldn't have,' she mumbled back, turning her gaze away.

'You are nothing more than a child. Let me help you,' Yakov persisted, feeling his soul starting to roast at the edges even as he said it.

'Stop it!' she wailed suddenly, springing to her feet and backing away. 'If I don't do this, no one will help us!'

'Have it your way,' sighed Yakov, sitting upright again. 'There is more to this than the casual murder of Menevon's brother. I do not yet know what, but I need your help to find out.'

'Why do you think so?' she asked, her defiance forgotten as curiosity took over.

'You say his throat was slit?' Yakov asked and she nodded. 'Why? Any court on Karis Cephalon will order a mutant hung on the word of a citizen, so why the murder? It must be because nobody could know who was involved, or why he died. I think he saw something or someone and was murdered so he couldn't talk.'

'But that means, if a master didn't do it...' Lathesia started before her eyes widened in realisation. 'One of us did this? No, I won't believe it!'

'You might not have to,' Yakov countered quickly, raising his hand to calm her. 'In fact it's unlikely. The only way we can find out is to go to where Menevon's brother died, and see what we can find.'

'He worked in one of the cemeteries not far from here, just outside the encampment boundary,' she told the preacher. 'We'll take you there.'

She half-ran, half-skipped to the open door and called through excitedly, 'Byzanthus! Byzanthus, fetch Odrik and Klain. We're going on an expedition tonight!'

* * *

The functional ferrocrete tombstones had little grandeur about them, merely rectangular slabs plainly inscribed with the name of the family. The moon was riding high in the sky as Yakov, Lathesia and the other mutants searched the graveyard for any sign of what had happened. Yakov entered the small wooden shack that served as the gravedigger's shelter, finding various picks and shovels stacked neatly in one corner. There was an unmistakable red stain on the unfinished planks of the floor, which to Yakov's untrained eye seemed to have spread from near the doorway. He stood there for a moment, gazing out into the cemetery to see what was in view. It was Byzanthus who caught his attention with a waved arm, and they all gathered on him. He pointed to a grave, which was covered with a tarpaulin weighted with rocks. Lathesia gave Byzanthus a nod and he pulled back the sheeting.

The grave was deep and long, perhaps three metres from end to end and two metres down. Inside was a plain metal casket, wrapped in heavy chains from which hung numerous padlocks.

'Why would anyone want to lock up a coffin?' asked Lathesia, looking at Yakov.

Yakov stood in one of the rooms just down the hall from where he had met Lathesia, gazing at the strange casket. The mutant leader was beside him looking at it too, a small frown creasing her forehead.

'What do you...' she started to ask before a loud boom reverberated across the building. Shouts and gunshots rang out along the corridor as the two of them dashed from the room. Byzanthus came tearing into view from the doors at the far end, a smoking shotgun grasped in his clawed hands.

'The SSA!' he shouted to them as he ran up the corridor.

'How?' Lathesia asked, but Yakov ignored her and ducked back into the room to snatch up his satchel. More gunfire rattled from nearby, punctuated by a low bellowing of pain. As the preacher returned to the corridor Byzanthus smashed him across the jaw with the butt of the shotgun, sending Yakov sprawling over the tiled floor.

'You betrayed us, governor's lapdog!' the mutant hissed, pushing the shotgun barrel into Yakov's chest.

'Emperor forgive you!' spat the preacher, sweeping a booted foot into one of Byzanthus's knees, which cracked audibly as his legs folded under him. Yakov pounced forward and wrestled the shotgun from his grip, turning it on Lathesia as she stepped towards him.

'Believe me, this was not my doing,' he told her, backing away. 'Save yourselves!'

He took another step back and then threw the shotgun to Lathesia. Sweeping up his bag, Yakov shouldered his way through the doorway that led to the sewer stairs as she was distracted. Yakov's heart was hammering as he pounded down the steps three at a time, almost losing his footing in his haste. At the bottom someone stepped in front of him and he lashed out with his fist, feeling it connect with a cheekbone. He spun the lockwheel on the door and splashed out into the sewers, cursing himself for ever getting involved in this mess. Two hundred years of penance wouldn't atone for what he had done. As the sounds of fighting grew closer he hurried off through the drips and puddles with long strides.

Yakov sat on his plain bed in a grim mood, brooding over the previous night's and day's events. He had spent the whole day a hostage to himself in the chapel, not daring to go out into the light, where some roving SSA man might recognise him from the raid on the rebels' hideout.

He had prayed for hours on end, tears in his eyes as he asked the Emperor for guidance. He had allowed himself to get involved in something beyond him. He was a simple preacher, he had no right to interfere in such matters. As his guilt-wracked day passed into evening, Yakov began to calm down. His dealings with the mutants may have been sinful, but he had discovered something strange. The chained coffin, and the murder of the mutant for what he knew about it, was at the heart of it. But what could he do? He had just decided to confess all to Prelate Kodaczka when footsteps out in the chapel attracted his attention.

Stepping into the shrine, he saw a figure kneeling before the altar, head bowed. It was Lathesia, and as he approached she looked up at him, her eyes red-rimmed from weeping.

'Byzanthus is dead, hung an hour ago,' she said dully, the black orbs of her eyes catching the light of the candle on the altar. 'He held off the agents to make sure I escaped. None of the others got out.'

'I did not betray you,' Yakov told her, kneeling beside her.

'I know,' she said, turning to him and laying a hand on his knee.

'I want to find out what is in that coffin,' Yakov said after a few moments of silence between them. 'Will you help me?'

'I watched them; they didn't take it anywhere,' she replied distractedly, wiping at a tear forming in her eye.

'Then will you go back there with me?' he asked, standing up again and reaching a hand down to help her up.

'Yes, I will,' she answered quietly. 'I want to know why they died.'

They took the overground route to the old aristocratic household, Lathesia leading him up a fire escape ladder onto a neighbouring rooftop. From there they could see two SSA stationed at the front entrance and another at the tradesman's entrance to the rear. She showed him the ropeline hung between the buildings, tied there for escape rather than entry, but suitable all the same. Yakov kept his gaze firmly on his hands as he pulled himself along the rope behind the lithe young rebel leader, trying not to think of the ten metre drop to the hard road beneath him. As she helped him onto the rooftop of her one-time lair, a gentle cough from the darkness made them freeze. Out of the shadows strolled a man swathed in a heavy coat, his breath carving mist into the chill evening air.

'A strange pastime for a preacher,' he said as he stepped towards them, hands in the pockets of his trenchcoat.

'Who are you?' demanded Lathesia, her hand straying to the revolver wedged into the waistband of her trousers at the small of her back.

'Please don't try and shoot me,' he replied calmly. 'You'll attract some unwanted attention.'

'Who are you?' Yakov repeated the question, stepping between the stranger and Lathesia.

'An investigator, for the Inquisition,' he told them stopping a couple of paces away.

'An inquisitor?' Lathesia hissed, panic in her eyes.

'Don't worry, your little rebellion doesn't concern me tonight,' he assured her, pulling his hands free from the coat and crossing his arms. 'And I didn't say I was an inquisitor.'

'You are after the casket as well?' Yakov guessed, and the man nodded slightly.

'Shall we go and find it, then?' the investigator invited them, turning and walking away.

The scene before Yakov could have been taken straight from a drawing in the Liber Heresius. Twelve robed and masked figures knelt in a circle around the coffin, five braziers set at the points of a star drawn around the casket. The air was filled with acrid smoke and the sonorous chanting of the cultists filled the room. One of them stood and pulled back his hood, and Yakov almost gasped out loud when he recognised the face of the governor. Holding his arms wide, he chanted louder, the words a meaningless jumble of syllables to the preacher.

'I think we've seen enough,' the investigator said, crouching beside Yakov and Lathesia on the patio outside the room. He drew two long laspistols from holsters inside his coat and offered one to Yakov. Yakov shook his head.

'Surely you're not opposed to righteous violence, preacher,' the stranger said with a raised eyebrow.

'No,' Yakov replied. Pulling his rucksack off, the preacher delved inside and a moment later pulled out a black enamelled pistol. With a deftness that betrayed years of practice he slipped home the magazine and cocked the gun. 'I just prefer to use my own weapon.'

Lathesia gasped in astonishment.

'What?' asked Yakov, annoyed. 'You think they call us the Defenders of the Faith just because it sounds good?'

'Shoot to kill!' rasped the stranger as he stood up.

He fired both pistols, shattering the windows and spraying glass shards into the room. A couple of the cultists pulled wicked-looking knives from their rope belts and leapt at them; the governor dived behind the casket shrieking madly.

Yakov's first shot took a charging cultist in the chest, punching him off his feet. His second blew the kneecap off another, his third taking him in the forehead as he collapsed. The investigator's laspistols spat bolts of light into the cultists fleeing for the door, while the boom of Lathesia's heavy pistol echoed off the walls. As Yakov stepped into the room, one of the cultists pushed over a brazier and he jumped to his right to avoid the flaming coals. A las-bolt took the traitor in the eye, vaporising half his face.

In a few moments the one-sided fight was over, all the cultists were dead, their blood soaking into the bare boards. Suddenly, the governor burst from his hiding place and bolted for the door, but Lathesia was quicker, tackling him to the ground. He thrashed for a moment before she smashed him across the temple with the grip of her revolver. She was about to pistol-whip him again but the stranger grabbed her wrist in mid-swing.

'My masters would prefer he survived for interrogation,' he told the girl, letting go of her arm and stepping back.

Lathesia hesitated for a moment before standing. She delivered a sharp kick to the governor's midriff before stalking away, emptying spent casings from her gun.

'I have no idea what is going on here,' Yakov confessed, sliding the safety into place on his own pistol.

'No reason you should,' the man assured him. 'I suppose I do owe you an explanation though.'

Slipping his laspistols back into his coat, the man leant back on the wall.

'The plague has been engineered by the governor and his allies,' the investigator told him. 'He wanted the mutants to rebel, to try to overthrow him. While Karis Cephalon remains relatively peaceful, the Imperial authorities and the Inquisition are content to ignore the more-or-less tolerant attitude to mutants found here. But should they threaten the stability of this world, they would be swift and ruthless in their response.'

The man glanced over his shoulder at Lathesia, who was studying the casket intently, then looked Yakov squarely in the eye before continuing quietly. 'But that's not the whole of it. So the mutants are wiped out, that's really no concern of the Inquisition. But the governor's motives are what concerns us. I, that is we, believe that he has made some kind of pact with a dark force, some kind of unholy elevation. His side of the deal was the delivery of a massive sacrifice, a whole population, genocide of the mutants. But he couldn't just have them culled; the entire economy of Karis Cephalon is based on mutant labour and no one would allow such a direct action to threaten their prosperity. So, he imported a virus which feeds on mutants. It's called Aether Mortandis and costs a lot of money to acquire from the Mechanicus.'

'And the coffin?' Yakov asked. 'Where does that fit in?'

'It doesn't, not at all!' the stranger laughed bitterly. 'I was hiding it when the gravedigger saw me. I killed him, but unfortunately before I had time to finish the burial, his cries brought an SSA patrol and I had to leave. It's just coincidence.'

'So what's so important about it then?' Yakov eyed the casket with suspicion. Lathesia was toying with one of the locks, a thoughtful look on her face.

'I wouldn't open that if I were you,' the stranger spoke up, startling the girl, who dropped the padlock and stepped back. The investigator put an arm around Yakov's shoulders and pulled him close, his voice dropping to a conspiratorial whisper.

'The reason the governor has acted now is because of a convergence of energies on Karis Cephalon,' the man told Yakov slowly. 'Mystical forces, astrological conjunctions are forming, with Karis Cephalon at its centre. For five years, the barrier between our world and the hell of Chaos will grow thinner and thinner. Entities will be able to break through, aliens will be drawn here, and death and disaster will plague this world on an unparalleled scale. It will be hell incarnate. If you wish, for your help today I can arrange a transfer to a parish on another world, get you way from here.'

Yakov looked at the man for a minute, searching his own soul.

'If what you say is true,' he said eventually, 'then I respectfully decline the offer. It seems men of faith will be a commodity in much need over the coming years.'

He looked up at Lathesia, who was looking at them from across the room.

'And,' Yakov finished, 'my parishioners will need me more than ever.'

THE LIVES OF FERAG LION-WOLF

Barrington J Bayley

Ferag Lion-Wolf, champion of Tzeentch, ruler of five worlds, rose from the slab of sparkling white alabaster on which he slept and prepared to receive his honoured visitor. Young maidens bathed him, anointing his body with pleasant-smelling oils so that he gave off an enchanting aroma. The same slave-girls dressed him in garments of shimmering heliotrope silk, decorated all over with the sinuous symbols of the greatest of the gods, and accoutred him with his weapons.

When they had finished, an officer wearing the uniform designed for the palace staff by Ferag himself entered and bowed, waiting for permission to speak.

'The chariot of Lord Quillilil has been sighted entering our planetary system, my great and gracious lord,' the officer announced, once Ferag had impatiently signalled him to continue. 'It will arrive within the hour.'

'And is everything ready?'

'All has been made ready, my great and gracious lord.'

'Good...' Ferag purred.

He dismissed the officer and then turned to examine himself in a full-length mirror. He could not help but be pleased with what he saw. Ferag Lion-Wolf had always been a striking figure, even before he found favour with the Changer of the Ways, to give the great god Tzeentch just one of his many titles. Rugged, strong and handsome, Ferag had earned the admiration of all on his home world, as well as on the many worlds where he had fought and adventured before becoming a champion of Chaos.

But now! Ferag was almost beside himself as he beheld the magnificent transformation wrought on him by the Great Conspirator's marks of favour. In place of his left arm was a powerful, flexing tentacle with twice the reach. His right foot was a scrabbling claw, particularly exciting to behold as it so much resembled the claw of a Chi'khami'tzann Tsunoi or Feathered Lord, the rank of daemon closest to Tzeentch himself! An extra pair of eyes was set in his forehead, above the others but closer together, giving his face a curiously watchful appearance, like the face of a lurking spider. Those eyes could look into someone's mind and see if plots were being laid there. They could also kill with a single baleful glance. His mouth was also changed. It could pucker into a long tube, half the length of his arm, with which to suck pure magical energy from the souls of others. Tzeentch had given him power and change! And this was not the end of the rewards he was to receive...

Ferag made a magical sign, causing a shimmering oval surface to appear in the air, looking like a vertical pool of water or maybe quicksilver. With his forefinger he traced runes in the Dark Tongue, which could only be spoken in the warp. The runes spelled out his Chaos name, so recently bestowed upon him by his greater daemon patron.

With another gesture he dissolved the writing screen.

And now to welcome Quillilil!

Ferag strode from the lofty-ceilinged chamber and on to the spacious balcony overlooking the extensive palace, looking around him and, as always, taking immense satisfaction in his accomplishments. He was ruler of an entire planetary system within the Imperium of Chaos, called by outsiders the Eye of Terror. Five of the system's eight planets were inhabited. Several billion beings all lived in dread, in obedience, in utmost respect and adoration, of Ferag Lion-Wolf.

Ferag had designed his palace to resemble what he imagined the heavenly palaces of Tzeentch and his Feathered Lords to be like. Tier upon tier of terraces rose to the cloud layer, sparkling and glowing in iridescent colours. Towers and minarets and convoluted galleries twisted and twined like snakes. But none of it, of course, was restricted by gravity. The towers and galleries jutted out at crazy angles, as if they had been constructed in space or – as was the impression Ferag had striven to create – the vast unknowable reaches of the warp.

His aides and guards gathered around him. It was time for Quillilil's chariot to arrive. A magnifier had been set up on the balcony. Through it, events in the upper atmosphere became visible as though they were only a short distance away. So they were able to watch as the chariot from the neighbouring planetary system, an elaborate, burnished affair decorated with gold and silver curlicues, appeared in the lemon-yellow sky and swooped through the upper air. Diving for the cloud layer, it descended towards the palace.

Ferag and his aides carefully watched the surrounding countryside, dotted with towns and villages whose privilege it was to share a landscape with their mighty ruler. Yes, there it was! The plot was afoot! Shark-like craft were hurtling over the horizon, three altogether, coming from different directions. In addition, from hidden places nearer at hand, a dozen wild-looking figures mounted on flying discs were soaring upwards, long hair flying behind them, waving weapons.

There was magic at work, or those discs would not have been able to fly here. They were K'echi'tsonae, steeds of Tzeentch, and their proper medium was the warp. Peering closely at the magnifier, Ferag could see the rows of teeth around their rims.

Both shark-craft and riders were converging on the interstellar chariot. Ferag had a consummate sense of timing. He raised a hand, staying his aides who were ready to release a barrage and destroy the raiders. Instead, he allowed the raiders to get closer to their prey.

'Let me deal with this,' Ferag murmured in his melodious baritone voice.

When it seemed there could be no help for the descending foreign vessel on its state visit, he pointed with all five fingers of his right hand. The air became charged with power. It crackled. All present felt the waves of prickling sensations over their entire bodies. And from the fingers of master magician Ferag Lion-Wolf there issued streams of raw magic, crossing the intervening miles instantaneously, sizzling, swaying, touching all three shark-craft and the dozen disc raiders.

For a brief moment the great stream of energy flickered around them, and then, in that same moment, they shivered and were gone.

Ferag Lion-Wolf smiled knowingly. Lord Quillilil's chariot settled itself onto a marbled landing bay further down the terrace. Ferag and his party had already made their way there when the ornate door of the chariot swung open. Flamboyantly clad guards emerged and took up station on either side, glancing nervously around them.

Lord-Commander Quillilil stepped down from the threshold. Unlike Ferag, he had never been a Space Marine, and so was much shorter in stature than the hulking Lion-Wolf. He wore a cloak of brilliant blue. His hands were small, with a shrivelled, talon-like look. In place of a mouth, he had a compact, curved beak, turquoise in colour. A straw-coloured plume sprouted from the top of his otherwise bald pate. His eyes were round and unblinking, and seemed unable to stare in any direction but straight ahead, so that he looked about him continually with sudden nervous movements.

'My Lord-Commander Quillilil!' Ferag greeted breezily, spreading arm and tentacle in welcome.

'My Lord-Commander Ferag!'

Quillilil's voice was high and chirping. He allowed Ferag to embrace him briefly, then stepped back to gaze at the palace around him. He was clearly impressed.

'I am happy to have been able to protect you, my lord Quillilil,' Ferag said. 'It appears some of your enemies have gathered here.'

Twittering laughter rose from Quillilil's throat. His eyes glittered. 'Yes! Subversives from my own planet who fled here some time ago. I knew my visit would flush them out! Why do you think I came here? You should be flattered, my lord Ferag, at the trust I have placed in you. My chariot is unarmed!'

'I, too, have used the occasion to my benefit,' Ferag told him. 'Your renegades could not have acted without help from some of my own subjects. They are now paying the penalty for their disloyalty.' He glanced at the surrounding countryside, taking pleasure in knowing of the death and torture being inflicted there.

'I have prepared a banquet for tonight,' he continued to tell his guest. 'You are particularly partial to human flesh, I believe?'

Quillilil clacked his beak rapidly, in eager affirmation.

'Skinned specimens have been marinading in spices for the past week. Tonight they will be roasted for your delectation. Tomorrow we will discuss a treaty between us. For the present, though, allow me to show you round my palace. But first–'

Ferag raised arm and tentacle and swept them through the air, making magical passes. There came an immense rumbling sound. The huge edifice all around them was coming apart. Towers, terraces, galleries, halls, all separated and began gyrating in the air, performing a gigantic dance. The landing bay on which they stood also took part in the display, whirling lazily through a cloud and back again.

Then, with meticulous precision, everything came together again. Stone block met stone block in silent harmony, mortared together as before. In seconds the palace had reassembled itself.

Quillilil trilled in feigned pleasure. 'Most impressive, my lord Ferag! And if you will allow me in return…'

He too made an elaborate sign with his hand. Further along the terrace, a jutting arcade detached itself, floated a short distance away into the ether and then began spinning at speed.

Quillilil made delicate pulling motions with his fingers. The minaret ceased spinning and returned to its place with a deep grinding of stone upon stone. There was a gentle murmur of approval from the assembled aides and retainers.

It was common for Tzeentchian magicians to show off to one another on first meeting. But for all his chirpiness, the visitor could not hide the fact that he had been bettered by his host.

Surreptitiously, Ferag cast his guest a passing glance with his upper pair of eyes, not wanting Quillilil to see the dark flash that would show he was looking into his mind. It was as he had expected. Quillilil was not happy at being ruler of a mere one-planet system. He envied Ferag his domains. The visit was but the first step in an elaborate, convoluted plan to take his place, stretching far into the future. Quillilil's brain was a maze of plot and counter-plot, intricate to the point of madness.

Which was as it should be in a champion of Tzeentch, the Great Conspirator and Master of Fortune. Quillilil would not, however, see his plans come to fruition. Ferag had laid a strategy to add his guest's planet to his own dominion. As for Quillilil himself, he would be disposed of as easily as one of the feeble humans he was about to feast upon.

Ushering his visitor from the landing bay, Ferag began conducting him through the great vaulted halls of the palace, pointing out feature after feature. But his mind was not on the task of being a tour guide. The promise made to him by his greater daemon patron recently – given to him at the same time as his Chaos name – had left Ferag in a state of pure exultation. It was not long, therefore, before he began talking instead of himself.

'Know, my friend, that I have lived a most eventful life, even for one of our kind,' he said seriously to Quillilil as they strode. 'Have you wondered at my name? Its meaning can tell you much about me. I was born on a primitive planet in the Imperium, outside of our Chaos realm. Life there was dangerous. What few human beings there were knew only how to make tools and weapons of stone, and they had it hard. Among my people one did not receive a permanent name at birth. One had to earn it as one grew to manhood. Now the lion-wolf is the most fierce animal on that planet. Standing twice the height of a human, with jaws that can crush a horse, able to outpace the fastest runner – it would take twenty armed warriors to defeat it! When I was eight years old, one of these beasts killed my father...'

The reminiscence took his mind back. He was a naked boy, standing on the dusty scrubland of the world of his birth. In the sky was the looming globe of its smouldering red sun.

And barely ten paces away, the lifeless body of his father was being tossed back and forth in the jaws of a lion-wolf! When the beast had come loping across the landscape towards them, they had both run for the protection of a rocky tor. But when he heard his father's stout timber spear clattering to the ground behind him, he had turned to witness the dreadful sight.

The boy hesitated. While the beast devoured its prey he could, perhaps, gain the summit of the tor and the fearsome animal might forget him.

But it had killed his father!

A screaming rage gripped him. He ran back and laid his hands on the spear. It was almost too heavy for him to lift, but he raised its fire-hardened point and yelled at the fearsome lion-wolf for all he was worth.

'You killed my father!'

The creature dropped the torn, mauled body and turned its massive face towards him, sniffing the air. He could smell its shaggy coat as it came towards him to investigate. He made jabbing motions with the spear, yelling and retreating. He was at the bottom of the tor now.

The lion-wolf gathered itself together and leaped!

The boy stood his ground, determined to gain revenge for the death of his father. He jammed the butt of the spear in a crevice in the rock and aimed the spearpoint at the gaping jaws of the lion-wolf as it sprang.

The lion-wolf had intended to bite off his head with one snap of its great teeth. Instead, the spear rammed itself down the beast's throat and bore the full impact of that huge body's momentum. Sprawled on the scrubland, the lion-wolf struggled to extract the offending shaft, coughing up great gouts of blood. The boy gave it no chance to do so. On he came, pushing with all his might – pushing the spear down and down, until he came within reach of those deadly claws! But by then it was too late for the animal. The spear had entered its heart.

Even so, the end was long coming. The lion-wolf did not die easily. It writhed and thrashed as its lifeblood poured from its mouth, watched by the fascinated, exultant, grieving eight-year-old...

'So then the tribe gave me my permanent name,' Lord-Commander Ferag said to his guest. 'In my native tongue "Ferag" means "killer", so I was known as "Killer of the Lion-Wolf". I have retained the first word out of respect for my original people.

'No other warrior had ever borne such a name, for no one else had killed a lion-wolf single-handed, and probably has not even now.'

'A stirring tale!' Lord Quillilil chirruped. 'When did you become inducted into the Adeptus Astartes?'

'No more than forty days later, a squad of Purple Stars Space Marines landed near our village. They were told of my courage with the lion-wolf. They tested me in every way, then took me back with them to their monastery.

'I served the Purple Stars for the next twenty years, learning all their ways, going on their campaigns as a Scout, as a messenger and in countless other roles. At the end of that time I was judged fit to be transformed into a Space Marine. I was given the extra organs, the progenoid glands, the sacred gene-seed. For two hundred years I served with the Purple Stars, and saw more action than I could hope to relate, eventually rising to the rank of company commander. I particularly distinguished myself in a raid on a tyranid hive ship...'

Once again Ferag Lion-Wolf found his mind regressing to the far past. A squad of Purple Stars Space Marines was cutting a way through the shell of a vast, snail-like form, its motive power crippled by laser fire so that it had become separated from the hive fleet. None of them knew what to expect on the inside, and what they did find was nothing they could have expected.

They were in a round tunnel which pulsed and throbbed like a living organ, branching at irregular intervals. A huge thumping sound was all around them, like the beating of a gigantic heart. The light was dim, blood-red, and seemed to seep from out of the very walls themselves.

Then, scrabbling down the tunnels which were scarcely large enough to contain them, came the tyranid warriors, huge bossed beasts, six-limbed, worse than the worst nightmare, each head a mass of razor-sharp teeth, each front pair of limbs whirling twin swords that could cut straight through a Space Marine's armour!

With horror Ferag saw his bolter shots bounce off the tyranids' armour while his men were butchered around him. There was no chance of retreating to the assault craft.

Then his mind flashed to the time he had fought the lion-wolf as a boy, and he took heart at the memory. He drew his chainsword in his left gauntlet. Sparks flew as he parried the tyranid boneswords, as he later came to know them. This enabled him to get close in – and the muzzle of his bolter went straight between the tyranid's massed teeth!

The monster jumped then slumped as the bolt exploded inside its body. Ferag let out a roar of laughter. He barked into his communicator.

'That's the way to do it, men! That's the way to do it!'

The heroic deed faded as Ferag brought his mind back to the present. 'The tactics I developed on that day became standard for fighting the foul tyranids at close quarters,' he finished.

He paused for a moment. 'Most warriors would be satisfied with such a life, I dare say, but I was not. The Imperium began to seem too confined for me – I wanted something grander, something to give scope to my abilities! In secret I began to study the ways of magic. I knew, of course, that there had once been a great heretical war, when fully half the original Space Marine Legions took refuge in our Imperium of Chaos. I became attracted to the study of Tzeentch. And eventually I did the unthinkable. I deserted my Chapter, and made my way here to devote myself to his service.' He grinned.

'And now I am his champion! Commander of five worlds! It has been a glorious time! I could not begin to regale you with my adventures, or say how long I have lived. In the Eye of Terror a day is a thousand years, a thousand years is but a day, and time means nothing, until death comes.'

'Your fame spreads far and wide, my dear lord commander,' his guest cooed.

'And so it should!' Ferag made a face. 'Do you know, my lord Quillilil, with what contempt I was treated at first? I am a Space Marine of the Second Founding, raised after the Horus war. The Chaos Legionaries are all of the First Founding. They thought themselves harder, and me as soft and weak. Well, they soon learned their mistake.'

Ferag's hand slashed through the air. 'I have killed thirty-five Traitor Marines in hand-to-hand combat! Twenty of them followers of Khorne, the berserker Blood God! And a dozen of those World Eaters, the most feared of all! There is no greater warrior than Ferag Lion-Wolf!'

His voice dropped and became more conciliatory. 'Forgive my boasting, my lord, but I only speak the truth.'

Quillilil twittered flattering laughter. 'It is no boasting at all, my fellow champion. Why, you are too modest. You almost deprecate yourself. Everyone knows of your great victory on the bowl planet.'

'Yesssss.' Ferag grinned. It was one of his most beloved memories, perhaps his greatest exploit since coming to the Eye of Terror.

A great army had been assembled, an unholy alliance between the forces of Khorne, the Blood God, and Nurgle, the Great Lord of Disease and Decay, also Tzeentch's most implacable enemy! The battle had been fought in a planet shaped like nothing so much as a shallow bowl, governed by its own special physical laws. It was, in fact, possible to fall off the rim of this bowl and into some inescapable hell.

Ferag had commanded a much smaller Tzeentch force. At first sight the twin hordes looked invincible. The Khorne core of Chaos Space Marines had drenched themselves in blood before the battle even began, butchering their own massed soldiery and driving them towards the enemy. As for the Nurgle horde… a vast, filthy Chaos daemon, a great unclean one, had been at its head, and he had come up with a special tactic. The millions-strong army had been rotted with amoeba plague. Its soldiery were no longer separate individuals, but combined into one sticky, putrid mass which came rolling on, engulfing everything in its path.

Against all this, Ferag had only the special strengths of Tzeentch: strategy and sorcery! It had been a battle of titanic proportions. The bowl world had glowed and seethed with magical forces for months. But in the end it was Ferag's tactical genius that had won the day. The vile hordes of Khorne and Nurgle had been driven over the planet's rim to go toppling into an eternal hell-world.

Ferag had gathered together what survived of the planet's original inhabitants and had given them a generations-long task – to erect in the middle of the bowl a monument to Tzeentch that towered above the rim itself.

It was no wonder, when he looked back over his life, that the Changer of the Ways appreciated his services. Further, was about to reward him with the greatest possible fulfilment. His greater daemon patron, appearing before him in person, had informed him that he was to receive the ultimate gift.

He was to become a daemon prince. He would be immortal, no longer subject to death, able to live forever in the heavens of the warp!

But there was still his guest. Almost reluctantly, Ferag Lion-Wolf returned his attention to the tour of inspection.

'Step this way, my lord Quillilil. There is a most delightful aerial esplanade through here.'

They walked under an ornate archway, through which shone the lemon-coloured sky. Ferag Lion-Wolf heard a grating sound overhead. Looking up, he saw that a block of stone had dislodged itself from the masonry and had begun to fall.

In that instant it occurred to him that perhaps this was the section of the palace upon which Quillilil had demonstrated his magic. But whether this was so or not, Ferag had no time to act. The stone block struck his head with great force, knocking him unconscious.

He recovered his senses in what seemed like a split second. He was standing on dusty scrubland, naked except for a rag made of woven grass tied loosely around his waist. A vast, murky red sun hovered near the horizon, producing a lurid sunset.

A circle of a dozen men stood around him. They were all looking at him with a sort of avid expectancy.

He looked back, searching one face after another, utterly bewildered.

Until the change came, sweeping through his mind in an unstoppable rush.

The memory of another life flooded into his mind. The life he had really lived. Not the life of the surgically adapted, battle-hardened ex-Space Marine he had thought himself to be, or of the glory-drenched champion of Tzeentch who for uncounted centuries had faithfully served his master.

He was not a warrior at all. He had never left his native planet. His name was not even Killer-of-the-Lion-Wolf. He never could have earned such a name, not even as a man, let alone as a boy! He was known as Ulf Dirt-Creeper, and he was acknowledged by all to be puny physically and a coward morally.

But he did belong to a Tzeentch coven. He had an aptitude for lying, cheating, and low cunning, for which the worshippers of the Change God found uses. Now, however he had been found wanting. It was a small matter, really – he had been sent to murder a man in his sleep, an enemy of the coven, also his sister's husband, and he had been unable to find the courage. Now he stood condemned.

Condemned to end his life as Chaos spawn.

But because he had been of service in the past, Tzeentch had rendered him a final gift. In the last instants before he descended into mindlessness, he had been allowed to stand at the end of a completely different life, one of glory and power. Of course, he could not be allowed to retain the delusion to the end. That would be un-Tzeentchian. The cruel truth had to be revealed.

The coven leader was intoning a formula redolent of untold power in a high-pitched voice. Ulf Dirt-Creeper felt a horrid crawling sensation within him. He whimpered and flailed miserably. Despite himself, his body bent double. His hands touched the earth and became flat, flappy feet. He felt his face swelling into a round, ridiculous travesty of anything thought of as human. His mouth elongated into a long, narrow tube, not for drawing magical force out of his adversaries, but for sucking up the worms and grubs which were to be his only food from now on.

The awful mutation continued, playing out before the disgusted yet fascinated gazes of his fellow cult members. Then Ulf Dirt-Creeper recalled having heard, so long ago now, another name for Tzeentch: the Great Betrayer. Sometimes, instead of the promised spiritual reward, would come the greatest betrayal of all. Not daemon prince but...

A burning question seized his petrified mind in the scant moments before it descended into gibbering insanity. Who was he, really? Ulf Dirt-Creeper or Ferag Lion-Wolf?

Which one is true?

Which one is true?

SNARES AND DELUSIONS

Matt Farrer

The town surrounds the obscenity, and the obscenity is eating the town. It has no name, this elegant pattern of buildings spread out beneath the wind on the dusty green hills. It is an oddity on this world, this town of dove-grey walls which seem to flow up out of the ground, their smooth lines and gentle angles forcing the eye to look in vain for any tool-marks or signs of shaping. Simplicity of shape and complexity of detail, like outcrops growing unworked from the soil, but natural rock could never grow in the delicate mandala of streets and paths, flowing across the hillside in a design so subtle that the eye can take it in for hours before it begins to understand how much the pattern delights.

Even the violence with which the obscenity has torn its way into the heart of the town has not eclipsed the art of its building, not yet. Despite the craters blasted into the buildings, the smoke in the streets, the dead scattered upon the ground, despite whatever invisible thing it is that is withering the grass and trees and silencing the song of the insects – the place still holds scraps of its beauty, for now.

The town has never needed a name. The Exodites speak of it as they ride their fierce dragons to and fro over the steppes and prairies, but they bring its uniqueness to mind without the coining of a label to go on a sign. For all that they are a warrior race of beast-riding and beast-hunting tribes, their language is the silky melody of all eldar and they are able to speak of the one little town on their world, its historians and artisans and seers, without its ever needing a name.

The obscenity is different. It drives its way out of the ground like the head of a murderous giant buried too shallow, buttresses bulging out from its walls like tendons pulled rigid on a neck as the head is thrown back to scream. Black iron gates gape and steel spines give an idiot glint from the parapets and niches. They are not there to defend. The thing leers and swaggers against the landscape in its power, sure that it is above attack. The spikes are there for cruelty, for execution and display. The obscenity is being built not for subjugating but for the pleasure of the subjugation.

It is growing. As small bands of figures grow from dots across the prairie, advance and join up and form into a procession through streets choked with the stink of death, they can see where buildings are being torn down and the earth beneath them ripped up to furnish more rock for the obscenity. There are rough patches, cavities along the side where new chambers and wings will be added, and the procession – the armoured figures gripping the chains, and the slim cloaked shapes staggering beneath the weight of them – passes the crowds of slaves, toiling in the dust, crying and groaning as the obscenity creeps outward and grows ever taller beneath their hands.

The town does not have a name, but the obscenity does. There is no eldar word for this red-black spear of rock, eating the town from within like a cancer, but it bears a name in the hacking, cawing language of the once-human creatures who drive the slaves ever harder to build it. It is called the Cathedral of the Fifth Blessing, and in its sick, buried heart its master is at prayers.

The air in the Deepmost Chapel was torn this way and that by the screams of the thralls, but Chaplain De Haan paid them no mind. The patterns on the warp-carved obelisk seemed to writhe, the lines and angles impossible by any sane geometry, and De Haan's eyes and brain shuddered as he tried to follow them. There had been times when he had relished or loathed the sensation in turn, even times when he had screamed when he looked at the pillar just as their mortal serfs were screaming now. That had been in the early days, when the Word Bearers had taken up the banner of Horus himself and Lorgar had still been crafting the great laws of faith in the Pentadict. Those laws had commanded contemplation of the work of Chaos as part of the Ritual of Turning, and now De Haan was calm as he felt the carvings send ripples though his sanity. *A lesson in self-disgust and abasement*, he had learned in his noviciate. *Realise that your mind is but a breath of mist in the face of the gale that is Chaos Undivided.* It was a useful lesson.

The time for contemplation was at an end, and he rose. The screams from the chapel floor, beneath the gallery where the Word Bearers themselves sat, went on. Although their mortal thralls were being herded out perhaps a dozen remained, those whose minds had not withstood the gaze at the column, who had begun to convulse on the floor and mutilate themselves. The slave-masters began to drag them toward the torturing pens; they would be adequate as sacrifices later. De Haan walked forward to the pulpit, turned to face the ranks of wine-dark armour and horned helms to begin his first sermon on this new world.

The cycle of worship laid down in the Pentadict decreed that sermon and prayers for that hour were to be about hate. There was a certain expectation in the air that plucked a little chord of pleasure at the base of the Chaplain's spine. Of all Lorgar's virtues hatred was the one De Haan prized most, the sea in which his soul swam, the light with which he saw the world. Some of his most beautiful blasphemies had been done in the name of hate. He knew he was revered as a scholar in the field.

The Sacristans moved to the dais below him and reached into the brocaded satchels they carried. They began to array objects on the dais: a banner of purple-and-gold silk tattered and scorched by gunfire in places; a slender eldar helmet and gauntlet in the same colours were set atop it. At the other end of the dais, a delicate crystal mask and a slender sword seemingly made from feather-light, smoky glass, a single pale gem set into the pommel. And beside them, carefully set exactly between the rest, a fist-sized stone, smooth and hard, that shone like a phoenix egg even in the dimness of the chapel. De Haan looked at them, heard the words in his mind: *All will be at an end.*

An exquisite shudder went through his body. He unclenched his right hand from the pulpit rail, gripped his crozius in his left and opened his mouth to preach. And something happened to the Revered Chaplain De Haan that had never happened to him in his millennia as a Word Bearer: he found himself mute.

High clouds had turned the sky dull and cool as De Haan stood on the jutting rampart outside his war room. His eyes narrowed behind his faceplate as if he were trying to stare through the curve of the planet itself.

'This race has been allowed to *go on*, Meer. It has been allowed to spread itself. They drink their wine on their craftworlds and stand under the sky on worlds like this. They crept out across the galaxy like the glint of mildew.'

Meer, chief among his lieutenants, knew better than to respond. He stood at the door which led out onto the rampart, hands folded respectfully before him. He had heard De Haan talk about the eldar many times.

'Not even the whining Emperor's puppies are like this. Nor the mangy orks. Tyranids, feh, beneath our dignity. But these things, these are an *affront*. To be assailed by them – ah! It gnaws at my pride.' His hand squeezed the haft of his crozius and the weapon's daemon-head hissed and cursed and spat its displeasure. Only during the rituals would the thing keep quiet. De Haan twisted it around and held it at a more dignified angle. It was a symbol of his office, a chaplaincy in the only Traitor

Legion to remember and revere the importance of Chaplains. It did not do to show it disrespect.

De Haan wondered why he had not been able to speak like this in the chapel, why he had stood grasping for words, trying to force thoughts to his lips. A sermon on hate, no less, and yet he had stumbled over the words, choked on maddening distractions, images, snatches of voices, the swirl of memories he was normally able to leave behind at prayer.

'The eyes of our Dark Master see far, Meer, and who am I to set myself up beside them?' Meer remained silent, but De Haan was speaking half to himself. 'The words fled me. My throat was dry and empty. I am wondering, Meer, was it an omen? Do they prey on my mind because they are so near? There was a… a feel to this world, something in the words of our prisoners and spies. Perhaps the Great Conspirator planned from the start that it would end here. To end here, Meer, to bring the sacrament into full flower! Imagine that.'

'I know you believe your enemy is here, revered,' came Meer's careful voice from behind him, 'but my counsel, and Traika's, is still that the time was not ripe for you to join us here.'

De Haan's fist tightened around the crozius again, and the head – now a fanged mouth and eye-stalk; it was always different each time he looked at it – yapped and spat again.

'The fortifications are still not complete, revered, and only threescore of our own brethren are in this citadel. The battle tanks and Dreadnoughts are still being readied, and the dissonance in this world's aura has made auguries hard. We still cannot scry far beyond what our own eyes could see. Our bridgehead is not secure, revered. Do you believe this is worth the risk? The reports we had of eldar here seem only to mean these savages, or perhaps mere pirates. We cannot be sure Varantha has passed near this system. We have seen no craftworld eldar here, or–'

De Haan spun around. 'And I told you, Meer, that it is not suspicions and rumours which have drawn us here this time. I could feel the slippery eldar filth singing to me when I first heard the reports. I saw their faces dancing in the clouds when I looked from the bridge of our ship. What could this psychic "dissonance" you complain of be, but the cowards trying to fog our minds and cover their tracks?'

'These eldar savages keep a thing called a world-spirit, revered. They–'

'I *know* what is a world-spirit – and what is the stink of a farseer!' De Haan's voice did not quite go all the way to a roar, but it did not have to. There was a jitter in his vision and a rustle far off in his hearing as the systems in his armour, long since come to a Chaotic life of their own, tried to recoil from his anger. 'You were not given the sacrament, Meer! You do not carry the Fifth Blessing! I do, and I command you with it. I tell you that Varantha is here, and this is our doorway to it! I have known it in my soul since we broke from the warp!'

Meer bowed, accepting the rebuke, and De Haan slowly, deliberately turned his back. High in his vision he could see a point of light, visible even while the sun was up: their orbiting battle-barge. A space hulk full of Chaos Marines and their slaves and thralls, cultists doped with Frenzon with their explosive suicide collars clamped to their necks, mutants and beastfolk from the Eye of Terror and traitors of every stripe. Seeing it focused his thoughts again.

'We shall bring down our brethren soon enough. The engines and Dreadnoughts too. For now, fetch Nessun. And have the latest prisoner train brought before me.'

There was a scrape of ceramite on stone as Meer bowed again and turned to go, and by the time Meer had reached the bottom of the stairs De Haan was sinking back into reverie.

He was thinking of the cramped, fetid tunnels within the walls of the giant canal-cities of Sahch-V, where he and Meer and Alaema and barely a half-dozen Word Bearer squads had lived like rats in burrows for nearly two years, as around them their covert missionaries moved out through the cities and along the canals which brought life to the basalt plains, beginning their quiet preaching, their mission schools with their drugs and brainwashing rooms. He remembered the small chamber beneath the thermic pumps outside Vana City where the three of them had listened to their agents' reports and pored over their ever-spreading web of traitors and catspaws.

He remembered cries in the tunnels, in particular the voice of Belg, the scrawny cleft-chinned cult emissary loud in the coffin-like burrows as he shouted down the passages: 'We are lost! The missions are dying. Our rebellion is clipped before it begins!' Someone had shot Belg down in a fury before De Haan had had a chance to hear more, but he remembered the word that had gone flying through the base as the reports began to come in.

Eldar!

And the second, the three syllables that had not yet – he could barely remember the feeling – become sweet poison in his brain, not yet become the black-burning obsession hanging in front of his eyes, the name they had not heard until the Warp Spiders had begun to hunt them through their chambers and drove them out to where the rest of the eldar lay waiting with shuriken and plasma-shot, fusion-beam and wraithcannon. Alaema had gone down with a lightning-wrapped witchblade through his gut, and De Haan had barely managed to drag himself and Meer away to the teleport point.

Varantha.

Oh, he remembered. Twenty-one centuries of remembering.

He remembered the sick anger that had seized him when he first spoke to the Imperial scholar they had captured as the wretch thrashed on the torture rack. Varantha meant 'Crown of our Steadfast Hopes'. Human traders spoke in awe of the gems it crafted, the rare flowers it bred, the beautiful metals its artisans worked. Varantha that passed through the western galactic margins, scraping the borders of the Halo where not even the Traitor Legions went, Varantha that was supposed to have passed through Hydraphur itself, the home of the Imperial Battlefleet Pacificus, coasting through the system's intricate double-ecliptic and away again before the whey-faced Imperials had even a suspicion it had been there.

Varantha that hated Chaos with a white heat. Varantha that had held off Karlsen of the Night Lords in his raids on the Clavian Belt until the Ultramarines had arrived, Varantha whose farseers had tricked and feinted to lure the orks of Waaagh-Chobog into falling on the Iron Hands' fortresses on Taira-Shodan instead of the Imperial and Exodite worlds around them, Varantha whose warriors had driven Arhendros the Silken Whisper off the three worlds he had claimed for Slaanesh.

And Varantha that had balked the Word Bearers on Sahch-V, had unravelled their plans and made sure the great citadels and halls they would have built could never be. A Varantha witch blade had cut down De Haan's mentor, Varantha wraithships had driven their battle-barges and strikers out of the system. And when they had broken free of the warp outside the Cadian Gate, ready for their final jump back to the Eye of Terror and sanctuary, it had been Varantha craft which had led the fleets of Ulthwe and Cadia, driving into the Chaos fleet like a bullet tearing into flesh.

Fighting Varantha, stalking the craftworld through a quarter of the galaxy, De Haan had discovered a capacity for hate he had never realised that even a Traitor Marine could possess. Every battle against the craftworld had been like a stroke of the bellows, fanning it ever hotter. The orbital refineries at Rhea, where the eldar had lured De Haan and his warband in – then disappeared, leaving the Word Bearers in the abandoned, genestealer-infested satellite compounds. The island chains of Herano's World where their Doomblaster had smashed the eldar psykers into the ocean at the campaign's opening, and De Haan had led a joyous hunt through the jungles, mopping up the scattered and leaderless Guardians.

And at the last, the farseer, staggering beneath the red-black clouds of Iante as artillery flashed and boomed across the distant horizon, watching De Haan as he circled it, stepping over its dead bodyguard. The calm resignation in its stance and the cold precision of its voice.

'So tell me then. What do you see for us, little insect?' De Haan had taunted.

'Why, you will set your eyes on the heart of Varantha, and all will come to an end,' it had replied, before a howling stroke of De Haan's crozius had torn it in half. He had felt the spirit stone shudder and pulse as he tore it free of the thing's breastplate with a sound like cracking bone, and he wondered every so often if the creature's soul was aware of who owned its stone now. He hoped it was.

It had not been long after that that he had been called to receive his sacrament, the Sacrament of the Fifth Blessing. The highest priests of his Chapter had recognised the depth of his spite and had praised him for it: the Fifth Blessing was hate, and the sacrament had appointed De Haan a holy vessel, freed him from his duties in order to lead a crusade that he might express that hate to the utmost, a great hymn to Lorgar carved across the galaxy in Varantha's wake. He could never think back on his sacrament without the hot red flames of pride flaring deep in what he thought was his soul.

He walked to the edge of his rampart and watched the slaves toiling at the walls far below. His arms convulsed, as though he could already feel eldar souls pulsing and struggling in his fingers, and the wave of malice which surged up his spine made him almost giddy.

'Revered?'

De Haan started at the voice and spun around. His crozius head, now some kind of grotesque insect, chittered something that sounded almost like words. He ignored it and found his concentration again.

'What have the threads of Fate brought us, Nessun?'

The other Space Marine hesitated. Nessun was no full-fledged sorcerer as the adepts of the Thousand Sons were, but by Lorgar's grace he had developed a spirit sight that could scry almost as well as the eldar warlocks they hunted. The mutation that had given him his warp eye had pushed it far out and up onto his brow, making an ungainly lump of his head. The ceramite of his armour had turned glass-clear over it, but De Haan and the others had long ago become used to the way the great milky eyeball pulsed and rolled between the horns of Nessun's helm.

'In the way of eldar, revered, there is little I can say for definite. I see shadows at the corners of my vision and echoes that I must interpret. You know that nothing is certain with these creatures.'

'Describe these shadows and echoes, Nessun. I am patient.'

'I have kept my gaze on the tribes here in the days since our first landing, revered, and watched as they fought our thralls and Brother Traika's vanguard force. There is a... texture to them that I have taught myself to recognise, by Lorgar's grace. But I have caught ripples, something dancing out of sight. I am not sure how I can explain it, revered. Imagine a figure standing just beyond the reach of light from a fire, so that sometimes its shape is touched by the firelight...'

'I think I understand.' De Haan wasn't aware that he had tensed until he felt his armour, alive like his helmet systems, shiver and creak as it tried to find a comfortable position.

'Revered, I am abased and humble before the foul glory of Chaos, but I must venture the guess that craftworld eldar may be here. Here on this world. I have dimly seen the patterns that the minds of farseers form when they assemble, and I have felt... gaps in my vision that I believe are warp gates, webway gates here and in orbit beyond the planet from our own ship, that have opened and closed and that they have not been able to hide...' He stopped short as De Haan drove gauntlet into fist, hissing with triumph, sending his armour shivering and flexing from the blow.

'An omen! My voice was bound in the chapel as an omen!' And he was about to speak again when Meer called from the war room.

'Most revered lord, the prisoners await you.'

There was something in Meer's voice that made De Haan almost run for the doorway.

Two eldar stood in the great hall, heads bowed as De Haan strode to his throne and sat down, crozius across his knees. The arm of one hung brokenly; blood matted the other's hair. Both were dressed in rough cloth and hide tunics, and their lasers, the power chambers smashed, had been hung around their necks. Traika, the commander of their vanguard and Raptors, bowed to De Haan and made the sign of the Eightfold Arrow with the hand that had fused to his chainsword. Traika's legs had warped and lengthened too, now bending backward like an insect's, the armour over them lumpy and stretched. It had made him fleet of foot but gave him an odd, tilted way of standing.

'We found these in the south-west quarter where the hills steepen. We thought we had cleansed the area, revered, but these were part of an ambush on one of our scouring forces. The fight was fierce but we carried the day.'

'Praise Lorgar's dark light and the great will of Chaos,' De Haan intoned, and the two were led away into the cathedral's cells. Traika gestured and a third alien was dragged up the steps, limping and tripping. The thrall holding its chains tossed a dead power-lance and a tall bone helm onto the floor. The prisoner did not react, standing slumped with its hair in its face, its long cloak of golden-scaled hide hanging limply around it.

'The last survivor of a group of Dragon Knights we believe were scouting the northern border of our controlled zone. I will attend the tormenting of this one personally, revered. I had felt sure that our deep raids had gutted the last of the Exodite resistance on the prairies. We must find out how this new raid was organised so soon.' The thrall began to drag the knight out, and Meer walked over to stand beside the throne.

'Revered, this is the final prisoner. It was badly wounded, and did not survive the journey back to be brought before you, but we believed you would want to see it. The Raptors brought it down in the river-valley to the south and our bikers brought it here with all haste.'

With a scraping groan of wheels the thralls pushed forward an iron frame with a figure stretched in it, a figure whose rich purple and gold armour caught the sunlight coming through the still-unglazed windows and gave off a burnished glow. Behind it four more – strong beastfolk these, whose muscles rippled and corded with their burden – dragged something into view and dropped it crashing to the floor, stirring the rock-dust that still coated the hall from its building. A jet bike, its canopy cracked open by bolt shells, the drive smashed and burnt from its crash, but the pennons hanging from its vanes perfectly clear: the stylised crown-and-starburst of Varantha.

For a long moment, De Haan was silent. Then he threw his arms wide as though he were about to embrace the corpse, and gave a bellow that echoed through the length of the hall.

'All will come to an end! Horus's eye, but the filthy little creature spoke the truth. The craftworld's heart! It is here! The sacrament ends here, my brethren! I will end it here!'

'Revered!' De Haan did not look back. His stride had lengthened as his pace had picked up, and he was practically jogging through the halls to the Deepmost Chapel, Meer and Nessun shouldering one another aside to keep up. The air in the fortress shivered as the great gongs they had hung over the barracks rang out again and again. Under the sound De Haan left a trail of angry murmurs in the air, curses and threats and dark prayers. Every so often he would slash his crozius viciously around him as if to knock the air itself out of his path.

He knew what Meer would be saying. More weak-spirited yapping, more about caution and rashness and the trickery of the eldar. But the warp gate was close. Varantha was close. The time when the heads of Varantha's farseers were set on spikes atop his Land Raider was a breath away.

Why, you will set your eyes on the heart of Varantha, and all will come to an end.

The heart of the craftworld, the very heart of Varantha! He wondered how it would feel, walking from the webway gate into Varantha itself. The domes where the most ancient of their farseers sat, their flesh crystallised and gleaming like diamond, waiting for the blow of an armoured fist that would send their souls screaming into the warp. The Grove of New Songs, that was what they called the forest-hall deep in Varantha where the few eldar children were born and weaned. De Haan had spent a hundred weeks agonising over whether he would kill the children or take them as slaves after he had poisoned and burned the trees. The infinity circuit, the wraithbone core which held the spirits of a billion dead eldar, had shone through his dreams like a galaxy aflame. Oh, to crack its lattice with his crozius and watch the warp tides pour in! It would need a special ceremony, the culmination of his crusade and sacrament, something he would have to plan.

And was Varantha possessed of engines, a world that could control its drift and sweep through space? He had never been able to discover that, but he began turning the idea over feverishly as he strode down the hallway to the chapel. To take command of Varantha, hollow out its core of eldar souls and fill them with sacrifices and the cries of daemons, to sail the fallen craftworld to the Eye of Terror itself! His head swam with the audacity: a world that would put their daemon-world fortresses and the asteroid seminaries at Milarro to shame. A corrupted world that would carry them through the galaxy, a great blight that would stand as a testament to their faith, their hate, their spite, their unholiness.

The rest of the Traitor Marines began to file in and take their places, and the slave-choir in their cells beneath the chapel floor raised a hymn of howls and cries as the choir-masters puffed drugs into their faces and yanked on the needles in their flesh. De Haan closed his eyes and could see the conquered Varantha still, a great twisted flower of black and crimson, sprawled against the stars. The shapes of the spires and walls, great plazas where the zealous would come to plead for the favour of Chaos, the cells and scriptoria where Lorgar's holy Pentadict would be copied and studied, the fighting pits where generations of new Word Bearers would be initiated. There would be pillars and statues greater than those they had raised after driving the White Scars from the island chains of Morag's World. There would be chamber after chamber of altars more richly decorated than those they had seized when they had sacked the treasury of Kintarre. There would be the slaughtering pens for the worship of Khorne, great libraries and chambers for meditating upon the lore of Tzeentch. There would be palaces of incense and music dedicated to Slaanesh, and cess-pits for the rituals of self-defilement dedicated to Nurgle. And all just parts, even as the Chaos Gods were just facets, all parts of the great treacherous hymn, an obscene prayer in wraithbone and carved ceramite. The Sacred City of Chaos Undivided.

De Haan cradled his vision lovingly in his mind, and saw that it was good.

'Lorgar is with us, Chaos is within us, damnation clothes us and none can stand against us.' Voices around the chapel echoed the blessing as De Haan held his rosarius aloft and made the sign of the Eightfold Arrow. For the second time that day he looked out over ranks of helms, leaned forward to look down at the bright eyes of the cultists and beast-folk crowded below him. But this time, his thoughts and his words were clear.

'Be it known to you, most devout of my comrades in Lorgar's footsteps, that we are gathered here once again in the observance of the Fifth Blessing of Lorgar, the blessing of hate. Bring your thoughts to the sacrament granted to me by the most high of our order, that I might light a dark beacon of spite for all the cosmos to see.' He paused, looked down again. The eldar artefacts had gone from the dais, locked away again by the Sacristans. It was not important – he did not need them now.

'Hatred earned me the great and honoured sacrament. Hatred has pleased the beautiful abomination of Chaos Undivided, and shone a light through the warp to Varantha. My beautiful hatred has brought us to their scent. After more than two millennia, the fulfilment of our sacred charter is near.' The memory of the Varantha Guardian, the knowledge of what they had found here, surged through him afresh: his head spun, his joints felt weak with exhilaration. His crozius head as he raised it was now a contorted nightmare-face, grimacing as if in ecstasy, mirroring his feelings.

'Soon we will be joined by our brothers, our fellow warriors and bearers of Lorgar's words. Even now the order goes out to land our machines of war, our bound Dreadnoughts. Within the week, my congregation, this world will have felt the full fury of our crusade and when the Exodites are scoured from it we shall march through the warp gate into the craftworld itself! Hone yourselves, my acolytes, hone your spite and fan your hate to the hottest, most bitter flame. None shall pass us in our devotion, none are as steeped in poisoned thoughts as we!' His voice hammered out and boomed against the walls of the chapel, intoxicating even with the power of its echoes. De Haan fought back an urge to laugh – this felt so right.

'In the beginning, even in the days before my pursuit earned me the sacrament, I had spoken to one of the degenerate farseers the eldar claim to revere. At its death the maggot spoke a prophecy that the blessed oracles of our high temples have sworn to be true. Brethren, as I lead you to battle I will set my eyes on the heart of Varantha and then all will come to an end. I will cut down their last farseer, I will break open the seals of their infinity circuit, I will shatter the heart and eye of their home!' His voice had risen to a roar. 'All will come to an end! Our crusade, our sacrament fulfilled! The eldar themselves have sworn it will be so. What honours, what glories we will build!'

Above him the gong rang again, and De Haan opened his eyes and leaned forward.

'Look to your weapons, brothers. I will lead you now in the Martio Imprimis. I tell you this: by the end of even this day we will be at war!'

The chant of the Martio Imprimis was an old song and a good one, crafted by Lorgar himself in the days before the Emperor had turned on his Word Bearers and when even De Haan had been only a youngblood initiate. The words were strange and their meanings almost lost, but they filled him with a beautiful, electric energy. It rang in De Haan's blood even now. The service in the Deepmost Chapel had been over for an hour but the Word Bearers had caught something of their Chaplain's mood and as the teleport beam sent thundercracks and sickly shimmers of light through the citadel's hangar, the Space Marines chanted still as they selected weapons and directed the thralls in moving the crates and engines away.

'Duxhai!' The crusade's chief artisan, still swaying a little from his teleport, turned as De Haan called him. He stepped back into a deep kneeling bow as De Haan strode across the hangar floor and left the moving of the icon-encrusted Razorback tanks to his seconds.

'Is it true, revered lord? I was told you have received omens and that Varantha itself is in our grip. They are singing hymns in all the halls and chambers of our fortress. Look!' The old Space Marine pointed to the nearest tank's turret, where splashes of blood glistened. 'They have already made sacrifices over our wargear.'

'It is true, Duxhai, and it is fitting that our brethren in orbit are making their thanks and obeisances. Lorgar has exalted us. I have been shown the way.'

Duxhai had worked on his armour himself over the centuries, making it a glorious construction of red and gold. Chaos had worked on it too: the studs and rivets on its carapace had all turned to eyes, yellow slit-pupilled eyes, which stared at De Haan now but rolled forward to watch Meer walk into the hangar. De Haan pointed to the Razorbacks.

'Give praise, Meer! See how Brother Duxhai's skills have transformed these? Captured barely a year ago, and already adorned and consecrated for service! These will carry Traika's vanguard squads into the teeth of the Varantha lines!'

'Our revered chaplain's own Land Raider will be brought down next,' put in Duxhai, 'and the transports are being readied to bring down the Dreadnoughts and Rhinos. We will be ready to move soon.'

'A dark blessing on you, brother, and thanks to the great foulness of Chaos. Revered, I must make a report.'

'Well?' De Haan was becoming nettled by Meer's manner, his shifty-eyed caution. He could see in the corner of his eyes that Duxhai had registered the offhand greeting also.

'Revered, we have lost contact with our patrols at the furthest sweep of the contested zone. I had our adepts move the communicators onto the outer balconies but there is still no way to raise them. The Raptors who went out to counterstrike at the areas where our own forces were ambushed cannot be reached either, and the bike squadron was due two hours ago but cannot be seen. The psychic haze has thickened, and Nessun's warp eye is almost blind. He reports a presence like a light through fog, but he cannot pinpoint it.'

'I will come to the war room, Meer. Wait for me there.' His lieutenant backed away, bowed and departed. 'Something in the air on this world turns my warriors to water, Duxhai. They whimper to me of "caution" and "fortification". Meer is a good warrior, but I should have made you my lieutenant for this world. I need your ferocity by me here.'

Duxhai bowed. 'I am honoured, revered. Lieutenant or no, I will gladly fight by your side. Allow me to prepare my weapons and I will meet you in the war room.'

De Haan nodded and waited a moment more, allowing the chanting of the Traitor Marines to soothe his ruffled nerves, before he strode away.

Nessun was standing quietly in the war room when De Haan entered, head bowed, warp eye clouded. Meer and Traika were pacing, almost circling each other, clearly at odds. De Haan ordered them to report.

'Something is coming, revered!' Meer began. 'The slaves are restless, there have been revolts on the building crews! The eldar know something! We must prepare for assault!'

'We must make the assault!' Traika's rasping voice. 'We are Word Bearers, not Iron Warriors! We do not skulk behind walls. We take Lorgar's blessing to our enemies, His blessings of hate and fire and blood and agony!' The obscenely long fingers of Traika's left hand flexed and clenched, as if to claw the tension out of the air.

Listening to them, De Haan hesitated. For the first time he felt a tug, a tilt at the back of his mind that he could not identify. He could not see with Nessun's precision, no seer he, but ten thousand years in the Eye of Terror had tuned him to the coarser ebbs and flows as it had them all. Something was near. He raised his crozius for silence – its crown a snarling hound's head now – and looked to Nessun.

'Speak, Nessun! Stare through these walls. Tell me what you see!'

'Revered, I... am not sure. There are patterns, something moving... a ring, a wall... closing or opening, I cannot say... a mind... shapes, silent... rushing air...' His voice was becoming ragged, and De Haan cut him off.

'It's clear enough. Meer, Traika: you are both right. The eldar know of us.' He fought back a chuckle. 'And they fear us. Catch us off-guard, would they? A quick strike at the head, was it? Drive me off their trail?' And now he did laugh, feeling the tension lifting from his back.

'Time for our sortie, my brothers! Have the Razorbacks lowered to the ramp. Traika, assemble your veteran squads! Meer, have our space command ready a bombardment for when we–'

That was when the first plasma blast hit the side of the cathedral with a sound like the sky being torn apart. The thunderous roar died away amid vast dust clouds, the groan of masonry, frenzied shouts from up and down the halls. De Haan stared straight ahead for one speechless moment, then hurled himself to the balcony, the others behind him. And then they could only stand and watch.

The world had filled with enemies. Sleek eldar jet bikes arrowed down from the sky to whip past the walls of the cathedral, and high above De Haan could hear the rumble of sonic booms as squadrons of larger alien assault craft criss-crossed over their heads. With sickening speed each distant blur in the air would grow and resolve into a raptor-sleek grav-tank, arcing in silently to spill a knot of infantry into the town before they rose and banked away again. In what seemed like a matter of heartbeats the fortress was ringed by a sea of advancing Guardians, their ranks dotted with gliding gun-platforms and dancing war-walkers, and the air swarmed with the eldar craft.

The aliens' assault started to be answered. Thumps and cracks came from the walls as the Word Bearers brought heavy weapons to bear and threads of tracer fire began reaching out to the purple-and-gold shapes that danced past on the wind. De Haan pushed to the edge of the balcony, heedless of the shapes above him and greedy for the sight of fireballs and smoke-trails, but he had time for no more than a glance before Meer and Traika pulled him away from the edge.

'Revered! With us! You must lead us. We cannot stay!' He cursed and almost raised his crozius to Meer, but the first laser beams had begun sweeping the balcony, carving at the rock and sending molten dribbles down the walls behind them. He nodded grimly and led them inside.

In the debris-swathed halls all was din and confusion. The slave-masters bellowed and flailed with their barbed whips, but their charges would not be ordered. De Haan realised someone had set off the Frenzon too early. Their thralls ran to and fro, shrieking and swinging their clubs, pistols spitting and making the stone chambers a hell of sparks and ricochets. Bullets spanged off De Haan's armour as he shouldered his way through the crowd of naked, bleeding berserkers.

'To me! They are upon us, we will cut them down here! To me!' and De Haan began the chant of the Martio Secundus. All around him Word Bearers turned and began to fall in behind him, dark red helms bearing down on him above the sea of bobbing cultist heads. Roars and growls began to mix with the cries of the mortals; the beastfolk were following too. De Haan gave a snarling grin behind his faceplate. *In Lorgar's name, we will make a fight of this yet.*

Reaching the great stair, they found that a whole part of the wall had gone, simply vanished leaving smooth stone edges where a piece had been erased. A distort-cannon crater – and the ceiling above it was already beginning to groan and send down streams of dust. He ignored the danger, sent his chant ringing out again and charged through the crater to the hall beyond; the hangar and teleport dais were close.

Then, swooping and darting though the breaches their cannon had made, came the eldar, Aspect Warriors all in blue, thrumming wings spreading from their shoulders. Lasers stabbed down into the throng underneath them and grenades fell from their hands like petals.

'Fight!' De Haan bellowed, and now that he was in battle he roared the Martio Tertius and sent a fan of bolt shells screaming through the squadron, smashing two Hawks backwards into the wall in clouds of smoke. His crozius, twisted into the head of a one-eyed bull, was belching streams of red plasma that hung in the air when he moved it; it had not boasted the blue power-field of the Imperial croziae for eight thousand years.

The remaining Hawks tumbled gracefully in the air and glided towards the ruined wall, now with other shots chasing them, but then the braying of the beastfolk changed note. De Haan whirled to see three of them, firing wildly, looking about them in panic, caught in a silvery mist. All three seemed to twitch and heave and fall oddly out of shape before they collapsed into piles of filth on the stone floor. Beyond them, the two Warp Spider warriors sucked the filament clouds back into the muzzles of their weapons. While shells from De Haan and Meer took one apart, the other stepped back. With a gesture, the air flowed around it like water and it was gone.

Down the hall and up the broad stairs, running hard, Duxhai came pounding out of the smoke, plasma gun clutched in his hands. The hangar was filled with smoke and flashes of light.

'The hangar is gone, lord, taken. We opened the gates to take the tanks down the ramp to the ground, but they drove us back with their strange weapons, and their heavy tanks are bombarding us. The teleport platform is destroyed. I have said the Martio Quartus for our fallen, and my brothers have dug in to hold them at bay. But we cannot stay here.'

De Haan almost groaned aloud. 'I will not be driven like an animal! This is my fortress, I will stand to defend it!' But his soldier's instincts had taken charge and were giving the lie to his words: he was already moving back down the stairs to meet the last of the Space Marines and a gaggle of thralls struggling up to meet him. He looked at them for a moment, and did not flinch as a Fire Prism fired through the hangar doors, opened a dazzling sphere of yellow-white fire over their heads.

'The Deepmost Chapel, then, and the Great Hall. We will cut them down as they enter, until our brothers can land. When the transports land the rest of our crusade the battle will turn soon enough.'

They hammered down the stairs. Beside them a glare came through the window-slits and then the rock wall flashed red-hot and crumbled as the Space Marines next to it hurled themselves away. The sleek alien tank which had opened the breach rose out of sight and the jet bikes behind it – no Guardian craft these but the smoky grey-green and bright silver of the Shining Spears – threw a delicate cat's cradle of lasers through the opening. Thralls yowled and fell, while the beastfolk sent bullets and shot blasting out of the opening as the jet bikes peeled off and rose out of sight.

Then the Word Bearers were in the chapel, the shadowy space and echoes calming De Haan, the familiar shape of the warp obelisk giving him strength. They fanned out into the chamber, around the upper gallery and the floor itself, needing no orders: within seconds the doors were covered. The pack of thralls and beastfolk huddled and muttered in the centre of the chamber, clutching weapons.

'Revered, we... we are beset on every side.' Nessun's voice was flat and hoarse with anger. 'I feel them at the gates, fighting our brothers and slaves. But they are above us too, they are breaching the upper walls and stepping onto the balconies from their grav-sleds. And, and... most revered lord...'

Suddenly Nessun's voice was drenched with misery, and even the heads of the warriors around him were turning. 'Our battle-barge. Our fortress. I see it reeling in space, revered... it is ringed by the enemy... their ships dance away from our guns... our brothers were preparing their landing, the shields had been lowered for the teleport to work. The eldar are tearing at it... my vision is dimming...'

There was silence in the chapel for a moment after Nessun's voice died away. De Haan thought of trying to reach the sensoria array in the spires above them, then pushed the useless thought away. The upper levels would be full of eldar scum by now, and by the time they could fight their way there his ship would indeed have been blasted from the sky.

He looked around. 'Alone, then. Alone with our hatred. I will hear no talk of flight. They will break against us as a wave against a cliff.'

'Lorgar is with us, Chaos is within us, damnation clothes us and none can stand against us.'

As they all said the blessing De Haan's eyes moved from one to the next. Meer cradling his bolter, seemingly deep in thought, Duxhai standing haughtily with plasma-gun held at arms, Traika glaring about him for any sign of weakness in the others, chainsword starting to flex and rev. De Haan raised his crozius and strode from the chapel, the others following, and as if on a signal they heard the bombardment outside begin again.

It was only fitting that De Haan and his retinue marched into the north end of the ruined Great Hall at the same time that the eldar filled its south. They had blown in the walls and shot the bronze doors apart and were fanning out through the ruins. De Haan leapt down the steps into the hall, letting the dust and smoke blur his outline as shots clipped the columns around him and his men returned fire from the archway. A plasma grenade exploded nearby, an instant of scorching whiteness that betrayed the eldar: in the instant that it blinded them the Word Bearers had launched their own advance, scrambling and vaulting over the rubble. There were insect-quick movements ahead and De Haan fired by reflex, plucking the Guardians out of their positions before he had consciously registered their location. The soft thrum of shuriken guns was drowned out by the hammer-and-yowl of the Word Bearers' bolt shells.

A stream of white energy flashed by De Haan's shoulder as Duxhai felled two more eldar, but there were Dire Avengers in the eldar positions now, with quicker reflexes and a hawk-eye aim to catch Duxhai before he could move again. The shuriken were monomolecular, too fast and thin to properly see, but the air around Duxhai seemed to shimmer and flash. Blood and ceramite gouted from his back as his torso flew apart, the eyes on his armour glazing over. He staggered back and De Haan jinked around him, launching himself into battle.

A grenade went off somewhere to his left and shrapnel clipped his armour. The Word Bearer felt the moist embrace of the plates around his body jump and twitch with the pain. He brought his crozius up and over, its wolf's head yowling with both joy and pain and belching thick red plasma. It caught the Avenger square on its jutting helmet and the creature twitched for a moment only before the glowing crimson mist ate it down to the bone. His bolt pistol hammered in his hand and two more eldar crashed backward, twitching and tumbling. Just beyond them, Traika cleared a fallen column in a great leap and landed among yellow-armoured Striking Scorpions whose chainswords sang and sparked against his own. In the rubble, Meer led the others in laying down a crossfire that strewed alien corpses across a third of the hall.

De Haan sang the Martio Tertius in a clear, strong voice and shot the nearest Scorpion in the back. Traika screamed laughter and swung at another, but as it back-pedalled another Scorpion, in the heavy intricate armour of an exarch, glided forward and whirled a many-chained crystalline flail in an intricate figure that smashed both Traika's shoulders and left him standing, astonished and motionless, for a blow that stove in his helm and sent ceramite splinters flying. De Haan bellowed a battle-curse and his crozius head became a snake that lashed and hissed. Two short steps forward and he lunged, feinted and struck the flail out of the creature's hand. It reeled back into Meer's sights, the plasma eating at it even as shells riddled it, but in the time it took for De Haan to strike down the last Scorpion the hall was alive with eldar again, and Meer and Nessun were forced back and away from him by a shower of grenades and sighing filament webs as the blast from a distort-cannon scraped the roof off the hall and let in the raging sky.

Even as De Haan charged, fired and struck again and again, some distant part of him groaned. Faint, maddening alien thoughts brushed his own like spider-silk in the dark, and shadows danced at the upper edge of his vision as jet bikes and Vypers circled. The air around him was alive with shuriken fire and energy bolts. The eldar melted away as he struck this way and that. Ancient stone burst into hot shards as he swung his crozius, but rage had taken his discipline and, like a man trying to snatch smoke in his fingers, he found himself standing and roaring wordlessly as the hall emptied once more and the shots died away.

There were no voices, no cries from his companions. De Haan did not have to turn to look to know that this last assault had taken them all.

Meer and Nessun were dead, and behind him he could hear the boom of masonry as his citadel began to crumble. The Prayer of Sacrifice and the Martio Quartus would not come to his numb lips, and he nodded to himself. Why should not his rites unravel along with everything else? The Chaos star set in his rosarius was dead, lacklustre. He looked at it dully, and that was when he began to feel something tugging at his mind.

It was like an electrical tingle, or the distant sound of crickets; the way the air feels before a storm, or the thrum of distant war-machines. De Haan's warp-tuned mind rang with the nearby song of power. He remembered Nessun speaking of the pattern that farseers' minds made when they assembled.

You will set your eyes…

Suddenly he was running again. No screams now, just a low moan in his throat, a tangle of savage emotions he could not have put a name to if he had tried. Blood trickled from his lips and his crozius thrummed and crackled. The gates of the cathedral hung like broken wings. He ducked between them to stand on the broad black steps of his dying fortress.

…on the heart of Varantha…

His crozius's head had fallen silent, and he looked at it in puzzlement. It had formed itself into a human face, mouth gaping, eyes wide. A face that De Haan recognised as his own, from back in the days before his helm had sealed itself to him.

Turn, De Haan. Turn And Face Me.

The voice did not come through his ears, but seemed to resonate out of the air and throughout his bones and brain. It was measured, almost sombre, but its simple force almost shook him to his knees. Slowly, he raised his head.

…and all will come to an end.

More than twice De Haan's height, the immense figure stood with its spear at rest. It took a step forward out of the smoke that had wreathed it, to the centre of the plaza. De Haan watched the blood drip from its hand and stain the grey stones on the ground. It stood and regarded him, and there was none of the expected madness or fury in the white-hot pits of its baleful eyes, only a brooding patience that was far more terrifying.

He took a step forward. All the fury had gone like the snuffing of a candle: now there was just wrenching despair which drove everything else from his mind. He wondered how long ago Varantha's farseers had realised he was hunting them, how long ago they had begun cultivating his hate, how long ago they had begun to set this trap for him. He wondered if the farseer whose prophecy he had thought to fulfil was laughing at him from within its spirit stone.

He stood alone on the steps, and the air was silent but for the hiss of heat from incandescent iron skin and the faint keening from the weapon in one giant hand.

Then the lines from the Pentadict danced through his mind, the lines with which Lorgar had closed his testament as his own death came upon him.

Pride and defiant hate, spite and harsh oblivion. Let the great jewelled knot of the cosmos unravel in the dust.

He looked up again, his mind suddenly clear and calm. He raised his crozius, but the salute was not returned. No matter. He took a pace forward and down the steps, that volcanic gaze on him all the time. He walked faster, now jogging. He worked the action on his pistol with the heel of his hand. Running, its eyes on him.

Charging now, feet hammering, voice found at last in a wail of defiance, Chaplain De Haan ran like a daemon across his last battlefield to where the Avatar of Kaela Mensha Khaine stood, its smoking, shrieking spear in its vast hands, waiting for him.

GATE OF SOULS

Mike Lee

Dirge was a cursed world.

It was a planet of bleak stone and black rock, and it didn't belong in the Hammurat system, of that much the Imperial surveyors were certain. It was a rogue world, one orphaned from its home star countless millions of years in the past, and it had wandered through the darkness of space for millions of years more before being trapped in the grip of Hammurat's three blazing suns. Where Dirge had come from – and what strange vistas it had crossed over the aeons – the surveyors didn't care to know. Its surface was a wasteland of deep craters and jagged peaks, shrouded in thick, poisonous air that howled and raged under the cosmic lash of Hammurat's suns.

What mattered was that Dirge was rich: a virtual treasure trove for the ever-hungry forge worlds of the Pyrus Reach subsector. The planet's crust was thick with valuable metals, radioactives and minerals, and the cometary impacts that had shattered Dirge's surface had brought with them even more exotic elements in amounts never before catalogued. When news of the discovery reached the subsector capital it touched off a frantic rush of prospectors and mining expeditions, eager to cash in on the new world's untapped riches. Within the space of a year, almost two million prospectors, miners, murderers and thieves had come to Dirge to feast upon its riches.

Little more than a year later three-quarters of them were dead.

Seething electrical storms burned out equipment and raging winds tossed fully-loaded ore haulers around like toys. Seismic activity collapsed tunnels or trapped gases exploded under the touch of plasma torches. Men were carved up in backroom brawls over claims too hazardous to mine. The outnumbered proctors mostly looked the other way, pocketing bribes equal to a year's salary on more settled worlds and counting the days until their transfers came through.

Sometimes prospectors would return to the crater-cities from the crags or the deep tunnels, bearing artifacts of polished stone inscribed with strange inscriptions. When the rotgut was flowing in grimy taverns all over Dirge, men would sometimes go quiet and whisper of things they'd seen out in the storms: strange, corroded spires and dark menhirs covered in symbols that made their blood run cold. No one paid the stories any heed. Prospectors loved to tell tales, and what difference did some strange stones make when there was money to be made?

And so the crater-cities grew, spreading like scabs across the deep impact wounds the comets left behind. Men died by the thousands every day, killed by storms, earthquakes, carelessness or greed. Still more lost their minds from metal poisoning, mounting debt, or simply snapped from the stress of constant danger and merciless quotas from corporate masters dozens of light-years away. They blinded themselves with homemade liquor or wasted away in the grip of drugs like black lethe and somna. Some sought comfort in the words of itinerant priests, putting their salvation in the hands of holy men who took their tithes and sent them back to their dormitories with empty prayers and benedictions.

In the end, nothing made a difference. Until a prospector named Hubert Lohr came down from the crags one day, sold off all his possessions and began preaching a new faith in the bars and back alleys of the crater-cities. Lohr accepted no tithes; instead he offered people the secrets of Dirge. He spoke to broken-down miners, diseased prostitutes and petty thieves and told them of the Lost Princes, who still wandered the void in search of their wayward world. The Lost Princes possessed powers greater than men – greater even than the God-Emperor, who offered nothing but mouldy catechisms and cruel exhortations for the men who lived and died beneath His gaze. Lohr told the fevered crowds that if they made an offering large enough it would shine like a beacon across the void and lead the Princes back to Dirge. And when they returned they would reward the faithful with gifts beyond their comprehension.

By the time the agents of the Ecclesiarchy and the planetary governor realised the peril in their midst it was already too late.

The battered Aquila lander had barely touched the plasteel tarmac before Alabel Santos was out of her seat and striding for the landing ramp. Even without the grim badge of the Inquisitorial rosette gleaming upon her breast she cut a fearsome figure in her ornate power armour. One hand rested on the butt of her inferno pistol and a sheathed power knife hung in a scabbard on her other hip. 'Get the gun-servitors ready,' she snapped at the portly, middle-aged man struggling with his own restraints while fumbling for his respirator mask. 'I don't plan on being here long.' Her man Balid bleated something in reply but she paid little heed, her armour's respirator system whining with strain as she headed swiftly out into the howling wind.

Purple lightning flared overhead, etching the bustling airstrip in sharp relief. Tech-adepts swarmed over a long line of parked Vulture gunships, tending fuel lines and reloading rocket pods for another fire support mission over Baalbek City. On the other side of the plasteel tarmac sat a cluster of Valkyrie air assault craft, red tags fluttering from the hellstrike missiles loaded on their stubby wings. A platoon of armoured storm troopers, part of the Guard regiment's mobile reserve, huddled near their parked transports, cursing the wind and waiting to be called into action.

Santos spotted the permacrete bunkers of the regimental field headquarters just a few hundred metres from the airstrip, the pale colour of the new structures standing out sharply from the dark grey terrain. The guards on duty raised their weapons at her approach, but hurriedly stepped aside when they saw what badge she wore. She cycled through the atmosphere lock then pushed past bewildered and tired staff officers before marching stiffly up to a broad planning table set with an old-fashioned paper map of Baalbek City. Grainy aerial reconnaissance picts were spread across the table, highlighting different city districts. Studying them was a short, broad-chested officer in the uniform of the Terassian Dragoons, surrounded by a pair of staffers and a tall, forbidding woman whose cold eyes glittered beneath the rim of her peaked commissar's cap.

The colonel glanced up at Santos's approach, a curt order on his lips, but his exhausted face went pale at the sight of the gleaming rosette. His gaze continued upwards. The inquisitor's head was held stiffly erect in a frame of brass, lending her stunning features the severe cast of a martyred saint. 'Colonel Ravin, I presume?' she said without preamble. Red light flashed balefully from her augmetic eye. 'I am Inquisitor Alabel Santos of the Ordo Hereticus. What is your situation?'

To his credit, the colonel didn't skip a beat, as though having an Imperial inquisitor arrive unannounced at his headquarters was all in a day's work. 'Two months ago dissident elements among the mining population engineered a planet-wide revolt, overwhelming the local proctors and PDF contingents–'

'I know why you're here, colonel,' Santos snapped. 'I've been reading your despatches since you arrived on Dirge.' She studied the picts scattered across the table and plucked one from the pile, sliding it over to the colonel. The aerial image showed a mob of citizens surrounding a bleached pillar of bone, their gloved hands raised in supplication before the blasphemous sigil at its peak.

'You aren't dealing with dissidents,' Santos replied coldly. 'They are something altogether worse.'

Colonel Ravin and the commissar eyed one another. 'They call themselves the Cult of the Black Stone,' the commissar said. 'That's all we've been able to learn so far.'

'Then I shall educate you further,' Santos said, leaning across the table. 'This is the symbol of the Word Bearers, colonel.' The inquisitor rapped the pict sharply with her knuckle for emphasis, causing the staff officers to jump. 'The Ruinous Powers have taken an active interest in Dirge, and I have reason to believe that one of their greatest champions is at work in Baalbek City. I've come halfway across the subsector to find out why.' And to stop him once and for all, Emperor willing, Santos thought grimly. You have much to answer for, Erebus.

Colonel Ravin's pallor deepened. 'But that's... that's incredible,' he stammered. 'Traitor Marines? *Here?* How do you know this?'

'Because it is the Inquisition's business to know such things,' Santos snapped, turning back to the picts. Out of the corner of her eye she saw the colonel stiffen, then with an effort she reined in her temper. You have enough enemies without needing to make more, she reminded herself.

'It's all in the reports, colonel,' she explained. 'I've been studying every status report, Administratum log and Ecclesiarchal dictum filed from Dirge for the last six months.' Santos picked up one of the picts: it showed the planetary governor's palace in Baalbek City. Like all city structures, it was low, broad and windowless, built to withstand the frequent cyclones that swept over the crater wall from the wastelands. The resolution of the pict was good enough that she could recognise the impaled figure of the planetary governor, suspended on a girder among an iron forest set on the palace roof. The inquisitor set the pict aside and reached for another.

'Four months before the uprising, merchant ships were reporting strange surveyor readings in the vicinity of the system's far asteroid belt,' Santos continued. 'The local port authority dismissed the reports as pirate activity, but curiously, there was a dramatic drop in pirate attacks in the system over the same time period. Shortly afterward, orbital traffic control detected a number of unidentified flights into and out of Dirge's atmosphere. Again, these reports were passed off as smuggling activity, but I have another theory – a Chaos warship entered the system and is likely still here, hiding in one of the system's asteroid fields.'

Santos studied an image of cultists dragging bloody corpses from a burning dormitory towards the base of one of the cult's sacrificial pillars. She set it aside with a frown of contempt. 'Then there are arrest reports from the local Arbites headquarters. In the days leading up to the uprising several cult figures were arrested and when put to the question they described their leaders as armoured giants – the "Lost Princes", according to one of the prisoners. The cultist described the greatest of these princes as a god among men, who wore the skins of his foes as testament to his power and bore a mighty talisman of his gods' favour.'

'The Chaos champion you spoke of,' the commissar declared. 'Who is he?'

But Santos shook her head. 'I dare not speak his name. I've placed your souls in peril just telling you this much.'

One pict after another showed cultists at work around hab units and municipal buildings across the city, carting out truckloads of debris and hauling them away. After the fourth such image she began to line them up on the map table in chronological order.

'If the prisoner was to be believed, there were no less than five Word Bearers present on Dirge, including the Chaos lord. That's an astonishing number for such a minor world.'

'Minor?' Ravin said. 'Dirge supplies more than half of the industrial materials used by forge worlds across the subsector.'

'The Word Bearers don't make war according to the *Tactica Imperium*,' Santos declared. 'They don't think in terms of lines of supply or resource interdiction. They fight for souls, spreading terror and debasement from world to world like a cancer. Dirge, however, is both isolated and sparsely populated. From their standpoint, it's a poor target.' The inquisitor studied the line of images and her frown deepened. 'Colonel, why did you order these images taken?'

Ravin looked over the picts and waved dismissively. 'We were trying to gauge the extent and composition of the enemy fortifications based on how much material they were excavating. Those work teams have been at it day and night since before we got here.'

Santos straightened. 'Excavations.' The inquisitor felt her blood run cold. 'These cultists aren't using floor panels and wall board to build fortifications, colonel. They're hollowing these buildings out to dig for something. That's why the Word Bearers are here. Why *he* is here. The rebellion was just a diversion so they could search the planet without interference.' Her hand was trembling slightly as she snatched up the last pict in the line. The time code in the corner indicated that the last excavation had begun almost three days ago. No new excavations since, she realised. They must think they've found what they're after.

'Colonel, I require the use of your mobile reserve and a flight of Vultures,' Santos declared in a steely voice. 'I'll brief the platoon leader en route.'

The building had formerly housed the local tithe assessor's office. Only three storeys tall, square, windowless and slab-sided, the structure was built like a treasure vault, which wasn't far from the truth. A small army of servitors and stooped scribes had toiled night and day within its cold, gloomy cells, recording the profits of the mining cartels and the independent prospectors and assessing the Emperor's due.

Now the square outside the building was piled with the guts of the Imperial tax collection machine. Large, ornate cogitators stood in drunken ranks, their wooden cabinets splintered and their brass gauges tarnishing in the corrosive air. Drifts of torn cables and mounds of flooring and wall board were plucked and pushed by the restless wind, and a pall of glittering dust swirled endlessly in the harsh construction lamps erected by the work crews outside the building.

Glass crunched like brittle bones beneath Erebus's armoured boots as he stepped through the narrow doorway. Just beyond the threshold a tiled floor extended for less than a metre before ending in a jagged cliff of permacrete and steel.

The miners of Dirge knew their trade well. Working day and night, they'd completely torn out the first two floors and the building's two sub-levels. Tangles of shorn wiring, crumpled metal ducting and shreds of wallboard hung like man-made stalactites from the gutted ceiling, painted white with a layer of grit that sparkled in the harsh light of the construction lamps.

All work had stopped in the pit below. More than two dozen men set aside their tools and prostrated themselves on the rocky ground at the Chaos lord's arrival. Erebus looked out over the fruit of their labours and was pleased.

Once the sub-levels had been removed the miners had dug another three metres into the grey, ashy soil before they'd found the first of the black stones. It had taken another day of careful work under difficult conditions to lift away millions of years of rock-hard encrustations that had covered the strange symbols carved into their surface. The work had gone slowly because the delicate sonic brushes would run out of power after only a few minutes in proximity to the rocks, and because the workers' brains disintegrated from prolonged exposure to the symbols themselves. Even from where Erebus stood he could feel the power of the warp rising like black frost from the surface of the accursed objects.

On the orders of Magos Algol, the tallest of the stones had been pulled upright again. It rose five metres into the air, casting a long, misshapen shadow across the excavation site. The surface of the object looked crude and rough-hewn, but the symbols carved into the rounded surface were sharp and precise. They climbed the stone in a kind of spiral, following the rules of a language that had died out before the birth of mankind. At the top of the stone the symbols ended at the base of a perfect sphere, haloed by an arch of stone wrought in the shape of twining tentacles.

Erebus smiled, revealing pointed teeth and the fearful demeanour of a cruel and vengeful god. The Chaos lord was clad neck to foot in the imposing armour of a Space Marine – but where its ancient engravings once extolled the might of the Emperor of Man, it now preached an altogether different faith. Blasphemous runes and symbols of ruin pulsed sickly from the Traitor Marine's breastplate and the edges of his pauldrons, and the skulls of defiled Imperial priests hung from a brass chain around Erebus's neck. Psalms of vengeance and depravity were scribed in blood upon the tanned hides of fallen Space Marine heroes and stretched between barbed spikes across the Chaos lord's pauldrons and from hooks at his waist. In his right hand Erebus held aloft a talisman of fearsome power – the dark crozius, symbol of his faith in the Chaos Gods.

A broad ramp, wide enough for two men to walk abreast, had been built from the ground floor to the base of the excavation. Its steel supports quivered slightly as Erebus descended slowly into the pit. His black gaze was fixed on the standing stone and the orb at its summit.

Erebus stepped unflinchingly into the stone's twisted shadow. The darkness that fell upon him was unnaturally cold, sinking effortlessly through the bulk of his daemonic armour. The Chaos lord felt his shrivelled insides writhe at the icy echo of the warp, and Erebus welcomed it, spreading his massive arms wide. His mind filled with visions of the Seething Gulf, the ocean of mad wonder that the servants of the false Emperor called the *Occularis Terriblus*. It was the font of godhood, the birthplace of universes. Amid the roiling sea of unfettered power, Erebus beheld a swollen red orb that glittered like a drop of congealing blood. He heard the cries of multitudes, the chorus of supplication sung at the feet of his unholy master, and he longed to join his voice to the song. *Lorgar!* His mind called into the void. *The time draws nigh, unholy one. Soon the gate will swing wide!*

Erebus chuckled to himself, the sound echoing in the cavernous space and causing the cultists to tremble in fear. He turned to the assembled multitude, his eyes alighting on two figures kneeling apart from the storm-suited labourers. One was a hulking giant in red armour similar to Erebus's own; the frail, elderly man hunched next to the Word Bearer looked as slight as a children's puppet, all slender sticks and grimy rags, too fragile to touch.

The Chaos lord favoured his servants with another dreadful smile. 'Arise, Phael Dubel,' he commanded gravely. 'And you, Magos Algol. Blessed are you in the eyes of the Gods Who Wait.'

The magos rose to his feet with an agility that belied his frail and aged appearance. His skin had the grey pallor of a corpse, his thin, wrinkled lips pulling back from gleaming steel teeth in an avaricious grin. His dark robes, once decorated with the fur mantle and chains of a Magos Archaeologis, now bore lines of depraved script that spoke of his allegiance to the Ruinous Powers. Algol's eyes glittered like black marbles in the shadows of his sunken eye sockets, bright with forbidden knowledge and reptilian cunning.

Dubel, one of the Chaos lord's chosen lieutenants, bowed deeply to his master and stepped to one side, turning so that he could keep the assembled workers and the open doorway in view at all times. One hand rested on the butt of his holstered bolt pistol. The other, clad in a fearsome, outsized gauntlet called a power fist, opened and closed in an unconscious reflex, as though the weapon hungered for a victim to crush in its grip.

Magos Algol walked a careful path around the sharp edges of the stone's shadow, looking up at Erebus with a calculating smile.

'You see, great one? It is just as the *Book of the Stone* described,' Algol's voice was harsh and quavering, like the sharp note of a plucked wire. 'I told you we would find it here.'

Erebus regarded the towering stone greedily. 'Have you deciphered the runes yet, magos? Does it tell us where the Orb of Shadows lies?'

'In time, in time,' the magos said, raising a wrinkled hand. 'The runes require careful study, great one. Their meanings, if interpreted without proper care, could be... explosive. But,' Algol added quickly, 'it does indeed speak of the orb. You will have the answer you seek.'

'Then do not let me keep you from your work, blessed magos,' Erebus said to the man. 'Inform me the instant that you have deciphered the text.'

The magos bowed to the Chaos lord and approached the stone, his hands fluttering eagerly as he began to contemplate the inscriptions. Erebus joined his lieutenant. 'Send word to the *Throne of Pain*,' he said quietly, referring to the cruiser hiding in Dirge's outer asteroid field. 'We will return to Ebok as soon as Algol has uncovered the location of the orb. Then our work will well and truly begin.'

Dubel looked back at the looming stone, his black eyes lingering on the sphere. 'Once we have the orb, what then?'

'Then we seek the Temple of Ascendancy,' Erebus replied. 'I believe it to be on Fariin, in the Elysiun System, but the orb will tell us for certain.'

The Traitor Marine stiffened, fixing his master with a suspicious stare. 'Ascendancy? You seek to follow the same path as Lorgar?'

Erebus returned his lieutenant's stare. 'I? No, Dubel. I am but a humble servant,' he said enigmatically. 'Perhaps I seek to blaze a path for Lorgar to follow *me*.'

Dubel's eyes widened in shock. Before he could reply, however, the ground shook beneath a drumbeat of thunderous explosions as Imperial rockets slammed into the side of the hollowed-out building.

One hand gripping a support strut just inside the Valkyrie's open hatchway, Alabel Santos leaned out into the assault craft's howling slipstream and watched the Vulture gunships streak over the flat roof of the target building. Fires were burning from rocket strikes in the debris-choked square and tendrils of smoke rose from craters blasted into the building's thick permacrete wall. The landing zone looked clear.

The three Valkyries of the mobile reserve platoon – plus an extra support craft carrying Balid and his gun-servitors – were howling along at roof height down one of the city's narrow streets, right on the heels of the gunships. She could already feel the Valkyries start to slow as they dropped toward the deck, preparing to flare their engines for tactical deployment.

Santos swung back into the passenger compartment and addressed the platoon commander. 'Once we hit the ground we're going to have to move fast. Have two of your squads form a perimeter around the Valkyries and I'll have my gun servitors provide support. You and the assault team go in with me. Once we're inside, don't hesitate. Don't think. Just kill everything that moves.'

The storm trooper lieutenant nodded at Santos, his face hidden behind a full-face tactical respirator that gave him the look of an automaton. His vox unit crackled. 'We're with you, inquisitor,' he said curtly. 'The Emperor protects.'

Santos drew her pistol just as the Valkyrie plummeted like a stone and then stopped less than a metre over the rubbish-strewn square with its engines shrieking. There was a stuttering roar as the door gunner let off a burst with his heavy bolter at some distant target. 'Go, go, go!' she shouted, leaping from the assault craft and heading for the building at a run. Behind her the storm trooper assault team deployed with speed and precision, hellguns covering the building's entrance. The lieutenant followed right behind Santos, a plasma pistol in one hand and a crackling power sword in the other.

The inquisitor pulled her power knife free from its scabbard and thumbed its activation rune. She rarely carried it; the knife was an heirloom weapon, given as a gift from her mentor Inquisitor Grazlen when she attained the rank of inquisitor.

Santos held the weapon in a white-knuckled grip as she charged into the building's narrow doorway. She was going to bury that burning blade in the Chaos lord's eye or die trying.

Chunks of broken permacrete and twisted plasteel continued to rain down from the gutted ceiling among Erebus and the cultists as turbofans shrieked and heavy weapons fire hammered outside. The Chaos lord looked for Magos Algol and found the corrupted scholar on his knees, coughing wetly amid falling drifts of dust. 'Finish your translation, magos!' Erebus thundered, then raised his accursed crozius before the huddled cultists and spoke in a piercing voice. 'Rise up, warriors of the faith! The servants of the false Emperor are upon us! The eyes of the gods are upon you – go forth and win their favour!'

With a lusty howl the cultists staggered to their feet and brandished the tools of their trade: heavy sonic drills, power mattocks and arc hammers. They knew from bitter experience what those tools could do to soft flesh and brittle bone.

Dubel drew his bolt pistol. There was a searing crackle as he ignited his power fist's disruption field. 'Death to the servants of the false Emperor!' he roared, and the cultists surged forward, racing up the ramp to the doorway just as the first of the attackers stepped into view.

An inquisitor, Erebus thought, catching sight of a woman in ornate power armour leading the charge. Her alabaster face was distorted in a snarl of almost feral rage, and she fixed him with such a black look of hate that he could not help but think they'd met somewhere before.

Erebus bared his teeth in challenge and spread his arms in welcome, words of blasphemous power hissing off his tongue.

There! The shock of seeing the Chaos lord again sent a bolt of pure, righteous fury through Alabel Santos. Erebus was mocking her, grinning like a devil, his arms open wide. I'll give you something to smile about, she thought, raising her inferno pistol. Just as she drew a bead on Erebus, another armoured shape rushed in front of the Apostle, bolt pistol raised. The mass-reactive rounds smashed into her shoulder and chest before her ears registered the flat boom of the pistol's report. The impacts spun her around, the servos in her power suit whining dangerously as they sought to compensate for the blows.

Footsteps thundered up the ramp towards Santos as a dozen cultists charged forwards, weapons ready. The lieutenant appeared beside the inquisitor, levelling his pistol and firing two quick shots into the oncoming mob. Bolts of superheated plasma blew the lead cultists apart. 'Flamer to the front!' the platoon leader ordered over his vox.

Armoured storm troopers fanned out on the narrow lip of permacrete to either side of the doorway, firing red bolts of las-fire into the charging cultists. Then a soldier stepped to the top of the ramp and fired a hissing stream of burning promethium point-blank at the charging miners. The cultists shrieked and fell back from the tongue of searing flame, setting the ramp alight with their tumbling, thrashing bodies.

Two storm troopers to Santos's right were blown off their feet by bolt pistol rounds, their carapace armour no match for the Traitor Marine's deadly fire. The inquisitor dropped to one knee, trying to peer through the thickening black smoke and strobing las-fire for another glimpse of the Chaos lord. She couldn't see him, but she could hear him, his deep, sonorous voice chanting terrible words that sent a shiver down her artificial spine. The Chaos lord's voice rose to a terrifying crescendo – and for a moment it felt as though the very air in the room was receding, drawing back from the battle as if in horror.

The screams of the burning cultists went silent all at once. Then Santos felt the fabric of reality come unravelled. She heard a chorus of screeching howls and tasted hot brass on her tongue, and before she could draw breath to shout a warning the daemons were upon them, charging straight through the fire.

They had faces like skinned wolves and their powerfully-muscled bodies gleamed with freshly-spilled blood. Their eyes, their fangs and their twisted horns were pure brass, bright from the forge, as well as the razor edges of their two-handed axes. Upon their sloped brows was carved the mark of the Blood God, and they had come for a bounty of skulls to lay at the foot of his throne.

Men screamed. The storm trooper carrying the flamer fell to one knee and toppled onto Santos, splashing the inquisitor with blood. Roaring an oath to the Divine Emperor, she pushed the corpse aside just as a blood-spattered figure loomed above her.

She didn't feel the blow. There was a hot wind against her face, and then there was the strange sensation of warm blood soaking through the bodyglove around her shoulder. Her left arm locked in place and Santos felt the sting of needles as the suit's medicae unit attempted to keep her from lapsing into shock. All she could think was *thank the Emperor it missed my head*, then she put her pistol against the daemon's midsection and pulled the trigger. A bolt of pure cyan, powerful enough to pierce the armour of a Land Raider, tore the daemon apart and then detonated with a thunderclap against the ceiling. The bloodletter dissolved in tatters of stinking, oily smoke.

Santos fell backwards, landing against the marble verge. As though in slow motion, she could see another daemon rushing at her, axe raised to strike. There were screams and the clash of steel somewhere nearby – and then, out of the corner of her eye, she saw the smoke shift and reveal the red-armoured form of the Dark Prophet, standing before a monolith of twisted stone.

Death approached on cloven feet. Santos could feel her strength fading, and between one heartbeat and the next she made her choice. Taking her eyes from the daemon, she steadied her pistol against the marble tiles. With a tic of her cheek, she activated her augmetic eye's laser sight. The needle-thin beam glittered in the smoke, tracing a merciless line across the open space and painting a bloody dot on the Chaos lord's forehead.

'This is for Krendan Hive,' she whispered, and pulled the trigger.

The bloodletter howled above her – and then staggered as a bolt of plasma smashed into its head. The daemon staggered, then the blade of a power sword sank into its chest. The lieutenant leapt over Santos's body as the daemon's form dissolved. 'Get the inquisitor to safety!' he ordered, taking aim on another daemon and shooting it in the face. 'The Emperor protects!' he bellowed, taking another step down the burning ramp.

Santos felt hands grab the collar of her armour. Darkness crowded at the edge of her vision. The thunderclap of her shot rang through the open space and she tried to catch a glimpse of Erebus again, but all she could see was the lieutenant advancing coolly into the face of the onrushing daemons and firing shot after shot from his plasma pistol. The weapon's discharge vents were glowing white-hot, and his armoured gauntlet was melting from the heat.

'The Emperor protects!' she heard him say as another daemon loomed before him. The lieutenant fired his pistol again – and this time the overheated power core exploded, consuming him and his foe in a ball of incandescent light.

Santos felt herself dragged across the stone floor and passed out in a fiery wave of pain.

Erebus saw the bright flare of the inferno pistol and for the briefest instant he feared that the Dark Gods had deserted him. His vision deserted him in a blaze of cyan, and a clap of terrible thunder dashed him to his knees.

By the time he regained his senses the battle was over.

The ramp was gone. Indeed, the entire front of the building had collapsed, sealing the doorway with tons of broken permacrete. A bare handful of flickering work lights still cast a fitful glow over the site.

After a moment, Erebus started to laugh. He raised his crozius and offered his thanks to the Ruinous Powers for their dark gifts. Nothing in this universe would keep him from reaching the Damnation Gate.

Still laughing, the Chaos lord turned to look for Magos Algol, and saw that the Dark Gods had been fickle with their blessings.

The inquisitor's bolt had missed Erebus and struck the monolith instead. Its dark surface had exploded, erasing the engravings in a storm of razor-edged shrapnel. Algol lay on his back at the foot of the ancient stone, his frail body shredded and a look of surprise etched on his bony face.

Erebus knelt by the body of the dead magos. Nearby, he heard a shifting of fallen rock, and glanced over to see Dubel picking himself up from the rubble. The Traitor Marine saw what had happened to Algol and hissed a vicious curse. 'We'll go back to Ebok empty-handed now,' the Traitor Marine spat.

The Chaos lord studied Algol's shocked face. 'I think not,' he said, taking the magos's head in his left hand. The man's thin neck snapped with an expert twist of his wrist; vertebrae popped in dry succession, and then Erebus held Algol's head up to the flickering light.

'The monolith is gone, but the eyes that beheld it still remain,' Erebus said. 'The eyes are the gateway to the soul, Dubel. And gates, once opened, will give up everything they contain.'

Erebus looked into Algol's eyes and laughed, seeing his future.

THE WRATH OF KHÂRN

William King

'Blood for the Blood God!' bellowed Khârn the Betrayer, charging forward through the hail of bolter fire, towards the Temple of Superlative Indulgence. The bolter shells ricocheting off his breastplate did not even slow him down. The Chaos Space Marine smiled to himself. The ancient ceramite of his armour had protected him for over ten thousand years. He felt certain it would not let him down today. All around him warriors fell, clutching their wounds, crying in pain and fear.

More souls offered up on the altar of battle to the Supreme Lord of Carnage, Khârn thought and grinned maniacally. Surely the Blood God would be pleased this day.

Ahead of him, Khârn saw one of his fellow berzerkers fall, his body riddled with shells, his armour cracked and melted by plasma fire. The berzerker howled with rage and frustration, knowing that he was not going to be in at the kill, that he would give Khorne no more offerings on this or any other day. In frustration, the dying warrior set his chainsword to maximum power and took off his own head with one swift stroke. His blood rose in a red fountain to slake Khorne's thirst.

As he passed, Khârn kicked the fallen warrior's head, sending it flying over the defenders' parapet. At least this way his fallen comrade would witness Khârn slaughter the Slaanesh worshippers in the few delicious moments before he died. Under the circumstances, it was the least reward Khârn could grant such a devout warrior.

The Betrayer leapt over a pile of corpses, snapping off a shot with his plasma pistol. One of the Slaanesh cultists fell, clutching the ruins of his melted face. Gorechild, Khârn's daemonic axe, howled in his hands. Khârn brandished it above his head and bellowed his challenge to the sick, yellow sky of the daemon-world.

'Skulls for the skull throne!' Khârn howled. On every side, frothing Berzerkers echoed his cry. More shells whined all around him. He ignored them the way he would ignore the buzz of annoying insects. More of his fellows fell but Khârn stood untouched, secure in the blessing of the Blood God, knowing that it would not be his turn today.

All was going according to plan. A tide of Khorne's warriors flowed across the bomb-cratered plains towards the towering redoubt of the Slaanesh worshippers. Support fire from the Chaos Titan artillery had reduced most of the walls around the ancient temple complex to just so much rubble. The disgusting murals painted in fluorescent colours had been reduced to atoms. The obscene minarets that crowned the towers had been blasted into well-deserved oblivion. Lewd statues lay like colossal, limbless corpses, gazing at the sky with blank marble eyes.

Even as Khârn watched, missiles blazed down from the sky and smashed another section of the defensive wall to blood-covered fragments. Huge clouds of dust billowed. The ground shook. The explosions rumbled like distant thunder. Sick joy bubbled through Khârn's veins at the prospect of imminent violence.

This was what he lived for, these moments of action where he could once again prove his superiority to all other warriors in the service of his exalted lord. In all his ten thousand year existence, Khârn had found no joy to touch the joy of battle, no lust greater than his lust for blood. Here on the field of mortal combat, he was more than in his element, he was at the site of his heart's desire. It was the thing that had caused him to betray his oath of allegiance to the Emperor of Mankind, his genetic destiny as a Space Marine and even his old comrades in the World Eaters Legion. He had never regretted those decisions even for an instant. The bliss of battle was reward enough to stay any doubts.

He jumped the ditch before the parapet, ignoring the poisoned spikes which lined the pit bottom and promised an ecstatic death to any that fell upon them. He scrambled up the loose scree of the rock face and vaulted over the low wall, planting his boot firmly into the face of a defender as he did so. The man screamed and fell back, trying to stem the flow of blood from his broken nose. Khârn swung Gorechild and ended his whining forever.

'Death is upon you!' Khârn roared as he dived into a mass of depraved cultists. Gorechild lashed out. Its teeth bit into hardened ceramite, spraying sparks in all directions. The blow passed through the target's armour, opening its victim from stomach to sternum. The wretch fell back, clutching at his ropy entrails. Khârn despatched him with a backhand swipe and fell upon his fellows, slaying right and left, killing with every blow.

Frantically the cultists' leader bellowed orders, but it was too late.

Khârn was among them, and no man had ever been able to boast of facing Khârn in close combat and living.

The numbers 2243, then 2244, blinked before his eyes. The ancient gothic lettering of the digital death-counter, superimposed on Khârn's field of vision, incremented quickly. Khârn was proud of this archaic device, presented by Warmaster Horus himself in ancient times. Its like could not be made in this degenerate age. Khârn grinned proudly as his tally of offerings for this campaign continued to rise. He still had a long way to go to match his personal best but that was not going to stop him trying.

Men screamed and howled as they died. Khârn roared with pleasure, killing everything within his reach, revelling in the crunch of bone and the spray of blood. The rest of the Khornate force took advantage of the destruction the Betrayer had caused. They swarmed over the walls in a howling mass and dismembered the Slaanesh worshippers. Already demoralised by the death of their leader, not even these fanatical worshippers of the Lord of Pleasure could stand their ground. Their morale broken, they panicked and fled.

Such pathetic oafs were barely worth the killing, Khârn decided, lashing out reflexively and killing those Slaanesh worshippers who passed too to close him as they fled. 2246, 2247, 2248 went the death counter. It was time to get on with his mission. It was time to find the thing he had come here to destroy – the ancient daemonic artefact known as the Heart of Desire.

'Attack!' Khârn bellowed and charged through the gaping mouth of the leering stone head that was the entrance to the main temple building.

Inside it was quiet, as if the roar of battle could not penetrate the walls. The air stank of strange perfumes. The walls had a porous, fleshy look. The pink-tinged light was odd; it shimmered all around, coming from no discernible source. Khârn switched to the auto-sensor systems within his helm, just in case there was some trickery here.

Leather-clad priestesses, their faces domino-masked, emerged from padded doorways. They lashed at Khârn with whips that sent surges of pain and pleasure through his body. Another man, one less hardened than Khârn, might have been overwhelmed by the sensation but Khârn had spent millennia in the service of his god, and what passed through him now was but a pale shadow compared to the battle lust that mastered him. He chopped through the snake-like flesh of the living lash. Poison blood spurted forth. The woman screamed as if he had cut her. Looking closer he saw that she and the whip were one. A leering daemonic head tipped the weapon's handle and had buried its fangs into her wrist. Khârn's interest was sated. He killed the priestess with one back-handed swipe of Gorechild.

A strange, strangled cry of rage and hate warned him of a new threat.

He turned and saw that one of the other Berzerkers, less spiritually pure than himself, had been overcome by the whip's evil. The man had torn off his helmet and his face was distorted by a sick and dreamy smile that had no place on the features of one chosen by Khorne. Like a sleepwalker he advanced on Khârn and lashed out with his chainsword. Khârn laughed as he parried the blow and killed the man with his return stroke.

A quick glance told him that all the priestesses were dead and that most of his followers had slain their drugged brethren. Good, thought Khârn, but part of him was disappointed. He had hoped that more of his fellows would be overcome by treachery. It was good to measure himself against true warriors, not these decadent worshippers of an effete god. Gorechild howled with frustrated bloodlust, writhing in his hand as if it would turn on him if he did not feed it more blood and sinew soon. Khârn knew how the axe felt. He turned, gestured for his companions to follow him and raced off down the corridor.

'Follow me,' he shouted. 'To the slaughter!'

Passing through a huge arch, the former Space Marines entered the inner sanctum of the temple and Khârn knew that they had found what they had come for. Light poured in through the stained glass ceiling. As he watched, Khârn realised that the light was not coming through the glass, but from the glass itself. The illustrations glowed with an eerie internal light and they moved. A riotous assembly of men and women, mutants and daemons enacted every foul deed that the depraved followers of a debauched god could imagine. And, Khârn noted, they could imagine quite a lot.

Khârn raised his pistol and opened fire, but the glass merely absorbed the weapon's energy. Something like a faint moan of pleasure filled the chamber and mocking laughter drew Khârn's attention to the throne which dominated the far end of the huge chamber. It was carved from a single gem that pulsed and changed colour, going from amber to lavender to pink to lime and then back through a flickering, random assortment of iridescent colours that made no sense and hurt the eye. Khârn knew without having to be told that this throne was the Heart of Desire. Senses honed by thousands of years of exposure to the stuff of Chaos told him that the thing fairly radiated power. Inside was the trapped essence of a daemon prince, held forever at the whim of Slaanesh as punishment for some ancient treachery. The man sitting so regally on the throne was merely a puppet and barely worth Khârn's notice, save as something to be squashed like a bug.

The man looked down on Khârn as if he had the temerity to feel the same way about Khorne's most devoted follower. His left hand stroked the hair of the leashed and naked woman who crouched like a pet at his feet. His right hand held an obscenely shaped runesword, which glowed with a blasphemous light.

Khârn strode forward to confront his new foe. The clatter of ceramite-encased feet on marble told him that his fellow berzerkers followed. In a matter of a hundred strides, Khârn found himself at the foot of the dais, and some odd, mystical force compelled him to stop and stare.

Khârn did not doubt that he was face-to-face with the cult leader. The man had the foul, debauched look of an ancient and immortal devotee of Slaanesh. His face was pale and gaunt; make-up concealed the dark shadows under his eyes. An obscene helmet covered the top of his head. As he stood, his pink and lime cloak billowed out behind him. Tight bands of studded leather armour girdled his naked chest, revealing lurid and disturbing tattoos.

'Welcome to the Heart of Desire,' the Slaanesh worshipper said in a soft, insinuating voice which somehow carried clearly across the chamber and compelled immediate, respectful attention. Khârn was instantly on his guard, sensing the magic within that voice, the persuasive power which could twist mortals to its owner's will. He struggled to keep the fury that burned eternally in his breast from subsiding under the influence of those slyly enthralling tones. 'What do you wish?'

'Your death!' the Betrayer roared, yet he felt his bloodlust being subdued by that oddly comforting voice.

The cult leader sighed. 'You worshippers of Khorne are so drearily predictable. Always the same tedious, unimaginative retort. I suppose it comes from following that mono-maniacal deity of yours. Still, you are hardly to be blamed for your god's dullness, I suppose.'

'When Khorne has devoured your soul, you will pay for such blasphemy!' Khârn shouted. His followers shouted their approval but with less enthusiasm than Khârn would have expected. For some reason, the man on the throne did not appear to be worried by the presence of so many armed men in his sanctum.

'Somehow I doubt it, old chap. You see, my soul has long been pledged to thrice-blessed Slaanesh, so unless Khorne wants to stick his talon down Slaanesh's throat or some other orifice, he'll have a hard time getting at it.'

'Enough of this prattle!' Khârn roared. 'Death is upon you!'

'Oh! Be sensible,' the cultist said, raising his hand. Khârn felt a tide of pleasure flow over him, like that he had felt from the whip earlier but a thousand times stronger. All around him he heard his men moan and gasp.

'Think! You can spend an eternity of pleasure being caressed by the power of Lord Slaanesh, while your soul slowly rots and sinks into his comforting embrace. Anything you want, anything you have ever desired, can be yours. All you have to do is swear allegiance to Slaanesh. Believe me, it's no trouble.'

As the cult leader spoke, images flickered through Khârn's mind. He saw visions of his youth and all the joys he had known, before the rebellion of Horus and the Battle for Terra. Somehow it all looked so clear and fresh and appealing, and it almost brought moisture to his tear ducts. He saw endless banquets of food and wine. For a moment, his palate was stimulated by all manner of strange and wonderful tastes, and his brain tingled with a myriad pleasures and stimulations. Visions of diaphanously clad maidens danced before his eyes, beckoning enticingly.

For a moment, despite of himself, Khârn felt an almost unthinkable temptation to betray his ancient oath to the Blood God. This was powerful sorcery indeed! He shook his head and bit his lip until the blood flowed. 'No true warrior of Khorne would fall for this pitiful trick!' he bellowed.

'All hail Slaanesh!' one of his followers cried.

'Praise to the great Lord of Pleasure!' shouted another.

'Let us grovel and adore him,' a third said, as the whole force cast themselves down onto their knees.

Khârn turned to look at his men, disbelief and outrage filling his mind. It seemed that they did not possess his iron-willed belief in Khorne's power, that they were prepared to betray him for a few tawdry promises of pleasure. In every face, in every posture, he saw slack-jawed worship of the posturing peacock on the throne. He knew that there was only one thing to be done under the circumstances.

The Slaanesh leader obviously felt the same. 'Kill him!' he cried. 'Offer up his soul to Slaanesh and unspeakable ecstasy shall be your reward!'

The first of Khârn's comrades raised his bolt pistol and squeezed the trigger. Khârn threw himself to one side and the shell whipped past his head. The Betrayer rewarded the traitor with a taste of Gorechild. The chain-axe screeched as it bit through armour in a mighty sweep that clove him clean in two. The warrior gave a muted whine as his Slaanesh-corrupted soul went straight to the warp.

Suddenly the rest of the berzerkers were upon him. Khârn found himself fighting for his immortal life. These were no mere Slaanesh cultists. Newly tainted though they might be, they had once been worthy followers of Khorne, fierce, deadly and full of bloodlust. Mighty maces bludgeoned Khârn. Huge chainswords threatened to tear his rune-encrusted armour. Bolter shells tore chunks from his chest-plate. Khârn fought on, undismayed, filled with the joy of battle, taking fierce pleasure every time Gorechild took another life. At last, these were worthy foes! The body count swiftly ticked on to 2460 and continued to rise.

Instinctively Khârn side-stepped a blow that tore off one of the metal skulls which dangled from his belt. The Betrayer swore he would replace it with the attacker's own skull. His return stroke made good his vow. He whirled Gorechild in a great figure-of-eight and cleared a space all around him, sending two more traitors to make their excuses to the Blood God. Insane bloodlust surged through him, overcoming even the soporific influence of the Heart of Desire and for a moment Khârn fought with his full unfettered power. He became transformed into an unstoppable engine of destruction and nothing could stand against him.

Khârn's heart pounded. The blood sang through his veins and the desire to kill made him howl uncontrollably. Bones crunched beneath his axe. His pistol blew away the life of its targets. He stamped on the heads of the fallen, crushing them to jelly. Khârn ignored pain, ignored any idea of self-preservation, and fought for the pure love of fighting. He killed and he killed.

All too soon it was over, and Khârn stood alone in a circle of corpses. His breathing rasped from his chest. Blood seeped through a dozen small punctures in his armour. He felt like a rib might have been broken by that last blow of the mace but he was triumphant. His counter read 2485. He sensed the presence of one more victim and turned to confront the figure on the dais.

The cultists' leader stood looking down at him with a faint expression of mingled disbelief and distaste on his face. The naked girl had fled. The throne pulsed enticingly.

'It's true what they say,' the man said with a delicious sigh. 'If you want anything done properly, you have to do it yourself.'

The insinuating voice drove Khârn's fury from him, and left him feeling tired and spent. The cultist strode down from the dais. Khârn felt almost too weary to parry his blow. He knew he must throw off this enchantment quickly. The runesword bit into his armour and a wave of mingled pain and pleasure passed through Khârn like poison. Summoning his last reserves of rage, he threw himself into the attack. He would show this effete fop who was the true warrior here.

Khârn hacked. Gorechild bit into the tattoos of the man's wrist. Gobbets of flesh and droplets of blood whirled away from the axe's teeth. The rank smell of hot bone filled the air as the hand separated from the arm – and began to crawl away with a life of its own. Khârn stamped on it and a rictus of pain appeared on its owner's face, as if the hand was still attached.

Khârn swung. The cultist's head separated from its shoulders. The body swung its blade, a puppet still controlled by the strings of its master's will. It bit into Khârn and the wave of sensation almost drove him to his knees.

'Nice trick!' roared Khârn, feeling the hand squirm beneath his boot. 'But I've seen it before.'

He brought his chain-axe down on the head and cleaved it in two. The body fell to the ground, a puppet with its strings cut. 2486, Khârn thought with some satisfaction.

The Betrayer advanced upon the throne. It pulsed enticingly before him. Within its multiple facets he thought he saw the face of a beautiful woman, the most beautiful he had ever seen – and the most evil. Her hair was long and golden, and her eyes were blue. Her lips were full and red, and the small, white fangs that protruded from her mouth in no way marred her perfection. She looked at Khârn beseechingly, and he knew at once he was face to face with the daemon trapped within the Heart of Desire.

Welcome, Khârn, a seductive voice said within his head. *I knew you would triumph. I knew you would be the conqueror. I knew you would be my new master.*

The voice was thrilling. By comparison, the cult leader's voice had been but a pale echo. But the voice was also deceptive. Proud as he was, mighty as he knew himself to be, Khârn knew that no man could truly be the master of a daemon, not even a fallen Space Marine like himself. He knew that his soul was once more in peril, that he should do something. But yet again he found himself enthralled by the persuasiveness of a Slaanesh worshipper's voice.

Be seated! Become the new ruler of this world, then go forth and blast those meddlesome interlopers from the face of your planet.

Khârn fought to hold himself steady while the throne pulsed hypnotically before him, and the smell of heavy musk filled his nostrils. He knew that once he sat he would be trapped, just as the daemon was trapped. He would become a slave to the thing imprisoned within the throne. His will would be drained and he would become a decadent and effete shadow of the Khârn he had once been. Yet his limbs began to move almost of their own accord, his feet slowly but surely carrying him towards the throne.

Once more, visions of an eternity of corrupt pleasure danced in Khârn's mind. Once more he saw himself indulging in every excess. The daemon promised him every ecstasy imaginable and it was well within its power to grant such pleasures. He knew it would be a simple thing for him to triumph on its behalf. All he had to do was step outside and announce that he had destroyed the Heart of Desire. He was Khârn. He would be believed, and after that it would be a simple matter to lure the Khorne worshippers to ecstatic servitude or joyful destruction.

And would they not deserve it? Already he was known as the Betrayer, when all he had done was be more loyal to his god than the spineless weaklings he had slaughtered. And with that the daemon's voice fell silent and the visions stopped, as if the thing in the throne realised its mistake, but too late.

For Khârn was loyal to Khorne and there was only room for that one thing within his savage heart. He had betrayed and killed his comrades in the World Eaters because they had not remained true to Khorne's ideals and would have fled from the field of battle without either conquering or being destroyed.

The reminder gave him the strength. He turned and looked back at the room. The reek of blood and dismembered bodies filled his nostrils like perfume. He remembered the joy of the combat. The thrill of overcoming his former comrades. He looked out on a room filled with corpses and a floor carpeted with blood. He was the only living thing here and he had made it so. He realised that, compared to this pleasure, this sense of conquest and victory, what the daemon offered was only a pale shadow.

Khârn turned and brought Gorechild smashing down upon the foul throne. His axe howled thirstily as it drank deep of the ancient and corrupt soul imprisoned within. Once more he felt the thrill of victory, and knew no regrets for rejecting the daemon's offer.

2487. Life just doesn't get any better than this, Khârn thought.

THE RETURNED

James Swallow

The skies above the Razorpeak range wept oil. Low cowls of cloud, grey as ancient stone, ranged from horizon to horizon, grudging to allow only a faint glow of sunlight to pierce them from the great white star of Gathis. The clouds moved upon the constant winds, the same gales that howled mournfully through the jagged towers of the mountains, the same heavy gusts that reached up to beat at the figure of Brother Zurus.

The slick rain, dark with the metallic scent of oceans and the tang of rotting biomass, fell constantly upon the landing platform where he stood. Zurus watched it move in wave fronts across the granite and steel. The storms hammered, as they always did, against the constructions men had built high up here in the tallest crags. The platform was only one of many extensions, cupolas and balconies emerging from the sheer sides of the tallest fell among the Razorpeaks. The earliest, most primitive tribes of Gathis II had christened it the Ghostmountain, a name not in honour of its white-grey stone, but in recognition of the many dead that haunted it, so lethal were its slopes. Thousands of years later and the name was, if anything, more fitting.

Once, before men had come from Terra to colonise this world, there had been a true peak atop the Ghostmountain, a series of serrated spires that rose high enough that they could pierce the cloud mantle. Now a great walled citadel stood in their place, the living rock of the peak carved and formed by artisans into halls, donjons and battlements of stark, grim aspect. At each point of the compass, a hulking tower rose, opening into the sculpted shape of a vast raptor screaming defiance at elements and enemies. These warbirds put truth to the name of the great fortress-monastery atop the Ghostmountain: the Eyrie.

One of the great eagles stood at his back, and like the raptor, Zurus was watchful. He peered out from under the hood of his heavy, rain-slick over-robe, waiting for the roiling, churning sky to release to him his responsibility. In the far distance, down towards the settlements of Table City and the lowhill coasts where the tribals lived, great jags of bright lightning flashed, and on the wind the grind of thunder reached his ears a few moments later, cutting through the steady hiss of the falling rains.

Zurus was soothed by the sound. He found it peaceful, and often when he was far from Gathis, perhaps upon the eve of battle at some distant alien battleground, he would meditate upon the sounds of the rainfall and find his focus in it. And so, when he had awoken at dawn this day, he had at once sensed something amiss. Zurus exited his sleeping cell and found only rays of weak sunlight reaching down the passages of the dormitoria; and outside, a break in the clouds, and a silence in the air.

A rare thing. By the ways of the Gathian tribes, an omen of ill fortune when the eternal tears of Him Upon The Throne ceased to fall, and with them the protection the God-Emperor of Mankind provided. After a time, the rain began again, as constant as it ever was, but Zurus had witnessed the moment of silence, and was on some level unsettled by it.

As he had crossed through the gate to venture out to the landing platform, a figure in red-trimmed robes was waiting for him in the lee of the entranceway.

Thryn, the Librarian Secundus. The old warrior's sallow, bleak features always measured Zurus whenever he turned to face him. The look in his eyes was no different from the expression he had shown when the battle brother had first seen the psyker, on the fateful day the Chapter had recruited Zurus into their fold. Many decades ago now.

Thryn nodded towards the open gate and the sky beyond. 'The rain returns,' he noted.

'It never leaves,' Zurus replied. The exchange of words had a ritual quality to them.

The Librarian's lip curled in something that a generous observer might have considered a smile. 'If only that were so. The light of naked sun upon the peaks... It does not bode well.'

Zurus gathered in his robes, unfurling the hood. 'I have no time for omens.'

Thryn's mouth twisted; the old warrior could sense a bald untruth even without the use of his witch-sight. 'You are ready for this, brother?' he asked, turning to stare out at the empty landing pad. 'You did not need to take on this duty alone. Other men–'

'It is right that I do it,' Zurus spoke over the Librarian. 'It is right,' he repeated.

Thryn turned back to study him for a long moment, then stepped away, out of his path. 'As you wish.' The Librarian banged his fist against the inner door of the gateway and halted. Metal gears began to grind as the saw-toothed hatchway drew open. When Thryn spoke again, he did not face him. 'But remember this, Zurus. What comes today, what you go to meet... You have not faced the like before.'

Something in the other warrior's tone chafed on him. 'If you think I will falter when .. *if* the time comes, you are mistaken. I do not shrink from death.'

Thryn gave a low chuckle. 'That much is certain. We are Doom Eagles, brother. Death is part of us.'

'I know the difference between friend and foe,' Zurus insisted. 'I know what the Archenemy looks like. I can tell a traitor when I see one.'

The inner gate clanged open. 'I have no doubt you believe that. But Chaos has faces it has never shown to you, kinsman. Do not forget that.' Thryn walked away, back into the fortress.

The thunder was closer now, sullen and deep enough to echo in his bones. His companion rains drew hard across the metal decking as if they were scouring it, preparing it for the arrival; and then it came to him that the tone of the storm-sound had changed, a new note growing loud, fast approaching.

Zurus looked up, following his hearing. The oily rain touched his face, streaking over an aspect that was a maze of scars. He saw a shape up there, only the suggestion of it really, a shadowed thing with broad wings and a hooked profile. A vast eagle, falling towards him, talons extending.

The sound was strident, and it opened the cowl of cloud cover for a brief instant. On pillars of orange fire and hard jet-noise, a gunmetal-silver drop-ship suddenly emerged from the haze, dropping fast. Rain sluiced from the steel wings and across the blocky, rigid angles of the Thunderhawk's blunt nose. Zurus's robes snapped and billowed as the thruster backwash buffeted him, but he did not move from his sentinel stance.

The drop-ship landed firmly, the slow impact resonating through the landing platform. Engines keening as they powered down, the craft settled on hydraulic skids, lowering itself to the deck as if it were thankful to have completed its journey. Zurus saw motion behind the windows of the cockpit, but nothing distinct. He found he was holding his breath, and chided himself, releasing it. The Astartes warrior resisted the urge to throw a glance over his shoulder, back towards the Eyrie. He had no doubt Thryn was at some gallery window far above him, watching.

With a crunch of cogs, the Thunderhawk's drop ramp unfolded, a mouth opening to show the dark interior of the transport craft. A servitor was the first to shamble out, head bobbing as it chewed on the punchcard containing its command strings. The machine-slave dragged a wheeled trolley behind it, half-covered by the tattered remains of a war cloak.

Zurus's gaze was momentarily drawn to the trolley as it was pulled past him; he saw the distinct and unmistakable shape of ceramite armour heaped within the wheeled container. The silver wargear, the trim of red and ebon, as familiar to him as the scar-patterns on his own face. Doom Eagle armour, but corroded and damaged in a fashion no son of Aquila would ever willingly countenance.

When he looked back there was a hooded man at the top of the ramp. He was looking down at his hands, and the streams of rainwater spattering off his upturned palms. He resembled a pilgrim accepting a benediction.

The Thunderhawk's sole passenger spoke, after a moment. 'The rains,' he began, in a low, crack-throated voice. 'I thought I might never see them again.' He took in a deep, long breath through his nostrils. 'On the wind. I smell Chamack.' There was a smile in the words.

Zurus nodded. Down in Table City, leagues away from the Eyrie, the great bio-matter refineries that fabricated lubricant oil from the fibres of the sinuous Chamack sea-plant worked night and day, and the heavy, resinous odour was always present in the air. Zurus only ever noticed it by its absence.

The moment passed and the new arrival bowed his head. He began to walk down the ramp, but in two quick steps Zurus had crossed to the bottom of the gangway and stood blocking his path. The other man faltered, then halted.

'Who are you?' said Zurus. 'Let the ghosts of the mountain hear your name.'

From beneath the other man's hood, eyes narrowed and became cold. 'The ghosts know who I am, brother. I am a Gathis-born son, as you are.'

'You must say the words,' insisted Zurus. 'For protocol's sake.'

Hands tightened into fists, before vanishing into folds of the dripping robes. 'The protocols of which you speak are for outsiders. *Strangers.*'

Zurus searched the face concealed beneath the hood for any sign of subterfuge or malice. 'Say the words,' he repeated.

The other man said nothing, and the moment stretched too long. Then finally, with a fall of his shoulders, the new arrival relented. 'My name is Tarikus. Warrior of the Adeptus Astartes. Brother-Sergeant of the esteemed Third Company of the Doom Eagles Chapter. And I have returned home.'

Tarikus. Zurus had been there on the day that name had been added to the Walls of Memory in the great Relical Keep. He had watched with due reverence as a helot carved the name into the polished black marble, etched there for eternity among the hundredfold dead of the Chapter. Zurus had been there to hear the Chaplains announce Tarikus's loss, and cement it in the annals of Doom Eagle history. Two whole Gathian cycles now, since he had been declared *Astartes Mortus*. Many seasons come and gone, his life become a revered memory among all the honoured fallen.

The other man drew back his hood for the first time and walked on, down towards the end of the drop ramp.

Zurus took a wary step backwards and met the gaze of a dead man.

'Is it him?'

Thryn did not turn away from the rain-slicked windowpane, watching the two men far below on the landing platform. He saw Brother Zurus step aside and allow the passenger from the Thunderhawk to stride back towards the gate. The Librarian clearly saw the tawny, battle-scarred aspect of the man, lit by a momentary pulse of high lightning. 'That remains to be seen, lord,' said Thryn, at length.

In the shadowed gloom of the observation gallery, Commander Hearon folded his arms across his barrel chest and his ever-present frown deepened. The answer was unsatisfactory to the Chapter Master of the Doom Eagles. 'I allowed him to be brought here on your advice, old friend,' Hearon rumbled. 'I did so because I thought you could give me the answer I wanted.'

'I will,' Thryn replied. 'In time.'

'Not too much time,' said the Chapter Master. 'Voices call for a swift end to the matter of this... return. Chief among them the Chaplains and your senior, Brother Tolkca.'

Thryn nodded. 'Yes, I imagine the Librarian Primus is ill-tempered at the thought of such a thing being placed in my hands.'

Hearon gestured at the air. 'He is at battle a sector distant. You are here. If he's irked by my decision, he may take it up with me on his return.' The commander leaned in. 'There is no precedent for this, Thryn. Death is the closure of all things, the last page in the passage of a life. For that book to be re-opened once we have written the final entry...' Hearon trailed off. 'This man... if that is what he is... must be put to the question. The truth of him must out.'

The Librarian nodded again, musing. Thryn had pored over the battle records and honours listed under the name of Tarikus. A veteran of bloody conflicts and engagements on worlds such as Thaxted and Zanasar, he had risen to the rank of Brother-Sergeant with command of a tactical squad under Consultus, the current captain of the Third Company. The Third had a history of ill fate; two commanders in succession had been lost to them during the last Black Crusade of the Archtraitor Abaddon, at Yayor and then again at Cadia, but Tarikus had survived them all – even the great massacre at Krypt, where the Doom Eagles had lost many men on the surface of that brutal, frigid planetoid.

It was only after the destruction of the planet Serek, on a voyage back to the Segmentum Tempestus, that the luck of Brother Tarikus had run dry. The medicae frigate he had been aboard was ambushed by the hated Red Corsairs, and torn apart. Tarikus had not been among the Astartes who made it to the saviour pods before the wrecked ship had plunged into a star. He was given the honour of a worthy end, and declared dead, with all the ritual and rite such a tribute entailed.

But now… Now a ghost walked the halls of the Eyrie.

Thryn was well aware that some brother Chapters of the Doom Eagles regarded their association with matters of death as unusual. *Morbid*, even *macabre*; he had heard these slights from warriors of the Space Wolves and the White Scars, even brothers of the Ultramarines, the very Legion his Chapter had been drawn from. Some viewed the character of the Doom Eagles and saw an *obsession* with fatality; but this was a short-sighted, narrow view.

The Doom Eagles were gifted with an understanding of the universe. They knew the truth, that all life is born dying, moment by moment. What others saw as fatalism, they saw as pragmatism, a manner born out of knowledge that life and joy were transient things, that the only constants in existence were despair, loss – and ultimately the embrace of death. *We are already dead*, so said the first words of the oath of the Chapter. The Doom Eagles understood that death was always close; and so they fought harder, strove longer, to perform their duties before the cloak of Final Sleep came upon them. They had no illusions.

Death was the end of all things. Nothing could come back from the void beyond it. This knowledge was the pillar upon which stood everything the Chapter believed in.

Tarikus, by his presence, his mere existence, challenged that.

Hearon spoke again. 'You have my authority to do as much as required in order to cut to the core of this circumstance.' The Chapter Master turned away. 'I ask you only be certain.'

Thryn felt a tightening in his gut as the full scope of Hearon's command became clear to him. 'And if I cannot be certain, my lord? What would you have me do then?'

'There is no scope for doubts, brother.' Hearon paused at the edge of the chamber's shadows and nodded towards the window. 'End him if you must. Our ghosts remain dead.'

Tarikus awoke, and his first reaction was one of shock. It faded quickly, to be replaced by a twinge of annoyance; ever since his escape from the prison on Dynikas V, each new slumber ended with the same tremor of fear and uncertainty, and it angered him.

Each time, he expected to find himself back in the searing metal cell, his ash-smeared skin slick with sweat against the hard surface of his sleeping pallet, the humid air about him resonating with heat. It was as if his subconscious mind could not willingly accept that he had found his freedom. He had experienced so many strange tortures during his imprisonment in that light-forsaken hell that even now, weeks after breaking out of the cursed place, some seed of doubt remained lodged in his thoughts, some tiny part of him too afraid to accept the reality presented to it for fear it would be torn away a moment later.

The stone and steel of the prison on Dynikas V was no more, his tormentors consumed by tyranid swarms, the prison itself scoured to the bedrock by Astartes lance fire; but the walls still stood in Tarikus's mind, and he wondered if they would ever fall.

With a sigh, he pushed such thoughts away, rose and moved to the simple fresher unit in the corner of his room. Perhaps there was an irony in the fact that this small chamber was also called a 'cell', but its function was dedicated to providing silence and peace, not confinement. He ran cold, brackish water over his face, glancing at the small circular window high in the wall. A simple pattern of acid-etching covered the glassaic; the shape of a spread-winged eagle and upon that the lines of a human skull. The sigil of his Chapter. Seeing it made Tarikus's chest tighten; the symbol meant so much to him. It had been his life for so long, and in the darkest moments of his incarceration, he had thought never to lay eyes upon it again.

Men of the steady and dour nature that characterised most of the Astartes of the Doom Eagles Chapter were not often given to moments of open excitement or joy, and yet Tarikus could not deny that he felt something close to those emotions deep within him, a strange elation at being home once more, but tempered with apprehension at what was to come next.

A day now since he arrived on the Thunderhawk. A day, after a sullen greeting from this Brother Zurus; none of his questions answered, mind, only the offer of a spartan meal and the room and rest. *A place where you can reflect*, Zurus had said. It was not lost on Tarikus that, although the door to his chamber had not been locked, a discreet gun-servitor had been stationed nearby. And he knew without needing to search for them that audial and visi-spectrum aura sensors were concealed in the covings above him.

They were watching him closely. He expected as much.

Should he have been affronted by such surveillance? On some level he was. On another, he understood the motivation behind it. Trust was a precious commodity in the Imperium of Mankind, and it was only in places where bonds of brotherhood and fealty ran strong that it could be spent. The ranks of the Adeptus Astartes were one such place, but when outsiders ventured into that circle – *outsiders and strangers*, Tarikus reminded himself – the wellspring quickly ran dry.

His own kinsmen did not trust him, and for reasons that a cursed fate had forced upon him.

Tarikus grimly considered the unfairness of it, the hard reality of callous outcome that was the way of his bleak universe. After Serek, where he and his squad had engaged a force of necrontyr and ultimately been compelled to flee a planet in its death throes, he had healed aboard a hospitaller ship. In a narthecia-induced slumber, his enhanced physiology working to repair the damage of a poor teleport reversion, he had slept the voyage away – at least until the Traitor-kin had ambushed them. Too weak to fight them all, Tarikus had been captured even as his brothers escaped, thinking him dead. From there, the whoreson Red Corsairs sold him like chained cattle to the master of the Dynikas prison – and he had remained in that place for month after month, year after year, confined with other Astartes stolen from battlefields or presumed dead. Forgotten men turned into laboratory animals, test subjects for the amusement of the Chaos primogenitor who called himself Fabius Bile.

Tarikus had expected to die there – but then he was a Doom Eagle, and Doom Eagles always expected death. Still, when the chance for freedom came, he embraced it with all his might, aware that his service to the Golden Throne was not yet over. In his soul, Tarikus knew that he was not ready to perish, not on Dynikas, not at the hands of Bile and his freak-army of modificate mutants. He had not been granted permission to die.

He heard footsteps out in the corridor, then a voice. 'Tarikus,' called Zurus, 'will you join me?'

The Doom Eagle gathered in his duty tunic and over-robe, then opened the cell door. 'Are we going somewhere?'

Zurus nodded once. 'I have something I wish you to see.'

They walked, and Zurus did his best to observe his charge without making his scrutiny an open challenge. Tarikus seemed no different from the man shown in his file picts, or captured by the imagers of servo-skulls in battle footage. He carried himself like an Astartes should, and with no prompting the warrior showed all the correct fealty and honour towards the sacrosanct statuary ringing the gates of the great circlet corridor, which ran the circumference of the Eyrie. If anything, Tarikus seemed almost moved to see the great carving of Aquila, first of the Doom Eagles and chosen of the Second Founding. Zurus looked up from his own deep bow a moment quicker than usual, examining the curve of the other man's shoulders.

Finally, Tarikus stood and straightened. 'Perhaps you wish to set an hourglass at my side, brother. That might be method enough to gauge my piety.'

'I am not an inquisitor,' replied Zurus, a little too swiftly. In truth, he wondered what the representatives of the Ordo Hereticus might have done if they knew of Tarikus and his circumstances – or indeed that of the other handful of Astartes, who had been liberated from Dynikas by brothers of the Blood Angels Chapter. To spend months, years even, in a gaol ruled by one of the most notorious traitors of the Heresy...

Could anyone, even a chosen warrior of the Emperor's Astartes, emerge untouched by the experience? Could a Space Marine survive such a thing and not be tainted in some fashion? Zurus held the question in his thoughts as he spoke again. 'You are among kinsmen here.'

'And who better to judge me?' Tarikus looked around, his hard gaze sweeping the ranges of the curving corridor, the galleries overhead and the gloomy alcoves where lume-light did not fall. 'Where are my other watchers? Nearby, I'd imagine.'

Zurus resisted the urge to look where Tarikus did. He knew full well that the Librarian Thryn was somewhere close at hand, studying them both. He wondered what Thryn thought of them; outwardly, the two Doom Eagles were similar in aspect, although Zurus's hairless scalp was paler – the legacy of his origin in the sea-nomad tribes, unlike Tarikus, who was a son of the high-mountain kindred. They were both as good an example of the aspect of a Son of Aquila as one could hope to find on the Ghostmountain; but it was what lay beneath that aspect that could not be quantified.

That which could not be valued in the weight of coin; this was what Zurus had to quantify. If Tarikus was found wanting, it would mean ignoble death – the worst of fates for a Doom Eagle to suffer.

A party of Scouts passed close, and Zurus guessed by their garb and weapons they had returned from a training sortie out in the equatorial island chains. He gave the youths a terse nod that was returned, but none of them acknowledged the presence of Tarikus, passing him by without making eye contact. Zurus saw him stiffen at the slight, but he said nothing. After a moment, he nodded to himself, as if accepting something.

'Where are my men?' said the other warrior, without meeting his gaze. 'It has been two years since I last saw them, and this question I have asked more than once. Do they live still?'

Zurus had been ordered not to speak of Tarikus's former comrades-in-arms, but the command sat poorly with him. He could not in good conscience remain silent on the matter. At length, he gave a nod. 'They live,' Zurus admitted. At Serek, Tarikus had led a number of good, steadfast Space Marines – Brothers Korica, Petius and Mykilus – each of whom had survived the Red Corsair attack on the medicae frigate.

'I wish to see them.'

Zurus shook his head. 'Perhaps later.'

Tarikus shot him a glare. 'Do not lie to me, brother. Grant me that, at least.'

He sighed. 'What do you expect me to say, Tarikus? What did you think would happen when you returned here?' Zurus gestured around. 'Did you think we would welcome you with open arms? Take you in as if nothing had happened? You said it yourself. Two years, brother. A long time in the heart of darkness.'

The other man's gaze dropped to the ornate stone floor, and despite himself, Zurus felt a pang of sympathy for him. 'I'm a fool, then,' said Tarikus. 'Naïve to think that I could return and pick up where I left off.' He shook his head. 'I only want to return. That is all.'

Zurus frowned and walked on. 'Come,' he told Tarikus, 'you must see this. You'll understand better when you do.'

The Eyrie's central feature was a great octagonal tower, tallest of the citadels that reached for the sky, deepest of those that plunged levels down into the heart-rock of the Ghostmountain. The Reclusiam was a million memorials to countless deaths across the galactic disc. Entire floors were given over to relics recovered from the sites of terrible battles and brutal wars across the entire span of the Imperium. Many were from conflicts in which the Doom Eagles had taken a direct part, but others were from atrocities so soaked in despair and fatality that warriors of the Chapter had been drawn to visit them.

The Doom Eagles were born from the Legion of the Ultramarines in the wake of the Horus Heresy, in the shadow of Great Aquila. He had been a warrior of Guilliman during the Siege of Terra, and along with the rest of the Ultramarines, battles fought during the race to reinforce humanity's home world waylaid them at a most crucial moment. As Chapter history told it, Aquila had been so wracked with guilt and despair at arriving too late to protect the Emperor from his mortal wounds at the hands of Horus, that he had sworn an oath never again to delay in defence of the Imperium. When the time of the Second Founding came, Aquila willingly broke away to forge the Doom Eagles and make his belief manifest in them. The first Master made it a tenet of his new Chapter that every Son of Gathis would understand the cost of hesitance, of failure – and with it, the great guilt that came in step.

He would have them see these things, know them first-hand. And so, the relics; gathered by brothers on pilgrimages to places of battle and failed wars, each item a piece of despair and calamity made solid and real.

Many levels of the Reclusiam were such grim museums, halls reverent with shards of stone and bone, glass and steel. Armageddon, Rocene, Malvolion, Telemachus, Brodra-kul, and countless other war-sites, all represented here. And in the hallowed core, brought to this place by Aquila himself, the silver-walled chamber where pieces of shattered masonry from the Imperial Palace lay alongside a feather from the wing of Sanguinius and a shard of the Emperor's own battle armour.

It was said that those with the witch-sight could hear the ghost-screams in the tower. If that were so, if these relics could indeed contain a fraction of the pain and anguish that had enveloped them, then Zurus was glad the great chorus of sorrow thundering silent in the air was hidden from him.

This was not their destination, however. With Tarikus quiet at his side, the Space Marine rode the grav-car that ran the brass rails following the length of the tower. They rode up and up, beyond the ranges of the death-relics of strangers and into the Hall of the Fallen.

The largest open space inside the Eyrie, the vast walls, floor and ceiling were sheathed in great tiles of polished obsidian, each the size of a Land Raider. Hanging at right angles from complex armatures, some from floor to ceiling, others suspended at differing heights, there were free-floating panels of the same dark stone. At a distance, the glassy black panes seemed clouded somehow, but as one drew closer, definition unfolded.

Each panel was perfectly laser-etched into thin strips; each strip sported a half-globe of glass, behind which lay a random item. Upon the strip, the name of a Doom Eagle claimed by death. Next to each name, inside the glass, a relic: a fragment of armour, an eye-lens, a bolt shell, an honour-chain. Every artefact, something touched by the dead. A piece of them, to be held in trust for as long as the Chapter existed.

The grav-car changed tracks, joining a conveyor that took them across the span of the hall, down and across in zigzag motions toward one of the tallest of the panels.

Zurus looked down towards the floor far below. Somewhere down there was the memorial of Aquila, and beside it a cracked helmet under glass. It had no dressing, no great and ostentatious detail to set it aside from every other marker. The First Master had ordered it so, knowing that in death, all men were in unity.

He glanced up and saw that Tarikus was also looking downward. Mimicking me, he wondered? Or is he feeling the reverence that I feel?

At last, the grav-car rattled to a halt some distance up the face of a suspended wall and Zurus gestured towards the pane that hung before them. Behind a glass bubble, an Astartes combat blade was visible, the fractal edge still bright and sharp even though the length of the knife was dirty and pitted with use.

Tarikus saw the weapon and took a half step towards it, then stopped dead. 'It's mine,' he said. The tone of his voice was peculiar; there was something like fear in it.

Zurus nodded and indicated the memorial panel. 'Look here, brother.'

There in gothic script, etched by the hand of some machine-slave stoneworker, letters lined in heavy silver. As if he had no control over the action, Tarikus reached out and ran his fingers over the shape of his name. 'No...' began the other Astartes, shaking his head.

Zurus nodded again. 'You were lost, brother. You know our laws and diktats. Your name was cast from the rolls. The ceremony of loss completed and sanctified. Your name, carved here, in memoriam. By the lights of the Chapter and all of Gathis–'

The other Doom Eagle turned abruptly to face him, a curious shade of emotion in his dark eyes. 'I am dead,' he said, finishing Zurus's sentence for him. 'I no longer exist.'

Tarikus strode from the gates of the Reclusiam across the processional bridge with such pace and intent that it was a long moment before he realised he had nowhere to go. He slowed and the grief he had tried to outrun caught up with him, as if it were only his swift tread that had kept it at bay.

In his darkest moments, trapped in that hated prison cell, Tarikus had encountered a great dread within himself that had shocked him with its potency. He had feared that he was *forgotten*; that after he was lost in deep space, the many sorties and battles he had fought, the honours he had earned, all would count for nothing among his brethren. He feared that all he had done would be meaningless.

But now he saw that the greater horror was this – that he had been *remembered*, in so final and damning a way as to make each breath he drew now a phantom. In the eyes of Great Aquila and his Chapter, Brother-Sergeant Tarikus had perished aboard that lost medicae frigate, years past. His kinsmen had counted him gone and made their peace with that fact.

Was it any wonder the Scouts had looked away from him, unsettled by his presence? For a Chapter so intimate with the manners of death, to see a warrior return from it must have shaken them to their core. Our ghosts remain dead, Tarikus thought, recalling the words written in the *Prayer Mortalis*.

Zurus called his name and he turned as the other Doom Eagle approached him, his pale face set like ice.

'This must be undone,' Tarikus began, but Zurus waved him into silence.

'Do you understand, brother?' Zurus demanded of him. 'You see now why your reappearance is... problematic?'

Tarikus felt a swell of anger inside him, and let it rise. 'Don't speak to me as if I am some whining neophyte. I am a battle-brother of this Chapter with honour and glory to my name!'

'Are you?' The question slipped from Zurus's lips.

He glared at the other warrior. 'Ah. I see. At first I thought you were concerned that my wits might have been dulled by my confinement, that perhaps you suspected my spirit damaged by my experiences... But it's more than that, isn't it?' Tarikus made a spitting sound and advanced on the other Doom Eagle. 'Can it be that you doubt the evidence of your own eyes, *brother*?' He put savage emphasis on the last word.

'The truth–'

Tarikus's anger was strong now, and he refused to let Zurus speak. 'What do you presume?' He spread his hands. 'Are you waiting for me to shed my skin, to transform into some hell-spawned Chaos daemon? Is that what you think I am?'

Zurus's gaze did not waver. 'That question has been asked.'

He took a quick step forward and prodded Zurus in the chest with his finger. 'I know what I am, kinsman,' snarled Tarikus. 'A warrior loyal to Holy Terra!'

'Perhaps,' said Zurus, 'or perhaps you are only a thing which believes that to be true. Something that only resembles Brother-Sergeant Tarikus.'

Muscles bunched in his arm, and for a long second Tarikus wavered on the verge of striking the other Space Marine across the face. That another Doom Eagle would dare to impugn the honour of a kinsman lit his fury still higher, reasons be damned.

And in that moment, through the lens of his cold anger, Tarikus discerned something else: a greasy, electric tingle across his skin and the sense of a hundred eyes staring at him. He relaxed his stance and turned away, glaring about across the length of the high marble bridge. The only sound was the clatter of heat exchangers working far below in the depths of the Ghostmountain.

To the air he spoke a demand. 'Show yourself, witch-kin.' Tarikus shot a look at Zurus, and the other warrior's expression confirmed his suspicions. He turned away again, ranging around. 'Come, brother. If you wish to damn my name, at least do me the courtesy of looking me in the eye when you do so,'

'As you wish.' The voice came from behind him, close and low. Tarikus found a figure in the lee of a carved support, swamped by red-trimmed robes. The Doom Eagle had looked in that direction only moments earlier, and there had been nothing there. Only shadows.

The psyker walked closer, dropping his hood. Cold, hard eyes bit into Tarikus, searching for any sign of weakness. He betrayed none.

'I am Thryn,' said the Librarian. 'My name is known.'

Tarikus nodded once. 'I have heard of you. A chooser of the faithful.'

'But not you,' Thryn replied. 'It was not my duty on the day you were picked from the aspirants to join this Chapter, all those decades ago. Perhaps, if it had been, this question would already be answered.'

'There is no question,' Tarikus retorted. 'What you see before you is all that I am. Doom Eagle. Adeptus Astartes. Son of Gathis.'

Thryn cocked his head. 'The enemy hides in plain sight. A tactic the followers of the Ruinous Powers are quite fond of. They have warped many a mind in the past. It is only sensible that we must be certain that has not happened here.'

Tarikus met Thryn's burning gaze and refused to look away. 'Do you know what kept me centred for all those months inside that hellhole, witch-kin? It was my faith in my brothers, my Chapter and my Emperor. Was I wrong to believe that? Have I been forsaken?'

'That is the question we must ask of you, Tarikus,' said Thryn.

'You dare ask me to prove myself?' The fury boiled inside him. 'After all that I have done in Aquila's name, you question *me*?' He advanced on the psyker until they were face to face. He could feel the prickling aura of the Librarian's controlled mind-force pressing on his flesh. 'This is your greeting for a lost brother, who by the grace of He That Is Most Mighty, has had the temerity to survive. Nothing but disdain and isolation. Accusations and disrespect.'

'This is the universe we live in,' offered Zurus.

Tarikus paused, holding Thryn's gaze. 'Perhaps you would have preferred it if I allowed myself to die in confinement.'

Thryn cocked his head. 'That would have brought a definite end to this matter, to be sure.'

'Then I apologise for daring to live,' Tarikus shot back. 'It must be very inconvenient for you.'

'There is still time,' said the psyker. 'But not much time.'

Tarikus was silent for a long moment, and with an effort, he calmed himself and shuttered away his annoyance. That there was some logic in the challenge posed by Zurus and Thryn only made matters worse; but rather than resist it, Tarikus drew in a breath and looked to his heart, to the soul and spirit that made him a Doom Eagle.

'So be it,' he said grimly. 'If I must be questioned, then I must be questioned. This is the way of things. I will face it and not flinch. Tell me what must be done to put this challenge to its end.'

'You're certain?' asked Zurus. 'It will be difficult. Some have been broken by less.'

'Tell me,' repeated Tarikus, glaring at the psyker.

Thryn looked back at him with a level, even gaze. 'There are rituals of purity. Rites of passage. You will be tested.' The psyker turned to leave. 'Tomorrow, at dawn–'

Tarikus's hand shot out and grabbed the Librarian's forearm, halting him instantly. 'No,' said the Doom Eagle. 'We will begin this now.'

Thryn studied him. 'You understand what you will face?'

'*Now*,' repeated Tarikus.

They began with the Talons.

A mechanism made of bright, polished steel, and as cold as polar ice, it wrapped around Tarikus and held the Doom Eagle in its grip. It resembled an artificer's vice, scaled up to the size of a giant. A great oiled screw turned, bringing knurled blocks of metal towards one another in an inexorable approach. From each block grew a fan of wicked barbs, claws modelled on the talons of the great raptors that rode the thermals of the Razorpeak range.

Tarikus stood between them, clad only in thin exercise robes. The muscles of his arms and legs bunched and became iron-solid as he settled in against the blocks. Only his strength and fortitude held back a crushing death. He breathed evenly, pacing himself, marshalling his strength rather than spending it all in a single effort.

The Talons pressed in. They never tired. The slow-turning gears pushed against the Space Marine's resistance, daring him to falter for just a moment; and there was the insidious thing about the trial. If the warrior relaxed, even for an instant, the blocks would lurch forward by a full hand's span, reducing the space between by a good measure – but in doing so, giving him a moment's respite from the struggle. Thus, the Talons preyed on fatigue and inattention. After hours, days between the blocks, a warrior might consider letting them close the distance a little, just to take a precious second of rest before they reached their stops and started to press in once again; but that was the route to failure. So it was said, Hearon himself once managed a lunar month in the Talons and never gave any quarter.

Tarikus was there for days. With no windows in sight, he could only make the most basic reckoning of the passing hours. And unlike Hearon's trial, Tarikus was not left alone with his struggle. From the shadows about the Talons, figures moved and called out to him, bombarding him constantly with questions and demands. They asked him to recite lines of catechism and Chapter rote, or they hectored him over every last point of the story he told of his confinement in Bile's prison. The interrogation went on and on, without end, circling his thoughts until he felt his mind going numb.

Thryn was among his questioners; perhaps he was only one of them, perhaps he was all of them, but as sweat dripped from Tarikus's limbs and acid slowly filled his veins, the warrior did not give the answers the Librarian wanted. He told the same story over and over, he recited his hymnals and prayers as he should have, all the while resisting the constant, blinding pressure. Denied food, denied water, denied release, he stood his ground.

Then without warning, a week into the trial, it ended. The Talons retracted, and Tarikus fell to the deck, his muscles twitching and cramping. It took him a moment to get back to his feet. Dimly, he was aware of figures in the cowled robes of Chapter serfs crowding towards him.

He frowned. This could not be the end of it. He had not suffered enough.

He was correct.

Tarikus was stripped naked and put into the hold of a rotorflyer. The aircraft left the Ghostmountain with a sudden upward lurch, and almost as quickly it began a steep downward arc. The Doom Eagle had barely enough time to register the howl of winds over the hull of the craft before the deck beneath him parted and he fell.

Tarikus landed hard on a shelf of icy rock, a harsh bombardment of sleet angling across it towards a sudden, sheer drop into the mist. He glanced up to see the flyer power away on flickering blades and caught sight of the Eyrie beyond it. They had deposited him on one of the nearby peak sides, little more than half a kilometre distant from the Ghostmountain as the eagle flew, but uncrossable without a jet pack or a wing-glider.

He cast around, searching for something to shield himself from the punishing weather, and found only a canted slab of rock. Aching from the strain of the Talons, Tarikus made it into the poor cover and found mud and lichen in the lee. The fungus he ate, the mud he smeared over his flesh to hold in his body heat.

He wondered if this was some kind of punishment. Had he failed the first test in some way that had not registered in his mind? Or had Thryn and those who sat in judgement of him tired of the game and made their choice, left him out here to die of exposure? Both seemed unlikely; a bolt shell to the back of his head would have ended him far faster than starvation or hypothermia, and the Doom Eagles were not given to cause suffering where it need not occur – there was enough of that to go around in the universe, without adding to the volume of it.

As he half-dozed behind his rough shelter, Tarikus imagined the scrutiny of distant eyes, watching him from the windows of the fortress-monastery he thought of as his home. He felt darkness crowd in on him, a numbness spreading through his body. Still they questioned him, only now it was without words, now it was with the force of ruthless nature. Now it was Gathis itself, the voice of the Ghostmountain and the Razorpeaks, that challenged him.

And still, the answer that was sought was not given. By the following dawn, Tarikus had died.

Thryn sensed his master's displeasure before he entered the observation gallery. It filled the space around him like a cold fog, present in everything and ready to become an ice-storm at a moment's notice.

Within he found Hearon at the heavy window, and off to one side the figure of Brother-Captain Consultus. The warrior was clad in his wargear, and he stood at stiff attention, eyes focused on a distant point beyond the far wall. Consultus looked like carved stone, immobile and rigid; but Thryn saw past that, reading the steady churn of emotions inside the captain of the Third.

The Luckless Third, so the other company commanders called them, but never to their faces. Thryn considered this and saw truth in it; the return of Tarikus was just one more piece of ill fortune laid at the boots of Consultus and his men.

Hearon threw a glance at the Librarian. 'You have an answer for me?'

'I do not, lord,' he replied.

'Where is he now?'

The psyker gestured with a nod. 'In the apothecarion. He was recovered before brain death could occur. He will live.'

'For what that is worth.' Thryn's master made a negative noise. 'Does your witch-sight fail you? Look into his soul, tell me what you see.'

'I have,' admitted the psyker, 'and I can draw no conclusion. Resilient as he is, his psyche was tormented by imprisonment and suffering, but that is to be expected. But this is not a case of black and white. There are many shades of grey.'

'I disagree,' Hearon replied. 'The question is a direct one. Is Tarikus to be trusted? Yes or no?'

'He has endured the trials,' ventured the captain. 'Survived, once again.'

'I know your opinion already,' Hearon snapped. 'Repeating it serves no purpose.' He looked back at Thryn.

'The captain is quite correct,' said the Librarian. 'His flesh withstands great punishment. He does not waver beneath chastisement that would kill a warrior of lesser courage.'

Hearon grimaced. 'That is a thing of meat and blood,' he said, with a terse gesture. 'And we know those can be controlled.' The Chapter Master shook his head. 'No, it is the question of Tarikus's spirit that tasks me. His soul is where the question lies.'

'His faith in the Emperor is strong.' Thryn paused, framing his words. 'His faith in his Chapter also.'

'*Even after we have done this to him*,' Hearon was looking at Consultus as he said the words. 'I don't need Thryn's powers to pluck that thought from your mind, brother-captain.'

'It is so, lord,' Consultus replied.

'Let no man here labour under the mistaken belief that I take pleasure in this,' Hearon grated. 'But Tarikus is one man. My responsibilities are to a Chapter one thousand strong, to a heritage of ten millennia. The Doom Eagles are my charge, and if I must shoulder the guilt of persecuting a single kinsman in order to protect them, I will do so without hesitation. It is only a grain of sand against the weight of Aquila's holy remorse.'

Thryn was silent for a moment. He knew full well why he had been called to this meeting, and why too Consultus, as Tarikus's former commanding officer, had been brought in as a witness. 'There is word from the Council of Eagles?'

Hearon nodded. Modelled after the High Council of Terra, the Doom Eagles encompassed a commission of men of highest rank who would draw together on matters of import facing the Chapter. The group would offer advice to the Chapter Master, and while ultimately Hearon held the sanction over all commands, he drew upon the knowledge and advice of all his company captains, his senior Chaplain, Apothecary, Forge Master and Librarian. 'The greater body of my warriors question the need to prolong this matter. The risk outweighs the gain. The damage that might be wrought by a single turncoat among our number is huge when compared against the value of one veteran sergeant.'

'Is it?' Consultus said quietly. 'Do we not damage the Chapter ourselves if we reject a warrior whose only crime was a failure to die?'

'The others believe he is tainted?' asked Thryn.

'The others suggest that Tarikus be put down,' said the captain, with no little venom.

Hearon ignored Consultus's interruption. 'I… am not convinced.'

'My lord?'

The Chapter Master returned to the window. 'The Doom Eagles have always been the most pragmatic of the Adeptus Astartes. We have no time for vacillation. That we may never again delay… Those words are etched on our hearts.' He paused. 'Some of our battle-brothers say we should excise this man and move beyond. End him, and confirm what has already been laid to stone; that Tarikus of the Third is dead and gone.'

Thryn cocked his head. 'And yet?'

'And yet…' repeated Hearon, glancing toward Consultus, 'I cannot in all good conscience end this in so cursory a manner. When death comes to claim me, I find myself asking how I could go to the Emperor's side and answer for this. That I would allow a Son of Gathis to meet the sword's edge all because of an unanswered question?' He shook his head. 'That will not stand.'

Thryn's eyes narrowed. 'There is another way, lord. A method I have yet hesitated to employ. A weirding, if you will.'

'Do what you must.' The Chapter Master looked over his shoulder at Thryn. 'You *will* bring me an answer, Librarian.'

'Even if Tarikus is destroyed by it?' said Consultus.

'Even if,' Hearon replied.

Zurus exited the south range after morning firing rites, and found the three of them waiting for him. He hesitated, for a moment uncertain how to respond, then beckoned the Space Marines to follow him. They moved to a worktable in the far corner of the arming hall, and he took the only stool and sat upon it. With careful, spare motions, Zurus dismantled his bolt pistol and set about the work of cleaning the weapon.

As he expected, it was Korica who spoke first. 'Lord,' he began, tension thick in his tone, 'we have talked amongst ourselves of… of this matter, and we have questions.'

'Indeed?' said Zurus, taking apart the trigger assembly. 'Questions seem to be the matter of the day.' From the corner of his eye, he saw the other two Doom Eagles exchange glances; one of them, his face dark and intense with old fire scarring, the other sallow of features with a single silver ring in his ear and the helix electoo of an Apothecary upon his neck. He read conflict in their aspects. It came as no surprise; he felt the same thing they did, to some degree.

'There is much talk in the galleries,' Korica went on, gesturing with his carbon-and-steel augmetic arm. 'Rumour and hearsay. We would know the truth.'

Zurus stopped and studied the pieces of his gun. 'Would you?' he said, a warning in his manner. 'Tell me, brother, would you also have me go against the express orders of the Chapter Master?'

'We would never disobey a legal command, brother-sergeant,' said the Apothecary. 'You know that.'

He nodded. 'Aye, Petius, I do.' Zurus glanced at the scarred warrior. 'Mykilus? As your kinsmen have spoken, I trust you must have something to venture as well?'

The other Doom Eagle gave a slow nod. 'Sir,' he began, 'you have commanded our squad for two cycles and we have been bound in blood and fire together. No disrespect to you is intended... but Tarikus was our sergeant for a long time. He saved each of our lives on one battleground or another. We thought him dead, and now we learn that he still lives...' Mykilus trailed off, unable to find the right words.

'Aquila's remorse runs strong in us,' said Korica. 'We believed Tarikus had been killed at the hands of the Red Corsairs. We brought back his knife. We share the guilt at giving up on him.' He shook his head. 'We let him down. We should have done more. Searched longer.'

Zurus looked up for the first time. 'No,' he said flatly. 'Do not torment yourselves. You could not have known.'

'We want to see him, sir,' said Petius.

'Impossible.' Zurus shot a glance at the Apothecary. 'It is forbidden. He is to remain in isolation until he has been judged.'

Korica's face twisted in anger. 'Tarikus is no traitor. We know the man better than any other battle-brother on the Ghostmountain! He is steadfast!'

Zurus studied the faces of the three men. 'Is that what you all think?' He got a chorus of nods in return – and yet, the warrior could sense some tiny inklings of doubt lurking behind the hard eyes of his men. The very same hesitation he himself experienced. 'I took on the mantle of Tarikus's stewardship for one reason,' Zurus went on. 'Because of what I knew of the man whom I had succeeded. I did it because of what you told me of him.' He didn't add that in truth, Brother Zurus had always felt as if he could not measure up to the shadow of the squad's former commander.

'Then tell us what you think, sir,' said Mykilus. 'If we cannot speak to him ourselves, tell us your thoughts.'

'Aye,' added Petius. 'You have looked him in the eye. What did you see?'

Zurus sighed. 'One of us.' His gaze dropped to the disassembled bolter. 'Or so it seemed.'

'Chaos does not lurk within the heart of Brother Tarikus,' grated Korica. 'I would stake my life on that.'

'Are you sure?' Zurus returned to his work. 'Trapped in the heart of madness, tormented every moment of every day by the foulest traitor-genius hell ever spawned? Could a man not be twisted under such pressure?'

'A man, perhaps,' said Petius. 'But not a Doom Eagle.'

'Not Tarikus,' insisted Korica.

Zurus was silent for a long time, carefully rebuilding the weapon. 'It is no wonder you wish Tarikus to be found pure,' he said, at length. 'Each of you carry the guilt of speaking his death when in fact he had only been lost. But that remorse will pale into nothing if he is proven to be tainted.'

'If that is so,' Mykilus began, his voice leaden, 'then we three will be the ones to send him into oblivion.'

'But it is *not*,' Korica insisted. 'And we three will be there to welcome him back once this mistrust is swept away!'

The gun went back together smoothly, and Zurus tested the action before returning it to his holster. Finally, he rose and walked away.

At the threshold of the chamber door he paused and glanced back at his men. *But not really my men*, he told himself. *Tarikus's men*.

'Are you coming?' he asked.

He was at peace.

Sleep, pure and real. Tarikus struggled to remember the last time he had rested so well, free from nightmares and horrific recollections. Sluggish amniotic fluid swathed him, and he drifted in a tiny, warm ocean of his own. His fingers brushed the inside of a glassy orb. No sound reached him here.

Peace. And all he had needed to do to find it was to die.

He knew that what he experienced now was not true death; he had known that even as the cold had crept into his flesh, tightening about his bio-implant organs, pushing him towards nothingness. No, this was the little-death of the healing trance, the strange state between where the engines of his Astartes physiology were left to work their chemical magicks. He had been here before. After the battle for Krypt. After the narrow escape from Serek–

Serek. Tarikus suppressed a shudder. Memory of that incident returned to him with harsh clarity. After Serek, he had been in a trance like this, repairing damage wrought by a forced teleport transition. And it had been inside a medicae tank such as this one that he had watched the Red Corsairs come to take him. It came back in hard punches of sense-memory – bolt shells cracking the glassaic, his body sluicing out with the liquid on to the deck, still broken, still unready. The renegades coming in to attack him. Blood mixed with the yellowish amnio-fluid. Fighting and killing; but ultimately, failing.

A shiver ran the length of him. Suddenly the warm liquid was as cold as the mountainside.

Tarikus took a breath of the oxygenated medium and felt the chill bore deeper. Out beyond the walls of the medicae tank shapes moved to and fro. They might have been other Astartes, perhaps come to observe this curiosity, this warrior back from the dead, this soul in limbo – or perhaps they were just servitors, going about their tasks, making sure Tarikus did not perish. Not yet.

He did not have permission to die. Aquila had not granted it.

The Doom Eagle looked inside himself and dared to wonder what a real death might feel like. He had been close to that abyss so many times, but never fallen to it; and now, in this moment of great darkness he dared to wonder if death would be the better end for him. If he had perished aboard the hospitaller ship, or perhaps in the cells of the Dynikas prison, then all that happened now would not have come to pass. Tarikus's Chapter would continue on, untroubled by the aberration of his chance survival. The pestilent questions would not have been asked. Constancy would not be challenged.

He felt hollow inside. In his prison cell, whenever he could snatch a moment away from the eyes of the mutant guards and the modificate freaks, he had prayed to the Golden Throne that he might live to see home once more. And in all that time, he had never once thought that he would not be trusted by his own kinsmen.

Conflict raged inside him. At once he hated Thryn and the others for daring to doubt him, but at the same moment he understood why they did so. If matters had been different, if it had been Zurus returning to Gathis and not Tarikus, then what choices would *he* have made in the same place? What questions would Tarikus have demanded answers for?

It came to him that the only way he would be able to prove himself would be to give up the last breath in his body. In death, truth could not be hidden.

The door to the psyker's sanctum opened on oiled pistons and a grave voice issued out from the darkness inside. 'Enter, Zurus. If you must.'

Zurus did as he was bid. Thryn's meditation chamber was little bigger than the accommodation cell where the sergeant laid his head, but it had the illusion of depth thanks to the strange jumble of shadows cast by electro-candles atop a series of iron stands, each at the corner of a mathematical shape carved into the floor.

Thryn rose from a kneeling cushion and pushed aside a fan of imager plates. Zurus glanced at them and saw only unreadable texts and oddly blurred images. He swallowed and failed to hide a grimace. The air in here was strange, almost oily, but with an acid tingle on the bare flesh of his face and hands.

Thryn glared at him. The psyker was in his wargear, and about his head in a blue-white halo, the crystalline matrix of a psionic hood glowed softly. 'You're interrupting my preparations, brother. And you have no good reason.'

Zurus met his hard look with one of his own. 'I have every reason–' he began.

'I'll save you the trouble of explaining yourself to me, shall I?' snapped the Librarian. 'You've been swayed by Tarikus. You've listened to his men, and felt their anxiety for their former commander's fate.' He turned away. 'And as you have never truly felt content as the leader of Tarikus's former squad, you wish to have him return to our fold so you can be free of your conflicts. Is that close to the truth?'

Zurus bristled at the other warrior's tone. 'You make us sound like mewling, weak children! You mock men who dare to show compassion and loyalty to their brothers!'

'Pragmatism is the watchword of the Doom Eagles,' Thryn continued. 'We do not let matters of sentimentality cloud our vision.'

'You think fidelity is something to be dismissed, witch-kin?' Zurus advanced on him. 'Is your warp-touched heart so empty that you forget your bonds of brotherhood?'

'I have forgotten nothing,' Thryn replied. 'But some must bear the burden to voice the questions that no others can utter. Some must dare to speak the hard words that no brother wishes to hear!' He turned to face him, the psy-crystals flickering. 'This obligation is mine. I will see it to its end.'

Zurus's shoulders sagged. 'How much further must this go? You have looked into his mind – tell me, have you sensed the taint of Chaos in his thoughts?'

Thryn shook his head. 'I have not.'

'And the testing of his flesh, first the Talons and then the wind and ice. Did his body belie the touch of the Archenemy at any time?'

'It did not,' intoned the Librarian.

'Then how can you let this go on? Tarikus is not corrupted!'

Thryn nodded. 'I agree.' It was not the answer Zurus was expecting. Before he could speak again, the psyker continued. 'I agree that his mind and his body are sound. But it is not those that I seek to test, brother. It is his soul. That which is the most ephemeral, yet the most powerful element of a life.' Thryn sighed, and something of the bleak aspect of his face softened. 'We know the insidious ways of Chaos, the Emperor blight them. Tarikus may carry a seed of darkness within him and never know it. It has happened before. He may live out a long life, and then one day, at an appointed time, or at some word of command, be transformed into something horrific. All that, if the smallest sliver of warp-stigma lies buried in his aura.'

Zurus frowned. 'The only way to be sure is to kill him, is that what you mean? If you end him and he erupts into some hell beast, you are proven right. If he dies, then he was innocent and just, and goes to the Emperor's side.' He snorted. 'A poor choice for Tarikus on either account.'

'This matter cannot be brought to a close while doubt still exists,' insisted Thryn.

'Then you'll do it?' Zurus snapped. 'And not just the little-death this time, but a cold-blooded murder?'

'Lord Hearon has granted me latitude to do whatever I must to end this uncertainty. And I will end it, this day.' Thryn returned to the centre of the room and knelt once more.

Zurus felt the tingle on his skin of psy-power in the air, the near-storm sense of it growing by the second. 'What will you do?'

Thryn bowed his head. 'Go now, brother. You will know soon enough.'

He lingered at the threshold for a long moment, then stepped through and allowed the hatch to close behind him. Cogs worked and seals fell into place, and Zurus stood outside, staring at the strange hexagrammatric wards etched into the metal, wondering what final trial Tarikus was about to face.

A sound came to him, echoing down the stone corridor. It sounded like thunder, but it could just as easily have been the report of distant shellfire.

Tarikus awoke, and he was in hell.

He fell hard, the rough metal plating of the floor rising up to slam into his knees and arms. He groaned and coughed up a river of stinging bile and thick amnio-fluid. Black streaks of blood threaded the ejecta from his lips. The warrior felt strange; his body seemed wrong, the impulses from his fingertips somehow out of synchrony with the rest of his nerves. He tried to shake himself free of the sensation but it would not leave him. Tarikus's flesh hung on him like an ill-fitting suit of clothes.

He looked up and blinked, his eyes refusing to focus properly. Lights and shadows jumped around him, blurring into shapes that he could not define. Something hove close and he perceived a hand reaching out to him, offering assistance.

'Here,' said a thick, resinous voice. 'To your feet. Come. There is much work to do.'

He took the grip, and felt peculiar talons where fingers should have been; but he was already rising, legs working, muscles tightening.

Light flashed, too slow to be storm-glow, the thunder-pulse with it too quick, too near. *Gunfire?* The sluggish thought trickled down through the layers of his awareness.

Tarikus jerked his hand away. 'Who are you? What is happening?'

Harsh laughter answered him. 'So many questions. Be still, warrior. All will be made clear.' One of the shadows came closer, looming large. 'Don't fight it, Tarikus. Let it happen.' He heard another low, callous chuckle. 'It will be less painful.'

There was heat at his back, burning and steady like the beating of a pitiless sun; and in the air about him, he perceived motes of dust falling in a slow torrent. He saw steel walls. Chains and broken glass. 'What is happening?' he shouted, but his words were lost in the blazing roar of a weapon. He knew that sound: a heavy bolter on full automatic fire, impacts cutting into flesh and ceramite.

'You have done well,' he was told. 'Better than we could have expected. You opened the way for us.' The shadow-man came closer. 'Our perfect weapon.'

'What?' Tarikus raised his hands in self-defence. 'I do not understand–'

'Then look at me,' said the voice. 'And know the truth.'

The light chose that moment to come again, and in its hard-edged, unflinching glare Tarikus saw a thing that resembled an Astartes, but one made of flayed meat, broken bone and corroded iron. A face of gallows-pale flesh leered at him and twisted in amusement. Beneath it, on the figure's chest, was the design of a star with eight razor-tipped points.

'Traitor!' Tarikus shouted the word.

The corrupted warrior nodded. 'Yes, you are.'

He stumbled backwards, shaking his head. His skull felt heavy and leaden. 'No...'

'Your hands. Look at your hands.'

Tarikus could not help but glance downward. The meat of his hard, calloused fingers was gone, and in its place were arcs of bone that glistened like black oil.

'The change is already upon you. It's coming now. Let it happen.'

Ice filled his gut and Tarikus thrashed at the air, smashing aside a support frame, crashing back into the opened medicae tank where he had been healing. He tried to give a wordless shout of denial, but the sound would not form in his constricting throat. His muscles bunched and he shuddered, losing balance. Tarikus could feel a wave of something terrible billowing up inside him, reordering the meat and blood of his body as it moved. He spat and acid flew from his lips, spattering the walls with tiny smoking pits where the droplets fell. He tried to reject it, and failed.

He could hear battle beyond the doors of the chamber now, fast and lethal. Thunder rumbled all around, echoing through the stone at his feet. The Eyrie was under attack.

The Traitor Marine took a step towards him. When it spoke again, there was almost concern in its words. 'The Primogenitor told me it would not be an easy transformation. But hold on, kinsman. You will be renewed in all but a moment. And then you will join us fully.'

'I am not your kinsman!' Tarikus roared, and the words were ragged animal sounds torn from the throat of some monster, not from his lips, not from the mouth of a Doom Eagle. 'What have you done to me?'

Another chuckle. 'You did this to yourself, Tarikus. Don't you recall?' The room seemed to contract, the walls closing in on them both. 'On

Dynikas. When you cast off your master. When you finally understood?'

'Understood… what?' All around him the stone of the medicae chamber flowed like wax into different shapes, and through the haze across his twitching vision the walls momentarily turned into planes of steel, vibrating with heat. The cell. The chains and the walls and the cell. *Did I never really leave? Have I always been there?*

The Traitor cocked its head. 'You understood that you had been discarded. Forgotten. That your corpse-god is ashes and lies. That you mean nothing to the men who tried to make you their slave.'

Tarikus stumbled away, shaking his head, denying every word. 'No!' He tried to launch himself towards the other warrior, but the sudden heat robbed him of every ounce of energy. In place of sweat, oily fluids seeped from his skin, draining his vitality with them.

'Don't you remember?' The Traitor gestured around, and Tarikus saw a distorted liquid mirror shimmer in the air. Upon it he saw himself in rags, kneeling before a towering figure in a coat made of human skin, a giant brass spider emerging from its back.

Fabius Bile.

'No…' he insisted. 'This is a trick! That did not happen! I would never break my oath!' Tarikus lurched back to his feet. 'I would not turn!'

'But you did,' said the voice. 'Because they hated you, forgot you.' The Traitor gestured and Tarikus saw a line of figures in tarnished silver armour standing high behind him. Their proportions were monstrous; they towered like Dreadnoughts, each one jeering and mocking him. They had faces he knew: Zurus and Thryn. At their shoulders: Korica, Mykilus and Petius. And above them all, as tall as a Titan, Aquila himself.

Tarikus reached out his mutating talon-hand and they shrank away; and then the worst of it. As one, all the Doom Eagles turned their backs on him, casting him aside.

Suddenly the room was tight and small about him, the space at the bottom of a pit that stretched up and away, walls too sheer to climb, light too far to reach.

'Poor Tarikus,' said the voice, soothing and unctuous. 'Is it any wonder you accepted the gift?'

Terror filled him at the words, but he could not stay silent. 'What gift?'

The Traitor opened its claw-hand and in it lay a feather, a small curl of plume alike to those that an eagle might leave behind in passing. It was ink-black, a colour so deep and strong that Tarikus immediately knew that to touch it would be poison to him.

No sooner had he laid eyes on the barb than his chest began to burn. Tarikus gasped and clawed at the wet strips of torn tunic shrouding his torso and ripped them away. His transformed talon hands caught the surface of his skin and great rents appeared in the meat of him. From the wounds he had made, no blood flowed; instead cascades of tiny black feathers issued out, spilling from his body. He roared and felt his throat filling with a swarming mass. Tarikus retched and spat a plug of wet, matted quills from his lips.

'Do you see now?' said the Traitor. 'A Chapter that rejected you, left you to perish in the cold, pitiless void. A cadre of false brothers who fled when their lives were in jeopardy. The lies you were told about fealty and honour, but all of it sand. Is it any wonder you were broken?' The other warrior leaned in. 'Is it any wonder you let us remake you in the Primogenitor's name?' He nodded. 'And now the last shroud is released from you, kinsman. Now you are free to be one of us... and our first act will be to grind this Ghostmountain to dust.'

Tarikus could not stop himself from trembling. The worst of it was not the visions, or the perhaps-memories, or the sense of his own body slipping away from him. No, the worst of it was that he could not be sure. The Traitor's words had the edge of truth to them.

How often in those long months in that cell had he lain in torment, one single question desperate on his lips. *Why have I been forgotten?* His every waking moment as an Adeptus Astartes had been in service of something greater than himself, and in return, in exchange for the surety of fate and death the Doom Eagles gave, Tarikus had the priceless gift of brotherhood. The certain knowledge of comradeship among his kindred, the knowing that he would never be lost, not so long as a single son of Gathis still drew breath. *So why did they never come for me? Why did they count me dead and be done, never to speak my name again?*

'Because it is a lie,' said the Traitor. 'And has ever been one.' He gestured around. '*We* will never lie to you, Tarikus. You will always know the truth with us.' The hand extended out to him once more. 'Take it.'

The thunder outside and the flashes of blue-white light coursed all around him. Tarikus looked up and saw the outstretched hand, the turncoat Astartes – and beyond, the shadows of the Doom Eagles.

They were judging him.

Time halted for Tarikus, and the questions that had bombarded him since he had returned to the Eyrie were echoing through his mind. The accusations welled up from within.

He could imagine a shade of himself – a weaker, broken Tarikus – who might have had the flaw of character to yield to the strain of his confinement on Dynikas. This ghost-Tarikus, this pale copy of him, made bitter by his abandonment, clawing in desperation for the one thing every Space Marine wanted... The bond of brotherhood. Without their comradeship, the Astartes were nothing. Everything they were was built upon that foundation. What horror it would be to lose that, to be cast adrift and counted as unkindred. A weakened soul, captured at the lowest moment, might be persuaded to bend the knee to a former foe for just a taste of that blessed bond once again. A fragile spirit, yes, who would willingly hide their new loyalty beneath the cloak of the old, and carry poison back to those who had deserted them. Poison and murder, all in the name of revenge.

Suddenly, events were moving again, and he was aware of the Traitor nodding. 'Yes. You see now, don't you?'

But that shade, that weakling who appeared in his thoughts... Whatever it was, it was not Tarikus, son of Gathis, scion of Aquila. He drew himself up and with a vicious shove, pushed the turncoat aside.

Tarikus glared up at the silent, condemning gazes of his Doom Eagle brethren, peering at the phantoms of their faces. 'I am not a heretic.' He spoke, and with each word that left his mouth, Tarikus felt his vitality returning to him. A sense of righteous power enveloped him, and with it the wrongness of his changed body bled away. Moment by moment, he began to feel *correct*. With every breath, he moved closer to the warrior he had always been – and with a surge of strength, Tarikus realised that he had not felt so certain of anything in years. Not since before he had been taken prisoner. 'Judge me if you will,' he shouted, 'I do not fear it! You will look inside my heart and see only fealty! I am Tarikus!'

The hazed faces of his former squad mates danced there in the wraithlight. Korica: impulsive and brave. Mykilus: steadfast and strong. Petius: taciturn and measured. They did not turn from him. They had not forgotten him.

Behind him, the Traitor was getting to its feet, coming towards him with murder in its eyes. 'Fool–'

He silenced the enemy by grabbing his throat and tightening his grip until the Traitor could only make broken gurgles. Gunfire-thunder rumbled louder and louder in his ears and Tarikus bellowed to make himself heard. 'I am a Doom Eagle! My fidelity will never falter!' He threw his enemy to the ground. 'I did not break! *I will never break!*'

A great pressure, silent but deafening, pushed out from inside his thoughts, and all at once the warped walls around him exploded like glass beneath a hammer.

Tarikus swept around; he was intact, unchanged. Everything that had happened in the phantom room was gone, vanished like shafts of sunlight consumed by clouds. He stood before the open healing tank, then turned and found the Librarian Thryn coming back to his feet. The psyker was nursing an ugly bruise forming at his throat. He spat and eyed the other Astartes.

'You?' said Tarikus. He sniffed the air, scenting the greasy tang of spent mind-power. 'You cast a veil over me... All of it illusions and game-play.'

'Aye,' Thryn replied, rough-voiced. 'And you almost tore the breath from me in the process.'

Tarikus advanced towards the psyker, his hands contracting into fists. Anger burned in his eyes, and the question of Thryn being clad in armour and himself not didn't cross his thoughts. 'I should beat an apology from you, witch-kin.'

'You should be thanking me,' Thryn retorted. 'At last, I finally saw into you. Saw what you hid from us.'

'I hid nothing,' Tarikus spat.

Thryn shook his head. 'Don't lie to me, not now. You hid your fear, Tarikus. The black and terrible fear that came upon you in the darkest moments of your confinement, when just for a moment, you wondered what would happen if you weakened.' The Librarian gave a crooked, unlovely smile. 'How very human of you.'

Gradually, Tarikus's fists relaxed. 'I looked into the darkness, across the edge of the abyss,' he said slowly. 'And I turned away.'

Thryn nodded. 'Indeed you did. And now I have the answer I wanted.' He offered his hand to the other Doom Eagle. 'Your integrity is assured. You are returned to us, brother. In body, mind... and in soul.'

Tarikus shook his hand in the old fashion, palm to wrist. 'I never left,' he said.

'When will there be an end to this?' grated Korica. He glared at Zurus, and the other warrior nodded slightly.

'I have no answer for you,' admitted the sergeant. He looked away, his gaze crossing the towering black marble fascias of the memorial towers, each reaching up and away towards the ornate ceiling far overhead. He saw something moving; a travel platform, dropping towards them.

Mykilus saw it too, and he pointed. 'Look there.'

Petius took a tentative step towards the edge of the gantryway, then halted. Like all of them, he was unsure of what meaning lay behind the urgent summons that had brought them to the relical.

In the next moment, the platform had arrived and a figure in duty robes stepped off, pushing past them.

'Tarikus?' Zurus could not keep the amazement from his voice. He had truly believed that he would never see the errant Astartes again. Thryn was not known for his leniency in matters of judgement. Then his thoughts caught up with him and Zurus allowed himself a small smile. He had been right about his lost brother; suddenly, all the doubts he had harboured about this duty and his part in Tarikus's ordeal were swept away, and it was as if a great weight fell from his shoulders.

Korica extended his augmetic arm towards Tarikus, but the veteran pushed past him, not slowing. The other Doom Eagles followed Tarikus down the length of the gantryway until he halted before a particular memorial slab.

Zurus knew what would come next the instant before it happened. The veteran's fist shot out and punched through the bubble of glassaic at the end of the panel and then folded around the death-remnant inside.

He watched the other warrior draw out a blood-streaked hand, and in it, a battle-worn combat blade. Tarikus looked down at the knife, and then up at them for the first time. His steady, clear-eyed gaze crossed each one of them in turn, ending with Zurus. The veteran opened his mouth to speak – and then thought better of it. Instead, Tarikus acted.

With a slow, steady draw of blade point over stone, he etched a heavy line through his own name, erasing the record of his death. He reclaimed his life. Mykilus was the first to speak. 'Welcome back, sir.' He bowed his head. 'If we had only known that the Red Corsairs had not killed you–'

'No.' Tarikus held up his hand. 'You will not speak of that again. And by my order, you will not carry any guilt over what happened.' He stepped forward and moved from brother to brother, tapping each on the shoulder in turn. 'I hold no malice. You did no wrong that day.'

Then he was looking at Zurus. The Doom Eagle sighed, and made a decision of his own. He reached beneath his robes and his hand returned with a fetter of black and silver links pooled in the palm; it was the honour-chain that signified his command of the battle squad. He offered it. 'This also belongs to you, I believe.'

Tarikus showed quiet surprise. 'The squad is yours, brother. You have made it so. These men are your men.'

Zurus shook his head. 'No. It has been my honour to lead them into battle in the name of the Emperor and Aquila, but I have never been their commander, not in the manner you were. I have only been… the caretaker of that post. You have seniority over me, the laurel and the honours. It is your right to reclaim your prior status.'

The veteran came closer, his brow furrowing. 'You are sure you wish to step down, Zurus? I know my brothers would not have followed you if you had not been worthy of it.' He nodded at the chain.

Zurus pressed the links into Tarikus's hand. 'I will not take that which by right is yours.' He stepped away. 'I will find another place in the Chapter.'

'You already have a place, sir,' said Korica. He glanced at Tarikus, and the veteran sergeant nodded.

'Aye,' said the other Doom Eagle. 'I have need of good men, who see clearly and fight well.' Tarikus held up the honour chain. 'I will accept this on condition that you remain in the squad as my second.'

Zurus thought on the offer, then nodded. 'That seems a fair bargain.'

Tarikus was silent for a long moment; then he wrapped the chain about the hilt of the knife and put it into his belt. 'Come, then, kinsmen. The enemy tasks me.' He gestured up towards the distant roof, where glimmers of constant storm-light flickered. 'I have been dead long enough.'

Zurus followed his commander's gaze upward to where the rain fell, steady and ceaseless as the Emperor's wrath.

A GOOD MAN

Sandy Mitchell

As the tide of war swept across the Sabbat Worlds, most of us could be forgiven for taking more notice of its rise than of its ebb. But after the battlefronts moved on, leaving rockpools of conflict and its aftermath beached by their withdrawal, the vital task of restoring the Pax Imperialis was only just beginning. On world after shattered world, a veritable second crusade of those with the necessary expertise to manage the reconstruction followed hard on the heels of the first.

Which was how Zale Linder came to Verghast, around the middle of 771, among a swarm of Administratum functionaries charged with the restoration of good order there. He wasn't much to look at, so typical of his brethren that he might have escaped notice altogether, had he not worked so assiduously at coming to my attention; but that was to be later, and to really appreciate his story, I suppose we'd better start at the beginning.

We can only imagine Linder's reaction to his surroundings when he first set foot on the shuttle apron at Kannack. Armed men were everywhere, in the uniforms of PDF regiments, or the Imperial Guard units left to garrison the planet, and the scars of the recent fighting were more than evident on the port facilities surrounding him. Come to that, as most of the shuttles approaching the Northern Collective overflew the glass-walled crater where Vannick had once stood, he'd probably seen some of the worst devastation even before his arrival.

For a man more used to the musty recesses of a scriptorium, the noise, bustle, and constant tang of combustibles from the surrounding manufactoria must have been disconcerting in the extreme. Nevertheless, by all accounts, he rallied at once, chivvying the small knot of brown-robed scribes towards the rail terminal, though few of them were quite so quick to adjust to their new surroundings as he was.

The echoing hall with its multitude of platforms, from which services departed to destinations throughout the North Col and beyond, probably seemed as alien to the Administratum adepts as the landing field had been, but they found a local service into Kannack itself without much trouble. The Verghastites had become used to off-worlders by this time, particularly bewildered-looking ones speaking strangely-accented Gothic, and the booking clerk who wrote out their tickets in a flowing copperplate hand directed them to the correct platform with all the polite deference due to customers he'd overcharged by about five per cent.

The train rattled its way to Kannack Hub in little more than an hour, affording Linder a few brief glimpses of the spoil heaps and outlying reclamation zones, before burrowing into the side of the Western Spine like a worm into an apple. The last couple of kilometres of track ran within the lower hab levels, through tunnels and caverns of steel and brick, some spaces large and open enough to seem like small towns in their own right, while in other places the enclosing walls whipped by disorientatingly just the other side of the window.

The Hub terminal was more crowded than anywhere they'd seen so far, and the little knot of off-world adepts navigated it in an apprehensive huddle, following the directions they'd been given as punctiliously as the curlicues of an ancient text being restored to legibility by a fresh layer of ink. Once again, Linder took the lead, although he was by no means the most senior member of the party; but he had more local knowledge than any of the others, furnished to him by a friend and colleague who'd arrived in an earlier wave a year or so before, and who had corresponded diligently in the interim. He already knew how to flag down one of the municipal charabancs thronging the outer concourse, and how to distinguish the combination of numeric and colour coding which marked one heading in the right direction. How grateful his colleagues were for being saved a five-kilometre walk, mostly in an upwards direction, isn't clear, but I presume the majority were relieved to find what seats they could among the shift-change crowds.

What really matters is that Linder eventually ended up where he belonged, at the Administratum Cloister; but the details of his journey are important to someone like me, to whom details are everything. In that relatively brief trip from the landing field, he demonstrated the single-mindedness and adaptability which set him apart from his colleagues, and which were to lead him down darker paths than he could ever have dreamed he would walk.

The first intimation that something was wrong would have been when he registered his arrival at the Codicium Municipalis, where he had been assigned to work, and enquired about the friend who had preceded him to Verghast.

'No record of that individual exists,' the junior Archivist on the other side of the polished wooden counter informed him, with the neutral inflection peculiar to lowly functionaries trying to appear not to relish the chance of making the lives of their superiors more difficult.

'Please check again,' Linder said calmly. He'd been navigating his way around the labyrinthine ways of the datastacks for most of his life, and was well aware that information could be lost or mislaid in a myriad of ways. 'Allow for misspellings, and cross-reference with the arrival records of the landing field.'

'The results are the same, honoured scribe,' the Archivist told him, after a wait no longer than Linder had expected. 'There is no reference to a Harl Sitrus in any of the informational repositories accessible from this cogitation node.'

'Then I suggest you commence an immediate archival audit,' Linder said, 'since the data I require has clearly been misfiled.'

'As you instruct, honoured scribe,' the Archivist said, suppressing any trace of irritation which might have entered his voice; there were worse ways of wasting his time, which Linder could easily impose if sufficiently irked. 'Would you like a summary of the results forwarded to your cubicle?'

'I would,' Linder said, and returned to his assigned task of tabulating the adjusted output of the Kannack manufactoria, which had altered appreciably in both volume and substance in response to the recent upheavals. The task was a painstaking one, consuming a good deal of time and the greater part of his attention, so he was faintly surprised to find the report he'd requested dropping from the pneumatic tube over the angled surface of his writing desk less than a week later.

Setting aside the work he was supposed to be doing, Linder began working his way through the thick wad of paper, annotating it as he went with an inkstick. The anonymous Archivist had been thorough, within the limits of his competence, but Linder's greater experience and expertise soon began to pay dividends, and by the time he was making excuses to the senior lexicographer for failing to finish his assigned task by the compline bell, he'd discovered a number of discrepancies in the archive records, each accompanied by marginalia in his elegantly cursive hand.

The majority of the anomalies he identified were in the files administered by the Bureau of Population Management, the department responsible for collating records of birth, death, and off-world migration, which it would then use to allocate resources where they were most urgently required. The devastation wrought on Verghast had rendered much of this material unreliable, so Linder was hardly surprised by this discovery, but one discrepancy perturbed him greatly. There was still no official record of Harl Sitrus's arrival on Verghast, even though the date was known to him; turning to his data-slate, he invoked Sitrus's first missive after landing.

We touched down at Kannack on 439 770, he read, frowning in perplexity. *That's a fair sized hive, one of the largest left standing after the razing of Vervun and the scouring of Ferrozoica. Klath got us to the scriptorium eventually, after a few wrong turnings...* Linder read on, skimming through the familiar words. Nothing else struck him as significant, but the date was unequivocal. The frown deepening, he turned back to the hardprint on his lectern, and paged through the summary of transits from orbit that day.

Shuttle Damsel's Delight, *grounded pad seventeen, Administratum charter. Twelve passengers, personal effects, cargo amounting to 497 tonnes (stationery sundries)*. That must have been the one.

To confirm the fact, he invoked the cogitator link, and examined the manifest in detail. Galen Klath, lexicographer, and eleven other names. Sitrus's was not among them.

Troubled, Linder spent a further few minutes in search of Klath's whereabouts. His personal quarters were listed as within the bounds of the Administratum Cloister, but Linder lacked the seniority to access their precise location. That didn't matter, though; the department the lexicographer was attached to was a mere thirty levels away, and a chance meeting would be easy enough to contrive. Perhaps he would be able to shed some light on the anomaly.

'Sitrus?' Klath asked, his face crumpling in perplexity. He was much as Linder remembered him, short and rotund, which, together with his hairless pate, made him look uncannily like an oversized toddler dressed for masquerade in adult clothes. 'Why do you ask?'

'I've been looking for him,' Linder said evenly. Having to explain the obvious was another thing he remembered about the plump lexicographer, which was one of the reasons he'd been so pleased to be transferred to his present duties, away from Klath's supervision. 'In his letters, he mentioned you were still colleagues.'

'I see.' Klath glanced round the crowded buttery, as though afraid of eavesdroppers. There were none Linder could see, just the usual crowd of men and women in inkstained robes, chattering idly as they grabbed some pottage or a mid-shift mug of caffeine before returning to their data-slates and hardprints. 'But I'm afraid I haven't seen him since the transfer.'

'He's transferred?' Linder asked.

Caught unawares by the brevity of the question, Klath nodded, chewed and swallowed, and replied with a stifled hiccup. 'To another department. He didn't say which.'

Linder echoed the nod, more slowly. There were over seven thousand separate bureaux within the cloister, dealing with everything from the disposition of tithing revenue to the certification of left-handed writing implements, and with nothing further to go on, his friend might just as well be on a different planet. 'Did he ever mention where he was living?' he asked, and Klath shook his head.

'He had a flat somewhere up on the Spine. Lots of people live outside the Cloister, if they can afford it. You young ones, anyway. Too much bustle if you ask me.'

Linder nodded again. He was still in the rooms assigned to him on his arrival, having little inclination to expose himself to the ceaseless activity of the wider hive, but Sitrus would have relished the proximity of taverns and bars, theatres and brawling pits. Ever since their first meeting, as callow Archivists, Sitrus had been hungry for experience, eager to meet life head-on, instead of vicariously through text and picts. It was an attitude uncommon within the sheltered precincts of the Cloister. Perhaps that was why Linder was so determined to see his friend again, instead of accepting that their paths had diverged forever when Sitrus boarded the first transport to Verghast over a year before.

'It must have taken everything he had,' he said. Rents on the Spine were high, the few adepts he'd met living outside the Cloister barely being able to afford a couple of rooms in a worker's hab.

Klath leaned closer, assuming a confidential air. 'Between you and me,' he said, 'I don't think he paid in cash. *Cherchez la femme*, and all that.'

'Really?' Linder considered this unexpected information. Sitrus had always enjoyed feminine company, he knew, but the only women he'd had any contact with before had been other Administratum adepts; which, given the circumscribed nature of the lives they led, had hardly been surprising. None of them could have afforded lodgings in the hive's most salubrious quarter, any more than Sitrus could. 'You mean he'd taken up with a local woman?'

Which would have been impossible, of course. Nothing in any of the letters he'd received had so much as hinted at such a liaison. But Klath was nodding slowly. 'I believe so,' he confirmed, with the self-satisfied air of someone passing on a juicy bit of scandal. 'For the last six months, at least.'

Six months in which Linder had received three missives from his friend. The first had dwelt at length on some interesting cross-referencing practices the Verghastite Archivists were continuing to cling to in the face of the filing protocols imposed by the new arrivals, and the compromise eventually arrived at to general satisfaction, before rambling off into a description of a few of the local festivals; the second had consisted mainly of enthusiastic comments about the local cuisine, which Sitrus appeared to be finding very much to his taste; and the third contained little apart from an account of an inspection of one of the protein reclamation plants, to which Sitrus had been attached to take notes, and which he'd enlivened with caustic pen portraits of the rest of the delegation. None had so much as hinted at a romantic liaison.

Klath had to be mistaken. Nevertheless, Linder supposed, he might as well follow it up, if only to eliminate the possibility. In that regard, the mind of a diligent bureaucrat isn't so far removed from the dispassionate pursuit of hidden truths peculiar to my own profession. Which meant that, from the moment Linder uttered his next remark, our paths would inevitably cross.

'Do you happen to remember her name?' he asked.

As it turned out, Klath wasn't sure, but a little more patient probing on Linder's part elicited the vague recollection that Sitrus had mentioned meeting someone called Milena once. That was little enough to go on, but for a fellow of Linder's skills and resources, it was sufficient; there were only so many women of that name living in the Spine, and not all of them were of the right age to be of romantic interest to Sitrus; and not all those remaining on the list were single. That didn't discount them entirely, of course, but Klath had implied that Sitrus was living with his inamorata, and a husband about the place would have put paid to so cosy an arrangement. Knowing his friend as he did, I'm sure Linder was able to eliminate a few more potential candidates without too much difficulty, but whatever other criteria he chose to apply, he didn't bother to share with me during our subsequent conversation on the subject.

Once he'd got the list down to an irreducible minimum, the streak of determination which had first surfaced during his eventful journey from the landing field displayed itself again. Undaunted by the scale of the task he'd set himself, he began using the limited amount of free time at his disposal to contact the remaining candidates, eliminating them one by one.

Most were polite, if puzzled, simply assuring him they weren't acquainted with his friend; an assurance he generally believed, as a lifetime spent in the service of the Administratum had left him able to detect evasion or unease in the harmonics of the voice. A few were clearly suspicious of his motives, and a handful decidedly hostile; these he annotated for possible further enquiry, if he reached the end of his list without any useful result. Whatever his reception, he plodded on, until one of the voices on the vox reacted in a fashion he'd not experienced before.

'Good shift-change,' he began, for the fifty-seventh time. 'Is that Milena Dravere?'

'Speaking.' The voice was brisk, brittle behind a sabre-rattle of confidence. 'And you would be...?'

'Zale Linder. We've never met, but we might have a friend in common. Do you know a scribe named Harl Sitrus?'

'You're a friend of Harl's?' The woman's voice cracked a little. 'Where is he? Is he all right?'

'I was hoping you could tell me,' Linder said, a fresh wave of bewilderment dousing the sudden flare of hope at her first words. 'I arrived on Verghast a few weeks ago, and I've been looking for him ever since.'

'Arrived?' The vox circuit hummed with speculative silence for a second or two. 'From off-world?'

'Khulan. I'm with the Reconstruction Administration.' Linder hesitated, wondering if this would be too much to take in. But it seemed to be the right thing to say.

'Oh, you're *that* Zale. Harl talked about you.'

'Did he?' Linder asked, conscious that the conversation seemed to be slipping away from him. 'What did he say?'

'That I could trust you.' The admission seemed a reluctant one. 'We should meet. Compare notes. Maybe we can find him together.'

'I could visit you,' Linder suggested, wondering if perhaps that was the wrong thing to say. The woman was clearly nervous, and might not feel comfortable about inviting him into her home. But she took the suggestion in her stride.

'Sixty-four Via Zoologica,' she said, barely hesitating. 'Can you find it?'

'I can,' Linder told her with confidence. He had a plan of the hive in his data-slate, newly updated with the latest alterations to roads and transit routes, where fresh construction was scabbing over the scars of Ferrozoican bombardment. 'But I won't be off shift until after compline.'

'An hour after compline, then,' Milena agreed, and broke the connection.

Cheered by the unexpected acquisition of an ally, Linder returned to work with his usual diligence, and had apparently made considerable progress in disentangling the cat's cradle of information on his desk when he was unexpectedly interrupted by a diffident knock on the door.

'What is it?' he asked, with some asperity, resenting the disruption of his concentration.

'There's someone here to see you, honoured scribe,' a pale-looking Archivist informed him, inserting just enough of his body across the cubicle's threshold to become visible.

'I'm busy. Tell them to wait.' Linder returned to his collection of slates and hardprints, already dismissing the matter from his mind.

'That won't be convenient,' I said, pushing past the Archivist, who promptly fled, his duty done. Linder turned back to the door, to find it clicking to, while I leaned casually against its inner surface. I extended a hand. 'Wil Feris, Adeptus Arbites.'

'Of course,' Linder said, as though my uniform hadn't already told him precisely what I was. Surprise was smeared across his face like a harlot's lipstick, but his handshake was firm, and once he'd registered that I was real and wasn't going away until I was good and ready, his expression became curious rather than alarmed. 'What can I do for you?'

'You've been looking for Harl Sitrus,' I said, resigning myself to leaning against the door for as long as the interview took. There was only one place to sit in the narrow room, and Linder showed no inclination to vacate it. 'So have I.'

'Do you know where he is?' Linder asked, and I shook my head.

'No,' I admitted, 'and that irks me. I'm not used to being hidden from. Not for this long, anyway.'

'Why would he be hiding?' Linder asked, an unmistakable frown appearing on his face. 'Surely you can't suspect him of anything?'

'Everyone's guilty of something,' I said. That was the first thing I'd learned on joining the Arbites, and before you ask, of course I include myself in that. But there are degrees of guilt, and culpability, and sometimes things aren't as clear cut as they seem.

'Not Harl,' Linder said, which surprised me; people usually react to that kind of insinuation by asserting their own innocence. 'Not of anything that would justify your interest, anyway.'

'I'm interested in a great deal,' I told him. Which was true; law enforcement on Verghast was in as big a mess as any of its other institutions, and the Arbitrators brought in to sort it out had been forced to take on cases which would have been handed to the locals on more smoothly functioning worlds. 'Including the falsification of records.'

'Harl would never do something like that,' Linder said, sounding genuinely angry. Most Administratum adepts would as soon profane the name of the Emperor as knowingly tamper with the data they were charged to protect.

'Don't you think it a little odd that so many records relating to him have disappeared?" I asked, refusing to raise my voice in return.

Linder looked thoughtful. 'That might be the result of tampering,' he conceded. 'But you've got no proof that Harl's responsible.'

'Nothing definite,' I agreed. 'But innocent men seldom disappear into thin air. Unless foul play's involved.'

Linder paled; clearly this possibility hadn't occurred to him. 'You think he's been murdered?' he asked at last.

'It's possible,' I said evenly, 'but I doubt it. I think he wiped his own records to cover his tracks, and hide whatever else he tampered with.'

'Harl wouldn't do a thing like that,' Linder said again, glaring at me with unmistakable dislike. 'And I'll prove it.'

'I'll be delighted if you can,' I told him. He clearly knew nothing of any use to me. 'In the meantime, if he should get in touch, or you find some trace of him, be sure to let me know.'

'You can count on it,' Linder said, in tones which made it clear he regarded the interview as over.

* * *

How much of his interrupted chain of thought Linder was able to pick up after my departure I can only guess, but given his stubborn streak, I imagine he'd pretty much completed his task for the day by the time he left the scriptorium and headed uphive to meet Milena Dravere. He found his way with little trouble, consulting his data-slate from time to time, but generally moving through the shift-change bustle with a resolute determination which left the local operatives I'd assigned to watch him scurrying to keep up; no mean feat, given that most of them were Kannack born and bred. True to the picture I was beginning to form of him, he took little notice of the barrage of noise and spectacle most men would have found distracting, but remained obdurately fixed on his goal.

The only time he showed any visible sign of surprise was when he reached the Via Zoologica itself, and realised that the road broke through into the open air. He paused for a moment, looking down the long, sloping flank of the hive shining like a beached galaxy below, then strode on, his shadow flickering in and out of existence as it merged momentarily with the patches of deeper darkness between the waylights. As he neared his destination, skirting a crowded tavern from which jaunty zither music floated incongruously on the night air, he slowed his pace, paying greater attention to the address plates screwed to the smog-eaten bricks of the overhanging housefronts.

At length he came to his destination, and knocked, a little hesitantly. After a few moments a woman opened the carved wooden door a wary crack.

'Milena?' he asked, unsure of his reception. 'It's me, Zale.'

'Then you'd better come in.' The door opened wider, and he stepped inside, finding himself in an airy, well-lit entrance hall. His hostess was petite, dark-haired, and carried a small-calibre autopistol in her left hand. Linder had never seen a genuine weapon before, and was taken aback; but before he could protest, Milena had closed and bolted the door, and deposited the gun on a nearby occasional table. From the number of faint scratches in the marquetry surface, Linder surmised that the gun generally rested there, where it could be picked up easily whenever the woman answered the door.

She motioned him through one of the arches leading off the hall, and he found himself in a comfortably appointed living room roughly the size of his entire lodgings. He looked around curiously, noting the opulent decor, the artful scattering of antiques and *objets d'art*, utterly unlike the contents of any room he'd ever been in before.

'You have a very elegant home,' he said, hoping to break the awkward silence.

'Thank you.' Milena perched on the edge of a sofa, opposite the armchair Linder had selected as seeming least likely to swallow him whole. He was astonished at how comfortable it was; the furniture he was used to was generally selected for its utility, rather than comfort. Milena glanced round, as though lost in her own house. 'Harl found it for me.'

'He did?' Linder prompted, hoping for more detail. He couldn't imagine Sitrus combing the property vendors, even on a friend's behalf. Perhaps his new department had something to do with accommodation allocation, and he'd found out about it that way.

'He's helped a lot of people,' Milena said. Her face was drawn and tense. 'He's a good man. Whatever some people say about him.'

'People like Feris?' Linder asked, and the woman nodded, suddenly tense again.

'How do you know Feris?' she asked, her left hand clenching as though closing on the butt of her gun. Her eyes fixed on Linder's, disturbing in their intensity. She shifted, almost imperceptibly, a few millimetres further away from where he sat.

'I don't,' Linder assured her, 'and I don't want to. He came to the scriptorium, not long after I voxed you, and threw his weight around.'

Milena nodded. 'I thought he was monitoring my vox calls. He's probably hoping Harl gets in touch with me.' A flash of panic illuminated her eyes. 'If he does, they'll be bound to catch him!'

'He's too clever for that,' Linder assured her. 'But why would the Arbites think he's been doing anything wrong? The idea's absurd.'

'Of course it is,' Milena said, her voice blazing with indignation. 'But Feris needs someone to blame, even if he can't prove anything. When Harl disappeared, he just jumped to the conclusion that he must be guilty.'

'More or less what he told me,' Linder agreed. He hesitated a little before going on. 'He did have another idea about what might have happened. But I'm afraid it's rather unpleasant.'

'Let me guess,' Milena said. 'He suggested Harl's been murdered, and someone's trying to cover it up.' She smiled, registering Linder's shocked expression. 'He tried the same trick on me. He doesn't believe that any more than we do.'

'Then why suggest it?' Linder asked.

Milena's posture became a little less hunched. 'To see if you'd let anything slip, of course. In case you were in on it.'

'In on what?' Linder began to feel completely out of his depth.

'Whatever he imagines Harl was involved in,' Milena said, as though explaining things to a child. I suppose it was at that point Linder first began to realise quite how out of his depth he was.

'Have you any idea what that might be?' he asked.

The woman regarded him steadily. 'Data falsification's about the worst thing an Administratum adept could be accused of, isn't it?'

Linder nodded. 'Short of heresy. I'm sure Harl told you that.'

'He did.' Milena's voice was low, as if, even here, they might be overheard. 'It wasn't a decision he took lightly.'

Linder felt the breath gush from his body, as though her words had been a physical blow. Slowly, he stood.

'I shouldn't have come here,' he said, biting back the angry words seething behind his tongue. 'I'm sorry to have intruded on you.'

'Sit down and listen, damn it!' Milena jumped up too, her fists clenched. 'I told you, he did nothing wrong!'

'You also just told me he falsified records,' Linder snapped back, 'and I've known him most of my life. Harl wouldn't do something like that, whatever the reason.'

'And I lived with him for more than half a year,' Milena said, her voice softening. 'Perhaps I saw a side of him you never did. But if you don't want to know the truth, then leave. You know where the door is.'

'All right.' Linder seated himself again. The desire to make sense of the data was ruling him, as it always would. 'I'm listening. But I don't promise to believe you.'

'Fair enough.' Milena breathed deeply, and began pacing the room. 'I told you Harl found this place for me. Before he did, I had nothing. Literally. I'm from Vannick, and I was in one of the outhabs when the nuke went off. I'd just stepped into an underpass, crossing the Vervunhive road, at the time. A few seconds either way, and I'd have been vaporised, like everything else above ground. All my idents went up in the fireball, along with my home and my family.' She took a long, shuddering breath, and Linder found himself wondering if she'd finished.

'That's...' he began, but Milena cut him off with a sharp hand gesture.

'Eventually, I made it here. It wasn't easy, and I had to do a lot of things I never want to think about again. But without idents I couldn't find a job, or a place to live. That limits your options, believe me.'

'So what happened?' Linder asked, not sure he wanted to know the answer.

'Harl did. We got talking in a bar I used to work. Don't get me wrong, he was never a client, but he used to drink there sometimes, and we got to know each other. One night I was in a bad way, and it all came pouring out. He never said much, but he listened, and the next time I saw him he gave me an ident. Genuine. Some Spiner girl who'd picked the wrong time to visit Vervunhive and never come back.'

'I see.' Linder thought about the unthinkable. In circumstances like that, the Sitrus he remembered might have been tempted to alter the records to help the woman. It would have been easy; he could even picture the expression on his friend's face as he shuffled the requisite pieces of data round the cogitator net, the sardonic smile which never quite became a sneer. He'd seen it many times in their early years as lowly Archivists, generally directed at him, as he failed to follow Sitrus in some minor transgression of the regulations. Sitrus would have relished the challenge of getting away with it, although the risk of being caught would have been relatively low. Dealing with any hardprint copies that existed would have been a little more difficult, but not too much so; a scribe's robe could hide a great deal more than a few sheets of paper, and once they were gone, it would be easy to ascribe their loss to the turmoil of the war. 'And something went wrong?'

'No.' Milena shook her head. 'No one noticed. Not at first.'

'At first?' Linder tried to get his reeling thoughts under control. 'What changed?'

'Harl did, I suppose. He must have got overconfident. After he helped me, he decided to rescue some of the other dispossessed.'

'Yes, he would.' Linder nodded. Once he'd crossed the line, and got away with it, Sitrus would have been unable to resist the impulse to carry on outwitting his superiors. He was constitutionally incapable of refraining from pushing his luck. Sometimes that had been an asset, propelling him up the Administratum hierarchy at a rate some of their contemporaries had been openly envious of, and sometimes a liability; Linder had seen him lose a month's remuneration on a single hand of cards before now.

'Like I said, he's a good man. And now Feris is treating him like a criminal!' Milena paced the room, her slight frame seeming too frail to contain her boiling rage.

'That must be why he wiped his records,' Linder said, considering the matter as dispassionately as he could. 'To protect you. With his access keys deleted from the system, there's no way of telling which files he accessed.'

He probably even believed that; a sufficiently devout tech-priest might be able to reconstruct them, given enough time to enact the proper rituals, but that kind of knowledge is well outside the purview of the Administratum.

'You won't tell Feris, will you?' Milena asked, twisting her hands together anxiously.

'Of course not,' Linder said, wondering if it was true. A lifetime of devotion to his calling was warring within him against the demands of friendship and compassion. It was all too much to take in.

'Thank you.' Milena smiled, with genuine warmth for the first time, the tension suddenly draining from her body. Then, to Linder's astonishment, she hugged him. 'I've been so afraid without Harl.'

'We'll find him,' Linder said, with a confidence he didn't feel, and hesitantly returned the embrace.

When he left, it was close to dawn, a faint greyish glow becoming visible through the clouds of smoke rising from the manufactoria below and to the east. The rumble of industry continued unabated in the background, mere distinctions of day and night irrelevant to the vast majority of Kannack's population. Up on the Spine, though, the affluent remained more aware of the diurnal round, and the streets were accordingly quiet, which forced my observers to keep their distance; otherwise things might have been concluded a great deal more quickly than they were.

'Take this,' Milena said suddenly, as Linder turned away from the closing door. He held out his hand automatically, and found his fingers wrapping themselves around the compact weight of the miniature autopistol she'd collected from the hall table before undoing the bolt. 'I've got another.'

'No thank you.' The metal was cold, smelling faintly of lubricants, and the wooden butt felt warm where she'd been gripping it. It seemed astonishingly heavy for something so small, and Linder fumbled, almost dropping it. 'I haven't a clue how it works anyway.'

'You point it and pull the trigger,' Milena said. 'It's been blessed by a tech-priest to ensure accuracy. But you need to flick the safety off first.' Noticing Linder's blank expression, she smiled indulgently. 'That's the switch by your thumb.'

Linder almost refused again, then stuffed the little firearm into the depths of his robe. The gift was well meant, and he didn't want to hurt her feelings. 'I'll be in touch,' he said instead, 'as soon as I find out anything else.' He wasn't sure how he was going to do that, but had a vague idea of seeing if Klath remembered anything else Sitrus might have said about people or places he knew.

'I'll be waiting,' Milena said. 'But come by anyway. I don't see many people now Harl's gone.'

'I will,' Linder promised, and was rewarded with another fleeting smile.

The predawn wind was chill, unwarmed by the thermal currents rising from the industrial sectors, and Linder huddled deeper inside his robe as he hurried back towards the tunnel mouth leading to the enclosed depths of the hive below. His footsteps echoed eerily in the unaccustomed quiet, and the shadows between the waylamps seemed impenetrable pools of darkness. The tavern was open again as he passed it, if it had ever closed, the indefatigable zither player still going strong; he considered the unlikelihood of that for a moment, before realising it must have been a recording. His attention attracted by the music, he paused, considering the prospect of a reviving mug of caffeine and a warm butter roll, then dismissed the idea; he would be cutting the time of his arrival at the scriptorium fine enough as it was.

But the brief hesitation was enough. As he listened to the echoes of his footfalls die away, another, caught unawares, smacked into the pavement at exactly the moment his next stride would have done.

'Who's there?' Linder looked round, seeking the source of the sound, but the shadows between the waylights kept their secrets. Unbidden, his hand sought the suddenly comforting weight of the gun. 'Come on out!'

No one answered. Feeling vaguely foolish, and inclined to blame his fears on an overactive imagination, Linder began walking again, listening to the steady beat of echoes against the enclosing brickwork. His hand curled round the butt of the autopistol, the small excrescence of the safety catch snuggled against the ball of his thumb.

Abruptly he turned, looking back the way he'd come, and was rewarded with a flash of movement, just leaving the pool of luminescence cast by the waylight behind him. Emboldened by the feel of the weapon in his hand, he took a step towards it, drawing the gun as he did so.

'Who are you?' he shouted. But the only answer he got was the slithering of shoe soles against cobbles, as his unseen pursuer turned and fled. A dark robe billowed for a moment in the cone of lamplight, and the diminishing echo of hurrying footsteps rebounded from the surrounding walls.

I suppose most men of Linder's profession would have resumed their journey at that point, perhaps with a brief prayer of thanks to the Throne for their deliverance, but, as I've noted before, he could be a stubborn fellow when the mood took him; and it took him then. Without any thought for his safety, he ran after the fleeting shadow, pausing now and then to catch his breath, and listen out for the fugitive echoes. The pursuit took him away from the thoroughfare he'd been following, ever deeper into a maze of alleyways, and thence inside the rising slope of the hive spine. He was vague about the details of the route he took, but I was able to reconstruct it later, bringing us to the market hall where he finally confronted his quarry.

At that hour it was still deserted, the stalls shuttered and empty, but the floodlamps in the ceiling had been kindled, ready for the vendors to set out their wares, and Linder blinked in the sudden brightness. As his dazzled eyes adjusted, he heard more footfalls echoing between the stands, and rounded the corner of the nearest row, aiming the gun ahead of him.

'Stop. Or I'll shoot.'

A hooded figure in a night-blue robe was crouched over a manhole cover in the middle of the aisle, frozen in the act of lifting it aside. It straightened slowly, and began to turn.

'Would you really, Zale?' The words were delivered in an amused drawl, as though the speaker was waiting for the punchline of a joke. 'You should never make a threat you're not prepared to carry out, you know. It makes you look weak.'

'Harl?' Linder lowered the weapon, stupefied with astonishment. 'What's going on?'

'I'm sure Milena filled you in,' Sitrus said, with a dismissive glance at the gun. 'You must have made quite an impression on her. She doesn't usually let other people play with her toys.'

'She told me what you did for her,' Linder said, tucking the weapon away, with a sudden flare of embarrassment.

Sitrus shrugged. 'It wasn't hard. I'd been thinking for some time about how you could match up a dormant identity with just about anyone, and she seemed the perfect person to give it a try.'

'Feris doesn't seem to feel that way,' Linder said, trying to assimilate this new and unexpected development. 'If he finds you, he'll charge you with record falsification at the very least.'

'Feris couldn't catch a cold showering naked in a blizzard,' Sitrus said, with tolerant amusement. He glanced down at the manhole next to his feet. 'But if you want to continue this conversation without interruption, we'd better get below. He's annoyingly persistent, and he's bound to have watchers trailing you.'

'Why me?' Linder asked, feeling his way down a rickety ladder. After a couple of metres his shoe soles scraped rockcrete, and he stepped aside to let his friend descend after him. The pillar of light from above cut off with a scrape and a clank as Sitrus replaced the iron cover, and the dimmer illumination of sparsely scattered glow-globes replaced it.

'Because you might lead him to me,' Sitrus said, the smile Linder had pictured so recently visible on his face as he stepped off the ladder into the gloom-shrouded tunnel. 'You really are out of your depth here, aren't you?'

'Of course I am!' Linder snapped. 'I'm a scribe, not some dreg from the underhive! I'm not used to this kind of thing.'

'You seem to have more of a knack for it than you think,' Sitrus said. 'Which is why I took the risk of bringing you here.'

'In case you hadn't noticed, I was chasing you,' Linder said.

Sitrus smiled again. 'It saved a lot of explanation. If I'd approached you in the open, you'd start asking questions, and we'd still be talking when Feris's plodders turned up. But I had intended getting a lot closer to this little bolthole before I let you see me.' He nodded appreciatively. 'You're full of surprises, Zale.'

'Then I'm not the only one.' Linder fell into step with his friend, strolling along the dank utility duct as though they were ambling through a garden together. 'What are you going to do now?'

'Keep my head down, and wait for Feris to die of old age.' Sitrus smiled again. 'I set up a nice new life for myself before I erased the old one. I've got money, and connections, and I can well afford a juvenat or two.'

'Then why do you want to talk to me?' Linder asked, as they descended a ramp into a vaulted brick gallery lined with humming power relays.

'Because I trust you,' Sitrus said, 'and you were able to find Milena. I'd like you to pass on a message for me.'

'Of course,' Linder said. 'She's worried sick about you.'

'Then you won't mind putting her mind at rest. Just tell her I'm safe, and I've left the hive. Can you do that?'

'Consider it done,' Linder said. They were crossing a deep channel of lichen-encrusted brick, along which some thick tarry liquid flowed sluggishly into the distance, their footsteps ringing on the metal mesh bridge spanning it. 'Is there anything else?'

'I doubt it,' Sitrus said, the half-contemptuous smile back on his face. 'You're already sticking your neck out more than you're comfortable with.'

'I'll decide what I'm comfortable with,' Linder snapped. For the last year he'd been living outside the shadow cast by his friend, and he'd forgotten how annoyingly superior he could sometimes seem.

'Good for you.' Sitrus stopped walking, and looked at him appraisingly in the light from a nearby glow-globe. They'd reached a nexus of tunnels, half a dozen radiating from the circular chamber they found themselves in. When he spoke again, his voice was lower. 'There are plenty more like Milena, you know. Desperate, with nowhere to turn; and I can't help them anymore. But if you're willing to take the risk, you could.'

'Me?' For a moment Linder was too stunned even to speak; when he forced the syllable out, it sounded more like a strangulated gasp than an intelligible word.

Sitrus nodded. 'You could give them their lives back, Zale.' Then he shrugged. 'Somebody's life, anyway. It's got to be better than the one they have now.'

'Falsify records?' Linder felt nauseous at the very idea. 'No, I couldn't.'

'No, I don't suppose you could.' Sitrus gave him the look again, and a flare of resentment took Linder by surprise. It had been like that for as long as he could remember, Sitrus taking it for granted that he lacked the guts to follow where he led.

'Suppose I was able to help,' he said, surprising himself almost as much as Sitrus, judging by the unfamiliar expression of astonishment on his friend's face. 'How would I go about it?'

'You'd have to go through me,' Sitrus said. 'At least to begin with. I've got the contacts in place, and the dispossessed trust me.' He looked at Linder appraisingly again. 'No offence, Zale, but these are damaged people, who don't give their confidence easily. You'll have to earn it.'

'None taken,' Linder said, before honesty compelled him to add, 'I'm not promising to do it, Harl. But I will think about it.'

'That's all I can reasonably expect.' Sitrus clapped him playfully on the back. 'You're a good man, Zale. I know you'll make the right choice.'

'I hope so.' Linder coughed uncomfortably. 'When I do decide, how do I let you know?'

'Ask Milena to hang something red from the second-floor balcony. When I hear it's there, I'll arrange a meeting, and we can discuss the details.'

'Something red. Right.' Linder nodded.

'Good.' Sitrus turned away, then paused, and indicated one of the tunnel mouths facing them. 'Head down that way for about three hundred metres, and you'll find a green access hatch. It opens into the tertiary storage area of the scriptorium.' Then he smiled again, the familiar mocking expression returning to his face. 'So you would have had time for that caffeine you were thinking about after all.'

Then he was gone, only the fading echo of his footsteps remaining.

'I'm a little disappointed,' I said, strolling into Linder's cubicle unannounced. 'I thought we had an agreement.'

'An agreement?' he responded, setting aside the hardprint he'd been annotating, with a deliberation which made it plain my visit was less of a surprise than I'd hoped.

I nodded, taking up my former position against the door. I didn't think he'd make a run for it, but there was no harm in closing off the option. 'To inform me if you heard from Harl Sitrus. I could count on it, apparently.'

'As you can see,' he returned, 'I'm rather busy. And I don't recall agreeing to speak to you immediately.'

'Fair enough,' I conceded. 'I should have emphasised the urgency of the matter. But you don't deny you spoke to him this morning?'

'No, I don't,' he returned levelly.

'And the substance of the conversation?'

'Was personal.' The fractional hesitation was enough to betray that he was holding something back, but they always do at first. 'He asked me to reassure Miss Dravere that he's safe and well, which I agreed to do.'

'How kind.' I shifted the focus of the questions. 'And did you discuss the charges against him?'

Linder nodded, reluctantly. 'We did. It seems I owe you an apology.'

'Accepted, of course,' I assured him. 'So he admitted it?'

'He told me he'd falsified a few records. As you can imagine, it came as rather a shock.'

'I imagine it did,' I said, trying to sound sympathetic. 'And was he any more specific than that?'

'He said he'd been giving the identities of people killed in the war to destitute refugees. I can't condone it, but he does seem to have been acting out of a misguided sense of altruism.'

'Then it seems he's been a little selective with his recollections,' I replied, wishing there was somewhere else to sit. 'Did he mention how we got on to his activities in the first place?'

Linder shifted uncomfortably in his seat. 'That didn't come up in the conversation,' he admitted.

'No,' I said, 'somehow I didn't think it would. It was when a man named Werther Geist returned to Kannack a couple of months ago, after an absence of nearly three years. Geist's quite wealthy as it happens, with interests all over Verghast, and the last anyone heard of him, he was visiting Vervunhive. So of course he was listed among the missing.' I paused, groping automatically in my pocket for a packet of lho-sticks, before remembering I was definitely giving them up again. Probably a bad idea to light one up surrounded by a million tonnes of paper anyway. 'The thing of it was, he left a couple of hours before the Ferrozoican attack, and ended up in Hiraldi, where he got mobilised along with a whole bunch of the local auxiliaries. And once the security situation eased, he got kicked back into civilian clothes again. Are you with me so far?'

Linder nodded. 'So when he returned to Kannack, he found another Geist already living in his house?'

'Got it in one,' I told him. 'But the thing is, they could both prove they were the genuine Geist. In the end we had to run a genetic comparison to find out who the imposter was.'

'Which I take it you did,' Linder said, sounding genuinely interested.

I nodded. 'The really interesting thing was who he turned out to be. He was a refugee, right enough. But from Ferrozoica.'

I watched Linder's face crumble. He shook his head. 'That can't be right. Harl would never help one of them.'

'But he did. I can show you the transcripts if you like.' In the end I did, just to prove the point, but I could see at the time he believed me. 'Once he realised we were going to turn the case over to the Inquisition, our suspect got positively voluble. Laid out the whole thing for us step by step. What Sitrus was doing, and how much he charged for the privilege.'

'How much?' Linder was getting angry again, but it didn't seem directed at me this time.

'Ten per cent of the assets the new identity had access to. Seems like a bargain to me,' I said.

'And how many ten per cents do you think he collected?' Linder asked, his voice thickening.

'I've no idea,' I admitted. 'I suspect his lady friend was one, but I can't prove it.'

'Then why haven't you arrested her?' Linder asked.

'Because the Arbites isn't the Inquisition,' I explained. 'We serve the law, and we operate within the letter of it at all times. Without evidence, I've no grounds to detain her. I've got a list of names as long as your arm who reappeared suddenly after being presumed dead, but I can't move against any of them either.'

'So you need Harl,' Linder said.

'I do.' I nodded slowly. 'And I'm open to suggestions.'

'Thank you,' Milena said. She was smiling, but there were tears on her face. 'Just to know he's all right...'

Linder shuffled his feet, uncomfortable with the display of emotion. 'I'm sure you'll see him again soon,' he said awkwardly.

'I don't have a soon,' Milena said, matter-of-factly.

'I'm sorry?' Linder felt his face twist in a frown of confusion.

'I'm dying, Zale. For Throne's sake, haven't you worked it out? I was only a couple of kilometres from a nuclear explosion!'

'The radiation,' Linder said, with sudden understanding.

'That's right.' Milena nodded. 'I'm getting the best care money can buy, but all it can do in the end is manage the pain.'

'How long?' Linder asked, regretting the question at once. But Milena didn't seem to mind.

'Who knows?' She shrugged. 'None of us do really. But I definitely won't see the end of the year.'

'I'm sorry.' Linder took her hand, hoping the gesture would convey what he couldn't find the words for. She smiled wanly, and returned the pressure for a moment, before withdrawing it.

'Thank you. Come to the funeral, if you can stand it. I'd like to think I'll have a friend there now Harl's gone.'

'I will,' Linder said. He probably hesitated after that, conscience, duty and friendship contending for the last time within him. Then he went on. 'Do you have something red in the house?'

Sitrus hadn't mentioned how he intended getting in touch again, so when a standard missive capsule dropped from the pneumatic tube over his desk, Linder's first thought was that it was simply another piece of paperwork to deal with. Only when he unrolled the scrip inside did he discover otherwise.

Tunnels behind the scriptorium, he read. The message was unsigned, but the handwriting was unmistakably Sitrus's. His heart hammering, he left the cubicle.

It took him several minutes to reach the green access hatch he remembered; when he did so it was ajar. Pulling it open enough to admit himself, he scrambled through, then drew it almost closed again behind him, leaving only a faint filament of light to sketch its position in the wall.

'Harl?' Only echoes answered him, chasing one another down the dimly lit passageways. Then he saw the fresh impression of an arrow, scored into the crumbling brickwork opposite the hatchway. It pointed in the opposite direction to the section he'd traversed before, but the corridor was broad and high enough to walk down unobstructed, so he followed the mute instruction without hesitation.

After a few moments it opened out into a wide, circular chamber, with passageways leading off from it at the cardinal points of the compass. It was high, with a ceiling of domed industrial brick some forty or fifty metres overhead, and a series of galleries circled the walls, connected by a pair of spiralling staircases which mirrored one another all the way up the shaft. Each gallery also gave on to a number of tunnel mouths, four or six generally, although a couple seemed to have as many as eight.

'You took your time,' Sitrus said, in what seemed no more than a normal conversational tone. Fooled by the acoustics, Linder glanced around, expecting to find his friend a few paces away; only when the words were followed by a chuckle of amusement did he look up, to find him leaning casually on the balustrade of a gallery three levels above.

'I came as quickly as I could,' Linder replied, without raising his voice either. The cavernous space lent it a faintly echoing timbre, but it carried clearly. He began to walk towards the nearest staircase. 'Interesting place for a meeting.'

'It works well,' Sitrus said. 'Plenty of exits if you didn't come alone.' He was strolling casually as he talked, keeping the width of the chamber between them, and scanning the tunnel mouth behind Linder with wary eyes.

'Who would I bring?' Linder asked.

'Well, it did cross my mind you'd invite Feris,' Sitrus said.

Linder began to climb the stairway. 'He came to see me. Same old story, with a few fresh embellishments. I think he was hoping I'd turn you in.'

'More than likely.' Sitrus began to climb the steps on the other side, maintaining the distance between them. 'So you thought about what I said.'

'I did.' Linder reached the first gallery, and began to circle it, tilting his head back to keep his friend in sight. 'But I'm still a little unclear about something.'

'And what might that be?' Sitrus asked, a wary edge entering his voice.

'Whether helping Milena was really the first time you'd falsified records. I checked her new idents, and the substitution was flawless.'

'I'd massaged a few files before,' Sitrus admitted, unabashed. 'It's easy once you know how. I'm surprised everyone doesn't do it.'

Linder fought down his instinctive revulsion, keeping his voice as calm as he could, thanking the Emperor for the echoes which helped him to conceal his feelings. 'And what files would those be? Your own personal ones?' Which would explain Sitrus's rapid rise to a position of influence within the Administratum.

'Of course,' Sitrus admitted. 'You know how it is. You need every little edge you can get if you want to get on.'

'And any others?' Linder persisted.

'A few. I smoothed a few career bumps for you, for instance.'

'Me?' This time Linder wasn't quite able to conceal his shock, prompting another indulgent chuckle from above.

'You surely didn't believe you got where you are on merit, did you?'

'It had crossed my mind,' Linder said, refusing to rise to the bait. Sitrus was goading him, that was all, trying to assess his trustworthiness. 'But if you helped, I won't be resigning on principle.'

'Good man,' Sitrus said. 'Anything else bothering you?'

'Just one thing,' Linder said, starting up the next staircase. 'Werther Geist. Did you know you were helping a Ferrozoican?'

Sitrus shrugged. 'Omelettes and eggs, Zale. You know how it is.'

'Yes, I'm afraid I do.' Linder shook his head. 'You know the worst part?'

'I'm sure you're going to tell me.' Sitrus was moving more quickly now, towards a tunnel mouth. It was now or never.

'I wanted to believe you.' Linder drew the little pistol Milena had given him. 'However convincing Feris was, I kept telling myself that at least you meant well.'

'I'll take that as a no, then, shall I?' The smile was back on Sitrus's face. 'I knew you'd be too spineless to go through with it. But I let myself hope a little too. So much we could have done together, Zale; so much money we could have made.' He waved, mockingly. 'Enjoy your files; it's all you were ever really fit for.'

'Stop or I'll shoot!' Linder shouted, seeing his former friend about to flee. Footsteps were hurrying along the tunnel behind him, and with a surge of relief he realised I'd got his message after all.

'Of course you will,' Sitrus said mockingly, turning to leave.

Linder never remembered firing the gun in his hand; just a loud report, which deafened him for a moment, and a jolt as though someone had punched him in the arm. To this day I'm convinced he never intended to hit his former friend, just startle him, but the tech-priest's blessing must have been a strong one; because, when he looked again, Sitrus was staggering, an expression of stunned disbelief on his face.

'Harl!' Linder ran for the stairs, as Sitrus took a couple of steps towards the nearest tunnel mouth, and collapsed to the floor. By the time I joined them, Sitrus's face was grey, and he was fighting for breath.

'Hell of a time to grow a backbone, Zale,' he said, the sardonic smile flickering on his face for the last time.

Linder turned an anguished face in my direction. 'Call a medicae!' he implored.

'On the way,' I said calmly, although if the voices in my comm-bead were right about their location, they'd find nothing but a corpse when they arrived. I knelt on the grubby brickwork, next to Sitrus. 'How many other Ferrozoicans did you give new identities to? You know every damn one of them will be tainted by Chaos. Do you want to face the Emperor with that on your conscience?'

'You're so clever, you work it out,' Sitrus said. Then he turned to Linder. 'Tell Milena I'll see her again sooner than we thought.'

'I'll tell her,' Linder said, his voice quaking; but I doubt that Sitrus ever heard.

I couldn't close the case without a formal identification of the body; and as the closest thing Sitrus had to next of kin on Verghast was Milena, I had to ask her. She held up well, all things considered, only showing signs of emotion when Linder gave her Sitrus's final message. She heard him out without speaking, then nodded curtly.

'Remember what I said about my funeral?' she asked.

'Of course,' Linder said.

'I'd rather you didn't come after all.' Then she swept out of the Sector House like a mourning-clad storm front.

'What now?' Linder asked, looking faintly dazed, which I could hardly blame him for.

'Now we do it the hard way,' I said. 'Go back to our list of suspects, and pull their records apart. Check for any anomalies, however small, that might indicate they're not who they say they are.' I looked at him appraisingly. 'Your expertise would be very useful, if the Administratum can spare you.'

'I'll make sure they can,' he said. 'But what about Milena? Aren't you going to bring her in?'

I shook my head. 'She's a low priority,' I said. 'We know she's not from Ferrozoica, so she'll keep. We'll get around to her case in a year or two.' Technically, I suppose, that was Obstruction of Justice, but there was no point in prosecuting her; she'd be dead before the case came to trial. Like I said, everyone's guilty of something, even me.

Linder looked at me strangely. 'You're a good man,' he said.

HELL NIGHT

Nick Kyme

It can't rain all the time...

The trooper's mood was sullen as he helped drag the unlimbered lascannon through the mire.

The Earthshakers had begun their bombardment. A slow and steady *crump-crump* – stop – *crump-crump* far behind him at the outskirts of bastion headquarters made the trooper flinch instinctively every time a shell whined overhead.

It was ridiculous: the deadly cargo fired by the siege guns was at least thirty metres at the apex of its trajectory, yet still he ducked.

Survival was high on the trooper's list of priorities, that and service to the Emperor of course.

Ave Imperator.

A cry to the trooper's right, though muffled by the droning rain, got his attention. He turned, rivulets teeming off his nose like at the precipice of a waterfall, and saw the lascannon had foundered. One of its carriage's rear wheels was sunk in mud, sucked into an invisible bog.

'Bostok, gimme a hand.'

Another trooper, Genk, an old guy – a *lifer* – grimaced to Bostok as he tried to wedge the butt of his lasgun under the trapped wheel and use it like a lever.

Tracer fire was whipping overhead, slits of magnesium carving up the darkness. It sizzled and spat when it pierced the sheeting rain.

Bostok grumbled. Staying low, he tramped over heavily to help his fellow gunner. Adding his own weapon to the hopeful excavation, he pushed down and tried to work his way under the wheel.

'Get it deeper,' urged Genk, the lines in his weathered face becoming dark crevices with every distant flash-flare of siege shells striking the void shield.

Though each hit brought a fresh blossom of energy rippling across the shield, the city's defences were holding. If the 135th Phalanx was to breach it – for the Emperor's glory and righteous will – they'd need to bring more firepower to bear.

'*Overload the generators,*' Sergeant Harver had said.

'*Bring our guns close,*' he'd said. '*Orders from Colonel Tench.*'

Not particularly subtle, but then they were the Guard, the Hammer of the Emperor: blunt was what the common soldiery did best.

Genk was starting to panic: they were falling behind.

Across a killing field dug with abandoned trenches, tufts of razor wire protruding like wild gorse in some untamed prairie, teams of Phalanx troopers dragged heavy weapons or marched hastily in squad formation.

It took a lot of men to break a siege; more still, and with artillery support, to bring down a fully functioning void shield. Men the Phalanx had: some ten thousand souls willing to sacrifice their lives for the glory of the Throne; the big guns – leastways the shells for the big guns – they did not. A Departmento Munitorum clerical error had left the battle group short some fifty thousand anti-tank, arrowhead shells. Fewer shells meant more boots and bodies. A more aggressive strategy was taken immediately: all lascannons and heavy weapons to advance to five hundred metres and lay void shield-sapping support fire.

Bad luck for Phalanx: wars were easier to fight from behind distant crosshairs. And safer. Bad luck for Bostok, too.

Though he was working hard at freeing the gun with Genk, he noticed some of their comrades falling to the defensive return fire of the secessionist rebels, holed up and cosy behind their shield and their armour and their fraggin' gun emplacements.

Bastards.

Bet they're dry too, Bostok thought ruefully. His slicker came undone when he snagged it on the elevation winch of the lascannon and he swore loudly as the downpour soaked his red-brown standard-issue uniform beneath.

There was a muted cry ahead as he fastened up the slicker and pulled his wide-brimmed helmet down further to keep out the worst of the rain – a heavy bolter team and half an infantry squad disappeared from view, seemingly swallowed by the earth. Some of the old firing pits and trenches had been left unfilled, except now they contained muddy water and sucking earth. As deadly as quicksand they were.

Bostok muttered a prayer, making the sign of the aquila. Least it wasn't him and Genk.

'Eye be damned, what is holding you up, troopers?'

It was Sergeant Harver. The tumult was deafening, that and the artillery exchange. He had to bellow just to be heard. Not that Harver ever did anything but bellow when addressing his squad.

'Get this fraggin' rig moving you sump rats,' he barracked, 'You're lagging troopers, lagging.'

Harver munched a fat, vine-leaf cigar below the black wire of his twirled moustache. He didn't seem to mind or notice that it had long been doused and hung like a fat, soggy finger from the corner of his mouth.

A static crackle from the vox-operator's comms unit interrupted the sergeant's tirade.

'More volume: louder Rhoper, louder.'

Rhoper, the vox-operator, nodded, before setting the unit down and fiddling with a bunch of controls. The receiver was amplified in a few seconds and returned with the voice of Sergeant Rampe.

'*...Enemy sighted! They're here in no-man's land! Bastards are out beyond the shield! I see, oh sh–*'

'Rampe, Rampe,' Harver bellowed into the receiver cup. 'Respond, man!' His attention switched to Rhoper.

'Another channel, trooper – at the double, if you please.'

Rhoper was already working on it. The comms channels linking the infantry squads to artillery command and one another flicked by in a mixture of static, shouting and oddly muted gunfire.

At last, they got a response.

'*...aggin' out here with us! Throne of Earth, that's not poss–*'

The voice stopped but the link continued unbroken. There was more distant weapons fire, and something else.

'Did I hear–' Harver began.

'Bells, sir,' offered Rhoper, in a rare spurt of dialogue. 'It was bells ringing.'

Static killed the link and this time Harver turned to Trooper Bostok, who had all but given up trying to free the lascannon.

The bells hadn't stopped. They were on this part of the battlefield too.

'Could be the sounds carrying on the wind, sir?' suggested Genk, caked in mud from his efforts.

Too loud, too close to be just the wind, thought Bostok. He took up his lasgun as he turned to face the dark.

Silhouettes lived there, jerking in stop-motion with every void impact flare – they were his comrades, those who had made it to the five hundred metre line.

Bostok's eyes narrowed.

There was something else out there too. Not guns or Phalanx, not even rebels.

It was white, rippling and flowing on an unseen breeze. The rain was so dense it just flattened; the air didn't zephyr, there were no eddies skirling across the killing ground.

'Sarge, do we 'ave Ecclesiarchy in our ranks?'

'Negative, trooper, just the Emperor's own: boots, bayonets and blood.'

Bostok pointed towards the flicker of white.

'Then who the frag is that?'

But the flicker had already gone. Though the bells tolled on. Louder and louder.

Fifty metres away, men were screaming. And running.

Bostok saw their faces through his gun sight, saw the horror written there. Then they were gone. He scanned the area, using his scope like a magnocular, but couldn't find them. At first Bostok thought they'd fallen foul of an earth ditch, like the heavy bolter and infantry he'd seen earlier, but he could see no ditches, no trench or fire pit that could've swallowed them. But they'd been claimed all right, claimed by whatever moved amongst them.

More screaming; merging with the bells into a disturbing clamour.

It put the wind up Sergeant Harver – Phalanx soldiers were disappearing in all directions.

'Bostok, Genk, get that cannon turned about,' he ordered, slipping out his service pistol.

The lascannon was well and truly stuck, but worked on a pintle mount, so could be swivelled into position. Genk darted around the carriage, not sure what was happening but falling back on orders to anchor himself and stave off rising terror. He yanked out the holding pin with more force than was necessary and swung the gun around towards the white flickers and the screaming, just as his sergeant requested.

'Covering fire, Mr Rhoper,' added Harver, and the vox-operator slung the boxy comms unit on his back and drew his lasgun, crouching in a shooting position just behind the lascannon.

Bostok took up his post by the firing shield, slamming a fresh power cell into the heavy weapon's breech.

'Lit and clear!'

'At your discretion, trooper,' said Harver.

Genk didn't need a written invitation. He sighted down the barrel and the targeting nub, seeing a flicker, and hauled back the triggers.

Red beams, hot and angry, ripped up the night. Genk laid suppressing fire in a forward arc that smacked of fear and desperation. He was sweating by the end of his salvo, and not from the heat discharge.

The bells were tolling still, though it was impossible to place their origin. The void-shrouded city was too far away, a black smudge on an already dark canvas, and the resonant din sounded close and all around them.

Cordite wafted on the breeze; cordite and screaming.

Bostok tried to squint past the driving rain, more effective than any camo-paint for concealment.

The flickers were still out there, ephemeral and indistinct... and they were closing.

'Again, if you please,' ordered Harver, an odd tremor affecting his voice. It took Bostok a few seconds to recognise it as fear.

'Lit and clear!' he announced, slamming in a second power cell.

'Not stopping, sir,' said Rhoper and sighted down his lasgun before firing.

Sergeant Harver responded by loosing his own weapon, pistol cracks adding to the fusillade.

Casting about, Bostok found they were alone; an island of Phalanx in a sea of mud, but the advanced line was coming to meet them. They were fleeing, driven wild by sheer terror. Men were disappearing as they ran, sucked under the earth, abruptly silenced.

'Sarge…' Bostok began.

Onwards the line came, something moving within it, preying on it like piranhas stalking a shoal of frightened fish.

Harver was nearly gone, just firing on impulse now. Some of his shots and that of Genk's lascannon were tearing up their own troops.

Rhoper still had his wits, and came forwards as the heavy weapon ran dry.

'F-f…' Harver was saying when Bostok got to his feet and ran like hell.

Rhoper disappeared a moment later. No cries for help, no nothing; just a cessation of his lasgun fire and then silence to show for the end of the doughty vox-officer.

Heart hammering in his chest, his slicker having now parted and exposing him to the elements, Bostok ran, promising never to bemoan his lot again, if the Emperor would just spare him this time, spare him from being pulled into the earth and buried alive. He didn't want to die like that.

Bostok must've been dragging his feet, because troopers from the advanced line were passing him. A trooper disappeared to his left, a white flicker and the waft of something old and dank presaging his demise. Another, just ahead, was pulled asunder, and Bostok jinked away from a course that would lead him into that path. He risked a glance over his shoulder. Harver and Genk were gone – the lascannon was still mired but now abandoned – fled or taken, he didn't know.

Some of the Phalanx were staging a fighting withdrawal. Gallant, but what did they have to hold off? It was no enemy Bostok had ever seen or known.

Running was all that concerned him now, running for his life.

Just reach the artillery batteries and I'll be fine.

But then a hollow cry echoed ahead, and Bostok saw a white flicker around the siege guns. A tanker disappeared under the earth, his cap left on the grille of the firing platform.

The fat lump of numbing panic in his chest rose into Bostok's throat and threatened to choke him.

Can't go back, can't go forwards…

He peeled off to the left. Maybe he could take a circuitous route to bastion headquarters.

No, too long. They'd be on him before then.

In the dark and the rain, he couldn't even see the mighty structure. No beacon-lamps to guide him, no searchlights to cling to. Death, like the darkness, was closing.

The bells were tolling.

Men screamed.

Bostok ran, his vision fragmenting in sheer terror, the pieces collapsing in on one another like a kaleidoscope.

Got to get away... Please Throne, oh pl–

Earth became swamp beneath his feet, and Bostok sank. He panicked, thinking he was about to be taken, when he realised he'd fallen into an earth ditch, right up to his chin. Fighting the urge to wade across, he dipped lower until the muddy water reached his nose, filling his nostrils with a rank and stagnant odour. Clinging to the edge with trembling, bone-cold fingers, he prayed to the Emperor for the end of the night, for the end of the rain and the cessation of the bells.

But the bells didn't stop. They just kept on tolling.

Three weeks later...

'Fifty metres to landfall,' announced Hak'en. The pilot's voice sounded tinny through the vox-speaker in the Chamber Sanctuarine of *Fire-wyvern*. Looking through the occuliport in the gunship's flank, Dak'ir saw a grey day, sheeting with rain.

Hak'en was bringing the vessel around, flying a course that would take them within a few metres of Mercy Rock, the headquarters of the 135th Phalanx and the Imperial forces they were joining on Vaporis. As the gunship banked, angling Dak'ir's slit-view downward, a sodden earth field riddled with dirty pools and sludge-like emplacements was revealed. The view came in frustrating slashes.

Dak'ir was curious to see more.

'Brother,' he addressed the vox-speaker, 'open up the embarkation ramp.'

'As you wish, brother-sergeant. Landfall in twenty metres.'

Hak'en disengaged the locking protocols that kept the Thunderhawk's hatches sealed during transit. As the operational rune went green, Dak'ir punched it and the ramp started to open and lower.

Light and air rushed into the gunship's troop compartment where Dak'ir's battle-brothers were sat in meditative silence. Even in the grey dawn, their bright green battle-plate flashed, the snarling firedrake icon on their left pauldrons – orange on a black field – revealing them to be Salamanders of the Third Company.

As well as illuminating their power armour, the feeble light also managed to banish the glare from their eyes. Blazing red with captured fire, it echoed the heat of the Salamanders' volcanic home world, Nocturne.

'A far cry from the forge-pits under Mount Deathfire,' groaned Ba'ken.

Though he couldn't see his face beneath the battle-helm he was wearing, Dak'ir knew his brother also wore a scowl at the inclement weather.

'Wetter too,' added Emek, coming to stand beside the hulking form of Ba'ken and peering over Dak'ir's broad shoulders. 'But then what else are we to expect from a monsoon world?'

The ground was coming to meet them and as Hak'en straightened up *Fire-wyvern* the full glory of Mercy Rock was laid before them.

It might once have been beautiful, but now the bastion squatted like an ugly gargoyle in a brown mud-plain. Angular gun towers, bristling with autocannon and heavy stubber, crushed the angelic spires that had once soared into the turbulent Vaporis sky; ablative armour concealed murals and baroque columns; the old triumphal gate, with its frescos and ornate filigree, had been replaced with something grey, dark and practical. These specific details were unknown to Dak'ir, but he could see in the structure's curves an echo of its architectural bearing, hints of something artful and not merely functional.

'I see we are not the only recent arrivals,' said Ba'ken. The other Salamanders at the open hatch followed his gaze to where a black Valkyrie gunship had touched down in the mud, its landing stanchions slowly sinking.

'Imperial Commissariat,' replied Emek, recognising the official seal on the side of the transport.

Dak'ir kept his silence. His eyes strayed across the horizon to the distant city of Aphium and the void dome surrounding it. Even above the droning gunship engines, he could hear the hum of generatoria powering the field. It was like those which protected the Sanctuary Cities of his home world from the earthquakes and volcanic eruptions that were a way of life for the hardy folk of Nocturne. The air was thick with the stench of ozone; another by-product of the void fields. Even the constant rain couldn't wash it away.

As *Fire-wyvern* came in to land with a scream of stabiliser-jets, Dak'ir closed his eyes. Rain was coming in through the hatch and he let it patter against his armour. The dulcet ring of it was calming. Rain – at least the cool, wet, non-acidic kind – was rare on Nocturne, and even against his armour he enjoyed the sensation. There was an undercurrent of something else that came with it, though. It was unease, disquiet, a sense of watchfulness.

I feel it too, a voice echoed inside Dak'ir's head, and his eyes snapped open again. He turned to find Brother Pyriel watching him intently. Pyriel was a Librarian, a wielder of the psychic arts, and he could read people's thoughts as they might read an open book. The psyker's eyes flashed cerulean-blue before returning to burning red. Dak'ir didn't like the idea of him poking around in his subconscious, but he sensed that

Pyriel had merely browsed the surface of his mind. Even still, Dak'ir looked away and was glad when the earth met them at last and *Fire-wyvern* touched down.

The cold snap of las-fire carried on the breeze as the Salamanders debarked.

Across the muddied field, just fifty metres from the approach road to Mercy Rock, a commissarial firing squad was executing a traitor.

An Imperial Guard colonel, wearing the red-brown uniform of the Phalanx, jerked spastically as the hot rounds struck him, and was still. Tied to a thick, wooden pole, he slumped and sagged against his bonds. First his knees folded and he sank, then his head lolled forward, his eyes open and glassy.

A commissar, lord-level given his rank pins and trappings, was looking on as his bodyguards brought their lasguns to port arms and marched away from the execution site. His gaze met with Dak'ir's as he turned to go after them. Rain teemed off the brim of his cap, a silver skull stud sat in the centre above the peak. The commissar's eyes were hidden by the shadow the brim cast, but felt cold and rigid all the same. The Imperial officer didn't linger. He was already walking away, back to the bastion, as the last of the Salamanders mustered out and the exit ramps closed.

Dak'ir wondered at what events had delivered the colonel to such a bleak end, and was sorry to see *Fire-wyvern* lifting off again, leaving them alone in this place.

'Such is the fate of all traitors,' remarked Tsu'gan with a bitter tang.

Even behind his helmet lens, Tsu'gan's stare was hard. Dak'ir returned his glare.

There was no brotherly love between the two Salamanders sergeants. Before they became Space Marines, they had hailed from opposite ends of the Nocturnean hierarchy: Dak'ir, an Ignean cave-dweller and an orphan, the likes of which had never before joined the ranks of the Astartes; and Tsu'gan, a nobleman's son from the Sanctuary City of Hesiod, as close to aristocracy and affluence as it was possible to get on a volcanic death world. Though as sergeants they were both equals in the eyes of their captain and Chapter Master, Tsu'gan did not regard their relationship as such. Dak'ir was unlike many other Salamanders, there was a strain of humanity left within him that was greater and more empathic than that of his brothers. It occasionally left him isolated, almost disconnected. Tsu'gan had seen it often enough and decided it was not merely unusual, it was an aberration. Since their first mission as Scouts on the sepulchre world of Moribar, acrimony had divided them. In the years that followed, it had not lessened.

'It leaves a grim feeling to see men wasted like that,' said Dak'ir. 'Slain in cold blood without chance for reparation.'

Many Space Marine Chapters, the Salamanders among them, believed in order and punishment, but they also practised penitence and the opportunity for atonement. Only when a brother was truly lost, given in to the Ruinous Powers or guilty of such a heinous deed as could not be forgiven or forgotten, was death the only alternative.

'Then you'd best develop a stronger stomach, *Ignean*,' sneered Tsu'gan, fashioning the word into a slight, 'for your compassion is misplaced on the executioners' field.'

'It's no weakness, brother,' Dak'ir replied fiercely.

Pyriel deliberately walked between them to prevent any further hostility.

'Gather your squads, brother-sergeants,' the Librarian said firmly, 'and follow me.'

Both did as ordered, Ba'ken and Emek plus seven others falling in behind Dak'ir whilst Tsu'gan led another same-sized squad from the dropsite. One in Tsu'gan's group gave Dak'ir a vaguely contemptuous look, before turning his attention to an auspex unit. This was Iagon, Tsu'gan's second and chief minion. Where Tsu'gan was all thinly-veiled threat and belligerence, Iagon was an insidious snake, much more poisonous and deadly.

Dak'ir shrugged off the battle-brother's glare and motioned his squad forwards.

'I could see his attitude corrected, brother,' hissed Ba'ken over a closed comm-link channel feeding to Dak'ir's battle-helm. 'It would be a pleasure.'

'I don't doubt that, Ba'ken,' Dak'ir replied, 'but let's just try and stay friendly for now, shall we?'

'As you wish, sergeant.'

Behind his battle-helm, Dak'ir smiled. Ba'ken was his closest ally in the Chapter and he was eternally grateful that the hulking heavy weapons trooper was watching his back.

As they marched the final few metres to the bastion gates, Ba'ken's attention strayed to the void shield on the Salamanders' right. The commissar lord, along with his entourage, had already gone inside the Imperial command centre. Overhead, the skies were darkening and the rain intensified. Day was giving way to night.

'Your tactical assessment, Brother Ba'ken?' asked Pyriel, noting his fellow Salamander's interest in the shield.

'Constant bombardment – it's the only way to bring a void shield down.' He paused, thinking. 'That, or get close enough to slip through during a momentary break in the field and knock out the generatoria.'

Tsu'gan sniffed derisively.

'Then let us hope the humans can do just that, and get us to within striking distance, so we can leave this sodden planet.'

Dak'ir bristled at the other sergeant's contempt, but kept his feelings in check. He suspected it was half-meant as a goad, anyway.

'Tell me this, then, brothers,' added Pyriel, the gates of the bastion looming, 'why are they falling back with their artillery?'

At a low ridge, just below the outskirts of the bastion, Basilisk tanks were retreating. Their long cannons shrank away from the battlefield as the tanks found parking positions within the protective outer boundaries of the bastion.

'Why indeed?' Dak'ir asked himself as they passed through the slowly opening gates and entered Mercy Rock.

'Victory at Aphium will be won with strong backs, courage and the guns of our Immortal Emperor!'

The commissar lord was sermonising as the Salamanders appeared in the great bastion hall.

Dak'ir noticed the remnants of ornamental fountains, columns and mosaics – all reduced to rubble for the Imperial war machine.

The hall was a vast expanse and enabled the Imperial officer to address almost ten thousand men, mustered in varying states of battle-dress. Sergeants, corporals, line troopers, even the wounded and support staff had been summoned to the commissar's presence as he announced his glorious vision for the coming war.

To his credit, he barely flinched when the Astartes strode into the massive chamber, continuing on with his rallying cry to the men of the Phalanx who showed much greater reverence for the Emperor's Angels of Death amongst them.

The Fire-born had removed battle-helms as they'd entered, revealing onyx-black skin and red eyes that glowed dully in the half-dark. As well as reverence, several of the Guardsmen betrayed their fear and awe of the Salamanders. Dak'ir noticed Tsu'gan smiling thinly, enjoying intimidating the humans before them.

'*As potent as bolt or blade,*' old Master Zen'de had told them when they were neophytes. Except that Tsu'gan deployed such tactics all too readily; even against allies.

'Colonel Tench is dead,' the commissar announced flatly. 'He lacked the will and the purpose the Emperor demands of us. His legacy of largesse and cowardice is over.'

Like black-clad sentinels, the commissar's storm troopers eyed the men nearest their master at this last remark, daring them to take umbrage at the defamation of their former colonel.

The commissar's voice was amplified by a loudhailer and echoed around the courtyard, carrying to every trooper present. A small cadre of Phalanx officers, what was left of the command section, were standing to one side of the commissar, giving off stern and unyielding looks to the rest of their troops.

This was the Emperor's will – they didn't have to like it; they just had to do it.

'And any man who thinks otherwise had best look to the bloody fields beyond Mercy Rock, for that is the fate which awaits he without the courage to do what is necessary.' The commissar glared, baiting dissension. When none was forthcoming, he went on. 'I am taking command in the late colonel's stead. All artillery will return to the battlefront immediately. Infantry is to be mustered in platoon and ready for deployment as soon as possible. Section commanders are to report to me in the strategium. The Phalanx will mobilise tonight!' He emphasised this last point with a clenched fist.

Silence reigned for a few moments, before a lone voice rang out of the crowd.

'But tonight is Hell Night.'

Like a predator with its senses piqued, the commissar turned to find the voice.

'Who said that?' he demanded, stalking to the front of the rostrum where he was preaching. 'Make yourself known.'

'There are things in the darkness, things not of this world. I've seen 'em!' A gap formed around a frantic-looking trooper as he gesticulated to the others, his growing hysteria spreading. 'They took Sergeant Harver, took 'im! The spectres! Just sucked men under the earth... They'll ta–'

The loud report of the commissar's bolt pistol stopped the trooper in mid-flow. Blood and brain matter spattered the infantrymen nearest the now headless corpse as silence returned.

Dak'ir stiffened at such wanton destruction of life, and was about to step forward and speak his mind, before a warning hand from Pyriel stopped him.

Reluctantly, the Salamander backed down.

'This idle talk about spectres and shadows haunting the night will not be tolerated,' the commissar decreed, holstering his still-smoking pistol. 'Our enemies are flesh and blood. They occupy Aphium and when this city falls, we will open up the rest of the continent to conquest. The lord-governor of this world lies dead, assassinated by men he trusted. Seceding from the Imperium is tantamount to an act of war. This rebellion will be crushed and Vaporis will be brought back to the light of Imperial unity. Now, prepare for battle...'

The commissar looked down his nose at the headless remains of the dead trooper, now lying prone.

'...and somebody clear up that filth.'

'He'll demoralise these men,' hissed Dak'ir, anger hardening his tone.

Two infantrymen were dragging the corpse of the dead trooper away. His bloodied jacket bore the name: Bostok.

'It's not our affair,' muttered Pyriel, his keen gaze fixed on the commissar as he headed towards them.

'The mood is grim enough, though, Brother-Librarian,' said Ba'ken, surveying the weary lines of troopers as they fell in, marshalled by platoon sergeants.

'Something has them spooked,' snarled Tsu'gan, though more out of contempt for the Guardsmen's apparent weakness, than concern.

Pyriel stepped forward to greet the commissar, who'd reached the Salamanders from the end of the rostrum.

'My lord Astartes,' he said with deference, bowing before Pyriel. 'I am Commissar Loth, and if you would accompany me with your officers to the strategium, I will apprise you of the tactical situation here on Vaporis.'

Loth was about to move away, determined to send the message that he, and not the Emperor's Angels, was in charge at Mercy Rock, when Pyriel's voice, resonant with psy-power, stopped him.

'That won't be necessary, commissar.'

Loth didn't looked impressed at he stared at the Librarian. His expression demanded an explanation, which Pyriel was only too pleased to provide.

'We know our orders and the tactical disposition of this battle. Weaken the shield, get us close enough to deploy an insertion team in the vicinity of the generatoria and we will do the rest.'

'I– that is, I mean to say, very well. But do you not need–'

Pyriel cut him off.

'I do have questions, though. That man, the trooper you executed: what did he mean by "spectres", and what is Hell Night?'

Loth gave a dismissive snort.

'Superstition and scaremongering – these men have been lacking discipline for too long.' He was about to end it there when Pyriel's body language suggested the commissar should go on. Reluctantly, he did. 'Rumours, reports from the last night-attack against the secessionists, of men disappearing without trace under the earth and unnatural denizens prowling the battlefield. Hell Night is the longest nocturnal period in the Vaporan calendar – its longest night.'

'Tonight?'

'Yes.' Loth's face formed a scowl. 'It's sheer idiocy. Fearing the dark? Well, it's just damaging to the morale of the men in this regiment.'

'The former colonel, did he supply you with these... *reports*?'

Loth made a mirthless grin.

'He did.'

'And you had him shot for that?'

'As my duty binds me, yes, I did.' Loth had a pugilist's face, slab-flat with a wide, crushed nose and a scar that ran from top lip to hairline that pulled up the corner of his mouth in a snarl. His small ears, poking out from either side of his commissar's cap, were ragged. He was stolid when he spoke next. 'There is nothing lurking in the darkness except the false nightmares that dwell in the minds of infants.'

'I've seen nightmares made real before, commissar,' Pyriel took on a warning tone.

'Then we are fortunate to have angels watching over us.' Loth adjusted his cap and straightened his leather frockcoat. 'I'll weaken the shield, be assured of that, nightmares or no.'

'Then we'll see you on the field, commissar,' Pyriel told him, before showing his back and leaving Loth to wallow in impotent rage.

'You really took exception to him, didn't you brother?' said Emek a few minutes later, too curious to realise his impropriety. They were back out in the muddy quagmire. In the distance, the sound of battle tanks moving into position ground on the air.

'He had a callous disregard for human life,' Pyriel replied. 'And besides… his aura was bad.' He allowed a rare smirk at the remark, before clamping on his battle-helm.

Overhead, the sky was wracked with jagged red lightning and the clouds billowed crimson. Far above, in the outer atmosphere of Vaporis, a warp storm was boiling. It threw a visceral cast over the rain-slicked darkness of the battlefield.

'Hell Night, in more than just name it seems,' said Ba'ken, looking up to the bloody heavens.

'An inauspicious omen, perhaps?' offered Iagon, the first time he'd spoken since landfall.

'Ever the doomsayer,' remarked Ba'ken under his breath to his sergeant. But Dak'ir wasn't listening. He was looking at Pyriel.

'Form combat squads,' said the Librarian, when he realised he was under scrutiny. 'Tsu'gan, find positions.'

Tsu'gan slammed a fist against his plastron, and cast a last snide glance at Dak'ir before he divided up his squad and moved out at a steady run.

Dak'ir ignored him, still intent on Pyriel.

'Do you sense something, Brother-Librarian?'

Pyriel eyed the darkness in the middle distance, the no-man's-land between the bastion and the shimmering edge of the far off void shield. It was as if he was trying to catch a glimpse of something just beyond his reach, at the edge of natural sight.

'It's nothing.'

Dak'ir nodded slowly and mustered out. But he'd detected the lie in the Librarian's words and wondered what it meant.

False thunder wracked the sky from the report of heavy cannons at the rear of the Imperial battle line. Smoke hung over the muddied field like a shroud, occluding the bodies of the Phalanx troopers moving through it, but was quickly weighed down by the incessant rain.

They marched in platoons, captains and sergeants hollering orders over the defensive fire of rebel guns and the dense *thuds* of explosions. Heavy weapons teams, two men dragging unlimbered cannons whilst standard infantry ran alongside, forged towards emplacements dug five hundred metres from the shield wall.

Incandescent flashes rippled across the void shield with the dense shell impacts of the distant Earthshaker cannons and from lascannon and missile salvoes, unleashed when their crews had closed to the assault line.

In the midst of it all were the Salamanders, crouched down in cover, at the edges of the line in five-man combat squads.

Librarian Pyriel had joined Dak'ir's unit, making it six. With the flare of explosions and the red sky overhead, his blue armour was turned a lurid purple. It denoted his rank as Librarian, as did the arcane paraphernalia about his person.

'Our objective is close, brothers. There...' Pyriel indicated the bulk of a generatorium structure some thousand metres distant. Only Space Marines, with their occulobe implants, had the enhanced visual faculty to see and identify it. Rebel forces, hunkered down in pillboxes, behind trenches and fortified emplacements, guarded it. In the darkness and the rain, even with the superhuman senses of the Astartes, they were just shadows and muzzle flashes.

'We should take an oblique route, around the east and west hemispheres of the shield,' Dak'ir began. 'Resistance will be weakest there. We'll be better able to exploit it.'

After Tsu'gan had secured the route, the Salamanders had arrived at the five hundred metre assault line, having stealthed their way to it undetected before the full Imperial bombardment had begun. But they were positioned at the extreme edges of the line – two groups east, two groups west – in the hope of launching a shock assault into the heart of the rebel defenders and destroying the generatoria powering the void shield before serious opposition could be raised.

'Brother Pyriel?' Dak'ir pressed when a response wasn't forthcoming.

The Librarian was staring at the distant void shield, energy blossoms appearing on its surface only to dissipate seconds later.

'Something about the shield... An anomaly in its energy signature...' he breathed. His eyes were glowing cerulean-blue.

For once, Dak'ir felt nothing, just the urge to act.

'What is it?'

'I don't know...' The psychic fire dimmed in the Librarian's eyes behind his battle-helm. 'Oblique assault – one primary, one secondary. East and west,' he asserted.

Dak'ir nodded, but had a nagging feeling that Pyriel wasn't telling them everything. He opened a comm-channel to the other combat squads.

'We move in, brothers. Assault plan *serpentine*. Brother Apion, you are support. We will take primary. Brother Tsu'gan–'

'We are ready, Ignean,' came the harsh reply before Dak'ir had finished. 'Assault vector locked, I am the primary at the western hemisphere. Tsu'gan out.'

The link was cut abruptly. Dak'ir cursed under his breath.

Taking out his plasma pistol and unsheathing his chainsword, running a gauntleted finger down the flat of the blade and muttering a litany to Vulkan, Dak'ir rose to his feet.

'Fire-born, advance on my lead.'

Emek's raised fist brought them to a halt before they could move out. He had his finger pressed to the side of his battle-helm.

'I'm getting some frantic chatter from the Phalanx units.' He paused, listening intently. 'Contact has been lost with several secondary command units.' Then he looked up. During the pregnant pause, Dak'ir could sense what was coming next.

'They say they're under attack... from *spectres*,' said Emek.

'Patch it to all comms, brother. Every combat squad.'

Emek did as asked, and Dak'ir's battle-helm, together with his brothers', was filled with the broken reports from the Phalanx command units.

'...ergeant is dead. Falling back to secondary positions...'

'...all around us! Throne of Earth, I can't see a target, I can't se–'

'...ead, everyone. They're out here among us! Oh hell, oh Emperor sa–'

Scattered gunfire and hollow screams punctuated these reports. Some units were attempting to restore order. The barking commands of sergeants and corporals sounded desperate as they tried to reorganise in the face of sudden attack.

Commissar Loth's voice broke in sporadically, his replies curt and scathing. They must hold and then advance. The Imperium would brook no cowardice in the face of the enemy. Staggered bursts from his bolt pistol concluded each order, suggesting further executions.

Above and omnipresent, the sound of tolling bells filled the air.

'I saw no chapel or basilica in the Phalanx bastion,' said Ba'ken. He swept his gaze around slowly, panning with his heavy flamer as he did so.

'The rebels?' offered Brother Romulus.

'How do you explain it being everywhere?' asked Pyriel, his eyes aglow once more. He regarded the blood-red clouds that hinted at the churning warp storm above. 'This is an unnatural phenomenon. We are dealing with more than secessionists.'

Dak'ir swore under his breath; he'd made his decision.

'Spectres or not, we can't leave the Phalanx to be butchered.' He switched the comm-feed in his battle-helm to transmit.

'All squads regroup, and converge on Phalanx command positions.'

Brother Apion responded with a rapid affirmative, as did a second combat squad led by Brother Lazarus. Tsu'gan took a little longer to capitulate, evidently unimpressed, but seeing the need to rescue the Guardsmen from whatever was attacking them. Without the support fire offered by their heavy guns, the Salamanders were horribly exposed to the secessionist artillery and with the shield intact they had no feasible mission to prosecute.

'Understood.' Tsu'gan then cut the link.

Silhouettes moved through the downpour. Lasgun snap-shot fizzed out from Imperial positions, revealing Phalanx troopers that were shooting at unseen foes.

Most were running. Even the Basilisks were starting to withdraw. Commissar Loth, despite all of his fervour and promised retribution, couldn't prevent it.

The Phalanx were fleeing.

'Enemy contacts?'

Dak'ir was tracking through the mire, pistol held low, chainsword still but ready. He was the fulcrum of a dispersed battle-formation, Pyriel to his immediate left and two battle-brothers either side of them.

Ahead, he saw another combat squad led by Apion, the secondary insertion group. He too had dispersed his warriors, and they were plying every metre of the field for enemies.

'Negative,' was the curt response from Lazarus, approaching from the west.

Artillery bombardment from the entrenched rebel positions was falling with the intense rain. A great plume of sodden earth and broken bodies surged into the air a few metres away from where Dak'ir's squad advanced.

'Pyriel, anything?'

The Librarian shook his head, intent on his otherworldly instincts but finding no sense in what he felt or saw.

The broken chatter in Dak'ir's ear continued, the tolling of the bells providing an ominous chorus to gunfire and screaming. The Phalanx were close to a rout, having been pushed too far by a commissar who didn't understand or care about the nature of the enemy they were facing. Loth's only answer was threat of death to galvanise the men under his command. The bark of the Imperial officer's bolt pistol was close. Dak'ir could make out the telltale muzzle flash of the weapon in his peripheral vision.

Loth was firing at shadows and hitting his own men in the process; those fleeing and those who were standing their ground.

'I'll deal with him,' promised Pyriel, snapping out of his psychic trance without warning and peeling off to intercept the commissar.

Another artillery blast detonated nearby, showering the Salamanders with debris. Without the Earthshaker bombardment, the rebels were using their shell-hunting cannons to punish the Imperials. Tracer fire from high-calibre gunnery positions added to the carnage. That and whatever was stalking them through the mud and rain.

'It's infiltrators.' Tsu'gan's harsh voice was made harder still as it came through the comm-feed. 'Maybe fifty men, strung out in small groups, operating under camouflage. The humans are easily spooked. We will find them, Fire-born, and eliminate the threat.'

'How can you be–'

Dak'ir stopped when he caught a glimpse of something, away to his right.

'Did you see that?' he asked Ba'ken.

The hulking trooper followed him, swinging his heavy flamer around.

'No target,' Ba'ken replied. 'What was it, brother?'

'Not sure...' It had looked like just a flicker of... *white robes*, fluttering lightly but against the wind. The air suddenly became redolent with dank and age.

'Ignean!' Tsu'gan demanded.

'It's not infiltrators,' Dak'ir replied flatly.

Static flared in the feed before the other sergeant's voice returned.

'You can't be sure of that.'

'I know it, brother.' This time, Dak'ir cut the link. It had eluded him at first, but now he felt it, a... *presence*, out in the darkness of the killing field. It was angry.

'Eyes open,' he warned his squad, the half-seen image at the forefront of his mind and the stench all too real as the bells rang on.

Ahead, Dak'ir made out the form of a Phalanx officer, a captain according to his rank pins and attire. The Salamanders headed towards him, hoping to link up their forces and stage some kind of counter-attack. That was assuming there were enough troopers left to make any difference.

Commissar Loth was consumed by frenzy.

'Hold your ground!' he screeched. 'The Emperor demands your courage!' The bolt pistol rang out and another trooper fell, his torso gaping and red.

'Forward, damn you! Advance for His greater glory and the glory of the Imperium!'

Another Phalanx died, this time a sergeant who'd been rallying his men.

Pyriel was hurrying to get close, his force sword drawn, whilst his other hand was free. In the darkness and the driving rain he saw... *spectres*. They were white-grey and indistinct. Their movements were jagged, as if partially out of synch with reality, the non-corporeal breaching the fabric of the corporeal realm.

Loth saw them too, and the fear of it, whatever this phenomenon was, was etched over his pugilist's face.

'*Ave Imperator*. By the light of the Emperor, I shall fear no evil,' he intoned, falling back on the catechisms of warding and preservation he had learned in the schola progenium. '*Ave Imperator*. My soul is free of taint. Chaos will never claim it whilst He is my shield.'

The spectres were closing, flitting in and out of reality like a bad pict recording. Turning left and right, Loth loosed off shots at his aggressors, the brass rounds passing through them or missing completely, driving on to hit fleeing Phalanx infantrymen instead.

With each manifestation, the spectres got nearer.

Pyriel was only a few metres away when one appeared ahead of him. Loth's shot struck the Salamander in the pauldron as it went through and through, and a damage rune flared into life on the Librarian's tactical display inside his battle-helm.

'*Ave Imp*–' Too late. The spectre was upon Commissar Loth. He barely rasped the words–

'*Oh God-Emperor…*'

–when a blazing wall of psychic fire spilled from Pyriel's outstretched palm, smothering the apparition and banishing it from sight.

Loth was raising his pistol to his lips, jamming the still hot barrel into his mouth as his mind was unmanned by what he had seen.

Pyriel reached him just in time, smacking the pistol away before the commissar could summarily execute himself. The irony of it wasn't lost on the Librarian as the bolt-round flew harmlessly into the air. Still trailing tendrils of fire, Pyriel placed two fingers from his outstretched hand onto Loth's brow, who promptly crumpled to the ground and was still.

'He'll be out for several hours. Get him out of here, back to the bastion,' he ordered one of the commissar's attendants.

The attendant nodded, still shaken, calling for help, and together the storm troopers dragged Loth away.

'And he'll remember nothing of this or Vaporis,' Pyriel added beneath his breath.

Sensing his power, the spectres Pyriel had seen had retreated. Something else prickled at his senses now, something far off into the wilderness, away from the main battle site. There was neither time nor opportunity to investigate. Pyriel knew the nature of the foe they were facing now. He also knew there was no defence against it his brothers could muster. Space Marines were the ultimate warriors, but they needed enemies of flesh and blood. They couldn't fight mist and shadow.

Huge chunks of the Phalanx army were fleeing. But there was nothing Pyriel could do about that. Nor could he save those claimed by the earth, though this was the malice of the spectres at work again.

Instead, he raised a channel to Dak'ir through his battle-helm.

All the while, the bells tolled on.

'The entire force is broken,' the captain explained. He was a little hoarse from shouting commands, but had rallied what platoons were around him into some sort of order.

'Captain…'

'Mannheim,' the officer supplied.

'Captain Mannheim, what happened here? What is preying on your men?' asked Dak'ir. The rain was pounding heavily now, and *tinked* rapidly off his battle-plate. Explosions boomed all around them.

'I never saw it, my lord,' Mannheim admitted, wincing as a flare of incendiary came close, 'only Phalanx troopers disappearing from sight. At first, I thought enemy commandos, but our bio-scanners were blank. The only heat signatures came from our own men.'

Malfunctioning equipment was a possibility, but it still cast doubt on Tsu'gan's infiltrators theory.

Dak'ir turned to Emek, who carried the squad's auspex. The Salamander shook his head. Nothing had come from the rebel positions behind the shield, either.

'Could they have already been out here? Masked their heat traces?' asked Ba'ken on a closed channel.

Mannheim was distracted by his vox-officer. Making a rapid apology, he turned his back and pressed the receiver cup to his ear, straining to hear against the rain and thunder.

'Not possible,' replied Dak'ir. 'We would have seen them.'

'Then what?'

Dak'ir shook his head, as the rain came on in swathes.

'My lord...' It was Mannheim again. 'I've lost contact with Lieutenant Bahnhoff. We were coordinating a tactical consolidation of troops to launch a fresh assault. Strength in numbers.'

It was a rarefied concept on Nocturne, where self-reliance and isolationism were the main tenets.

'Where?' asked Dak'ir.

Mannheim pointed ahead. 'The lieutenant was part of our vanguard, occupying a more advanced position. His men had already reached the assault line when we were attacked.'

Explosions rippled in the distance where the captain gestured with a quavering finger. These were brave men, but their resolve was nearing its limit. Loth, and his bloody-minded draconianism, had almost pushed them over the edge.

It was hard to imagine much surviving in that barrage, and with whatever was abroad in the killing field to contend with too...

'If Lieutenant Bahnhoff lives, we will extract him and his men,' Dak'ir promised. He abandoned thoughts of a counter-attack almost immediately. The Phalanx were in disarray. Retreat was the only sensible option that preserved a later opportunity to attack. Though it went against his Promethean code, the very ideals of endurance and tenacity the Salamanders prided themselves on, Dak'ir had no choice but to admit it.

'Fall back with your men, captain. Get as many as you can to the bastion. Inform any other officers you can raise that the Imperial forces are in full retreat.'

Captain Mannheim motioned to protest.

'Full retreat, captain,' Dak'ir asserted. 'No victory was ever won with foolish sacrifice,' he added, quoting one of Zen'de's Tenets of Pragmatism.

The Phalanx officer saluted, and started pulling his men back. Orders were already being barked down the vox to any other coherent platoons in the army.

'We don't know what is out there, Dak'ir,' Ba'ken warned as they started running in Bahnhoff's direction. Though distant, silhouettes of the lieutenant's forces were visible. Worryingly, their las-fire spat in frantic bursts.

'Then we prepare for anything,' the sergeant replied grimly and forged on into the churned earth.

Bahnhoff's men had formed a defensive perimeter, their backs facing one another with the lieutenant himself at the centre, shouting orders. He positively sagged with relief upon sighting the Emperor's Angels coming to their aid.

The Salamanders were only a few metres away when something flickered into being nearby the circle of lasguns and one of the men simply vanished. One moment he was there, and the next... gone.

Panic flared and the order Bahnhoff had gallantly established threatened to break down. Troopers had their eyes on flight and not battle against apparitions they could barely see, let alone shoot or kill.

A second trooper followed the first, another white flicker signalling his death. This time Dak'ir saw the human's fate. It was as if the earth had opened up and swallowed him whole. Except the trooper hadn't fallen or been sucked into a bog, he'd been *dragged*. Pearlescent hands, with thin fingers like talons, had seized the poor bastard by the ankles and pulled him under.

Despite Bahnhoff's efforts his platoon's resolve shattered and they fled. Several more perished as they ran, sharing the same grisly fate as the others, dragged down in an eye-blink. The lieutenant ran with them, trying to turn the rout into an ordered retreat, but failing.

Emboldened by the troopers' fear, the things that were preying on the Phalanx manifested and the Salamanders saw them clearly for the first time.

'Are they daemons?' spat Emek, levelling his bolter.

They looked more like ragged corpses, swathed in rotting surplices and robes, the tattered fabric flapping like the tendrils of some incorporeal squid. Their eyes were hollow and black, and they were bone-thin with the essence of clergy about them. Priests they may once have been; now they were devils.

'Let us see if they can burn,' snarled Ba'ken, unleashing a gout of promethium from his heavy flamer. The spectres dissipated against the glare of liquid fire coursing over them as Ba'ken set the killing fields ablaze, but returned almost as soon as the fires had died down, utterly unscathed.

He was about to douse them again when they evaporated like mist before his eyes.

An uncertain second or two passed, before the hulking Fire-born turned to his sergeant and shrugged.

'I've fought tougher foes–' he began, before crying out as his booted feet sank beneath the earth.

'Name of Vulkan!' Emek swore, scarcely believing his eyes.

'Hold him!' bellowed Dak'ir, seeing white talons snaring Ba'ken's feet and ankles. Brothers Romulus and G'heb sprang to their fellow Salamander's aid, each hooking their arms under Ba'ken's. In moments, they were straining against the strength of the spectres.

'Let me go, you'll tear me in half,' roared Ba'ken, part anger, part pain.

'Hang on, brother,' Dak'ir told him. He was about to call for reinforcements, noting Pyriel's contact rune on his tac-display, when an apparition materialised in front of him. It was an old preacher, his grey face lined with age and malice, a belligerent light illuminating the sockets of his eyes. His mouth formed words Dak'ir could not discern and he raised an accusing finger.

'Release him, hell-spawn!' Dak'ir lashed out with his chainsword, but the preacher blinked out of existence and the blade passed on harmlessly to embed itself in the soft earth behind him. Dak'ir raised his plasma pistol to shoot when a terrible, numbing cold filled his body. Icy fire surged through him as his blood was chilled by something old and vengeful. It stole away the breath from his lungs and made them burn, as if he had plunged naked beneath the surface of an arctic river. It took Dak'ir a few moments to realise the crooked fingers of the preacher were penetrating his battle-plate. Worming beyond the aegis of ceramite, making a mockery of his power armour's normally staunch defences, the grey preacher's talons sought vital organs in their quest for vengeance.

Trying to cry out, Dak'ir found his larynx frozen, his tongue made leaden by the spectral assault. In his mind his intoned words of Promethean lore kept him from slipping into utter darkness.

Vulkan's fire beats in my breast. With it I shall smite the foes of the Emperor.

A heavy pressure hammered at his thunderous hearts, pressing, pressing...

Dak'ir's senses were ablaze and the smell of old, dank wood permeated through his battle-helm.

Then a bright flame engulfed him and the pressure eased. Cold withered, melted away by soothing heat, and as his darkening vision faded Dak'ir saw Pyriel standing amidst a pillar of fire. At the periphery, Ba'ken was being dragged free of the earth that had claimed him. Someone else was lifting Dak'ir. He felt strong hands hooking under his arms and pulling him. It was only then as his body became weightless and light that he realised he must've fallen. Semi-conscious, Dak'ir was aware of a fading voice addressing him.

'Dragging your carcass out of the fire again, Ignean...'

Then the darkness claimed him.

The strategium was actually an old refectory inside the bastion compound that smelled strongly of tabac and stale sweat. A sturdy-looking cantina table had been commandeered to act as a tacticarium, and was strewn with oiled maps, geographical charts and data-slates. The vaulted ceiling leaked, and drips of water were constantly being wiped from the various scrolls and picts layering the table by aides and officers alike. Buzzing around the moderately sized room's edges were Departmento Munitorum clerks and logisticians, counting up men and materiel with their styluses and exchanging dark glances with one another when they thought the Guard weren't looking.

It was no secret that they'd lost a lot of troops in the last sortie to bring down the void shield. To compound matters, ammunition for the larger guns was running dangerously low, to 'campaign-unviable' levels. Almost an hour had passed since the disastrous assault, and the Imperial forces were no closer to forging a battle-plan.

Librarian Pyriel surveyed the tactical data before him and saw nothing new, no insightful strategy to alleviate the graveness of their situation. At least the spectres had given up pursuit when they'd entered the grounds of Mercy Rock, though it had taken a great deal of the Epistolary's psychic prowess to fend them off and make retreat possible.

'What were they, brother?' said Tsu'gan in a low voice, trying not to alert the Guard officers and quartermaster who had joined them. Some things – Tsu'gan knew – it was best that humans stayed ignorant of. They could be weak-minded, all too susceptible to fear. Protecting humanity meant more than bolter and blade; it meant shielding them from the horrifying truths of the galaxy too, lest they be broken by them.

'I am uncertain.' Pyriel cast his gaze upwards, where his witch-sight turned timber and rockcrete as thin as gossamer, penetrating the material to soar into the shadow night where the firmament was drenched blood-red. 'But I believe the warp storm and the spectres are connected.'

'Slaves of Chaos?' The word left a bitter taste, and Tsu'gan spat it out.

'Lost and damned, perhaps,' the Librarian mused. 'Not vassals of the Ruinous Powers, though. I think they are... *warp echoes*, souls trapped between the empyrean and the mortal world. The red storm has thinned the veil of reality. I can *feel* the echoes pushing through. Only, I don't know why. But as long as the storm persists, as long as Hell Night continues, they will be out there.'

Only a few metres away, oblivious to the Salamanders, the Guard officers were having a war council of their own.

'The simple matter is, we cannot afford a protracted siege,' stated Captain Mannheim. Since Tench's execution and the commissar's incapacitation, Mannheim was the highest ranking officer in the Phalanx. His sleeves were rolled up and he'd left his cap on the tacticarium table, summiting the charts.

'We have perhaps enough munitions for one more sustained assault on the void shield.' The quartermaster was surveying his materiel logs, a Departmento Munitorum aide feeding him data-slates with fresh information that he mentally recorded and handed back as he spoke. 'After that, there is nothing we possess here that can crack it.'

Another officer, a second lieutenant, spoke up. His jacket front was unbuttoned and an ugly dark sweat stain created a dagger-shaped patch down his shirt.

'Even if we did, what hope is there while those things haunt the darkness?'

A patched-up corporal, his left eye bandaged, blotched crimson under the medical gauze, stepped forward.

'I am not leading my platoon out there to be butchered again. The secessionists consort with daemons. We have no defence against it.'

Fear, Tsu'gan sneered. Yes, humans were too weak for some truths.

The second lieutenant turned, scowling, to regard the Salamanders who dwelt in the shadows at the back of the room.

'And what of the Emperor's Angels? Were you not sent to deliver us and help end the siege? Are these foes, the spectres in the darkness, not allied to our faceless enemies at Aphium? We cannot break the city, if you cannot rid us of the daemons in our midst.'

Hot anger flared in Tsu'gan's eyes, and the officer balked. The Salamander snarled with it, clenching a fist at the human's impudence.

Pyriel's warning glance made his brother stand down.

'They are not daemons,' Pyriel asserted, 'but warp echoes. A resonance of the past that clings to our present.'

'Daemons, echoes, what difference does it make?' asked Mannheim. 'We are being slaughtered all the same, and with no way to retaliate. Even if we could banish these... *echoes*,' he corrected, 'we cannot take on them *and* the void shield. It's simple numbers, my lord. We are fighting a war of attrition which our depleted force cannot win.'

Tsu'gan stepped forward, unable to abstain from comment any longer.

'You are servants of the Emperor!' he reminded Mannheim fiercely. 'And you will do your part, hopeless or not, for the glory of Him on Earth.'

A few of the officers made the sign of the aquila, but Mannheim was not to be cowed.

'I'll step onto the sacrificial altar of war if that is what it takes, but I won't do it blindly. Would you lead your men to certain death, knowing it would achieve nothing?'

Tsu'gan scowled. Grunting an unintelligible diatribe, he turned on his heel and stalked from the strategium.

Pyriel raised his eyebrows.

'Forgive my brother,' he said to the council. 'Tsu'gan burns with a Nocturnean's fire. He becomes agitated if he cannot slay anything.'

'And that is the problem, isn't it?' returned Captain Mannheim. 'The reason why your brother-sergeant was so frustrated. Save for you, Librarian, your Astartes have no weapons against these echoes. For all their strength of arms, their skill and courage, they are powerless against them.'

The statement lingered, like a blade dangling precariously over the thread of all their hopes.

'Yes,' Pyriel admitted in little more than a whisper.

Silent disbelief filled the room for a time as the officers fought to comprehend the direness of their plight on Vaporis.

'There are no sanctioned psykers in the Phalanx,' said the second lieutenant at last. 'Can one individual, even an Astartes, turn the tide of this war?'

'He cannot!' chimed the corporal. 'We need to signal for landers immediately. Request reinforcements,' he suggested.

'There will be none forthcoming,' chided Mannheim. 'Nor will the landers enter Vaporis space whilst Aphium is contested. We are alone in this.'

'My brother was right in one thing,' uttered Pyriel, his voice cutting through the rising clamour. 'Your duty is to the Emperor. Trust in us, and we will deliver victory,' he promised.

'But how, my lord?' asked Mannheim.

Pyriel's gaze was penetrating.

'Psychics are anathema to the warp echoes. With my power, I can protect your men by erecting a psy-shield. The spectres, as you call them, will not be able to pass through. If we can get close enough to the void shield, much closer than the original assault line, and apply sufficient pressure to breach it, my brothers will break through and shatter your enemies. Taking out the generatoria first, the shield will fail and with it the Aphium resistance once your long guns have pounded them.'

The second lieutenant scoffed, a little incredulous.

'My lord, I don't doubt the talents of the Astartes, nor your own skill, but can you really sustain a shield of sufficient magnitude and duration to make this plan work?'

The Librarian smiled thinly.

'I am well schooled by my Master Vel'cona. As an Epistolary-level Librarian, my abilities are prodigious, lieutenant,' he said without pride. 'I can do what must be done.'

Mannheim nodded, though a hint of fatalism tainted his resolve.

'Then you have my full support and the support of the Phalanx 135th,' he said. 'Tell me what you need, my lord, and it shall be yours.'

'Stout hearts and steely resolve is all I ask, captain. It is all the Emperor will ever ask of you.'

Tsu'gan checked the load of his combi-bolter, re-securing the promethium canister on the flamer element of the weapon.

'Seems pointless, when we cannot even kill our foes,' he growled.

The bellicose sergeant was joined by the rest of his brothers at the threshold to Mercy Rock, in the inner courtyard before the bastion's great gate.

Behind them, the Phalanx platoons were readying. In the vehicle yards, the Basilisks were churning into position on their tracks. Anticipation filled the air like an electric charge.

Only two Salamanders were missing, and one of those was hurrying to join them through the thronging Guardsmen from the makeshift medi-bay located in the bastion catacombs.

'How is he, brother?' Emek asked, racking the slide to his bolter.

'Unconscious still,' said Ba'ken. He'd ditched his heavy flamer and carried a bolter like most of his battle-brothers. Dak'ir had not recovered from the attack by the spectre and so, despite his protests, Ba'ken had been made de facto sergeant by Pyriel.

'I wish he were with us,' he muttered.

'We all do, brother,' said Pyriel. Detecting a mote of unease, he asked, 'Something on your mind, Ba'ken?'

The question hung in the air like an unfired bolt-round, before the hulking trooper answered.

'I heard Brother-Sergeant Tsu'gan over the comm-feed. Can these things even be fought, brother? Or are we merely drawing them off for the Guard?'

'I saw the Ignean's blade pass straight through one,' Tsu'gan muttered. 'And yet others seized upon Ba'ken as solid and intractable as a docking claw.'

Emek looked up from his auspex.

'Before they attack, they corporealise; become flesh,' he said, 'Although it is flesh of iron with a grip as strong as a power fist.'

'I had noticed it too,' Pyriel replied. 'Very observant, brother.'

Emek nodded humbly, before the Librarian outlined his strategy.

'Our forces will be strung out across the killing field, four combat squads as before. I can stretch my psychic influence to encompass the entire Phalanx battle line but it will be a comparatively narrow cordon, and some of the spectres may get through. Adopt defensive tactics and wait for them to attack, then strike. But know the best we can hope for is to repel them. Only I possess the craft to banish the creatures into the warp and that won't be possible whilst I'm maintaining the psychic shield.'

'Nor then will you be able to fight, Brother-Librarian,' said Ba'ken.

Pyriel faced him, and there was an unspoken compact in his low voice. 'No, I'll be temporarily vulnerable.'

So you, brothers, will need to be my shield.

The severity of the mission weighed as heavy as the weather. Captain Mannheim had been correct when he'd spoken in the strategium: for all their strength of arms, their skill and courage, they *were* powerless against the spectres. Almost.

Pyriel addressed the group. 'Fire-born: check helm-displays for updated mission parameters and objectives.'

A series of 'affirmatives' greeted the order.

'Switching to tac-sight,' added Tsu'gan. A data stream of time-codes, distances and troop dispositions filled his left occulobe lens. He turned to Pyriel just as the great gates to Mercy Rock were opening. 'I hope you can do what you promised, Librarian, or we are all dead.'

Pyriel's gaze was fixed ahead as he donned his battle-helm.

'The warp storm is unpredictable, but it also augments my own powers,' he said. 'I can hold the shield for long enough.'

On a closed channel, he contacted Tsu'gan alone.

'My psychic dampener will be low,' he warned. 'If at any moment I am compromised, you know what must be done.'

If I am daemonically possessed by the warp, Tsu'gan read between the Librarian's words easily enough.

A sub-vocal 'compliance' flashed up as an icon on Pyriel's display.

'Brothers Emek, Iagon?' the Librarian asked with the gates now yawning wide. The gap in the wall brought lashing rain and the stench of death.

Emek and Iagon were interrogating overlapping scan patterns on their auspexes in search of warp activity in the shadows of the killing field.

'Negative, brother,' Emek replied. Iagon nodded in agreement.

The way, for now at least, was clear.

Despite the rain, a curious stillness persisted in the darkness of Hell Night. It was red and angry. And it was waiting for them. Pyriel was drawn again to the patch of wilderness, far off in the distance.

Just beyond my reach...

'Into the fires of battle...' he intoned, and led the Salamanders out.

Dak'ir awoke, startled and awash with cold sweat. He was acutely aware of his beating hearts and a dense throbbing in his skull. Disorientating visions were fading from his subconscious mind... An ashen world, of tombs and mausoleums lining a long, bone-grey road... The redolence of burning flesh and grave dust... Half-remembered screams of a brother in pain...

...Becoming one with the screams of many, across a dark and muddied field... The touch of rain, cold against his skin... and a bell tolling... 'We are here...' 'We are here...'

The first was an old dream. He had seen it many times. But now new impressions had joined it, and Dak'ir knew they came from Vaporis. He tried to hold onto them, the visions and the sense memories, but it was like clutching smoke.

With the thinning of the unreal, the real became solid and Dak'ir realised he was flat on his back. A wire mattress with coarse sheets supported him. The cot groaned as he tried to move – so did Dak'ir when the daggers of pain pierced his body. He grimaced and sank back down, piecing together the immediate past. The attack by the spectral preacher came back to him. A remembered chill made him shiver.

'You're pretty well banged up,' said a voice from the shadows. The sudden sound revealed just how quiet it was – the dull reply of heavy artillery was but a faint thudding in the walls. 'I wouldn't move so quickly,' the voice advised.

'Who are you?' rasped Dak'ir, the dryness in his throat a surprise at first.

A high-pitched squeal grated against the Salamander's skull as a Phalanx officer sitting in a wheelchair rolled into view.

'Bahnhoff, my lord,' he said. 'You and your Astartes tried to save my men in the killing field, and I'm grateful to you for that.'

'It's my duty,' Dak'ir replied, still groggy. He managed to sit up, despite the horrendous pain of his injuries and the numbness that lingered well after the preacher had relinquished his deathly grip. Dak'ir was gasping for breath for a time.

'*Lieutenant* Bahnhoff?' he said, remembering; a look of incredulity on his face when he saw the wheelchair.

'Artillery blast got me,' the officer supplied. 'Platoon dragged me the rest of the way. Took *me* off the frontline too, though.'

Dak'ir felt a pang of sorrow for the lieutenant when he saw the shattered pride in his eyes.

'Am I alone? Have my brothers gone to battle without me?' Dak'ir asked.

'They said you were too badly injured. Told us to watch over you until they returned.'

'My armour...' Dak'ir was naked from the waist up. Even his torso bodyglove had been removed. As he made to swing himself over the edge of the cot, enduring still further agonies, he saw that his battle-plate's cuirass was lying reverently in one corner of the room. His bodyglove was with it, cut up where his brothers had needed to part it to treat his wounds. Dak'ir ran his finger over them. In the glow of a single lume-lamp they looked like dark bruises in the shape of fingerprint impressions.

'Here... I found these in a storage room nearby.' Bahnhoff tossed Dak'ir a bundle of something he'd been carrying on his lap.

The Salamander caught it, movement still painful but getting easier, and saw they were robes.

'They're loose, so should fit your frame,' Bahnhoff explained.

Dak'ir eyed the lieutenant, but shrugged on the robes nonetheless.

'Help me off this cot,' he said.

Together, they got Dak'ir off the bed and onto his feet. He wobbled at first, but quickly found his balance, before surveying his surroundings.

They were in a small room, like a cell. The walls were bare stone. Dust collected in the corners and hung in the air, giving it an eerie quality.

'What is this place?'

Bahnhoff wheeled backwards as Dak'ir staggered a few steps from the cot.

'Mercy Rock's catacombs. We use it as a medi-bay,' the lieutenant's face darkened, 'and morgue.'

'Apt,' Dak'ir replied with grim humour.

A strange atmosphere permeated this place. Dak'ir felt it as he brushed the walls with his finger-tips, as he drank in the cloudy air.

We are here...

The words came back to him like a keening. They were beckoning him. He turned to Bahnhoff, eyes narrowed.

'What is that?'

'What is *what*, my lord?'

A faint scratching was audible in the sepulchral silence, as a quill makes upon parchment. Bahnhoff's eyes widened as he heard it too.

'All the Munitorum clerks are up in the strategium...'

'It's coming from beneath us,' said Dak'ir. He was already making for the door. Wincing with every step, he betrayed his discomfort, but gritted his teeth as he went to follow the scratching sound.

'Are there lower levels?' he asked Bahnhoff, as they moved through a shadowy corridor.

'Doesn't get any deeper than the catacombs, my lord.'

Dak'ir was moving more quickly now, and Bahnhoff was wheeling hard to keep up.

The scratching was getting louder, and when they reached the end of the corridor the way ahead was blocked by a timber barricade.

'Structurally unsafe, according to the engineers,' said Bahnhoff.

'It's old...' Dak'ir replied, noting the rotten wood and the gossamer webs wreathing it like a veil. He gripped one of the planks and tore it off easily. Compelled by some unknown force, Dak'ir ripped the barricade apart until they were faced by a stone stairway. It led into a darkened void. The reek of decay and stagnation was strong.

'Are we going down there?' asked Bahnhoff, a slight tremor in his voice.

'Wait for me here,' Dak'ir told him and started down the steps.

'Stay within the cordon!' bellowed Tsu'gan, as another one of Captain Mannheim's men was lost to the earth.

An invisible barrier stretched the length of the killing ground that only flared incandescently into existence when one of the spectres struck it and recoiled. Like a lightning spark, the flash was born and died quickly, casting the scene starkly in its ephemeral life. Gunnery teams slogged hard to keep pace and infantry tramped hurriedly alongside them in long thin files, adopting firing lines once they'd reached the two hundred metre marker. Las-bursts erupted from the Phalanx ranks in a storm. Barking solid shot from heavy bolters and autocannon added to the sustained salvo. So close to the void shield, the energy impact returns were incandescently bright and despite the darkness, made several troopers don photoflash goggles. For some, it was just as well that their vision was impeded for shadows lurked beyond Librarian Pyriel's psychic aegis and not everyone was immune to them.

The barrier was narrow, just as Pyriel had warned, and as the Phalanx had tried to keep pace with the Salamanders on the way to the advanced assault line some stepped out of it. A muted cry and then they were no longer seen or heard from again. By the time the firing line was erected, some several dozen troopers were missing. The Salamanders, as yet, had not succumbed.

Tsu'gan saw the flickering white forms of the warp echoes through the Librarian's psychic shield. They lingered, angry and frustrated, ever probing to test the limits of Pyriel's strength. Though he couldn't see his face through his battle-helm, Tsu'gan knew by the Epistolary's juddering movements that he was feeling the strain. He was a vessel now for the near-unfettered power of the warp. Like a sluice gate let free, the energy coursed through him as Pyriel fought hard to channel it into the shield. One slip and he would be lost. Then Tsu'gan would need to act quickly, slaying him before Pyriel's flesh was obtained by another, heralding the death of them all, Salamanders or no.

One of the creatures breached the barrier wall, corporealising to do it, and Tsu'gan lashed out with his fist.

It was like striking adamantium, and he felt the shock of the blow all the way up his arm and into his shoulder, but did enough to force the creature back. It flashed briefly out of existence, but returned quickly, a snarl upon its eldritch features.

'Hard as iron you said,' Tsu'gan roared into the comm-feed as the weapons fire intensified.

Overhead the Earthshaker shells were finding their marks and the void shield rippled near its summit.

Emek battered another of the spectres back beyond the psychic cordon, the exertion needed to do it evident in his body language.

'Perhaps too conservative,' he admitted.

'A tad, brother,' came Tsu'gan's bitter rejoinder. 'Iagon,' he relayed through his battle-helm, 'what are the readings for the shield?'

'Weakening, my lord,' was Iagon's sibilant reply, 'but still insufficient for a break.'

Tsu'gan scowled.

'Ba'ken…'

'We must advance,' the acting sergeant answered. 'Fifty metres, and apply greater pressure to the shield.'

At a hundred and fifty metres away, the danger from energy flares cast by void impacts and friendly fire casualties from the Earthshakers was greatly increased, but then the Salamanders had little choice. Soon the bombardment from the Basilisks would end when they ran out of shells. The void shield had to be down before then.

'Brother-Librarian,' Tsu'gan began, 'another fifty metres?'

After a few moments, Pyriel nodded weakly and started to move forwards.

Tsu'gan turned his attention to the Phalanx.

'Captain Mannheim, we are advancing. Another fifty metres.'

The Phalanx officer gave a clipped affirmative before continuing to galvanise his men and reminding them of their duty to the Emperor.

Despite himself, the Salamander found he admired the captain for that.

The bells tolled on as the Imperial forces resumed their march.

The stairs were shallow and several times Dak'ir almost lost his footing, only narrowly avoiding a plunge into uncertain darkness by bracing himself against the flanking walls.

Near the bottom of the stairwell, he was guided by a faint smudge of flickering light. Its warm, orange glow suggested candles or a fire. There was another room down here and this was where the scratching sound emanated from.

Cursing himself for leaving his weapons in the cell above, Dak'ir stepped cautiously through a narrow portal that forced him to duck to get through and into a small, dusty chamber.

Beyond the room's threshold he saw bookcases stuffed with numerous scrolls, tomes and other arcana. Religious relics were packed in half-open crates, stamped with the Imperial seal. Others, deific statues, Ecclesiarchal sigils and shrines were cluttered around the chamber's periphery. And there, in the centre, scribing with ink and quill at a low table, was an old, robed clerk.

The scrivener looked up from his labours, blinking with eye strain as he regarded the giant, onyx-skinned warrior in his midst.

'Greetings, soldier,' he offered politely.

Dak'ir nodded, uncertain of what to make of his surroundings. A prickling sensation ran through his body but then faded as he stepped into the corona of light cast by the scrivener's solitary candle.

'Are you Munitorum?' asked Dak'ir. 'What are you doing so far from the strategium?' Dak'ir continued to survey the room as he stepped closer. It was caked in dust and the grime of ages, more a forgotten storeroom than an office for a Departmento clerk.

The scrivener laughed; a thin, rasping sort of a sound that put Dak'ir a little on edge.

'Here,' said the old man as he backed away from his works. 'See what keeps me in this room.'

Dak'ir came to the table at the scrivener's beckoning, strangely compelled by the old man's manner, and looked down at his work.

Hallowed Heath – a testament of its final days, he read.

'Mercy Rock was not always a fortress,' explained the scrivener behind him. 'Nor was it always alone.'

The hand that had authored the parchment scroll in front of Dak'ir was scratchy and loose but he was able to read it.

'It says here that Mercy Rock was once a basilica, a temple devoted to the worship of the Imperial Creed.'

'Read on, my lord...' the scrivener goaded.

Dak'ir did as asked.

'"...and Hallowed Heath was its twin. Two bastions of light, shining like beacons against the old faiths, bringing enlightenment and understanding to Vaporis,"' he related directly from the text. '"In the shadow of Aphium, but a nascent township with lofty ambitions, did these pinnacles of faith reside. Equal were they in their fervour and dedication, but not in fortification–"' Dak'ir looked around at the old scrivener who glared at the Salamander intently.

'I thought you said they were not fortresses?'

The scrivener nodded, urging Dak'ir to continue his studies.

'"–One was built upon a solid promontory of rock, hence its given appellation; the other upon clay. It was during the Unending Deluge of 966.M40 when the rains of Vaporis continued for sixty-six days, the heaviest they had ever been in longest memory, that Hallowed Heath sank down beneath a quagmire of earth, taking its five hundred and forty-six patrons and priests with it. For three harrowing days and nights the basilica sank, stone by stone, beneath the earth, its inhabitants stranded within its walls that had become as their tomb. And for three nights, they tolled the bells in the highest towers of Hallowed Heath, saying, "We are here!", "We are here!" but none came to their aid."'

Dak'ir paused as a horrible understanding started to crawl up his spine. Needing to know more, oblivious now to the scrivener, he continued.

'"Aphium was the worst. The township and all its peoples did not venture into the growing mire for fear of their own lives, did not even try to save the stricken people. They shut their ears to the bells and shut their doors, waiting for a cessation to the rains. And all the while, the basilica sank, metre by metre, hour by hour, until the highest towers were consumed beneath the earth, all of its inhabitants buried alive with them, and the bells finally silenced."'

Dak'ir turned to regard the old scrivener.

'The spectres in the killing field,' he said, 'they are the warp echoes of the preachers and their patrons.'

'They are driven by hate, hate for the Aphiums who closed their ears and let them die, just as I am driven by guilt.'

Guilt?

Dak'ir was about to question it when the scrivener interrupted.

'You're near the end, Hazon, read on.'

Dak'ir was compelled to turn back, as if entranced.

'"This testament is the sole evidence of this terrible deed – nay; it is my confession of complicity in it. Safe was I in Mercy Rock, sat idle whilst others suffered and died. It cannot stand. This I leave as small recompense, so that others might know of what transpired. My life shall be forfeit just as theirs were, too."'

There it ended, and only then did Dak'ir acknowledge that the old man had used his first name. He whirled around, about to demand answers... but he was too late.

The scrivener was gone.

The Earthshaker barrage stopped abruptly like a thumping heart in sudden cardiac arrest. Its absence was a silent death knell to the Phalanx and their Adeptus Astartes allies.

'It's done,' snarled Tsu'gan, when the Imperial shelling ended. 'We break through now or face the end. Iagon?'

'Still holding, my lord.'

They were but a hundred metres from the void shield now, having pressed up in one final effort to overload it. Without the heavy artillery backing them up, it seemed an impossible task. All the time, more and more Phalanx troopers were lost to breaches in the psychic shield, dragged into dank oblivion by ethereal hands.

'I feel... *something*...' said Pyriel, struggling to speak, 'Something in the void shield... Just beyond my reach...'

Despite his colossal efforts, the Librarian was weakening. The psychic barrier was losing its integrity and with it any protection against the warp echoes baying at its borders.

'Stand fast!' yelled Mannheim. 'Hold the line and press for glory, men of the Phalanx!'

Through sheer grit and determination, the Guardsmen held. Even though their fellow troopers were being swallowed by the earth, they held.

Tsu'gan could not help but feel admiration again for their courage. Like a crazed dervish, he raced down the line raining blows upon the intruding spectres, his shoulders burning with the effort.

'Salamanders! We are about to be breached,' he cried. 'Protect the Phalanx. Protect your brothers in arms with your lives!'

'Hail Vulkan and the glory of Prometheus!' Ba'ken chimed. 'Let Him on Earth witness your courage, men of the Phalanx.'

The effect of the sergeants' words was galvanising. Coupled with Mannheim's own stirring rally, the men became intractable in the face of almost certain death.

Tsu'gan heard a deep cry of pain to his left and saw Lazarus fall, impaled as Dak'ir had been by eldritch fingers.

'Brother!'

S'tang and Nor'gan went to his aid as Honorious covered their retreat with his flamer.

'Hold, Fire-born, hold!' Tsu'gan bellowed. 'Give them nothing!'

Tenacious to the end, the Salamanders would fight until their final breaths, and none so fiercely as Tsu'gan.

The battle-hardened sergeant was ready to make his final pledges to his primarch and his Emperor when the comm-feed crackled to life in his ear.

'You may have cheated death, Ignean,' snapped Tsu'gan when he realised who it was. 'But then survival over glory was always your–'

'Shut up, Zek, and raise Pyriel right now,' Dak'ir demanded, using the other Salamander's first name and mustering as much animus as he could.

'Our brother needs to marshal all of his concentration, Ignean,' Tsu'gan snapped again. 'He can ill afford distractions from you.'

'Do it, or it will not matter how distracted he becomes!'

Tsu'gan snarled audibly but obeyed, something in Dak'ir's tone making him realise it was important.

'Brother-Librarian,' he barked down the comm-feed. 'Our absent brother demands to speak with you.'

Pyriel nodded labouredly, his hands aloft as he struggled to maintain the barrier.

'Speak...' the Librarian could scarcely rasp.

'Do you remember what you felt before the first assault?' Dak'ir asked quickly. 'You said there was something about the shield, an anomaly in its energy signature. It is psychically enhanced, brother, to keep the warp echoes *out*.'

Through the furious barrage a slim crack was forming in the void shield's integrity, invisible to mortal eyes but plain as frozen lightning to the Librarian's witch-sight. And through it, Pyriel discerned a psychic undercurrent straining to maintain a barrier of its own. With Dak'ir's revelation came understanding and then purpose.

'They want vengeance against Aphium,' said Pyriel, beginning to refocus his psychic energy and remould it into a sharp blade of his own anger.

'For the complicity in their deaths over a thousand years ago,' Dak'ir concluded.

'I know what to do, brother,' Pyriel uttered simply, his voice drenched with psychic resonance as he let slip the last of the tethers from his psychic hood, the crystal matrix dampener that protected him psychically, and laid himself open to the warp.

'In Vulkan's name,' Dak'ir intoned before the link was overwhelmed with psychic static and died.

'Brother Tsu'gan...' Pyriel's voice was deep and impossibly loud against the battle din. A tsunami of raw psychic power was coursing through him, encasing the Librarian in a vibrant, fiery aura. '...I am about to relinquish the barrier...'

Tsu'gan had no time to answer. The psychic barrier fell and the warp echoes swept in. Thunder split the heavens and red lightning tore across boiling clouds as the warp storm reached its zenith.

Already, the breach Pyriel had psychically perceived was closing.

'Maintain positions!' roared Mannheim, as his men were being taken. 'Keep firing!'

Secessionist fire, freed up from mitigating the Imperial artillery barrage, was levelled at the Phalanx. Mannheim took a lucky las-round in the throat and was silenced.

Tsu'gan watched the officer fall just as Pyriel burst into violent conflagration. Running over to Mannheim, he scooped the fallen captain up into his arms, and watched as a bolt of flame lashed out from Pyriel's refulgent form. It surged through the void shield, past the unseen breach, reaching out for the minds of the Librarian's enemies...

Deep in Aphium rebel territory, in an armoured bunker sunk partially beneath the earth, a cadre of psykers sat in a circle, their consciousnesses locked, their will combined to throw a veil across the void shield that kept out the deeds of their ancestors. It was only around Hell Night when the blood storm wracked the heavens and brought about an awakening for vengeance, a desire for retribution, that their skills were needed.

One by one they screamed, an orange fire unseen by mortal eyes ravaging them with its scorching tendrils. Flesh melted, eyes ran like wax under a hot lamp, and one by one the psyker cadre burned. The heat inside the bunker was intense, though the temperature gauge suggested a cool night, and within seconds the psykers were reduced to ash and the defence of Aphium with it.

Upon the killing field, Tsu'gan detected a change in the air. The oppressive weight that had dogged them since mustering out for a second time on Hell Night had lifted, like leaden chains being dragged away by unseen hands.

Like mist before the rays of a hot sun, the warp echoes receded into nothing. Silence drifted over the killing field, as all of the guns stopped. The void shield flickered and died a moment later, the absence of its droning hum replaced by screaming from within the city of Aphium.

'In Vulkan's name...' Tsu'gan breathed, unable to believe what was unfolding before his eyes. He didn't need to see it to know the spectres had turned on the rebels of Aphium and were systematically slaying each and every one.

It wasn't over. Not yet. Pyriel blazed like an incendiary about to explode. The Librarian's body was spasming uncontrollably as he fought to marshal the forces he'd unleashed. Raging psychic flame coursed through him. As if taking hold of an accelerant, it burned mercilessly. Several troopers were consumed by it, the mind-fire becoming real. Men collapsed in the heat, their bodies rendered to ash.

'Pyriel!' cried Tsu'gan. Cradling Captain Mannheim in his arms, he raised his bolter one-handed.

...you know what you must do.

He fired into Pyriel's back, an expert shot that punctured the Librarian's lung but wasn't fatal. Pyriel bucked against the blow, the flames around him dwindling, and sagged to his knees. Then he fell onto his side, unconscious, and the conflagration was over.

'Tsu'gan. Tsu'gan!'

It took Tsu'gan a few seconds to realise he was being hailed. A curious stillness had settled over the killing field. Above them the red sky was fading as the warp storm passed, and the rain had lessened. On the horizon, another grey day was dawning.

'Dak'ir...'

Stunned, he forgot to use his derogatory sobriquet for the other sergeant.

'What happened, Zek? Is it over?'

Mannheim was dead. Tsu'gan realised it as the officer went limp in his arms. He had not faltered, even at the end, and had delivered his men to victory and glory. Tsu'gan's bolter was still hot from shooting Pyriel. He used it carefully to burn an honour marking in Captain Mannheim's flesh. It was shaped like the head of a firedrake.

'It's over,' he replied and cut the link.

A faded sun had broken through the gathering cloud. Errant rays lanced downwards, casting their glow upon a patch of distant earth far off in the wilderness. Tsu'gan didn't know what it meant, only that when he looked upon it his old anger lessened and a strange feeling, that was not to last in the days to come, spilled over him.

Rain fell. Day dawned anew. Hell Night was ended, but the feeling remained.

It was peace.

AT GAIUS POINT

Aaron Dembski-Bowden

I

The memory of fire. Fire and falling, incineration and annihilation.
 Then darkness.
 Absolute silence. Absolute nothing.

II

I open my eyes.
 There before me, outlined by scrolling white text across my targeting display, is a shattered metal wall. Its architecture is gothic in nature – a skeletal wall, with black steel girders like ribs helping form the wall's curvature. It is mangled and bent. Crushed, even.
 I do not know where I am, but my senses are awash with perception. I hear the crackle of fire eating metal, and the angry hum of live battle armour. The sound is distorted, a hitch or a burr in the usually steady thrum. Damage has been sustained. My armour is compromised. A glance at the bio-feed displays shows minor damage to the armour plating of my wrist and shin. Nothing serious.
 I smell the flames nearby, and the bitter rancidity of melting steel. I smell my own body; the sweat, the chemicals injecting into my flesh by my armour, and the intoxicatingly rich scent of my own blood.
 A god's blood.
 Refined and thinned for use in mortal veins, but a god's blood nevertheless. A dead god. A slain angel.

The thought brings my teeth together in a grunted curse, my fangs scraping the teeth below. Enough of this weakness.

I rise, muscles of aching flesh bunching in unison with the fibre-bundle false muscles of my armour. It is a sensation I am familiar with, yet it feels somehow flawed. I should be stronger. I should exult in my strength, the ultimate fusion of biological potency and machine power.

I do not feel strong. I feel nothing but pain and a momentary disorientation. The pain is centralised in my spinal column and shoulder blades, turning my back into a pillar of dull, aching heat. Nothing is broken – bio-feeds have already confirmed that. The soreness of muscle and nerve would have killed a human, but we are gene-forged into greater beings.

Already, the weakness fades. My blood stings with the flood of adrenal stimulants and kinetic enhancement narcotics rushing through my veins.

My movement is unimpeded. I rise to my feet, slow not from weakness now, but from caution.

With my vision stained a cooling emerald shade by my helm's green eye lenses, I take in the wreckage around me.

This chamber is ruined, half-crushed with its walls distorted. Restraint thrones lie broken, torn from the floor. The two bulkheads leading from the chamber are both wrenched from their hinges, hanging at warped angles.

The impact must have been savage.

The... impact?

The crash. Our Thunderhawk crashed. The clarity of recollection is sickening... the sense of falling from the sky, my senses drenched in the thunder of descent, the shaking of the ship in its entirety. Temperature gauges on my retinal display rose slowly when the engines died in exploding flares that scorched the hull, and my armour systems registered the gunship's fiery journey groundward.

There was a final booming refrain, a roar like the carnosaurs of home – as loud and primal as their predator-king challenges – and the world shuddered beyond all sanity. The gunship ploughed into the ground.

And then... Darkness.

My eyes flicker to my retinal display's chronometer. I was unconscious for almost three minutes. I will do penance for such weakness, but that can come later.

Now I breathe in deep, tasting the ashy smoke in the air but unaffected by it. The air filtration in my helm's grille renders me immune to such trivial concerns.

'Zavien,' a voice crackles in my ears. A momentary confusion takes hold at the sound of the word. The vox-signal is either weak, or the sender's armour is badly damaged. With the ship in pieces, both could be true.

'Zavien,' the voice says again.

This time I turn at the name, realising it is my own.

Zavien strode into the cockpit, keeping his balance on the tilted floor through an effortless combination of natural grace and his armour's joint-stabilisers.

The cockpit had suffered even more than the adjacent chamber. The view window, despite the thickness of the reinforced plastek, was shattered beyond simple repair. Diamond shards of the sundered false-glass twinkled on the twisted floor. The pilot thrones were wrenched from their support columns, cast aside like detritus in a storm.

Through the windowless viewport there was nothing but mud and gnarled black roots, much of which had spilled over the lifeless control consoles. They'd come down hard enough to drive the gunship's nose into the earth.

The pilot, Varlon, was a mangled wreck sprawled face-down over the control console. Zavien's targeting reticule locked onto his brother's battered armour, secondary cursors detailing the rents and wounds in the deactivated war plate. Blood, thick and dark, ran from rips in Varlon's throat and waist joints. It ran in slow trickles across the smashed console, dripping between buttons and levers.

His power pack was inactive. Life signs were unreadable, but the evidence was clear enough. Zavien heard no heartbeat from the body, and had Varlon been alive, his gene-enhanced physiology would have clotted and sealed all but the most grievous wounds. He wouldn't still be bleeding slowly all over the controls of the downed gunship.

'Zavien,' said a voice to the right, no longer over the vox.

Zavien turned from Varlon, his armour snarling in a growl of joint-servos. There, pinned under wreckage from the collapsed wall, was Drayus. Zavien moved to the fallen warrior's side, seeing the truth. No, Drayus was not just pinned in place. He was impaled there.

The sergeant's black helm was lowered, chin down on his collar, green eyes regarding the broken Imperial eagle on his chest. Jagged wreckage knifed into his dark armour, the ravaged steel spearing him through the shoulder guard, the arm, the thigh and the stomach. Blood leaked through his helm's speaker grille. The biometric displays that flashed up on Zavien's visor told an ugly story, and one with an end soon to come.

'Report,' Sergeant Drayus said – the way he always said it – as if the scene around them were the most mundane situation imaginable.

Zavien kneeled by the pinned warrior, fighting back the aching need in his throat and gums to taste the blood of the fallen. Irregular and weak, a single heartbeat rattled in Drayus's chest. One of his hearts had shut down, likely flooded by internal haemorrhaging or burst by the wreckage piercing his body. The other pounded gamely, utterly without rhythm.

'Varlon is dead,' Zavien said.

'I can see that, fool.' The sergeant reached up one hand, the one not half-severed at the forearm, and clawed with unmoving fingers at the collar joint beneath his helm. Zavien reached to help, unlocking the helmet's pressurised seals. With a reptilian hiss, the helmet came free in Zavien's hands.

Drayus's craggy face, ruined by the pits and scars earned in two centuries of battle, was awash in spatters of blood. He grinned, showing blood-pinked teeth and split gums. 'My helm display is damaged. Tell me who is still alive.'

Zavien could see why it was damaged – both eye lenses were cracked. He discarded the sergeant's helm, and blink-clicked the runic icon that brought up the rest of the squad's life signs on his own retinal display.

Varlon was dead, his suit powered down. The evidence of that was right before Zavien's eyes.

Garax was also gone, his suit transmitting a screed of flat-line charts. The rangefinder listed him as no more than twenty metres away, likely thrown clear in the crash and killed on impact.

Drayus was dying, right here.

Jarl was...

'Where's Jarl?' Zavien asked, his voice harsh and guttural through his helm's vox speakers.

'He's loose.' Drayus sucked in a breath through clenched teeth. His armour's failing systems were feeding anaesthetic narcotics into his blood, but the wounds were savage and fatal.

'My rangefinder lists him as a kilometre distant.' Even with its unreliability compared to a tracking auspex, it was a decent enough figure to trust.

The sergeant's good hand clenched Zavien's wrist, and he glared into his brother's eye lenses with a fierce, bloodshot stare. 'Find him. Whatever it takes, Zavien. Bring him in, even if you have to kill him.'

'It will be done.'

'After. You must come back, after.' Drayus spat onto his own chest, marking the broken Imperial eagle with his lifeblood. 'Come back for our gene-seed.'

Zavien nodded, rising to his feet. Feeling his fingers curl in the need to draw weapons, he stalked from the cockpit without a backward glance at the sergeant he would never see alive again.

Jarl had awoken first.

In fact, it was truer to say that Jarl had simply not lost his grip on consciousness in the impact, for his restraints bound him with greater security than the standard troop-thrones. In the shaking thunder of the crash, he had seen Garax hurled through the torn space where a wall had been a moment before. He had heard the vicious, wet snap of destroyed vertebrae and ruined bone as Garax had crashed into the edge of the hole on the way out. And he had seen Zavien thrown from his restraint throne to smash sidelong into the cockpit bulkhead, sliding to the floor unconscious.

Enveloped in a force cage around his own restraint throne, Jarl had seen these things occurring through the milky shimmer-screen of electrical force, yet had been protected against the worst of the crash.

Ah, but that protection had not lasted for long. With the gunship motionless, with his brothers silent, with the Thunderhawk around him creaking and burning in the chasm it had carved in the ground, Jarl tore off the last buckles and scrambled over the wreckage of what had been his power-fielded throne. The machine itself, its generator smoking, reeked of captivity. Jarl wanted to be far from it.

He glanced at Zavien, stole the closest weapons he could find in the chaos of the crash site, and ran out into the jungle.

He had a duty to fulfil. A duty to the Emperor.

His father.

Zavien's blade and bolter were gone.

Without compunction, he took Drayus's weapons from the small arming chamber behind the transport room, handling the relics with none of the care he would otherwise have used. Time was of the essence.

The necessary theft complete, he climbed from the wreck of the gunship, vaulting down to the ground and leaving the broken hull behind. In one hand was an idling chainaxe, the motors within the haft chuckling darkly in readiness to be triggered into roaring life. In the other, a bolt pistol, its blackened surface detailed with the crude scratchings of a hundred and more kill-runes.

Zavien didn't look at the smoking corpse of his gunship in some poignant reverie. He knew he would be back to gather the gene-seed of the fallen if he survived this hunt.

There was no time for sentiment. Jarl was loose.

Zavien broke into a run, his armour's joints growling at the rapid movement as he sprinted after his wayward brother, deep into the jungles of Armageddon.

III

They call it Armageddon.

Maybe so. There is nothing to love about this planet.

Whatever savage beauty it once displayed is long dead now, choked under the relentless outflow of the sky-choking factories that vomit black smog into the heavens. The skies themselves are ugly enough – a greyish-yellow shroud of weak poison embracing the strangled world below. It does not rain water here. It rains acid, as thin, weak and strangely pungent as a reptile's piss.

Who could dwell here? In such impurity? The air tastes of sulphur and machine oil. The sky is the colour of infection. The humans – the very souls we are fighting to save – are dead-eyed creatures without passion or life.

I do not understand them. They embrace their enslavement. They accept their confinement within towering manufactories filled with howling machines. Perhaps it is because they have never known freedom, but that is no true excuse to act as brain-killed as a servitor.

We fight for these souls because we are told it is our duty. We are dying, selling our lives in the greatest war this world has ever known, to save them from their own weakness and allow them to return to their lightless lives.

The jungle here... We have jungles on my home world, yet not like this.

The jungles of home are saturated with life. Parasites thrive in every pool of dark water. Insects hollow out the great trees to build their chittering, poisonous hives. The air, already swarming with stinging flies, is sour with the reptilian stench of danger, and the ground will shake with the stalking hunts of the lizard predator-kings.

Survival is the greatest triumph one can earn on Cretacia.

The jungle here barely deserves the name. The ground is clinging mud, leaving you knee-deep in sulphuric sludge. What ragged life breathes the unclean air is weak, irritating, and nothing compared to the threats of home.

Of course, the jungles here possess a danger not even remotely native to the planet itself. They swarm with the worst kind of vermin.

With the planet locked in the throes of invasion, I am all too aware of what brought down our Thunderhawk.

A pack of them hunted up ahead.

As soon as he heard their piggish snarls and barking laughter, Jarl's tongue ached with a raw, coppery urgency. His teeth itched in their sockets, and he felt his heartbeat in the soft tissue around his incisors.

His splashing sprint through the jungle became a hunched and feral stride, while the chainblade in his grip growled each time he gunned the trigger. Small arms fire rattled in his direction even before he cleared the line of trees. They knew he was coming, he made sure of that.

Jarl ignored the metallic rainfall of solid rounds clanging from his war plate. The trees parted and revealed his prey – six of them – hunkered around a tank made of scavenged, rusted scrap.

Greenskins. Their fat-mouthed pistols crashing loud and discordant, their brutish features illuminated by the flickering of muzzle flashes.

Jarl saw none of this. His vision, filtered through targeting reticules, saw only what his dying mind projected. A far greater enemy, the ancient slaves of the Ruinous Powers, feasting on the bodies of the loyal fallen. Where Jarl ran, the skies were not the milky-yellow of pus, but the deep blue of nightfall on ancestral Terra. He did not splash through black-watered marshland. He strode across battlements of gold while the world ended around him in a storm of heretical fire.

Jarl charged, his scream rendered harsh and deafening by his helm's vocalisers. The chainsword's throaty roar reached an apex in the moment before it was brought down onto the shoulder of the first ork.

The killing fury brought darkness again, but the blackness now was awash with blessed, sacred red.

Zavien heard the slaughter. His pace, already at a breakneck sprint through the vegetation, intensified tenfold.

If he could catch Jarl, catch him before his brother made it to Imperial lines, he would avert a catastrophe of innocent blood and the blackest shame.

His red and black war plate – the dark red of arterial blood, the black of the void between worlds – was a ruined mess of burn markings, silver gougings where damage in the crash had scored away the paint from the ceramite's surface, and mud-spattered filth as he raced through the swamp.

Yet when one carries the pride of a Chapter on one's shoulders, necessity lends strength to aching limbs and the false muscles of broken armour.

Zavien burst into the clearing where his brother was embattled. His trigger fingers clenched at once – one unleashing a torrent of bolter shells at his brother's back, the other gunning the chainaxe into whirring, lethal life.

'Jarl!'

Treachery.

What madness was this? To be struck down by one's own sons? Sanguinius, the Angel of Blood, turns from the twisted daemons he has slain and dismembered. One of his own sons screams his name, charging across the golden battlements while the heavens above them burn.

The primarch cries out as his son's weapon speaks in anger. Bolt shells crack against his magnificent armour. His own son, one of his beloved Blood Angels, is trying to kill him.

This cannot be happening.

And, in that moment, Sanguinius decides it is not. There is heresy at work here, not disloyalty. Blasphemy, not naked betrayal.

'What foulness grips you!' the Angel cries at his false son. 'What perversion blackens the soul of a Blood Angel and warps him to serve the Archenemy?'

'Sanguinius!' the traitor son screams. 'Father!'

Zavien roared Jarl's name again, not knowing what his brother truly heard. The cries that returned from his brother's vox-amplifiers chilled his blood – a bellowed, clashing litany of archaic High Gothic and the tongue of Baal that Jarl had never learned.

Surrounded by the ravaged bodies of dead greenskins, the two brothers came together. Zavien's first blow was blocked, the flat of Jarl's chainblade clashing against the haft of his axe. Jarl's armour was pitted and cracked with smoking holes from the impact of bolt shells, yet his strength was unbelievable. Laughing in a voice barely his own, he hurled Zavien backwards.

Unbalanced by his brother's insane vigour, Zavien fell back, rolling into a fighting crouch, shin-deep in marshwater.

Again, Jarl shouted in his unnerving, ancient diction – words Zavien recognised but did not understand. As with Jarl, he had never learned Baalian, and never studied the form of High Gothic spoken ten thousand years before.

'Let this not be your end, my son. Join me! We will take the fight to Horus and drown his evil ambitions in the blood of his tainted warriors!'

Sanguinius removes his helm – a sign of honour and trust despite the war raging around them – and smiles beneficently at his wayward son. His benevolence is legendary. His honour without question.

'It need not be this way,' the Angel of Blood says through his princely smile. 'Join me! To my father's side! For the Emperor!'

Zavien stared at his brother, barely recognising Jarl's face in the drooling, slack-jawed grin that met his gaze. His brother's features were red; a shining wetness from eyes that cried blood.

A meaningless screed of syllables hammered from Jarl's bleeding mouth. It sounded like he was choking on his own demented laughter.

'Brother,' Zavien spoke softly. 'You are gone from us all.'

He rose to his feet, casting aside the empty bolt pistol. In his red gauntlets, he clutched the chainaxe two-handed, and stared at the brother he no longer knew.

'I am not your son, Jarl, and I am no longer your brother. I am Zavien of the Flesh Tearers, born of Cretacia, and I will be your death if you will not let me be your salvation.'

Jarl heaved a burbling laugh, bringing bloody froth to his lips as he wheezed in a language he shouldn't know.

'You disgrace my bloodline,' the Angel said with infinite sorrow, his godlike heart breaking at the blasphemy before his eyes. 'The Ultimate Gate calls to me. A thousand of your masters will fall by my blade before they gain entrance to the Emperor's throne room. I have no more patience for your puling heresy. Come, traitor. Time to die.'

Sanguinius unfurled his great white wings, pearlescent and sunlight-bright in the firestorm wreathing the battlements. With tears in his eyes, tears of misery at the betrayal of one of his own sons, he launched forward to end this blasphemy once and for all.

And I realise I cannot beat him.

When we are shaped into what we are, when we are denied our humanity to become weapons of war, it is said that fear is purged from our physical forms, and triumph is bred into our bones. This is an expression, an attempt at the kind of crude verse forever attributed to the warrior-preachers of the Adeptus Astartes.

It is true that defeat is anathema to us.

But I cannot beat him. He is not the warrior I trained with for decades, not the brother whose every move I can anticipate.

His chainblade, still wet with green gore, arcs down. I block, barely, and am already skidding back in the sulphuric mud. His strength is immense. I know why this is. I am aware of the... the genetic truths at play. His mind cannot contain his delusional fury. He is using everything he has, *everything*, powering his muscles with more force and expending more energy than a functioning mind can allow. I can smell the alkaline reek of his blood through the damage in his armour – combat narcotics are flooding his system in lethal quantities. In his madness, he cannot stem the flood of battle narcotics fusing with his bloodstream.

His strength, this godly power, will kill him.

But not quickly enough.

A second deflected slice, a third, and a fourth that crashes against my helm; a blocked headbutt that crunches into my bracer and dulls my arm; a kick that hammers into my chestplate even as I lean aside to dodge.

A thunderclap. My vision spins. Fire in my spine.

I think my back is broken. I try to say his name, but it comes out as a scream.

Rage, black and wholesome, its tendrils bearing the purest intent, creeps in at the edge of my vision.

I hear him laughing and damning me in a language he shouldn't know.

Then I hear nothing except the wind.

Sanguinius lifts the traitor with contemptuous ease.

Held above his head, the blasphemer thrashes and writhes. The Angel of Blood stalks to the edge of the golden battlements, laughing and weeping all at once at the carnage below. It is a tragedy, but it is also beautiful. Mankind using its greatest might and achievements as it attempts to engineer its own demise. Titans duel in their hundreds, with millions of men dying around their iron feet. The sky is on fire. The entire world smells of blood.

'Die,' the Angel curses his treacherous son with a beauteous whisper, and hurls him from the battlements of the Imperial Palace into the maelstrom of war hundreds of metres below.

Freed of his burden and his bloodline's honour restored, the Angel in gold makes haste away.

His duty is not yet done.

IV

Consciousness returned with the first impact.

A jarring crunch of armour against rock jolted Zavien from his lapse into the murky haze of near-unconsciousness. Feeling himself crashing down the cliff side, he rammed his hand down hard into the rock – a claw of ceramite clutching at the stone. The Astartes grunted as his arms snapped straight, taking his weight, arresting his tumbling fall.

Damage runes flicked up on his retinal display, a language of harsh white urgency. Zavien ignored them, though it was harder to ignore the pain throughout his body. Even the injected chemical anaesthetic compounds from his armour and the nerve-dulling surgery done to him couldn't entirely wash it away. That was a bad sign.

He clawed his way back up the cliff, teeth clenched, gauntlets tearing handholds into the stone where nature hadn't provided any.

Once at the top, the Flesh Tearer retrieved the chainaxe that had flown from his grip, and broke into a staggering run.

He almost killed me.

That is a hard truth to swallow, for we were evenly matched for all of our lives. My armour is damaged, operating at half capacity, but it still lends me strength as I run. Behind me, the wrecked greenskin tank remains alone, its crew slain, the rest of its missiles aiming into the sky with no one to fire them.

Curse those piggish wretches for bringing down our gunship.

I run on, gathering speed, slowing only to hack hanging vegetation from my path.

I recall the topography of this region from the hololithic maps at the last war council. The mining town of Dryfield is to the east. Jarl's rage-addled mind will drive him to seek out life. I know where he is going. I also know that unless something slows him down...

He will get there first.

Sister Amalay D'Vorien kissed the bronze likeness of Saint Silvana, and let the necklace icon fall back on its leather cord. The weak midday sun, what brightness penetrated the gauzy, polluted cloud cover, was a dull presence in the heavens, only occasionally reflecting glare off the edges of Promethia, the squad's Immolator tank.

Her own armour was once silver, now stained a faint, dull grey from exposure to the filthy air of this world. She licked her cracked lips, resisting the desire to drink from the water canteen inside the tank. Second Prayer was only an hour before, and she'd slaked her thirst with a mouthful of the brackish water, warmed as it was by the tank's idling engine.

'Sister...' called down Brialla from the Immolator's turret. 'Did you see that?'

Amalay and Brialla were alone while the rest of their squad patrolled the edges of the jungle. Their tank idled on the dirt road, with Amalay circling the hull, bolter in hand, and Brialla panning her heavy flamers along the tree lines.

Amalay whispered a litany of abasement before duty, chastising herself for letting her mind wander to thoughts of sustenance. Her bolter up and ready, she moved around to the front of the Immolator.

'I saw nothing,' she said, eyes narrowed and focused. 'What was it?'

'Movement. Something dark. Remain vigilant.'

There was a tone colouring Brialla's voice, on the final words. A suggestion of disapproval. Amalay's laxity had been noticed.

'I see nothing,' Amalay spoke again. 'There's... No, wait. *There.*'

The 'something' broke from its crouch in the vegetation at the tree line. A blur of crimson and black, with a chainblade revving. Amalay recognised an Astartes instantly, and the threat a moment later. Her bolter barked once, twice, and dropped from her hands to clatter to the dirt. The gun crashed once more from its vantage point on the ground, a loud boom that hammered a shell into the tank's sloped armour plating.

Even as this last shot was fired, Amalay's head flew clear of her shoulders, white hair catching the wind before the bleeding wreckage rolled into the undergrowth.

Brialla blasphemed as she brought the flamer turret around on protesting mechanics, and wrenched the handles to aim the cannons low.

The Astartes was cradling Amalay's headless body, speaking to it in a low snarl. Her sister was already dead. Brialla squeezed both triggers.

Twin gouts of stinking chemical flame roared from the cannons, bathing Amalay and the Astartes in clinging, corrosive fire. She was already whispering a lament for her fallen sister, even as she blistered the armour and skin from Amalay's bones.

It was impossible to see through the reeking orange miasma. Brialla killed the jets of flame after seven heartbeats, knowing whatever had been washed in the fire would be annihilated, purged in the burning storm.

Amalay. Her armour blackened, its joints melted, her hands reduced to blackened bone. She lay on the ground, incinerated.

A loud thud clanged on the tank's roof behind Brialla. She turned in her restraint throne, the slower turret cycling round to follow her gaze. Already, she was trying to scramble free of her seat.

The Astartes was burning. Holy fire licked at the edges of his war-plate, and his joints steamed. He eclipsed the sun, casting a flickering shadow over her. His armour was black, charred, but not immolated. As she hauled herself out of her restraints, he levelled a dripping chainsword at her face.

'The Flesh Tearers!' she screamed into the vox-mic built into her armour's collar. 'Echoes of Gaius Point!'

In anciently-accented Gothic, her killer said six whispered words.

'You will pay for your heresy.'

I watch from the shadows of the trees.

The Sororitas are tense. While one of them performs funerary rites over the destroyed bodies of their sisters, three others stalk around the hull of their grey tank, bolters aimed while they stare into the jungle through gunsights.

I can smell the corpses beneath the white shrouds. One is burned, cooked by promethium chemical fire. The other had bled a great deal before she died, torn to pieces. I do not need to see the remains to know this is true.

For now, I hide, crouched and hidden. The jungle masks the ever-present charged hum of my armour from their weak, mortal ears, while I listen to fragments of their speech.

Jarl's trail has grown cold, even the smell of his potent blood lost in the billion scents of this sulphuric jungle. I need focus. I need direction.

But as soon as I draw near enough to see the sisters' steel-grey armour and the insignias of loyalty they each wear, I curse my fortune.

The Order of the Argent Shroud.

They were with us at Gaius Point.

Echoes of that battle will haunt us all until the Chapter's final nights.

'My auspex senses something,' I hear one of them say to her sisters. I make ready to move again, to taste shame and flee. I cannot confront them like this. They must not know of our presence. 'Something alive,' she says. 'And with a power signature.'

'Flesh Tearer!' one of the sisters calls out, and my blood freezes in my veins. It is not fear I feel, but true, sickening dread as she uses our Chapter's sacred name. *How can they know?*

'Flesh Tearer! Show yourself! Face the Emperor's judgement for the barbarity of your tainted Chapter!'

My teeth clench. My fingers quiver, then grip the chainaxe tighter. *They know.* They know a Flesh Tearer did this. Their wretched slain sisters must have warned them.

Another female voice, the one carrying the auspex scanner, adds to the first one's cries. 'We were at Gaius Point, decadent filth! Face us, and face retribution for your heresy!'

They know what happened at Gaius Point. They saw our shame, our curse, and the blood that ran that day.

They believe I butchered two of their sisters here, and now lay the sins of my brother Jarl upon my shoulders.

Gunfire rings out. A bolter shell slices past my pauldron, shredding vegetation.

'I see him,' a female voice declares, 'There!'

My trigger finger strokes the Engage rune on the chainaxe's haft. After a heartbeat's hesitation, I squeeze. Jagged, whirring teeth cycle into furious life. The weapon cuts air in anticipation of the moment it will eat flesh.

They *dare* blame me for this...

They open fire.

I am not a heretic.

But this must end.

V

Zavien reached Dryfield just as the sun was setting.

He had left the jungle behind three hours before. The lone warrior's run came to an end at the fortified walls – outside the mining settlement, he heard no sound from within, only the desperate howl of the wind across the wasteland.

Hailing the walls, calling for sentries, earned him no response.

The settlement's gates were sealed: a jury-rigged amalgamation of steel bars, flakboard and even furniture piled high behind the double doors in the wall ringing the village. These pitiful defences were the colony's attempts to reinforce their walls against the ork hordes sweeping across the planet.

With neither the time nor the inclination to hammer the gates open through force, Zavien mag-locked his axe to his back and punched handholds in the metal wall itself, dragging himself to the ramparts fifteen metres above.

The village was a collection of one-storey buildings, perhaps enough to house fifteen families. A dirt track cut through the village's centre like an old scar; evidence of the supply convoys that made it this far out from the main hives, and the passage of ore haulers who came to profit from the local copper mine. Low-quality metal would be in great demand by the planet's impoverished citizens, who could afford no better.

The largest building – indeed, the only one that was more than a hut made from scrap – was a spired church bedecked in crudely-carved gargoyles.

Zavien acknowledged all of this in a heartbeat's span. The Astartes scanned the ramshackle battlements around the village, then turned to stare at the settlement itself.

No sign of movement.

He walked from the platform, falling the fifteen metres to the ground and landing in a balanced crouch.

He came across the first body less than a minute later.

A woman. Unarmed. Slumped against the wall of a hovel, a

blood-smear decorating the wall behind her. She was carved in half, and not cleanly.

The wide streets between the ramshackle huts and homes were decorated with trails of blood and the tracks of weight dragged through the dirt. All of these led to the same place. Whomever had come here and slain the colonists had dragged the bodies to the modest church with its shattered windows and corroded walls of flakboard and red iron.

Zavien's retinal locator display was finally picking up faint returns from Jarl's war plate. His brother was inside, no longer running. And from the silence, no longer killing.

The Flesh Tearer stalked past the weaponless corpse, limp in its lifeless repose, slain by his own sword in his brother's hands. Zavien had seen such things before – they were images he would never forget while he still drew breath.

He felt cold, clinging shame run through his blood like a toxin. Just like at Gaius Point.

It wasn't supposed to happen.

At Gaius Point.

It was never supposed to happen.

That night, they had damned themselves forever.

It should have been a triumph worthy of being etched onto the armour of every warrior that fought there.

The Imperial front line was held by the Point's militia and the Order of the Argent Shroud, who had rallied the people of the wasteland town into an armed fighting force and raised morale to fever pitch through their sermons and blessings in the name of the God-Emperor.

The greenskins descended in a swarm of thousands, hurling themselves at the town's barricades, their mass forming a sea of bellowing challenges, leathery flesh and hacking blades.

At the battle's apex, the Sisters and the militia were on the edge of being overwhelmed. At last, and when it mattered most, Gaius Point's frantic distress calls were answered.

They came in Thunderhawks, boosters howling as they soared over the embattled horde. The gunships kissed the scorched earth only long enough to deploy their forces: almost two hundred Astartes in armour of arterial red and charcoal black. The rattling roar of so many chainblades came together in a ragged, ear splitting chorus, sounding like the war-cry of a mechanical god.

Zavien was in the first wave. Alongside Jarl and his brothers, he hewed left and right, his blade's grinding teeth chewing through armour and bloody, fungal flesh as the sons of Sanguinius reaped the aliens' lives.

The orks were butchered in droves, caught between a hammer and anvil, being annihilated from behind and gunned down from the front.

Zavien saw nothing but blood. Xenos blood, stinking and thick, splashing across his helm. The smell of triumph, the reek of exultant victory.

He was also one of the first to the barricades.

By then, he couldn't see. He couldn't think. His senses were flooded by stimuli, all of it aching, enticing and maddening. He tried to speak, but it tore from his lips as a cry aimed at the polluted skies. Even breathing did nothing but draw the rich scent of alien blood deeper into his body, disseminating it through his system. To be so saturated by xenos taint ignited a fire in his mind, tapping into the gene-deep fury that forever threatened to overwhelm him.

Driven on by the ceaseless urge to drown his senses in the purity of enemy blood, Zavien disembowelled the last ork before him, and vaulted the barricade. He had to kill. *He had to kill.* He was born for nothing else.

He and his brothers had been fighting in ferocious hand-to-hand battle for two hours. The enemy was destroyed. The joyous cheers of the militia died in thousands of throats as, in a wave of vox-screams and howling chainswords, half of the Flesh Tearers broke the barricades and ran into the town.

With no foes to slay, the Astartes turned their rage upon whatever still lived.

The Angel mourned the slain.

Their deaths were a dark necessity on the path to redemption. The prayers he chanted to the ceiling of the Emperor's throne room inspired tears in his eyes, and tears in the eyes of the thousands of loyal soldiers staring on.

'We must burn the slain,' he whispered through the silver tears. 'We must forever remember those who died this day, and remember the foulness that turned their hearts against us.'

'Sanguinius!' a voice cried from behind. It echoed throughout the chamber, where a million banners hung in the breezeless air, marking every regiment ever sworn to fight and die for the young Imperium of Man.

The Angel tilted his head, the very image of patient purity.

'I thought I killed you, heretic.'

'Jarl!'

Wheezing, mumbling, with bloody saliva running in strings from his damaged mouth grille, Jarl staggered around to face his brother.

What burbled from his mouth was a mixture of languages, wet with the blood in his throat. The chemical reek of Jarl's body assaulted Zavien's senses even over the smell of his brother's burned armour and the reek of the slain. The combat narcotics flooding Jarl's body were eating him alive.

Zavien did nothing but stare for several moments after he called his brother's name. The dead were everywhere, piled all across the floor of the church, a slumbering congregation of the slaughtered. Perhaps a hundred of them, all dragged here after the carnage. Perhaps many of them had been found here in worshipful service, and only half the village had needed to be dragged. Trails of streaked, smeared blood marked the floor.

'Burn the bodies,' Jarl said in grunted Cretacian, the tongue of their shared home world, amongst a screed of words Zavien couldn't make out. 'Purge the sin, burn the bodies, cleanse the palace.'

Zavien raised his chainaxe. In sickening mirror image, his blood-maddened brother raised his dripping chainsword.

'This ends now, Jarl.'

There was a bark of syllables, a drooling mess of annihilated words.

The Angel raised his golden blade.

He had been so foolish. This was no mere heretic. Had he been blinded all along? Yes... the machinations of the tainted traitors had shrouded his golden eyes from the truth. But now... Now he saw everything.

'Yes, Horus,' he said with a smile that spoke of infinite regret. 'It ends now.'

VI

The brothers met in the defiled church, their boots struggling to grip the mosaic-laid floor, awash as it was with innocent blood. The whining roar of chainblades was punctuated by crashes as the weapons met. Jagged teeth shattered with every block and parry, clattering against nearby wooden pews as they were torn from their sockets.

Zavien's blood hammered through his body, tingling with the electric edge of combat stimulants. Jarl was a shadow of the warrior he had been – frothing at the mouth, raving at allies that didn't exist, and half-crippled by the lethal battle-drug overdose that was burning out his organs.

Zavien blocked his brother's frantic, shaking cuts. Every time his axe fell, he'd carve another chasm into Jarl's armour. Ultimately, only one warrior was aware enough to know this would never be settled by chainblades.

With a last block and a savage return, Zavien smashed Jarl's blade aside and kicked it from his grip. Its engine stuttered to a halt, resting on the tiled ground. Jarl watched it fly from his grip with delayed, bleeding vision.

Before he could recover, Zavien's hands were at his throat. The Flesh Tearer squeezed, his hands crunching into Jarl's neck, collapsing the softer joint-armour there and vicing into the flesh beneath.

Jarl fell to his knees as his brother strangled him. His gene-enhanced physiology was poisoned by both the curse and the narcotics, and his sight began to darken as his body could take no more punishment.

Darken, yet clear.

Deprived of air, unable to even draw a shred of breath, he mouthed a voiceless word that never left the confines of his charred helm.

'Zavien.'

Zavien wrenched his grip to the side, snapping the bones of his brother's spine, and still strangling.

He stood like this for some time. Night had fallen before the warrior's gauntlets released their burden and Jarl's body finally slumped to the ground.

There the madman rested, asleep among those he had slain.

'It is done,' Zavien spoke into his squad's vox channel, his eyes closed as only silence replied.

'Jarl is dead, brothers. It is done.'

He chose to finish what his brother had begun. Even in madness, there sometimes hides a little sense.

The bodies had to be burned. Not to purify any imagined heresy, but to hide the evidence of what had happened here.

It was never supposed to happen. Here, or at Gaius Point. They had damned themselves, and all that remained was to fight as loyally as they could before righteous vengeance caught up with them all.

As the church burned, pouring thick black smoke into the polluted sky, the sound of engines grumbled from the horizon.

Orks. The enemy was finally here.

Zavien stood among the flames, immune to them, his axe in his hand. The fire would draw the aliens closer. There was no way he could defend the whole village against them, but the thought of shedding and tasting their blood before he finally fell ignited his killing urge.

His fangs ached as the vehicles pulled in to a halt outside.

No.

Those engine sounds were too clean, too well-maintained. It was the enemy. But it was not the greenskins.

I walk from the church, the broken axe in my hand.

There are twenty of them. In human unison, impressive enough even if it lacks the perfection of Astartes unity, they raise their bolters. The Sisters of the Order of the Argent Shroud. The silver hulls of their tanks and their own armour are turned a flickering orange-red in the light of the fire that should have hidden our sins.

Twenty guns aim at me.

The thirst fades. My hunger to taste blood trickles back into my throat, suddenly ignorable.

'We were at Gaius Point,' the lead sister calls out. Their eyes are narrowed at the brightness of the flame behind me.

I do not move. I tell them, simply:

'I know.'

'We have petitioned the Inquisition for your Chapter's destruction, Flesh Tearer.'

'I know.'

'That is all you have to say for yourself, heretic? After Gaius Point? After killing the squad of our sister Amalay D'Vorien? *After massacring an entire village?*'

'You came to pass judgement,' I tell her. 'So do it.'

'We came to defend this colony against your wretched blasphemy!'

They still fear me. Even outnumbered and armed only with a shattered axe, they still fear me. I can smell it in their sweat, hear it in their voices, and see it in their wide eyes that reflect the flames.

I look over my shoulder, where Jarl's legacy burns. Motes of amber fire sail up from the blaze. My brother's funeral pyre, and a testament to what we have all become. A monument to how far we have fallen.

We burn our dead on Cretacia. Because so many are killed by poisons and beasts and the predator-king reptiles, it is a mark of honour to die and be burned, rather than be taken by the forest.

It was never meant to be like this. Not here, and not at Gaius Point.

Twenty bolters open fire before I can look back.

I don't hear them. I don't feel the wet, knifing pain of destruction.

All I hear is the roar of a Cretacian predator-king, the fury rising from its reptilian jaws as it stalks the jungles of my home world. A carnosaur, black-scaled and huge, roaring up to the clear, clean skies.

It hunts me. It hunts me now, as it hunted me so long ago, at the start of this second life.

I reach for my spear, and...

Zavien clutches the weapon against his chest.

'It is death itself,' *he grunts to his tribal brothers as they crouch in the undergrowth. The tongue of Cretacia is simple and plain, little more than the rudiments of true language.* 'The king-lizard is death itself. It comes for us.'

The carnosaur shakes the ground with another slow step closer. It breathes in short sniffs, mouth open, jaws slack, tasting the air for scents. A grey tongue the size of a man quivers in its maw.

The spear in his steady grip is the one he made himself. A long shaft of dark wood with a fire-blackened point. He has used it for three years now, since his tenth winter, to hunt for his tribe.

He does not hunt for his tribe today. Today, as the sun burns down and bakes their backs, he hunts because the gods are in the jungle, and they are watching. The tribes have seen the gods in their armour of red metal and black stone, always in the shadows, watching the hunting parties as they stalk their prey.

If a hunter wishes to dwell in paradise among the stars, he must hunt well when the gods walk the jungles.

Zavien stares at the towering lizard-beast, unable to look away from its watery, slitted red eye.

He shifts his grip on the spear he crafted.

With a prayer that the gods are bearing witness to his courage, he throws the weapon with a heartfelt scream.

The Flesh Tearer crashed to the bloodstained ground, face down in the dust.

'Cease fire,' Sister Superior Mercy Astaran said softly. Her sisters obeyed immediately.

'But he still lives,' one of them replied.

This was true. The warrior was dragging himself with gut-wrenching slowness, one-armed and with a trembling hand, through the dirt. A dark trail of broken armour and leaking lifeblood pooled around him.

He raised his shaking hand once more, dug the spasming fingers into the ground, and dragged himself another half-metre closer to the burning church's front door.

'Is he seeking to escape?' one of the youngest sisters asked, unwilling to admit her admiration for the heretic's endurance. One arm lost at the elbow, both legs destroyed from the knees down, and his armour a cracked mess that leaked coolant fluids and rich, red Astartes blood.

'It is hardly escape to crawl into a burning building,' another laughed.

'He wishes to die among the blasphemy he caused,' Astaran said, her scowl even harsher in the firelight. 'End him.'

A single gunshot rang out from the battle-line.

Zavien's fingers stopped trembling. His reaching hand fell into the dust. His eyes, which had first opened to see the clear skies of a distant world, closed at last.

'What should we do with the body?' Sister Mercy Astaran asked her commander.

'Let the echoes of this heresy remain as an example, at least until the greenskins take control of the surrounding wastelands. Come sisters, we do not have much time. Leave this wretch for the vultures.'

MIDNIGHT ON THE STREET OF KNIVES

Andy Chambers

Commorragh is a city like no other in the universe. It exists outside space and time in the unknowable depths of the Sea of Souls, the realm beyond our realm that idiot savants argue gave birth to all that we know. Commorragh's makers, or rather architects as they would claim, did not fashion the city as one place. Rather each of them used ways unimaginable to lesser beings to fashion their own secret enclaves out of the Immaterial Realm to serve as fortress, sanctum, pleasure palace or arena according to their whim. In time the hubris of these 'architects' grew so great that they created something that breached the very walls between realms. As all crashed into ruins they fled to their enclaves like rats into their holes. In time, as they grew ever more fearful of the dreadful child they had sired together, those that survived the tempest strove to connect their realms. So steeped in torture and murder were they that they had no choice. They must do so to feed one upon another and whomever else they could bring beneath their hand. And so the eternal city was born.

– Adept Xalinis Huo, Hereticus Majoris.

It was midnight on the Street of Knives when Kharbyr spotted his mark heading straight towards him not six stalls up. The street was dark and crooked but it was virtually deserted and the gaunt figure of Bellathonis's servant stood out in freeze-frame in the stark flicker of the furnaces. Kharbyr had been lucky, oh yes, but he'd made the right choice of where to hunt in the first place and that made him feel extremely smug. He was cleverer than the others and he would be the one to claim the promised reward. He treated himself to a pinch of agarin while he waited, savouring the clean bite of it in his nostrils and the shiver it sent down his spine. Oh, this was going to be fun.

The whisper had come that Bellathonis's servant had left the Red House carrying the package in a hurry and, most importantly, alone. When he'd heard that, Kharbyr had gambled that the haemonculus's minion would cut through here. The Street of Knives was a safe run for as long as it lasted, at least as safe as it got anywhere in the city. The Archon of Metzuh suffered no fractious incidents here that might impede the productivity of her weaponsmiths and artisans.

To underscore her displeasure at such activities, the Street of Knives was patrolled by her incubi, their mere presence enough to deter most troublemakers. The initial excitement of seeing his prey had sent Kharbyr's hand shooting toward his blade of its own volition, but a pair of grim, armoured incubi already had him under scrutiny as if they could sense his intentions. The bodies of the truly foolhardy young blades – the ones who just couldn't take a hint – were hanging on chains from the jagged eaves of the weapon shops. They were left there as hellion-bait to clarify the point to others to curb their instincts in this part of the city.

With a conscious effort of will, Kharbyr unwrapped his fingers from the polished bone grip and calmly turned to examine a display of wickedly curved hydraknives as the servant hurried past. Naturally, fighting still occurred this close to the Archon's palace, but only over matters of import that were orders of magnitude above this one.

Kharbyr got his first good look at the servant as he passed: a pale, haggard face with red, staring eyes, a heavy jaw and a morose scowl that looked to be a permanent fixture. It was a fitting face for the minion of a haemonculus, a creature of vivisections and interrogations. Thick brows beneath the servant's hairless pate were currently knotted with concern and a kind of mulish determination.

A long, ribbed coat of dark hide flapped from the servant's narrow shoulders with all the panache of partially sloughed skin. No weapons were obvious, but he was clutching the package so fiercely that it looked as if he feared it might make a break for freedom at any moment. He was also muttering incoherently and smelled appallingly of ether and offal. The servant was certainly going to be easy to shadow. Kharbyr let the noisome fool get a little further ahead and then wandered innocently after him.

Xagor clutched the hide-wrapped jar of pineal glands tighter to his chest. As he scurried along he tried to balance speed against drawing too much attention to himself. It was unlikely anyone would try to steal the jar here, but the master would not happy if Xagor so much as let it out of his sight or, worse still, he lost it. Those that displeased the master were soon begging for death. Xagor knew this for certain as he'd attended them himself on many occasions. With a haemonculus as skilled as the master, death was always a long time coming. No, handling the jar was bad enough, but what he'd heard while he was getting it at the Red House made it all so much worse.

Master Bellathonis was always hungry for news. He instructed all his servants most specifically on the importance of relaying to him any scrap of information, speculation, gossip or rumour as soon as it reached their lowly ears. The master had even gone so far as to demonstrate the alterations he made to servants who proved too slow or stupid to abide by this simple but cardinal rule.

Yes, Master Bellathonis took news very seriously indeed and now Xagor had suffered the misfortune of being told a piece of news that could change everything. A Dysjunction! His hand gripped the neck of the jar tighter as he fantasised about choking the life out of Matsilier for telling him in the first place. The crones predicted a Dysjunction before the year was out. The idiot had been so full of himself he couldn't wait to share a secret and show how important he was. That had made it even worse. Who knew how many others he'd told, or how soon it would get back to the master or whether it had already done so and he, Xagor, the best and most trusted of the master's servants, would presently be excreting from all the wrong orifices.

So here he was, scurrying down the Street of Knives, frantically trying to work out how to get this unwelcome lump of knowledge and an intact jar of glands to the master's manse before someone else got there first. It was big news. A Dysjunction would send the fragile peace in the city tumbling into anarchy, the wardings would all shift and whole tiers could be inundated. It could even be the big one, the end of the city itself. His guts twisted queasily at the prospect. Everyone in Commorragh knew that they lived on the edge of the abyss, but chose to ignore it in a very determined fashion. Being confronted with the fact was an uncomfortable sensation.

Xagor briefly toyed with the idea of fleeing on the assumption that it was already too late, but he prided himself on having a more pragmatic viewpoint. If there was one thing that all the fickle masters of Commorragh could agree upon, it was that runaways were singled out for especially imaginative punishment in order to set an example. In a society that had whiled away countless millennia raising the infliction of pain and misery to a high art form, that meant things far worse than one of Master Bellathonis' comparatively mild bouts of scatological humour. In this regard Xagor had to concede the policy was effective.

No, the correct course was to obey his first instinct and hurry back to face the consequences. If he was too late, well, the master could be almost... indulgent in his punishments if he believed you had tried your best. The master might even reward him. Xagor also prided himself on his sense of optimism. Sadly, that was sorely tested by the idea of

Dysjunction. They had occurred before, though not in Xagor's lifetime, and the idea that something as permanent as the city could have whole tiers shift and revolve like some great orrery was anathema to him. The master would surely know what to do.

Unfortunately in another sixty paces the Street of Knives would split into three diverging alleyways. These quickly mired themselves in the under-warren beneath the slave mills like streams entering a swamp. The marginal safety afforded by the incubi terminated there. Entering the under-warren alone was a tacit admission that you were tired of life and expected to be relieved of it soon. It was something that the lurking mandrakes to be found there would apply themselves to most industriously for only the scant payment of your death scream.

There was nothing for it but to take the Short Stairs to the canal and gamble on reaching the Beryl Gate. If he were lucky he'd just be ignored, but the epicureans were always so unpredictable.

Kharbyr glided along on the trail of the oblivious servant. He felt elated, almost giddy, as he slipped through the shadows. He had to fight the urge to skip forward and plunge his blade between those unsuspecting shoulder blades. The dead swung on their chains above him and grinned down with their rictus grins approvingly. Come and join us, they seemed to smile, we couldn't master our murder-lust either. Always room for one more.

Kharbyr swallowed and tried to focus. The instructions had been regarding the package. There was no smear of shame in trailing the mark to watch and listen while he carried it. Many had an interest in Bellathonis and wanted to hear about the comings and goings of his minions. There might be a meeting or exchange that he could report back on.

Still, something in Kharbyr chafed at such a dull assignment. Perhaps if the servant were carrying something important then murdering him could pay off anyway, or he might be forced to divulge something useful before he expired. Unfortunately, a haemonculus's servant would doubtless laugh at the kind of excruciations Kharbyr could inflict on the spot in some alley, but if he could be kidnapped...

Kharbyr was so caught up in his musings that it took him a moment to register that the servant had vanished. Momentary panic edged with irrational fury swept over him. Fool! Strike when you can – never hesitate!

Xagor went bounding down the elegantly sculpted Short Stairs like a goat down a mountainside, clinging to his jar for dear life as he took the curving steps three at time. Just before he'd turned off, he'd had the unpleasant feeling that someone really was following him and that it was not just his well-developed paranoia at work this time. The stairs would be a good place to try and lose any shadows, providing he didn't do so at the cost of breaking his own neck.

The Short Stairs wandered between gates into the Hy'Kran and Metzuh tiers of the city in a fanciful curlicue of stone, metal and glass that jutted right out over the smooth, dark silk of the Metzuh's Grand Canal in several places. Other steps, spirals and esplanades branched irregularly from it following their own unfathomable logic. They were called the Short Stairs because they only connected two tiers, whereas the Long Stairs beyond Hy'Kran crossed half a dozen. Xagor had heard a story once that the Short Stairs formed a word or message when seen from a distance, but no one seemed to agree on what it said.

Xagor was soon forced to moderate his pace. There were plenty of open landings where the Short Stairs simply stopped in open air to afford a stunning view of the Grand Canal and its drifting pleasure barges. A much closer view of the canal awaited those who neglected to spot such sudden drop-offs. On the positive side, there were more subjects here and that was what he needed right now. He slowed right down as he started to pass amongst them, trying not to imagine what would happen on the Short Stairs during the Dysjunction when the tiers began to move.

He was among slaves here, or valued servants like himself hurrying after their master or mistress's bidding. But there were highborn here too, strolling individually and in groups. The crisscrossing streams of slaves and servants parted around the highborn like water around stones, carefully keeping out of immediate striking range. Xagor adjusted his descent to head toward two of the larger groups of highborn coming up from below.

Kharbyr sprinted heedlessly back along the Street of Knives, casting around for Bellathonis's servant. The two incubi were regarding him with distinct interest by the time he came to steps leading down. He darted onto the Short Stairs and stopped short, regarding the noisome masses he found there with disdain. Scrawny, half-naked slaves were streaming up and down it like rats.

He could see the servant, heading down towards a fistful of warriors bearing marks of The Scarlet Edge. Kharbyr found himself sprinting again, furious that this stupid, easy-to-follow piece of dross was being such a pain. He had to accept a galling loss of face as he passed other highborn and they made cutting remarks about him to his back. In their place he would have done the same, but letting the taunts go unanswered was a humiliation almost too much to be borne. He cut down a particularly dim-witted slave that couldn't move out of the way fast enough and that made him feel slightly better. The loathsome haemonculus's creature was going to die for this, Bellathonis's servant or not. He could worry about the consequences later.

It was dark by the canal, so dark that Xagor had to navigate last spiral of the stair virtually by touch, all the time terrified that a misstep would make him drop the jar. The gaily-lit pleasure barges outside seemed to emphasise rather than mitigate the gloom as they glided past.

The Grand Canal ran in a broad, lazy circuit all the way around Metzuh tier, bounded by the warding on one bank and the palaces of Metzuh on the other. Supposedly, the canal had once been filled with a pure, sweet-smelling narcotic oil but now it was such a strange mélange of drugs, wastes, chemicals and excreta that it defied classification. The scent alone could be overpoweringly hallucinogenic, a dip in the stuff brought madness or oblivion.

The promenade along the canal bank had long since become the exclusive territory of those Metzuh highborn most given to hedonism and sensuality as their current diversion of choice – the epicureans. Any slave foolish enough to venture down here would be taken for sport in the blink of an eye and it was not a wise place for servants to tarry. Opulent dens and flesh halls cluttered the bottom of the tier and sprawled out across the broad tiles of the promenade very much like their patrons. The odd docks and piers periodically jutting out from the canal side played host to a number of fanciful craft.

Beyond the curve of the canal and out of sight at present, Xagor knew there was a slender bridge that pierced the warding at the Beryl Gate. Through the gate were the Aviaries of Malixian, who some called 'the Mad'. The noble Archon Malixian was one of Bellathonis's most favoured patrons, in no small part thanks to the suite of laboratories the archon had granted him. Such was a true mark of distinction when so many haemonculi had to make do with whatever garret or basement they could find to set up shop. The Aviaries would give safe passage all the way to the Screaming Tower where Bellathonis currently conducted his work.

Kharbyr paused to let a pair of masked revellers move past before swarming down a trellis into the welcoming darkness on the promenade. He sank himself deeper into the shadows while he looked around for signs of his mark. The gloom fitted his mood. He was coming to the disquieting realisation that he had lost the trail. If the servant was meeting someone along the canal, he could be hidden inside any one of a dozen salons or dens by now. He might have even boarded a barge and be so well out of reach he may as well have grown wings and flown away.

Weighing the options, Kharbyr considered what little he knew. The servant had left the Red House carrying something he hadn't had when he arrived. He'd been alone and he'd left in a hurry. The last two facts didn't really fit with him going to meet someone. He wouldn't be hurrying if things had been pre-planned and Bellathonis was unlikely to entrust anything important to a lone servant in any event. Something unexpected must have happened inside the Red House to send the servant haring off like that without waiting for an escort. So where would

the servant really be going? Kharbyr felt his spirits lift at the realisation.
The servant was running straight to his master.

Xagor hugged the jar to himself and strode along with what he hoped looked like a purposeful gait. His hands were sending sharp needles of pain up his arms with every step but he welcomed them. Those who would serve pain must first learn how to endure it and then how to love it, so said Bellathonis as he had tortured Xagor for the first time. To some a haemonculus is nothing but a torturer, but those with the calling know that even the lowliest of them aspires to something much greater.

The promenade was almost quiet. High pitched wails and screams floated down from above, seemingly muffled by billows of sweetly-scented mist from the canal. Xagor had already slipped past one duel between two highborn and a less formal affair between two groups of revellers over some real or imagined slight, but that was quiet by the standards of the area. The high-arched bridge to the Beryl Gate was coming into sight but the loose groups of epicureans were coalescing more and more into a crowd. There was some kind of disturbance up ahead that seemed to be getting closer. A barbed metal spine could be seen rising above even the tallest highborn in that direction and it was steadily forging a path through the mass towards him.

Kharbyr carefully made his way along the canal edge blending in as best he could. He struggled not to sneer at the antics of the epicureans every time he saw them fighting with one another. Their skills were like those of children in their fifth year of training, all showy hack and slash with no hint of finesse. He was sure he could take any of them easily and was sorely tempted to try his hand, but there wasn't time. He had to get to the bridge and through the gate. A small bribe to the guards would soon tell him if the servant had got there first and if he hadn't then Kharbyr could simply slip inside and choose his spot for ambush.

A commotion behind him made him turn and stop in his tracks. A murder engine was edging out onto the promenade, its jewelled snout swinging back and forth like a beast searching for spoor. Epicureans flinched away with unseemly haste as the hideous contraption approached. Kharbyr wondered if it had been set on the trail of anyone in particular or had just slipped its leash to inflict some random carnage of its own volition. As the epicureans scattered, one figure stood unmoving. With a shock Kharbyr realised that it was his mark, the haemonculus's servant, who was just standing there holding the package and gaping at the multi-bladed death machine gliding smoothly towards him.

Xagor recognised the workmanship of the barbed sting even before he could see the magnificent engine itself. It was one of Vlokarion's Coven of Thirteen, a matched set of Talos built for the amusement of Archon

Yrdiir Xun by the legendary haemonculus Vlokarion four millennia ago. The device whispered forward on unseen grav-motors, evidently searching for a new client to embrace inside its cage of filigreed bone. Jointed, insectile-looking arms rose from its flanks, poised with exquisite malice to display their array of blades, saws, hooks and probes. Most of the highborn moved more discreetly out of its path, not wishing to attract its attention now it was fixed on him. Xagor simply stood mesmerised by the glittering beauty of it.

It drifted closer, seemingly intrigued by his immobility. Theoretically, a Talos was nothing more than a mobile torture machine with no mind of its own. Its sentience, its *anima* was drawn entirely from the client it embraced and kept in a permanent state of agony. The symbiosis was complete: the Talos gained awareness and personality from the client, the client gained the will and the ability to share their suffering with whomever the Talos chose. Xagor could see that the current client was coming to the end of their journey and wondered how long they had been incarcerated. A well-made Talos was as skilful as a surgeon in its work. Those built by Vlokarion were said to keep their clients alive for centuries. They were also said to have grown to have their own strange kind of sentience in the millennia since their creator's demise.

Now the machine floated there before him and seemed to regard him with its gleaming sensors. The pitiable-looking client shifted and mewled feebly within their cage. Without thinking, Xagor slowly prised one hand away from his jar to reach out and stroke the curving metal prow. Weapons slid partway from pits in the Talos's gleaming skin and then back again uncertainly as his hand came close.

Kharbyr slipped deeper into the crowd. Once a healthy space had been cleared, there were plentiful spectators jostling to watch the torture engine go to work. In what was sure to be a disappointment to them, but a relief for Kharbyr, the thing hadn't started ripping the little idiot in front of it into confetti yet. He was going to lose his mark – and the package too – once the murder machine got going. Right now it seemed bemused that anyone would have the temerity to just stand there in front of it when it was on the hunt, but that wasn't going to last.

He surreptitiously felt through his belt loops for a vial containing faerun. When used on a blade, faerun would make even shallow cuts inflict such nerve-shredding agony that the recipient would be utterly terrorised. Typically, he would use it on someone already restrained because it was liable make a victim run like the hounds of hell were after them.

Luck was with him and he found he still had a few drops of faerun left. He used it lavishly on his blade in a quick, practised move while glancing around for a likely victim. There was a youngish-looking female nearby, pierced, tattooed and naked to the waist. Kharbyr sauntered past and delivered a quick slice across her unprotected ribs without even breaking his stride. Only then did it strike him that the effects of the faerun might get totally altered by whatever concoctions were already coursing through the epicurean's system

He heard a gasp and a little cry as he let the crowd swallow him up, but not the kind of shrieks he had hoped would distract the torture engine. Just then the crowd scattered as the machine rose higher and then surged forward as the girl started running. His mark was left standing there, dumbly watching the machine go. Kharbyr decided to keep the fool in sight from now on; who knew how many other ways the servant might find to get himself killed while Kharbyr was waiting to kill him in the Aviaries?

Xagor wistfully watched the Talos leave. To be excruciated by such a device would have been a life-long honour for a devotee of pain like him. Tragically, that made Xagor a most unsuitable client from the Talos's point of view.

Xagor realised that something was wrong as he climbed the arching bridge towards the Beryl Gate and what should be sanctuary. The warding between Metzuh and the Aviaries was clearly visible this close to the gate, a swirling, translucent boundary of sickly colours curving away in all directions. The high, caged peaks of the largest Aviaries could be seen beyond, rendered hazy by the warding as if they had been sunk underwater. Xagor twisted his jar between aching hands and kept going. He was so close now that he had to go on; the only alternative way to the master's tower from here didn't bear contemplation.

Traffic seemed unusually sparse and that was worrying. He was a lot closer to the gate before he realised that everyone ahead of him was being turned back and a corner of his mind started gibbering with panic. A knot of Archon Malixian's warriors were standing in front of the gate in full panoply and letting no one through, as far as Xagor could tell. He considered asking one of those being sent back what was going on, but he decided that would just make him look suspicious and anger the warriors. Malixian's followers often shared the Archon's distaste for what most in Commorragh would commonly frame as 'sanity.'

He licked his lips and approached the warriors. They didn't swing the jagged maws of their splinter rifles to cover him so that was a good sign. They weren't moving out of the way either, so that was not so good. He stopped respectfully a few paces short of them.

'I–' Was all Xagor got out before one of the warriors laconically cut him off.

'None may pass.'

'I'm about my master's business, it's very urgent,' Xagor wheedled with an uncomfortable feeling of taking his life in his hands.

'None. May. Pass.'

The warrior's face was unreadable behind his masked helm, but he spread his fingers upright as he spoke and ticked off the words with his fingers to create a crude gesture for emphasis. The other warriors sniggered and aimed their splinter rifles at him.

'I serve Master Bellathonis!' Xagor squeaked.

'Well that makes all the difference, doesn't it? In you go,' the warrior said with disarming civility. He stepped aside and the jagged weapon maws dropped away. Xagor sensed a trap.

'Might I ask what's going on, why you're turning the other people back?' Xagor asked as politely as he could manage. Archon Malixian and the master had been as thick as thieves recently, hopefully that still held true.

'You might, and if you did I'd tell you that you don't want to be in the Aviaries right now.'

'Oh, no.'

'Oh, yes.'

'It's going on right now? It isn't about to start or nearly over?' Xagor held onto a shred of hope, they might escort him if he was lucky.

'Not a chance, if anything the blood's going to be well and truly up by now.'

'But I have to get to my master's tower right away! I'm sure he'd reward you!'

'Not. A. Chance.' He did the finger thing again before thoughtfully adding, 'I'm sure the Aviatrix will welcome the extra meat if you fancy your chances of getting through on foot.'

The Beryl Gate was misnamed really, Kharbyr mused. The tonnes of silvery metal used in its construction heavily outweighed the twisted ornamental pillars that gave it its name. Kharbyr hung back while the servant talked to the warriors at the gate. Eventually they let the servant through, although the servant looked reluctant to go on. After a few heartbeats Kharbyr headed over to the warriors himself. Kharbyr weighed his chances against them if it came to a fight. They had rifles and that would count against them up close, but that probably wouldn't be enough to offset their numbers and protection.

'None may pass.'

When the challenge came the warriors seemed wary. Had that servant said something to set them on edge? Told them he was being pursued? Kharbyr suddenly felt like a slave being pinned out for examination. He decided to take the offensive.

'Out of my way, I have important business in the Aviaries,' he said.

The warriors looked at each other with theatrical surprise at his boldness. One of them spoke up.

'With who?'

Kharbyr's mind raced with possibilities. He plumped for sticking with the easiest lie.

'On behalf of the haemonculus Bellathonis, I was engaged to protect his servant.'

Some subtle body language passed between the warriors at that, but Kharbyr couldn't read it. They stepped aside and one of them waved him through the gate with a mocking bow.

'Then go along inside. I'm sure you'll join him presently,' the way the warrior said it implied a permanent and fatal appointment awaited them both. Kharbyr scrunched his face up sourly. There must be a hunt in progress.

Xagor shivered behind a bush and listened to the hideous calls wafting through the Aviary spires that rose on every side of him. A few moments later he saw the silhouettes of a pair of hellions slicing through the air high above. There was a hunt going on all right, and it sounded like a lively one.

Archon Malixian's fondness for flying beasts of all kinds was legendary, and on occasion he saw fit to exercise his pets. A few score of slaves would be released into the Aviaries' grounds and allowed to scatter, and then the cages would be opened to release clawed, fanged and poisoned death in a variety of winged guises. The archon's Kabal would go aloft with their master to enjoy the pain and terror of the dying slaves as the hunt proceeded. They also dealt with any prey deluded enough to try to hide or desperate enough to fight back.

He made a dash for another dark corner closer to his goal. He tried to move in short dashes. Running in the open made him conscious of being precisely the sort of tasty morsel being hunted and the cumbersome jar was starting to weigh heavily in his hands. As he caught his breath he started to worry about running into released slaves. They would be looking for the darkest corners to hide in too, and Archon Malixian liked to use healthy specimens so that his pets would get a proper workout. An inhuman shriek cut through the darkness, closer than any he'd heard so far. He was more worried still when he heard some rustling in the bushes nearby.

A few desperate slaves would ordinarily be no concern, but under the circumstances Xagor was extremely vulnerable. He couldn't defend himself while encumbered with the jar, and any noise might attract the attention of far deadlier foes from above. Malixian's kabal wasn't likely to recognise a stray servant of Bellathonis when their bloodlust was in full swing, and his pets wouldn't care.

Xagor was about to move again when the flap and snap of leathery wings made him freeze. A half dozen arrow-headed predators were rising in a lazy spiral from behind a building-sized cage on his left. The long dark shape of a raider craft slid smoothly after them, its crew clearly visible hanging over its open sides as they scanned the ground beneath.

* * *

Kharbyr was sweating despite himself. Each time he readied himself to sprint out of cover and take the servant unawares, the damned fool would run off ahead of him. The idea of capturing the servant had reoccurred to him but that was looking worse and worse. At this rate the mark was going to simply slip through his fingers yet again and leave him with nothing for his efforts. That was all assuming that they could both stay clear of Malixian's pets and cronies.

The distant crack of weapon fire gave him the answer. The blade was always more satisfying but Kharbyr did carry a long, elegant splinter pistol of his own. He would shoot the servant down with it and quickly search the body. The package the servant was carrying might go some way towards repaying the indignities Kharbyr had suffered in the pursuit. If not, then at least vengeance would have been meted out and he could get out of here with some sense of pride intact.

He drew his pistol and aimed it at the servant. Between the range and the gloom it was going to be a difficult shot. The servant suddenly froze as a Raider hove into view, and Kharbyr inwardly cursed. The Raider's crew would spot the flash of a shot for sure. Anyone on ground level was going to be prey to them and prey armed with a pistol was liable to bring the whole kabal down to investigate. With a long-suffering sigh he drew his knife in his other hand and started creeping closer again.

A shrill whistle went up and the predator flock darted downwards. The raider shot after them, disappearing out of sight again behind the cages. Flashes licked behind the bars and the distant crackle of splinter fire reached Xagor just a moment later. Someone must be getting feisty. He almost jumped out of his skin when a shot smacked into the cage right beside him. He spun around, bobbling the jar in his surprise. There was a figure in a dark cloak not thirty paces away pointing something glittery at him. Xagor ran for his life.

The pistol cracked twice more and a splinter shrieked past, close enough to feel its passage. Xagor skidded around a corner to put something between himself and his attacker before desperately looking around. He spotted a low bridge between two vast cages up ahead and ran for the inviting shadows to be found underneath it.

Xagor was trying to look in all directions at once, so he stumbled right over the body in the mouth of the tunnel. The jar flew out of his hands as if it had been greased and went pin-wheeling off into the darkness. His cry of despair morphed into one of terror as clawed shapes rose up and reached for him out of the shadows. His last thoughts were of surprise that mandrakes would be bold enough to conduct their own hunt in the Aviaries of Malixian the Mad.

Kharbyr had fired his pistol almost by reflex when he heard shots nearby, but he told himself that taking a snap shot was weighed against the sound of it being hidden by the other firing. Whatever dark fates were conspiring against him meant he missed his mark and only gave away his presence instead. The servant gaped at him stupidly and then took off running for his life. Kharbyr took careful aim and pulled the trigger again just as something smashed into him from behind.

Kharbyr was sent sprawling by the blow but a lifetime of experience rolled him into a ball that brought him back onto his feet in a heartbeat. Another blow, sensed more than seen, came swinging out of the darkness. He ducked under it and fired his pistol into the half-seen shape before him. It gave a surprised grunt and fell away in a hot spray of blood.

Another attacker came for him then and he realised that they were slaves, naked and armed only with whatever crude weapons they had been able to find. Contempt boiled up inside him, contempt and a spurt of fury at their temerity in attacking him. He laid open the second slave's arm from wrist to elbow and the faerun made the ugly thing scream like its arm had been dipped in molten metal. Kharbyr had the presence of mind to cut the slave's legs out from under it before it could start to run.

The slave's suffering was just too delicious and Kharbyr lingered for a moment to properly appreciate it. Its face contorted fantastically and its soul gave a little shiver as it struggled free. Kharbyr drank it all in greedily and abandoned himself to let the anguish wash away his ennui for a few precious seconds.

Composing himself, Kharbyr saw no sign of his mark nor of Malixian's hunters closing in. He hurried to the corner where the servant had disappeared. Peering cautiously around it, he saw nothing but an apparently empty lawn between several huge cages beyond. Then he spied a dark tunnel mouth between two of the cages, exactly the kind of place an idiot on the run would make for.

He smelled blood before he reached the shadows, and that made him pull up short and advance more warily. Dark shapes were moving in the tunnel, something only visible as blacker silhouettes in the gloom – mandrakes. One was crouched over what was unmistakably the body of the haemonculus's servant; more of them lurked beyond, and they had seen him just as he saw them. Kharbyr levelled his pistol and fired without hesitation. Quite apart from the fact that the mandrakes had stolen his mark, they would most likely try to take Kharbyr himself for dessert.

Kharbyr's shots failed to connect with anything substantial in the gloom. They did, however, bring one of the mandrakes out into the open to challenge him. A smoky, half-seen shape that seemed to flicker and shift constantly stepped forth. Kharbyr went after the thing with his blade. If this one could be beaten, the others might give up their kill; then he could at least search the servant's body and retrieve the package.

It was like fighting smoke. Every cut he made only showed the mandrake to be somewhere else. Its own attacks seemed to come out of nowhere and it took every ounce of Kharbyr's skill to keep them at bay. Even then it felt uncomfortably as if he were being toyed with, and that was not a sensation Kharbyr enjoyed. He realised that the mandrake was gradually driving him toward the tunnel mouth, backing him towards where the other mandrakes were waiting in ambush.

A piercing shriek suddenly intruded into their duel and Kharbyr saved his own life by instantly diving to one side. Razor-sharp blades whickered past him not a hand's span away as a hellion shrieked by. Kharbyr rolled desperately as a second hellion swept down to take a cut at him with a hooked glaive. Sparks flew from the hellion's armour as he desperately snap-fired a barrage of splinters at it. One of the tiny slivers found a weak point and punched through.

The hellion pitched backward and its skyboard ploughed into the ground a few strides away. Kharbyr leapt for it desperately. The mandrake had disappeared but the first hellion was curving back around for another attack run. Odds were that the rest of Malixian's kabal wouldn't be far behind.

Kharbyr clamped his feet into the skyboard's restraints and took to the air with a cry of anguish on his lips. Everything had gone wrong; all was lost and now he had to hope that he could escape with his life. At least the worthless servant was dead. He could console himself with that.

A mandrake was crouched on Xagor's chest, one razor-sharp claw resting lightly against his throat. He desperately wanted to swallow, but dared not. Shapes moved around him in the darkness and then the mandrake suddenly dropped flat on top of him. Xagor was too shocked to react, unable to believe that the mandrakes were going to abuse him on the spot. A crackle of splinter shots a moment later confused him even more. All he could think to do was to close his eyes. More shots and the ringing of blades came to his ears.

A long time seemed to pass before the weight eased from his chest with no apparent harm done. Xagor opened his eyes cautiously. The mandrake was squatting nearby watching him. It laid one long finger where its lips would be to shush him and pointed out of the tunnel mouth. Xagor craned around to look with hope rushing unbidden into his heart. The cloaked figure that had been chasing him was out there, mounting a stolen skyboard and racing away. The air was filled with the high-pitched whine of anti-grav units as Malixian's kabal took up the chase. Xagor was saved.

Or not. Of course the mandrakes might think that it was Xagor's bodyguard that had just fled and left him to their tender ministrations. They might simply be mocking him in their weird, silent way. He looked back at the mandrake for a clue, but its shadow-skinned face was unreadable. A second mandrake seemed to coalesce out of the darkness. It was carrying something in one hand that it extended towards him and Xagor tensed involuntarily. With a shock he realised that it was handing him his jar back.

The Screaming Tower had never felt more like a sanctuary. Xagor entered as quietly as he could, so as to not disturb the master – an infraction that carried its own considerable risks. The tall, lanky form of Bellathonis was bent over some consoles that spilled a profusion of wiring connected to three subjects strapped into examination frames. Bellathonis straightened and pressed a control. All three subjects simultaneously erupted in modulated howls of pain.

'What do you have for me, Xagor? The materials I wanted from the Red House, I trust?' Bellathonis said without looking around.

Xagor was taken off guard and quailed a little in spite of himself. The master was fond of modification and had recently implanted extra eyes with fully functioning optic nerves into his shoulder-blades. 'All the better to watch my rivals with' he had said. The idea that the master could be looking at you when his back was turned was somehow deeply disturbing to Xagor.

'I have the jar from the Red House, master,' Xagor called, 'but also news of tremendous import.'

That caught the master's attention in no uncertain terms. His hooked nose and sharp chin turned to Xagor and made him feel like he was back in the Aviaries being regarded as a morsel to be consumed by one of Malixian's pets.

'I'll be the judge of its import, Xagor, and if it's truly important you'd better not have tarried on your way back to me.' Bellathonis's tone was jocular but the cruel glitter in his eyes told a different story.

'A Dysjunction, master. Matsilier at the Red House talks to all the clients and he told me that the crones have predicted a Dysjunction in the city. Soon!' Xagor finished in a rush.

'A Dysjunction, eh? Oh, how very interesting. Our lovely crones have read the fates and seen that our little abode of the damned is due for a shake up. It must be all over the city by now.' The last was sharp; Xagor wondered how much Bellathonis already knew.

'I came straight back, master! I didn't even wait for a guard. I was pursued, there was a Talos and a-a hunt...' It all sounded like an increasingly weak string of excuses to Xagor's soon-to-be-modified ears.

'Yes, yes,' Bellathonis waved away his excuses. 'But here you are, so the mandrakes I sent looking for you obviously did their job.'

Xagor gawped. He had never heard the master talk of employing mandrakes before. Bellathonis elegantly plucked the jar from his nerveless hands.

'Don't look so surprised. I knew there was a hunt in the Aviaries and it seemed likely that you would go that way with the "news" you were so desperate to bring to me.'

'You already knew, master?' A crushing weight descended on Xagor as Bellathonis let the moment stretch out. The haemonculus eventually gave him a chilling smile.

'Only suspected, oh faithful servant. Certain factions have been making preparations and it seemed likely that you would hear something at the Red House. Well done; this is very important news. A Dysjunction will change all the old alliances and rivalries beyond recognition, something which has long been overdue. I've only witnessed three in my considerable lifespan and they all made for very interesting times, let me tell you.' Bellathonis continued as he unsealed the lid of the jar. 'Yes, you've done well by bringing this to my attention so promptly, Xagor. I do believe you've earned yourself a reward. Extra pineal gland, perhaps?'

Bellathonis dipped a long-fingered hand into the jar, but what emerged looked suspiciously like a dripping, shrunken head to Xagor. Bellathonis held it by snaky black locks and tutted as he wiped slime from the face of the thing.

'Master, I don't understand.'

'Allow me to introduce you. Xagor, this is Angevere; Angevere this is Xagor.'

Bellathonis held the head out for Xagor to see. The face was pinched and lined. The eyes and lips were crudely sutured shut but Xagor could see that they were still moving, the face contorting.

'Angevere the crone,' Bellathonis murmured as he connected the head to one of the consoles he'd been working on as Xagor entered. 'Now come over here and when I nod to you, twist this dial half a turn to the right and then back again.'

Xagor's heart swelled with pride. He was being asked to assist! Just him and the master, working together like old comrades. The other servants would be incandescent with jealousy. Bellathonis pushed a final needle into the neck stump of Angevere and nodded to Xagor, who twisted the dial with gusto. A triple scream burst from the three subjects again, this time curiously intermingled as if they cried out with one voice. As Xagor twisted the dial back to its start position the three subjects spoke for the first time.

'*What have you done to me?*' they said together.

'Made you my guest, you dreadful old monster,' Bellathonis cackled with radiant self-satisfaction. 'For the duration of the Dysjunction at least, or perhaps longer if you misbehave. We can while away the time delightfully with these three fresh subjects I've connected you to.'

Bellathonis's nod was almost imperceptible but Xagor was drinking in every moment and he caught it. He twisted the dial clinically and was rewarded by another chorus of screams and a faint smile from the master.

'What do you want?' the three voices gasped.

'Ah, the correct question – and there's nothing so precious in any discussion. We'll talk about the future and what you know about it in due course, Angevere.'

'*There will be consequences,*' the voices said.

'Desperate times mean desperate measures, witch. If I'm right, it won't matter soon,' Bellathonis said with an air of finality. He turned to his servant with a look of apparently genuine concern. 'Poor Xagor, you look exhausted. There's a young man out in the vestibule waiting to see me, ask him to step in here and then go straight to your quarters. Get some rest; we're going to be very busy later.'

'They tore my face!' the young man shouted.

'So they did. Dear me, I should take a look at that,' said Bellathonis. 'Take a seat.'

'Damn right you'll fix it! I was about your business and I demand some kind of recompense for this farce.'

'Of course, getting this injury does mean that you got outwitted by birds, doesn't it?' Bellathonis remarked as he selected something long and sharp from a tray. 'And my business, as I recall, was receipt of a package that got here with precious little help from you – apart from the Talos, of course.'

'I–'

'Hush now, Kharbyr, and let's see what we can do with that face.'

THE CARRION ANTHEM

David Annandale

He was thinking bitter thoughts about glory. He couldn't help it. As he took his seat in the governor's private box overlooking the stage, Corvus Parthamen was surrounded by glory that was not his. The luxury of the box, a riot of crimson leather and velvet laced with gold and platinum thread, was a tribute, in the form of excess, to the honour of Governor Elpidius. That didn't trouble Corvus. The box represented a soft, false glory, a renown that came with the title, not the deeds or the man. Then there was the stage, to which all sight lines led. It was a prone monolith, carved from a single massive obsidian slab. It was an altar on which one could sacrifice gods, but instead it abased itself beneath the feet of the artist. It was stone magnificence, and tonight it paid tribute to Corvus's brother. That didn't trouble Corvus, either. He didn't understand what Gurges did, but he recognised that his twin did, at least, work for his laurels. Art was a form of deed, Corvus supposed.

What bothered him were the walls. Windowless, rising two hundred metres to meet in the distant vault of the ceiling, they were draped with immense tapestries. These were hand-woven tributes to Imperial victories. Kieldar. The Planus Steppes. Ichar IV. On and on and on. Warriors of legend, both ancient and contemporary, towered above Corvus. They were meant to inspire, to draw the eye as the spirit soared, moved by the majesty of the tribute paid by the music. The works of art in this monumental space – stone, image and sound – were supposed to entwine to the further glory of the Emperor and his legions.

But lately, the current of worship had reversed. Now the tapestry colossi, frozen in their moments of triumphant battle, were also bowing before the glory of Gurges, and that was wrong. That was what made Corvus dig his fingers in hard enough to mar the leather of his armrests.

The governor's wife, Lady Ahala, turned to him, her multiple necklaces rattling together. 'It's nice to see you, colonel,' she said. 'You must be so proud.'

Proud of what? he wanted to say. Proud of his home world's contributions to the Imperial crusades? That was a joke. Ligeta was a joke. Of the hundred tapestries here in the Performance Hall of the Imperial Palace of Culture, not one portrayed a Ligetan hero. Deep in the Segmentum Pacificus, far from the front lines of any contest, Ligeta was untouched by war beyond the usual tithe of citizens bequeathed to the Imperial Guard. Many of its sons had fought and fallen on distant soil, but how many had distinguished themselves to the point that they might be remembered and celebrated? None.

Proud of what? Of his own war effort? That he commanded Ligeta's defence regiment? That only made him part of the Ligetan joke. Officers who were posted back to their home worlds developed reputations, especially when those home worlds were pampered, decadent backwaters. The awful thing was that he couldn't even ask himself what he'd done wrong. He knew the answer. *Nothing*. He'd done everything right. He'd made all the right friends, served under all the right officers, bowed and scraped in all the right places at all the right times. He had done his duty on the battlefield, too. No one could say otherwise. But there had been no desperate charges, no last-man-standing defences. The Ligetan regiments were called upon to maintain supply lines, garrison captured territory, and mop up the token resistance of those who were defeated but hadn't quite come to terms with the fact. They were not summoned when the need was urgent.

The injustice made him seethe. He knew his worth, and that of his fellows. They fought and died with the best, when given the chance. Not every mop-up had been routine. Not every territory had been easily pacified. Ligetans knew how to fight, and they had plenty to prove.

Only no one ever saw. No one thought to look, because everyone knew Ligeta's reputation. It was the planet of the dilettante and the artist. The planet of the song.

Proud of *that*?

Yes, that was exactly what Ahala meant. Proud of the music, proud of the song. Proud of Gurges. Ligeta's civilian population rejoiced in the planet's reputation. They saw no shame or weakness in it. They used the same logic as Corvus's superiors, who thought they had rewarded his political loyalty by sending him home. Who wouldn't want a pleasant command, far from the filth of a Chaos-infested hive-world? Who wouldn't want to be near Gurges Parthamen, maker not of song, but of *The* Song?

Yes, Corvus thought, Gurges had done a good thing there. Over a decade ago, now. The Song was a hymn to the glory of the Emperor. Hardly unusual. But *Regeat, Imperator* was rare. It was the product of the special alchemy that, every so often, fused formal magnificence with populist appeal. The tune was magisterial enough to be blasted from a Titan's combat horn, simple enough to be whistled by the lowliest trooper and catchy enough that, once heard, it was never forgotten. It kept up morale on a thousand besieged worlds, and fired up the valour of millions of troops charging to the rescue. Corvus had every right, every *duty*, to be proud of his brother's accomplishment. It was a work of genius.

So he'd been told. He would have to be satisfied with the word of others. Corvus had amusia. He was as deaf to music as Gurges was attuned to it. His twin's work left him cold. He heard a clearer melody line in the squealing of a greenskin pinned beneath a Dreadnought's foot.

To Lady Ahala, Corvus said, 'I couldn't be more proud.'

'Do you know what he's offering us tonight?' Elpidius asked. He settled his soft bulk more comfortably.

'I don't.'

'Really?' Ahala sounded surprised. 'But you're his twin.'

'We haven't seen each other for the best part of a year.'

Elpidius frowned. 'I didn't think you'd been away.'

Corvus fought back a humiliated wince. 'Gurges was the one off-planet,' he said. Searching the stars for inspiration, or some other pampered nonsense. Corvus didn't know and didn't care.

Hanging from the vault of the hall were hundreds of glow-globes patterned into a celestial map of the Imperium. Now they faded, silencing the white noise of tens of thousands of conversations. Darkness embraced the audience, and only the stage was illuminated. From the wings came the choir. The singers wore black uniforms as razor-creased as any officer's ceremonial garb. They marched in in their hundreds, until they filled the back half of the stage. They faced the audience. At first, Corvus thought they were wearing silver helmets, but then they reached up and pulled down the masks. Featureless, eyeless, the masks covered the top half of each man's face.

'How are they going to see him conduct?' Elpidius wondered.

Ahala giggled with excitement. 'That's nothing,' she whispered. She placed a confiding hand on Corvus's arm. 'I've heard that there haven't been any rehearsals. Not even the choir knows what is going to be performed.'

Corvus blinked. 'What?'

'Isn't it exciting?' She turned back to the stage, happy and placid before the prospect of the impossible.

The light continued to fade until there was only a narrow beam front and centre, a bare pinprick on the frozen night of stone. The silence was as thick and heavy as the stage. It was broken by the solemn, slow *clop* of boot heels. His pace steady as a ritual, as if he were awed by his own arrival, Gurges Parthamen, Emperor's bard and Ligeta's favourite son, walked into the light. He wore the same black uniform as the musicians, but no mask. Instead…

'What's wrong with his face?' Ahala asked.

Corvus leaned forwards. Something cold scuttled through his gut. His twin's face was his own: the same severe planes, narrow chin and grey eyes, even the same cropped black hair. But now Corvus stared at a warped mirror. Gurges was wearing an appliance that flashed like gold but, even from this distance, displayed the unforgiving angles and rigidity of adamantium. It circled his head like a laurel wreath. At his face, it extended needle-thin claws that pierced his eyelids, pinning them open. Gurges gazed at his audience with a manic, implacable stare that was equal parts absolute knowledge and terminal fanaticism. His eyes were as much prisoners as those of his choir, but where the singers saw nothing, he saw too much, and revelled in the punishment. His smile was a peeling back of lips. His skin was too thin, his skull too close to the surface. When he spoke, Corvus heard the hollow sound of wind over rusted pipes. Insects rustled at the frayed corners of reality.

'Fellow Ligetans,' Gurges began. 'Before we begin, it would be positively heretical of me not to say something about the role of the patron of the arts. The life of a musician is a difficult one. Because we do not produce a tangible product, there are many who regard us as superfluous, a pointless luxury the Imperium could happily do without. This fact makes those who value us even more important. Patrons are the blessed few who know the artist really can make a difference.'

He paused for a moment. If he was expecting applause, he did not receive it; the knowledge and ice in his rigid gaze stilled the audience. Unperturbed, he carried on. 'I have, over the course of my musical life, been privileged to have worked with more than my share of generous, committed, sensitive patrons. It is thanks to them that my music has been heard at all.' He lowered his head, as if overcome by modesty.

Corvus would have snorted at the conceit of the gesture, but he was too tense. He dreaded the words that might come from his brother's rictus face.

Gurges looked up, and now his eyes seemed to glow with a light the colour of dust and ash. 'Yes,' he said, 'the generous patron is to be cherished. But even more precious, even more miraculous, even more worthy of celebration, is the patron who *inspires*. The patron who opens the door to new vistas of creation, and pushes the artist through. I stand before you as the servant of one such patron. I know that my humble tribute to the Emperor is held in high regard, but I can now see what a poor counterfeit of the truth that effort is. Tonight, so will you. I cannot tell you what my patron has unveiled for me. But I can *show* you.'

The composer's last words slithered out over the hall like a death rattle.

Gurges turned to face the choir. He raised his arms. The singers remained unmoving. The last light went out. A terrible, far-too-late certainty hit Corvus; he must stop this.

Then Gurges began to sing.

For almost a minute, Corvus felt relief. No daemon burst from his brother's mouth. His pulse slowed. He had fallen for the theatrics of a first-rate showman, that was all. The song didn't sound any different to him than any other of Gurges's efforts. It was another succession of notes, each as meaningless as the next. Then he noticed that he was wrong. He wasn't hearing a simple succession. Even his thick ears could tell that Gurges was singing two notes at once. Then three. Then four. The song became impossible. Somehow still singing, Gurges drew a breath, and though Corvus heard no real change in the music, the breath seemed to mark the end of the refrain.

It also marked the end of peace, because now the choir began to sing. To a man, they joined in, melding with Gurges's voice. The song became a roar. The darkness began to withdraw as a glow spread across the stage. It seeped from the singers. It poured like radiation fog into the seating. It was a colour that made Corvus wince. It was a kind of green, if green could scream. It pulsed like taut flesh.

It grinned like Chaos.

Corvus leapt to his feet. So did the rest of the audience. For a crazy moment of hope, he thought of ordering the assembled people to fall upon the singers and silence them. But they weren't rising, like him, in alarm. They were at one with the music, and they joined their voices to its glory, and their souls to its power. The roar became a wave. The glow filled the hall, and it showed Corvus nothing he wanted to see. Beside him, the governor and his wife stood motionless, their faces contorted with ecstasy. They sang as if the song were their birthright. They sang to bring down the sky. Their heads were thrown back, their jaws as wide as a snake's, and their throats twitched and spasmed with the effort to produce inhuman chords. Corvus grabbed Elpidius by the shoulders and tried to shake him. The governor's frame was rigid and grounded to the core of Ligeta. Corvus might have been wrestling with a pillar. But the man wasn't cold like stone. He was burning up. His eyes were glassy. Corvus checked his pulse. Its rhythm was violent, rapid, irregular. Corvus yanked his hands away. They felt slick with disease. Something that lived in the song scrabbled at his mind like fingernails on plastek, but couldn't find a purchase.

He opened the flap of his shoulder holster and pulled out his laspistol. He leaned over the railing of the box, and sighted on his brother's head. He felt no hesitation. He felt only necessity. He pulled the trigger.

Gurges fell, the top of his skull seared away. The song didn't care. It roared on, its joy unabated. Corvus fired six more times, each shot dropping a member of the choir. Finally, he stopped. The song wasn't a spell and it wasn't a mechanism. It was a plague, and killing individual vectors was worse than useless. It stole precious time from action that might make a difference.

He ran from the box. In the vestibule, the ushers were now part of the choir, and the song pursued Corvus as he clattered down the marble steps to the mezzanine and thence to the ground floor. The foyer, as cavernous as the Performance Hall, led to the Great Gallery of Art. Its vaulted length stretched a full kilometre to the exit of the palace. Floor-to-ceiling glassaics of the primarchs gazed down on heroic bronzes. Warriors beyond counting trampled the Imperium's enemies, smashing them into fragmented agony that sank into the pedestals. But the gallery was no longer a celebration of art and glory. It was a throat, and it howled the song after him. Though melody was a stranger to him, still he could feel the force of the music, intangible yet pushing him with the violence of a hurricane's breath. The light was at his heels, flooding the throat with its mocking bile.

He burst from the grand doorway onto the plaza. He stumbled to a halt, horrified.

The concert had been broadcast.

Palestrina, Ligeta's capital and a city of thirty million, screamed. It convulsed.

The late-evening glow of the city was stained with the Chaos non-light. In the plaza, in the streets, in the windows of Palestrina's delicate and coruscating towers, the people stood and sang their demise. The roads had become a nightmare of twisted, flaming wreckage as drivers, possessed by art, slammed into each other. Victims of collisions, not quite dead, sang instead of screaming their last. Everywhere, the choir chanted to the sky, and the sky answered with flame and thunder. To the west, between the towers, the horizon strobed and rumbled as fireballs bloomed. He was looking at the space port, Corvus realised, and seeing the destruction caused by every landing and departing ship suddenly losing all guidance.

There was a deafening roar overhead, and a cargo transport came in low and mad. Its engines burning blue, it ploughed into the side of a tower a few blocks away. The ship exploded, filling the sky with the light and sound of its death. Corvus ducked as pieces of shrapnel the size of meteors arced down, gouging impact craters into street and stone and flesh. The tower collapsed with lazy majesty, falling against its neighbours and spreading a domino celebration of destruction. Dust billowed up in a choking, racing cloud. It rushed over Corvus, hiding the sight of the dying city, but the chant went on.

He coughed, gagging as grit filled his throat and lungs. He staggered, but started moving again. Though visibility was down to a few metres, and his eyes watered and stung, he felt that he could see clearly again. It was as if, by veiling the death of the city from his gaze, the dust had broken a spell. Palestrina was lost, but that didn't absolve him of his duty to the Emperor. Only his own death could do that. As long as he drew breath, his duty was to fight for Ligeta, and save what he could.

He had to find somewhere the song had not reached, find men who had not heard and been infected by the plague. Then he could mount a defence, perhaps even a counter-attack, even if that were nothing more than a scorched-earth purge. There would be glory in that. But first, a chance to regroup. First, a sanctuary. He had hopes that he knew where to go.

He felt his way around the grey limbo of the plaza, a hand over his mouth, trying not to cough up his lungs. It took him the best part of an hour to reach the far side of the Palace of Culture. By that time, the worst of the dust had settled and the building's intervening bulk further screened him. He could breathe again. His movements picked up speed and purpose. He needed a vehicle, one he could manoeuvre through the tangled chaos of the streets. Half a kilometre down from the plaza, he found what he wanted. A civilian was straddling his idling bike. He had been caught by the song just before pulling away. Corvus tried to push him off, but he was as rigid and locked down as the governor had been. Corvus shot him. As he hauled the corpse away from the bike, he told himself that the man had already been dead. If Corvus hadn't granted him mercy, something else would have. A spreading fire. Falling debris. If nothing violent had happened, then...

Corvus stared at the singing pedestrians, and thought through the implications of what he was seeing. Nothing, he was sure, could free the victims once the song took hold. So they would stand where they were struck and sing, and do nothing else. They wouldn't sleep. They wouldn't eat. They wouldn't drink. Corvus saw the end result, and he also saw the first glimmer of salvation. With a renewed sense of mission, he climbed on the bike and drove off.

It was an hour from dawn by the time he left the city behind. Beyond the hills of Palestrina, he picked up even more speed as he hit the parched mud flats. Once fertile, the land here had had its water table drained by the city's thirst. At the horizon, the shadow of the Goreck Mesa blocked the stars. At the base of its bulk, he saw pinpricks of light. Those glimmers were his destination and his hope.

The ground rose again as he reached the base. He approached the main gate, and he heard no singing. Before him, the wall was an adamantium shield fifty metres high – a sloping, pleated curtain of strength. A giant aquila was engraved every ten metres along the wall's two-kilometre length. Beyond the wall, he heard the growl of promethium engines, the report of firing ranges, the march of boots. The sounds of discipline. Discipline that was visible from the moment he arrived. If the sentries were surprised to see him, dusty and exhausted, arriving on a civilian vehicle instead of in his staff transport, they showed no sign. They saluted, sharp as machines, and opened the gate for him. He passed through into Fort Goreck and the promise of salvation.

On the other side of the wall was a zone free of art and music. A weight lifted from Corvus's shoulders as he watched the pistoning, drumming rhythm of the military muscle. Strength perfected, and yet, by the Throne, it had been almost lost too. A request had come the day before from Jeronim Tarrant, the base's captain. Given the momentous, planet-wide event that was a new composition by Gurges Parthamen, would the colonel authorise a break in the drills, long enough for the men to sit down and listen to the vox-cast of the concert? Corvus had not just rejected the request out of hand, he had forbidden any form of reception and transmission of the performance. He wanted soldiers, he had informed Jeronim. If he wanted dilettantes, he could find plenty in the boxes of the Palace of Culture.

On his way to the concert, he had wondered about his motives in issuing that order. Jealousy? Was he really that petty? He knew now that he wasn't, and that he'd been right. The purpose of a base such as this was to keep the Guard in a state of perpetual, instant readiness, because peace might become war in the passing of a second.

As it had now.

He crossed the parade field, making for the squat command tower at the rear of the base, where it nestled against the basalt wall of the mesa. He had barely dismounted the bike when Jeronim came pounding out of the tower. He was pale, borderline frantic, but remembered to salute. Discipline, Corvus thought. It had saved them so far. It would see them through to victory.

'Sir,' Jeronim said. 'Do you know what's going on? Are we under attack? We can't get through to anyone.'

'Yes, we are at war,' Corvus answered. He strode briskly to the door. 'No one in this base has been in contact with anyone outside it for the last ten hours?'

Jeronim shook his head. 'No, sir. Nothing that makes sense. Anyone transmitting is just sending what sounds like music–'

Corvus cut him off. 'You listened?'

'Only a couple of seconds. When we found the nonsense everywhere, we shut down the sound. No one was sending anything coherent. Not even the *Scythe of Judgement*.'

So the Ligetan flagship had fallen. He wasn't surprised, but Corvus discovered that he could still feel dismay. The fact that the base had survived the transmissions told him something. The infection didn't take hold right away. He remembered that the choir and the audience hadn't responded until Gurges had completed a full refrain. The song's message had to be complete, it seemed, before it could sink in.

'What actions have you taken?' he asked Jeronim as they headed up the staircase to the command centre.

'We've been sending out requests for acknowledgement on all frequencies. I've placed the base on heightened alert. And since we haven't been hearing from anyone, I sent out a distress call.'

'Fine,' Corvus said. For whatever good that call will do, he thought. By the time the message was received and aid arrived, weeks or months could have elapsed. By that time, the battle for the soul of Ligeta would have been won or lost. The singers would have starved to death, and either there would be someone left to pick up the pieces, or there wouldn't be.

The communications officer looked up from the auspex as Corvus and Jeronim walked into the centre. 'Colonel,' he saluted. 'A capital ship has just transitioned into our system.'

'Really?' That was fast. Improbably fast.

'It's hailing us,' the master vox-operator announced.

Corvus lunged across the room and yanked the headphones from the operator's skull. 'All messages to be received as text only until further notice,' he ordered. 'No exceptions. Am I clear?'

The operator nodded.

'Acknowledge them,' Corvus went on. 'Request identification.'

The soldier did so. Corvus moved to the plastek window and looked out over the base while he waited. There were five thousand men here. The position was elevated, easily defensible. He had the tools. He just had to work out how to fight.

'Message received, colonel.'

Corvus turned to the vox-operator. His voice sounded all wrong, like that of a man who had suddenly been confronted with the futility of his existence. He was staring at the data-slate before him. His face was grey.

'Read it,' Corvus said, and braced himself.

'Greetings, Imperials. This is the *Terminus Est*.'

Typhus entered the strategium as the ship emerged into the real space of the Ligetan system.

'Multiple contacts, lord,' the bridge attendant reported.

Of course there were. The Imperium would hardly leave Ligeta without a defending fleet. Typhus moved his bulk towards the main oculus. They were already close enough to see the swarm of Imperial cruisers and defence satellites. 'How many are on attack trajectories?' Typhus asked. He knew the answer, but he wanted the satisfaction of hearing it.

The officer looked twice at his hololithic display, as if he doubted the reports he was receiving. 'None,' he said after a moment.

'And how many are targeting us?'

Another brief silence. 'None.'

Typhus rumbled and buzzed his pleasure. The insects that were his parasites and his identity fluttered and scrabbled with excitement. His armour rippled with their movement. He allowed himself a moment to revel in the experience, in the glorious and terrible paradox of his existence. Disease was an endless source of awe in its marriage of death and unrestrained life. It was his delight to spread the gospel of this paradox, the lesson of decay. Before him, the oculus showed how well the lesson was being learned. 'Bring us in close,' he commanded.

'At once, lord.' The bridge attendant was obedient, but was a slow learner himself. He was still thinking in terms of a normal combat situation, never mind that the Imperial fleet's lack of response to the appearance of a Chaos capital ship was far from normal. 'We are acquiring targets,' he reported.

'No need, no need,' Typhus said. 'See for yourselves. All of you.'

His officers looked up, and Typhus had an audience for the spectacle he had arranged. As the *Terminus Est* closed in on the glowing green-and-brown globe of Ligeta, the enemy ships gathered size and definition. Their distress became clear, too. Some were drifting, nothing more now than adamantium tombs. Others had their engines running, but there was no order to their movements. The ships, Typhus knew, were performing the last commands their crews had given them, and there would be no others to come.

'Hail the Imperials,' he ordered. 'Open all frequencies.'

The strategium was bathed in the music of disease. Across multiple channels came the same noise, a unified chaos of millions upon millions of throats singing in a single choir. The melody was a simple, sustained, multi-note chord of doom. It became the accompaniment to the view outside the *Terminus Est*, and now the movement of the fleet was the slow ballet of entropy and defeat. Typhus watched two cruisers follow their unalterable routes until they collided. One exploded, its fireball the expanding bloom of a poisonous flower. The other plunged towards Ligeta's atmosphere, bringing with it the terrible gift of its weapons payload and shattered reactor.

Typhus thought about its landfall, and his insects writhed in anticipation.

He also thought about the simplicity of the lesson, how pure it was, and how devastating its purity made it. Did the happenstance that had brought Gurges Parthamen into his grasp taint that purity, or was that flotsam of luck an essential piece of the composition's beauty? The composer on a self-indulgent voyage, getting caught in a localised warp storm, winding up in a near-collision with the *Terminus Est*; how could those elements be anything other than absolute contingency? His triumph could so easily have never even been an idea. Then again, that man, his ambition that made him so easily corruptible, the confluence of events that granted Typhus this perfect inspiration – they were so improbable, they could not possibly be chance. They had been threaded together by destiny.

Flies howled through the strategium as Typhus tasted the paradox and found it to his liking. Chaos and fate, one and the same.

Perhaps Gurges had thought so, too. He had put up no resistance to being infected with the new plague. Typhus was particularly proud of it. The parasitic warp worm laid its eggs in the bloodstream and attacked the brain. It spread itself from mind to mind by the transmission of its idea, and the idea travelled on a sound – a special sound, a song that was an incantation that thinned the walls between reality and the immaterium, and taught itself to all who had ears to hear.

'My lord, we are being hailed,' said the attendant.

Typhus laughed, delighted, and the boils on the deck quivered in sympathy. 'Send them our greeting,' he ordered.

Now he had an enemy. Now he could fight.

Corvus rejected despair. He rejected the odds. There was an enemy, and duty demanded combat. There was nothing else.

Corvus stood at the reviewing stand on the parade grounds, and, speakers turning his voice into Fort Goreck's voice, he addressed the assembled thousands. He explained the situation. He described the plague and its means of contagion. Then he laid down the rules. One was paramount. 'Music,' he thundered, 'is a disease. It will destroy us if it finds the smallest chink in our armour. We must be free of it, and guard against it. Anyone who so much as whistles will be executed on the spot.' He felt enormous satisfaction as he gave that order. He didn't worry about why.

Less than a day after his arrival, Typhus witnessed the apotheosis of his art. The entire planet was one voice. The anthem, the pestilence; the anthem that was pestilence, had become the sum total of existence on Ligeta. Its population lived for a single purpose. The purity was electrifying.

Or it would have been, but for one single flaw. There was that redoubt. He had thought it would succumb by itself, but it hadn't. It was still sending out desperate pleas to whatever Imperials might hear. Though Typhus could amuse himself with the thought that this one pustule of order confirmed the beauty of corruption, he also knew the truth. Over the course of the next few days, the song would begin a ragged diminuendo as its singers died. If he didn't act, his symphony would be incomplete, spoiled by one false note.

It was time to act.

The attack came on the evening of the second day. Corvus was walking the parapet when he saw the sky darken. A deep, unending thunder began, and the clouds birthed a terrible rain. The drop pods came first, plummeting with the finality of black judgement. They made landfall on the level ground a couple of kilometres from the base. They left streaks in the air, black, vertical contrails that didn't dissipate. Instead, they grew wider, broke up into fragments, and began to whirl. Corvus ran to the nearest guard tower, grabbed a marksman's sniper rifle and peered through its telescopic sight. He could see the movement in the writhing clouds more clearly. It looked like insects. Faintly, impossibly, weaving in and out of the thunder of the pods and the landing craft that now followed on, Corvus heard an insidious buzz.

The darkness flowed from the sky. It was the black of absence and grief, of putrefaction and despair, and of unnameable desire. Its touch infected the air of the landing zone, then rippled out towards the base. It was a different disease, one Corvus had no possible defence against. Though no tendrils of the blackness itself reached this far, Corvus felt something arrive over the wall. The quality of the evening light changed. It turned brittle and sour. He sensed something vital becoming too thin, and something wrong start to smile.

All around him, Fort Goreck's warning klaxons sounded the call to arms. The din was enormous, and he was surprised and disturbed that he could hear the buzzing of the Chaos swarms at all. That told him how sick the real world was becoming, and how hard he would have to fight for it.

The drop pods opened, their venomous petals falling back to disgorge the monsters within. Corvus had never felt comfortable around Space Marines, his Ligetan inferiority complex made exponentially worse by their superhuman power and perfection. But he would have given anything to have one beside him now as he saw the nightmare versions of them mustering in the near distance. Their armour had long since ceased to be simple ceramite. It was darkness that was iron, and iron that was disease. They assembled into rows and then stood motionless, weapons at the ready. Only they weren't entirely still. Their outlines writhed.

Landing craft poured out corrupted infantry in ever greater numbers. At length, the sky spat out a leviathan that looked to Corvus like a Goliath-class transport, only so distorted it seemed more like a terrible whale. Its hull was covered with symbols that tore at Corvus's eyes with obscenities. Around it coiled things that might have been tendrils or tentacles. Its loading bay opened like a maw, and it vomited hordes of troops and vehicles onto the blackening soil of Ligeta.

The legions of plague gathered before Corvus, and he knew there was no hope of fighting them.

But still he would. *Down to the last man*. Though there might be no chance of survival, there would, he now realised with a stir of joy, be the hope of glory in a heroic last stand.

Night fell, and the forces of the *Terminus Est* grew in numbers and strength. The host was now far larger than was needed to storm Fort Goreck, walls or no, commanding heights or no. But the dark soldiers didn't attack. They stood, massed and in the open. Once disembarked, they did nothing. Heavy artillery rumbled out of the transport and then stopped, barrels aimed at the sky, full of threat but silent. The rumble of arrivals stopped. A clammy quiet covered the land.

Corvus had returned to the command centre. He could watch just as well from there, and the low buzzing was less noticeable on this side of the plastek.

'What are they waiting for?' Jeronim muttered.

The quiet was broken by the distant roar of engines. Corvus raised a pair of magnoculars. Three Rhinos were moving to the fore. There were rows of rectangular shapes on the top of the Rhinos. They were horned metal, moulded into the shape of screaming daemons. Loudspeakers, Corvus realised.

Dirge Casters.

If the Rhinos broadcast their song, Fort Goreck would fall without a shot being fired.

Corvus slammed a fist against the alarm trigger. The klaxons whooped over the base. 'Do not turn these off until I give the order,' he told the officers. Still not loud enough, he thought. He turned to the master vox. He shoved the operator aside and flipped the switches for the public address system. He grabbed the mic and ran over to the speaker above the doorway to the command centre. He jammed the mic into the speaker. Feedback pierced his skull, mauled his hearing and sought to obliterate all thought. He gasped from the pain, and staggered under the weight of the sound.

The men around him were covering their ears and weaving around as if drunk. Corvus struggled against the blast of the sound and shook the officers. 'Now!' he screamed. 'We attack now! Launch the Chimeras and take out those vehicles!'

He would have given his soul for a battery of battle cannons, so he could take out the Rhinos from within the safety of the noise shield he had just erected. But this would have to do. He didn't think about how little he might gain in destroying a few speakers. He saw the chance to fight the opponent.

He saw the chance for glory.

He took charge of the squads that followed behind the Chimeras. He saw the pain of the men's faces as the eternal feedback wore at them. He saw the effort it took them to focus on the simple task of readying their weapons. He understood, and hoped that they understood the necessity of his actions, and saw the heroism of their struggle for the Emperor. Gurges had been a fool, Corvus thought. What *he* did now was worthy of song.

The gates opened, and the Chimeras surged forwards. The Rhinos had stopped halfway between their own forces and the wall, easily within the broadcast range of the Dirge Casters. The song was inaudible. Corvus felt his lips pull back in a snarl of triumph as he held his laspistol and chainsword high and led the charge. The courage of the Imperium burst from the confines of the wall. Corvus yelled as he pounded behind the clanking, roaring Chimeras. The feedback whine faded as they left the base behind, but the vehicles had their own din, and Corvus still could hear no trace of the song.

Then something spoke with the voice of ending. The sound was enormous, a deep, compound thunder. It was the Chaos artillery, all guns opening up simultaneously, firing a single, monumental barrage. The lower slope of Fort Goreck's rise exploded, earth geysering skywards. A giant made of noise and air picked Corvus up and threw him. The world tumbled end over end, a hurricane of dirt and rocks and fire. He slammed into the ground and writhed, a pinned insect, as his flattened lungs fought to pull in a breath. When the air came, it was claws and gravel in his chest. His head rang like a struck bell.

When his eyes and ears cleared, he saw the wreckage of the Chimeras and the rout of his charge. The vehicles had taken the worst of the hits, and were shattered, smoking ruins of twisted metal. Pieces of men were scattered over the slope: an arm still clutching a lasgun, a torso that ended at the lower jaw, organs without bodies, bodies without organs. But there were survivors, and as the enemy's guns fell silent, the song washed over the field. Men picked themselves up, and froze as the refrain caught them. A minute after the barrage, Corvus was the only man left with a will of his own. He picked up his weapons and stumbled back up the slope towards the wall. As he ran, he thought he could hear laughter slither through the ranks of the Chaos force.

The gates opened just enough to let him back inside. The feedback blotted out the song, but wrapped itself around his brain like razor wire. He had lost his cap, and his uniform was in tatters. Still, he straightened his posture as he walked back through the stunned troops. Halfway across the grounds, a conscript confronted him. The man's eyes were watering from the hours of mind-destroying feedback and his nose was bleeding. 'Let us go,' he pleaded. 'Let us fight. We'll resist as long as we can.'

Corvus pushed him back. 'Are you mad?' he shouted over the whine. 'Do you know what would happen to you?'

The trooper nodded. 'I was on the wall. I saw.'

'Well then?'

'They look happy when they sing. At least that death isn't pointless torture.'

Corvus raised his pistol and shot the man through the eye. He turned in a full circle, glaring at his witnesses, making sure they understood the lesson. Then he stalked back to the command centre.

A night and a day of the endless electronic wail. Then another night of watching with nerves scraped raw. Corvus plugged his ears with cloth, but the feedback stabbed its way through the pathetic barrier. His jaw worked, his cheek muscles twitched, and he saw the same strain in the taut, clenched faces of his men. The Rhinos came no closer, and there were no other enemy troop movements. Fort Goreck was besieged by absolute stillness, and that would be enough.

The third day of the siege was a hell of sleeplessness and claustrophobic rage. Five Guardsmen attempted to desert. Corvus had them flogged, then shot.

As the sun set, Corvus could see the end coming. There would be no holding out. The shield he had erected was torture, and madness would tear the base apart. The only thing left was a final, glorious charge that would deny the enemy the kind of triumph that they clearly desired. But how to make that attack if the troops would succumb to the anthem before they even reached the front lines?

Corvus covered his ears with his hands, trying to block the whine, to dampen it just enough so that he could think. Silence would have been the greatest gift the Emperor could bestow upon him.

Instead, he was granted the next greatest: inspiration.

The medicae centre was on the ground floor of the command block. Corvus found the medic, and explained what was required. The man blanched and refused. Corvus ordered him to do as he said. Still the medic protested. Corvus put his laspistol to the man's head, and that was convincing enough. Just.

The process took all night. At least, for the most part, the men didn't resist being rendered deaf. Some seemed almost relieved to be free of the feedback whine. Most submitted to the procedure with slack faces and dead looks. They had become creatures of stoic despair, held together and animated by the habits of discipline. Corvus watched yet another patient, blood pouring from his ears, contort on a gurney. At least, he thought, he was giving the soldiers back their pride for the endgame.

There wasn't time to inoculate the entire base contingent against the anthem, so Corvus settled on the best, most experienced squads. That would be enough. They were Imperial Guard, and they would give the traitor forces something to think about.

Morning came quickly, and though one more enemy gunship had landed during the night, the enemy's disposition otherwise remained unchanged. His eyes rough as sand from sleeplessness, Corvus inspected his assembled force. The soldiers looked like the walking dead, unworthy of the glory they were about to find. He would give it to them anyway, Corvus thought, and they could thank him in the Emperor's light.

He glanced at the rest of the troops. He would be abandoning them to their fate. He shrugged. They were doomed regardless, and at least he had enforced loyalty up to the last. He could go to his grave knowing that he had permitted no defection to Chaos.

He had done his duty.

He had earned his glory.

'Open the gates,' he roared, and wished he could hear the strength of his shout over the shriek of the feedback. The sentries couldn't hear him either, but his gesture was clear, and the wall of Fort Goreck opened for the last time.

There are songs that have been written about the final charge of Colonel Corvus Parthamen. But they are not sung in the mess halls of the Imperial Guard, and they are not stirring battle hymns. They are mocking, obscene doggerel, and they are snarled, rather than sung, with venomous humour, in the corridors of dark ships that ply the warp like sharks. A few men of the Imperium do hear it, in their terminal moments, as their positions are overrun by the hordes of Chaos. They do not appreciate it any more than Corvus would have.

The charge was a rout. The men ran into las-fire and bolter shells. They were blown to pieces by cannon barrage. They were shredded by chainswords and pulped by armoured fists. Still, they made it further down the hill than even Corvus could have hoped. A coherent force actually hit the Chaos front lines and did some damage before being annihilated. Their actions might have seemed like glorious heroism born of nothing-to-lose desperation. But the fact that not a single man took cover – that not one did anything but run straight ahead, weapon firing indiscriminately – revealed the truth. They were running to their deaths, and were glad of the relief.

Corvus was the last. It took him a moment to notice that he was alone, what with the joy of battle and the ecstasy of being free of the whine. He was still running forwards, running to his glory, but he wondered now why there didn't seem to be any shots aimed at him. Or why the squad of Chaos Space Marines ahead parted to let him pass. He faltered, and then he saw who was waiting for him.

The monster was huge, clad in what had once been Terminator armour, but was now a buzzing, festering exoskeleton. Flies swarmed from the funnels above his shoulders and the lesions in the corrupted ceramite. His single-horned helmet transformed the being's final human traces into the purely daemonic. His grip on his giant scythe was relaxed.

Corvus saw just how powerful disease-made flesh could be. He charged anyway, draining his laspistol, then pulling his chainsword. He swung at the Herald of Nurgle. Typhus whipped the Manreaper around. The movement was as rapid as it was casual and contemptuous. He hit Corvus with the shaft and shattered his hip. Corvus collapsed in the dirt. He bit down on his scream as Typhus loomed over him.

'Kill me,' Corvus spat. 'But know that I fought you to the end. I have my own victory.'

Typhus made a sound that was the rumble of giant hives. Corvus realised he had just heard laughter. 'Kill you?' Typhus asked. His voice was deep. It was smooth as a deliquescent corpse. 'I haven't come to kill you. I have come to teach you my anthem.'

Through his pain, Corvus managed his own laugh. 'I will never sing it.'

'Really? But you have already. You believe you serve order and light, but, like your carrion Emperor, everything you do blasts hope and rushes towards entropy. Look what you did to your men. You have served me well, my son. You and your brother, both.'

Corvus fought against the epiphany, but it burst over his consciousness with sickly green light. The truth took him, and infected him. He saw his actions, he saw their consequences, and he saw whose glory he had truly been serving. As the pattern took shape for him, so did a sound. He heard the anthem, and he heard its music. There was melody there, and he was part of it. Surrender flooded his system, and the triumphant shape of Typhus filled his dying vision. Corvus's jaw snapped open. His throat contorted with ecstatic agony, and he became one with Ligeta's final choir.

PLAYING PATIENCE

Dan Abnett

I

West of Urbitane, the slum-tracts begin, and one descends into a ragged wilderness of dispiriting ruins where the only signs of life are the armoured manses of the narcobarons, projecting like metal blisters above the endless rubble. This is a destitute realm, a great and shameful urban waste, stalked by the Pennyrakers and the Dolors and a myriad other gangs, where Imperial authority has only the most tenuous grip.

A foetid wind blows through the slum-tracts, exhaled like bad breath from the sumps and stacks of the massive city. This miasmal air whines through the rotting habitats and moans in the shadows.

And those shadows are permanent, for the flanks of Urbitane rise behind the tracts, eclipsing all daylight. Flecked with a billion lamps, the rockcrete stacks of the sweating hive city ascend into the roiling clouds like the angular shoulders of some behemoth emerging from chthonic depths, and soar as a sheer cliff above the slums that litter the lightless ground at its foot.

Sub-orbitals cross the murky sky, their trace-lights blinking like cursors on a dark screen. Occasionally the slums tremble as a bulk-lifter passes particularly low overhead on its final approach into the canyons of the hive, the bass rumble of its engines shivering the air.

Where, in the west, the hive stacks come tumbling down to meet the slums, shelving like giant staircases in bad repair, there is a patched stonework tower that houses the Kindred Youth Scholam. It is a meagre place, supported by charitable works, teetering on the brink between city and slum. Humble, crumbling, it faces west, its many window-slits barred, for the safety of the pupils.

At the start of of the year 396 Imperial, there were, amongst the scholam's many inhabitants, three sisters called Prudence, Providence and Patience.

The night I arrived on Sameter, the rigorists had locked Patience in the scholam's oubliette.

II

Sameter is a dismal place, and its morose air matched our mood. A slovenly, declining agrochemical world in the heartlands of the Helican subsector, it had seen better days.

So had we. My companions and I were weary and dejected. Pain clung to us like a shroud, so tightly none of us could express our grief. It had been that way for six months, since Majeskus. The only thing that kept us together and moved us along was a basic desire for revenge.

We had been forced to make the voyage to Sameter aboard a privately hired transport. The *Hinterlight* was dry-docked for repairs half a subsector away, and its mistress, Cynia Preest, had pledged to rejoin us as soon as the work was done. But I knew she was rueing the day she had ever agreed to assist my mission. When I had last spoken with her, she had confided, bitterly, that another incident like Majeskus would surely make her break her compact with me and return to the life of a merchant rogue in the Grand Banks.

She blamed me. They all blamed me, and they were damn well right. I had underestimated Molotch. I had given him the opening. My blind confidence had led to the disaster. Throne, what a fool I had been! Molotch was the sort of enemy one should never underestimate. He was Cognitae, perhaps the brightest and best to emerge from that infernal institution, which took genius as a basic prerequisite.

Our lander skimmed down through the filthy air above the Urbitane isthmus, bumping in the crosswind chop, and cycled in towards one of the hive's private landing gantries on the north side of the city. As the breaking jets fired, sudden, intense gravity hung upon us. Even inside my suspensor field, I felt its weight. I had linked one of my chair's data cables to the lander's systems, and so saw everything that the shuttered cabin denied my friends. The looming piles of the hive, the shelf-like stacks, each one kilometres wide, the bristling lights, the smog. Hive towers rose up, as vast and impassive as tombstones, etched with lit windows. Chimneys exhaled skeins of black smoke. The lower airways buzzed with small fliers and ornithopters, like gnats swarming up on a summer evening. There, the spires of the Ecclesiarch Basilica, gilded like a crown; beyond, the huge glass roofs of the Northern Commercia, so high that the clouds of a microclimate weather system had formed beneath their vault. There, the Inner Consul, the radiating rings of the transit system, the wrought-iron pavilions of the Agriculture Guild.

We touched down at sunset. Great, shimmering doughnuts of gas-flame were issuing from the promethium refineries along the isthmus, bellying up like small, fireball suns against the curdled brown undercast.

The private landing gantry was high up in the twisted mass of the inner hive-towers. Leased by the local ordos to provide convenient access to the city, it was a creaking metal platform trembled by the windshear. Even so, exhaust vapour from our dented, scabby lander pooled in an acrid haze inside the rusting safety basket of the pad. The lander, a gross-utility vehicle three hundred years old, reclined on its pneumatic landing claws like a tailless lizard. It had been painted red, a long time ago, but the colour was only a memory now. Steam hissed from the rapidly cooling hydraulics, and a disturbing quantity of lubricant and system fluid gushed out of its underside from joints and cracks and fissures.

Without asking, Kara Swole took hold of my chair's handle and pushed me out down the open ramp. I could have done it myself but I sensed that Kara, like all of them, wanted something to do, just to keep busy. Harlon Nayl followed us out, and walked to the edge of the safety cage to stare out into the foggy depths of the hive. Carl Thonius lingered in the hatchway, paying the pilot his fee and tip and making arrangements for future services. Harlon and Kara were both dressed in bodygloves and heavy jackets, but Carl Thonius was, as ever, clad in exquisite, fashionable garments: buckled wedge shoes, black velvet pantaloons, a tailored jacket of grey damask tight around his thin ribs, a high collar tied with a silk bow and set with a golden pin. He was twenty-four years old, blond-haired, rather plain of face, but striking in his poise and manners. I had thought him too much of a dandy when the ordos first submitted him as a possible interrogator, but had quickly realised that behind the foppish, mannered exterior lay a quite brilliant analytical mind. His rank marked him out amongst my retainers. The others – Nayl and Kara, for example – were individuals I hired because of their skills and talents. But Carl was an inquisitor in training. One day, he would aspire to the office and signet of the sublime ordos. His service to me, as interrogator, was his apprenticeship, and every inquisitor took on at least one interrogator, training them for the duty ahead. I had been Gregor Eisenhorn's interrogator, and had learned an immeasurable amount from that great man. I had no doubt that, in a few years, Carl Thonius would be well on his way to that distinguished rank.

Of course, for reasons I could not have ever imagined, that would not be the case. Hindsight is a worthless toy.

Wystan Frauka emerged from the lander, lighting his latest lho-stick from the stub of the last. He had his limiter turned on, of course, and it would remain on until I told him otherwise. He looked bored, as usual, detached. He wandered over to where a servitor was unloading our luggage from the lander's aft belly-hatch and looked for his own belongings.

Harlon remained at the edge of the safety cage, deep in thought. A heavyset man, thick with corded muscle, his head shaved, he had a dominating presence. Born on Loki, he'd been a bounty hunter for many years before gaining employment with my mentor Eisenhorn because of his skills. I had inherited him, so to speak. There was no man I would rather have at my side in a fight. But I wondered if Harlon Nayl *was* at my side any more. Not since… the event. I'd heard him talk about 'going back to the old game', his defeated tone the same as Cynia Preest's. If it came down to it, I would let him go.

But I would miss him.

Kara Swole trundled me over to the gantry edge until we were facing the safety basket too. We stared out across the city.

'See anything you like?' she asked. She was trying to be light and funny, but I could taste the pain in her voice.

'We'll find something here, I promise,' I said, my voice synthesised, expressionless, through the mechanical vox-ponder built into my support chair. I hadn't mind-talked to any of them for a long time now, not since Majeskus, probably. I despised the vox-ponder's menacing flatness, but telepathy seemed too intimate, too intrusive at a time when thoughts were raw and private.

'We'll find something here,' I repeated. 'Something worth finding.'

Kara managed a smile. It was the first I had seen her shape for months, and it warmed me briefly. She was trying. Kara Swole was a short, voluptuous redhead whose rounded build quite belied her acrobatic abilities. Like Harlon, I had inherited her from Eisenhorn. She was a true servant of the ordos, as hard as stone when she needed to be, but she possessed a gentleness as appealing and soft as her curves. For all her dexterity, her stealth, her confidence with weapons, I think it was that gentleness that I most valued her for.

Molotch had faded into the void after his crimes above Majeskus, leaving no trace. Sameter, benighted planet, offered us the vestige of a clue. Three of Molotch's hired guns, three of the men we had slain in the battle on the *Hinterlight*, had proved, under forensic examination, to have come from Sameter. From this very place, Urbitane, the planet's second city.

We would find their origins and their connections, and follow them through every tenuous twitch and turn, until we had Molotch's scent again.

And then…

Carl had finished his transactions with the lander pilot. As I turned, I saw the pilot looking at me, staring at me the same way he and the other crew members had stared since they had first seen me come aboard. I didn't have to reach out with my mind to understand his curiosity.

The wounds of Chaos had left me a mangled wreck, a disembodied soul locked forever within a grav-suspended, armoured support chair. I had no physical identity anymore. I was just a lump of floating metal, a mechanical container, inside which a fragment of organic material remained, kept vital and pulsing by complex bio-systems. I knew the very sight of me scared people, people like the pilot and the rest of his crew. I had no face to read, and people do so like a face.

I missed my face. I missed my limbs. Destiny had left me one virtue, my mind. Powerfully, alarmingly psychic, my mind was my one saving grace. It allowed me to carry on my work. It allowed me to transcend my pitiful state as a cripple in a metal box.

Molotch had a face. A handsome visor of flesh that was, in its way, as impassive as my sleek, matt-finished metal. The only expression it ever conveyed was a delight in cruelty. I would take great pleasure in burning it off his shattered skull.

'Do we have the names and physiologues?' I asked.

'Nayl's got them,' Kara replied.

'Harlon?'

He turned and walked over to join us, pulling a data-slate from the hip-pocket of his long, mesh-weave coat.

He flipped it on.

'Victor Zhan. Noble Soto. Goodman Frell. Biogs, traces, taints and histories. All present and correct.'

'Let's do what we came here to do,' I said.

III

Oubliette. A place where things or persons are put so that they may be forgotten about. Or, as Patience preferred to think, a place where one might sit awhile and forget.

The scholam's oubliette was a cavity under the lower hall, fitted with a bolted hatch. There was no light, and vermin scuttled around in the wet shadows. It was the punishment place, the area where those pupils who had committed the worst infractions were sent by the rigorists. But it was also one of the few places in the Kindred Youth Scholam where a pupil could enjoy some kind of privacy.

According to its register, the scholam was home to nine hundred and seventy-six young people, most of them slum orphans. There were thirty-two tutors, all privately employed, and another forty servants and ancillary staff, including a dozen men, all ex-Guard, known as the *rigorists*, whose duties were security and discipline.

Life in the scholam was austere. The old tower, built centuries earlier for some purpose no one could now remember, was chilly and damp. The tower itself clung for support to the side of a neighbouring stack, like a climbing plant against a wall. The floors of its many storeys were cold ouslite dressed with rush-fibre, the walls lime-washed and prone to trickles of condensation. A murmur from the lower levels reminded the inhabitants that there was a furnace plant working down there, but it was the only clue, for no heat ever issued from the thumping pipework or the corroded radiators.

The regime was strict. An early rise, prayers, and an hour of ritual examination before breakfast, which was taken at sunrise. The morning was spent performing the many chores of the scholam – scrubbing floors, washing laundry, helping in the kitchen – and the afternoon was filled with academic classes. After supper, more prayers, ablutions in the freezing wash-house, and then two hours of liturgical study by lamplight.

Occasionally, trusted older pupils were allowed to accompany tutors out of the tower on trips into the nearby regions of the hive, to help carry purchased food stocks, fabrics, ink, oil and all the other sundry materials necessary to keep the scholam running. They were a distinctive sight in the busy streets of the western stacks: a grim, robed tutor leading a silent, obedient train of uniformed scholars, each one laden down by bundles, bales, bags and cartons. Every pupil wore a uniform, a unisex design in drab grey with the initials of the scholam stitched onto the back.

Few pupils ever complained about the slender comfort of their lives, because almost all of them had volunteered for it. Strict it might be, but life in the Kindred Youth Scholam was preferable to the alternative outside in the tracts. Existence in the wastelands west of the hive offered a lean choice: scavenge like an animal, or bond into a gang. Either way, life expectancy was miserably low. Municipally-sponsored scholams, offering a bed, food and a basic education that emphasised the values of the Throne, represented an escape route. Reasonably healthy, lice-free, qualified youngsters could leave such institutions with a real prospect of securing an apprenticeship to one of the hive guilds, a journeyship, or at least a decent indenture.

Patience had been at the scholam for twelve years, which meant she was twenty-two or twenty-three years old and by far the oldest pupil registered at that time. Most pupils left the care of the charity around their majority, when their age gave them a legal identity in the eyes of the guilds. But Patience had stayed on because of her sisters. Twins, Providence and Prudence were fifteen, and Patience had promised them she would stay and look after them until they turned eighteen. It was a promise she'd made to her sisters, and to her dying mother, the day their mother had brought the three of them to the scholam and asked the tutors to take them in.

Patience was not her birth name, no more than Prudence's was Prudence or Providence's Providence. They were scholam names, given to each pupil at their induction, symbolic of the fresh start they were making.

Except for Patience, few pupils were made to suffer the oubliette. She had now been in there nineteen times.

On this occasion, she was in for breaking the nose of Tutor Abelard. She'd punched the odious creep for criticising her work in the laundry. The crack of cartilage and the puff of blood had been very satisfying.

Cooling down, in the dark, Patience recognised that it had been foolish to strike the tutor. Just another mark against her record. For this, she was missing the graduation supper taking place in the vaults many floors up. There was an event like it every few months, when distinguished men of consequence – guild masters, merchants, manufactory directors and mill owners – came to the scholam to meet and examine the older pupils, making selections from the best and contracting apprenticeships. By morning, Patience knew, many of her long-term friends would have left the scholam forever to begin new lives in the teeming stacks of Urbitane.

The fact was, she'd been there too long. She was too old to be contained by the scholam, even by the hardline rigorists, and that was why she kept running into trouble. If it hadn't been for her promise, and her two, beloved sisters, she'd have been apprenticed to a hive mill long since.

Something bristly and locomoting on more than four legs scuttled across her bare hand. With a twitch of her gift, she hurled it away into the dark.

Her gift. Only she had it. Her sisters showed no sign of it. Patience never used her gift in front of the tutors, and she was fairly certain they knew nothing about it.

It was a mind thing. She could move things by thinking about them. She'd discovered she could do it the day her mother left them at the scholam gates. Patience had been practising ever since.

In the dark of the black stone cell, Patience tried to picture her mother's face, but couldn't. She could remember a warm smell, slightly unwashed but reassuring, a strong embrace, a hacking cough that presaged mortality.

The face, though, the face...

It had been a long time. Unable to form the image in her head, Patience turned her mind to something else. Her name. Not Patience. Her real name. The tutors had tried to rid her of it, forcing her to change her identity, but she still hung on to it. It was the one private piece of her that nothing and no one could ever steal. Her true name.

It kept her alive. The very thought of it kept her going.

The irony was, she could leave the oubliette whenever she chose. A simple flick of her gift would throw back the bolt and allow her to lift the trapdoor. But that would give her away, convince the tutors she was abnormal.

Patience reined her mind in and sat still in the darkness.

Someone was coming. Coming to let her out.

* * *

IV

Harlon Nayl's eyes didn't so much as blink as the fist came at him. His left hand went out, tilting inwards, captured the man's arm neatly around the inside of the wrist, and wrenched it right round through two hundred degrees. A bone may have snapped, but if it did, the sound was masked by the man's strangled squeal, a noise which ended suddenly as Nayl's other hand connected with his face.

The man – a thickset lhotas-eater with a mucus problem – shivered the deck as he hit it. Nayl kept hold of his wrist, pulling the man's arm straight and tight while he stood firmly on his armpit. This position allowed for significant leverage, and Nayl made use of it. Harlon was in a take-no-prisoners mood, I sensed, which was hardly useful given our objective.

A little leverage and rotation. A ghastly scream, vocalised through a face spattered with blood.

'What do you reckon?' asked Nayl, twisting a little more and increasing the pitch. 'Do you think I can get top C out of him?'

'Should I care?' replied Morpal Who Moves with mannered disinterest. 'You can twist Manx's arm right off and beat him round the head with it, he still won't tell you what you want. He's a lho-brow. He knows nothing.'

Nayl smiled, twisted, got another shriek. 'Of course he is. I worked that much out from his scintillating conversation. But one of you does. One of you knows the answer I want. Sooner or later his screams will aggravate you so much you'll tell me.'

Morpal Who Moves had a face like a crushed walnut. He sat back in his satin-upholstered buoy-chair and fiddled with a golden rind-shriver, a delicate tool that glittered between his bony fingers. He was weighing up what to say. I could read the alternatives in his forebrain like the label on a jar.

'This is not good for business–'

'Sir, this is my place of business, and I don't take kindly to–'

'Throne of Earth, who the frig d'you think you are–'

Morpal's place was a four-hectacre loading dock of iron, stock-brick and timber hinged out over the vast canyon gulf of the West Descent, an aerial thoroughfare formed by the gap between two of the hive's most colossal stacks. Beneath the reinforced platform and the gothic buttresses that supported it, space dropped away for almost a vertical kilometre to the base of the stacks. Ostensibly, this was a ledge where cargo-flitters and load-transporters – and many thousands of these craft plied the airways of the West Descent – could drop in for repairs, fuel, or whatever else the pilots needed. But Morpal was a fence and racketeer, and the transience of the dock's traffic gave him ample opportunity to steal, replace, backhand, smuggle and otherwise run his lucrative trade.

More than twenty men stood in a loose group around Harlon. Most were stevedores and dock labourers in Morpal's employ. The others were flit-pilots, gig-men, hoy-drivers and riggers who'd stopped in for caffeine, fuel and a game of cards, many of them regulars who were into Morpal for more than a year's salary each.

All this and more was visible from their collective thoughts, which swirled around the loading dock like a fog. I was five kilometres away, in a room in a low-rent hotel. But it was all clear enough. I knew what Mingus Futir had eaten for breakfast, what Fancyman D'cree had stolen the night before, the lie Gert Gerity had told his wife. I knew all about the thing Erik Klass didn't want to tell Morpal.

Wystan Frauka sat beside me, smoking a lho-stick, his limiter activated. He was reading a tremendously tedious erotic novel on his slate.

Surface was easy. Deep mind was harder. Morpal Who Moves and his cronies were well-used to concealing their secrets.

That was why Harlon had gone in first.

Morpal finally arrived at a decision. He had determined, I sensed, to take the moral high ground. 'This is not how things are done on my platform,' he told Harlon. 'This is a respectable establishment.'

'Yeah, right,' snorted Nayl. 'One last time. What can you tell me about Victor Zhan? He worked here once, before he went off planet. I know he worked here, because I had the records checked out. So tell me about Victor.'

'Victor Zahn hasn't been around in five years,' Morpal said.

'Tell me about him anyway,' Nayl snapped.

'I really don't see any reason to do that.'

'I'll show you one.' Nayl reached his free hand into his hip pocket, took something out and threw it down onto the cup-ringed, grimy tabletop. His badge of authority. The signet crest of the Inquisition.

Immediately all the men took a step beck, alarmed. I felt Morpal's mind start in dismay. This was the kind of trouble no one wanted.

Unless...

'Damn it,' I said.

Frauka looked up from the midst of his book's latest loveless tryst. 'What's up?'

'Morpal Who Moves is about to make a miscalculation.'

'Oh dear,' said Frauka, and turned back to his novel.

Morpal had run the dock for forty-six years. For all his misdeeds and misdemeanours, some of them serious, he'd never run foul of the law, apart from the odd fine or reprimand. He actually thought he could deal with this and get away with it.

+Harlon. Morpal's signal will be a double finger-click. Your immediate threat is the grey-haired gig-man to your left, who has a dart-knife. To his right, in the leather apron, the rigger has a pivot-gun, but he will not be able to draw it as fast. The flit-pilot in green wants to prove himself to Morpal, and he won't hesitate. His friend, the one with the obscura-tinted eyes, is less confident, but he has a boomgun in his cab.+

'Well?' Harlon Nayl asked.

Morpal Who Moves clicked both middle fingers.

I flinched at the sudden flare of adrenaline and aggression. A great part of it came from Nayl.

The rigger in the leather apron had drawn his pivot-gun, but Nayl had already stoved the table in with the face of the grey-haired gig-man and relieved him of his dart-knife. Nayl threw himself around as the pilot in green lunged forward, and slam-kicked him in the throat. The pilot went down, choking, his larynx crushed, as the pivot-gun finally boomed. The home-made round whipped high over Nayl's head as he rolled and triggered the dart-knife. The spring-propelled blade speared the rigger through the centre of his leather apron, and he fell over on his back, clawing at his belly.

Others ploughed in, one striking Nayl in the ribs with an eight wrench.

'Ow!' Nayl grunted, and laid the man out. The obscura fiend was running across the platform towards his hoy. Nayl threw another man aside, and grabbed the edges of Morpal's buoy-chair. The Mover yelled in dismay as Nayl slung the frictionless chair sideways. It sped across the platform like a quoit, knocking two of the stevedores over, and slammed hard against the dock's restraining rail. The serious impact dazed Morpal. He slumped forward.

Nayl backfisted a man in the nose, and then punched out another who was trying to flee anyway. Two front teeth flew into the air. The obscura fiend had his hoy's door open, reaching in.

A stevedore with a hatchet swung at Nayl, forcing him to jump back. Nayl blocked the next swing with his forearm, fractured the man's sternum with a jab, and threw him with a crash into the nearby row of porcelain samovars.

The obscura addict turned from his cab and racked the grip of his boomgun. He brought it up to fire.

Nayl slid the Hecuter 10 from his bodyglove and calmly shot him through the head at fifteen metres.

Blood splashed up the rusted fender of the hoy. The man cannoned backwards, dropping the boomgun from dead fingers.

The rest of them scattered.

Kara ran onto the platform, her weapon raised. It had taken her just thirty seconds to move out of cover at my command to back up Nayl, but the fight was already done.

'Don't leave any for me, then,' she complained.

'You should have been here,' Nayl said. He walked over to the rig and picked up the fallen boomgun, examining it.

'Nice,' he said.

+Harlon...+

Nayl looked over at Morpal, who was just coming round, the back of his buoy-chair rammed against the platform's rail. He saw Nayl, saw him aiming the weapon...

+Harlon! No!+

But Nayl's blood was up. The need for vengeance, suppressed for so long, was finally finding an outlet.

Nayl fired. Morpal had ducked. The shot exploded the seat-back above him, and the rail behind. The force of the impact drove the buoy-chair backwards.

Intact, unscathed, but still sitting in his chair, Morpal Who Moves went backwards, toppled, and fell into the inter-stack gulf.

'Well, damn,' Nayl hissed.

+For Throne's sake, Nayl! I told you not to–+

Thonius had just walked into the hotel room behind me.

'Good book?' he asked Frauka.

'Saucy,' Frauka replied, not looking up.

+Nayl's just ruined our lead.+

'Never mind,' Thonius grinned, a smug satisfaction on his face. 'It was pointless anyway. I've found a much better one.'

V

She knew for certain it was Rigorist Knill even before he opened the oubliette hatch. Just part of her gift, the same thing that allowed her to win at cards or guess which hand a coin was in.

'Come, you,' he said. A glow-globe coded to Knill's bio-trace bobbed at his shoulder and cast its cheap yellow light into the cell.

Patience got up and stepped out into the hallway, making a big show of dusting down her garments.

'They'll be dirtier yet,' Knill remarked, closing the heavy, black iron door. 'The dinner's over, and the Prefect wants the pots doing.' Knill chuckled and pushed her on down the hallway. The glowglobe followed obediently.

There was little to like about Rigorist Knill. In his days as an Imperial Guardsman, he had been big and powerful, but age and a lack of exercise had sunk his muscles into slabby fat, hunching him over. His teeth were black pegs, and a scarred, concave section of his skull explained both the end of his soldiering career and his simpleton's nature. Knill was proud of his past, and still wore his medal on his chest. He liked to regale the pupils with accounts of the glorious actions he had seen, and got angry when they mocked him and pointed out inconsistencies in his stories. But he wasn't the worst by a long way. Skinny Rigorist Souzerin had such a short temper and love of the flail that the pupils believed he had once been a commissar. Rigorist Ocwell was rather too fond of the younger girls. And then there was Rigorist Ide, of course.

'So I'm to wash pots?' Patience asked.

'Get on,' Knill grumbled, and gave her a cuff. Like all the rigorists,

Knill wore a knotted leather flail and a longer wooden baton suspended from his wide leather belt. The flail was for minor punishments, the baton a more serious disciplinary tool. Knill, who trusted his fists, seldom used either. Many of Prefect Cyrus's long morning sermons revolved around the symbology of the rigorists' twin instruments, likening them to the paired heads of the holy aquila, voices of different pitch and measure through which the dogmas of the Golden Throne might be communicated in complementary ways. In the Kindred Youth Scholam, most lessons seemed to require some corporal component.

They ascended the draughty stone stairs, and passed through the unlit lesson halls of the seventh remove. The narrow hallways between classrooms were formed by partly-glazed wooden partitions. The glass in the frames was stained the colour of tobacco by the passage of the years.

Then Knill unlocked the door to the next ascent.

'I thought I was wanted for scullion duties,' Patience said.

'The Prefect would clap eyes on you first,' replied Knill, and jerked his head upwards.

Patience sighed, and began to trudge up the winding stairs ahead of Knill's light. She knew what that meant. A quiz from the Prefect on the error of her ways. If she was lucky, she'd get away with an apology to Tutor Abelard, and a few *Lachrymose Mea* in the chapel under the Prefect's instruction before she spent the night in the potroom, freezing her hands in the greasy sop-tubs.

If she was unlucky, there would be Souzerin and his flail. Or Ide.

It took them over twenty minutes to climb the meandering tower to the upper vaults. In the main chamber there, servants and a few chosen pupils were clearing the last dregs of the feast. The air was still warm, and scented with rich cooking smells. Prefect Cyrus did not stint when important visitors came to the scholam. He even provided wine and amasec, and did not complain when manufactory directors lit up pipes and lho-sticks. Patience could smell the spicy smoke lingering in the long room. Two young pupils form the sixth remove were team-folding the white cloths from the feast tables. A tutor, Runciman, was supervising them, and explaining the geometry of the correct fold-angles.

'Wait,' Knill told her, and left her in the doorway. He shambled off down the length of the long, beamed hall, his light tagging along after him like a willowisp. Patience waited, edgy, arms folded. Three young children ran out past her, their arms full of candlesticks, napkin rings threaded around their tiny wrists. One glanced up at her, eyes wide.

Knill reached the far end of the room. Prefect Cyrus was sitting at the high table still, a swell-glass in his hand, talking quietly with a stranger in a dark red robe. One of the night's visitors, a guilder or a mill owner perhaps. Clearly a man of wealth and breeding, well-groomed. He was listening to the Prefect intently, sipping something from a tall crystal beaker. To his left, apart from the conversation, sat another man, another stranger. This man was short, but powerfully made, his cropped hair ginger in the lamplight, his bodyglove traced with silver. He was smoking a lho-stick, and gazing with half-interest at the ancient, flaking murals on the chamber walls. From her vantage point, Patience could see the ginger-haired man wore an empty holster on his hip. Prefect Cyrus did not permit firearms inside the scholam, but that holster suggested the ginger-haired man was a bodyguard, a paid protector. The man in red was evidently even more important than she had first suspected, if he could afford his own muscle.

Then Patience saw Ide. The rigorist was standing at the far end of the chamber, waiting. He was staring right at her. She shuddered. Tall, strong, Ide was a brute. His eyes were always half-open, and he wore his white-blond hair in a long, shaggy mane, secured at the nape by a silver buckle. Ide was the only rigorist who never bragged about his Guard days. Patience had a nasty idea why.

Knill spoke briefly to the prefect, who excused himself to the man in red, and walked down to the centre of the hall, Knill at his heels. The Prefect gestured that Patience should come join him. She approached obediently, until they were face to face.

Prefect Cyrus was anything between forty and four hundred. Slim and well-made, he had undergone many programs of juvenat work, making his flesh over-tight and his skin hideously smooth and pink. His eyes were violet and, Patience believed, deliberately sculpted by the augchemists to appear kind and fatherly. His blue robes were perfectly pressed and starched. When he smiled, his implanted teeth were as white as ice.

He was smiling now.

'Patience,' he whispered. She could smell the oil of cloves he wore to scent his body.

'My Prefect,' she answered with effort.

'You flinch. Why do you flinch?'

She could not say it was because Rigorist Ide had just taken the first few steps on his way to join them. 'I broke the rules, and committed an affront to the person of Tutor Abelard. I flinch as I await my punishment.'

'Patience,' the Prefect said. 'Your punishment is over. You've been set in the oubliette, have you not?' He looked round at Knill. 'She has been in the oubliette all night, hasn't she, Knill?'

'That is so, Prefect,' replied Knill with a nod.

'All done, then. No need to flinch.'

'Then why am I here?' Patience asked.

'I have good news,' the prefect said, 'and I wanted to share it with you as soon as possible. Good, good news, that I'm sure will lift your heart as surely as it has lifted mine.'

'What is it?'

'Patience, places have been secured this night for your dear sisters. Serving in the hall this evening, they so won the admiration of a merchant lord, one of our guests, he offered them indenture on the spot.'

Patience blinked. 'My sisters?'

'Have taken wing at last, Patience. Their particulars are all signed and contracted. Their new life has already begun.'

'No. That's not right,' Patience said sharply. 'They're too young. They haven't yet reached maturity. I won't allow it.'

'It is already done,' the Prefect said, his face showing no sign of annoyance.

'Then undo it,' Patience said. 'Right now! Undo it! I should've been consulted! They are in my charge!'

'Patience, you were detained in the oubliette, for your own wrong-doings. I decided the matter. Your sisters are already long departed, and I trust you will wish them well in your prayers this night.'

'No!' she shouted.

'Shut your hole!' warned Knill, stepping forward, his light bobbing after him.

'No need for that, Knill,' said Cyrus. The Prefect gazed at Patience. 'I am rather surprised by your response, Patience. I had thought you would be pleased.'

She glowered at him. 'You cheated me. You knew I wasn't around to object. This is wrong! They are too young–'

'I tire of this, Patience. There is no rule or law that says girls of your sisters' age may not be contracted. Such an agreement is in my power.'

'It isn't! You can only authorise a contract of employ in the case of an orphan lacking the appropriate blood-kin! That's the law! I've only stayed here this long to supervise their well-being! You bastard!'

'Take her away, Knill,' said the Prefect.

'Don't even think about it, Knill,' Patience warned. 'I want his name, Cyrus. The name of this man who has taken my sisters.'

'Oh, and for what good?'

'I am of majority. I can leave this stinking tower whenever I choose. Give me the name... now! I will find him and secure the release of my sisters!'

Prefect Cyrus turned to Knill. 'Another period in the oubliette, I feel.'

'Yes, sir.'

'Oh, no,' said Patience, backing away. 'You can't touch me now. Not now. I've stuck by the scholam's frigging rules this long, one way or another, for the good of my sisters, but you have no hold on me! I am an adult, with the rights of an adult! Go frig yourself, Cyrus, I'm leaving!'

'Double the period for that vile language!' Cyrus barked.

'Double this, stink-breath!' Patience cried, making a gesture one of the pot-boys had taught her.

Knill lunged at her, arms wide. She ducked sideways, putting a little of her gift into the kick she slammed at the old soldier's belly. Knill lurched away and crashed into a table, knocking pewterware onto the floor, anxiously steadying himself against the table's edge in surprise.

Somehow, Ide had got behind her. The blow from his baton, swung two-handed, caught her across the back of the skull and dropped her to her hands and knees. Patience blacked out for a brief moment, and blood streamed out down her nose onto the flagstones. She felt Ide's big hand crush her left shoulder as it grabbed her.

'Never did live up to your name,' she heard Ide murmur.

Her name. Her *name*. Not Patience. The one little piece of her life she still owned entirely.

Ide was swinging the baton down again to smack her shoulders. She froze his hand. Ide gasped, sweating, terrified, as an invisible force slowly pulled his powerful arm back and drew the baton away from her. She let it smash Ide in the face.

He staggered back with an anguished cry, blood spurting from his mangled nose. Then she was up, on her feet, flicking her head back hard so that the blood from her nose spattered out in a shower. Knill was coming for her. So was the Prefect. Someone was crying an alarm.

Patience looked at Knill and he flew backwards through the air, slamming into the table again so hard it went over with him. She looked at Cyrus, and snarled as she simultaneously burst all the blood-vessels in his face. He fell down on his knees, whimpering.

'You bastards!' she was screaming. 'My sisters, you bastards!'

Ide swung at her again. He was crazy-mad now, trying to kill her. Patience held out a hand and Ide went sprawling over on his back... and continued to slide down the length of the hallway until his skull crashed into the stone doorpost.

Rigorist Souzerin had appeared from somewhere, his flail raised as he ran at her. Knill was clambering to his feet.

Patience ducked Souzerin's first slash, then hurled him backwards a few steps with a twitch of her mind. She was getting tired now. Knill thundered forward.

'I'll take that,' Patience said, and ripped the medal from Knill's tunic with a mental flick. She slapped her outspread palms against Knill's dented skull and blasted him away into the murals. The ancient plasterwork cracked under the heavy impact and Knill fell limp onto the floor.

Souzerin came in again. Knill's medal was still hanging in the air. Patience whipped it around and buried it in Souzerin's cheek. He fell down with a wail of pain, blood pouring from the long gouge.

'I've seen enough,' said the man in the red robe.

The ginger-haired man rose to his feet and turned off his limiter.

Patience shrieked as her gift went away completely. It was as if her strength had been shut off. A hard vacuum formed and popped in her soul. She had never met an untouchable before.

Staggering, she turned. The ginger-haired man came towards her, his hands open and loose.

'Let's go, darling,' he said.

She threw a punch at him. She felt so weak.

He caught it, and hit her in the face.

The blow seemed effortless, but she fell hard, barely conscious. The ginger-haired man leaned over and pinched a nerve point that left her paralysed.

Blind, helpless, she heard Prefect Cyrus being helped back onto his feet.

'You were right, Cyrus,' she heard the man in red say. 'An excellent subject. An unformed telekine. The gamers will pay well for this. I have no objection to meeting your price of ten thousand.'

'Agreed, Loketter,' the Prefect sniffed. 'Just... just get her out of my sight.'

VI

Carl Thonius was patently pleased with himself. 'Consider the names again. Victor Zhan. Noble Soto. Goodman Frell. The forenames are all names, yes, but they're also all simple, virtuous. The sort of solid, strong, aspirational names a highborn master, for example, might give to his slaves.'

'These men were slaves?' Kara asked.

'Not exactly,' said Carl. 'But I think they're all *given* names. Not birth names.'

Carl had a particular talent in the use of cogitators and logic engines. Since our arrival, he had spent many hours in the census archives of Urbitane. 'I've been tracing the file records of all three men. It's laborious work, and the records are, no tittering at the back, incomplete. The names are officially logged and genuine, but they are not connected to any local bloodlines. Soto, Zhan and Frell are all common names here on Sameter, but there is no link between any of these men and any family or families carrying those names. In other words, I believe they chose the surnames themselves. They chose common local surnames.'

'Fake identities,' Nayl shrugged. 'Not much of a lead then.'

'Says the man who pushed our last decent lead off a kilometre high ledge,' Carl mocked. Nayl gave him a threatening look, and the interrogator shrugged. 'No, not fake identities. The evidence points to the fact that all three men were orphans, probably from the slums. They were raised in a poorhouse or maybe a charitable institution, where they were given their virtuous forenames. On leaving the poorhouse, as young adults, they were obliged to choose and adopt surnames so that they could be registered on the citizenry roll and be legally recognised.'

'Odd that he employed three men with the same background,' Kara said. She could not bring herself to utter Molotch's name.

'Curious indeed,' I agreed. 'Carl, I don't suppose you managed to identify the institutions that raised them?'

'Throne, you don't want much do you?' Carl laughed. He beamed, like a conjuror showing off a sleight-of-hand marvel. 'Of course I did. And they all came from the same one. A darling little place called the Kindred Youth Scholam.'

Nayl left the hotel room almost immediately and headed off to scare up some transport for us. For the first time in months, I felt my team moving with a sense of focus, so refreshingly different from the blunt-edged vengeance that had spurred them since Majeskus. Carl deserved praise. He had diligently uncovered a trail that gave us refined purpose once again.

We had been so squarely and murderously outplayed by the heretic Zygmunt Molotch. I had been pursuing him for a long time, but at Majeskus, he stopped running and turned to face me.

The ensuing clash, most of which took place aboard my chartered starship, the *Hinterlight*, left over half the crew dead. Amongst them, trapped by Molotch's malicious evil, were three of my oldest, most trusted retainers: Will Tallowhand, Norah Santjack and Eleena Koi. Badged with their blood, triumphant, the bastard Molotch had escaped.

I had lost friends before. We all had. Serving the ordos of the Holy Inquisition was a dangerous and often violent calling. I myself, more than most, can vouch for the cost to life and limb.

But Majeskus was somehow a particularly searing blow. Molotch's assault had been ingeniously vicious and astoundingly callous, even by the standards of such vermin. It was as if he had a special genius for spite. I had vowed not to rest until I had found him again and exacted retribution in full.

In truth, when I came to Sameter, I do not think I was an Imperial inquisitor at all. I am not ashamed to admit that for a brief while, my duty to the God-Emperor had retreated somewhat, replaced by a more personal fire. I was Gideon Ravenor, burning to avenge his friends.

The same, I knew, was true of my four companions. Harlon and Kara had known Eleena Koi since their days together in the employ of my former master Eisenhorn. Harlon had also formed a particular bond of friendship with the mercurial Will Tallowhand. In Norah Santjack, Thonius had enjoyed the stimulating company of a mind as quick and clever as his own. There would be no more devilish games of regicide, no more late-night debates on the respective merits of the later Helican poets. And Thonius was yet young. These were the first comrades he had lost in the line of duty.

Even Wystan Frauka was in mourning. Louche and taciturn, Frauka was an unloved, unlovely man who made no friends because of his untouchable curse. But Eleena Koi had been an untouchable too, one of nature's rare psychic blanks and the last of Eisenhorn's Distaff.

There had been a relationship there, one neither of them ever chose to disclose, presumably a mutual need created by their shared status as outsiders, pariahs. He missed her. In the weeks after Majeskus, he said less than usual, and smoked all the time, gazing into distances and shadows.

Aboard the hired transport – a small, grey cargo-gig with whistling fan-cell engines – we moved west through the hive city. Carl linked his data-slate to my chair's input and I reviewed his information concerning the scholam.

It had been running for many years, ostensibly a worthy charity school struggling to provide housing and basic levels of education for the most neglected section of Urbitane's demographic. There were millions, nay billions, of institutions like it all across the Imperium, wherever hives rose and gross poverty loomed. Many were run by the Ecclesiarchy, or tied to some scheme of work by the Departmento Munitorum or the Imperial Guard itself. Some were missionary endeavours established by zealous social reformers, some political initiatives, some just good, four-square community efforts to assist the downtrodden and underprivileged.

And some were none of those things. Carl and I inspected the records of the Kindred Youth Scholam carefully. On the surface, it was respectable enough. Its register audits were a matter of public record, and it applied for and received the right grants and welfare support annually, which meant that the Administratum subjected it to regular inspection. It was approved by the Munitorum, and held all the appropriate stamps and marques of a legitimate charitable institution. It had an impressive portfolio of recommendations and references from many of Urbitane's worthies and nobles. It had even won several rosettes of distinction from the Missionaria.

But scratch any surface…

'You'll like this,' said Carl. 'The Prefect, he's one Berto Cyrus. His official file is spotless and perfectly in order. But I think it's a graft.'

A graft. A legitimate dossier that has been expertly designed to overfit previous records and eclipse them. Done well – and this had been done brilliantly – a graft would be more than adequate to bypass the Administratum. But we servants of the holy ordos had greater and more refined tools of scrutiny to bring to bear. Carl showed me the loose ends and rough edges that had been tucked away to conceal the basic deception, the long, tortuous strands of inconsistency that no one but the Inquisition would ever think to check, for the effort would be too labour-intensive. That was ever the failing of the Imperium's monumental Administratum. Overseeing hives the size of Urbitane, even an efficient and ordered division of the Administratum could only hope to keep up with day to day processing. There was no time for deeper insight. If one wanted to hide something from the Imperial Administratum, one simply had to place it at the end of a long line of diversions and feints, so far removed from basic inspections that no Administry clerk would ever notice it.

'He's older than he pretends to be,' said Carl. 'Far older. Here's the give away. Three digits different in his twelve digit citizenry numeric, but changed here, at birth-registry date, where no one would ever go back to look. Berto Cyrus was actually a stillborn infant. The Prefect took over the identity.'

'Which makes him?'

'Which makes him eighty-eight years older than his record states. And therefore makes him, in fact, Ludovic Kyro, a cognitae-schooled heretic wanted on five worlds.'

'Cognitae? Throne of Earth!'

'I said you'd like it,' Carl smiled, 'and here's the other thing. Its implications are not very pleasant.'

'Go on.'

'Given the scholam's throughput of pupils over the years, very, very few are still evident in the city records.'

'They've disappeared?'

'That's too strong a word. *Not accounted for* would be a better term. The ex-pupils have dropped off the record after their time at the scholam, so there's no reason anyone scrutinising the school's register in an official capacity should question it. Pupils leave, sign up indentures, contracts, hold-employs, but then these documents lead nowhere.'

'From which you deduce what?' I asked, though I could see Carl had the answer ready in the front of his mind.

'The scholam is a front. It's… laundering children and young adults. Raising them, training them, nurturing them, and then moving them as a commodity into other hands. The fact that the pupils are known only by their scholam names means that they can be slipped away unnoticed. It's quite brilliant.'

'Because they take in anonymous children, give them new identities to provide them with legal status, and then sell them on under cover of perfectly correct and perfectly untraceable paperwork?'

'Just so,' said Carl.

'What do they do with them?' I wondered.

'Whatever they like, would be my guess,' said Wystan, glancing up from his tawdry book. I hadn't even realised he'd been listening. 'Those three we're tracking, they ended up as hired guns, probably because they were handy in that regard. Strong guys get muscle work. Pretty girls…'

'Whatever else we do,' I said, 'we're closing that place down.'

VII

The cell was a metal box and smelled of piss. The ginger-haired man opened the hatch and dragged Patience out. She tried to resist, but her limbs were weak and her mind muddy. The ginger-haired man still had his limiter off.

His name was DaRolle, that much she had learned, and he worked for a man called Loketter.

'On your feet, darling,' DaRolle said. 'They're waiting for you.' He prodded her along the dim hallway. Patience didn't know where she was, but she knew it was at least a day since she had been taken from the scholam by these men.

'It's Patience, right?' the ginger-haired man said. 'Your trophy name?'

'My what?'

'Trophy name. The scholam gives you all trophy names, ready for the game. And yours is Patience, isn't it?'

'Where are my sisters?' she asked.

'Forget you ever had any.'

Loketter, the man in red, was waiting for them in a richly appointed salon at the end of the hallway. There were other men with him, all distinguished older males just like him, sitting around on couches and buoy-chairs, smoking lho and sipping amasec. Patience had seen their type so many times before at graduation suppers. Men of wealth and status – mill owners and merchants, shipmasters and guilders – and Patience had dreamed of the day when one of them would select her for service, employment, a future.

How hollow that seemed now. For all their grooming, for all their fine clothes and fancy manners, these men were predators. The scholam which she had trusted for so long had simply been their feeding ground.

'Here she is,' smiled Loketter. The men applauded lazily.

'Still in her scholam clothes,' a fat man in green said with relish. 'A nice touch, Loketter.'

'I know you like them fresh, Boroth. Her name is Patience, and she is a telekine. I'm not sure if she realises she is a telekine, actually. Do you, my dear? Do you know what you are?'

Loketter addressed the last part of his question at her. Patience flushed.

'I know what I am,' she said.

'And what is that?'

'Trapped amongst a bunch of perverts,' she said.

The men laughed.

'Oh, such spirit!' said Boroth.

'And pretty green eyes too!' said another man, swathed in orange furs.

'The wager is seven thousand crowns per half hour of survival,' Loketter announced.

'Very high,' said the man in furs. 'What is the area, and the jeopardy?'

'Low Tenalt,' replied Loketter, and several of the men laughed. 'Low Tenalt,' Loketter repeated. 'And the jeopardy is the Dolors. Although, if she's nimble, she might make it to Pennyraker territory, in which case the wager increases by another hundred and fifty.'

'How many pawns?' asked a tall, bearded man in a selpic blue doublet.

'Standard rules, Vevian. One per player. Open choice. Body weapons only, although I'll allow a gun per pawn for jeopardy work. Guns are not to be used for taking the quarry, as I have no need to remind you. Gunshot death or disintegration voids the game and the pot goes to the house.'

'Observation?' asked a thin man in grey robes.

'Servo-skull picter, as standard. House will supply eight. You'll each be allowed two of your own.'

'Will she be armed?' Boroth asked.

'I don't know. Would you care to chose a weapon?' Loketter asked Patience.

'What is the game?' she replied.

More laughter.

'Life, of course,' Loketter said. 'A weapon, Patience? DaRolle, show her.'

The ginger-haired man walked over to a varnished hardwood case set on a side table, opened it and revealed the numerous polished blades and exotic killing devices laid out on the velvet cushion.

'Choose, darling,' he said.

Patience shook her head. 'I'm not a fighter. Not a killer.'

'Darling, if you're going to live for even ten minutes, you'll have to be both.'

'I refuse,' said Patience. 'Frig you very much, "darling".'

DaRolle tutted and closed the case.

'Unarmed?' Boroth said. 'I'll take the wager, Loketter. In fact, I'll double you.'

'Fourteen taken and offered,' Loketter announced.

'Taken,' said a man in pink suede.

'I'm in,' said the bearded man Loketter had called Vevian.

Four of the others agreed too, opening money belts and casket bands and tossing piles of cash on the low, dished table at Loketter's feet. In ten seconds there was a thousand times more money in that baize bowl than Patience had ever even imagined.

'Begin,' Loketter said, rising to his feet. 'Pawns to the outer door for inspection and preparation. Drones will be scanned prior to release. I know your tricks, Boroth.'

Boroth chuckled and waved a pudgy hand.

'The game will commence in thirty minutes.' Loketter walked over to face Patience. 'I have great faith in your abilities, Patience. Don't let me down. Don't lose me money.'

She spat in his face.

Loketter smiled. 'That's exactly what I was looking for. DaRolle?'

The ginger-haired man grabbed Patience by the arms and marched her out of the room. They went down a maze of long, brass tunnels and finally up some iron steps into what seemed like a loading dock or an air-gate.

'Go stand by the doors, darling,' he said.

'What happens now?' Patience asked.

'Now you run for your life until they get you,' DaRolle said.

Patience put her hands against the rusted hatchway, and then pulled them away as the hatch rumbled open.

She didn't know what to expect when she looked out. Beyond the hatchway, the shadowy wastes of the slum-tracts stretched away into the distance.

'I won't go out there,' she growled.

DaRolle came up behind her and shoved her outside. Patience fell into the dirt.

'Word of advice,' called the ginger-haired man. 'If you want it, anyway. Watch for the Dolors. They use the shadow. Don't trust black.'

'I don't t–' Patience began.

But the hatch slammed shut.

Patience got to her feet. Gloom surrounded her. A hot, stinking wind blew in through the nearby ruins, smelling of garbage and city rot.

Somewhere, something whooped gleefully in the darkness. A lifter rumbled overhead, its lights flashing. When she turned, she saw the immensity of the hive filling the sky behind her like a cliff, extending up as far as she could see.

She started to run.

VIII

There was something wrong with Prefect Cyrus's face: a blush of burst blood vessels that even careful treatment with a medicae's dermo-wand had failed to conceal. He was trying to be civil, and was clearly impressed by his visitor's apparel, but he was also put out.

'This is irregular, I'm afraid,' he fussed as he led them into a waiting room where Imperial teachings were writ in gold leaf on the darkwood panels. 'There are appointed times for inspection, and also for apprenticeship dealings. Take a seat, won't you?'

'I apologise for the difficulties I'm causing,' Carl replied. 'But time is rather pressing, and you came highly recommended.'

'I see,' said Cyrus.

'And I have... resources to make it worth your while.'

'Indeed,' smiled Cyrus. 'And your name is?'

'I'd prefer not to deal in names,' Carl smiled.

'Then perhaps I should show you out, sir. This is a respectable academy.'

Sitting cross-legged on the old couch, his fur-trimmed mantle turned back over his shoulder to expose the crimson falchapetta lining, Carl Thonius beckoned with one gloved hand to Kara, who stood waiting in the doorway. Kara was robed and cowled like some dumb servitor, and carried a heavy casket. As she approached, Carl leaned over and flipped the casket lid open.

'Lutillium. Twenty ingots, each of a weight of one eighth. I'll leave it to you to calculate the market price, Prefect.'

Cyrus licked his lips slightly. 'I, ah… what is it you want, sir?'

'Two boys, two girls. No younger than eleven, no older than thirteen. Healthy. Fit. Comely. Clean.'

'This is, ah…'

'I'm sorry, I'm being very direct,' said Carl. 'I should have said this before. This is a matter of *the most pleasant fraternal confidence*.'

'I see,' said Cyrus. Carl had just used one of the cognitae's private recognition codes, by which one graduate knew another. 'I'll just see what's taking those refreshments so long to arrive.'

The Prefect bustled out of the room and hurried down a gloomy hallway to where Ide was waiting.

'Bring the others in,' Cyrus whispered to him. 'Do it quickly. If this is on the level, we look to earn well. But I have a feeling.'

Ide nodded.

In the waiting room, Carl sat back and winked at Kara.

+The Prefect's suspicious.+

'Really?' Carl said softly. 'And I thought I was bringing such veracity to the part.'

+Get ready. Nayl?+

Harlon Nayl grunted as he drove another crampon into the crumbling outer brick of the tower's side, and played out his line to bring him closer to a ninth floor window. A terrible updraft from the stack-chasm below tugged at his clothing.

'Ready enough,' he replied.

+Harlon's in position. Carl? You can do the honours.+

'Thank you, sir,' he whispered. 'It'll be a pleasure.'

Cyrus came back into the room, smiling broadly. 'Caffeine and cusp cake is just on its way. The cake is very fine, very gingery.'

'I can't wait,' Carl said.

+They're closing in. Four now arriving at the west door. Three on the stairs behind Kara. Two more approaching from the floor above. All ex-Guard. Armed with batons. And I read at least one firearm.+

Carl rose to his feet. 'Oh, Prefect? There is one other thing I did want to say.'

'And that is?' asked Cyrus.

Carl smiled his toothiest smile. 'In the name of the Holy Inquisition, you motherless wretch, surrender now.'

Cyrus gasped and began to back away. 'Ide! Ide!' he screamed.

Kara hurled the casket and it slammed into Cyrus's midsection, felling him hard. He grunted in pain and several of the heavy ingots scattered across the floor.

+Move!+

Kara threw off her drab robe and flew forward as the first rigorist came in through the doorway. Guns were forbidden in the scholam, but that didn't prevent this man from carrying one. Weapon scanners around the entry gate screened visitors for firearms. But lutillium, apart from its monetary worth, had value as a substance opaque to scanners.

Rigorist Ide raised his handgun as he came in. Kara, on her knees, reached into the fallen casket and produced the Tronsvasse compact hidden between the layers of ingots.

'Surprise,' she said, and buried a caseless round in his forehead. The rear part of Ide's skull burst like a squeezed pimple and he fell on his back.

She got up, shot the sprawled Cyrus once through the back of the thigh to make sure he wasn't going anywhere, and swung to face the door. The next two rigorists burst in on Ide's heels, batons raised, and she shot out their knees. Thonius winced and covered his ears.

In the hall outside, the other rigorists backed in terror from the sound of gunfire. Then a shaped charge blew out the casement behind them in a blizzard of glass and leading, and Harlon Nayl swung into the hallway. He had a large automatic pistol in his left fist.

'Any takers?' he asked.

One ran, and Nayl shot him through the heel. The others sank to their knees, hands to their heads.

'Good lads,' Nayl said. He took a neural disruptor from his belt in his right hand and walked over to them, cracking each one comatose with a fierce zap from the blunt device.

In the waiting room, the air threaded with gun-smoke, Kara turned to face the opposite doors as other alerted rigorists crashed in from the stairs. Knill led them, and didn't even blink at the sight of the small woman with the handgun. He flew at her.

'Ninker!' she complained, and shot him. The round penetrated his torso and didn't slow him. He crashed into her and knocked her flat.

Souzerin and another rigorist named Fewik were right behind Knill. Fewik knocked Carl over with a blow from his baton, and Souzerin raised the battered bolt pistol that he carried since his days in the commissariat. He fired at Kara, but managed only to blow off Knill's left foot and his left arm at the elbow.

Nayl appeared at the opposite door and yelled a warning that Souzerin answered by lifting his aim and blasting at the doorway. Brick chips and wooden splinters exploded from the jamb. Kara reached out from under Knill's deadweight and shot Souzerin up through the chin. The rigorist left the ground for a moment, then crashed back down dead. Nayl reappeared and put a round through Fewik's back as he turned to flee.

Nayl helped Kara out from under the half-dead brute.

'Nobody help me up then,' Carl complained.

Panic had seized the scholam. I could feel it, breathe it. Hundreds of children and young adults, terrified by the explosions and gunshots.

And a deeper panic, a deeper dread, that emanated from the minds of the rigorists and tutors.

I hovered towards the main gate, Wystan at my side, and ripped the ancient doors off their hinges with a brisk nudge of my mind. Inside the entrance way, half a dozen tutors and rigorists were running towards us, hoping for a speedy exit.

+I am Inquisitor Ravenor of the holy ordos! Remain where you are!+

I don't think they understood the manner of the command, though several involuntarily defecated in fear as the telepathic burst hit them. All they saw was a lone man approaching beside a strange, covered chair.

+Now!+

My psi-wave threw them all backwards violently, like the pressure blast of a hurricane. Windows shattered. They tumbled over, robes shredding, flying like dolls or desperately trying to grip onto the floor.

Wystan lit a lho-stick. 'What I like about you,' he said, 'is that you don't muck around.'

'Thank you.'

I had switched to vox-ponder and now I activated my built in vox-caster. 'This is Ravenor to Magistratum Fairwing. Your officers may now move in and secure the building as instructed.'

'Yes, inquisitor.'

'Do not harm any of the children.'

IX

I had expected to find many things within the scholam: evidence of abuse and cruelty certainly, damaged souls, perhaps even answers, if I was lucky.

I had not expected to find traces of psyker activity.

'What's the matter?' Kara asked me.

+I'm not sure.+

We moved down the long hallways, past the frightened faces of pupils herded along by the Magistratum officers, past whimpering tutors spread against the old walls as they were patted down for concealed weapons. The traces were slight, ephemeral, fading, like strands of gossamer clinging to the brickwork. But they were there.

+There was a psyker here.+

Kara stiffened.

+Relax. He... no, I believe it was a she. She's not here anymore. But she was here for a long time and she left only recently.+

'When you say a long time, you mean?'

+Years.+

'And when you say recently..?'

+Days, maybe less.+

We explored the tower. For Kara, this was a curious process. She could not see or feel, taste or smell the traces that were so evident to me. She just followed me around, one empty room after another. I could sense her boredom and her frustration. She wanted to be with the others, active, rounding up the last of the scholam's inhabitants.

'Sorry. This must be tedious for you,' I said.

'It's fine,' she replied. 'Take your time. I can be patient. Patience is a virtue.'

'Indeed.' We entered a large dining hall in the upper reaches of the tower. The traces were strongest and freshest there.

'Telekine,' I said. 'I'm in no doubt. A telekine, raw but potentially strong.'

'We have to find her,' Kara said. 'If this damn place really was grooming subjects for the cognitae, she could be a lead. A direct connection to a cognitae procurer.'

Kara was right. Amongst their many crimes, the cognitae prided themselves on recruiting and retaining unlicenced psykers for their own purposes.

'Go and find Carl for me, Kara,' I requested. 'I want to get him working on discovering who this psyker was and where she might have gone.'

'Because of the cognitae link,' she nodded.

'Yes, because of that,' I replied. 'But even if no link exists, we still have to find her. An unsanctioned psyker, lose on Sameter. That cannot be permitted. We must track her down. And dispose of her.'

X

'I'm sorry,' Carl Thonius said. 'Sir, I'm very sorry.'

The device was very small, no larger than a hearing aid implant.

'I should have searched him right there, but with all the shooting and screaming.'

'Don't worry about it, Carl,' I said.

'I think I will, sir. Everything's blanked.'

The device was a trigger switch, coded to Cyrus's thumb print. An advanced piece of tech. Down on the floor, helpless from the wound Kara had delivered to his leg, Cyrus had plucked this device from his pocket and activated it. And the scholam's entire data archive had been erased.

'Can you recover anything?' I asked.

'It's a fairly comprehensive wipe. I might be able to recode the last few days worth of material. The stuff most recently processed might still exist in the codification buffer.'

'Do what you can,' I advised. Privately, I was annoyed with his lapse. But we had, with the assistance of local law-enforcement, rounded up dozens of tutors and scholam elders, including Cyrus himself. And who could say what the poor pupils themselves might be able to tell us?

Besides, it was hardly surprising. Carl was so poor in circumstances of violence. I don't believe he had ever fired a shot in anger, though he performed well enough in weapons drill.

'I'll get to work, sir,' Carl said. 'I'm so very sorry–'

'So you bloody should be,' Nayl snorted.

'Enough, Harlon!' I rebuked. 'Carl is my interrogator and you will address him with respect.'

'I'll do that,' Nayl replied, 'when he earns it.'

'Do what you can, Carl,' I said. 'But remember, your priority is to find out all there is to know about the unsanctioned psyker they had here. Who she was, where she went. She has to be found and dealt with, quickly.'

'Yes, sir.'

As Carl moved away, the senior magistratum approached. His enforcement officers, clad in black and silver, were still clearing the scholam floor by floor. I could sense his unease. He was an experienced criminologist, but he'd never had his entire station house requisitioned to assist the Inquisition before. He was terrified of screwing up. He was terrified of me.

'Problems?' I asked.

'A few scuffles, sir. You'd rather taken the wind out of their sails.'

'I want all the children to be given medical checks, and then safe-housed until statements can be taken from them all. Inform the Administration that welfare assistance will be required, but not yet. No one is to be rehoused or re-homed unless they've been examined. Why do you frown?'

The magistratum started a little. 'There are over nine hundred children, sir...' he began.

'Improvise. Ask the local temples for alms and shelter.'

'Yes, sir. May I ask... is this an abuse case, sir?'

'Indirectly. I can't say more. The staff I'll interview here, now. I'll need some of your men to assist in guarding them while the interrogations are underway. Once I'm done, I will file charges, and you can begin to process them.'

'Yes, sir.'

'I'll start with the Prefect.'

A magistratum first-aider had patched Cyrus's leg wound, and they'd shackled him to a chair in one of the refectories. He was in pain, and very frightened, which would make it easier to extract information.

Cyrus stared at me as I rolled in to face him. Nayl followed me in, but sat his ominous bulk down at the far end of the long table from Cyrus, a threat waiting to happen.

'I... I have rights,' Cyrus began. 'In the eyes of Imperial Law, I have–'

'Nothing. You are a prisoner of the Inquisition. Do not ask for or expect anything.'

'Then I'll tell you nothing.'

'Again, you are mistaken. You will tell me everything I ask you to tell me. Harlon?'

From the far end of the table, Nayl began to speak. 'His name is Ludovic Kyro, Cognitae-trained, wanted on five worlds for counts of heresy and sedition...'

Cyrus closed his eyes as the words came out. We already knew his true identity. What else did we have?

'Tell me about Victor Zahn.'

Cyrus frowned. 'I don't know a Victor Zahn...' I was watching his mind. It wasn't the truth, but it wasn't an outright lie either. Cyrus didn't immediately recognise the name.

+Tell me about Victor Zahn.+

Cyrus blinked as the telepathy slapped him. My interrogative was accompanied by an image of Zahn's corpse in the *Hinterlight*'s morgue which I dropped into his mind like a slide into a magic lantern.

'Oh Throne!' he murmured.

'You know him, then?'

'He was a pupil here, years ago.'

+And Goodman Frell? And Noble Soto?+

Two more graphic images.

'Oh, Holy! They were pupils too. This was years ago. Five or more.'

'And you groomed them,' said Nayl. 'You and your staff. Groomed them like you groom all the poor strays who wind up here. Sold them on.'

'No, this is a respectable place and–'

'So respectable,' I said, 'that you wipe all your records so we can't see them.'

Cyrus bit his lip.

'Zahn. Frell. Soto. Who did you sell them too?'

'T-to a merchant, as I remember.'

Lie. Bald and heavy. And well formed, not just vocally, but mentally too. A layer of mendacity cloaked Cyrus's thoughts, like a cake of dried mud. A mind-trick, one of the many taught by the Cognitae. I had been expecting as much. For all his fear, Cyrus was still a product of that heretical institution, and therefore had to be unlocked with precision. If I'd just burst into his mind telepathically from the outset, I might have damaged or destroyed many of his locked engrams. But now I had a solid lie out of him, and that lie revealed the way his mind-shields worked: their focus, their strengths, their inclination.

'Who did you sell them too?'

'I told you, a merchant. A free trader.'

+Who?+

He squealed as the psi-jab rattled his mind. He was utterly unprepared for the sharpness of it.

'That was a demonstration of how things will be if you resist,' I said. 'Now I'm going to ask the question once more...'

XI

Patience heard the buzzing, not with her ears but with her mind, and slid into cover behind a crumbling rockcrete wall. Moments later, a varnished human skull hovered past through the gloom. Tech implants decorated the back of its cranium, and lights shone in its hollow orbits. A sensor drone, sweeping for her. She'd heard the bastards talking about them before her release. This was the first physical proof that men were actually after her.

Men. Hunters. Killers.

The skull hovered on the spot for a moment, circled once, and then sped away into the shadows. Patience stayed low. After another minute, a second drone – this one built around the skull of a dog or cat – skimmed past and made off in another direction.

She slowed her breathing, and deliberately encouraged her mind to do the sort of tricks that usually happened unbidden. She reached out. She could feel the area around her in a radius of ten metres, forty, sixty. The shape of the geography: the sloping trench to her left, the broken columns ahead, the line of burned-out habs to her right. Behind her, the sewer outfall pouring sludge into a cracked storm drain. She sensed bright sparks of mental energy, but they were just rats scuttling in the ruins.

Then she sensed one that wasn't.

This spark was bigger, human, very controlled and intense. Right ahead, beyond the columns, moving forward.

Moving slowly so as not to dislodge any loose stones, she turned and began to creep away around the storm-drain chute towards a jumble of plasteel ruins. Her left toe kicked a rock and it rolled away off the drain's edge and started to fall. Patience caught it neatly with her mind and lifted it up into the silence of her hand.

The brief delay had been to her advantage. Now she sensed three or four human mind-traces in the ruins ahead of her. Not focused like the other one, feral. In the shadows.

Don't trust the black, that's what DaRolle had said to her. Trouble was, could she trust DaRolle's advice?

She crouched low, and stayed there until she could see them. Ragged human shapes, barely visible, moving like animals through the ruins. Gangers, members of the notorious Dolor clan. She could see three, but was sure there were more. The hunter was closing from the right, now almost at the rockcrete wall.

Patience lifted the rock in her hand and threw it, sending it far further than her arm alone could have managed. It landed in the trench with a loud clatter.

The hunter turned and made for it immediately. She got a glimpse of a man in an armoured jack and high boots scurrying towards the lip of the trench.

Then the Dolors saw him too.

A pivot-gun roared and the hunter was knocked off his feet. The gangers rushed forward at once, baying and yelling, crude blade weapons flashing in their dirty hands.

The hunter's jack had stopped the worst of the ball round. He leapt back up, and shot the closest Dolor through the neck with his handgun. The savage figure spasmed and went down thrashing. Then the others cannoned into the hunter and they all went over into the trench.

Patience started to run. She heard another shot behind her. A scream.

She scrambled over a rusted length of vent-ducting, and dropped into the cavity of a roofless hab...

...where a man was waiting for her.

Patience gasped. There had been no spark off him at all. Either he was shielded, or his mind just did not register to her gift like regular human minds.

He was tall and thin, clothed head to foot in a matt-black, skin-tight body suit. Only his eyes were visible through a slit in the tight mask, but she saw the way the fabric beneath them stretched to betray the smile that had just crossed his face. He held a long, slender spike-knife in each hand.

Patience stretched out with her mind, hoping to push him away, but the tendrils of her gift slipped off his black suit, unable to purchase. He lunged at her, the twin blades extended, and she was forced to dive sideways, grazing her palms and knees on the rough ground. She started to roll, but he was on her at once, the tip of one blade slicing through the flesh of her left shoulder.

Patience cried out, but the pain gave her strength. She kicked out, and as the man jumped back, she flipped onto her feet. She backed as he circled again. She could hear him chuckle, feel the blood running down her arm.

He lunged again, leading with his right-hand blade. She ducked it, and came out under his arm, but the other blade raked across the back of her right hand as she tried to fend him off. She punched at him. He struck her in the side of the head with the ball of his right hand and knocked her onto the ground.

There was a rushing sound in her head. She thought of her sisters, and the mother she could no longer picture. In desperation, she lashed out with her gift, but the killer's black skin-suit again rendered him proof against her power. It was too slippery. She couldn't get hold of anything except–

The man stumbled backwards in surprise as the knives flew out of his hands. He might have been armoured against a telekine, head to toe, but his blades were good, old-fashioned solid objects.

Patience pulled them both in until they were slowly orbiting her body as she rose. It would the matter of a moment to toss them both away out of the hunter's reach.

But she had a much better idea.

With a bark of effort, she drove them point-first towards his eye-slit and nailed his skull against the back wall of the hab.

* * *

XII

Carl Thonius knocked on the refectory door and waited for a response. From inside, the oddly modulated screams and yelps of Prefect Cyrus shivered the air. As he waited, Carl glanced round at the four magistratum troopers guarding the hallway. They were clearly unnerved by the strange sounds of human pain echoing from the refectory. Carl smiled breezily, but got no response. He knocked again.

The screams ebbed for a moment, and the door flew open. Nayl peered out.

'What?' he spat.

'I need a word, dear fellow. With the boss.'

'Don't "dear fellow" me, frig-face. Is this important? He's busy!'

'Well,' Carl stammered. He was always edgy when he had to deal with the big ex-bounty hunter. 'It is, sort of.'

Nayl sneered. 'Sort of doesn't cut it.' He slammed the door in Carl's face.

Carl cursed and knocked again. Nayl threw the door back open.

'Don't do that,' Carl snapped. 'Don't treat me like that–'

'Oh, go away you frig-wipe...'

Carl looked Nayl in the eyes. 'Know your place, Nayl. You may not like me, but I am his interrogator. I want to see him now.'

Nayl looked Thonius up and down. 'Balls after all,' he said, grudgingly. 'Okay.'

Carl walked into the room. Cyrus was slumped forward in his chains, wheezing, blood leaking from his tearducts. Kara sat on a chair just inside the door, her face grim.

'Carl?' I said softly. 'This isn't really time for an interruption.'

'Sir, I've been trying to recover the lost data. The erased data. There's really not much to get back, I'm afraid. I doubt we'll ever find out what happened to most of the poor children laundered through this place.'

'Your incompetence could have waited,' Nayl said.

'Stop ragging on him, Nayl,' Kara hissed.

Carl shot Nayl a dark look. I could tell there was something more.

'I told you I might be able to recode the last few days worth of material. Uh, recently processed material still existing in the codification buffer.'

'Yes, Carl.'

He cleared his throat. 'There was one item there. A record of a transaction made two nights ago. An older female pupil named Patience. Groomed by these bastards partly because of her spirit, and mostly because she was a latent telekine.'

I swung round to face him. 'Are you sure?'

'Yes, sir.'

'A telekine?'

He nodded. 'The recoding is pretty clear. I think she was the psyker you were looking for.'

'Did you say her name was Patience?' Kara asked quietly.

'Yes, why?' Carl replied. She shrugged. She was holding something back.

'Kara?' I nudged.

'It's nothing,' she said. 'Just, when you were looking around, for traces of her, you thought I was bored and I said–'

'Patience is a virtue,' I finished.

Kara nodded. 'Yeah, Patience is a virtue. Spooky.'

'Coincidence,' Nayl muttered.

'Believe me, Harlon,' I said, 'in the length and breadth of this great Imperium of Man, there is no such thing as coincidence. Not where psyk is involved.'

'Duly noted,' he replied, not caring or believing.

'Where did this Patience go, Carl?' I asked.

'She was sold for ten thousand to a narcobaron cartel who purchased her for use in a game they like to play.'

'A game?' I asked.

'The record implies this is not the first subject the scholam has sold to the cartel for this purpose. I say game, it's more sport. They release the purchased child into the slum-tracts and then... then they gamble on how long he or she will survive. Once they send their hunters out.'

'So what?' asked Nayl. 'They'll clean up our little psyk-witch loose end without us having to break a sweat.'

'If the records are true,' I warned. 'Consider this. There might be a game. There might be a narcobaron with a taste for barbaric gladiatorial sport. On the other hand, all those things might be a substitution code to conceal an act of purchase to a Cognitae procurer.'

'I actually don't know which would be worse,' Kara said.

I turned back to Cyrus. He whined as my mind re-entered his. He was still weak and reeling from our initial session, and by rights I should have left him a while to be sure of getting accurate responses. But there was no time. An unsanctioned menace was loose somewhere, or already leaving the planet under close watch.

I tried a few key phrases – 'the psyker', 'the telekine', 'Patience' – pushing them at his mind in the way a child rams shaped blocks at a box, hoping to find the right hole to fit. He responded with various recurring words: *Loketter, the game, trophy worth*...

I wasn't sure how hard to push. I wasn't sure if I was slamming him back against the limits of truth, where there is nowhere left for sanity to go, or simply meeting some form of substitution. Substitution was another standard Cognitae mind ploy. Anticipating psychic interrogation, the brotherhood mnemonically learned to replace the details of true memories with engrammatic euphemisms. *Narcobaron*, for example, could stand for *procurer*. *Game* might stand for *purpose*. It was a simple but almost unbreakable deceit. Well-schooled, a Cognitae brother could mask memories with metaphors. He could not be caught out in a lie, because he wasn't lying. The truth had been erased and replaced with other facts. Using such techniques, a member of the brotherhood might withstand the most serious psyk-scrutiny, because the truth was no longer there to uncover.

'He's giving me nothing,' I cursed, turning away. 'Unless it is the truth. Do you have an active lead, Carl?'

Thonius nodded.

Kara got to her feet. 'Let's go and find her,' she said. 'If the story's real, I mean if there is this frigging barbaric game actually going on, there's a girl out there who really, really needs help right now.'

'Throne! Let her die!' Nayl barked. 'Frigging psyker! What? What?' Kara and Thonius were already heading for the door.

'One life, Harlon,' I said as I slid past him. 'I learned many things from Eisenhorn, but ruthlessness was not one of them. Thousands may die, millions even, unless Molotch is found and brought to justice. But any count of a million starts with one, and to ignore one life when there is still a chance of saving it, well, one might as well give up on the other nine hundred and ninety-nine thousand nine hundred and ninety-nine as well.'

'Whatever,' said Nayl.

'Thank you for your vote of confidence,' I said. 'Kara, inform the magistratum that these interviews are suspended until we return.'

XIII

The armoured manse did indeed belong to the man named Loketter, and nineteen counts of narco-traffic were outstanding on his name. The manse was a brass mushroom that dominated a long slope of rubble scree above the shadowland of the slum-tracts. Down here, with the monolithic bulk of Urbitane behind us, the immensity of the urban squalor and ruin was shocking to see.

The manse was ferro-armoured, and shielded, but our scanners lit with the buzz of electromag activity inside.

'Signals!' Kara reported. 'They're running drones out into the slum.'

'Can you track them?' I asked.

'Working...' She adjusted some dials. 'I've got a lock on nine. Covering a hex-grid twelve by ten. Map comparison... Throne, these archives are so old! Here we go. An area known as Low Tenalt.'

'Details?'

'Serious slum-land,' Carl said, speed-viewing the data on his codifier. 'Basically wreckage. High probability of gang activity. Territorially, the gangs are the Dolors and, to the west, the ruin-burbs are run by the so-called Pennyrakers. Magistratum advice is to avoid this area.'

'Really?'

Carl shrugged. 'Magistratum advice is a blanket "avoid the slum-tracts", so what the hey?'

'How far?' I asked.

At the helm of the cargo-gig, Nayl consulted the gyro-nav built into the stick. 'Eight spans to the Low Tenalt area from here, on boost.'

'Do it,' I said.

'You don't want to level this manse first?' Nayl asked.

'They can wait. This girl can't.'

Nayl nodded reluctantly, and hit the boosters. He wasn't in this like the rest of us were. Running low, like a pond-fly skating the surface, we zipped through the ruined landscape, skipping rubble heaps, ducking under shattered transit bridges, running fast and low along the brick-waste gouges that had once been hab-streets.

Everything was a grey gloom, caught in the immense shadow of the city. Such ruin, such endless ruin...

'Coming up, point three,' reported Nayl, hauling on the stick. The engines whined shrill. 'Two... one... setting down.'

The gig thumped and slithered as it settled on the loose brick.

Carl, Nayl and Kara were already up, arming weapons.

'Sit down, Carl,' I said. 'I need you to run scope from here.'

'Oh,' he said.

'I want full scanner input,' I said as I hovered towards the opening hatch behind Kara and Harlon. 'Wystan can watch your back.'

'You're going yourself?' Wystan asked, surprised. It was one of the few times I'd ever heard emotion in his voice.

'Yes,' I said.

Kara and Harlon looked at me.

'Yes, I'm coming with you,' I said. 'Have you got a problem with that?'

'It's just–' Kara began.

'You don't usually...' Nayl finished.

'This isn't usually,' I said, and powered out past them into the chilly gloom.

Nayl leapt out after me, his Urdeshi-made assault gun cinched high around his broad frame. Kara paused and looked back at Wystan and Thonius. 'Lock the door,' she grinned. 'And don't open it unless you know it's us. Even then, keep your powder dry.'

She jumped out, raised her Manumet 90 riot gun, and ran to join us.

Carl swallowed. Wystan Frauka got up, and locked the hatch shut. He looked at Carl, lit yet another lho-stick and patted the handgun tucked into his belt. 'I got your back, Carly,' he said.

'Great,' said Thonius. He turned to regard the sweeping screens of the scanner and adjusted his vox mic.

'Getting this?' he called.

'Loud and obnoxiously clear,' Nayl crackled back.

'A ha ha. Funny. Not. Move west, two hundred metres, then head north along the axis of the old fuel store. The drones seem to be gathering there.'

'Thank you, Carl,' I responded.

We moved through the wasteland. It was one of the few times my state allowed me speedier and quieter access than my able-bodied friends. Nayl and Kara followed, clambering over the dunes of rubble.

'See anything you like?' Kara said.

'I don't frigging believe we're doing this,' Nayl grumbled.

'Move left. Left!' Carl's voice rasped over the vox. 'I've got drones moving now. Gunshots.'

'I heard them,' Nayl said, and started away to the left.

'Flank him wide, Kara,' I said, and she moved away in the opposite direction.

'Throne,' I heard Carl say. 'I think we were right. I think this is some kind of frigging game.'

I propelled myself forward. Both Kara and Harlon were out of sight now, though I could sense them just fifty metres away, each side of me.

The twisted ruins of the tracts rose up on left and right. I tasted life-signs.

'Hello?' I transponded.

The Dolors appeared out of the gloom. Ragged, emaciated, filthy, feral. There were twenty of them.

Blackened teeth bared in wild grins. They raised their cudgels and spears and charged.

'Your mistake,' I said.

XIV

The barons were laughing. Most of them were drunk, or out of their heads on lhotas and obscura.

DaRolle looked up from the drone relay.

'Have we got the bitch yet?' Boroth demanded.

'You wish,' DaRolle said. He walked across the lounge and crouched down beside Loketter.

'What?' asked the man in red.

'New players just entered the game,' DaRolle said.

Loketter sat up. 'Show me.'

DaRolle held out his data-slate. 'Three on the ground. A gig too, grounded there.'

'What the hell is this?'

'Problem, Loketter?' asked Vevian.

Loketter rose and smiled. 'Not a problem, but a bonus element to our game today. Look at your scans. See? Newcomers.'

'Who the frig are they?' Gandinsky blurted.

'Interlopers,' Loketter said. 'House will pay two thousand for each one killed. Firearms permitted.'

The intoxicated crowd applauded this energetically.

Loketter looked at DaRolle. 'The ones on the ground I can get these fools to mess with,' he whispered. 'You go and fry up this gig.'

'Yeah?'

'Yeah. Find out who these fools are. Then burn it and every one on it.'
DaRolle nodded. 'Pleasure,' he said.

XV

Patience was still running. The Dolors, invisible in the shadows but everywhere now, were jeering and caterwauling, their strangled cries echoing around the ragged walls and shattered windows.

They were calling out to her, taunting her, abusing her with obscene words and suggestions, many of which, thankfully, were so choked by the gang-argot they made no sense.

Occasionally, stones or pieces of trash came flying out of the darkness at her, and she deflected all those she could. Some found her, especially the stinging stone bullets launched from catapults and slings.

Her instinct was to head back towards the colossal city, but no matter how much ground she managed to cover, it seemed not to get any closer. Its sheer scale made the distance hard to judge. It was probably kilometres away still.

She reached the ruins of a manufactory, its ply-steel roof collapsed. Seas of garbage and rubble spread out from its eastern side, and she began to pick her way across the weed-choked waste. Behind her, she could hear the gangers scurrying through the manufactory ruins. A few missiles flew out after her.

A figure suddenly appeared ahead of her, across the sea of trash. A small male, or perhaps a female, who'd been down in cover behind the remains of a yard wall, hidden by a chameleon cloak. Glancing up, Patience cursed as she saw a hunter drone that had obviously been shadowing her for several minutes.

Patience changed course, and began to run away from the figure. She ran wide across the overgrown trash. The figure started to follow, trying to cut her off, running hard, but neither made particularly good going. The trash and rubble was so uneven, so treacherous. Patience kept tripping, stumbling, turning her ankles.

As soon as the hunter appeared, the jeering from the invisible Dolors grew more ferocious. Catapult missiles and even the occasional arrow whipped out from the manufactory at the hunter.

The hunter – and it was clearly a female – stopped in her tracks, and produced an autopistol. She slammed in a clip and fired three times at the manufactory.

The shells must have been high-ex, because each impact went up like a grenade. Sections of the manufactory ruin blew in, and the Dolors went very quiet suddenly.

Patience was still running. The hunter put the gun away and resumed the chase.

A second drone zoomed into view suddenly, circled Patience once and then headed for the hunter. The woman stopped again, looking round frantically as she reached for her sidearm. Patience half-heard her shout a question into her vox-set.

There was a loud crack, a peripheral flash of light, and the female hunter jolted suddenly as a las-round went clean through her torso. She crumpled without a sound.

Her killer appeared, directly ahead of Patience. She skidded to a halt. He was big, and wore segmented plating over a coat of green hide. A glowing augmetic implant covered one eye. He had a las-carbine in his hands.

He stared at Patience for a moment, then put the carbine away in the leather boot over his shoulders. Then he drew a large dagger with a twisted black blade and took a step towards her.

'Make it easy now, and I promise you won't feel nothing,' he said.

Patience was breathing hard from the running. It made it easier somehow to summon up her gift. The man thought the first couple of stones that came flying at him were from the gangers, but then more came, and more, larger rocks, pieces of trash, chunks of garbage. Debris started showering off the ground all around her, whipping at him.

He cried out, shielding his face with his hands, and backed away. She heard him cry again, in pain, as a greasy lump of broken-off machinery hit him in the chest. He staggered, trying to fend the blizzard away. Then a piece of cinder block caromed off the side of his head, and he fell down on his knees, holding his head. Two more large rocks struck his face and forehead, and he slumped over entirely.

Patience sighed, and the rain of trash subsided, pieces bouncing off the ground as they landed. Silence.

She gave the body one last look, and started to run again. Behind her, in the manufactory, and all along the outer fence line, the invisible gangers started to whoop and holler again.

XVI

I had just seen off a second assault by the slum-gangers when I felt the telekinetic burst. Fierce, unfocused, not too far away.

'Turn west,' I voxed.

'Understood,' Kara responded.

'I read that,' came Nayl. 'I just heard bolter fire from that direction too.'

I slid through the ruins, my mind wide open. There were psi-traces all around me, at least a dozen as close as fifty metres. Most were the feral impulses of the hidden Dolors. But there. One other. Harder.

Two las-rounds struck the front of my chair and fizzled off harmlessly. I found the hunter as he was about to fire again, and picked him up. He yelled in fear as he left the ground, dragged up into the air ten metres, twenty. Then I let him go.

I didn't even bother to watch him land. The sharp light of his mind went out abruptly.

'I heard shots,' Kara voxed. 'Are you all right?'

'Fine,' I replied. 'Kara, it is a game. An obscene hunting game. We have to find this girl, whatever she is, before they do.'

'Understood. Absolutely.'

Kara was about a third of a kilometre away to my right.

'I've got a drone active in your vicinity,' Carl told her over the link.

Kara acknowledged, and glanced around. That was when the two hunters, twins clad in silver-grey skin sleeves, pounced. One pinned her arms from behind, the other came at her with a chainfist. She rolled her body back, using the man pinning her as a back-brace, and bicycle-kicked the other in the face. He went over in the rubble, rolling.

But the man pinning Kara from behind rammed forward and head-butted her in the back of the skull.

+Kara!+

Even at that distance, I felt her pain and sensed that she had blacked out. They'd have her gutted before she could come round.

I knew I had no choice. I had to ware her. It wasn't something she – or anyone else I knew – enjoyed, but it was necessary. Besides, we had trained for this. Kara Swole was a particularly receptive candidate.

The wraithbone pendant around her neck lit up with psychic energy. Kara's body suddenly animated again, but it was me moving her. I had taken her physical form over, put it on like a suit of clothes.

Blank-eyed, Kara's body twisted hard and broke the pinning hold. She tore clear, landed well, and swept out the legs of the hunter with the chainfist so he went over on his backside.

Then she turned, raising a forearm block against the other's attack, following the block with two rapid jabs to his face and a side-stamp that caught and dislocated his right knee.

He howled in pain. Kara/I grabbed his flailing arms and swung him bodily around right into his partner, who was returning to the fight for the second time.

The partner's forward-thrust chainfist, which had been sweeping at Kara/me met the ribs of his fellow hunter instead. The whirring bite-blades of the gauntlet weapon punched clean through the man's side in a shocking welter of blood and torn tissue. He screamed as he died, his whole body quivering in time to the rending vibrations of the glove's cycling blades.

His partner and accidental killer screamed too: in outrage and horror at what he had just done. He wrenched the glove out, but it was too late. His twin, a huge and awful excavation yawning in the side of his torso, stopped quivering and dropped. A film of blood covered everything in a five metre radius.

Berserk, the remaining hunter hurled himself at Kara/me. We leapt, boosted by a touch of telekinesis, and executed a perfect somersault over his head.

He swung around. But by then Kara/I had grabbed up her fallen riot gun. Her puppet hand racked the slide. A single, booming shot blew the hunter backwards eight metres.

We heard a sound behind us, and turned, bringing the pumpgun up.

'Steady!' Nayl warned.

'What are you doing here?' Kara/I demanded.

'You were in trouble, Kara!' he said. 'I heard it over the vox. I came as fast as I could.'

'What about the girl? What about the girl we're looking for?'

Nayl shrugged. 'Kara?'

'No, it's me, dammit!' I said with Kara's voice. 'Catch her for Throne's sake, I'm coming out.'

Nayl hurried forward and took Kara's limp form into his arms as I ceased waring her. She was semiconscious, and the trauma of being a ware subject would leave her disorientated and sick for a good while.

+Guard her, Harlon. In fact, get her back to the transport.+

'Where are you going?' he asked the empty air.

+To find the girl.+

XVII

Closed back into the womb-like nowhere of my support chair, I impelled it forward again, trying to reacquire the raw psychic-pulse I'd felt before. I felt edgy. Having to ware someone was a curious thing to deal with, and the feelings always left me conflicted. I was aware that the subject loathed the sensation, and it was also most usually done in moments of extremis, involving violence and furious levels of adrenaline. But for me it was a brief delicious escape, a cruel reminder of what I had lost. I despised myself for deriving pleasure from such painful, demeaning moments.

+Carl?+

'Yes, sir?'

+Do you have a fix on me?+

'Yes, sir. I've got two more drone tracks about half a kilometre ahead, converging. Please hurry, sir.'

+I'm hurrying.+

Back in the gig, Carl looked up from his scanner displays, fidgeting with his cuffs nervously. He looked at Wystan, who was reading his data-slate again.

'Don't you care?' Carl asked.

The untouchable nodded at his book. 'It's just getting interesting.'

Outside, DaRolle scurried forward, keeping low behind a half-fallen wall. He checked the area, unshipped his laspistol, and deactivated his limiter.

Then he began to run, head down, towards the parked transport.

XVIII

Her breathing was coming in short, sharp bursts. Patience had run as hard and as fast as she could. There was at least one person very close to her now, but the psychic-trace was faint and hard to place. She was worn out, exhausted, and her gift was weak from over-use.

She clambered down into a cavity behind a ruined pumping station, crawling into a cave formed by the overhang of the fallen roof. She curled up against the back wall, her arms around her knees. Outside, the Dolors were still jeering and shouting, but it was more distant now.

She'd gone as far as she could. Now it was just a matter of waiting. Waiting for the end.

+Patience.+

She started, and looked around, not daring to speak.

+Patience. Stay calm. Stay where you are. I'm coming to help you. I want to help you.+

'Where are you?' she hissed in fear.

+Don't speak. They'll hear you. Think your answers.+

'What do you mean? Where the frig are you?'

+Don't be scared. Try not to speak aloud. They'll hear you.+

'This is another trick. You're one of them! One of the frigging hunters!'

+No. Patience, my name is Gideon. I swear by the God-Emperor himself I mean you no harm. I'm trying to help you. You're hearing me because I am speaking directly to your mind, psychically.+

'You lie!'

+Try me. Think of something I couldn't know.+

Patience closed her eyes and moaned softly.

+Prudence. And Providence.+

She gasped.

+Your sisters. You're worried about them. They were taken… wait… yes, they were taken from the scholam. Without your consent.+

'Just kill me, you bastard, or leave me alone!'

+Please, Patience, don't speak. They'll hear you.+

I was moving fast now. The jagged ruins of the slum-tracts slid by me on either side. Rocks and catapult bullets occasionally clattered off my chair's armour. Where was she? Where was she?

+Patience? Can you still hear me?+

'Leave me alone!' she sobbed, crawling deeper into the damp cavity. 'I can't do this! I can't do this any more!'

+Yes, you can! Just keep it together! Focus! Focus on something!+

Patience twisted in panic, clawing at the sides of her head. I was scaring her. My voice. Something about my voice. Not just the fact that it was coming, disembodied, into her mind. Something else.

What?

As I steered my chair out across a long sea of trash and debris, I gently peered into her mind, into the panic and turmoil. Into the fear.

I saw it. It was my voice itself. I sounded like a middle-aged, well-educated male. Reasonable, polite, refined. Exactly the sort of man who had betrayed her entire life, her fellow pupils, her sisters. I saw she had formed a picture of me already. It was part Cyrus, part Ide, part Loketter, part some ginger-haired man. It was all of these, blended into one monster.

Immediately, I switched the focus of my telepathy.

+Kara?+

I found her at once, bleary and sick. Nayl was helping her along a rubble ledge back towards the gig.

'What?' she asked.

+I'm sorry, Kara, but I need to ware you again.+

'Throne, no!' she whimpered.

'She's had enough, boss,' Nayl said.

+It's important. Really important. I need her voice.+

Kara looked at Nayl and nodded wearily. He caught her as her wraithbone pendant flashed and she fell.

I left her body limp in Nayl's arms, and put on her personality like a skin-suit. My psychic-voice became Kara Swole's soft, reassuring tones.

+Patience?+

'What? What?'

+Patience, my name is Kara. My good friend Gideon has asked me to talk to you. Time is very short, Patience, and you need to listen to me if you want to stay alive. Trust Gideon. Do exactly as I say.+

I could feel the girl giving way to panic.

+Patience, focus! Hold on! There must be something you can hold onto! Something you can hold onto so you can keep going! Your sisters, maybe? Your mother? Patience?+

She had found it at last. It was something so small and dark and hard in her mind that even my telepathy could not unlock it. She held onto it, tight, tight, as the dark closed in.

Her panic waned. Her breathing slowed. I was close now. I could reach her.

Patience opened her eyes. A skull, eyes bright, hovered at arm's reach in front of her, gazing at her. A drone.

I was too late. She had made too much noise.

The hunters had found her.

XIX

'Throne!' cried Carl, leaning back from his auspex station in alarm. 'What the hell did you do?'

'I might have broken wind,' admitted Wystan Frauka. 'Sorry.' He turned back to his book.

'Check your limiter, dear boy,' Thonius demanded.

'Why?'

'Why? I was just listening in, and Ravenor suddenly went off-line!'

'The vox?'

'The vox is still live! I mean his telepathic link just scrambled! Was that you?'

Wystan Frauka frowned and put down his data-slate. He checked his device. 'No, it's on. I'm blocked.'

'Then what?'

'Relax, Carly. I'll take a look.'

'Please–' Carl began

Frauka patted the handgun in his belt again. 'I told you, I've got your back.'

'No, it's just… could you not call me "Carly"?'

Frauka frowned. 'Okay. What about "Thony" then?'

'No!'

Frauka held up his hands. 'All right. Throne! I was just being pally. The boss said I was too aloof. Too aloof, can you believe it? He suggested I should try being more friendly. He said it would help with team building, and–'

'Frigging hell, Frauka!'

'What? Emperor's tits, you guys are so uptight! I'll go look! I'll go look! I got your back, remember?'

Frauka turned. DaRolle's laspistol was aimed directly at his face. The ginger-haired killer grinned.

'On a side note,' Frauka said, 'it would have been nice if you'd got my back too, Carly.'

XX

'Out!' said the hunter in grey-scale armour. He gestured with his double-bladed harn knife. Patience got up, and slowly came out of the pumping station cavity. The hunter's drone circled her, purring softly.

'Gonna fight?' he asked.

She shook her head.

'Good girl. Step out here.'

She came out.

The hunter keyed his vox-link. 'This is Greyde. I've got her. Game's done. Tell Loketter that my master Vevian will want his winnings in small bills, so he can pay me off nice and handsome.'

The hunter looked at Patience. 'Why are you smiling?'

'No reason.'

He settled his grip on the alien blade. 'Sure you're not thinking of trying something dumb? I'd hate that. It'd make me take a lot longer with you.'

'I won't fight,' Patience said.

'Good.'

'Because Kara told me I didn't have to any more.'

'Who? Who's Kara?'

'The girl who told me her friend was coming. She told me to have patience, because patience is a virtue.'

The hunter, Greyde, looked around edgily. 'No one here but us, girl. No sign of any friend of yours.'

Patience shrugged. 'He's coming.'

A wind picked up, stirring the dust and the grit around them, billowing the filth up in swirling clouds. Like an exhalation from the sumps of the towering city.

Except it wasn't.

Larger pieces of trash lifted and fluttered through the air. Pebbles rolled on the ground. It was like a hurricane was gathering over the slums.

No hurricane.

Alarmed, Greyde grabbed the girl, viced her neck with one powerful arm, and raised the harn blade to deliver the kill-stab.

+Kuming Greyde. I know you. I know everything about you. I know the nine counts of murder that you are wanted for, and the fifty-seven other killings you have on your clammy soul. I know you killed your own father. I know you understand only hard cash and killing.+

'What? What?' the hunter wailed in terror as the tempest of wind engulfed him and his prey.

+I don't carry cash. No pockets. I guess it's going to be killing then.+

I turned on my chairs stablights, so I became visible as I ploughed in through the tumult of dirt and dust. The hunter screamed, but the dust choked him. Gagging, he threw Patience aside, and drew his Etva c.II plasma cannon, a pistol-sized weapon more than capable of burning clean through my armoured chair.

Staggering, half-blinded, he aimed it at me.

With a simple tap of my mind, I fired my chair's psy-cannon. The hunter's corpse slammed back through the wall of the pumping station. Even before it had hit the wall, every bone in that body had been pulped by concussive force, every organ exploded.

The wind dropped. Grit pattered off the sealed body of my chair.

+Patience?+

She got up. I wasn't using Kara Swole's voice any more.

+Are you all right?+

She nodded. She was singularly beautiful, despite the dirt caking her and the tears in her clothing. Tall, slender, black-haired, her eyes a piercing green.

'Are you Kara's friend?' she asked.

+Yes.+

'Are you Gideon?'

+Yes.+

She stepped forward, and placed her right hand flat on the warm canopy of my support chair. 'Good. You don't look anything like I imagined.'

XXI

'So, we're dead? Yeah, of course we are,' Frauka said softly.

'You'd be dead already,' replied DaRolle. 'I just wanted to find out which bastard was running you. Who is it? Finxster? Rotash? That'd be right. Rotash always wants a slice of the boss's game-play.'

'Neither, actually,' Frauka smiled.

'Frauka…' Carl began, terrified. He'd backed away as far as the gig's scan-console would allow, and even then knew there was no hope. This killer had them both cold. Carl wondered where he'd left his weapon. The answer – 'in the cabin lockers' – did not cheer him up.

'Who, then?'

'You won't know him. His name's Ravenor.'

DaRolle sniffed. 'Never heard of the frig.'

'Untouchable?' Frauka asked, casually indicating the limiter around DaRolle's throat.

'Uh huh. You too?'

Frauka smiled. 'Made that way, so help me. Still, the pay's decent. Always someone who needs a good blunter, right?'

'I hear that,' DaRolle grinned.

'Oh well,' Frauka sighed. 'Do me a favour, okay? Make it clean and quick. Back of the head, no warning.'

'Sure.'

'I mean, one blunter doing a favour for another? We gotta stick together, right, even if we are working for rival crews?'

'No problem,' said DaRolle.

'Okay,' Frauka said, and turned his back. 'Any time you like.'

DaRolle aimed his pistol again.

'I don't suppose…' Frauka began. Then he shook his head. 'No, I'm taking the piss now.'

'What?' asked DaRolle.

'Yeah, what?' Carl squeaked in frozen terror.

'One last stick? For a condemned man?'

DaRolle shrugged. 'Go on.'

Frauka took out his lack, set a lho-stick to his lips and lit it with his igniter. He breathed in the smoke and smiled. 'Oh, tastes good. Real mellow. Want one?'

'No,' said DaRolle.

'Real smooth,' said Frauka, inhaling a long drag. 'These things'll kill you, you know.'

'I wouldn't worry about that,' DaRolle smiled.

'I don't frigging believe this!' Carl whined.

'Hey,' said Frauka, glancing over his shoulder. 'Why don't you do him now while I'm smoking this baby? Save time. I never did like him.'

'Oh Throne!' Carl cried out and fell into a foetal position under the console.

'Frig, what a baby!' DaRolle laughed.

'Tell me about it,' Frauka said. He stubbed out his smoke. 'Okay, ready.' He held up the squashed butt. 'Know what that was, my friend?'

'Don't tell me,' smirked DaRolle. 'Best smoke of your life?'

'No,' said Frauka quietly. 'It was delaying tactics.'

DaRolle swung round. The hulking shape of Harlon Nayl filled the hatch behind him. Nayl's Hecuter 10 boomed once.

'Everyone alive?' Nayl asked, stepping in over the twisted body of the ginger-haired man.

'Saw you approaching on the scanners,' Frauka said. 'Thought I'd keep him talking.'

Carl Thonius got to his feet, shivering with anger and fright. 'You're unbelievable, Frauka,' he hissed.

'Thank you, Carl,' Frauka smiled, and sat down with his book again. 'See? Now you're team building too.'

XXII

I led the girl back to the gig, where the others were waiting.

'Hello, Patience, I'm Kara,' Kara said.

'Good to know you,' Patience replied.

By the time we raided Loketter's manse, backed up by a full squad of magistratum troopers, the narcobaron and his cronies had cleared out. There are warrants out for all of them. I understand Loketter is still on the run.

We returned to the Kindred Youth Scholam, and resumed the interrogations. It took several weeks, but by the end of it, I'd wrung some precious facts out of Cyrus and his staff.

There wasn't much. No, that's a lie. There was enough to ensure that Cyrus would face further interrogation at the Inquisition facility on Thracian Primaris, and enough to make sure the scholam's tutors and rigorists would remain incarcerated in the penitentiaries of Urbitane for the rest of their natural lives.

And a lead. Not much, but a start. From Cyrus, just before his mind finally snapped, I learned that Molotch was heading for the outworlds. Sleef, perhaps. Maybe even deeper than that. I instructed Nayl and Kara to provision for what could be a long, dangerous pursuit.

The day before we were due to leave Sameter, I met with Carl in one of the scholam's old, faded classrooms. Most of the staff had been shipped out by then, in magistratum custody.

'Did you trace what I wanted?' I asked.

He nodded. 'It's very little. With the records wiped–'

'What have you got?'

'Pupils Prudence and Providence were sold to a free trader who called himself Vinquies. The name was false, of course. No other records remain, and the name doesn't match any excise log I can get from Sameter Out Traffic.'

'The man himself?'

'There was a picture in Cyrus's mind, and in the minds of several of the other tutors present at the supper, but they're not reliable. I've fed them through both the local magistratum files and the officio itself. Nothing.'

'So... so, they're lost?'

Carl nodded sadly. 'I suppose, if we dedicated the rest of our careers to trying to find them, we might turn up some clue. But in all reality, they're long gone.'

'I'll tell her,' I said, and slid out of the room.

Patience was in the oubliette. By choice. The hatch was open. She sat inside, in the semi-dark, sliding her hands over the stones. She was still wearing her torn and filthy uniform. She'd refused to take it off.

'Patience?'

She stared out at me. 'You can't find them, can you?'

I thought for a moment, and decided it was better to lie. Better a lie now than a lifetime of hopeless yearning.

'Yes, Patience, I found them.'

'They're dead, aren't they?'

'Yes.'

She coiled up, and I felt her hold onto that small black nugget in her mind again.

+Patience.+

'Yes, Gideon?'

+I'm sorry. I truly am. We have to leave soon. I'd like you to come with us.+

'With you? Why?'

+I'll be honest. I can't leave you here. You know about your gift? What it means?+

'Yes.'

+You're a psyker. A telekine. You can't be allowed to remain in public. But I can look after you. I can train you. You could come to serve the God-Emperor of Mankind at my side. Would you like that?+

'Better than an apprenticeship to a mill,' she said. 'Will Kara be there?'

+Yes, Patience.+

'All right then,' she said, and stepped out of the oubliette to join me.

+If you follow me, it will be hard at times. I will demand a lot of you. I will need to know everything about you. What do you think to that?+

'That's fine, Gideon.'

+I'll be asking you questions, probing you, training your gift, unwrapping who you are.+

'I understand.'

+Do you? Here's a test question, the sort of thing I'll be asking you. What was it that you held on to? When the hunters were closing. I felt it as a dark secret part of you, something you wouldn't let go.+

'It was my name, Gideon,' she said. 'My true name, my real name. It was always the single thing my mother gave me that I didn't ever give away to the bastards in this place.'

+I see. That makes sense. Good, thank you for being so honest.+

+Gideon, do you want me to tell you my real name? I will, if you want.+

'No,' I said. 'No, not now, not ever. I want you to hold onto it. It's your secret. Keep it safe and it will keep you sane. It'll remind you what you've come through. Promise me you'll keep it safe.'

+I will.+

'Patience is a fine name. I'll call you that.'

'All right,' she replied, and started to walk down the hallway at my side.

'I'll need a surname, though,' she said at length.

'Choose one,' I replied.

She looked down at the monogram embroidered on her ragged scholam-issue clothes.

'Kys?' she suggested. 'I'll be Patience Kys.'

ABOUT THE AUTHORS

Dan Abnett is the author of the hugely successful Gaunt's Ghosts, Eisenhorn and Ravenor series, along with several Horus Heresy novels, most recently *The Unremembered Empire*, which follows on from the *New York Times* bestselling *Know No Fear*.

David Annandale wrote the Space Marine Battles novel *The Death of Antagonis* and the novella *Yarrick: Chains of Golgotha*. He is currently working on more tales of Commissar Yarrick.

Barrington J Bayley (1937-2008) was a British science fiction author. His Black Library work included the novel *Eye of Terror* and several short stories.

Braden Campbell's Black Library credits include a number of short stories and the novella *Shadowsun: The Last of Kiru's Line*.

Author of *The Gildar Rift*, *Accursed Eternity* and *Valkia the Bloody*, **S P Cawkwell** continues to write about the Silver Skulls and the Gorequeen.

Andy Chambers is the author of the popular dark eldar series, consisting of *Path of the Renegade*, *Path of the Incubus* and the forthcoming *Path of the Archon*, along with a number of short stories and the novella *The Masque of Vyle*.

Ben Counter is best known for the Soul Drinkers and Grey Knights series, but has recently been busy telling tales of the Imperial Fists, such as *Malodrax* and *Seventh Retribution*.

Aaron Dembski-Bowden wrote the Night Lords trilogy, the Space Marine Battles book *Armageddon* and the Horus Heresy novels *The First Heretic*, which was a *New York Times* bestseller, and *Betrayer*.

Matthew Farrer lives in Australia. He has written several Warhammer 40,000 novels, including the Enforcer series, and the Horus Heresy short story 'After Desh'ea'.

By day, **John French** licenses products for Games Workshop. By night, he writes. His credits include *Ahriman: Exile* and the Horus Heresy novella *The Crimson Fist*.

Jonathan Green has been writing for Black Library since its inception. He is the author of the Black Templars Armageddon novels and a pair of Path to Victory gamebooks, amongst many other credits.

Andy Hoare is the author of the Space Marine Battles novel *Hunt for Voldorius* as well as the Imperial Guard novel *Commissar* and several tales set in the Damocles Gulf.

Paul Kearney is a fantasy and science fiction author from Northern Ireland. His works for Black Library are the short stories 'The Last Detail' and 'Broken Blood'.

William King is the author of the Tyrion and Teclis trilogy and the Macharian Crusade series. He wrote the first seven books in the long-running *Gotrek & Felix* series as well as the first four tales of Ragnar Blackmane.

Nick Kyme is the author of the Salamanders series, the Space Marine Battles novel *Damnos*, several Warhammer 40,000 audio dramas, including *Perfection* and *Veil of Darkness*, and the Horus Heresy novel *Vulkan Lives*.

Mike Lee wrote the Time of Legends trilogy The Rise of Nagash and the Horus Heresy novel *Fallen Angels*. He also co-wrote the five-volume Darkblade series with Dan Abnett.

George Mann's Black Library work focuses on the Raven Guard and Brazen Minotaurs and includes the novella *The Unkindness of Ravens* and the audio dramas *Helion Rain* and *Labyrinth of Sorrows*.

Graham McNeill writes the long-running Ultramarines series and is a regular contributor to the Horus Heresy. His novel *A Thousand Sons* was a *New York Times* bestseller.

Writer of the long-running Ciaphas Cain series, **Sandy Mitchell** has also worked on various other novels and short stories for Black Library, including the tale 'A Good Man' in the *Sabbat Worlds* anthology.

Author of the novels *Gunheads* and *Deathwatch*, **Steve Parker** sleeps, eats, trains and writes in Tokyo, Japan. He is working on more tales of the Deathwatch.

Hailing from Australia, **Anthony Reynolds** is best known for the Word Bearers and Bretonnian Knights series. He has also contributed to the Horus Heresy.

Rob Sanders wrote the Space Marine Battles novel *Legion of the Damned*, along with *Atlas Infernal* and *Redemption Corps*. He has also written short stories and a novella for the Horus Heresy.

Andy Smillie is the author of numerous tales of the Flesh Tearers, including the Space Marines Battles novella *Flesh of Cretacia* and audio drama *Blood in the Machine*.

James Swallow is the author of the Blood Angels and Sisters of Battle series and the *New York Times* bestselling Horus Heresy novels *Nemesis* and *Fear to Tread*.

Gav Thorpe is currently writing the Dark Angels: Legacy of Caliban series, which began with *Ravenwing*, and a series of Horus Heresy novellas featuring the primarch Corax.

Author of the Space Marine Battles novel *Siege of Castellax*, **C L Werner** also wrote the Time of Legends series The Black Plague and the Thanquol and Boneripper novels.

Richard Williams penned the novels *Relentless* and *Imperial Glory*. He is also a theatre actor and director.

Chris Wraight is currently writing the Space Wolves series, including *Blood of Asaheim* and *Stormcaller*, co-writing the Time of Legends series The War of Vengeance and penning the serialised Horus Heresy novel *Scars*.

Henry Zou is the author of the Bastion Wars novels *Flesh and Iron*, *Blood Gorgons* and *Emperor's Mercy*.

READ IT FIRST
EXCLUSIVE PRODUCTS | EARLY RELEASES | FREE DELIVERY
blacklibrary.com

Available from *blacklibrary.com*

Hobby Centres
and all good bookshops

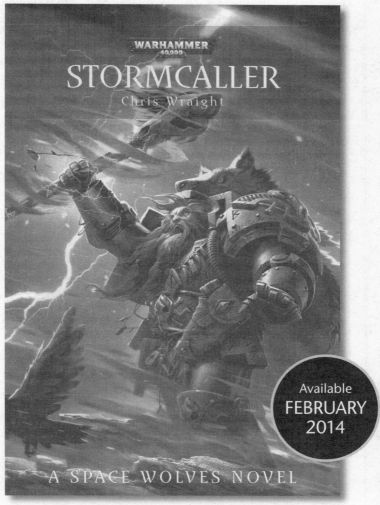

Available from *blacklibrary.com*

Hobby Centres
and all good bookshops

THE HERESY STARTS HERE...

Discover the truth behind the legendary conflict that shaped the Warhammer 40,000 universe. The *New York Times* bestselling novel series begins in **Horus Rising** by Dan Abnett.

Available from

blacklibrary.com and all good bookshops